# STONE
# OF
# TEARS

TERRY GOODKIND

# STONE
# OF
# TEARS

TOR
fantasy ®

A TOM DOHERTY ASSOCIATES BOOK

NEW YORK

G-00
C 1

STONE OF TEARS
Copyright © 1995 by Terry Goodkind
All rights reserved, including the right to reproduce this book, or portions
thereof, in any form.

This book is printed on acid-free paper.

*Edited by James Frenkel*
*Maps by Terry Goodkind*
*Jacket art by Keith Parkinson*

A Tor Book
Published by Tom Doherty Associates, Inc.
175 Fifth Avenue
New York, N.Y. 10010

Tor Books on the World-Wide Web: http://www.tor.com

Tor® is a registered trademark of Tom Doherty Associates, Inc.

Library of Congress Cataloging-in-Publication Data
Goodkind, Terry.
    Stone of tears / Terry Goodkind.
       p.    cm. — (The Sword of truth ; bk. 2)
    ''A Tom Doherty Associates book.''
    ISBN 0-312-85706-3
    1. Wizards—Fiction.  I. Title.  II. Series: Goodkind, Terry.
  Sword of truth ; bk. 2.
  PS3557.05826S76    1995
  813'.54—dc20                                95-30303
                                                           CIP

First Edition: October 1995
Printed in the United States of America

0 9 8 7 6 5 4 3 2 1

*For my parents, Natalie and Leo*

I would like to thank my editor, James Frenkel, for having the integrity to settle for no less than my best effort; my British editor, Caroline Oakley, for her continuing support and encouragement; my friends Bonnie Moretto and Donald Schassberger M.D., for their expert advice; and Keith Parkinson for the outstanding cover art.

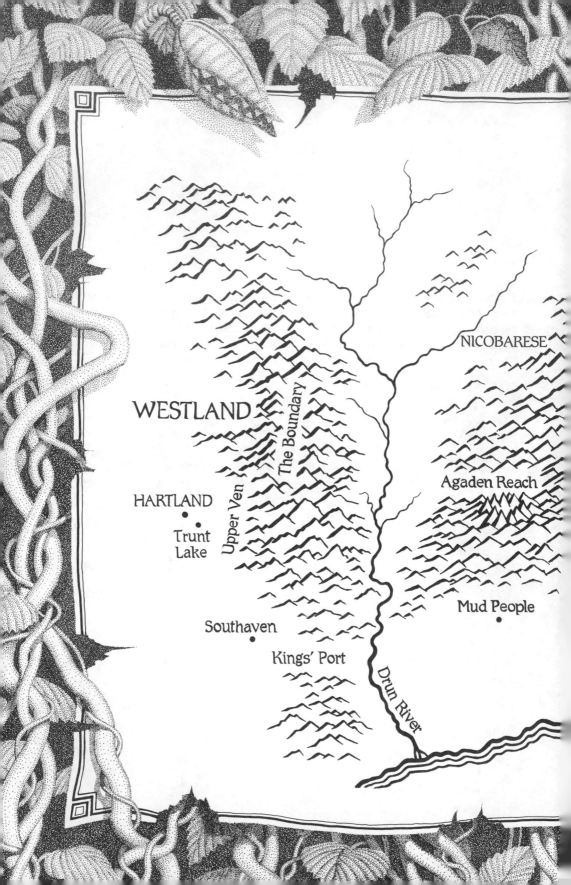

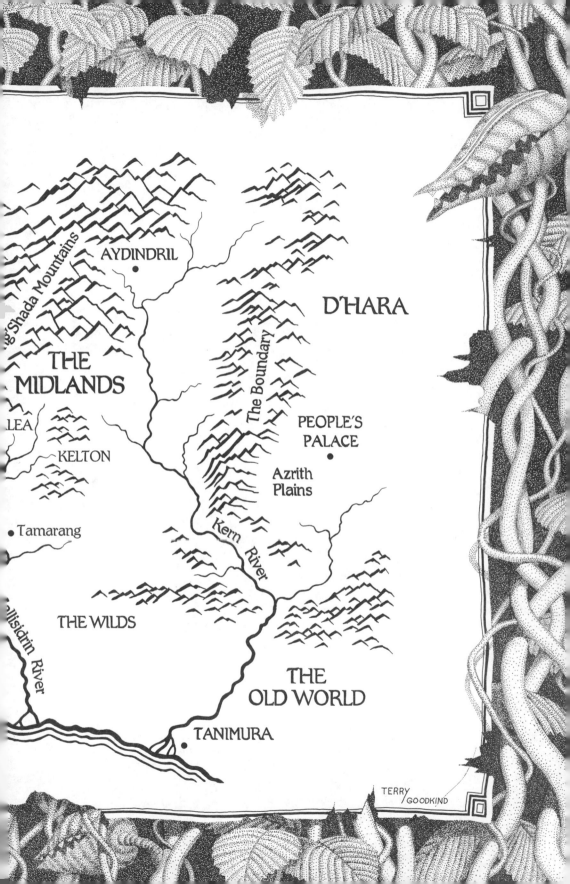

# STONE
## OF
## TEARS

Rachel clutched her doll tighter to her chest and stared at the dark thing watching her from the bushes. At least she thought it was watching her. It was hard to tell because the eyes were as dark as the rest of it, except when the light caught them just right; then they gleamed a golden color.

She had seen animals in the woods before, rabbits and raccoons and squirrels and such, but this was bigger. It was as big as her, maybe bigger. Bears were dark. She wondered if it could be a bear.

But this wasn't exactly the woods, since it was indoors. She had never been in an indoor woods before. She wondered if indoor woods had animals like the outdoor woods did.

She might have been afraid if Chase wasn't there with her. She knew she was safe with him. Chase was the bravest man she ever saw. Still, she was a little afraid. Chase had told her she was the bravest little girl he knew. She didn't want him to think she was afraid of some big rabbit.

Maybe that's all it was, some big rabbit, sitting on a rock or something. But rabbits had long ears. Maybe it really was a bear. She put her doll's foot in her mouth.

She turned and looked down the path, across the pretty flowers and short walls covered with vines, and across the grass to where Chase was talking to Zedd, the wizard. They were standing by a stone table, looking at the boxes, and talking about what to do with them. Rachel was glad that that mean Darken Rahl didn't get them and that he wasn't ever going to be able to hurt anyone again.

Rachel turned back to make sure the dark thing wasn't coming any closer to her. It was gone. She looked around, but didn't see it anywhere.

"Sara, where do you think it could have gone?" she whispered.

Her doll didn't have an answer. Rachel bit down on Sara's foot and started walking toward Chase. Her feet wanted to run, but she didn't want Chase to think she wasn't brave. He had said she was brave, and that made her feel good. She looked over her shoulder as she walked, checking, but she didn't see the dark thing anywhere. Maybe it lived in a hole, and it had gone there. Her feet still wanted to run, but she didn't let them.

When Rachel got to Chase, she pushed up against him and hugged his leg. He and Zedd were talking, and she knew it was impolite to interrupt, so she sucked on Sara's foot while she waited.

"So what could happen if you just shut the lid?" Chase was asking the wizard.

"Anything!" Zedd stuck his skinny arms up in the air. His wavy white hair was smoothed down but it still stuck out in places. "How should I know? Just because

I know what the boxes of Orden are doesn't mean I know what to do with them now that Darken Rahl has opened one. The Magic of Orden killed him for opening it. It could have destroyed the world. It could kill me for closing it. Or worse."

Chase sighed. "Well, we can't just leave them sitting around, can we? Don't we have to do something?"

The wizard frowned and looked at the boxes while he was thinking. After more than a minute of quiet, Rachel tugged on Chase's sleeve. He looked down at her.

"Chase . . ."

" 'Chase'? I told you the rules." He put his hands on his hips and twisted his face up, trying to make it look mean, until she giggled and hugged his leg tighter. "You've only been my daughter for a few weeks, and already you're breaking the rules. I told you before, you are to call me 'Father.' None of my children are allowed to call me Chase. Understand?"

Rachel grinned and nodded. "Yes, Ch . . . Father."

He rolled his eyes and shook his head. Then he mussed her hair. "What is it?"

"There's some big animal in the trees. I think it might be a bear, or worse. I think you might need to take out your sword and go have a look."

He laughed. "A bear! In here?" He laughed again. "This is an indoor garden, Rachel. There aren't any bears in an indoor garden. Maybe it was a shadow. The light does odd things in here."

She shook her head. "I don't think so, Ch . . . Father. It was watching me."

He smiled and mussed her hair again and put his big hand on the side of her face and hugged her head to his leg. "Then you just stay by me and it won't bother you."

She sucked Sara's foot and nodded as he held her head to his leg. She didn't feel so afraid now that his hand was on her, and so looked over to the trees again.

The dark thing, mostly hidden by one of the vine-covered walls, darted closer. Rachel bit down harder on Sara's foot and let out a little whimper as she looked up at Chase. He was pointing at the boxes.

"And just what is that thing, that stone, or jewel or whatever it is? Did it come out of the box?"

Zedd nodded. "It did. But I don't want to say what I think it is until I'm sure. At least not out loud."

"Father," Rachel whined, "it's coming closer."

He looked down. "Good. You just keep your eye on it for me." He looked back to the wizard. "What do you mean you don't want to say? Do you think it has something to do with what you said about the veil to the underworld possibly being torn?"

Zedd frowned while he rubbed his smooth chin with his skinny fingers and looked down at the black jewel sitting in front of the open box. "That's what I'm afraid of."

Rachel looked over to the wall to watch where the dark thing was. She gave a start when she saw the hands reach over the edge of the wall. It was a lot closer.

But they weren't hands. They were claws. Long curved claws.

She looked up at Chase, at all his weapons, just to be sure he had enough. He had knives, a lot of knives, around his waist, a sword strapped over the back of his shoulder, a big axe hooked to his belt, a few other things that looked like clubs, with sharp spikes sticking out of them, hanging from his belt, too, and a crossbow on his back. She hoped it was enough.

All the weapons scared other men, but they didn't seem to be scaring the dark thing that was coming closer. And the wizard didn't even have a knife. He just wore that plain, tan robe. And he was so skinny. Not big like Chase. But wizards had magic. Maybe his magic could scare the dark thing away.

Magic! Rachel remembered the magic fire stick Wizard Giller had given her. She reached into her pocket and put her fingers around it. Maybe Chase would need her help. She wouldn't let that thing hurt her new father. She would be brave.

"Is it dangerous?"

Zedd looked up at Chase from under his eyebrows. "If it's what I think it is, and it were to fall into the wrong hands, 'dangerous' wouldn't even begin to describe it."

"Then maybe we should drop it down a deep hole, or destroy it."

"Can't. We may need it."

"What if we hide it?"

"That's what I'm thinking. The problem is where. There are things to take into consideration. I need to take Adie to Aydindril and study the prophecies with her before I know for sure what to do with the stone, and what to do about the boxes."

"And until then? Until you know for sure?"

Rachel looked over to the dark thing. It was closer, as close as the wall came to them. With its claws over the top of the wall, it lifted its head up and looked right into her eyes.

The thing grinned at her, showing long, sharp teeth. Her breath caught in her throat. Its shoulders shook. It was laughing. Rachel's eyes were as big as they would go. She could hear her heartbeats making a whooshing sound in her ears.

"Father . . ." she whined in a small voice.

He didn't look down. He just shushed her. The thing put its leg over the wall and dropped down in front, still looking at her, still laughing. Its shiny eyes looked at Chase and Zedd. It hissed and then laughed as it hunched down.

Rachel tugged Chase's pant leg and strained to make her voice work. "Father . . . it's coming."

"All right Rachel. Zedd, I still don't know . . ."

With a howl the dark thing sprang into the open. It ran like a streak, just a blur of black. Rachel screamed. Chase spun just as it hit him. Claws flashed through the air. Chase fell to the ground as the thing leapt on Zedd.

The wizard's arms flailed about. Flashes of light shot from Zedd's fingers, bouncing off the dark thing and tearing up dirt or stone where they hit. The thing knocked Zedd to the ground.

Laughing in a loud howl, it jumped back on Chase as he was pulling his axe from his belt. Rachel screamed again as the claws tore at Chase. The thing was faster than any animal she had ever seen. Its claws were just a blur.

Rachel was terrified Chase was being hurt. It flung the axe out of Chase's hand, laughing that awful laugh. It was hurting Chase. Rachel had the fire stick in her hand.

She jumped forward and put the fire stick on its back. She screamed the magic words to make the fire stick work. "Light for me!"

The dark thing burst into flames. It made a horrible scream as it spun to her. Its mouth opened wide, teeth snapping as flames burned all over it. It laughed again, but not like people laughed when they thought things were funny. Its laugh made

15

her skin prickle. It hunched over and started walking toward her, still on fire, as Rachel backed up.

Chase let out a grunt as he threw one of the clubs with the sharp spikes sticking out of it. The club hit the thing's back, and stuck in its shoulder. It looked around at Chase and laughed as it reached behind and pulled the club from its back. It started for Chase again.

Zedd was up. Fire flew from his fingers, covering the thing with even more flames. It laughed at Zedd. All the fire went out. Smoke rose from it. Its body looked the same now as before it got burned. In fact, it had looked like it was dark from being burned even before Rachel had set it on fire.

Chase was on his feet, and there was blood on him. Rachel got tears at seeing that. Chase snatched the crossbow off his back and in a blink he shot an arrow. It stuck in the thing's chest. With that terrible laugh it snapped the arrow off.

Chase threw aside the crossbow and yanked out the sword from over his shoulder, then ran for the thing, jumping over it as he stabbed with the sword. The thing moved so fast Chase missed. Zedd did something that sent the thing tumbling across the grass. Chase put himself in front of Rachel, pushing her back with one hand while he held the sword out in the other.

The thing sprang to its feet again, looking at each of them.

"Walk!" Zedd yelled at them. "Don't run! Don't stand still!"

Chase grabbed Rachel's wrist and started walking backward. Zedd started walking backward, too. The dark thing stopped laughing and looked at each of them, blinking. Chase was breathing hard. His chain-mail shirt and the tan leather tunic under it had big rips from the claws. Rachel got more tears at all the blood on him. Blood was running down his arm onto her hand. She didn't want him to be hurt. She loved him something fierce. She clutched Sara and the fire stick tighter.

Zedd stopped. "Keep walking," he told Chase.

The dark thing looked at Zedd standing there, and a big grin with sharp teeth came to its face again. It laughed that awful laugh and tore at the ground as it started in a rush toward the wizard.

Zedd threw his hands up. Dirt and grass flew up in the air around the thing. It was lifted into the air. Bolts of blue lightning struck it from all around before it hit the ground. It howled in laughter as it thudded to the ground, smoking.

Something else happened, Rachel couldn't tell what, and the thing stopped with its arms stretched out, like it was trying to run, but its feet were stuck. It howled and twisted, but couldn't move. Zedd's arms swirled around in circles and he threw them out once more. The ground shook as if from thunder and there were flashes of light hitting the thing. It laughed and there was a breaking sound, like wood snapping, and the thing started toward Zedd.

Zedd began walking again. The thing stopped and frowned. Then the wizard stopped and threw his arms out again. A terrible ball of fire went through the air toward the thing as it ran for Zedd. The ball of fire made a loud scream and grew bigger as it flew toward the dark thing.

The fire hit so hard it made the ground shake. The blue and yellow light was so bright Rachel had to squint as she was walking backward. The ball of fire stayed in that one place as it burned and made a loud roar.

Smoking, the dark thing stepped out of the fire, its shoulders shaking as it laughed. The flames went out in little sparks that flew around in the air.

"Bags," the wizard said as he started walking backward.

Rachel didn't know what "bags" meant, but Chase had told Zedd not to say it in front of little ears. She didn't know what that meant either. The wizard's wavy, white hair was all messed up and sticking out in clumps.

Rachel and Chase were on the path through the trees, almost to the door. Zedd was walking backward toward them as the dark thing watched. Zedd stopped and the thing started coming again.

Walls of flame shot up in front of it. The air smelled like smoke and roared with noise. The thing stepped through the wall of fire. Zedd made another, and it stepped through that, too.

When the wizard started walking again, it stopped by a short, vine-covered wall, watching. Fat vines ripped off the wall by themselves and grew suddenly longer. They whipped around the dark thing as it stood there, tangling all around it. Zedd was almost up with them.

"Where are we going?" Chase asked him.

Zedd turned. He looked tired. "Let's see if we can shut it in here."

The thing tore at the vines as they pulled it to the ground, and was slicing through them with its sharp claws as the three of them went through the big doorway. Chase and Zedd each took one of the golden metal doors and pushed it shut.

From the other side came a howl, and then a loud crash. A big dent popped out in the door, knocking Zedd to the ground. Chase put a hand on each door and put all his weight against them as the thing pounded from the other side.

Horrible screeches came through the metal as the thing clawed at the door. Chase was covered with sweat and blood. Zedd jumped to his feet and helped Chase hold the doors closed.

A claw stuck through the crack between the two doors and slid down; then another came out from underneath. Through the door, Rachel could hear the thing laughing. Chase grunted as he pushed. The doors creaked.

The wizard stood back and held out his arms, with his fingers up, like he was pushing against the air. The creaking stopped. The thing howled louder.

Zedd grabbed Chase's sleeve. "Get out of here."

Chase backed away from the doors. "Is that going to hold it?"

"I don't think so. If it comes for you, walk. Running or standing still attracts its attention. Tell anyone else you see."

"Zedd, what is that thing?"

There was another loud crash and another big dent popped out in the door. The tips of claws broke through the metal and made rips in the door. The noise it made hurt Rachel's ears.

"Go! Now!"

Chase snatched her up with an arm around her waist and started running down the hall.

Zedd idly fingered the stone through the coarse cloth of his robe, where it was nestled in an inner pocket, as he watched the claws pull back through the rips in the metal. He turned and watched the boundary warden carrying Rachel down the hall. They hadn't gone more than a few dozen strides when one of the doors flew off its hinges with a horrific boom. The strong hinges shattered as if they were made of clay.

Zedd dove out of the way, the gold-clad iron door just missing him as it flew across the hall and crashed against the polished granite wall, sending shards of metal flying and stone dust boiling down the hall. Zedd rolled to his feet and ran.

The screeling bounded out of the Garden of Life and into the hall. Its body was hardly more than a squat skeleton covered in a veneer of dry, crisp, blackened skin. Like a corpse that had dried in the sun for years. White bone stuck out in places where the skin, hanging in flaps here and there, had been torn in the fight, but that didn't seem to bother the creature; it was a thing of the underworld, and not hindered by all the frailties of life. There was no blood.

If it could be torn up enough, or hacked apart, maybe it could be stopped, but it was awfully quick. And magic certainly wasn't doing it much harm. It was a creature of Subtractive Magic; Additive Magic was just being absorbed into it like a sponge.

Maybe it could be harmed with Subtractive Magic, but Zedd had nothing of that half of the gift. No wizard in the last few thousand years did. Some might have had the calling for the Subtractive—Darken Rahl was proof of that—but none had had the gift for it.

No, his magic wasn't going to stop this thing. At least, the wizard thought, not directly. But maybe indirectly?

Zedd walked backward as the screeling watched with blinking, bewildered eyes. *Now,* he thought, *while it's standing still.*

Concentrating, Zedd gathered the air, making it dense, dense enough to lift the heavy door. He was tired; it took an effort. He pushed the air with a mental grunt, crashing the door onto the back of the screeling. Dust rolled up and across the hall as the door slammed the creature to the ground. It howled. Zedd wondered if it was howling in pain, or anger.

The door lifted, stone chips sliding off. The screeling held the heavy door up with one clawed hand as it laughed, a woody tendril of the vine he had tried to strangle it with still coiled around its neck.

"Bags," Zedd muttered. "Nothing is ever easy."

Zedd kept walking backward. The door crashed to the floor as the screeling stepped out from underneath it and followed. It was starting to learn that the people who walked were the same ones who ran or stood still. This was an unfamiliar world to it. Zedd had to think of something before it learned any more. If only he wasn't so tired.

Chase went down a wide marble stairway. Zedd followed him at a quick walk. If he had been sure it wasn't Chase or Rachel the screeling was after, he would have gone a different way, drawing the danger away from them, but it could just as easily go after them, and he didn't want to leave Chase to fight it alone.

A man and a woman, both in white robes, were coming up the stairs. Chase tried to turn them around but they slipped past him.

"Walk!" Zedd yelled at them. "Don't run! Go back or you will be killed!" They frowned at him in confusion.

The screeling was shuffling along toward the stairs, its claws clicking and scraping on the marble floor. Zedd could hear it panting with that nerve-jarring near laughter.

The two people saw the dark thing and froze, their blue eyes going wide. Zedd shoved them, turning them around, and forced them back down the stairs. They both suddenly broke into a run, bounding down the stairs three at a time, their blond hair and white robes flying.

"Don't run!" Zedd and Chase yelled at the same time.

The screeling rose up on its clawed toes, attracted by the sudden movement. It let out a cackling laugh and darted to the stairs. Zedd threw a fist of air, hitting it in the chest, knocking it back a pace. It hardly noticed. It peered over the carved stone railing at the top and saw the people running.

With a cackle, it grasped the railing and leapt over, dropping a good twenty feet to the two running, white-robed figures. Chase immediately put Rachel's face to his shoulder and reversed direction, coming back up the stairs. He knew what was going to happen, and there was nothing he could do about it.

Zedd waited at the top. "Hurry, while it's distracted."

There was a very brief struggle, and screams that were just as brief. Howling laughter echoed in the stairwell. Blood splattered in an arc up the white marble, almost to where Chase was charging up the stairs. Rachel hid her face against him and hugged his neck tight, but didn't make a sound.

Zedd was impressed by her. He had never seen one so young use her head as well as she did. She was smart. Smart and gutsy. He understood why Giller had used her to try to keep the last box of Orden away from Darken Rahl. The way of wizards, Zedd thought—using people to do what must be done.

The three ran down the hall until the screeling appeared at the top of stairs; then they slowed to a backward walk. The screeling grinned with bloodred teeth, its deathless black eyes momentarily reflecting golden in the sunlight coming in a tall, narrow window. It winced at the light, licked the blood off its claws, and then loped after them. They went down the next stairway. The creature followed, sometimes stopping briefly in confusion, seemingly unsure if it was them it was after.

Chase held Rachel in one arm and a sword in his other hand. Zedd stayed between them and the screeling as they backed down a small hall. The screeling climbed up the walls, scratching the smooth stone, and sprang across tapestries, tearing them with its claws as it followed the three.

Polished walnut side tables, each with three ornate legs carved in vines and dotted with gilded blossoms, tipped over into the hall as the screeling pushed at them with a claw, grinning and laughing at the sound of cut-glass vases shattering on the stone floor. Water and flowers spilled over carpets. The screeling hopped down and tore a priceless blue and yellow Tanimuran carpet to shreds as it howled in laughter and then skittered up the wall to the ceiling.

It advanced along the ceiling like a spider, head hanging down, watching them. "How can it do that?" Chase whispered.

Zedd only shook his head as they backed into the immense central halls of the People's Palace. The ceiling here was well over fifty feet high, a collection of four-pointed ribbed vaults held up by a column at the corner of each vault.

Suddenly the screeling sprang along the ceiling of the small hall it was in and leapt at them.

Zedd released a bolt of fire as the creature flew through the air. He missed, the fire boiling up the granite wall, leaving a trail of black soot before it dissipated.

For the first time, Chase didn't miss. With a solid strike his sword lopped off one of the screeling's arms. For the first time the screeling howled in pain. It tumbled around on the ground and darted behind a green-veined gray marble column. The severed arm lay on the stone floor, twitching and grasping.

Soldiers came running across the vast hall, their swords to hand, the clatter of their armor and weapons reverberating off the vaulted ceilings high overhead, their boot strikes echoing off the tiles around the devotion pool as they skirted it. D'Haran soldiers were a fierce lot, and they looked all the more so at finding there was an invader in the palace.

Zedd felt an odd sort of apprehension at the sight of them. A few days ago they would have dragged him off to the former Master Rahl to be killed; now they were the loyal followers of the new Master Rahl, Zedd's grandson, Richard.

As Zedd saw the soldiers coming, he realized the halls were filled with people. The afternoon devotion had just ended. Even if the screeling did have only one arm, this could be a bloodbath. The screeling could kill a few dozen of them before they even thought to run. And then it would kill more when they did. They had to get all these people away.

The soldiers rushed up around the wizard, eyes hard, searching, ready, looking for the cause of the commotion. Zedd turned to the commander, a heavily muscled man in leather and a polished breastplate with the ornate letter *R* embossed on it: the symbol of the House of Rahl. The scars of rank were incised on upper arms covered only with coarse mail sleeves. Intense blue eyes glowered out from under his gleaming helmet.

"What's going on here?" he demanded. "What is it?"

"Get these people out of this hall. They are all in danger."

The commander's face reddened behind the cheek plates of his helmet. "I'm a soldier, not a bloody sheepherder!"

Zedd gritted his teeth. "And a soldier's first duty is to protect people. If you don't get these people out of this hall, Commander, I will see to it you become a sheepherder!"

The commander's fist snapped to his heart in salute, his voice suddenly controlled at realizing who he was arguing with. "By your command, Wizard Zorander." He turned his anger instead on his men. "Get everyone back! Right bloody now! Spread rank! Sweep the hall!"

The soldiers fanned out, pushing a wave of startled people before them. Zedd hoped they could get them all clear, and then maybe, with the soldiers' help, they could bottle up the screeling and hack it to pieces.

But then the screeling launched itself from behind the column, a black streak tearing across the floor. It tumbled into a bunched knot of onlookers the soldiers were herding back, toppling many over one another to the floor. Shrieks and wails and the screeling's hideous laughter erupted from across the hall.

Soldiers fell upon the creature and were flung back, bloodied, as more came to their aid. In the panicked clump of people, the soldiers couldn't swing a sword or axe with any effect as the screeling tore a bloody path through the bodies. It had no more caution for the armed soldiers than unarmed innocents. It simply ripped at anyone close enough.

"Bags!" Zedd cursed. He turned to Chase. "Stick close to me. We have to draw it away." He looked around. "Over there. The devotion pool."

They ran to the square pool of water that was situated under an opening in the roof. Sunlight streamed down, reflecting in rippling patterns on the column at one of its corners. A bell perched on the dark pitted rock that sat off-center in the water. Orange fish glided through the shallow pool, unconcerned with the mayhem above.

Zedd was getting an idea. The screeling certainly wasn't bothered by fire; the most it did when hit with it was steam a little. He ignored the sounds of pain and dying and stretched his hands out over the water, gathering its warmth, preparing it for what he was going to do. He could see shimmering waves of heat just above the surface of the water. He held the rising heat at that point, just below ignition.

"When it comes," he told Chase, "we have to get it in the water."

Chase nodded. Zedd was glad the boundary warden wasn't one who always needed to have things explained to him, and knew better than to waste precious seconds with questions. Chase set Rachel on the floor. "Stay behind me," he told her.

She, too, asked no questions. She nodded and hugged her doll close. Zedd saw she was clutching the fire stick in her other hand. Gutsy indeed. He turned to the uproar across the hall, lifted a hand, and sent tickling tongues of flame into the flailing dark thing in its center. The soldiers fell back.

The screeling straightened, turning, dropping a disembodied arm from its teeth as it did so. Steam rose where the flames had licked it. It hissed a cackling laugh at the wizard standing still in the sunlight by the pool.

The soldiers were pushing the remaining people down the halls, although the people no longer needed the encouragement. Zedd rolled balls of fire across the floor. The screeling batted them out of the way and they sparked out. Zedd knew the fire wouldn't harm it; he only wanted to draw its attention. It worked.

"Don't forget," he said to Chase, "in the water."

"You don't mind if it's dead when it goes in, do you?"

"All the better."

With a clatter of claws against stone, the screeling charged across the hall. The tips of the claws scratched into the floor, sending little spurts of stone dust behind along with flakes and chips. Zedd hit it with compacted knots of air, hammering it down, keeping its attention, trying to slow it down enough so they might be able to handle it. It came to its feet in a rush each time, charging onward. Chase crouched a little lower in readiness, now holding a six-bladed mace in his fist instead of the sword.

The screeling made an impossible leap through the air at the wizard, landing on him with a howl before he had a chance to turn it aside. As he was thrown to the floor, Zedd wove webs of air to keep the thrashing claw at bay. Teeth snapped viciously at his throat.

Man and beast rolled over once, and when the screeling came up on top, Chase swung the mace at its head, hitting a glancing blow. It spun to him and he slammed it square in the chest, knocking it off the wizard. Zedd could hear bones snapping with the blow. The screeling seemed hardly to notice.

Its one arm swept out, yanking Chase's legs out from under him, and then sprang on his chest as he hit the floor with a hard grunt. Zedd struggled to regain his wits. Rachel laid the fire stick on the screeling's back, and flames burst up. Zedd pushed it with air, trying to knock it in the water, but the screeling held on to Chase with its claw to keep from being pushed. Angry black eyes glared out from behind the fire. Lips curled back in a snarl.

Chase brought the mace up with both hands, catching the powerful creature square in the back. The impact knocked the screeling into the pool. Hissing steam rose upon the contact of flame and water.

Instantly, Zedd ignited the air above the water, using the heat in the water to feed it. The wizard's fire sucked all warmth from the water. The entire pool froze into a solid block of ice. The screeling was encased. The fire sputtered out when the heat feeding it was exhausted. There was sudden quiet, except for the moans from the injured across the hall.

Rachel fell on Chase, her voice choked with tears. "Chase, Chase, are you all right?"

He put an arm around her as he levered himself into a sitting position. "That I am, little one."

Zedd could see that that wasn't entirely true. "Chase, go sit on that bench. I have to help those people, and I don't want little eyes to see what's over there."

He knew this appeal would work better than telling Chase he didn't want him walking around with his injuries until they could be seen to. Still, Zedd was a little surprised when Chase nodded without protest.

The commander and eight of his men rushed up. A few of them were bloody; one had ragged claw cuts right through the metal of his breastplate. They all cast an eye to the screeling frozen in the pool. "Nice bit of work, Wizard Zorander." The commander gave a small nod and smile of respect. "There are a few over there who are still alive. Is there anything you can do for them?"

"I'll have a look. Commander, have your men use their battle-axes to hack that thing to pieces before it figures out how to melt the ice."

His eyes went wide. "You mean it's still alive?"

Zedd gave a grunt to indicate that it was so. "The sooner the better, Commander."

The men already had their crescent axes unhooked from their belts, waiting for the order. The commander gave them a nod and they charged onto the ice, swinging before they slid to a stop.

He lowered his voice. "Wizard Zorander, what is that thing?"

Zedd looked from the man's face over to Chase, who was listening intently. He held the boundary warden's gaze. "It's a screeling." Chase didn't show any reaction; the boundary warden rarely did. Zedd turned back to the commander.

The big man's blue eyes were wide. "The screelings are loose?" he whispered. "Wizard Zorander . . . you can't be serious."

Zedd studied the man's face. He saw scars he hadn't seen before, scars earned

22

in battles to the death. For a D'Haran soldier, there rarely was any other kind. This was a man not used to letting fear show in his eyes. Even in the face of death.

Zedd sighed. He hadn't slept in days. After the quads had come and tried to capture Kahlan, and she thought Richard had been killed, she had gone into the Con Dar, the blood rage, killing their attackers. She, Chase, and Zedd had walked for three days and nights to reach the palace, for her to extract vengeance. There was no stopping a Confessor in the grip of the Con Dar, that ancient mix of magics. Then they had been captured, and discovered Richard alive. That was only yesterday, but it seemed forever ago.

Darken Rahl had worked all night drawing forth the Magic of Orden from the three boxes as they had watched, helpless, and only this morning was he killed by opening the wrong box. Killed by the Wizard's First Rule, wielded by Richard. Proof that Richard had the gift, even if Richard didn't believe it, for only one with the gift could use the Wizard's First Rule on a wizard of Darken Rahl's talent.

Zedd glanced over momentarily at the men hacking at the screeling in the ice. "What is your name, Commander?"

The man stiffened proudly to attention. "Commander General Trimack, First File of the Palace Guard."

"First File? What are they?"

Pride stiffened the man's jaw even more. "We are the ring of steel around Lord Rahl himself, Wizard Zorander. Two thousand strong. We fall to a man before harm gets a glance at Lord Rahl."

Zedd nodded. "Commander General Trimack, a man in your position knows that one of the responsibilities of rank is to bear the burden of knowledge in silence and solitude."

"I do."

"Your knowledge that this creature is a screeling is one of those burdens. For the time being anyway."

Trimack let out a heavy breath and gave a nod. "I understand." He looked over to the people on the floor across the hall. "About the injured, Wizard Zorander?"

Zedd had respect for a soldier who held concern for wounded innocents. His disregard before had been duty, not callousness. His instinct had been to meet the attack.

Zedd started across the hall with Trimack at his side. "You know Darken Rahl is dead?"

"Yes. I was in the grand courtyard earlier today. I saw the new Lord Rahl before he flew away on the red dragon."

"And you will serve Richard as loyally as you have served in the past?"

"He is a Rahl, is he not?"

"He is a Rahl."

"And he has the gift?"

"He does."

Trimack nodded. "To the last man. Before harm gets a glance at him."

Zedd glanced over. "He will not be an easy man to serve under. He's headstrong."

"He is a Rahl. That says the same thing."

Zedd smiled in spite of himself. "He is also my grandson, although he doesn't know it yet. As a matter of fact, he doesn't even know he is a Rahl. Or the Lord Rahl. Richard might not take well to the position he finds himself in. But someday, he is going to need you. I would take it as a personal favor, Commander General Trimack, if you would give him a little understanding."

Trimack's eyes surveyed the area, ever ready for any new danger. "I would give him my life."

"I think understanding would serve him better in the beginning. He thinks of himself as nothing more than a woods guide. He is a leader by nature and by birth, but not by his own appraisal. He will not want anything to do with it, but it has come to him nonetheless."

At last a smile came to Trimack's face. "Done." He stopped and turned to the wizard. "I am a D'Haran soldier. I serve the Lord Rahl. But the Lord Rahl must also serve us. I am the steel against steel. He must be the magic against magic. Without the steel, he may still survive, but without the magic, we will not. Now tell me what a screeling is doing out of the underworld."

Zedd sighed and gave a nod. "Your former Lord Rahl was meddling with dangerous magic. Underworld magic. He tore the veil between this world and the underworld."

"Bloody fool. He's supposed to serve us, not take us into eternal night. Someone should have killed him."

"Someone did. Richard."

Trimack grunted. "Then Lord Rahl is already serving us."

"A few days ago, some would have viewed that thought as treason."

"It is a greater treason to deliver the living to the dead."

"Yesterday you would have killed Richard to keep him from harming Darken Rahl."

"And yesterday he would have killed me to get at his foe. But now we serve each other. Only a fool walks into the future backward."

Zedd nodded and offered a small, but warm, smile of respect, but then his eyes narrowed as he leaned closer. "If the veil is not closed, Commander, and the Keeper is loosed on the world, everyone will share the same fate. It won't be just D'Hara, but the whole of the world that is consumed. From what I have read of the prophecies, Richard may be the only one who can close the veil. You just remember that, if harm tries to get a glance at Richard."

Trimack's eyes were ice. "Steel against steel, that he may be the magic against magic."

"Good. You have it right."

Zedd surveyed the dead and dying as he approached. It was impossible to avoid walking through the blood. His heart ached at seeing the hurt. Only one screeling. What if more came?

"Commander, send for some healers. There are more here than I can tend to."

"Already done, Wizard Zorander."

Zedd nodded and began checking the living. Soldiers of the First File were spread out among the bodies, pulling the dead, many of whom were their own, out of the way, and comforting the hurt. Zedd put his fingers to the sides of foreheads to feel the injuries, to feel what a healer could care for and what required more.

He touched a young soldier laboring to breathe through a gurgle of blood. Zedd grunted at what he felt. He glanced down and saw rib bones pulled through a fist-sized hole in his breastplate. Zedd's stomach wanted to erupt. Trimack knelt on the other side of the young man. The wizard's eyes flicked up at the commander, and the other nodded his understanding. The young man's remaining breaths of life numbered in the few dozen.

"Go on," the commander said in a quiet voice, "I'll stay with the lad."

Zedd moved on as Trimack gripped the young man's hand in his own and began telling a reassuring lie. Three women in long brown skirts sewn with rows of pockets came up in a rush. Their mature faces took in the scene without flinching.

With bandages and poultices pulled from their big pockets, the three women descended on the wounded and began stitching and administering potions. Most wounds were within the skill of the women to heal, or else beyond the skill of the wizard. Zedd asked one of the three, the one who looked least likely to pay heed to protests, to go see to Chase. Zedd could see him sitting on the bench across the hall, his chin against his chest, Rachel sitting on the floor with her arms wrapped around his leg.

Zedd and the other two healers moved among the people on the floor, helping where they could, passing on where they couldn't. One of the healers called to him. She was hunched over a middle-aged woman who was trying to wave her away.

"Please," she was saying in a weak voice, "help the others. I am fine. I need only to rest. Please. Help the others."

Zedd felt the wetness of his blood-soaked robes against his knees as he knelt beside her. She pushed his hands away with one of hers. The other held her guts from spilling out of a ripping wound in her abdomen.

"Please. There are others who should be helped."

Zedd lifted an eyebrow to her ashen face. A fine gold chain through her hair held a blue stone against her forehead. The blue stone matched her eyes so, that it almost made her look to have three eyes. The wizard thought he recognized the stone, and wondered if it could be true, or only a bauble bought on a whim. He had not seen one wearing the Stone as a calling in a very long time. Surely one this young couldn't know what it proclaimed.

"I am wizard Zeddicus Zu'l Zorander. And who are you, child, to give me orders?"

Her face paled even more. "Forgive me, wizard. . . ."

She calmed as Zedd touched his fingers to her forehead. The pain caught his breath so sharply that he jerked his fingers away. He had to struggle to keep the tears of hurt from showing.

He knew without a doubt now: she wore the Stone in calling. The Stone, to match the color of her eyes, and worn over the forehead, as if the mind's eye, was a talisman to proclaim her inner vision.

A hand snatched at the back of his robes, tugging.

"Wizard!" came a sour voice from behind. "You will tend to me first!" Zedd turned to a face that matched the voice, and maybe outdid it a little. "I am Lady Ordith Condatith de Dackidvich, House of Burgalass. This wench is nothing but my body servant. Had she been as quick as she should have been, I wouldn't be suffering so! I could have been killed, as slow as she was! You will tend to me first! I could expire at any moment!"

Zedd could tell without touching her that her injuries were minor. "Forgive me, my lady." He made a show of putting his fingers to her head. As he thought: a hard bruise to her ribs, a few lesser to her legs, and a small gash on her arm, requiring at most a stitch or two.

"Well?" She clutched at the silver ruffles at her neck. "Wizards," she muttered. "Next to worthless if you want to know the truth of it. And these guards! I think they were asleep at their posts! Lord Rahl shall hear of this! Well? What of my injuries?"

"My lady, I'm not sure there is anything I can do for you."

"What!" She snatched the neck of his robe and gave it a snug yank. "You had better see that there is, or I will see that Lord Rahl has your head on a pike! See what good your lazy magic does you then!"

"Of course, my lady. I will endeavor to do my best."

He ripped the small gash in the dark maroon satin fabric of the sleeve, making it a huge, hanging flag, then put a hand back on the shoulder of the woman with the blue stone. She moaned as he blocked some of her pain and gave her strength. Her ragged breathing evened. He kept his hand on her, trickling in a little magic of reassurance and comfort.

Lady Ordith shrieked. "My dress! You've ruined it!"

"Sorry, my lady, but we can't risk the wound festering. I would rather lose the dress than the arm. Wouldn't you agree?"

"Well, yes, I guess. . . ."

"Ten or fifteen stitches should do it," he said to the sturdily built healer bent over between the two women on the floor. Her hard, blue-gray eyes glanced to the small wound and then back to the wizard.

"I am sure you would know best, Wizard Zorander," she said in an even voice, betraying only in her gaze to him that she understood his true intent.

"What! You are going to let this ox of a midwife do your work for you?"

"My lady, I'm an old man. I've never had any talent for sewing, and my hands shake something awful. I'm afraid I would do more damage than I would repair, but if you insist, I will try my best. . . ."

"No," she sniffed. "Let the ox do it."

"Very well." He looked up to the healer. No emotion touched her features, but splotches of red colored her cheeks. "I fear there is only one hope for her other injuries, considering the pain she is in. Do you have any wattle root in those big pockets of yours?"

She gave a little frown of puzzlement. "Yes, but . . ."

"Good," he cut her off. "I think two cubes should be sufficient."

Her eyebrow lifted. "Two?"

"Don't you try to be skimpy with me!" Lady Ordith screeched. "If there isn't enough to go around, then someone of lesser importance will just have to go short! You give me the full dose!"

"Very well." Zedd glanced up at the healer. "Administer her the full dose. Three cubes. Shredded, not whole."

The healers eyes opened a little wider, and she incredulously mouthed, *shredded*? Zedd squinted and nodded his insistence. The corners of her mouth curled up in a tightly controlled smile.

Wattle root would take away the pain of the minor injuries, but it needed only be swallowed whole. One small cube was all that was needed. Shredded, and that much of it, would set Lady Ordith's plumbing afire. The good lady was going to be spending the better part of the next week in her privy.

"What is your name, my dear?" he asked the healer.

"Kelley Hallick."

Zedd let out a tired sigh. "Kelley, are there any others that are beyond your considerable talents?"

"No, sir. Middea and Annalee are finishing with the last of them."

"Then will you please take Lady Ordith somewhere where she will not . . . where she will be more comfortable while you tend to her."

Kelley glanced down at the woman Zedd had a comforting hand to, to the rip across her abdomen, and back up to his eyes. "Of course, Wizard Zorander. You look to be very tired. If you would come to me later, I will fix you a stenadine tea." The small smile touched the corners of her mouth again.

Zedd couldn't keep a grin from his own face. Besides restoring alertness, stenadine tea was also used to give lovers stamina. By the glint in her eye, he judged her to be a fine brewer of stenadine tea.

He gave Kelley a wink. "Perhaps I will." Any other time he might have given it serious consideration—Kelley was a handsome woman—but right now that was just about the farthest thing from his mind.

"Lady Ordith, what is your body servant's name?"

"Jebra Bevinvier. And a worthless girl she is, too. Lazy and impudent."

"Well, you will not be burdened with her inadequate service any longer. She is going to need a long time to recover, and you are shortly going to be leaving the palace."

"Leaving? What do you mean leaving?" She put her nose in the air. "I have no intention of leaving."

"The palace is no longer safe for a lady of your importance. You will have to leave for your own protection. As you said yourself, the guards are asleep half the time. You will have to be on your way."

"Well, I simply have no intention of . . ."

"Kelley"—he gave her a firm look—"please help Lady Ordith to a place where you can tend to her."

Kelley was dragging the Lady Ordith off like a load of wash before she had a chance to cause any more trouble. Zedd turned a warm smile to Jebra and brushed some of her short, sandy hair back off her face. She held one arm across her grievous wound. Zedd had managed to halt most of the bleeding, but that wasn't going to save her; what was outside had to be put back in its place inside.

"Thank you, sir. I'm feeling much better now. If you could help me to my feet, I will be out of your way."

"Lie still, child," he said softly. "We must talk."

With a hard glance, he moved onlookers back. Soldiers of the First File had only to see that one brief look and they were already pushing people away.

Her lip trembled as her breast rose and fell more rapidly. She gave a little nod. Her eyes blinked. "I'm going to die, aren't I?"

"I won't lie to you, child. Your wound is at the limit of my talents were I well rested. You don't have the time for me to rest. If I don't do something, you will die. If I try, I might hasten the end."

"How long?"

"If I do nothing, maybe hours. Maybe the night. I could ease the pain enough to at least make the last of it tolerable."

She closed her eyes as tears seeped from the corners. "I never thought I cared to live."

"Because of the Seer's Stone you wear?"

Her eyes snapped open. "You know? You recognize the Stone? You know what I am?"

"I do. The time is long past when people knew a Seer by the Stone, but I am old. I have seen such before. That is why you didn't want me to help you? You fear what the touch might do to me?"

She nodded weakly. "But I find I suddenly care to live."

Zedd patted her shoulder. "That is what I wanted to know, child. Worry not about me. I am a wizard of the First Order, not some novice."

"First Order?" she whispered, wide-eyed. "I did not know one was left. Please, sir, do not risk yourself on the likes of me."

Zedd smiled. "Not much of a risk, only a little pain. And my name is Zedd."

She thought a moment; then her free hand clutched his arm. "Zedd . . . if I am to have a choice . . . I choose to try for life."

Zedd smiled a little and stroked her cold, sweaty forehead. "Then I promise to give you my most earnest effort." She nodded as she gripped his arm, gripped her only chance. "Is there anything you can do, Jebra, to hold aside the pain of the visions?"

She bit her lower lip and shook her head as tears sprang anew. "I'm sorry," she whispered, barely audible. "Perhaps you shouldn't . . ."

"Hush, child," he comforted.

Zedd took a deep breath and laid a hand over the arm that held her guts back. He put the palm of his other hand gently over her eyes. This was not something he could fix from the outside. It had to be repaired from within, with her own mind's aid. It could kill her. And him.

He braced himself and released the barrier in his mind. The impact of pain took

28

the wind from his lungs. He didn't dare to spare the energy to draw a breath. He gritted his teeth and fought it with muscles hardened to stone with the strain. And he hadn't even touched the pain of the wound yet. He had to deal with the pain of her visions, get past them, before he could cope with that problem.

Agony sucked his mind into a river of blackness. Specters of her visions swirled past. He could only guess at their meaning, but the pain of their reality was all too vivid. Tears flooded from his tightly closed eyes; his whole body shook as he struggled to fight through the torrent of anguish. He knew he couldn't allow himself to be pulled along with it, or he would be lost, consumed.

The emotions of her visions buffeted him as he was swept deeper into her mind. Dark thoughts just beyond the surface of perception clawed at his will, trying to drag him into the depths of hopeless abandon. His own painful memories washed to the surface of his consciousness to join with Jebra's lifetime of sorrow in a convergence of terrible agony and madness. Only his experience and resolve kept his sanity, his free will, from being pulled into the bottomless waters of bitterness and grief.

At last, he broke through to the calm, white light at the center of her being. Zedd reveled in the comparatively mild pain of her life-threatening wound. Reality could seldom match the imagination, and in the imagination, the pain was real.

All around the calm center, the cold darkness of eternal night encroached on the waning warmth and light of her life, impatient to shroud forever Jebra's spirit. Zedd pulled back that shroud, to let the light of his gift warm her spirit with life and vitality. The shadows receded before the power of his Additive Magic.

The strength of that magic, its exigency for the well-being of life, drew the exposed organs back to where the Creator intended them. Zedd didn't yet dare to spare anything to block her suffering. Jebra's back arched. She wailed in pain. He, too, felt her pain. His own abdomen flamed with the same agony she felt. He shook with the searing sharpness of it.

When the hardest, that which was beyond his comprehension, was finished, he at last spared a portion of the magic to block her pain. Jebra sagged against the floor with a moan of relief. He felt the relief in his own body.

Directing the flow of magic, Zedd finished the healing. He used his power to pull her wound together, letting tissue knit to tissue, flesh to flesh, layer upon layer, up to the surface of skin, joining as if it had never been parted.

Finished at last, Zedd had only to escape her mind. That was as dangerous as entering, and his strength was nearly gone; he had given it over to her. Rather than wasting any more time worrying about it, he released himself into the flow of agony.

Nearly an hour after he had begun, he found himself on his knees, hunched over, weeping uncontrollably. Jebra was sitting up, with her arms around him, holding his head to her shoulder. As soon as he was aware that he was back, he managed to bring himself under control and straighten. He glanced around the hall. Everyone had been pushed back a goodly distance, beyond earshot. None had any interest in being near a wizard when he was wielding magic that left people screaming as Jebra had done.

"There," he said, at last, with a modicum of restored dignity, "that wasn't so bad. I believe all is well now."

Jebra laughed a quiet, shaky laugh and hugged him tight. "I was taught a wizard couldn't heal a Seer."

Zedd managed to get a bony finger in the air. "No ordinary wizard can, my dear. But I am Zeddicus Zu'l Zorander, wizard of the First Order."

Jebra wiped a tear from her cheek. "I have nothing of value to repay you with, except this." She unhooked the gold chain that ran through her hair and brought it down, putting it in his hand. "Please, accept this humble offering."

Zedd looked down at the chain with the blue stone. "That is very kind of you, Jebra Bevinvier. I'm touched." Zedd felt a pang of guilt for having planted the impulse in her mind. "It's a fine chain, and I will accept it in humble gratitude." He used a thread-thin stream of power to separate the stone from its mounting. He handed the Stone back; he only needed the chain. "But the chain is payment enough. Keep your Stone; it's yours by right."

She closed her fingers around the Stone with a nod and gave him a kiss on the cheek. He accepted the peck with a smile.

"And now, my dear, you will need to rest. I have used a good deal of your strength to put things right. Maybe a few days of bed rest, and you will be as good as new."

"I fear that you have not only left me healed, but also without employment. I must find work to feed myself." She looked down at the bloody, shredded rip in her green dress. "And to clothe myself."

"Why were you wearing the Stone, if you were the servant of the Lady Ordith?"

"Not many know what the Stone signifies. Lady Ordith didn't. Her husband, the duke, did. He wanted my services, but his wife would never have allowed a woman in his employ, so he had me placed as her servant.

"I know it is not the most honorable thing, for a Seer to place herself covertly, but there is much starvation in Burgalass. My family knew of my ability and closed their doors to me, afraid of the visions I might have of them. Before my grandmother passed on, she put her Stone in my hand, saying if I wore hers she would be honored."

Jebra pressed the fist with the Stone to her cheek. "Thank you," she whispered, "for not accepting it. For understanding."

Zedd felt a renewed pang of guilt. "And so this duke had you taken in and used you for his own purposes?"

"Yes. Maybe a dozen years ago. Because I was Lady Ordith's body servant, I was almost always present at any meeting or function. The duke would come to me later and I would tell him what I saw of his adversaries. With my help, he made more of his power and wealth.

"Virtually no one anymore knows of the Stone of a Seer. He disdained people who ignored the old knowledge. He mocked his opponents' ignorance by having me wear the Stone openly.

"He also had me keep an eye to the Lady Ordith. It prevented her from succeeding at making herself a widow. So she now contents herself with being absent from the duke's house whenever she can. She will not be displeased to be rid of me; the duke used his strings of power to keep me employed when the Lady Ordith would have wished it otherwise."

"Why would she be displeased with your service?" He grinned. "Are you lazy and rude, as she claims?"

Jebra smiled back, the fine wrinkles at the corners of her eyes deepening. "No. It's the visions. Sometimes when I have them, well, you felt some of the hurt when

30

you healed me, though it is not as bad as that for me, I think. But sometimes the hurt keeps me from her service for a time."

Zedd rubbed his chin. "Well, since you are out of employment, you will be a guest here at the People's Palace until you are recovered. I have some little influence around here." He marveled at the sudden truth of that, and pulled a purse from a pocket in his robes. He gave it a jingle. "For your expenses, and wage, if I could convince you to take up a new employer."

She hefted the purse in her palm, testing its weight. "If this be copper, it is insufficient for any but you." She smiled and leaned a little closer, her eyes merry and scolding at the same time. "And if it be silver, it is too much."

Zedd gave her a grave expression. "It's gold." Startled, she blinked. "But it is not me, mainly, you will be working for."

She stared at the purse of gold in her hand, then looked back at him. "Who then?"

"Richard. The new Lord Rahl."

Jebra paled and shook her head vigorously, her shoulders hunching up. She shoved the purse back in Zedd's hands. "No." Even paler, she shook her head again. "No. I'm sorry. I don't want to work for him. No."

Zedd frowned. "He is not an evil person. He's quite kindhearted, in fact."

"I know that."

"You know who he is?"

She looked down at her lap and nodded. "I know. I saw him yesterday. The first day of winter."

"And you had a vision when you saw him?"

Her voice was weak and filled with fear. "Yes."

"Jebra, tell me what you saw. Every bit of it. Please? It's important."

She looked up at him from under her eyebrows for a long moment, then back down at her lap as she chewed her lower lip.

"It was at the morning devotion, yesterday. When the bell rang, I went to a square, and he was standing there, looking into the pool. I noticed him because he was wearing the sword of the Seeker. And because he was tall and handsome. And he wasn't kneeling as the others were. He stood there, watching the people gathering, and as I approached, his eyes passed across my sight. Just for an instant. The power coming from him took my breath away.

"A Seer can sense certain kinds of power, like the gift, emanating from a person." She looked up at Zedd. "I have seen those with the gift before. I have seen their auras. They have all been like yours; there is a warmth to them, a gentleness. Your aura is beautiful. His was different. It had that, but more, too."

"Violence," Zedd said in a soft voice. "He is the Seeker."

She nodded. "It could be. I don't know; I've never seen the like of it before. But I can tell you what it felt like. It felt like having my face pushed into a basin of icy water before I had a chance to get a breath.

"Sometimes I never get a vision from a person. Sometimes I do. I can never tell when it's going to come. Sometimes when a person is in distress, they throw off auras and visions more strongly. He was throwing off auras like lightning in a thunderstorm. He was in great emotional pain. Like an animal in a trap trying to chew its own leg off. He felt the horror of having to betray his friends to save them. I didn't understand that. It didn't make any sense.

"There was an image of a woman, a beautiful woman with long hair. Maybe a

31

Confessor, although I don't know how that could be. The aura flamed so strongly with anguish for her that I felt my face, fearing I would find the skin burned. If I hadn't been at devotion, I would have fallen to my knees anyway from the agony of the auras.

"I almost rushed to him, to comfort him, when two Mord-Sith approached, and noticed him standing, and not kneeling. He felt no fear, but he went to his knees anyway, out of resignation to the terrible betrayal he had been forced into. I was relieved when he knelt; I thought that would be the end of it. I was thankful I had seen only auras, for the most part, and not true visions. I didn't want to see any visions from that man." She stared off, seemingly lost in the memory of it.

"But that wasn't the end of it?"

Her eyes came back to where she was. "No. I thought the worst of it was over, but what I had seen didn't touch what was to come."

Jebra dry-washed her hands for a moment. "We were saying the chant to Father Rahl, and all of a sudden he sprang up. He had a smile on his face. He had solved the puzzle that trapped him. The last piece had snapped into place. The woman's face and his love for her filled the aura."

She shook her head. "I pity the person who ever puts a finger between those two. They will lose the finger, maybe the hand, and maybe the whole arm before they have the time to think to pull it back."

"Her name is Kahlan," Zedd said with a little smile. "And then what happened?"

Jebra crossed her arms across her abdomen. "Then the visions started. I saw him killing a man, but I couldn't tell how. Not with blood, but killing him just the same. And then I saw the man he was going to kill: Darken Rahl. And then I saw that it was his father, but he didn't know it. That was when I knew who he was: the son of Darken Rahl, the soon to be new Master Rahl. The aura was flashing in terrible conflicts. Commoner to king."

Zedd put a comforting hand to her shoulder. "Darken Rahl wanted to rule the world with a frightful magic. By stopping him, Richard saved a great many from torture or death. Even though killing is terrible, by doing so he has saved the lives of many more. Surely you would not be frightened of Richard because of that."

She shook her head. "No. It was by what came next. The two Mord-Sith stood, because he was going to leave a devotion. One raised her Agiel, threatening him. I was surprised to see he wore one at his neck, red, just like theirs. He held it out in his fist. He told them that if they didn't let him pass, he would kill them. The aura of violence around him took my breath away. He wanted them to try. They sensed it and let him pass.

"As he turned to leave . . . that was when I saw the other visions." She put a hand to her heart as tears ran down her cheeks. "Zedd . . . my visions are not always clear. Sometimes, I don't know what they mean. Once I saw a farmer's vision. Birds were pecking at the stomachs of him and his family. I didn't know what it meant. It turned out that a flock of blackbirds came and ate the seed he had just planted. He was able to replant, and guard the field. But he and his family could have starved if he hadn't."

She wiped her fingers at the tears on her cheeks. "Sometimes I can't tell what the visions mean, or if they will turn out to be true; not all of that kind do." She fussed with her hair. "But sometimes they come to pass exactly as I see them. I can tell when they are true, and will happen without a doubt."

Zedd patted her shoulder. "I understand, Jebra. Visions are a form of prophecy, and I know how confusing prophecy can be. What kind of vision did you see from Richard? The confusing kind, or the ones that are clear?"

She shared a deep gaze with his eyes. "I saw every kind. I saw every kind of vision I have ever had, from the confusing to clear; from the possible to the certain. They came in a rush. They have never done that before. Mostly I only have a single vision, and I either know what it means and that it is true, or I don't understand it and can't tell if it will come to pass. The visions from this man came in a torrent. They rushed past like wind-driven rain. But every one was pain and hurt and danger.

"The ones that stood out the hardest, and I knew to be true, were the worst. One was of something around his neck. I couldn't tell what, but it was something that will cause him great pain, and take him from the woman . . . Kahlan, you said her name was . . . take him from everyone he loves. Lock him away."

"Richard was captured by a Mord-Sith, and tortured by her. Perhaps that is what you saw," Zedd offered.

Jebra shook her head vehemently. "It wasn't what was; it was what will be. And not the pain of a Mord-Sith. Different. I am sure of it."

Zedd nodded in thought. "What else?"

"I saw him in an hourglass. He was on his knees in the bottom half, crying in anguish, the sand falling all around him, but not a grain touching him. The gravestones of all those he loved were in the top half, where he couldn't reach them against the fall of the sand.

"I saw a knife at his heart, a killing knife, held in his own shaking hands. Before I could see what would happen, another vision came—they are not always in order of events. He was in his fine red coat, the one with gold buttons and brocade trim. He was facedown . . . a knife in his back. He was dead, but at the same time, he wasn't. His own hands reached down to roll him over, but before I saw his dead face, another vision came.

"It was the worst. The strongest." The tears welled up again, and she began to sob softly. Zedd squeezed her shoulder to encourage her to go on. "I saw his flesh burning." She wiped at the tears and rocked back and forth a little as she cried. "He was screaming. I could even smell the burning skin. Then, whatever was burning him—I couldn't tell what it was—when it pulled back, he was unconscious, and there was a mark upon him. A mark burned into him."

Zedd worked his tongue in his mouth, trying to wet it. "Could you see what the mark was?"

"No, not what it looked like. But I knew what it was as surely as I know the sun when I see it. It was the mark of the dead, a mark of the Keeper of the underworld. The Keeper had marked him to be his own."

Zedd worked to steady his breathing, his trembling hands. "Were there more visions?"

"Yes, but not as strong and I didn't understand them. They rushed by so fast I couldn't grasp their form, only their pain. Then he was gone.

"While the Mord-Sith were turned, watching him go, I ran back to my room and locked myself in. I lay on the bed for hours, crying uncontrollably with the hurt of what I had seen. The Lady Ordith banged at my door, wanting me, but I called to her that I was sick and she finally went away in a huff. I cried until my insides were jelly. I saw virtue in that man, and I wept in fear of the evil I saw snatching for him.

"Though the visions were all different, they were the same. They all had the same feel: danger. Danger presses in around that man as tightly as water presses around a fish." She regained some of her composure as Zedd sat silently watching her. "That is why I will not work for him. The good spirits protect me, I don't want anything to do with the danger around that man. With the underworld."

"Maybe you could help him, with your talent, help him to avoid the danger. That is what I was hoping anyway," Zedd said in a quiet voice.

Jebra dabbed her cheeks dry with the back of her sleeve. "Not for all the duke's gold and power would I want to be in Lord Rahl's wake. I am no coward, but I am no heroine in a song, and no fool either. I did not wish my guts put back to have them ripped out again, and this time my soul with them."

Zedd quietly watched her sniffling herself back under control, putting the frightening visions away. She took a deep breath and sighed. Her blue eyes finally looked to his.

"Richard is my grandson," he said simply.

Her eyes winced shut. "Oh, good spirits forgive me." Her hand covered her mouth for a long moment; then her eyes came open, her eyebrows wrinkled together in horror. "Zedd . . . I'm so sorry for telling you what I saw. Forgive me. Had I known, I never would have told you." Her hands trembled. "Forgive me. Oh please, forgive me."

"The truth is the truth. I am not one who would shut a door in your face for seeing it. Jebra, I am a wizard; I already know of the danger he is in. That is why I asked you to help. The veil to the underworld is torn. That thing that ripped you open escaped into the world of the living through the tear. If the veil tears enough, the Keeper will escape. Richard has done things that the prophecies say mark him as maybe the only one able to close the tear."

He lifted the purse of gold and slowly settled it in her lap, her eyes following it down. He withdrew his empty hand. Her gaze stayed on the purse as if it were a beast that might bite.

"Would it be very dangerous?" she asked at last in a weak voice.

Zedd smiled when her eyes came up. "No more dangerous than going for an afternoon stroll in a fortress palace."

With a reflex jerk, her hand clutched her abdomen where the wound had been. Her eyes rose to look off down the wide, resplendent halls, as if seeking escape, or maybe fearing an attack. Without looking to him she spoke.

"My grandmother was a Seer, and my only guide. She told me once that the visions would bring me a lifetime of hurt, and there was nothing I would ever be able to do to stop them. She said that if ever I was presented with the opportunity to use the visions for good, to take the chance, and it would make up for some of the burden. That was the day she put her Stone in my hand."

Jebra lifted the purse and set it back in Zedd's lap. "I will not do it for all the gold in D'Hara. But I will do it for you."

Zedd smiled and patted her cheek. "Thank you, child." He put the gold back in her lap, the coins making a muffled clink. "You will be needing this. You will have expenses. What is left is yours. That is the way I wish it."

She nodded resignedly. "What must I do?"

"Well, first we must both get a good night's sleep. You will need to rest for a few days to regain your strength. And then you have some traveling to do, Lady Bevinvier." He smiled at the way one of her eyebrows lifted. "We are both very tired right now. Tomorrow after I have rested, I must be off on important business.

Before I leave, I will come to you and we will talk more of this. But starting right now, I would ask you not to wear the Stone where it can be seen. No good can come of declaring your talent to eyes in the shadows."

"So my new employer shall use me covertly too? Not the most honorable of things."

"The ones who would recognize you now are not vying for gold. They serve the Keeper. They want much more than gold. If they discover you, you will wish I had not saved you today."

She winced before finally nodding.

Zedd stood with the aid of a hand to his knee. He helped Jebra up. As he expected, she was unable to stand without leaning heavily on him. She apologized for the burden. He made her smile by telling her he would use any excuse to have his arm around the waist of a pretty maiden.

People were starting to go back to their business, engaged in hushed conversation as their eyes darted about the suddenly not so safe palace. Those hurt had been helped away, and the dead carried off. Maidservants in heavy skirts worked tearfully at the task of cleaning up the blood, sloshing mops in buckets of reddening water. Soldiers of the First File were spread out everywhere. Zedd motioned to Commander Trimack across the hall.

"Anyway, I shall be glad to be away from this place," Jebra said. "I have seen auras here that make me sweat in my sleep."

As the officer started toward them, Zedd asked, "Do you see anything of this man coming toward us?"

She studied him a moment as he strode toward them, checking the placement of his men. "A faint aura. Duty." She frowned as she stared. "It has always been a burden for him. He is daring to hope that maybe he will now find pride in it. Does that help you any?"

Zedd smiled a little. "Yes it does. Any visions?"

"No. Just the faint aura."

The wizard nodded in thought, then brightened. "By the way, why has a woman as lovely as you not found herself a husband?"

She gave him a sidelong glance. "Three have asked. As each was on bended knee before me, I saw a vision of them lying with another woman."

Zedd grinned. "Did they ask why you said no?"

"I didn't say no. I only slapped them so hard it made their heads ring like a bell."

Zedd laughed until she was caught up in it.

Trimack came at last to a halt before them. "Commander General Trimack, may I introduce the Lady Bevinvier." Trimack gave a smart bow. "As are you, as am I, this lady is one who is at the task of keeping harm from getting a glance at Lord Rahl. I would like her to have a heavy guard at all times while she is in the palace. Lord Rahl needs her help, and I don't want her life risked again as it was today."

"While she is in the palace she will be as safe as a babe in her mother's arms. By my honor." He turned and gave a coded tap to his shoulder. A good two dozen men of the First File came at a dead run, freezing to a halt at attention, not even breathing hard. "This is the Lady Bevinvier. Every one of your lives before hers."

With a sharp snap, every fist came to an armored heart as one. Two of them took Jebra's weight from Zedd. She kept one hand tightly closed around the Stone. The purse of gold bulged in a pocket of her long, green skirt. It was covered most of the way down with dried blood.

Zedd addressed the men holding her up. "She will need suitable quarters, and meals brought in. Please see to it she is not disturbed by anyone but me." He looked at her tired blue eyes and gently touched her arm. "Rest well, child. I will visit you in the morning."

She smiled weakly. "Thank you, Zedd."

As the soldiers helped her away, the wizard turned his attention to Trimack. "There is a woman staying in the palace, a Lady Ordith Condatith de Dackidvich. Lord Rahl is going to have enough trouble without her kind around. I want her out of here before the day is finished. If she refuses to leave, offer her the choice of a carriage or a noose."

Trimack grinned wickedly. "I will see to it personally."

"If there are any others you know of about the palace, who are of her temperament, feel free to make them the same offer. New rule brings change." Zedd couldn't see auras, but he was sure that if Jebra had been standing there, she would have seen Trimack's brighten.

"Some are uncomfortable with change, Wizard Zorander."

The man had spoken more than his simple words. "Are there any above you in command in the palace? Other than Lord Rahl?"

Trimack clasped his hands behind his back as his eyes swept the hall. "There is one named Demmin Nass, commander of the quads, who gave orders to all but Darken Rahl."

Zedd let out a heavy breath at that memory. "He is dead."

Trimack nodded with what might have been relief. "Below the palace, quartered in the chambers of the plateau, there are perhaps thirty thousand men of the army. Their generals outrank me in the field, but in the palace the word of the commander general of the First File is law. Some of them I know will welcome the change. Some will not."

"Richard is going to have a difficult enough time being the magic against magic— underworld magic—without troubles from steel. You have a free hand, Commander, to do as you see fit to protect him. Err on the side of duty."

Trimack grunted acknowledgment, then went on. "The People's Palace, one roof though it may be, is a city. Thousands live here. Merchants and supplies, trains of wagons to lone peddlers, come and go in an endless stream in all directions except to the east, across the Azrith Plains. The roads in are the arteries that feed the heart of D'Hara—the People's Palace.

"The inside of the plateau is chambered with twice the number of rooms of the palace above ground. As with any city of this size, the motives of the multitudes coming here are beyond our ability to judge with absolute certainty.

"I will have the great inner doors closed and seal off the palace above ground. It is something that has not been done in a few hundred years, and it will cause worry among the people of D'Hara, but I would risk the worried talk. The only way to the palace itself, if not through the inside entrances, is up the cliff road on the east side. I will keep the bridge up.

"That still leaves us with thousands in the palace proper. Any of them could have designs not to our liking. Worse, there are thousands of battle-tested soldiers in the belly of the palace, many led by men I would not want getting a glance at Lord Rahl. I have a feeling the new Lord Rahl is not the kind of Rahl they are used to dealing with, and they are not going to like the change.

"D'Hara is a vast empire, the supply routes long. Perhaps it is time some of these divisions were sent out to see to the safety of these routes, especially the ones to the far south, near the wilds, where I have heard rumor there is unrest and trouble. And perhaps from the ranks of the ones I trust, the size of the First File could be increased threefold."

Zedd studied Trimack's face as the man continued to scan the hall. "I am no soldier, but your ideas make sense. The palace must be made as secure as possible. How you do it is up to you."

"I will give you a list then, in the morning, of the generals to be trusted and those to worry about."

"Why would I need such a list?"

Trimack's intense gaze was steady. "Because orders such as these must come from one with the gift."

Zedd shook his head, muttering, "Wizards should not be ruling people. It's not right."

"It is the way in D'Hara. Magic and steel. I want to protect Lord Rahl. This is what I think needs to be done."

Zedd stared off into the distance, feeling the ache of exhaustion in his bones. "Do you know, Trimack, that I have fought and killed wizards who wanted to take it upon themselves to rule?"

When an answer didn't come, Zedd turned back to the officer. Trimack was studying him. "Given the choice, Wizard Zorander, I would choose to serve one who bears command as a burden, to one who wears the mantle as a right."

Zedd sighed and nodded. "In the morning then. There is one other matter, the most important of all: I want the Garden of Life guarded. That is where the screeling first attacked. I don't know if there will be more. There is a door up there that will have to be fixed. Put a ring of steel around the garden. Enough men that they have room only to swing an axe. No one, no one at all, is to be allowed to go in except myself or Richard, or by our order.

"Anyone attempting to go into that room is to be viewed as harm trying to get a look at Lord Rahl. Even one who tells you he is there only to pull weeds. And you can bet your mother's honor that anything trying to get out is harm trying to have more than a look."

Trimack clapped his fist to his armored chest. "To the last man, Wizard Zorander."

"Good. Lord Rahl may need what's in that room. I don't dare to move those things for the time being. They are extremely dangerous. Take very seriously the guarding of that room, Commander. More screelings could come. Or worse."

"How soon?"

"I would not have thought we would have seen the first for a year or more. At least months. That the Keeper could have loosed one of his assassins so soon is a great worry. I don't know who it was sent for. It's possible it was simply sent to kill whoever was around. The Keeper needs no reason to kill. I must leave the palace tomorrow to learn what I can before we are surprised again."

Trimack pondered this with troubled eyes. "Do you know when Lord Rahl will return?"

Zedd shook his head. "No. I thought I was going to have time to teach him some of what he must know, but now I must send for him at once to meet me in Aydindril and see if we can discover what must be done. He is in great danger and knows nothing of it. Events have outpaced me. I have no idea what the Keeper is going to do next, but I now fear how deep his tendrils may be. That they were around Darken Rahl even before the veil was torn means I have already been an ignorant fool in this business.

"If Richard should happen to return unexpectedly, or if anything happens to me . . . help him. He sees himself as a woods guide, not the Lord Rahl. He will be distrustful. Tell him I said to trust you."

"If he is distrustful, how shall I convince him to trust me?"

Zedd smiled. "Tell him I said it is the truth. The toasted toads' truth."

Trimack's eyes widened with incredulity. "You wish the Commander General of the First File to say such a childish thing to the Lord Rahl?"

Zedd straightened his face and cleared his throat. "It's a code, Commander. He will understand it."

Trimack nodded, but looked skeptical. "I had better see to the Garden of Life, and the rest of it. No disrespect intended, but you look like you could use some rest." He tilted his head toward where the army of maidservants were still cleaning blood off the marble floor. "All the healing you did looks to have tired you."

"It did. Thank you, Commander Trimack. I will take your advice."

Trimack's fist snapped to his heart, the salute softened by the hint of a smile. He began to turn, but hesitated. His intense blue eyes looked back to the wizard.

"May I say, Wizard Zorander, that it's a pleasure to at last have one with the gift in the palace who is more concerned with putting people's guts back inside, than with spilling them out. I've never seen the like of it."

Zedd didn't smile. His voice was quiet. "I am sorry, Commander, that I could do nothing for that lad."

Trimack gave a sorrowful nod. "I know that to be the truth, Wizard Zorander. The toasted toads' truth."

Zedd watched the commander stride across the hall, drawing armored men to him like a huge magnet. The wizard brought his hand up, staring at the gold chain looped over his sticklike fingers. He gave a pained sigh. Wizard business—using people. And now for the worst of it. He brought the black, tear-shaped stone from a pocket deep in his robes. The spirits be cursed, he thought, for the things a wizard must do.

He held the mounting where the blue Stone had been, and pressed the point of the smooth, black stone to it. Elemental power flowed from the fingers of each hand, joining in the middle, welding the stone to the mount.

Hoping he was wrong, Zedd brought forth a painful memory of his long-dead wife. With the way Jebra's mind had shredded his barriers, it wasn't difficult. When a tear ran over his cheek, he wet his thumb in it, and shut the memory away with the greatest of effort. He smiled a little at the irony that wizards had to use even themselves, and that the horrible memory at least brought with it one with a little pleasure to balance it.

Holding the black stone in the palm of one hand, he buffed its surface with the tear-dampened thumb. The stone turned a clear amber as he rubbed it with his thumb. His heart sank a little. There was no doubt now as to what it was.

Resigned to what must be done, Zedd wove a wizard's web around the stone. The spell would work to hide the true nature of the stone from everyone, except Richard. More important, the web would draw Richard's attention to the stone. If he ever saw it, the attraction would be planted firmly in his mind.

He glanced over at Chase, who was stretched out on his back on a marble bench across the hall. One foot was planted on the floor, and Rachel was sitting on the ground, an arm wrapped around his calf, her head against his knee. His other foot was on the bench. A bandaged forearm rested across his forehead.

Zedd sighed and started across the polished marble floor. He wondered for a moment what the boundary warden was supposed to guard, now that the boundary was gone. He stopped, standing over the two.

Without removing his forearm from his eyes, Chase spoke. "Zedd, my old friend, if you ever again have some ruthless, strong-armed witch of a healer pour a concoction that tastes that spirits-be-cursed foul down my gullet, I'll twist your head around so you have to walk backward to see where you're going."

Zedd grinned. Now he knew he had picked the right woman for the job.

"Did the medicine taste really awful, Chase?" Rachel asked.

He lifted his arm a little, letting it hover over his eyes as he looked down at her. "If you call me Chase again, you may find out."

"Yes, Father." She grinned. "I'm sorry she made you drink that awful medicine." Her face turned to a pout. "But it scares me something fierce to see blood on you." He grunted.

She peered at him. "Maybe the next time, if you take your sword out when I tell you to, you wouldn't get blood on you and have to drink awful medicine."

Zedd marveled at the childlike innocence of the perfectly delivered, stinging rebuke. Chase held his head up a little off the bench, with his arm frozen in the air several inches above his eyes, as he glowered at the little girl. Zedd had never seen a man struggle so mightily to keep from laughing. Rachel's nose wrinkled up and she giggled at the strained face he was making.

"May the good spirits be mercifully kind to your future husband," Chase said, "and at least grant him a few years' peace until you lay your eyes on the poor, doomed fool."

She frowned. "What does that mean?"

Chase swung his leg down and sat up. He scooped her up and plopped her down on his knee. "I'll tell you what it means. It means that there's a new rule. And this one you better not break."

"No, Father, I won't. What is it?"

"From now on," he said with a scowl, his face close to hers, "if you need to tell me something important, and I don't listen to you, you are to kick me. Hard as you can. And you just go on kicking me until I listen. Got it?"

She smiled. "Yes, Father."

"I'm not joking. I mean it."

She nodded earnestly. "I promise, Chase."

The big man rolled his eyes and swept her to his chest with one arm, holding her to him the way she held her doll to herself. Zedd swallowed back the lump in his throat. At that moment, he didn't like himself very much, and he liked the alternatives a lot less.

The wizard fell to one knee before her. The dried blood made his robes stiff at his knees. "Rachel. I must ask you to do something for me."

She nodded. "What is it, Zedd?"

He brought his arm up, the gold chain hanging from his fingers. The stone swung back and forth under his hand. "This belongs to someone else. Would you wear it for now? Keep it safe? Someday Richard may come and get it from you, to take it where it belongs, but I don't know when that will be."

Chase's fierce, hawkish eyes looked like what Zedd imagined a mouse must see an instant before the end.

"It's very pretty, Zedd. I never wore such a pretty thing."

"It's also very important. As important as the box that Wizard Giller gave you to look after."

"But Darken Rahl is dead. You said so. He can't hurt us anymore."

"I know, child, but this is still important. You did such a good and brave job with the box that I think you would be the best one to wear this necklace until the one it belongs to comes for it. You must wear it always until then. Don't let anyone else even try it on for play. This is not something to play with."

Her expression turned serious at the mention of the box. "I'll take good care of it, Zedd, if you say it's important."

"Zedd," Chase hissed as he pulled Rachel's head to himself, cupping his hand over her ear so she couldn't hear, "what do you think you're doing? Is that what I think it is?"

Zedd gave him a forbidding look. "I'm trying to keep all the children of the world from having very bad nightmares. For eternity."

Chase gritted his teeth. "Zedd, I don't want . . ."

Zedd cut him off. "Chase, how long have you known me?" Chase didn't answer. He only glared. "In all the time you've known me, have you ever known me to bring harm to another, especially a child? Have you ever known me to put another at risk for anything foolish?"

"No," Chase said in a voice like grating stone. "And I don't want to see you start now."

Zedd kept his own voice firm. "You will have to trust that I know what I'm doing." His eyes flicked to where the screeling had killed the people. "What has happened today doesn't even begin to touch what is about to happen. If the veil isn't closed, the suffering and death will be beyond your comprehension. I'm doing what I must, as a wizard. As a wizard, I recognize this little one, just as Giller recognized her. She is a ripple in the pond. She is destined to do important things.

"When we were in the tomb of Panis Rahl, earlier, checking to see that they were walling it in properly, I studied some of the runes on the walls. They weren't all melted yet. They were in High D'Haran, and I don't understand much of it, but I understood enough. They were instructions on going to the underworld. You know that stone table in the Garden of Life? It's a sacrificial altar. Darken Rahl used it to go to the underworld, to travel under the boundaries."

"But he's dead. What does . . ."

"He killed children, and offered their unsoiled souls as a gift to the Keeper of the underworld to gain himself passage. Do you understand what I'm saying? He made pacts with the Keeper.

"That means the Keeper has been using people in this world. Where he has used

41

one, he has surely used more. And now the veil is torn. That a screeling was here proves it beyond question.

"Many of the oldest prophecies, I believe, are about what's beginning to happen now, and about Richard. Whoever wrote them was intending to send him help across time. I believe they are meant to aid him in the fight against the Keeper. But much has happened in the last few thousand years to muddy those words. I fear that it is the Keeper's patient work that has obfuscated the meaning of the prophecies.

"He has no more important skill than patience. He has an eternity of it. He has probably been sending careful tendrils into this world to influence people, wizards, like Darken Rahl, to do his bidding. The fact that we need the prophecies so much right now, and that there are no wizards left who understand them, can't be coincidence. I have no idea where the Keeper's eyes lurk, or what he intends next."

Chase's eyes still had fire in them, but it was different from the kind they held before. "Tell me how to help. What would you like me to do?"

Zedd smiled sadly and patted the big man's shoulder. "I would like you to teach this child to be like you. I know she is smart. Bring it out in her. Make her your student. Teach her how to use every weapon you know. Teach her to be strong, and quick."

Chase sighed and gave a nod. "Such a little warrior."

"In the morning, I must leave to get Adie and take her to Aydindril. I would like you to go to the Mud People. Ride hard, fast as you can go. Richard and Kahlan and Siddin will be with the dragon tonight, and tomorrow she will take them there. It will take you weeks to reach him. We can't afford to waste any time.

"Tell Richard and Kahlan to come to me in Aydindril at once. Tell them of the danger as I have told you. Then maybe you should take this child to safety. If there is any such thing."

"Isn't there anything else I can do?"

"The most important thing is to get to Richard. I've been a fool for thinking we would have time. I never should have let him out of my sight." Zedd rubbed his chin a moment in thought. "Maybe you could tell him I am his grandfather, and that Darken Rahl was his father. Maybe that will give his anger time to cool before he reaches me."

Zedd lifted an eyebrow and smiled. "Do you know what the Mud People call him? They call him 'Richard With The Temper.' Imagine that. Richard of all people. He is one of the gentlest people I've ever known. But I fear the Sword of Truth has brought out his other side."

Chase flashed a rare, reassuring look. "He won't be angry to learn you are his grandfather. He loves you."

Zedd sighed. "Maybe so, but I don't think he will be pleased to know who his father really is. And that I hid that knowledge from him. George Cypher raised him and they loved each other deeply."

"That's the truth, and this doesn't change it."

Zedd nodded. He held the necklace up. "Will you trust me?"

Chase appraised the wizard for a moment, then sat Rachel up straight on his knee. "Let me latch the clasp for you."

After Chase hooked it around her neck, Rachel picked up the amber stone in her small hands, bending her face down to see it. "I'll take good care of it for you, Zedd."

The wizard ruffled her hair. "I'm sure you will." He put a finger to each side of her forehead, letting the magic flow into her, and gave her the thought of how important the necklace was, that she was not to talk to people about it or where she got it, and that she must protect it as she had the box of Orden.

He removed his fingers, and she opened her eyes and smiled. Chase picked her up with a hand on each side of her waist and set her down to stand on the bench next to him. He searched through the arsenal of knives at his waist and found the strap for the smallest. He untied the leather thong and pulled the sheathed blade free. He held it up in front of her face.

"Since you are my daughter now, you will wear a knife, just like me. But I don't want you taking it out until I teach you about it. You could cut yourself badly. I will teach you how to use it in a safe manner. I'm going to teach you how to protect yourself so you will be safe. All right?"

Rachel beamed. "You'll teach me to be like you? I would like that ever so much, Chase."

Chase grunted as he tied the leather strap at her waist. "I don't know how good I'll be at teaching you. Seems I can't even teach you to call me Father."

She smiled shyly. "Chase and Father mean the same thing to me."

Chase shook his head, a resigned grin on his face. Zedd came to his feet and straightened his robes. "Chase, If you need anything, Commander General Trimack will see to it. Take as many men as you would like."

"I wouldn't like any. I'm in a hurry, I don't need the extra baggage to tend, and besides, I think a man and his daughter would draw less attention. Isn't that the whole idea?" He glanced pointedly at the stone around Rachel's neck.

Zedd smiled, appreciating the boundary warden's sharp mind. Those two were going to make quite a pair. "I will travel with you, until I reach the route toward Adie. I must do some things in the morning, and then we can be on our way."

"Good. You look like you could use some rest before we start out."

"I think you're right."

Zedd suddenly realized why he was so tired. He had thought it was because he hadn't slept in days, but that wasn't it. It was because they had struggled for months to stop Darken Rahl, and just when he thought it was over, that they had finally won, he now knew it had only begun. And this wasn't just a dangerous wizard they were fighting; it was the Keeper of the underworld.

With Darken Rahl he had known most of the rules, how the boxes of Orden worked, how much time they'd had. He knew next to nothing now. The Keeper could win in the next five minutes. Zedd felt hopelessly ignorant. He sighed inwardly. He guessed he knew some things; he would just have to build on that knowledge.

"By the way," Chase said as he straightened the knife at Rachel's waist, "one of the other healers—Kelley, she said her name was—she gave me a message for you." He leaned back and fished around in his pocket with two big fingers, bringing out a small piece of paper. He handed it to the wizard.

"What's this?" The paper said *West Rim, North Highland Way, Third Tier.*

Chase pointed at the paper as Zedd held it out, reading it. "She said that is where you could find her. She said to tell you that she thought you needed rest, and that if you would come to her, she would make you a stenadine tea, and that she would brew it weak so you would sleep well. Does that make any sense to you?"

Zedd smiled just a little to himself as he crumpled the note in his fist. "A bit." He tapped his lower lip in thought. "Get yourself some rest. If you think the pain of the wounds will keep you from sleeping, I could have one of the healers brew you up some . . ."

Chase held a hand up. "No! I'll sleep fine."

"Very well." He patted Rachel's arm and Chase's shoulder and started off. A thought came to him and he turned back. "Have you ever seen Richard wearing a red coat? A red coat with gold buttons and brocade?"

Chase gave a snort of a laugh. "Richard? Zedd, you half raised him. You should know better than I that Richard doesn't have a red coat like that. He has a feast-day coat that's brown. Richard is a woods guide. He favors earth colors. I've never even seen him wear a red shirt. Why?"

Zedd ignored the question. "When you see him, tell him I said not to wear a red coat." He shook a finger at Chase. "Ever! It's very important, don't forget. No red coat."

Chase nodded. "Done." He knew when not to press the old man.

Zedd gave Rachel a smile and a quick hug before starting off down the hall. He wondered idly if he could remember where a dining hall was. It had to be almost past dinnertime.

A thought occurred to him: he didn't know where he was going. He hadn't done anything about finding himself a place to sleep. Well, no matter, he thought, the palace had guest rooms. He had told Chase about them. He could go there too.

He unfolded the crumpled piece of paper in his hand and looked at it. A distinguished man with a neatly trimmed gray beard and dressed in official gold robes was walking past. Zedd snagged him gently.

"Excuse me, but could you tell me where . . ." He looked at the paper. "Where 'West Rim, North Highland Way, Third Tier' is located?"

The bearded man gave a polite bow of his head. "Of course, sir. Those are the healers' quarters. It is not far. Let me guide you partway there, and give you direction for the rest of it."

Zedd broke into a smile. He suddenly didn't feel quite so tired. "Thank you. That is very kind of you."

**A**s Sister Margaret turned the corner at the top of the stone steps, an old maidservant carrying a mop and bucket saw her and fell to her knees. The Sister paused momentarily to touch the top of the old woman's bowed head.

"The Creator's blessing on His child."

The woman looked up, her face wrinkling into a warm, toothless smile. "Thanks be to you, Sister, and blessings to you in His work."

Margaret smiled back and watched as the old woman lugged her heavy bucket on down the hall. Poor woman, she thought, having to work in the middle of the night. But then, here she was herself, up and about in the middle of the night.

The shoulder of her dress pulled uncomfortably. She looked down and saw that in her haste she had misaligned the top three buttons. She redid them before pushing open the heavy oak door out into the darkness.

A pacing guard saw her and came at a run. She held the book over her mouth to hide her yawn. He lurched to a halt.

"Sister! Where's the Prelate? He's been yelling for her. Runs shivers up my spine, it does. Where is she?"

Sister Margaret scowled at the guard until he remembered his manners and dropped a quick bow. When he came back up she started off down the rampart with the man at her heels.

"The Prelate does not come simply because the Prophet roars."

"But he called out for her specifically."

She stopped and clasped her hand over the one holding the book. "And would you like to be the one to bang on the Prelate's bedchamber door in the middle of the night and wake her, simply because the Prophet shouts for it?"

His face paled in the moonlight. "No, Sister."

"It is enough that a Sister must be dragged out of bed for his nonsense."

"But you don't know what he's been saying, Sister. He's been yelling that . . ."

"Enough," she cautioned in a low tone. "Need I remind you that if a word he says ever touches your tongue, you will lose your head?"

His hand went to his throat. "No, Sister. I would never speak a word of it. Except to a Sister."

"Not even to a Sister. It must never touch your tongue."

"Forgive me, Sister." His tone turned apologetic. "It's just that I've never heard him cry out so before. I've never heard his voice except to call for a Sister. The things he said alarmed me. I have never heard him speak such things."

"He has contrived to get his voice through our shields. It has happened before. He manages it sometimes. That is why his guards are sworn on an oath never to repeat anything they should happen to hear. Whatever you heard, you had best forget it before this conversation is over, unless you want us to help you forget."

He shook his head, too terrified to speak. She didn't like frightening the man, but they couldn't have him wagging his tongue over a mug of ale with his fellows. Prophecies were not for the common mind to know. She laid a gentle hand on his shoulder.

"What is your name?"

"I am Swordsman Kevin Andellmere, Sister."

"If you will give me your word, Swordsman Andellmere, that you can hold your tongue about whatever you heard, to your grave, I will see about having you reassigned. You are obviously not cut out for this duty."

He dropped to a knee. "Praise be to you, Sister. I'd rather face a hundred heathens from the wilds than have to hear the voice of the Prophet. You have my oath, on my life."

"So be it, then. Go back to your post. At the end of your duty, tell the captain of the guards that Sister Margaret ordered you reassigned." She touched his head. "The Creator's blessing on His child."

"Thank you for your kindness, Sister."

She walked on, across the rampart, to the small colonnade at the end, down the winding stairs, and into the torchlit hall before the door to the Prophet's apartments. Two guards with spears flanked the door. They bowed together.

"I hear the Prophet has been speaking out, through the shield."

Cold, dark eyes looked back at her. "Really? I haven't heard a thing." He spoke to the other guard while holding the Sister's gaze. "You hear anything?"

The other guard leaned his weight on his spear and turned his head as he spat. He wiped his chin with the back of his hand. "Not a thing. Been quiet as a grave."

"That boy upstairs been waggin' his tongue?" the first asked.

"It has been a long time since the Prophet found a way to get anything other than a call for a Sister through our shields. He has never heard the Prophet speak before, that's all."

"You want we should make it so's he don't hear nothin' again? Or speak it?"

"That won't be necessary. I have his oath, and have ordered him reassigned."

"Oath." The man made a sour face at the word. "An oath is nothin' more than babbled words. A blade's oath is truer."

"Really? Am I to assume that your oath of silence is nothing more than 'babbled words,' too? Should we see to your silence, then, in a 'truer' way?" Sister Margaret held his dark gaze until it at last broke with a downward glance.

"No, Sister. My oath is true enough."

She nodded. "Has anyone else been about to hear him yelling?"

"No, Sister. As soon as he started in calling for the Prelate, we checked the area, to be sure there were none of the staff, or anyone else, about. When we found everything was clear, I posted guards at all the far entrances and sent for a Sister. He's never called for the Prelate before, only a Sister. I thought it should be up to a Sister, not me, to decide if the Prelate was to be awakened in the middle of the night."

"Good thinking."

"Now that you're here, Sister, we should be off to check the others." His expression darkened again. "To make sure no one heard anything."

She nodded. "And you had better hope Swordsman Andellmere is careful and doesn't fall off a wall and break his neck, or I will come looking for you." He gave an annoyed grunt. "But if you hear him repeat so much as a single word of what he heard tonight, you find a Sister before you stop to take another breath."

Through the door and halfway down the inner hall, she stopped and felt the shields. She held the book to her breast in both arms as she concentrated, searching for the breach. She smiled when she found it: a tiny twist in the weave. He had probably been picking at it for years. She closed her eyes and wove the breach together, binding it with a barb of power that would thwart him if he tried the same thing again. She was ruefully impressed by his ingenuity, and his persistence. Well, she sighed to herself, what else had he to do?

Inside his spacious apartments the lamps were lit. Tapestries hung on one of the walls, and the floors were generously covered with the local colorful, blue and yellow carpets. The bookshelves were half empty. Books that belonged on them lay open everywhere; some on the chairs and couches, some facedown on pillows on the floor, and some stacked in disheveled piles next to his favorite chair beside the cold hearth.

Sister Margaret went to the elegant, polished rosewood writing table to the side of the room. She sat at the padded chair and, opening the book on the desktop, flipped through it until she came to a clean page at the end of the writing. She didn't see the Prophet anywhere. He was probably in the garden. The double doors to the small garden were open, letting in a gentle breath of warm air. From a drawer in the desk she took an ink bottle, pen, and a small sprinkle box of fine sand, setting them beside the open book of prophecies.

When she looked up, he was standing in the half light in the doorway to the garden, watching her. He was in black robes with the hood drawn up. He stood motionless, his hands in the sleeves of the opposite arms. He filled the doorway not just with his size, but with his presence.

She wiggled the stopper from the ink bottle. "Good evening, Nathan."

He took three strong, slow strides out of the shadows and into the lamplight, pushing back the black hood to uncover his full head of long, straight, white hair that touched his broad shoulders. The top of the metal collar just barely showed at the neck of his robes. The muscles in his strong, clean-shaven jaw tightened. White eyebrows hooded his deep, dark, azure eyes. He was a ruggedly handsome man, despite being the oldest man she had ever known.

And, he was quite mad. Or he was quite clever, and wanted everyone to think he was mad. She wasn't sure which was true. No one was.

Either way, he was probably the most dangerous man alive.

"Where is the Prelate?" he asked in a deep, menacing voice.

She picked up the pen. "It is the middle of the night, Nathan. We are not going to wake the Prelate simply because you throw a fit, demanding she come. Any Sister can write down a prophecy. Why don't you sit down and we can begin."

He came to the desk, opposite her, towering over her. "Don't test me, Sister Margaret. This is important."

She glowered up at him. "And don't you test me, Nathan. Need I remind you that you will lose? Now that you have gotten me out of my bed in the middle of the night, let's get this over so I may return to it and try to salvage a part of a night's sleep."

"I asked for the Prelate. This is important."

"Nathan, we have yet to decipher prophecies you gave us years ago. It could not possibly make any difference if you give this one to me and she reads it in the morning, or next week, or next year for that matter."

"I have no prophecy to give."

Her anger rose. "You have called me from my bed for company?"

A broad smile spread on his lips. "Would you object? It's a beautiful night. You are a handsome enough woman, if a little tightly wound." He cocked his head to the side. "No? Well, since you have come, and must have a prophecy, would you like me to tell you of your death?"

"The Creator will take me when He chooses. I will leave it to Him."

He nodded, staring off over her head. "Sister Margaret, would you have a woman sent to visit me? I find I am lonely of late."

"It is not the task of the Sisters to procure harlots for you."

"But they have seen to a courtesan for me in the past, when I have given prophecies."

With deliberate care, she set the pen on the desk. "And the last one left before we could talk to her. She ran back half naked and half mad. How she got through the guards, we still don't know.

"You promised not to speak prophecies to her. You promised, Nathan. Before we could find her she had repeated what you had told her. It spread like a wild fire. It started a civil war. Nearly six thousand people died because of what you told that young woman."

His worried, white eyebrows went up. "Really? I never knew."

She took a deep breath and spoke in a soft voice to control her anger. "Nathan, I myself have told you this three times now."

He looked down with sad eyes. "I'm sorry, Margaret."

"*Sister* Margaret."

"Sister? You? You are far too young and attractive to be a Sister. Surely you are but a novice."

She stood. "Good night, Nathan." She closed the cover on the book and started to pick it up.

"Sit down, Sister Margaret," came his voice, again full of power and menace.

"You have nothing to tell me. I am returning to my bed."

"I did not say I had nothing to tell you. I said I had no prophecy to give."

"If you have had no vision and have no prophecy, what could you possibly have to tell me?"

He withdrew his hands from his sleeves and placed his knuckles on the desk, leaning close to her face. "Sit down, or I won't tell you."

Margaret contemplated using her power, but decided that it was easier, and quicker, to simply make him happy and sit down. "All right, I'm sitting. What is it?"

He leaned over even more, his eyes going wide. "There has been a fork in the prophecies," he whispered.

She felt herself rising out of the chair. "When?"

"Just today. This very day."

"Then why have you called me in the middle of the night?"

"I called out as soon as it came to me."

"And why have you not waited until the morning to tell us this? There have been forks before."

He slowly shook his head as he smiled. "Not like this one."

She didn't relish telling the others. No one was going to be happy about this. No one but Warren, that is. He would be in a state of glee to have a piece to fit into the puzzle of the prophecies. The others, though, would not be pleased. This meant years of work.

Some prophecies were "if" and "then" prophecies, bifurcating into several possibilities. There were prophecies that followed each branch, prophecies to foretell events of each fork, since not even the prophecies always knew which events would come to pass.

Once one of these kind of prophecies came to pass and resolved which fork was to be true, and one of the alternatives took place, a prophecy had forked, as it was called. All the prophecies that followed down the path that had been voided now became false prophecies. These themselves multiplied, like the branches of a tree, clogging the sacred prophecies with confusing, contradicting, and false information. Once a fork had occurred, the prophecies they now knew to be false had to be followed as far as could be traced, and pulled out.

It was a formidable task. The further the event in question was from the fork, the more difficult it was to know if it was of the false fork, or of the true. Worse, it was difficult to tell if two prophecies, one following another, belonged together, or if they were to happen a thousand years apart. Sometimes the events themselves helped them to decipher where it was to be placed chronologically, but only sometimes. The further in time from the fork, the more difficult was the task of relating them.

The effort would take years, and even then, they could be sure only of accomplishing part of it. To this day, they could not know with confidence if they were reading a true prophecy, or the descendant of a false fork in the past. For this reason, some considered the prophecies unreliable at best, useless at worst. But if they now knew of a fork, and more importantly, knew the true and the false branches, they would have a valuable guide.

She sank back into the chair. "How important is the prophecy that forked?"

"It is a core prophecy. There could be none more important."

Decades. It wouldn't take years, it would take decades. A core prophecy touched almost everything. Her insides fluttered. This was like going blind. Until the tainted fruit of the false fork could be culled, they couldn't trust anything.

She looked up into his eyes. "You do know which it was that forked?"

He smiled proudly. "I know the false fork, and the true. I know what has come to pass."

Well, at least there was that. She felt a ripple of excitement. If Nathan could tell her which fork was true, and which was false, and the nature of each branch, it would be valuable information indeed. Since the prophecies were not in chronological order, there was no way to simply follow a branch, but this would be a very good start: they would know right where to begin. Better yet, they had learned of it as it happened, and not years later.

"You have done well, Nathan." He grinned like a child who had pleased his mother. "Bring a chair close, and tell me of the fork."

Nathan seemed drawn up in the excitement as he pulled a chair to the side of the desk. He flounced down in it, squirming like a puppy with a stick. She hoped she wouldn't have to hurt him to get this stick out of his mouth.

"Nathan, can you tell me the prophecy that has forked?"

His eyes twinkled with mischief. "Are you sure you want to know, Sister Margaret? Prophecies are dangerous. The last time I told one to a pretty lady, thousands died. You said so yourself."

"Nathan, please. It's late. This is very important."

The mirth left his face. "I don't remember the words, exactly."

She doubted the truth of that; when it came to prophecies, Nathan's mind saw the words as if they were written on a stone tablet. She put a reassuring hand on his arm. "That is to be understood. I know it is difficult to remember every word. Tell it as best you can."

"Well, let's see." He looked at the ceiling as he stroked his chin with his thumb and fingertips. "It is the one that says something about the one from D'Hara who would shadow the world by counting shadows."

"That's very good, Nathan. Can you remember more?" She knew he probably remembered it word for word, but he liked to be coaxed. "It would be a tremendous help to me."

He eyed her a moment and then nodded. "*By winter's breath, the counted shadows shall bloom. If the heir to D'Hara's vengeance counts the shadows true, his umbra will darken the world. If he counts false, then his life is forfeit.*"

A forked prophecy indeed. This had been the first full day of winter's season. She didn't know what the prophecy meant, but she knew of it. This one was the matter of much study and debate down in the vaults, and worry over which year this prophecy might come to pass. "And which fork has the prophecy taken?"

His face turned grim. "The worst one."

Her fingers fumbled with a button. "We are to fall under the shadow of this one from D'Hara?"

"You should study the prophecies closer, Sister. The following prophecy goes on to say: *Should the forces of forfeit be loosed, the world will be shadowed yet by darker lust through what has been rent. Salvation's hope, then, will be as slim as the white blade of the one born True.*" He leaned closer and whispered. "The only one of darker lust, Sister Margaret, would be the Lord of Anarchy."

She whispered a prayer. "May the Creator shelter us in his light."

His smile was mocking. "The prophecy says nothing about the Creator coming to our aid, Sister. If it is protection you seek, you had better follow the true fork. It is in that way He has offered you a glimmer of hope for defense from what will be."

She smoothed the folds of her dress on her lap. "Nathan, I don't know what this prophecy means. We can't follow the true and false forks if we don't know what it means. You said you know those forks. Can you tell me? Can you tell me a prophecy on each fork, one that leads each way, so we may follow their path?"

"*Vengeance under the Master will extinguish every adversary. Terror, hopelessness, and despair will reign free.*" He peered at her intently with one eye. "This one leads down the false fork."

She wondered how it was possible for the true prophecy to be worse. "And one of the true fork?"

"A close prophecy after the true fork says: *Of all there were, but a single one born of the magic to bring forth truth will remain alive when the shadow's threat is lifted. Therefore comes the greater darkness of the dead. For there to be a chance at life's bond, this one in white must be offered to her people, to bring their joy and good cheer.*"

Margaret pondered these two prophecies. She didn't recall either. The first seemed simple enough to understand. They could follow the false branch, for a ways, anyway, from this one. The second was more oblique, but seemed as if it could be deciphered with a little study. She recognized it as a prophecy about a Confessor. The reference to "one in white" meant the Mother Confessor.

"Thank you Nathan. This will make the false fork easier to follow. The other, the true fork, will be a little harder, but with this prophecy to lead the way, we should be able to reason it out. We will just have to look for prophecies leading away from this event. Somehow she is to bring happiness to her people." That brought a small smile to her lips. "It sounds as if maybe she is to be wed, or something of that nature."

The Prophet blinked at her, then threw his head back and howled. He rose to his feet, roaring in laughter until he coughed and choked. He turned back to her, his face red.

"You pompous fools! The way you Sisters strut around as if what you do is meaningful, as if you even knew what you were doing! You remind me of a yard of chickens, cackling to one another as if they thought they understood higher mathematics! I cast the grain of prophecy at your feet, and you cluck and scratch at the dirt, and then peck at gravel!"

For the first time since she became a Sister, she felt small and ignorant. "Nathan, that will be quite enough."

"Idiots," he hissed.

He lurched toward her so quickly it frightened her. Before she knew it, she had released a bolt of power. It dropped him to his knees. He clutched at his chest as he gasped. Margaret recalled her power almost instantly, sorry she had reacted in this manner: out of fear.

"I apologize, Nathan. You frightened me. Are you all right?"

He grasped the chair back, drawing himself up into it as he gasped. He nodded. She sat still, ill at ease, waiting for him to recover.

A grim smile spread on his lips. "Frightened you, did I? Would you like to be really frightened? Would you like me to *show* you a prophecy? Not tell you the words, but show it to you? Show it to you the way it was meant to be passed on? I have never shown a Sister before. You all study them and think you can decipher their meaning from the words, but you don't understand. That is not the true way they work."

She leaned forward. "What do you mean that is not the way they work? They are meant to foretell, and that is what they do."

He shook his head. "Only partly. They are passed on by ones with the gift, ones like me: prophets. They are intended to be read and understood through the gift, by ones with the gift, ones like me, not to be picked over by the likes of your power."

As he straightened himself, pulling the aura of authority around himself again, she studied his face. She had never heard of such a thing. She wasn't sure if he was telling the truth, or just talking out of anger. But if it was the truth . . .

"Nathan, anything you could tell me, or show me, would be a great help. We are all struggling on the side of the Creator. His cause must prevail. The forces of the Nameless One struggle always to silence us. Yes, I would like you to show me a prophecy the way it is meant to be passed on, if you can."

He drew himself up, peering at her with burning intensity. At last he spoke softly.

51

"Very well, Sister Margaret." He leaned toward her, his expression so grave it nearly took her breath away.

"Look into my eyes," he whispered. "Lose yourself in my eyes."

His gaze drew her in, the deep, azure color spreading in her vision until it seemed she was looking up into the clear sky. She felt as if he were drawing every breath for her.

"I will tell you the prophecy of the true fork again, but this time, I will show it to you as it is meant to be." She floated as she listened. *"Of all there were, but a single one born of the magic to bring forth truth will remain alive . . ."*

The words melted away, and instead, she saw the prophecy as if seeing a vision. She was pulled into it. She was no longer in the palace, but in the vision itself.

She saw a beautiful woman with long hair, dressed in a satiny white dress: the Mother Confessor. Margaret saw the other Confessors being killed by quads sent from D'Hara and she felt the blinding horror of it. She saw the woman's best friend and sister confessor die in her arms. She felt the grief of the Mother Confessor.

Then, Margaret saw the Mother Confessor before the one from D'Hara who had sent the quads to kill the other Confessors. The handsome man in white stood before three boxes. To Margaret's surprise, each box cast a different number of shadows. The man in white robes performed rituals, cast evil spells, underworld spells, late into the night, through the night, until the sun rose. As the day brightened, somehow Margaret knew that it was this day. She was seeing what had happened this very day.

The man in white had finished with the preparations. He stood before the boxes. Smiling, he reached out and opened the one in the center, the one that cast two shadows. Light from within the box bathed him in its brilliance at first, but then in a flash of power, the magic of the box swirled about him and snuffed out his life. He had chosen wrong; he forfeited his life to the magic he sought to claim.

She saw the Mother Confessor with a man. A man she loved. She felt her happiness. It was a joy the woman had never experienced before. Margaret's heart swelled with the bliss the Mother Confessor felt at the side of this man. It was a vision of what was happening at this very moment.

And then Margaret's mind swept forward in a swirl. She saw war and death sweep across the land. She saw death brought by the Keeper of the underworld, to the world of the living with a wicked lust that choked her with terror.

Again the prophecy swept her forward to a great crowd. At the center was the Mother Confessor, standing on a heavy platform. The people were excited and in a celebratory mood.

This was the joyous event that would bring the fork of the prophecy, one of the forks that must be passed correctly to save the world from the darkness snatching at it. She was caught up in the festive mood of the crowd. She felt a tingle of expectant hope, wondering if the man the Mother Confessor loved was to be the one she was to wed, and if that was the happy event the Prophecy spoke of that would bring joy to the people. Her heart ached for it to be so.

But something wasn't right. Margaret's warm delight cooled until her flesh prickled with icy bumps.

With a wave of worry, Margaret saw that the Mother Confessor's hands were bound, and next to her stood a man, not the man she loved, but a man in a black hood. He held a great axe. Margaret's worry turned to horror.

A hand forced the Mother Confessor to kneel, seized her hair and laid her face to the block. Her hair was short now, not long as it had been before, but it was the same woman. Tears seeped from the Mother Confessor's closed eyes. Her white dress shimmered in the bright sunlight. Margaret couldn't breathe.

The great crescent axe rose into the air. It flashed through the sunlight, thunking solidly into the block. Margaret gasped. The Mother's Confessor's head dropped into the basket. The crowd cheered.

Blood gushed and spread down the dress as the headless, lifeless corpse collapsed to the wooden floor. A pool of bright blood spread under the body, turning the white dress red. So much blood. The crowd roared with elation.

A wail of horror escaped Margaret's throat. She thought she might vomit. Nathan caught her as she fell forward, crying and sobbing. He held her to him as a father would a frightened child.

"Ah, Nathan, is that the event that will bring joy to the people? Is this what must happen if the world of the living is to be saved?"

"It is," he said softly. "Almost every prophecy down this true branch is a fork. If the world of the living is to be saved from the Keeper of the underworld, then every event must take the correct branch. In this prophecy, the people must rejoice at seeing the Mother Confessor die, for down the other fork lies the eternal darkness of the underworld. I don't know why it is so."

Margaret sobbed into his robes as his strong arms held her tight against him. "Oh dear Creator," she cried, "take mercy on your poor child. Give her strength."

"There is no mercy when fighting the Keeper."

"Ah, Nathan, I have read prophecies of people dying, but it was only words. To see it as real has wounded my soul."

He patted her back as he held her. "I know. How well I know."

Margaret pushed herself up, wiping tears from her face. "This is the true prophecy that lies beyond the one that forked today?"

"It is."

"And this is the way they are meant to be seen?"

"It is so. This is the way they come to me. I have shown you the way I see them. The words, too, come with the prophecy, and those are what are to be written down, so those not meant to see the prophecies will not see them as they truly are, but those who are meant to will see them when they read the words. I have never before shown anyone a prophecy."

"Then, why have you shown me?"

His sad eyes regarded her a moment. "Margaret, we are in a battle with the Keeper. You are meant to know the danger we are in."

"We are always in a battle with the Keeper."

"I think, perhaps, this is different."

"I must tell the others. I must tell them what you can show them. We must have your help to understand the prophecies."

"No. I will show no other what I have shown you. No matter the pain they would think to inflict upon me, I will not cooperate. I will never again do this for you, or another Sister."

"But why not?"

"You are not meant to see them. Only to read them."

"But that can't be. . . ."

"It is meant to be; otherwise, your gift would work to unlock them. You are not

53

meant to see them, just as you often tell me others with common minds are not meant to hear them."

"But they could help us."

"They would help you no more than the one I told that girl helped her, or the thousands who died. Just as you keep me a prisoner here, so others may not hear what they are not meant to hear, so I must keep all but another prophet a prisoner of their ignorance. It is the will of He who has given the gift, and all else. Had He meant you to, He would have given you the key with your gift, but He has not."

"Nathan, there are others who would hurt you until you revealed it to them."

"I will not reveal it to them, no matter how much they hurt me. They will kill me before I do so." He tilted his head toward her. "And they won't try, unless you tell them."

She stared at him, seeing him differently than she had ever seen him before. None before had ever been as devious as he. He was the only one they had never been able to trust. All the others had told the truth about their gift and its capabilities, but they knew Nathan lied, knew he was not telling them all he was able to do. She wondered what he knew, what he was capable of.

"I will go to my grave with what you have shown me, Nathan."

He closed his eyes and nodded. "Thank you, child."

There were other Sisters who would have hurt him for addressing a Sister so. She was not one of them. She stood and straightened her dress.

"In the morning, I will tell those in the vaults of the prophecy that has forked, and of the ones on the false and on the true branches. They will have to decipher them as best they can, with what the Creator has given them."

"That is the way it is meant to be."

She returned the ink, pen, and sand shaker to the desk drawer. "Nathan, why did you want the Prelate to come? I don't recall you ever asking for her before."

When she looked up, he was studying her with cool detachment.

"That, too, Sister Margaret, is not for you to know. Do you wish to bring me pain, to attempt to make me tell you?"

She picked up the book of prophecy off the desk. "No, Nathan, I will not do that."

"Then, will you deliver a message to the Prelate for me?"

She nodded, sniffling back the tears that still burned at her eyes. "What would you have me tell her?"

"Will you take this, too, to your grave, and tell no other but the Prelate?"

"If you wish it, although I don't see why. You can trust the Sisters. . . ."

"No. Margaret, I want you to listen to me. When it is the Keeper you battle, you must not trust anyone. I am taking a dangerous chance in trusting you, and the Prelate. Trust no one." His bunched eyebrows gave him a frightening look. "Only those you trust can betray you."

"All right, Nathan. What is the message?"

He peered intently at her. At last his words came in a whisper. "Tell her that the pebble is in the pond."

Margaret blinked at him. "What does that mean?"

"You have been frightened enough, child. Don't tempt your endurance again."

"Sister Margaret, Nathan," she said softly. "I am not 'child,' but Sister Margaret. Please treat me with the respect I am accorded."

He smiled. "Forgive me, Sister Margaret." Sometimes his eyes ran shivers up her spine. "One more thing, Sister Margaret."

"What is it?"

He reached out and brushed a tear from her cheek. "I don't really know of your death." She sighed inwardly with relief. "But I do know something else of importance pertaining to you. Of importance in the battle with the Keeper."

"If it will help me to bring the Creator's light upon the world, then tell me."

He seemed to draw himself inward, looking out at her as if from a great distance. "A time will come, soon, when you stumble upon something, and you will have need to know the answer to a question. I don't know the question, but when you have the need to find the answer, come to me, and that, I will know. This, too, you must tell no other."

"Thank you, Nathan." She reached out and touched his hand. "The Creator's blessing on His child."

"No thank you, Sister. I do not wish anything more from the Creator."

She stared at him in surprise. "Because we keep you locked in here?"

His small smile returned. "There are many different kinds of prisons, Sister. As far as I am concerned, His blessings are tainted. The only thing worse than being touched by the Creator is being touched by the Keeper. And of that, I am not even resolved."

She took her hand back. "I will still pray for you, Nathan."

"If you care so much for me, then free me."

"I'm sorry, I can't do that."

"You mean, you won't do that."

"Look at it how you will, but you must remain here."

At last he turned away from her. She started for the door.

"Sister? Would you send a woman to visit me? To spend a night or two with me?"

The pain in his voice almost made her weep. "I thought you would be beyond that age."

He slowly turned to her. "You have a lover, Sister Margaret."

She reeled at this. How could he know? He didn't know; he was guessing. She was young, and thought attractive by some. Of course she would be interested in men. He was only guessing. But then, none of the Sisters knew what he was able to do.

He was the only wizard they couldn't trust to be truthful about his powers.

"You listen to gossip, Nathan?"

He smiled. "Tell me, Sister Margaret, do you have the day planned out in advance, when you will be too old for love, even if it is only for a time as fleeting as a night? Exactly how old, Sister, is it, when we lose the need for love?"

She stood silent, ashamed, for a time. "I will go myself, Nathan, into the city, and bring back a woman to visit you for a time. Even if I must pay her price myself. I can't pledge she will be beautiful to your eyes, as I don't know what your eyes fancy, but I can vow she will not be empty between the ears, as I think you value this more than you will admit."

She saw a single tear fall from the corner of his eye. "Thank you, Sister Margaret."

"But Nathan, you must promise me you will tell her no prophecy."

He bowed his head slightly. "Of course, Sister. I swear it on my word as a wizard."

"I mean it, Nathan. I do not wish to have a part in being responsible for people dying. Not only men died in those battles, but women, too. I could not bear having a part in it."

His eyebrows lifted. "Not even, Sister Margaret, if one of those women would bear, had she lived, a boy child who would grow into a brutal tyrant who would go on to torture and slaughter tens of thousands upon tens of thousands of innocent people, women and children among them? Not even, Sister, if you had a chance to choke off this fork of a terrible prophecy?"

She stood stunned, frozen. At last she made herself blink. "Nathan," she whispered, "are you saying . . ."

"Good night, Sister Margaret." He turned and strode off to the solitude of his small garden, pulling up his black hood as he went.

T he wind ripped at her, tugging at her clothes and snapping the loose ends. After yesterday's tangled mess, Kahlan was at least glad she had thought to tie back her hair. She clung to Richard for dear life, pressing the side of her face against his back as she squeezed her eyes tightly shut.

It was happening again—the thick feeling of growing heavy that made the knot in the pit of her stomach sink lower of its own accord. She thought she might be sick. She was afraid to open her eyes; she knew what always happened when she felt heavy like this. Richard called back for her to look.

She opened her eyes just a little, peeking through narrow, squinting slits. As she suspected, the world was tilted at a crazy angle. Her head spun sickeningly. Why did the dragon have to tip over whenever it made a turn? She could feel herself being pressed against the red scales. She couldn't understand why she wasn't falling off.

Richard had told her he had figured out that it was just like when you swung a bucket of water around over your head and the water didn't fall out. She had never swung a bucket of water over her head and wasn't entirely sure he was telling the truth about the water not falling out. She looked longingly at the ground and saw what Richard was pointing at—the Mud People's village.

Siddin squealed with glee from his place in Richard's lap as Scarlet's huge, leathery wings caught the air and pulled them into a tight spiral. As the red dragon plummeted earthward, the knot of Kahlan's stomach felt as if it were coming up in her throat. She didn't understand how they could like doing this. They enjoyed it. They actually enjoyed it! Arms stuck up in the air, they were both laughing with delight, acting like little boys. Well, one was a little boy, and she guessed he had a right.

She suddenly smiled and then laughed herself. Not at flying on a dragon, but at seeing how happy Richard was. She would fly on a dragon every day just to see him laughing and happy. She stretched up and kissed the back of his neck. He brought his hands down and rubbed one on each of her legs. She clasped them tighter around him and forgot a little about feeling sick.

Richard called forward for Scarlet to land in the open field in the center of the village. The sun was almost down, making the tan, plastered, mud-bricked buildings in the circle of the village stand out brightly in the slanting light. Kahlan could smell the sweet smoke from the cooking fires. The long shadows trailed the people running for cover. Women ran from the cooking shelters and men from their weapons making, all shouting and calling out.

She hoped they wouldn't be too frightened. The last time Scarlet had come here she had carried Darken Rahl, and when he didn't find Richard he had killed people. These people didn't know Rahl had forced Scarlet to fly him around after he had stolen her egg. Of course, even without Darken Rahl riding her, no one ever thought of a red dragon as anything but a deadly threat. She herself would have run for her life at seeing a red dragon. The red were the most fearsome of all the dragons, and no one would ever imagine doing anything with a red dragon except trying to kill it, or running for his life.

No one but Richard, that is. Who else but Richard would think to befriend one? He had risked his life to get her egg free from Rahl's control so she would help him, and in the process had made a friend for life, although Scarlet still professed her intent to eat him someday. Kahlan suspected it was some private joke between the two, as Richard laughed whenever she said it. At least Kahlan hoped it was only a joke—she wasn't entirely sure. Kahlan looked down at the village and hoped the hunters didn't start shooting poison arrows before they saw who was riding the red dragon.

Siddin suddenly recognized his home. He pointed excitedly, and jabbered to Richard in the Mud People's language. Richard couldn't understand a word of it but smiled and nodded and ruffled Siddin's hair. They both gripped the spikes on Scarlet's back as she pulled out of the steep descent. Dust swept up around them, lifted by the fluttering of Scarlet's huge wings as she settled on the ground.

Richard grabbed hold of Siddin and sat the little boy up on his broad shoulders, then stood up on Scarlet's back. The stiff, cold breeze carried the dust away to reveal a ragged ring of hunters, their bows drawn, poison arrows pointing up at the three of them. Kahlan held her breath.

Grinning, Siddin waved both hands over his head, as Richard had told him to. Scarlet held her head down so the Mud People could get a clear view of who was riding her. The hunters, astonished, cautiously lowered their bows. Kahlan exhaled when she saw the tension come off the bowstrings.

A figure in buckskin pants and tunic stepped through the ring of hunters. Long silver hair hung down, spreading over his shoulders. It was the Bird Man, his sun-browned face a picture of shock.

"It's me, Richard! I have returned! With your help, we have defeated Darken Rahl. And, we have brought Savidlin and Weselan's son back."

The Bird Man looked to Kahlan as she translated. A beaming grin spread on his face. *"We welcome you both back to your people with open arms."*

Women and children were gathering among the ring of hunters, their dark, mud-slicked hair framing amazed faces. Scarlet lowered her bulky body to the ground and Richard slid off her shoulder, landing on his boots with a thump. He held Siddin in one arm as he reached up with the other and helped Kahlan down. She was quietly joyful to have her feet on the earth again.

Weselan pushed through the throng, running to them, Savidlin right at her heels. She wailed her son's name. Siddin held his arms out gleefully and practically leapt into her arms. Weselan alternated between crying and laughing as she tried to hug her son and Richard and Kahlan all at once. Savidlin rubbed his boy's back and looked to her and Richard with wet eyes.

*"He was brave as any hunter,"* Kahlan told him.

He gave a single, firm, pride-filled nod. He appraised her for a moment and then stepped closer, giving her a gentle slap. *"Strength to Confessor Kahlan."*

Kahlan returned the slap and greeting, and then he threw his arms around her and squeezed her tight for a long time. When finished with hugging her, he straightened his elder's coyote hide on his shoulders and looked up at Richard. He shook his head in wonderment. And then he gave Richard a powerfully hard whack across the jaw, a demonstration of his heartfelt respect for Richard's strength.

*"Strength to Richard With The Temper."*

Kahlan wished he hadn't done that. She could tell by Richard's eyes that he had a headache. He had had it since yesterday, and she had hoped it would be better after a good sleep the night before in Scarlet's cave. Siddin had played with the little red dragon until he was dead tired, and then had cuddled between them and gone to sleep.

Having not slept for days, she thought she would have no trouble sleeping, but she found she didn't want to stop looking at Richard. She had finally put her head on his shoulder, held his hand in both of hers, and fallen asleep smiling. They had all needed the rest. Bad dreams had caused Richard to jerk awake several times in a cold sweat, and even though he had said nothing, she could see in his eyes that he still had the headache. Richard didn't let it bother him, though, and returned Savidlin's slap in kind.

"Strength to Savidlin. My friend."

Properly greeted, souls protected, Savidlin let his grins and backslaps fly. After they had exchanged greetings with the Bird Man, Richard addressed the crowd.

"This brave and noble dragon, Scarlet," he called out in a voice for all to hear, even though they couldn't understand the words, "has helped me kill Darken Rahl and avenge our murdered people. She has brought us here so Siddin could be returned before his parents could fear for him another night. She is my friend, a friend to the Mud People."

Everyone was dumbfounded as Kahlan translated. The hunters, at least, puffed up at hearing that an enemy of the Mud People had been killed by one of their own—even if he was one of their own by proclamation and not by birth. The Mud People honored strength, and to them killing one who harmed their people meant strength.

Scarlet's head swung down, her ears twitching. One yellow eye frowned at Richard. "Friend! Red dragons are friends to no people! We are feared by all!"

"You're my friend." Richard smiled. "I'm a person."

Scarlet snorted a puff of smoke at him. "Paah. I will eat you yet."

Richard's grin widened. He pointed at the Bird Man. "You see this man? He gave me the whistle that I used to save your egg. If not for that whistle, the gars might have eaten your little one." He stroked a hand on the bright red snout. "And a wonderful little one it is."

Scarlet tilted her head, blinking a big yellow eye at the Bird Man. "I guess he would make a meager snack." She peered back at Richard, a chuckle rumbling in her throat. "The whole of the village wouldn't make a decent meal. More trouble than it would be worth." She brought her head closer to him. "If they are your friends, Richard Cypher, they are my friends, too."

"And Scarlet, this one is called the Bird Man because he loves creatures that fly."

Scarlet's scaly eyebrows lifted. "Really?" She swung her head close to the Bird Man, inspecting him anew. The proximity of Scarlet's big head caused a few close to him to back away a step or two. The Bird Man held his ground. "Thank you,

Bird Man, for helping Richard. He has saved my young one. The Mud People have nothing to fear from me. On my dragon's honor."

The Bird Man looked to Kahlan as she translated, smiled to Scarlet, and then turned to his people. *"As Richard With The Temper says, this noble dragon, Scarlet, is a friend to the Mud People. She may hunt our land, and we will bring no harm to her, nor her to us."*

Cheering erupted from the crowd. For a people to have a dragon as a friend was taken as an honor to their strength. Everyone seemed to be shouting with excitement. They waved their arms in the air and stamped around in little dances. Scarlet joined in the merriment by throwing her head back and sending a roaring column of flame skyward. The people cheered louder.

Kahlan noticed Richard glancing off to the side. She followed the direction of his gaze to a small band of hunters standing together. None of them were cheering. She recognized their leader. He was the one who had blamed Richard for bringing trouble to their village—blamed Richard for the deaths of Mud People at the hands of Darken Rahl.

As the hooting and hollering went on, Richard motioned Scarlet toward him. When she lowered her head, he put his face right in her ear. She listened to whatever he was saying and then pulled her head back, regarding him with a big yellow eye. She nodded.

Richard held out the carved bone whistle hanging from a leather thong at his neck as he turned to the Bird Man. "You gave me this as a gift, but told me it would never aid me because I could only call all the birds at once. I think maybe the good spirits wanted it that way. This gift helped me save everyone from Darken Rahl. It helped me save Kahlan. Thank you."

The Bird Man smiled at the translation. Richard whispered in Kahlan's ear that he would be back in a short time, and then climbed up on Scarlet.

"Honored elder, Scarlet and I would like to give you a small gift. We would like to take you up in the air, so you may see where your beloved birds fly." He extended a hand to the Bird Man.

The elder, upon hearing the translation, looked apprehensively at Scarlet. Her vibrant red scales were glossy in the late-afternoon sun, undulating with her breathing. Her tail reached nearly to the mud-brick homes across the field. The dragon unfolded her wings and lazily stretched them. He looked at Richard, who was still offering his hand to him. A little-boy grin lit the elder's face. It made Kahlan laugh. He clasped Richard's arm and hoisted himself up.

Savidlin strode over and stood by Kahlan as the dragon rose into the air. The people cheered their approval as they watched the dragon lifting their honored elder into the air. Kahlan wasn't seeing the dragon. She saw only Richard. She could hear the Bird Man laughing as Scarlet carried them up and away. She hoped he was still laughing after Scarlet made a turn.

Savidlin glanced at her. *"He is a rare person, Richard With The Temper."*

She smiled and nodded. Her gaze went across the way, to the man who wasn't cheering or happy. *"Savidlin, who is that man?"*

*"Chandalen. He blames Richard for Darken Rahl coming here and killing people."*

The Wizard's First Rule came to her mind: People will believe anything. *"If it wasn't for Richard, Darken Rahl would rule us all now, the same Darken Rahl who killed those people."*

Savidlin shrugged. *"Not everyone who has eyes can see. Remember the elder you killed? Toffalar? That was his uncle."*

She nodded absently. *"Wait here."*

Kahlan walked across the field, pulling the tie from her hair as she went. She was still dazed by the knowledge that Richard loved her and that he couldn't be harmed by her magic. It was hardly possible to believe she, a Confessor, could ever experience love. It went against everything she had ever been taught. She just wanted to take Richard somewhere alone and kiss him and hug him until they were old.

There was no way she was going to allow this man, Chandalen, to bring any harm to Richard. Now that she and the man she loved could somehow, magically, be together, she wasn't going to allow anything to jeopardize that.

The mere thought of anyone harming Richard brought the Blood Rage, the Con Dar, boiling up inside her. She had never known about the Con Dar before, had never known it was part of her magic, until she brought it forth when she thought Richard had been killed. Since then, she felt it within her, just as she always felt the rest of the Confessor's magic.

With his arms folded across his chest, Chandalen watched her come. His hunters stood behind him, leaning on spears planted butt-first in the ground. Apparently, they had just returned from a hunt; their lean bodies were still smeared with sticky mud. They stood easy but alert. Bows were slung over their shoulders and quivers hung at one side of their belts, long knives at the other. There were smears of blood on some of the men. Grass tied in bands at their upper arms and around their heads helped make them invisible in the surrounding grassland when they chose to be. Kahlan stopped in front of Chandalen, looking into his dark eyes.

She slapped him. *"Strength to Chandalen."*

He pulled his glare from her, arms still folded, turned his head, and spat. His fierce eyes came back to hers. *"What do you want, Confessor?"*

The hunters' mud-streaked faces all took on small, tight smiles. The Mud People's land was probably the only place where it was an insult not to be slapped. *"Richard With The Temper has sacrificed more than you could ever know to save our people from Darken Rahl. Why do you hate him?"*

*"The two of you have brought trouble to my people. You will bring it again."*

*"Our people,"* she corrected. Kahlan unbuttoned the cuff of her shirt and drew the sleeve up to her shoulder. She pushed her arm up in front of his face. *"Toffalar cut me. This is the scar he left as he tried to kill me. That was before I killed him. Not after. He killed himself by attacking me. I did not go after him."*

Without emotion Chandalen's gaze rose from the scar to her eyes. *"Uncle never was very good with a knife. Pity."*

Kahlan's jaw clenched rigid. She couldn't back down now.

She kissed the end of her fingers as she held his gaze. Reaching out, she touched the kissed fingers to his cheek where she had slapped him. The hunters broke into angry whispers, yanking their spears from the ground. Chandalen's face twisted into a hateful glare.

This was the worst insult you could give a hunter. He had given a disrespectful slight by not slapping her. It did not admit to having no respect for her strength, only that he didn't wish to show it if he did. By placing a kiss where she had offered a slap of respect, she had withdrawn her respect for his strength. The touch of the kiss said she had no respect for his strength and considered him no more than a foolish child. She had as much as spat on his honor publicly.

While this was a dangerous thing to do, it was more dangerous among the Mud People to show weakness to an enemy. That would be an invitation to be murdered in your sleep. Showing weakness denied you the right to face an adversary in the light. Honor required that strength be challenged openly. Since she had done this to him in the view of others, honor required any challenge from him be the same.

"*From now on,*" she said, "*if you want my respect, you must earn it.*"

Chandalen's white-knuckled fist jerked back to his ear, preparing to strike her.

Kahlan held her chin out for him. "*So. You have decided to show your respect for my strength?*"

His glare flicked to something behind her. His hunters flinched and reluctantly thrust the butts of their spears into the ground. Kahlan turned and saw about fifty men with drawn bows. Every arrow was leveled at Chandalen or one of his nine men.

"*So,*" Chandalen sneered, "*you are not so strong. You must ask others to back you.*"

"*Lower your weapons,*" she called back to the men. "*No one is to raise a weapon to these men for me. No one. This is between Chandalen and me only.*"

Reluctantly, all the bows lowered, and the arrows rattled back into quivers.

Chandalen folded his arms once more. "*You are not so strong. You will hide behind the Seeker's sword, too.*"

Kahlan slapped her hand onto his forearm and gripped it tightly. Chandalen's eyes widened a little as he froze. For a Confessor to place her hand on someone in this manner was an overt threat, and he recognized it as such. Defiant or not, he knew better than to move a muscle; he couldn't move as fast as her thought, and that was all she needed.

Her voice was a low hiss. "*In the last year, I have killed more men than you have falsely boasted to have killed in the whole of your life. If you ever try to harm Richard, I will kill you.*" She leaned closer. "*If you even dare to express the thought out loud, and it reaches my ears—I will kill you.*"

She took in the hunters with a deliberate sweep of her gaze. "*My hand will always be extended to each of you in friendship. If any hand extends to me with a knife, I will kill you as I killed Toffalar. I am the Mother Confessor—don't think I can't. Or won't.*"

She held the gaze of each hunter in turn until they nodded in acknowledgment. Her hard eyes came at last to Chandalen. Her grip tightened. He swallowed. At last he, too, nodded.

"*This is a matter between us. I will not speak to the Bird Man of it.*" She took her hand from his arm. In the distance, the dragon roared its return. "*We are on the same side, Chandalen. We both fight for the Mud People to live. That part of you, I respect.*"

She gave him a very small slap. She offered him no opportunity to return it, or to fail to, and instead turned her back to him. The slap had given him back a small amount of his respect in the eyes of his men, and would make him look foolish and weak if he chose to press an attack now. It was a small offering, but it had shown she acted honorably. She would leave it up to his men to decide if he had. Bullying a woman brought no honor.

But then, she was no mere woman; she was a Confessor.

Kahlan let out a deep breath as she returned to Savidlin and turned to watch the dragon land. Weselan stood next to him, still hugging Siddin tightly. For his part, Siddin didn't look to want anything else in the world but to be rocked in his mother's arms. Kahlan gave a mental shudder at the thought of what might have happened to him.

Savidlin turned to her and lifted an eyebrow. *"You would make a good elder, Mother Confessor. You could give lessons in honor, and leadership."*

*"I would prefer the lessons weren't necessary."*

Savidlin grunted his agreement. Dust and wind kicked up by the dragon's wings fluttered past in fits that billowed her cloak. Kahlan was buttoning her cuff when the two men slid off Scarlet.

The Bird Man looked a little green, but he was grinning from ear to ear. He stroked a red scale respectfully and beamed at the yellow eye that watched him. Kahlan approached, and the Bird Man asked her to translate a message to Scarlet.

She smiled and looked up at the dragon's huge head, at its ears, which were now turning toward her. "The Bird Man would like you to know that this has been one of the greatest honors of his life. He says you have given him the gift of a new vision. He says that from this day forward, if you or your young one ever need refuge, you will always be welcome and safe in this land."

Scarlet gave a sort of dragon grin. "Thank you, Bird Man. I am pleased." She lowered her head to speak to Richard. "I must leave now. My young one has been alone long enough, and will be hungry."

Richard smiled as he stroked a red scale. "Thank you, Scarlet. For everything. Thank you for showing us your little one. It is even more beautiful than you. Take care of the both of you. Live free."

Scarlet spread her jaws wide and reached into the back of her mouth. There was a snap, and she brought a tooth point out, held in her black-tipped talons. It was only a point, but a good six inches long.

"Dragons have magic," she told him. "Hold out your hand." She dropped the tooth point in Richard's palm. "You seem to have a knack for getting yourself in trouble. Keep this safe. If you ever have great need, call me with it, and I will come. Be certain, as it will only work once."

"But how can I call you with it?"

Her head floated closer to him. "You have the gift, Richard Cypher. Just hold it in your hand and call to me. I will hear. Remember, great need."

"Thank you Scarlet, but I don't have the gift."

Scarlet threw her head back and rumbled in laughter. The ground shook. The scales on her throat vibrated. When her fit of laughter died out in spurts, she tilted her head to look at him with one yellow eye. "If you don't have the gift, then no one does. Live free, Richard Cypher."

Everyone in the village watched in silence as the red dragon grew smaller in the golden sky. Richard put his arm around Kahlan's waist, pulling her close against him.

"I hope that I've finally heard the last of this nonsense about me having the gift," he muttered half to himself. "I saw you from up in the air." He pointed with his chin across the clearing. "You want to tell me what that was all about with our friend over there?"

Chandalen was making a point of not looking at her. "No. It's not important."

"Are we ever going to get to be alone?" Kahlan asked with a coy smile. "Pretty soon I'm going to have to start kissing you in front of all of these people."

Dusk was bringing a cozy, fading light to the impromptu feast. Richard glanced around the grass-roofed shelter at the elders in their coyote hides. They were all smiles and chatter. Their wives and a few children had joined the group. People were stopping by the shelter to welcome the two of them back, smiling and exchanging gentle slaps.

Little children across the way were chasing brown chickens that wanted nothing more than to find a place to roost for the night. The chickens squawked as they made flapping escapes. She couldn't understand how the children could stand to be naked, as cold as it was. Women in bright dresses were bringing woven trays of tava bread and glazed pottery bowls of roasted peppers, rice cakes, long boiled beans, cheese, and roasted meats.

"You really think they're going to let us get away before we tell them the whole story of our great adventure?"

"What great adventure? All I remember is being scared to death all the time and being in more trouble than I knew how to get out of." Her insides twisted in pain at the memory of learning he had been captured by a Mord-Sith. "And thinking you were dead."

He smiled. "Didn't you know? That's what an adventure is: being in trouble."

"I've had enough of adventure to last me the rest of my life."

Richard's gray eyes looked distant. "Me, too."

Her gaze went to the red leather rod, the Agiel, which hung on a gold chain around his neck. She reached back and took a piece of cheese from a platter. Her face brightened. She put the cheese to his mouth. "Maybe we can just make up a story that sounds like a proper adventure. A short adventure."

"Suits me," he said, and then bit off a chunk of the cheese as she held it to his mouth.

Immediately, he spit the cheese into his hand and made a sour face. "This is awful!" he whispered.

"Really?" She sniffed the piece she still held. She took a tiny bite. "Well, I don't like cheese, but it doesn't taste any worse than usual to me. I don't think it has gone bad."

He was still making the face. "Tastes like it has to me."

Kahlan thought a minute, and then frowned. "Yesterday at the People's Palace, you didn't like the cheese there either. And Zedd said there was nothing wrong with it."

"Nothing wrong with it! It tasted rotten! I ought to know, I love cheese. I eat it all the time. I know bad cheese when I eat it."

"Well, I hate cheese. Maybe you're just picking up my habits."

He rolled a roasted pepper in a piece of tava bread and grinned. "I could think of a worse fate."

As she returned the smile, she saw two hunters approaching. Her back stiffened. Richard noticed her reaction and sat up straighter. "These are two of Chandalen's men. I don't know what they want." She gave him a wink. "Be a good boy? Let's not have an adventure."

Without smiling or answering, he turned and watched the two come. The hunters stopped in front of her at the edge of the platform. They planted the butts of their spears firmly in the ground, leaning on them with both hands. They both assessed her with slightly narrowed eyes and small, tight smiles that weren't entirely unfriendly. The one closest pushed his bow a little farther up on his shoulder and then extended an open hand to her, palm up.

She looked down at the hand. She knew what it meant—an open hand offered without a weapon in it. She glanced up at him in confusion. *"Does Chandalen approve of this?"*

*"We are Chandalen's men. Not his children."* He kept the hand out.

Kahlan looked at it a moment and then stroked her palm over his. His smile widened a little and he gave her a gentle slap.

*"Strength to Confessor Kahlan. I am Prindin. This is my brother, Tossidin."*

She gave Prindin a slap and wished him strength. Tossidin held his palm open to her. She stroked it with hers. He gave her a slap and added his wish of strength. He had a handsome smile that matched his brother's. Surprised by his friendliness, she returned his slap and greeting. Kahlan glanced to Richard. The brothers noticed the look, and in response both gave Richard a slap and greeting.

*"We wanted to tell you that you spoke with strength and honor today,"* Prindin said. *"Chandalen is a hard man, and a hard man to get to know, but he is not a bad man. He cares deeply for our people and wants only to protect them from harm. That is what we do—protect our people."*

Kahlan nodded. *"Richard and I are Mud People, too."*

The brothers smiled. *"The elders have proclaimed it for all to know. We will protect you both, the same as any other of our people."*

*"Will Chandalen?"*

Both grinned, but neither answered. They pulled their spears up, readying to leave.

"Tell them I said they have fine bows," Richard said.

She glanced sideways to see him watching the two. She told his words to Prindin. They smiled as they nodded. *"We are very good with them."*

Richard's expressionless gaze stayed on the two brothers. "Tell them I think their arrows look to be well made. Ask if I may see one."

Kahlan frowned at him before translating for the hunters.

The brothers beamed with pride. Prindin pulled an arrow from his quiver and handed it to Richard. Kahlan noticed that the elders were all quiet. Richard rolled the arrow in his fingers. Betraying no emotion, he looked at the nock and then turned it around and looked at the flat, metal point.

He handed the arrow back. "Very fine work."

As Prindin replaced the arrow in his quiver, Kahlan told him what Richard had said. He slid a hand partway up his spear and leaned a little of his weight on it. *"If you know how to shoot a bow, we would invite you to come with us tomorrow."*

Before she could translate, Savidlin spoke to her. *"Richard told me before, when you were here last, that he had to leave his bow behind in Westland, and that he missed it. As a surprise, I made him one, for when you both came back. It is a gift to him for teaching me how to make roofs that do not leak. It is at my home. I was going to give it to him tomorrow. Tell him, and tell him that if he agrees, I would like to take some of my hunters and go with him tomorrow."* He smiled. *"We will see if he is as good a shot as our hunters."*

The brothers grinned and nodded their enthusiasm. They looked to be confident of the results of the contest. Kahlan told Richard what Savidlin had said.

Richard was surprised, and seemed to be moved by what Savidlin had done. "The Mud People make some of the finest bows I have ever seen. I am honored, Savidlin. That is generous of you. I would like very much to have you there with me." He grinned. "We can show these two how to shoot."

The brothers laughed at the last part of the translation. *"Tomorrow then,"* Prindin said as they left.

Richard had a dark look on his face as he watched the two walking away.

"What was that all about with the arrows?" she asked.

He finally looked over at her. "Ask Savidlin if I could have a look at his arrows, and I'll show you."

Savidlin handed over his quiver. Richard pulled out a handful of arrows, sorting through the ones with thin, hardened wooden points. Kahlan knew them to be poisoned. Richard took an arrow with a flat, metal point and put the rest back.

He handed the arrow to her. "Tell me what you see."

She rolled it in her fingers as he had done with the other. She didn't know what that was supposed to tell her, so she looked at the point and the nock.

She shrugged. "It looks just like an ordinary arrow to me. Just like any other."

Richard smiled. "Just like any other?" He plucked an arrow out of the quiver by the nock end, holding the small round point up for her to see. He raised an eyebrow. "Does it look like this one?"

"Well, no. That point is small, long, thin, and round. But this one has a metal point. It's just like the one Prindin had."

Richard slowly shook his head. "No. It's not." He put the wooden pointed arrow back and took the one she had, holding the nock toward her. "See here? Where the string goes? It goes on the string like this, with the notch up and down. Does that tell you anything?" She frowned and shook her head. "Some arrows have spiraled feathers so the arrows rotate. Some people believe that increases their power. I don't know if that is true or not, but it's beside the point. All the Mud People's arrows are fletched with straight feathers. That keeps them steady in flight. They hit in the same attitude as they are fired."

"But I still don't see how this arrow is different from Prindin's."

Richard put his thumbnail in the nock. "This is the way the arrow goes on the string. With the notch up and down like this. When the arrow is in the bow, and when it hits, it is just like this. Now, look at the blade. See how it's up and down, too? Just like the notch. The blade and the string are in the same plane. Savidlin's bladed arrows are all like this.

"The reason for it is that he uses these bladed arrows to hunt large animals, like wild boar, and deer. The rib bones in animals go up and down, just like the blade does. That gives the arrow a better chance of passing between the ribs, rather than being stopped by them."

He leaned a little closer to her. "Prindin's arrows are different. The blades are turned ninety degrees. When his arrows are nocked, the blade is horizontal. His arrows aren't made to pass through the ribs of animals. The blades are horizontal because he hunts something different. Something with ribs that are horizontal. People."

Kahlan felt bumps ripple up her arms. "Why would they do that?"

"The Mud People are very protective of their land; they don't often allow outsiders in. I would guess that Chandalen and his men are the ones who guard their borders from encroachment. They are probably the fiercest hunters among the Mud People, and the best shots. Ask Savidlin if they are good with their bows."

She conveyed his question.

Savidlin chuckled. *"None of us ever beats Chandalen's men. Even if Richard With The Temper is good, he is going to lose. But they are careful not to humiliate us too badly. They will be gracious winners. Richard should not worry, he will enjoy the day. They will teach him to shoot better. That is why I wish to take my men: Chandalen's men always teach us to be better. Among the Mud People, being the best, winning, means you have a responsibility to those you have beaten. You must teach them to be better. Tell him he cannot back out, now that he has accepted the challenge."*

"I always thought it did people good to learn something," Richard said. "I won't back out."

Richard's intense gaze made her smile until her jaws hurt. Smiling himself, he turned, pulled his pack across the plank floor, and took out an apple. He cut the apple in half, removed the seeds, and handed half to her.

The elders fidgeted nervously. In the Midlands, red fruit was poison, the result of an evil magic. They didn't know that in Westland, where Richard was from, you could eat red things like apples. They had seen him eat an apple once before, when he had tricked them into not making him take a wife from their village by convincing them that his eating it might make his seed poisonous to his bride, but they sweated as they watched the two of them doing it again.

"What are you doing?" Kahlan asked him.

"Just eat your apple and then translate for me."

When they finished, Richard stood, motioning her up next to him. "Honored elders, I have returned from stopping the threat against our people. Now that it is over, I would like to ask your permission for something. I hope you find me worthy. I would like to ask your permission to have a Mud Woman as my wife. As you can see, I have taught Kahlan to eat these things as I do. She will not be harmed by it, or by me, and in the same way, though she is a Confessor, I will not be harmed by her. We would like to be together, and we would like to be wedded by our people."

Kahlan could hardly get the last of the words out past the tightness in her throat, and she could hardly keep from throwing her arms around him. She could feel her eyes burning and filling with tears, and had to clear her throat to finish the words. She put her arm around Richard's waist to steady herself.

The elders suddenly beamed with surprise. The Bird Man wore a wide grin. *"I think you are finally learning to be Mud People,"* he said. *"Nothing could please us more than for you two to be wed."*

Richard didn't wait for the translation, but gave her a kiss that took her breath away. The elders and their wives applauded.

It was all the more special to her that they would be wedded before the Mud People. Kahlan felt at home here. When they had come before, seeking help in their struggle to stop Rahl, Richard had shown the Mud People how to make roofs that didn't leak. They had made friends, had fought battles together, with lives saved, and lost. In the process, the two of them had bonded with these people. In honor of their sacrifices, the Bird Man had proclaimed them Mud People.

The Bird Man stood and gave Kahlan a fatherly hug that felt as if he were saying that he understood everything she had been through and was happy she had at last found happiness. She shed a few tears against his shoulder as he held her in his strong arms. Their adventure, a long ordeal, had taken her from the depths of pain and despair to the heights of joy. The fight had ended only yesterday. It didn't seem possible it could be over at last.

As they went on with the feast, Kahlan wished more than ever that it could end soon so she could be alone with Richard. He had been held prisoner for over a month, and had only rejoined her the day before. She hadn't even really had a chance to talk with him. Or hug him nearly enough.

Children danced and played around the small fire while the adults gathered around torches, eating and talking and laughing. Weselan scooted down next to her, hugged her, and said she would make her a proper wedding dress. Savidlin kissed her cheek and slapped Richard's back. She found it difficult to look away from Richard's gray eyes. She didn't want to. Ever.

The hunters who had been out on the plain the day the Bird Man had tried to teach Richard how to call specific birds with the special whistle he had given Richard as a gift, wandered by the elders' platform. All Richard could do that day was make a sound that called all the birds at once, but not different species individually. The hunters had laughed endlessly that day.

As they listened now, Savidlin made Richard show the whistle and tell again how he had used it to call all the birds that roosted in the valley filled with gars. The thousands of hungry birds had eaten the gars' blood flies, creating a panic. The diversion had enabled Richard to rescue Scarlet's egg.

The Bird Man laughed, even though he had already heard the story three times by now. Savidlin laughed and slapped Richard's back. The hunters laughed and slapped their thighs. Richard laughed as he watched them react to Kahlan's translation.

Kahlan laughed at seeing Richard laugh. "I think we have found an adventure that satisfies them." She thought about it and frowned. "How did Scarlet land you close enough to the egg without being seen by the gars?"

Richard looked away and was silent a moment. "She landed me on the valley on the other side of the hills around Fire Spring. I went through the cave."

He didn't look at her. Kahlan hooked some hair behind an ear. "And was there really a beast in the cave? A Shadrin?"

He let out a deep breath as he looked across the open area. "That there was. And more." As she put her hand on his shoulder, he took it and kissed the back of it, still staring off. "I thought I was going to die there, alone. I thought I would never see you again." He seemed to shake off the memory and leaned back on an elbow, gazing at her with a lop-sided smile on his face.

"The Shadrin left some scars that aren't healed yet. But I would have to take off my pants to show them to you."

"Really?" Kahlan gave a throaty laugh. "I think I better have a look . . . to see if everything is all right."

As she looked deep his eyes, she abruptly realized most of the elders were watching them. Suddenly she felt her face warm. She snatched up a rice cake and took a quick bite, relieved to know they couldn't understand their words. She hoped others couldn't understand the look in their eyes. She chided herself to pay more attention to where she was. Richard sat up again. Kahlan reached over to a small bowl of roasted ribs that looked to be wild boar, and set it down in his lap.

"Here. Have some of these."

She looked over at a group of the wives. She held up the rice cake and smiled. *"These are very good."* They nodded their satisfaction. She looked back to Richard. He was staring down at the bowl of meat. His face was white.

"Take it away," he whispered.

Kahlan frowned and lifted the bowl from his lap, setting it behind her. She scooted closer to him. "Richard, what's wrong?"

He was still staring at his lap, as if the bowl were still there. "I don't know. I looked down at the meat, and then I could smell it. It made me feel sick. It just seemed like a dead animal to me. Like I was about to eat some dead animal lying there in front of me. How could anyone eat some dead animal that was just lying there?"

Kahlan didn't know what to say. He didn't look well. "I think I know what you mean. I was sick once and they fed me some cheese. I threw it all back up. They thought it would be good for me, and every day fed me more, and I would throw it up, until I was well again. That is why, to this day, I don't like cheese. Maybe it's something like that, because you have a headache."

"Maybe," he said in a weak voice. "I spent a long time at the People's Palace. They don't eat meat there. Darken Rahl doesn't—didn't—eat meat, so none was served at the palace. Maybe I just got used to not eating meat."

She rubbed his back as he put his head in his hands, running his fingers through his hair. First cheese, and now meat. His eating habits were becoming as peculiar as . . . a wizard's.

"Kahlan . . . I'm sorry, but I need to go somewhere where it's quiet. My head really hurts."

She put her hand on his forehead. His skin was cold and clammy. He looked about ready to fall over. Her insides fluttered with worry.

Kahlan squatted in front of the Bird Man. *"Richard doesn't feel well. He needs to go somewhere quiet. Is that all right?"*

At first he thought he knew why they wanted to leave. His smile faded when he saw the anxiety on her face. *"Take him to the spirit house. It is quiet there. No one will bother him. Get Nissel if you think there be need."* A little of his smile came back. *"Maybe he has spent too much time on the dragon. I thank the spirits my gift of flight was short."*

She nodded, unable to manage much of a smile, and said a quick good night to the others. Picking up both their packs, she put a hand under Richard's arm and helped him to his feet. His eyes were squeezed shut, his eyebrows wrinkled together in pain. The pain seemed to pass a little, and he opened his eyes, took a deep breath, and started off with her across the open area.

The shadows were thick among the buildings, but the moon was up, giving them enough light to see their way. The sounds of the feast faded into the background, leaving only the slow scrape of Richard's boots scuffing on the dry ground.

He straightened a little. "I think some of it has passed."

"Do you get headaches often?"

He smiled over to her in the moonlight. "I'm famous for my headaches. My father told me that my mother used to get headaches like the ones I get, where you feel sick to your stomach because your head hurts so much. But this one is different. I've never had ones like this before. It's like something inside my head is trying to get out." He took his pack from her and hoisted it to his shoulder. "It hurts more than my other headaches."

They passed from the narrow passageways to the wide space around the spirit house. It sat by itself, moonlight reflecting off the tile roof Richard had helped the Mud People build. Wisps of smoke rose from the chimney.

Around the side, by the door, a row of chickens roosted on a low wall. They watched as she pulled the door open for him, starting a little at the squeak of the hinges, and settled down as the two of them passed inside.

Richard flopped down in front of the fireplace. Kahlan pulled out a blanket and made him lie back, bunching the blanket under his head. He rested the back of his wrist over his eyes as she sat, cross-legged, next to him.

Kahlan felt helpless. "I think I should go get Nissel. Maybe a healer can do something for you."

He shook his head. "I'll be all right. I just need to be away from all the noise." He smiled, his arm still over his eyes. "Have you ever noticed how badly we do at parties? Every time we are at a party something happens."

Kahlan thought back to every gathering they had been at together. "I think you're right." She rubbed a hand on his chest. "I think the only solution is for us to be alone."

Richard kissed her hand. "I would like that."

She enfolded his big hand in both of hers, wanting to feel the warmth of him as she watched him rest. It was dead quiet in the spirit house, except for the slow crackling of the fire. She listened to his slow, steady breathing.

After a while, he slid his hand away, and looked up at her. Firelight reflected in his eyes. There was something about his face, his eyes; something her mind was trying to tell her. He looked like someone else she had met, but who? A name whispered in the back of her thoughts, but she couldn't quite hear it. She stroked his hair back off his forehead. His skin didn't feel quite so cold.

He sat up. "I just thought of something. I asked the elders for permission to marry you, but I haven't really asked you."

Kahlan smiled. "No, you haven't."

Suddenly he looked embarrassed and unsure of himself. His eyes wandered a little. "That was really stupid. I'm sorry. That wasn't the right way to do it. I hope you're not angry. I guess I'm not very good at this. I've never done it before."

"Me neither."

"And I guess this isn't the most romantic place to do it. It should be someplace beautiful."

"Wherever you are is the most romantic place in the world to me."

"And I guess I must look pretty silly asking you something like this when I'm lying here with a headache."

"If you don't ask me pretty soon, Richard Cypher," she whispered, "I'm going to choke it out of you."

His eyes finally found hers, found hers so intently it nearly took her breath away. "Kahlan Amnell, will you marry me?"

Quite unexpectedly, she found she couldn't speak. She closed her eyes and kissed his soft lips as a tear rolled down her cheek. His arms closed around her, hugging her tight against the heat of him. She pulled back breathlessly. Her voice at last returned. "Yes." She kissed him again. "Please, yes."

Kahlan laid her head against his shoulder. Richard gently stroked her hair as she listened to his breathing and the crackle of the fire. He held her tenderly and kissed the top of her head, there being no need for words. She felt safe in his arms.

Kahlan let loose her pain: the pain of loving him more than life itself and thinking he had been tortured to death by the Mord-Sith before she could tell him how much she loved him; the pain of having thought she could never have him because she was a Confessor and her power would destroy him; the hurt of how much she needed him, how uncontrollably she loved him.

As her anguish expended itself, it was replaced by her joy in what lay ahead: a lifetime, together. The breathless excitement of it seeped into her. She clutched at him, wanting to melt into him, wanting to be one with him.

Kahlan smiled. That was what being married to him would be: being one with him, as Zedd had told her once—like finding the other half of herself.

When she finally looked up, there was a tear on his face. She wiped the tears from her cheeks, and he did the same. She hoped his tears meant he had let his demons go, too.

"I love you," she whispered.

Richard pulled her tight against him. His fingers traced a trail down the bumps of her spine.

"I feel so frustrated that there aren't any better words than 'I love you,' " he said. "It doesn't seem enough for the way I feel about you. I'm sorry there aren't any better words to tell you."

"They are words enough for me."

"Then, I love you, Kahlan. A thousand times, a million times, I love you. Forever."

She listened to the snap and pop of the fire, and to his heart beating. To her own heartbeat. He rocked her gently. She wanted to stay there in his arms forever. Suddenly the world seemed a wonderful place.

Richard grasped her shoulders and held her away to better see her. A wonderful smile spread across his face. "I can't believe how beautiful you are. I have never seen anyone as beautiful as you." He ran a hand down her hair. "I'm so glad I didn't cut your hair that time. You have beautiful hair. Don't ever change it."

"I'm a Confessor, remember? My hair is a symbol of my power. Besides, I can't cut it. Only another can do that."

"Good. I would never cut it. I love you the way you are, power and all. Don't ever let anyone cut it. I've liked your long hair ever since the first day I saw you, in the Hartland Woods."

She smiled as she remembered that day. Richard had offered her help in escaping from the quads. He had saved her life. "It seems so long ago. Will you miss that life? Being a simple, carefree woods guide?" She smiled coquettishly. "And single?"

Richard grinned. "Single? Not with you as my wife. But a woods guide? Maybe a little." He stared off at the fire. "I guess that for better or worse, I am the true Seeker. I hold the Sword of Truth, and the responsibilities that go with it, whatever they are. Do you think you can be happy being the wife of the Seeker?"

"I would be happy living in a tree stump, if you were there with me. But Richard, I'm afraid I'm still the Mother Confessor. I have responsibilities, too."

"Well, you told me what it meant to be a Confessor, how when you touch someone with your power it forever destroys who they were, replacing it with absolute, magical devotion to you, to your wishes, and in that way you can have them confess the truth of their crimes, or for that matter you can make them do anything you would wish, but what other responsibilities do you have?"

"I guess I never told you about everything else that it means to be the Mother Confessor. It wasn't important at the time; I didn't think we could ever be together.

71

I thought we would die, or even if we somehow won, you would go home to Westland and I would never see you again."

"You mean the part about it meaning that you are more than a queen?"

She nodded. "The Central Council of the Midlands in Aydindril is made up of representatives of the more important lands of the Midlands. Together, the Central Council more or less rules the Midlands. Even though the lands are independent, they still bow to the word of the Central Council. In that way, through the Confederation of Lands, common goals are protected and peace is maintained. It keeps people talking instead of fighting. If one land were to attack another, it would be viewed as an attack against unity, against all, and all would put the aggression down. Kings, queens, rulers, officials, merchants, and others come to the Central Council to petition for what they want: trade agreements, boundary treaties, accords dealing with magic—an endless list of wants and wishes."

"I understand. It's something like that in Westland. The council rules in much the same way. Although Westland isn't nearly big enough to have kingdoms, there are districts that govern themselves, but are represented by councilors in Hartland.

"Since my brother was a councilor, and then First Councilor, I was around the dealings of government. I saw the councilors coming from different places to ask for things. Being a guide, I was always leading them to and from Hartland. I learned a lot about it from talking to them."

Richard folded his arms. "So what is the Mother Confessor's part in it?"

"Well, the Central Council rules the Midlands . . ." She cleared her throat as she looked down at her hands in her lap. ". . . and the Mother Confessor rules the Central Council."

His arms came unfolded. "You mean to say that you rule all the kings and queens? All the lands? You rule the Midlands?"

"Well . . . yes, in a way, I guess. You see, not all the lands are represented on the Central Council. Some are too small, like Queen Milena's Tamarang, and the Mud People, and a few others are lands of magic, the land of the night wisps, for example. The Mother Confessor is the advocate for these lesser lands. Left to their own wishes, the council would decide to carve up these smaller lands. And they have the armies to do it easily. Only the Mother Confessor stands for those who have no voice.

"The other problem is that these lands are often in disagreement. Some have been bitter adversaries for as long as anyone can remember. The council is often deadlocked as rulers or their representatives each stubbornly demands his own way, to the detriment of the greater interests of the Midlands. The Mother Confessor has no interest but the good of the Midlands.

"Without leadership the different lands, through the Central Council, would only be interested in vying for power. The Mother Confessor counters these parochial interests with a larger view, with direction and leadership.

"Just as the Mother Confessor is the final arbiter of truth through her magic, she is also the final arbiter of power. The word of the Mother Confessor is law."

"So it is you who tells all the kings and queens, all the lands, what to do?"

She took one of his hands and held it. "I, and most of the Mother Confessors before me, let the Central Council decide for themselves what they wish, how they want the Midlands ruled. But when they fail to come to agreement, or to a just agreement, it is to the disadvantage of those not represented. Only then do I step in and tell them how it shall be."

"And they always do as you say?"

"Always."

"Why?"

She took a deep breath. "Well, they know that if they don't bow to the Mother Confessor's leadership, they will be alone and vulnerable to any stronger neighbor who craves power. There would be war until the strongest among them crushed all the rest, as Darken Rahl's father, Panis Rahl, did in D'Hara. They know that ultimately it is in their own interest to have an independent council leader, who sides with no land."

"But it's not in the best interest of the strongest. Something other than a good heart or common sense must keep the strongest of these lands in line."

She nodded with a smile. "You understand the games of power well. You are right. They know that if they were bold enough to allow their ambitions a free rein, I, or any of the Confessors, could take their ruler with our magic. But there is more. The wizards back the Mother Confessor."

"I thought wizards didn't want anything to do with power."

"They don't, exactly. The threat of their intervention makes it unnecessary. Wizards call it the paradox of power: if you have power, and are ready, able, and willing to use it, you don't need to exercise your power. The lands know that if they don't work together, and use the impartial leadership of the Mother Confessor, then the wizards are always in the background, ready to teach the disadvantages of being unreasonable or greedy.

"The whole thing is a very complex, interwoven relationship, but what it all comes down to is that I rule the Central Council, and if I'm not there to do so, the weak, the defenseless, and the peaceful will eventually be overrun, and the rest will be drawn into a war until all but the strongest are crushed."

Richard sank back to contemplate this with a slight frown on his face. She watched the firelight play on his features. She could feel what he was thinking about: he was remembering the way she had, with only a gesture of her hand, demanded that Queen Milena fall to her knees, kiss the Mother Confessor's hand, and swear loyalty. She wished she hadn't had to show him the power she wielded, and how much she was feared, but what she had done had been necessary. Some deferred only to power. When necessary, a leader had to show that power, or be cut down.

When he looked up at last, his face held a serious cast. "There is going to be trouble. The wizards are all dead; they killed themselves before they sent you looking for Zedd. The threat backing the Mother Confessor is gone. The other Confessors are all dead, killed by Darken Rahl. You are the last. You have no allies. There is no one to take your place if anything happens to you. Zedd told us to meet him in Aydindril, he must know this too.

"From what I have seen of powerful people, from councilors in my homeland, even my own brother, to queens here, to Darken Rahl, they will view you as a lone obstacle in their way. If the Midlands is to be kept from being torn apart, the Mother Confessor must rule, and you are going to need help. You and I both must serve the truth. I'm going to help you."

A sly smile parted his lips. "If those councilors were afraid to plot against the Mother Confessor, or give her trouble, because of the wizards, wait until they meet the Seeker."

Kahlan touched her fingers to his face. "You are a rare person, Richard Cypher.

73

You are with the most powerful person in the Midlands. Yet you make me feel as if I am riding your coattails to greatness."

"I'm nothing more than the one who loves you with all my heart. That is the only greatness I wish to live up to." Richard sighed. "It seemed a lot simpler when it was just you and me all by ourselves in the woods, and I cooked you dinner on a stick over an open fire." He gave her a sidelong glance. "You are still going to let me cook you dinner, aren't you, Mother Confessor?"

"I don't think Mistress Sanderholt would like that. She doesn't like anyone in her kitchens."

"You have a cook?"

"Well, I've never seen her cook anything, come to think of it. Mostly she just whisks all about, ruling her domain with a wooden spoon she wields like a scepter, tasting food and scolding cooks, assistants, and scullions. She is the head cook.

"She frets something awful when I come down to the kitchens to cook. Mistress Sanderholt begs me to take up another interest. She says I scare her people. She says they shake for the rest of the day whenever I come to the kitchens and ask for pots. So I try not to do it too often. But I do so like to cook."

Kahlan smiled at the memory of Mistress Sanderholt. It was long months since she had been home.

"Cooks," Richard muttered to himself. "I've never had anyone cook for me. I always cooked for myself." His smile returned. "Well, I guess this Mistress Sanderholt will be able to make a little room for me if I want to cook you something special."

"I would wager that you will soon have her doing whatever it is you wish."

He squeezed her hand. "Will you promise me one thing? Promise me that one day you will let me take you back to Westland and show you some of the beautiful places in the Hartland woods, places that only I know of. I've dreamed of taking you to them."

"I would like that," Kahlan whispered.

Richard leaned forward to kiss her. Before his lips touched hers, before his arms could embrace her, he winced in pain. His head sagged forward against her shoulder as he moaned. Kahlan clasped him to her in fear, then laid him back down as he clamped his arms to his head, unable to breathe. Panic gripped her. He pulled his knees up to his chest as he rolled onto his side.

She braced her hand on his shoulder as she leaned over him. "I'm going to get Nissel. I'll go fast as I can."

He could only nod as he shook.

Kahlan ran to the door, pushing it open, out into the still night. She could see her ragged breaths in the frigid air as she pushed the door closed. Her eyes flicked over the short wall. Moonlight washed the top of it with a silver cast.

The chickens were gone.

A dark shape hunched, still, behind the wall.

It moved a little in the moonlight, and there was a quick flash of shiny, golden eyes.

The dark thing rose up, claws rasping over the top of the short wall. It laughed a low cackle that sent goose bumps up her arms to the base of her neck. Kahlan froze. Breath caught in her throat. The form was a black void in the pale moonlight. After the brief flash, the eyes had vanished into a pool of night.

Her mind raced, trying to fit what she knew with what she was seeing. She wanted to run, but didn't know which way. Toward Richard, or away?

Though she couldn't see the eyes, she could feel them, like cold death. The tiniest of sounds rose from her throat. With a howling laugh, the dark shape leaped to the top of the wall.

The heavy door crashed open behind her, banging against the wall of the spirit house. At the same time, she heard the distinctive ring of the Sword of Truth being drawn in anger. The black head snapped toward Richard, the eyes flashing golden again in the moonlight. Richard reached out, snatching her by the arm, and tossed her back through the doorway. As the door rebounded from hitting the wall, he kicked it shut behind himself.

From beyond the door, Kahlan heard a howling laugh, and then there was a crash against the door. She came to her feet, pulling her knife. Through the door she could hear the sword tip whistle, and bodies thudding against the wall of the spirit house. She could hear the screaming howls of laughter.

Kahlan threw her shoulder against the door and rolled out into the night. As she sprang to her feet she saw a small, dark form hurtling toward her. She slashed with her knife and missed.

It came again, but before it was on her, Richard kicked it, slamming it back against the short wall. In the moonlight the Sword of Truth flashed toward the shadow. The blade caught only the wall. A shower of mud-brick fragments and plaster exploded into the air. The thing howled in laughter.

Richard snatched her back just as the dark shape flew past. She caught it with her blade, ripping through something hard—bone hard. A claw flashed past her face, the sword following, missing.

She could hear Richard panting as he searched the darkness. The shadow came out of nowhere and knocked him to the ground. Dark forms tumbled across the dirt. She couldn't tell which was Richard and which was the attacker. Claws flung dirt into the air as it flailed at him.

With a grunt, Richard heaved it over the wall. Instantly it sprang to the top, and stood there, eyes flashing golden in the moonlight, cackling that awful laugh as the two of them backed away. It fell silent as it watched them walking backward.

The air was suddenly alive with the zip of arrows. Within the space of a heartbeat, a dozen thudded into the black body. Not one missed. A breath later an equal number followed. The thing panted in laughter. It stood on the wall looking like a black pincushion.

Kahlan's jaw dropped as she saw it snap off a handful of arrows that stuck out of its chest. The thing snarled a cackling laugh at them, then blinked as it watched them backing away. She couldn't understand why it just stood there. Another flight of arrows thudded into the black body. It paid no attention, but dropped from the wall to the ground.

A dark figure ran forward, spear in hand. From the shadow of the wall, the thing sprang at the runner. The hunter let the spear fly. With impossible speed, the black form ducked to the side and with its teeth snatched the spear from the air. Laughing, it bit the shaft in half. The hunter who had thrown it backed away, and the thing seemed to lose interest, turning to again watch her and Richard.

"What in the world is it doing?" Richard whispered. "Why did it stop? Why is it just watching us?"

With a cold shock, she knew.

"It's a screeling," Kahlan whispered more to herself than to him. "Oh, dear spirits protect us, it's a screeling."

She and Richard were clutching each other's shirtsleeves as they walked backward, watching the screeling.

*"Get away!"* she yelled at the hunters. *"Walk! Don't run!"*

They answered with another useless flight of arrows.

"This way," Richard said. "Between the buildings, where it's dark."

"Richard, that thing can see better in the dark than we can see in the light. It's from the underworld."

He kept his eyes on the screeling standing in the open, in the moonlight. "I'm listening. What else can we do?"

She shook her head. "I don't know. But don't run, and don't stand still. That attracts its attention. I think the only way to kill it may be to hack it apart."

He looked over to her, his eyes angry in the moonlight. "What do you think I've been trying to do?"

Kahlan looked around at the small passageway they were entering. "Maybe we should go through here after all. Maybe it will stay there and we can get away. If not, at least we can lead it away from the others."

The screeling watched them backing away, and then started loping after them, panting a wicked laugh.

"Nothing is ever easy," Richard muttered.

They backed through the narrow passageway of smooth, plastered walls, the screeling following. Kahlan could see the dark knot of hunters following it in, could feel the pounding of her heart.

"I wanted you to stay in the spirit house. Why didn't you stay there where you were safe?"

She recognized the tone of rage from the sword's magic. Her hand holding his shirtsleeve felt wet and warm. She looked over and saw blood running down his arm, over her hand. "Because I love you, you big ox. And don't you dare do anything like that again."

"If we get out of this alive, I'm going to put you over my knee."

They kept backing down the twisting passageway. "If we get out of this alive, I will let you. What happened to your headache?"

Richard shook his head. "I don't know. One second I could hardly breathe, and the next, it was gone. As soon as it was gone, I could feel that thing on the other side of the door, and I heard it make that awful laugh."

"Maybe you just thought you could sense it because you heard it."

"I don't know. That could be. But it was the strangest feeling."

She pulled him by his shirtsleeve down a side passage. It was darker. Moonlight fell high up on a wall to their left. With a start, she saw the dark shape of the screeling skittering across the moonlit wall, like some huge, black bug. Kahlan had to force herself to draw a breath.

"How can it do that?" Richard whispered.

She had no answer. Behind them, torches appeared. Hunters were closing in around them, trying to bottle up the attacker.

Richard looked around. "If these people try to get this thing, its going to kill the lot of them." They stepped into a moonlit intersection of passageways. "Kahlan, I can't let that happen." He looked to his right, down toward a group of hunters coming with torches. "Go to those men. Get behind them."

"Richard, I'm not leaving. . . ."

He shoved her. "Do as I say! Now!"

His tone made her jump. Involuntarily, she backed away. Richard stood still in the moonlight, holding the sword in both hands, the tip resting on the ground. He looked up at the screeling hanging on the wall. It howled a laugh, as if suddenly recognizing the figure standing before it.

The screeling let go with its claws, dropping straight down, landing in the darkness with a thud.

Kahlan could see the angry set of Richard's jaw as he watched the blur racing toward him, kicking up a cloud of dust. The sword's tip stayed on the ground.

This can't be happening, she thought, it just can't. Not when everything is finally right. This thing could kill him. It could really kill him. It could be the end of everything. The thought stopped her breath. Her Confessor's Blood Rage roared to the surface. Her flesh tingled.

The screeling sprang into the air toward Richard. The sword tip snapped upward, impaling the dark, flailing form. She could see a good foot and a half of steel sticking from its back, glinting in the moonlight. The screeling again howled its terrible laughter. It clawed at the sword, pulling itself up by the blade toward Richard. It severed some of its own clawed fingers as it clutched at the blade, thrashing ahead. Richard gave the sword a mighty swing. The screeling slid off, slamming against the wall.

Without pause it sprang for him again. Already Richard was swinging the sword. Kahlan felt a rush of panicked anger. Without even realizing what she was doing, she had her arm up, her fist toward the thing trying to kill Richard, the man she loved; the only man she would ever love.

The screeling was nearly upon him, the sword completing its swing. Kahlan felt the power surge through her in a choking rush. She released it. Eerie blue light exploded from her fist, rending the night with a blinding flash of blue daylight.

The sword and the bolt of blue lightning hit the screeling at the same time. The screeling burst apart in a shower of bloodless, black pieces. Kahlan had seen the Sword of Truth do the same thing to living flesh. She didn't know if it was the sword or the blue lightning that had done it this time.

The crack of thunder from the bolt left her ears ringing in the sudden silence.

She ran to Richard and threw her arms around him as he hunched, panting. "Are you all right?"

He hugged her with his free hand, nodding. She held him for a long minute as shouting hunters with torches circled around them. Richard slid the sword back into its scabbard. In the torchlight, she could see a ragged gash on his upper arm. She tore off a strip of his shirtsleeve and tied it around the bleeding wound.

She looked around at the hunters, all of whom held either nocked arrows or spears. *"Is everyone safe?"*

Chandalen stepped into the torchlight and spoke to Kahlan. *"I knew you would bring trouble."*

She peered hard at his face, then merely thanked him and his men for trying to help.

"Kahlan, what was that thing? And what in the world did you do?" Richard was slumping.

She slipped her arm around his waist. "I think it's called a screeling. And I'm not entirely sure what I did."

"A screeling? What is a . . ."

His hands came to the sides of his head as his eyes winced shut. He sank to his knees. Kahlan wasn't able to hold his weight. Savidlin was there and reached for him, but before he could get an arm around him, Richard fell forward on his face. He cried out in the dirt.

*"Savidlin, help me get him back to the spirit house, and send someone for Nissel. Please, tell them to hurry."*

Savidlin shouted for one of his men to run for the healer. He and some of the others lifted Richard. Leaning on his spear, Chandalen only watched.

A torchlit procession wound its way back to the spirit house. Savidlin and the men carrying Richard went inside with Kahlan. They laid Richard in front of the fire, lowering his head to the blanket. Savidlin sent his men out, but stayed with her.

Kahlan knelt next to Richard and with trembling hands felt his forehead. He was ice cold and drenched in sweat. He appeared to be nearly unconscious. She bit her lip and tried not to cry.

*"Nissel will make him well,"* Savidlin said. *"You will see. She is a good healer. She will know what to do."*

Kahlan could only nod. Richard mumbled incoherently as his head twisted about, as if seeking some position that brought no pain.

They sat in silence until Savidlin asked, *"Mother Confessor, what was that you did? How did you make lightning?"*

*"I'm not sure how I did it. But it is part of the Confessor's magic. It is called the Con Dar."*

Savidlin studied her a moment as he squatted on his feet with his sinewy arms wrapped around his knees. *"I never knew a Confessor could call down lightning."*

She glanced over. *"I have known for only a few days myself."*

*"And what was the dark thing?"*

*"I think it may be a creature from the underworld."*

*"From the place the shadows came from, before?"* Kahlan nodded. *"Why would it come now?"*

*"I'm sorry, Savidlin; I don't have an answer. But if any more come, tell the people to walk away from them. Don't stand still, and don't run. Just walk away, and come get me."*

In silence he contemplated what she had said. At last the door squeaked open and a stooped figure flanked by two men with torches entered.

Kahlan sprang up and ran to her, taking her hand. *"Nissel, thank you for coming."*

Nissel smiled and patted her shoulder. *"How is the arm, Mother Confessor?"*

*"Healed, thanks to you. Nissel, something is wrong with Richard. He has terrible headaches. . . ."*

Nissel smiled. *"Yes, child. We will have a look at him."*

One of the men with Nissel handed her a cloth bag as she knelt beside Richard. The objects in the bag clinked against one other as she set it on the ground. She told the man to bring the torch around. She took off the bloody bandage and, with her thumbs, pressed open the wound. Nissel glanced to Richard's face to see if he felt it. He didn't.

*"I will tend to the wound first, while he sleeps."*

She cleaned the gash and stitched it while Kahlan and the three men watched in silence. The torches spit and hissed, lighting the inside of the nearly empty spirit house with harsh, flickering light. On the shelf, the skulls of ancestors watched along with the rest of them.

Sometimes talking to herself as she worked, Nissel finished sewing, packed the wound with a poultice that smelled of pine pitch, and wrapped the arm with a clean bandage. Rummaging around in her bag, she told the men they could leave. As he went past, Savidlin touched Kahlan's shoulder sympathetically and told her he would see them in the morning.

After they were gone, Nissel halted her pawing in the bag and looked up at Kahlan. *"I hear you are to be mated to this one."* Kahlan nodded. *"I thought you couldn't have a love, because you are a Confessor, that your power would take him . . . when you make babies."*

Kahlan smiled across Richard to the old woman. *"Richard is special. He has magic that protects him from my power."* They both had promised Zedd they would never reveal the truth—that it was his love for her that protected him.

Nissel smiled, and her weathered hand touched Kahlan's arm. *"I am happy for you, child."* She bent back to her bag and finally pulled out a handful of little stoppered pottery bottles. *"Does he get these headaches often?"*

*"He told me he gets bad headaches sometimes, but that this is different, that it hurts more, like something is trying to get out of his head. He said he has never had any like it before. Do you think you can help him?"*

"We will see." Pulling stoppers, she waved the bottles one at a time under his nose. One of them finally brought Richard awake. Nissel smelled the bottle herself to see what it was. She nodded and mumbled and went back into her bag.

"What's going on?" Richard groaned.

Kahlan bent over and kissed his forehead. "Nissel is going to do something for your headaches. Lie still."

Richard's back arched as he squeezed his eyes shut against the pain. He put his shaking fists to the sides of his head.

The healer pressed his chin down with her fingers, forcing his mouth open, and with her other hand shoved in some small leaves. *"Tell him to chew. Keep chewing."*

"She says to chew the leaves; they will help you."

Richard nodded and rolled to his side in agony as he chewed. Kahlan combed his hair back with her fingers, feeling helpless, wishing she could do more. It terrified her to see him in pain.

Nissel poured a liquid from a skin into a large cup and mixed into it powders from other jars. She and Kahlan helped Richard sit up to drink the concoction. When he finished, he flopped back down, breathing hard, but still chewing the leaves.

Nissel stood. *"The drink will help him to sleep."* Kahlan came to her feet and Nissel handed her a small bag. *"Have him chew more of these leaves when he needs them. They will help the pain."*

Kahlan hunched over a little, so as not to tower over the old woman quite so much. *"Nissel, do you know what is wrong?"*

Nissel pulled the stopper from the little bottle and sniffed it, then held it under Kahlan's nose. It smelled of lilacs and licorice. *"Spirit,"* she said simply.

*"Spirit? What do you mean?"*

*"It is a sickness of his spirit. Not of his blood, not of his balance, not of his air. Spirit."*

Kahlan didn't know what any of that meant, but it wasn't really what she wanted to know. *"Will he be all right? Will the medicine, and the leaves, will they cure him?"*

Nissel smiled and patted Kahlan's arm. *"I would like very much to be there when you are wed. I will not give up. If this doesn't work, there are other things to try."*

Kahlan took her arm and walked her out the door. *"Thank you, Nissel."* Kahlan saw Chandalen standing near the short wall. Some of his men stood farther off in the darkness. Prindin was close, against the spirit house. She went to him. *"Would you escort Nissel home, please?"*

*"Of course."* He took the healer's arm respectfully and guided her into the night.

Kahlan shared a long look with Chandalen, and then went over to him. *"I appreciate you and your men guarding us. Thank you."*

He regarded her without emotion. *"I am not standing guard for you. I am guarding our people from you. From what you may bring next."*

Kahlan brushed dirt from her shoulders. *"Either way, if something else comes, don't try to kill it yourself. I don't want any Mud People to die. That includes you. If something comes, you must not stand still, or run. If you do, it will kill you. You must walk. Come and get me. Don't try to fight it by yourselves. Understand? Come and get me."*

He still showed no emotion. *"And you will call down more lightning?"*

She looked at him coolly. *"If I have to."* She wondered if she could; she had no idea how she had done it. *"Richard With The Temper is not well. He may not be able to shoot arrows with you and your men tomorrow."*

He looked smug. *"I thought he would think of an excuse to back out."*

Kahlan took a deep breath through gritted teeth. She didn't want to stand here and trade insults with this fool. She wanted to go back inside to be with Richard. *"Good night, Chandalen."*

Richard was still on his back, chewing the leaves. She sat beside him, heartened to see that he looked more alert.

"These things are starting to taste better."

Kahlan stroked his forehead. "How do you feel?"

"A little better. The pain comes and goes. I think these leaves are helping. Except they are making my head spin."

"But better to spin than to pound?"

"Yes." He put his hand on her arm and closed his eyes. "Who were you talking to?"

"That fool, Chandalen. He's guarding the spirit house. He thinks we may bring more trouble."

"Maybe he's not such a fool. I don't think that thing would have been here without us. What did you call it?"

"A screeling."

"And what is a screeling?"

"I'm not sure. Nobody I know has ever seen one, but I've heard them described. They're supposed to be from the underworld."

Richard stopped chewing and opened his eyes to look at her. "The underworld? What do you know about this screeling thing?"

"Not much." She frowned. "Have you ever seen Zedd drunk?"

"Zedd? Never. He doesn't like wine. Just food. He says that drinking interferes with thinking, and there is nothing more important than thinking." Richard smiled. "He says that the worse a man is at thinking, the better he is at drinking."

"Well, wizards can get pretty scary when they're drunk. One time when I was little, I was in the Keep, studying my languages. They have books of languages there. Anyway, I was studying, and four of the wizards were reading a book of prophecy together. It was a book I had never seen before.

"They were leaning over it, and started getting all worked up. They were talking in hushed tones. I could tell they were frightened. At the time it was a lot more fun to watch wizards than to read my languages.

"I looked up and they had all turned white as snow. They all stood up straight at the same time, and flipped the cover shut. I remember it banged and made me jump. They all stood there, quiet for a while, and then one went away and came back with a bottle. Without saying a word, he passed out cups and poured out the drink. They all drank it down in one swallow. He poured more and they did the same thing again. They sat down on stools around the table the big book was on and kept drinking until the bottle was empty. By that time they were pretty happy. And drunk. They were laughing and singing. I thought it was tremendously interesting. I had never seen anything like it.

"They finally saw me watching them, and called me over. I didn't really want to go, but they were wizards, and I knew them pretty well, so I wasn't afraid and I went over to them. One set me up on his knee and asked if I wanted to sing with them. I told them that I didn't know the song they were singing. They looked at each other and then said they would teach me. So we sat there for a long time and they taught me the song."

"So, do you remember it?"

Kahlan nodded. "I've never forgotten that song." She rearranged herself a little and then sang it for him.

> The screelings are loose and the Keeper may win.
> His assassins have come to rip off your skin.
> Golden eyes will see you if you try to run.
> The screelings will get you and laugh like it's fun.
>
> Walk away slow or they'll tear you apart,
> and laugh all day long as they rip out your heart.
> Golden eyes will see you if you try to stand still.
> The screelings will get you, for the Keeper they kill.
>
> Hack 'em up, chop 'em up, cut 'em to bits,
> or else they will get you while laughing in fits.

If the screelings don't get you the Keeper will try,
to reach out and touch you, your skin he will fry.

Your mind he will flail, your soul he will take.
You'll sleep with the dead, for life you'll forsake.
You'll die with the Keeper till the end of time.
He hates that you live, your life is the crime.

The screelings might get you, it says so in text.
If screelings don't get you the Keeper is next,
lest he who's born true can fight for life's bond.
And that one is marked; he's the pebble in the pond.

Richard stared at her when she finished. "Pretty gruesome song to teach a child."
Finally, he resumed chewing the leaves.

Kahlan nodded with a sigh. "That night, I had terrible nightmares. My mother
came into my room and sat on my bed. She hugged me and asked what I was
having nightmares about. I sang her the song the wizards had taught me. She climbed
into my bed and stayed with me that night.

"The next day she went to see the wizards. I never knew what she did or said to
them, but for the next few months, whenever they saw her coming they turned and
hurried off the other way. And for a good long time they avoided me like death itself."

Richard took another leaf from the little bag and put it in his mouth. "The
screelings are sent by the Keeper? The Keeper of the underworld?"

"That's what the song says. It must be true. How could anything of this world
take that many arrows and just laugh?"

Richard thought in silence a moment. "What is 'the pebble in the pond'?"

Kahlan shrugged. "I've never heard of it before or since."

"What about the blue lightning? How did you do that?"

"It's something to do with the Con Dar. I did it before when it came over me
the first time." She took a deep breath at the memory. "When I thought you were
dead. I'd never felt the Con Dar before, but now I feel it there all the time, just as
I can always feel the Confessor's magic. The two are somehow connected. I must
have awakened it. I think it's what Adie warned me about that time we were with
her. But Richard, I don't know how I did it."

Richard smiled. "You never fail to amaze me. If I just found out I could call
down lightning, I don't think I would be sitting there so calmly."

"Well, you just remember what I can do," she warned, "if some pretty girl ever
bats her lashes at you."

He took her hand. "There are no other pretty girls."

The fingers of her other hand combed through his hair. "Is there anything I can
do for you?"

"Yes," he whispered. "Lie down next to me. I want you close. I'm afraid of
never waking, and I want to be close to you."

"You will wake," she promised cheerfully.

She took out another blanket and pulled it over the two of them. She cuddled
close, her head on his shoulder and an arm over his chest, and tried not to worry
about what he had said.

When she woke, her back was against the warmth of him. Light was seeping in around the edges of the door. She sat up, rubbed the sleep from her eyes, and looked down at Richard.

He lay on his back, staring up at the ceiling, taking slow, shallow breaths. She smiled at the familiar pleasure of his face. He was so handsome it made her ache.

Suddenly she realized with a jolt what it was about him that looked so familiar to her. Richard looked like Darken Rahl. Not the same kind of impossible perfection—the flawlessly smooth, uninterrupted sweep of features that were too exactly right, like some precisely perfect statue—but more rugged, rougher; more real.

Before they'd defeated Rahl, when Shota, the witch woman, had appeared to them as Richard's mother, Kahlan had seen her looks in Richard's nose and mouth. It was as if Richard had Darken Rahl's face with some of his mother's features making it better than Rahl's cruel perfection. Rahl's hair was fine, straight, and blond, while Richard's was coarser and darker. And Richard's eyes were gray instead of Rahl's blue, but they both possessed the same penetrating intensity—the same kind of raptor's gaze that seemed as if it could cut steel.

Though she didn't know how it could be possible, she knew Richard had Rahl blood. But Darken Rahl was from D'Hara, and Richard from Westland; that was about as far apart as you could get. It must be, she finally decided, a connection in the distant past.

Richard was still staring at the ceiling. She put her hand on his shoulder, giving it a squeeze. "How is your head?"

Richard jumped hard. He looked around and blinked at her. He rubbed his eyes. "What? . . . I was asleep. What did you say?"

Kahlan frowned. "You weren't asleep."

"Yes I was. Sound asleep."

Kahlan felt a flutter of apprehension. "Your eyes were wide open. I was watching you." She left unsaid that as far as she knew, only wizards slept with their eyes open.

"Really?" He looked around. "Where are those leaves?"

"Here. Does it still hurt bad?"

"Yes." He sat up. "But it's been worse." He put some of the leaves in his mouth and ran his fingers through his hair. "At least I can talk." He smiled at her. "And I can smile without my face feeling like it's going to break."

"Maybe you shouldn't go shoot arrows today if you don't feel well enough."

"Savidlin said I couldn't back out. I'm not going to let him down. Besides, I really want to see this bow he made for me. It's been . . . well, I don't even remember how long it's been since I shot a bow."

After he chewed some of Nissel's leaves for a while, they folded up the blankets and went looking for Savidlin. They found him at his home, listening to Siddin telling stories of what it was like to ride a dragon. Savidlin liked listening to stories. Even though it was a little boy telling them, he listened with the same interest he would accord a hunter returning from a journey. Kahlan noted with pride that the little boy was giving a remarkably accurate rendition, without fanciful embellishment.

Siddin wanted to know if he could have a dragon for a pet. Savidlin told him the red dragon was not a pet, but a friend to their people. He told him to find a red chicken, and he could have that.

Weselan was cooking a pot of some sort of porridge with eggs mixed in. She asked Richard and Kahlan to join them and passed each a bowl as they sat on a skin on the floor. She gave them flat tava bread to fold and use as a scoop for the porridge.

Richard had her ask Savidlin if he had a drill of any kind. Savidlin leaned way back, and with a finger and thumb pulled a thin rod from a pouch beneath a bench. He handed the rod to Richard, who had the dragon's tooth out. Richard turned the rod around with a puzzled look, put it at the base of the tooth, and twisted it experimentally.

Savidlin laughed. *"You want a hole in that?"* Richard nodded. Savidlin held out his hand. *"Give it to me. I will show you how it is done."*

Savidlin used his knifepoint to start a small hole and then held the tooth between his feet as he sat on the floor. He placed a few grains of sand in the hole, followed by the rod. He spat in his palms and then spun the rod back and forth rapidly between his hands, stopping occasionally to drop a few more grains of sand down the hole and wipe a little spittle into the opening. In a little while, he had drilled all the way through the tooth. He used his knife to clean the burrs from where the drill went through the other side of the tooth, and then held it up, grinning, showing off the hole. Richard laughed and thanked him as he strung a leather thong to the tooth. He hung it around his neck with the Bird Man's whistle and the Mord-Sith's Agiel.

He was getting quite a collection. Some of it she didn't like.

Wiping out his porridge bowl with a piece of tava bread, Savidlin asked, *"Is your head better?"*

"It's better, but still hurts something fierce. Nissel's leaves help. I'm embarrassed I had to be carried back last night."

Savidlin laughed. *"One time, I had a bad hurt, here."* He pointed at a round scar in his side. *"I was carried home by women."* He leaned closer and lifted an eyebrow. *"Women!"* Weselan cast a disapproving eye toward him. He made a point of not noticing. *"When my men found out I was carried home by women, they had a good laugh over it."* He put the last of the tava bread in his mouth and chewed for a few minutes. *"Then I told them which women carried me home, and they stopped laughing and wanted to know how to get a hurt like mine so they too could be carried home by those women."*

*"Savidlin!"* Weselan scolded in a scandalized tone. She turned to them. *"If he didn't already have a hurt, I would have given him one. A good one."*

"So how did you get this hurt?" Richard asked.

Savidlin shrugged. *"Like I told my men: it was easy. You just stand there like a surprised rabbit while a trespasser puts a spear through you."*

"And why didn't he finish you?"

*"Because I put a few ten-step arrows in him."* He pointed at his throat. *"Here."*

"What's a ten-step arrow?"

Savidlin reached to the side and pulled a barbed, fine-pointed arrow from his quiver. *"One of these. See the dark stain? Poison. Ten-step poison. When it sticks you, you get only ten steps, and then you are dead."* He laughed. *"My men decided to think of a different way to get those women to carry them."*

Weselan leaned over and stuffed the rest of her tava bread in her husband's mouth. She turned to Kahlan. *"Men enjoy telling the most awful stories."* She broke into a shy smile. *"But I worried for him until he was well. I knew he was well when he came to me and made Siddin. Then I did not worry anymore."*

Kahlan realized she had translated before she had paid attention to the meaning of the words. She felt her ears burn. Instead of looking at Richard, she paid close attention to eating her porridge. She was glad her hair covered her ears, at least.

Savidlin gave Richard a look of a put-upon male. *"You will find that women, too, like to tell stories."*

Kahlan tried desperately to think of a new direction for the conversation. She couldn't. Thankfully, Savidlin did. He leaned back, looking out the door.

*"It will soon be the time to go."*

"How do you know what time we are to go?"

Savidlin shrugged. *"I am here, you are here, some of the men are here. When they are all here, that is the time to go."*

Savidlin went to the corner and retrieved a bow that was taller than the one Kahlan had seen him use before. Taller for Richard. With the aid of his foot, Savidlin stretched the cord to the bow.

Richard had a wide grin on his face. He told Savidlin it was the finest bow he had ever seen. Savidlin beamed with pride and gave him a quiver full of arrows.

Richard tested the weight of the draw. "How did you know how strong to make the pull? It's just right."

Savidlin pointed at his chin. *"I remembered how strong your respect for my strength was when we first met. It is too heavy for me, but I estimated it was right for you."*

Kahlan stood up next to Richard. "Are you sure you want to go? How does your head feel?"

"Terrible. But I have the leaves; they help a little. I think I'll be all right. Savidlin is looking forward to this. I don't want to disappoint him."

She rubbed her hand on his shoulder. "Should I come with you?"

Richard kissed her forehead. "I don't think I'll need anyone to translate to tell me how badly I'm being beaten. And I don't think I want to give Chandalen's men any excuse to humiliate me any worse than they are already going to."

"Zedd told me you were pretty good. In fact, he told me you were better than good."

Richard stole a look at Savidlin, who was stringing his own bow. "It's been a long time since I've shot a bow. Zedd was just trying to stir up trouble, I'll bet."

He stole a kiss while Savidlin was finishing and then went out the door with him. Kahlan leaned against the doorframe, still feeling the print of his lips on hers as she watched him walking away.

Showing no emotion, Chandalen stared up from sighting down one of his arrows. Prindin and Tossidin flashed sly smiles. They were looking forward to this. Richard glanced around, meeting the eyes of all the men as he walked past. They fell in behind him. He was a good head taller than any of them. They looked like a bunch of children following an adult. But these children had poison arrows, and some of them didn't hold any favor for Richard. Suddenly she didn't like this.

Weselan stood next to her, watching the men go. *"Savidlin said he will watch Richard's back. Don't be concerned, Chandalen would not do anything foolish."*

*"I worry about what Chandalen considers foolish."*

Weselan wiped her hands on a cloth, turning back to keep a watchful eye on Siddin. Siddin wanted to go out, and was sitting, poking a finger along the ground, looking dejected because his mother said she wanted him to stay inside. Weselan stood over him a long moment watching. He looked up, his chin resting in one palm. She gave him a gentle snap with the cloth.

*"Go outside and play."* Weselan sighed as he tore through the door with a squeal of glee. She shook her head to herself. *"The young don't know how dear life is. Or how fragile."*

*"Maybe that is why we all wish we were young again."*

Weselan nodded. *"Maybe so."* A handsome smile came to her tanned face. Her dark eyes sparkled. *"What color would you like to wear when you wed your man?"*

With both hands, Kahlan pulled her long hair back over her shoulders and thought a minute. A smile welled up from within. *"Richard favors blue."*

Weselan twined her fingers together. *"Oh, that would be just right, then. I have just the thing. I have been saving it for something special."*

She went into her small bedroom and came back with a bundle. Sitting on the bench next to Kahlan, she carefully unfolded it in her lap. The cloth was finely woven, a rich blue with a print of lighter blue flowers dappled across it. Kahlan thought it would make a gorgeous dress.

She tested the weave between her finger and thumb. *"It's beautiful. Where did you get it?"*

*"I traded for it."* She flicked her hand over her head. *"With people from the north. They like the bowls I make. I traded with them for it."*

Kahlan knew fine cloth when she saw it. Weselan would have had to make many bowls for this cloth. *"I wouldn't feel right using it, Weselan. You worked hard for this. It is yours."*

Weselan held up the corners of the blue fabric, giving it a critical appraisal. *"Nonsense. You two come here and teach our people how to make roofs that don't leak. You save Siddin from those shadow things, and in the process rid us of an old fool and make it so Savidlin can be one of the six elders. He has never been so happy. When Siddin is carried off, you find him and bring him back to us. You destroy the man who would have enslaved us. You two are guardians to our people. What is a piece of cloth?*

*"I will be proud the Mother Confessor of all the Midlands is wedded in a dress I make. Me, just a simple woman. For you, my friend, from all those faraway places, with all those grand things that I cannot even imagine. You would not be taking something from me. You would be giving me something."*

Kahlan's eyes filled with tears. Her lower lip trembled. *"You can't know the joy you have given me, Weselan. To be a Confessor is to be feared. My whole life, people have feared and shunned me. No one has ever treated me as just a woman, talked to me as a woman. Only as a Confessor. No one before Richard ever saw me as a person. No woman before you ever welcomed me into her home. No woman has ever let me hold her child."* She wiped away some of the tears. *"It will be the most beautiful dress I have ever worn, the most treasured dress I will ever have. I will wear it, proud that a friend made it for me."*

Weselan gave her a sidelong look. *"When your man sees you in this dress, he will make you a child of your own."*

Kahlan laughed and cried and hugged her. She had never dared to dream that all these things could happen in her life, that she could ever be treated as anything but a Confessor.

Kahlan and Weselan spent the better part of the morning starting the dress. Weselan seemed as excited about making the dress as Kahlan was about wearing it. The seamstresses back in Aydindril had nothing over Weselan with her fine bone needles. They settled on a simple design fashioned something like a kirtle.

They had a light lunch of tava bread and chicken broth. Weselan said she would work on the dress later, and asked what Kahlan wanted to do in the afternoon. Kahlan said she really would like to cook something.

Kahlan never ate meat when she was here before on official business because she knew the Mud People ate human flesh, ate their enemies to gain their knowledge. To avoid offending them, she had always used the excuse that she didn't eat meat. The night before, Richard had reacted strangely to eating meat, so Kahlan didn't say anything to change the menu when Weselan suggested a vegetable stew.

The two of them cut up tava, some other rust-colored roots Kahlan didn't recognize, peppers, beans, some nutty kuru, and then added greens and dried mushrooms into the big iron kettle hanging over the little fire in the corner cooking hearth. Weselan pushed a few sticks of hardwood into the fire as she told Kahlan the men probably wouldn't be back until dark. She suggested they go to the common area with the other women and bake some tava bread in the ovens.

*"I would like that,"* Kahlan said.

*"We will talk about the wedding with them. Talk of weddings always makes for good conversation."* She smiled. *"Especially when there are no men around."*

Kahlan was happy to find that the young women talked to her now. In the past they had always been too shy. The older women wanted to talk about the marriage. The younger women wanted to talk about faraway places. They wanted to know if it was really true that men followed her orders, that they did as she said.

Their eyes were wide as Kahlan told them about the Central Council and how she protected the interests of peoples like the Mud People from the threat of invasion by more powerful lands so the Mud People and others in small communities could live as they wished. She explained that although she was able to command people, she did so only because she was the servant to all the people. When they asked if she commanded armies of men in battle, Kahlan told them that it wasn't like that; that what she did was try to help the different lands work together so there wouldn't be fighting. They wanted to know how many servants she had and what sorts of fabulous dresses she had. The questions were beginning to make the older women nervous, and to frustrate Kahlan.

She flopped a ball of dough down on the board, sending up a little cloud of flour. She looked the younger women in the eye.

*"The prettiest dress I will ever have will be the dress Weselan is making me, because she is doing it out of friendship, and not because I commanded her to make it. There is no possession to compare to friendship. I would give up everything I have, and live in rags, and grub for roots, just to have one friend."*

That seemed to quiet the young girls, and settle the older women. The chatter

drifted back to the subject of the wedding, and Kahlan was happy to let it. She tried
to keep out of it, to let the older women lead the talk.

Near the end of the afternoon, Kahlan saw a commotion across the field. She saw
a taller figure, Richard, taking long strides toward Savidlin and Weselan's home.
Even from a distance, she could tell he was angry. A throng of hunters followed in
his wake, trotting at times to keep pace.

Kahlan wiped her flour-covered hands on a cloth. She threw the cloth on a table
as she stepped off the plank floor of the shelter and jogged the distance to the men.
She caught them as they went down a wide passageway.

Pushing through the hunters, she finally caught up with Richard just before he
reached Savidlin's doorway. Chandalen was right at his heels, along with Savidlin.
Chandalen had blood down his shoulder, with some kind of mud pack over a wound
on top. He looked to be in a mood to chew rocks.

She grabbed Richard's sleeve. He spun around with a hot expression that cooled
a little when he saw it was her. He removed his hand from the hilt of the sword.

"Richard, what's wrong?"

He glared around at the men, mostly Chandalen, then settled his gaze back on
her. "I need you to translate. We had a little . . . 'adventure' . . . this afternoon. I
haven't been able to make them understand what happened."

"*I want to know how he could dare to try to kill me!*" Chandalen was saying
over Richard's words.

"What's he talking about? He wants to know why you tried to kill him."

"Kill him! I saved his fool life. Don't ask me why! I should have let him get
killed! The next time I will!" He ran his fingers through his hair. "My head is killing
me."

Chandalen pointed angrily at the wound on the top of his shoulder. "*You did
this deliberately! I saw how you shoot! It could not have been an accident!*"

Richard threw his hands in the air. "Idiot!" he said to the sky. He lowered his
glare to Chandalen's fierce eyes. "Yes, you saw me shoot! Do you have any doubt
that if I wanted to kill you, you would not be breathing right now! Of course I did
it deliberately! It was the only way to save you!" He reached over her shoulder,
putting his hand close to Chandalen's face, holding his first finger and thumb half
an inch apart. "This is all the room I had! At the most! If I didn't take it, you would
be dead!"

"*What do you mean?*" Chandalen demanded.

Kahlan put a hand on his arm. "Calm down, Richard. Just tell us what happened."

"He couldn't understand me. None of them could. I couldn't explain it to them."
He looked at her in frustration. "I killed a man today."

"What!" she whispered. "You killed one of Chandalen's men?"

"No! That's not what they're angry about. They're happy I killed him. I was
saving Chandalen's life! But they think . . ."

She collected herself. "Just calm down. I will explain your words to them."

Richard nodded and rubbed his eyes with the heels of his hands. He looked down
at the ground as he combed the fingers of both hands through his hair. He looked
back up. "I'm only going to explain this once, Chandalen. If you can't get it through
your thick head, then we are going to stand at opposite ends of the village and

shoot arrows at each other until we can't argue anymore. And I will only need one arrow."

Chandalen lifted an eyebrow and folded his muscular arms. *"So explain."*

Richard took a deep breath. "You were standing a long way off. For some reason, I knew he was there, behind you. I spun around. All I could see of him . . . here, like this." He grabbed Kahlan by her shoulders and turned her around, facing Chandalen. He held her shoulders and ducked down behind her. "Like this. I couldn't see any of him but the top of his head. He had his spear ready. In one second more, he would have put it through your back. I had only one chance to keep him from killing you. Only one chance. I couldn't see enough of him; there was nothing else to shoot at from where I was. Only the very top of his head.

"The top of his forehead sloped back. If I hit it too high, the arrow would have deflected off, and he would have killed you. The only way to stop him, to kill him, was to let the arrow nick the top of your shoulder."

He held his finger and thumb half an inch apart again. "This is all I had. If I put the arrow that much lower, your bone would have deflected the arrow, and he would have had you. If I would have put it that much higher, just enough not to nick you, he would have lived, and you would be dead. I knew Savidlin's bladed arrow could pass through a little of your flesh and allow me to kill him. There was no time for anything else. I·had to shoot instantly. I think a dozen stitches is a light price to pay for your life."

Chandalen's eyes looked a little less sure. *"How do I know you are telling the truth?"*

Richard shook his head, muttering. He suddenly thought of something. He snatched a cloth sack from one of Chandalen's men. He thrust his hand in the sack and pulled out a head, lifting it by blood-soaked, matted hair.

Kahlan gasped. She put a hand over her mouth as she turned away. But before she did, she saw an arrow jutting from the center of the forehead, the blade end sticking from the back of the head.

Richard held the head behind Chandalen's shoulder and laid the feathers of the shaft on his shoulder, next to the wound.

"This is all I saw. If it were not as I say, if he had been standing straighter, and I put the arrow where I did, it would not have touched you."

The hunters all started nodding and whispering among themselves. Chandalen looked down at the shaft of the arrow lying on his shoulder. He looked back at the head. He thought about it a minute and then unfolded his arms and took the head, stuffing it back in the sack.

*"I have been stitched before. A few more will not hurt me. I will take your words as true. This time."*

Richard put his fists on his hips as he watched Chandalen and his men walking away. "You're welcome," he called after them.

Kahlan didn't translate that. "Why do they have that head?"

"Don't ask me. It wasn't my idea. And you don't want to know what they did with the rest of him."

"Richard, that seems a risky shot to me. How far were you when you shot that arrow?"

The heat left his voice. "Not risky at all, believe me. And I was at least a hundred paces."

"You can shoot an arrow that accurately at a hundred paces?"

He sighed. "I'm afraid I could have done it at twice that distance. Three times that distance." He looked down at the blood on his hands. "I have to go wash this off. Kahlan, in about two minutes my head is going to explode. I have to sit down. Could you please go get Nissel? Yelling at that idiot was the only thing keeping me on my feet."

She put a hand on his arm. "Of course. Go on inside, I'll go get her."

"I think Savidlin is angry with me too. Please tell him that I'm sorry I ruined so many of his arrows."

She frowned as Richard went inside, closing the door. Savidlin looked as if he was about to speak to her. She took him by the arm.

*"Richard needs Nissel. Come with me, and tell me what happened."*

Savidlin cast a glance over his shoulder at the door to his home as they hurried away. *"Richard With The Temper seems to be living up to his name."*

*"He is upset because he killed a man. It is not an easy thing to live with."*

*"He didn't tell you all of the story. There was more to it."*

*"So tell me."*

He looked over with a grave expression. *"We were shooting. Chandalen was angry, because of the shots Richard was making. He said Richard was a demon and went off and stood in the tall grass by himself. The rest of us were standing off to the other side, watching Richard shoot. The things he was doing did not seem possible. He nocked an arrow. Suddenly, he spun around toward Chandalen. Before we could even shout, Richard shot an arrow at Chandalen as he stood there with his arms folded. He had no weapon in his hand. None of us could believe Richard would do this.*

*"As the arrow was still flying toward Chandalen, two of his men, who had arrows nocked, drew their bows. The first one shot a ten-step arrow at Richard before his own arrow even reached Chandalen."*

Kahlan was incredulous. *"He shot at Richard, and missed? Chandalen's men don't miss."*

Savidlin's voice was low, and trembled slightly. *"He would not have missed. But Richard spun, pulling his last arrow from his quiver, a bladed arrow, and shot. I have never seen anyone do such a thing so fast."* He hesitated, as if he didn't think she would believe him. *"Richard's bladed arrow met the other in the air and split it in half. Each half went to one side of Richard."*

Kahlan halted Savidlin with a hand on his arm. *"Richard hit the other arrow while it was in the air?"*

He nodded slowly. *"And then the other man shot. Richard had no more arrows. He stood, his bow in one hand, and waited. It too was a ten-step arrow. I could hear it ripping the air."*

Savidlin looked around, as if not wanting anyone else to hear. *"Richard snatched it right out of the air with his hand. He had his fist around its middle. He put the man's arrow in his own bow and drew it on Chandalen's men. He was yelling at them. We couldn't understand his words, but they dropped their bows on the ground and put their arms out to the sides, to show him their empty hands. We all thought Richard With The Temper had become crazy. We thought he might kill us all. We were all very afraid.*

*"Then Prindin called out. He had found the man behind Chandalen. We all saw then, that Richard had killed a trespasser who was armed with a spear. We realized Richard had been trying to kill the invader, not Chandalen. Chandalen, though,*

*was not so certain. He thought Richard cut him with his arrow on purpose. Chandalen became even angrier when his men all went and gave Richard slaps of respect."*

Kahlan stared at him. She couldn't believe the things she was hearing. Most of it sounded impossible. *"Richard wanted me to tell you he was sorry he ruined your arrows. What was he talking about?"*

*"Do you know what a shaft shot is?"*

Kahlan nodded. *"It's when you shoot an arrow through another already in the center of the target, and split the shaft of the first. The Home Guard in Aydindril gave ribbons for doing it. I have seen a few men with a half dozen ribbons. I knew one with ten."*

Savidlin reached around and pulled a fat bundle from his quiver. Every arrow was split. *"It would be easier to give Richard With The Temper a ribbon if he ever missed. He would have no ribbons. He ruined over a hundred arrows today. Arrows take time to make. They are not to be wasted, but the men kept wanting him to do it again, because they had never seen anything like it before. One time, he put six arrows through the first, one right on top of the other.*

*"We shot rabbits, and cooked them over a fire. Richard sat with us, and then when we started eating, he wouldn't eat with us. He looked sick, and went off and shot arrows by himself until we were finished. Later, after we ate, is when he killed the man."*

She nodded. *"We better hurry and get Nissel."* She glanced over as they walked along. *"Savidlin, why did those men have that head? How can they be so gruesome?"*

*"Did you see that there was black painted over the eyes of the dead man? That was to hide him from our spirits, so he could sneak up on us. A man who comes onto our land with black over his eyes comes for only one reason: to kill. Chandalen's men put the heads of men like that on poles at the edge of our land to warn others who would paint black on their eyes.*

*"It may seem gruesome to you, but in the end it makes for much less killing. Do not think less of Chandalen's men for taking a head. They do it today not because they like it, but so there will be less killing tomorrow."*

Kahlan suddenly felt foolish. *"I guess that, just as Chandalen, I am guilty of judging too quickly. Forgive me, Elder Savidlin, for thinking things about your people that were wrong."*

He gave her a one-arm hug around her shoulders.

When they came back with the healer, they found Richard huddled in a corner, his fingers intertwined over his head. His skin was white, cold, and wet. Nissel gave him something to drink. After a few minutes, she gave him a small cube of something to swallow. Richard smiled when he saw it. He must have known what it was. Nissel sat on the floor next to him and felt his pulse for a long time. When a little of his color came back, she made him put his head back and open his mouth. She twisted a clove of something over his mouth, dripping the juice in. He made a face. Nissel smiled at that without comment.

She turned to Kahlan. *"I think these things will help him. Tell him to keep chewing the leaves. Come get me if he needs me."*

*"Nissel, is he going to get better soon? Shouldn't he be getting better?"*

The stooped old woman glanced down at Richard. *"Spirit has a mind of its own. It doesn't always listen. I think his does not want to listen."* She suddenly brightened at seeing the stricken look on Kahlan's face. *"Don't worry, child. I can make even the spirit listen."*

Kahlan nodded. Nissel gave her a warm smile and a pat on the arm before she went on her way.

Richard looked up at Kahlan and Savidlin. "Did you tell him? Did you tell him I'm sorry about ruining all his arrows?"

Kahlan smiled a little to Savidlin. *"He is worried about ruining so many arrows."*

Savidlin grunted. *"It is my own fault. I made your bow too good."* Richard managed a laugh. *"Weselan is off making bread. I must go see to some things. Rest well. We will be back when it is time to eat. We will eat together. It smells like my wife has made some good stew."*

After Savidlin left, Kahlan sat on the floor, tight against him.

"Richard, what happened today? Savidlin told me how you shot arrows today. You haven't always been that good, have you?"

He wiped sweat off his brow with the back of his hand. "No. I've split arrows before, but not more than a half dozen in one day."

"You've shot that many in one day before?"

He nodded. "On a good day, when I can feel the target. But today was different."

"How?"

"Well, we went out on the plain, and my head was really starting to hurt. The men set up targets of bundled grass. I didn't think I would even be able to hit a target, because my head hurt so much. But I didn't want to disappoint Savidlin, so I tried anyway. When I shoot, I call the target to me."

"What do you mean, you call the target to you?"

Richard shrugged. "I don't know. I used to think everyone did it when they shot. But Zedd told me they don't. I look at the target, and just sort of pull it to me. When I'm doing it right, it blocks out everything else. It's only me and the target, as if it comes closer. Somehow, I know exactly how the arrow must be held to hit the target. When I'm doing it right, I can feel that the arrow is in the right place before I release the bowstring.

"When I learned that I always hit the target when I had that certain feeling, I quit shooting arrows. I would just aim, trying to bring on the correct feel. I knew when I had it I wouldn't miss, so I didn't bother shooting. I would nock another arrow and try for the feel again. Over time, I learned to do it more often."

"How was it different today."

"Well, like I said, my head really hurt. I watched some of the other men shoot. They were very good. Savidlin started slapping me on the back, so I knew it was my turn. I figured I might as well get it over. My head felt as if it was going to split open. I drew the bow, and called the target to me."

Richard ran his fingers through his hair. "I don't know how to explain it. I called the target, and instantly, my headache was gone. No pain at all. The target came to me as it never had before. It felt like there was a notch in the air where I needed only to lay the arrow. I have never felt it so strongly before. It was as if the target was huge. I knew it would be impossible to miss.

"After a while, just for variation, instead of splitting the arrows already there, I would just shave off the red outside feather. When I did that, the men thought I had missed splitting the arrow already there. They had no idea I was doing something more difficult."

"And your headache was completely gone?" He nodded. "Do you have any idea why all this was happening?"

Richard pulled his knees up and rested his forearms on them. He looked away from her face. "I'm afraid I do. It was magic."

"Magic?" Kahlan whispered. "What do you mean?"

His eyes came back to her. "Kahlan, I don't know what your magic feels like inside you, but I have felt magic. Every time I draw the Sword of Truth, magic flows into me, becomes part of me. I know what that magic feels like. I've felt it often enough, and in different ways, depending on how I use it. But because I have joined with the sword, I can sense the the magic from it, even as it sits in its scabbard on my hip. Now I can call forth its magic without even having to draw the sword. I can sense it, like a dog at my heel, ready to jump for me.

"Today, when I drew the bow and called the target, I also called something else: magic.

"When Zedd touched me before, to heal me, and when you touched me when you were in the Con Dar, I felt the magic. This was something like that. I knew it was magic. It felt different from yours and Zedd's, but I recognized the texture of magic. I could feel the life of it, like a second breath. Alive." Richard put a fist in the center of his chest. "I could feel it coming from inside me, building until I released it to call the target."

Kahlan recognized in herself the feelings he was describing. "Maybe it has something to do with the sword."

He shook his head. "I don't know. I suppose it could be. But I couldn't control it. After a while, it simply went away, like a candle blown out in the wind. It felt like suddenly being in darkness, as if I was suddenly blind. And the headache came back.

"I couldn't hit the target, and I couldn't call it to me, so I just let the others shoot. The magic would come and go. I could never tell when it was going to happen. Then when the men started eating meat, I felt sick, and had to go away from them. I shot while they ate, and sometimes I could summon the magic and the headache would go away."

"What about when you caught the arrow out of the air?"

He gave her a sidelong glance. "Savidlin told you about that, did he?" She nodded. Richard let out a deep breath. "That was the strangest of all. I don't know how to explain it. Somehow, I made the air thicker."

She leaned closer, studying his face. "Made the air thicker?"

He nodded again. "I knew I had to slow the arrow down, and the only thing I could think of was that if the air was thick, like it was those times with the sword, when the air got thick and stopped the sword, then maybe I had a chance. Otherwise, I was going to die. It just all came into my head at once, the idea, and the doing. Instantly.

"I have no clue as to what I did. I just had the thought and I saw my hand snatch the arrow out of the air."

He fell silent. Kahlan rubbed her thumb on the side of her boot heel. She didn't know what to say. Fear was nibbling at the fringes of her mind. She flicked her eyes up for a glance at him. He was staring off into space.

"Richard," she whispered, "I love you."

His answer was a long moment in coming. "I love you too." He turned to her. "Kahlan, I'm afraid."

"Of what?"

"Something is going on. A screeling shows up, I have these headaches, you call down lightning, I do what I did today. The only thing I can think to do is to go to Aydindril and find Zedd. All these things have something to do with magic."

She didn't think he was necessarily wrong, but put some other answers to them anyway. "Me calling down the lightning has to do with my magic. Not you. Though I don't know how I did it, I did it to protect you. The screeling, I think, is from the underworld. That has nothing to do with us. It is just something evil. The magic with you today . . . well, that could have something to do with the magic from the sword. I just don't know."

"And the headaches?"

"I don't know," she admitted at last.

"Kahlan, the headaches might kill me. I don't know how I know that, but I know it's true. It's not just a simple headache. It's something else. I don't know what."

"Richard, please don't say that. You're scaring me."

"Scares me, too. One reason I was angry at Chandalen was because I fear he may be right about me. About me bringing trouble."

"Maybe we should start thinking about getting out of here. Getting to Zedd."

"And what about the headaches? Much of the time, I can't even stand. I can't stop every ten paces to shoot an arrow."

She swallowed past the lump in her throat. "Maybe Nissel can find an answer."

He shook his head. "She can help only a little, and only for a time. Soon, I don't think she is going to be able to do anything. I'm afraid I might die."

Kahlan started crying. Richard leaned back against the wall, put his arm around her shoulders, and pulled her against him. He started to say something else, but she put her fingers over his lips. She pressed her face against him as she cried, clutching at his shirt. It seemed as if everything was slowly starting to unravel. He held her and let her cry.

Kahlan began to realize she was being selfish. It was him these things were happening to. He was the one in pain, in danger. She should be comforting him, not the other way around.

"Richard Cypher, if you think this is going to get you out of marrying me, you had better think again."

"Kahlan, I'm not . . . I swear . . ."

She smiled and gently touched his cheek as she kissed him. "I know. Richard, we've solved problems a lot bigger than this one. We will figure it out. I promise. We have to; Weselan has already started my dress."

Richard put some of Nissel's leaves in his mouth. "Really? I bet you are going to look beautiful in it."

"Well, if you want to find out, you are just going to have to marry me."

"Yes, ma'am."

Savidlin, Weselan, and Siddin returned a short time later. Richard had closed his eyes and rested as he chewed the leaves, and he said his head felt a little better. Siddin was excited. He was a local celebrity, having ridden on a dragon. He had spent the better part of the day telling other children what it had been like. Now he wanted to sit in Kahlan's lap and tell her about how he had been the center of attention.

She listened with a smile while they all ate stew and tava bread. Like her, Richard didn't want any cheese. Savidlin offered him a piece of smoked meat. Richard politely declined.

As they were finishing their meal, a grim-faced Bird Man, ringed by men with spears, showed up at the door. Everyone set their bowls down and stood. Kahlan didn't like the look on his face.

Richard stepped forward. "What is it? What's happened?"

The Bird Man took in everyone with a sweep of his eyes. *"Three women, strangers, have come on horses."*

Kahlan wondered why three women would bring men with spears around the Bird Man. *"What do they want?"*

*"They are difficult to understand. They speak only a little of our language. I believe they want Richard. They seemed to say they want Richard and they want to see his parents."*

"My parents! Are you sure?"

*"I think that is what they were trying to say. They said for you not to try to run any more. That they have come for you, and you must not run. They told me I must not interfere."*

Richard unconsciously loosened his sword in its scabbard, his brow taking on a hawklike set. "Where are they?"

*"I had them wait in the spirit house."*

Kahlan hooked some hair behind her ear. *"Did they say who they are?"*

The Bird Man's long silver hair gleamed in the light of the setting sun coming from behind him. *"They called themselves the Sisters of the Light."*

Kahlan's breath caught in her throat; goose bumps rippled up her arms. Her insides felt as if they had been twisted into an icy knot.

She couldn't make her eyes blink.

Richard frowned. "Well? Who are they? What did he say?"

Still, she couldn't make her eyes blink. She could only manage a whisper. "He said they are the Sisters of the Light."

He stared at her a long moment. "Who are the Sisters of the Light?"

Finally, she blinked and looked over at him. "I don't know a whole lot about them. No one does. Richard, I think we should leave." Kahlan clamped both hands on his arm. "Please? Let's go. Right now."

Richard's gaze glided over the men with spears, stopping on the Bird Man. "Thank him for coming to us. Tell him we will take care of it."

After the Bird Man nodded and he and his men left, and they had told Savidlin they would go alone, Richard led her outside by the arm. They went around a few corners and he pushed her gently up against a wall, holding her by her upper arms.

"All right, you may not know a lot about them, but you know something. Tell me what it is. I don't need to be a mind reader to tell you know something, and you're afraid."

"They have something to do with wizards. With those with the gift."

"What do you mean?"

Kahlan put her hands on his arms the way he had his on hers. "One time when I was traveling with Wizard Giller, we were sitting around talking. You know, about life, dreams, things like that. Giller was a wizard by calling. He didn't have the gift, just the calling. Being a wizard had been his lifelong ambition, his calling. Zedd had taught him to be a wizard. Only, because of the wizard's web Zedd put over everyone when he left the Midlands, Giller didn't remember Zedd. No one did. No one even remembered his name.

"Anyway, I asked him if he ever wished he had more than the calling. If he wished he had the gift. He smiled and daydreamed about it a minute. Then his smile went away. His face turned white, and he said no, he didn't wish he had the gift.

"I was puzzled by the look of fear on his face. Wizards don't often get a look like that over a simple question. I asked him why he wouldn't want to have the gift. He said because if he had the gift, he would have to face the Sisters of the Light.

"I asked him who they were, but he wouldn't tell me anything about them. He said it was best not to even mention their name aloud. He begged me not to ask him any more on the subject. I still remember how much the look on his face scared me."

"Do you know where they're from?"

"I've been almost everywhere in the Midlands. I've never heard of them being seen anywhere. And I've asked."

Richard let go of her and put a fist on his hip. With his other hand, he squeezed his lower lip to a point as he thought. Finally he folded his arms and turned around. "The gift. So we're back to the gift. I thought we were done with this nonsense. I don't have the gift!"

She knitted her fingers together. "Richard please, let's just get away. If a wizard was afraid of the Sisters of the Light . . . Let's just get away from here."

"And what if they follow? What if they catch up with us when the headache has me flat on my back, when I'm defenseless?"

"Richard, I don't know anything about them. But if a wizard is that afraid of them . . . What if we are defenseless right now?"

"I am the Seeker. I am not defenseless. But I might be later. Better to meet them on my terms than theirs. And I'm tired of hearing about the gift! I don't have it and I'm going to put an end to this nonsense right now."

She took a deep breath and nodded. "All right. I guess the Seeker and the Mother Confessor are not without defenses."

He gave her a stern look. "You're not coming."

"Do you have a rope?"

Richard frowned. "No. Why?"

She lifted an eyebrow. "You will have a hard time stopping me if you don't have a rope to tie me up."

"Kahlan, I'm not letting you . . ."

"And I'm not giving you a chance to have a look at a woman you might fancy more than me, without being there to give her a whack."

He watched her with an exasperated expression, and then leaned forward and kissed her. "All right. But let's not have an 'adventure'?"

She smiled. "We will just tell these three you don't have the gift, send them on their way, and then I'm going to give you a serious kiss."

The sky was darkening into a deep blue when they reached the spirit house. Three strong horses were tethered a short distance away. Their saddles were different from any she had seen before, with high pommels and cantles. As they paused in front of the door, the air was cold enough to show their breath. Richard and Kahlan gave each other a smile and a squeeze of the hand. Richard checked that the sword was clear in its scabbard. He took a deep breath and pulled open the door. Kahlan wore her Confessor's face, as her mother had taught her.

The inside of the spirit house was lit by a small fire and two torches in brackets, one to each side of the fireplace. Their packs still sat to the side. The air smelled of pitch and the balsam-scented sticks that were always burned in the spirit house to make the ancestors' spirits welcome. Torchlight flickered on the skulls of ancestors sitting on a single shelf. The dirt floor was dry, since Richard had used the spirit house to teach the Mud People to make roofs that didn't leak.

The three women stood straight and tall in the center of the single-roomed, windowless building. Their brown, heavy wool cloaks hung almost to the ground. The hoods were up, partly shadowing their faces. They wore long, divided riding skirts of different, dark, muted colors, and simple white blouses.

They pushed back their hoods. The one in the middle, a few inches taller than the other two, but not as tall as Kahlan, had brown hair with some curl and body to it. The one to her right had straight, black, shoulder length hair, and the other's was curly, short, and dark, with streaks of gray. Each had her hands clasped at ease in front of her.

It was the only thing at ease about them. Their mature faces wore looks that reminded Kahlan of the headmistress of the maidservants back in Aydindril. It was a countenance of authority they appeared to have held so long that it had worn permanent creases. Kahlan took a second glance at their hands to see if they were empty; they looked like they should be carrying switches. Their eyes watched, as if ready to silence any impudence.

The woman in the middle spoke. "You two are Richard's parents?" Her voice wasn't quite as harsh as Kahlan expected, but still carried a clear tone of authority.

Richard glowered at them, looking as if just his look might push the three back a pace. He waited until the glare caused them to blink, before he spoke. "No. I am Richard. My parents are dead. My mother since I was young, and my father since the end of summer."

The three exchanged sidelong glances.

Kahlan saw the anger in his eyes. He was bleeding magic from the sword without even drawing it. She could tell the sword was only a blink away from coming out. She could see by the look in his eyes that he would not hesitate if these women did anything wrong.

"That is not possible," the taller one in the center said. "You are . . . old."

"Not as old as you," Richard snapped.

Their cheeks colored. The woman's eyes flashed an angry scowl, but she quickly softened it. "We did not mean to say you are old, we meant to say you are older than we expected. I am Sister Verna Sauventreen."

The black-haired woman to her right spoke. "I am Sister Grace Rendall."

"I am Sister Elizabeth Myric," the third said.

Sister Verna turned her stern expression on Kahlan. "And who would you be, child."

Kahlan didn't know if it was Richard's attitude causing it, but she felt her blood heating, too. She gritted her teeth. "I am not your 'child.' I am the Mother Confessor." Kahlan's tone could carry authority, too, when she wished it to.

It was almost imperceptible, but the three flinched. Together, they bowed their heads slightly.

"Forgive us, Mother Confessor."

The air of threat in the spirit house was still palpable. Kahlan realized her hands were fists. It came to her that she felt this way because they were a threat to Richard. She decided it was time to act like the Mother Confessor.

"Where are you three from?" she asked in an icy voice.

"We are from . . . far away."

Kahlan's glare was beginning to match Richard's. "In the Midlands, a bow to the Mother Confessor is done on at least one knee." It was a custom she almost never had any interest in enforcing, but she felt the need now.

The three leaned back as one, standing straighter. Their indignant frowns deepened.

It was enough to bring out the sword.

The distinctive ringing of steel hung in the air. Richard said nothing; he simply stood holding the sword in both hands. Kahlan could see his muscles straining to be released. The Sword of Truth's magic danced dangerously in his eyes. She was glad his glower wasn't directed at her; it was frightening. The three didn't appear to be as frightened by it as she would have expected, but they turned to her, and together, went to one knee, bowing their heads again.

"Forgive us, Mother Confessor," Sister Grace said. "We are not familiar with your customs. We meant no offense." They kept their heads down.

Kahlan waited the appropriate period, and then added a few long seconds. "Rise, my children."

When they came to their feet they clasped their hands in front again.

Sister Verna took a deep, impatient breath. "We are not here to frighten you, Richard. We are here to help you. Put the sword away." The last held a harsh hint of command to it.

Richard didn't move. "I was told you said you came for me, whatever that means, and that I must not run. I haven't been running. I am the Seeker. I will decide when to put away the sword."

"The Se . . ." Sister Elizabeth almost shouted. "You are the Seeker?"

The three exchanged looks again.

"State your business," Richard said. "Now."

Sister Grace took an impatient breath this time. "Richard, we are not here to harm you. Are you that afraid of three women?"

"Even one woman is cause enough for fear. I have learned that lesson the hard way. I no longer harbor foolish inhibitions about killing women. Last time offered: state your business, or this conversation is ended."

She glanced to the Agiel around his neck. "Yes, we can see you have learned some lessons." Her face softened a little. "Richard, you need our help. We have come because you have the gift."

Richard looked at each of them before he again spoke. "You have been seriously misinformed. I don't have the gift nor do I want anything to do with it."

He slid the sword back into its scabbard. "I'm sorry you have come a long way for nothing." He took Kahlan's arm. "The Mud People don't like outsiders. Their weapons are tipped with poison, and they are not shy about using them. I will tell them to grant you safe passage out of their land. I advise you not to test their restraint."

Richard led Kahlan by the arm toward the door. She could feel the rage radiating from him, could see the anger in his eyes, and something else, too: his headache. She could see the pain he suffered.

"The headaches will kill you," Sister Grace said quietly.

Richard froze in his tracks, his chest heaving as he stared ahead at nothing. "I've had headaches all my life. I'm used to them."

"Not like these," Sister Grace pressed. "We can see it in your eyes. We recognize the headaches of the gift. It's our job."

"There is a healer here who is taking care of them. She is very good. She has already helped me, and I am confident she will soon cure me of them."

"She can't. No one can but us. If you don't let us help you, the headaches will kill you. That is why we're here; to help you, not to bring you to harm."

Richard's hand stretched for the latch. "You needn't concern yourselves about me. I'm not cursed with the gift. Everything is under control. Safe journey to you, ladies."

Kahlan gently put her hand on his arm, preventing him from reaching the latch. "Richard," she whispered. "Maybe we should at least listen to them. What harm can there be in listening to them? Perhaps you could learn something useful to help the headaches."

"I don't have the gift! I don't want anything to do with magic! Magic has caused

me nothing but trouble, nothing but pain. I don't have the gift and I don't want it."
He reached for the latch again.

"And I suppose you are going to tell us that your eating habits haven't changed,
all of a sudden," Sister Grace said. "I would say in just the last few days."

Richard froze again. "Everyone has changes in mood about what they want to
eat."

"Has anyone watched you sleep?"

"What?"

"If anyone has watched you sleep, they will have noticed that you now sleep
with your eyes open."

Kahlan felt a cold wave of goose bumps. Everything was starting to connect.
Wizards all had odd, specific eating habits, and they all slept with their eyes open,
sometimes; even those without the gift. In those with the gift, like Zedd, it was
more often.

"I don't sleep with my eyes open. You are wrong."

"Richard," Kahlan whispered, "maybe we should listen to them. Hear what they
have to say."

He looked to her, as if pleading for her to help him escape this. Pleading for her
help. "I don't sleep with my eyes open."

"Yes, you do." She put a hand on his arm. "I have seen you sleeping for months
as we were trying to stop Rahl. When I stood watch, I often saw you sleep. Only
since we left D'Hara have I seen you sleep with your eyes open, just like Zedd
does."

Richard still had his back to the three women. "What do you want? How can
you help me with the headaches?" he called to them.

"If we are to discuss this, we are not going to talk to the back of your head."
Sister Verna's tone was like one used when talking to an obstinate child. "You will
address us properly."

It was the wrong tone to use on Richard at that moment. He yanked the door
open and slammed it as he went out. Kahlan thought the door might come off its
hinges, but it didn't. She felt heartsick about what she had said to him. He had
wanted her to take his side; he was in no mood to hear the truth.

She was puzzled by his attitude. Richard was not one to avoid the truth. But he
was deathly afraid of something. She turned and looked at the three women.

Sister Grace separated her hands and let them hang at her sides. "This is no
game, Mother Confessor. If he isn't helped by us, he is going to die. He doesn't
have much time."

Kahlan nodded, her anger gone, replaced by an empty sadness. "I will go talk
to him," she said in a small voice that was almost lost in the large room. "Please
wait here. I will bring him back."

Richard was sitting on the ground, leaning against the short wall, right under
where his sword had cut a swath the night before when the screeling had come.
His elbows were on his knees, his hands over his head, fingers locked together. He
didn't look up. Kahlan sat tight against him.

"Your head hurts pretty bad right now, doesn't it?"

He nodded. She pulled the dry shaft of a weed and held it between her hands
as she rested her forearms on her knees. As if what she had said reminded him, he
took some leaves out of his shirt pocket and put them in his mouth.

Kahlan stripped a little leaf off the stem. "Richard, tell me, what are you afraid of?"

He chewed the leaves a moment, and then lifted his head, leaning back. "Do you remember when the screeling came, and I said I sensed it, and you said maybe it was just that I heard it?" She nodded. "When I killed that man today, I sensed him too, just like the screeling. It was just the same. Danger. I didn't know what either was, but I sensed the danger. I knew there was trouble, but I didn't know what kind."

"What does that have to do with the three in there?"

"Before we went in the spirit house, to see those women, I had the same sensation: danger. I don't know what it means, but it's the same feeling. Somehow, I know those women are going to come between us."

"Richard, you don't know that. They said only that they want to help you."

"I do know. Just as I knew the screeling was there, and the man with the spear was there. These women are somehow a danger to me."

Kahlan felt a lump growing in her throat. "You also said you know the headaches might kill you. Richard, I'm afraid for you."

"And I'm afraid of magic. I hate magic. I hate the magic of the sword. I wish I could be rid of it. You can't imagine the things I've had to do with it. You don't know what it took to turn the blade white. Darken Rahl's magic killed my father, and took my brother. It hurt a great many people." He let out a deep breath. "I hate magic."

"I have magic," she said softly.

"And it almost kept us apart forever."

"But it didn't. You figured out how to make it work. Without my magic, I would never have met you." She rubbed his arm. "Magic also gave Adie back her foot, and has helped a lot of others. Zedd is a wizard; he has the gift. Would you say that is bad? Zedd has always used his gift to help people.

"Richard, you have magic too. You have the gift. You as much as admitted it. You used it to sense the screeling. You saved me. You used it to sense the man that was going to kill Chandalen. You saved him."

"I don't want to have magic."

"It seems to me you are thinking of the problem, and not the solution. Isn't that what you always say: think of the solution, not the problem?"

Richard thumped his head back against the wall and closed his eyes. He let out an exasperated breath. "Is this what being married to you is going to be like? For the rest of my life, you always telling me when I'm being stupid?"

She smiled. "Would you have me let you delude yourself?"

He scrubbed his hands on his face. "I guess not. My head hurts so much, I guess it's keeping me from thinking straight."

"Then let's do something about it? Let's go in and at least talk to the sisters, and hear what they have to say? They said they want to help."

He gave her a dark look. "So did Darken Rahl."

"Running away is not the solution. You didn't run from Darken Rahl."

He looked at her a long moment and then nodded. "I'll listen."

The three were standing where Kahlan had left them. They gave her small smiles of appreciation, apparently pleased she had brought him back. Richard and Kahlan stood close together in front of the three women.

"We will listen—listen—to what you have to say about my headaches."

Sister Grace looked to Kahlan. "Thank you for your help, Mother Confessor, but we will speak with Richard alone now."

Richard's anger flared again, but he kept his tone in check. "Kahlan and I are to be married." The three gave each other the look again. It was a little more serious this time. "What you have to say to me affects her, too. If you want to talk to me, she will stay and hear it too. Both of us, or neither. Choose."

The looks were still passing between the three. At last Sister Grace spoke. "Very well."

"And the first thing you should know is that I don't like magic, and I'm not convinced I have the gift. If I do, I am not pleased about it, and only want to be rid of it."

"We are not here to please you; we are here to save your life. To do that we must teach you to use the gift. If you don't learn to control it, it will kill you."

"I understand. I had a similar problem with the Sword of Truth."

"The first thing you must learn," Sister Verna said, "is that just as the Mother Confessor is to be treated with deference, so are we. We have worked long and hard to become Sisters of the Light, and expect to be treated with due respect. I am *Sister* Verna, this is *Sister* Grace, and this is *Sister* Elizabeth."

Richard glared at them. At last, he bowed his head. "As you wish. Sister Verna." He regarded each in turn. "And who are the Sisters of the Light?"

"We are the ones who train wizards, those with the gift."

"Where are the Sisters of the Light from?"

"We all live and work at the Palace of the Prophets."

Kahlan frowned. "Sister Verna, I've never heard of the Palace of the Prophets. Where is it?"

"In the city of Tanimura."

Kahlan's frown deepened. "I know every city in the Midlands. I've never heard of Tanimura."

Sister Verna held Kahlan's gaze for a moment. "Nonetheless, that is where we are from."

"Why were you surprised when you found out how old I am?"

"Because," Sister Grace said, "it is almost unheard of for one with the gift not to come to our attention when he is still young."

"How young?"

"At the very most, a third your age."

"And why do you think I did not come to your attention?"

"Obviously, you have been hidden from us, somehow."

Kahlan recognized that Richard was slipping into his Seeker's role, seeking answers to his questions before he gave them anything they wanted.

"Did you train Zedd?"

"Who?"

"Zeddicus Zu'l Zorander, wizard of the First Order."

The look passed between them again. "We don't know First Wizard Zorander."

"I thought it was your business to know of ones with the gift. Sister Verna?"

They stiffened. "You know this wizard of the First Order?"

"I do. Why don't you?"

"Is he old?" Richard nodded. "Perhaps he was before our time."

"Perhaps." Richard, with a fist on his hip, strolled a few steps away and stopped with his back to them. "How do you know about me? Sister Elizabeth."

"It is our business to know about those with the gift: wizards. Though you were obviously hidden from us, when you triggered the gift, we knew."

"What if I don't want to be a wizard?"

"That is your business. Ours is to teach you to control the magic. We are not here to force you to be a wizard, only to help you control the magic so you will live. Then you may be what you wish."

Richard marched back and put his face close to Sister Verna. "How do you know I have the gift?"

"We are the Sisters of the Light. It is our business to know."

"You thought I would be young. You thought I would be with my parents. You didn't know I was the Seeker. You don't know who the First Wizard is. You seem to be slipping in your business. Besides these errors, perhaps you are also mistaken about me having the gift, Sister Verna? Your mistakes do not inspire confidence. Does your position of respect tolerate such mistakes?"

Each woman's face was crimson. Sister Verna controlled her voice with an effort. "Richard, our job, our calling, is to help those with the gift. We have devoted our lives to it. We are from far away. What we have learned has been done at a great distance. We don't have all the answers. The matters you speak of are not important. What is important is that you have the gift, and if you don't let us help you, you will die.

"One reason we help those with the gift when they are young, and we wanted to see your parents, is because of the very difficulty we are having right now. If we can talk to the parents, we can help them see what is best for their son. Parents are more interested in the well-being of their children than one of your age is in himself. Teaching one of your age is going to be difficult. People are more easily taught when they are young."

"Before they are able to think for themselves, Sister Verna?" She was silent. "I will ask again. How do you know I have the gift?"

Sister Grace smoothed her straight black hair. "When one is born with the gift, it lies dormant, and is harmless. We strive to find these boys when they are young. We have a number of ways of knowing who they are. It has happened that one with the gift does things that trigger its growth, its evolution. When that happens it becomes a threat to them. How you managed to slip by our knowledge is something we can't answer.

"Once triggered, the power begins to evolve. It cannot be stopped. It must be mastered or you will die. This is what has happened to you. It is exceedingly rare for it to happen this way. To be honest, though we have been taught it has happened before, none of us has personal knowledge of it. Back at the Palace of the Prophets there will be old records of this in others, and we will look into it. But that doesn't change what matters: you have the gift, it has been triggered, and the evolution has begun.

"We have never had to teach one of your age before. I fear the trouble it is going to cause at the palace. Teaching the gift requires discipline. One of your age has obvious difficulty with this."

Richard softened his tone, but his gaze hardened. "Sister Grace, I will ask for the last time. How do you know I have the gift?"

She stood up a little straighter and let out a noisy breath. She flicked a glance to Sister Verna. "Tell him."

Sister Verna gave a resigned nod and pulled a small black book from behind her belt. With a frown, she began leafing through it. "Those with the gift have some use of it throughout their life, in little ways, even though it lies dormant. Perhaps you have noticed how you could do some things that others could not, yes? The evolution of the gift is triggered by the specific use of the magic. Once triggered, it cannot be undone. This is what you have done."

She continued turning pages, running her finger down them. "Ah. Here it is." She lowered the book and looked up. "There are three things that must be done, in a specific manner, to trigger the gift. We don't fully understand the precise nature of these things, but we understand their general principles. You have done these three things. First, you must use the gift to save another. Second, you must use the gift to save yourself. Third, you must use the gift to kill another with the gift. Perhaps you can see the difficulty in accomplishing them, and why we haven't seen this before?"

"And what is written about me in that book?"

She looked once more to the book, then glanced up, lifting an eyebrow, to make sure he was paying attention before consulting the pages as she spoke. "First, you used the gift to save the life of one who was being pulled back into the underworld. Not physically, but by her mind. You drew her back. Without you, she would have been lost." She looked up from under her eyebrows. "You understand, yes?"

Kahlan looked at Richard. They both understood. She was the one he had saved. "In the wayward pine," she said, "the first night we met. When you kept the underworld from taking me back."

Richard nodded to Sister Verna. "Yes, I understand."

Sister Verna put her finger back to the book. "As for saving yourself with the gift . . . let's see . . . I saw it here a minute . . . ah! Yes, here it is." She looked up from under her eyebrows again. "Second, you used the gift to save your own life." She tapped the book with a finger. "You partitioned your mind. You understand, yes?"

Richard's eyes closed. "Yes, I understand," he said in a weak voice. Kahlan didn't understand that one.

Sister Verna went back to the book. "Third, you used the gift to kill a wizard. His name was Darken Rahl. You understand, yes?"

"Yes." He opened his eyes. "How do you know these things?"

"The things you have done used magic, specific magic, that leaves an essence because of who you are and because you are untrained. Were you trained, it would not leave this essence, and we would not know. We have ones back at the Palace of the Prophets who are sensitive to such events."

Richard glared at her. "You have violated my privacy, spied on me. And as for the third of your three things, I didn't exactly kill Darken Rahl. Not technically."

"I can understand how you feel," Sister Grace said quietly. "But it is only done to help you. If you wish to stand here and argue with us about whether or not these things qualify as the three triggers, I will put your doubts at ease. Once they are done, you begin the process of becoming a wizard. You may not believe it, or choose to be a wizard, but there is no doubt it has happened. We do not place this burden on you. We are only here to help you deal with it."

"But . . ."

"But nothing. When the magic is triggered, at least three changes come about. First, you begin to have fetishes about food. It may be things you crave, or things you have always eaten that you now refuse to eat. We have studied this, and don't understand its cause, but it has something to do with influences at the time the gift comes to life.

"Second, you begin to sleep, at least some of the time, with your eyes open. All wizards do this, even ones who only have the calling. It has something to do with learning to use the magic. If you have the gift, that brings it about as you use it to do these three things. If you have only the calling, the teaching brings it on.

"Third, the headaches come. The headaches are lethal. There is no cure for them other than learning to control the magic. If you don't, sooner or later, they will kill you."

"How soon? How much time do I have if I refuse your help?"

Kahlan put a hand on his arm. "Richard . . ."

"How much time!"

Sister Elizabeth spoke. "It is said that one lived with the headaches for a few years before he died. It is also said that another was dead within several months. We believe the time you have depends upon how strong your power is; the stronger the power, the stronger the headaches, and the shorter the time. But possibly within as little as a month they will begin to be strong enough to render you unconscious at times."

Richard gave her an even look. "They already have been that strong."

The three Sisters' eyes widened, and they exchanged the look again.

"We began looking for you before you did these three things. Since we left the palace, you have done all three," Sister Verna said. "This book is magic. When messages are written in its twin back at the palace, they appear to us here. That is how we know you have done them. How long since you have done the third— since you have killed this Darken Rahl?"

"Three days. But I was unconscious on the second night after I killed him."

"The second . . . !" Again they gave each other the look.

His irritation was back. "Why do you keep looking at each other like that?"

Sister Verna's voice came in a soft tone. "Because you are a very rare person, Richard. In many ways. We have never encountered so many unexpected things wrapped up in one person."

Kahlan slipped an arm around his waist. "You're right; he is a rare person. A person I love. What can you do to help him?" She was worried that he was frightening them and they wouldn't want to help.

"There are specific rules he must follow. We all must; they are inviolate. There is no room for negotiation. He must put himself in our hands and must come with us to the Palace of the Prophets." Sister Grace's eyes were sad as she said, "Alone."

"For how long?" Richard demanded. "How long does it take?"

Sister Grace's black hair shone in the torchlight as she turned her head to him. "It depends on how quickly you learn. It takes as long as it takes. You have to stay until it is finished."

Kahlan felt a tightness in her chest as Richard slipped his arm around her waist. "Can I visit him?"

Sister Grace shook her head slowly. "No. And there is more." Her eyes flicked to the Agiel for an instant. She reached into her cloak and pulled something out. It was a ring of metal, hardly more than a hand across. Even though it seemed unbroken, Sister Grace did something and it unlatched, opening into hinged half circles. Its dull silver color reflected the firelight. She held it up in front of Richard. "This is called the Rada'Han. It is a collar. You must wear it."

Richard took a step back, his hand coming away from Kahlan's waist and going to his throat. His face paled and his eyes widened. "Why?" he asked in a whisper.

"The rules begin. Discussion is over." Sister Verna and Sister Elizabeth moved behind Sister Grace as she spoke, standing with their hands at their sides as the black haired woman held the collar out in her hands. "This is no game. From now on, it can go only by the rules. Listen carefully, Richard.

"You will be offered three chances to take the Rada'Han; three chances to take our help, a Sister for each chance. There are three reasons for the Rada'Han, a Sister to reveal each. Before each offer, and chance to refuse, a different Sister will give you one of the reasons. After each reason, you will be offered the chance to accept or refuse.

"After the third refusal, as I hope you never learn, there are no more chances. You will receive no further help from the Sisters of the Light. You will die from the power of the gift."

Richard's hand still clutched at his throat. His voice was still hardly more than a whisper. "Why do I have to wear a collar?"

Sister Grace stiffened with authority. "No discussion. You will listen. You must put the Rada'Han around your neck yourself, of your own free will. Once it is on, you will not be able to remove it. It can only be removed by a Sister of the Light. It will stay on until we say it comes off. We will only say that when you are trained. Not before."

Richard's chest heaved with each labored breath. His stare was fixed on the collar. His eyes had a strange, wild, haunted look Kahlan had never seen before. She was frozen at seeing his terror, at her own terror.

Sister Grace held his eyes with a vengeance when he looked up at her. "Your first offer is at hand. Each offer comes from a different sister. The first offer comes from me.

"I, Sister of the Light, Grace Rendall, give the first reason for the Rada'Han, give the first chance to be helped. The first reason for the Rada'Han is to control the headaches and open your mind so you may be taught to use the gift.

"You now have the chance to accept or to refuse. I strongly advise you to accept the first offer of our help. Please believe me, it will only be much more difficult for you to accept the second time, and worse yet the third time.

"Please, Richard, accept the offer now, on the first of the three reasons and offers. Your life depends on this."

She stood still, waiting. His gaze went back to the dull silver collar. He looked on the verge of panic. The room was dead quiet except for the slow crackle of the fire and the soft hiss of the torches.

He looked up, and his mouth opened, but no words came as he stared unblinking at her intense gaze.

At last he blinked and spoke in a hoarse whisper. "I will not wear a collar. I will never again wear a collar. For anyone. For any reason. Never."

She straightened a little, lowering the collar, looking genuinely surprised. "You refuse the offer and the Rada'Han?"

"I refuse."

Sister Grace stood a while, staring with what seemed to be a mix of sadness and worry. Pale, she turned to the two Sisters behind her. "Forgive me, Sisters, I have failed." She handed the Rada'Han to Sister Elizabeth. "It is upon you now."

"The Light forgives you," Sister Elizabeth whispered as she kissed Sister Grace on each white cheek.

"The Light forgives you," Sister Verna whispered, giving the same kisses.

Sister Grace turned back to Richard, her voice less steady. "May the Light cradle you always with gentle hands. May you someday find the way."

Holding Richard's gaze, she brought her hand up, giving it a flick. A knife appeared from her sleeve. But rather than a blade, it had what seemed to be a pointed, round rod coming from the silver handle.

Richard leapt back, drawing the sword in one swift, smooth motion. Its distinctive ring sounded in the air.

Deftly, Sister Grace flipped the knife in her hand so it stopped with the blade pointing not toward Richard, but toward herself. She held it with practiced grace, without taking her eyes from Richard.

And then she plunged the knife between her breasts.

There was a flash of light that seemed to come from within her eyes, and she collapsed to the ground, dead.

Richard and Kahlan both took a step back in wide-eyed shock and horror. Sister Verna bent and pulled the knife from the dead woman. She stood and looked at Richard.

"As we told you: this is no game." She slipped the silver knife into her cloak. "You must bury her body yourself. If you let another do it for you, you will have nightmares for the rest of your life; nightmares caused by magic. There is no cure for them. Don't forget, you must bury her yourself." Both Sisters pulled their hoods up. "You have been offered the first of three chances, and refused. We will return."

The two Sisters glided to the door and were gone.

The sword's point slowly settled to the ground. Richard stared at the dead woman, tears running down his face.

"I won't wear a collar again," he whispered to no one but himself. "Not for anyone."

With labored movements, he retrieved a small shovel and a handle from his pack, and hooked them onto his belt. He then rolled Sister Grace onto her back, folded her hands across her, and lifted her lifeless form in his arms. One arm slipped from its place, loose, swinging. Her head hung down, limp. Her dead eyes stared. Black hair dangled. There was a small blossom of blood on the front of her white blouse.

Richard's pained eyes sought Kahlan. "I'm going to bury her. I would like to go alone."

Kahlan nodded and watched him shoulder the door open. After it had been pushed shut, she sank to the ground and started crying.

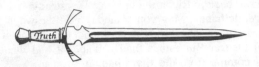

She was sitting, staring into the fire, when Richard came back. He had been gone a long time. After Kahlan had stopped crying, she had gone to tell Savidlin and Weselan what had happened, and then came back to the spirit house to wait for Richard. They had told her to come get them if she needed anything.

Richard sat down next to her and put his arms around her, his head on her shoulder. She ran her fingers through the back of his hair and held him close. She wanted to say something, but was afraid to say anything, so she just held him.

"I hate magic," he whispered at last. "It's going to come between us again."

"We won't let it. We just won't. We will think of something."

"Why did she have to kill herself?"

"I don't know," Kahlan whispered.

Richard took his arms away and fingered some of Nissel's leaves out of his shirt pocket. He sat chewing them as he gazed into the fire, a slight frown of pain on his face.

"I feel like running away, but I don't know where to go. How do you run away from something inside you?"

Kahlan rubbed her fingers back and forth on his leg. "Richard, I know this is hard for you to hear, but please listen. Magic isn't bad." He didn't object, so she went on. "How people use it is sometimes bad. Like the way Darken Rahl used it. I have had magic all my life. I've had to learn to live with who I am. Do you hate me because I have magic?"

"Of course not."

"Do you love me despite my magic?"

He thought a minute. "No. I love everything about you, and your magic is part of you. That was how I got past the Confessor's magic. If I had loved you despite your power, I wouldn't have been accepting you for who you are. Your magic would have destroyed me."

"So you see? Magic isn't all bad. The two people you love most in the world have magic. Zedd and me. Please listen. You have the gift. It is called a gift, not a curse. It is a wonderful, rare thing. It could be something used to help others. You have already used it to help others. Maybe you should try to think of it in this way, instead of trying to fight something that can't be fought."

He stared into the fire a long time as she smoothed his pant leg. She could hardly hear him when at last he spoke.

"I won't wear a collar again."

Kahlan's gaze went to the Agiel. The red leather rod hung from a fine gold chain at his neck, swinging slightly with his breathing. She knew the Agiel was used to torture people, but she didn't know how. She only knew she didn't like him wearing it.

Kahlan swallowed. "Did the Mord-Sith make you wear a collar?"

He stared unblinking at the fire. "Her name was Denna."

She turned to him, but he didn't respond. "Did she . . . Did Denna make you wear a collar?"

"Yes." A tear ran down his cheek. "She used it to hurt me. It had a chain on it. She hooked the chain to her belt and led me around by that collar like an animal. When she would attach the chain to some resting place, I couldn't move it. She controlled the magic that gives me pain when I use the sword to kill. She could amplify the magic, the pain. It prevented me from so much as putting tension on the chain. I tried. I tried hard. You can't imagine how much it hurt. Denna made me put the collar around my own neck. She made me do a lot of things."

"But the headaches will kill you. The Sisters said the collar will stop the headaches and help you learn to control the gift."

"They said that was one of the reasons. They also said there are two more reasons for the collar. I don't know what those other two reasons are. Kahlan, I know you think I'm being foolish. I think I'm being foolish, too. My head tells me the same things you are saying. But my insides tell me something altogether different."

Kahlan reached out and took the Agiel in her fingers, rolling it back and forth. "Because of this? Because of what Denna did?" He nodded, still staring at the fire. "Richard, what does this do?"

Richard looked to her at last. He gripped the Agiel in his fist. "Touch my hand. Don't touch the Agiel, just my hand."

Kahlan reached out and put her fingers against his fist.

She jerked back with a yelp of pain. She shook her wrist, trying to ease the sting. "Why didn't it hurt before when I touched it?"

"Because it was never used to train you."

"Then why isn't it hurting you to hold it?"

Richard still had his fist around the middle of the red leather rod. "It is. It hurts whenever I hold it."

Kahlan's eyes widened. "You mean it's hurting you right now, like when I touched your hand?"

The pain of the headache was in his eyes. "No. My hand was shielding you from what it really feels like."

She reached out again. "I want to know."

He dropped the Agiel. "No. I don't want it to hurt you like that. I don't want anything to ever hurt you like that."

"Richard, please? I want to know. I want to understand."

Richard stared into her eyes, and then let out a breath. "Is there anything you ask I wouldn't do?" He took the Agiel in his fist again. "Don't grip it; you may not be able to let go quick enough. Just touch it. Hold your breath and keep your teeth together so you don't bite your tongue. Tense your stomach muscles."

Kahlan's heart was pounding as her hand went toward the Agiel. She didn't want to feel the pain. It had hurt enough just to touch his hand, but she wanted to know because it was part of who he was now. She wanted to know everything about him. Even the things that hurt.

It felt like touching a bolt of lightning.

The pain shot up her arm, exploding in her shoulder. She screamed as the shock threw her on her back. She rolled over on her face, gripping her shoulder with her other hand. She couldn't move her arm. Her hand tingled and shook. She was shocked and frightened by the sheer power of the pain. She cried into the dirt as Richard's hand touched her back in sympathy. She cried, too, because now she understood, just a little, what had been done to him.

When at last she was able to sit up, he was still watching her, still holding the Agiel in his fist. "It hurts like that for you to hold it?"

"Yes."

She hit him on the shoulder with her fist. "Let go of it!" she cried. "Stop it!"

He released the Agiel, letting it hang again. "It helps distract me from the headaches, sometimes, to touch it. Believe it or not, it helps."

"You mean the headache hurts more than that?"

He nodded. "If it wasn't for what Denna taught me about pain, I would be unconscious right now. Denna taught me how to control pain, how to tolerate it, so she could give me more."

She tried to hold back the tears. "Richard, I . . ."

"What you felt was the least of what the Agiel can do." He picked it up again and touched the tip to the inside of his other forearm. Blood gushed from under the Agiel. He took it away. "It can strip the flesh right off you. It can break your bones. Denna liked to use it to crack my ribs. She would press it against me and I could hear the bone crack. They still aren't healed; it still hurts to lie down, or when you hug me tight enough. It can do a lot of other things too. It can even kill with a touch."

He stared at the fire. "Denna shackled my wrists, and later locked my arms behind me, and held me up with a rope from the ceiling. She used the Agiel on me for hours at a time. I would beg until I was hoarse, for her to stop. She never did. Not once.

"There was no way for me to fight back, nothing I could do to stop her. She trained me, she taught me, until I sometimes thought I had no blood or breath left. I begged her to kill me, to end the pain. I would have done it myself, but she used magic to prevent it. She had me kneel in front of her and beg her to use the Agiel. I would have done anything she said. She had a friend who came along sometimes, so they could share the . . . fun."

Kahlan sat frozen, hardly able to breathe. "Richard, I . . ."

"Every day, she led me by the collar to a place where she could hang me up by a rope, a room where she could use the Agiel on me without distraction, where it didn't matter so much if my blood got everywhere. Sometimes she did it from the first thing in the morning until night. And then at night . . .

"That is what wearing a collar means to me. You can tell me about how much sense it makes, about how it will help me, and about how I have no choice, but that is what wearing a collar means to me.

"I know exactly what your shoulder feels like right now. It feels like the skin has been burned, and the muscle has been torn, and bone is splintered. That is what it feels like to wear a Mord-Sith's collar. Only everywhere on your body all at once, and all day long. Add to that the thought that you are helpless to stop it, that you can never escape, that you'll never again see the only person you will ever love.

"I would rather die than put a collar around my neck again."

Kahlan rubbed her shoulder. It felt just as he had described it. She couldn't think of anything to say. She hurt too much, inside, to say anything. So she sat and watched him look at the fire as tears ran down her face. She ached for him.

And then she heard herself ask something she had promised herself she wasn't ever going to ask. "Denna took you for her mate, didn't she." She wished she could call the words back, and at the same time, she didn't.

Richard didn't flinch. "Yes," he whispered as he stared at the fire. Another tear ran down his cheek. "How did you know?"

"Demmin Nass brought two quads to take me. He had a spell-web from Darken Rahl to protect him from Zedd's magic. From mine too. Zedd couldn't do anything; he was frozen by a web. Demmin Nass told me what had happened to you. He said you were dead. That was when I called forth the Con Dar and killed him."

Richard's eyes closed as another tear ran down. "There was no way for me to stop her. I swear, Kahlan . . . I tried. You can't imagine what Denna did to me for trying to stop her. There was no way for me to fight back. She could do anything she wanted. It wasn't enough for her to hurt me just in the day. She wanted to hurt me at night, too."

"How can anyone be that evil?"

Richard stared at the Agiel as he slowly grasped it in his fist again. "She was captured when she was twelve. They trained her with this Agiel. This very one. Everything she did to me, they had done to her. Over and over. For years. They tortured her parents to death in front of her. There was no one to help her.

"She grew into a woman at the end of this Agiel, surrounded only by people who wanted her to hurt. There was no one to give her even a single word of hope, of comfort, of love.

"Can you imagine her terror? They gave her a life of endless pain. They raped her body and her spirit. They broke her. They made her one of them. Darken Rahl, personally, made her one of them.

"The whole time she used this Agiel on me, it hurt her. The same as it hurts me to hold it now. There's some magic for you.

"One day, Darken Rahl beat her, for hours, because he thought she wasn't hurting me enough. He flailed the skin right off her back."

Richard's head hung as he cried. "And then at the end of all that, at the end of a life of pain and madness, I come along, turn the Sword of Truth white, and run it through her. The only thing she asked before I killed her was for me to wear her Agiel and remember her. I was the only one who understood her pain. It was the only thing she wanted: for someone who understood to remember her.

"I promised, and she hung it around my neck. And then she just sat there as I pushed my sword through her heart. She had been hoping I would be the one with the power to kill her.

"That is how someone can be that evil. If I had the power, I would bring Darken Rahl back to life so I could kill him again."

Kahlan sat stunned, motionless, caught in a vortex of conflicting emotions. She hated this Denna for hurting Richard, she was unaccountably jealous of her, and at the same time, she felt unexpected, wrenching sorrow for her. Finally, she turned away and wiped the tears from her face.

"Richard, why didn't they win? Why wasn't Denna able to break you? How did you keep your sanity?"

"Because, as the Sisters said, I partitioned my mind. I don't know how to explain it. I didn't even know exactly what it was I was doing, but that's how I saved myself. I put the core of myself away and sacrificed the rest. I let her do what she would. Darken Rahl said that I have the gift because I did that. That was when I first heard the word—partitioned."

Richard lay back, resting his arm over his eyes. Kahlan pulled out a blanket and bunched it under his head. "I'm so sorry, Richard," she whispered.

"It's over. That is what matters." He took his arm from his eyes and at last smiled up at her. "It's over and we are together. In some ways, it was good. If she hadn't taught me, I wouldn't be able to deal with this headache. Maybe Denna has helped me. Maybe I can use what I know to get out of this."

She winced in sympathy. "Is it really bad right now?"

He nodded a little. "But I'll die before I ever put a collar around my neck again."

She understood now, though she wished she didn't. She lay down snug against him. The fire was a watery blur.

T he next day the sky was a cold gray and the wind icy as the two of them went out alone on the plain. Richard wanted to be away from people, away from buildings. He wanted to see the sky and the earth, he said. The brown grass bowed in the stiff gusts that flapped and tugged their cloaks as they walked along in silence. Richard wanted to shoot his bow to make the headache go away for a while. Kahlan just wanted to be with him.

It seemed that the eternity, which a few days ago she had felt belonged to them, was slipping through her fingers. She wanted to fight back, but didn't know how. Everything that was so right was suddenly going wrong.

She didn't think that Richard would put on the Rada'Han, the collar, no matter what the Sisters said. He might accept learning to use the gift, but she didn't think he would wear a collar. And if he didn't, he would die. After what he had told her—and worse, the things she knew he hadn't—how could she expect him to wear it? Or ask him to?

It did feel good, though, to be away from the village, away from people and away from Chandalen's eyes following them everywhere. How could she blame him? It did seem as if the two of them kept bringing trouble, but it irritated her that he acted as if they did it on purpose. She was tired of trouble. It seemed as if it would never end. Well, she decided, for today, at least, they would be away from trouble, and just enjoy being together.

Kahlan had told him she used to shoot a bow. She couldn't draw his because it was too heavy, so Richard encouraged her to borrow one and bring it along so he could teach her how to shoot better. They found the bundled grass targets the men had set up before, standing head high like a group of scarecrows on guard over the vast, flat grassland. A few even had balled grass for heads. Each had an X made of grass for a target. The targets with heads had an X there as well. Richard thought the Xs were too fat, so he took them off and made ones of single grass stalks.

They stood a long way off; so far, in fact, that she could hardly see the bundled grass, much less the Xs. Richard strapped on a simple leather bracer Savidlin had made for him along with the bow, and shot arrows until his headache was gone.

Richard was a picture of stillness, of smoothness; he was one with the bow. She smiled at how good he looked, and that he was hers. It made her heart ache with joy to see his gray eyes sparkle without the pain of the headache in them. They moved closer so she could shoot.

"Don't you want to go check where your arrows hit?"

He smiled. "I know where they hit. You shoot now."

She shot a few arrows, getting the feel again. He set one end of his bow on the ground, rested both hands over the other end, and watched her. She had been a girl the last time she used a bow. Richard watched her shoot a few more times, and then came and stood behind her. His arms came around her, and he adjusted her hand on the bow and put his fingers on the string.

"Here. Do this. You can't get any power or be steady enough holding the arrow with your thumb and the knuckle of your first finger that way. Hold the bowstring back with your first three fingers, like this, nesting the arrow between the first two. And pull with your shoulder too. You don't need to pull on the arrow, just concentrate on holding back the string. The arrow will take care of itself. See? Isn't that better?"

She grinned. "It is with your arms around me."

"Pay attention to what you're doing," he scolded.

Kahlan took aim and shot. He said it was better and told her to try again. She shot a few more arrows, and thought she might have even hit the bundled grass once. She drew the bowstring again, trying to hold the bow steady. Suddenly, he tickled her stomach. She doubled over squealing and laughing, trying to get his fingers off her.

"Stop it!" She laughed breathlessly, trying to twist away from him. "Stop it! Richard! I can't shoot when you're doing that!"

He put his fists on his hips. "You have to be able to."

She frowned up at him as she panted. "What do you mean?"

"Besides being able to hit what you want, you have to be able to shoot no matter what is happening. If you can't shoot when you're laughing, how can you shoot when you're afraid? Just you and the target, that's all there is. Nothing else matters. You have to be able to block everything else out.

"If a wild boar is charging you, you can't think about how afraid you are, or what will happen if you miss. You have to be able to make the shot under pressure. Or else have a tree close by you can climb."

"But, Richard, you can do it because you have the gift. I can't do that."

"Nonsense. The gift has nothing to do with it. It's simple concentration. Here, I'll talk you through it. Nock an arrow."

He stood behind her again, pulling her hair off her neck, leaning close, looking over her shoulder, and whispering in her ear as she drew the bowstring back. He whispered what she should feel, how she should breathe, where she should look, what she should see. He talked in a way that made the words melt into nothingness, and instead made images form in her head. Only three things existed: the arrow, the target, and his words. She was in a world of silence.

When everything else winked out, the target seemed to grow larger in her vision, drawing the arrow to it. His words made her feel it, made her do things without understanding them. She relaxed and exhaled, holding herself still without taking another breath. She could feel it, feel the target. She knew when it was time, when it was right.

Lightly, like a breath of air, the arrow left of its own accord, as if it had decided to go on its own. In the quiet, she could see the feathers clear the bow, feel the string hit the bracer; she could see the target pulling the arrow, she could hear the arrow hit the X. She felt air rush back into her lungs.

It was almost like when she released her Confessor's power. It was magic, Richard's magic. His words were magic. It was like having a new vision.

She felt as if she were coming awake from a dream. The world came back. She almost fell against him.

Kahlan turned and threw her arms around his neck, still gripping the bow in one hand. "Richard, that was wonderful. The target came to me!"

"See? I told you you could do it."

She kissed his nose. "I didn't do it, you did it. I was just holding the bow instead of you."

He smiled. "No. You did it. I just showed your mind how. That's what teaching is. I was simply teaching you. Do it again."

Kahlan had lived around wizards all her life. She knew the way wizards did things. That was the way Richard had done it. He spoke to her the way wizards spoke. It was the gift speaking, she knew, even if he wouldn't admit it.

As she shot more arrows, he talked less. Without his words guiding her, it was harder to get the feel, but now and again she did. She could tell when she was doing it herself, without him. It seemed to be as he said, like intense concentration.

As she started to learn to block the world out as she aimed, he began to do things to try to distract her. At first he just rubbed her stomach. It made her smile until he told her to stop thinking about what he was doing and think only about what she must do. After a few hours, she could shoot while he tickled her. Sometimes. It was an exhilarating feeling to be able to feel where the arrow needed to be. She couldn't do it very often, but when it happened it felt wonderful. Addictive.

"It's magic," she told him. "That's what you're doing. Magic."

"No, it's not. Everyone can do it. Chandalen's men are doing it when they shoot. Everyone who gets good enough does it. It's your own mind doing it. I just helped by showing you. If you had practiced long enough, you would have learned it by yourself before now. Just because you don't know how something is done doesn't make it magic."

She gave him a sidelong glance. "I'm not so sure. You shoot. Let me tickle you while you try to shoot."

"After we have something to eat. And you practice some more."

They flattened a circle of grass, like a nest, and lay on their backs, watching the birds wheel in the sky as they ate tava bread wrapped around greens, handfuls of kuru, and drank water from a skin. The surrounding grass protected them a little, so the wind didn't feel quite so cold. She laid her head on his shoulder as they watched the sky in silence. She knew they were both wondering what they were going to do.

"Maybe," Richard said at last, "I could partition my mind again, to control the headaches. Darken Rahl said that was what I had done."

"You talked to him? You talked to Darken Rahl?"

"Yes. Actually, he did most of the talking. I mostly listened. He told me a lot of things. I don't believe all of them. He told me George Cypher wasn't my father. He told me I had partitioned my mind, and that I have the gift. He told me I had been betrayed. Because of what Shota said—that you and Zedd would both use your magic against me—I thought one of you had betrayed us. I never thought of my brother.

"Maybe if I could figure out how to partition my mind again, I could control the headaches so they wouldn't kill me. Maybe that's what the Sisters teach. I've already done it once, so if I could do it again, I might be able to save myself without . . ."

He rested an arm over his eyes, not wanting to finish the thought out loud. "Kahlan, maybe I don't have the gift. It could just be the Wizard's First Rule."

"What do you mean?"

"Zedd told us that much of what people believe is wrong. The First Rule can make you believe something is true either because you want it to be true, or because you're afraid it might be. I'm afraid of having the gift, and that fear makes me accept the possibility that what the Sisters say is true. It could be there are other reasons the Sisters want me to think I have the gift, and that it isn't true. Maybe I don't have it."

"Richard, do you really think you can dismiss all the other things that have happened? Zedd said you have the gift, Darken Rahl said you have the gift, the Sisters say you have the gift, even Scarlet says you have the gift."

"Scarlet doesn't know what she is talking about, I don't trust the Sisters, and do you think I would believe anything Darken Rahl said?"

"And what about Zedd? Do you think Zedd is lying? Or that he doesn't know what he is talking about? You have told me you think he is the smartest man you know. Besides, he is a wizard of the First Order. Do you really think a wizard of the First Order wouldn't know the gift when he saw it?"

"Zedd could be wrong. Just because he's smart, that doesn't mean he knows everything."

Kahlan thought a while about his reluctance to accept that he had the gift. She wished, for his sake, that it could be the way he wanted it, but she knew the truth.

"Richard, at the People's Palace, when I touched you with my power, and we all thought it had taken you, and didn't know you had figured out how not to be consumed by the magic, you recited the Book of Counted Shadows to Darken Rahl, didn't you?" He nodded. "I couldn't believe you did that. How did you know it? Where did you ever learn the book?"

Richard sighed. "When I was young, my father took me to a place where he had it hidden. He told me it was being guarded by a beast sent by covetous hands, to watch over it, until that person could come for the book. So he rescued it. I know now that they were the hands of Darken Rahl, but at the time we didn't know that; my father said he had to take it because otherwise it would be stolen by those hands.

"He feared that person might eventually find it, so he had me memorize it. All of it. He said I had to know every word, so that someday I could return the knowledge to the keeper of the book. He didn't know that Zedd was the book's keeper. It took me years to memorize every word of the book. He never looked in it, he said that was for only me to do. After I had learned it all perfectly, we burned the book. I'll never forget that day. Light and sound and strange forms came forth as the book burned."

"Magic," she whispered.

He nodded as he rested his wrist over his eyes again. "My father died keeping the book from Darken Rahl. He was a hero. He saved us all by his actions."

Kahlan tried to think of how to put words to the things she was thinking, the things she knew. "Zedd told us the Book of Counted Shadows was kept in his keep. How did your father get it?"

"He never told me that."

"Richard, I was born and raised in Aydindril. I spent a good portion of my life in the Wizard's Keep. It's a huge fortress. In times long ago, hundreds of wizards lived there. When I grew up, there were only the six, and none were wizards of the First Order.

"It is not an easy place to enter. I was able to because I'm a Confessor, and needed to learn from books kept there. All the Confessors had access to the keep. But it was protected, by magic, from any others entering."

"If you're asking, I don't know how my father did it. He was a pretty smart man; he must have figured it out."

"If the book was in the Keep itself, maybe. There were wizards and Confessors coming and going, and at times others were permitted to enter. Perhaps someone could have found a way to sneak in. Even once inside, there are areas protected more strongly by magic. Areas even I could not enter.

"But Zedd said the Book of Counted Shadows was an important book of magic, very important. He said he kept it in *his* keep: the wizard of the First Order's keep. That is altogether different. It's separate from the rest, part of the larger Keep, but set off by itself.

"I've walked the long ramparts to the First Wizard's Keep. There is a beautiful view of Aydindril from there. Just walking the ramparts, I could feel the awesome power of the spells that protect that place. It made your skin crawl. If you went close enough, the power of the protection spells made the hair lift off your shoulders and stick out in all directions, popping and snapping with little sparks. If you went closer still, the spells filled you with a sensation of dread so strong you couldn't force your feet to take another step, or your lungs to draw another breath.

"Since Zedd left the Midlands, before we were born, none had entered the First Wizard's keep. The other wizards tried. To enter, there is a plate you must touch. It is said touching the plate is like touching the frozen heart of the Keeper himself. If the magic doesn't recognize you as one permitted entry, you cannot gain entrance. Touching the plate without at least the protection of your own magic, or even just getting close enough to the spells themselves, can be death.

"Since I was young, and first went to the Keep to learn from the books, the wizards had been trying to get in. They wanted to know what was inside. The First Wizard was gone, and they thought they should take an inventory, thought they should at least know what was in there.

"They never succeeded. Not one of them was ever able to so much as place a hand to the plate. Richard, if five wizards of the Third Order, and one of the Second, could not get in, how did your father?"

He sighed. "I wish I had an answer for you, Kahlan, but I don't."

She didn't want to dash his hopes, give irrefutable life to his fears, but she had to. The truth was the truth. He had to know that truth about himself.

"Richard, the Book of Counted Shadows was a book of instruction for magic. It was magic."

"I have no doubt of that. I know what I saw when we burned it."

She stroked the back of his hand with her finger. "There were other books of instruction for magic in the Keep: less important ones. The wizards let me look at them. When I would read them, I would get to a place in the books, and a strange thing would happen, sometimes after only a few words, sometimes after a few pages: I would forget what I had just read. I couldn't remember a word of it. Not a single word. I would go back and read it again, and the same thing would happen.

"The wizards would smile watching me, and then they would laugh. After a while of trying to read the books, and not knowing what I had just read, I finally got frustrated and asked what was happening. They told me that books of instruction for magic are protected by powerful spells invoked at certain words in the books. They said none but one with the gift could read a book of magic instruction and

117

remember so much as a single word. Those six wizards were wizards by calling, not by the gift. Even they couldn't read all the books and know what they said, only the less important ones, and only then because of their training.

"Zedd told us that the Book of Counted Shadows was one of the most important books in the Keep, so important it was kept in the First Wizard's enclave.

"Richard, you would never have been able to memorize it if you didn't have the gift. There is no other way. Somehow, your father must have known, that is why he chose you to learn it."

Her head was still resting on his shoulder, and she felt his breathing halt for a moment as he realized the significance of what she had told him. "Richard, do you still remember the book?"

His voice came low and distant. "Every word."

"Though I heard you recite it, and I know you spoke it all, I cannot remember a word of what you said. The magic of certain words erased it all from my mind. I don't know how you used it to defeat Darken Rahl."

"The first of the book said that if the words were being told to the one who controlled the boxes of Orden, and not read by that person, then the only way that person could know the words were true was with the use of a Confessor. Rahl thought you had taken me with your power, and so he thought I was speaking all the words true. I did speak the words true, but I left out an important part at the end so he would pick the box that would kill him."

"You see? You still remember the words. You could not do that if you didn't have the gift; the magic would prevent it. Richard, if we are going to get out of this, we have to at least face the truth, and then think of what to do about it.

"My love, you have the gift. You have magic. I'm sorry, but that is the truth of it."

He let out an exasperated breath. "I guess I just so badly didn't want it to be that I have been trying to talk myself out of it. But things don't work that way. I hope you don't think me a fool. Thank you for loving me enough to make me see the truth."

"You are no fool. You are my love. We will think of something." She kissed the back of his hand and they watched the sky in silence. It was a dark, cold gray, a mirror to her mood.

"I wish you could have met my father. He was a special person. I guess even I never knew how special. I miss him." He stared off into his own thoughts. "What of your father?"

Kahlan twisted a strand of her hair around her finger. "My father was mate to my mother; mate to a Confessor. He was not a father in the way a man is a father to other children. He had been taken by her power, and there was nothing to him but his devotion to her. He paid heed to me only to please my mother, only because I was born to her. He didn't see me as myself, but only as a part of the Confessor he was bonded to."

Richard pulled a piece of long grass and flattened the end of it between his front teeth as he thought, at last asking, "Who was he before she took him with the magic?"

"He was Wyborn Amnell. King of Galea."

Richard pushed himself up on an elbow, looking down at her with surprise. "King! Your father was a king?"

Without realizing she was doing it, her expression slipped into the calm exterior that showed nothing: a Confessor's face.

"My father was mate to a Confessor. That was all that was in him. When my mother was dying of a terrible wasting illness, he was in a constant state of panic. One day the wizard and the healer who had been tending her came to us and said there was nothing more they could do, that the spirits would soon take her to be with them, that she would soon pass from life.

"With a wail of anguish like none I have ever heard, my father clutched his chest and fell to the floor, dead."

Richard gazed into her eyes. "I'm sorry, Kahlan." He bent and kissed her forehead. "I'm sorry," he whispered.

He lay back once more and put the stalk of grass back between his teeth.

"It was a long time ago."

"So, what does that make you? Are you a princess, or a queen, or something?"

She laughed a little at the question, at how strange all this must seem to him. He still knew little of her life, her world. "No. I am the Mother Confessor. The daughter of a Confessor is a Confessor, not the daughter of her father." She felt uncomfortable about seeming to belittle her father. It was not his fault her mother had chosen and taken him. "Do you wish to know about him?"

He shrugged. "Sure. You are part of him, too. I like knowing all about you."

She thought a moment about what his reaction would be. "Well, he was the husband to Queen Bernadine when my mother chose him as her mate."

"Your mother chose a man who was already married?"

She felt Richard's eyes on her. "It is not as it must seem to you. The marriage between him and the queen was arranged. He was a warrior, a great commander. The marriage wedded his realm to the lands ruled by Queen Bernadine, creating the land of Galea. He did it for his people, to make a united land under a crown that could stand against hostile neighbors.

"The queen was a wise and respected leader. She married my father for the good of Galea, not for herself. She and my father had no love for each other. He gave her, gave the people of Galea, a fine, strong daughter, Cyrilla, and a then a son, Harold."

"Then you have a half sister and brother."

She shrugged. "In a way. But not in the way you think of it. I am a Confessor, not a knot in the string of royalty. I have met both Cyrilla and Harold. They are fine people. Cyrilla is the Queen of Galea now. Her mother died a few years back. Prince Harold is the commander of the army, as was his father. They don't think of me as kin, nor I them. I am of the Confessors; of the magic."

"What about your mother? When did she come into all this?"

"She had just become the Mother Confessor at the time. She wanted a strong mate, one who would give her a daughter with strength. She had heard the queen was not happy in her marriage, and went to speak with her. Queen Bernadine told my mother that she did not love her husband, that he was a cuckold. Even though she loved another, she respected Wyborn as a strong man, as a leader, and as a cunning warrior, and would not condone my mother taking him with her power.

"While my mother was thinking on what she would do, Wyborn caught the queen in the bed of that lover. He nearly killed her. When my mother heard of this, she returned to Galea and solved everyone's problems before he could add the murder of the lover to the beating he had given his wife.

"Though a Confessor has many things to fear, being struck by her husband is not one of them."

"It must be hard to have to choose a mate without loving him."

She smiled and pressed her head against him. "In my whole life, I never thought I would be able to have anyone I love. I wish my mother could have known this joy."

"What was it like having him as your father?"

She folded her fingers together against her stomach. "He was as a stranger to me. He had no emotion except for my mother, no real feelings, except for devotion to my mother. She wished him to spend time with me, to teach me the things he knew, so he was overjoyed to do so, but for her sake, not mine.

"He spent time teaching me what he knew: war. He taught me the tactics of his enemies, how to steal victory from a much larger and confident force, and most importantly, how to survive, and triumph, by using your head instead of rules. My mother would sit sometimes and watch as he taught me. He would look up and ask her if he was teaching me correctly. She told him he was; to teach me so that I might know the skills of war he knew, in the hope I'd never need them, and if I did, so that I might survive.

"He taught me that the most important quality in a warrior is ruthlessness. He said that he prevailed many times by being ruthless. He said terror could overwhelm reason, and it was a leader's job to bring that manner of terror to the enemy.

"The things he taught me helped me survive when other Confessors died. Because of what he taught me, I was able to kill when there was need. He taught me not to be afraid of doing the things that must be done to survive.

"For the things he taught me, I loved him, and I hated him."

"Well, I love him, for teaching you to how to survive, so that you could be with me now."

Kahlan shook her head slightly as she watched a small bird chasing away a raven. "The things he knew were not the horror; those who make you do them to survive are. He never wrongly took war to others. I shouldn't fault him for knowing how to triumph when he was forced to fight a war. Richard, perhaps we should start thinking about surviving now."

"You're right," he said, slipping an arm around her. "You know, I was thinking, we're sitting here like those targets; just sitting here waiting for an arrow to come and shoot us, waiting to see what will happen to us."

"What do you think we should do?"

He shrugged. "I don't know. But if we keep sitting here, sooner or later we're going to get shot. Sooner or later the Sisters are going to come back. Why should we just wait for them to come to us? I don't have the answers, but I can't see how sitting here is going to help."

She crossed her arms under her breasts, burying her hands to get them warm. "Zedd?"

Richard nodded. "Zedd would know what to do, if anyone would. I think we need to see him."

"What about the headaches? What if you get them when we're traveling? What if they get worse, and you don't have even Nissel to help?"

"I don't know." He sighed. "But I think we have to try. Otherwise, I don't have a chance."

"Then let's leave right away, before they get worse. Let's not wait for anything else to happen."

He squeezed her shoulders. "Soon. But we have to do something first. Something important."

Kahlan twisted her head around, looking up at him. "What?"

He smiled down at her. "We have to get married," he whispered. "I'm not leaving until I get to see this dress I keep hearing so much about."

She turned and hugged him. "Oh, Richard, it's going to be so beautiful. Weselan smiles the whole time she sews on it. I can't wait for you to see me in it. I know you will love it."

"Of that, my wife-to-be, I have no doubt."

"Everyone is looking forward to it. A wedding feast among the Mud People is a big party. Dancing, music, actors. The whole village joins in. Weselan said it will take a week or so to prepare everything, once we give the word to start."

He pulled her closer. "Word is given."

She had her eyes closed as she kissed him, but even so, she could tell his headache was back.

"Come on," she said, catching her breath, "let's shoot some arrows so your head will stop hurting."

They took turns for a while. Kahlan squealed in delight when they went to retrieve their arrows and she found she had put one of hers through one of his.

"Wait until the Home Guard hears about this! They will turn green, having to give the Mother Confessor a ribbon for making a shaft shot. They may even turn green just seeing me with a bow in my hands!"

Richard laughed as he pulled arrows from the targets. "Well, you'd better keep practicing. They might not believe you, and you may have to prove it to them. And I'm not taking the blame for this one with Savidlin." He turned to her suddenly. "What did you say? What did you say, before, last night, about the quad? Rahl sent them with a spell so Zedd couldn't stop them?"

Kahlan was a little surprised at his sudden change of subject. "Yes, his magic wouldn't work against them."

"That's because Zedd has only Additive Magic. That's all any wizard with the gift has: just the Additive. Darken Rahl had the gift for Additive but he had somehow learned to use Subtractive. Zedd had no defense against Subtractive Magic. Neither did you. Wizards created the Confessor's magic, and wizards have only Additive Magic." She nodded with a frown for him to go on. "So then how did you kill them?"

"I went into the Con Dar." She shrugged. "It's part of the Confessor's magic, but I had never before known how to use it. It was something to do with rage. It means 'Blood Rage.' "

"Kahlan, do you realize what you're saying? You had to have used Subtractive Magic. Otherwise, how could you have defeated them? Zedd's magic didn't work, and your regular magic didn't work, because those men were protected from Additive Magic. You must have Subtractive Magic. But if wizards of long ago created your Confessor's magic, how can it have an element of Subtractive to it?"

She stared at him. "I don't know. I never thought about it, but it must be as you say. Maybe when we get to Aydindril, Zedd can explain it."

With a frown, he pulled another arrow from the bundled grass. "Maybe. But why would Confessors have Subtractive Magic?" His frown deepened. "I wonder if that was what you did with the lightning."

Richard with the gift, and her with Subtractive Magic. Two frightening thoughts. She shivered, but not from the cold.

They shot arrows the rest of the afternoon, until the daylight began to dim. Her shoulders and arms were weary from pulling the bowstring. She told him she couldn't shoot another arrow if her life depended on it, and told him to shoot some arrows before they went back, so his headache would be gone for a while. As she watched him, it occurred to her she hadn't tried to distract him while he shot, and he had promised she could try.

Kahlan stepped up close behind him. "Time to see if you are really as good as you think you are."

When he drew back the bowstring, she tickled his ribs. He didn't flinch; he shot the same as before. But he laughed and squirmed after the arrow was away. She kept trying as he shot, but wasn't able to distract him. She became more determined. If tickling wouldn't work, she would just have to try something else.

Kahlan pressed up against his back as he concentrated on aiming, and smoothly unbuttoned the top three buttons of his shirt. She slipped her hand inside and ran it over his chest. His skin was taut over his hard muscles. He felt good. Warm. Strong. Hard.

She unbuttoned more buttons to better extend her reach. She ran the fingers of one hand through the back of his hair as the other roamed across his stomach. Richard kept shooting.

She started to forget about distracting him as she kissed the back of his neck. He giggled and hunched his shoulders after the arrow was away. He nocked another arrow. At last, she had all the buttons undone and was feeling all of the front of his torso, all the way down to his belt. Kahlan pulled the shirttails out of his pants and ran both hands over his body, one high, one low. It didn't keep him from hitting the target. She couldn't break his concentration. Her breathing quickened.

She decided she was going to win this game. She smiled as she pressed harder against him and reached farther.

"Kahlan!" he gasped. "Kahlan . . . that's not fair!" He still had the bowstring drawn, but his aim was starting to wander. He worked to steady it.

She drew his earlobe gently between her teeth and kissed his ear. "You said you have to be able to shoot no matter what is happening," she whispered as she pushed her hand farther.

"Kahlan . . ." His voice was high and strained. "That isn't fair . . . that's cheating!"

"No matter what. Those were your exact words. You have to be able to make the shot under pressure." She ran her tongue into his ear. "Is this enough pressure, my love? Can you do it? Can you make the shot?"

"Kahlan . . ." he panted. "You're cheating. . . ."

She gave a throaty laugh and squeezed. He gasped and released the bowstring. By its flight, she knew that was one arrow they would never find.

"I think you missed," she breathed in his ear.

He twisted around in her arms, dropping his bow. His face was red as he enclosed her in his arms.

He kissed her ear. "Not fair," he whispered, his breath hot. "You cheat." The touch of his lips on her ear made her gasp.

She held on tight as he pulled her hair away and put his warm mouth to her neck. It made her shiver. She hunched her shoulder against his face and half moaned, half laughed as the world tilted and she found herself on the ground under him. She managed to get out most of "I love you" before his lips covered hers and she wrapped her arms around his neck. She couldn't get her breath. She didn't want to.

Just as she was starting to wonder when his hands were going to get even for what she had done, Richard leapt to his feet.

He drew his sword in a rush.

The passion in his eyes had been replaced by rage. Anger from the Sword of Truth flashed in his expression. The ring of steel was carried away by the wind. He stood with his shirt open, his chest exposed and heaving with fury. She pushed herself up on her elbows.

"Richard, what is it?"

"Something is coming. Get behind me. Now!"

Kahlan sprang to her feet, snatched up her bow, and nocked an arrow. "Some *thing*?"

A ways off, she saw the grass moving, and it wasn't the wind.

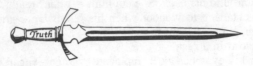

A splotchy gray head bobbed toward them through the long grass. Whatever it was, it wasn't very tall. Kahlan wondered if it could be another screeling. At that thought, she drew her bowstring back until the arrow's point was at her grip on the bow and the string against her cheek. She frantically worried if she could make the shot if it came at them. Although, from what she had seen of a screeling before, an arrow, she realized, would do no good. She wondered if she could call the lightning again.

Richard lifted his arm in front of her. "Wait."

A squat, hairless figure with long arms and big feet, dressed only in pants held up with straps, broke through the grass in front of them. Blinking yellow eyes gazed up at her pointing the arrow between them.

A sharp-toothed grin split its face. "Pretty lady."

It was the witch woman Shota's companion.

"Samuel!" Richard growled. "What are you doing here?"

The beastly creature hissed and reached for the sword. "Mine! Gimme!"

Richard brandished the blade menacingly and Samuel, pouting, snatched his arm back. Richard laid the sword's tip on the gray folds of skin at Samuel's neck. "I asked, what are you doing here?"

Hateful eyes peered up. "Mistress wants you."

"Well, you can just go home by yourself. We're not going to Agaden Reach."

He regarded Richard with one yellow eye. "Mistress not in the Reach." He turned, stretching up on his toes to look over the grass, and pointed a long, thick finger back toward the Mud People's village. "Mistress waits for you there. Where those people live together." He glared back at Richard. "She said if you don't come, she will kill them, and Samuel can cook them in a stew." His grin returned.

Richard gritted his teeth. "If she has hurt anyone . . ."

"She said she will not hurt them . . . if you come to her."

"What does she want?"

"You."

"What does she want with me?"

"Mistress not tell Samuel. Tells me only to get you."

Kahlan had relaxed half the tension on the bowstring. "Richard, Shota said she would kill you if she ever saw you again."

He kept his eyes on Samuel as he spoke. "No. She said she would kill me if I ever went back to Agaden Reach. She's not in the Reach."

"But . . ."

"If I don't go, she said she will kill people. Do you doubt her?"

"No . . . but she still might kill you."

He grunted and then smiled. "Kill me? I don't think so. She likes me. I saved her life. Indirectly at least."

Kahlan bristled. Shota had once tried to bewitch him, and she didn't like that one bit. Other than the Sisters of the Light, the witch woman was just about the last person Kahlan ever wanted to see again. "I don't like it."

Richard stole a quick glance at her. "If you have a better idea, put words to it."

Kahlan let out an angry breath. "I guess we have no choice. But you just keep her hands off you."

Richard gave her a startled look, then turned to the witch woman's companion. "You take the lead, Samuel, and don't forget who's carrying the sword. And remember what I told you the last time. I might still have some Samuel stew if you try doing anything to harm us."

Samuel eyed the blade a moment. Without another word he turned and started off, glancing over his shoulder to make sure they followed. Richard kept the sword out, slung his bow over his shoulder, and put himself between Kahlan and Samuel. The anger of the sword's magic blazed in his eyes. Samuel loped through the grass ahead of them, turning back occasionally to hiss at them.

Kahlan stayed close on Richard's heels. "She'd better not put snakes on me again. No snakes!" she said emphatically. "And I mean it."

"As if we have a choice," Richard muttered.

It was near dark by the time they reached the village. They came in from the east, and noticed immediately that the entire population of the village was clustered at the south end of the common field, shielded by armed hunters standing shoulder to shoulder. Kahlan knew the Mud People were deathly afraid of the witch woman. They wouldn't even speak her name aloud.

For that matter, everyone she ever knew was deathly afraid of the witch woman—including her. Shota would have killed her the last time if Richard hadn't used a wish Shota had granted him, to save her. She didn't think Shota would be granting Richard any more wishes.

Samuel led them through the narrow passageways, toward the spirit house, walking as if he had lived here all his life. He gurgled his odd laugh as he bounded along, giving them an occasional glance. He grinned with bloodless lips, as if he knew something they didn't. When his grin showed too many teeth and Richard prodded him with the sword, Samuel growled and hissed, his yellow eyes glowing in the fading light.

Samuel laid his long-fingered hand on the latch to the spirit house. "Pretty lady waits here. With me. Mistress wants only Seeker."

"Richard, I'm going in too," Kahlan said firmly.

He gave her a sidelong glance and then looked at Samuel. "Open the door."

One powerful arm drew the door back, as shining yellow eyes glowered at him. Richard held his sword out, indicating that he wanted her to go in. The door squeaked closed behind them, with a sour-faced Samuel on the other side.

In the center of the room sat a tall, elegant throne. Torchlight danced and flared on the carved, gold-leaf vines, snakes, cats, and other beasts that covered every inch of the stately structure. A canopy draped with heavy red brocade and trimmed with gold tassels jutted out overhead. The throne itself sat atop three square, white marble platforms that served as steps. The whole thing was massive and imposing. Tufted red velvet covered the seat, the back, and the tops of the arms. Kahlan couldn't imagine how it could have possibly fit through the door. Or how many men it must have taken to carry it.

Shota sat regally, her impassive almond eyes watching Richard. She reclined slightly, against the red velvet, one leg crossed over the other, her arms resting on the chair's high, wide-spaced arms, with hands draped haughtily over gold gargoyles. The gargoyles licked her wrists while she clicked one long, lacquered fingernail against a thumbnail. Luxuriant auburn hair cascaded over her shoulders.

Shota redirected her ageless eyes to Kahlan. The long, rock-solid gaze felt as if it paralyzed her, penetrated her. A red, white, and black banded snake slumped down, hanging from the canopy. It flicked its tongue at Kahlan, hissing, and then dropped into Shota's lap, coiling up like a contented cat.

It was a message to say that she had not been invited, and was now warned of what would happen if Shota became displeased. Kahlan swallowed, trying not to let it show. After what seemed an eternity, and after the witch woman seemed satisfied that the message was understood, she turned her unblinking eyes back to Richard.

"Put your sword away, Richard." Shota's voice was like smooth velvet rubbed the right way. Kahlan didn't think it was fair that anyone that beautiful should also be graced with a voice that could melt butter, or a man's heart.

"From the impression you left when we parted, I fear you might try to kill me." His voice, also, was annoyingly smooth.

"If I decide to kill you, my dear boy, and I may, your sword will not help you." Richard suddenly yelped and dropped the sword as if it was a hot coal. He stared down at the sword as he comforted his hand. "Now, put it away." That time the quality of her voice was more of velvet rubbed the wrong way.

From under his eyebrows, Richard looked up at Shota on her throne, before bending to retrieve his sword and slide it back into its scabbard.

A self-satisfied smile spread across Shota's full lips. She lifted the snake from her lap and set it aside. Shota watched Richard a moment longer and then stood, leaning forward enough in the process to offer her breasts the opportunity to fall out of her wispy, low-cut, variegated gray dress. How they managed not to, Kahlan didn't know. A little stoppered bottle tumbled from its snug place between her breasts and swung on a fine silver chain.

Kahlan's face heated as Shota gracefully descended the three platforms, never taking her eyes from Richard. The loose points of the dress floated gently, as if in a light breeze. But there was no breeze inside the spirit house.

That fabric, Kahlan decided, was definitely too thin for a dress. She wondered what she would look like in it, and blushed at the mental image.

Once standing on the ground, Shota turned and pulled the stopper from the little bottle. The entire throne wavered, like something seen through heat waves. Abruptly it turned to gray smoke and swirled in a circle, diminishing all the time in size, and sucked itself into a fine line that went into the little bottle. Shota replaced the stopper, tucked the bottle back between her breasts, and with a finger, pushed it so far down it could no longer be seen. Kahlan took a deep, noisy breath.

Shota's gaze glided from Richard's eyes and took in his open shirt with what might have been amusement. Or satisfaction. Richard's face reddened.

Shota's smile widened. "How delightfully indecent." She ran one of her long, red nails all the way down his chest to his navel, and then she gently patted his stomach. "Button your shirt, Richard, or I may forget why I'm here."

His face turned a deeper red. Kahlan moved deliberately closer to his side as he began redoing the buttons.

"Shota," he said as he tucked the tails in his pants, "I have to thank you. You may not know it, but you really helped me before. Helped me to figure it out."

"It was my intention to help you."

"You don't understand. I mean you helped me figure out how to be with Kahlan. You helped me figure out how we could be together. How to love her." He smiled. "We're going to be married."

There was a moment of icy silence.

"That's right," Kahlan said, holding her chin up, "we love each other . . . and can be together now . . . Forever." She hated the way Shota made her feel explanations were necessary, and the way she fumbled with them.

Shota's intense gaze slid to her and her smile slowly evaporated, making Kahlan have to swallow again. "You ignorant children," Shota whispered as she slowly shook her head. "You foolish, ignorant children."

Richard's expression was becoming heated. "We may be ignorant, but we are not children, and we love each other. And we are going to be married. I was hoping you would be happy for us, Shota, since you played a small part in it."

"What I told you, dear boy, was that you needed to kill her."

"But that's all over," Kahlan protested. "The problem has been solved. It's all right for us now. Everything is all right."

Kahlan gasped as she felt her feet lift off the ground. Both she and Richard were flung across the room and up against the wall. The impact knocked the wind from her lungs. Little points of light floated and danced before her eyes. She looked down, trying to clear her vision.

She and Richard were flattened against the mud-brick wall, a good three feet off the ground. She could hardly breathe. The only thing she could move was her head. Even her clothes were flattened. Her cloak lay against the wall as if it were the floor. Richard was as helpless as she. They both struggled, twisting their heads, but it was useless; they were stuck tight.

Shota glided across the room toward them, her eyes hot and dangerous. She stopped in front of Kahlan. "He didn't need to kill you? And it's all right now, is it, Mother Confessor?"

"Yes," Kahlan managed, trying to sound confident as she hung helpless.

"Did it ever occur to you, Mother Confessor, that perhaps there are reasons behind what I say?"

"Yes, but that has all . . ."

"Did it ever occur to you, Mother Confessor, that there is a reason why Confessors are not supposed to love their mates? And perhaps another reason he should have killed you?"

Kahlan couldn't answer. Her mind raced with frantic thoughts.

"What are you talking about?" Richard demanded.

Shota ignored him. "Did it, Mother Confessor?"

Kahlan's throat was so dry, she had to swallow twice before she could speak. "What do you mean? What reason?"

"Have you lain with this man you love? Have you done that yet, Mother Confessor?"

It was Kahlan's turn to blush. "What kind of question is that to ask someone!"

"Answer the question, Mother Confessor," Shota hissed, "or I will skin you right now and use your hide to make myself something pretty. I am of a mind to do it anyway. You had better not even think of lying to me."

"I . . . We . . . No! And what business is it of yours anyway!"

Shota stepped closer. Her eyes sent a silent shriek through Kahlan. "Maybe you'd better think twice before you do, Mother Confessor."

"What do you mean?" she breathed, wide-eyed.

Shota folded her arms across her breasts. Her voice became more menacing. "Confessors are not supposed to love their mates, because if they bear a male child, she has to ask the husband to kill the baby. The husband is supposed to have been taken by the Confessor's power, so that he will do whatever she asks. Without question."

"But . . ."

Shota stepped even closer, her eyes filled with fury. "If you love him, how could you ask that of him! How could you ask Richard to kill his son? Do you think he would? Would you? Would you kill the son of the man you love? Would you, Mother Confessor?"

Shota's words knifed into Kahlan's heart and soul, leaving her barely able to whisper the answer. "No."

She felt her hopes and happiness collapsing. In the joy of finding she could be with Richard, she hadn't given any thought to the future. To the consequences. To children. She had thought only of Richard and her being together.

Shota was screaming at her. "And then what, Mother Confessor! You will raise him? And you will visit upon the world a male Confessor? A male Confessor!" She unfolded her arms, her white-knuckled fists dropping to her sides. "You will bring the world to the dark times again! The dark times! Because of you! Because you love this man! Did you ever think of that, you ignorant child?"

The lump in Kahlan's throat threatened to choke her. She wanted to run from Shota, but she couldn't move. "Not all male Confessors are that way."

"Almost every one is! Almost every one!" She pointed a single finger at Richard without looking at him. "Are you going to risk the world, because you love this man? Risk sending everyone into the terror of the dark times, just because you would selfishly want the son of this man to live?"

"Shota," Richard's voice was surprisingly calm. "Most Confessors bear girls. You are worrying about something that probably won't even happen. We may not even have children. Not all couples conceive. You are extending your worries along a lot of forks in the road."

Richard suddenly slid down the wall, landing with a grunt. In a rage, Shota grabbed his shirt in her fists and lifted him, slamming him against the wall, knocking the wind from his lungs. "Do you think I am as stupid as you? I know the flow of time! I am a witch woman! I told you before, I know how certain events flow and unfold! If you lie with this woman, she will have a male child! She is a Confessor! Every Confessor bears a Confessor! Always! If you give her a child, it will be a boy!"

She slammed him against the wall again. Kahlan winced at the sound of his head hitting the wall. Shota's behavior was frightening, and seemed out of character. She had impressed Kahlan before as menacing in the extreme, but she also seemed intelligent and reasonable. At least to an extent. She seemed different now, unstable.

Richard didn't try to remove her hands, but Kahlan could see he was getting angry. "Shota—"

She slammed him up against the wall again. "Keep your tongue still or I will cut it out!"

Richard's rage looked to match Shota's. "You were wrong before, Shota! Wrong! There are many ways for events to flow forward in time. Had I listened to you the last time, and killed Kahlan when you wanted me to, Darken Rahl would rule us all now! And it would have been because I followed your stupid advice! It was through her that I defeated Darken Rahl! If I had done as you wished, we would have lost!"

His chest heaved as he glared at her. "If you have come all this way to threaten us about some perceived threat, you have wasted your time. I didn't do it your way the last time, and I will not do it your way now! I will not kill her nor will I give her up on your word! On anyone's!"

Shota stared at him a moment and then removed her hands from his shirt. "I did not come here about some 'perceived' threat to the future," she whispered. "I did not come here to argue with you about making babies with Confessors, Richard Rahl."

Richard jerked back in shock. "I'm not . . ."

"I came here, because I may want to kill you for what you have done, Richard Rahl. That you two ignorant children want to go make babies is a flea on the back of the true monster you have already created."

"Why are you calling me that?" Richard whispered.

Shota studied his pale face. "Because that is who you are."

"I am Richard Cypher. George Cypher was my father."

"You were raised by a man named Cypher. You were sired by one named Darken Rahl. He raped your mother."

Richard's face turned whiter. Kahlan ached for him. She understood now, knew it was true. This was what she had seen in him; she had seen the face of his father, Darken Rahl. She tried desperately to free herself, to go to him, but couldn't.

Richard shook his head. "No. That's not true. It just isn't possible."

"True," Shota snapped. "Your father was Darken Rahl. Your grandfather is Zeddicus Zu'l Zorander."

"Zedd?" he whispered. "Zedd is my grandfather?" He straightened. "Darken Rahl . . . No, he can't be. It's not true."

He turned and looked up at Kahlan. He saw it in her face, saw that she knew it was. He turned back to Shota. "Zedd would have told me. He would have. I don't believe you."

"I don't care," she said in a flat tone. "I don't care what you believe. I know the truth." Her emotion came back. "And the truth is you are the bastard son of a bastard son of a bastard son! And each one of those bastard sons, all the way back, had the gift. Worse, Zedd has the gift. You have the gift, but it is from two bloodlines of wizards." She glared at his wide eyes. "You are a very dangerous person, Richard Rahl." Richard looked like he might fall down. "You have the gift. In this case, I would be more inclined to call it a curse."

"I would agree with you about that," Richard whispered.

"You know you have the gift? We are going to have no argument about that?" Richard could only nod. "The rest of it I could not care less about. You are the son of Darken Rahl, and on the other side, the grandson of Zeddicus Zu'l Zorander. He is the father of your mother. If you choose to ignore the truth of that, I don't care.

Believe as you will. Delude yourself as you will. I am not here to argue your ancestry."

Richard leaned back until the wall stopped him. He ran his fingers through his hair. "Go away, Shota. Please, go away." His voice sounded as if all life had gone out of him. "I don't want to hear anything else you have to say. Just go away. Leave me alone."

"I am disappointed in you, Richard."

"I don't care."

"I didn't know you were this stupid."

"I don't care."

"I thought George Cypher meant something to you. I thought you had some kind of honor."

His head came up. "What do you mean?"

"George Cypher raised you. Gave you his time, his love. He taught you, cared for you, provided for you. Shaped you. And you would throw that away because someone else raped your mother? That is what is important to you?"

Richard's eyes lit with fire. His hands started coming up. Kahlan thought he was going to try to strangle Shota, but then his hands sank back to his sides. "But . . . if Darken Rahl is my father . . ."

Shota threw her arms up in the air. "What? You are suddenly going to start acting like him? You are going to spontaneously start doing vile things because you now know? You fear you will go out and kill innocent people because you learned your real father is Darken Rahl? You will ignore the things you learned from George Cypher because you find your name is Rahl? And you call yourself the Seeker. I am disappointed in you, Richard. I thought you were your own man. Not the reflection of others' impressions of your ancestors."

Richard hung his head as Shota frowned angrily and watched him in silence. At last he took a deep breath. "I'm sorry, Shota. Thank you for not letting me be any more stupid than I already am." His eyes were wet as he turned to Kahlan. "Please, Shota, let her down."

Kahlan felt the pressure lift, and she slid down the wall, her boots thumping against the ground. The glare Shota gave her made her stay where she was, even though she wanted to go to Richard. He stared at his boots.

Shota put her fingers under his chin and lifted his head. "You should be happy; your father was not ugly. Some of his looks are the only thing of his you have. That, and a bit of his temper. And the gift."

Richard pulled his chin away from her fingers. "The gift. I don't want the gift. I don't want anything to do with it. I wouldn't call anything I got from Darken Rahl a gift. I hate it! I hate magic!"

"It comes from Zedd, too," Shota said with surprising compassion. "From both sides. That is the way you get the gift; it is passed down, sometimes skipping one, or even many generations. Sometimes not. You received it from both sides. In you, it is more than a single dimension. It is a very dangerous mix."

"Passed down. Like any other deformity."

With a sneer, Shota gripped his face in her long fingers. "Remember that before you lie with her. From Kahlan, the boy would be a Confessor. From you—he would have the gift. Can you even fathom the danger of that? Can you conceive of a Confessor with the gift? A male Confessor? I doubt you can. You should have killed

130

her when I told you to, you ignorant child, before you found a way to be with her. You should have killed her."

Richard glared at her. "I've heard enough of that talk. I intend to hear no more of it. I told you before; it is through Kahlan I defeated Darken Rahl. Had I killed her, he would have won. I hope you didn't waste your journey here just to repeat this nonsense."

"No," Shota said quietly. "None of these things matter. That is not why I am here. I came because of what you have done, not because of what you might do someday. What you have already done, Richard, is worse than anything you could ever do with this woman. No monster you conceive with her could equal the monster you have already created."

Richard frowned. "I stopped Darken Rahl from ruling the world. I killed him. I created no monster."

She shook her head slowly. "The Magic of Orden killed him. I told you; he mustn't open a box. You didn't kill him, you let him open one of the boxes of Orden. The Magic of Orden killed him. You were supposed to kill him before he opened one of the boxes."

"I couldn't! That was the only way! There was no other way to kill him! And what difference does it make anyway? He's dead!"

"It would have been better if you had let him win than let him open the wrong box."

"You're crazy! What could be worse than Darken Rahl gaining the Magic of Orden and ruling the world unchallenged!"

Her eyebrows lifted. "The Keeper," she whispered. "It would have been better to let Darken Rahl rule us, or behead us, or even torture us to death, than what you have allowed to happen."

"What are you talking about?"

"The Keeper of the underworld is kept in his place, kept from the world of the living, by the veil. The veil holds him and his minions back. Holds the underworld back. It keeps the dead from the living. What you have done has torn that veil. Already, some of the Keeper's assassins have been loosed."

"The screelings . . ." Richard whispered.

Shota nodded. "Yes. By freeing the Magic of Orden, you have allowed its magic to somehow tear the veil to the underworld. If it tears enough, the Keeper will be freed. You can't even conceive of what that means." Shota lifted the Agiel at his neck. "It will make what was done to you with this seem like a lover's kiss compared to what he will do. To everyone. It would have been better to have let Darken Rahl win, than to have let this happen. You have condemned everyone to a fate beyond horror."

She gripped the Agiel in her fist. "I should kill you for what you have done. I should make you suffer unspeakably. Do you have any idea how much the Keeper would like to settle his gaze upon one with the gift? Do you have any idea how much he wants those with the gift? Or how much he wants witch women?"

Kahlan saw tears run down Shota's cheeks. With a flush of understanding that sent an icy ripple of panic through her, Kahlan realized Shota wasn't angry. She was afraid.

That was why she was here: not because she was angry at Kahlan being alive, or at them having a child. She was here because she was terrified. The idea of

Shota, a witch woman, being afraid was worse than anything her own mind could conjure.

Richard stared at her, his eyes wide. "But . . . there must be something we can do, some way to stop it."

"We?" she screamed, jabbing her finger at his chest. "You! Only you, Richard Rahl! Only you! Only you can fix it!"

"Me! Why me?"

"I don't know," she cried through gritted teeth. "But you are the only one with the power." She pounded her fist against his chest. "You!" She kept hitting his chest as he just stood there. "You are the only one who has a chance! I don't know why, but only you can fix it. Only you can repair the tear in the veil." Shota was sobbing now. "Only you, you stupid, foolish child."

Kahlan was dazed by the magnitude of what was happening. The idea of the Keeper being loose was beyond comprehension. The dead in the world of the living; she couldn't imagine the horror of it, but seeing Shota's fear put dimension to the dread.

"Shota . . . I don't know anything about it. I don't have any idea of how to . . ."

Shota was still hitting his chest as she cried. "You must. You must find a way. You have no idea what the Keeper would do to me, what he'd do to a witch woman. If you won't do it for me, do it for yourself. He would be no easier on you than me. And if you won't do it for yourself, do it for Kahlan. He would have her for an eternity of pain for no other reason than that you love her. He would do it to her just to make it worse for you. We will all be held on the cusp between life and death for all eternity, twisting in anguish." She was sobbing uncontrollably now. "Our souls will be stripped from us . . . He will have our souls . . . forever."

Shota hit Richard's chest again. He put his arms around her and pulled her against him, comforting her as she cried. "Forever, Richard. Soulless minds trapped by the dead. An eternity of torment. You are too stupid to even comprehend it. You could never even imagine the horror of it, until it happens."

Kahlan stood next to Richard, putting her hand reassuringly on his shoulder. She felt no anger at the sight of him comforting Shota. She could see how terrified the witch woman was. Kahlan couldn't share the same level of terror, because she didn't know the things Shota knew. But in some ways, seeing Shota's reaction was knowing enough.

"Screelings came into the Reach," she cried.

Richard looked down at her. "Screelings! In Agaden Reach?"

"Screelings, and a wizard. A particularly nasty wizard. Samuel and I escaped with little more than our lives."

"A wizard!" With his hands on her shoulders, Richard pushed her away. "What do you mean a wizard? There are no other wizards."

"There is one in the Reach. The screelings and the wizard are in Agaden Reach now. They are in my home. My home!"

Kahlan couldn't hold her tongue. "Shota, are you sure it was a wizard? Could it be someone pretending to be a wizard? There are no more wizards. Except Zedd. They are all dead."

Shota gave a tearful frown. "Do you think anyone could deceive me about having magic? I know a wizard when I see one, and I know a wizard with the gift. I know wizard's fire. This one is a wizard with the gift, young though he is. I don't know where he came from, or why no one knew of him. But he was with screelings. Screelings!

"That can mean only one thing. This wizard has given himself over to the Keeper. He is doing the Keeper's bidding. He is working to tear the veil the rest of the way for the Keeper. It means the Keeper has agents in this world. Darken Rahl was probably one of them. That is why he was able to use Subtractive Magic."

Shota turned to Richard. "That the Keeper is using wizards means that it must take a wizard to tear the veil. You have the gift. You are a wizard. A stupid wizard, but a wizard nonetheless. I don't know why, but you are the only one with a chance to close the tear."

Richard brushed a tear from Shota's cheek. "What are you going to do?"

The fire came back to Shota's eyes. Her teeth clenched. "I am going back to the Reach. I am going to take back my home."

"But they chased you out."

"They took me by surprise," she snapped. "I only came here to tell you how stupid you are. And that you must do something about it. You must close the tear, or we are all . . ."

Shota turned her back to them. "I am going back to the Reach. The Keeper is going to lose his agent. I am going to take the gift from him. Do you know how to remove the gift from a wizard?"

"No." Richard looked interested. "I didn't know it could be done."

"Oh yes, it can be done." She turned and arched an eyebrow. "If you rip their skin off, the magic bleeds from them. That is the only way to remove the gift from a wizard. I am going to hang him up by his thumbs, and then I am going to skin him alive. Every inch of him. Then I am going to use his skin to cover my throne. Then I am going to sit on my throne, on his skin, and watch him scream to death as the magic bleeds from him." She made a fist. "Or I am going to die trying."

"Shota, I need some help. I don't know anything about all this."

Shota stared off flexing her fists. At last her hands relaxed and opened. "There is nothing I can tell you that will help."

"You mean there is something you can tell me, but it won't help." Shota nodded. Richard sighed. "What is it?"

She folded her arms against her stomach. Her eyes were wet again. "You will be trapped in time. Don't ask what that means, because I don't know. You will have no chance of closing the veil unless you escape the trap. It will keep you locked away, and the Keeper will escape unless you are able to free yourself. Unless you learn something of the gift, you have no chance for either."

Richard walked to the far side of the room. He stood with his back to them, one hand on a hip, his other combing through his hair. Kahlan didn't look at Shota. She didn't want to meet the witch woman's gaze if she didn't have to.

"Is there anything else?" Richard called over his shoulder. "Anything you can tell me? Anything?"

"No. And believe me, if there was I would be more than anxious to offer it. I don't wish to meet the Keeper's gaze."

Richard thought by himself for a time. At last, he came back and stood before Shota. "I am having headaches. Bad headaches."

Shota nodded. "The gift."

"Three women came. They call themselves the Sisters of the Light. They said I

133

have to come with them to learn to use the gift, or the headaches will kill me."
Richard studied her face. "What do you know about them?"

"I am a witch woman. I don't know much about wizards. But the Sisters of the
Light have something to do with wizards. With training them. That is all I know. I
don't even know where they are from. They come once in a great while, when they
find one has been born with the gift."

"What if I don't go with them? Will I die, as they say?"

"If you don't learn to control the gift, the headaches will kill you. That much I
know."

"But are they the only way?"

Shota shrugged. "I don't know. But I know you must learn to use the gift, or
you will not escape the trap, or be able to close the veil—or even survive the
headaches."

"So you are saying you think I should go?"

"No. I said you must learn to use the gift. There may be another way."

"What way?"

"I don't know, Richard. I don't even know if there is another way. I'm sorry,
but I can be of no help in this. I just don't know. Only a fool will give advice about
something she doesn't understand. I can give you no advice in this."

"Shota," Richard pleaded, "I'm lost. I don't know what to do. I don't understand
any of it, the Sisters, the gift, or the Keeper. Isn't there anything you can tell me
to help me?"

"I have told you everything I know. I feel as lost as you. Worse. I have no ability
to influence what will happen. At least you have that. Dim as the chance is." Shota's
eyes glistened. "I fear I am going to look into the Keeper's dead eyes. Forever. I
haven't been able to sleep since I learned these things. If I knew anything, I would
help. I just don't know anything about the world of the dead. It is not something
the living have faced yet."

Richard stared at the ground. "Shota," he whispered. "I don't have any idea what
to do. I'm afraid. I'm very afraid."

She nodded. "So am I." She reached out and touched his face. "Good-bye,
Richard Rahl. Don't fight who you are. Use it." She turned to Kahlan. "I don't
know if you can help him, but if there is a way, I know you will do your best."

Kahlan nodded. "That I will, Shota. I hope you get your home back."

Shota gave her a small smile. "Thank you, Mother Confessor."

She turned and glided to the door, her wispy dress flowing behind. She pushed
the door open. Samuel was waiting on the other side, his yellow eyes shining. Shota
stopped in the doorway and stiffened.

"Richard, if you should happen to somehow close the veil, and save me from
the Keeper, save everyone from the Keeper, I will be forever grateful to you."

"Thank you, Shota."

Her back was still to them. "But know this: if you give the Mother Confessor a
child, it will be a boy. It will be a Confessor. Neither of you will have the strength
to kill him, even though you know the consequences." She paused a moment. "My
mother lived in the dark times." Her voice was like ice. "I have the strength. And,
I will use it. You have my word on that. But know that it will not be personal."

The door squeaked closed behind her. The spirit house felt suddenly very empty.
Very quiet.

Kahlan felt numb. She looked down at her hands. They were shaking. She wanted

Richard to hug her, but he didn't do it. He was staring at the door. His face was white as snow.

"I don't believe this," he whispered. He still stared at the door. "How can this be happening? Am I dreaming all this?"

Kahlan felt as if her knees were about to buckle. "Richard, what are we going to do?"

Richard turned to her, his eyes distant. They filled with tears. "This has to be a nightmare."

"If it is, I'm having the same one. Richard, what are we going to do?"

"Why does everyone ask me that? Why does everyone always ask me? What makes everyone think I am the one who knows?"

Kahlan stood woodenly, trying to make her mind work. She couldn't seem to form a coherent thought. "Because you are Richard. You are the Seeker."

"I don't know anything about the underworld, the Keeper. The world of the dead."

"Shota says no one living does."

Richard seemed to come out of his daze. Abruptly he grabbed her shoulders. "Then we must ask the dead."

"What?"

"The ancestors' spirits are dead. We can talk to them. I can ask for a gathering and ask them questions. We can learn from them. Maybe we can find out how to close the veil. Maybe I can find out how to stop the headaches, how to use the gift." He gripped her arm. "Come on."

Kahlan almost smiled. He was indeed the Seeker. Richard pulled her through the passageways, running when they could see well enough. Clouds hid the moon and it was dark between the buildings. The air was like ice on her face, making tears run from the corners of her eyes.

When they reached the open field, there was light. Torches lit the people gathered there. They were all still bunched together with hunters shielding everyone; they didn't know the witch woman was gone. The entire village watched in silence as the two of them crossed the opening, the hunters parting for them as they approached the Bird Man and the other six elders. Chandalen stood to their side.

*"Everyone is safe,"* Kahlan reassured them. *"The witch woman is gone."*

There was a collective sigh of relief.

Chandalen thumped the butt of his spear on the ground. *"Again you bring trouble!"*

Richard ignored him and asked her to translate. He took in the elders and let his gaze settle on the Bird Man. "Honored elder. The witch woman was not here to harm anyone. She was here to warn me about a great danger."

*"You claim,"* Chandalen snapped. *"We do not know this to be true."*

Kahlan knew Richard was struggling to keep calm. "Do you doubt that if she wanted to send you to the spirit world, she could have done it?"

Chandalen answered only with a glare.

The Bird Man gave Chandalen a look that seemed to shrink him a few inches. He looked to Richard. *"What danger?"*

"She says we are in danger of the dead escaping into the world of the living."

*"They cannot come into the world of the living. The veil keeps them back."*

"You know of the veil?"

*"Yes. Each level of the dead, the underworld as you call it, is sealed with a veil.*

135

When we hold a gathering, we invite our ancestors' spirits to visit us, and they are able to come through the veil for a short time."

Richard studied the Bird Man's face a moment. "What else can you tell me about the veil?"

The other shrugged. *"Nothing. We know only what our ancestors' spirits have told us about it: that they must pass through it to come to us when we call them, and that it holds them back the rest of the time. They tell us that there are many levels of the underworld, the dead, and that they are in the uppermost level, and so they can come. Those who are not honored are in lower levels, and may not come. Their spirits are locked away forever."*

Richard met the eyes of all the elders. "The veil is torn. If it isn't sealed again, the world of the dead will swallow us all." Gasps spread back through the gathered people. Fearful whispering broke out. Richard's gaze went back to the Bird Man. "Please, honored elder, I request a gathering. I must have the help of our ancestors' spirits. I must find a way to seal the veil before the Keeper of the dead escapes. The spirit ancestors may be able to help. I must know if they can help."

Chandalen thumped his spear. *"Lies! You carry us the lies of a witch woman. We should not call the honored spirits of our ancestors for the words of a witch woman! The spirits of our ancestors are called only for our people, not a witch woman! They will strike all our people dead for such blasphemy!"*

Richard glared at him. "They are not being called by a witch woman. It is I who makes the request, and I am one of the Mud People. I ask for the gathering to help me keep our people from being harmed."

*"You bring death to us. You bring strangers. You bring the witch woman. You only wish to help yourself. How did this veil become torn?"*

Richard unbuttoned his sleeve and pushed it up his arm. He slowly pulled the Sword of Truth. Holding Chandalen's glare, he drew the sword across his forearm, turning it to wipe both sides in the blood. He jammed the point in the ground and rested both hands over the hilt.

"Kahlan, I want you to translate something. Don't leave out a single word." Richard returned his glare to Chandalen. His voice was calm, almost gentle, but his eyes shone with lethal intent. "Chandalen, if I hear one more word from you tonight, even if it is to agree with me and offer your help, I will kill you. Some of the things the witch woman told me have put me in the mood to kill. If you give me any more reason—it will be you I kill."

The eyes of all the elders widened. Chandalen opened his mouth to say something, but at seeing the look on Richard's face, he shut his mouth and folded his arms. His glower was fierce, but no match for Richard's. At last he glanced to the ground.

Richard spoke again to the Bird Man. "Honored elder, you know my heart. You know I would do nothing to harm our people. I would not ask this if it were not important, or if I had any other choice. Please, may I have a gathering so I may ask our ancestors' spirits how I can stop this threat to our people?"

The Bird Man turned to the other elders. Each nodded in turn. Kahlan knew they would; it was only a formality. Savidlin was their friend, and the others had dealt with Richard before; there was not one of them who wanted to challenge him. The real decision was the Bird Man's. He watched each elder nod, and then turned back to Richard.

*"This is bad business. I do not like calling the ancestors to ask about their world. It is our world they come to help us with. They may be displeased. They may be*

136

*angered. They may say no."* He watched Richard a moment. *"But I know your heart. I know you are a savior to our people, and you would not ask if you had any other choice."* He laid a firm hand on Richard's shoulder. *"Granted."*

Kahlan sighed in relief. Richard nodded his thanks. Kahlan knew he didn't look forward to meeting the ancestors' spirits again. The last time had been devastating to him.

Suddenly, there was a flutter of shadow in the air. Kahlan threw her hands up protectively. Richard was knocked back a step as something hit him on the head. People shouted in confusion. A dark shape thumped to the ground between Richard and the Bird Man. Richard straightened, putting his fingers to his scalp. Blood trickled down his forehead.

The Bird Man squatted down over a dark form, and then straightened. He was holding a dead owl cradled in his hands. The head lolled to the side. The wings fell open. The elders all looked at one another. Chandalen's frown deepened, but he said nothing.

Richard inspected the blood on his fingers. "Why in the world would an owl hit me like that? And what killed it?"

The Bird Man gently smoothed the dead bird's feathers. *"Birds live in the air, a different level than us. They live in two levels—land and air. They can travel between their level and ours. Birds are closely connected to the spirit world. To the spirits. Owls more than most birds. They see in the night, where we are blind, just as we are blind to the spirit world. I am a spirit guide for our people. Only a Bird Man can be a spirit guide, because he can understand such things."*

He held the dead bird a little higher. *"This is a warning. I have never witnessed an owl bringing a spirit message before. This bird gave its life to warn you. Richard, please reconsider your request for a gathering. This warning means the gathering will be dangerous, dangerous enough for the spirits to send this message."*

Richard looked from the Bird Man's face to the owl. He reached out and stroked its feathers. No one made a sound. "Dangerous for me, or for the elders?"

*"For you. You are the one calling for the gathering. The owl brought the message to you. The warning was for you."* He glanced up at Richard's forehead. *"A blood warning. One of the worst kinds. The only thing worse than an owl, would have been if a raven had brought the message. That would have meant sure death."*

Richard took his hand back and wiped his fingers on his shirt. He stared down at the dead owl. "I don't have any choice," he whispered. "If I don't do something, the veil will be torn, and the Keeper of the dead will escape. Our people, everyone, will be swallowed into the world of the dead. I must learn how to stop it. I must try."

The Bird Man nodded. *"As you wish. It will take three days to prepare."*

Richard looked up. "You did it in two days before. We can't spare any time."

The elder took a deep breath and sighed. *"Two days."*

"Thank you, honored elder." Richard turned to her, his eyes were filled with pain. "Kahlan, please, find Nissel, and bring her? I'm going to the spirit house. Ask her to bring something stronger?"

She squeezed his arm. "Of course. I'll hurry."

Richard nodded. He pulled his sword from the ground and walked off into the darkness.

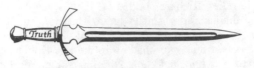

$\mathcal{C}$ause of death. She looked up in thought, pressing the round end of the plain, wooden-handled pen to her lower lip. The small, modest room was dimly lit with candles set among and on top of the disheveled piles of papers on her desk. Scrolls were balanced precariously in stacks between fat books. The dark patina of the desktop was only visible in a small area in front of her, framing the waiting report.

Odd objects of magic stood jammed together collecting dust on the shelves behind her. The ever-present and diligent cleaning staff was not allowed to touch them, and so the task of dusting them was left to her, but there was never enough time, or inclination. Besides, they looked less important to curious eyes when covered in a mask of dust.

Heavy drapes were drawn against the night. The only splash of color in the room was one of the local blue-and-yellow carpets she had placed on the other side of the desk. Visitors usually spent their time in her office staring down at it.

Cause of death. Reports were such a bother. She sighed. But a necessary bother. For now, anyway. The Palace of the Prophets required reams of reports. There were Sisters who spent their whole lives in the libraries, cataloging reports, pampering them, keeping records of every useless word they thought might someday be important.

Well, there was nothing for it but to think up a suitable cause of death. The truth would never do. Her Sisters would have to have a satisfactory explanation as to the cause of death. They valued highly those with the gift. Fools.

Training accident? She smiled. Yes, a training accident. She hadn't used that one in many years. She pursed her lips as she dipped the pen in the ink bottle and began writing. *The cause of death was a training accident with the Rada'Han. A twig, as I have often warned the other Sisters, no matter how young and tender, will break if bent too far.*

Who could question? Let them wonder where among them the fault lay. It would keep them from digging too deeply, lest the blame fall on them. As she blotted the paper, there was a soft rap at the door.

"One moment, please." She touched the corner of the boy's letter to the candle flame and, when it was nearly consumed, tossed it in the cold hearth. The broken seal melted into a molten red puddle. He would be writing no more letters. "Come."

The heavy, round-topped door opened enough to admit a head.

"Sister, it's me," came a whisper from the shadow.

"Don't stand there like a novice, come in and close the door."

The woman entered, closing the door quietly, after putting her head back out to check the hall. She didn't look down at the carpet. "Sister . . ."

With a finger across lips, and an angry scowl, she was silenced. "No names when we are alone. I've told you before."

The other looked about at the walls, as if expecting someone to pop out. "But surely you've shielded your room."

"Of course it's shielded. But it is always possible the breeze could carry words to the right ears. If that ever happened, we wouldn't want our names carried with the words, now would we."

The other's eyes flicked around at the walls again. "Of course not. Of course you are right." She scrubbed her hands together. "Someday this won't be necessary. I hate that we must remain hidden. Someday we will be able to . . ."

"What have you found out?"

She watched as the woman straightened her dress at the hips and then put her fingers to the desk, leaning over a little. Her eyes had a fierce intensity. They were strange eyes, pale, pale blue, with dark violet flecks. She always found it hard not to stare at those eyes.

She leaned closer, and whispered. "They've found him."

"You saw the book?"

She nodded slowly. "I saw it. At dinnertime. I waited until the others were at dinner." She gave an even look. "He refused the first offer."

She slapped her hand down on the desk. "What! Are you sure?"

"That's what the book said. And not only that, there was more. He's grown. Grown into a man."

"Grown!" She took a heavy breath as she watched the Sister standing before her. "Which Sister was it?"

"What difference does it make? They are all ours."

"No, they weren't. I wasn't able to send three of our own. Only two. One is a Sister of the Light."

The other's eyes widened. "How could you let that happen? Something as important as this . . ."

She slapped her hand down on the desk again. "Silence!"

The other straightened, knitting her fingers together. A small pout came to her face. "It was Sister Grace."

She closed her eyes and leaned back in the chair. "Sister Grace was one of ours," she whispered.

The other leaned over the desk again. "Then, only one of the two remaining is ours. Who is it? Sister Elizabeth, or Sister Verna?"

"That is not for you to know."

"Why not? I hate never knowing. I hate not knowing if the Sister I'm talking to is a Sister of the Light, or one of us, a Sister of the Dark. . . ."

She slammed her fist on the desk and gritted her teeth. "Don't you ever say that out loud again," she hissed, "or I will send you to the Nameless One in pieces."

This time the other stared down at the carpet as her face paled. "Forgive me," she whispered.

"There isn't a Sister of the Light alive who believes we are anything but myth. If that name ever reaches their ears, they could begin to wonder. That name is never, ever, to be spoken aloud by you! If the Sisters were to ever discover you, or who you serve, they would have a Rada'Han around your neck before you had a chance to scream."

The other's hands went to her throat as she let out a small gasp. "But I . . ."

"You would claw your own eyes out, for fear of seeing them come to question you every day. That is why you are not to know the names of the others: so you can't give them over. That is why they don't know your name: so they can't give you over. It is to protect us all, so we may serve. The only name you know is mine."

"But Sister . . . I would bite my own tongue off before I ever gave them your name."

"You say that now. But were there a Rada'Han around your neck, you would be begging to give me up just to have it off. . . . And it isn't my forgiveness that matters. If you fail us, the Nameless One will not be forgiving. When you meet his eyes, it will make whatever could be done to you with the Rada'Han while you were alive seem a pleasant time at tea."

"But I serve . . . I am sworn . . . I have given the oath."

"Those who serve well will be rewarded when the Nameless One is free of the veil. Those who fail him, or fight him, will have an eternity to regret their mistake."

"Of course, Sister." She was staring furiously at the carpet now. "I live only to serve." She knitted her fingers back together. "I will not fail our Master. On my oath."

"On your soul."

Her defiant, violet flecked eyes came up. "I have given my oath."

She nodded as she sank back in the chair. "As have we all, Sister. As have we all." She stared at the other's eyes a moment. "Did the book say anything else?"

"I didn't have time to search it thoroughly, but there were some other things I caught. He is with the Mother Confessor. He is promised as her mate."

She frowned. "The Mother Confessor." She waved her hand. "That is no problem. What else."

"He is the Seeker."

She slapped her hand on the desk. "Curse the Light!" She let out a noisy breath. "The Seeker. Well, we can deal with that. Anything more?"

The other nodded slowly, leaning closer. "He is strong, and grown, yet only two days after he triggered the gift the headaches made him unconscious."

She rose slowly out of her chair. This time it was her eyes that went wide. "Two days," she whispered. "Are you sure? Two days?"

The other shrugged. "I am only telling you what the book said. I'm sure of what it said. I'm not sure it is true. I don't see how it could be."

She sank back into her chair. "Two days." She stared at her desk. "The sooner we get a Rada'Han around his neck, the better."

"Even the Sisters of the Light would agree with you about that. There was a message sent back. From the Prelate."

She lifted an eyebrow. "The Prelate herself sent orders?"

The other nodded. "Yes." Under her breath, she added, "I wish I knew if she was with us, or against us."

She ignored the comment. "What did she say?"

"That if he refuses the third offer, Sister Verna is to kill him herself. Have you ever heard of such an order? If he is really this strong, and he refuses the third time, he would be dead in a few weeks anyway. Why would she give such an order?"

"Have you ever heard of anyone refusing the first offer?"

"Well, no, I guess I haven't."

"It is one of the rules. If one with the gift refuses all three offers, they are to be killed, to spare them the suffering at the end, the madness. You have never seen such an order before because you have never heard of anyone refusing the first offer.

"I have spent time in the archives, looking through the prophecies. That is where I saw reference to the rule. The Prelate knows all the obscure rules, the old rules. And she is afraid; she has read the prophecies too."

"Afraid?" she asked, wide-eyed. "The Prelate? I have never seen her afraid of anything."

She nodded up at the woman. "She is afraid now. Either way suits our purposes. Either he is collared, or he is dead. If he is collared, we will deal with him, in our way, as we have always done. If he is dead, we won't have to. Maybe better he were dead. Maybe better he were dead before the Sisters of the Light find out what he is, if they don't already know."

The other leaned over the desk again, lowering her voice. "If they know, or find out, there are those among the Sisters of the Light who would kill him."

She studied the violet flecks a moment. "Indeed there are." A smile spread across her face. "What a dangerous dilemma for them. What a glorious opportunity for us." Her smile faded. "What of the other matter?"

The woman straightened. "Ranson and Weber are waiting where you wanted them." She folded her arms beneath her breasts. "They were pretty cocky, because they have passed all the tests, and tomorrow are to be released." A sadistic grin came to her thin lips and flecked eyes. "I gave them a little reminder that they still wear the collar. I'm surprised we can't hear their knees knocking together all the way up here."

She ignored the other's smile. "I have lessons to give. You will go in my place. Tell them I had reports to work on. I'll go see to our two friends. They may have passed all the Prelate's tests, but they have not yet passed all of mine. One has an oath to give. And the other . . ."

She leaned halfway over the desk, hunger in her flecked eyes. "Which one? Which one are you going to . . . Oh, I so wish I could watch. Or help. Promise me you will tell me everything?"

She smiled at the other's eagerness. "Everything. I promise. From beginning to end. Every last scream. Now go see to my lessons for me."

The woman danced through the doorway like a giddy schoolgirl. She was too eager. That kind of eagerness was dangerous. That kind of lust made one forget to be careful, made one take chances. She pulled a knife from a drawer, and made a mental note to use her less in the future, and keep an eye on her.

She tested the edge gingerly with a thumb and, satisfied it was razor sharp, tucked the knife up her sleeve, the sleeve without the dacra. She plucked a small, dusty statue from the shelf, and slipped it into a pocket. Before she was around the desk and through the door, she remembered one more item, and turned back to pick up the stout rod leaning against the side of her desk.

It was late, and the halls were quiet and mostly empty. Despite the heat, she pulled her short, thin, blue cotton cloak tighter across her shoulders. Thoughts of this new one with the gift gave her a chill. Grown. A man.

She shook her head as she walked silently over the long carpets, past lamps set in wall brackets centered in the raised cherry paneling, past tables set with dried flowers, and past heavily draped windows looking out over the bailey and courtyard below. Lights of the city in the distance twinkled like a carpet of stars. Slightly rank air drifted in the windows. Must be near low tide, she thought.

The cleaning staff, polishing a chair-rail molding here, or a banister there, dropped into deep curtsies as she swept past. She hardly noticed them, and certainly didn't acknowledge them. They were beneath her attention.

Grown. Into a man.

Her face heated with anger at the thought. How could this be? Someone had made a serious mistake. A mistake. An oversight. It had to be that.

A maidservant on her hands and knees, concentrating on wiping at a spot on a carpet, looked up just in time to leap back out of the way with a "Forgive me, Sister." On her hands and knees, she touched her head to the floor with another apology.

Grown. It would have been difficult enough to turn this one if he were still a boy. But a man? She shook her head again. Grown. She smacked the rod against her thigh in frustration. Two maidservants nearby jumped at the sound and fell to their knees, burying their tightly closed eyes behind prayerful hands.

Well, grown or not, he would have a Rada'Han around his neck, and a whole palace full of Sisters to watch over him. But even wearing a Rada'Han, he was still grown into a man. And the Seeker. He might be difficult to control. Dangerously difficult.

If necessary, she guessed, he could always have a "training accident." If not that, there were certainly enough other dangers to one with the gift, dangers that could leave a man worse than dead. But if she could turn him, or use him, that would make all the trouble worthwhile.

She turned into a hall she at first thought empty, then noticed a young woman standing in the shadows between lamps, gazing out a window. She thought she recognized her. One of the novices. She stopped behind the young woman and folded her arms. The novice tapped her toe on the carpet as she leaned on her elbows through the opened window, looking at the gates below.

She cleared her throat. The young woman spun, gasped, and dropped into a curtsy.

"Forgive me, Sister, I didn't hear you coming. A good evening to you."

When the big brown eyes came up, she put the end of the rod under the young woman's chin and lifted it a little more. "Pasha, isn't it?"

"Yes, Sister. Pasha Maes. Novice, third rank. Next in line to be named."

"Next in line," she sniffed. "Presumption, my dear, does not befit a Sister, and less so a novice. Even one of the third rank."

Pasha cast her eyes down and gave a curtsy, as best she could with the rod still under her chin. "Yes, Sister. Forgive me."

"What are you doing here?"

"Just watching, Sister. Watching the night."

"Watching the night. I would say you were watching the gates. Am I wrong, novice?"

Pasha tried to look down, but the rod lifted her chin, keeping her eyes to her superior. "No, Sister," she admitted, "you are not wrong. I was watching the gates." She licked her full lips several times.

At last she spilled out the words. "I heard the talk, the talk among the girls. They say, well, they say three of the Sisters have been gone a long time now, and that could only mean they are bringing back one with the gift. A new one. In all the years I have been here, I have never seen a new one brought in." She licked her lips again. "Well, I am . . . I mean . . . I hope to be next in line. And if I am to be named, I will have to be assigned a new one." She knitted her fingers together. "I so want to be named a Sister. I have studied hard, worked hard. Waited and waited. And no new one has come yet. Forgive me Sister, but I just can't help being excited, and hopeful, that I will be worthy. So . . . yes, I was watching the gate, hoping I would see him brought in."

"And you think you are strong enough to handle the job? To handle a new one?"

"Yes, Sister. I study and practice my forms every day."

She looked down her nose at the novice. "Is that so? Show me."

As they stared at each other, she felt her feet rise off the ground a few inches. Solid grip of air, strong. Not bad. She wondered if the novice could handle interference. With that thought, fire ignited at both ends of the hall, sweeping with a howl toward the two women. Pasha didn't flinch. The fire hit a wall of air before reaching them. Air was not the best for fire. A small error Pasha quickly corrected. Before the fire burned through, the air became moist, dripping. The fire hissed out.

Although she didn't try to move, she knew she couldn't. She could feel that the grip held her firmly. She turned it cold, brittle, with ice, and broke it. When she was free, she lifted Pasha from the floor. Defensive webs from the girl wove through her snaking onslaught, but failed to break the grip. Her feet rose again. Impressive— the girl could counter even while being held.

Spells tangled together, conflicting, fighting, snarling into knots. Each matched and defended, striking back at any opportunity. The silent, motionless battle raged on for a time, the two of them hanging inches off the ground.

At last, she tired of the sport, and severed herself from the webs, tying them to the girl, locking them on. She settled gently to the ground, and left Pasha with the whole weight of the load to juggle. A simple, if devious, escape: giving the opponent not only the attacking spells to deal with, but dumping her own back on her. Pasha hadn't been expecting this, and wasn't able to defend against it; it was not the way she had been taught.

Sweat ran down the novice's face as she grimaced slightly. The force radiating through the hall made carpets curl up at their corners. Lamps chattered in their brackets. Pasha was getting angry. Her brow wrinkled. With a loud crack that shattered a mirror far off down the hall, she broke the spells. Her slippered feet settled to the ground.

Pasha took a few deep breaths. "I have not seen that done before, Sister. It is not . . . by the rules."

She put the rod back under the other's chin. "Rules are for children's games. You are no longer a child. When you are a full Sister, you must deal with situations where there are no rules. You must be prepared for that. If you always stick to somebody's 'rules,' you may find yourself at the point of a very sharp knife, held by a hand that doesn't know about your 'rules.' "

Pasha didn't flinch. "Yes, Sister. Thank you for showing me."

She smiled inwardly, but kept it off her face. This one had a spine, if a small one. A rare commodity in a novice, even one of the third rank.

She let her eyes take in Pasha again: soft brown hair that just touched her shoulders, big brown eyes, attractive features, lips of the sort men stared at, proud, upright shoulders, and a sweep of curves that even a novice's dress failed to conceal.

She let the rod trail from Pasha's chin, down her neck, down into the heart of her exposed cleavage.

Grown into a man.

"And since when, Pasha," she said in a quiet voice that could have been taken for either threatening, or kind, "have novices been allowed to wear their dresses unbuttoned like this?"

Pasha blushed furiously. "Forgive me, Sister. It's such a warm night. I was alone . . . I didn't think there was anyone about. I just wanted to let the breeze cool my skin." Her face turned a deeper red. "I sweat so, there. I never meant to offend anyone. I'm so embarrassed. Forgive me."

Pasha's hands rushed to the buttons. With the rod, she gently pushed the hands away from the swell of the young woman's bosom.

"The Creator made you this way. You should not be embarrassed of what He has chosen, in his wisdom, to bestow upon you. You should never be ashamed, Pasha, of what He has graced you with. Only those of questionable loyalty to the Creator would scorn you for being proud of showing the Maker's hand in all its magnificence."

"Why . . . thank you, Sister. I never looked at it in quite that way." A frown wrinkled her brow. "What do you mean, 'questionable loyalty'?"

She pulled the rod away and lifted an eyebrow. "Those who worship the Nameless One don't hide in the shadows, my dear. They could be anywhere. Why, even you could be one. Even me."

Pasha fell to a knee, bowing her head. "Oh, please, Sister," she implored, "don't say such a thing of yourself, even in jest. You are a Sister of the Light, and we are in the Palace of the Prophets, safe, I pray, from the whispers of the Nameless One."

"Safe?" With her rod, she motioned the novice up. After she was on her feet, she gave her a stern look. "Only a fool assumes she is safe, even here. Sisters of the Light are not fools. Even they must always be alert to the dark whispers."

"Yes, Sister. I will remember."

"Remember it, any time someone would make you ashamed of how the Creator has formed you. Ask yourself why they blush at seeing the Maker's hand. Blush, as the Nameless One would."

"Yes, Sister. . . . Thank you," she stammered. "You have given me things to think on. I have never thought about the Creator in this way before."

"He has reasons for the things He does. Is this not true?"

"What do you mean?"

"Well, when He gives a man a strong back, what does that say?"

"Everyone knows that. He was given the strong back to use. It means the Creator has given him the strong back so that he might work to feed his family. Work to make his way. Work to make the Creator proud. And not waste the Creator's gift by being lazy."

She whisked the rod up and down in front of Pasha. "And what do you think the Creator had in mind when he gave you this body?"

"I . . . don't know . . . exactly. That I should use it to . . . make the Creator proud of His work . . . in some way?"

She nodded. "You think on it. You think on your reason for being here. Being here at this time. We are all here for a reason. The Sisters of the Light are here for a reason, are they not?"

"Oh, yes, Sister. We are here to teach the ones with the gift, teach them to use

144

it, and guide them so they may not hear the whispers of the Nameless One, that they may hear only the Creator."

"And how are we able to do that?"

"We were given the gift of being sorceresses, so that we may be able to guide them in their gift."

"And if the Creator was wise enough to give you that gift, the gift of being a sorceress, do you not think He may have given you your looks for a reason too? Maybe to be a part of your calling as a Sister of the Light? To use your looks to serve Him?"

Pasha stared. "Why, I never thought of it that way before. In what way are my looks to be of aid?"

She shrugged. "We cannot always know what the Creator has intended. When He wishes, it will be revealed."

"Yes, Sister." Her voice was unsure.

"Pasha, when you see a man that the Creator has graced with good looks, a finely shaped body, what do you think? What do you feel?"

Pasha blushed. "I . . . sometimes . . . it makes my heart race. I guess. It makes me feel . . . good. Feel longings."

At last she allowed a small smile. "There is no need to blush, my dear. It is a longing to touch what the Creator's hand has wrought. Don't you suppose it pleases the Creator that you appreciate His work? Don't you think He wants you to like what He has done? To enjoy it? Just as you must know that men enjoy witnessing your beauty and long to touch the work of the Creator's hand. It would be a crime against the Creator not to use, in your service to Him, what He has given you."

Pasha smiled shyly. "I never thought about it in that way. You have given me new eyes, Sister. The more I learn, the more it seems I don't know. I hope that someday I will be a Sister of the Light half as wise as you."

"Knowledge comes as it will, Pasha. Life's lessons come at the most surprising times. Like tonight." She swished the rod toward the window. "Here you are, looking out a window, hoping to learn one thing, and you have learned something more important."

Pasha touched her arm. "Oh, thank you, Sister, for taking the time to teach me. No Sister has spoken so frankly to me before."

"This is one lesson, Pasha, that is outside the palace curriculum. It is a lesson the Nameless One would be angry you learned, so keep it to yourself. As you think on what I have told you, and the Creator's hand is revealed, you will understand better how it is to work for Him. And if you need more understanding, I will always be here to help guide you. But keep our talk from others. As I said, you can never tell who listens to the whispers of the Nameless One."

Pasha curtsied. "I will, Sister. Thank you."

"A novice is given many tests. Tests of the palace's devising. There are rules to them. The final test to be named a Sister of the Light is being charged with a new one. In this, the final test, there are not always rules. New ones can be difficult to control. But that does not mean they are bad."

"Difficult?"

"Of course. They come here, plucked from the only life they knew, and are thrust into a new place, with new demands they don't understand. They can be rebellious, difficult to control. It is because they are afraid. We must have patience."

"Afraid . . . ? Of the Sisters? And the palace?"

"Weren't you afraid, when you first came here? Just a little?"

"Well, maybe just a little. But it was my dream to come. I wanted it more than anything."

"For the new ones, it is not always their dream. They are confused about their power. With you, it grew as you grew. You were accustomed to it; it was part of you. With them, it is sometimes sudden, unexpected. Not what they planned or wanted. The Rada'Han can ignite the power, and it is new to them. It can be frightening. That fear makes them fight it, sometimes. Fight us.

"Your job, the responsibility of a novice of the third rank, is to control them, for their own good, until they can be taught by the Sisters. In all your other lessons, there have been rules. In this, there sometimes are no rules. The new ones don't know of our rules yet. They can be difficult to control if you follow only the rules you know. Sometimes the collar is not enough. You must use whatever the Creator has given you. You must be able to do whatever it takes to control the will of these untrained wizards. That is the true, and final test to be a Sister. Novices have failed in this final test, and been put out of the palace."

Pasha's eyes were wide. "I have never heard such things."

She shrugged. "Then I have been of aid to you. I am pleased the Creator has chosen me to help. Perhaps others have not wanted so strongly for you to succeed, and have held back. Perhaps you would do well to bring to me your questions about any new one you are assigned."

"Oh, yes. Thank you for your help, Sister. I must admit it worries me to learn that new ones can be difficult. I guess I always imagined they would be eager to learn, and that it would be a joy to show them and to help teach them."

"They are all different. Some are as easy as a babe in a crib. Let us hope you are given one like that. Some will test your wits. Why, I have even seen old records that tell of ones that have triggered the gift before we could get to them, before we could get a Rada'Han on them and help them."

"No . . . That must be frightening for them—to have the power awakened without guidance from us."

"Indeed. And fear can make them troublesome, as I have said. I have even seen an old report of one who refused the collar on the first offer."

Pasha's fingers covered her mouth as she gasped. She took them away. "But . . . that means . . . one of the Sisters . . ."

She nodded solemnly. "It is a price we are all prepared to pay. We bear a heavy responsibility."

"But why wouldn't the parents make him accept the offer?"

She leaned closer, lowering her voice. "In the report I saw, the one with the gift was grown. A man."

Pasha stared in wide-eyed disbelief. "A man . . .?" she whispered. "If a boy can be difficult to control . . . what of a grown man?"

She gave the novice an even look. "We are here to serve in the Creator's work. You can never tell what the Creator has in His plan, why you are given what you have. A novice in charge of a new one must use whatever the Creator has given her. The collar is not always enough. You can never tell what you might need to do. The rules don't always work.

"Do you still want to be a Sister of the Light? Even knowing you may be given a new one who could be more difficult than any other novice has ever been given?"

"Oh, yes! Yes, Sister! If the new one is difficult, I know it is a test from the

Creator himself, to see if I am truly worthy. I will not fail. I will do whatever must be done. I will use everything I have learned, everything the Creator has given me. I will be on guard that he may be from a strange land, or have strange customs, and be afraid, or troublesome, or difficult. And that I may have to make my own rules to succeed." She hesitated. "And if you are so kind as to mean what you said about helping me, then I know I will have your wisdom backing me, and I will not fail."

She nodded with a smile. "I have given my word. It holds, no matter the difficulty." She frowned in thought. "Perhaps, it could be that you are graced with your looks so a new one might see the beauty of the Creator through you, through his work. Perhaps, this is how you are to show a new one the way."

"It would be an honor, in any way, to show a new one the light of the Creator's hand."

"You are right in that, my dear." She straightened, clasping her hands. "Now. I want you to go to the mistress of the novices, and tell her that you have too much free time, and that starting tomorrow, you need to be assigned some chores. Tell her you have been spending too much of your time looking out windows."

Pasha bowed her head and curtsied again. "Yes, Sister," she said meekly.

She smiled when the novice looked up. "I too, have heard that three of the Sisters are searching for one with the gift. I think it will be a while before they return with him, if at all, but when they return, and if they bring him, I will remind the Prelate that you are next in line, and are ready for the task."

"Oh, thank you, Sister! Thank you!"

"You are a fine young woman, Pasha. The Creator has truly shown the beauty of his work in you."

"Thank you, Sister," she said without blushing.

"Thank the Creator."

"I will, Sister. Sister? Before the new one is brought in, could you teach me more about what the Creator has intended for me? Help me to understand?"

"If you wish."

"Oh, I do. I really do."

She patted Pasha's cheek. "Of course, my dear. Of course." She stood up straight. "Now, off to the mistress of the novices with you. I won't have soon-to-be-Sisters with nothing better to do than stare out windows."

"Yes, Sister." Pasha curtsied with a smile and rushed off down the hall. She stopped and turned. "Sister . . . I am afraid I don't know your name."

"Go!"

Pasha flinched. "Yes, Sister."

She watched the swell of Pasha's hips sway as she walked quickly off down the hall, kicking the rolled edges of carpets back down as she went. The girl had exquisite ankles.

Grown into a man.

She collected her thoughts and started off again, down the halls and stairs. As she descended, the wooden stairs changed to stone. The heat lessened, although not the stuffiness, or the smell of the tide flats. The warm glow of lamps was replaced by the flickering shadows of widely spaced torches. The cowering palace staff diminished in number until she saw no one. She continued down to the lowest floors, below dusty storerooms, down below the servants' quarters and workshops.

The torches became more widely spaced until there were no more. She ignited a ball of flame in her palm, and held it up to see by as she continued on.

When she reached the proper door, she sent the flame into a cold torch set in a bracket next to the doorway. The stone-walled room was small, an abandoned cellar of some sort, empty except for moldy straw on the floor, a lit torch, and the two wizards. The smell was unpleasant: burning pitch and damp mold.

At her entrance, the two stood, swaying slightly. Both wore the plain robes befitting their high rank. Each had a stupid half grin on his face. They weren't cocky, she realized; they had been drinking. Probably celebrating their last night in the Palace of the Prophets. Their last night with the Sisters of the Light. Their last night wearing the Rada'Han.

The two men had been friends since they had been brought to the palace as boys, almost at the same time. Sam Weber was a plain man of average height, with curly, light brown hair and a clean-shaven jaw that seemed too big for the rest of his soft face. Neville Ranson was slightly taller, with straight black hair cut short and smoothed neatly down. He wore a short, well-kept beard that was just beginning to show flecks of gray. His eyes were almost as dark as his hair. His features seemed all the more sharply formed, standing next to his soft friend.

She had always thought he had grown into a handsome man. She had known him since he had come to the palace as a small boy. She had been a novice then, and he had been the one assigned to her, put in her care; her final test before becoming a Sister of the Light. That had been a long time ago.

Wizard Ranson swept his arm across his middle and gave a dramatic, although wobbly, bow. He came back up with a widening grin. His grin always made his face look boyish, despite his years and the beginnings of gray.

"A good evening to you, Sister . . ."

Hard as she could, she backhanded him across the face with her rod. She could feel his cheekbone break. He fell back to the floor with a cry.

"I have told you before," she hissed through gritted teeth, "never to use my name when we are alone. Being drunk does not excuse the order."

Wizard Weber stood stone still, his eyes wide, his face white, his grin gone. Ranson rolled over on the ground with his hands to his face, leaving blood on the straw.

The color came back to Weber's face in a red rush. "How dare you do this? We have passed all the tests! We are wizards!"

She sent a cord of power into the Rada'Han. The impact threw him back against the wall, where the collar stuck to the stone like a nail to a magnet. "Passed the tests!" she screamed. "Passed the tests! You have not passed my tests!" She twisted on the pain until Weber was choking in agony. "Is this how you address a Sister! Is this the way you show respect!"

She snipped off the cord and he fell to the floor, giving a grunt when he hit. He pushed himself up on his knees with an effort.

"Forgive me, Sister," he said in a pained, hoarse voice. "I beg you forgive our disrespect." His eyes rose cautiously to meet her glare. "It was only the drink speaking. Forgive us? Please?"

With her fists on her hips, she stood watching him. She pointed with the rod at the one rolling and moaning on the floor. "Heal him. I don't have time for this nonsense. I have come to give you both your test, not to watch him whine and complain about a little slap."

Weber bent to his friend, rolling him gently over on his back. "Neville, it's all right. I'll help you. Lie still."

He took the man's shaking hands away and replaced them with his own. He began talking and healing. She waited impatiently with her arms folded. It didn't take long; Weber was talented at healing. Weber helped his friend sit up and, with a handful of straw, wiped the blood from the healed wound.

Ranson pushed himself to his feet. His eyes flashed anger, but he kept any speck of it out of his voice. "Forgive me, Sister. What is it you want?"

Weber came up beside him. "Please, Sister, we have done everything the Sisters have asked. We are finished."

"Finished? Finished? I don't think so. Have you forgotten our talks? Have you forgotten what I told you? Did you think I would forget? Simply let the two of you dance out of here? Free as birds? No man walks out of here without seeing me or one of mine. There is the matter of an oath."

The two glanced at each other, retreating a half step.

"If you will just let us go," Weber offered, "we will give you our oath."

She watched them a moment, her voice coming quietly at last. "My oath? It is not an oath to me, boys. It is an oath to the Keeper. You know that." They both paled a little. "And the oath comes only after one of you has passed the test. Only one of you has to give the oath."

"One of us?" Ranson asked. He swallowed. "Only one of us has to give the oath, Sister? Why only one of us?"

"Because," she whispered, "the other will have no need to give an oath. He is going to die."

They both gave a little gasp and moved closer together.

"What is this test?" Weber asked.

"Take off your robes, and we will begin."

They glanced at each other. Ranson lifted his hand a little. "Our robes, Sister? Now? Here?"

She looked to each. "Don't be bashful, boys. I have seen you both swim naked in the lake since you were only this big." She held her hand out just below her waist.

"But that was when we were boys," Weber complained. "Not since we have grown into men."

She glowered at them. "Don't make me have to tell you again. The next time, I will burn them off you."

They both flinched and began pulling their robes over their heads. She made a deliberate point of looking each up and down, just to show them her displeasure with their argument. Each man's face turned red in the torchlight.

With a flick of her wrist, she brought her knife to her hand. "Up against the wall. Both of you."

When they didn't move quickly enough, she used the collars to slam them against the wall. With a thin stream of power to each Rada'Han, she immobilized them against the stone. They were flattened against the wall and helpless to lift a finger.

"Please, Sister," Ranson whispered, "don't kill us. We'll do anything. Anything."

She looked over at him. "Yes, you will. One of you anyway. But we haven't gotten to the oath yet. Now still your tongue or I will do it for you."

As the two were held helpless, she moved to Weber first. Putting the knife tip against his upper chest, she drew it slowly down, carefully cutting through the skin

149

and no more. Sweat poured from Weber's face as he gritted his teeth. His jowls shook. After she had made a cut, about a forearm long, she went back to where she had begun and made another next to it, so the two cuts were about a finger's width apart. Small, high-pitched sounds escaped from the man's throat as she drew the knife along. The ends of the parallel lines drew together to a point. Small trickles of blood ran down his chest. She worked the knifepoint under the top, between the cuts, separating the skin from him until there was a generous flap of it hanging down.

She moved over to Ranson and made the same twin cuts, with a flap of skin hanging away at the top. Tears ran down his face with the sweat, but he said nothing. He knew better. When finished, she straightened and inspected her work. They looked the same. Good. She tucked the knife back up her sleeve.

"One of you two is going to have the Rada'Han taken off tomorrow, and be free to go. As far as the Sisters of the Light are concerned, anyway. Not as far as I, or more importantly, the Keeper, are concerned. It will be the beginning of your service to him. If you serve well, you will be rewarded when he is free of the veil. If you fail in your tasks . . . well, you wouldn't want to know what would happen to you if you should fail him."

"Sister," Ranson asked in a shaky voice, "why only one of us? We could both give the oath. We could both serve."

Weber's sudden glare shifted to his friend. He didn't like being spoken for. He always had been obstinate.

"The oath is a blood oath. One of you will have to pass my test to earn the privilege of taking it. The other is going to lose the gift tonight, lose his magic. Do you know how a wizard loses the gift?"

They both shook their heads.

"When they are skinned, the magic bleeds from them." She said it as if she were discussing peeling a pear. "Bleeds away until it's all gone."

Weber stared at her, his face gone white. Ranson closed his dark eyes and shook.

At the same time, she wrapped the flap of skin on each man around her first fingers. "I'm going to ask for a volunteer. This is just a little demonstration of what is in store for the one who volunteers. I don't want either of you to think dying is going to be the easy way out." She gave them a warm smile. "You have my permission to scream, boys. I believe this is going to hurt."

She yanked the strips of skin off their chests. She waited patiently for the screams to stop, and even a little while longer while they sobbed. It was always good to let a lesson sink in.

"Please, Sister, we serve the Creator, as the Sisters have taught us," Weber cried. "We serve the Creator, not the Keeper."

She regarded him coolly. "Since you are so loyal to the Creator, Sam, I will give you first choice. Do you want to be the one to live, or to die tonight?"

"Why him?" Ranson demanded. "Why does he get to choose first?"

"Keep your tongue still, Neville. You will speak when spoken to." She slid her gaze back to Weber. She lifted his chin with a finger. "Well, Sam? Who dies, you or your best friend?" She folded her arms across her breasts.

He looked up at her with hollow eyes. His skin was ashen. He didn't look over at his friend. His voice came in a flat whisper.

"Me. Kill me. Let Neville live. I won't give an oath to the Keeper. I would rather die."

She looked back into his empty eyes a moment and then turned to Ranson. "And what have you to say, Neville? Who lives? Who dies? You, or your best friend in the world. Who gives the Keeper their oath?"

He glanced to Weber, who didn't look back. He licked his lips. His dark eyes came back to her.

"You heard him. He chooses to die. If he wants to die, let him. I choose to live. I will give the Keeper my oath."

"Your soul."

He nodded slowly, his eyes flashing fierce determination. "My soul."

"Well then"—she smiled—"it seems you two friends have come to an agreement. Everyone is happy. So be it. I am pleased, Neville, that it is to be you with us. You have made me proud."

"Do I have to be here?" Ranson asked. "Do I have to see it?"

"See it?" She raised an eyebrow. "You have to do it."

He swallowed, but the hard look stayed in his eyes. She had always known it would be him. Oh, not that there hadn't been doubts, but she had known. She had taught him well. She had spent a great deal of time on him, bending him to her way.

"May I be granted one request?" Weber whispered. "May I have the collar off before I die?"

"So that you may make Wizard's Life Fire and take your own life before we have a chance to take it from you? Do you think I am stupid? A stupid, soft woman?" She shook her head. "Denied."

She released both Rada'Han from the wall. Weber sank to his knees, his head hanging. He was alone in the room, and knew it.

Ranson stood and straightened his shoulders. He pointed at the bloody wound down his chest. "What about this?"

She turned her gaze to Weber. "Sam. Stand up." Weber stood, his eyes staying to the ground. "Your good friend has an injury. Heal him."

Without a word, Weber finally turned and put his hands on Ranson's chest, and began healing. Ranson stood tall, waiting for the pain to be taken away. She walked to the door and leaned her back against it, watching Weber do his work. His last work.

When he finished, he didn't look at either her or Ranson, but went to the far wall and slid his back down it until he sat on the floor. He buried his head between his knees and folded his arms around them.

The healed but still naked wizard strode up to her and stopped, waiting. "What is it I am to do?"

She flicked her wrist, bringing the knife to her hand once more. She gave it a quick, sharp toss in the air, catching it by the blade. She held the handle out to him.

"You are to skin him. Alive."

She pushed the handle against him until his hand came up and took it.

Ranson's eyes left her steady gaze. He stared at the knife in his hand. "Alive," he repeated.

She reached into a pocket and pulled out the small item she had brought: a pewter figure of a man on one knee, holding a crystal over his head. His tiny bearded face was turned up to it in wonder. The crystal was slightly elongated, coming to faceted points. Inclusions floated frozen inside, like a sky of constellations. She

151

wiped the dust off it with the corner of her light cloak and held the small statue out to Ranson.

"This is magic, and a receptacle of magic. The crystal is called quillion. It will absorb the magic as it bleeds from your friend, after he is skinned. When, and only when, all his magic has bled into the quillion, it will give off an orange glow. You will bring the crystal to me to prove you have done the job."

Ranson swallowed. "Yes, Sister."

"Before I leave tonight, you will give the oath." She pushed the figure with the crystal toward him until he took it. "This will be your first task after giving the oath. Fail it, or fail any of the tasks to follow, and you will wish you could trade places with your friend. You will wish it for all eternity."

He stood gripping the knife in one hand and the small figure in the other. "Yes, Sister." He stole a quick glance over his shoulder at the man crouched on the floor against the wall. He lowered his voice. "Sister, could you . . . could you still his tongue. I don't know if I could bear him talking while I do it."

She raised an eyebrow. "You have a knife, Neville. If his words bother you, cut out his tongue."

He swallowed and closed his eyes for a moment. They came open. "What if he dies before the magic is all bled away?"

"With the quillion present, he will live as long as there is any significant trace of it in him. After it's all in the crystal, it will begin to glow. In that way you will know it is finished. After that, I don't care what you do with him. If you want, you may finish him quickly."

"What if he tries to prevent what I do?" He leaned a little closer. "With his magic."

She smiled and gave a nod. "That I will still, with his collar. He will not be able to stop you. After he's dead, there will be no life force to hold the Rada'Han on him. It will open. Bring it with you and give it to me when you bring the crystal."

"And what about the body?"

She gave him a hard look. "You know how to wield the Subtractive. I have spent a good deal of time teaching you, as have others." She darted a glance at Weber. "Use it. Get rid of the body with Subtractive Magic. Every last scrap of it. Every last drop of blood."

Ranson straightened a little and nodded. "All right."

"After you have finished here, and before you come to me at dawn, there is one more task you will perform this night."

Ranson took a deep breath, letting it out slowly. "Another task? Must I do another task this night?"

She smiled and patted his cheek. "This second task you will enjoy. It's a reward for doing a good job with the first. Serving the Keeper well has its rewards, as you will find out. Failing him has its punishments, as I hope you never discover."

He looked suspicious. "And what is this second task?"

"You know a novice named Pasha?"

He let out a grunt. "There isn't a man in the palace who doesn't know who Pasha Maes is."

"And how well do these men 'know' her?"

Ranson shrugged. "She likes to give a kiss and a cuddle in a corner."

"Any more than a 'kiss and a cuddle'?"

"I know a few men who have had their hand up her skirt. I've heard them talk about what fine legs she has, how they would give up the gift just to have those legs around them. But I don't think any have. Some of the men watch out for her, as if she were a defenseless kitten. One in particular, young Warren, keeps a watchful eye on her."

"Warren is one of the men she likes to kiss and cuddle?"

"I don't think she would know him if he was standing in front of her." He chuckled softly. "If he could even work up enough courage to take his nose out of the archives and look her in the face." He frowned. "So what is the task?"

"When you are finished here, I want you to go to her room. Tell her how you are to be released tomorrow, and that when you passed all your tests, the Creator came to you in a vision. Tell her that the Creator told you in this vision that you were to go to her and teach her how to use the glorious gift of her figure that He had given her, how she was meant to use this gift to please men, so that when the special task He has for her is revealed, she will be prepared.

"Tell her the Creator said it was to help her deal with her new one, as he would be the most difficult any novice has ever been given. Tell her the Creator revealed to you that He made this night hot, so she would sweat between her breasts, over her heart, to awaken her to His wishes." She gave him a smooth smile. "Then, I want you to teach her how to please a man."

He stared incredulously at her. "What makes you think she will believe any of this, or go along?"

Her smile widened. "You tell her what I told you to tell her, Neville, and you will have a great deal more than your hand up her skirt. She will probably have her legs around you before you finish talking."

He nodded dumbly. "All right."

She glanced deliberately down at him. "I'm glad to see that you are . . . up to the task." She looked back to his eyes. "Teach her everything you can think of to please a man. At least everything you can teach her by dawn. Teach her well. I want her to know how to make a man happy, and keep him coming back for more."

He smiled. "Yes, Sister."

She put the tip of the rod under his chin, lifting it a little. "You be gentle with her, Neville. I don't want you to hurt her in any way. I want this to be a very pleasant experience for her. I want her to enjoy it." She looked down at him again. "Well, do the best you can with what you have."

"I've never had any complaints," he snapped.

"Idiot. Women don't complain to men's faces about that. They complain to the backs of their heads. Don't you dare jump on her, please yourself, and then fall asleep. You have until dawn. I don't want you sleeping tonight. You make sure this is an experience she remembers fondly. You teach her well. Everything you know."

She pushed up with the rod a little more. "This may be a pleasant task, but it is a task for the Keeper just the same. Fail in this, as in any other, and your service will end abruptly. But your pain will go on and on. Keep alert when you are with her. In the morning, I expect a detailed report of everything you have taught her. You will report every bit of it. I need to know what she knows so I may guide her."

"Yes, Sister."

She glanced past him to the man against the wall. "The sooner you finish here, the sooner you can be with Pasha, and the more time you will have to teach her."

He nodded with a grin. "Yes, Sister."

153

She took the rod away and he let out a breath. With a gesture, she made his robe float to her hand. She shoved it at him.

"Put this on. You're embarrassing yourself." She watched as he began gathering the material and pulling it over his head. "Tomorrow the real work, the real task, begins."

His head poked through the robe, his arms following one at a time. "What work? What task?"

"After you are released, you must be off at once, in the service of your homeland. You do remember your homeland, don't you? You are going to go to Aydindril, as an advisor to High Prince Fyren. You have things to do there. Important things."

"Like what?"

"We will talk about it in the morning. But now, before you can do the first task, and the second, and the rest of it, you have an oath to give. Is this of your free will, Neville?"

She watched his eyes. They darted briefly to his friend huddled against the wall. Then he turned to glance at the knife and the quillion. She saw his dark eyes go out of focus, and she knew he was thinking about Pasha. He answered her in a whisper.

"Yes, Sister."

She nodded. "Very good, Neville. Kneel. The time of the oath is upon you."

As he went to his knees, she lifted her hand. The flame of the torch puffed out, plunging the room into total blackness.

"The oath to the Keeper," she whispered, "is given in the darkness that is his homeland."

Gently, Kahlan pulled the door open. He was awake and sitting in front of the fire. When the door closed, it shut out some of the eerie sound of the boldas and the drums coming from the center of the village. She stood next to him and tipped his head against her leg and then combed her fingers through his hair.

"How is your headache?"

"It's all right. The rest and that last drink Nissel gave me helped." He didn't look up. "They want me out there, don't they?"

Kahlan sank down to sit on the ground next to him. "Yes. It is time." She rubbed his shoulder. "Are you sure you want to eat the meat, knowing this time what it is?"

"I have to."

"But it's still meat. Will you be able to eat it?"

"If I want a gathering, I have to eat it. The way is the way. I will eat it."

"Richard, I'm worried about this gathering. I'm not so sure you should go through with it. Maybe there's another way. The Bird Man is afraid for you too. Maybe you shouldn't do it."

"I have to."

"Why?"

He stared into the fire. "Because this is all my fault. I am responsible. It is my fault the veil is torn. That's what Shota said. My fault. I caused it."

"Darken Rahl caused it . . . somehow."

"And I am a Rahl," he whispered.

Kahlan glanced over, but he didn't look back. "The crimes of the father, passed on to the son?"

He smiled a small smile. "I don't believe that old line. But maybe there is a little snip of truth to it." His eyes turned to her. "You remember what Shota said? That only I could restore the veil? Maybe because Darken Rahl tore it through the Magic of Orden, and my intervention, I have to restore it."

She watched the firelight flicker in his eyes. "So you think . . . what? That maybe since a Rahl tore it, it takes a Rahl to close it?"

He shrugged. "Maybe. That could explain why only I can close it. It may not be the reason, but it's the only one I can think of." He smiled. "I'm glad I'm marrying a smart woman."

She grinned. It made her happy to see him smile. "Well, this smart woman can't see how that could be the reason."

"It might not be, but it's a possibility I have to consider."

"Then why do you have to go through with the gathering?"

His eyes lit up with excitement as he gave her a boyish grin. "Because I figured it out. I figured out what we're going to do."

He rearranged himself, turning toward her and folding his legs. "Tomorrow night, we'll have the gathering and find out what we can that will help us, then, the next morning when it's over . . ." He snatched the dragon's tooth up in his fist and held it up to her as the grin grew on his face. "Then I call Scarlet—with this. That's how we get to Zedd. That's how we can get to Aydindril without the headaches stopping me on a long journey by land. Scarlet flies with magic; her magic allows her to cover vast distances in little time.

"We'll be gone before the Sisters can stop us, and it will take them a long time to follow. I won't have to turn them down, for now; I can get to Zedd first. He will know what to do. About the headaches, I mean. After the gathering, I'll call Scarlet. It will probably take her the better part of the day to reach us." He leaned toward her and gave her a quick kiss. "While we're waiting, we'll be married."

Her heart leapt. "Married?"

"Yes, married. All in the same day. Day after tomorrow. We'll do it all and be away before the day is out."

"Oh, Richard . . . I would like that. But, let's do it now. Call Scarlet now. We can be married in the morning when she gets here. I know the Mud People would do it quickly for us. We can get to Zedd and he will know what to do and you won't have to risk a gathering."

He shook his head. "We have to have the gathering. Shota said only I could close the veil. Not Zedd. What if he doesn't have any idea what to do? He has said he doesn't know much about the underworld. No one does. No one knows about the world of the dead.

"But the ancestors' spirits do. I have to find out whatever I can to help. We can't waste the time going to Zedd, only to find out he doesn't know what to do. I have to find out what I can first, then go to Zedd. Shota said only I could close the veil. Maybe it's because I am the Seeker. I have to do my job and find the answers. Even if they mean little to me, they might be significant to Zedd, and then he might know what to do, know what I can do."

"What if we beat Zedd to Aydindril? If we travel on Scarlet, she will get us there in a day; Zedd may not be there yet."

"If he isn't there, we know he's going there, and we'll find him. He will be able to see Scarlet."

She watched him a moment. "Your mind is made up about all this, isn't it?"

He shrugged. "If anyone could poke holes in my idea, it would be you. You have any better ideas?"

She shook her head at last. "I wish I did, but I don't. I like all of it but the gathering."

Richard's face softened with a gentle smile. "I would really like to see you in the wedding dress Weselan is making. Can she have it done that soon? We could spend our wedding night in Aydindril, in your home."

Kahlan couldn't keep the smile back. "She can. And there doesn't have to be a big wedding party. Anyway, there's not time to prepare, with the banquet for the gathering going on. But the Bird Man will be pleased to marry us without it." She looked at him coyly. "We would have a real bed, in Aydindril. A big comfortable bed."

His arm circled around her waist and pulled her against him. He gave her lips a soft kiss. She didn't want it to end, but she gently pushed back and glanced away.

"Richard . . . what about the other things Shota said? About a child?"

"Shota was wrong before, about a lot of things. Even the things she was right about didn't turn out how we expected. I'm not going to give you up on her word. Remember what you said to me one time? About never letting a beautiful woman pick your path for you when there was a man in her line of sight? And besides, we will be able to talk to Zedd first. Confessors and the gift are something he does know a lot about."

She ran her finger down his chest. "You seem to have an answer for everything. How did you get so smart?"

He pulled her to him and kissed her again, harder this time.

"I will find an answer to anything that tries to keep me from you and your big comfortable bed. I would go to the underworld and fight the Keeper himself to be with you."

She cuddled against his shoulder. It seemed like forever since he had found her in Westland, being chased by a quad. It seemed a lifetime ago, not a mere few months. They had been through so much. She was so tired of being afraid, and being chased, hunted. It wasn't fair that just when it was over, it was starting again.

She gave herself a mental shake. That was the wrong way to see things. It was the problem, not the solution. She forced herself to look at the new problem in its own light, and not color it with what had happened in the past.

"Maybe it won't be so hard this time. Maybe we can do as you say, and find out what needs to be done, and be finished with it." She kissed his neck. "We'd better get out there; they are waiting. And besides, if I stay here with you any longer, we won't make it to my big comfortable bed."

They left the quiet of the spirit house and walked hand in hand through the dark pathways between the buildings of the village. She felt safe holding his hand. From the first day they met, and he offered his hand to her to help her up, she had liked having her hand in his. No one had ever done that before; people were afraid of Confessors. She wanted this over, so they could be together and live in peace. So they could hold hands whenever they wanted, and not ever have to run.

The sound of the people, the dancing, the conversation, and the children grew louder until the two of them passed into the firelit field. Musicians stood on open, grass-roofed platforms, swaying as they drew paddles up and down the carved ripples on the boldas, sending the haunting strains out over the surrounding flat grassland. Arms a blur, men pounded on drums, sending frantic, echoing beats across the village to others who answered or joined in. Dancers in costumes followed one another around in circles, stopping and turning as one, jumping and stomping, acting out stories for the gleeful children and adults who crowded around them. Cooking fires sent sweet-smelling smoke and wonderful aromas drifting to them.

As they walked past, large fires roared and crackled in the center of the field, warming one side of her with their heat. Men proudly wore their finest skins, and women their brightest dresses. All had their hair freshly slicked down with sticky mud. Woven trays of tava bread, roasted peppers, onions, long beans, cabbage, cucumber and beets, bowls of stewed meats, fish, and chicken, as well as platters of boar and venison, were carried by young women from the cook fires to people gathered at various shelters. The whole village was in joyful celebration to welcome the ancestors' spirits.

Savidlin stood at their approach, welcoming them onto the elders' platform. He looked dignified with his official coyote hide around his shoulders. The Bird Man and the other elders gave the two of them smiles and nods. As soon as she and Richard sat cross-legged, the young women brought woven trays and platters of food. They both took pieces of tava bread and rolled them around peppers, careful to put them to their mouths with the right hand only. A boy brought pottery mugs and a jug of water mildly flavored with spices.

When he was satisfied they were comfortably settled, the Bird Man nodded to a group of women at a nearby shelter. Kahlan knew what this meant. The women were special cooks, the only ones allowed to prepare the banquet specialties. Richard's eyes watched as one of them came with a woven platter filled with dried meat, neatly arranged in a circular pattern. He gave no sign of his feelings.

There would be no gathering if he didn't eat this meat. Worse, this was not just any meat. She knew, though, that he was determined, and would eat it.

The woman bowed her head, holding the platter out to the Bird Man, and then the other elders. After each took some, she offered it to the elders' wives. A few took a piece. She turned and held the platter out to Richard. He looked at it a moment, and then reached up and took one of the larger pieces. He held it in his fingers, looking at it as the woman left after Kahlan declined the offer.

*"I know it is difficult for you,"* the Bird Man said to Richard, *"but it is necessary for you to have the knowledge of our enemies."*

Richard pulled off a big bite with his teeth. "The way is the way." He chewed and swallowed without showing any emotion. He looked off into the distance. "Who is it?"

The Bird Man watched him a moment after Richard looked back to him. *"It is the man you killed."*

"I see."

He took another bite. He had taken a big piece, and was eating the whole thing to show them his determination to have the gathering, to show them that despite the warning from the spirits, he was resolved to go through with it. He watched the dancers as he chewed, washing each swallow down with a drink from his mug. The elders' platform was an isolated island of quiet in the sweep of noise and activity.

Richard abruptly stopped chewing. His eyes widened. He sat up straighter. His head snapped around to the elders.

"Where's Chandalen?"

They looked at one another after studying his face a moment.

Richard sprang to his feet. "Where's Chandalen!"

*"He is here, somewhere,"* the Bird Man said.

"Find him! Right now! Bring him here!"

The Bird Man sent one of the nearby hunters to search. Richard hopped down off the platform without a word and went to the shelter with the banquet cooks. He found the woman with the platter of meat and took a piece.

Kahlan turned to the Bird Man. *"Do you have any idea what is going on?"*

He nodded solemnly. *"He has had a vision; a vision from our enemies' flesh. It happens sometimes. That is why we do this—to know what is in our enemies' hearts."*

Richard returned and paced back and forth in front of the elders' platform, waiting.

"Richard, what is it? What do you see?"

He stopped pacing. The expression on his face was agitated. "Trouble." He resumed his pacing. She asked what sort of trouble, but he didn't seem to even notice the question.

At last the hunter returned with Chandalen and his men.

*"What would make Richard With The Temper ask for me?"*

Richard shoved the piece of meat at him. "Eat this. Tell me what you see."

Chandalen watched Richard's eyes as he ate the strip of dried meat. Richard went back to his impatient pacing, pulling off another bite with his teeth. He chewed and paced.

Finally he could wait no longer. "Well? What do you see?"

Chandalen watched warily. *"An enemy."*

Richard let out an exasperated breath. "Who was this man? From what people?"

*"He was Bantak, from the east."*

Kahlan jumped up. *"Bantak!"* She hopped down off the platform and stood next to Richard. *"Bantak are peaceful. They would never attack anyone. It is against their way."*

*"He was a Bantak,"* Chandalen repeated. *"He had black painted on his eyes. He attacked us."* He redirected his gaze to Richard. *"At least, that is what Richard With The Temper claims."*

Richard went back to pacing. "They're coming," he muttered. He stopped and grabbed Chandalen by the shoulders. "They're coming! They're coming to attack the Mud People!"

Chandalen frowned. *"The Bantak are not fighters. It is as the Mother Confessor says, they are peaceful. They plant crops, herd goats and sheep. We trade with them. This one that attacked us must have been sick in the head. The Bantak know the Mud People are stronger than they. They would not attack us."*

Richard hardly heard the translation. "Get your men together. Get more men. We have to go stop them."

Chandalen studied him. *"We have nothing to fear from the Bantak. They would not attack us."*

Richard nearly exploded. "Chandalen, you are charged with protecting our people! I am telling you there is a threat to them! You must not ignore me in this!"

He ran his fingers through his hair, calming himself. "Chandalen, don't you think it a little strange that one man would have attacked all of us? Would you, as brave as you are, have come into the open and attacked that many men, by yourself? You, with only a spear, and they with bows?"

Chandalen only glared. The Bird Man led the other elders off the platform and stood next to Chandalen, facing Richard. *"Tell us what our enemy has revealed to you. Tell us what you have seen."*

"This man . . ." Richard held the piece of meat up in front of the Bird Man's face. "This man was the son of their spirit guide."

The elders broke into worried whispers. The Bird Man didn't move his eyes from Richard. *"Are you sure of this? Killing the son of a spirit guide is a grave offense. Even in self-defense. It would be the same if someone killed my offspring, had I one."* He lifted an eyebrow. *"Grave enough to start a war."*

Richard nodded hurriedly. "I know. That's what they had planned. For some reason, they thought the Mud People were suddenly dangerous to them. To be sure, they sent the son of their spirit guide, knowing that if we killed him, it would be a sign of our hostile intent. They were planning on watching for his head on a pole, to see if they were right. If he didn't return, and they found the head, they were going to attack."

He waved the meat in front of the elders' faces again. "This man, for some reason, had bitterness in his heart. He wanted there to be a war. He attacked us, knowing he would be killed, wanting it, so it would start the war, and his people could kill all the Mud People. Don't you see? With the banquet going on, they will hear the sounds of it far out onto the plain. They will know we are not prepared to defend ourselves, that we are diverted. They are coming! Now!"

The elders all leaned back a little. The Bird Man turned to Chandalen.

*"Richard With The Temper has had a vision from our enemy. Have each of your men gather ten others. We must not allow the Bantak to harm our people. You will stop them before they reach the village."*

Chandalen's eyes flashed to Richard, and then back to the Bird Man. *"We will see if his vision is true. I will lead our men east. If they are coming, we will stop them."*

"No!" Richard screamed when Kahlan translated. "They will come from the north!"

*"North!"* Chandalen glared at him. *"The Bantak live to the east, not the north. They will come from the east."*

"They will expect you to defend to the east. They think the Mud people want to kill them. They expect it. They will flank you and come from the north!"

Chandalen folded his arms. *"The Bantak are not fighters. They do not know of such tactics. If they are going to attack us, as you say, they will simply come straight in. As you said, they will hear the banquet; they will know we will be unprepared. They have no reason to go all the way around and come in from the north. It would only slow them down for no reason."*

Richard glared at him. "They are coming from the north."

*"Was this part of your vision?"* the Bird Man asked. *"Did you see this too, from eating the meat?"*

Richard forced out a breath and looked down. "No. I didn't see it with the rest of the vision." He ran his fingers through his hair. "But I know it's true. I don't know how, but I know. They are coming from the north."

The Bird Man turned to Chandalen. *"Perhaps you could split the men. Take some to the east, and some to the north."*

Chandalen shook his head. *"No. If the vision proves true, we will need all our men together. One strike, with surprise, with all our men, and with luck, will end it. If there are enough of them, as he seems to think, then they might defeat a number that small, and then they would be upon our people before we could turn them back. Many women and children would be killed. The whole village could fall. It is too dangerous."*

The Bird Man nodded. *"Chandalen, a vision has been presented to us. It is your job to keep our people safe. Since the vision did not say which way they would come, only that they would come, I leave it to you to protect us as you see best. You are the smartest fighter among us, I will trust your fighting judgment."*

He frowned and leaned closer to the man. *"But know that it had better be a fighting judgment, and not a personal one."*

Chandalen showed no emotion. *"It is my opinion the Bantak would attack from the east."* He glanced at Richard. *"If they really come."*

Richard put a hand on Chandalen's folded arm. "Chandalen, please listen to me." His voice was quiet and worried. "I know you don't like me. Maybe you are justified in your feelings. Maybe you are right that I have brought trouble to our people. But trouble is coming now, and it is coming from the north. Please, I beg you, believe me. The lives of all our people depend on this. Hate me all you want, but don't let any of them die because of that hate."

Richard drew the Sword of Truth and held out the hilt. "I will give you my sword. Go north. If they come from the east, and I am wrong, you may kill me with it."

Chandalen looked down at the sword, and back up to Richard's face. A small smile spread on his own. *"I will not let you trick me. I will not let our people be devastated, just for a chance to kill you. I would rather let you live among us, than let my people be killed. I go to the east."* He turned and strode off, shouting instructions to his men.

Richard stood watching him go, then slid the sword back into its scabbard.

"That man is a fool," Kahlan said.

Richard shook his head. "He is just doing what he thinks best. He wants to protect his people more than he wants to kill me. If I had to pick one man to fight beside me, as much as he hates me, it would be him. I am the fool, for not being able to make him see the truth." He turned to her. "I have to go north. I have to stop them."

Kahlan looked around. "There are some other men here. We will gather all we can and—"

He shook his head, cutting her off. "No. There wouldn't be enough. Besides, we need every man able to hold a bow or spear here, to defend the village if I fail. The elders must go on with the banquet. We must have the gathering. That is what's most important. I'll go alone. I'm the Seeker. Maybe I can stop them. Maybe they will listen to one man, see that he isn't so much of a threat."

"All right. Wait here. I'll be right back."

"Why?"

"I have to put on my Confessor's dress."

"You're not going!"

"I have to. You can't speak their language."

"Kahlan, I don't want . . ."

"Richard!" She snatched a fistful of his shirt. "I'm the Mother Confessor! There will be no war under my nose while I have a say in it! You will wait here!"

She released his shirt and stormed off. The Mother Confessor didn't wait for answers to her instructions; she expected them to be carried out. She suddenly regretted yelling at Richard, but she was furious at Chandalen for not listening.

She was furious, too, at the Bantak. She had been to their village before and always found them to be a gentle people. Whatever their reasons, as long as she was around there was going to be no war. The Mother Confessor was supposed to

161

stop wars, not sit by and watch them start. This was her responsibility, her job, not Richard's.

At Savidlin and Weselan's home, in the dark with all the noise going on outside, she slipped into her white Confessor's dress. All Confessors wore dresses cut the same, square at the neck, long, simple, free of embellishment, and satiny smooth, but of black fabric.

Only the Mother Confessor's was white. It was a mantle of power. In the dress, she was not Kahlan Amnell; she was the Mother Confessor, a symbol of the power of truth. With all the other Confessors now dead, the weight of defending the Midlands, those without power, was upon her shoulders.

It made her feel different now to wear the dress. Before, it had seemed the normal thing to do. Now, since she had met Richard, it seemed a heavier responsibility. Before, she had always felt alone in her job, but now, with him, she felt more of a connection to the people of the Midlands, more one of them, more responsible to them. She knew now what it was to love someone, and to fear for him. She was not going to allow anyone to start a war, not as long as she was the Mother Confessor. She grabbed their heavy cloaks and went back through the passageways to the festivities.

The elders were standing in front of their platform, where she had left them. Richard was still waiting. She tossed his cloak to him and addressed the elders.

*"Tomorrow night is the gathering. It must go on. We will be back well before then."* She turned to the wives. *"Weselan, we wish to be married the next day. I'm sorry there isn't more time to prepare, but we must leave as soon as it is done. We must go to Aydindril. We must stop the threat to the Mud People and everyone else."*

Weselan smiled. *"Your dress will be ready. I wish we could give you a big wedding feast, but we understand."*

The Bird Man put a hand on her shoulder. *"If Chandalen is wrong . . . Be careful. The Bantak are peaceful, but maybe things have changed. Tell them we wish their people no harm. We do not want war with them."*

Kahlan nodded and flung her cloak around her shoulders as she started off. "Let's go."

Richard fell in beside her without objection. Without speaking, they left the village and went north out onto the flat, open grasslands. As they walked, the sounds of the people and boldas and drums faded steadily into the night. The moon wasn't near full, but it gave them enough light to see by as they walked through the waist-high, dry grass. They hoped that it was dark enough to make them poor targets.

Richard finally glanced over. "Kahlan, I'm sorry."

"For what?"

"For forgetting who you are. That you are the Mother Confessor, and that this is your job. I was just worried for you."

She was surprised by his apology. "I'm sorry I yelled at you. I shouldn't have done that. I just don't want there to be any fighting. I'm supposed to keep the people of the Midlands from fighting. It makes me angry when they insist on killing one another. Richard, I'm so tired of seeing people killed. I thought it was over. I can't bear it anymore. I swear I can't."

He put an arm around her. "I know. Me, too." He gave her shoulder a squeeze as they walked. "The Mother Confessor will put a stop to it." He looked over. She thought he was frowning, but it was too dark to be sure. "With my help."

She grinned. "With your help." She leaned her head against him a moment. "From now on, always with your help."

They walked a long way from the village without seeing anything but the black ground and starlit sky. Richard would stop once in a while to watch the surrounding grassland and take out a few of Nissel's leaves to chew. Sometime past the middle of the night they came to a slight depression in the landscape. He looked around again and then decided they should wait where they were. It would be better for the Bantak to come upon them, he said, than for the two of them to walk into a surprise.

Richard flattened out a small patch of grass and they sat down to wait. They each took turns taking little naps while the other watched to the north. With her hand over his, she watched him sleep and scanned the horizon, and thought about all the times they had done this before, one standing watch, the other sleeping. She longed for the day they could just sleep, and not have to watch. Sleep together. It would happen, she decided, soon enough. Richard would figure out how to close the veil, and then it would be over. They could be at peace.

Kahlan slept nuzzled against him with her cloak wrapped tight against the cold. His warmth made her all the more sleepy. She began to wonder if he was right, if the Bantak would come from the north. If they came from the east, there would be a lot of killing. Chandalen would show no mercy. She didn't want the Mud People to be hurt, but she didn't want the Bantak hurt either. They, too, were her people. She drifted into worried sleep, her last thoughts of Richard.

He brought her awake, pressing his arm around her and his hand over her mouth. The sky was just beginning to lighten to their right, to the east. Thin wisps of dark purple clouds bunched near the horizon, as if trying to mask the sunrise with their dark hue. Richard was watching to the north. She was lower than he, and couldn't see anything, but she knew by the tenseness of his muscles that someone was coming.

They lay still, close to the ground, waiting. Gentle breezes rustled the dry grass around them. Kahlan quietly, slowly, slid the cloak from her shoulders. She didn't want there to be any mistake about who she was. The Bantak would recognize her long hair, but she wanted them to see her Confessor's dress, too. She didn't want there to be any doubt who she was and that she was here as the Mother Confessor. Richard shrugged his cloak off his shoulders. Shadows slid through the grass around them.

When there seemed to be men all around, the two of them stood up. Men with spears and bows closest leapt back and screamed yells of surprise. The Bantak were spread out in a long, thin line, advancing toward the Mud People's village.

There were excited shouts. Men swept in from the line, a few surrounding them, most bunched in front. Kahlan stood tall, her hands at her sides. She wore her Confessor's face, a calm that showed nothing, as her mother had taught her. Richard was tight at her side, his hand on the hilt of his sword. Most of the men, in simple hide clothes trimmed with grass, leveled weapons at the two of them. They were clearly nervous about doing so.

"You would dare to threaten the Mother Confessor?" she called out. "Lower your weapons. Now."

Eyes flicked around, looking to see if the two of them were alone. The men seemed to become less sure about pointing spears and arrows at the Mother Confessor; they were doing something unheard of, and they knew it. They looked as if they couldn't decide to keep doing what they were doing, or drop their weapons and fall to their knees. A few of them crouched lower, in half bows.

Kahlan took an aggressive stride toward them. "Now!"

The men flinched, cowering back a little. The points of all the weapons moved from her—to Richard. They appeared to hope this would be an acceptable compromise. It was not what she had expected.

She stepped in front of Richard. All the weapons were once again pointing at her.

"What do you think you are doing," he whispered to the back of her head.

"Just stay quiet. Let me try to do this. We don't have a chance if we can't get them to lower their weapons and talk."

"Why are they doing this? I thought everyone was afraid of the Mother Confessor."

"They are afraid, but they are used to seeing a wizard with me. They may be more bold because they don't see one now. Even so, they shouldn't be doing this." She took another step forward. "Who speaks for the Bantak? Who among you takes responsibility for allowing the Bantak to threaten the Mother Confessor?"

Not being able to point their weapons at Richard with her in the way, the Bantak lost a bit of their confidence and lowered the points a little. Not all the way, but a little.

At last, an old man approached, pushing through, stopping in front of her. He wore simple hide clothes like the other men, but around his neck hung a gold medallion worked with Bantak symbols. She knew him. He was Ma Ban Grid, the Bantak's spirit guide. His scowl made his heavily wrinkled loose skin seem even more deeply creased than she remembered. She also didn't remember him scowling like this; she remembered only his easy smile.

*"I speak for the Bantak,"* Ma Ban Grid said. He had only two bottom teeth in front. His jaw wobbled easily with the difficult-to-pronounce Bantak words. He glanced at Richard. *"Who is this one?"*

Kahlan returned Ma Ban Grid's scowl. *"Now Ma Ban Grid would question the Mother Confessor before she is welcomed before his eyes?"*

The Bantak men shuffled their feet uneasily. Ma Ban Grid did not. His gaze was solid and unwavering. *"These are not right times. These are not our lands. We are not here to welcome visitors before the eyes of the Bantak. We have come to kill the Mud People."*

*"Why?"*

Ma Ban Grid peered down his nose at her. *"They have invited war, as our spirit brethren have warned us they would. They have proven it by killing one of mine. We must kill them before they can kill us all."*

"There will be no war! There will be no killing! I am the Mother Confessor and I will not allow it! The Bantak will suffer by my hand if they do this!"

The band of men broke into worried whispers and moved back a pace. The spirit guide stood his ground.

*"The spirit brethren have also told me that the Mother Confessor no longer holds command over the people of the Midlands. They say that as proof, she has been stripped of the company of a wizard."* He gave her a smug look. *"I see no wizard. As always, the spirits speak true to Ma Ban Grid."*

Kahlan stared speechless at the old man.

Richard leaned toward her. "What are they saying?" Kahlan told him what Ma Ban Grid had said. He stepped up next to her. "I want to speak to them. Translate for me?"

Kahlan noded. "They wanted to know who you are. I didn't tell them."

Richard's eyes turned cold with menace. "I will let them know who I am." His voice took on the same cold quality as his eyes. "And they aren't going to like it."

He turned his hawklike glare on the men, deliberately ignoring Ma Ban Grid, and she saw in those eyes the rage of the sword's magic. He was calling the magic forth even as the sword sat in its scabbard. "You men are following an old fool, an old fool by the name of Ma Ban Grid, who is not wise enough to know true spirits from false spirits." The men gasped at the insult. Richard turned his penetrating gaze to Ma Ban Grid. "Is this not true, old fool?"

Ma Ban Grid stammered with anger a moment before he could get any words out. *"Who are you to dare to insult me like this!"*

Richard glared at him. "Your false spirits told you the Mud People killed one of yours. The false spirits lied to you, and you, in your foolishness, believed them."

*"Lie! We found his head! The Mud People killed him! They want war with us! We will kill them all. Every last one! They have killed one of mine!"*

"I am growing tired of talking to one as stupid as you, old man. The Bantak are a witless people if they put one such as you in charge of talking to the spirit brethren."

"Richard, what are you doing?" she whispered.

"Translate."

When she did, Ma Ban Grid's face reddened more with each word. He looked ready to burst into flames.

Richard leaned closer to him. "The Mud People didn't kill the one that was yours. I did."

"Richard! I can't tell them that. They will kill us."

He continued to glare at Ma Ban Grid as he spoke softly to her. "Something is frightening these people into doing this. They are going to kill us and then go and kill a lot of the Mud People unless I can make them even more frightened of us. Translate."

She let out a noisy breath at him and then told the Bantak what Richard had said. The weapons came back up.

*"You! You killed one of mine!"*

Richard shrugged. "Yes." He pointed at his forehead. "I put an arrow right here. One arrow. Right here. Right through his head, as he was about to put his spear in the back of a man. A man who had no hate in his heart for the Bantak. I killed him as I would kill a coyote sneaking up to steal one of my lambs. One who would take a life by such cowardice deserves to die. One who would listen to false spirits, and send one of his own to do such a thing, does not deserve to lead a people."

*"We will kill you!"*

"Really? Maybe you will try, but you cannot kill me." Richard turned his back to the old man and walked about twenty paces away, the men opening up to let him pass. He turned back. "I used one arrow to kill one of yours. Use one arrow to try to kill me, and we will see who the good spirits protect. Pick any man you wish. Have him do to me as I did to yours. Shoot me with an arrow." He pointed angrily at his forehead again. "Right here, where I shot the coward who would kill for false spirits!"

"Richard! Have you lost your mind? I'm not going to tell them to shoot you."

"Kahlan, I can do this. I can feel it."

"You did it once. What if it doesn't work this time? I'm not going to stand here and let you be killed."

"Kahlan, if we don't stop these people, here, now, both of us are going to be killed, and then the Keeper is going to escape. Tonight is the gathering; that is what's important. I'm using the Wizard's First Rule; the first step to believing is wanting to believe something is true, or being afraid it is. Up until now, they have been believing something because they wanted to. I have to make them afraid that what I am going to say is true."

"What are you going to say?"

"Hurry up. Translate before I lose their interest and they decide to kill us and then go after the Mud People."

She turned back to Ma Ban Grid and, reluctantly, translated. The men all started shouting that they wanted to be the one to shoot the arrow. Ma Ban Grid's eyes moved among them as they yelled and waved their arms.

He smiled. *"All you men may shoot this evil one who has killed one of mine. Everyone! Shoot him!"*

The bows came up. Richard glared. "Coward! Do you men see how foolish this old man is? He knows he listens to false spirits! He would have you listen to them also! He knows the good spirits protect me in my challenge. He is afraid to have you see he is a fool. This proves it!"

Ma Ban Grid's jaw tightened. He held his arm up for his men to halt. At last he turned to a man with a bow and snatched it from his hands. *"I will show you the spirits I hear are true! You will die for killing one of mine! For saying our spirit brethren are false spirits!"*

He drew a poison arrow back and in a blink shot it at Richard. A cheer rose from the men. Kahlan's breath caught in her throat. She went cold with fear.

Richard snatched the arrow out of the air right in front of his face.

The men gasped and then fell silent as Richard marched back to the spirit guide, the arrow in his hand, and fire in his eyes. He stopped before Ma Ban Grid and snapped the arrow in front of his face to the sound of fearful murmurs.

His voice was deadly. "The good spirits protect me, old fool. You listen to false spirits."

*"Who are you?"* Ma Ban Grid whispered, wide-eyed.

Richard slowly drew the Sword of Truth. The soft ring of steel filled the quiet dawn. He placed the sword's point at Ma Ban Grid's throat.

"I am Richard, the Seeker. Mate to the Mother Confessor." Worried whispers drifted through the cold air. "And, I am a wizard. Her wizard."

Eyes as far as she could see widened. Jaws dropped. Ma Ban Grid's face slackened a little. He glanced to the sword.

*"Wizard? You?"*

"Wizard!" Richard's angry glare swept across the gathered men. "Wizard. I command the magic. The gift. It would seem, old fool, your false spirits have lied to you. They said the Mother Confessor had no wizard. They sent one of yours to start a war the Mud People do not want. They have used you for their own purposes. Perhaps a wise spirit guide would have known this, perhaps an old fool would not." Grumbling broke out among the men. "If you persist in this, if you disobey the Mother Confessor, I will use my magic to destroy you. I will use terrible magic to burn the Bantak's land to ashes and put a blight upon it for all time. Each Bantak will die a horrible death; a death by my magic. I will kill every last Bantak. Young, and old." His cold gray eyes returned to Ma Ban Grid. "But I will start with the old."

*"Magic?"* Ma Ban Grid whispered. *"You would kill us with magic?"*

Richard leaned closer. "If you disobey the Mother Confessor, I will kill you all with magic more frightful than anything you can imagine." As the men all listened in rapt attention to her translation, Richard recited a litany of horrors he would bring to them. Most of the things she remembered Zedd telling a mob that had come to kill him when they thought he was a witch. Richard was using the same things now to scare the Bantak. The more he spoke, the wider their eyes became.

Ma Ban Grid's gaze left the sword and returned to Richard's face. He looked less sure of himself, but wasn't entirely ready to concede. *"The spirits told me there was no wizard with the Mother Confessor. Why should I believe you are a wizard?"*

All of the anger left Richard's face. She had never seen him hold the sword without the fury of the sword's magic in his eyes. There did seem to be something in his eyes, but it wasn't hate, or rage; he looked at peace. Somehow, it was more frightening than the anger. It was the peace of a man committed to a course.

In the dim dawn light, the blade of Richard's sword changed. It began to glow white. White hot with magic. It brightened until no one could miss seeing the bright white luminescence.

Richard was using the only magic he knew and could depend on. The magic of the sword.

It was enough. Fear swept the crowd. Men fell to their knees, dropping their weapons, muttering for forgiveness, beseeching the spirits to protect them. Others stood frozen, not knowing what to do.

"Forgive me, old man," Richard whispered, "but I must kill you to save a great many more lives. Know that I forgive you, and regret what I must do."

As she translated, Kahlan put a hand on Richard's arm to keep him from doing anything. "Richard, wait. Please, give me a chance?"

He nodded slightly. "One chance. Fail, and I kill him."

She knew he was trying to scare the Bantak, to break the spell they seemed to be under, but he was scaring her too. He was beyond the rage of the sword, to something worse. She looked back to the spirit guide.

*"Ma Ban Grid, Richard will kill you. He does not lie about this. I have asked him to wait, so I may grant you my forgiveness, if you will see the truth of what we say. I can ask him not to kill you, and he will do as I ask. But only once. After that, I will have no control over him. If you are insincere in your change of heart, there will be much death and suffering. Richard is a man of his word. He has made a promise to you, and if you try to trick him with your answer, he will keep his promise.*

*"I give you this one chance to hear the truth. It is not yet too late. The Mother Confessor does not want any of her people to die. Every life in the Midlands holds dear value in my heart. But sometimes, I must let a few lose their lives, so that many more may live. I will hear your answer."*

The men all stood stooped and still. They looked as if they had gotten themselves into something they no longer wanted. The Bantak were a peaceful people and they seemed to regret their foray, even seemed confused by it. Richard had succeeded in giving them a bigger fright than whatever brought them to this.

The breeze fluttered the dry grass and in its passing pulled a stray wisp of hair across her face. Kahlan reached up and pulled it back as she waited. With eyes that seemed to have gone empty of passion, Ma Ban Grid searched her face. The spell had been broken.

His voice came soft and sincere. *"I heard the spirits speak. I thought they were speaking the truth. It is as he says. I am an old fool."* He looked around at his silent men. *"The Bantak have never before sought to bring death to others. We will not start now."*

He bowed his head and pulled his medallion over his wispy gray hair. He brought it up in both hands, offering it to her. *"Please, Mother Confessor, give this to the Mud People. Tell them it is given in peace. We will start no war with them."* He glanced over. Richard returned the sword to its scabbard. Ma Ban Grid looked back to her. *"Thank you for stopping us, for stopping me, from listening to false spirits and doing a terrible thing."*

Kahlan bowed her head to the old man. *"I am thankful I was able to serve in time to prevent anyone from being hurt."*

Richard glanced to her. "Ask him how the spirits convinced him to do something against the nature of his people."

*"Ma Ban Grid, how did the spirits put the lust for war in your heart? The lust for killing?"*

He stared off, unsure. *"Their whispers came to me in the night. Made me feel*

168

*the need. I have felt an urge to violence before, but never acted on it. This time, it seemed I could not hold it back. I had never felt this need so strongly before."*

"The veil to the underworld, the spirit world, is torn." Whispers spread back through the men as she told them Richard's words. "False spirits may seek to speak to you again. Be on guard against them. I understand how you were tricked, and will hold no anger against you for it. But I expect you to be more cautious now that you have learned the truth and have been warned."

*"Thank you, wizard."* Ma Ban Grid nodded. *"I will make it so."*

"Did the spirits voices tell you anything else?"

The old man frowned in thought. *"I don't really remember their voices telling me what must be done. It was more of a feeling that filled me with the need. My son"*—he looked up—*"the one who died . . . he was with me, and heard them also. I felt that the spirits spoke differently to him, somehow. His eyes were wild with hate. Even more than mine. He went as soon as we were visited by the spirits."* His gaze sank to the ground.

Richard regarded the spirit guide a long moment. His voice came softly. "I am sorry, Ma Ban Grid, that I had to kill your son. It wounds my heart to have done so. Know that had there been any other path, I would have taken it."

The old man nodded, but couldn't bring forth words. He looked around at his men. He seemed suddenly ashamed. *"I don't know what we are doing here,"* he whispered. *"This is not the Bantak way."*

"It is the fault of false spirits. I am glad we were here to help you see the truth of it," Richard said.

He nodded again and turned to his men, looking about at them, and then walked off toward their homeland. Kahlan let out a heavy sigh. Richard watched warily as the Bantak plodded off into the sunrise, dragging spears behind.

"What do you make of that?" she asked when he turned to her at last.

He rested his hand on the hilt of the sword and turned to watch the Bantak. "The Keeper is getting ahead of us." He looked back to her eyes. "He has taken the effort to discredit you. To discredit the Mother Confessor. He is laying traps for us. He has plans, and I don't have the slightest idea what they are."

"What are we going to do?"

"What we planned to do. Tonight we have the gathering, and tomorrow we are married and leave for Aydindril."

She studied his face. "You really are a wizard," she said softly. "You used magic to break the Keeper's spell."

His expression didn't change. "No, I'm not. It was just a little trick Zedd taught me. He said once that people are more afraid to die from magic than anything else, as if they would somehow be more dead. I used that fear and the Wizard's First Rule to make them believe it. It was a stronger fear than the one the spirits gave them."

"And what of turning the Sword of Truth white?"

He regarded her a long moment. "Do you remember when Zedd showed us how the sword works? How it couldn't harm anyone you think innocent?" She nodded. "Well, he was wrong. When it is white, you can kill anyone. Anyone. Even one you know to be innocent. Even one you love." His eyes hardened. "I hate magic."

"Richard, the gift has just helped you save the lives of many people."

"At what cost?" he whispered. "Whenever I even think of turning the sword white, all I can remember is how I did it to you, how I almost killed you with it."

169

"But you didn't. Almost doesn't make bread rise."

"That doesn't stop the pain of it. Or of having killed with the sword's white magic, and of knowing what I am capable of. It makes me feel like a Rahl." He let out a heavy breath and changed the subject. "I think we had better be very careful at the gathering tonight."

"Richard . . . this puts a new light on things. We have been warned twice now of the danger of dealing with the spirits. Won't you reconsider the gathering?"

He looked away. "What choice do I have? The Keeper seems to be ahead of us. Events are moving fast. The more we find out, the more we realize we don't know. We must learn what we can."

"But maybe the ancestors' spirits won't be able to help us."

"Then we will have learned something. We can't pass up the chance; too much is at risk. We have to try." He gently took her hand. "Kahlan . . . I can't allow myself to be responsible for this. To know it's my fault."

She waited until his eyes came up. "Why? Because Darken Rahl is your father? You think you are responsible because you are a Rahl?"

"Maybe. But Rahl or not, I can't be responsible for the Keeper having everyone. For having you. I have to find a way to stop it. Darken Rahl haunts me from the grave. Somehow I have caused this. I don't know how, but it's my fault. I have to do whatever it takes to stop it, or everyone will suffer. And the Keeper will have you, forever.

"That thought scares me more than anything in my life has ever scared me. It wakes me with nightmares. There isn't anything I wouldn't do to stop him from getting you. I won't take a chance of missing anything, no matter the risk. I have to have the gathering." His gaze held hers. "Even though I fear it might be a trap, I have to try."

"A trap? . . . You think it might be a trap?"

"It could be. We have been warned. At least we can be alert for it." He looked down at her hand in his. "I won't have the sword in the gathering. Do you think you can call down the lightning if you have to?"

Kahlan shook her head. "I don't know, Richard. I don't know how I did it. It just happened. I don't know how to control it."

He nodded as he rubbed the back of her hand with his thumbs. "Well, maybe you won't have to try. Maybe the ancestors' spirits will be able to help us. They helped us before."

Richard reached up and gripped the Agiel. His gray eyes were filled with the pain of the headache. He sank down and put his head in his hands as she sat next to him. "I have to rest awhile before we go back. This headache is killing me."

She feared he was right, that the headache really was killing him. She ached for the next day, when they could get to Zedd, get to help.

It was late afternoon by the time they returned to the celebration, the banquet. Richard's head was a little better, but still hurt him enough to leave the pain in his eyes. The elders stood as the two of them approached the open pole shelter. The Bird Man stepped forward.

*"What of the Bantak? Did you see them? There has been no word from Chandalen."*

Kahlan held the gold medallion out to him and let it drop in his hand when it came up.

*"We found them, to the north, as Richard said we would. Ma Ban Grid sent this as a gift to tell the Mud People that the Bantak will not make war with them. They made a mistake, and are sorry. We made them see that the Mud People mean them no harm. Chandalen has also made a mistake."*

The Bird Man nodded solemnly, and turned to a hunter standing nearby, telling him to bring back Chandalen and his men. Kahlan didn't think he looked as pleased as she thought he would be.

*"Honored elder, is something wrong?"*

His brown eyes seemed heavy. He glanced to Richard and back to her. *"Two of the Sisters of the Light have returned. They wait in the spirit house."*

Kahlan's heart jumped. She had hoped they wouldn't be back so soon. What had it been, only a few days? She turned to Richard.

"The Sisters of the Light are waiting in the spirit house."

Richard sighed. "Nothing is ever easy." He addressed the Bird Man. "Tonight is the gathering. Will you be ready?"

*"Tonight the spirits will be with us. We will be ready."*

"Be careful. Take nothing for granted. All our lives depend on it." He took her arm. "Let's see if we can put a stop to this."

They walked together across the field, past the roar of the fires. People were still everywhere, eating, dancing, playing the boldas and drums. There were fewer children about. Some were off napping, but some still managed to dance and play.

"Three days," he muttered.

"What?"

"It's been three days, almost, since they were here last. I will send them away, and tomorrow, we will be gone. When they come back in another three days, we will have been in Aydindril for two."

She stared ahead as they walked. "That is if they keep to the same schedule. Who says they won't show up for the third time after only one day. Or one hour."

She could feel his eyes on her, but she didn't look over when he spoke. "Are you trying to make a point?"

"You only get three chances, Richard. I'm afraid for you. I'm afraid of the headaches."

This time, she did look over, but he didn't. "I won't wear a collar. Not for any reason. Not for anyone."

"I know," she whispered.

He yanked the door open and strode into the spirit house. His jaw was set with determination. His eyes fixed on the two women standing in the center of the dimly lit room as he marched up to them. Both wore their cloaks with the hoods pushed back. Their faces, in mild frowns, seemed almost calm.

Richard stopped in front of the two. "I have questions, and I want answers."

"We are glad to see you are still well, Richard," Sister Verna said. "Still alive."

"Why did Sister Grace kill herself? Why did you allow it?"

Sister Elizabeth stepped in front of Sister Verna. She held the open collar in her hands. "We told you before, discussion is over. It is by the rules now."

"I have rules too." With his fists on his hips, he looked to each woman in turn. "My first rule is that neither of you is going to kill herself today."

They ignored him. "You will listen. I, Sister of the Light, Elizabeth Myric, give the second reason for the Rada'Han. Give the second chance to be helped. The first of the three reasons for the Rada'Han is to control the headaches and open your mind so you may be taught to use the gift. You have refused the first chance to be helped. I bring the second reason and offer."

She watched his eyes as if to be sure she had his full attention. "The second reason for the Rada'Han is so that we may be able to control you."

Richard glared at her. "Control me? What does that mean, to control me?"

"It means what it says."

"I'm not putting a collar around my neck so you may 'control' me." He leaned a little closer. "Or for any other reason."

Sister Elizabeth held the collar up. "As you were told before, it is more difficult for you to accept the second offer. Please believe us, you are in great danger. Your time is running out. Please Richard, accept the second offer now, on the second of the three reason and offers. It will only be much more difficult to accept on the third of the three reasons."

There was something in his eyes Kahlan had seen only once before—the last time the collar was held out to him. Something alien, something frightening. It sent a chill through her. Goose bumps rose on her arms. The anger left his voice.

"I told you before," he whispered. "I will not wear a collar. For anyone. For any reason. If you want to teach me to use the gift, to control it, we can talk about it. There are things going on you know nothing about: important things, dangerous things. I have responsibilities as the Seeker. I am not a child like you are used to dealing with. I am an adult. We can talk about it."

Sister Elizabeth stared at him with fierce intensity. Richard retreated a half step. His eyes closed, and he shook slightly. At last, he straightened. His eyes came open as he took a deep breath. He returned the Sister's stare. Something had happened, and Kahlan had no idea what it was.

The strength in Sister Elizabeth's eyes waned. Her hands lowered the collar. Her voice came in a fearful whisper. "Will you accept the offer and the Rada'Han?"

Richard stood staring at her. The power was back in his voice. "I refuse."

Sister Elizabeth went pale as she stared back for a moment before turning to the woman behind her. "Forgive me, Sister, I have failed." She put the Rada'Han in Sister Verna's outstretched hand. Her voice came in a whisper. "It is upon you now."

Sister Verna kissed her on each cheek. "The Light forgives you, Sister."

Sister Elizabeth turned back to Richard, her face gone slack. "May the Light cradle you always with gentle hands. May you someday find the way."

Richard stood with his fists on his hips as he watched her eyes. She lifted her chin. As Sister Grace had done, she brought her arm up and with a flick of her wrist brought the silver-handled knife to her hand. Richard continued to watch her as she flipped it around toward herself. Kahlan watched, holding her breath, spellbound, as the woman prepared to kill herself. The silence seemed thick. For a heartbeat, everyone was stone still.

The instant the knife began to move, Richard did too. His speed was shocking. Before Sister Elizabeth realized what had happened, Richard had her by her wrist. His other hand came up and began prying the odd knife from her fingers as she struggled to keep ahold of it. She was no match for his strength.

"I told you my rule. You are not allowed to kill yourself today."

Her face twisted with futile effort. "Please! Let go—"

Her body flinched. Her head jerked back. There was a flash of light that seemed to come from within her, from within her eyes. Sister Elizabeth crumpled forward to the ground, Sister Verna pulling her own knife from the woman's back as she fell.

Sister Verna's gaze rose from the dead woman to Richard. "You must bury her body yourself. If you let another do it for you, you will have nightmares for the rest of your life, nightmares caused by magic. There is no cure for them."

"You killed her! You murdered her! What's the matter with you! How could you kill her!"

She tucked her knife up her sleeve as she glared at him. She reached out, snatching the silver knife from his hand, and slipped it in her cloak.

"You killed her," Sister Verna whispered.

"Your hands have the blood on them!"

"So does the executioner's axe, but it doesn't wield itself."

Richard lunged for her throat. She didn't move; she simply continued to stare at him. His hands stopped before reaching her. Richard shook, straining against an invisible barrier as she watched him.

In that instant, Kahlan knew what the Sisters were.

Richard relaxed the pressure of pushing against the barrier. He pulled his hands back a little. He visibly relaxed. Gently, his face gone calm, he reached one hand toward Sister Verna. His fingers clutched around her throat. Her eyes went wide with shock.

"Richard," she whispered angrily, "take your hand from me."

"As you have said, this is no game. Why did you kill her?"

His weight came off his feet. Richard floated a few inches into the air. He tightened his grip on her throat. When he didn't release her, fire ignited all around them, roaring to life, a whorl of flame closing around him.

"I said, take your hand from me."

In a moment more, the fire would consume Richard. Before she realized what she was doing, Kahlan had her fist out toward the Sister. Blue light crackled all around her wrist and hand. Little threads of blue lightning escaped from the sides as she struggled to restrain herself from releasing the bolt of power. Wisps of blue fire sizzled forth, throughout the spirit house, up the walls, across the ceiling and floor, everywhere except where the other two stood. She shook with the strain of holding back the power.

"Stop it!" The threads of blue lightning sucked the fire into them. "There will be no more killing today." The blue light extinguished.

Silence again filled the room as Sister Verna stared at Kahlan. A hard edge of anger stole into her eyes. Richard settled to the ground and took his hand from the woman's throat.

"I wouldn't have harmed him. I only meant to frighten him into releasing me." She turned her glare to Richard. "Who taught you to break a web?"

"No one taught me. I taught myself. Why did you kill Sister Elizabeth!"

"You taught yourself," she mocked. "I told you. This is no game. It must go by the rules." Her voice lost its edge. "I have known her for many years. If you had ever turned that sword of yours white, you would understand what it took for me to do as I did."

Richard didn't tell her he had turned the sword white. "You would expect me to put myself in your hands, after what you have done?"

"Your time is running out, Richard. After what I have seen today, I would be

173

surprised if the headaches don't soon kill you. I don't know why it is that the pain hasn't already put you down. Whatever is protecting you won't last much longer. I know you don't like to see anyone die. Neither do we, but please believe that what is done is done for you, to save you."

She turned to Kahlan. "Be very careful with that power of yours, Mother Confessor. I doubt you have the slightest idea how dangerous it is." Sister Verna pulled her hood up as her brown eyes turned to Richard. "You have been offered the first and second of three chances, and refused. I will return." She leaned a little closer. "You only have one chance left. If you refuse it, you will die. Think on it carefully, Richard."

After the door closed behind Sister Verna, Richard squatted next to the dead Sister. "She was doing something to me. Magic. I could feel it."

"What did it feel like?"

Richard shook his head a little. "The first time they were here, I thought I felt something pulling me to accept their offer, but I was so afraid of the collar, I paid it no attention. This time, it was much stronger. It was magic. The magic was trying to force me to say yes, to accept the offer from the Sisters. I just thought about the collar until the force left and I was able to say no."

He looked up at her. "You have any idea what's going on? What she was doing, and what Sister Verna did, with the fire, and the rest of it?"

Kahlan's hand still tingled from the blue lightening. "Yes. The Sisters are sorceresses."

Richard rose smoothly to his feet. "Sorceresses." He watched her eyes for a long moment. "Why would they kill themselves when I said no?"

"I think it is to pass their power on to the next Sister, to make her stronger for when they try again."

He looked down at the body. "Why would I be so important, that they would kill themselves to get me?"

"Maybe it is as they say. To help you."

He glanced at her out of the corner of his eye. "They don't want one man, a stranger, to die, yet two of them have already died trying to get me to accept their help so a life wouldn't be lost? How does that add up?"

"I don't know, Richard, but I'm so scared it hurts. I'm afraid they could be telling the truth: that you don't have much time, and the headaches are killing you. I'm afraid you won't be able to control them much longer." Her voice broke with emotion. "I don't want to lose you."

Richard slipped his arms around her. "It will be all right. I will bury her. The gathering will be in a few hours. Tomorrow we will be in Aydindril and then I will be safe. Zedd will know what to do."

She could only nod against his shoulder.

**K**ahlan sat naked in the circle with eight naked men. Richard was to her left, painted, as were she and the elders, with the black and white mud except in a small circle in the center of his chest. In the dim light coming from the small fire behind her, she could see the wild jumble of lines and swirls sweeping diagonally across his face. They all wore the same mask, so that the ancestors' spirits might see them. She wondered if she looked as savage to him as he looked to her. The unfamiliar, acrid smell from the fire made her nose itch. None of the elders scratched their noses; they only stared at nothing and chanted sacred words to the spirits.

The door slammed shut by itself, making her jump.

The Bird Man's distant eyes came up. *"From now, until we are finished, near dawn, no one may go out, no one may come in. The door is barred by the spirits."*

Kahlan didn't like the idea that, as Richard had said, this could be a trap. She squeezed his hand more tightly. He returned the squeeze. At least, she thought, she was with him. She hoped she could protect him. She hoped she could call the lightning if she had to.

The Bird Man fished out a frog and then passed the woven basket to the next elder. Kahlan stared at the skulls arranged in a circle in the center as each elder took a frog and began rubbing its back against the bare circle of skin on his chest. As they did so, each rolled his head back and chanted different words. Without looking over, Savidlin passed her the basket.

Closing her eyes, she reached inside and finally caught a squirming, kicking spirit frog. Its smooth, slimy skin was revolting. Swallowing hard, and taking a mental grip on her Confessor's power to try to keep from releasing it unintentionally, she pressed the frog's back to the skin between her breasts as she passed the basket to Richard.

Tingling tightness spread across her skin. She freed the frog and took up Richard's hand once more as the walls began to waver, as if seen through heat and smoke. Her mind tried in vain to hold on to the images of the spirit house around her. They drifted away as she felt herself spinning around the skulls.

Soft sensations caressed her skin. Light danced from the skulls in the center and filled her eyes. Sounds of the boldas and drums and chanting filled her ears. The pungent smell from the fire filled her lungs. As once before, the light from the center brightened, taking them into it, into the silken void, spinning them around.

And then there were shapes around them. Kahlan remembered them, too, from before: the ancestors' spirits. She felt a gossamer touch on her shoulder: a hand; a spirit hand.

The Bird Man's mouth moved, but it wasn't his voice. It was the joined voices of the ancestors' spirits, flat, hollow, dead.

*"Who calls this gathering?"*

Kahlan leaned toward Richard, and whispered, "They want to know who calls this gathering."

He nodded. "I do. I call this gathering."

The touch left her shoulder and the spirits all floated from behind them into the center of the circle.

*"Speak your name."* The echo of their voices sent ripples of pain along the skin of her arms. *"Your full and true name. If you are certain that you wish this gathering, despite the danger, speak the request after your name. You get but this one warning."*

Richard stared at her translation. "Richard, please . . ."

"I have to." He looked back to the spirits in the center and took a deep breath. "I am Richard . . ." He swallowed and closed his eyes for a moment. "I am Richard Rahl, and I request this gathering."

*"So be it,"* came the empty whispers.

The door to the spirit house crashed open.

Kahlan jumped with a little shriek. She felt Richard's hand flinch, too. The doorway stood open, a black maw in the soft light around them. The elders all looked up, their eyes no longer glazed with the distant vision. They seemed confused, dazed.

The spirit voices came again, this time not through the elders, but from the center, from the spirits themselves. The sound of it was even more painful than before.

*"All but the one who calls the ancestors' spirits may leave. Leave while you still can. Heed our warning. Those who remain behind with him risk forfeiting their souls."* They turned as one to Richard. Their voices were a hiss. *"You may not leave."*

The elders' frightened eyes flicked around to each other as she translated for Richard. Kahlan knew: this had never happened before.

"Everyone out," Richard whispered. "Have everyone get out. I don't want them hurt."

Kahlan looked to the Bird Man's worried eyes. *"Please. All of you, leave now. While you can. We don't want harm to come to any of you."*

The elders all looked to the Bird Man. He stared at her a moment, glanced at Richard, and then back to her.

*"I can offer you no guidance, child. This has never happened before. I don't know what it means."*

Kahlan nodded. *"I understand. Go now, before it is too late."*

Savidlin touched her shoulder, and then the elders vanished as they walked through the black void of the doorway. She sat in the quiet with Richard; with the spirits.

"Kahlan, I want you out of here, too. Go. Now." His voice was calm, almost cold. Fear danced in his eyes. And magic.

She watched his face as he stared at the spirits.

"No," she whispered. She turned once more to the center. "I will not leave you. Not for any reason. Though no words have been spoken over us, we are joined in our hearts, by my magic. We are one. What happens to one, happens to both. I am staying."

Richard didn't look over. He continued to stare at the spirits as they floated in the center of the room, above the skulls. She thought he would yell at her to leave. He didn't. His voice came soft and gentle.

"Thank you. I love you, Kahlan Amnell. Together, then."

The door banged closed.

Kahlan jumped, and a little sound escaped from her throat before she could catch it. Her heart pounded in her ears. She tried to slow her breathing, but couldn't. She swallowed instead.

The image of the spirits dimmed. *"What you have called forth, Richard Rahl, we cannot stay to witness. We are sorry."*

Their forms seemed to evaporate as she watched. As they vanished, the light went with them, until the two of them were left in total blackness. She could hear the slow crackle of the fire off beyond that blackness, Richard's quick breathing, her own breathing, and nothing else. Richard's hand found hers. In the darkness, they sat together, alone, naked.

As Kahlan began to think, to hope, that nothing was going to happen, she became aware of a slight brightening in front of her. There was light beginning to glow.

Green light.

A shade of green light she had seen from only one place.

The underworld.

Her breaths came in ragged pulls. The green light brightened, and with it, distant wails.

From the air all about came an earsplitting crack, like a clap of thunder, sudden, hard, painful. The ground shook with the impact of it.

From the center of the green light, a white brilliance oozed through, to coalesce into a form and stand before them. Her breath caught in her throat. The fine hairs on the back of her neck stood out stiffly.

The white form took a step closer. She only dimly realized Richard's grip on her hand was hurting her. Kahlan knew the white robes, the long blond hair, the painfully handsome face that stood before them, smiling that small, gruesome smile.

"Dear spirits protect us," she whispered.

It was Darken Rahl.

As one, she and Richard came slowly to their feet. The glowing blue eyes watched them rise. Relaxed, unhurried, Darken Rahl brought a hand up and licked his fingertips.

"Thank you, Richard, for calling me back." His cruel smile widened. "How thoughtful of you."

"I . . . didn't call you back," Richard whispered.

Darken Rahl laughed a quiet laugh. "Once again, you make a mistake. Call me back you did. You called a gathering. A gathering of ancestors' spirits. I am your ancestor. Only you could have brought me back, through the veil. Only you."

"I denounce you."

"Denounce me all you will." He held his arms out, out in the white light around him. "I am still here."

"But I killed you."

The glowing, shimmering, white robed form laughed again. "Killed me? So you did. And, you used magic to send me to a different place. A place where I am known. A place where I have . . . friends. And now you have called me back. Again with magic. Not simply called me back, Richard, but torn the veil further to do so." He slowly shook his head. "Is there no end to your stupidity?"

Darken Rahl seemed to float, and at the same time walk, toward Richard. Richard let go of Kahlan's hand as he backed away. She couldn't make her legs move to go with him.

Richard's eyes were wide. "I killed you. I defeated you. I won. You lost."

The blond head nodded slowly. "You won a small battle, in a timeless war, by using the gift, and the Wizard's First Rule. But in your ignorance, you violated the Wizard's Second Rule, and in so doing, you have lost it all." His slow, wicked smile came back. "Such a shame. Didn't anyone ever tell you? Magic is dangerous. I could have taught you. Could have shared it all with you." He shrugged. "But it doesn't matter. You have helped me win even without being taught. I couldn't be more proud of you."

"What is the Wizard's Second Rule? What did I do!"

Rahl's eyebrows lifted as he took another step closer.

"Why, Richard, don't you know? You should," he whispered. "You have broken it a second time, today. And in violating it a second time, you have torn the veil once more, a second time, and brought me here, so that I might tear it the rest of the way and free the Keeper." His mocking smile returned. "All by yourself." He gave a taunting laugh. "My son. You should never have meddled in things you don't understand."

"What do you want!"

Rahl drifted closer. "You, my son. You." His hand began to rise toward Richard. "You sent me to another world, and now, in turn, I am going to send you there. You are for the Keeper. He wants you. You are his."

Without even realizing it, Kahlan's fist was up, the Con Dar igniting in the depths of her being. Rage exploded through her, and blue lightning erupted from her fist. The dark void around them was ripped away in a fury of light and sound that shook the ground under her feet. The spirit house was back, lit by the blue bolt as it arced toward Darken Rahl.

Effortlessly, his hand came up, deflecting the strike. The bolt of lightning split. One shaft blasted through the roof, into the black sky, sending a shower of tile fragments raining down. The other fork struck the ground, throwing dirt hurtling everywhere.

Darken Rahl's eyes met hers. His gaze seared her very soul. He smiled the most wicked smile she had ever seen. It seemed to make every fiber of her being ache. She tried to call forth the power again, but nothing happened. He had done something. Kahlan tried, but she couldn't move a muscle. Richard seemed as paralyzed as she.

Her world was collapsing in a frightening rush. *Richard*, she wailed in her mind. *My Richard. Oh, dear spirits, don't let this happen.*

His eyes burning with rage, Richard managed to take a step forward, but Darken Rahl put his hand to the left side of his chest, above his heart, stopping him stone still.

"I mark you, Richard. For the Keeper. With the Keeper's mark. You are his."

Richard threw his head back. His scream seemed to rend the very fabric of the air, and tear her heart and soul with its despair. Kahlan felt as if she died a thousand deaths in that instant.

As Darken Rahl held his hand to Richard's chest, wisps of smoke curled away. Kahlan's nostrils filled with the stench of burning flesh.

Darken Rahl pulled his hand back. "The price of ignorance, Richard. You are marked. You are the Keeper's, now. Now, and forever. The journey begins."

Richard collapsed like a puppet whose strings had been cut. Kahlan didn't know if he was unconscious, or dead. Something held her up, but it wasn't her legs. It was the strings held by Darken Rahl.

He glided closer to her. He loomed over her, crushing her in blinding brilliance. Kahlan wanted to shrink away, to close her eyes, but she could not.

Finally, she regained her voice. "Kill me too," she whispered. "Send me where you have sent him. Please."

His glowing hand reached toward her. The agony in her heart tore her mind senseless. His fingers fanned open. His touch on her flesh sent fire and ice through her in a wave of shock.

The hand pulled back.

"No." Darken Rahl's pitiless smile spread anew. "No. That would be too easy. Better to let him see what happens to you. Better to let him watch, helpless." The smile showed teeth for the first time. "Better to let him suffer it." His eyes had an intensity that seemed to impale her. It was the same frightening glare Richard had inherited.

"You live, for now. Soon enough, you will twist in a different pain, living, and dead," he whispered in a measured, merciless tone. "He will watch. Forever. I will watch. Forever. The Keeper will watch. Forever."

"Please," she cried, "send me with him."

A finger reached out and touched a tear. The pain of the touch made her flinch. "Since you love him so much, I will give you a gift." He turned and drew his arm smoothly through the air in Richard's direction. His frightening blue eyes returned to her. "I will let him live a short time longer. Long enough for you to watch as the Keeper's mark bleeds the life from him. Bleeds his soul from him. Time is nothing. The Keeper will have him. I give you this spark of time in forever to watch the one you love die."

He leaned toward her. She struggled to back away, but couldn't. His lips left a kiss on her cheek. The pain of it sent a silent shriek through her and filled her mind with a vision of being raped. Luminous fingers lifted her hair from her neck. His mouth was by her ear.

"Enjoy my gift," he whispered intimately. "In time, I will have you, too. Forever. Between life and death. Forever. I would like to tell you how much you will suffer, but I am afraid you would not be able to comprehend it. Soon enough, I will show you." He gave a whispering laugh in her ear. "After I have torn the veil the rest of the way, and freed the Keeper."

As she stood helpless, he left another kiss on her neck. The horror of the visions it seared through her mind left her feeling defiled beyond anything she had thought possible. "Just a tiny taste. Good-bye, for now, Mother Confessor."

As he turned from her, she was able to move again. She snatched desperately for the power. It wouldn't come. She cried and shook as she watched him glide through the doorway of the spirit house and disappear.

And then she collapsed to the ground with a wail of agony. Convulsing in ragged sobs, she clawed across the dirt to Richard.

He lay on his side, away from her. She pulled him over on his back. His arm flopped to his side, limp. His head rolled toward her. He looked ashen, dead. On his chest was a burned handprint—the Keeper's mark. The blackened skin was cracked and bleeding. His life, his soul, was bleeding away.

She fell on him, clutched at him, as she wept and shook uncontrollably.

Kahlan gripped her fingers into a fist in his hair and pressed her face against his cold cheek. "Please, Richard," she cried in choking sobs, "please don't leave me. I would do anything for you. I would die in your place. Don't die. Don't leave me. Please, Richard. Don't die."

She crouched against him, her world ending. Dying. She could think of nothing to do, other than cry that she loved him. He was dying, and she could do nothing to stop it. She could feel his breathing slow.

She willed herself to die with him, but death wouldn't come. She lost all sense of time. She didn't know if she had been there a few minutes, or a few hours. She didn't know what was real anymore. It all felt like a nightmare. With trembling fingers, she stroked his face. His skin was dead cold.

"You would be Kahlan."

She spun around, sitting up, at the sound of the woman's voice coming from behind her. The door to the spirit house was closed again. In the darkness, a white, spiritlike glow towered over her. It appeared to be a spirit, a woman, her hands clasped in front of her. She watched with a pleasant smile. Her hair, as best as Kahlan could make of it, was plaited in a single braid.

"Who are you?"

The figure sank down to sit in front of her. The spirit had no clothes Kahlan could make out, but didn't appear to be naked either. The woman looked at Richard. A glaze of both longing and anguish came over her fair features. The spirit turned to Kahlan.

"I am Denna."

The shock of the name, and her proximity to Richard, brought Kahlan's fist up in a jerk. Lightning screamed to be released. Before Kahlan could let it go, Denna spoke again.

"He is dying. He needs us. Both of us."

Kahlan hesitated. "You can help him?"

"We both can, maybe. If you love him enough."

Kahlan's hopes flared. "I would do anything. Anything."

Denna nodded. "I hope so."

Denna looked back to Richard and tenderly stroked his chest. Kahlan was a blink away from releasing the power. She didn't know if Denna was trying to hurt him, or help him. She hoped against hope. This was her only chance to save Richard. Richard took a deep breath. Kahlan's heart leapt.

Denna withdrew her hand and smiled. "He is still with you."

Kahlan lowered her fist a little, and wiped tears from her cheek with the fingers of her other hand. She didn't like the look of longing Denna had as she watched Richard. Not one bit. "How did you get here? Richard couldn't have called you; you are not his ancestor."

Denna turned, her small, dreamy smile fading. "It would be impossible to relate it to you accurately, but perhaps I could explain it enough that it would help you to understand. I was in a place of darkness and peace. It was disturbed as Darken Rahl passed through. His passing through is something that is not supposed to happen. As he neared, I sensed that Richard had somehow called him, and enabled him to pass from where he was, held by a veil, and to come here.

"I know Darken Rahl all too well, and I knew what he would do to Richard. So I followed him. I would never have been able to pass through my own veil, but by latching on to him, I was able to come through, too, to follow in his wake. I came

180

because I knew what Darken Rahl would do to Richard. I don't know how to explain it better."

Kahlan nodded. She wasn't seeing a spirit; she was seeing a woman who had taken Richard as her mate. The power boiled angrily inside her. She struggled to put it down, telling herself that this was to save Richard. She didn't know any other way; she had to let Denna help, if she could. Kahlan had said she would do anything, and she meant it. Even if it was not to try to kill someone who was already dead. Someone she wanted to kill a thousand times and then another thousand.

"Can you help him? Can you save him?"

"The Keeper's mark has been placed upon him. The mark will take the holder to the Keeper. If another's hand is placed over the mark, it will transfer to them, and take them instead, in his place. Richard will not then be pulled to the Keeper. He will live."

Kahlan knew in that instant what she must do. Without hesitation, she leaned over Richard, stretching her hand out. "Then I will take the mark. I will go in his place so that he will live." She spread her fingers to match the black mark. Her hand was only a scant inch above it.

"Kahlan, don't do that."

She looked over her shoulder. "Why? If it will save him, then I am willing to go in his place."

"I know you are, but it is not that simple. We must talk first. It will not be easy, for either of us. It will hurt both of us to really help him."

Kahlan reluctantly sat back down and nodded. She would have agreed to anything, paid any price, even talking to this . . . woman. She put a hand protectively on Richard as she sat facing Denna. "How do you know who I am?"

Denna grinned, almost laughed. "To know Richard is to know who Kahlan is."

"He told you about me?"

Denna's smile faded. "In a way. I heard your name countless times. When I hurt him until he was delirious, he cried your name. Never another. Not his mother's, nor his father's. Only yours. I hurt him until he didn't know his own name, but he always knew yours. I knew he would find a way to be with you despite your Confessor's power." A little of her smile came back. "I think Richard could find a way to make the sun rise at midnight."

"Why are you telling me this?"

"Because I am going to ask you to help him, and I want you to understand exactly how much you will be hurting him before you agree to it. You must understand what it is you will have to do in order to save him. I won't trick you into doing it. It must be with your full knowledge. Only in that way will you know how to save him. If you don't understand, you could fail.

"He is in danger from more than this mark. He is sick with a madness, madness I put there. It will kill him as surely as will the Keeper's mark."

"Richard is probably the most sane person I know. He has no madness. It is the mark we must remove."

"He is marked in other ways: he has the gift. I knew from the moment he came to kill me. I can see it in him now, the aura of it. I know it is killing him, and I know his time is very short. I don't know how long, only that there is not much time left. We can't save him from the Keeper just to have him die anyway from the gift."

Kahlan nodded as she wiped her nose on the back of her hand. "The Sisters of the Light say they can save him. They say he must put a collar on to save himself. Richard will not put it on. He told me what you did to him, why he won't wear a collar. But Richard is not crazy. He will see in the end what must be done, and do it. That is the way he is. He will see the truth."

Denna shook her head. "What he told you does not scratch the surface of it. You cannot imagine what he has not told you. I know his madness. He will not tell you the rest of it. I must."

Kahlan's anger boiled. "I don't think it would be wise for you to tell me. If he doesn't want to tell me, then I don't think I should know it."

"You must. You must understand him if you are to help him. In some ways, I understand him better than you. I have taken him to the edge of madness, and beyond. I have seen him in a wasteland of insanity.

"I have stood over him and held him there."

Kahlan glared. She recognized the look in Denna's eyes when she looked at Richard. She didn't trust her. "You love him."

Denna stared at her. "He loves you. I used that love to hurt him. I took him to the brink of death and held him there, on the cusp. Others would bring a man to the edge faster, but they couldn't hold him there. They always went one step too far, too quickly, and killed them, ending it before they could extract the most exquisite pain, inflict the cruelest of the insanity. Darken Rahl chose me because I had a talent for keeping them alive and giving them that pain, and then more, and then even more. Darken Rahl himself taught me.

"I had to sit for hours, sometimes, and wait, knowing that if I touched him just once more with the Agiel, it would be one touch too many; it would kill him. As I sat, waiting for him to recover enough so that I might hurt him more, he would whisper your name, over and over, for hours. He wasn't even aware he was doing it.

"You were the thread that kept him alive. It was the one thread that allowed me to give him that extra pain. Allowed me to take him further toward death, deeper into madness. I used his love for you to punish him beyond anything otherwise possible.

"As I would sit there, listening to him whisper your name, I wished it would once, just once, have been my name he called out. It never was. I hurt him more for that than for anything else."

Tears ran down Kahlan's cheeks, falling from her face. "Please, Denna, I don't want to hear any more. I can't bear to hear any more—to know I made it possible for you to do what you did."

"You must. I have not yet even begun to tell you what you must hear if you want to help him. You must understand how I used magic against him; why he hates the magic within himself. I understand, because what I did to him was also done to me, by Darken Rahl."

As Kahlan sat shaking, staring blankly at nothing, almost in a trance, Denna began telling her what she had done to Richard. How she used the Agiel. She flinched at the description of every kind of touch, at everything it could do. Kahlan remembered all too well what its touch felt like, the maddening pain. She learned that what she had felt was the least of it.

She cried as Denna told her how Richard had hung in shackles as she pulled his head back by his hair and made him stay perfectly still while she pushed the Agiel in his ear, or risk damage inside his head. And how he had been able to do it because of his love for Kahlan. She shook, when she heard the horrifying description of what it did to him, what the magic did to him; what his own magic did to him. She couldn't look at Denna as the other spoke. Couldn't meet her eyes. And that was only the beginning.

She clutched her stomach and held a trembling hand to her mouth to keep from vomiting as Denna described one unspeakable act after another. Kahlan couldn't make herself stop crying. She gagged as she closed her eyes tight.

As she listened, she prayed to the good spirits that Denna wouldn't tell her the one thing she knew she couldn't bear to hear.

But then Denna told her. Told her what a Mord-Sith did to her mate, why their mates didn't live long. Every intimate detail. And what she had done to Richard that she had done to no other mate.

With a wail, Kahlan turned away, crawled a short distance, and started throwing up. With one hand holding herself up, and the other across her abdomen, she cried and heaved and gagged. Denna's hands were there, holding her hair back as Kahlan emptied the contents of her stomach onto the dirt. She vomited until her insides were heaved dry.

She felt Denna's warm tingling touch on her back. She wanted to call forth the lightning, but was too sick to find the power. She was torn between wanting to throw herself on Richard and comfort him, and ripping this woman apart with the magic of the Con Dar, the Blood Rage.

Between gagging, and panting, and crying, Kahlan managed to get the words out. "Take . . . your hands . . . off me." The hand holding her hair slipped away. The one on her back lifted. Her stomach heaved again in a dry convulsion. "How many times did you do that to him?"

"Enough. It does not matter."

Kahlan turned in a rage, clenching her fists as she screamed. "How many times!"

Denna's voice was soft and calm. "I'm sorry, Kahlan, I don't know. I didn't keep a tally. But he was with me a long time. Longer than any other mate. I did it almost every night. The things I did, I did to no other, because none had the strength Richard did, the strength of his love for you. The others would have died the first time. He fought me, for a long time. I did it enough, that's all. Enough."

"Enough! Enough for what!"

"Enough to drive a part of him mad."

"He's not mad! He's not! He's not!"

Denna watched as Kahlan shook with pain and rage. "Kahlan, listen to me. Anyone else would have been broken by what I did. Richard saved himself by partitioning his mind. He locked the core of himself away where I couldn't get to it, where the magic couldn't get to it. He used the gift to do that. It saved the core of himself from the insanity. But in the darkest corners of his mind lurks madness. I used his magic against him, to drive him insane. He couldn't protect all of himself from the things I did.

"I told you what I did so you could see the truth of his madness. He had to sacrifice that part to save the rest. To save the rest for you. I wish I could have done the same when it was done to me."

Kahlan lifted Richard's hand in hers, holding the back of it to her heart. "How could you do those things?" she cried. "Oh, my poor Richard. How could you? How could you do that to anyone?"

"We all have our own little bits of insanity. Some more than others. My life was a darkness of it."

"Then how could you! How could you, knowing what it was like!"

Denna watched her from under her eyebrows. "You have done terrible things too. You have used your power to hurt people."

"But they were people guilty of horrible crimes!"

"All of them?" she asked quietly. "Every one?"

Kahlan's breath caught with the memory of using her power against Brophy.

"No," she whispered. "But I didn't do it because I wanted to. I had to. It is my job. Who I am. What I am."

"But you did it. And what of Demmin Nass?"

The words cut through her. Her mind flooded with the memory, the sweet memory, of castrating that beast of a man. She sank forward with a wail. "Oh, dear spirits, am I no better than you?"

"We all do what we must, whatever the reasons." Her glowing, diaphanous fingers lifted Kahlan's chin. "I do not tell you these things to hurt you, Kahlan. The telling of them wounds me more than you can know. I tell you because I want to save Richard, so that he doesn't die before his rightful time, and so that the Keeper does not escape."

Kahlan clutched Richard's hand tighter to her breast as she wept. "I'm sorry, Denna . . . but I don't have it in me to forgive you. I know Richard does . . . but I do not. I hate you."

"I would not expect you to forgive me. I only wish you to understand the truth of what I am telling you, the truth of Richard's madness."

"Why! To what purpose!"

"So that you will understand what you must do. Wearing a collar is the core of that insanity. It symbolizes everything I did to him. In his mind, magic is madness, torture. A collar is madness, torture. Insanity.

"The thought of having a collar around his neck brings that madness out of the darkest corners of his being, brings out his deepest fears. He is not exaggerating when he says he would rather die than put a collar around his neck. He will not do it to save himself. If he doesn't, he will die. There is only one thing in the world that will make him put on the collar."

Kahlan's head snapped up. Her eyes were wide. "You want me to ask him to put a collar around his neck." She went weak with dread. "You would have me do that to him? After what you have told me?"

Denna nodded. "He will do it if you tell him to. He will not do it for any other reason. None."

Richard's limp arm slipped from Kahlan's shaking hands. Her fingers covered her mouth. Denna was right. After what she knew now, what she had heard, she knew Denna was right.

She knew now what it had been that she had seen in Richard's eyes when he looked at the collar the Sisters held out to him. It had been madness. Richard would never put a collar around his neck of his own accord. Never. She knew that now. Really knew it.

A small cry escaped her throat. "If I make him put on the collar, he will think I have betrayed him. In his madness, he will think I want to hurt him." Pain welled up inside her, and she started to cry all over again. "He will hate me."

Denna's voice came in a soft whisper. "I am sorry, Kahlan. That could be the truth of it. We can't know for sure, but he may very well see it that way. I don't know how much the madness will take over when he knows he must put on the

184

collar, when you tell him he must. But he loves you more than life itself, and will put it on for no other reason."

"Denna, I don't know if I could do that to him. Not after what you have told me."

"You must, or he will die. If you love him enough, you must do this. You must be strong enough in your love for him to force him to do it, knowing the pain it will bring him. You may have to act as I would have acted, to frighten him enough to do as you say. You may have to bring the madness to full flower, make him think the way he did when he was with me, when he would have done anything he was told.

"You may lose his love. He may hate you forever. But if you really love him, you will see that you are the only one who can help him; the only one who can save him."

Kahlan snatched desperately for a way out. "But in the morning, we were going to go to Zedd, a wizard, who might be able to help him control the gift. Richard thinks Zedd will know what to do; that he will be able to help him."

"That may be true. I'm sorry, Kahlan, I don't know the answer to that. It may work. But I do know that the Sisters of the Light have the power to save him. If they come, and he turns them down for the third time, he will forever lose the opportunity to get their help. If it turns out that this wizard can't help Richard, then he will die. His time is short, days at most.

"Do you understand what that means, Kahlan? He won't just die; the Keeper will have him, have everyone. Richard is the only one who can close the veil."

"How? Do you know how he can close it?"

"I'm sorry, I don't. I know only that it must be torn the rest of the way from this side. That is why the Keeper has agents on this side. That is why Darken Rahl came here. Somehow, Richard is the only one who can stop them, and also the only one with the power to repair what has been rent.

"If he turns the Sisters down, and this wizard can't help him, then he dies, soon, and it will be as if the mark itself took him to the Keeper. If he can get to this wizard before he turns the Sisters down for the third time, he can learn whether he can be helped without them . . . without the collar. But if they come before he can get to Zedd, I must have your promise you will do what must be done to save him."

"There is time. The Sisters won't be back for at least a few days. We can get to Zedd first. There is time!"

"I hope you are right, I really do. I'm sure you won't believe me, but I don't want Richard to ever have to wear a collar, to ever face that madness again. But if you can't get to Zedd, then you must promise me you won't allow him to miss the chance at life the Sisters offer."

Tears streamed from Kahlan's burning eyes. Richard would hate her if she made him put on the collar; she knew he would. He would think she had betrayed him.

"But what of the mark? He still has the mark on him."

Denna watched her a long time. Her voice came so softly Kahlan could scarcely hear it. "I will take the mark. I will go to the Keeper in his place." A shimmering tear ran down her cheek. "But I will only do it, I will only give up my soul, if I know it gives him a chance."

Kahlan stared incredulously. "You would do that for him?" she whispered. "Why?"

"Because after all I had done to him, he cared about my pain. He is the only one who ever did anything to stop my pain. When Darken Rahl beat me, he cried, and he made a potion to take away my pain, though I had never once stopped torturing him no matter how much he begged. Not once.

"And after all the things I have told you I did to him, he forgave me. He understood what I had suffered. He took my Agiel to wear around his neck and promised to remember me, to remember that I was more than a Mord-Sith; to remember that I was once just Denna."

Another shimmering tear ran down. "And because I love him. Even in death, I love him. Though I know my love will never be requited, I still love him."

Kahlan looked at Richard as he lay on his back, unconscious, helpless, with the Keeper's mark, black and bleeding, on his chest. The black and white mud painted everywhere on him made him look wild, savage, but he wasn't; he was the gentlest person she had ever known. She realized then that she would do anything to save him. Anything.

"I will do it," she whispered. "I promise. If we can't find Zedd before the Sisters come back for the third time, I will make him put on the collar, no matter what it takes. Even if it makes him hate me. Even if it kills me."

Denna's hand reached out to her. "An oath then, between the living and the dead, to do what must be done to save him."

Kahlan stared at the hand before her. "I still can't forgive you. I won't forgive you."

The hand stayed where it was, waiting. "The only forgiveness I need has already been granted."

Kahlan stared at the hand, and then reached out and took it. "An oath then, to save the one we love."

They clasped hands, and shared a silent joining.

Denna took away her hand. "Time is short for him. It must be now." Kahlan nodded. "When it is done, get help for him. Though the pull of the mark will be removed, the wound will still be there, and it is a serious one."

Kahlan nodded. "There is a healer here. She will help him."

Denna's eyes were filled with compassion. "Thank you, Kahlan, for loving him enough to help him. May the good spirits be with you both." She gave a small, frightened smile. "Where I am going, I will never see any of them, or I would send them to help you."

Kahlan touched the back of the other's hand, offering a silent prayer for strength.

Denna returned the touch to Kahlan's cheek, and then knelt next to Richard. Her hand went to the mark, covering it, dissolving into it. Richard's chest heaved.

Denna's features twisted in pain. She threw her head back with a piercing scream that shot through Kahlan.

And then she was just gone.

Richard groaned. Kahlan bent over him, caressing him. Crying.

"Kahlan?" he moaned. "Kahlan, what happened? It hurts. It hurts so . . ."

"Lie still, my love. Everything is all right. You are safe, with me. I'll get help."

He nodded and she ran to the door, throwing it open. The elders were sitting in a small circle in the dark, just outside the door. They looked up expectantly.

*"Help me!"* she screamed. *"Carry him to Nissel! There's no time to get her!"*

## CHAPTER 17

**W**hen he stirred, Kahlan lifted her head.

His gray eyes blinked and searched around the small room until they found her face. "Where are we?"

She gave his shoulder a little squeeze. "At Nissel's. She tended your burn."

His right hand came up and touched the bandage-covered poultice. He winced. "How long . . . What time is it?"

Kahlan looked up from where she was crouched on the floor next to him, rubbed her eyes, and squinted out the partly opened door at the gray light. "It has been light for an hour or two. Nissel is in the back room, sleeping. She was up most of the night, tending your wound. The elders are all outside, watching over you. They haven't left since we brought you here."

"When? When did you bring me here?"

"In the middle of the night."

Richard looked around again. "What happened? Darken Rahl was there." His big hand grasped her arm. "He touched me. He . . . marked me. Where did he go? What happened after he touched me?"

She shook her head. "I don't know. He just left."

His hand squeezed her arm painfully. His eyes were wild. "What do you mean he left! Did he go back into the green light? Back into the underworld?"

She pulled at his fingers. "Richard! You're hurting me."

He let go. "I'm sorry." He cradled her head to his good shoulder. "I'm sorry. I didn't mean to. I'm sorry." He let out a noisy breath. "I can't believe how stupid I am."

She kissed his neck. "It didn't hurt that much."

"That's not what I mean. I mean I can't believe how stupid I was to call him back from the underworld. I can't believe I did something that stupid. I was warned. I should have thought. I should have figured it out. I let myself focus on one thing so strongly that I didn't look around and see what was coming from a different direction. I must be mad to have done that."

"Don't say that," she whispered. "You're not mad." She pushed herself up and looked down at him. "Don't you ever say that about yourself."

He blinked, then pushed himself up to sit facing her. He winced when he touched the bandage again. He reached out to run his hand down her cheek, through her hair. He smiled the smile that made her heart melt.

He sought her eyes. "You are the most beautiful woman in the world. Did I ever tell you that?"

"All the time."

"Well, you are. I love your green eyes, your hair. You have the most beautiful hair I ever saw. Kahlan, I love you more than anything in the world."

She forced herself to hold back tears. "I love you more than anything else, too. Please, Richard, promise me you won't ever doubt my love. Promise me that no matter what happens, you won't ever doubt how much I love you."

He cupped her cheek. "I promise. I promise I will never doubt your love. No matter what. All right? What's the matter?"

She leaned against him, laid her head on his shoulder, and wrapped her arms carefully around him so as not to hurt him. "Darken Rahl frightened me, that's all. I was so afraid when he burned you with his hand. I thought you were dead."

He stroked her shoulder. "So what happened? I remember him telling me how he got here, because I called him, and he was my ancestor, and then he said something about marking me for the Keeper. Then I don't remember anything else. What happened?"

Kahlan's mind raced. "Well . . . he said he was going to mark you, kill you, that the mark would send you to the Keeper. He said he was here to tear the veil the rest of the way. He put his hand against you. Burned you. But before he could do it enough, before he could kill you, I called the lightning, the Con Dar."

He missed a breath. "I don't suppose that we could be lucky enough that it killed him, or destroyed him, or whatever it is that can be done to a spirit."

She shook her head. "No. It didn't destroy him. He was able to block it, partly anyway. But I think it frightened him. He left. Not back into the green light, but out the door. Before he could finish what he was going to do to you. He just left, that's all."

He grinned and hugged her tighter. "My heroine. You saved me." He was quiet a moment. "Here to tear the veil," he whispered to himself. His brow was set in a thoughtful frown. "And then what happened?"

Kahlan steeled herself for the lie of omission. But she couldn't bear the scrutiny of his eyes. She nestled her face against his shoulder, frantically trying to think of a way to get him off the subject. "And then the elders and I carried you here, so Nissel could tend to your burn. She said that it's bad, but that the poultice will make it well. You have to leave it on for a few days, until it begins to heal over enough."

She angrily shook a finger at him. "I know you. You will want to take it off sooner. You always think you know best. Well, you don't. You will just leave it on like I tell you, Richard Cypher."

His smile faded a little. "Richard Rahl."

She stared at him. "I'm sorry," she whispered. "Richard Rahl." She forced a smile. "My Richard. Maybe you could change it when we're married. You could be Richard Amnell. Mates to Confessors sometimes take their wife's family name."

He grinned. "I like it. Richard Amnell. Husband to the Mother Confessor. Devoted husband. Loving husband." The haunted look returned to his eyes. "Sometimes I fear I don't know who, or what, I am. Sometimes I think . . ."

"You are part of me, and I am part of you. That's all that is important."

He nodded absently, his eyes glistening with tears. "I wanted to help, with a gathering. I wanted to find a way to stop all this. Instead, as Darken Rahl said, I've only made it worse. He was right; I am stupid. It's going to be my fault . . ."

"Richard, stop it. You've been hurt. You're just exhausted. When you've rested, you'll figure it out. You'll know what to do."

He gave himself a mental shake. He threw the blanket off and looked down. "Who washed the mud off me and dressed me?"

"The elders washed off the mud. Nissel and I were going to dress you," she said, as his face turned red, "but you were too big and heavy for us. The elders did that too. They had quite a time of it. It took all of them."

He nodded absently; he had stopped listening. He reached up to the spot on his chest where the whistle, Scarlet's tooth, and the Agiel usually hung, but didn't find them. "We have to get out of here. We have to get to Zedd. Right now, before anything else happens. I need Zedd's help. Where is Scarlet's tooth? I have to call her. Where's my sword?"

"All of our things are in the spirit house."

He scrubbed his hands over his face, thinking, then combed his fingers through his hair. "All right." His solid gaze came to her eyes. "I'll go get the tooth and call Scarlet, and get our things together, get them ready to leave." He gently squeezed her upper arm. "You go to Weselan, and put on your wedding dress. While we wait for Scarlet to come, we can be married. We'll leave when Scarlet gets here." He kissed her cheek. "We will be married, and we'll be in Aydindril with Zedd before dark. Everything will be all right, you'll see. Everything will be all right. I'll find out what I did wrong, and fix it. I promise."

She put her arms around his neck. "We will fix it," she corrected. "Together. Always together."

He laughed quietly in her ear. "Together. I need you. You light my way."

She slipped away from him, and looked at him sternly. "Well, I have instructions for you, and you are going to do as you are told. You are going to wait here until Nissel says you can get up. She said that when you wake, she has to change the poultice and bandage and give you medicine. You are going to stay here until she is finished. Understand? I don't want you getting sick and dying on me now, not after I have gone to all the trouble of saving you; and a great deal of trouble it was.

"I'll go to Weselan so she can finish fitting my dress. When Nissel is finished with you, then"—she shook a finger at him—"and only then, may you leave to go call Scarlet. When you are finished here with Nissel, and when you have called Scarlet and gotten our things together, come get me, and I will marry you." She kissed the end of his nose. "If you also promise to love me always."

"Always," he said with a grin.

She rested her wrists on his shoulders, to each side of his strong neck, and clasped her fingers together behind his head. "I'll wake Nissel, and ask her to hurry with you. But please, Richard, don't waste any time after that. Call Scarlet quickly, quick as you can. I want to get away from here. I want to get away before Sister Verna even comes close. I don't want to take any chances, even if she isn't supposed to be back for a few days. I want us away from here. Away from the Sisters of the Light. I want to get you to Zedd so he can help you with the headaches before they can get any worse."

He gave her a boyish, lopsided smile. "What about your big bed in Aydindril? Don't you want to get to that in a hurry, too?"

With a finger, she gently squashed his nose flat. "I've never had anyone else in my big bed before. I hope I don't disappoint you."

He gripped her waist in his strong hands and pulled her to him hard enough to make her grunt. He pushed her hair back off her neck and gave it a tender kiss— right where Darken Rahl's lips had been. "Disappoint me? That, my love, is the only thing in the world it would be impossible for you to do." He gave her neck one more tickling kiss. "Now, go get Nissel. We are wasting time."

Kahlan pulled on the fabric, trying to bring it up as much as she could. *"I've never worn anything cut this low. You don't think it . . . shows too much?"*

Weselan looked up from the floor where she was fussing with the hem of the blue dress. She took the fine bone needle from her mouth as she rose to appraise her client's fit. She studied the expanse of flesh a moment.

*"You don't think he will like it?"*

Kahlan felt her face flush. *"Well, I think he will. I hope so, but . . ."*

Weselan leaned a little closer. *"If you are worried about him seeing that much, maybe you had better reconsider this."*

Kahlan lifted an eyebrow. *"He is not the only one who will be looking. I've never worn anything like this before. I'm . . . worried that I don't do it justice."*

Weselan smiled and patted Kahlan's arm. *"You wear the dress well. It looks beautiful on you. It's perfect."*

Kahlan still fretted as she glanced down at herself. *"Really? Are you sure? I fill it out properly?"*

Weselan's smile widened. *"Really. You have fine breasts. Everyone says so."*

Kahlan felt her face redden. She was sure of the truth of the casual statement. Among the Mud People, commenting favorably on a woman's breasts, in public, was no more odd than a man elsewhere telling a woman she had a pleasant smile. It was an uninhibited attitude that more than once had caught her off-guard.

Kahlan held the skirt out to the sides. *"It's the most beautiful dress I've ever worn, Weselan. Thank you for all your hard work. I will treasure it always."*

*"Maybe someday, if you have a daughter, she will wear it when she weds."*

Kahlan smiled and nodded. *Please, dear spirits*, she was thinking, *if a child comes, let it be a daughter and not a son.* She reached up and touched the delicate necklace she wore, her fingers turning the small, round bone strung among a few red and yellow beads.

Adie, the bone woman, had given her the necklace to protect her from the beasts that dwelt in the pass through the boundary that at the time had separated Westland from the Midlands. The old woman had told her it would help protect her child one day.

Kahlan dearly loved the necklace. It was just like the one her mother had received from Adie, and had, in turn, given to Kahlan. Kahlan had buried it with her closest childhood friend, Dennee. Since Dennee's death she had missed her mother's necklace.

This one was all the more special because the night before they had gone through the pass, Richard had added his oath to the necklace, to protect any future child she might have. Neither she nor Richard had suspected at the time that there was any way that child might possibly be his.

*"I hope so. Weselan, will you stand with me?"*

*"Stand with you?"*

Kahlan pulled some of her hair self-consciously over her half-exposed chest. *"Where I come from, it is the custom to have a friend stand by you when you wed.*

*To stand as a representative of the good spirits watching over the joining. Richard would like Savidlin to stand with him. I would like it if you stood by me."*

*"That seems a strange custom. The good spirits always watch over us. But if it is your custom, I would be honored to be the one who stands by you."*

Kahlan beamed. *"Thank you."*

*"Now stand up straight. I am almost finished."*

Weselan again bent to her task at the hem. Kahlan tried to stand with her back straight. It hurt from sitting on the floor next to Richard the last half of the night. She wished she could sit, or lie down, she was that sleepy. But mostly, her back hurt.

Suddenly, she wondered how much Denna was hurting right now.

She didn't care, she told herself. Whatever was happening to her would never be enough, after what she had done to Richard. Her stomach lurched at the memory of what Denna had told her.

Kahlan could still feel the place on her neck where Darken Rahl had put his lips. A shiver ran up her spine at the memory.

She remembered the mask of agony on Denna's face the instant before she disappeared. It didn't matter: she deserved it.

It could have been Richard, though. If it hadn't been for Denna, it could have been Richard.

*"Don't be afraid, Kahlan."*

*"What?"* She focused her eyes. Weselan was standing in front of her, smiling. *"I'm sorry. What did you say?"*

Weselan reached out and wiped a tear from Kahlan's cheek. *"I said not to be afraid. Richard is a good man. You will have a happy life with him. It is natural to fear being wedded, but do not worry. It will be fine, you will see. I cried too, before I wedded my Savidlin. I didn't think I would, because I wanted him so, but I found myself crying, just like you."* She winked. *"I never had reason to cry again. Sometimes I find reason to complain, but never to cry."*

Kahlan wiped the other cheek. What was the matter with her? She didn't care what was happening to Denna; she didn't. Not one bit.

She nodded to Weselan and forced a smile. *"That would be my greatest hope in life. Never to cry again."*

Weselan gave her a comforting hug. *"Would you like something to eat?"*

*"No, I'm not . . ."*

Savidlin came bursting through the door. He was sweating and panting. Kahlan went cold with fright at the look on his face. She started shaking even before his words came.

*"When Nissel finished with Richard, I went with him to the spirit house, like you told me to, so he could call the dragon. The Sister of the Light came for him. She is there, with him. I didn't understand his words, but I knew their meaning, and your name. He wanted me to come for you. Hurry."*

*"Noooo!"* Kahlan wailed, as she shot past him and out through the doorway.

As she ran, she held the hem of her dress up in her fists so she wouldn't trip on it. She had never run so fast. Her breath couldn't keep pace as she raced down the narrow passageways. Her hair streamed behind her as she ran. The winter air was frigid on her skin. The sound of Savidlin running behind her faded away.

She couldn't form a thought, except that she must get to Richard. This couldn't be happening. It was too soon. The Sister shouldn't be here. The two of them were leaving, almost gone. It wasn't fair at all. Richard.

Big white snowflakes drifted down; not enough to turn the ground white, but enough to bring an icy foreboding of the winter that was coming—the winter that was here. The wet flakes melted instantly as they touched her hot skin. Some caught in her lashes until she blinked them away. A light breeze curled around a corner, swirling into a white curtain. Kahlan flew through it and down a passageway.

She skidded to a stop and looked around. It was the wrong way. She ran back and took the correct turn. Tears ran down her face with the melted snowflakes. It was too much. It couldn't be.

Panting and desperate, she broke from the buildings, into the clearing around the spirit house. The Sister's horses were tethered on the other side of the short wall, the wall with the gash through it from when Richard had tried to kill the screeling.

People were standing around, but she didn't see them. Everything except the door to the spirit house grayed in her vision. She ran desperately for it.

It took forever, as if she were running in a dream and couldn't make any headway. Her legs ached with the strain. Her hand stretched for the latch. Her heart pounded in her ears.

"Please, dear spirits," she begged, "don't let me be too late."

Grunting through gritted teeth, she yanked the door open and threw herself through.

Kahlan jerked to a halt. She gulped air. Richard stood before Sister Verna, beneath the hole ripped through the roof by the lightning. The two of them stood in a shaft of gray light, in the gently drifting snowflakes floating down. The rest of the room dimmed into darkness around them. At his hip, Richard's sword glinted in the light. He didn't have the tooth, or whistle, or Agiel around his neck. He hadn't had time to call Scarlet yet.

In one hand, Sister Verna was holding the collar out to him. Her gaze went to Kahlan in silent warning for a moment, and then slid back to Richard. "You have heard the three reasons for the Rada'Han. This is your last chance to be helped, Richard. Will you accept the offer?"

Richard left the Sister's steady gaze, and turned slowly toward Kahlan, toward where she stood panting. His bright gray eyes followed down her dress and came back up to her face. His voice was gentle, reverent. "Kahlan . . . that dress . . . is beautiful. Beautiful."

Kahlan couldn't find her voice. Her heart was pounding, breaking. Sister Verna spoke his name in a tone of serious warning.

For the first time, Kahlan saw that Sister Verna held something in her other hand. It was the silver knife. But she wasn't pointing it at herself; it was held toward Richard. Kahlan knew: if he didn't accept, she intended to kill him. He didn't even seem to be aware of the knife as it flashed in the dim light. Kahlan wondered if she had used a spell to block it from his vision.

Richard turned back to the Sister. "You have done your best. You have tried your best. It is not enough. I told you before, I will not . . ."

"Richard!" Kahlan took another step toward him as he turned to the sound of her shriek. Her eyes locked on his. "Richard," she whispered as she took another step. Her voice broke. "Accept the offer. Take the collar. Please."

Sister Verna didn't move. She watched calmly.

Richard frowned a little. "What? Kahlan . . . you don't understand. I told you, I won't . . ."

"Richard!" He fell silent as he looked at her in puzzlement. She glanced at the Sister standing motionless, the knife still in her hand. She watched as Kahlan stepped closer. Their eyes met. Kahlan knew: the other would wait to see what would happen. There was a hardness in those eyes that spoke of what she was prepared to do if Kahlan didn't change Richard's mind. "Richard, listen carefully to me. I want you to accept the offer."

His frown deepened. "What . . . ?"

"Take the collar."

His eyes flashed anger. "I told you before. I will not . . ."

"You said you loved me!"

"Kahlan, what's the matter with you? You know I love . . ."

She cut him off. "Then you will accept the offer. If you really love me, you will take the collar and put it on. For me."

He stared at her in disbelief. "For you . . .? Kahlan, I can't . . . I won't . . ."

"You will!" She was being too gentle, and knew it. It was only confusing him. She had to be stronger. She had to act more like Denna if she was to save him. *Dear spirits*, she begged in her mind, *please give me the strength to do this, to save him.*

"Kahlan, I don't know what's gotten into you. We can talk about it later. You know how much I love you, but I'm not going to . . ."

She clenched her hands into fists and screamed at him. "If you love me, you will! Don't stand there and tell me you love me if you aren't willing to prove it! You disgust me!"

He blinked in surprise. The way his voice sounded made her ache. "Kahlan . . ."

"You aren't worthy of my love if you aren't willing to prove it! How dare you say you love me!"

His eyes were filling with tears.

With madness.

With the memory of what Denna had done to him.

He sank slowly to his knees. "Kahlan . . . please."

She leaned over him as she held out clenched fists. "Don't you dare talk back to me!" His arms flinched up, covering his head. He thought she was going to strike him. He really thought she was going to strike him. Her heart felt as if it ripped. Tears streamed down her face as she let the rage loose. "I told you to take the collar! How dare you talk back to me! If you love me you will take it!"

"Kahlan, please," he cried. "Don't do this. You don't understand. Don't ask me to . . ."

"I understand perfectly well!" she screamed. "I understand that you say you love me! But I don't believe you! I don't believe you! You're lying to me! Your love for me is a lie if you won't take the collar! A lie! A filthy lie!"

He couldn't look up at her, look up at her as she stood over him in the blue dress she was to wed him in. He struggled to get the words out as he fixed his eyes on the ground. "It's not . . . it's not a lie. Please, Kahlan, I love you. You mean more to me than anything in the world. Please believe me. I would do anything for you. But please . . ."

Dying inside, she grabbed a fistful of his hair and jerked his head up, making

193

him look at her. Madness danced in his eyes. He was gone. But only for now, she prayed. Please dear spirits, only for now.

"Words! That's all you offer me! Not love! Not proof! Just words! Worthless words!"

As she held him by his hair, she drew her other hand back to slap him. His eyes winced shut. She couldn't make herself do it; she couldn't hit him. It was all she could do just to stay on her feet, not to fall to her knees and throw her arms around him and tell him how much she loved him, that everything was all right.

But it wasn't all right. If he didn't do this, he would die. She was the only one who could save him. Even if it killed her.

"Don't hit me anymore," he whispered. "Please, Denna . . . Don't."

Kahlan swallowed back the wail that tried to escape her throat and made herself speak. "Look at me." He did as she ordered. "I'm not going to tell you again, Richard. If you love me, you will accept the offer and put on the collar. If you don't, I will make you regret disobeying me more than anything you have ever regretted in your life. Do it now, or it's over. Everything is over." His eyes faltered. She gritted her teeth. "I'm not going to tell you again, my pet. Put on the collar. Now!"

Kahlan knew, knew that "my pet" was what Denna had called him. Denna had told her with the rest of it. She knew what those two words meant to him. She had hoped she wouldn't have to use them. Whatever link he had to sanity dissolved in that instant. She saw it in his eyes: the thing she feared more than death.

Betrayal.

She released her grip on his hair as, on his knees, he turned to Sister Verna. She lifted the collar a little, holding it out to him. It looked dull, gray, dead in the cold light. Richard stared at it. Snowflakes drifted down in the still, quiet light. Expressionless, Sister Verna watched him.

"All right," he whispered. His shaking hand reached for the collar. His fingers touched it, curled around it. "I accept the offer. I accept the collar."

"Then put it around your neck," Sister Verna said in a soft voice, "and close it."

He turned to Kahlan. "I would do anything for you," he whispered.

Kahlan wanted to die.

His hands shook so much she thought he might drop the collar as he took it from Sister Verna. He held it, staring at it.

But then his hands stopped shaking. He took a deep breath and put the collar around his neck. It closed with a snap, and the seam disappeared, leaving a smooth ring of metal.

The shaft of light dimmed as if to twilight even though it was still day. Deep, ominous thunder rumbled in every direction out across the grasslands. It didn't sound like any thunder Kahlan had ever heard before. She could feel it in the ground beneath her feet. She thought that maybe it had something to do with the magic of the collar, something to do with the Sisters.

She knew, when she glanced at Sister Verna and saw her eyes glide around, that it wasn't.

Richard smoothly rose to his feet before the Sister. "You may find, Sister Verna, that holding the leash to this collar is worse than wearing it." He gritted his teeth. "Much worse."

Sister Verna's voice remained calm. "We only want to help you, Richard."

He nodded slightly. "I take nothing on faith. You will have to prove it."

194

In a panic, a sudden thought came to Kahlan. "What is the third reason? What is the third reason for the collar?"

Richard turned to her with a glare that even his father could not have matched. For a moment, she forgot how to breathe.

"The first reason is to control the headaches and open my mind so that I may be taught to use the gift. The second reason is to control me." His hand came up and grabbed her by the throat. His eyes sliced through her. "The third reason is to give me pain."

She closed her eyes with a wail. "No! Dear spirits, no!"

He released her throat. His expression went slack, lost. "I hope I have proven my love for you, Kahlan. I hope you believe me now. I have given you everything. I hope it is enough; I have nothing else to offer. Nothing."

"You have. More than you could ever realize. I love you more than anything in the world, Richard."

She reached out to touch his cheek. He pushed her hand away. His eyes said it all; she had betrayed him.

"Do you?" He looked away. "I would like to believe you."

She tried to swallow the painful, burning lump in her throat. "You promised me you would never doubt my love."

He nodded slightly. "So I did."

If she could have called lightning down on herself, she would have done it. "Richard . . . I know you don't understand right now, but I only did what I had to—to help you live. To keep you from being killed by the headaches, the gift. I hope that someday you will understand. I will always wait for you; I love you with all my heart."

He nodded tearfully. "If that's true, then find Zedd. Tell him what you have done. Tell him."

Sister Verna's voice broke in. "Richard, take your things and go wait with the horses."

Looking back at her, he nodded. He went to the far corner and picked up his cloak, bow, and pack. Reaching in, he pulled out the three leather thongs, the one with the Bird Man's whistle, the one with Scarlet's tooth, and the one with Denna's Agiel. As Kahlan watched him hang the three of them around his neck, she wished she had something of her own to give him. She tried desperately to think of something.

As he went past her, she put a hand to his arm and stopped him. "Wait." Kahlan pulled the knife from his belt. She held out a long lock of her hair and severed it with the knife. She didn't even think about what she was doing, what happened when Confessors cut their own hair.

With a scream of pain, she found herself on the ground. The magic seared through her, burning every nerve in its passing. She fought to remain conscious as she gulped for air. She struggled against the wrenching pain of it.

She had to remain conscious, or Richard might leave before she could give it to him. She thought of only that, and forced herself to her feet. As she did so, the pain finally abated.

Still panting, Kahlan pulled a small blue ribbon from the waist of the dress, cut it too, and after wrapping the long strand of hair around two fingers, tied it together in the middle with the ribbon. As he watched, she returned the knife to its sheath at his belt and put the lock of hair in his shirt pocket.

"To remind you always that my heart is with you . . . that I love you."

Expressionless, he looked at her a long moment. "Find Zedd" was all he said before turning and going through the doorway.

Kahlan stood, staring at the door after he was gone. She felt numb, empty, lost.

Sister Verna stopped next to her, watching the door with her. "That was probably the most courageous act I have ever witnessed," she said softly. "The people of the Midlands are fortunate to have you as their Mother Confessor."

Kahlan continued to stare at the door. "He thinks I betrayed him." She turned and looked at the Sister, tears welling up in her eyes. "He thinks I betrayed him."

The Sister studied her face for a time. "You have not. I promise you that in time I will help him to see the truth of what you have done this day."

"Please," she begged, "don't hurt him."

Sister Verna clasped her hands in front of herself and took a deep breath. "You have just hurt him to save his life. Would you have me do any less?"

A tear ran down her cheek. "I guess not. And I doubt you could do anything as cruel as what I have just done."

Sister Verna nodded. "I fear you are right. But I will give you my promise that I will personally watch over him, and see to it that what is done is only what is necessary. I promise you that I will not let it go one inch beyond that. Not one breath. On my word as a Sister of the Light."

"Thank you." She looked down at the knife in the other's hand. The sister pushed it back up her sleeve. "You would have killed him. If he said no, you would have killed him."

She nodded. "If he had said no, the pain and madness at the end would have been grotesque. I would have spared him that. But it doesn't matter now. You have saved his life. Thank you, Mother Confessor . . . Kahlan."

Sister Verna stepped toward the door. "Sister? How long? How long will you have him? How long will I have to wait?"

The Sister didn't turn. "I'm sorry, I can't say. It takes as long as it takes. Much of it is up to him. It depends on how fast he learns."

Kahlan smiled for the first time. "I think you will be surprised at how fast Richard learns."

Sister Verna nodded. "That is what I fear most. Knowledge before wisdom. It frightens me more than anything else."

"I think, too, that Richard's wisdom may surprise you."

"I pray you are right. Good-bye, Kahlan. Don't try to follow, or he will die."

"Sister, one more thing." The cold danger in her own voice surprised her. "If you are lying to me about any of it, if you kill him, I will hunt down every Sister of the Light. I will kill every last one. But not before each of you begs endlessly to die."

The Sister stood still as stone a moment before nodding and then going on her way.

Kahlan followed her out and stood with the people outside as she watched the sister mount her horse. Richard already sat tall on a big bay gelding. His back was to her as he waited.

Kahlan's heart was breaking. She wanted to see his face one more time, but he didn't turn as the two of them started away.

Kahlan sank to her knees. "Richard," she cried. "I love you."

He seemed not to hear her as he and Sister Verna disappeared into the snowy grasslands. Kahlan sat on the ground, in her wedding dress, her head hanging down, crying. Weselan put an arm around her, comforting her.

Kahlan remembered what he had said: Find Zedd. She forced herself to her feet. The elders were all there. She looked around at them all.

"I must leave at once. I must get to Aydindril. I need some men to go with me, to help me, to be sure I make it."

Savidlin came up next to her. "I go. And as many of my hunters as you wish. All of them, if you wish. We will take a hundred."

Kahlan put a hand on his shoulder and gave him a little smile. "No. I do not wish it to be you, my friend, or your hunters. I will take only three men." Everyone mumbled in confusion. "More would bring attention, maybe trouble. It will be easier with three to slip unnoticed. It will take less time that way."

Kahlan took the hand away and pointed at a man who stood watching, glaring. "I choose you, Chandalen." The two brothers were standing to his side. "And you, Prindin and Tossidin."

Chandalen stormed forward. "Me! Why would you want me!"

"Because I must not fail. I know that if I took Savidlin, he would try his hardest, but if he failed, the Mud People would know he did his best. You are a better hunter of men. Richard told me once that if he had to pick one man to fight beside him, it would be you, even though you hate him.

"Where we go, men are the danger. If I don't make it, if you fail me, everyone will think it is because you didn't try your hardest. They will always think you let me die—let another Mud Person die—because you hate me and Richard. If you let me be killed, you will never be welcomed back to the Mud People. Your people."

Prindin stepped forward, his brother right next to him. "I will go. My brother, too. We will help you."

Chandalen glared. "I will not! I will not go!"

Kahlan looked to the Bird Man. His brown eyes met hers, and then he turned an iron gaze on Chandalen. "Kahlan is a Mud Person. You are the bravest, most cunning fighter among us. It is your responsibility to protect us. All of us. You will do this. You will go with her. You will follow her orders and you will get her safely to where she wishes to go. Or, you will leave now, and never return. And Chandalen, if she is killed, don't come back. If you do, we will kill you as we would kill any outsider with black painted on his eyes."

Chandalen shook with rage. He threw his spear on the ground. Seething, he put fists to his hips. "If I am to leave our land there will have to be a ceremony to call the spirits to protect us on our journey. It will take until tomorrow. We leave then."

All eyes went to Kahlan. "I leave in one hour. You will be with me. You have until then to prepare."

Kahlan turned to the spirit house to change out of her wedding dress, into her traveling clothes, and to get her things together. She gratefully accepted Weselan's offer to help.

Fat, wet flakes of snow drifted down. Sometimes they fell harder, gathering in gusts and swirling into white curtains. Richard rode in a numb haze, behind Sister Verna. The third horse was tethered to his and trotted along behind. When the snow swept down in dense flurries, the Sister was no more than a gray shape ahead of him.

It never occurred to him to wonder where they were going, or to close his cloak against the cold, biting wind. It didn't matter; nothing mattered.

His thoughts seemed to float and dance with the snow, unable to settle. He had never loved anything in his life the way he loved Kahlan. She had become his life.

And she had sent him away.

He hurt too much to think of anything else. He was stunned that she would doubt his love, that she would send him away. Why would she send him away?

His mind drifted in and out of dense, desperate thoughts. He couldn't understand how she could ask him to put on a collar to prove his love. He had told her what wearing a collar meant to him. Maybe he should have told her all of it. Maybe then she would have understood.

His chest ached where Darken Rahl had burned him. When he reached up and touched the bandage, he finally noticed that the snow flurries had stopped. The low, scudding clouds were broken in places, letting shafts of sunlight shine through. The grassland was a flat, dead brown, and the clouds a dull, dead gray. The landscape was colorless, empty.

By the angle of the sun he realized it was getting to be late afternoon. They had been riding for a long time, in silence; Sister Verna had said nothing to him.

He reached up and experimentally touched the collar for the first time. It was smooth, seamless, cold. He had said he would never wear a collar again. He had promised himself. Yet here he was wearing one. Worse, he had put it on himself, put it on because Kahlan had asked him to. Because she doubted him.

For the first time since he had put it on, he forced himself to think of something else. He couldn't think about Kahlan anymore, couldn't stand the pain. He was the Seeker; he had other things to think about, important things. With a gentle squeeze of his lower legs to the horse's girth, he urged it ahead, pulling it close beside the Sister's chestnut gelding.

Richard reached up to push back the hood of his cloak, and realized it wasn't even up, so he ran his fingers through his wet hair instead. He looked over at Sister Verna.

"There are some things we have to talk about. Important things you don't know about."

She glanced over without emotion. The edge of her hood partially blocked her face. "And what would those things be?"

"I am the Seeker."

She looked away, returning her eyes to where they had been. "That is hardly something I don't know."

Her calm, unconcerned attitude annoyed him. "I have responsibilities. I told you before: there are important things going on you know nothing about. Dangerous things." She didn't respond. It was as if he hadn't spoken. He decided to cut right to the heart of it. "The Keeper is trying to escape the underworld."

"We do not speak his name. You are not to speak it as you have just done. It brings his attention. When we must speak of him, he is addressed as the Nameless One."

She was talking to him as if he were a child. Kahlan's life was in danger and this woman was treating him like a child. "I don't care what you call him, he's trying to get out. And I assure you, I already have his attention."

At last she looked over, unconcerned. "The Nameless One is always trying to get out."

Richard took a deep breath and tried again. "The veil to the underworld is torn. He is going to get out."

Sister Verna turned to him once more, this time pulling the edge of the hood back to get a better look. Curly brown hair peeked out the edge of the dark, heavy hood. She had an odd frown. A frown of amusement. There was a wisp of a smile at the corners of her mouth.

"The Creator himself put the Nameless One where he is. The Creator himself placed the veil with His own hand to keep him there." Her smile swelled a little as her eyebrows came closer together, creasing her weathered brow. "The Nameless One cannot escape the prison the Creator has placed him in. Do not be afraid, child."

Exploding in rage, Richard wheeled his bay mare around toward the Sister. The two horses jostled, whinnying and tossing their heads. Richard firmly snatched the reins of the Sister's surprised horse to keep it from rearing, or bolting.

He leaned toward her, his chest heaving in fury. "I will not be called names! I will not have names put to me because I wear a collar! I am Richard! Richard Rahl!"

Sister Verna didn't flinch. Her voice remained calm and smooth. "I'm sorry, Richard. It was only force of habit. I am used to dealing with ones much younger than you. I meant nothing demeaning by it."

The way she stared at him made him feel suddenly foolish, embarrassed. Made him feel like a child. He released the reins. "I apologize for yelling. I'm not in a very good mood."

She frowned again. "I thought your name was Cypher."

He tugged his cloak over his chest where the bandage covered his burn. "It's a long story. George Cypher raised me as his son. I only found out a short time ago that I am in truth the son of Darken Rahl."

Her frown deepened. "Darken Rahl. The one with the gift you killed? You killed your father?"

"Don't look at me like that. You didn't know him. You have no idea what kind of man he was. He imprisoned and tortured and killed more people than you or I could imagine. The idea of him being with my mother makes me sick. But that is the truth of it. I am his son. If you expect me to be sorry I killed him, you will have longer than eternity to wait."

Sister Verna shook her head with what seemed genuine concern. "I'm sorry, Richard. Sometimes the Creator weaves a tangled cloth for our lives, and we are left to wonder why. But I am sure of one thing: He has reasons for what He does."

Babble. He was getting babble from this woman. He urged his horse around and started out again. "I'm telling you, the veil is torn, and the Keeper is going to get out."

Her voice lowered dangerously. "The Nameless One."

He glanced over, annoyed. "Fine. The Nameless One. I couldn't care less what you want to call him, but he is going to get out. We are all in great danger."

Kahlan was in great danger.

He didn't care if this sorceress of a Sister burned him to a cinder; his life meant nothing to him anymore. His only concern was Kahlan's safety.

Sister Verna's quizzical frown and smile returned. "Who told you such a thing?"

"Shota, a witch woman, she told me the veil was torn." He left out that Shota had also told him he was the one who had torn it. "She said it was torn and if it wasn't fixed, the Kee—the Nameless One would escape."

Sister Verna smiled. Her eyes sparkled. "A witch woman." She laughed a little. "And you believed her? You believed a witch woman? You think witch women speak the truth in such simple fashion?"

Fuming, Richard glanced at her from the corner of his eye. "She seemed pretty sure of it to me. She wouldn't lie about something this important. I believe her."

Sister Verna seemed to think the whole thing amusing. "If you had ever had occasion to deal with a witch woman before, Richard, you would know that they have an odd view of the truth. They can be well intentioned at times, but witch women speak in words that rarely come to pass the way they sound."

The truth of that took some of the steam out of him. Sister Verna certainly seemed to know about witch women. In fact, she seemed to share his own view of them. "She seemed pretty sure of what she was saying. She was afraid."

"I am sure she was. A wise person is always afraid of the Nameless One. But I wouldn't put much stock in what she says."

"It's not just what she says. Other things have happened, too."

She looked over curiously. "Such as?"

"A screeling."

She set her calm brown eyes back ahead. "A screeling. You have seen a screeling, yes?"

"Seen it! It attacked me! Screelings are from the underworld. They are sent by the Nameless One. It was sent through a tear in the veil, to kill me!"

Her smile returned. "You have quite an imagination, Richard. You have listened to too many children's songs."

He restrained his renewed anger. "What do you mean?"

"Screelings are indeed from the underworld, as are other beasts. The heart hounds, for example. But they are not 'sent.' They simply escape. We live in a world that lies between good and evil; between the light and the dark. The Creator did not intend this to be a perfect world, safe from all harm. We cannot understand His reasons, always, but He has them, and He is perfect. Perhaps the screelings are meant to show us the dark side. I don't know. But I do know they are simply an evil that sometimes comes. I have seen this happen before to ones with the gift. It is possible that the gift draws them. A test perhaps. A warning, perhaps, of the rancid evil that awaits those who stray from the light."

"But . . . there are prophecies that say they are sent when the veil is torn, sent by the Nameless One."

"How could that be, Richard? Has the veil ever been torn before?"

"How should I know?" He thought a minute. "But I don't see how it could have been. If it were, how could it have been mended? And it wouldn't have gone unnoticed. What are you getting at?"

"Well, if the veil has never been torn, how could the screelings have been sent before? How would we know what they were? How could they have a name already put to them?"

It was Richard's turn to frown. "Maybe we only know them as screelings because they have been named in the prophecy."

"You have read this prophecy?"

"Well, no. Kahlan told it to me."

"And she read it herself, with her own eyes, yes?"

"No. She learned it when she was young." Richard's irritated frown deepened. "In a song. She learned it from wizards."

"In a song." Sister Verna didn't look over, but her smile widened. "Richard, I do not mean to belittle your fears, but things repeated, over and over, especially in a song, have a way of changing.

"As for prophecies, well, they are harder to understand than a witch woman. We have vaults full of them at the palace. As part of your studies, perhaps you will be allowed to work with them. I have read all of them we have, and I can tell you that they are beyond the minds of most. If you aren't cautious, you can find a prophecy that will say whatever you want to hear. Or at least you will think it is what you want to hear. Some wizards devote their lives to the study of them, and yet even they understand only a tiny fraction of their truth."

"This is a danger not to be taken so lightly."

"Do you think the veil is torn that simply? Have faith, Richard. The Creator placed the veil. Have faith in Him."

Richard rode in silence for a time. Sister Verna did seem to make sense. He felt as if his understanding of the world was tilting.

But it was difficult for him to think too hard on the subject; Kahlan kept creeping back into his mind. His anguish at her wanting him to put on a collar to prove his love, knowing it would take him from her, tore at his heart. The betrayal burned painfully in his chest.

He picked at the reins with his thumbnail. At last he turned once more to the Sister. "That's not all. I haven't told you the worst of it."

She smiled a motherly smile. "There is more? Tell me then. Perhaps I can put your fears to rest."

Richard let out a deep breath, trying to release at least a little of the pain with it. "The man I killed, Darken Rahl, my father, well, when he died, he was sent to the underworld. To the Kee . . . the Nameless One. Last night, he escaped. Escaped through the tear in the veil. He is back in this world, back to tear the veil the rest of the way."

"And you know he was sent to the Nameless One. You were in the underworld to see him arrive there, at the side of the Nameless One, yes?"

The woman had a way of poking his temper awake. He tried to ignore the sting of the jab. "I talked to him when he came back to this world. He told me. He told me he was here to tear the veil the rest of the way. He said the Keeper would have us all. A dead man, come back to this world. Do you see? The only way his spirit could be here is if he came through the veil."

"You were just sitting there, and this dead man walked up and spoke to you, yes?"

Richard frowned deeply at her, but she didn't look over to see it. "It was at a gathering, with the Mud People. I was trying to talk to their ancestors' spirits, to try to find out how to close the veil, and he appeared."

"Ahhh." She nodded in satisfaction. "I see."

"What does that mean!"

Sister Verna's face set into an expression of tolerance, born of explaining things to children. "Did the Mud People have you drink or eat some sacred potion before you saw this spirit?"

"No!"

"You simply sat down with them and saw spirits, yes?"

"Well, not exactly. There is a banquet first. For a couple of days. The elders eat and drink special things. But I never did. Then we were painted with mud, and then I went into the spirit house with the seven elders. We sat in a circle, and they chanted awhile. Then they passed around a basket and we took out a spirit frog, and rubbed the slime from its back onto our skin. . . ."

"Frogs." Sister Verna looked over. "Red frogs, yes?"

"Yes. Red spirit frogs."

With a smile she looked back ahead. "I know of them. And it made your skin tingle, yes? And it is then you saw spirits?"

"That's a pretty simplistic version, but I guess you could distill it down like that. What are you trying to say?"

"You have traveled the Midlands often? You have seen many of her peoples?"

"No. I'm from Westland. I don't know much about the people of the Midlands."

She nodded to herself again. "There are many peoples in the Midlands, unbelievers, who do not know of the light of the Creator. They worship all sorts of things. Idols and spirits and such. They are savages who hold to customs of worship centered around these false beliefs. They mostly have one thing in common. They use sacred food or drink to help them 'see' their 'spirit protectors.' "

She looked over to make sure he was paying attention. "The Mud People apparently use the substance on the red frogs to help them have these visions of what they wish to see."

"Visions?"

"The Creator has placed many plants and animals in our world for us to use. The power of these things work in invisible ways. A tea, for example, of the bark of willow can help reduce a fever. We can't see it work, but we know it does. There are many things that if eaten will make us sick, even kill us. The Creator gave us minds to learn the difference. There are some things that if eaten, or in the case of the red frogs, rubbed into our skin, will make us see things, just as we see things when we dream.

"Savages who don't know better think the things they see are real. That is what happened to you. You rubbed the slime of a red frog into your skin and it gave you visions. Your rightful fear of the Nameless One made it all the more real to you.

If these 'spirits' were real, why would you need to use some special plant, or food, or drink, or in this case, red frogs, to see and talk to them?

"Please don't think I am mocking you, Richard. The visions can seem very real. When you are under their influence, they can seem as real as anything. But they are not."

Richard was reluctant to believe the Sister's explanation, but he understood what she was talking about. From a young age, Zedd had taken him into the woods to find special plants to help people: aum to take away pain and help minor wounds heal faster, and wattle root to ease the pain of deeper wounds. Zedd had showed him other plants that would help fevers, digestion, the pain of childbirth, dizzy spells, and he had also told him about plants to avoid, plants that were dangerous, and plants that would make people see things that weren't there: visions.

But he didn't think he had imagined Darken Rahl. "He burned me." Richard tapped his shirt where the bandage was. "I couldn't have been having visions. Darken Rahl was there, he reached out and touched me, and it burned my skin. I'm not imagining that."

The Sister gave a little shrug. "That could be one of two things. After you rubbed the frog on your skin, you couldn't see the room you were in, could you?"

"No. It just seemed to disappear into a dark void."

"Well, see it or not, it was still there. And I'm sure the savages would have had a fire burning when you had this gathering. And when you were burned, you were not sitting in the same place, but you were standing, moving about, yes?"

"Yes," he admitted reluctantly.

She pursed her lips. "In the deluded state you were in, you probably fell and burned yourself on a stick in the fire and imagined that it was this spirit doing the burning."

Richard was beginning to feel decidedly foolish. Could the Sister be right? Was it all this simple? Was he really this gullible?

"You said it could be two things. What is the other?"

The Sister rode in silence for a moment. When her voice came, it came lower, darker, than it had before. "The Nameless One always seeks to have us side with him. Though he is locked behind the veil, his tentacles can still reach into this world. He can still harm us. He is dangerous. The dark side is dangerous. When ignorant people dabble in things dark, they can call forth danger, call forth the attention of the Nameless One or his minions. It is possible you really were touched, burned, by one of the evil ones." She glanced over. "There are dangerous things people are too foolish to avoid. Sometimes, those things can kill."

Her voice brightened a bit. "That is one of our jobs; trying to teach those who have not yet seen the light of the Creator to go toward that light, and stay away from the things dark, and dangerous."

Richard couldn't think of anything to counter the Sister's explanations of events. The things she said made sense. If she were right, that would mean that Kahlan wasn't really in danger; that Kahlan was safe. He wanted to believe that. He desperately wanted to believe that. But still . . .

"I will admit that you could be right, but I'm not sure. There seems to be more to it than I can put into words."

"I understand, Richard. It's hard to admit we have been wrong. No one wants to admit they have been tricked, or made to look the fool. That view of ourselves hurts. But part of growing, learning, is being able to hold the truth above all else, even when it means we must admit to having held foolish ideas.

"Please believe me, Richard, I do not see you as a fool for having believed as you did. Your fear was understandable. The mark of a wise person is being able to reach beyond for the truth, to admit they can learn more than they already know."

"But all of these things are connected . . ."

"Are they? A wise person doesn't string together the beads of unrelated events into a necklace simply to have something they wish to see. A wise person sees the truth even if it is something unexpected. That is the most beautiful necklace to wear—the truth."

"The truth," he muttered to himself. He was the Seeker. The truth was what the Seeker was all about. It was woven in gold wire into the hilt of his sword: the Sword of Truth. Something about the things that had happened were more than he could put into words for her. Could it be as she said? Could he simply be fooling himself?

He remembered the Wizard's First Rule: people will believe anything, either because they want it to be true, or are afraid it might be. He knew from experience that he was as susceptible to it as anyone else. He wasn't above believing a lie.

He had believed Kahlan loved him. He had believed she would never do anything to hurt him. And she had sent him away. Richard felt the lump rising in his throat again.

"I'm telling you the truth, Richard. I am here to help you." He didn't answer. He didn't believe her. As if to answer his thoughts, she asked, "How are your headaches?"

The question stunned him. Not the question so much as the realization. "They're . . . gone. The headache is completely gone."

Sister Verna smiled and nodded in satisfaction. "As I promised you, the Rada'Han would take away the headache. We only want to help you, Richard."

His eyes turned to watch her. "You also said the collar is to control me."

"So we may teach you, Richard. You must have a person's attention to teach them. That's all it is for."

"And to hurt me. You said it is to give me pain."

She shrugged, opening her palms to the sky, the reins woven through her fingers. "I have just given you pain. I showed you how you were believing in something foolish. Does that not give you pain? Does it not hurt you to learn you have been wrong? But isn't it better to know the truth than to believe a lie? Even if it hurts?"

He looked away, thinking of the truth of Kahlan making him put on a collar, sending him away. That truth hurt more than anything: the truth that he wasn't good enough for her. "I guess so. But I don't like wearing a collar. Not one bit."

He was sick of talking. His chest hurt. His muscles were all cramped. He was tired. He missed Kahlan. But Kahlan had made him put on a collar and sent him away. He let his horse and the one tethered to his saddle fall back to trail behind the Sister's once more as tears ran down his cheeks, feeling like ice on his skin.

He rode in silence. His horse tore off wads of grass and chewed as it plodded along. Ordinarily, Richard wouldn't have let his horse eat while it had a bit in its mouth. It couldn't chew properly with the bit, and could end up with colic. You could lose a good horse to colic. Instead of stopping it, Richard stroked its warm neck and gave reassuring pats.

It felt good to have company that didn't tell him he was stupid; company that didn't judge or make demands. He didn't feel like doing the same to the horse. Better to be a horse than a man, he thought. Walk, turn, stop. Nothing more. Better to be anything than what he was.

Despite what Sister Verna said, he knew he was nothing more than a captive. Nothing she said could change that.

If he was ever going to be set free, he would have to learn to control the gift. Once the Sisters were satisfied he could control the gift, maybe they would free him. If Kahlan didn't want him, at least he would be free.

That was what he would do, he decided. Learn to use the gift as fast as he could, so he could get the collar off and be set free. Zedd had always told him he was a fast learner. He would learn everything. Besides, he had always liked learning. He had always wanted to know more. There was never enough for him. He brightened the slightest bit at the idea. He liked learning new things. Maybe it wouldn't be so bad. He could do it. Besides, what else was there?

He thought of the way Denna trained him, taught him.

His mood sank. He was just deluding himself. They would never set him free. He wasn't going to learn because he wanted to, or what he wanted to; he was going to learn what the Sisters of the Light wanted him to learn, and he didn't necessarily believe that what they taught was the truth. They were going to teach him about pain. It was hopeless.

He rode with his dark, brooding thoughts. He was the Seeker. The bringer of death.

Every time he killed someone with the Sword of Truth, he knew that that was what he was. That was what the Seeker did, what the Seeker was: the bringer of death.

As the sky began flaming into pinks, yellows, and golds, he noticed white patches in the distance ahead. It wasn't snow; the snow hadn't stuck. Besides, these things moved. Sister Verna didn't say anything about them; she simply rode along. The sun at their backs sent long shadows ahead of them. For the first time, Richard realized they were traveling east.

When they were closer, he recognized the white forms spread across their way, turning pink in the last rays of the sun. It was a small flock of sheep. As they passed among them, Richard saw that the people tending the animals were Bantak. He recognized their manner of dress.

Three Bantak men approached to the side of Richard, ignoring Sister Verna. They mumbled something he didn't understand, but their words and faces seemed to hold a certain reverence. The three dropped to their knees and bowed down, stretching their arms out, their hands on the ground toward him. Richard slowed his horse to a walk as he looked down at them. They came back up on their knees, chattering at him, but he didn't understand the words.

Richard lifted his hand in greeting. It seemed to satisfy them. The three broke into grins and bowed a few more times as he rode past. They came to their feet and trotted next to his horse, attempting to push things into his hands: bread, fruit, strips of dried meat, a drab, dirty scarf, necklaces made of teeth, bone and beads, even their shepherd's crooks.

Richard forced a smile and, with signs he thought they would understand, tried to decline the offers without offending the men. One of the three was particularly insistent he take a melon, offering it repeatedly. Richard didn't want trouble, so he took the melon and bowed his head several times. They seemed proud, nodding and bowing as he rode on. He gave them a last bow from his saddle as he rode past, and slipped the melon into a saddlebag.

Sister Verna had her horse turned toward him, waiting for him to catch up. She scowled as she waited. Richard didn't hurry his horse along; he simply let it go at its own pace. What now, he wondered.

When he finally reached her, she leaned toward him. "Why are they saying those things!"

"What things? I don't understand their language."

She gritted her teeth. "They think you are a wizard. Why would they think that? Why!"

Richard shrugged. "I would guess it's because that's what I told them."

"What!" She pushed the hood of her cloak back. "You are not a wizard! You have no right telling them you are! You lied!"

Richard folded his wrists over the high pommel of the saddle. "You're right. I'm not a wizard. Yes, I told them a lie."

"Lying is a crime against the Creator!"

Richard heaved a weary sigh. "I did not do it to play at being a wizard. I did it to stop a war. It was the only way I could keep a lot of people from dying. It worked and no one was hurt. I would do the same thing again if it would prevent killing."

"Lying is wrong! The Creator hates lies!"

"Does this Creator of yours like killing better?"

Sister Verna looked like she was ready to spit fire at him. "He is everyone's Creator. Not just my Creator. And He hates lies."

Richard calmly appraised her heated expression. "Tell you that himself, did he? Come right up and sit down next to you and say 'Sister Verna, I want you to know I hate lies'?"

She ground her teeth and growled the words. "Of course not. It is written. Written in books."

"Ahh," Richard nodded. "Well then, of course it is the truth. If it is written in books, then it has to be true. Everyone knows that if something is written down and attributed, then it must be true."

Her eyes were fire. "You treat lightly the Creator's words."

He leaned toward her, some of his own heat surfacing. "And you, Sister Verna, treat lightly the lives of people you consider heathens."

She paused and with an effort calmed herself a little. "Richard, you must learn that lying is wrong. Very wrong. It is against the Creator. Against what we teach. You are as much a wizard as an infant is an old man. Calling yourself a wizard when you are not is a lie. A filthy lie. It is a desecration. You are not a wizard."

"Sister Verna, I know very well that lying is wrong. I am not in the habit of going around telling lies, but in perspective, I consider it preferable to people being killed. It was the only way."

She took a deep breath and nodded, causing the curls in her brown hair to spring up and down a little. "Perhaps you are right. So long as you know that lying is wrong. Don't make a habit of it. You are no wizard."

Richard stared at her as his grip tightened on the reins. "I know I'm not a wizard, Sister Verna. I know exactly what I am." He gave his horse's ribs a squeeze with his legs, urging it ahead. "I'm the bringer of death."

Her hand darted out and snatched a fistful of his shirtsleeve, yanking him around in his saddle. He snugged the reins back as he was pulled around to her wide eyes.

Her voice was an urgent whisper. "What did you say? What did you call yourself?"

He gave her an even look. "I'm the bringer of death."

"Who named you that?"

Richard studied her ashen face. "I know what wearing this sword means. I know what it is to draw it. I know it better than any Seeker before me has known. It is part of me, I am part of it. I used its magic to kill the last person who put a collar around my neck. I know what it makes me. I lied to the Bantak because I didn't want people to be killed. But there is another reason. The Bantak are a peaceful people. I did not want them to learn the horror of what it means to kill. I know all too well that lesson. You killed Sister Elizabeth; perhaps you know, too."

"Who named you 'bringer of death'?" she pressed.

"No one. I named myself, because that is what I do, what I am. I am the bringer of death."

She released her grip on his shirt. "I see."

As she began turning her horse around, he called out her name in a commanding tone. It brought her to a halt. "Why? Why do you want to know who named me that? Why is it so important?"

Her anger seemed to have vanished, and left a shadow of fear in its passing. "I told you I read all the prophecies at the palace. There is a fragment of one that contains those words. 'He is the bringer of death, and he shall so name himself.'"

Richard narrowed his eyes. "And what does the rest of the prophecy say? Did it also say that I will kill you, and anyone else I have to, to get this collar off?"

She looked away from his glare. "Prophecies are not for the eyes or ears of the untrained."

With a sharp kick, she surprised her horse and sent it surging ahead. As he followed behind, Richard decided to let the matter drop. He didn't care about prophecies. They were nothing more than riddles as far as he was concerned, and he hated riddles. If something was important enough to need saying, why couch it in riddles? Riddles were stupid games, and not important.

As he rode, he wondered how many people he was going to have to kill to get the collar off. One, or a hundred, it didn't matter. His rage boiled at the thought of being led around by the Rada'Han. He gritted his teeth at the thought. His jaw muscles flexed at the thought. His fists tightened on the reins.

Bringer of death. He would kill as many as it took. He would have the collar off, or he would die trying. The fury, the need to kill, surged through every fiber of his being.

With a start, he realized he was calling forth the magic from the sword, even as it sat in its scabbard. He no longer had to hold the sword to do it. He could feel its wrath tingling through him. With an effort, he put it down and calmed himself.

Besides the rage of hate from the sword, he also knew how to call forth its opposite side, its white magic. The Sisters didn't know he could do that. He hoped he would have no reason to teach them. But if he had to, he would. He would have the collar off. He would use either side of the sword's magic, or both, to have the collar off his neck. When the time came. When the time came.

In the violet afterglow of twilight, Sister Verna brought them to a halt for the night. She had said nothing further to him. He didn't know if she was still angry, but he didn't really care.

Richard walked the horses a short distance to a line of small willows at the bank of a creek and removed their bridles, replacing them with halters. His bay tossed her head, glad to have the bit out of her mouth. Richard saw it was an aggressive spade bit. Few bits were more cruelly punishing.

People who used them, it seemed to him, were people who thought horses were nothing more than beasts humans had to conquer and control. He thought maybe they should have to have a bit in their mouths to see how they liked it. Properly trained, a horse needed nothing more than a jointed snaffle. If it was properly trained, and given a little understanding, it didn't even need a bit. He guessed some people preferred punishment to patience.

He reached up experimentally to stroke the horse's black-tipped ear. It lifted its head firmly away from his hand. "So," he muttered, "they like to twitch your ear, too." He scratched and patted the horse's neck. "I won't do that to you, my friend." The horse leaned against his scratching.

Richard retrieved water in a canvas bucket and let each horse have only a few swallows, as they weren't cooled down. In one of the saddlebags, he found brushes, and took his time carefully currying each of them and then picking their hooves clean. He took longer than he needed to, because he preferred their company to the Sister's.

After he finished, he cut a section of rind from the melon the Bantak had given him, and gave each horse a piece. Horses loved few things in life as much as a melon rind. Each showed eagerness for the treat. It was the first eagerness any of them had shown. After seeing the spade bits, he knew why.

When he decided his chest hurt too much to stand around any longer, he went over to where Sister Verna sat on a small blanket and put his own blanket on the ground opposite her. He folded his legs as he sat and pulled a piece of the flat tava bread from his pack, more for something to do than because he was hungry. She accepted his offer of a piece. He cut up the melon and put the remaining rind aside, saving it for later. Richard offered Sister Verna a piece of melon.

She looked at it coolly as he held it out. "It was given under false pretenses."

"It was given as thanks for preventing a war."

She took it at last, but not eagerly. "Perhaps."

"I'll take first watch, if you wish," he offered.

"There is no need to stand watch."

He appraised her in the near darkness as he chewed a juicy piece of melon. "There are heart hounds in the Midlands. Other things, too. I could draw another screeling. I think a watch would be wise."

She pulled off a piece of tava bread without looking up. "You are safe with me. There is no need for a watch."

Her voice was flat. It wasn't angry, but it wasn't far from it, either. He ate in silence for a while, and then decided to try to lighten the mood. He tried to make his voice sound cheerful, even though he felt no cheer.

"I'm here, you're here, I'm wearing the Rada'Han, how about if you start teaching me to use the gift?"

She looked up from under her eyebrows as she chewed. "There will be time enough to teach you when we reach the Palace of the Prophets."

The air felt as if it had suddenly cooled. His anger heated. The sword's anger tugged at him to be released. Richard put it down. "As you wish."

Sister Verna lay down on her blanket, pulling her cloak tightly around herself. "It's cold. Build a fire."

He put the last bite of tava bread in his mouth and waited until he had swallowed before speaking softly. Her eyes watched him.

"I'm surprised you don't know more about magic, Sister Verna. There is a word that is magic. It can accomplish more than you might think. Maybe you have heard it before. It is the word 'please.' " He rose to his feet. "I'm not cold. If you want a fire, build it yourself. I'm going to go stand watch. I told you before, I will take nothing on faith. If we are killed in the night, it won't be without warning on my watch."

He turned his back to her without waiting for a response. He didn't want to hear anything she had to say. Walking off a good distance through the dry grass, he found a mound of dirt around a ground-hog hole and flopped down on top of it to watch. To think.

The moon was up. It stared down at him and cast a pale silver light upon the surrounding empty land, enough light to enable him to see without any trouble. He looked out over the deserted countryside, brooding. As much as he tried to think of other things, it did no good. He could think of only one thing: Kahlan.

He drew up his knees and wrapped his arms around them, after he had wiped some tears from his face. He wondered what she was doing, where she was, whether she would get Zedd. He wondered if she still cared for him enough to go get Zedd.

The moon moved slowly across the sky as it stared down on him. What was he going to do? He felt lost.

He pictured Kahlan's face in his mind. He would have conquered the world to see her smile at him. To bask in the warmth of her love. Richard studied her face in his mind. He pictured her green eyes, her long hair. Her beautiful hair.

At that thought, he remembered the lock of her hair she had put in his pocket. He pulled it out and looked at it in the moonlight. It was a circle she had pulled together and tied in the middle with the ribbon from her wedding dress, so that it reminded him of a figure eight turned sideways, as he held it in his fingers. Turned sideways like that, it was also the symbol for infinity.

Richard rolled the lock of hair between his finger and thumb, watching it as it spun. Kahlan had given it to him to remember her by. Something to remember her by. Because he would never see her again. Racking grief choked his breathing.

He gripped the Agiel as hard as he could, until his fist shook with the effort. The pain from the Agiel, and his heartache, twisted together into burning agony. He let it distort his perception until he could stand it no longer, and then he let it go on longer yet, let it go on until he collapsed to the base of the dirt mound, barely conscious.

He gasped for air. The pain had swept all the thoughts from his mind. If only for a few minutes, his mind had been free of the anguish. He lay on the ground a long time, recovering.

When he was finally able to sit up once more, he found the lock of hair still in his hand. He stared at it in the moonlight, remembering what Sister Verna had said to him, that he had told the Bantak a lie. A filthy lie. Those had been Kahlan's words. She had said that his love for her was a "filthy lie." Those words hurt more than the Agiel.

"It's not a lie," he whispered. "I would do anything for you, Kahlan."

But it wasn't good enough. Putting on the collar wasn't good enough. He wasn't good enough. Son of a monster. He knew what she wanted. What she really wanted.

She wanted to be free of him.

She wanted him to put on the collar so he would be taken away. So she would be free.

"I would do anything for you, Kahlan," he cried.

He stood up and looked out over the empty grassland. The dark horizon wavered in a watery blur.

"Anything. Even this. I set you free, my love."

Richard threw the lock of Kahlan's hair as far as he could out into the night.

He sank to his knees and fell face-first to the ground, sobbing. He cried until he could cry no more. He continued to lie on the cold ground, groaning in agony until he realized he was gripping the Agiel again. He let it go and at last sat up, flopping back in exhaustion against the dirt mound.

It was over, finished. He felt empty. Dead.

After a time he rose to his feet. He stood a moment, and then slowly drew the Sword of Truth.

Its ring was a soft song in the cold air. The anger came out with the steel, and he let it fill the void in him, rage freely through him. He welcomed the anger into himself, letting it fill him until he was submerged in its wrath. His chest heaved with lethal need.

His eyes glided to where the Sister lay sleeping.

He could see the dark hump of her body as he approached silently. He was a woods guide; he knew how to stalk silently. He was good at it.

His eyes carefully watched the ground as he moved fluidly, watched the sleeping form of Sister Verna as he closed the distance. He didn't hurry. There was no need to hurry. He had as much time as he needed. He tried to slow his breathing to keep from making noise. He was nearly panting with all-consuming fury.

The thought of wearing a collar again fed the raging fire within him, fueled the inferno.

Rage from the sword's magic seared through him like molten metal. Richard recognized the feeling all too well, and gave himself over to it. He was beyond reason, beyond being stopped. Nothing short of blood would now satisfy the bringer of death.

His knuckles were white on the hilt. His muscles knotted with restrained need aching to be set free. But they wouldn't be restrained for long. The magic of the Sword of Truth screamed to do his bidding.

Richard stood, a silent shadow, over Sister Verna, looking down at her. The fury pounded in his head. He drew the sword along the inside of his forearm, wiping both sides in the blood, giving the steel a taste of it. The dark stain ran down the fuller, dripping from the tip. It ran wet and warm down his arm. His chest heaved as he gripped the hilt in both hands again.

He felt the weight of the collar around his neck; the blade rose, glinting in the moonlight.

He watched the sleeping Sister at his feet. She was drawn up almost into a ball. She was cold, and she shivered as she slept.

He stood with the blade raised, watching her as he gritted his teeth and shook with raging need. Kahlan didn't want him. Son of a monster.

No. Just monster. He saw himself standing over the sleeping woman, his sword in the air, ready to kill.

He was the monster.

That was what Kahlan saw. And she had sent him away away in a collar to be tortured. Because he was a monster that needed to be collared, a beast.

Tears ran down his face. The sword slowly sank until the tip touched the ground. He stood staring at the Sister as she slept, shivering with the cold. He stood a long time, watching.

Richard finally slid the sword quietly back into its scabbard. He retrieved his blanket and laid it over Sister Verna, tucking it carefully around her, being gentle so as not to wake her. He sat and watched until she stopped shivering and then he lay down, wrapping himself in his cloak.

He was exhausted, and he hurt all over, but he couldn't sleep. He knew they were going to hurt him. That was what the collar was for. When she got him to the palace, they were going to hurt him.

What difference did it make?

Memories danced and darted through his mind, memories of what Denna had done to him. He remembered the pain, the helpless agony, the blood: his blood.

The visions went on and on. As long as he lived he would never be able to forget them. It had only just ended, and now it was going to start all over again. There would never be an end to it.

There was only one thought in all the turmoil of his mind that comforted him. He had learned from Sister Verna that he was wrong about the Keeper escaping. That meant Kahlan was safe. She was safe, and that was all that really mattered. He tried to keep everything else away and think only of that. That thought allowed him to drift, at last, into sleep.

Lis eyes opened. The sun was just breaking the horizon. When he sat up, the pain from his burn caught his breath short. He put his hand over his shirt, where the bandage was, and held it there until that pain subsided. The residual effects of the Agiel left the rest of him feeling as if he had been beaten with a club. He ached everywhere. He remembered from the time when Denna had "trained" him using the Agiel, feeling a lot worse when he awoke, only to have her start using the Agiel on him all over again.

Sister Verna was sitting on her blanket, her legs folded beneath her, watching him as she chewed something. She had her cloak around her shoulders with the hood down. Her curly brown hair looked freshly brushed.

She had neatly folded Richard's blanket, and placed it back next to where he slept. She said nothing about it. Richard pushed himself to his feet, taking a moment to steady himself and stretch his hurting, cramped muscles. The sky was a clear, cold, deep blue. The grass smelled sweet and damp with dew. The vapor of his breath drifted lazily in the still, crisp air.

"I'll go saddle the horses, and we can be on our way."

"Don't you want something to eat?"

He shook his head. "I'm not hungry."

"What happened to your arm?" she asked without looking up.

There was dark, dried blood all down his arm and hand. "I was polishing my sword. It was dark. I cut myself. It's nothing."

"I see." She glanced up as he scratched the stubble on his face. "I hope you are more careful when you shave your neck."

Richard decided in that instant that as long as he was held captive in a collar, he would not shave. It would be his way of proclaiming to them that a collar was unjust, that he knew he was nothing more than their prisoner, and that he would not believe their spurious protestations to the contrary. There could be no justification for a collar, and there would be no compromising of that basic truth—none, not ever.

Richard glowered at the Sister. "Prisoners don't shave." He turned toward the horses.

"Richard." He looked over his shoulder. "Sit down." Her voice was gentle, but he glared at the order nonetheless. She gestured to a place in front of her. "Sit down. I was thinking about what you said. You are here; I am here. Sit down and I will begin teaching you how to control the gift."

He was caught off-guard. "Now? Here?"

"Yes. Come and sit."

He didn't really care about using the gift; he hated magic. He had only asked about it before because he had been trying to ease the tension. His eyes darted about before he finally sat and folded his legs, imitating the way she was sitting.

"What do you want me to do?"

"There is much to teach you about using the gift. You will learn about balance in all things, especially magic. You must heed all our warnings, and follow what we tell you. There are dangers to using magic. Perhaps you already know this from using the Sword of Truth, yes?" Richard didn't move. She went on. "There is greater danger in using the gift. It can have unanticipated results. Results that can be disastrous."

"I have already used the gift. You said I used it in three specific ways."

She leaned forward a little. "And look what happened. It brought an unanticipated result. It resulted in you having that collar around your neck."

Surprised, Richard stared at her. "That wasn't a result of my using the gift. You were already looking for me; you said so. If I hadn't used the gift, the result would have been the same."

Sister Verna slowly shook her head; her eyes stayed on his. "We had been looking for you for years. Something hid you from us. If you hadn't used the gift in the ways you did, I doubt we ever would have found you. Using the gift put that collar around your neck."

Years. They had been searching for him for years. All that time he had lived peaceably in Westland, first with his brother and father and Zedd, and then on his own as a woods guide, they had been looking for him, and he never knew it. The thought gave him a chill. He brought it on himself, by using magic. He hated magic.

"Although I would agree that that is disastrous, for me, how could you? It's what you want."

"It is what we had to do. But you have threatened my life. You have threatened the lives of anyone else who keeps that collar around your neck. That would be all the Sisters of the Light. I never take the warnings of wizards, even untrained wizards, lightly. Your use of the gift, allowing us to find you, could end up being a disaster for all of us."

He felt no satisfaction that his threats had not gone unnoticed. He felt nothing. "Then why are you doing this?" he whispered. "Making me wear it?"

"To help you. You would have died otherwise."

"You have already helped me. The headaches are gone. You have my thanks. Why can't you let me go now?"

"If the collar is removed too soon, before you learn enough of controlling the gift, they will come back. You will die."

"Then teach me, so I can get it off."

"We must be cautious in teaching magic. You must have patience in your studies. We are careful in our training because we know more of the dangers of magic than you, and we don't want you to be hurt through ignorance. But that is not a problem for now, because it will take time before you are advanced enough to really use the gift and risk these dangers, as long as you adhere to what we say. You can have patience, yes?"

"I have no desire to use magic; I guess that could be construed as patience."

"Good enough, for now. We will begin then." She squirmed a little, rearranging her legs. "There is a force within us all. It is the force of life. We call it Han." Richard frowned. "Lift your arm." He did as she asked. "That is the force of life, given us by the Creator. It is encased within you. You have just used Han. Those with the gift can extend that force outside themselves. Such an external force is called a web. Those with the gift, like you, have the ability to cast a web. With the web, you can do things outside your body, much as the life force can do within your body."

"How can that be?"

Sister Verna picked up a small stone in her fingers. "Here, my mind is using Han to make my hand lift the stone. My hand is not doing it of its own accord, but rather, my mind is directing the life force to use my hand to accomplish what my mind wishes done." She set the stone back on the ground and folded her hands in her lap. The stone floated into the air and hung between them. "I have just accomplished the same thing, only this time I did it by projecting the life force outside of my body. That is the gift."

"You can do what a wizard can?"

"No. Only some of it. That is how we are able to teach its use. We understand the feel of it. The Sisters have some control of the life force, and the gift, but nothing like a wizard who knows how to control his Han."

"How do you get this life force to go outside your body?"

"That can't begin to be explained until you learn to recognize the force within yourself, learn to touch the Han."

"Why?"

"Because every person is different. Every person uses the force differently. It isn't used the same in any two people. Love is a form of Han being projected outside one's self, into another. It is, though, a very mild, weak form. Even though love is universal, it is used and felt differently by all. Some use it to bring out the best of the Han in another. Some use it to bring out the best in themselves. Some use it to control, to dominate another. It can heal or wound.

"Once we understand how the gift works within you, how you use it, we can guide you through exercises called forms. The forms are a method of practice that will help you learn to control the power once it is free of your body. But for now, that is not important. First you must learn to feel the Han within yourself, before you can project it anywhere outside your body.

"After you are able to touch the Han, then we must discover what it is you can do with it. Every wizard is different, and uses Han differently. Some can use it only through the use of mind, like wizards who study the prophecies. The use of their Han to understand prophecies is the major way the gift manifests itself with them. It is their unique talent. Some can only use their Han to create beautiful, inspiring objects. Some use their Han to create things invested with magic. It is their unique talent, how they are able to express Han. Some are able to use their thoughts to influence the world about them, as I showed you when I lifted the rock. Some can do other things with Han. Some are able to do a little of everything."

Her frown returned. "The truth is of the utmost importance in this, Richard. You must be completely truthful in telling us how the Han feels within you. Lying will cause grave difficulty." She relaxed a bit. "But first, you must be able to call upon your Han before we can discover what sort of wizard you are."

"I told you: I don't want to be a wizard. I just want to learn to control the gift so I can stop the headaches and get this collar off my neck. You said I didn't have to be a wizard."

"Controlling Han, with the gift, is what it means to be a wizard. When you learn to control it, you will be a wizard. That is the very essence of a wizard. But *wizard* is only a word. You should not fear a word. If you choose not to use the gift, that is your business, we can't force you, but a wizard you will be."

"Teach me what I need to know, but I'll not be a wizard."

"It is not something evil, Richard. It is just learning to know yourself, what you are capable of, what your talents are."

Richard sighed. "Fine. So how do I control it?"

"Teaching control of the gift is a process taken in steps. I cannot explain it to you all at once because you would be unable to understand steps further along. Each step must be mastered before you can move on to the next.

"Before we can show you how to project the Han outside yourself, you must first recognize it, and then be able to touch it, join with it within yourself. You must know what it is. You must be able to feel it. You must be able to reach for it, touch it, at will. You understand what I am saying, yes?"

Richard nodded. "A little, I guess. So what is it? How will I know it? What is it like to know it, to touch it?"

Sister Verna's eyes became distant, seeming to go out of focus. "You will know it," she whispered. "It is like seeing the light given off by the Creator. It is almost like joining with Him."

Richard watched her glazed expression. She seemed enthralled by what she was seeing within herself.

"So how do I find it?" he asked at last.

Her eyes focused on him. "You must search for it, within yourself."

"How?"

"You simply sit, and search within. You put all other thoughts aside, and seek the quiet, the calm, within yourself. At first, it is helpful if you close your eyes, breathe slowly, evenly, and let yourself find the peace of nothingness. In the beginning, it helps to focus on a single thing, in order to exclude all distracting thoughts."

"A single thing? Like what?"

She shrugged. "Whatever you wish. It is only a device to help you reach the end, not the end in itself. Everyone is different. Some use a single word, repeating it over and over to the exclusion of all else. Some use a mental picture of a simple object, using it to bring their mind into focus. Eventually, after you learn to recognize the power, to touch it and become one with it, you won't need to focus on a device first. You will know the nature of Han, and be able to reach directly for it. It will become second nature to you. I know it sounds strange and difficult to you now, Richard, but in time you will find it as easy as it is for you to call forth the magic of your sword."

Richard had the uneasy feeling that he already knew what she was talking about. He could almost understand what she was saying. The words seemed strange, but they described something that was somehow familiar, yet different.

"So you just wish me to sit and close my eyes and seek the quiet within?"

She nodded. "Yes." Sister Verna pulled her heavy brown cloak tighter around her shoulders. "You may begin."

Richard let out a breath. "All right."

He closed his eyes. It seemed his thoughts were scattering in all directions at once. He tried to herd them away. He tried to think of a word or a picture to focus on. He thought of Kahlan's name before anything else. He let it flow like liquid through his mind. Kahlan. He rejected the idea. He hated his magic, and didn't want to associate her with anything he hated. Besides, the thought of her only brought pain, the pain of loving her enough to give her what she wanted, of having set her free.

He thought of simple words, simple objects, but none held any interest for him. He calmed his mind and relaxed his breathing. He sought peace within himself, a calm center, the way he had always done when he needed to think of a solution to a problem. In the quiet, he tried to think of an image he could use. It popped into his mind, almost of its own accord.

The Sword of Truth.

It was already magic, and therefore he wouldn't be tainting it. It was a simple image. It seemed to fit the requirements. It was settled. It would be the Sword of Truth.

Richard pictured it floating by itself on a field of black. He studied the details he knew so well: the polished blade with the fuller down its length, the aggressive, downswept crossguards, the hilt covered in fine, twisted silver wire with twisted gold wire woven through it forming the raised letters of the word *Truth*.

As he pictured it, fixing it in his mind, floating on a black background, something fought him. It was the background, not the sword. Around the edge of the black was white, forming the black into a square. Richard remembered it from before.

It was one of the instructions in the Book of Counted Shadows, the book he had memorized when he was a boy. *Clear your mind of all thought, and in its place put nothing but the image of white with a square of black in its center.* It was part of the instructions for removing the covers from the boxes of Orden and using the magic of the book. He had used that magic to show Darken Rahl how to remove the cover from a box to prove to him he truly did know the book. But why would it be in his mind now? Just a random memory forcing its way to the surface, he decided.

It was as good a background as any to put the sword on. After all, he was trying to use magic. If his mind wanted to use it, it made no difference to him; he would let it be. At that thought, the image of the sword and a square black background with white around it solidified and became still.

Richard concentrated on the mental image of the sword against the black square with the white border. He concentrated as hard as he could. Something began to happen.

The sword, the black square, and the white border all began to shimmer as if seen through heat waves. The solid form of the sword softened. It became transparent, and then it was gone. The background dissolved. He was looking into a place he knew.

The Garden of Life, at the People's Palace.

Richard thought it odd, and somewhat annoying, that he wasn't able to hold his concentration enough to keep the image of the sword in his mind. The memory of the place where he killed Darken Rahl must have been so strong that it forced its way into his mind while he was relaxed.

He was about to try to force the image of the sword to come back when he smelled something. Burned flesh. The stench made his nostrils flare. He almost gagged. His stomach turned sickeningly.

He searched the image of the Garden of Life. It was like looking through a dirty windowpane. There were bodies lying over the short walls, fallen, partly hidden, in bushes, and sprawled on the grass. All were hideously burned. Some held weapons, swords or battle-axes, in charred fists. Others lay with open hands, their weapons resting where they had tumbled as their owners fell dead. Choking apprehension swelled in Richard's chest.

Richard saw the back of a white, glowing figure standing before the stone altar, before the three boxes of Orden. One of the boxes stood open, as Richard remembered. The white figure with long blond hair lifted his face away from the boxes.

Darken Rahl turned and looked right into Richard's eyes. His blue eyes glowed. A smile spread slowly on his lips. It seemed as if Richard was helplessly pulled closer. Closer to the grinning face.

Darken Rahl lifted a hand to his mouth and licked the tips of his fingers. "Richard," he hissed. "I'm waiting for you. Come watch while I tear the veil."

Unable to draw a breath, Richard slammed the image of the sword back into his mind, like slamming a door. He held it there, rigidly, without the background, as he tried to make himself breathe.

It was just a stray memory, and his fear, making him see the image, he told himself. He concentrated on the sword as he finally decided that what he had seen wasn't real, but maybe a manifestation of his heartache over Kahlan, and his lack of sleep.

That's what it had to be. It couldn't have been real. That would be impossible. He would have to be insane to believe it had been real.

He opened his eyes. Sister Verna was sitting calmly watching him. She gave a heavy sigh—he thought maybe out of displeasure.

Richard swallowed. "I'm sorry. Nothing happened."

"Don't be discouraged, Richard. I did not expect anything to happen. It takes a long time to learn to touch the Han. It will happen when it happens. There is no way to rush it. It does no good to push too hard; it comes from finding the inner peace and not by force. That is long enough for today."

"A few minutes? That's all you want me to try?"

She lifted an eyebrow. "You have had your eyes closed for over an hour."

He stared at her, and then glanced to the sun. It seemed to have jumped up into the sky. Over an hour. How was that possible? A tingle of apprehension spread through him.

She cocked her head. "It seemed only a few minutes to you?"

Richard stood. He didn't like the frown on her face. "I don't know. I wasn't paying any attention. I guess it did feel like an hour."

He started packing the few things he had taken out. The more he thought about what he had seen, the more unreal it seemed. It began to feel like a dream after waking, the fear, the hard edges, the reality, fading. He began to feel foolish for being so frightened by a dream.

A dream? He hadn't been sleeping. How could he have been dreaming when he was awake?

Maybe he hadn't been awake. He had been dead tired. Maybe while he was sitting there concentrating on the sword, he had fallen asleep. That's how he went to sleep, sometimes: by concentrating on something until he drifted off. That was the only explanation for the time going so fast. He was asleep, and the rest of it had been a dream.

He let out a heavy breath. He felt silly for having been so frightened, but he felt relieved, too. When he turned, Sister Verna was still watching him.

"Do you wish to shave now? Now that I have shown you I only wish to help you."

Richard straightened. "I told you: prisoners don't shave."

"You are not a prisoner, Richard."

He stuffed his blanket into his pack, tucking in the corners to make it fit. "Will you remove the collar?"

Her answer was slow in coming, but firm. "No. Only when it is time."

"May I leave, and go where I wish?"

She sighed impatiently. "No. You must go with me."

"And if I don't, if I try to leave you?"

Her eyes narrowed a little. "Then I would be forced to prevent it. You would find you did not like that."

Richard nodded solemnly. "That fits my definition of a prisoner. As long as I'm a prisoner, I will not shave."

The horses nickered at his approach, their ears pricking toward him. Sister Verna eyed them suspiciously. He returned the greeting with gentle words and a stiff scratch to the side of each horse's neck. Taking out the brushes, he gave each a quick grooming, paying particular attention to their backs.

Sister Verna folded her arms. "Why are you doing that? You groomed them last night."

"Because horses like to roll in the dirt. They could have something under where the saddle goes. Feels kind of like walking around with a rock in your boot, only worse; it could give them a sore, and then we won't be able to ride them. So, I like to check them over before I put their saddles on."

When he finished, he cleaned the brushes against each other. "What are their names?"

Sister Verna gave a sour frown. "They don't have names. They are just horses. We don't give names to dumb animals."

He pointed with the curry brush at the chestnut gelding. "You don't even give your own a name?"

"He is not my own. They all belong to the Sisters of the Light. I ride whichever one is available. The bay you rode yesterday is the one I rode before you came with me, but it makes no difference. I simply ride whichever one is available."

"Well, from now on, they're going to have names. Avoids confusion. Yours is the chestnut, and he will be Jessup, my bay will be Bonnie, and the other bay will be Geraldine."

"Jessup, Bonnie, and Geraldine," she huffed. "No doubt from *The Adventures of Bonnie Day.*"

"Glad to hear you read something other than prophecies, Sister Verna."

"As I told you before, ones with the gift who come to the palace are brought when they are young. One boy brought *The Adventures of Bonnie Day* with him. I read it to see if it was appropriate for young minds, and to see if it was of good moral teachings. I found it to be a preposterous story of three people who would have had no troubles if a one of them had been blessed with brains."

Richard smiled a little. "Perfect names for 'dumb animals' then."

She scowled at him. "It was a book of no intellectual value. No value of any kind. I destroyed it."

Richard's smile tried to fade, but he didn't let it. "My father . . . well, the man who raised me as his son, and who I think of as my father, George Cypher, well, he traveled often. One time, when he came home, he brought me *The Adventures of Bonnie Day*, as a gift for learning to read. It was the first book I ever had. I read it many times. It brought me pleasure, and made me think, each time I read it. I, too, thought the three heroes did foolhardy things, and I always vowed not to repeat the same mistakes they made. You may have seen no value in it, but it taught me things. Things of value. It made me think. Perhaps, Sister Verna, that is something you don't like your students to do?"

He turned away from her and started taking apart the bridles. "My real father, Darken Rahl, came to my house, just this autumn, looking for me. He wanted to cut my belly open and read my entrails—to kill me. Just as he killed George Cypher." He stole a quick glance over his shoulder. "Anyway, I wasn't at home, and while we was waiting for me, he tore that book apart and threw the pages all around. Maybe he didn't want me learning any of its lessons or thinking for myself either."

Sister Verna didn't say anything, but he could feel her eyes watching him take the bridles apart, undo the headstalls and reins from the bits. After he had them apart, he packed the headstalls away and flipped the reins over his shoulder.

He could hear her let out a little, angry breath. "I'll not be calling horses by names."

Richard stacked the three spade bits atop one another on the dirt, where the horses had pawed the ground bare. "You might want to reconsider the wisdom of that, Sister Verna."

She stepped out to the side of him, where he could see her, pointing at the ground. "What are you doing? Why did you take the bridles apart? What are you doing with those bits?"

Richard drew the sword. Its distinctive ring filled the cold, bright air. The rage of the magic instantly flooded through him. "I'm destroying them, Sister."

With a scream of fury, and before she could make a move, he brought the sword down with a powerful swing. The tip whistled through the air. The blade shattered the three bits into flying shards of hot metal.

She rushed forward, her cloak flapping. "What's the matter with you! Have you lost your mind! We need those bits to control the horses!"

"Spade bits can be cruel. I won't allow you to use them."

"Cruel! They are just stupid beasts! Beasts that need to be controlled!"

"Beasts," he muttered, shaking his head and sliding his sword back into its scabbard. He snugged up the halter on Bonnie and began attaching the reins to the side rings. "You don't need a bit to control a horse. I'll teach you how. Besides, without a bit in their mouths they can eat while we travel. They'll be happier that way."

"That's dangerous! Spade bits give you control over a headstrong beast."

He arched an eyebrow to her. "With horses, as with many other things, Sister, you often get what you expect to get."

"Without bits, you don't have any control."

"Nonsense. If you ride properly, you control with your legs and body. You just have to teach the horse to pay attention and trust you."

She stepped close, commanding his attention. "That's foolish! And dangerous! There are dangers out here. If you get into a dangerous situation, and the horse is frightened, it could bolt. Without a spade bit you won't be able to stop a runaway horse."

He halted what he was doing and looked to her intense brown eyes. "Sometimes, Sister, we get the opposite of what we intend. If we do get in a dangerous situation, and you get overanxious, and jerk too hard on a spade bit, you could tear the horse's mouth. If you do that, the pain, terror, and anger can be so intense that he won't respond to anything you do. He won't understand. He will only know that you hurt him, and that you're hurting him more with each pull on the reins. You'll be the threat. He will throw you in a heartbeat.

"Then, if he is simply frightened, he will bolt. Worse, he could be angry. Angry horses are dangerous. In trying to avoid danger with a spade bit, you will have brought it upon yourself." He held her startled eyes in his gaze. "If we get to a town or something, and can find a jointed snaffle bit, I'll let you use that. But I will not allow you to put a spade bit in any horse's mouth as long as I'm with you."

She took a deep breath, releasing it carefully as she folded her arms again. "Richard, we can't control them without a bit. It's that simple."

He gave her a one-sided smile. "Sure we can. I'll teach you. The worst thing that can happen without a bit is that he can run away with you, and you'll have a time of stopping him, but sooner or later, you will be able to. Your way, you and the horse could be hurt, or killed."

He turned and scratched Bonnie's neck. "First thing you have to do is make friends with them. They have to trust you not to hurt them, or let anything happen to them, though you are in charge. If you're their best friend, they won't let anything happen to you. They'll do what you ask.

"It's surprisingly easy; all you have to do is show them a little respect and kindness along with a firm hand. If they're going to be your friend, they need names, to get their attention, and so they know when you're talking to them."

He scratched a little harder, the horse leaning into it. "Isn't that right, Bonnie? You're a good girl, aren't you? Sure you are." He looked over his shoulder at the Sister. "Jessup likes it when you scratch under his chin. Give it a try, show him you want to be friends." He gave her a humorless grin. "Like it or not, Sister, we don't have the bits anymore. You need to learn a new way."

Sister Verna stared at him with a cold look. At last she unfolded her arms and went over to the chestnut gelding. She stood in front of him a moment and then reached out and stroked the side of his head, finally moving her hand under his jaw to give him a scratch. "There's a good boy," she said in a flat tone.

"You may think horses are dumb, Sister Verna, because they don't understand most of your words, but they understand tone of voice. If you want him to believe you, you had better at least pretend you're sincere."

She moved her hand up and rubbed his neck. "You are a dumb beast," she said in a syrupy sweet voice. "Happy?" she snapped over her shoulder.

"As long as you're nice to him. You need to gain his trust. Horses aren't as dumb as you think. Look at the way he's standing; he doesn't trust you. From now on, I'm assigning you to Jessup. You'll tend to all his needs. He must come to depend on you, to trust you. I'll take care of Bonnie and Geraldine. You'll be the only one to groom Jessup, and you will do it after he is ridden, and before he is ridden the next morning."

"Me! Most certainly not! I'm in charge. You are quite capable of grooming all three, and will do so."

"This has nothing to do with who's in charge. Among other things, grooming helps build a bond between you and the horse. I already told you: the bits are gone, you need to learn a new way. I need to teach you how, for your own safety." He handed her a set of reins. "Tighten up the halter and attach these to this ring, here."

While she was doing it, he cut up the leftover melon rind into small pieces. "Talk to him. Call him by name, and let him know you like him. It doesn't matter what you say, you can describe what you're doing if you want, but make it sound like he's important to you. If you have to, pretend; treat him like he's one of your little boys."

She glared over her shoulder at him, then turned back to hooking up the reins. She started talking, softly, so Richard couldn't hear her, but he could tell it was gentle. When she finished, he handed her some of the pieces of melon rind.

"Horses love this. Give him a piece, tell him what a good boy he is. The idea is to change his feelings about having the reins on. Let him know it's going to be pleasant, instead of that bit he hates."

"Pleasant," she repeated in a flat tone.

"Sure. You don't need to show him how much you can hurt him to make him do as you wish. That's counterproductive. Just be firm but gentle. The idea is to try to win him over with kindness and understanding, even if it isn't sincere, and not by using force."

Richard's smile vanished, and he let his features slide into a glare. He leaned closer to her as she stood looking up at him. "You should be able to do that, Sister Verna; you seem pretty good at it. Just treat him like you treat me."

Her stunned expression hardened. "I swore on my life to bring you back to the Palace of the Prophets. When they see you at last, I fear I may be hung for doing my duty."

She turned and gave the melon rind to the eager horse, stroking his neck and encouraging him with motherly pats. "There's a good fellow. Good boy. You like that, Jessup? Good boy."

Her voice was heavy with compassion and tenderness. The horse liked it. Richard knew it lacked sincerity. He didn't trust her, and wanted her to know it. He didn't appreciate people thinking they were so easily fooling him. He wondered if her attitude toward him would change, now that he had let her know he hadn't swallowed her act.

Kahlan had told him that Sister Verna was a sorceress. He had no idea what she was capable of, but he had felt the web she had thrown around him in the spirit house. He had seen the fire she started with a thought. She could have easily started a fire the night before, without telling him to do it. He had the strong feeling she could break him in half with her Han, if she so chose.

She was just trying to train him; get him accustomed to doing as she said, without thinking. Just like training a horse. Or a "beast," as she had called it. He doubted she had any more respect for him than she did for her horses.

But instead of using a spade bit to control him, she had the Rada'Han around his neck, and that was much worse. But he would have it off, when the time came. Even if Kahlan didn't want him and had sent him away, he would have it off.

While Sister Verna was making friends with Jessup, Richard started saddling the horses. "How far to the Palace of the Prophets?"

"It is a long way to the southeast. A long and difficult way."

"Well, then we will have plenty of time to teach you how to handle Jessup without a bit. You won't have as hard a time as you think. He will defer to and follow Bonnie. Bonnie is the dominant horse."

"The male is dominant."

Richard lifted the saddle up onto Bonnie. "A mare is always at the top of the hierarchy. Dams teach and protect the foals; their influence lasts a lifetime. There isn't a stallion a mare can't intimidate and chase away. Mares can run off any unwanted stallion. A stallion may drive a predator away from the herd, but a mare will chase it and try to kill it. A male horse will always defer to the authority of the lead mare. Bonnie is the lead mare. Jessup and Geraldine will follow her and do as she does, so I'll take the lead. Just follow me, and you won't have any trouble."

She swung herself up into the saddle. "The beam in the central hall. It's the highest. Everyone will be able to see it."

"What are you talking about?"

She gave him a solemn look. "The beam in the central hall. That is where they will probably hang me from."

Richard swung up into his saddle. "It's your choice, Sister. You don't have to take me there."

She sighed. "Yes, I do." She gave him her most gentle and concerned look. He thought it quite convincing, if a little strained. "Richard, I only wish to help you. I want to be your friend. I think you need a friend right now. Very much."

Richard bristled. "That is a kind offer, Sister Verna. But I decline. You seem a little too quick to put that knife you keep up your sleeve in the back of your friends. Did it bother you at all, Sister Verna, to steal the life from Sister Elizabeth, a friend and companion? It didn't seem so. I decline to offer you my friendship, Sister. Or my back.

"If you're sincere in your wish to be my friend, then I would advise you to truly commit to it before I call upon you to prove it. When the time comes, you are only going to get one chance. There are no shades of gray in this matter. Only friends and enemies. Friends don't keep a friend in a collar, and hold them prisoner. I intend to have this collar off. When I decide it's time, any friend will help me. Those who try to stop me won't be my friends; they will be dead enemies."

Sister Verna shook her head and urged Jessup in behind him as he started away. "The beam in the central hall. I'm sure of it."

**T**he sound of her heart pounded in her ears. Struggling to control her panicked breathing, she ducked behind the fat trunk of an old pine, pressing up against the rough bark. If the Sisters had discovered she was following them . . .

The dark, damp air filled her lungs in ragged pulls. Her lips moved soundlessly with prayers to the Creator beseeching protection. With eyes as big as gold pieces, she stared into the darkness and swallowed, trying to wet her throat.

The dark form glided silently closer. She could just see it as she peeked out past the edge of the tree. She suppressed the urge to scream, to run, and prepared herself to fight. She reached for the sweet light; she embraced her Han.

The shadow slipped closer, hesitating, searching. One more step, just one more, and she would spring. She would have to do it right—make sure there was no chance to raise an alarm. It had to be fast, and it would take different kinds of webs, all thrown at once, but if she could be precise and quick, there would be no chance of a scream, no alarm, and she would know for sure who it was. She held her breath.

The dark shape finally took another step. Spinning out from behind the tree, she threw the webs. Cords of air, strong as dock line, whipped around the form. As the mouth came open, she jammed a solid knot of air into it, gagging it, before it had a chance to cry out.

She slumped a little with relief when no sound came forth, but her heart still raced nearly out of control as she gasped for air. With an effort, she managed to bring calm back to her mind, although she maintained a firm grip on her Han, fearful to let her caution slip; there could be others about. She took a deep breath and stepped closer to the immobilized shape. When she was close enough to feel its breath on her face, she extended her palm up, and in its center released a thread of fire, to light a tiny flame, just enough to see the face.

"Jedidiah!" she whispered. She pressed her hand to the back of his neck, her fingers feeling the smooth, cool metal of the Rada'Han, and leaned her forehead against his as she closed her eyes. Tears ran down her cheeks. "Oh, Jedidiah. You gave me a such a fright."

She opened her eyes and looked up at his terrified face, lit by the tiny, flickering flame. "I will release you," she whispered softly, "but you must be very quiet. Promise?"

He nodded, as best he could, considering how tightly she had him bound. She slipped off the webs, pulling out the gag of air. Jedidiah sagged with relief.

"Sister Margaret," he whispered in a shaky voice, "you very nearly made me soil myself."

She laughed soundlessly. "I'm sorry, Jedidiah, but you very nearly did the same to me."

She snipped the thin thread of Han fueling the small flame and they both sank to the ground, leaning against one another, recovering from the fright. Jedidiah, several years younger, was bigger than she, a handsome young man. Painfully handsome, she thought.

She had been assigned to him when he had first come to the palace and she had been a novice. He had been eager to learn, and had studied hard. He had been a pleasure from the first day. She knew others had been difficult, but not Jedidiah. He had done everything she had asked of him. She had only to ask, and he threw himself into it.

Others thought he was more eager to please her than to please himself in what he did, but none could deny that he was a better student than any other, and was becoming a better wizard, and that was all that mattered. This was one area where the results were what counted, not the method, and she had quickly earned her full Sisterhood for the way she had brought him along.

Jedidiah had been more proud of her than she had been of herself when she had been named a Sister of the Light. She was proud of him, too; he was probably the most powerful wizard the palace had seen in a thousand years.

"Margaret," he whispered, "what are you doing out here?"

"Sister Margaret," she corrected.

"No one is around." He kissed her ear.

"Stop that," she scolded. The tingle from the kiss ran all the way down her spine; he had added a wisp of magic to the kiss. Sometimes she wished she hadn't taught him that. But other times she ached to have him do it. "Jedidiah, what are you doing here? You have no business following me, following a Sister, out of the palace."

"You're up to something, I know you are, and don't you try to tell me you're not. Something dangerous. At first, I was only a little concerned, but when I realized you were headed out into the Hagen Woods, I became frightened for you. I'm not going to let you go wandering into a dangerous place like this. Not by yourself anyway. Not without going along to protect you."

"Protect me!" she whispered harshly. "Might I remind you of what just happened? You were helpless in a heartbeat. You weren't able to fight off even a single one of my webs. You weren't able to break one of them. You are hardly able to touch your Han, much less use it effectively. You have a lot to learn before you are wizard enough to go around protecting anyone. It's all you can do at this point to keep from stepping on your own feet!"

The rebuke silenced him. She didn't like to reprimand him so harshly, but this was far too dangerous for him to be involved in, if what she suspected was true. She feared for him, and didn't want him hurt.

The things she had said weren't entirely true, either. He was already more powerful than any Sister, when he could bring everything together properly, even though that wasn't often. Already, there were Sisters who were afraid to push him too far. She could feel him look away.

"I'm sorry, Margaret," he whispered. "I was afraid for you."

Her heart ached at the hurt in his voice. She kept her head close to his so they could speak in soft whispers. "I know you are, Jedidiah, and I appreciate your concern, I really do. But this is Sister business."

"Margaret, the Hagen Woods are a dangerous place. There are things in here that could kill you. I don't want you in here."

The Hagen Woods were indeed dangerous. They had been for thousands of years, and had been left that way by decree of the palace. As if they could do anything about it.

It was said the Hagen Woods were a training ground for a very special kind of wizard. That kind of wizard was not sent there, but went in by choice. Because he wanted to. Craved to . . . needed to.

But that was only what was said. She knew of no wizard going off to spend time in the Hagen Woods, at least not for the last few thousand years. If it was true any ever did. The tales said that in ancient times there were wizards of that kind, with that much power, and that they went into the Hagen Woods. Few ever came out, it was also said. But there were rules, even to this place.

"The sun didn't set while I was here. I came after dark. If you don't let the sun set on you in the Hagen Woods, you can leave, and I don't intend to stay long enough for the next sun to set on me. It's safe enough. For me, anyway. I want you to go home. Right now."

"What's so important that you would go in here? What are you doing? I expect an answer, Margaret. A truthful answer. I won't be put off. There is danger for you in this and I won't be put off."

She fingered the finely worked gold flower she kept on a chain around her neck. Jedidiah had made it for her himself, not with magic, but with his own hands. It was a morning glory, meant to represent his awakening awareness of the gift, an awareness she had helped to blossom. That little gold flower meant more to her than anything else she had.

She took up his hand and leaned against him. "All right, Jedidiah, I will tell you. But I can't tell you all of it. It's too dangerous for you to know everything."

"What's too dangerous? What can't you tell me?"

"Be quiet and listen, or I will send you back right now. And you know I can do it."

His other hand went to the collar. "Margaret, you wouldn't do that. Tell me you wouldn't do that, not since we have been . . ."

"Hush!" He fell silent. She waited a moment to be certain he was going to stay hushed before she went on. "I have suspected for a time that some of the ones with the gift who have gone away, or died, have not done so as it has been put to us. I think they have been murdered."

"What!"

"Keep your voice down!" she whispered angrily. "Do you want to get us killed, too?" He fell silent once more. "I think something awful is going on in the Palace of the Prophets. I think some of the Sisters murdered them."

He stared at her in the darkness. "Murdered? By Sisters? Margaret, you must be crazy to even suggest such a thing."

"Well, I'm not. But everyone would think I was if I were to say such a thing aloud inside the palace walls. I have to figure out a way to prove it."

He thought a moment. "Well, I know you better than anyone, and if you say it's true, then I believe you. I'll help. Maybe we could dig up the bodies, find something to go against what was said about their deaths, find somebody who saw something. We could carefully question the staff. There are ones I know who . . ."

"Jedidiah, that's not the worst of it."

"What could be worse?"

She held the gold flower in the crook of a finger and rubbed her thumb against it. Her voice came even lower than before. "There are Sisters of the Dark in the palace."

Even without being able to see him in the darkness, she knew bumps were running up his arms. The night bugs chirped around them as she watched the dark shape of his face. "Margaret . . . Sisters of the . . . that can't be. There is no such thing. That is only a myth . . . a fable."

"It is no myth. There are Sisters of the Dark in the Palace."

"Margaret, please don't keep saying that. You could be put to death for making an accusation like that. If you accuse a Sister of that, and can't prove it, you would be put to death. And you can't prove it because it isn't possible. There is no such thing as a Sister of the . . ."

He couldn't even say the words. The thought of it frightened him so much, he couldn't even say it out loud. She knew his fear. She had felt it herself until she had happened on things she could no longer ignore. She wished she hadn't gone to see the Prophet that night, or at least not listened to him.

The Prelate had been angry that Margaret wouldn't give the Prophet's message to one of her aides. When she had finally granted an audience, the Prelate had only stared blankly at her and asked what the "pebble in the pond" was. Margaret didn't know. The Prelate had lectured her sternly for bothering her with Nathan's nonsense. Margaret had been furious at Nathan when he had denied remembering giving any such message for the Prelate.

"I wish it were as you say, but it is not. They're real. They are among us. They are in the palace." She watched the dark shadow of him a moment. "That's why I'm out here. To get the proof."

"How are you going to do that?"

"They're out here. I followed them. They come out into the Hagen Woods to do something. I'm going to find out what."

His head turned about, searching the darkness. "Who? Which Sisters? Do you know which ones?"

"I know. Some of them anyway."

"Which ones are they?"

"Jedidiah, I can't tell you. If you knew, and you made even the slightest mistake . . . you would not be able to defend yourself. If I'm right and they really are Sisters of the Dark, they would kill you for knowing. I can't bear the thought of you being hurt. I won't tell you until I go to the Prelate's office with the proof."

"How do you know they are Sisters of the . . . And what proof have you? What proof could you get?"

She searched the darkness for any sign of danger. "One of the Sisters has something. A thing of magic. A thing of dark magic. I saw it in her office. It's a little statue. I noticed it one time because she has a number of things, old things everyone thinks are just ancient curiosities. I had seen it before, and like all the rest of the things, it was covered with dust.

"But this one time, after one of the boys died, I went to her office to talk to her about it, about her report. That little statue was tucked back in a corner, with a book leaning against it, hiding it, and it wasn't covered with dust. It was clean."

"That's it! This Sister dusted a statue, and you think . . ."

"No. No one knows what that statue is. After I saw she had dusted it, I had reason to question what it was. I had to be careful, not let anyone know what I was up to, but I finally found out what it is."

"How? How did you find out?"

She remembered her visit to Nathan, and her vow never to reveal how she had learned what that statue was. "Never you mind. That is not for you to know."

"Margaret, how could you . . ."

She cut him off. "I said I'm not telling you. And it isn't important anyway. What is important is what the statue is, not how I found out about it. It's a man holding up a crystal. The crystal is quillion."

"What's quillion?"

"It's an exceedingly rare magic crystal. It has the power to bleed the magic from a wizard."

The surprise of that left him speechless for a moment. "How do you know it's quillion, if it's so rare? How would you be able to recognize it? Maybe it is just some other crystal that looks similar."

"That might be true if it hadn't been used. When quillion is used to bleed the magic from a wizard, it glows orange with the power of his gift, his Han. For just a brief second as I left her office, I saw that statue, all clean, hiding behind that book. The quillion was glowing orange. But that was before I knew what it was. After I found out, I went back, to take it to the Prelate, as proof, but it no longer was glowing."

"What could that mean?" he whispered in a fearful voice.

"It means that the wizard's power had passed out of the crystal, into somebody. A host. Quillion is just a vessel for the gift until it can be placed into someone else. Jedidiah, I think the Sisters are killing those with the gift, and stealing it for themselves. I think they are absorbing the power into themselves."

His voice trembled. "On top of what they already are? They now have the power of a wizard's gift?"

She nodded. "Yes. That makes them more dangerous than we could even believe, more powerful than we can imagine. That's what scares me the most, not being put to death for making the accusation, but being found out by these Sisters. If they really are taking the power into themselves, I don't know how we can stop them. None of us can match them.

"I need proof, so the Prelate will believe me. Maybe she will know what to do. I certainly don't.

"What I can't understand is how the Sisters are absorbing the gift from the quillion. The gift of a wizard, his Han, is male. The sisters are female. A female can't just absorb the male Han. It's not that simple; otherwise they would simply have bled the Han into themselves when they killed him. If they are really taking the Han from the males into themselves, I don't know how they're doing it."

"So what are you doing out here?"

She folded her arms against an inner chill, even though the air was warm. "Do you remember the other day, when Sam Weber and Neville Ranson had completed all the tests and were to have their collars off and leave the palace?"

He nodded in the dark. "Yes. I was really disappointed because Sam had promised to come say good-bye, and show me he had his Rada'Han off. I wanted to wish him well after he was a true wizard. He never came. They told me he left in the night, because he didn't want any tearful good-byes, but Sam was my friend, he was a gentle person, a healer, and it just wasn't like him to leave in that fashion, without telling me good-bye. It just wasn't. I was hurt he didn't come by. I really wanted to wish him well."

"They killed him."

"What?" He sagged down a little. "Oh, dear Creator, no." His voice broke with tears. "Are you sure? How do you know?"

She put a comforting hand on his shoulder. "The day after he supposedly left in such a strange manner, I suspected something terrible had happened. I went to see if the quillion was glowing again, but the door was shielded."

"That doesn't prove anything. Sisters shield their rooms or offices sometimes. You do it yourself when you don't want to be disturbed, like when we are together."

"I know. But I wanted to see the quillion, so I waited around a corner, until the Sister came to her office. I came out from where I waited, timing it so that as I walked past, she would be entering. As I went by, and just before she closed the door behind herself, I saw into her dark office. I saw the statue on the shelf behind the book. It was glowing orange. I'm sorry, Jedidiah."

His voice lowered with anger. "Who was it? Which Sister?"

"I'm not going to tell you, Jedidiah. Not until I can take proof to the Prelate. It's too dangerous."

He thought a moment. "If this crystal really is quillion, and it would prove what she is, why wouldn't she hide it better?"

"Maybe because she didn't think there was a chance of anyone knowing what it was. Maybe because she isn't afraid and doesn't take the time to be any more careful than she thinks necessary."

"Then let's go back, break the shield, get the cursed thing and take it to the Prelate. I can break the shield, I know I can."

"I was going to do that myself. I went back to do it tonight, but the room wasn't shielded anymore. I snuck in to take the statue, but it was gone. That was when I saw her leaving the palace, and I saw others leaving too. I followed them out here.

"If I can steal the quillion while it's glowing, I can prove they are Sisters of the Dark. I have to stop them before they can suck the life out of anyone else. Jedidiah, they're murdering people, but worse, I fear the reason they are doing it."

He let out a soft sigh. "All right. But I'm going with you."

She gritted her teeth. "No, you are going back."

"Margaret, I love you, and if you send me back to worry all alone, I will never forgive you. I'll go to the Prelate myself and make the accusation, to bring you help. Though I may be put to death for making the accusation, I know it would raise suspicions, and maybe an alarm. That's the only other way I'll be able to protect you. Either I go with you, or I go to the Prelate; I promise you I will."

She knew he was telling the truth. Jedidiah always kept his promises. Powerful wizards always did. Rising to her knees, she leaned over and put her arms around his neck. "I love you too, Jedidiah."

She kissed him deeply as he rose up on his knees to meet her. His hands went under the back of her dress and he gripped her bottom, pulling her against him. The feeling of his hands on her flesh made her moan softly. His hot lips kissed her neck and then her ear, sending shimmers of magic tingling through her. His knee forced her legs apart, giving his hands access to her. She gasped at the contact.

"Come away with me now," he whispered in her ear. "Let's go back, and you can shield your room and I'll give you more until you scream. You can scream all you want and no one will hear you."

She pushed away from him and pulled his hands out from under her dress. He was breaking down her resistance. She found she had to force herself to stop him. He was using his magic to seduce her away from the danger, trying to save her by drawing her away. She knew that if she let it go on for another second, it would work.

"Jedidiah," she panted in a hoarse whisper, "please don't make me have to use the collar to stop you. This is too important. Lives are at stake." He tried to reach out to her once more, but she sent a cord of power through her hands on his wrists to stop him. She firmly held his hands away.

"I know, Margaret. Your life is one of them. I don't want anything to harm you. I love you more than anything in the world."

"Jedidiah, this is more important than my life. This is about the lives of everyone. I think this is about the Nameless One."

He froze stiff. "You can't be serious."

"Why do you think these Sisters want this power? What do they need with it? Why would they be willing to kill for it? To what end? Who do you think Sisters of the Dark serve?"

"Dear Creator," he whispered slowly, "don't let her be right." His hands came up and held her by her shoulders. "Margaret, who else knows these things? Who have you told?"

"Only you, Jedidiah. I know who four, maybe five, of the Sisters of the Dark are. But there are others, and I don't know who they are. I don't know who I can trust. There were eleven I followed out here tonight, but there could easily be more."

"What about the Prelate? Maybe you shouldn't go to her, she could be with them."

She shook her head with a sigh. "You may be right, but it's the only chance we have. There is no one else I can think of who can help me. I have to go to her." She touched her fingertips to his face. "Jedidiah, please go back. If anything were to happen to me, then you would be able to do something. There would be someone who knew."

"No. I won't leave you. If you make me go back, I will tell the Prelate. I love you. I would rather die than live without you."

"But there are others to think of. Other lives at stake."

"I don't care about anyone else. Please, Margaret, don't ask me to leave you to this danger."

"Sometimes you can be infuriating, my love." She took his hands up in hers. "Jedidiah, if we are caught . . ."

"If we are together, then I accept the risk."

She twined her fingers through his. "Then be my husband? As we have talked about? If I die tonight, I want it to be as your wife."

He put a hand behind her head and drew her against him. Pulling her hair away from her ear he whispered softly into it. "That would make me the happiest man in the world. I love you so much, Margaret. But how can we be married here, now?"

"We can say the words. Our love is all that counts, not some other person saying words for us. Words coming from our hearts will bond us better than anyone else could do."

He squeezed her tight. "This is the happiest moment in my life." He pulled back,

229

taking up her hands again. In the darkness they looked at each other. "I, Jedidiah, pledge to be your husband, in life and in death. I offer you my life, my love, and my eternal devotion. May we be bonded in the Creator's eyes and heart, and in our own."

She whispered the words back to him as tears streamed down her cheeks. She had never been so afraid and so happy in all her life. She shook with the need of him. When they finished the words, they kissed. It was the most tender, loving kiss he had ever given her. Tears continued to run down her face as she pressed against him, against his lips. Her hands clutched the back of his broad shoulders, holding him to her. His arms around her made her feel safer and more loved than she had ever felt. At last, they parted.

She struggled to catch her breath. "I love you, my husband."

"I love you, my wife, always and forever."

She smiled. Even though she couldn't see it in the dark, she knew he was smiling, too. "Let's go see if we can get some proof. Let's see if we can put a stop to the Sisters of the Dark. Let's make the Creator proud of the Sisters of the Light, and a wizard-to-be."

He squeezed her hand. "Promise me you won't do anything foolish. Promise me you won't try to do anything that might get you killed. I want to spend some time with you in bed, not the woods."

"I need to see what they are up to. See if I can find a way to prove all this to the Prelate. But they are more powerful than I am, to say nothing of the fact that there are at least eleven of them. On top of that, if they truly are Sisters of the Dark, they have the use of Subtractive Magic. We have no defense against that.

"I don't know how we are to get the quillion away from them. Maybe we will see something else that will help us. If we just keep our eyes open, and let the Creator guide us, maybe He will reveal what it is we can do. But I don't want either of us taking any more of a chance than we have to. We must not be discovered."

He nodded. "Good. That's the way I want it too."

"But Jedidiah, I'm a Sister of the Light. That means I have responsibilities, responsibilities to the Creator, and all his children. Though we are now husband and wife, it's still my job to guide you. In this, we are not equals. I'm in charge, and I will only allow you to go with me if you promise to abide by that. You are not yet a full wizard. If I tell you something, you must obey. I'm still better with my Han than you are with yours."

"I know, Margaret. One reason I wanted to be your husband is because I respect you. I wouldn't want a weak wife. You have always guided me, and that will not change now. You've given me everything I have. I will follow you always."

With a smile, she shook her head. "You are a marvel, my husband. A marvel of the best kind. You will make a remarkable wizard. Truly remarkable. I've never told you, because I always feared you would let the knowledge swell your head, but some of the Sisters say that they think you may prove to be the most powerful wizard in a thousand years."

He didn't speak, and she couldn't see his face, but she was sure he was blushing. "Margaret, your eyes are the only ones I need to see filled with pride."

She kissed his cheek, and then took his hand. "Let's go see how we can put a stop to this."

"How do you know where they went? How can we follow them? It's dark as pitch in these woods. The trees hide the moon."

She pinched his cheek. "A trick my mother taught me. I've never shown it to anyone. When I saw them leaving the palace, I cast a pool of my Han at their feet. They stepped through it. It leaves tracks of my own Han. Only I can see them. Their footprints are as bright as the sun on a pond to me, but to no other."

"You must teach me this trick."

"Someday, I promise. Come on."

She led him by the hand as she followed the glow of the Sisters' footprints through the dense woods. Distant night birds called in haunting voices, owls hooted, and other creatures made low screams and clicks. The ground was uneven, tangled with roots and brush, but the glowing footprints helped her to see the way.

The damp heat made her sweat, causing her dress to cling to her wet skin. When she got home, she would shield her room and she would have a bath. A long bath. With Jedidiah. Then she would let him use his magic on her, and she would use hers on him.

They went deeper into the Hagen Woods, deeper than she had ever gone before. Vapor drifting from boggy areas carried the pervasive stench of rotting vegetation. They passed through dark gullies veiled with hanging roots and moss that brushed against her face and arms, making her flinch at the unexpected contact. The footprints led up and over sparsely wooded, rocky ridges.

At the top of one, standing in the still, damp air, she looked back, out across the somber landscape. In the far distance, she could see the flickering lights of Tanimura, and set among the lights, rising up in the silvery moonlight, the Palace of the Prophets, its dark shape blocking out the lights of the city beyond.

She longed to be back there, to be home, but this was something that had to be done. There was no one else to do it. The lives of everyone depended on her. The Creator was depending on her. Still, she longed to be home, and safe.

But home was no longer safe. It was as dangerous as the Hagen Woods, if there really were Sisters of the Dark. Even with as much as she knew, it was difficult for her to accept the idea. The Prelate had to believe her, she just had to. There was no one else she could turn to for help. She wished there were even just one Sister she could trust, confide in, but she didn't dare trust anyone. Nathan had warned her not to trust anyone.

Even though she wished Jedidiah were home, and safe, she was glad to have him with her. She knew there was nothing he could do to help, but it still felt good to have him to confide in. Her husband. She smiled at the thought. She would never forgive herself if anything happened to him. She would protect him with her life, if she had to.

The ground pitched into a descent. Through gaps in the trees, she could see they were going down into a deep bowl in the earth. The edge was steep and they had to move slowly so as not to send any rocks tumbling through the woods. One started to slide as her foot touched it, and she quickly used a handful of air to stop it, and then push it firmly into the ground. She sighed in relief.

Jedidiah followed her, a silent, comforting shadow. Her tension relaxed a little when they passed from the loose rock, back into denser woods where the ground was mossy and silent to step on.

The faint sound of chanting drifted to them through the thick woods, carried on heavy, fetid air. Low, rhythmic, guttural tones of words she couldn't understand resonated in her chest. Even without understanding the words, she felt revulsion at them, as if they made the air reek.

231

Jedidiah gripped her upper arm, dragging her to a halt. He put his mouth close to her ear. "Margaret, please," he whispered, "let's go back now, before it's too late. I'm afraid."

"Jedidiah!" she growled as she reached up and snatched him by the collar. "This is important! I'm a Sister of the Light. You're a wizard. What do you think I've been training you for? To stand on a street down in the market and perform tricks? To have people throw coins at you? We serve the Creator. He has given us everything we have so we may use it to help others. Others are in danger. We must help. You're a wizard. Act like one!"

She could just see his wide eyes in the faint light. He sagged slightly as the tension went out of his muscles. "I'm sorry. You're right. Forgive me. I will do what I must, I promise."

Her anger cooled. "I'm afraid, too. Touch your Han, keep a firm grip on it, but not too tight. Hold it so you can release it in an instant, as I've taught you. If anything happens, don't hold back. Don't be afraid of how much you might hurt them. If you do need your power, anything less than all of it will not be enough. If you keep your head, you're strong enough to defend yourself. You can do it, Jedidiah. Have faith in what I've taught you, what all the Sisters have taught you. Have faith in the Creator, in what He has given you. You have it for a reason, we all do. This may be the reason. Tonight may be what you've been called for."

He nodded again and she turned back to the glowing footprints, following them into the thick forest. They wandered through the trees toward the center of the bowl, toward where the chanting was coming from. The closer they got, the more the voices made her skin prickle. The voices were Sisters'. She thought she recognized some of them.

*Dear Creator*, she prayed, *give me the strength to do what I must to help you. Give Jedidiah strength, too. Help us serve you, to help others.*

Little flickers of light came through the leaves. They crept closer. The trees around her were huge. The two of them glided from one trunk to another, no longer following the footprints. They could see glimpses now of something through openings in the underbrush. Slowly, they tiptoed forward across the open forest floor beneath large, spreading spruce trees. The needles were soft and quiet to walk on. Shoulder to shoulder, they slid behind low, heavy brush at the edge of woods. It was as close as they could go. Beyond lay a flat, round, open area.

At least a hundred candles were set on the ground in a ring, like a fence, or boundary, as if holding back the dark forest. Inside the candles was a circle drawn on the ground. It looked to be made of white sand that sparkled with little points of prismatic light. It looked like the descriptions of sorcerer's sand she had heard, although she had never actually seen any. It stood out clearly in the candlelight, and the light of the moon overhead.

Symbols were drawn with the same white sand. They were inside the circle, points of them touching the outer boundary of the circle at irregular intervals. Margaret had never seen the symbols before, but she knew some of the elements of them from an old book. They spoke to the underworld.

About halfway in from the outer white line and candles, eleven sisters sat in a circle. Margaret stared harder, trying to see in the dim, flickering light. It looked as if each had a hood over her head, with holes cut for the eyes. They chanted in unison. Shadows from the Sisters extended inward to a point in the center.

In the center lay a woman, naked, except for a hood like the others. She lay on her back, her hands crossed over her breasts, her legs pressed together.

Twelve. With the one in the center, that made twelve. She searched the circle of Sisters again. Even with the candles, it was still dark, and the candles were to the Sisters' backs.

Her eyes stopped on a form on the opposite side of the circle. Her breath caught in her throat. That form was larger than the rest. It was hunched, its head lowered, and without a hood. It sat at a convergence of lines in the symbols.

It was not a Sister. With a start, she saw the faint orange glow. The statue with the quillion was resting in its lap.

She and Jedidiah crouched, frozen, watching the circle of Sisters as they chanted. After a time, one of them, to the side of the hunched form, stood. The chanting stopped. She spoke short, sharp words in a language Margaret didn't know. At points in the speech, her hand shot into the air, flinging sparkling dust over the naked woman in the center. The dust ignited, bathing the hooded Sisters with brief, harsh light. At the flash, they all answered with odd, rhyming words. She and Jedidiah exchanged looks, her own confused, frightened feelings reflected in his eyes.

The standing Sister flung both hands up, calling out a list of strange words. She went to the naked woman, stood at her head, and threw up her arms again. The sparkling dust caught fire once more. This time, the orange glow from the quillion brightened.

The head of the hunched form slowly rose. Margaret made a silent gasp when she saw the face of the beast. Its fanged mouth opened with a low growl. The Sister drew a delicately wrought silver scepter from her cloak, and gave it sharp shakes as she chanted again, sprinkling water over the prone woman.

Something was happening to the quillion. It brightened, and then dimmed. The dark eyes of the beast watched the naked woman. Margaret stared, wide-eyed. Her heart pounded so hard it felt as if it would tear a hole in her chest.

As the quillion faded, the beast's eyes began to glow orange—the same color orange as the quillion. As the quillion dimmed, the glow in the beast's eyes intensified, until the little statue was dark, and the thing's eyes shined bright.

Two more Sisters stood. They moved to each side of the first.

The first knelt. Her hooded head lowered, looking down to the naked woman. "It is time, if you are sure. You know what must be done; the same as has been done to us. You are the last to be offered the gift. Do you wish to accept it?"

"Yes! I'm entitled. It's mine. I want it."

Margaret thought she knew both voices, but she wasn't sure because the hoods muffled their words.

"Then it shall be yours, Sister." The other two knelt beside her as she pulled a cloth from her cloak, twisting it between her fists. "You must pass this test of pain to gain the gift. We cannot touch you with our magic while it is being done, but we will help you as best we can."

"I will do anything. It's mine. Let it be done."

The naked woman spread her arms. The sisters to each side leaned with all their weight on her wrists.

The Sister at her head held the twisted cloth over the hooded face. "Open your mouth, and bite down on this." She put the cloth between the woman's teeth. "Now, open your legs. You must keep them open. If you try to close them, it will be a rejection of what you are being offered, and you will lose the chance. Forever."

233

The naked woman stared fixedly up at nothing. She panted with fear, her breast heaving. Slowly, she spread her legs.

The beast stirred, giving a low grunt.

Margaret gripped Jedidiah's forearm, her fingers digging into him.

The beast sniffed the air. As it slowly unfolded itself, Margaret saw that it was larger than it had looked when it was all hunched over. It was powerfully built, looking mostly like a man. Flickers of candlelight reflected off sweat-slicked, knotted muscles of its arms and chest. Downy hair started at the narrow hips, growing coarser farther down the legs, to the ankles, where it was the longest, thickest. But the head was something other than a man. It was a horror of anger and fangs.

A long, thin tongue flicked out, tasting the air. The eyes glowed orange in the dim light, orange with the power of the gift it had absorbed from the quillion.

As it stretched out on its hands and knees toward the naked woman, Margaret almost gasped aloud; she recognized the beast. She had seen a drawing of it in an old book. The same book in which she had seen drawings of some parts of the spells before her. She wanted to scream.

It was a namble. One of the Nameless One's minions.

*Oh, dear Creator*, she prayed fervently, *please protect us*.

Growling in a low rumble, its powerful muscles flexing, its haunted eyes glowing orange, the namble edged like a huge cat toward the woman on the ground. Head low, it crawled between her legs. In a state of ragged fear, the woman still stared up at nothing.

The namble sniffed at her crotch. Its long tongue flicked out, running over her. She flinched, making a small jerk of a sound against the cloth in her teeth, but she kept her legs open. Her eyes did not move. She did not look at the namble. The Sisters in the circle began a soft chant. The namble licked her again, slower, grunting this time as it did so. She squealed against the rag. Beads of sweat shimmered on her flesh. She kept her legs wide apart.

Rising up on its knees, the beast gave a throaty roar to the black sky. Its pointed, barbed, erect phallus stood out, plainly silhouetted against the candles beyond. Muscles bulged in knotted cords along its arms and shoulders as the namble bent forward, putting a fist to each side of the woman. Its tongue licked out around her throat as it gave a vibrating rumble of a growl, and then it lowered itself, covering her with its massive form.

Its hips hunched forward. The woman's eyes winced shut as she screamed against the cloth in her teeth. The namble gave a quick, powerful thrust and her eyes snapped open in a panic of pain. Even with the cloth clenched in her teeth, her screams could be heard over the chanting each time the beast knocked the wind from her, adding more force to the shrieks.

Margaret had to force herself to take a breath as she watched. She hated these women; they had given themselves over to something unspeakably evil. Still, they were her Sisters, and she could hardly bear to watch one being hurt. She realized she was shaking. She clenched the gold flower at her neck in one fist and Jedidiah's arm with her other as tears streamed down her face.

The beast thrashed at the Sister on the ground as the three Sisters held her. Her muffled screams of torment ripped at Margaret's heart.

The Sister holding the cloth finally spoke. "If you want the gift, you must encourage him to give it to you. He will not surrender it unless you overcome his control—unless you take it from him. You must win it from him. Do you understand?"

Crying, her eyes shut tight, the woman nodded.

The Sister pulled the cloth away. "Then he is yours now. Take the gift, if you will."

The other two released her arms and the three of them returned to their places in the circle, taking up the chanting with the others. The woman let out a wail that turned Margaret's blood to ice. It made her ears hurt.

The woman flung her arms and legs around the namble, clutching herself to it, moving with it, moving with the chanting. Her screams died away as she panted with the effort.

Margaret could watch no longer. She closed her eyes and swallowed back a wail of her own that tried to force itself from her throat. But even with her eyes closed, it was no better. She could still hear it. *Please, dear Creator*, she begged in her mind, *let it end. Please let it end.*

And then, with a husky grunt, it did. Margaret opened her eyes to see the namble still, its back hunched. It shuddered, and then slowly went limp. The woman struggled to breathe under its weight.

With strength that seemed impossible, she at last pushed the namble off her. Chest heaving, it rolled to its hands and knees and slunk back to its place in the circle, folding itself into a dark bundle. The chanting had stopped. The woman lay on the ground for a time, panting, recovering. She was covered with a glistening sheen of sweat that reflected the yellow light of the candle flames.

Taking one last, deep breath, the woman came smoothly to her feet. A dark stain of blood ran down her legs. With a calm awareness that sent a chill up Margaret's spine and caught her breath short, the woman turned to face her, pulling off her hood.

The menacing orange glow in her eyes faded, and they returned to the pale blue with dark violet flecks that Margaret knew so well.

"Sister Margaret." Her tone was as mocking as the smile on her thin lips. "Did you enjoy watching? I thought you might."

Wide-eyed, Margaret rose slowly to her feet. Across the circle, the Sister who had held the cloth also rose, and pulled off her hood. "Margaret dear, how nice of you to show such interest in our little group. I didn't know you were that stupid. Did you think I let you see the quillion in my office by accident? That I wasn't aware someone was interested? I had to know who was skulking about, looking into things that were none of their concern. I let you see it. I wasn't sure though, until you followed us." Her smile froze Margaret's breathing. "Think we are fools? I saw the pool of Han you cast for us to step in. I obliged you. Such a shame. For you."

Margaret's hand was clutched tightly around the gold flower at her neck, her fingernails digging into her palm. How could they have seen the pool of her Han? She had underestimated them, that was how. Underestimated what they could do with the gift. It was going to cost her her life.

But only her. Only her. Please, dear Creator, only her. She could sense Jedidiah close at her side.

"Jedidiah," she whispered, "run. I'll try to hold them off while you escape. Run, my love. Run for your life."

His powerful hand came up and gripped her upper arm. "I don't think so, 'my

235

love.' " Her eyes were captured by his cruelly empty expression. "I tried to save you, Margaret. I tried to get you to turn back. But you wouldn't listen." He glanced to the Sister across the clearing. "If I got her oath, couldn't we just . . ." The Sister glared back. He sighed. "No, I suppose we couldn't."

He gave her a strong shove into the clearing. She came to a stumbling stop at the edge of the candles. She had gone numb. Her mind refused to work. Her voice refused to work.

The Sister across the circle clasped her hands together, looking to Jedidiah. "Has she told anyone else?"

"No. Just me. She was looking for proof before she went to anyone else for help." His eyes returned to her. "Isn't that right, my love?" He shook his head again, the smirk of a smile touching his lips. Lips she had kissed. She felt sick. She felt like the biggest fool the Creator had ever seen. "Such a shame."

"You have done well, Jedidiah. You will be rewarded. And as for you, Margaret . . . well, tomorrow Jedidiah will report that after trying to avoid the insistent affections of an older woman, he finally and firmly rejected you for good, and you ran away in shame and humiliation. If they come here and find your bones, it will confirm their fears that you chose to end your life because you felt unworthy to live any longer as a Sister of the Light."

The dark-flecked eyes glided back to Margaret. "Let me have her. Let me test my new gift. Let me taste it."

Those eyes kept Margaret frozen, her hand still clutching the gold flower at her neck. She could hardly breathe through the numbing agony of knowing Jedidiah had betrayed her.

She had prayed to the Creator to give Jedidiah strength, strength to help others. She had had no idea who those others would be. The Creator had answered her prayers, foolish as they had been.

When the Sister consented, the thin lips widened in a greedy grin. Margaret felt naked, helpless, in the penetrating gaze of those flecked eyes.

At last, Margaret made her mind work. Her thoughts sprang to a terrified groping for a way of escape. She could only think of one thing to do, before it was too late. With panicked abandon, she let her Han explode through every fiber of herself, and brought forth a shield; the most powerful shield she knew—a shield of air. She made it hard as steel. Impenetrable. She poured her hurt and hate into it.

The thin smile never left. The flecked eyes didn't move. "Air, is it then? With the gift, I can see it now. Shall I show you what I can do with air? What the gift can do with it?"

"The Creator's power will protect me," Margaret managed.

The thin smile turned to a sneer. "You think so? Let me show you the Creator's impotence."

Her hand came up. Margaret expected a ball of Wizard's Fire. It wasn't; it was a ball of air so dense she could see it, see it coming. It was so dense it distorted what was seen through it. Margaret could hear the whoosh of its approach, the wail of its power. It went through her shield like flaming pitch through paper.

It shouldn't have been able to do that; her shield was air. Air should not have been able to break a shield of air, not a shield as strong as she had made. But this was air made not by a mere Sister, but one with the gift. A wizard's gift.

Confused, Margaret realized she was lying on the ground, looking up at the stars, pretty stars: the Creator's stars. She couldn't draw a breath. Simply couldn't.

She thought it odd; she didn't remember the air hitting her. Only her breath being ripped violently from her lungs. She felt cold, but there was something warm against her face. Warm and wet. It was a comfort.

Her legs didn't seem to work. Try as she might, she couldn't make them move. With the greatest of effort, she managed to lift her head a bit. The Sisters hadn't moved, but now somehow, they were farther away. They all watched her. Margaret looked down at herself.

Something was terribly wrong.

Below her ribs, there was mostly nothing there. Just the shredded, wet remains of her insides, and then nothing. Where the rest of her should have been, there was nothing. Where had her legs gone? They must be somewhere. They had to be somewhere.

There they were. They lay a little distance away, where she had been standing.

So. That was why she couldn't take a breath. Air shouldn't have been able to do that. It was impossible. At least air wielded by a Sister shouldn't have been able to do that. It was a wonder.

*Dear Creator, why have you not helped me? I was doing your work. Why have you let this be done?*

It should hurt, shouldn't it? Shouldn't it hurt to be ripped in half? But it didn't. It didn't hurt the least little bit.

Cold. She felt only cold. But the warm rope of her guts lying against her face felt good. Warm. She took comfort in the warmth.

Maybe it didn't hurt because the Creator was helping her. That must be it. The Creator had taken her pain. *Dear Creator, thank you. I did my best. I am sorry I failed you. Send another.*

Boots were near: Jedidiah. Husband Jedidiah; monster Jedidiah.

"I tried to warn you, Margaret. I tried to keep you away. You can't say I didn't try."

Her arms lay sprawled out to her sides. In her right hand she could feel the little gold flower. She hadn't let go of it. Even as she was torn in half, she never let go. She tried to now, but she couldn't make her hand open. She wished she had the strength to open her hand. She didn't want to die with that in her hand. But she just couldn't open her fingers.

*Dear Creator, I have failed in this, too.*

Since she couldn't release it, she did the only other thing she could think of. She sent the rest of her power into it. Maybe someone would see, and ask the right question.

Tired. She was so very tired.

She tried to close her eyes, but they wouldn't close. How could a person die, if they couldn't close their eyes?

There were a lot of stars. Pretty stars. There seemed to be fewer than she remembered. Hardly any at all. She thought her mother had told her once how many there were. But she couldn't remember.

Well, she would just have to count them.

One . . . two . . .

How long?" Chase asked.

The seven fierce-looking men that were squatted down in a half circle before her and Chase just stared at him and blinked. None of the seven had any weapons except belt knives, and one didn't even have that. But there were a lot of other men standing behind them, and they all had bows or spears, or both.

Rachel tugged her thick, brown, woolen cloak tighter around herself and shifted her weight as she squatted, wiggling her toes, wishing her feet weren't so cold. They were starting to tingle. She stroked her fingers over the big, amber stone hanging on the chain from her neck. Its smooth teardrop shape felt warm against her fingers.

Chase mumbled something Rachel couldn't understand as he pushed his heavy black cloak back over his shoulders and then pointed with a stick at the two people drawn in the dirt. All the leather belts for his weapons creaked as he leaned forward on boots big enough for any of the other men to fit both of their feet into just one. He tapped his stick on the ground again, then turned and pushed his hand out toward the grassland.

"How long?" He pointed at the drawing and pushed his hand out a few more times. "How long since they left?"

They chattered something Chase and she couldn't understand, and then the man with long silver hair falling down around his sun brown face, the one who didn't have a coyote hide around his shoulders but wore only simple buckskin clothes, drew another picture in the dirt. She could tell what it was easy this time. It was the sun. He made marks under it. Chase watched as the man drew three rows of marks under the picture of the sun. He stopped.

Chase stared at the picture. "Three weeks." He looked up at the man with the long hair. "Three weeks?" He pointed at the sun on the ground and held up most of his fingers three times. "They've been gone three weeks?"

The man nodded and made some more of those funny words.

Siddin handed her another piece of flat bread with honey. It tasted wonderful. She tried to eat it slowly, but it was gone before she knew it. She had tasted honey only once before, back at the castle when she lived there as the Princess's playmate. The Princess never let her have honey, said it wasn't for the likes of her, but one of the cooks had given her some once.

Her stomach fluttered at the memory of how mean the Princess had been to her. She never wanted to live in a castle again. Now that she was Chase's daughter, she would never have to. Every night she lay in her blankets, before she went to sleep, and wondered what the rest of her new family was like.

Chase said she would have sisters and brothers. And a real mother. He said she would have to mind her new mother. She could do that. It was easy to mind when someone loved you.

Chase loved her. He never really said it, but it was easy to tell. He put his huge arm around her, and stroked her hair, when she was afraid of sounds in the dark.

Siddin smiled at her as he licked the honey off his fingers. It was nice to see him again. When they had first come here she thought there was going to be trouble. Scary men, all painted with mud, and with grass stuck all over themselves, came up to them when they were still out on the grassland. She didn't even see where they came from. They were just there all of a sudden.

Rachel was afraid at first, because the men pointed arrows at them, and their voices sounded scary and she couldn't understand what they said, but Chase just got off the horse and held her in his arms while he watched them. He didn't even draw his sword or anything. She didn't think anything scared him. He was the bravest man she ever saw. The men had looked at her as she stared at them, and Chase stroked her hair and told her not to be afraid. The men stopped pointing the arrows at them, and led them to the village.

When they got here, she saw Siddin. Siddin knew her and Chase, from before when Kahlan had saved him from Queen Milena back in the castle. Zedd, Kahlan, Chase, Siddin, and she had all been together when they were running with the box. She couldn't speak Siddin's language, but he knew them, and told his father who they were. After that, everyone was real nice to them.

Chase pointed with one finger to one of the pictures of a person, the finger of his other hand to the other picture, and then held the fingers together and pointed away, moving his hands like they were going over hills. "Richard and Kahlan left three weeks ago, and they went north? To Aydindril?"

The men all shook their heads and started jabbering again. Siddin's father held up his hand for quiet. He pointed at himself and the other men and held up three fingers, then he pointed at the picture on the ground that had a dress and said Kahlan's name, and then he pointed north.

Chase pointed at the picture of the sun, then the picture of Kahlan, then at the men, holding up three fingers, then north. "Three weeks ago, Kahlan and three of your men went north, to Aydindril?"

The men all nodded and said "Kahlan" and "Aydindril."

Chase put a knee to the ground as he leaned forward, tapping the picture of the other person. "But Richard went, too." He pointed north again. "Richard went to Aydindril too. With Kahlan."

The men all turned to the man with the long silver hair. He looked at Chase and then shook his head. The carved piece of bone hanging from a leather thong around his neck swung back and forth. He pointed down at the picture of the man with a sword, and then pointed in a different direction.

Chase stared at the man for a long minute; then he frowned, as if he didn't understand. The man leaned over with the stick and drew three more people, each with a dress. He looked up from under his eyebrows as if he wanted to make sure Chase was watching, and then he drew an X across two of the figures. His eyes returned to Chase again as he folded his arms over his knees, waiting.

"What does that mean? Dead? Is that what you mean, they are dead?" The men stared, not moving. Chase pulled a single finger, like a knife, across his throat. "Dead?"

The man with the silver hair gave one nod and said "dead," but it sounded a little funny, the way he made the word seem longer than it should. He pointed with his stick to the picture of the sun, then the picture of Kahlan, and then he pointed over his shoulder to the way they went. He pointed to the sun again, then at the picture of Richard, then at the picture of the woman without the X, then he pointed in a different direction.

Chase stood. His chest rose and then fell as he let out the deep breath. He was awfully tall. He stared in the direction the man with the silver hair said Richard had gone. "East. That's deeper into the wilds," he whispered to himself. "Why isn't he with Kahlan?" He rubbed his chin. Rachel thought he looked worried. It couldn't be that he looked scared. Nothing scared Chase. "Dear spirits, why would Richard go deeper into the wilds? What could possess Kahlan to let that boy go into the wilds? And who is he with?" The men all glanced at each other, as if they were wondering why Chase was talking to the air.

Chase squatted back down, all his leather creaking, and pointed at the drawing of the third woman and frowned and shrugged at the men. He pointed at the picture of Richard and the woman and pointed east again. He held the palms of his hands up near his shoulders as he shrugged and made faces to show he didn't understand.

The man with the long silver hair gave Chase a sad look as he let out a long breath. He pointed at the third woman, the one without an X, and then he turned and took a rope from a man behind him. He wrapped the rope around his own neck. He looked to Chase's frown and then he pointed to the picture of Richard. When Chase looked up and their eyes met, the man pulled the rope tight with a snap. He pointed east. He touched the stick to the picture of Kahlan and then pulled his fingers down his cheeks, from the corners of his eye, like tears, then pointed north.

Chase stood. It was almost a jump. His face was pale. "She took him," he whispered. "This woman captured Richard, and took him into the wilds."

Rachel stood next to him. "What does it mean, Chase? Why didn't Kahlan go with him?"

He looked down at her. His face had an odd, still look that made her stomach knot up. "She went for help. She went to Aydindril. To get Zedd."

No one made a sound. He stared back out to the east as he hooked a thumb behind his big silver belt buckle.

"Dear spirits," he whispered to himself, "if Richard really did go into the wilds, turn him north. Don't let him go to the south, or even Zedd won't be able to help him."

Rachel hugged her doll tight. "What's the wilds?"

"A very bad place, little one." He stared out unblinking toward the darkening sky. "A very bad place."

The way he said it, all calm and quiet, gave her goose bumps.

Zedd could feel the muscles in the horse's back flexing under him as he ducked beneath a branch while slowing the animal. Zedd favored riding bareback. If he needed to ride a horse, he preferred to let the animal feel as unencumbered as possible. He thought it only fair. Most seemed to appreciate his consideration, this one especially. She gave him more than she ever would have under a saddle, and he had taken everything she had given.

He had proffered his saddle and the rest of the tack to a man named Haff. Haff had the biggest ears Zedd had ever seen. How a man with ears the like of those had ever found a wife was a wonder. But have a wife he did, and four children, too, and he looked to have more need of the tack than Zedd. Not to ride, of course, but to sell. His crops and stores had been carried off by soldiers of the D'Haran army.

It was the least Zedd could do. After all, Rachel was soaked to the bone, and Haff offered them a dry place to sleep, even if it was in a dilapidated little barn, and his wife offered them a cabbage soup, thin as it was, asking nothing in return. It was worth a saddle just to see the look on Chase's face when Zedd said he wasn't hungry.

The big man ate enough for three men, though, and he should have known better. There was going to be much hunger this winter. The tack wouldn't bring its worth, not with hunger spreading like a dark wind before a thunderhead, but it would bring something, maybe enough to take the hardest edge off the winter.

Zedd saw Chase put a coin in each of the four children's pockets, when he thought no one was looking, growling at them in a tone that would make a grown man blanch, but which for some odd reason made children only smile, not to look in the pocket until he was gone. He hoped it wasn't gold. The boundary warden could smell a thief open a window in the next town and probably tell you his name, too, but he had no wits about him around children.

Haff suspiciously wanted to know what he was to do in return for the tack. Zedd told him he was to swear his undying loyalty to the Mother Confessor, and the new Lord Rahl of D'Hara, both of whom had put a stop to things the like of which had been done to him. The man had stared at him, his big ears sticking out under that ridiculous knit hat with a tassel on each side that only served to draw attention where it wasn't needed, and had said, "Done," with a firm nod.

A small start: one loyal, for the price of a saddle. That it would all be so easy. But that was weeks ago. Now, he was alone.

The sweet smell of a birch fire drifted to him through the thick woods, the horse lifting her nose to it as she stepped carefully along the narrow path. In the still air, gathering darkness sent deepening shadows across the way. Even before the small house came into view, he could hear the racket: the sound of furniture being overturned, the crash of pots and pans, and demons being cursed. The horse's ears pricked toward the commotion as they rode down the twisting trail. Zedd gave her a reassuring pat on the neck.

The little house, wood walls dark with age, and a roof thickly layered with ferns and dry pine needles, was set back into the towering trees, nestled among rough trunks dark in the day's end. He dismounted to the side of the brown, dead ferns spreading like a garden in front of the house. The horse rolled her eyes toward him as he came around to give her a scratch under her jaw.

"Be a good girl and find yourself something to eat." He put a finger under the horse's chin, forcing her head up. "But stay close?" The horse nickered. With a smile, Zedd rubbed her gray nose. "Good girl."

From inside the house came a low growl interspersed with angry clicks. Something heavy thudded to the floor, accompanied by a thick oath in a foreign tongue.

"Come out from under there, you vile beast!"

Zedd grinned at the sound of the familiar, raspy voice. He watched the horse stroll off a ways to graze on tufts of dry grass, lifting her head, while she chewed, to look back toward the house at each sharp thump.

Zedd sauntered up the curving walk toward the house. He paused, turning full around twice to admire the beauty of the surrounding woods. They truly were a wonder, calm and peaceful in a place that had been a pass through one of the most dangerous spots in the world: the boundary. But the boundary was gone now. Yet, the woods were a serene refuge, imbued with an almost palpable tranquillity that Zedd knew wasn't natural. They had been infused with those qualities at the skilled hands of the woman who at that very moment was throwing curses bold enough to make a battle-hardened Sandarian lancer blush.

And he had seen one of those curse his own queen into a dead faint. That, of course, had only earned the man the rope. The fellow had had a few things to say to the hangman, too, which in turn didn't bring him a clean drop, but did offer him the opportunity to get off one last eloquent, if vulgar, oath. The other lancers seemed to think the trade worth the price.

For her part, the queen never seemed to fully recover her delicate air, and thereafter always flushed a fabulous red at the mere sight of one of her lancers, needing to be fanned furiously by her attendants in order to remain conscious. She would probably have had them all hanged had they not saved her throne, to say nothing of her dainty neck, on more than one occasion. But that was a long time ago, in another war.

Clasping his hands together behind himself, Zedd inhaled deeply, relishing the clean, crisp air. Bending over, he plucked a dry, wilted wild rose, and with a wisp of magic brought it to fresh bloom. The yellow petals spread and swelled with new vitality. Closing his eyes, he took a deep whiff of the flower and then idly stuck it in his robes, over his breast. He was in no hurry.

It was not wise to interrupt a sorceress in a snit.

Through the open door came a more serious curse as the object of the sorceress's ire was at last brought to account. With a whack from the blunt end of an axe, the thing was sent flying through the doorway. The small, armored beast landed on its back at Zedd's feet. Wobbling, it clicked and growled as it raked the air with its claws, trying to right itself. It appeared no worse for the axe, or for its brief flight and rough landing.

Filthy gripper. It was a gripper that had attached itself to Adie's ankle before. Once a gripper had you, there was virtually no way to get it off. It held on with those claws and rasped its teeth into you, down to bone, sucking your blood with its puckered, fang-ringed mouth. They never let go as long as there was blood to feed on, and that armor shed any counterattack.

Adie had used an axe to chop off her foot where the gripper had been attached, chopped off her own foot to save her life. Thinking about it turned his stomach. He watched the beast at his feet for a moment, then gave it a casual kick, sending it a goodly distance. Landing right side up, it waddled off into the woods in search of easier prey.

Zedd looked up at the figure standing in the doorway, scowling at him with her completely white eyes, her breast still heaving. She wore robes the same light burlap color as his, but unlike his, hers were decorated at the neck with yellow and red beads sewn in the ancient symbols of her profession. She put her fists on her hips. The scowl held a firm grip on her features, not that it diminished in the least how handsome they were.

She still held the axe in one hand, though, a worrisome sign. Best not to trouble her too quickly with what he wanted.

Zedd smiled. "You really shouldn't play with grippers, Adie. That's how you lost your foot the last time, you know." He plucked the yellow rose from its place at his chest. His thin lips pushed his wrinkled cheeks back farther as his smile widened. "Got anything to eat? I'm starving."

She watched him silently for a moment without moving, then slipped the axe head to the floor and leaned the handle against the wall just inside the door. "What do you be doing here, wizard?"

Zedd stepped onto the tiny porch and gave a dramatic bow. When he came up, he offered her the flower as if it were a priceless jewel. "I just couldn't stay away from your tender embrace, dear lady." He flashed his most irresistible smile.

Adie studied him a moment with those white eyes. "That be a lie."

Zedd cleared his throat and pressed the flower closer. He thought maybe he needed to practice his smile. "Is that stew I smell?"

Without taking her gaze from him, she accepted the flower, sticking it in her straight, jaw-length black and gray hair. She truly was handsome. "It be stew."

Her soft, thin hands took his. A small smile stole onto her finely wrinkled face, and she gave a slight nod. "It be good to see you again, Zedd. For a time, I feared I never would. I spent many a night in a sweat, knowing what would happen had you failed. When winter came and the Magic of Orden didn't sweep the land, I knew you had succeeded."

Zedd was encouraged that his best smile hadn't been wasted after all, but he was careful with his answer. "Darken Rahl has been defeated."

"What of Richard and Kahlan? Do they be safe?"

Zedd puffed up with pride. "Yes. In fact, Richard was the one who defeated Darken Rahl."

She nodded again. "I think there be more to the story."

He shrugged, trying to make it seem less important than it was. "A bit of a tale."

Though the small smile still rested easily on her face, her white eyes seemed to be weighing his soul. "And there be a reason you be here. A reason I fear I won't like."

He pulled his hands out of hers and pushed some of his unruly, wavy white hair back while frowning. "Bags, woman, are you going to feed me any of that stew or not?"

Adie finally withdrew her white eyes from him and turned back into her home. "I think there be enough stew, even for you. Come in and shut the door. I do not wish to see another gripper tonight."

Invited in. Well, things were going smoothly. He wondered how much he was going to have to tell her. Not all, he hoped. Wizard's work: using people. The worst of it was using people he liked. Especially people he liked deeply.

As Zedd helped her right the chairs and table, and pick up the pots and tin plates strewn about the floor, he began telling her of the things that had happened since he had been with her last. He started with the harrowing tale of going through the pass, protected, somewhat, by the bone she had given him to hide him from the beasts. He still had the bone on a thin leather thong around his neck, seeing no need to be rid of it after he had gotten safely through.

She listened without comment as he wove the tale, and when he told of Richard's capture by the Mord-Sith, she didn't turn to show her face, but he saw the muscles

243

in her shoulders tense for the briefest of moments. With no small amount of emphasis to make his point, he related how Darken Rahl had taken the night stone from Richard, the night stone she had given him to see him safely through the pass.

He scowled at her back as she picked a plate off the floor. "I was nearly killed by that stone. Darken Rahl used it to trap me in the underworld. I escaped by the thinnest of hairs. You almost got me killed, giving that thing to Richard."

"Do not be a thickheaded fool," she scoffed. "You be smart enough to save yourself. Had I not given the night stone to Richard, he would have died in the pass, and then Darken Rahl would have won, and right now would no doubt be torturing you. You would soon be dead. By giving the stone to Richard, I saved your life."

He shook a leg bone of some sort at the glance she cast over her shoulder. "That thing was dangerous. You shouldn't go handing out dangerous things as if they were a stick of candy. Not without warning people, anyway." He had a right to be indignant. He had been the one sucked into the underworld by that wretched stone. The woman could at least pretend to be contrite.

Zedd went on with the story of how Richard had escaped, although he had a web around him hiding his identity, and how the quads had attacked Chase, Kahlan, and himself. He had to make an effort to control his voice at the telling of what had almost happened to Kahlan, and how she had called forth the Con Dar and killed their attackers. He finished with how Richard had tricked Darken Rahl into opening the wrong box. He told her how the Magic of Orden had taken Darken Rahl for his mistake. Zedd smiled to himself as he reached the end of his story, telling her that Richard had somehow gotten past Kahlan's power, that they were free to love each other—he wasn't about to tell her how, that was not for anyone to know—and they were happily together now.

He was pleased that he had managed to tell the story without having to delve too deeply into some of the more painful events. He didn't want to have to revisit some of those hurts. She didn't ask any questions, but came and put a hand on his shoulder, saying that she was relieved all of them had survived, and won.

Zedd was silent after the telling, at least as much as he wanted to tell, of the tale. He set to stacking the pile of loose bones into the corner where she said they belonged. By the way they were scattered about, the gripper must have sought refuge in them. A sorry mistake.

That people called Adie the bone woman was small wonder; the house had little else in it. Her life seemed devoted to bones. A sorceress dedicated to bones was a troubling concept. He saw little evidence of potions, powders, or the usual type of charms, any of the typical things he knew to expect from a woman of her talents. He knew *what* she was probing into, just not *why*.

Sorceresses usually confined their concerns to things living. She was a searcher into things dark and dangerous. Things dead. Unfortunately, that was what he was doing, too. If you wanted to know about fire, you had to study it, he guessed. Of course, it was a good way to get burned. He knew he didn't like the analogy the moment it popped into his head.

He looked up from the bone pile as he placed the last of them. "If you don't want grippers in your house, Adie, you should keep your door closed."

His perfectly apt, scolding frown was wasted, as she didn't turn from her task of stacking the firewood back in its bin at the side of the hearth. "The door be closed. And bolted," she said in her dry rasp, in a tone seemingly meant to wither his unseen scowl. "This be the third time."

Picking up a bone that had been hiding behind a stick of firewood, she straightened and carried it to him. "Before, the grippers never came near my house." Her voice lowered as if in a threat to unseen ears. "I saw to that." She handed over the thick, white rib bone, peering down at him as he squatted on the floor next to the bone pile. "Now, since winter, they come near. The bones no longer seem to keep them away. The reason be a mystery to me."

Adie had lived in this pass a long time. No one knew as well as she its dangers, its quirks, its vagaries. None knew better than she what it took to be safe here, to live on the cusp between the world of the living and the world of the dead, at the edge of the underworld. Of course, the boundary was gone now. It should be safe here now.

He wondered what else was going on that she wasn't telling him; sorceresses never told all they knew. What was she doing still living here with strange, and dangerous, things happening? Stubborn women, sorceresses, the lot of them.

Adie limped slightly as she walked across the room lit only by the fire. "Light the lamp?"

Following behind, Zedd swept a hand in the direction of the table. The lamp lit itself, adding a soft glow to that of the fire in the large hearth made of smooth river stones, and helped illuminate the dark walls of the room. Every wall held white bones. Shelves lined one wall, and were stuffed to overflowing with the skulls of dangerous beasts. Many of the bones had been made into ceremonial objects, some had been made into necklaces, decorated with feathers and beads, and some had been inscribed with ancient symbols. Some had spells drawn on the wall around them. It was the oddest collection he had even seen.

Zedd pointed a bony finger down at her foot. "Why are you limping?"

Adie gave him a sidelong glance as she stopped and lifted a spoon from a hook set into the mortar at the side of the fireplace. "The new foot you grew me be too short."

Zedd stood with one hand on a knobby hip, and the sticklike fingers of the other holding his smooth chin as he looked down at her foot. He hadn't noticed it wasn't long enough when he had grown it back; he had needed to leave soon after it was done. "Maybe I could grow the ankle a little longer," he wondered aloud. He took his hand from his chin and flourished it in the air. "Make them even."

Adie glared over her shoulder as she stirred the stew. "No, thank you."

Zedd arched an eyebrow. "Wouldn't you appreciate having them both even?"

"I appreciate you growing my foot back for me. Life be easier with two of them. I did not realize how much I hated that crutch. But the foot be fine the way it is." She lifted the long-handled spoon to her lips, blowing on the hot stew.

"It would be easier if they were even."

"I said no." She tasted the stew.

"Bags, woman, why not?"

Adie tapped the spoon clean on the edge of the iron kettle and hung it back on its hook, then lifted a dented tin from the side of the mantel, unscrewing the lid. Her voice was quiet, her rasp softer. "I do not wish to revisit that pain. Had I known what it would be like, I would have chosen to live the rest of my life without the foot." Reaching her hand into the tin, she took a three-finger-and-thumb pinch of five-spice and flung it into the stew.

245

Zedd tugged at his ear. Perhaps she was right. Growing the foot back for her had nearly killed her. He hadn't expected what had happened, her reaction to his using that much magic on her. Still, he had been successful, and managed to draw away the pain of the memories, though he still didn't know what they had been about. But he should have taken into account that she could have had memories that held that much pain.

He should have taken the Wizard's Second Rule into account, but he had been intent on doing something good for her. That was the way it worked with the second rule; it was usually hard to tell if you were violating it.

"You know the price of magic, Adie, almost as well as a wizard. And besides, I made it up to you. For the pain, I mean." He knew it wouldn't take as much magic to make the ankle longer as it had to grow the foot back, but after what she had suffered, he could understand her reluctance. "Perhaps you are right. Maybe I have done enough."

Her white eyes settled on him again. "Why be you here, wizard?"

He gave her an impish grin. "I wanted to see you. You are a hard woman to forget. And I wanted to tell you about Darken Rahl being defeated, by Richard. That we won." He frowned at her stare. "Why do you think the grippers are coming here?"

She shook her head with a sigh. "You talk like a drunk man walks: in every direction but where he be headed." She flicked a finger toward the table, indicating that she wanted him to get the bowls. "I already knew we won. The first day of winter has come and past. Had Rahl won, things wouldn't be so peaceful as they are. Though I be pleased to see your bones again."

Her voice lowered, became even more raspy. "Why be you here, wizard?"

He strode over to the table, glad to elude the scrutiny of those eyes for a moment. "You didn't answer my question. Why do you think the grippers are coming here?"

Her voice lowered into a deeper, harsher rasp, bordering on anger. "I think the grippers be here for the same reason you be here: to cause an old woman trouble."

Zedd grinned as he returned with bowls. "My eyes don't see an old woman. They see only a handsome woman."

She regarded his grin with a helpless shake of her head. "I fear your tongue be more dangerous than a gripper."

He handed her a bowl. "Have the grippers ever come here before?"

"No." She turned and began spooning stew into the bowl. "When the boundary be in place, the grippers stayed in the pass, with other beasts. After the boundary went down, I not see them for a time, but when winter came, so did the grippers. That not be right. I think something be wrong."

He exchanged the empty bowl for the full, holding it to his nose and inhaling the aroma. "Maybe when the boundary finally failed, there was no longer any hold over them, and they simply came out of the pass."

"Maybe. When the boundary failed, most of the beasts went with it, back into the underworld. Some were freed of their bonds and escaped into the surrounding country. I never saw any grippers until the winter came, nearly a month ago. I fear something else happened, for them to be here."

Zedd knew very well what had happened, but didn't say so. Instead, he asked, "Adie, why don't you leave? Come away with me. To Aydindril. It would be . . ."

"No!" Her mouth snapped closed. She seemed almost surprised by her own voice. She smoothed her robe with her hand, letting the anger leave her face and then took the spoon out of the hand with the bowl and returned to dishing out stew. "No. This be my home."

Zedd watched silently as she worked over the kettle. When finished, she carried her bowl to the table, set it down, and retrieved a loaf of bread from over the counter, from a shelf behind a blue-and-white-striped curtain. She pointed with the bread to the other empty chair. Zedd set his bowl on the table and sat, hiking his robes up as he folded his legs underneath himself. Adie lowered herself into the chair opposite him and sliced off a chunk of bread, using the knifepoint to push it across the table before she looked up to meet his eyes.

"Please, Zedd, do not ask me to leave my home."

"I am only worried for you, Adie."

Adie dunked a chunk of bread in her stew. "That be a lie."

He looked up from under his eyebrows as he picked up his bread. "It's not a lie."

She ate without lifting her head. " 'Only' be a lie."

Zedd went back to his stew and ate in earnest. "Umm. Thish ish womerful," he mumbled around a hot chunk of meat. She nodded her thanks. He ate until his bowl was empty, then took it to the fireplace and filled it once more.

On his way back to the table, he swept his hand around at the room, pointing with his spoon. "You have a lovely home, Adie. Quite lovely." He sat and picked up the bread she passed to him. He put his elbows on the table, his sleeves slipping up his forearms as he broke the bread in half. "But I don't think you should be living here, all alone. Not with the grippers and all." He gestured with the bread to the north. "Why don't you come with me to Aydindril? It's a lovely place, too. You would like it there. There's plenty of room. Kahlan could see to it you have your choice of places to live. Why, you could even stay at the Keep, if you preferred."

Her white eyes stayed on her meal. "No."

"Why not? We could have a good time there. A sorceress could have a grand time in the Keep. There are books and . . ."

"I said no."

He watched her as she went back to eating stew. He pushed his sleeves up farther and did the same. He couldn't eat long. He set the spoon in the bowl and looked up from under his eyebrows.

"Adie, there is more to the story, more I haven't told you."

She lifted an eyebrow. "I hope you do not expect me to look surprised. I not be good at pretending." She bent back over her bowl.

"Adie, the veil is torn."

Her hand paused with the spoon halfway to her mouth. She didn't look up. "Baa. What do you know of the veil. You do not know what you speak of." The spoon completed its journey.

"I know it's torn."

She scooped up the last piece of potato from her bowl. "You speak of things that are not possible, wizard. The veil not be torn." She stood, picking up her empty bowl. "Be at ease, old man, if the veil be torn, we would have a lot more than grippers to be worried about. But we don't."

Zedd turned, putting a hand on the back of his chair, watching her limp toward the kettle hanging from the crane in the fireplace. "The Stone of Tears is in this world," he said in a quiet voice.

Adie halted. Her bowl fell to the floor, clattering in the thick silence, and rolled away. Her hands were held out before her as if she still held it. Her back was stiff. "Do not say such a thing aloud," she whispered, "unless you be certain beyond doubt. Unless you be certain on your honor as First Wizard. Unless you be willing to offer your soul to the Keeper if you be lying."

Zedd's fierce, hazel eyes watched her back. "I pledge my soul to the Keeper if I'm telling you a lie. May he take me this instant. The Stone of Tears is in this world. I have seen it."

"Dear spirits, protect us," she whispered weakly. Still, she did not move. "Tell me what fool thing you have done, wizard."

"Adie, come and sit down. First, I want you to tell me what you are doing living here, in the pass, or what used to be the pass. What you have been doing living at the edge of the underworld, and why you won't leave."

She spun to face him, one hand gripping the skirt of her robe. "That be my business."

With his hand on the chair back, Zedd pushed himself to his feet. "Adie, I must know. This is important. I must know what you have been doing, so that I may know if it can be a help.

"I know very well the pain you live with. I saw it, remember? I don't know what caused it, but I know how deep it is. I would ask you to share the story with me. I ask you as a friend to confide in me. Please don't make me ask as First Wizard."

Her eyes rose to meet his at the last of what he said. The flash of anger faded and she nodded. "Very well. Perhaps I have kept it to myself too long. Perhaps it would be a relief to tell someone . . . a friend. Perhaps you will not want my help, after you hear. If you still do, I expect you tell me all that has happened." She thrust a finger in his direction. "All."

Zedd gave her a small smile of encouragement. "Of course."

She limped to her chair. Just as she sat down, the largest skull on the shelves suddenly thudded to the floor. Both stared at it. Zedd walked over and picked it up in both hands. His thin fingers stroked tapered, curved fangs as long as his hand. The skull was flat on the bottom; it shouldn't have been able to roll off the shelf. He replaced it solidly as Adie watched.

"It seems," she said in her rasp, "that the bones want to be on the floor lately. They keep falling down."

Zedd returned to his chair after a final frown to the skull. "Tell me about the bones, why you have them, what you do with them; everything. Start at the beginning."

"Everything." She folded her arms across her lap, briefly looking as if she wanted to run for the door. "It be a painful story to tell."

"Not a word of it will ever touch my lips, Adie."

**A**die drew a long breath. "I be born in the town of Choora, in the land of Nicobarese. My mother did not have the gift of sorcery. She be a skip, as it be called. My grandmother Lindel be the one before me to have it. My mother be grateful to the good spirits she be a skip, but bitter at them that I be gifted.

"In Nicobarese, those with the gift be loathed and distrusted. It be thought the gift be allied to the the flows of power not only from the Creator, but also from the Keeper. Even ones using the gift for good be suspected of being a baneling. You know of the banelings, yes?"

Zedd tore off a piece of bread. "Yes. Ones turned to the Keeper. Sworn to him. They hide in the light, as well as the shadows, serving his wishes, working to his ends. They can be anyone. Some work for good for years, hiding, waiting to be called. But when they are called, they do the Keeper's bidding.

"They are also called by different names, but they are all agents of the Keeper. Some books call them that: agents. Some are important people, like Darken Rahl, used for important tasks. Some are everyday people, used for dirty little deeds. Those with the gift, like Darken Rahl, are the most difficult for the Keeper to turn. Those without it are easier, but even they are rare."

Adie's eyes widened. "Darken Rahl be a baneling?"

Zedd lifted an eyebrow as he nodded. "Admitted it to me himself. He said he was an agent, but it's the same thing, whatever the word, and I've heard any number. They all serve the Keeper."

"This be dangerous news."

Zedd sopped up some stew with the piece of bread. "I bring very little of any other kind. You were saying about your grandmother Lindel?"

"In the time of Grandmother Lindel's youth, sorceresses be put to death for anything that fate brought: sickness, accidents, still births. Put to death, wrongly, for being banelings. Some of the gifted fought back at being wrongly persecuted. They fought well. It deepened the hatred, and only served to confirm the fears of many of the Nicobarese people.

"At last, there was a truce. Nicobarese leaders agreed to let the gifted women be, if they would give a soul oath, as a way of proving they not be banelings, an oath not to use their power unless permission be granted by a governing body, the king's circle of their town, for instance. It be an oath to the people. An oath not to use the gift and bring the Keeper's notice."

Zedd swallowed a mouthful of stew. "Why would people think sorceresses were banelings?"

"Because it be easier to blame a woman for their troubles than to admit the truth, and more satisfying to accuse than to curse the unknown. Those with the gift use power that can help people, but it can also be used to harm them. Because it can be used to harm, it be believed the power must be given, at least in part, by the Keeper."

"Superstitious nonsense," he growled.

"As you well know, superstition needs no grounding in truth, but once rooted, it grows a strong though twisted tree."

He grunted his assent. "So no sorceress used her power?"

Adie shook her head. "No. Unless it be for some common good, and they went before the king's circle of their town first and asked permission. Every sorceress went before the circle of their town or district and swore an oath to the people, an oath on her soul, to abide by the wishes of the people. Swore a solemn oath not to use her power on or for another unless asked to do so by the agreement of the circle."

Zedd put his spoon down in disgust. "But they had the gift. How could they not use it?"

"They used it, but only in private. Never where anyone could see, and never on another."

Zedd leaned back in his chair, shaking his head in silent wonder at the Wizard's First Rule, at the things people would believe, while Adie went on.

"Grandmother Lindel be a stern old woman who lived by herself. She never wanted anything to do with teaching me about using the gift. She told me only to let it be. And my mother, of course, could teach me nothing. So I learned on my own as I grew, as the gift grew, but I knew very well the wickedness of using it. I be lectured on that almost every day. To use the gift in a manner not permitted was made to seem like touching the taint of the Keeper himself, and I believed it so. I feared greatly going against what I be taught. I be a fruit of the tree of that superstition.

"One day, when I be eight or nine, I be in the town square with my mother and father, on market day, and across the square, a building caught fire. There be a girl, about my age, on the second floor, trapped by the flames. She screamed for help. No one could reach her because the fire be all through the first floor. Her screams of terror burned every nerve in me. I started to cry. I wanted to help. I could not stand the screams." Adie folded her hands in her lap and looked down at the table. "I made the fire to go out. The girl be saved."

Zedd watched her placid expression as she stared at the table. "I don't suppose anyone, except the girl and her parents, were happy?"

Adie shook her head. "Everyone knew I had the gift. They knew it be me who had done it. My mother stood and cried. My father just stood looking the other way. He would not look at me, at an agent of the Keeper's evil.

"Someone went for Grandmother Lindel; she was respected because of how she stood by the oath. When Grandmother Lindel came, she took me and the girl before the men of the king's circle. Grandmother Lindel switched the girl who I saved. She bawled a good long time."

Zedd was incredulous. "She beat the girl! Why?"

"For letting the Keeper use her to bring forth the use of the gift." Adie sighed. "The girl and I had known each other, had been friends, of a sort. She never spoke to me again."

Adie hugged her arms across her stomach. "And then Grandmother Lindel stripped me naked in front of those men, and switched me until I was covered with welts and blood. I screamed more than the girl had in the fire. Then she marched me, naked and bloody, through the town, to her house. The humiliation be worse than the beating.

"When we got to her house, I asked how she could be so cruel. She looked down her nose at me, looked at me with that puckered, angry face of hers, and said, 'Cruel, child? Cruel? You got not one switch more than you deserved. And not one less than what it took to keep you from being put to death by those men.'

"Then she made me give the oath. 'I swear on my hope of salvation, never to use the gift on another, for any reason, without the permission of the king or one of his circles, and upon forfeit of my soul to the Keeper, should I ever use the gift to harm another.' And then she shaved my head bald. I be kept bald until I grew to the age of a woman."

"Bald? Why?"

"Because in the Midlands, as you know, the length of a woman's hair shows her social standing. It be meant to show me, and everyone else, that there be no one lower than I. I had used the gift, publicly, without permission. It be a constant reminder of the wrong I had done.

"I lived with Grandmother Lindel from then on. I only rarely saw my mother and father. At first, I missed them greatly. Grandmother Lindel taught me how to use the gift, so I would be able to know it well, to be able to know what I was not to do.

"I did not like Grandmother Lindel much. She be a cold woman. But I respected her. She be fair, after a fashion. If she punished me, and she did, it be only because I broke her rules. She switched me, hard, but only for an infraction I be warned of. She taught me, she guided me in the gift, but she never gave me a kindness. It be a hard life, but I learned discipline.

"Most of all, I learned to use the gift. For that, I will always be thankful to her, for that be my life. The gift be touching something higher, something more noble than what I be."

"I'm sorry, Adie." He started eating his cold stew because he didn't know what else to do. He wasn't hungry anymore.

Adie rose from her chair and walked to the fireplace, staring into the flames for a time. Zedd waited silently for her to find the words.

"After I reached the age of a woman, I be allowed to let my hair grow." She smiled a small smile. "At that age, as I filled into my form, I be thought an attractive woman."

Zedd pushed the bowl of stew away and went to stand by her, putting a hand on her shoulder. "No less attractive now, dear lady."

She put a hand over his without looking from the flames. "In time, I fell in love with a young man. His name be Pell. He be an awkward young man, but a good and noble man, and he be kindness itself to me. He would have brought me the ocean, one spoonful at a time, if he thought it would please me. I thought the sun rose to show me his face, and the moon came out to let me taste his lips. Every beat of my heart be for him.

"We wanted to be wed. The king's circle of Choora, led by a man named Mathrin Galliene, had other ideas."

She took her hand away and gripped a knot of robes at her stomach. "They had decided I was to be wed to a man from the next town, the son of their mayor. I was a prize to the people of Choora. Having a sorceress bonded to a people by her oath was seen as a sign of the virtue of those people. To give me to an important man from a larger town was cause for excitement, joy, expectation. It would seal our towns in many ways, not the least of which was valuable trade.

"I be in a panic. I went to Grandmother Lindel and begged her to intercede for me. I told her of my love for Pell, and that I did not wish to be a prize in return for trade. I told her the gift was mine, and not to be used to bind me into slavery. A sorceress not be a slave. Grandmother Lindel was a sorceress. The gift in her be disdained, but people respected her because she be devoted to her oath, and they held more than a healthy respect for her: she be feared. I pleaded for her help."

"Doesn't seem like the kind of person to help you."

"There be no one else to turn to. She made me leave her for one day, so she could think on it. It be the longest day of my life. When I came to her at the end of the day, she told me to kneel before her, and give the oath. She told me I had better mean it more than any time I had ever said it before, and she had made me say it often. I knelt and said the oath, meaning every word.

"When I finished, I held my breath and waited. I still be on my knees. She looked down her nose at me, that sour frown of hers still on her face. And then she said, 'Though you be wild of spirit, child, you have worked to tame it. The people have asked for your oath, and you have given it. May I not live to see you break it. You owe no debt beyond that. I will take care of the circle and see to Mathrin Galliene. You will wed Pell.' I wept into the hem of her dress."

Adie was silent, staring into the fire, lost in the memories. Zedd lifted an eyebrow. "Well, did you wed your love?"

"Yes," she whispered in her soft rasp. She took the spoon off its hook and stirred the stew while Zedd watched her. At last, she hung it back at its place. "For three months, I thought life be beyond bliss."

Her mouth worked soundlessly as she stared into nothingness. Zedd put an arm around her shoulder and gently led her back to the table. "Sit, Adie. Let me bring you a cup of tea."

She was still sitting, her hands folded together on the table, staring off, when he returned with the steaming cups. He placed one in her thin hands as he sat opposite her. He didn't press her to go on before she was ready.

At last, she did. "One day, the day of my birth and nineteen years, Pell and I had taken a walk in the country. I be with child." She lifted the cup in both hands and took a sip. "We spent the day walking past farms, thinking of names for our child, holding hands, and . . . well, you know the foolishness of love at that age.

"On our way back, we had to walk past the Choora mill, just outside of town. I thought it strange no one be there. Someone always be at the mill." Adie closed her eyes for a moment and then took another sip of tea. "As it turned out, there be people there. The Blood of the Fold. They be waiting for us."

Zedd knew of them. In the larger cities of Nicobarese, the Blood of the Fold were an organized corps of men who hunted banelings; rooted out evil, as they saw it. In other lands, there were men like them, who went by other names, but they were the same. None were especially picky about proof. A corpse was the only proof they need show of their job well done. If they said the body was that of a baneling, then it was. In the smaller towns, the Blood were usually self-appointed toughs and thugs. The Blood of the Fold were widely feared. With good reason.

"They took us . . ." Her voice broke, but only that once. . . . "into separate rooms in the bottom of the mill. It be dark, and smelled of the damp stone walls and grain dust. I did not know what be done to Pell. I be almost too terrified to breathe.

"Mathrin Galliene said Pell and I be banelings. He said I would not wed as I should have because I wished to bring the Keeper's notice to Choora. There be a sickness, a fever, in the country that summer, and it brought death to many a family. Mathrin Galliene said Pell and I brought the sickness. I denied it be so, and spoke the oath to show proof." Adie turned the cup in her fingers as she stared at it.

Zedd touched her hand. "Drink, Adie. It will help you." He had put a pinch of cloud leaf into her tea, to help relax her.

She took a long swallow. "Mathrin Galliene said Pell and I be banelings, and the graveyard be full of the proof of that. He said he wanted only for Pell and I to tell the truth, to confess. The other men of the Blood be growling like hounds around a rabbit, ready to tear us apart. I be terrified for Pell.

"As they beat me, I knew they would be doing worse to him, to make him name me a baneling. Nothing be better for the Blood than to have someone name a loved one as a baneling. They would not listen when I denied it." She looked up into his eyes. "They would not listen."

"Anything you said," Zedd offered quietly, "would have made no difference, Adie. It wouldn't have mattered. When you are in a leghold trap, reasoning with the steel does no good."

She nodded. "I know." Her face was a calm mask over a thunderhead. "I could have stopped it, had I used the gift, but it be against everything I be taught, believed. It be as if using the gift would prove to myself that what the men said be true. I felt it would have been blasphemy against the Creator. I be as helpless while the men beat me as if I did not have the gift."

She drained the tea from her cup. "Even as I screamed, I could hear Pell's screams echoing from another room."

Zedd went to the fire and brought the pot back, filling her cup again. "It wasn't your fault, Adie. Don't blame yourself."

She flicked a glance up at him as he poured himself another cup. "They wanted me to name Pell as a baneling. I told them I would not, that they could kill me, but they could not make me say that it be so.

"Mathrin bent close to me, put his face close to mine. In my head, I can still see his smile. He said, 'I believe you, girl. But it doesn't matter, because it not be you we want to name the baneling. It be Pell we want to speak the name of the baneling. It be you we want Pell to name. You be the baneling.'

"Then the men held me down. Mathrin tried to pour something down my throat. It burned my mouth. He held my nose. It be swallow or drown. I wished to drown, but I swallowed without wanting to. It burned my throat like swallowing fire. I could not speak. I could not make a sound. I could not even scream. No sound be there. Only burning pain. More pain than I had ever known." She took a sip of tea, as if to soothe her throat.

"Then the men took me in the room with Pell and tied me to a chair in front of him. Mathrin held me by my hair so I could not move. It broke my heart to see what they had done to my Pell. His face be white as snow. They had cut off most of his fingers, one knuckle at a time." Her own fingers tightened around her cup as she stared into the vision.

"Mathrin told Pell that I had confessed that Pell be a Baneling. Pell's eyes be big, looking at me. I tried to scream that it not be true, but no sound came. I tried to shake my head that it not be true, but Mathrin held me so I could not.

"Pell told them he did not believe them. They cut off another finger. They told him they only do it because I named him. Only do it on my word. Pell kept his eyes on me as he shook, and kept telling them he did not believe them. They told Pell I had told them I wished him to be killed because he be a baneling. Still Pell said he did not believe them. He said he loved me.

"Then he told Pell I had named him a baneling, and that if it not be so, I could deny it and they would let us both go free. He told Pell that I had promised I would not deny it because he be a baneling, and I wanted him to die for it. Pell screamed for me to tell them. Screamed for me to deny it. He screamed my name, screamed for me to say something.

"I tried, but I could say nothing. My throat be fire. My voice did not work. Mathrin held me by my hair; I could not move. Pell's eyes be big as he stared at me. As I sat silent.

"Then Pell spoke to me. 'How could you do that to me, Adie? How could you name me a baneling?' Then he cried.

"Mathrin asked him to name me a baneling. He said that if he did, they would believe him over me, because I had the gift, and he would be freed. Pell whispered, 'I will not say that of her to save my life. Even though she has betrayed me.' Those words broke my heart."

As she stared off at nothing, Zedd noticed a candle on the counter behind her melt into a puddle. He could feel the waves of power radiating from her. He realized he was holding his breath. He eased it out.

"Mathrin cut Pell's throat," she said simply. "He severed Pell's head and held it before me. He said he wanted me to see what following the Keeper had brought on Pell. He said it be the last thing he wanted me to ever see. The men held my head back and pulled my eyes open. Mathrin poured the burning liquid in them.

"I be blinded.

"In that moment, something happened inside me. My Pell was gone, he died thinking I had betrayed him, my life was about to end. I suddenly realized how it be my own fault, for holding to an oath. The life of my love, for an ignorant oath, for a foolish superstition. Nothing mattered anymore; everything be gone to me.

"I turned the gift loose, turned the rage loose. I broke my oath not to use the gift to harm another. I could not see, but I could hear; I could hear their blood hit the stone walls. I struck out wildly. I shredded every living thing in that room, be it man or mouse. I could not see, so I simply struck at any life I could feel. I could not tell if any had escaped. In a way, I be glad to be blind, or seeing what I be doing, I might have stopped before I finished.

"When all be still, dead, I felt my way around the room, counting the bodies. One be missing.

"I crawled to my grandmother Lindel's. How I made my way, I cannot imagine, except to think the gift guided me. When she saw me, she be furious. She pulled me to my feet and demanded to know if I had broken my oath."

Zedd leaned forward. "But you couldn't speak. How did you answer?"

Adie smiled a small, cold smile. "I picked her up by the throat, with the power of the gift, and slammed her against the wall. I walked up to her and nodded my head. I squeezed her throat in anger. She fought me. She fought me with all her power. But I be stronger, much stronger. I never knew until that moment that the gift be different in different people. She be as helpless as a stick doll.

"But I could not hurt her, as much as I wished to for her asking that question before any other. I released her and sagged to the floor; I could stand no longer. She came to me and began tending to my wounds. She told me I had done wrong, by breaking my oath, but that what was done to me was a more grievous wrong.

"I never feared Grandmother Lindel again. Not because she be helping me, but because I had broken the oath, I be beyond the laws I had been taught, and because I knew I was stronger than she. From that day on, she be afraid of me. I think she helped me because she wanted me well, so I could leave.

"A few days later, Grandmother Lindel came home to tell me that she had been called before the king's circle and questioned. She said all the men at the mill, all the Blood of the Fold, be dead, except Mathrin. He had escaped. She told the circle she had not seen me. They believed her, or said they did because they did not want to confront her and additionally a sorceress who had killed that many men in such a shocking manner, so they let her go about her business."

Some of the tension seemed to ease from her shoulders. She studied the tea cup a moment and then took another sip. She held the cup out for him to warm. Zedd poured a little more. He idly wished he had put some of the powdered cloud leaf in his own tea. He didn't think that was the end of the story.

"I lost my child," Adie said in a soft rasp.

Zedd looked up. "I'm sorry, Adie."

She looked up to meet his eyes. "I know." She took one of his hands in both hers after he set down the kettle. "I know." She took her hands back. "My throat healed." She touched her fingers lightly to her neck, then knitted them together. "But it left me with a voice like dragging iron over rock."

He smiled at her. "I like your voice. Iron fits the rest of you."

The ghost of a smile passed across her face. "My eyes, though, did not grow better. I be blind. Grandmother Lindel not be as strong as me, but she be old, and had seen many a trick with the gift. She taught me to see without my eyes. She taught me to see with the gift. It not be the same as eyes, but in some ways, it be better. In some ways, I see more.

"After I be healed, Grandmother Lindel wanted me to leave. She not be fond of living with one who had broken the oath, even though I be of her blood. She feared I would bring trouble. Whether from the Keeper, for breaking my oath, or from the Blood of the Fold, she did not know, but she feared trouble would come because of me."

Zedd leaned back in his chair, stretching his tense muscles a bit. "And did trouble come?"

"Oh, yes," Adie hissed, raising her eyebrows as she leaned forward. "Trouble came. Mathrin Galliene brought them: twenty Blood of the Fold. Ones paid by the Crown. Professionals. Battle-hard men; big men, grim-faced, savage men, all pretty on horseback in neat ranks with swords, shields, and banners, every spear held just so, at the same angle. All pretty in their chain mail and polished breastplates shining with the embossed crest of the Crown, and all wearing helmets with red plumes that flicked as they rode. Every horse white.

"I stood on the porch and watched with the eyes of the gift as they spread rank before me with perfect precision, like they be performing for the king himself. Every horse put every foot the same, stopping in a line at the lifting of a finger from the commander. They be spread out before me, ready, eager, to do their grisly duty. Mathrin waited behind them on his horse, watching. The commander called out to me, 'You be under arrest as a baneling, and are to be executed as such.' "

Adie lifted her head from the specters of her memory, her eyes meeting Zedd's. "I thought of Pell. My Pell."

Her expression hardened into an iron mask. "Not one sword cleared a scabbard, not one spear be leveled, not one foot touched the ground, before they died. I swept the line, from left to right, one man at a time, everything I had, into each in turn, quick as a thought. Thump thump thump. Every one, except the commander. He sat still and stone-faced upon his white horse as men in armor crashed to the ground to each side of him.

"When it be finished, when the last shield had clattered into silence, I met his eyes. 'Armor,' I told him, 'be of no use against a true baneling. Or a sorceress. It only be of use against innocent people.' Then I told him he was to deliver a message to the king for me, from one sorceress named Adie. In a calm, firm voice, he asked the message. I said, 'Tell him that if he sends another of the Blood of the Fold to take me, it will be the last living order he ever gives.' He looked at me for a moment without a hint of emotion in his cold eyes, and then he turned his horse and walked it away without looking back."

Her gaze sank to the table. "My grandmother turned her back to me. She told me to leave the shelter of her roof and never to return."

A little wince touched Zedd's face before he caught it, at the thought of a sorceress with enough power to kill men in that fashion. It was exceedingly rare for a sorceress to be that strong in the gift. "What of Mathrin? You didn't kill him?"

She shook her head. A humorless smile played across her lips.

"No. I took him with me."

"Took him with you?"

"I bonded him to me. Bonded his life to mine. Bonded him so that he always knew where I be, and so that every new moon he was compelled to come to me, no matter where I be, no matter what he wished. He had to follow me, at least close enough so that he could come to me every new moon."

Frowning, Zedd studied the dregs in his tea cup. "I met a man, once, in Winstead, the capital and Crown seat of Kelton. His name was Mathrin. He was a begger, missing the fingers on one hand, as I recall. He was blind. His eyes had been . . ." Zedd's eyes suddenly fixed on hers. She was watching him. "His eyes had been gouged out."

Adie nodded. "Indeed they had." Her face was iron again. "Every new moon, he came to me, and I cut something off him, letting his screams try to fill the emptiness in me."

Zedd leaned back, his hands pressed to the tabletop. Iron indeed. "So you made a new home in Kelton?"

"No. I made no home. I traveled, seeking out women with the gift, ones who could help me in my studies. None knew very much of what I sought, but each knew at least a little that others did not.

"Mathrin followed, and every new moon he came to me, and I cut something else from him. I wanted him to live forever, to suffer forever. He be the one who beat me, down there, with his fists, so I would lose Pell's child. He be the one who killed Pell. He be the one who blinded me."

Her white eyes shone red in the lamplight as she stared off again. "He be the one who made Pell believe I had betrayed him. I wanted Mathrin Galliene to suffer forever."

Zedd gestured vaguely with his hand. "How long did he . . . last?"

Adie sighed. "Not long enough, and too long." Zedd frowned. "One day, a thought occurred to me: I had never used the gift to prevent Mathrin from killing himself. Why would he still come to me? Let me make him to suffer like I did? Why would he not simply end it? So, the next time he came, and I cut something else off, I also cut the bond. Cut his need to come the next time. But I did it in a way so as he would not notice, so he could simply forget about me, if he wished."

"So that was the last you saw of him?"

She gave a grim shake of her head. "No. I thought it would be, but he returned with the next new moon. Returned when he needn't have. It made my blood run cold, to wonder why. I decided that it be time for him to pay with his life for what he had done to me, and Pell, and all the others. But I resolved that before he gave me his life, he would give me the answer.

"In my travels, I had learned many things. Things for which I thought I would never have use. That night I found use. I used them to learn what torture Mathrin feared above all others. The trick be used to learn fears, but be useless to learn other secrets. Against his will, the words tumbled out of him, his fears spilled out.

"I left him to sweat all that night and the whole next day while I went in search of the things I needed: the things he feared above all else. When I finally returned with them, he be nearly insane with fright. His fears be well founded. I asked him to confess his secret. He said no.

"I dumped out the sack, put the little cages and the other things in front of him as he sat naked and helpless on the floor. I picked up each, held it before his sightless face, and described it, told him what be in each little cage or basket or jar. Again I asked him to confess. He be sweating and panting and shaking, but he said no. Mathrin thought I be bluffing, that I did not have the courage. Mathrin be wrong.

"I steeled myself, and brought his worst fears to life for him."

Zedd's brow bunched up into wrinkles. Curiosity won out over dread. "What did you do?"

She lifted her head to look into his eyes. "That be the one thing I will not tell you. It not be important anyway.

"Mathrin would not talk, and suffered so much that I almost stopped several times. Each time I wanted to stop, I thought about the last thing my eyes had seen before he blinded me: Pell's head held in Mathrin's fist before me." Adie swallowed, her voice so low Zedd could hardly hear her. "And I remembered Pell's last words: 'I will not say that of her to save my life. Even though she has betrayed me.' "

She closed her eyes for a moment. They came open and she went on. "Mathrin be on the edge of death. I thought he was not going to tell me why he came to me. But just before he died, he became still, despite what was being done to him. And then he said he would tell me, because he be about to die, because this, too, had been by plan. I asked him again why he had come back.

"He leaned toward me. 'Don't you know, Adie?' he asked me. 'Don't you know what I be? I be a baneling. I have been hiding right under your nose all this time. You have kept me near you all this time, and the Keeper knew right where you be. The Keeper lusts for those with the gift above all else.' I had thought that that be it, that he be a baneling. I told him he had failed, it had done him no good, as he be about to die for his crimes.

"He smiled at me." She leaned forward. "Smiled! And he said, 'You be wrong Adie. I have not failed. I have done the Keeper's bidding. I have fulfilled my task. Perfectly. All this be by plan. I have made you do exactly as he wished. I shall be rewarded. I be the one who started the fire when you be little. I be the one who did those things to Pell. Not because I thought him or you a baneling. I be the baneling, I did it to make you break your oath. To make you welcome the Keeper's hate into your heart.

" 'Breaking your oath be the first step, and look what you have done since. Look at what you be doing right now. Look at how far you have slipped toward him. You be within his grasp now. You may not have given him your oath, but you do his bidding. You have become what you hate. You have become me; you be a baneling. The Keeper smiles upon you, Adie, and thanks you for welcoming him into your heart.' Mathrin slumped, and fell back, dead."

Adie dissolved into tears, her head sagging into her hands. Zedd unlocked his joints and swept around the table, holding her to him as he stood next to her, holding her head against his stomach, stroking her hair, comforting her as she cried.

"Not so, dear lady. Not so at all."

She wept against his robes, shaking her head. "You think you be so smart, wizard? You not be so smart as you think. You be wrong about this."

Zedd knelt beside her chair, holding her hands in his, looking up into her stricken face. "I'm smart enough to know that the Keeper, or one of his minions, would not let you have the satisfaction of knowing you had won a battle against him."

"But I . . ."

"You fought back. You struck out from your hurt, not for a lust of the things you did. Not for a want to help the Keeper."

Her brow wrinkled together with her effort to stop the tears. "You be so sure? Sure enough to trust one such as I?"

Zedd smiled. "I'm sure. I may not know everything, but I know you are no baneling. You are the victim, not the criminal."

She shook her head. "I not be so sure as you."

"After Mathrin died, did you go on killing? Seeking vengeance against any innocent?"

"No, of course not."

"Had you been an agent, you would have given yourself over to the Keeper, to his wishes, and gone on to hurt those who fought him. You are no Baneling, dear lady. My heart weeps for the things the Keeper took from you, but he did not take your soul, that is still yours. Put those fears aside."

He held her hands and gave them soft squeezes. She didn't try to take her hands back, but let them stay in his, as if to soak up the comfort as they trembled.

Adie wiped the tears from her cheek. "Pour me some more tea? But no more powdered cloud leaf, or I will fall asleep before I can finish the story."

Zedd arched an eyebrow. She had known what he had done. He patted her shoulder as he rose to his feet. He poured her tea and then pulled his chair forward and sat again while she sipped.

After she drank half of her cup, she looked to have regained her control. "The war with D'Hara be burning hot, but it be near the end. I felt the boundary go up. Felt it come into this world."

"So you came here right after the boundary went up?"

"No. I studied with a few women first. Some taught me a few things about

258

bones." She pulled a little necklace from under her robes. She fingered the small, round bone, with red and yellow beads to each side. It was just like the one she had given him to get him through the pass. He still wore it around his neck. "This be a bone from the base of a skull like that on the shelf over there; the one that fell on the floor. The beast be called a skrin. Skrin be guardian beasts to the underworld, something like the heart hounds, except they guard in both directions. The best way to explain it is that they be part of the veil, though that not be accurate. In this world they be solid, have form, but in the other, they be only a force."

Zedd frowned. "Force?"

Adie held out her spoon and let it drop on the table. "Force. We cannot see it, but force be there. It makes the spoon drop, and keeps it from flying up into the air. It cannot be seen, but it be there. Something like that with the skrin.

"On rare occasions, in their duty to repel all from the cusp where the world of the living and the world of the dead touch, they be pulled into this world. Few people know of them because it so rarely happens." Zedd was frowning. "It be very complex. I will explain it better another time. The important thing be that this bone from the skrin hides you from them."

Adie took a sip of her tea while Zedd pulled his necklace out of his robes, taking a new look at it. "And it must hide you from other beasts, too, to get through the pass?" She nodded. "How did you know about the pass? I put the boundary up, and I didn't know the pass existed."

She turned the teacup around and around in her fingers. "After I left my grand-mother, I sought out women with the gift, women who could teach me things about the world of the dead. After Mathrin died, I studied harder, with more urgency. Each woman could tell me only what small bit she knew, but they usually knew one who knew more. I traveled the Midlands, going among them, gathering knowledge. I collected all those bits of knowledge, piecing them together. In this manner, I learned a little of how the worlds interact.

"By putting up a boundary across parts of this world, it be a little like stoppering up a teakettle and then putting it on the fire. Without a vent, something will blow off. I knew that if there be magic wise enough to know how to bring the underworld into this, it must have a way to equalize each side of the boundary. A vent of some sort. A pass."

Zedd lifted an eyebrow, staring off into his thoughts, as he drew his thumb down his chin. "Of course. That makes sense. Balance. All force, all magic, must be balanced." He focused his eyes on her. "When I brought up the boundary, I was using magic I didn't fully understand. It was in an ancient book, from the wizards of old, who had more power than I can fathom. Using their instructions to bring up the boundary was an act of desperation."

"It be hard for me to imagine you being desperate."

"Sometimes, that's all life is: one desperate act after another."

Adie nodded. "Perhaps you be right. I was desperate to hide from the Keeper. I remembered what Mathrin had said: he be hiding right under my nose. I reasoned that the safest place for me to hide from the Keeper would be where he wouldn't look: right under his nose, right at the edge of his world. So I came to the pass.

"The pass did not be this world, yet it did not be the underworld either. It be a mix of both. A place where both worlds boiled together a little bit. With the bones, I be able to hide from the Keeper. He and the beasts from his world could not see me."

"Hide?" The woman had more iron in her than the kettle hanging on the fire. If he knew Adie, there was more to it. Zedd gave her a stern stare. "You came here, simply to hide?"

She averted her eyes as she fingered the small, round bone on her necklace, and then at last tucked it back into her robes. "There be another reason. I made an oath. To myself. I swore I would find a way to contact my Pell, to tell him I did not betray him." She took a long swallow of tea. "I have spent most of my life here, in the pass, trying to find a way to reach into the world of the dead, to tell him. The pass be part of that world."

Zedd pushed at his cup with a finger. "The boundary, the pass, is gone, Adie. I need your help in this world."

She laid her arms on the table. "When you grew my foot back for me, it brought back everything that had happened, made it fresh, as if I be reliving it. It made me remember some things I had forgotten for a long time. It made me remember hurts that still be there, though time had dimmed them."

"I'm sorry, Adie," he whispered. "I should have taken your past into consideration, but I didn't suspect you had lived through that much pain. Forgive me."

"There be nothing to forgive. You gave me a gift by giving me my foot back. You did not know the things I have done. It not be your fault I did them. You did not know I be a baneling."

He cast her a harsh glare. "You think that because you have fought back against wickedness, you have become wicked?"

"I have done worse than a man like you can understand."

Zedd nodded slightly. "Is that so. Let me tell you a little story. I had a love once, like your Pell. Her name was Erilyn. My time with her was like your time with Pell." A slow smile came to his lips, as his memory touched the mist of those pleasant times. The smile withered. "Until Panis Rahl sent a quad after her."

Adie reached out and laid a hand on his. "Zedd, you do not need to . . ."

Zedd brought his other fist down on the table, making the cups jump. "You can't imagine what the four of them did to her." He leaned forward, his face standing out red against his white hair. He ground his teeth together. "I hunted them down. What I did to each of them would make whatever you did to Mathrin seem a lark. I went after Panis Rahl, but couldn't reach him, so I went after his armies. For every man you killed, Adie, I killed a thousand. Even my own side feared me. I was the wind of death. I did what was needed to stop Panis Rahl. And maybe more."

He settled his weight back in the chair. "If there is such a thing as a man of virtue, you do not sit with him now."

"You did only what you had to. That does not diminish your virtue."

He arched an eyebrow. "Wise words, spoken by a wise woman. Perhaps you should listen to them." She remained silent. He put his elbows on the table and idly picked up the cup, rolling it in his palms as he went on. "In a way, I was luckier than you. I had more time with my Erilyn. And I didn't lose my daughter."

"Panis Rahl did not try to kill your daughter, too?"

"Yes. Indeed, he thought he had. I . . . cast a death spell. To make them think they had seen her death. It was the only way to protect her, to keep them from trying until they succeeded."

"A death spell . . ." Adie whispered a benediction in her native tongue. "That be a dangerous web. I would not reproach you for doing such a thing, you had cause, but such a thing does not go unnoticed by the spirits. You be lucky it worked, and it saved her. You be very fortunate the good spirits be with you on that day."

"I guess sometimes it's hard to tell which side of luck you're looking at. I raised her without a mother. She had grown into a fine young woman when it happened.

"Darken Rahl had been standing next to his father when I sent the Wizard's Fire through the boundary. He was standing next to his father when my fire found him. Some of it burned Darken Rahl. He spent his growing years learning, so he could finish what his father had started, and extract his vengeance. He learned how to cross the boundary; he was coming into the Midlands, and I never knew.

"He raped my daughter.

"He didn't know who she was—everyone thought my daughter was dead—or he would have killed her sure. But he hurt her." He pressed his palms together. The cup shattered. He turned his hands up, to see if they had been cut, and was a little surprised they weren't. Adie said nothing.

"After that, I took her to Westland, to hide, to protect her. I never knew if it was more of that bad luck, or if somehow wickedness found her, but she died. Burned to death in her house. Though I always suspected the irony was more than coincidence, I never found proof it was so. Perhaps, after all, the good spirits hadn't been with me on the day I cast her death spell."

"I be sorry, Zedd," Adie said in a soft rasp.

He waved off her pity with a flourish of his hand. "I still had her boy." With the side of his finger, he pushed the shards of the cup into a little pile in the center of the wooden tabletop. "Darken Rahl's son. The spawn of an agent of the Keeper. But my daughter's son too, and my grandson. Innocent of the crimes that brought him to be. A fine boy."

He looked up at her from under his bushy eyebrows. "I believe you know him. His name is Richard."

Adie lurched forward in her chair. "Richard! Richard is your . . ." She leaned back, shaking her head. "Wizards and their secrets." She scowled a little, but then softened her expression. "Perhaps you had just cause for a secret such as this. Does Richard have the gift?"

Zedd lifted his eyebrows as he nodded. "Indeed he does. That was one reason I hid him in Westland. I feared he had the gift, though I wasn't sure, and I wanted him to be safe from danger. As you said, the Keeper lusts for those with the gift more than any other. I knew that if I began teaching him, used magic very much myself, the gaze of danger would settle on him.

"I wanted to let him grow, become strong of character, before I tested him, and if he had the gift, taught him. I had always suspected he had the gift. Sometimes, I hoped he did not. But I now know he does. He used it to stop Darken Rahl. Used magic."

He leaned forward. "I suspect he has the gift from both his grandfather and his father. From two different lines of wizards."

"I see" was all she said.

"But we have more important things to worry about right now. Darken Rahl used the boxes of Orden. He opened one, the wrong one, for him anyway. But maybe the wrong one for us too. There are books back at the Keep that speak of it. They warn that if the boxes are used, if the Magic of Orden is used, and even if the person who put them in play makes a mistake and it kills him, it can still tear the veil.

261

"Adie, I don't know as much about the underworld as you. You have been studying it most of your life. I need your help. I need you to come to Aydindril with me to study the books to see what can be done. I've read many of them and don't understand much of their meaning. Perhaps you will. Even if you only see one thing I miss, it could be important."

She stared at the table with a bitter expression. "I be an old woman. I be an old woman who has welcomed the Keeper into my heart."

Zedd watched her, but she didn't meet his eyes. He pushed his chair back and stood. "An old woman? No. A foolish woman, maybe." She didn't reply. Her gaze stayed pointedly on the table.

Zedd strolled across the room and inspected the bones hanging on the wall. He clasped his hands behind his back as he studied the talismans of the dead.

"Maybe I am just an old man then. Hmm? A foolish old man. Maybe I should let a young man do this work." He glanced over his shoulder. She was watching him. "But if a young man is good, then even younger would be better. In fact, why not let a child do it? That would be better yet. Maybe there is a ten-year-old-boy somewhere who will be willing to do something to stop the dead from swallowing the living."

He threw his hands up in the air. "According to you, it would seem, knowledge is of no use, only youth."

"Now you are being foolish, old man. You know what I mean."

Zedd stepped back to the table and gave a shrug of his bony shoulders. "If you just sit here in this house instead of helping with what you know, then you might as well be the thing you fear most: an agent of the Keeper."

He put his knuckles to the table and glowered as he leaned over her. "If you don't fight him, then you help him. That is what his plan has been all along. Not to turn you to him, but to make you fear stopping him."

She looked into his eyes, uneasiness stealing into her expression. "What do you mean?"

"He has already done all he needed, Adie. He made you afraid of yourself. The Keeper has an eternity of patience. He doesn't need you to work for him. It takes effort to turn one with the gift. You weren't worth the trouble. He needed only for you not to work against him. He did all that was necessary. He didn't waste an effort to do more.

"In some ways he is as blind to this world as we are to his. He has only so much influence here; he must choose his tasks carefully. He doesn't spend what power he has here frivolously."

Realization took the place of unease. "Perhaps you not be such an old fool."

Zedd smiled as he pulled the chair forward and sat. "That has always been my opinion."

Hands nestled in her lap, Adie studied the tabletop as if hoping it would come to her aid. The house was silent, except for the slow crackle of the fire in the hearth. "All these years, the truth be hiding right under my nose." She lifted her head, giving him a puzzled frown. "How did you come to be so wise?"

Zedd shrugged. "But one of the advantages of having lived so long. You view yourself as just an old woman. I see a striking, dear lady, who has learned much in her time in this world, and has gained wisdom from what she has seen."

He pulled the yellow rose from her hair and held it before her. "Your loveliness is not a mask, layered over a rotten core. It blossoms from the beauty inside."

262

She lifted the flower from his fingers and laid it on the table. "Your clever tongue cannot cover the fact that I have wasted my life. . . ."

Zedd shook his head, cutting her off. "No. You have wasted nothing. You simply have not seen the other side of things yet. In magic, in all things, there is a balance if we look for it. The Keeper did as he did, sending a baneling to you, to keep you from interfering in his work, and to plant a seed of doubt in you that would perhaps turn you to him one day.

"But in that too, there was something to balance what he did. You came here to learn about the world of the dead in order to contact your Pell. Don't you see, Adie? You were manipulated to prevent you from interfering with the Keeper's plans, but in so doing, the balance is that you have learned things that might be of aid in stopping him. You must not surrender to what he had done to you; you must strike back with what he has inadvertently given you."

Her eyes glistened as she cast her gaze about her house, looking to the bone pile, the walls covered with talismans of the dead she had collected over the years, and to the shelves holding more yet. "But my oath . . . my Pell. I must reach him, tell him. He died thinking I betrayed him. If I cannot redeem myself in his eyes, then I be lost, my heart be lost. If I be lost, then the Keeper will find me."

"Pell is dead, Adie. Gone. The boundary, the pass, is gone. You would know better than I if it would have ever been any use in what you wanted, but in all these years, you have not found a way to make it so. If you wish to continue the pursuit of your oath, you will find no help here. Perhaps in Aydindril, you will.

"Helping to stop the Keeper does not mean you must break your oath to yourself. If my knowledge and help can be of any aid in what you seek, I offer it gladly. Just as you know things I do not, I know things you don't. I am, after all, the First Wizard. Perhaps what I know will help you. Pell would not want you to bring him your message that you did not betray him, if it meant you must betray everyone else."

Adie picked up the yellow flower, twirling it between her finger and thumb a moment before setting it down again. Gripping the edge of the table, she pushed herself to her feet. She stood a moment, and then lifted her head to gaze with her white eyes around the room once more.

Smoothing her robes at her hips, as if to make herself presentable, she limped around the table to stand behind his chair. Zedd felt her hands rest on his shoulders. Unexpectedly, she leaned over and kissed the top of his head and smoothed his unruly hair with gentle fingers. Zedd was relieved the fingers hadn't gone around his throat. He thought they might, after some of the things he had said.

"Thank you, my friend, for hearing my tale, and for helping me to find the meaning in it. My Pell would have liked you. You both be men of honor. I accept your word that you will help me tell my Pell."

Zedd twisted around in his chair and raised his face to her soft smile and kind eyes. "I will do whatever I can to help you keep your oath. You have my oath on that."

Her smile widened as she smoothed down a stray lock of his white hair. "Now. Tell me of the Stone of Tears. We must decide what is to be done with it."

T he Stone of Tears? Well, it is hidden."

She gave a single, firm nod. "Good. It not be something to be loose in this world." Her brow wrinkled in a little frown. "It be hidden well? It be safe?"

Zedd winced a little. He didn't want to tell her, he knew what she would say, but he had promised. "I put it on a chain. Put it on a chain and hung it around the neck of a little girl. I don't know . . . exactly . . . where she is right now."

"You touched it!" Adie's eyes widened. "The Stone of Tears? You touched it, and hung it around the neck of a little girl!"

She gripped his chin firmly in her suddenly powerful fingers and leaned close to his face. "You have hung the Stone of Tears, the Stone that it be told was hung by the Creator Himself around the Keeper's neck to lock him in the underworld . . . you hung that around a little girl's neck? And let her wander off!"

Zedd scowled defensively. "Well, I had to do something with it. I couldn't just leave it lying about."

Adie smacked the palm of her hand to her forehead. "Just as he makes me think him wise, he shows me he be a fool indeed. Dear spirits, save me from the hands you have placed me in."

Zedd shot to his feet. "And just what would you have done with it!"

"Well, I would have certainly given it more thought than you seem to have done. And I wouldn't have touched it! It be a thing from another world!" She turned her back to him, shaking her head and whispering things in her foreign tongue.

Zedd shifted his robes, straightening them with a firm tug. "I didn't have the luxury of time to give it any thought. We were attacked by a screeling. If I had left it there . . ."

Adie spun around. "A screeling! You be full of good news, old man." She jabbed a finger against his chest. "That still be no good excuse. You still should not have . . ."

"Not have what? Not have picked it up? I should have let the screeling pick it up, instead?"

"Screelings be assassins. They not be there to take the Stone."

Zedd jabbed a finger right back at her. "You know that? Are you so sure? Would you have been willing to have risked everything on it? And if you were wrong, let the Keeper have the Stone to do with as he would? Are you so sure, Adie?"

Her hand dropped to her side as she stared at his frown. "No. I guess not. It could be as you say. There be a chance the screeling may have taken it. Perhaps you did the only thing you could do." She shook the finger at him. "But to hang it around the neck of a little girl . . .!"

"And where would you have had me keep it? In my pocket? In the pocket of a wizard? In the pocket of one with the gift, where the Keeper is sure to look first? Or perhaps you would have had me hide it, in a place only I knew, where, if a baneling gets his hands on me and somehow makes me talk, I could tell him it would be, so he could go and collect it?"

Adie folded her arms with a muttered curse. At last her expression relaxed. "Well . . . perhaps . . ."

"Perhaps nothing. I had no choice. It was an act of desperation. I did the only thing I could do, given the circumstances."

She let out a tired sigh, then nodded. "You be right, wizard. You did the best you could have done." She patted the top of his shoulder. "Foolish as it be," she added under her breath. Her hand gave a gentle push. "Sit. Let me show you something."

Zedd sat as he watched her limp across the room toward the shelves. "I would rather have done anything else, Adie," he said sorrowfully, "than what I had to do."

She nodded as she walked. "I know. . . ." She stopped and turned. "A screeling, you say?" Zedd nodded. "You be sure it be a screeling?" He arched an eyebrow. "Yes, of course you be sure." Her brow creased in thought. "Screelings be the Keeper's assassins. They be singleminded, and extremely dangerous, but they not be very smart. They must have something to show them the one they be after, a way to find them. They not be good at searching in this world. How could the Keeper know where you be? How could the screeling know to find you? Know it be you he be after?"

Zedd shrugged. "I don't know. I was where the boxes had been opened. But it had been some time since it had happened. There would be no way to know I was still there."

"And did you destroy the screeling?"

"Yes."

"That be good. The Keeper will not waste the effort to send another, not after you have proven you be able to defeat it."

Zedd threw his hands up. "Oh yes, just wonderful. Screelings are sent to eliminate a threat to the Keeper. It was probably sent to rid the Keeper of my meddling, just as the Keeper sent a baneling to rid himself of your interference. You're right: he will not send another screeling, now that I've proven that I can defeat one. He will send something worse."

"If indeed it be sent for you." She touched a finger to her lower lip as she mumbled to herself. "Where be the Stone when you found it?"

"Next to the box that had been opened."

"And where came the screeling?"

"In the same room as the boxes, as the Stone."

She shook her head in puzzlement. "Perhaps it could be as you say, that it came to get the Stone, but it makes no sense for a screeling to come for the Stone. I wonder how he found you." She limped on toward the shelves. "Something had to guide him."

Balancing on her toes, she peered to the back of a shelf, carefully pushing aside various objects, at last retrieving what she sought. Holding it in one hand, she limped back and placed it carefully on the table. It was a little bigger than a hen's egg, round, and age-darkened with a deep patina that was a brownish black in the recesses. It was masterfully carved into the shape of a vicious beast, all balled up, but glaring with eyes that seemed to watch you no matter which way it was held. It looked to be bone, and very old.

Zedd picked it up, testing its weight. It was much heavier than he thought it should have been. "What's this?"

"A woman, a sorceress, gave this to me when I went to her, to learn. She be on her deathbed. She asked if I knew of the skrin. I told her what I knew. She sighed with relief, and then said something that made my skin prickle. She said she had been waiting for me, as the prophecies had told her to do. She placed this in my hand, saying it be carved from the bone of a skrin."

Adie flicked her hand toward the walls, and then toward the bone pile. "I have a whole skrin here, among the bones. I did battle with one once, in the pass. His bones be here. His skull be on the shelf. It be the one that fell on the floor."

She put a thin finger on the carved bone sphere in Zedd's hand as she leaned toward him and lowered her raspy voice. "This, the old one said, must be guarded, by one who understands. She told me it be of ancient magic, made by wizards of old, possibly with their hand guided by the Creator Himself. Made because of prophecies.

"She said it may be the most important thing of magic I would ever touch. That it be invested with more power than she or I would ever understand. She said that it be of skrin bone, and of skrin force, that it be a talisman that be of importance if the veil ever be in danger.

"I asked how it was to be used, how the magic worked, and how it had come into her hands. She be very exhausted from the excitement of my coming to her, and said she must rest. She told me to come back to her in the morning and she would tell me everything she knew. When I returned, she had died." Adie gave him a meaningful look. "Her death be a little too timely to suit me."

Zedd had had the same thought. "But you have no idea what it is, or how it is to be used?"

"No."

Already, Zedd was using magic to lift it on a cushion of air, floating it in space, watching it slowly spin. The whole time the finely carved eyes of the beast peered back as the ball revolved before him. "Have you tried using any magic on it?"

"I be afraid to try."

Zedd held his bony hands to each side of the floating carving, probing gently with different kinds of force, different sorts of magic, letting them shift and slide over the round bone, testing, searching gingerly for a crack, a shield, a trigger.

It had the oddest feel to it. The magic reflected back as if it had touched nothing, as if the thing weren't there at all. Perhaps it could be a shield he had never seen before. He increased the force. It slipped against the carving like new shoe leather on ice.

Adie wrung her hands. "I do not think you should be . . ."

The flame of the lamp puffed out. A thin thread of greasy smoke curled from the abruptly dead wick. The room was left to the flickering shadows cast from the fire in the hearth. Zedd frowned at the dark lamp.

A sudden crash brought both their heads jerking around. The skull rolled across the floor toward where they sat. Halfway there, it wobbled and rocked to a stop, right side up. Empty eye sockets stared up at the two of them. Long fangs rested on the wood floor.

The carved bone ball thumped to the table, bouncing twice, as Zedd and Adie came to their feet.

"What foolish thing did you do, old man?"

Zedd stared at the skull. "I didn't do anything."

More bones tumbled from the shelves. Bones hanging on the wall clattered to the floor, some bouncing and flipping back into the air as they struck.

Zedd and Adie both turned to a racket behind them. The bone pile rattled apart, bones toppling and spilling over one another as the pile pulled itself apart. Some of the bones, as if alive, slid or rolled across the floor, toward the skull. Sliding along the floor, a rib bone caught the leg of a chair and spun around, but continued on.

Zedd twisted to Adie, but she was hurrying to the shelf above the counter behind the table, the one covered with the blue-and-white-striped cloth.

"Adie, what are you doing? What's going on?"

Bones collected in increasing number around the skull.

She yanked the cloth away, ripping it from its hooks. "Leave! Before it be too late!"

"What's going on!"

Jars and tins clanged together as she shoved them aside. She pushed her hand farther along the shelf, fingers searching blindly. Canisters thudded to the floor. A jar tumbled out, shattering on the edge of the counter, throwing sparkling shards cf glass over the table and chairs. A thick, dark mass from the jar oozed over the edge of the counter, carrying splinters of glass with it, making it look like nothing more than a melting porcupine.

"Do as I say, wizard! Leave! Now!"

Zedd rushed toward her, glass crunching under his feet. He jerked to a halt when he glanced over his shoulder toward the skull.

It was level with his eyes, bones collecting and assembling under it as it rose into the air. A few rib bones ranked themselves, vertebrae slipped into line, talons tipped claws, leg bones erected to the side of each flank. The jaw snapped into place as the skull rose toward the ceiling.

Zedd spun toward Adie, snatched her by the arm, yanking her toward him. She came away from thc counter clutching a small tin in her other hand.

"Adie, what's happening!"

Her head tilted up toward the skull brushing the ceiling. "What do you see?"

"What do I see! Bags, woman! I see a bunch of bones come to life!"

The shoulders of the skrin hunched as the thing grew with the addition of more bones. More yet were sliding across the floor toward it.

Adie gaped at him. "I don't see bones. I see flesh."

"Flesh! Bags! I thought you said you killed that thing."

"I said I battled it. I do not know that a skrin can be killed. I do not think they be alive. You be right about one thing, wizard: since you be able to defeat a screeling, the Keeper sent worse."

"How did he know where we were? How does the skrin know where we are? All these bones are supposed to hide us!"

"I do not know. I cannot understand how . . ."

A skeletal arm swept toward them. Zedd lurched back, pulling her with him. Yet more bones assembled. Adie was frantically unscrewing the tin as he dragged her around the back of the table. The lid came off, dropping to the floor, spinning like a top. The skrin lunged, bringing an arm down. With a loud crack, the table shattered into splinters.

The round, carved ball bounced across the floor. Zedd tried to snatch it with a magic, but it was like trying to pinch a pumpkin seed with greased fingers. He tried to scoop it up with air compressed around it, but it slipped away and rolled into the corner.

The skrin skeleton leapt at them. They both went down in a heap as he yanked her back. Zedd hauled her to her feet as she thrust her hand into the little tin. The skrin was having trouble moving quickly; it had grown too large to fit beneath the ceiling.

The jaws of the beast opened wide, as if to roar. No sound came forth, but Zedd could feel a blast of air. It made their robes flap and fly as if in a wind.

Adie's hand came out of the tin, flinging sparkling white sand at the beast.

Sorcerer's sand. The fool woman had sorcerer's sand.

The skrin staggered back a step, shaking its head. It recovered in an instant, lurching forward again. Zedd unleashed a ball of fire. It passed among the bones to splatter liquid flame against the far wall. The tongues of flame sputtered out, leaving behind a sooty splotch. Zedd tried air, since fire didn't work. It had no effect.

The two of them sidestepped across the room as the beast whirled to attack again. Zedd tried different elements of magic while he pulled Adie along with him. She ignored the danger as she poured the rest of the sorcerer's sand into her hand. When the skrin made another silent roar, she flung the sand with a foreign incantation. The blast of air from the roar died as she spoke the words. The skrin seemed to inhale, taking in the sparkling white sand. The jaws snapped closed as the head drew back.

"That be all I have," she said. "I hope it be enough."

The skrin shook its head, then spat out the sand in a cloud of sparkles. It came for them again, but when he tugged on her sleeve she yanked her arm away. Zedd tried sending logs and chairs flying into the bone beast, trying to distract it while she scurried around behind it. They simply bounced off.

Stabbing a hand into a pocket, he brought out a handful of sparkling dust of his own. With a quick flick, he sent it into the center of the bone collection standing before him. It had no more effect than had Adie's sorcerer's sand. Nothing he could do seemed to be much of a distraction, and it soon turned its attention to Adie. She was snatching an ancient bone from the wall. Feathers dangled from one end, strings of red and yellow beads from the other.

Zedd grabbed a bone arm, but the beast flung him away.

As the skrin reeled to her, she shook the bone at the thing, casting spells in her own tongue. The skrin snapped at her. She yanked her hand back just in time to save it, but not the bone talisman. It was splintered in half.

That was it. He had no idea how to fight the thing, and Adie wasn't having any success. He dove under the head toward her, rolling to his feet.

"Come on! We have to get out of here!"

"I can't leave. There be things of great value here."

"Grab what you can, we're leaving."

"Get the round bone I showed you."

Zedd tried to dodge and lunge toward the corner, but the skrin snapped and swept talon-tipped claws at him. He fought back with blasts of every kind of magic he had. Before he realized it, he was losing ground, and had nowhere to retreat.

"Adie, we have to get out now!"

"We cannot leave that bone! It be important for the veil!"

She ran for the corner. Zedd grabbed for her but missed. The skrin almost did, too. It caught her with a claw, ripping a gash down her arm. She cried out as she was flung against the wall, rebounding to sprawl facedown on the floor. More bones crashed down around her.

Zedd caught a handful of the hem of her robe, dragging her back as talons raked the wall, just missing his head. Adie clawed at the floor, trying to get away from him, to get to the round bone in the corner.

The skrin reared back with a silent roar. The ceiling ripped open as the beast stood to its full height. Huge chunks and splinters of wood rained down. Claws raked wildly, tearing the wood of the walls. Fangs ripped at the roof. Zedd pulled Adie toward the door as she fought him.

"There be things here I must take! Important things! It has taken me a lifetime to find them!"

"There's no time, Adie! We can't save them now!"

She tore away from his grasp, lunging toward the bone talismans on the wall. The skrin went for her. Zedd used magic to yank her back. He grabbed her in both arms and fell backward with her through the doorway just as a claw splintered it.

They rolled to their feet. Zedd scrambled into a run, pulling her along as she fought him. She tried using magic on him, but he shielded against it. The night air was frigid. Clouds of their breath streamed away with the cold wind as they both ran and fought each other.

Adie wailed like a mother watching her child being slaughtered. Her arms, one soaked with blood, stretched toward the house. "Please! My things! I must not leave them! You do not understand! They be important magic!"

The skrin tore at the walls to get out, to get at the two of them.

"Adie!" He pulled her face close to his. "They are no good to you dead. We will come back for them, after we get away from that thing."

Her chest heaved. Tears welled up in her eyes. "Please, Zedd. Please, my bones. You don't understand. They be important. They have magic. They may help us to close the veil. If they fall into the wrong hands . . ."

Zedd whistled for the horse. He was moving again, pulling her along with him. She protested every step of the way.

"Zedd, Please! Don't do this! Don't leave them!"

"Adie! If we die, we can't help anyone!"

The horse galloped up, skidding to a stop. Her wide eyes rolled in near panic as she saw the thing pulling itself through the walls of the house, splintering and snapping boards and beams. She gave a frightened scream, but held her ground as Zedd gripped her mane and threw himself on her back, hauling Adie up behind.

"Go! Fly like the wind, girl!"

Hooves flung chunks of dirt and moss high into the air as the horse leapt out, fangs snapping at her flanks. Zedd crouched forward, Adie clutching him around the waist as they galloped into the darkness. The skrin wasn't ten strides behind, and looked to be as fast as the horse. At least it wasn't faster. Zedd could hear the teeth snapping. The horse squealed when they did, stretching to run with everything she had. He wondered who could run the longest, the horse or the skrin, and he was afraid he knew the answer.

Richard's eyes opened. "I think someone is coming."

Sister Verna was sitting on the other side of the small fire, writing in the little book she kept tucked behind her belt. She looked up from under her eyebrows. "You have touched your Han, yes?"

"No," he admitted. His legs ached. He must have been sitting without moving for at least an hour. "But I'm telling you, I think someone is coming."

They did this every night, and it was no different this time. He would sit and picture the sword, on a blank background, and try to reach that place within himself that she said was there, but he could not find, while she watched him, or wrote in her little book, or touched her own Han. He had not visualized the sword on a black square with a white border since the first night. He had no desire to chance revisiting that nightmare.

"I am beginning to think I'm not able to touch my Han. I'm trying my best, but it just isn't working."

She drew the book close to her face in the moonlight and resumed writing. "I have told you before, Richard, it is something that takes time. You have not yet begun to have had enough practice. Do not be discouraged. It comes when it comes."

"Sister Verna, I'm telling you, someone is coming."

She kept writing. "And if you are not able to touch your Han, Richard, how would you know this? Hmm?"

"I don't know." He raked his fingers through his hair. "I've spent a lot of time alone in the woods. Sometimes I can just feel when someone is near. Don't you ever know when someone is near? Haven't you ever felt someone's eyes on you?"

"Only with the aid of my Han," she said as she wrote.

He watched as firelight flickered across her dispassionate face. "Sister Verna, you said we were in dangerous lands. I'm telling you, someone is coming."

She leafed back through the book, squinting as she read in the dim light. "And how long have you known this, Richard?"

"I told you as soon as I had the feeling, just a moment ago."

She lowered the book to her lap and looked up. "But you say you did not touch your Han? You felt nothing within yourself? You felt no power? Saw no light? Did not sense the Creator?" Her eyes narrowed. "You had better not be lying to me, Richard. You had better never lie to me about touching your Han."

"Sister Verna, you're not listening! Someone is coming!"

She closed the book. "Richard, I have known since you began your practice that someone approaches."

He stared at her in surprise. "Then why are we just sitting here?"

"We are not just sitting here. You are practicing reaching your Han, and I'm tending to my business."

"Why haven't you said anything? You told me this land is dangerous."

Sister Verna sighed and began tucking her book back behind her wide belt. "Because they were still some distance off. There was nothing else for us to do but to continue. You need the practice. You must keep trying until you are able to touch your Han." She shook her head with resignation. "But I suppose you are too agitated now to continue. They are still ten or fifteen minutes away; we may as well begin packing our things."

"Why now? Why didn't we leave as soon as you sensed them?"

"Because we had been spotted. Once we have been discovered, there is no way to escape these people. This is their land; we would not be able to outrun them. It's probably a sentinel who has found us."

"Then why do you want to pack to leave now?"

She regarded him as if he were hopelessly thick. "Because we can't spend the night here after we kill them."

Richard leapt to his feet. "Kill them! You don't even know who is coming, and already you plan to kill them?"

Sister Verna stood, drawing herself up straight, and peered into his eyes. "Richard, I have done my best to prevent this. Have we seen anyone else before now? No. Even though these people cover this land like a swarm of angry ants, we have seen no one. I have led us between anyone I could sense with my Han, in an effort to avoid contact. I have done my best to avoid trouble. Sometimes, even when you do your best, trouble cannot be avoided. I do not want to kill these people, but they are intent on killing us."

That certainly explained why they had been traveling such a peculiar route. Although they had been heading steadily southeast for weeks, they had done so in an odd fashion. Without ever explaining, she had directed them first one way, then another, occasionally backtracking, but always, relentlessly, southeast.

The barren land had become progressively rockier and more desolate. He had not bothered asking about their route because he didn't think she would tell him, and because he didn't care. Wherever they went, he was still a prisoner.

Richard scratched his new beard as he started kicking dirt over the fire. It was a warm night, as most had been lately. He wondered what had happened to winter. "We don't even know who they are yet. You can't just go killing anyone that shows up."

"Richard." She clasped her hands together. "Not all the Sisters who try to return are successful. Many are killed trying to cross these lands. In every case, there were three Sisters. I am but one. Not good odds."

The horses nickered and began moving about, tossing their heads and pawing their hooves. Richard strapped the baldric over his shoulder. He checked that the sword was clear in its scabbard.

"You were wrong, Sister, not to try to get away as soon as you knew. If you have to fight, it should be because there is no other way. You didn't even try."

Hands still clasped together, she watched him. Her voice was soft but firm. "These people are intent upon killing us, Richard. Both of us. If we had tried to run, this one would have alerted the others, and brought hundreds, thousands, to bring us down. I have not run so as to embolden this one into trying to take us himself, so we can end the threat."

271

"I'm not killing people for you, Sister Verna."

As they glared at each other, he heard a scream: a woman's scream. He stared out into the night, trying to see into the shadows of the rocky spires, trying to see where the scream came from. He couldn't see anyone, but the screams and cries were coming closer.

Richard kicked dirt over the last of the flames and sprinted to the horses, calming them with reassuring words and gentle strokes. He didn't care what she said, he wasn't killing people on her word. The woman was crazy not to want to try to escape.

She probably wanted a fight, just to see what he would do. She was always watching him as if he were a bug in a box. She questioned him every time he practiced trying to touch his Han. Whatever the Han was, he hadn't been able to sense it, much less touch it or call it forth. Just as well, as far as he was concerned.

Richard was starting toward the saddlebags, to gather the rest of their things, when a woman came running out of the night. Cloak flying behind, and crying in terror, she ran headlong into their camp. She let out a wail and dashed desperately for him.

"Please!" she cried out. "Please help me! Please don't let them get me!"

Her loose hair streamed behind as she ran. The naked fear on her face ran a shiver up Richard's spine. She stumbled as she reached him. Richard caught her frail form in his arms. Her dirty face was streaked with sweat and tears.

"Please, sir," she sobbed, looking up at him with dark eyes, "please don't let them get me. You don't know what those men will do to me."

Richard's mind filled with the fright of remembering Kahlan being pursued by the quads. He remembered how terrified she had been of those men, and how she had spoken almost the same words: *You don't know what those men will do to me.*

"No one is going to get you. You are safe now."

The woman's arms came out from under her cloak, slipping around him. Her dark eyes stayed on his as he held her weight.

She opened her mouth as if to speak, but instead gave a little grunt and jerked. Light seemed to flash from within her eyes. She went slack and heavy in his arms.

Richard looked up into Sister Verna's unwavering gaze as she yanked the silver knife from the woman's back. Richard felt himself letting the dead weight slip to the ground. The woman slumped fluidly and rolled onto her back.

The night air rang with the sound of steel as Richard drew the sword.

"What's the matter with you?" he hissed. "You have just murdered this woman."

Sister Verna returned his glare in kind. "I thought you said you held no foolish prohibitions against killing women."

The wrath of the sword's magic pounded through him, raging to be set free. "You are mad." He was rushing toward a lethal precipice. The sword's point rose in anger.

"Before you would think to kill me," Sister Verna said in a measured tone, "you had better make sure you are not making a mistake." Richard didn't answer. He was incapable of speaking through the fury. "Look in her hand, Richard."

He looked down at the lifeless body. Her hands were covered by her heavy woolen cloak. Using the sword, he flicked the cloak back off her arm to reveal a knife still gripped in her dead fist. The point had a dark stain on it.

"Did she scratch you with the knife?"

Richard's chest still heaved with anger. "No. Why?"

"Her knife is coated with poison. All it would take is a scratch."

"What makes you think it was meant for me! She was probably hoping to defend herself from the men who are chasing her!"

"There are no men chasing her. She is a sentry. You are always telling me to stop treating you like a child, Richard. Stop acting like one. I know about these people, how they do things. She meant to kill us."

He could feel the muscles in his jaw flex as he gritted his teeth. "We could have tried to get away when she first spotted us."

She nodded. "Yes, and we would have died. I am telling you, Richard, I know these people. The wilds are layered like an onion with different peoples, all of whom will kill us if they find us. Had we let her reach her kind, they would have caught us and killed us.

"Don't let the anger of your sword close your eyes. She has a poison knife in her hand, she had it to your back, and she fell into your arms to be able to get close enough to use it. You foolishly let her do so." She turned a little and swept an arm behind. "Where are the ones chasing her?" She let the arm drop to her side. "There is no one else. I could sense them with my Han if there were. She was alone. I have just saved your life."

He drove the Sword of Truth back into its scabbard. "You have done me no great favor, Sister Verna."

He didn't know what to believe. He knew only that he was sick of magic, and weary of death. "What is that knife you keep up your sleeve? What's the light in their eyes when you kill with it?"

"It's called a dacra. I guess it could be compared to the poison blade she was carrying. With the dacra it's not the wound itself that kills; the dacra extinguishes the spark of life." Her eyes lowered. "It's a painful thing to steal a life. Sometimes, it is the only way. This, tonight, was the only way to save our lives, whether you choose to believe it or not."

"All I know, Sister Verna, is that you use it without hesitation, and that you didn't even try anything else." He started to turn away. "I'm going to bury her."

"Richard." She smoothed her skirt. "I hope you understand, and that you don't misinterpret our actions, but when we reach the palace, we may have to take the Sword of Truth from you. For your own good."

"Why? How could that be for my own good?"

She clasped her hands together again. "The prophecy that you have invoked, the one that says 'He is the bringer of death, and he shall so name himself,' is a very dangerous prophecy. It goes on to say that the holder of the sword is able to call the dead forth, call the past into the present."

"What does that mean?"

"We don't know."

"Prophecies," he muttered. "Prophecies are just stupid riddles, Sister. You invest too much concern in them. You admit that you don't understand them, yet try to follow them. Only a fool follows blindly what he doesn't understand. If it were true, I would call the dead forth and give this woman's life back to her."

"We know a lot more about them than you think. I believe it would be for the best if we took the sword, just for safekeeping, until we understand the prophecy better."

"Sister Verna, if someone took the dacra from you, would you still be a Sister?"

"Of course. The dacra is simply a tool to help us in our job. It doesn't make us who we are."

He smiled a cold smile. "It's the same with the sword. With or without it, I am still the Seeker. I would be no less a danger to you. Taking it away from me will not save you."

Her fists tightened. "It is not the same."

"You are not taking the sword," he said flatly. "You could never understand how much I hate this sword, hate its magic, and how much I wish to be rid of it, but it was given to me when I was named Seeker. It was given to me to be mine for as long as I wish to hold it. I am the Seeker, and I, not you, or anyone else, will decide when I am to give it up."

Her eyes narrowed. "*Named* Seeker? You did not find the sword? Or purchase it? It was given by a wizard? You were *named* Seeker? A real Seeker? By a wizard?"

"I was."

"Who was this wizard?"

"The one I told you of before: Zeddicus Zu'l Zorander."

"You met him just this once, when he gave you the sword?"

"No. I have spent my whole life with him. He practically raised me. He is my grandfather."

There was a long moment of dead silence. "And he named you Seeker, because he refused to teach you to control the gift? To be a wizard?"

"Refused! When he realized I have the gift, he practically begged to teach me to be a wizard."

"He offered?" she whispered.

"That's right. I told him I didn't want to be a wizard." Something was wrong. She seemed disturbed by this news. "He said the offer still stands. Why?"

She rubbed her hands absently. "It is just . . . unusual, that's all. Many things about you are unusual."

Richard didn't know if he believed her. He wondered if maybe he didn't need the collar, if Zedd could have helped him without it.

But Kahlan had wanted it on him. She had wanted him taken away. His insides twisted with that pain.

The sword was the only thing he had of Zedd. It was given to him when he was still back in Westland, when he was home. He missed his home, his woods. The sword was the only thing left of Zedd, and home.

"Sister, I was named Seeker, and given this sword, for as long as I wish to keep it and be Seeker. I will be the one to decide when the time has come to give it up. If you wish to take it away from me, then try to do it now.

"If you try, one of us is going to die in the attempt. At the moment, I don't much care which one of us it is. But I intend to fight to the death. It's mine by right, and you are not taking it as long as there is a breath of life in me."

He listened to the distant howl of an animal dying a sudden, violent death, and then to the long, empty silence that followed.

"Since you were given the sword, and did not simply find it, or purchase it, you may keep it. I will not take it from you. I cannot speak for the others, but I will try to see to your wishes. It is the gift we must tend to. It is that magic we must teach you to control."

She drew herself up and regarded him with an expression of such cold danger it made him have to fight the urge to shrink back. "But if you ever again draw it against me, I will make you rue the day the Creator let you take your first breath." Her jaw muscles tightened. "Do we understand each other?"

"What's so important about me that you would kill to capture me?"

Her cold composure was more frightening than if she had yelled at him. "Our job is to help those with the gift, because the gift is given by the Creator. We serve the Creator. It is for him we die. I've lost two of my oldest friends because of you. I've wept myself to sleep with grief for them. I've had to kill this woman tonight, and I may have to kill others before we reach the palace."

Richard had the feeling it would be best to keep quiet, but he couldn't. She had a way of stirring the coals of his anger to flame. "Don't try to assuage your guilt over what you've done at my expense, Sister."

Her face heated with color that he could see, even in the moonlight. "I've tried to be patient with you, Richard. I've given you leeway because you've been pulled from the only life you have known, and been thrust into a situation you fear and don't understand, but my patience is near its end.

"I've tried my best not to see the lifeless bodies of my friends when I look into your eyes. Or when you tell me I'm heartless. I've tried not to think about you being the one standing at their burial, not me, and about the things I would have said over their fresh graves. There are things going on that are beyond my understanding, beyond my expectations, beyond what I was led to believe. Were it up to me, I'm of a mind to grant you your wish and remove your Rada'Han, and let you die in madness and pain.

"But it's not up to me. It is the Creator's work I do."

Although the hot coals of his temper hadn't been doused, they had cooled. "Sister Verna, I'm sorry." He wished she would scream at him. That would be better than her calm anger, her quiet displeasure.

"You are angered because you think I treat you as a child, and not as a man, and yet you have given me no reason to do otherwise. I know where you stand, in your abilities, and where you have yet to travel. In that journey you are no more than a babe who bawls to be turned loose in the world, yet cannot even walk.

"The collar you wear is capable of controlling you. It is also capable of giving you pain. Great pain. Up until now, I have avoided using it, and have tried instead to encourage you in other ways to accept what must be done. But if I have to, I will use it. The Creator knows I've tried everything else.

"We will soon be in a land much more dangerous than this. We will have to deal with the people there to get through. The Sisters have arrangements with them, to be allowed to pass. You will do as I tell you, as they tell you. You will do the things you are told, or there will be a great deal of trouble."

Richard's suspicion flared anew. "What things?"

She glared at him. "Do not test me further tonight, Richard."

"As long as you understand you're not getting my sword without a fight."

"We are only trying to help you, Richard, but if you draw a weapon on me again, I will see to it you greatly regret it." She glanced to the Agiel hanging at his neck. "Mord-Sith hold no monopoly in giving pain."

Cold confirmation of his suspicions spread through his gut. They intended to train him the way a Mord-Sith trained him. That was the real reason for the collar. That was how they intended to teach him: with pain. For the first time, he felt as if she had inadvertently let him see the bones of her intentions.

She pulled the little book from her belt. "I have some work to do before we leave. Go bury her. And hide her body well; if it's found, it will tell them what happened, and they will be after us, and then I will have killed for nothing."

She sat in front of the cold jumble of firewood. With a smooth sweep of her hand over the dark coals, it burst into flame. "After you've buried her, I want you to go for a walk and let your temper cool. Do not return until it has done so. If you try to wander away, or if you don't bring some reason into that thick head of yours by the time I'm ready to leave, I will bring you back by the collar." She gave him a menacing look from under her eyebrows. "You will not like it if I have to do that. I promise you, you will not like it one bit."

The dead woman was slight, and little burden to carry. He hardly noticed the weight as he walked away from the camp into the low, rocky hills. The moon was up and the way easy to see. His mind swirled with his brooding thoughts as he trudged along, kicking an occasional stone.

Richard was surprised at his pang of pain for Sister Verna. She had never before revealed how heartsick she was over the deaths of Sisters Grace and Elizabeth. He had thought that because she hadn't said anything, she was callous. He felt sorry for her now, sorry for her anguish. He wished she hadn't let him know. It was easier to rail against his situation when he thought she was heartless.

He found himself a long way from their camp, at the crest of a hump of ground, with rocky walls and spires rising around him. His mind came out of his twisting thoughts and returned to the body he carried on his back. Though the stab wound from the dacra might not have been what had killed her, blood had nonetheless seeped down her back, matting her hair and soaking his shoulder. He felt sudden revulsion at carrying a dead woman around on his back.

He laid the body gently on the rocky ground and looked about, searching for a place to lay her to rest. He had a small shovel hooked to his belt, but there didn't look to be easy digging anywhere. Maybe he could wall her up in one of the rocky crags.

While he peered into the shadowed gullies, he absently rubbed the still sore burn on his chest. Nissel, the healer, had given him a poultice, and every day he spread it on before covering the wound once more with a bandage. He didn't like looking at it. He didn't like seeing the scar of a handprint burned into his flesh.

Sister Verna had said it could have been that he had burned himself in the fireplace in the spirit house, or that they might have indeed called forth the dark minions of the Nameless One. It obviously wasn't a burn from the fire; it was the mark of the underworld. Of Darken Rahl.

He was somehow ashamed of it, and never let Sister Verna see it. The scar was a constant reminder of his father's true identity. It seemed an affront to George Cypher, the man he thought of as his father, the man who had raised him, trusted and taught him, given him his love, and whom he had loved in return.

The mark was also a constant reminder of the monster he really was—the monster Kahlan had wanted collared and sent away.

Richard swatted at a bug buzzing around his face. He looked down. They were buzzing around the dead woman, too. He went cold with a jolt of fright even before he felt the sting of a bite on his neck.

Blood flies.

He drew his sword in a rush as the huge, dark shape lunged from behind the rock. The ringing sound of steel was drowned out by a roar. Wings spread wide, the gar dove for him. For an instant, he thought he saw a second, hunched in the shadows behind the first, but his attention was immediately seized by the immense thing descending on him, by the fierce, glowing, green eyes locked on him.

It was too big to be a long-tailed gar, and by the way it anticipated and avoided his first stab, too smart. It would have to be a short-tailed gar, he cursed silently. It was thinner than short-tailed gars he had seen before, probably the result of poor hunting in this desolate land, but thin or not, it was still huge, towering half again as tall as he.

Richard stumbled and fell over the dead woman as he lurched back to escape the swipe of a massive claw. He came up swinging the sword in fury, letting the anger of the sword's magic surge through him. The tip of the sword sliced a gash across the smooth, taut, pink stomach. The gar howled in rage as it rushed him again, unexpectedly batting him to the ground with a leathery wing.

Richard rolled to his feet, whirling the sword as he came up. The blade flashed in the moonlight, taking off a wingtip in a spray of blood. That only enraged the gar into lunging toward him. Long, wet fangs ripped at the night air. Its eyes were ablaze with a furious green glow. The howling roar hurt his ears. Claws swept in to each side of him.

The magic pounded through him, demanding blood. Instead of dodging the advance, Richard ducked. He sprang up, driving the sword through the chest of the great, fur-covered beast. He yanked the blade back with a twisting cut to the sound of a scream of mortal pain.

Richard pulled the sword behind, prepared to take the hideous head off with a powerful stroke, but the gar didn't come at him. Claws clutched to the gushing wound at its chest, it teetered a moment, and then toppled heavily onto its back, bones in its wings snapping as it fell on them.

A keening wail came from the shadows. Richard retreated a few paces. A small, dark form darted across the ground, to the vanquished monster, falling on top of it. Little wings wrapped around the heaving chest.

Richard stared in disbelief. It was a baby gar.

The wounded beast lifted a shaking claw to clutch weakly at the whimpering form. It drew a gurgling breath that lifted the little gar sprawled atop its chest. The arm dropped to the side. Faintly glowing green eyes drank in its little one, and then looked up at Richard with pleading pain. A froth of blood bubbled as it expelled its last, rattling breath. The glow in its eyes waned, and then it was still. With plaintive cries, the little creature seized small fistfuls of fur.

Little or not, Richard thought, it is still a gar. He stepped close. He had to kill it. The rage pounded through him. He lifted the sword over his head.

The little gar drew a trembling wing over its head as it shrank back. As frightened as it was, it would not leave its mother. It whimpered in anguish and fear.

A terrified little face peered over the trembling wing. Wide, wet, green eyes blinked up at him. Tears ran down the deep creases in its cheeks as it sobbed in distress with a purling wail.

"Dear spirits," Richard whispered, as he stood paralyzed, "I can't do this."

The little gar quivered as it watched the sword's point sink to the ground. Richard turned his back and closed his eyes. He felt sick, both from the sword's magic, which inflicted upon him the pain of his vanquished foe, and from the dreadful prospect of what he had been ready to do.

As he replaced the sword, he drew a deep breath to steady himself, then lifted the dead woman over his shoulder and started off. He could hear the choking sobs of the little gar as it clung to its still mother. He couldn't kill it. He just couldn't. Besides, he told himself, the sword wouldn't allow it. The magic only worked against threat. It wouldn't allow him to kill the little gar. He knew it wouldn't.

Of course, it would work if he turned the blade white, but he couldn't bear that pain. He would not subject himself to that agony, not for no more purpose than to kill a defenseless pup.

He carried the dead woman's body toward the next rise as he listened to the whimpers grow faint. Laying the body down again, he sat to catch his breath. He could just see the great beast in the moonlight, a dark blotch against the light-colored rock, and the small form atop it. He could hear the slow sounds of anguish and confusion. Richard sat a long time, watching, listening.

"Dear spirits, what have I done?"

The spirits, as usual, had nothing to say.

Out of the corner of his eye, movement caught his attention. Two distant silhouettes passed in front of the big, bright moon. They banked into a slow turn, and began to descend. Two gars.

Richard came to his feet. Maybe they would see the baby and help it. He found himself cheering them on, and then realized how absurd it was to hope a gar would live. But he was beginning to feel an odd sympathy for monsters.

Richard ducked down. The two gars overhead came close to him as they swept in a wide circle around the scene on the next hill. Their spiral tightened.

The little gar fell silent.

The dark shapes dove down, landing a ways apart with a flutter of wings. They moved cautiously around the dead gar and its offspring. Wings held open, they suddenly leapt toward the silent baby gar. It broke its silence with a scream. There was a flurry of wings, vicious roars, and frightened shrieks.

Richard stood. Many animals ate the young of another of their own kind. Especially males, and especially if food was scarce. They weren't going to save it; they intended to eat it.

Before he even realized what he was doing, Richard was racing down the hill. He ran heedless of the foolishness he intended. He pulled the sword free as he charged up the hill to the little gar. Its terrified wails urged him on. The savage snarls of its attackers ignited the wrath of the sword's magic.

Steel first, he rushed into the fur and claws and wings. The two gars were bigger than the one he had killed, confirming his suspicion that they were males. His blade caught only air as they leapt back, but one of them dropped the little gar. It skittered across the ground and clutched its mother's fur. The other two circled him, charging and darting and swiping with their claws. Richard swung and stabbed with the sword. One of them snatched at the baby. Richard scooped it away with his free arm and quickly retreated a dozen paces.

They fell on the dead gar. With a cry, the baby stretched its arms toward its mother, its wings flapping against his face in an effort to free itself. In a frenzy, the two gars tore at the carcass.

Richard made a calculated decision. As long as the dead gar was there, the pup wouldn't leave it; the pup would have a better chance at survival if it had nothing to hold it to this place. It squirmed mightily in his arm. Though fully half his size, at least it was lighter than he would have thought.

He feigned a charge to hurry the two along. They snapped at him, too hungry to be frightened off without a meal. They fought each other. Claws slashed and pulled, ripping the body asunder. Richard charged again as the little gar tore free, running ahead of him with a shriek. The two leapt into the air, each with half a prize. In a moment they were gone.

The little gar stood where its mother had been, keening as it watched the two disappear into the dark sky.

Panting and weary, Richard returned his sword to its scabbard and then slumped down on a short ledge, trying to catch his breath. His head sunk into his hands as tears welled up. He must be losing his mind. What in the world was he doing? He was risking his life for nothing. No, not for nothing.

He raised his head. The little gar was standing in the blood where its mother had been, its trembling wings held out limply, its shoulders slumped, and its tufted ears wilted. Big green eyes watched him. They stared at each other for a long moment.

"I'm sorry, little one," he whispered.

It took a tentative step toward him. Tears ran down the gar's face. Tears ran down his. It took another small, shaky step.

Richard held his arms out. It watched, and then with a miserable wail, fell into them.

It clutched its long, skinny arms to him. Warm wings wrapped around his shoulders. Richard hugged it tightly to himself.

Gently stroking its coarse fur, he hushed it with comforting whispers. Richard rarely had seen a creature in such misery, a creature so in need of comfort that it would even accept it from the one who had caused its pain. Maybe, he thought, it was only recognizing him as the one who had saved it from being eaten by two huge monsters. Maybe, given the terrible choice, it chose to see him as a savior. Maybe the last impression, of saving it from being eaten, was simply the strongest.

The little gar felt like nothing more than a furry sack of bones. It was half starved. He could hear its stomach grumbling. Its faint musky odor, while not pleasant, was not repulsive either. He cooed succor as the thing's whimpering slowed.

When it had at last quieted with a heavy, tired sigh, Richard stood. Sharp little claws tugged at his pant leg as it looked up to his face. He wished he had some food to leave with the pup, but he hadn't brought his pack and had nothing to offer.

He pulled the claw from his pants. "I have to go. Those two won't come back now. Try to find yourself a rabbit or something. You'll have to do the best you can on your own now. Go on."

It blinked up at him, its wings and one leg slowly stretching as it yawned. Richard turned and started off. He looked over his shoulder. The little gar followed after.

Richard stamped to a halt. "You can't come with me." He held his arms out and shooed it away. "Go on. Be off with you." He started walking backward. The gar followed. He stopped again and shooed it more firmly. "Go! You can't come with me! Go on!"

The wings wilted again. It took a few shaking steps back as Richard started off again. This time it stayed put as he went on his way.

Richard had the woman's body to bury, and he needed to get back to camp before Sister Verna decided to use the collar to bring him back. He had no desire to give her an excuse; he knew she would find one soon enough. He glanced behind to make sure the gar hadn't followed. He was alone.

He found the body, laid on its back, where he had left it. He noted with relief that there were no blood flies about. He had to find either a patch of ground soft enough to dig a hole, or else a deep crevice of some sort to hide her body in. Sister Verna had been explicit about hiding it well.

As he was surveying the scene, there was a soft flutter of wings and the little gar thumped to the ground nearby. He gave a quiet lament as the creature folded its wings and squatted comfortably before him, peering up with big green eyes.

Richard tried to shoo it away again. It didn't move. He put his hands on his hips. "You can't come with me. Go away!"

It tottered to him and clutched his legs. What was he going to do? He couldn't have a gar tagging after him.

"Where are your flies? You don't even have any blood flies of your own. How can you expect to catch your dinner without your own blood flies?" He gave a rueful shake of his head. "Well, it's not my concern."

The small, wrinkled face peeked around his legs. A low growl came from its throat as its lips pulled back to reveal sharp little fangs. Richard looked around. It was growling at the dead woman. He closed his eyes with a groan. The pup was hungry. If he buried the body, the gar would dig it up.

Richard watched as the gar hopped over to the body, pawing at it as its growls grew louder. Richard tried to swallow back the dryness in his throat, or maybe the things he was thinking.

Sister Verna had said to get rid of the body. They mustn't know how the woman had died, she had said. He couldn't stand the thought of the remains being eaten. But even if he buried it, it would be eaten anyway—by worms. Why were worms better than a gar? Another ghastly thought came to him: who was he to judge—he had eaten human flesh. Why was that any different? Was he any better?

And besides, if the pup was busy eating, he could be off, and they would be gone before it had time to follow. It would be on its own then. He would be rid of it.

Richard watched as the little gar cautiously inspected the body. It experimentally tugged at an arm with its teeth. The pup wasn't experienced enough to know what to do with a kill. It growled louder. The sight made Richard sick.

The teeth dropped the arm and the gar looked at him, as if to ask for help. The wings fluttered with excitement. It was hungry.

Two problems at once.

What difference did it make? She was dead. Her spirit had departed her body and wouldn't miss it. It would solve two problems at once. Gritting his teeth at the task in mind, he drew the sword.

Pushing back the hungry gar with a leg, Richard took a mighty swing, slashing open a great rent. The little gar pounced.

Richard walked quickly away without looking back. The sounds turned his stomach. Who was he to judge? Light-headed, he broke into a trot back to the camp. Sweat soaked his shirt. The sword had never felt so heavy at his hip. He tried to put the whole incident out of his head. He thought about the Hartland Woods and wished he were home. He wished he could still be who he had once been.

Sister Verna had just finished currying Jessup and was lifting on his saddle. She eyed him with a sidelong glance before moving to her horse's head, speaking softly

280

and privately to him as she scratched his chin. Richard took up the curry comb and brushed quickly at Geraldine's back, cautioning her sharply to stand still and quit turning about. He wanted to be away quickly.

"Did you make sure they wouldn't find the body?"

His hand with the comb froze on Geraldine's flanks. "If they find what's left, they won't know what happened. I was attacked by gars. They got the body."

She thought this over silently for a moment. "I thought I heard gars. Well, I guess that will do." He went back to brushing as she spoke again. "Did you kill them?"

"I killed one." He considered not telling her, but decided it didn't matter. "There was a baby gar. I didn't kill it."

"Gars are murderous beasts. You should have killed it. Perhaps you should go back and finish it."

"I can't. It . . . won't let me get close enough."

With a little grunt she pulled the girth strap tight. "You have a bow."

"What difference does it make? Let's just be off. All by itself, it will probably die anyway."

She bent, checking that the strap wasn't pinching her horse. "Perhaps you're right. It would be best if we were away from here."

"Sister? Why haven't the gars bothered us before?"

"Because I shield against them with my Han. You were too far away, beyond my shields, and so they came for you."

"So this shield will keep all gars away from us?"

"Yes."

Well, at least there was one thing the Han was good for. "Doesn't that take a lot of power? Gars are big beasts. Isn't it hard?"

The question brought a small smile to her lips. "Yes, gars are big, and there are other beasts I must shield against, too. All this would take much power. You must always search for the way to accomplish the task using the least amount of Han."

She stroked her horse's neck as she went on. "I keep the gars away not by repelling the beasts themselves, but by shielding against their blood flies. It's much easier. If the flies can't get through the shield, the gars won't think there is anything worthwhile and so won't come to us either. It uses little of my strength this way, yet achieves my aim."

"Why didn't you use this shield against the people here? Against the woman tonight?"

"Some of the people in the wilds have charms against our power. That's why many Sisters die trying to cross. If we knew how these charms or spells worked, we might be able to counter them, but we don't. It's a mystery to us."

Richard finished saddling Geraldine and Bonnie in silence. The Sister waited patiently. He thought she had more to say, about their argument before he had gone to bury the woman, but she remained silent. He decided to speak first, and get it over with.

"Sister Verna, I'm sorry about Sisters Grace and Elizabeth." He idly stroked Bonnie's shoulder as he studied the ground. "I said a prayer over their graves. I just wanted you to know that. A prayer to the good spirits to watch over them and treat them well. I didn't want them to die. You may think otherwise, but I don't want anyone to die. I'm sick of death. I can't even eat meat anymore because I can't stand the thought of anything having to die just to feed me."

"Thank you for the prayer, Richard, but you must learn that it is only the Creator we must pray to. It is His light that guides. Praying to spirits is heathenish." She seemed to think better of her harsh tone, and softened it. "But you are unschooled, and would not know that. I can't fault you for doing the best you could. I'm sure the Creator heard your prayer, and understood its benevolent intent."

Richard didn't like her narrow-minded attitude. He thought that perhaps he knew more about spirits than she did. He didn't know much about this Creator of hers, but he had seen spirits before, both good and bad. He knew you ignored them at your own peril.

Her dogmas seemed as foolish to him as the superstitions of the country people he knew when he had been a guide. They had been full of stories of how people came to be. Each remote area he had visited had its own version of man created from this or that animal or plant. Richard had liked listening to the stories. They were filled with wonder and magic. But they were just stories, rooted in a need to understand how the teller fit into the world. He was not going to accept on faith the things the Sisters said.

He did not think that the creator was like some king, sitting upon a throne, listening to every petty prayer to come his way. Spirits had been alive once, and they understood the needs of mortals, understood the exigencies of living flesh and blood.

Zedd had taught him that the creator was simply another name for the force of balance in all things, and not some wise man sitting in judgment.

But what did it matter? He knew people held tightly to their doctrines and were closed-minded about it. Sister Verna believed what she did and he wasn't going to change it. He had never faulted people for the beliefs they held; he was not about to start now. Such beliefs, true or not, could be a balm.

He pulled the baldric off over his head and held the sword out to her. "I've thought about the things you said before. I've decided I don't want the sword anymore."

Her hands came up and he laid the weight of the sword, scabbard, and baldric in them.

She showed no emotion. "Do you really mean this?"

He nodded. "I do. I am finished with it. The sword is yours now."

He turned to check his saddle. Even without the sword at his hip, he could still feel the tingle of its magic. He could give up the sword, but the magic was still within him; he was the true Seeker, and could not be rid of that. At least he could be rid of the blade, and thereby the things he did with it.

"You are a very dangerous man, Richard," she whispered.

He looked back over his shoulder. "That's why I'm giving you the sword. I don't want it any longer, and you do, so it's yours. We'll see now how you like killing with it."

He tucked the end of the girth strap through the buckle and drew it tight. He gave Bonnie a gentle pat before turning around. Sister Verna was still holding out the sword.

"Until now I had no idea just how dangerous you are."

"Not anymore. You have the sword now."

"I cannot accept it," she whispered. "It was my duty to take the sword from you when you came back—to test you. There was only one thing you could have done to prevent losing it. And you have done it." She lifted the sword to him. "There is no man more dangerous than one who is unpredictable. There is no way to forecast what you will do when pushed. It is going to be great trouble. For you. For us."

Richard didn't know what she was talking about. "There's nothing unpredictable about it. You wanted the sword, and I'm weary of the things I do with it, so I gave it to you."

"You understand, because it is the way you think. Others don't think that way. You're an enigma. Worse, your inexplicable behavior comes at the times you need it most. That is the gift at work. You're using your Han without understanding what you are doing. That is dangerous."

"One reason for the collar is to open my mind to the gift. That's what you said. If I'm using the gift, which is what you want me to do, and if it is what I need, then I don't see how that is dangerous."

"What you need and what's right are not necessarily the same. Just because you want something, that does not make it right." She nodded to the sword. "Take it back. I cannot accept it now. You must keep it."

"I told you, I don't want it."

"Then throw it in the fire. I cannot take it. It's tainted."

Richard snatched it out of her hands. "I'm not throwing it in the fire." He put his head through the baldric and straightened the scabbard at his hip. "I think you're too superstitious, Sister. It's just a sword. It is not tainted."

She was wrong. It was the magic that was tainted, and he had not offered that to her. Even if he wanted to be rid of its magic, all magic, he could not. It was part of him. Kahlan had seen that, and she had rid herself of it. Of him.

She turned from him and mounted Jessup. Her voice was cold and distant. "We must be on our way."

Richard settled into his saddle and followed after. He hoped the little gar would have a chance at life, after the meal it had needed. He said a silent good-bye to it as he rode into the night behind Sister Verna.

Though he had meant what he said about giving her the sword, he felt strangely relieved to have it back. It belonged with him, and somehow made him whole. Zedd had given it to him; it was what had changed him, but it was also all he had to remind him of his friend and home.

The horse was exhausted, but still ran with wild abandon. Adie held a tight grip on Zedd's waist as he leaned over the horse's withers, clutching her mane. Muscles bunched and flexed rhythmically beneath him. Trees in the dense forest flashed by in an endless blur. The horse leapt over rocks and logs without pause.

The skrin was only a heartbeat behind. Being taller than the horse, it struck branches as it ran. Zedd could hear the limbs snap and splinter. He had tried felling trees across the way right behind them, but it didn't slow the bone beast. He had tried tricks and spells and wizardry of every sort. None had worked, but he refused to admit defeat. Admitting defeat established a mental state of resignation that would make it certain.

"I fear the Keeper has us this time," Adie called at his back.

"Not yet he doesn't! How did he find us? The bones of the skrin have been in your house, hiding you, for years! If they have been hiding you, then how did he find us?"

She had no answer.

They were running the path where the boundary had been, headed toward the Midlands. Zedd was thankful the boundary walls were no longer there, or they could have inadvertently run into the underworld by now. Boundary or not, this couldn't go on for much longer, and then the skrin would have them. Boundary or not, the underworld would have them. The Keeper would have them.

*Think*, he ordered himself.

Zedd was using magic to lend strength and stamina to the horse, but even so, heart, lungs and sinew could not endure long past their natural limits. He was nearly as weary as the frightened animal. This couldn't go on much longer.

He had to stop trying to slow the skrin, and put his mind to solving the problem. But that could be a dangerous shift in tactics. It could be that although what he was doing wasn't stopping the skrin, it was keeping it from them.

He thought he saw a flash of green light to the left. A shade of green he had seen from only one place: the boundary. From the underworld. Impossible, he thought. The horse's hooves thundered on.

"Adie! Do you have anything with you that the skrin would recognize?"

"Like what?"

"I don't know! Anything! It has to have found us by something. Something to connect us to the underworld."

"I have nothing. It must have found us by the bones at my house."

"But the bones have been what have been hiding you!"

There was no mistaking the flash of green light this time. It was to the right. Another came to the left.

"Zedd! I think the skrin be bringing up the underworld, to force us into it!"

Bones.

"Can it do that?"

Her voice wasn't as loud this time. "Yes."

"Bags," he muttered into the cold wind at his face.

Eerie green light flickered between the trees. It was closer. If he didn't think of something, they were going to die.

*Think.*

Suddenly the green light seemed to ignite into a solid wall to each side. It made a thump he could feel deep in his chest when it arrived, whole, in this world. The horse galloped down the path between them. The way between the walls was narrowing.

Bones.

Skrin bones.

"Adie! Give me the necklace around your neck!"

The luminous green walls of the boundary pressed in to each side. They were out of time. They were out of options.

Adie pulled off her necklace and put her arm around him again, holding out the bone necklace. Her hand was slick with blood. Zedd yanked his own necklace over his head and snatched hers in the same hand.

"If this doesn't work, I'm sorry, Adie. I just want you to know I've enjoyed sharing time with you."

"What are you going to do?"

"Hold tight!"

The green walls of the boundary closed together ahead of them. Zedd held the horse firmly and gave her a silent command.

She dug in her hooves and spun around to a halt just before the trail ended in a wall of the underworld.

Zedd flung the two necklaces made with skrin bone into the green light, between a wide gap in the trees.

The skrin was upon them. Without pause, it followed the necklaces as they sailed into the boundary, into the green light. There was a flash, and a booming clap, like a lightning strike, as the skrin went through.

The green light, and the skrin, flickered and were gone. The dark forest was silent but for ragged breathing.

Adie laid her head wearily against his back. "You be right, old man. Your life be one act of desperation after another."

Zedd patted her knee before sliding off the sweaty horse. The poor animal was so exhausted it was at the brink of death. Zedd held its head between his hands and gave it a dose of strength, and his sincere thanks. He laid the side of his face against her nose as he closed his eyes and gave reassuring strokes to her cheeks for a moment before going to check on Adie.

Blood still oozed from the wound on her arm. The size of the horse made Adie appear smaller than she really was. Her slumped shoulders and hanging head didn't help diminish the illusion. She didn't acknowledge any pain as Zedd inspected the wound.

"I be a fool," she said. "The whole time I thought I be hiding under the Keeper's nose, he be hiding under mine. He knew where I be the whole time. All these years."

"We can take solace in the fact that it earned him no profit. He has wasted his investment. Now hold still. I must tend to this wound."

"There be no time for that. We must get back to my house. I must get my bones."

"I said be still."

"We must hurry."

Zedd scowled up at her. "We will go back when I'm finished, but the horse is exhausted; she must be walked. I'll walk and let you ride, if you give me no further trouble. Now be still or we will be here the whole night quibbling."

By the time they reached Adie's house, dawn was breaking, offering a cold, weak light. It was a sad sight. The skrin had torn the place to splinters. Adie disregarded the leaning, holed walls as she rushed inside, stepping over debris, picking up bones, holding them in the crook of her other arm, as she worked her way toward the corner where they had last seen the round, carved bone.

Zedd was inspecting the ground outside when he heard her calling to him.

"Come help me find the round bone, wizard."

He stepped over a fallen beam. "I don't expect you will find it."

She pushed a board aside. "It be here somewhere." She stopped, looking back over her shoulder. "What do you mean, you don't expect we will find it?"

"Someone has been here."

She looked around at the ruin. "You be sure?"

Zedd waved his arm vaguely toward where he had been studying the ground. "I saw a footprint, over there. It isn't ours."

She let the bones in her arm drop to the floor. "Who?"

He laid his hand on a beam that hung from the ceiling, its end resting on the floor. "I don't know, but someone has been here. It looks to be a woman's boot, but it isn't yours. I suspect she will have taken the round bone."

Adie pawed through the rubble in the corner, searching. At last she stopped. "You be right, old man. The bone be gone." She turned, seeming to inspect the very air with her white eyes. "Banelings," she hissed. "You be wrong about the Keeper wasting his effort."

"I fear you're right." Zedd brushed his hand clean on the side of his leg. "We had better get away from here. Far away."

Adie leaned toward him, her voice low but firm. "Zedd, we must have that bone. It be important for the veil."

"She has covered her trail with magic. I don't have any idea where she went. I only saw one footprint. We must be be away from here; the Keeper might expect us to return. I'll cover our trail, also so no one will know where we're going."

"You be so sure about that? The Keeper seems to know where we be, and sends his minions for us at will."

"He tracked us by the necklaces we wore. He will be blind to us for the time being. But we must get away from here. He may have eyes watching, the same eyes that took the bone."

Her head sunk lower as she closed her eyes. "Forgive me, Zedd, for endangering you so. For being a fool."

"Nonsense. No one knows everything. You can't expect to walk through life without stepping in the muck now and again. The important thing is to maintain your footing when you do, and not fall on your face and make it worse."

286

"But that bone be important!"

"It's gone. We can do nothing about it now. At least we foiled the Keeper; he didn't get us. But we must be away from here."

Adie bent to pick up the bones she had dropped. "I will hurry."

"We can't take anything, Adie," he said quietly.

She straightened. "I must take my bones. Some of them be important. Some have powerful magic."

Zedd took up her thin hand. "Adie, the Keeper knew where we were by one of the bones. He's been watching you. We can't know if he would recognize any of these, too. We must leave them, but we can't risk having someone else taking them; they must be destroyed."

Her mouth worked for a moment before she found words. "I will not leave them. They be important. They were extremely difficult to obtain. It took me years to find some of them. The Keeper could not have marked them. He could not know the trouble I went to."

Zedd patted her hand. "Adie, he wouldn't have placed one he wanted you to have, to mark you, right in your path. He would have made you struggle for it, so you would value it and keep it close."

She yanked her hand back. "Then he could have marked anything!" She pointed. "How do you know this horse was not given by a baneling?"

Zedd gave her a level look. "Because it was not the one offered. I took another."

Tears welled up in her eyes. "Please, Zedd," she whispered. "They be mine. They be how I was going to reach my Pell."

"I will help you get your message to your Pell. I have given you my word, but this is not the way to do it; it hasn't worked yet. I'll help you find a new way."

She limped a step closer to him. "How?"

He regarded her stricken face with sympathy. "I have a way to bring spirits through the veil for a brief time, to speak with them. Even if I can't bring Pell through, I might be able to get a message to him. But Adie, you must listen to me; we can't do it now. We must wait until the veil is closed."

Her trembling fingers touched his arm. "How? How can such a thing be done?"

"It can be done. That is all you must know."

"Tell me." Her fingers tightened on his arm. "I must know you speak the truth. I must know it can be done."

He weighed the decision a long moment. He had used the wizard's rock his father had given him to call the spirits of his father and mother to himself, but they had told him explicitly not to call them again until this was finished, or they would risk tearing the veil apart. Using the rock in such a fashion was dangerous even in the best of times, and he had been cautioned not to do it except in the gravest circumstances.

Opening a path to the spirits was always a great risk. You never knew what you could be letting through, unintended. Enough dark things were getting through without his helping them.

Even though Adie was a sorceress, this use of the wizard's rock was not for her to know. It was a secret, like many others, that wizards must keep. His heart felt heavy with that responsibility.

"You will have to trust my word that it can be done. I've given my word that I'll help you, and when it is safe, I'll try."

Her fingers still dug urgently into his arm. "How can such a thing be? Are you sure? How could you know such a thing?"

He straightened his shoulders. "I'm a wizard of the First Order."

"But are you sure?"

"Adie, you must take my word. I don't give it lightly. I'm not sure it will work, but I believe it may. Right now the important thing is to use what we know, what you and I know, to stop the Keeper from tearing the veil. It would be wrong to use what I know for selfish reasons and thus endanger the safety of everyone else. Maintaining the veil requires a delicate balance of forces; this could disturb it. It could even be that such a use would tear the veil."

She took her hand from his arm and wiped a stray strand of gray hair from her face. "Forgive me, Zedd. You be right. I have studied the cusp between the worlds for most of my life. I should know better. Forgive me."

He smiled as he hugged her around her shoulders. "I'm gratified that you hold your vows to be so important. It means that you are a person of honor. There's no better ally than a person of honor."

She looked around her shattered home. "It just be that . . . I have spent my life gathering these things. I have been their caretaker for so long. Others have entrusted them to me."

Zedd walked her out of the rubble. "Others have invested their trust in you to use the gift you were given to protect those without power. They are the ones who wrote the prophecies. You have been brought to this point for a reason. That's the trust you must keep."

She nodded, rubbing a thin hand on his back as they walked away from the remains of her home.

"Zedd, I think several other bones be missing, too."

"I know."

"They be dangerous in the wrong hands."

"I know that too."

"Then what do you plan to do about it?"

"I plan to do what the prophecies say is the only thing that gives us a chance at closing the veil."

"And what be that, old man?"

"Helping Richard. We must find a way to help him, for the prophecies say he is the only one who can close the veil."

Neither looked back as fire roared to life, roiling and racing through the ruins, dancing through the bones.

Queen Cyrilla held her head high. She refused to acknowledge how much the coarse fingers of the brutes who held her were hurting her arms. She didn't resist as they walked her down the filthy corridor. Resistance was hopeless, anyway, and would bring her no aid. She would conduct herself now as always: with dignity. She was the queen of Galea. She would endure with dignity what was to come. She would not show her terror.

Besides, it was not what was being done to her that mattered. It was what was going to happen to the Galean people that grieved her.

And what had already happened.

Nearly one hundred score of the Galean guard had been murdered before her eyes. Who could have foreseen that they would be set upon in this, of all places: on neutral ground? That a few had escaped was no solace. They, too, would probably be hunted down and killed.

She hoped that her brother, Prince Harold, had been among those who had escaped. If he had gotten away, perhaps he could rally a defense against the worse slaughter that was yet to come.

The brutal hands on her arms brought her to a halt next to a hissing torch set in a rust-encrusted bracket. The fingers twisted so painfully that a small cry escaped her lips despite her will to stifle it.

"Are my men hurting you, my lady?" came a mocking voice from behind.

She coolly denied Prince Fyren the satisfaction of an answer.

A guard worked keys at a rusty lock, sending a sharp, metallic sound echoing down the stone corridor when the bolt finally drew. The heavy door groaned on its hinges as it was pulled open. The viselike hands forced her on, through the doorway and down another long, low passageway.

She could hear the swish of her satin skirts, and to the sides and behind, the men's boots on the stone floor, splashing occasionally through stagnant, foul-smelling water. The dank air felt cold on her shoulders, which were unaccustomed to being uncovered.

Her heart threatened to race out of control when she thought about where she was being taken. She prayed to the dear spirits that there wouldn't be rats. She feared rats, their sharp teeth, their clutching claws, and their cunning, black eyes. When she was very little she had nightmares about rats, and would wake screaming.

It an effort to bring her heart back under control, she tried to think of other things. She thought about the strange woman who had sought a private audience with her. Cyrilla wasn't at all sure why she had granted it, but she now wished she had paid more heed to the insistent woman.

What was her name? Lady something. A glimpse of her hair beneath the concealing veil had shown it to be too short for someone of her standing. Lady . . . Bevinvier. Yes, that was it: Lady Bevinvier. Lady Bevinvier of . . . someplace. She couldn't will her mind to remember. It didn't matter anyway; it was not where the woman was from, but what she had said, that mattered.

*Leave Aydindril*, Lady Bevinvier had warned. *Leave at once.*

But Cyrilla had not come all this way, in the teeth of winter, to leave before the Council of the Midlands had heard her grievance, and acted upon it. She had come to demand that the council do its duty to bring an immediate halt to the transgressions against her land and people.

Towns had been sacked, farms burned, and people murdered. The armies of Kelton were massing to attack. An invasion was imminent, if not already under way. And for what? Nothing but naked conquest. Against an ally! It was an outrage!

It was the council's duty to come to the defense of any land being attacked, no matter by whom. The whole point of the Council of the Midlands was to prevent just such treason. It was their duty to direct all the lands to come to the aid of Galea, and put down the aggression.

Though Galea was a powerful land, it had been gravely weakened by its defense of the Midlands against D'Hara, and was not prepared for another costly war. Kelton had been spared the brunt of the D'Haran conquest, and had reserves aplenty. Galea had paid the price of resistance in their stead.

The night before, Lady Bevinvier had come to her, and had begged that she leave at once. She had said Cyrilla would find no help for Galea from the council. The Lady Bevinvier said that if the queen stayed, she would be in great personal danger. At first, when pressed, Lady Bevinvier refused to explain herself.

Cyrilla thanked her but said she would not turn away from her duty to her people, and would go before the council, as planned. Lady Bevinvier broke down in tears, begging that the queen heed her words.

She at last confided that she had had a vision.

Cyrilla tried to draw the nature of the vision out of the woman, but she said that it was incomplete, that she didn't know any details, only that if the queen didn't leave at once, something terrible would happen. Though Cyrilla trusted well the powers of magic, she had little faith in fortune-tellers. Most were charlatans, seeking only to fatten their purse with a clever turn of a phrase, or a vague hint of danger to be avoided.

Queen Cyrilla was touched by the woman's seeming sincerity, though she reasoned it might be nothing but deception, meant to trick her out of a coin. A ruse for money seemed strange coming from a woman of such seeming wealth, but times had been hard, and she knew the wealthy were not immune to losses. After all, if gold and goods were to be seized, it only made sense to seek them from those who had them. Cyrilla knew many who had worked hard all their lives, only to lose everything in the war with D'Hara. Perhaps Lady Bevinvier's short hair was the result of that loss.

She thanked the woman, but told her that the mission was too important to be turned aside. She pressed a gold piece into the woman's hand, only to have Lady Bevinvier throw the coin across the room before rushing off in tears.

Cyrilla had been shaken by that. A charlatan did not refuse gold. Unless of course she sought something more. Either the woman had been telling the truth, or she was working in aid of Kelton, trying to prevent the council from hearing of the aggression.

Either way, it didn't matter; Cyrilla was resolute. Besides, she was influential in the council. Galea was respected for its defense of the Midlands. When Aydindril had fallen, councilors who had refused to swear the allegiance of their land to D'Hara had been put to death and replaced by puppets. Those councilors who had collaborated were allowed to retain their position. Galea's loyal ambassador to the council had been executed.

How the war had ended was a puzzle; D'Haran forces were told that Darken Rahl was dead and all hostilities were ended. A new Lord Rahl had succeeded, and the troops were simply called home, or ordered to help those they had conquered. Cyrilla suspected Darken Rahl had been assassinated.

Whatever had happened was good by her; the council was now back in the hands of the people of the Midlands. The ones who collaborated, and the puppets, had been arrested. Things were said to be set back to the way they had been before the dictator. She expected the council would come to the aid of Galea.

Queen Cyrilla, too, had an ally on the council, the most powerful ally there was: the Mother Confessor. Although Kahlan was her half sister, that held no sway. Galea, and the queen, supported the independence of the different lands, and the peace of the Midlands through the council. Galea had always advocated unity of purpose. The Mother Confessor respected that steadfastness, and that was what made her Galea's ally.

Kahlan had never shown Cyrilla any favoritism, and that was as it should have been; favoritism would have weakened the Mother Confessor, threatening the alliance of the council, and therefore peace. She respected Kahlan for putting the unity of the Midlands above any power games. Such games were a shifting bog anyway; one was always better off in the end when dealt with fairly, rather than by favor.

Cyrilla had always been secretly proud of her half sister. Kahlan was twelve years younger, smart, strong, and, despite her young age, an astute leader. Though they were related by blood, they almost never spoke of it. Kahlan was a Confessor, and of the magic. She was not a sister who shared the blood of a father, but a Confessor, and the Mother Confessor of the Midlands. Confessors were blood to no one but Confessors.

Still, having no family of her own, save her beloved brother, Harold, she had often longed to take Kahlan in her arms as kin, as a little sister, and speak of the things they shared. But that was not possible. Cyrilla was the queen of Galea, and Kahlan was the Mother Confessor; two women who were virtual strangers who shared nothing save blood and mutual respect. Duty came before the heart. Galea was Cyrilla's family; the Confessors, Kahlan's.

Though there were those who resented Kahlan's mother taking Wyborn as a mate, Cyrilla was not among them. Her mother, Queen Bernadine, had taught her and Harold of the need for Confessors, their need for strong blood in that line of magic, and how it served the greater cause of the Midlands in keeping peace. Her mother had never spoken bitterly of losing her husband to the Confessors, but explained instead the honor Cyrilla and Harold had of sharing blood with the Confessors, even if it was mostly unspoken. Yes, she was proud of Kahlan.

Proud, but also perhaps a bit wary. The ways of Confessors were a mystery to her. From birth they were trained in Aydindril, trained by other Confessors, and by wizards. Their magic, their power, was something they were born with, and in a way they were slaves to it. In some ways it was the same with her; born to be queen, without much choice. Though she had no magic, she understood the weight of birthright.

From birth until their training was completed, Confessors were kept cloistered, like priestesses, in a world apart. Their discipline was said to be rigorous. Though Cyrilla knew they must have emotions like anyone, Confessors were trained to subjugate them. Duty to their power was all. It left them no choice in life, save choosing a mate, and even that was not for love but for duty.

Cyrilla had always wished she could bring a little of the love of a sister to Kahlan. Perhaps, she also wished Kahlan could have brought a little of that love to her, too. But it could never be. Maybe Kahlan had loved her from afar, as Cyrilla had Kahlan. Perhaps Kahlan had been proud of her, too, in her own way. She had always hoped it was so.

The thing that pained her the most was that though they both served the Midlands, she was loved by her people for doing her duty, but Kahlan was feared and hated for it. She wished Kahlan could know a people's love; it was a comfort that in part made up for the sacrifice. But a Confessor never could. Perhaps, she thought, that was why they were taught to subjugate their emotions and needs.

Kahlan, too, had tried to warn her of the danger from Kelton.

It had been at the midsummer festival, several years ago, the first summer after the death of Cyrilla's mother. The first summer Cyrilla had been queen. The first summer, too, since Kahlan had ascended to Mother Confessor.

That Kahlan had became the Mother Confessor at such a young age spoke of both the strength of her power and of her character. And perhaps of a need. Since the selection was made in secrecy, Cyrilla knew little about the succession of Confessors, except that it was done without animosity or rivalry, and had to do with the strength of power weighed against age and training.

To the people of the Midlands, age was irrelevant. They feared Confessors in general, regardless of age, and the Mother Confessor in particular. They knew she was the most powerful of Confessors. Unlike most people, however, Cyrilla knew that power in and of itself was not necessarily something to fear, and Kahlan had always been fair. She had never sought anything but peace.

That day the streets of Ebinissia, the Crown city of Galea, had been filled with festivities of every sort. Not even the lowest stableboy had failed to find welcome at the tables of the fair, or at the games, or around the musicians, acrobats, and jugglers.

Cyrilla, as queen, had presided over the contests, and given ribbons to the victors. She had never seen so many smiling faces, so many happy people. She had never felt so contented for her people, or been made to feel so loved by them.

That night there was a royal ball at the palace. The great hall was filled with nearly four hundred people. It was dazzling to see everyone in their most elegant dress. Food and wine were arrayed on the long tables in abundant and stunning variety—only fitting for the most important day of the year. It was grand beyond any ball that had come before, for there was much for which to be thankful. It was a time of peace and prosperity, growth and promise, new life and bounty.

The music trailed off in thin, discordant notes, and the loud drone of the gathering fell suddenly dead silent as the the Mother Confessor strode purposefully into the hall, her wizard at her heels, his silver robes flying behind. Her regal-looking white dress stood out among the confusion of color like the full moon among the stars.

Bright color and fancy dress had never looked so unexpectedly trivial. Everyone bowed low at her passing. Cyrilla waited with her advisors beside the table on which sat a large, cut-glass bowl of spiced wine.

Kahlan crossed the hushed room, followed by every eye, and drew to a halt before the queen, giving a prompt bow of her head. Her expression was as still as ice. She didn't wait for the formality of the bow to her office to be returned.

"Queen Cyrilla. You have an advisor named Drefan Tross?"

Cyrilla held her open hand out to the side. "This is he."

Kahlan's emotionless gaze moved to Drefan. "I would speak with you in private."

"Drefan Tross is a trusted advisor," Cyrilla interrupted. He was more than that. He was a man she was very fond of, a man she was just beginning to fall in love with. "You may speak to him in my presence." She didn't know what this was about, but thought it best if she were privy to it. Confessors did not interrupt banquets except for trouble. "This is neither the time nor place to conduct business of this sort, Mother Confessor, but if it cannot wait, then let it be done and finished with here and now."

She thought that would put it in abeyance until a more appropriate time. Without expression, the Mother Confessor considered this a moment. The wizard at her back was anything but expressionless. He appeared quite agitated, in fact. He bent toward Kahlan to speak, but she raised her hand to silence him before he could begin.

"As you wish. I am sorry, Queen Cyrilla, but it cannot wait." She returned her attention to Drefan. "I have just taken the confession of a murderer. In his confession, he also revealed himself to be an accomplice to an assassin. He named you as that assassin, and your target as Queen Cyrilla."

There were astonished whispers from those near enough to overhear. Drefan's face went red. The whispers died into brittle silence.

Cyrilla could scarcely follow what happened next. A blink of the eye and it would have been missed. One instant Drefan stood as he had, with his hand in his gold and deep blue coat, and the next he was driving a knife toward the Mother Confessor. Standing tall, she moved only her arm, catching his wrist. Seemingly at the same time, there was a violent impact to the air—thunder but no sound. The cut-glass bowl shattered, flooding red wine over the table and floor. Cyrilla flinched with the sudden flash of pain coursing through every joint in her body. The knife clattered to the floor. Drefan's eyes went wide, his jaw slack.

"Mistress," he whispered reverently.

Cyrilla was numb with shock to see a Confessor use her power. She knew only of its aftereffects, and had never seen it being used. Few had. The magic seemed still to sizzle in the air a long moment.

The crowd pressed closer. A warning glare from the wizard changed their curiosity to timidity, and they moved back.

Kahlan looked drained, but her voice betrayed no weakness. "You intended to assassinate the queen?"

"Yes, Mistress," he said eagerly, licking his lips.

"When?"

"Tonight. In the confusion when the guests were departing." Drefan looked to be in torment. Tears welled up and ran down his cheeks. "Please, Mistress, command me. Tell me what you wish. Let me carry out your command."

Cyrilla was still in shock. This was what had been done to her father. This was how he had been taken as a mate to a Confessor. First her father, and now a man she held dear.

"Wait in silence," Kahlan ordered. Hands hanging at her sides, she turned to Cyrilla, her young eyes now heavy with sorrow. "Forgive me for disturbing your celebration, Queen Cyrilla, but I feared the results of delay."

Her face burning, Cyrilla twisted to face Drefan. He stood gaping at Kahlan. "Who ordered this, Drefan! Who ordered you kill me!"

He didn't even seem to be aware she had spoken.

"He will not answer you, Queen Cyrilla," Kahlan said. "He will only answer me."

"Then you ask!"

"That would not be advisable," the wizard offered quietly.

Cyrilla felt a fool. Everyone knew of her fondness for Drefan. Everyone saw now that she had been duped. No one would ever forget this midsummer festival.

"Do not presume to advise me!"

Kahlan leaned closer and spoke softly. "Cyrilla, we think he may be protected by a spell. When I asked his accomplice that question, he died before he could answer. But I believe I know the answer. There are oblique ways of getting the information that might possibly circumvent the spell. If I could take him somewhere alone and question him in my own way, we might be able to get the answer."

Cyrilla was near tears with fury. "I trusted him! He was close to me! He has betrayed me! Me, not you! I will know who sent him! I will hear it from his own lips! You stand in my kingdom, in my home! Ask him!"

Kahlan straightened, her face returning to the calm mask that showed nothing. "As you wish." She redirected her attention to Drefan. "Was what you intended to do to the queen of your own volition?"

He dry-washed his hands in anxious anticipation of pleasing the Mother Confessor. "No, Mistress. I was sent."

If it was possible, Kahlan's face seemed to become even more placid. "Who sent you?"

One hand rose, and his mouth opened, as if in an attempt to do her bidding. All that came from his throat was a gurgle of blood before he collapsed.

The wizard gave a knowing grunt. "As I thought: the same as the other."

Kahlan picked up the knife and offered it handle-first to Cyrilla. "We believe there to be a conspiracy of great magnitude brewing. Whether or not this man was part of it I don't know, but he was sent by Kelton."

"Kelton! I refuse to believe that."

Kahlan nodded at the knife in Cyrilla's hand. "The knife is Keltish."

"Many people carry weapons forged in Kelton. They are some of the finest made. That is hardly proof enough for such an accusation."

Kahlan stood unmoving. Cyrilla was too upset at that moment to wonder what thoughts could have been going on behind those green eyes. Kahlan's voice finally came without emotion. "My father taught me that the Keltans will strike for only two reasons. First out of jealousy, and second when they are tempted by weakness. He said that either way, they will always first test by trying to kill the strongest, highest-ranking, of their opponents they can. Galea is now the strongest it has ever been, thanks to you, and the midsummer festival is the mark of that strength. You are the cause of that jealousy, and a symbol of that strength.

"My father also said that you must always keep an eye to the Keltans, and never offer them your back. He said that if you thwart them in the first attempt, it deepens their hunger for your blood, and they will always lie in wait for any weakness so they may strike."

Cyrilla's smoldering rage at being beguiled by Drefan made her lash out without considering her words. "I would not know what our father said. I never had the benefit of his teachings. He was taken from us by a Confessor."

Kahlan's face transformed from the calm, cold blankness of a Confessor to a look of ageless, knowing benevolence that seemed well beyond her years.

"Perhaps, Queen Cyrilla, the good spirits chose to spare you the things he would have taught you, and had him teach me instead. Be thankful they have looked kindly upon you. I doubt the things he taught would have brought you any joy. They bring me none, save perhaps that they have helped me preserve your life this night. Please do not be bitter. Be at peace with yourself, and cherish what you do have: the love of your people. They are your family, one and all."

Kahlan started to turn away, but Cyrilla gently caught her arm and drew her aside as men bent to carry the body from the hall.

"Kahlan, forgive me." Her fingers worked a ribbon at her waist. "I have wrongly directed my anger over Drefan to you."

"I understand, Cyrilla. In your place, I would probably have reacted the same. I could see your feelings for Drefan in your eyes. I would not expect you to be happy over what I have just done. Forgive me for bringing anguish to your home on a day that should be only joyful, but I greatly feared the results of delay."

Kahlan had made *her* feel like the younger sister. She looked anew at the tall, beautiful young woman standing before her. Kahlan was of the age to have a mate. Perhaps she had already chosen one, for all she knew. Her mother must have been about this old when she took Cyrilla's father as hers. So young.

Looking into those depthless green eyes, Cyrilla let go of some of her anger over Drefan. This young woman, her sister, had just saved her life, knowing full well it would bring no thanks, and would probably earn her only deeper fear, and possibly undying hatred, from her half sister. So young. Cyrilla felt shame at her own selfishness.

She smiled at Kahlan for the first time. "Surely, the things Wyborn taught you weren't all grim?"

"He taught me only killing. Whom to kill, when to kill, and how to kill. Be thankful you know no more of his lessons, and that you have never needed what he taught. I have, and I fear I have only begun to use what he taught me."

Cyrilla frowned. Kahlan was a Confessor, not a killer. "Why would you say such a thing?"

"We believe we have uncovered a conspiracy. I will not speak of it until I know its nature, and have proof, but I think it may bring a storm beyond any you or I have ever seen before."

Cyrilla touched her sister's cheek, the only time in her life she had ever done so. "Kahlan, please stay? Enjoy at my side what is left of the festival? I would love to have you with me."

Kahlan's face returned to the calm mask of a Confessor. "I cannot. It would only ruin your people's light heart to have me present. Thank you for the offer, but you should be able to enjoy your day with your people, without my spoiling it further."

"Nonsense. It would spoil nothing."

"I would like nothing more than that it were so, but it is not. Remember what our father said: keep a wary eye to the Keltans. I must be gone. There is trouble gathering and I must see that the Confessors find its cause. Before I return to Aydindril I will pay a visit to Kelton and deliver my suspicions, and a warning that what has happened not be repeated. I will inform the council of the trouble of this day, so that all eyes will be on the Keltans."

What did they teach in Aydindril that could turn what looked to be porcelain to iron?

"Thank you, Mother Confessor" was all she had been able to say, to offer her sister the honor of her office, as she watched her stride off, her wizard in tow. That had been the most intimate conversation she had ever had with her half sister. The midsummer festival had not held much joy for her after Kahlan had left. So young, yet so old.

At the council today, Cyrilla had been surprised to find that the Mother Confessor was not presiding over the council. No one knew where she was. It was to be expected she would have been absent when Aydindril fell; she was frequently gone in her capacity as a Confessor, and had probably been doing what she could to halt the threat from D'Hara. All the Confessors had fiercely fought the hordes from D'Hara. She was sure Kahlan would have done no less, using in part what her father had taught her.

But that she had not immediately returned to Aydindril when D'Hara withdrew was worrisome. Perhaps she had not yet had time to return. Cyrilla feared Kahlan might have been killed at the hands of a quad. D'Hara had sentenced all the Confessors to death, and hunted them relentlessly. Galea had offered refuge to the Confessors, but the quads, implacable, and without mercy, had found them anyway.

Worse, absent the Mother Confessor, there had not been a wizard overseeing the council meeting. Cyrilla's flesh had prickled with apprehension at seeing no wizard. She recognized that the absence of a Confessor and a wizard created a dangerous vacuum in the council chambers.

But when she saw who presided over the council session, her apprehension sharpened to alarm. Sitting in the first chair was High Prince Fyren, of Kelton. The very man she had come to seek deliverance from sat in judgment. To see him sitting in the chair that had always belonged only to the Mother Confessor was startling.

The council, it would seem, had not been put back to the way it should have been.

Nonetheless, she ignored him and instead pressed her demands to the rest of the council. In turn, Prince Fyren stood and accused her of treason against the Midlands. He had the unmitigated gall to accuse her of the very thing of which he was guilty.

Further, Prince Fyren assured the council that Kelton was committing no aggression but was acting only in self-defense against a greedy neighbor. In a tirade, he lectured them on the evils of women in positions of power. The council took his word for everything. They allowed her to present no evidence.

She stood stunned and speechless as the council heard Fyren's charges, and without pause found her guilty, sentencing her to be beheaded.

Where was Kahlan? Where were the wizards?

Lady Bevinvier's vision had proven true. Cyrilla should have listened, or at least taken some precaution. Kahlan's warning, too, had proven true; Kelton had first tried to strike out of jealousy, and now, years later, they had renewed the attack when they saw tempting weakness.

The Galean guard stood in the great courtyard, ready to immediately escort

Cyrilla home. She had needed to set about readying Galea's defenses until the forces expected to be sent by the council could arrive. But it was not to be.

At the pronouncement of sentence, she heard the terrible shouts of battle outside. Battle, she thought bitterly. It was not a battle, but a slaughter. Her troops had waited in the great courtyard without their weapons, as a sign of respect and deference, an open gesture of acquiescence to the rule of the Council of the Midlands.

Queen Cyrilla stood at the window, a guard at each arm, shaking in horror as she watched the slaughter. A few of her men managed to take up weapons by overpowering their attackers, and put up a valiant struggle, but they had no chance. They were outnumbered five to one, and were, by and large, without means to defend themselves. She couldn't tell if in the chaos any escaped. She hoped they had. She prayed Harold had.

The white snow that lay upon the ground was turned to a sea of red. She was aghast at the butchery. There was mercy only in its swiftness.

Cyrilla had been made to kneel before the council as Prince Fyren took up her long hair in his fist, and with his own sword sliced it away. She had knelt in silence, her head held proudly up in honor of her people, in honor of the men she had just seen murdered, while he cut her hair as short as the lowest kitchen scullion.

What an hour before had seemed to be the near end of her people's ordeal had become instead the mere beginning.

The powerful fingers on her arms jerked her to a halt before a small iron door. She winced in pain. A crude ladder twice her height lay on its side against the wall on the opposite side of the corridor.

Again the guard with the keys came forward to work the lock. He cursed the mechanism, complaining that its lack of use made it stiff. All the guards seemed to be Keltans. She had seen none of the Aydindril Home Guard. Most, she knew, had been killed in Aydindril's fall to D'Hara.

At last the man drew back the door to reveal a dark pit. Her legs felt as if they wanted to turn liquid. Only the hands gripping her arms held her up. They were going to put her in that dark pit. With the rats.

She willed her legs solid again. She was the queen. But her pulse would not slow.

"How dare you put a lady in a rat-infested hole!"

Prince Fyren stepped close to the black maw. One hand on a hip held back his unbuttoned, royal blue coat. With his other hand he hefted a torch from a bracket.

"Rats? Is that what worries you, my lady? Rats?" He gave her a derisive smile. He was too young to be so well schooled at insolence. Had her arms been free she would have slapped him. "Let me allay your fears, Queen Cyrilla."

He tossed the torch into the blackness. As it dropped, it illuminated faces. A husky fist caught the torch. There were men in the pit. At least six, maybe ten.

Prince Fyren leaned into the doorway, his voice echoing into the hole. "The queen worries there may be rats down there."

"Rats?" came a coarse voice from the pit. "There be no rats down here. Not anymore. We et them all."

A hand with white ruffles at the wrist still rested on Prince Fyren's hip. His voice taunted with feigned concern. "There, you see? The man says there are no rats. Does that ease your apprehension, my lady?"

Her eyes darted between the flickering torchlight below and Fyren. "Who are those men?"

"Why, just a few murderers and rapists awaiting their beheading, same as you. Quite vile animals, actually. What with all I've had to attend to, I haven't had time to see to their sentences. I'm afraid being down in the pit for so long puts them in an ugly disposition." His grin returned. "But I'm sure having a queen among them will mellow their mood."

Cyrilla had to force her voice to come. "I demand my own cell."

The grin vanished. An eyebrow lifted. "Demand? You demand?" He suddenly struck her across the face. "You demand nothing! You are nothing but a common criminal, a loathsome murderer of my people! You have been tried and convicted!"

Her cheek burned with the sting of his handprint.

"You can't put me in there—with them." Her whispered entreaty was hopeless, she knew, but she couldn't keep it from her lips.

Fyren rolled his shoulders, straightening his back and coat as he regained his composure. His voice rose to those below. "You men wouldn't defile a lady, would you?"

Soft laughter echoed up from the pit. "Why, course not. We wouldn't want to be beheaded twice." The coarse voice deepened into cold menace. "We'll treat her real nice like."

Cyrilla could taste warm, salty blood at the corner of her mouth. "Fyren, you can't do this. I demand to be beheaded at once."

"There you go again: demanding."

"Why can't it be done now! Let it be done now!"

He drew his hand back to slap her again, but then let it lower as his simper returned. "You see? At first you proclaimed your innocence, and didn't want to be executed, but already you are reconsidering. After a few days down there, with them, you will be begging to be beheaded. You will eagerly confess your treason before all those gathered to witness your punishment. Besides, I have other matters to attend to. I can't be bothered right now. You will be put to death when I deem I have the time."

With rising terror, she was only now beginning to grasp the full extent of the fate that awaited her in the pit. Tears burned her eyes.

"Please . . . don't do this to me. I'm begging you."

Prince Fyren smoothed the white ruffles at his throat and spoke softly. "I tried to make it easy for you, Cyrilla, because you're a woman. Drefan's knife would have been quick. You would have suffered little that way. I would never have allowed a man in your place such mercy. But you wouldn't have it the easy way. You allowed the Mother Confessor to interfere. You allowed yet another woman to infringe on the dominion of men!

"Women don't have the stomach for ruling. They're ill suited to the task. They should never be allowed to command armies or to meddle in the affairs of nations. Things had to be set right. Drefan died trying to do it the easy way. Now we do it the other way."

He nodded to a man behind him. The guard hauled the ladder to the doorway to lower an end into the pit as the hands on her arms moved her to the edge. The other men drew swords, apparently to prevent any in the pit from thinking to come up the ladder.

Cyrilla could think of no way to stop this. She voiced a protest, knowing it was foolish, but unable to check her panic. "I am a queen, a lady, I will not be made to scurry down a rickety ladder."

Prince Fyren blinked at her ludicrous objection, but then motioned with his hand for the man to pull the ladder back from the doorway.

He gave a mocking bow. "As you wish, my lady."

He rose, giving a slight nod to the men holding her arms. They released her. Before she thought to move a muscle, he rammed the heel of his hand into her chest, between her breasts.

The painful blow knocked her off balance. She toppled backward through the opening. Down into the pit.

As she plummeted, she fully expected to strike the stone floor and be killed. She resigned to it with a last gasp as the futile flow of her past glory whirled before her mind's eye. Had it all come to this? All for nought? To have her skull cracked like an egg fallen from a table to the floor?

But hands caught her. Hands were everywhere upon her, unexpectedly upon the most indecent places. Her eyes opened to see the light of the doorway go dark with a loud, reverberating clang.

Faces were all around her in the haunting, flickering torchlight. Scruffy, whiskered faces. Ugly, sweaty, wicked faces. Cunning black eyes played over her. Hungry, humorless grins showed crooked, sharp teeth. So many teeth. Her throat clenched shut, locking her breath in her lungs. Her mind refused to function, and flashed with confusing, useless images.

She was pressed to the floor. The stone was cold and painfully rough against her back. Grunts and low squeals assailed her from every side. Men were tight together above her. Against her struggles, her limbs were pushed and pulled as the men willed.

Clutching, clawlike hands ripped at her fine dress and pinched brutally at suddenly, shockingly, exposed flesh.

And then Cyrilla did something she hadn't done since she was a little girl.

She screamed.

Except for her thumb and forefinger idly turning the smooth, round bone on her necklace, Kahlan stood motionless as she studied the sprawling city. The surrounding rugged slopes seemed to tenderly cradle the buildings that filled nearly the length and breadth of the gently rolling valley. Steeply pitched slate roofs pricked the land within the ribbon of wall, with the higher peaks of the palace off to the northern end, but not so much as a wisp of smoke rose from the hundreds of stone chimneys into the clear air. She saw no movement. The arrow-straight south road leading to the main gate, the smaller, meandering roads that branched off to end at the lesser gates, and those which bypassed the outer walls altogether to lead north, were deserted.

The sloping mountain meadow before her lay buried beneath a white winter blanket. A light breeze liberated the burden of snow from a sagging branch of a nearby pine, freeing a sparkling cloud to curl away. The same breeze ruffled the white wolf fur of the thick mantle snugged against her cheek, but she hardly noticed.

Prindin and Tossidin had made the mantle for her, to keep her warm on their way northeast through the bitter winter storms that raked the bleak land they had traveled. Wolves were fearful of people, and rarely let themselves be seen, so she knew little of their habits. The brothers' arrows had found their mark where she saw nothing. If she hadn't seen Richard shoot, she would have thought the shots impossible. The brothers were almost as good as he.

Though she had always held a vague enmity for wolves, she had never actually been harried by them. Since Richard had told her of their close family packs, she had come to feel an affection for them. She hadn't wanted the two brothers to kill wolves to make the warm cape, but they insisted that it was necessary and, in the end, she had acquiesced.

It had sickened her to watch the carcasses being skinned, revealing the red muscle beneath, and white of bone and sinew, the substance of being, so elegant when filled with life and spirit, so suddenly morbid when left with neither.

As the brothers went about the grisly task, she could think only of Brophy, the man she had touched with her power, only to have it prove him innocent. He had been turned to a wolf by her wizard, Giller, to release him from the power of a Confessor's magic, so he could start over in a new life. She had wondered at how saddened these wolves' families must have been when they never returned, as she knew Brophy's mate and pack must have been when he was killed.

She had seen so much killing. She was weary nearly to tears of it, at the way it seemed to go on without an end in sight. At least the three men had felt no pride or joy at having killed the magnificent animals, and had said a prayer to the spirits of their brother wolves, as they had called them.

*"We should not be doing this,"* Chandalen grumbled.

He was leaning on his spear, watching her, she knew, but she didn't take her eyes from the silent city below, the too-still scene. His tone was not as sharp as it usually was. It betrayed his awe at seeing a city the size of Ebinissia.

He had never before been far from the Mud People's lands, had never seen this many buildings, especially none of such grand scale. When he had first taken in the size of it, his brown eyes had stared in silent wonder he could not conceal, and his acid tongue, for once, had forsaken him. Having lived his whole life in the village out on the plains, it must look to him as if he were seeing the result of magic, not mere human effort.

She felt a small pang of sorrow for him and the two brothers, that their simple view of the outside world had to be shattered. Well, they would see more, before this journey was ended, that would astonish them further.

"Chandalen, I have spent a great effort, nearly every waking moment, teaching you and Prindin and Tossidin to speak my language. No one where we go will speak yours. It is for your own good that I do this. You are free to believe that I am being spiteful, or that I am doing as I say: being mindful of your safety outside your land, but either way, you will speak to me in the tongue I have taught you."

His tone tightened, but still could not disguise how humbled he was at seeing a great city for the first time. It was far from the greatest he would see. Perhaps, too, it betrayed something she had never before sensed from him: fear.

"I am to take you to Aydindril, not this place. We should not be using our time at this place." His inflection implied he thought a place such as this could be only evil.

Squinting against the blindingly bright sun on white snow, she saw the two figures, far below, starting up the slope. She let the round bone slip from her fingers. "I'm the Mother Confessor. It's my duty to protect all the people of the Midlands, the same way I work to safeguard the Mud People."

"You bring no help to my people, only trouble."

His protest seemed more habit than a heartfelt challenge. She answered it in a quiet, tired murmur. "Enough, Chandalen."

Thankfully, he didn't press the argument, but turned his anger elsewhere. "Prindin and Tossidin should not come up the hill in the open like that. I have taught them not to be so stupid. If they were boys, I would strike their bottoms. Anyone can see where they go. Will you do as I say, and come out of the open now?"

She let him shepherd her back into the shroud of trees, not because she thought it necessary, but because she wanted to let him know she respected his efforts to protect her. Despite his animosity at being forced to go on this journey, he had done his duty, watching over her constantly, as had the two brothers, they with smiles and concern, he with a scowl and suspicion. All three made her feel like a precious, fragile cargo that must be tended at all times. The brothers, she knew, were sincere. Chandalen, she was sure, saw his mission only as a task that must be performed, no matter how onerous.

"We should go quickly from here," he pressed, again.

Kahlan withdrew a hand from under the fur mantle and pulled a stray strand of her long hair back from her face. "It is my duty to know what has happened here."

"You said your duty was to go to Aydindril, as Richard With The Temper asked."

Kahlan turned away without answering, moving deeper into the snow-crusted trees. She missed Richard more than she could bear. Every time she closed her eyes, she saw his face as it had looked when he thought she had betrayed him. She wanted to drop to her knees and let out the scream that seemed to be always there, trapped just below the surface, trying to find a way past her restraint, a scream born of her horror at what she had done.

But what else could she have done? If what she had learned was true, and the veil to the underworld was torn and Richard was in fact the only one who could close it, and if the collar was the only thing that could save his life and give him the chance to close the veil, then she had had no choice. How could she have made any other decision? How could Richard ever respect her if she didn't face her responsibilities to the greater good? The Richard she loved would eventually realize that. He had to.

But if any of it was not true, then she had delivered the man she loved into his worst nightmare, for nothing.

She wondered again if Richard often looked at the lock of her hair she had given him, and thought of her. She hoped that he could find it in himself to understand and forgive her. She wanted so much to tell him how much she loved him. She yearned to hold him to her. She wanted only to get to Aydindril, to Zedd, for help.

But she had to know what had happened here. She stiffened her back with resolve. She was the Mother Confessor.

She had intended to skirt Ebinissia, but for the last two days they had been coming across the frozen corpses of women. Never any men, only women, from young to old, children to grandmothers. Most were half naked, some without clothes at all. And in the dead of winter. While most had been alone, a few were together, huddled in frozen death, too exhausted, or too frightened, or too disoriented to have sought shelter. They had run from Ebinissia not in disorderly haste, but in panic, choosing to freeze to death rather than remain.

Most, too, had been badly abused before they had scattered in every direction into the mountainous countryside. Kahlan knew what had been done to them, what had made them make the choice they did. The three men knew, too, but none would voice it aloud.

She pulled her warm mantle tighter around herself. This atrocity couldn't have been at the hands of the armies from D'Hara; it was far too recent. The troops from D'Hara had been called home. Surely, they wouldn't have done this after they had been told the war was ended.

Unable to stand for another moment not knowing what fate had befallen Ebinissia, she pushed her bow farther up on her shoulder and started down the hillside. Her leg muscles were at long last used to the wide-footed gait needed to walk on the snowshoes the men had made from willow and sinew. Chandalen charged after her.

"You must not go down there. There could be dangerous."

"Danger," she corrected as she hitched her pack up higher. "If there was danger, Prindin and Tossidin would not be out in the open. You may come, or you may wait here, but I'm going down there."

Knowing argument was useless, he followed in a rare fit of silence. The bright afternoon sun brought no warmth to the bitterly cold day. There was usually wind at the fringe of the Rang'Shada Mountains, but thankfully there was little this day, for a change. It hadn't snowed for several days, and they had been able to make better time in the clear weather. Still, with every breath she took, the air felt as if it were turning the inside of her nose to ice.

She intercepted Prindin and Tossidin halfway down the slope. They brought themselves to a halt before her, leaning on their spears, breathing heavily, which was unusual for them as nothing seemed to tire them, but they were unaccustomed to the altitude. Their faces were pale, and their handsome twin smiles long gone.

"Please, Mother Confessor," Prindin said, pausing to catch his breath from the strenuous climb, "you must not go to that place. The ancestor spirits of those people have abandoned them."

Kahlan untied a waterskin from her waist and pulled it from under her mantle, where her body's heat kept the water from freezing. She held it up to Prindin, urging him to take a drink before questioning him.

"What did you see? You didn't go into the city, did you? I told you not to go inside the walls."

Prindin handed the waterskin to his panting brother. "No. We stay hidden, as you told us. We do not go inside, but we do not need to." He licked a drop of water from his lower lip. "We see enough from outside."

She took back the waterskin when Tossidin finished, and replaced the stopper. "Did you see any people?"

Tossidin stole a quick glance over his shoulder, down the hill. "We see many people."

Prindin wiped his nose on the back of his hand as he looked from his brother to her. "Dead people."

"How many? Dead from what?"

Tossidin tugged loose the thong holding his fur mantle tight at his neck. "Dead from fighting. Most are men with weapons: swords and spears and bows. There are more than I know the words to count. I have never seen that many men. In my whole life, I have not seen that many men. There has been war here. War, and killing of those defeated."

Kahlan stared at them for a moment as horror threatened to choke off her breath. She had hoped that somehow the people of Ebinissia had escaped, that they had fled.

A war. Had the D'Haran forces done this after the war was ended? Or was it something else?

Her muscles at last unlocked and she started down the hill, the mantle billowing open, letting in the icy air. Her heart pounded with dread at what had befallen the people of Ebinissia. "I must go down there to see what has happened."

"Please, Mother Confessor, do not go," Prindin called after her. "It is bad to see."

The three men jumped to follow as she marched down the hill, the slope speeding her effort. "I have seen dead people before."

They began encountering the sprawled corpses—apparently the sites of skirmishes—a good distance from the city walls. Snow had drifted against them, partially covering them. In one place, a hand reached up from the snow, as if the man below were drowning, and reaching for air. Most had not been touched by animals or birds, there being an overabundance for scavengers. All were soldiers of the Galean army, frozen in death where they had fallen, blood-soaked clothes frozen rock-solid to them, ghastly wounds frozen open.

At the south wall, where huge oak doors crisscrossed with iron strapping had stood, was a gaping hole through the stone, its edges melted and burned black. Kahlan stood staring at rock melted like wax from a candle that had guttered. She knew of only one power that could do that: wizard's fire.

303

Her mind fought to understand what she was seeing. She knew what the results of wizard's fire looked like, but there were no more wizards. Except Zedd and, she guessed, Richard. But this would not have been Zedd's deed.

Outside the walls, off to either side, headless corpses were heaped in huge, frozen mounds. Heads stared out from less orderly piles of their own. Swords and shields and spears were discarded to separate heaps, looking like great, dead, steel porcupines. This had been a mass execution, carried out at a number of stations at once to handle the numbers more efficiently. All were Galean soldiers.

As she stared in numb shock at the splayed limbs draped over their fellows under them, Kahlan spoke softly to the three men behind her. "The word you did not know to use to count this many is *thousand*. There are perhaps five thousand dead men here."

Gently, Prindin planted the butt end of his spear in the snow, giving it an uneasy twist. "I did not know there was a word needed to count this many men." His fist twisted the spear again, and his voice lowered to a whisper. "This will be a bad place when the warm weather comes."

*"It is a bad place now,"* his brother murmured to himself in his own tongue.

Kahlan knew this was the least of the dead. She knew the tactics of defense for Ebinissia. The walls were not secure fortifications, the way they had been in times long ago. As the city had grown in the prosperity of the Midlands alliance, the older, stronger, fortified walls had been torn down, and the stone used to build these newer, more encompassing outer walls. But they had been built less secure than in the past. They were more a symbol of the size and pride of the Crown city than a strong defensible perimeter.

Under attack, the gates would have been closed, with the toughest, most experienced troops on the outside to stop the attackers before they had a chance to reach the walls. The real defense for Ebinissia was the surrounding mountains, whose narrow passes prevented a broad attack.

Under Darken Rahl's order, D'Haran forces had laid siege to Ebinissia for two months, but the defenders outside the walls were able to hold them back in the surrounding passes, pin them down, and harry them relentlessly until the attackers finally withdrew, licking their wounds, in search of easier prey. Though the Ebinissians had prevailed, it had been at a great cost of lives to the defenders. Had Darken Rahl been less concerned with finding the boxes, he could have sent greater numbers and maybe overrun the defenders in the passes, but he didn't. This time, someone had.

These headless men were a part of that outer defensive ring. Backs to the wall, they had been defeated and captured, and then executed before the walls were breached—apparently as a demonstration to those still inside, to terrorize them, to panic them into an ineffectual defense. She knew that what was inside the walls would be worse. The dead women they had been finding told her that much.

Out of habit, and without even realizing it, she had put on the calm face that showed nothing: the face of a Confessor, as her mother had taught her.

"Prindin, Tossidin, I want you two to go around the outside of the walls. I want to know what else is on the outside. I want to know everything about what has happened here. I want to know when this was done, where the attackers came from, and where they went when they were finished. Chandalen and I will go inside. Meet us back here when you are finished."

The brothers went quickly at her direction, their heads close together as they whispered to one another while pointing, analyzing tracks and signs they understood with hardly more than a glance. Chandalen walked silently at her side, his bow, with an arrow nocked and tension to the string, at the ready as she stepped over rubble and moved on through the yawning hole.

None of the three men had objected to her instructions. They were, she knew, astonished at the size of the city, but more than that, they were overwhelmed at the enormity of what had happened here; they respected her obligation to the dead.

Chandalen's eyes ignored the bodies that lay everywhere and watched instead the shaded openings and alleyways among the small daub-and-wattle houses that were homes to the farmers and sheepherders who worked the land closer to the city. There were no fresh prints in the snow; nothing alive had been here recently.

Kahlan chose the proper streets and Chandalen stayed close at her right shoulder, half a step behind. She didn't stop to inspect the dead laying everywhere. All looked to have died the same way: killed in a fierce battle.

"These people were defeated by great numbers," Chandalen said in a quiet tone. "Many thousands, as you called it. They had no chance to win."

"Why do you say that?"

"They are bunched together between the buildings. This is a bad place to have to fight, but in a closed-in place like this, that is the only way. That is the way I would try to defend against a larger number—by blocking the enemy from spreading out behind me to trap me. Greater numbers would not be as much good in the small passageways. I would try to keep the enemy from spreading out, and come at them from all sides so they could not attack as they wished, but must be always in fear of where I would be next. You must not meet the enemy as they wish you to, especially when they greatly outnumber you.

"There are old men, and boys, among the soldiers. Boys and old men would not come to fight beside Chandalen unless they saw it was a war to the death and I was greatly outnumbered. For these men to stand and fight against vastly greater numbers, they must have been brave. Old men and boys would not have come to help such brave men if the enemy were not so great."

She knew Chandalen was right. Everyone had seen or heard the executions outside the walls. They knew defeat was death.

The bodies were felled like reeds before a great wind. As they ascended the rise to where the old city walls had stood, the dead were more numerous. It looked that they had fallen back, trying to make a stand from higher ground. It had done them no good; they had been overrun.

All the dead were defenders; none were the corpses of attackers. Kahlan knew that some believed leaving the dead where they fell in defeating an enemy augured ill luck in future battles, and further, that it abandoned their spirits to retribution by the spirits of those defeated. Likewise, they believed that if they left their dead at the site of a defeat, the spirits of their fallen comrades would live on to plague their enemies. Whoever had done this must have believed such, and dragged their own dead away from the bodies of those they had vanquished. Kahlan knew of several peoples who believed that the act of dying in battle could bring about such thaumaturgy. One nation, above all, sat at the head of her roster.

As they skirted an overturned wagon, its load of firewood spilled in a heap, Chandalen paused beneath a small wooden sign carved with a leafy plant next to a mortar and pestle. With a hand, he shielded his eyes from the sunlight and looked

305

into the long, narrow shop set back a few feet from the buildings to each side. "What is this place?"

Kahlan walked past him, through the splintered doorframe. "It's an herb shop." The counter was covered with broken glass jars and dried herbs, all scattered together in a useless mess. Only two glass lids remained unbroken among the pale green debris. "This is where people went to get herbs and remedies."

Behind the counter, the wall cabinet, which reached from floor to ceiling and almost the entire length of the narrow shop, had held hundreds of small wooden drawers, their patina darkened by the countless touches of fingers. The ones still left in place were smashed in with a mace. The drawers and their contents on the floor had been crushed underfoot. Chandalen squatted and pulled open the few drawers near the bottom that had remained untouched, inspecting briefly their stores before sliding each drawer closed again.

"Nissel would be . . . *how do you say 'astonished'?*"

"Astonished," Kahlan answered.

"She would be astonished, to see this many healing plants. This is a crime, to destroy things that help people."

She watched him pull open drawers and then slide them closed. "A crime," she agreed.

He pulled open another drawer, and gasped. He squatted, motionless, for a moment, before reverently lifting a bundle of miniature plants, tied at their stems with a bit of string. The tiny, dry leaves were a dusky greenish brown with crimson veining.

A low whistle came from between his teeth. "*Quassin doe,*" he whispered.

Kahlan eyed the shadowed back of the shop as her vision adjusted to the darkness. She saw no bodies. The proprietor must have fled before he was killed, or maybe he was one who had stood with the army against the invaders. "What is *Quassin doe?*"

Chandalen turned the bundle over in his palm, his eyes fixed unblinking on it. "*Quassin doe* can save your life if you take ten-step poison by mistake, or, if you are quick enough, when shot by an arrow with the poison on it."

"How can you take it by mistake?"

"Many poison *bandu* leaves must be chewed, for a long time, and made wet in your mouth, before being cooked until they become a thick paste. Sometimes, if you swallow some of the wetness in your mouth by accident, or chew too long, it can make you sick."

He opened a buckskin waist pouch and showed her a small, carved bone, lidded box. Inside was a dark paste. "This is ten-step poison we put on our arrows. We make it from the *bandu.* If you ate a very little of this, it would make you sick. If you ate a little more you would be a long time to die. If you ate more, you would die quick. But no one would eat it after it is made and put in here." He slipped the box of poison back in his pouch.

"So you could take some of the *quassin doe,* and it would make you well if you accidentally swallowed some of the *bandu* when you were chewing its leaves to make the poison?" He nodded in answer to her question. "But if you were shot with a ten-step arrow, wouldn't you die before you could take the *quassin doe?*"

Chandalen turned the bundle of plants in his fingers. "Maybe. Sometimes, a man will scratch himself with his own ten-step arrow, by not meaning to, and he can take the *quassin doe,* and he will be well again. If you are shot with a poison arrow, sometimes you will have time to save yourself. Ten-step arrows only work quick if you are shot in the neck. Then you have no time to take the *quassin doe*, you will die too quick. But if you are shot in another place, maybe your leg, the poison takes longer to work, and you have time to take the *quassin doe*."

"What if you aren't near to Nissel, so she could give it to you? You would die if you were out on the plains hunting and you scratched yourself accidentally with a poison arrow."

"All hunters used to carry a few leaves with them, so they may take it if they scratched themselves, or were shot with an arrow and had time. If there is not much poison on the arrow, like if it has not much on it because it is used to hunt small animals, you have longer. In times long ago, when there was war, our men would swallow *quassin doe* just before a battle, so the enemy's ten-step arrows would not poison them."

He shook his head sadly. "But this is much trouble to get. The last time we traded for this much, every man in the village had to make three bows, and two fists of arrows, and all the women had to make bowls. It is gone now, for a long time. Years. The people we traded with have been able to find no more. Two men have died since we no longer have it. My people would trade much to have this much again."

Kahlan stood over him, watching him gently place it back in the drawer. "Take it, Chandalen. Give it to your people. They have need of it."

He slowly slid the drawer closed. "I cannot. It would be wrong to take it from another people, even if they are dead. It does not belong to my people, it belongs to the people here."

Kahlan squatted down next to him, pulled open the drawer, and lifted out the little bundle. She found a square of cloth lying on the floor nearby, used for packaging purchases and wrapped the *quassin doe* plants. "Take it." She pushed the bundle into his hand. "I know the people of this city. I will repay them for what I have taken. Since I will pay for it, it belongs to me now. Take it. It is my gift for the trouble I have caused your people."

He stared at the cloth parcel in his hand. "It is too valuable for a gift. A gift of such great value would bind us to an obligation to you."

"Then it is not a gift, but my payment, to you and Prindin and Tossidin, for guarding me on this journey. You three are risking your lives to protect me. That is a debt I owe you that is greater than this payment. You will owe me no more obligation."

With a frown, he studied the bundle a moment, and then bounced it twice in his hand before tucking it in the buckskin pouch at his waist. He tied the flap closed by its rawhide thong and stood. "Then this is in trade for what we do. We owe you no obligation beyond this journey."

"None," she said, sealing the bargain.

The two of them walked on through the silent streets, past the shops and inns of the old city quarter. Every door, every window, was broken in. Shards of glass sparkled in the sunlight, shimmering tears for the dead. The invading horde had swept through every building, searching out anything alive.

"How do this many thousands, all living in this one place, find land to feed their families? There could not be enough game to hunt, or fields for all to plant."

Kahlan tried to see the city through his eyes. It must be a great puzzle to him. "They don't all hunt, or plant the land. The people who lived here specialized."

307

"Specialized? What is this?"

"It means that different people have different jobs. They work at one thing. They use silver or gold to buy the things they need that they don't grow or make themselves."

"Where do they get this silver or gold?"

"People who want the thing they specialize in pay for it with silver or gold."

"And where do these others get this silver or gold?"

"They get it from people who pay them for the things they do."

Chandalen looked at her skeptically. "Why do they not trade? It would be easier to trade."

"Well, in a way, it is trading. Often, the person who wants what you have has nothing you want, so they give you money—silver or gold made into flat, round disks called coins—instead. Then you can use the money to buy things you need."

"Buy." Chandalen seemed to test the strange word with his tongue as he looked off down a street to their right while shaking his head in disbelief. "Why would people work, then? Why would they not just go and get this silver or gold money?"

"Some do. They hunt silver and gold. But that is hard work, too. Gold is hard to find and dig out of the ground. That is why it is used for money: because it is rare. If it were easy to find, like grains of sand, then no one would take it in trade. If money were easy to get, or to make, it would become worthless, and then in the end this system of trade, with worthless money, would fail, and everyone would starve."

He came to a halt with a frown. "What is this money made from? What is this silver or gold you speak of?"

She didn't stop with him, and he had to take a few bounding steps to catch back up with her. "Gold is . . . The medallion, the necklace, that the Bantak gave as a gift to the Mud People, to show they did not wish to make war, that is made of gold." Chandalen nodded with a knowing grunt. Kahlan halted this time. "Do you know where the Bantak got that much gold?"

Chandalen swept his gaze across the slate rooftops. "Of course. They got it from us."

Kahlan gripped his arm covered with his mantle and pulled him around. "What do you mean, they got it from you?"

He tensed at her touch. He didn't like her hand—a Confessor's hand—on him. That the fur mantle separated actual contact of flesh was of no consequence; their flesh was close enough. If she relaxed her restraint of the power, that thin piece of hide would be no impediment; Kahlan had loosed her power through armor before. She released her grip and he visibly relaxed. "Chandalen, where did the Mud People get that much gold?"

He looked at her as if she were a child asking where you might find dirt. "From the holes in the ground. In our land, to the north where it is rocky and nothing much will grow or live, there are holes in the ground. They have this gold in them. It is a bad place. The air is hot and bad. It is said that men die if they stay too long in the ground. The yellow metal is in these deep holes. It is too soft to make good weapons, so it is of no use."

He dismissed its importance with a wave of his hand. "But the Bantak say their ancestors' spirits like the look of the yellow metal, and so we let them come onto our land and go in the holes so they may get it to make things their ancestors' spirits may like to look upon when they come to this world."

"Chandalen, do others know of these holes in the ground, of the gold that is in them?"

He shrugged. "We do not let outsiders come to our land. But I told you, it is too soft to make weapons with, so it is of no use. It pleases the Bantak, and they are good traders with us, so we let them take what they want. They do not take much, though, because it is a bad place to go into. No one would want to go there, except the Bantak, to please their ancestors' spirits."

How could she explain it to him? He didn't understand the ways of the outside world. "Chandalen, you must never use this gold." He made a face that said he had already explained how useless it was, and no one would want it. "You may think it is useless, but others would kill to get it. If people knew you had gold on your land, they would swarm over you to get it. The craving for gold makes men crazy, and they would do anything to get it. They would kill Mud People."

Chandalen straightened with a smug expression. He took his hand from the bowstring and tapped his chest. "I, and my men, protect our people. We would keep the outsiders away."

Kahlan swept her arm around, taking in the hundreds upon hundreds of dead around her. "Against this many? Against thousands?" Chandalen had never seen this many people. He understood little of the numbers that lived outside his lands. "Thousands who would never stop coming until they swept you aside?"

His eyes followed the arc her arm had taken. His brow wrinkled with the frown of a worry unfamiliar to him, his arrogance evaporating as he took in the dead. "Our ancestors' spirits have warned us not to speak of the holes in the ground with the bad air. We only let the Bantak go there, no one else."

"See that it stays that way," she said. "Or they will come and steal it."

"That would be wrong, to steal from a people." He put renewed tension to the bowstring as she let out a noisy breath of frustration. "If I make a bow to trade, everyone knows it is the work of Chandalen, because it is such a fine bow. If anyone steals it, everyone knows what it is and where it came from, and the thief would be caught, and be made to give it back. Maybe he would be sent away from his people. How do these people tell who the money belongs to, if it is taken by a thief?"

Kahlan's mind reeled from the effort of trying to explain such things to Chandalen. At least it was keeping her from having to think about the dead all about her. She started walking again through the snow, having to step over a man's back because there was no way around, they were fallen so close.

"It is difficult. Because of this, people guard their money. If anyone is caught stealing, the punishment is severe, to discourage thieving."

"How are thieves punished?"

"If they didn't steal much, and are lucky, they might be locked in a small room until their family can make reparations for what they stole."

"Locked? What is this?"

"A lock is way of barring a door. The stone rooms that thieves are placed in have a door they are not able to open from the inside. It has a lock on it, and you must have a key, the right key, to open it, so they cannot get out."

Chandalen checked the side street beyond a silversmith's shop as they continued up the main road. "I would rather be put to death than be locked in a room."

"If the thief stole from the wrong person, or is unlucky, that is what happens to him."

Chandalen grunted. She didn't think she was doing a very good job of explaining things to him. He seemed to think the whole scheme unworkable.

"Our way is better. We make what we want. Everyone makes what they need. This specializing way is not our way. We trade only for a few things. Our way is better."

"You do the same as these people, Chandalen. You may not realize it, but you do."

"No. Each person knows many things. We teach all our children to know how to do everything they need."

"You specialize. You're a hunter, and more than that, you're a protector to your people." She nodded once again to the dead around her. Some stared back with flat eyes. "These men were soldiers. They specialized at protecting their people. They gave their lives trying to protect their people. You're the same as they: a soldier. You're strong, you are good with a bow and a spear, and you are good at discovering and preparing to thwart the various ways others would try to harm your people."

Chandalen thought this over a moment as he stopped briefly to knock a heavy clump of snow from the binding of his snowshoe. "But that is only me. Because I am so strong, and wise. Others of my people do not specialize."

"Everyone specializes, Chandalen. Nissel, the healer, she specializes at helping sick or injured people. She spends most of her time helping others. How does she feed herself?"

"Those she helps give her what she needs, and if there is no one to help so she can be offered food by them, then others who have enough offer some of theirs so Nissel will be well fed and ready to help us."

"You see? Those she helps pay her with tava bread, but it's the same thing almost as they do here with money. Because she specializes in a service to the village, everyone helps a little so she will be there for the village when there is need of her. Here, that's called a tax, when everyone pays a little toward the good of the group, to help support those who work for all the people."

"Is this how you get your food? The people all give for you, like we do when you come to make trouble for us?"

She was relieved that for the first time he didn't say it with enmity. "Yes."

Chandalen eyed empty second-floor windows as they walked on among buildings that were becoming larger and more ornate. The double, iron-strap-hinged doors to an inn on their left were broken in, and tables, chairs, pots, dishes, and linen embroidered with red roses—apparently to echo the inn's name, the Red Rose— had been thrown into the street, where they were half covered over with the snow. Through the empty doorway she could see the body of an apron-clad kitchen boy sprawled on the floor, his eyes staring up at the ceiling, frozen with the terror of his last vision. He couldn't have been over twelve.

"But that is just the hunters, and Nissel," Chandalen added, after some thought. "Others of us do not do this specializing."

"Everyone does, to some degree. The women bake the tava bread, the men make the weapons. Nature is that way, too. Some plants grow where it is wet, some where it is dry. Some animals eat grass, some leaves, some bugs, and some other animals. Every thing plays its part. Women have the babies, and men . . ."

She halted, fists at her sides, staring at the countless bodies fallen all around her. She swept her arm out.

"And men, it would seem, are here to kill everything. You see, Chandalen? Women's specialty is to bring forth life, and men's specialty is to take it away."

Kahlan clenched her fist against her stomach. She was dangerously close to losing her composure. Nausea swept through her. Her head spun.

Chandalen stole a glimpse at her from the corner of his eye. "The Bird Man would say not to judge all by what some do. And women do not make life alone. Men are part of that, too."

Kahlan gulped cold air. With a struggle, she started off again, shuffling her snowshoes ahead. Chandalen let her set a quicker pace as he walked beside her. She turned them up a street lined with fine shops. As she moved up and then down a snowdrift, he pointed with his bow, seeming to look for an excuse to change the subject.

"Why do they have wooden people here?"

A headless mannequin rested at an angle against a windowsill, tipped halfway out of a shop. The elaborate blue dress the mannequin wore was trimmed with white beads draped in layers about the waist. Glad to have a diversion from the thoughts swirling in her head, Kahlan changed direction a little, toward the mannequin in the blue dress.

"This is a tailor's shop. The people who owned this shop specialized in making clothes. This wooden person is simply a form to display what they make, so others may know the fine work they do. It's a demonstration of pride in their work."

She stopped before the large window. All the panes of glass were broken out. A few of the yellow-painted mullions hung crookedly from the top of the frame. The shade of blue of the gorgeous gown reminded Kahlan of her wedding dress. She could feel the blood pounding in the veins of her neck as she swallowed back a cry. Chandalen watched both directions up and down the street as her hand slowly reached out to touch the frozen, blue fabric.

Her vision focused past the mannequin, into the shop, where a square of sunlight fell across the snow-dusted floor and up and over a low work counter. Her hand faltered. A dead man with a balding head was pinned to the wall by a spear through his chest. A woman lay sprawled facedown over the counter, her dress and underskirts bunched up around her waist, exposing blue flesh. A pair of tailor's scissors jutted from her back.

In the gloom at the far end of the room stood another mannequin, in a fine man's coat. The front of the dark coat was shredded with hundreds of small cuts. The soldiers had evidently used the mannequin as a target for knife throwing while they waited their turn on the woman. Apparently, when they were finished with her, they stabbed her to death with her scissors.

Kahlan twisted away from the shop to find herself face-to-face with Chandalen. His was red. There was menace in his eyes.

"Not all men are the same. I would cut the throat of any man of mine if he did such a thing."

Kahlan had no answer for him, and suddenly wasn't in the mood to talk. As she started off again, she loosened the mantle at her neck, needing the feel of cold air.

In silence, but for the low, baleful moan of the breeze between the buildings, they slogged past stables of horses, their throats all cut, and past inns and grand houses, their cornices high overhead shading them from the bright, slanting sunlight. Fluted, wooden columns to each side of one door had been hacked at with a sword, seemingly for no purpose but to deface the elegance of the home.

It was colder in the shade, but she didn't care. They stepped over corpses that lay facedown in the snow with wounds in their backs, and around overturned wagons and coaches and dead horses and dead dogs. It all melted into a meaningless madness of destruction.

Eyes cast to the ground before her, she trudged on through the snow. The cold air bit into her flesh, and she pulled her mantle closed once more. The cold was sapping her of not only warmth, but strength. With grim determination she put one foot in front of the other, continuing on toward her destination, hoping, somehow, that she would never reach it.

With the frozen dead of Ebinissia all about, she filled her crushing loneliness with a silent prayer.

*Please, dear spirits, keep Richard warm.*

**N**aked under the sun's fury, the parched, dead flat ground stretched endlessly before them, in the distance offering up shimmering images to waver and dance in the sun's furnace glare, like phantom hostages surrendered to an omnipotent foe. Behind, the fractured hills ended in a bank of rocky rubble. The silence was as oppressive as the heat.

Richard wiped sweat from his brow on the back of his sleeve. The leather of his saddle creaked as he shifted his weight while he waited. Bonnie and the other two horses waited, too, their ears pricked ahead, as they occasionally pawed the cracked, dry earth and voiced apprehensive snorts.

Sister Verna sat motionless atop Jessup, scrutinizing the nothingness of the distance as if viewing an event of great import. Except for the way her brown curls hung limp, she didn't appear to be affected by the heat.

"I don't understand this weather. It's winter; I've never heard of it being hot like this in winter."

"The weather is different in different places," she murmured.

"No it's not. When it's winter, it's cold. It's only hot like this in high summer."

"Have you ever seen snow on mountaintops in the summer?"

Richard reversed the positions of his hands resting on the pommel. "Yes. But that's just on mountaintops. The air is colder up there. We're not on a mountaintop."

Still she did not move. "Not just mountaintops have different weather. In the south the weather is not so cold as it is in the north. But this place is different still. It's like an inexhaustible well of heat."

"And just what is this place?"

"The Valley of the Lost," she whispered.

"Who was lost in it?"

"Those who created it, and whoever enters." At last she turned a bit to peer at him. "It's the end of the world. Your world, anyway."

He shifted his weight to the other side when Bonnie did the same. "If it's the end of the world, why are we here?"

Sister Verna held her hand up to the land behind. "Just as there is Westland, where you were born, separated from the Midlands, and the Midlands from D'Hara, so, too, are those lands separated from what lies on the far side of this place."

Richard frowned. "And what lies on the other side of here?"

She turned back to the expanse before them. "You lived in the New World. Across this valley lies the Old World."

"The Old World? I never heard of the Old World."

"Few in the New World have. It has been sealed away and forgotten. This valley, the Valley of the Lost, separates them, much the same way the boundary used to separate the three lands of the New World. The last of the country we have been crossing has been inhospitable, a desert wasteland. Anyone venturing through it and into this valley never returns. People think there is nothing beyond, that this is the southern end of the Midlands and D'Hara, with nothing beyond but what you see here: an endless waste, where one could die of thirst and hunger and you could have your bones baked by the heat of the sun."

Richard eased Bonnie up next to the Sister. "So, what is beyond? And why can't anyone cross? And if no one can cross, how can we?"

She looked over out of the corner of her eye. "Simple questions, but not simply answered." She relaxed back in her saddle a little. "The land between the New and the Old Worlds narrows somewhat, with the sea to each side."

"The sea?"

"You have never seen the ocean?"

Richard shook his head. "In Westland, it lies far to the south, and people don't live there. Or, so I've been told. I've heard others speak of the ocean, but I've never seen it. They say it's more vast than any lake ever imagined."

Sister Verna gave him a little smile. "They speak true." She turned ahead, pointing off to the right. "Some distance that way lies the sea." She pointed left, to the southeast. "Off even farther in that direction is also the sea. Though the land is vast between them, it is still the narrowest place between the New and the Old Worlds. Because of that, a war was fought here. A war between wizards."

Richard straightened in his saddle. "Wizards? What war?"

"Yes, wizards. It was ages ago, when there were many wizards. What you see before you is the result of that war. It's all that remains, as a reminder, of what wizards who have more power than wisdom can conjure."

He didn't like the accusing look she gave him. "Who won?"

At last she folded her hands over the pommel of her saddle and let her shoulders relax a bit. "No one. The two sides were separated by this land between the seas. Though the fighting may have stopped, no one prevailed."

Richard leaned around for a waterskin. "How about a drink?"

With a small smile, she took the skin as he handed it over and took a long draw. "This valley is an example of what can happen when your heart, rather than your head, rules your magic." Her smile evaporated. "Because of what they did, the peoples of the two worlds are separated for all time. It is one reason the Sisters of the Light work to teach those with the gift—so they will not act out of foolishness."

"What were they fighting about?"

"What do wizards ever fight about? They fought over which wizards should rule."

"I was told something about a wizard's war over whether or not wizards should rule at all."

She handed back the waterskin and wiped her lips with one finger. "That was a different war, yet part of the same. After this place separated the two sides, some of each camp were trapped on the New World side. Both groups had gone to enforce their rule on those who had traveled to live in the New World, and on those who had always lived there.

"Once trapped, one side went into hiding for centuries and worked to build their strength before they attempted to seize power over all the New World. The war that had burned long ago flared again, until their force was defeated, except for a few who fled into their stronghold in D'Hara." She lifted an eyebrow to him. "Kin of yours, I believe."

Richard glared at her for a long moment before finally taking a swig of the hot water. He dribbled a little on a strip of cloth—something Kahlan had taught him—and tied it around his head, both to cool his brow and hold back his lengthening hair. Richard hooked the waterskin back on his saddle. "So what happened here?"

She swept her hand once from the southeast to the southwest. "Where the land was narrowest, here, not only armies but wizards did battle, and sought to prevent one another from advancing. The wizards laid down spells, conjuring every sort of magic, in an attempt to snare their opponents. Both sides, equally, unleashed wickedness of unspeakable horror and danger. That is what lies ahead."

Richard stared at her glazed expression. "You mean to say that their magic, their spells, are still out there?"

"Unabated."

"How can that be? Wouldn't they wear away? Fade?"

"Perhaps." She sighed. "But they did more. To maintain the power of their spells they built structures to sustain the force."

"What structures could do that?"

Sister Verna still stared out at nothing, or perhaps, to things he couldn't see. "The Towers of Perdition," she whispered.

Richard stroked Bonnie's neck and waited. At last, Sister Verna seemed to dismiss her private thoughts with a deep breath and continued.

"From one sea to the other, both sides built opposing lines of these towers, invested with their power and wizardry. They were begun at the sea, and came together here, in this valley. But because of the force of the towers each side built, neither side could get close enough to complete the last tower in their own line. What they had wrought ended in a stalemate, with each side prevented from completing their last tower. It allowed a weakened place in the magic. A gap."

Richard shifted uneasily in his saddle. "If there's a gap, then why can't people cross."

"It's only a lessening in the full strength of the line. To each side, all the way across the hills and mountains, to land's end, and beyond, out into the sea where it somewhere diminishes, Perdition's line is impenetrable. To enter is to be claimed by the storms of spells, the magic. Any who enter would be killed, or worse—they could wander the brume forever.

"Here, in this valley, the deadlock prevented the completion of the last tower on each side that would have sealed the line. But the spells wander and drift between the gap, like thunderclouds drifting on the wind, clashing and coming together in places. Because of the weakness in this place, there is a maze that can be passed through by those with the gift. The clear passages are always shifting, and the spells cannot always be seen. They must be felt, with the gift. Still, it is not easy."

"So that's why the Sisters of the Light can make it through? Because they have the gift?"

"Yes. But only twice at most. The magic learns to find you. Long ago, Sisters who went through to the New World and returned were sent again, but none ever returned a second time." Her gaze left his, seeking the distant emptiness. "They are in there, never to be found, or saved. The Towers of Perdition and its storms of magic claimed them."

Richard waited until her eyes came back to him. "Perhaps, Sister, they became disaffected, and chose not to return. How would you know?"

Her expression sobered. "We know. Some who have been through have seen them"—she inclined her head toward the shimmering distance—"in there. I, myself, saw several."

"I'm sorry, Sister Verna." Richard thought about Zedd. Kahlan might find him, and tell him what had happened. He had to push away the painful memory of Kahlan. "So, a wizard could make it through."

"Not a wizard of his full power. After we teach those with the gift to control it, they must be allowed to return before their power is fully developed. The whole purpose of the line is to prevent wizards from getting through. The fully developed power of a wizard would draw the spells as a magnet draws iron filings. It is they that the magic seeks; it is for them that the towers were built. They would be lost, just as would anyone who didn't have some use of the gift to feel the gaps in the spells. Too little, or too much, and you are lost. That is why those who created the line could not complete it; the domain of the spells from the other side prevented them from entering. Their creation ended in deadlock."

Richard felt his hopes sag. If Kahlan carried out his request to seek out his old friend, Zedd could not do anything to help him. Swallowing back the numbing loss of hope, he reached up and felt the dragon's tooth hanging on the leather thong at his chest. "What about going over? Could something fly over?"

She shook her head. "The spells extend up into the air, as they extend out into the sea. Anything that can fly cannot fly high enough."

"What about by sea? Could you sail far enough out to go around?"

Sister Verna shrugged. "I have heard tell that a few times throughout the ages it has been accomplished. In my life I have seen ships leave to attempt it, but I have never seen one return."

Richard glanced back over his shoulder, but saw nothing. "Could . . . someone follow you through?"

"One or two, if they stayed close enough, as you must. Greater numbers would surely be lost. The pockets between spells are not large enough to allow many to follow."

Richard thought in silence, at last asking, "Why hasn't anyone destroyed the towers, so the spells could dissipate?"

"We've tried. It cannot be done."

"Just because you haven't found a way, Sister, that doesn't mean it can't be done."

She gave him a sharp look. "The towers, and the spells, were created with the aid of not only Additive but also Subtractive Magic."

Subtractive Magic! How could the wizards of old have learned to use Subtractive Magic? Wizards didn't have command of Subtractive Magic. But then, Darken Rahl did. Richard gentled his tone. "How can the towers keep the spells from dissipating?"

Sister Verna worked her thumbs on the reins. "Each tower has a wizard's life force in it."

Despite the heat, Richard felt a chill. "You mean to say that a wizard gave his life force into the towers?"

"Worse. Each tower contains the life force of many wizards."

Richard stared in numb shock at the thought of wizards giving up their lives to invest the towers with their life force. "How close are the towers?"

"It is said some are miles apart, some only yards. They are spaced according to the fabric of lines of power within the earth itself. We don't understand the sense of this alignment. Since entering the line to find them would be death, we don't even know how many towers there are. We know of only the few in this valley."

Richard squirmed in his saddle. "Will we see any of the towers when we cross?"

"There's no way to tell. The gaps shift constantly. Occasionally, on the way through, the openings take you close to a tower. I saw one on my first journey through. Some Sisters never saw one. I hope never to see another."

Richard realized he was gripping the hilt of his sword with his left hand. The raised letters of the word TRUTH bit into his flesh. He relaxed his hand, releasing the hilt.

"So, what can we expect to see?"

Sister Verna broke her gaze into the distance and redirected it to him. "There are spells of every sort. Some are spells of despair. To be snared in one is to have your soul wander in despair for all time. Some are spells of joy and delight, in which one is lost in enchantment for all time. Some are pure destruction, and will tear you apart. Some will show you things you fear, to make you run into the clutches of things that lurk behind. Some tempt with things you hope for. If you give in to the desire . . ." She leaned closer to him. "You must stay close to me, keep going. You must ignore any desire you have, both fear and longing, to do otherwise. Do you understand?"

Richard finally nodded. Sister Verna returned her gaze to the shimmering forms. She sat motionless, watching. In the distance, beyond the wavering light, he thought he saw thunderheads, dark and ominous, drifting across the horizon. He felt more than heard their thunder. Somehow, he knew it wasn't clouds, but magic. When Bonnie tossed her head, Richard gave her a reassuring pat on her neck.

After watching awhile, he looked over to the Sister. She sat still and tense.

"What are you waiting for, Sister? Courage?"

She answered without moving. "Exactly. I am waiting for courage, child."

He felt no anger this time at her calling him "child," but rather that it might be an appropriate characterization, as far as his abilities were concerned.

In a whisper, and still without looking away from the sunbaked inferno ahead, she went on. "You were still in swaddling clothes when I came through, but I remember every detail as if it happened yesterday. Yes, I am waiting for courage."

He gave Bonnie a squeeze with his legs, urging her ahead. "The sooner we start, the sooner we're through."

"Or lost." She walked her horse after him. "So anxious to be lost, Richard?"

"I'm already lost, Sister."

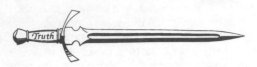

They were confronted by steps, twenty strides wide, that revealed themselves for what they were only at the far right, where the wind had funneled down next to the sweeping, pink marble balustrade and kept the snow clear. Pausing for only a moment as she realized they had reached her destination, Kahlan set her snowshoes firmly into the snowdrift that covered the steps, and ascended to the portico, its fascia decorated with a row of statues swathed in cut stone that mimicked the drape of cloth so well it seemed as if it might move in the light breeze. Ten white columns to each side held the massive entablature at a dizzying height above the arched entrance. Bodies fallen in a desperate battle were sprawled atop one another all over the snow-covered lawns, and sat as if in repose against the walls of the domed exterior entrance hall.

The ornate doors, displaying delicately carved royal shields of the House of Amnell, held aloft by twin mountain lions, lay in splinters on the floor of the vestibule. Flanking the rope-carved stone arch at the far end stood life-size statues of Queen Bernadine and King Wyborn, each holding a spear and shield in one hand, the queen a sheaf of wheat in the other, and the king a lamb. The queen's breasts were broken away; flakes of stone and stone dust littered the rust colored marble tiles. Both statues were without their heads.

With nearly numb fingers, Kahlan untied the bindings of her snowshoes and leaned them against the queen's statue. Chandalen followed her example before following her into the reception hall lined with broken mirrors and torn tapestries. She pulled her mantle tight around herself as clouds of their breath rose lazily into dead still air that was somehow much colder than that outside.

"What is this place used for?" Chandalen asked in a whisper, as if afraid he might wake the spirits of the dead.

She had to force herself not to whisper. "It is the home of the queen of this land. Her name is Cyrilla."

His doubting voice echoed down the stone hall. "One person lives in a place such as this?"

"Many people live here. There are advisors, much like the elders among your people, and others that are responsible for governing the needs of the land, and people who tend to their needs so they may perform their duties. Many people call this their home, but the queen is the head of the household, as she is the head of her land. She is above them all."

Chandalen followed silently as she began to search the palace. His eyes slid from one wondrous object to another; from elaborately carved furniture that now lay everywhere in splinters, to the heavy red, blue, gold, or green draperies that adorned the ten-foot-tall, square-top windows, all broken now.

She descended a flight of stairs to the lower rooms, the oak treads creaking with every step in the cold. He insisted on entering each room first, pushing doors open with a foot and gliding in behind a fully drawn ten-step arrow, before allowing her to search inside.

They found only the dead. In a few of the rooms they found some of the staff, who had been lined up against a wall and pincushioned with arrows. In the kitchens it looked as if after executing the cooks, cook's helpers, wine stewards, assistants, dishwashers, potboys, spit boys, and scullions, the invaders had sat down and had a drunken feast. The ale and wine casks were empty. It appeared they had thrown more food at the walls than they had eaten.

While Chandalen checked the ransacked larder, Kahlan's eye was caught by the bodies of two young women, kitchen help, on the floor behind a long chopping block. One was completely naked, and the other had but one brown, woolen stocking, bunched down around her thin ankle. Her first assumption had been wrong. Not all the help had been killed before the drunken feast.

Her face as still as those of the dead women, she turned and strode from the kitchen and started up the servants' stairs to check the upper floors. Chandalen's thumping footfalls came charging up behind as he took three steps at a time to catch her.

She knew he didn't like it that she had left without him, but he didn't voice it. "There is salted meat. Maybe we could take a little? I do not think these people would think it wrong for us to do so. They would not deny us a little food."

Kahlan put her hand to the railing as she climbed with a steady cadence, but then pulled the hand back inside her mantle, because the polished maple was so cold to the touch it stung her fingers. "If you eat the meat, you will die. They will have poisoned it, so that if any of the dead's countrymen return to this place and eat any of the food here, they, too, will die."

They found the main floor clear of bodies. It looked to have been used as an army headquarters. Empty barrels of wine and rum lay about the ballroom floor. Food scraps, mugs and cups, broken dishes, pipe ashes, bloody bandages, oily rags, broken or bent swords, spears and maces, dark wood shavings from a walnut table leg someone had whittled away until it was nothing but a stub, basins of frozen water, dirty linen, bedsheets ripped into strips, and filthy, quilted bedcovers of every color littered the carpeted floor. Dirty bootprints were everywhere, even on the tabletops. By the swirling scratches, it looked as if men had danced atop them.

Chandalen walked through the rubble, inspecting various bits. "Two, maybe three days they were here."

She nodded her agreement as her eyes cast about. "It looks that way."

He rolled a wine barrel back and forth with his foot, testing if it was empty. It was. "I wonder why they stayed so long? Just to drink, and dance?"

Kahlan sighed. "I don't know. Maybe they were resting and tending to their wounded. Maybe they just went on a drunken binge to celebrate their victory over these people."

He looked up sharply. "Killing is not a thing to celebrate."

"It is, for the people who did this killing."

Reluctantly, Kahlan at last climbed the stairs to the top floor. She didn't want to look up there. That was where the bedchambers were.

They checked the west wing first: the men's apartments. They looked to have been used by the troops as sleeping quarters. With an army of as many men as had to have done this, they would have had many men of rank. The officers probably stayed here, in the fine rooms. The soldiers under their command would have used the inns and more common houses.

With a deep breath to strengthen her resolve, she set her jaw and crossed the central hall, with its balcony that overlooked the grand staircase, to the east-wing rooms. Chandalen, close at her heels, wanted to open the doors for her and check the rooms first, but here she wouldn't allow it. Her hand paused for a moment on the doorknob, then finally opened the first door. She stood for a time, staring at the scene inside. She went to the next door and flung it open, and then to the next.

All the rooms were occupied. Each bedchamber had women in it, none clothed. Room after room after room were all the same. By the filthy condition of the carpets, there looked to have been a steady stream of traffic. Wood shavings lay in little piles about the floor, where a man had passed the time whittling on whatever was handy while he waited his turn.

"Now we know why they spent several days here," Kahlan said without meeting Chandalen's eyes. He remained silent. She couldn't bring forth more than a whisper. "So they could do this."

Those few days had undoubtedly been the longest of these women's lives. Kahlan prayed that their spirits were at peace, now.

She reached the door at the end, the door to the room the younger women shared. Slowly, she opened it, and stood looking in, Chandalen close behind her looking past her shoulder.

Stifling a gasp, she turned and put a hand to his chest. "Please, Chandalen, wait here."

He nodded as he furiously studied his boots.

Kahlan closed the door behind herself and stood with her back against it for a time. One hand at her side, and the other covering her mouth, she skirted an overturned, wrecked wardrobe, and walked the length of the frigid room, between the rows of beds, looking from one side to the other. The precious hand mirrors, brushes, combs, and pins that at one time had been arranged with loving care on tables between the beds now lay scattered about the floor. The blue moire curtains billowed slightly in the icy air coming through the broken windows.

These were the queen's ladies-in-waiting. Young women of fourteen, fifteen, and sixteen, a few a little older. These were not just nameless corpses; Kahlan knew many of these young women.

The queen had taken them with her when she had traveled to Aydindril to speak before the council. Kahlan could not have failed to notice them, their vibrancy, their wide-eyed excitement at being in Aydindril. Seeing the grandeur of Aydindril through their young eyes had given Kahlan new vision of the things around her, and brought a smile to her lips. She had longed to give them a tour, personally, but being with the Mother Confessor would have frightened them, and so she hadn't. But she had admired them from afar, and envied their lives of possibility.

Kahlan stopped at various beds, her back stiff, her head held high, her jaw rigid, as she reluctantly cast her eyes down at faces she knew. Juliana, one of the youngest, had always been self-confident and assertive. She knew what she wanted and wasn't timid about going after it. She had always been smitten with young men in uniform: soldiers. One time, it had brought her to grief with her chaperone, Mistress Nelda. Kahlan had surreptitiously interceded on her behalf, informing Mistress Nelda that despite Juliana's dalliances, the Aydindril Home Guard were all men of impeccable honor, and would never lay a finger on a queen's lady. Her wrists were now tied to the headpost, and by the way they had bled, looked to have been that way through the whole of her ordeal. Kahlan silently cursed the spirits for their cruel humor in giving the young innocent what she had thought she wanted.

Little Elswyth was in the next blood-soaked bed. Her breasts had been stabbed countless times, and her throat slit, as were many of the rest, like hogs at slaughter. At the end of the room, Kahlan stopped at the foot of the last bed. Ashley, one of the older teenagers, had each ankle tied to a footpost. She had been strangled with a curtain tieback. Her father was one of the Galean aides to the ambassador in Aydindril. Her mother had been thrilled to tears when Queen Cyrilla had agreed to take Ashley on as one of her ladies-in-waiting. How would she ever find the words to tell Ashley's father and mother what had happened to their little girl while in the service of their queen?

As Kahlan retraced her steps through the length of the room, taking a last look at each dead body, at each face frozen in horror or in blank submission, she idly wondered why she wasn't crying. Shouldn't she cry? Shouldn't she fall to her knees, scream in anguish, pound her fists, and cry until she drowned in tears? But she didn't. She felt as if there were no tears to be had.

Perhaps there were too many. Perhaps she had seen so many that day that it had simply numbed her to it. Like when you get into a tub of water for a bath, and at first you feel that it is too hot to stand, that surely you are being scalded, but after a few minutes it seems only warm.

She softly pulled the door closed. Chandalen stood in the exact same spot she had left him. His knuckles were white on his bow. Kahlan walked past him, expecting him to follow. He didn't.

"Most women would cry," he said as he stared at the door.

She felt a flush of heat in her cheeks. "I am not most women."

Chandalen didn't take his eyes from the door. "No, you are not."

His eyes finally left the door to look down at his bow. The tension left his shoulders as he pulled a deep breath, as if it was the first he had taken in a while. "I wish to tell you a story."

Kahlan waited a few paces away. "I do not wish to hear a story right now, Chandalen. Perhaps later."

He turned his fierce brown eyes to her. "I wish to tell you a story," he repeated, a little louder this time.

She sighed. "If it's important to you, then tell me."

Holding her gaze, he closed the distance between them. He was a scant inch shorter than she, but right then he looked taller to her. "When my grandfather was as young, and strong"—he tapped his puffed-up chest—"as I am now, he already had a wife, and two sons. Many peoples came to our village to trade. We let all come. We kept no one away. All were welcome. The Jocopo were one of these people who came to trade."

"Who are the Jocopo?" Kahlan knew every people in the Midlands, but had never heard of these.

"People who lived to the west, closer to where the boundary was."

Kahlan frowned as her mind searched a mental map. "No one lives to the west of the Mud People. That land is deserted."

Chandalen watched her from under his eyebrows. "The Jocopo were big people." He held his hand a head higher than he was, before letting it fall to his side. "But they were always peaceful. Like the Bantak. Like our people. Then they made war on us. We do not know the reason. But our people were very afraid. They would shake at night, in the fear that the Jocopo might come again the next day. They would come to our village, and cut the men's throats, and take women, and do these things to them." He flicked his hand self-consciously at the door.

"Rape," she said in an even tone. "It is called rape."

He nodded. "The Jocopo would do this to our women. They stole many women, and did this rape to them." He glanced at the door again. "In the way it was done to these women. Do you understand?"

"They were raped by many men and tortured and murdered."

He nodded, relieved that he didn't have to elaborate. "The Mud People did not have fighters, like we do now, like me." His chest swelled again, and his chin came up. At last, the wind left his lungs. "We never had to fight with anyone. None of our people wanted to fight others. They thought it was wrong. But the Jocopo made us want to fight.

"They stole my grandmother. My grandfather's wife. The mother to my father. My grandfather gave an oath to send the Jocopo to the spirit world. He gathered men together, men who had their wives, or sisters, or mothers taken, and . . ." He wiped his forehead as if he were sweating, but in the cold he was not.

Kahlan put a hand on his arm. He didn't flinch this time. "I understand, Chandalen."

"My grandfather called for a gathering, and was visited by our ancestors' spirits. He wept for his wife before the spirits, and asked if the ancestors' spirits would teach him how to stop the Jocopo. They told him that first he must stop weeping until after the fighting was done."

Kahlan took her hand back and absently stroked the fur at her neck. "My father taught me something very much like that. He said, 'Don't shed tears over those already in the ground, until after you have brought vengeance to those who put them there. There will be time enough, then.'"

Chandalen appraised her approvingly. "Then your father was a wise man."

Kahlan waited silently until at last he seemed to mentally gather up the memories of the stories, and go on.

"The ancestors' spirits came to my grandfather every night in a gathering. They taught him what he must do, how to kill. He taught these men what he had learned. He taught them how to put mud on themselves, and tie grass to themselves, so not to be seen. Our men became like the shadows. The Jocopo could not see them if they stood as close as we do now.

"My grandfather and his men made war with the Jocopo. Not war the way the Jocopo made war, but the way the spirits taught. The Jocopo made war in the day, because they were many, and had no fear of us. The spirits told grandfather that he must not fight the Jocopo the way they wanted, but must make them fear the night, and the empty grassland, and every call of a bird or frog or bug.

"For every one of the Mud People, there were five Jocopo. At first, they were not afraid of us, because of their numbers. We killed Jocopo when they hunted food, when they tended their crops, when they cared for their animals, when they went for water, when they went to squat, when they slept. Any Jocopo. Every Jocopo. We did not try to fight them; we only killed them. Until there were no more Jocopo in this world, only in the spirit world."

She wondered briefly if he meant that they had killed the children, too, but she knew the answer; there were no more Jocopo. Something else her father had taught her came to mind: *If war is brought to you, then it is incumbent upon you to show no mercy. Surely you will be shown none, and you will be a traitor to your people and as good as their enemy if you let any clemency slip its bounds, for your people will pay for your mistake with their lives.*

"I understand, Chandalen. Your people did the only thing they could. Your grandfather did what was necessary to protect his people. My father also taught me, 'If war is brought to you, then let there be war like your enemy has never imagined in his most frightening nightmares. Anything less, and you hand victory to your foe.'"

"Your father, too, must know the spirits of his ancestors. He did well to teach you their lessons." His voice lowered sympathetically. "But I know they are harsh lessons to live by, and can make you look hard to others."

"I know the truth of that. Your grandfather brought honor to the Mud People, Chandalen. I'm sure that when it was done, he shed many tears for those of his people who were murdered."

Chandalen untied the thong at his neck and shrugged back his mantle, letting it drop to the floor. He wore a heavy buckskin tunic and pants. At each shoulder, held with a band made of woven prairie cotton around his upper arm, was a bone knife. The lower end was sharpened to a point, and the knuckle at the other end was covered with the same woven cotton for a better grip. Black feathers hung from the top.

He tapped one of the bones. "This is of my grandfather." He touched the other. "This is of my father. One day, when I have a strong son, he will wear one of me, and of my father, and the one of my grandfather will be put to rest in the ground."

When Kahlan had first seen the bone knives, when they had left the Mud People village, she had thought they were ceremonial. With terrible certainty, she now knew they were not. They were real weapons: spirit weapons.

"What are the feathers?"

He stroked the glossy black feathers on the one at his right shoulder. "The Bird Man we had then, when this was made, placed these." He touched the ones on his left shoulder. "The Bird Man we have now placed these. They are raven."

The raven was a powerful spirit to the Mud People. Its image invoked death. While she thought the idea of wearing a knife made from your grandfather and father's arm bone was gruesome, she knew it was an honor to Chandalen, and so didn't say anything to insult his beliefs. "It brings me honor, Chandalen, that you would bring the spirits of your ancestors to protect me."

He didn't look happy. "The Bird Man says you are Mud People, too, and must be protected, so I wear these. It is my duty."

He stroked his grandfather's bone again. "My grandfather taught my father, and my uncle, Toffalar, the man you killed, to be protectors of our people." He touched his father's bone. "My father taught me. I will teach my son, when he comes, and someday he will carry my spirit with him as he protects our people.

"Since the time we killed the Jocopo, we have not let many come onto our land. Our ancestors' spirits teach us that to invite others to come as they wish is to invite death. The spirits speak true. You brought Richard With The Temper to us, and because of him, Darken Rahl came and killed many of our people."

So it came down to this. Chandalen was supposed to be a protector of his people, but they had been killed and he hadn't been able to stop it. "The ancestors' spirits helped us to save the Mud People, Chandalen, and countless others. They saw that Richard's heart was true, that he was risking his life, the same as you, to save others who did not want war."

"He stayed in the spirit house while Darken Rahl killed our people. He did not try to stop him. He did not fight. He let our people die."

"Do you know why?" She waited as he stood stone-faced, but when he didn't reply, she resumed. "The spirits told him that if he went out to fight Darken Rahl, he would be fighting the way Darken Rahl fought, and Richard would die, never to help anyone. They told him that if he wanted to defeat Darken Rahl and save the rest of the Mud People, he must not fight the way Darken Rahl did, but wait and fight his own way, later, just as the spirits told your grandfather."

He regarded her skeptically. "This is his story."

"I was there, Chandalen. I heard them say this. Richard wanted to fight. He wept with frustration when the spirits told him he must not. There was nothing that could have been done to stop Rahl just then. It was not Richard's fault, nor was it yours. You could have done nothing to stop it, the same as Richard could have done nothing. If he had tried, he would be dead, and Darken Rahl would have won."

He leaned a little closer. "If you had not brought him, it would not have happened. Darken Rahl would not have come looking for him."

She drew herself up straight. "Chandalen, do you know what I do? What my specialty is?"

"Yes. Like all Confessors, you make people afraid of you, so you may tell them what to do, and because they are afraid, they will do as you say."

"In a way. I lead the Council of the Midlands. I represent all the people and protect their rights. I make it possible for those like the Mud People to live as they wish."

"We protect ourselves."

She gave him a sober nod. "You think so? For every one of the Mud People, there were five Jocopo. Your grandfather was brave, and defeated an enemy that outnumbered him. But for every man, woman, and child of the Mud People, there are over a hundred dead soldiers here, and this is only one city of this land. They were defeated as if they were nothing. One hundred fighting men for every Mud Person, and they fought bravely, you said so. What chance do you think you would have against an army that could defeat this many? Against an army half that size?"

Chandalen shifted his weight without answering.

"There are lands, Chandalen, that have no say, like the Mud People, and the Bantak. They are not represented on the council. The larger lands, like this one, and the one that defeated them, are very powerful, yet Darken Rahl conquered them. I speak for the lands that have no voice on the council. I protect your wish to be left alone, and forbid others to come onto your land.

"Without me to make them afraid, and tell them what to do, they would take your land for themselves. You have seen the country we have traveled through. Much of it is difficult to plant. People would take your land for farms, and to raise animals. Your sacred grasslands would be burned and tilled and planted with crops to trade for gold.

"As brave and strong as you are, you would not be able to protect your people. These outsiders would blacken your land with their numbers. Just because your are brave, and strong, does not mean you will win. The soldiers here were brave, and strong, and a hundred times your number, and look what happened to them. And this is only one city. There are many larger.

"Being brave does not mean you have to be stupid, Chandalen. You saw what was done here. How long do you think you could fight against an army like that which did this? Even if every one of your men killed fifty, they would hardly notice. You would be like the Jocopo, gone. Every last one of you."

Kahlan jabbed a finger at her own chest. "I am the one who tells them they may not. They do not fear you, but they fear me, and the alliance I represent. There are good people in the Midlands, people who are willing to fight to protect others who are less powerful. The dead here are one of those peoples. They are one that has always backed me when I said no land may attack another to gain land.

"I head the Council of the Midlands and hold together the lands that want peace. Under me they would fight any who would make war on others. Yes, I make people afraid, so they will do what I say. But not to have the glory of power. I hold power to keep the people of the Midlands—including the Mud People—free of oppression. These people here have fought before to keep all the people of the Midlands free to live as they wished. They have fought for you, for your rights, though you have never known of the blood they have shed on your behalf."

She clutched her mantle more tightly. "You have never before had to fight for them, until Darken Rahl threatened all. I came to the Mud People, with Richard, to seek help. Your ancestors' spirits saw the truth of our struggle, and they helped us so that the Mud People, and all others, could live free. For the first time, Mud People had to shed blood for the Midlands. Your ancestors' spirits saw the truth of this, and they helped us.

"The people of the Midlands owe the Mud People a debt for their sacrifice, but you also owe them.

"Richard With The Temper put his life at risk for your people. He lost loved ones in the struggle, the same as you. He suffered things you could never understand. You could not imagine what was done to him by Darken Rahl before Richard killed him."

Kahlan stood in fury, clouds of her hot breath rising into the cold air.

"I make people afraid of me so you may continue to be blind and stubborn. Richard and I have fought to keep all the people of the Midlands, including the Mud People, from being murdered, as the Jocopo murdered Mud People, even though you would deny us your help, or simple gratitude."

Silence echoed around them.

Chandalen walked slowly to the railing, idly running a finger along its polished surface. She watched each slow cloud of his breath dissipate, to be followed by another. He spoke softly. "You see me as stubborn. I see you, too, as stubborn. Maybe our fathers should have also taught us to see that sometimes people do as they do, not because they are stubborn, but because they fear for those they protect. Maybe you and I should be able to see each other not as harsh, but as doing the best we know, to keep our people safe."

A small smile came unexpectedly to Kahlan's lips. "Perhaps, Chandalen is not so blind as I thought. I will try, myself, to see better, see you for the man of honor you are."

He gave a nod, and a small smile of his own. "Richard With The Temper is not a stupid man." He put his hands to the railing, looking out over the first floor. "He said that if he had to pick one man to fight beside him, he would pick Chandalen."

"You speak the truth," she said softly. "He is not a stupid man."

"Richard also sacrificed himself as your mate. He has saved our men from being chosen, as surely you would have picked one of us, because we are so strong." His voice rose with pride. "You would probably have picked me, so that you might have the strongest mate. Richard has saved me."

Kahlan smiled again in spite of herself as he stared out over the railing. "I'm sorry you feel the task of being my mate is so onerous a thing."

Chandalen came back to her. He stood a moment, studying her eyes, and then began untying the band at his right arm. He pulled the band and bone knife free, holding it out before her.

"Grandfather would be proud to protect you, one of his own, one of his Mud People." He flipped her mantle back over her left shoulder.

"Chandalen, I cannot accept this. It holds the spirit of your grandfather."

He ignored her words and tied the band to her left arm. "I have the spirit of my father with me, and I am strong. You fight to protect our people. Grandfather would want to be with you in your fight. You do him an honor."

She held her chin up as he slipped the bone knife into the band. "I'm honored, then, to have your grandfather's spirit with me."

"This is good. You have the duty now to fight as my grandfather fought to protect your people. All of your people." He lifted her right hand and placed it on the bone knife. "Swear to carry this duty in your heart."

"I have already sworn to protect the Mud People, and the others of the Midlands. I have already fought and will continue to fight for all of you."

He squeezed her hand tighter to the bone. "Swear to Chandalen."

She studied his grim expression a long moment. "You have my vow, Chandalen. I swear it before you."

He smiled as he pulled her mantle back over her shoulder, over the bone knife. "Chandalen will thank Richard With The Temper, when I see him again, for saving me from being chosen as the mate to the Mother Confessor. I will wish him no bad fortune. He fights, too, for the Mud People, as the Bird Man has told us."

Kahlan bent to pick up his mantle. "Here. Put this back on, I don't want you to freeze. You must still get me to Aydindril."

He nodded, still wearing the small, tight smile, as he threw the mantle over his shoulders. His smile died as he glanced at the doors. "Someone has been here since this was done."

Kahlan frowned. "What makes you think that?"

"Why did you close the doors after you had looked?"

"Out of respect for the dead."

"When we came to them, they were closed. Those who did this rape had no respect. They would not have closed all the doors. They wanted anyone who came to see what they had done. Someone else has been here, and closed the doors."

Kahlan glanced to the doors, seeing the meaning of what he said. "I think you're right." She shook her head. "Those who did this would not have closed the door."

Chandalen leaned on the railing again, looking down at the wide stairs. "Why are we here?"

"Because I had to know what happened to these people."

"You saw that outside. Why are we here, in this house?"

Kahlan glanced at the steps leading up to the top floor. "Because I have to know if the queen was killed, too."

He looked over his shoulder toward her. "She means something to you?"

Kahlan was suddenly aware of the pounding of her heart. "Yes. Do you remember the statues near the door we entered?"

"A woman, and a man."

She nodded. "The statue of the woman is a statue of her mother. My mother was a Confessor. The statue of the man is a statue of her father. King Wyborn. He was also my father."

Chandalen lifted an eyebrow. "You are sister to this queen?"

"Half sister." Summoning courage, she started for the stairs. "Let's see if she is here, and then we can be on our way to Aydindril."

Kahlan's heart was still pounding as she stood before the door to the queen's chambers. She couldn't bring herself to open it. It smelled dreadful in the hall, but she hardly noticed.

"Do you wish me to look for you?"

"No," she said. "I must see with my own eyes."

She turned the knob. The door was locked, the key still in place. She touched the icy metal plate. "This is a lock, the thing I told you of before," she lectured as she pulled the key out and held it up. "This is a key." Replacing the key, she twisted it with shaking fingers. "If you have a key, you can open the lock, and then the door."

Someone had obviously locked the door, out of respect for the queen.

The windows were intact, as was the furniture. The room was as freezing cold as the rest of the palace, but the smell made them suddenly gag and hold their breath.

Human excrement covered everything in the outer sitting room. The two of them stared in shock. Dark piles dotted the carpets and sat on the desk and table. The blue velvet chairs and couches were soaked with yellow, frozen urine. Someone had even squatted neatly in the fireplace.

Holding their mantles across their noses, they stepped carefully across the room to the next closed door. The queen's bedchamber was worse. There was hardly a place to put a foot without stepping in it. But as covered as the floor was, the worst was the bed; it was heaped with feces. Delicately painted floral scenes on the walls were smeared with it. If everything hadn't been frozen solid, they would have been driven from the room by the stench. As it was, it was barely tolerable.

Thankfully, there were no bodies. The queen was not here.

The names on Kahlan's mental roster of who could have done all this fell away, and only one nation was left. The ones who had been at the top, before.

"Keltans," she hissed to herself.

Chandalen was dumbfounded. "Why would these men do this? Are they children who do not know better?"

After a last look around, Kahlan led them back out into the hall, locking the door once more, at last taking a full breath. "It's a message. It's meant to show their disrespect for the people who lived here. It says that they have nothing but scorn for these people, and anything that's theirs. They've soiled their foe's honor in every way they could think of."

"At least your half sister is not here."

Kahlan snugged the thongs of her mantle tight at her neck. "At least there is that."

She descended the steps, pausing to look once more at the closed doors on the second floor. Chandalen watched her after he, too, glanced to the row of doors.

She sought to fill the silence. "We must go and find Prindin and Tossidin."

His face was lined with ire. "Does this not make you angry?"

She realized only then that she was wearing her Confessor's face. "It would do no good for me to show my anger right now. When the time is right, you will know just how angry I am."

In a cramped daub-and-wattle house next to the hole in the city's wall, Kahlan watched as Chandalen built a small fire for her in the central pit. The two brothers were nowhere to be seen.

"Warm yourself," he said. "I will see if Prindin and Tossidin are close, and tell them where we wait."

After he had left, she drew off her mantle, even though she knew it wasn't a good idea to get too used to the warmth because it would only make the cold seem worse later. Drawn by the lure of the fire, she squatted close, rubbing her hands together over the flames, shivering as the warmth seeped into her bones.

The small room was one of only two that had been a large part of some family's world. The table was broken but the crude bench sitting against the wall was not. A few pieces of clothing were scattered about, along with bent tin plates and a broken spinning wheel. Three bobbins were crushed into the dirt floor.

Kahlan retrieved a dented pot from among the rubble, deciding it was easier to use it than to unpack one of their own. She heaped it full of snow from outside the door, placed the pot on three stones in the fire, then warmed her icy fingers again, finally pressing them against the cold flesh of her face. There was tea in a crushed canister in the corner, but she instead pulled her own from her pack while she waited for the snow to melt, and the men to return.

Try as she might, she couldn't get the faces of the dead young women out of her mind.

Several times, she added snow as that in the pot melted down. As the water was just starting to bubble, Prindin came through the door. He leaned his bow against the wall and with a sigh slumped down heavily on the bench.

Kahlan stood and glanced to the empty doorway. "Where's your brother?"

"He should be here soon. We took different ways back, to be able to look at more tracks." He craned his neck, looking through the doorway into the second room. "Where is Chandalen?"

"He went to find you and Tossidin."

"Then he will be back soon. My brother is not far."

"What did you find?"

"More dead people."

He didn't seem to want to talk about it at the moment, so she decided to wait until Chandalen returned with Tossidin before questioning him.

"I was just warming water. We'll have some hot tea."

He nodded, flashing her his handsome smile. "It would be good to have hot tea."

Kahlan bent over the pot, shaking tea from a leather pouch with one hand, and holding her long hair back from her face with the other.

"You have a fine-looking bottom," came his voice from behind.

She straightened and turned to him. "What did you say?"

Prindin pointed toward her middle. "I said you have a fine-looking bottom. It is a good shape."

Kahlan had learned not to be startled or insulted by the strange customs of different peoples of the Midlands. Among the Mud People, for example, a man complimenting a woman on her breasts was the same as saying she looked to be capable of being a fit and healthy mother, able to nurse her future children. It was a compliment that brought smiles of pride from the flattered woman's family, and was a sure way for a suitor to make friends with her father. At the same time, asking to see a woman with the sticky mud washed from her hair was likely as not to raise drawn bows—it was tantamount to asking the young woman for improper favors.

The Mud People treated matters of sex in an especially casual manner. Kahlan had more than once been brought to blushing by Weselan's unexpected and cavalier descriptions of coupling with her husband. Worse, she was as likely as not to do it in his presence.

As she stared at Prindin, the visions of the young women's faces, too, floated before her eyes.

Though Prindin had not complimented her on her breasts, it seemed to her that a woman's hips could be construed to carry the same maternal compliment. She knew he meant no disrespect, but still, his beaming smile made the hairs on her arms stand on end. Maybe it was just the inappropriate timing, with the dead all about, that unnerved her. But he hadn't seen the dead young women.

Prindin's smile faded only a little as a frown came to his brow. "You look surprised. Doesn't Richard With The Temper ever tell you how fine your bottom is?"

Kahlan fumbled for words, not sure how to bring this to an honorable halt. "He has never mentioned it, specifically."

"Other men must have told you this before. It is too fine for them not to notice. The shape of your body is very good to look at. It fills me with desire to . . ." He frowned in puzzlement. "I don't know your word for . . ."

Blood went to her face in a red rush as she took a step toward him. "Prindin!" She relaxed her fists and brought her voice back in check. "Prindin. I am the Mother Confessor."

He nodded, his grin returning, but not quite as confident. "Yes, but you are a woman, too, and your shape . . ."

"Prindin!" He blinked at her as she ground her teeth. "In your land it may be proper to speak to a woman in this fashion, but in other places in the Midlands, it is not. In other places, speaking in this manner is offensive. Very offensive. More than that, I'm the Mother Confessor, and it's not proper to speak to me in this way."

His smile vanished. "But you are now one of the Mud People."

"That may be true, but I'm still the Mother Confessor."

His face blanched. "I have offended you." He leapt up from the bench and fell to his knees before her. "Forgive me, please. I meant no disrespect. I meant only to show my favor for you."

Her red face glowed in embarrassment. She had done it now; she had humiliated him.

"I understand, Prindin. I know your words are harmless, but you must not speak this way outside your land. Others would not understand your ways and would be greatly offended."

He was nearly in tears. "I did not know. Please say you forgive Prindin." He clutched at her pants, and gripped her upper thighs with his powerful fingers.

"Yes . . . of course . . . I know you meant no harm." She took hold of his wrists, pulling them gently from her legs. "I forgive you. . . ."

Chandalen came through the door, his face set in a grim cast. He took a quick glance at Prindin before looking up into her eyes.

"What is this?"

"Nothing." She hastily helped Prindin to his feet as his brother entered the room. "But we're going to have to have a talk about the proper way to speak to ladies in the Midlands. There are things you three will need to be taught, to keep you out of trouble." She smoothed her pant legs and the lingering sting of where Prindin's strong fingers had been, and then straightened herself. "Tell me what you've found."

Chandalen cast a withering glare at Prindin. "What have you done?"

Prindin took a half step back, diverting his eyes. "I did not know it would be wrong. I told her she had a fine . . ."

"I said it was nothing," Kahlan said, cutting him off. "It's just a small misunderstanding. Forget about it." She turned to the fire. "I made hot tea. Get some cups—there are some we can use on the floor over there—and we will have some tea while you tell me what you found."

Tossidin made for the cups, thumping the back of his brother's head along the way, adding a whispered reprimand. Chandalen shrugged off his mantle and squatted before the fire, warming his hands. The brothers brought the cups, Prindin rubbing the back of his head, and passed them around.

In an attempt to let them all know Prindin hadn't lost any honor in her eyes, Kahlan directed her attention and first question to him. "Tell me what you found."

Prindin glanced briefly at the other two before setting his face with a serious expression. "Ten, maybe twelve days ago, this killing was done. The enemy came mostly from the east, but there were many, and some came from farther to the north and south. They had war in the narrow places in the mountains with men from this city. Those men from the city not killed ran away as they were overrun and gathered their numbers here, and tried to make a stand. While they ran to here, they were chased by their enemy, fighting and dying as they ran."

More and more of the invaders poured through the passes, sweeping around to the south, here, where they had a battle. After they defeated those men, and killed the ones they captured, the enemy came through the wall. When they were finished in this city, all of them, together, went east again."

Tossidin leaned in a little. "Before they left, they took their dead from the city. They used wagons; there are many tracks from the wheels. It took them maybe two days to take all their dead from here. Many thousands. The people here must have fought like demon spirits. The ones who did this lost more men than they killed."

"Where are the bodies?" she asked.

"In a bowl in a pass to the east," Prindin said. "The wagons took the dead along the road, and then they were thrown down into the low place. They are piled so deep we do not know how low the ground is there."

"What did they look like?" She took a sip of tea, holding the tin cup with both hands wrapped around it, soaking up the warmth. "How were they dressed?"

Prindin reached under his shirt and pulled out a folded cloth. He handed her the bloodred bundle. "There were poles, with these on them. Many of the men wore clothes with the same symbols on them, but we did not want to take the clothes from the dead."

Kahlan unfolded the banner and stared in shock at the long red triangle draped over her hands. In the center was a black shield with an ornate silver letter on it. The letter *R*. It was a war banner, with the shield and symbol of the House of Rahl.

"D'Haran soldiers," she whispered. "How could that be?" She looked up. "Were there Keltans, too?"

The three men looked at one another. They didn't understand. They didn't know the Keltans.

"There were some with other clothes," Prindin said. "But most had this symbol on them, or on their shields."

"And they went east?"

Tossidin nodded. "I do not know the way to tell you their numbers, but there were so many that if you stood in the same spot on the wide road they took, you would be there all day watching them pass."

"Also," Prindin said, "as they were going, others joined them, from the north where they had been waiting, and went with them."

Kahlan's eyes narrowed as she frowned in thought. "Did they have many wagons? Big wagons?"

Prindin snorted a laugh. "They must have hundreds. These men do not carry anything. They use wagons. They have victory, because they are many, but they are lazy. They ride in wagons, or use them to carry their things."

"It takes a lot of supplies," she said, "to support an army that big. And if they ride in wagons it keeps them fresh for fighting."

"It also makes them soft," Chandalen said defiantly. "If you carry what you need, like we do, then you grow strong. If you walk without carrying what you need, or ride in wagons, or on horses, then you grow soft. These men are not strong, like us."

"They were strong enough to crush this city," Kahlan said, looking up from under her eyebrows. "They were strong enough to win the battle and destroy their opponent."

"Only because they are many," Chandalen argued, "like the Jocopo, not because they are strong, or good fighters."

"Large numbers," she said, quietly, "has a strength all its own."

None of the three men disagreed with that.

Prindin downed the last of his tea before speaking. "Their numbers are all gone now. They stay together as they go east."

"East." She thought a moment while the three waited. "Did they go through a pass that has a thin rope bridge stretched above it? A bridge that can only be crossed by one person at a time, on foot?"

The brothers nodded.

Kahlan stood. "Jara Pass," she whispered to herself as she turned to stare out the door. "It's one of the few big enough for their wagons."

"There is more," Tossidin said as he stood, too. "Maybe five days after they left, more men came here." He held up the spread fingers of both hands. "This many did the killing here." He closed all but a lone little finger on his right hand. "This many came here after it was done."

332

Kahlan glanced to Chandalen. "The ones who closed the doors."

He nodded as the two brothers frowned.

"They searched the city," Tossidin went on. "There were no people left here to kill, so they followed the tracks, followed those that went east, to join with them."

"No," Kahlan said. "They were no allies of those who did this. They didn't go to join them. They're going after them, though."

Prindin considered this a moment. "Then if they catch the ones who did this, then they, too, will die. They have no numbers like those they chase. They will be like fleas trying to eat a dog."

Kahlan snatched up her mantle and flung it around her shoulders. "Let's get going. Jara Pass is wide and easy enough for large wagons, but it's also very long and meandering. I know small passes—like the one that takes that rope bridge over the Jara, and then up through Harpies Cleft—that an army cannot travel, but we can, and it's much shorter. What they travel in three or four days, we can travel in one."

Chandalen stood, but did so in an easy manner. "Mother Confessor, following these men will not take us to Aydindril."

"We have to go over one of the passes to get us to Aydindril. Harpies is as good as any."

Chandalen still made no move to recover his mantle. "But that way lies an army of thousands. You wanted to get to Aydindril with as little trouble as possible. That way lies trouble."

Kahlan squatted with her boot over a snowshoe, and began lacing on the binding. The faces of the dead young women wavered before her eyes. "I'm the Mother Confessor. I will not allow this to happen in the Midlands. It's my responsibility."

The men glanced uneasily at one another. The brothers moved to retrieve their snowshoes. Chandalen did not.

"You said your responsibility was to go to Aydindril as Richard With The Temper asked. You said you must do as he asked."

Kahlan paused her work at the binding of the second snowshoe. Anguish seared though her. She considered Chandalen's words, but only briefly. "I'm not abandoning that responsibility." She finished the binding and stood. "But we're Mud People. We have other responsibilities, too."

"Other responsibilities?"

Kahlan tapped the bone knife that was tied to her arm, under her mantle. "To the spirits. The Jocopo, the Bantak, and now these men, have listened to spirits that would have them do great evil—spirits that come through the tear in the veil. We have responsibilities to the spirits of our ancestors, and their living descendants."

She knew that to close the veil, she needed to reach Zedd, to get help for Richard. It was possible that Richard was the only one who could close the veil. Chandalen was right; they must reach Aydindril.

But the faces of the young women still filled her mind. The horror of what had been done to them still coursed through her.

The two brothers were sitting on the bench putting on their snowshoes. Chandalen stepped close to her and lowered her voice.

"What good will come of us catching this army? It is wrong."

She looked into his brown eyes. They were not filled with defiance as they had been in the past, but with genuine concern.

"Chandalen, the men who did this killing, and went east, are perhaps fifty thousand strong. The ones who closed the doors in the palace and are chasing that army are perhaps five thousand. They are filled with anger, but if they catch the ones they're chasing, they'll be slaughtered, too. If I have a chance to prevent five thousand men from dying, then I must try for that chance."

He lifted an eyebrow. "And if you are killed in this, then what greater evil will break its bounds?"

"That's what you three are supposed to prevent—my being killed."

She started for the door. Chandalen gently gripped her arm and brought her to a halt. He spoke calmly.

"It will be dark soon. We can rest here tonight, and cook food. We can leave in the morning after we are rested."

"The moon will be up soon to light our way. We have no time to waste." She leaned toward him. "I'm going on, now. If you're as strong as you say, you'll go with me. If you're not, you may rest here."

Chandalen put his hands on his hips. His lips tightened as he let out a deep breath. He appraised her with frustration.

"You cannot walk more than Chandalen. We go, too."

Kahlan gave him a quick, tight smile, and swept through the door. The brothers snatched up their bows and jumped to fall in behind her while Chandalen bent to tie on his snowshoes.

**R**ichard watched the horses eating grass that wasn't there, and scratched his itchy beard. The surface of the valley was baked and barren, but the horses seemed contented in their grazing, as if there were lush green grass beneath their feet. Illusion, it seemed, deluded and enticed even the horses. He wondered what wasn't there that he was going to see.

Sister Verna at last moved, pulling up on Jessup's lead line, pulling him away from his browsing. "This way."

Ominous, dark clouds hugged the ground ahead, boiling as if alive and eagerly awaiting them. Richard pulled the other two horses on, following after the Sister. She had told them that they must walk because the horses could be suddenly spooked by things unseen and could carry them, helpless, into a spell.

Sister Verna abruptly altered her course across the featureless ground, taking them a little to the right. The dark cloud of dust and dirt lifted and tumbled, driven by the gusts that, as of yet, didn't touch them. Sister Verna looked over her shoulder, her expression as dark as the cloud.

"Whatever you see, you ignore it. Whatever it is, it isn't real. You just ignore it. Do you understand?"

"What am I going to see?"

She redirected her attention to the way ahead. Her white blouse was damp with sweat, as was his shirt. "I can't tell you. The spells seek those things in your own mind you fear or long for, so everyone sees different things. Yet some visions are the same. Some fears are the same in all of us. Some of the magic we will see is not visions, but real. Like those clouds of dust."

"And what did you see the last time that you're so afraid of?"

She walked in silence for a time. "One I loved."

"If she was a loved one, why would you be afraid to see her?"

"Because he tried to kill me."

Richard blinked at the stinging sweat in his eyes. "He? Do you have a man you love, Sister?"

She watched the ground as she walked. "Not anymore." Her voice was soft with sorrow. She glanced up at him a moment, before seeking the ground once more with her eyes. "When I was young, I had a love. Jedidiah."

She was silent, so he asked. "He is not your love anymore?" She shook her head. "Why not?"

Pausing only a moment, she wiped her brow with a finger before moving on. "I was young, perhaps younger than you, when I left the Palace of the Prophets. Left to find you. We didn't know if you had been born yet. We knew that if you had not been, you would be, but we didn't know when, so three Sisters were sent.

"But that was many years ago. I've spent better than half my life away from the palace. From Jedidiah." She stopped again, peering first right, then left, before starting ahead once more. "He will have long ago forgotten me, and found another."

"If he really loved you, Sister, he won't have forgotten you and found another. You haven't forgotten him."

She gave a tug on her horse's line, pulling him away from something he wanted to investigate. "Too many years have passed. We've grown older apart. I have grown old. We are not the same people we were. He is one with the gift, and has his own life. It would not include me."

"You're not old, Sister. If you really love each other, time shouldn't matter." He wondered if he was talking about her, or himself.

Sister Verna gave a soft, private laugh. "Youth. Youth holds much hope, but not much wisdom. I know the ways of people. Of men. He has been too long from my skirts. He will long ago have sought another."

Richard felt himself blushing in the heat. "Love has more to it than that."

"Ah, so you know so much of love, yes? You, too, will soon be searching the charms of a new pair of pretty legs."

Richard was about to vent a rush of sudden anger when Sister Verna stopped. She looked up. The dark cloud swirled in, closing in on them.

From somewhere, Richard heard the faint sound of someone screaming his name.

"Something is wrong," Sister Verna whispered to herself.

"What is it?"

She ignored him, pulling Jessup to the left. "This way."

Lightning lit the air about them. A blinding bolt struck the ground ahead, sending a shower of the chalky earth skyward. The ground shook with the impact. Every muscle flinched from the nearness of the strike.

When the lightning tore the dark wall open for an instant, Richard saw Kahlan. She was standing, watching him. And then she was gone.

"Kahlan?"

Sister Verna reversed course. "This way. Now! Richard, I told you, it is not real. Whatever you saw, you must ignore it."

He knew it was an illusion, but the sight ran a sharp pang of longing through him. He groaned inwardly. Why did the magic have to attract him with visions of her? His own mind, Sister Verna had said, would bring forth the things he feared, or those for which he longed. Which was this, he wondered, fear or longing?

"Is the lightning real?"

"Real enough to kill us. But it's not lightning in the sense of what you know. This is a storm of spells that are battling each other. The lightning is a discharge of their power as they fight each other. At the same time, it also seeks to destroy any intruder. Our way is among the gaps in their battle."

Again, he heard the distant scream of his name, but it wasn't Kahlan's voice. It was a man's voice.

Another lightning bolt struck directly in front of them. He and the Sister both protectively threw an arm up before their faces. The horses didn't start. It must be as the Sister said; horses would have panicked had it been real lightning.

As the dirt thrown up by the lightning rained down around them, Sister Verna turned and snatched him by his shirtsleeve.

"Richard, listen to me. Something is wrong. The way is shifting too fast. I'm not able to feel it as I should be able to."

"Why would that be? You've been through here before. You were able to do it before."

"I don't know. We don't know a great deal about this place. It's tainted with magic we don't entirely understand. It could be that the magic has learned to recognize me, from when I was here before. Going through more than twice is not possible. Going through the second time is said to be more difficult than the first. It could just be that. But it might be something else."

"What something else? You mean me?"

Her eyes glanced past him to things she was seeing, but he knew weren't there. She refocused her gaze on him. "No, not you. If it were you, I would still be able to feel the pass as I did before, but I can't. I can only feel it some of the time. I think it's because of what happened with Sisters Elizabeth and Grace."

"What do they have to do with it?"

The dark storm was all about them now, swirling and howling. Their clothes flapped in the gusts. He had to squint against the dust.

"In their death, they passed on their gift. That is the reason they gave their lives when you refused the offer, to pass their gift to the next, to make her stronger so she might succeed at the next try."

That was why he had felt the pull to accept the collar more strongly each time the offer had been made. Kahlan had said that that might have been the reason they killed themselves when he refused—to add to their power, make them stronger.

"You mean you have the power, the Han, of the other Sisters?"

She nodded as her eyes darted about. "It gives me the power of all three." Her eyes came back to his. "It could be that I have too much power to make it through." She clutched his shirt tighter and pulled him closer to her face. "If I don't make it, you must go on alone, try to make it on your own."

"What! I don't know how to make it through. I don't feel anything of the spells about us."

"Don't argue with me! You felt the lightning. You felt that much of it. One without the gift would not feel it until it was too late. You must try."

"Sister, you will be all right. You will sense the way."

"But if I don't, you must try. Ignore anything you see that tempts you. Richard, if I die, you must try to make it through, to the Palace of the Prophets."

"If anything happens to you, I'll try to make it back to the Midlands. It's closer."

She gave a sharp tug on his shirt. "No! Must you always challenge what I tell you?" She scowled at him a moment before letting her expression cool. "Richard, if you don't have a Sister to teach you to control the gift, you will die. The collar alone will not save you. You must have a sister for the Rada'Han to be of use. Without a Sister, it would be like having lungs, but no air to fill them. We are the air. Some of us have already given our lives to help you. Don't let them die in vain."

He took her hand from his shirt and gave it a gentle squeeze. "You're going to make it. I promise you, you'll make it. If there is anything I can do to help, I'll try. Don't be afraid. Ignore what you're seeing. Isn't that what you said?"

She released an exasperated breath and then took her hand back, turning away. "You don't know the things I see." She looked over her shoulder, squinting at him. "Don't test me, Richard, I'm not in the mood. You do as you're told."

Richard heard the thunder of horse's hooves as Sister Verna quickly led them ahead. The darkness swirled around them as lightning crackled through it. He found it difficult to accept the calmness of the horses. Could it be that he really was using the gift to feel it?

To his left, the wall of dust lifted. Light beyond shone through. Richard stared at the sight. It was the Hartland Woods, the woods he knew, longed to return to. They were here before him. He had only to step through. The peace of the place he stared at made him ache with longing, as if stepping through to them would be his salvation.

But he knew it was an illusion, a spell of longing meant to trap him, and let him wander for all time in ensorcellment. He wondered what would be so bad about that, even if it wasn't real. If it was a place he loved, and he would be happy there, what would be so bad about that?

He heard his name called again, again in a scream. Horses' hooves were almost upon him. He spun around, realizing it was Chase's voice screaming his name.

"Ignore it, Richard," came the Sister's growl. "Keep moving."

Richard longed for his friend as much as he longed for the Hartland Woods. He walked backward, watching.

Chase was riding at a full gallop, his black cloak flying behind, his weapons glinting in the light of the merciless sun. The horse was covered with lather. Someone else was with him, in his lap. Richard squinted, trying to see better, and realized it was Rachel. That was natural; Rachel would be with Chase. Rachel was screaming his name, too. Richard watched the illusion as it bore down upon him.

Something about Rachel riveted his attention. Something about her gave Richard the strong sense of Zedd's presence. His eyes were lured to an amber stone hanging by a gold chain about her neck. The sight of the stone drew Richard's interest as if it were Zedd himself calling to him.

"Richard!" Chase was screaming. "Don't go in there! Don't go in there! Zedd needs you! The veil is torn! Richard!"

Chase suddenly drew the horse to a skidding stop. Richard took slow, backward steps as he watched the illusion. Chase had gone calm, and was no longer screaming. With Rachel in his arms he dismounted, looking about in wonder. The dust was passing between them again, and Richard was having difficulty seeing his old friend. Chase set Rachel down and took her hand as they both turned about, staring off at nothing. Richard thought that an odd thing for a vision to do, but then decided it must just be a way of trying to entice him to go see what they were looking at.

Richard turned to the Sister as she called his name. "Come on, or I'll make you wish I had left you here! You mustn't stop!" She surveyed each side as she moved ahead. "This opening is closing around us. Hurry, before we're trapped."

Richard glanced behind. The vision was disappearing beyond the swirling darkness. Chase and Rachel appeared to be walking off toward something. The roiling clouds passed between Richard and the vision of his friends, and they were gone.

Richard trotted to catch up with Sister Verna. He wondered at the reason for such an odd vision. Why would the magic pick those two from his mind to tempt him? They had seemed so real. It had felt as if he could have reached out and touched the two of them. Perhaps the magic was trying to seduce him in to following someone he trusted with his life. But it had seemed so real; Chase had looked so desperate.

He cautioned himself to pay attention. Of course it seemed real to him. That was

338

the whole purpose of the magic: to appear real in order to fool you, to draw you in. It wouldn't be very effective magic if it didn't seem real.

Richard put a hand to Jessup's flanks as he came up behind him, to let him know he was there and keep from startling him. He ran the hand along the length of the muscular horse as he trotted by, pulling Bonnie and Geraldine along by their lines in his other hand.

Richard gave Jessup a pat on the neck as he went past. Jessup dropped his head and once again browsed at grass that wasn't there, his lead line dragging the ground. Richard froze in his tracks.

Sister Verna was gone.

Lightning exploded in every direction with deafening noise. A bolt blasted the ground at his feet. He leapt to the side to avoid the next strike. His hair seemed to stand on end as the lightning hit. He could feel the searing heat. His vision was laced with blue-white afterimages of the jagged flashes.

Richard screamed out the Sister's name as he gathered up the lead lines, pulling the horses on as he frantically scanned about. The lightning seemed to follow him, striking the ground repeatedly where seconds ago he had been.

Balls of flame ignited in the air, shrieking as they came apart. It seemed as if the very air burned. The wail of the fire was everywhere. Richard ran toward the gaps left after each dissipated, dodging the lightning and the flames, covering his head with a hand, even though he knew that if the magic hit him, that hand wouldn't save him. The cacophony seemed enough to drive a person mad. The dark dust clouds prevented him from seeing anything, if indeed there was anything to see. He ran on, heedless of direction, just trying to avoid the blue bolts and yellow flames.

Abruptly, the corner of white, polished marble walls loomed up before him. Lurching to a panting halt, he looked up, but couldn't see the top; it disappeared into the dark cloud above. A strike that was too close for comfort started him running again, pulling the three horses behind. The middle of the wall had an arched opening in it. Rounding the corner, he found that that wall, too, held an arched opening.

As he ran, he counted. Each of the five sides of the structure was about thirty strides. In the center of each wall was an arched opening six strides wide, and about as tall. He stopped, catching his breath, outside one of the openings. It was empty inside, and through the opening he could see each arch in the other walls.

Lightning hammered the ground, flinging dirt into the air. He threw his arms up in front of his face. The strikes marched toward him, their sound thundering in his ears. He had nowhere to go. He let go of the horses and dove through the arch, rolling across the sandy ground inside.

Silence echoed in his ears as he sat up, leaning back on his hands. Inside the structure was barren, empty. The air wasn't sweltering, as it had been outside, but felt almost cool in comparison, and smelled sweet, like a grassy meadow.

Through the arched openings he could see the boiling black clouds that hugged the ground. The lightning arced violently, but its sound was only a dim rumble. The horses wandered slowly, grazing on the grass that wasn't there.

This must be one of the Towers of Perdition Sister Verna had told him about. The interior of the walls soared up into the darkness high above, and were black with the results of Wizard's Life Fire. Richard ran a finger through the black grit and tasted it. He winced at the bitter tang it left on his tongue. The wizard who had died to give his life to this fire had not done so willingly; he had done it to save himself the torture of what they had intended to do to him, or perhaps what they were doing to him.

The ground was covered with white sand that sparkled with prismatic light. It was drifted into the corners, like snow. Richard remembered seeing sand like this before. It was in the People's Palace, in the Garden of Life, in a circle in the center of the room. Darken Rahl had drawn spells in that sparkling white sand when he had been trying to open the boxes of Orden.

Richard paced around the inside of the tower, trying to decide what to do. It seemed safe in this place, but for how long? Surely, sooner or later, the magic would find him. Maybe the seeming safety of this place was simply an enchantment meant to trap him, keep him here for all time, afraid to venture out.

He couldn't stay. He had to find the Sister. She needed his help. She was afraid. He had told her she would make it through.

But why should he want to help her? She kept him prisoner. If he left her here, he would be free. But free to do what? If she didn't help him learn to control the gift, he would die. Or so she said.

Richard turned at a sound from behind. Kahlan stepped out of the darkness of an archway. Her long hair didn't flow over her shoulders, but was tied back in a single braid. Instead of her white Confessor's dress, she wore the red leather of a Mord-Sith.

Richard stood stiffly, his chest heaving. "Kahlan, I refuse to think of you in this way, even in an illusion drawn from my own mind."

She arched an eyebrow. "But isn't this what you fear most?"

"Change it, or be gone."

The red leather shimmered and became the white Confessor's dress he knew so well. The braid came undone.

"Better, my love? I'm afraid it still won't save you. I have come to kill you. Die with honor. Defend yourself."

Richard drew the Sword of Truth. The unique ring of its steel echoed throughout the tower. Wrath surged through him as the magic was loosed. He endured with detached misery the sensation of murderous need while looking upon the face of the only person who made his life worth living.

His knuckles tightened on the braided, wire hilt, on the bumps of the word *Truth*. His jaw muscles flexed as he gritted his teeth. He felt a rush of understanding at how the wizards could have made Life Fire, and have given themselves into it, rather than endure what was to be done to them. Some things were worse than death.

Richard tossed the sword to the ground at Kahlan's feet.

"Not even in an illusion, Kahlan. I would rather die."

Her green eyes shone with a sad, timeless, knowing look. "Better you had died, my love, that you wouldn't see what I have come to show you. It will bring you more pain than death."

Her eyes closed as she sank to her knees, leaning forward, bending into a deep bow. The whole of the time she was slumping forward, her hair shortened. By the time her head touched the sparkling white sand, her hair looked as if it had been chopped short, close to the nape of her neck.

"This must be, or the Keeper will escape. Stopping it will aid him, and he will have us all. Speak if you must these words, but not of this vision." Without looking up, she spoke in a detached rote.

*"Of all there were, but a single one born of the magic to bring forth truth will remain alive when the shadow's threat is lifted. Therefore comes the greater darkness of the dead. For there to be a chance at life's bond, this one in white must be offered to her people, to bring their joy and good cheer."*

As Richard stood staring at the illusion, at the back of her head, a ring of blood blossomed around her neck. Richard's breath halted. As if it had been cleaved off, Kahlan's head tumbled away. Her body fell to its side, blood gushing, spreading in a pool beneath it, turning the white sand and white dress to red.

Richard drew a gasp of a breath.

"Noooo!"

His chest heaved. He felt his fingernails cutting into his palms. His toes curled in his boots.

It's an illusion, he told himself as he shook. An illusion. Nothing more. An illusion meant to terrorize him.

Kahlan stared up at him with flat, dead green eyes. Though he knew it had to be an illusion, it nonetheless was working. Panic paralyzed his legs; fright raced recklessly through his mind.

The image of Kahlan wavered and then vanished suddenly as Sister Verna stormed through an archway to the side.

"Richard!" she shrieked in fury. "What are you doing in here! I told you to stay with me! Can't you follow the simplest instructions? Must you always act like a child!"

She took two strides forward, her face red with rage.

His heart thumped violently with the pain of what he had just seen. He blinked at Sister Verna. He was in an ill humor to tolerate the surly side of her disposition. "You were gone. I couldn't find you. I looked but . . ."

"Don't talk back to me!" Her curls sprang up and down as she yelled. "I've had all the talk from you I can stomach. I told you I was in no mood for it. My patience is at an end, Richard."

He opened his mouth to speak, but the collar yanked him backward, his feet leaving the ground. It felt as if he had been jerked by a rope around his neck. With a grunt he slammed into the wall. The impact knocked the wind from his lungs and the sense from his head. He hung, his feet clear of the ground, pinned to the wall by the Rada'Han. The collar was choking him. He tried to focus his eyes, but his vision only blurred uselessly.

"It's time you had a lesson I should have given long ago," the Sister said in a growl as she stalked toward him. "I have suffered enough of your disobedience. I will suffer it no longer."

Richard struggled to breathe. Each breath burned as he drew it through the constriction at his neck. His vision cleared and finally focused on Sister Verna's face. His anger heated.

"Sister . . . don't . . ."

Pain took his words. It ignited in his chest with such intense burning force it made his fingers tingle. He couldn't draw a breath to scream.

"I've had enough of your words. I will hear no more. No more of your excuses, your arguments, your harsh judgments. From now on, you will do as you are told, when you are told, and you will offer me no more of your insolence."

She took another step toward him. Her expression twisted with menace. "Do we understand each other!"

She somehow made the pain worse. He shook with the crushing hurt in his chest. Stinging tears flooded from his wide eyes.

"I asked you a question! Do we understand each other!"

Air rushed into his lungs. "Sister Verna . . . I'm warning you . . . don't do this or . . ."

"You are warning me! You are warning me!"

White-hot pain knifed through his chest, twisting tighter with each breath. A scream ripped from his lungs. His worst fears were coming to life. This was what wearing a collar had brought him to, again. This was what the Sisters had in mind for him. This was his fate, if he allowed it.

Richard called the sword's magic.

Summoned by its master, the power swept into him, hot with promise, hot with wrath, hot with need. Richard welcomed it, embraced it, letting his own rage join with the rage of the sword and spiral through him. His fury consumed the pain, using it to draw power.

"Don't you dare fight me, or I will make you rue the day you were born!"

Fiery flames of agony bloomed anew. Richard drew them into the wrath. Though he wasn't touching the sword, he didn't need to. He was one with the magic, and he called forth all its force now.

"Stop this," he managed through gritted teeth. "Or I will."

Sister Verna, with her fists at her side, stepped closer.

"Now you threaten me? I warned you before about threatening me. You have made your last mistake, Richard."

Though he was nearly blinded by the pain she suddenly unleashed into him, he was able to see one thing. The Sword of Truth. It lay in the sand, near the Sister.

The Seeker focused the sword's magic into the power that bound him to the wall. With a loud crack, the bond broke and he tumbled away from the wall, rolling through the sand.

His hands found the sword.

Sister Verna charged toward him. He came up swinging the sword in an arc. The need for her blood seared through his soul, beyond retrieval. Nothing else mattered.

Bringer of death.

He didn't try to direct the track of the blade, but simply focused his need to kill into the power of its swing.

The sword's tip whistled through the air.

Bringer of death.

The blade exploded through the Sister at shoulder level. The cool air erupted with a spray of hot blood, the smell of it filling his nostrils as the sight of it filled his vision. Her head and part of her shoulders tumbled up into the air as the blade severed her in two. Blood and bone hit the walls. The lower half of her body collapsed fluidly to the ground. Blood soaked into the white sand, spreading beneath her. What was left of her shoulders and head hit the ground a good ten feet away, sending up a spray of white sand. The gore of her insides glistened in a line away from the body.

Richard collapsed to his knees, panting, the pain finally gone. He had told himself he would not allow this to be done to him again. He had meant it.

Like a distant memory, his insides ached with the pain of what he had done. It had all happened so fast, before he had had time to think. He had used the sword's magic to take a life, and the magic would want its due.

He didn't care. It was nothing to compare to the pain of what she had been doing to him, what she would have done to him. As he focused on the rage, the pain evaporated and was gone.

But what was he going to do now? He needed the Sisters to teach him how to keep the gift from killing him. He would die without Sister Verna's help. How could he go to the other Sisters and ask for their help, now? Had he just sentenced himself to death, too?

But he would not allow them to hurt him any more. He would not.

He knelt, recovering, resting on his heels, trying to think. In front of him, near the side of Sister Verna's body, lay the little book she had kept tucked behind her belt. It was the little book in which she was always writing.

Richard picked it up and thumbed through the pages. It was blank. No, not entirely. Near the back, there were two pages with writing.

*I am the Sister in charge of this boy. These directives are beyond reason if not absurd. I demand to know the meaning of these instructions. I demand to know upon whose authority they are given.*
*—Yours in the service of the Light, Sister Verna Sauventreen.*

Richard reflected on the fact that Sister Verna had been temperamental even in her writing. He looked to the next page. It was in a different hand.

*You will do as you are instructed, or suffer the consequences. Do not presume to question the orders of the palace again.*
*—In my own hand, The Prelate.*

Well, it looked as if Sister Verna had managed to raise the ire of someone besides himself. He tossed the book back on the ground next to her. He sat staring at her body, at what he had done. What was he going to do now?

He heard a sigh, and lifted his head to see Kahlan, in her white Confessor's dress, standing again in an archway. With a sad expression, she slowly shook her head.

"And you wonder why I would send you away."

"Kahlan, you don't understand. You don't know what she was going to . . ."

A quiet laugh drew his attention to the other side of the room. Darken Rahl stood in another archway, his white robes aglow.

Richard felt the scar of his father's handprint on his chest tingle and burn with heat.

"The Keeper welcomes you, Richard." Darken Rahl's grim smile widened. "You make me proud, my son."

With a scream, Richard tore across the sand, the rage ignited anew. Sword first, he launched himself at Darken Rahl.

The glowing form evaporated as Richard flew through the archway. Laughter echoed and then faded.

Outside the tower, the lightning went wild. Three hot bolts traced through the darkness toward him. Instinctively, he lifted the sword as a shield. The lightning struck the sword, flashing and twisting like a snake in a snare. Thunder jarred the ground beneath his feet.

Richard squinted against the blinding light. He gritted his teeth with the strain

343

of forcing the sword downward, taking the flaring, liquid lines of fire with it. They dulled and diminished as they were dragged to the ground, where they writhed, hissing as if in death, until at last they faded and were gone.

"Enough of these visions."

Richard angrily sheathed his sword and collected the horses from their grazing. He didn't know where he was going to go, but he was getting away from this tower, away from the dead Sister. Away from what he had done.

The lightning didn't come anymore. The clouds still roiled around him, but the lightning didn't come. He walked without giving thought to where he was going. When he felt inexplicable danger, he skirted it. To the sides, visions tempted him to look, but he stoically ignored them.

Almost not seeing it at first, because of the dark clouds, he came upon another tower. It looked like the first, except it was a glossy black. At first thinking he would avoid it, he found himself walking to one of the arches and peering in. The ground inside was covered with sand that was drifted into the corners, the same as the last tower, but it was black instead of white. It glimmered with the same prismatic light as the white sand.

Curiosity overcame caution and he reached inside, running a finger through the black grit covering the walls. It tasted sweet.

The wizard who had given his life into this fire had done so to save another, not to save himself torture. This wizard had been altruistic, the other ignoble.

If having the gift meant he was a wizard, Richard wondered which kind he was. He would like to think of himself as high-minded, but he had just killed another to save himself from torture. But was he not within his rights to kill to protect his life? Must he wrongly die to be honorable?

Who was he to judge which of these wizards had been wiser, or which had done what was within his rights?

The sparkling black sand fascinated him. It seemed to draw light from nowhere and reflect it about the inside of the tower in winking colors. Richard retrieved an empty spice tin and scooped it full of the black sand. He tucked the tin back in his pack hanging from Geraldine's saddle while he whistled for Bonnie—she was off browsing again.

Her ears swiveled toward him as her head came up. Dutifully, she trotted over and joined him and the other two horses, pushing her head against his shoulder in hopes of a neck scratch. As they left the tower behind, he gave her the scratch she wanted.

His shirt was soaked with sweat as he hiked quickly across the barren ground. He wanted to be out of this valley and away from the magic, the spells, and the visions. Sweat rolled from his brow as he walked, trying to ignore familiar voices that called to him. He ached with desire to see the faces of loved ones who called his name, but he didn't look. Other voices hissed with menace and threat, but he kept moving. At times, the spells tingled against his flesh, burning with pricks of heat or cold or pain, and he rushed away from them even faster.

As he wiped sweat from his eyes, they focused on the baked earth before him and he saw tracks. His own. He realized that in trying to avoid the feelings of danger, the visions, and the voices, he must have been walking in circles, if in fact the footprints were real.

He began to have the queasy feeling that the magic was trapping him. Maybe all this time he had been walking, he had not been making any headway out of the Valley of the Lost. Maybe he, too, was lost. How was he going to find a way out? He tugged the horses on and kept moving, but with a rising sense of panic.

Unexpectedly, out of the dark fog before him came a vision that startled him into a dead stop. It was Sister Verna. She was wandering aimlessly, her hands clasped prayerfully, her eyes skyward, and a blissful smile upon her lips.

Richard staked toward her. "Be gone! I've had enough of these specters! Leave me alone!" She didn't seem to hear him. That was impossible; she was easily close enough to hear him. He stepped closer, the air feeling abruptly thick and sparkling around him as he did so, until he seemed to step beyond it. "Do you hear? Listen to me! I said be gone!"

Distant brown eyes focused on him. She held her arm out, her hand held up in forbidding. "Leave me. I have found what I seek. Leave me to my peace, my bliss."

As she turned away, Richard felt an apprehensive, tingling sensation all the way down to his toes. She wasn't trying to entice him, as the other visions had.

His hair tried to stand on end.

"Sister Verna?"

Could it be true? Could she be alive? Maybe he hadn't really killed her. Maybe it had all been a vision. "Sister Verna, if it really is you, talk to me."

She regarded him with a puzzled frown. "Richard?"

"Of course Richard."

"Go," She whispered as her eyes turned up once more. "I am with Him."

"Him? Him who?"

"Please, Richard, you are tainted. Go away."

"If you're a vision, then you go away."

She regarded him with pleading. "Please, Richard. You're disturbing Him. Don't ruin what I've found."

"What have you found? Is it Jedidiah?"

"The Creator," she said in a hallowed tone.

Richard peered skyward. "I don't see anyone."

She turned her back to him and strolled away. "Leave me to Him."

Richard didn't know if this was the real Sister Verna, or an illusion. Or maybe the dead Sister's spirit. Which was true? How could he tell?

He had promised the real Sister that she would make it through, that he would help her. He followed after her before she could disappear into the dark fog.

"What does the Creator look like, Sister Verna? Is he young? Old? Does he have long hair? Short? Does he have all his teeth?"

She turned in a rage. "Leave me!"

The menace in her expression froze him in his tracks.

"No. Listen to me, Sister Verna. You're coming with me. I'm not leaving you trapped in this spell. That's all you see: an enchantment spell."

He reasoned that if she was a specter, and he took her with him, she would vanish when they left the magic of the valley. If she was real, well then he would be saving her. She would be alive. Though he wished to be free of her, he wished more that she was alive, and that she wouldn't really do to him what she had done back in the tower. He didn't want that to be the true Sister Verna. He started toward her again.

Her hand came up, as if to push him, even though he was a good ten paces away. The force of the impact threw him to the ground. He rolled over, clutching his chest, clutching at the receding agony. It felt like what had been done to him in the tower—hard, burning pain—but it faded faster.

Wincing, he sat up, quickly gathering his wits as he gasped for breath. He looked up to check where the Sister was in case she was about to hurt him again. What he saw halted his breath only half out of his lungs.

As the Sister once again stared skyward, the dark fog around them swirled and coalesced into forms, the forms of wraiths: insubstantial figures, seething, simmering with death. Their faces churned with steaming, shifting shadows that conjoined into glowing red eyes set in inky faces—hot tongues of flame alive with hate, glowering out from eternal night.

Bumps rippled and tingled across the backs of his shoulders. When he had been in the spirit house and felt the screeling on the other side of the door, when he had sensed the man about to kill Chandalen, and when he had first encountered the Sisters, he had felt an overwhelming, inexplicable sense of danger. He felt that danger now.

There wasn't the slightest doubt in his mind that these things were part of the magic of this valley, and that that magic had at last found an intruder. Him.

"Verna!" he screamed.

She scowled down at him. "I told you, Richard, I am to be addressed as *Sister* Verna. . . ."

"Is that what you do to your charges? Hurt them with your power?"

She looked startled. "But I . . ."

"Is this your eternal Paradise? Quarreling with people? Hurting them?" He rushed to his knees, eyeing the drifting forms about them. "Sister, we have to get out of here."

"I wish to stay with Him. I have found my bliss."

"This is your idea of Paradise? Giving pain? Answer me, Sister Verna! Is that what your Creator wishes of you? To hurt the people you are responsible for?"

She gaped at him, quickness suddenly coming to her movements as she rushed to him. "Did I hurt you?" She gripped his shoulders. "Oh, child, I'm sorry. I didn't mean to."

He came the rest of the way to his feet and shook her. "Sister, we have to get out of here! I don't know how! Tell me how to get out of here before it's too late!"

"But . . . I wish to stay."

"Look around, Sister Verna! What do you see?"

She jerked her head woodenly about, from one dark form to another, then to him. "Richard . . ."

Richard angrily pointed skyward. "Look, Sister! That's not the Creator! It's the Keeper."

She peered where he directed. With a gasp, her fingers flew to her mouth.

The red glow in the eyes of one of the dark, shifting forms intensified into burning embers. The sense of danger flamed through Richard's very soul. The sword was out in a blink. The vaporous wraith solidified into solid bone and muscle, claws and fangs, into a frightening beast covered with a dark, cracked, leathery hide dappled with hideous, suppurating sores. It descended upon him in a terrifying rush.

347

With the sword gripped in both hands, Richard screamed with unleashed fury, driving the sword through the beast's chest as it rushed at him. Soft flesh and hard bone hissed at contact with the blade. The monster slid from the sword and hit the ground like a bucket of slop, its hide not entirely able to contain its contents. A drop of blood splattered on Richard's arm, burning through his shirt and into his flesh. From the inside, the beast boiled and frothed. Worms wriggled from the abscessed sores.

Sister Verna stared wide-eyed at the bubbling, smoking mass. He grabbed her curly hair in his fist and twisted her head to look at the forms that were closing in. "Is this your idea of Paradise? Look! Look at them!"

He dragged her backward with him as the dark, watery blood running from the beast ignited, sending acrid, oily black smoke curling from the flames. Richard halted when he remembered what she had told him before, about backing into worse danger. He smelled burning flesh and, realizing it was his own, spat on the painful, smoking spot of the beast's blood on his arm.

He took in a quick sweep of the area. There were more of the forms behind. Another of them solidified into a beast, this time with cloven hooves and a broad snout. Razor-sharp tusks sprouted, growing into long, curved weapons.

Snorting, it charged them. Richard drove his sword downward through the thing's skull as it tried to gore him. With a squeal, the beast collapsed heavily. By the time the bulky body hit the ground, it had mutated to a writhing mass of snakes. They tumbled and rolled as they hit, the tangled pile of them wriggling apart. Hundreds of hooded red eyes glowered up at him. Red tongues flicked the air as the yellow-and-black-banded bodies slithered toward the two of them.

Richard didn't think they were mere incorporeal illusions; the place on his arm where the drop of blood had splattered burned painfully. The snakes hissed. Some coiled to strike, revealing dripping fangs.

"Richard, we have to get out of here. Come, child."

They turned and ran, the floating, red-eyed forms following. Richard felt the thick air as he went through. The air around him sparkled.

Sister Verna cried out. He turned to see her on the ground before the snakes. She sprang to her feet and tried again, but could not pass through. To her, the air was solid.

She stood silently a moment, going calm. She clasped her hands. "Richard, I am trapped in this spell. I cannot leave it. It is me the spell captured, and recognizes. It is too late for me. Save yourself. Run. Without me, you may have a chance. Hurry. Go."

There seemed to be a lot more snakes than Richard had seen at first. The ground was alive with them. They were surrounding him. He struck as they did, and beheaded three that came too close.

The headless bodies writhed and then disassembled into hundreds of huge, glossy, black-and-brown-banded bugs. They skittered in every direction. Some ran up his pant leg. He frantically shook his legs trying to get them out. Each bite felt like a hot coal on his flesh. He stomped his feet to get them off. From the ground where he had killed the snakes, more of the bugs poured out, their hard-shelled bodies tumbling over each other, rustling like the sound of dry leaves blowing across parched earth.

Dancing among the clicking bugs and between the squirming snakes, he stepped back into the sparkling air. "Without you I don't have a chance. You're coming with me."

He enfolded her in his arms and threw himself sword-first at the sparkling barrier. The wall seemed hard at first, but then the air about them exploded in glittering flashes. Lines of light, like crazed glass, shot in every direction. The air erupted in a burst of sparkles and a crack of thunder. The darting sparkles slowed and then drifted to earth, like fat flakes of snow, their light extinguishing when they touched the ground. The two of them moved past the vanished barrier, free of the spell.

The dark forms followed. The snakes followed. Bugs popped and crunched under his boots.

Richard's grip tightened on the sword. "Let's get out of here."

She took two strides and then froze.

"What's wrong?"

"I can't feel the way," she whispered. "Richard, I can't feel the gaps." She turned to him. "Do you feel anything?" He shook his head. "Try! Richard, try to feel where there is less danger."

He stomped his feet to knock the bugs off his legs and swiped off one that had made it to his face. Snakes were still pouring from the ground where the monster had fallen. They boiled up like water from a spring. "I can't. I feel danger all about. It's the same everywhere. Which way!"

She clutched her skirt in a fist. "I don't know."

Richard heard a scream. The familiar voice wrenched his attention before he could stop himself. Kahlan was standing where the snakes poured from the ground. They slithered up and over her as if she were a rock in a living stream of snakes. She held her arms out to him.

"Richard! Help me! You said you would love me always! Please, Richard! Don't leave me to this! Help me!"

His own voice came in a shaky whisper. "Sister Verna, what do you see?"

"Jedidiah," she answered quietly. "There are snakes all over him. He wants my help. May the Creator have mercy on us."

"Why should he start now?"

"Do not speak blasphemy."

He forced himself to turn from the vision. Gripping the Sister's arm, he led her away. They sidestepped as they watched the forms drifting around them. They avoided the snakes, but it was impossible not to step on the huge bugs. He knew that moving anywhere without knowing where to go could be more dangerous than standing still, now that the magic had found them. Even so, he couldn't make his feet stop. Finally they reached ground that was clear of snakes and bugs, for the moment.

"We're running out of time. Do you feel anything yet? Do you feel the way yet?"

"Nothing. I'm sorry, Richard. I have failed in my duty, failed the Creator. I've killed us both."

"Not yet."

Richard whistled for the horses. They came at a trot, ignored by the dark forms. Bonnie nuzzled her head against him, forcing him back a step. Sister Verna took up the lead line and started leading Jessup away.

"No!" Richard leapt up onto Bonnie. He swatted two clicking bugs from his pant leg. "Mount up. Hurry."

Sister Verna stared at him. "Richard, we can't ride the horses. I told you that. They are just dumb animals. They will be spooked and take us into a storm of spells. We can't control them without bits!"

"Sister, you told me you read *The Adventures of Bonnie Day*. Do you remember when the three heroes were taking the injured people to safety, and they came to the poison river that couldn't be crossed? What did they say? They said that the people just had to have faith that it could be done. Bonnie, Geraldine, and Jessup led them across the river. Have faith, Sister. Mount up. Hurry."

"You want me to do something I know will get us killed because of some fool thing you read in a book! We must walk!"

Bonnie tossed her head and danced about. Richard took up the slack in the reins to keep her in place. "You don't know the way. I don't know the way. If we stay we die."

"Then what good is riding going to do!" She had to give a sharp tug to keep Jessup still. He was roused by Bonnie's excitement.

"Sister, what have the horses been doing all day, whenever we let them?"

"Browsing on grass that isn't there. They're having visions!"

"Are they? Do you know that? What if what we're seeing is the illusion? Maybe they see what's really here. Now let's go!"

The dark forms were closer, their eyes glowing a brighter red. Sister Verna glanced at them, and then pulled herself up onto the saddle. "But—"

"Have a little faith, Sister." Bonnie pranced sideways, eager to be off. "I promised you I would save you, and I intend to. I'll lead. Don't hold back."

Richard gave his horse a sharp kick in the ribs with his heels while shouting the command. She leapt out into a dead run. The other two horses sprang to follow. He leaned forward over Bonnie's withers as she stretched into the gallop. He let her have free rein, without giving her any hint of direction. He focused on her ears, instead of what lay ahead, not wanting to influence her.

"Richard!" Sister Verna screamed from behind. "In the name of the Creator, watch where you're going! Don't you see what you're leading that horse into!"

"I'm not leading her," he called out over the sound of thundering hooves. "She is picking her own course."

The Sister galloped up beside him, her eyebrows knit together in fury. "Are you insane? Look at where you're headed!"

Richard snatched a glance. They were rushing headlong for the edge of a cliff.

"Close your eyes, Sister."

"Have you lost your . . ."

"Close your eyes! It's a vision. A vision of a fear we all have in common—falling. Just like we both saw snakes."

"The snakes were real! If you're wrong we will be killed!"

"Close your eyes. If it's really there, the horses won't run over the edge of a cliff." He hoped he was right about that.

"Unless it's really there, and the magic shows them a vision of flat ground so as to kill us!"

"If we stay, we die! We have no choice!"

He heard a growled curse from her as she hauled in on her left rein, trying to turn her horse, but Jessup stayed with Bonnie. Bonnie was leading; Jessup and Geraldine wouldn't leave her.

350

"I told you destroying those bits was foolish! We can't control them! They're running away with us!"

"I told you I would save you. Destroying those bits is what will save you. My eyes are closed. If you want to live, close yours!"

Sister Verna was silent as the three horses thundered on. Richard's eyes were squeezed shut. When he judged they should be at the brink, he held his breath. He prayed that the good spirits would be with him this time.

His legs tingled in anticipation of plummeting over a cliff. He tried not to think of what it would be like on the way down. Shared fear, that's all it was. He realized he was holding Bonnie's mane in a death grip. He relaxed his fingers but kept his eyes closed.

The plunge didn't come.

The three horses galloped on. He did nothing to slow them, but let them run as they would. They were in a frisky mood from grazing all day, and he could tell they were enjoying the run. They were running for the sheer joy of it.

After a time, Richard realized that the sound of their hooves was changing. It wasn't as sharp; it had grown softer.

"Richard! We're out of the valley!"

He looked back over his shoulder to see the wisp of dark storm clouds boiling at the edge of the horizon. The golden sun hung low in the sky over the grassy, undulating ground beneath them. Their horses slowed to a canter.

"Are you sure? Are you sure we're away from it?"

She nodded. "This is the Old World. I know this place."

"But it could still be an illusion, to give us confidence, and trap us before we're clear."

"Must you always question what I tell you? I can feel it with my Han. This is no illusion. We are safely out of the valley and away from its magic. It cannot reach us now."

Richard wondered briefly if she could still be an illusion. But he, too, sensed that the danger was no longer there. He leaned forward and gave Bonnie's warm neck a big hug.

The immense hills they were entering were barren of trees, covered with clumps of grass and wildflowers, the low places sprinkled throughout with sandy-colored rocks. The sun shined warmly, but it no longer scorched the land. Richard laughed into the wind at his face.

He grinned at Sister Verna, but she wasn't smiling. Her brow was creased with a scowl as she scanned the sweep of hills before them.

"Wipe that grin off your face," she snapped.

"I'm just happy we made it. I'm happy you're alive, Sister."

"If you had any idea how angry I am with you right now, Richard, you would not be quite so pleased I am still with you. Take this advice seriously: you would be doing yourself a great favor, right now, if you kept that tongue of yours still."

He could only shake his head.

Y ou must cut off my arm."

Zedd drew the sleeve of the sky blue, satin robe down her arm, covering the wound that wouldn't heal, and the faint green glow of her flesh.

"I'm not cutting off your arm, Adie. How many times do I have to tell you?"

He set the cut-glass lamp back on a side table inlaid with silver worked in floral patterns, next to the tray of brown bread and half-eaten lamb stew, and strolled across the carpets to draw the heavy, embroidered curtains back a bit with a thin finger. He peered, without seeing, out the frost-laced window, at the dark street. The glow from the fire in the outer room cast a warm, dim light through the open double doors. The rooms were fairly quiet, considering the size of the crowd down in the dining room.

The Ram's Horn did a bustling business despite it being the dead of winter, or perhaps because of it. The open road was no place to sleep in this cold and snow, and trade couldn't stop simply because of the season. Merchants, drivers, and travelers of every sort filled this inn, as well as all the others in Penverro.

He and Adie had been lucky to find lodging. Or perhaps the innkeeper had been the lucky one, lucky that someone would come along who was willing to pay the outrageous price he asked for his finest rooms.

But the price of the rooms did not concern Zedd; producing the required price in gold was no problem for a wizard of the First Order. He had real problems, though. The gash where the skrin had cut Adie with its claw wasn't healing. In fact, it was getting worse. And it would do no good trying to use more magic to cure the wound; magic was the trouble.

"Listen to me, old man." Adie levered herself up in the bed, onto one elbow. "It be the only way to stop it. You have tried, and I do not fault your efforts. But if we don't stop it, I will die. What be one arm, compared to my life? If you do not have the courage, then give me a knife. I can do the work myself."

He scowled over his shoulder. "Of that, dear lady, I have no doubt. But it would do no good, I'm afraid."

"What do you mean?" she asked in a low rasp.

He plucked a cold chunk of lamb from the gold-rimmed bowl and popped it in his mouth before he hiked his lavish robes up a bit and sat on the edge of the bed. He took up her good hand as he chewed. It seemed thin and frail, but he knew her to be more the stuff of iron.

"Adie, do you know anyone with knowledge of this sort of taint?"

She ignored his question. "Why do you say it will do no good?"

Zedd patted her hand. "Answer the question. Do you know anyone who would know anything about this?"

"I would have to think on it some, but I do not think there be anyone still alive who would have such knowledge. You be a wizard, who would know better than you? Wizards be healers." She took back her hand. "And what do you mean cutting off the arm would do no good?" She was silent a moment, and then her eyes widened. "You mean it be too late . . .?"

Zedd stood and turned away from her. He put a hand on his bony hip as he considered the options. There was not much to consider.

"Think on it, Adie, and do so with haste. This is beyond my knowledge, and it is serious."

He heard the bed squeak as Adie sank back down onto the pillows. She released a tired sigh.

"Then I be dead. At least my spirit will be with my Pell, at last. You must go on now. Do not waste any more time. I have already slowed you too much, been in this bed too many days. You must get to Aydindril. Please, Zedd, don't let me be responsible for what will happen if you don't get to Aydindril. Go help Richard, and leave me to my end."

"Adie, please do as I ask, and think. Who would be able to help us?"

Too late, he realized he had just made a mistake. He winced and waited for what he knew what was coming.

He heard the bedsprings squeak again. "Us?"

"I simply mean . . ."

She snatched the sleeve of his fine robes and spun him around. Her brow was set in a serious scowl. She gave a firm tug, forcing him to sit on the bed next to her. Her eyes seemed more pink than white in the lamplight, yet he could see the dim haze of green in them.

"Us?" she repeated. This time it came out in a growling rasp. "And you complain about the small secrets a sorceress would choose to keep to herself! Out with it, or I will make you sorry you dragged me along with you."

Zedd gave a tired sigh. It was just as well; he couldn't keep it from her much longer anyway. He drew the dark sleeve of his robe up his arm.

The flesh of his upper arm, in the same place where her arm had been cut, was blotched with cloudy black circles about the size of gold coins, and had the same faint green glow as her arm. She stared at it without reaction.

"Wizards use the magic of empathy to cure people. We take the pain and the essence of the discordance, the sickness or injury, into ourselves. We have passed the test of pain, so in this, as in other things, we are able to endure what we take from another. We use the gift to sustain us, and to give strength to the person, allowing the magic to cure what is out of order. The harmony within us corrects the disharmony. Sickness and injury is an aberration, and the magic restores the flows of power in a person to what it is intended to be." He stroked her hand. "Within limits, of course. We are not the hand of Creation. But from it, we have the gift to use when it is appropriate."

"But . . . why be your arm like mine?"

"The actual transfer of the sickness or injury is blocked. Only the pain and disharmony of it is taken on, so we may pass strength, healing, and wellness to the one we are helping." He took hold of the silver brocade at the cuff and drew the sleeve back down his arm. "Somehow, the taint of the skrin passed through that barrier."

Concern creased her features. "Then we must both lose our arms."

Zedd worked his tongue to wet it. "No. I'm afraid that wouldn't help. When I try to cure someone, I can sense where the injury or sickness, the disharmony, lies." He stood again, turning his back to her. "Though the wound is on your arm, the taint of the skrin's magic is evident throughout your body." His voice dropped to a whisper. "It is also throughout me, now."

Zedd could hear the muffled laughter from down in the dining room. Merry music seemed to ooze up through the elegant, richly colored carpets. A bard was singing a bawdy tale about a princess masquerading as a serving wench. Her father and king had pledged her to a prince she loathed. After having exposed the suitor as a scoundrel and greedy opportunist, she found that, despite having to endure her bottom being pinched, she preferred the occupation of serving wench to that of princess, and went on to live a life of singing and dancing. The crowd roared their approval, thumping their mugs in time with the tune.

Adie's voice came softly from behind him. "We be in a great deal of trouble, old man."

He nodded absently. "Indeed."

"I be sorry, Zedd. Forgive me for what I have brought upon us."

He dismissed her regrets with a wave of his hand. "What's done is done. It's not your fault, dear lady. If anything, it's mine, for not thinking before I used magic on this; the price of using your heart before using your head." The price, too, for violating the Wizard's Second Rule, he thought, but did not voice it.

The heavy folds of his robes swirled around him as he turned back to face her. "Adie, think. There must be someone who would know about this taint, someone who knows about the skrin. Is there anyone you visited when searching knowledge of the underworld who would know something? Even if it's just a little, it might give me the clue I need to rid us of this."

Her weight settled deeper into the pillows as she frowned in thought. Finally, her head rolled from side to side.

"When I visited the women with the gift, I be young. They be old, at least older than I. They would all be dead by now."

Zedd stepped closer. "Did any have daughters? Daughters with the gift?"

Adie's eyes came to his, her eyebrows lifted, and a smile grew on her finely wrinkled face. "Yes! One who taught me some of the most important things about the skrin had daughters." She propped herself up on her good elbow. "Three daughters." Her grin grew. "They all had the gift. They be little at the time, but they had the gift. They would not be nearly as old as I. If their mother lived long enough, she would have taught them what she knew. That be the way of a sorceress."

Despite the dull ache of a foreign magic in his bones, Zedd's step was lively with excitement. "Then we must go to them! Where are they?"

Adie winced as she sank back down on the pillows. She drew the blanket up to her chest. "Nicobarese. They be in a remote part of Nicobarese."

"Bags." Zedd let out a sigh. "That's a long way in the wrong direction." He stroked a thumb and finger down opposite sides of his smooth jaw. "Can you think of anyone else?"

Adie whispered to herself as, one at a time, she lifted open the fingers of a closed hand. "Sons," she muttered. "She had only sons." She lifted open another finger. "No, she didn't know anything of the skrin." Finally, she lifted open the last finger. "No children." Her hands fell limp to her sides. "I be sorry, Zedd. The three sisters be the only ones who might know something, and they be in Nicobarese."

"And this woman, their mother, where did she learn these things? Maybe we could go there."

Adie smoothed the blanket against her stomach. Her hand slipped away to rest at her side. "The light only knows. The only place I know we can go to seek answers be Nicobarese."

Zedd pointed a bony finger skyward. "Then we go to Nicobarese!"

Adie looked at him dubiously. "Zedd, there be Blood of the Fold in Nicobarese. My name be remembered there. And not remembered fondly."

"That was an awfully long time ago, Adie. Two kings ago."

"Time means nothing to the Blood."

He rubbed his chin as he thought. "Well, no one knows who we are; we've been hiding our identity to remain out of the Keeper's sight. We will simply continue to be two wealthy travelers." He scowled at her. "I'm already wearing this ridiculous outfit." The lavish robes they both wore had been her idea, and not one he enjoyed.

Adie shrugged. "It would appear we have no choice. What must be done, must be done." She grunted with the effort of sitting up in the bed. "We must be on our way."

Zedd waved his hand dismissively. "You are weak and need rest. I will secure us transportation. It's too difficult to ride horseback anymore. I'll hire us a coach, or something." He lifted an eyebrow as he gave her a sly smile. "After all, if we're going to wear these garish outfits, and feign being wealthy travelers, it would be best to play the part with a coach."

She watched as he scrutinized himself in front of the tall, standing mirror. He held the full robes out, examining their volume. The robe was a heavy, maroon fabric, with black sleeves and cowled shoulders. The cuffs of the sleeves had three rows of silver brocade. Around the neck and down the front were bands of gold brocade woven in a coarser design. The waist was held with a flashy, red satin belt set with a gold buckle. The whole effect was so ostentatious it made him groan inwardly.

Well, necessary was necessary. Zedd swept his arm across his middle while bowing dramatically.

"How do I look, dear lady?"

Adie plucked a slice of brown bread from the tray. "Foolish."

He straightened in a rush and finally shook a finger at her. "May I remind you that you picked it out!"

She shrugged. "Revenge. You picked mine. I thought it only fitting to seek redress."

He strode across the expanse of carpets in a huff, muttering that he thought she had gotten the better of the bargain by far. "You get a little rest. I'll see about our transportation."

Adie tore a chunk of bread off with her teeth and spoke around the mouthful as he headed for the door. "Don't forget your hat."

Zedd froze with a wince. He spun on the balls of his feet. "Bags, woman! Must I wear the hat, too!"

She chewed a moment and then swallowed. "The man who sold us the outfit said it be all the rage among noblemen."

Zedd forced out a noisy breath and then snatched the limp, red hat off the marble tabletop beside the double doors to the outer room. He plopped it atop his wavy white hair. "Better?"

"The feather be crooked."

He clenched his fists. At last he reached up and rearranged the floppy hat, straightening the long peacock feather.

"Happy?"

She smiled—at his expense, he presumed. "Zedd, I said you look foolish only because you be such a handsome man that the fancy clothes look silly in trying to improve upon perfection."

A grin stole back onto his face. He gave another quick bow. "Why, thank you, madam."

She pulled the piece of bread in half. "And Zedd, be careful." He cocked his head with a questioning frown. "Masquerading in that outfit, like the princess in the song, you may get your bottom pinched."

Zedd gave her a mischievous wink. "I won't let any stray wench trespass on your territory."

He canted his hat to a jaunty angle and, humming a merry tune, swept through the doors. A cane, he thought. Perhaps he should have a cane. An ornate one, of course. It seemed to him that a gentleman should have a proper cane.

Warm air ascended the stairs from the dining room along with the buzz of the packed room. The aroma of roasting meats drifted in from the kitchen to mix pleasantly with the sweet tang of pipe smoke. Zedd rubbed his stomach as he descended the stairs, wondering if he might spare the time to sample a plate.

On the landing sat a tall basket holding three canes. Zedd pulled the most ornate, a straight black cane with an elaborate head worked in silver, from the basket. He tapped the flamboyant cane on the wood landing, testing its length and heft. Seemed a tad heavy, he thought, but it would do as a proper accessory.

The proprietor, Master Hillman, a rotund man with his white shirtsleeves rolled up above his dimpled elbows and wearing a sparkling white apron, spied him as he reached the bottom of the steps and immediately rushed across the room, shoving men out of his way. The man's round, pink cheeks plumped out farther as his small mouth spread with a familiar grin.

"Master Rybnik! So good to see you again!"

Zedd almost turned to see to whom the man was speaking before he remembered that was the name he had given. He had told the innkeeper that his name was Ruben Rybnik, and had given Adie's name as Elda, saying she was his wife. Zedd had always favored the name Ruben. Ruben. He rolled the sound pleasantly through his mind. Ruben.

"Please, Master Hillman, call me Ruben."

The man's head bobbed. "Of course, Master Rybnik. Of course."

Zedd held out the cane. "I find I have need of a cane, of late. Could I convince you to part with this one?"

The man opened his arms in a wide gesture. "For you, Master Rybnik, anything. My nephew makes them, and I let him display them here for my discriminating guests. But this one is special, and costly." He came forward at Zedd's skeptical expression, lifting the cane. He leaned close to speak confidentially. "Let me demonstrate, Master Rybnik. I don't show this to anyone. Might give them the wrong impression of my establishment, you know. Here. You see? You twist, and here at the silver band, it comes open."

He separated the two parts a few inches to reveal a gleaming blade. "Nearly two feet of Keltish steel. Discreet protection for a gentleman. But I'm not sure that for your simple purposes you would want such a costly . . ."

Zedd pushed thin blade away and gave a twist, the finely worked mechanism emitting a soft click as the parts locked together. "It will do nicely. I like its looks. Not too flashy. Add the cost to my tally for the room." Wealthy gentlemen weren't supposed to ask the price.

Master Hillman bowed his head up and down. "Of course, Master Rybnik. Of course. And a fine choice, I might add. Quite dashing." He wiped his clean, meaty hands on the apron's corner and then held an arm out to the room. "May I offer you a table, Master Rybnik? Let me clear a table for you. I will have someone move. Let me see to it. . . ."

"No, no." Zedd gestured with his new cane. "That empty one in the corner, near the kitchen, will do splendidly."

The man looked with worry to where Zedd had pointed. "There? Oh no, sir, please, let me get you a better table. Perhaps near the bard. You would like to hear a lively tune, I'm sure. He knows any tune you could name. Let me know your favorite and I will have him play it for you."

Zedd leaned close and gave the man a wink. "I much prefer the wonderful aromas coming from your kitchen to the singing."

Master Hillman beamed with pride and then swept his arm in the direction of the empty table, ushering Zedd toward it. "You do me such honor, Master Rybnik. I have never had anyone swoon over my cooking as do you. Let me get you a plate."

"Ruben, please. Remember? And I would be delighted to sample a slice of that roast I smell."

"Yes, Master Rybnik, of course." Wringing the corner of his apron, he leaned over the table as Zedd sat against the wall. "How is Mistress Rybnik? I hope she is feeling better. I pray for her every day."

Zedd sighed. "Much the same, I'm afraid."

"Oh dear, oh dear. I'm so sorry. I'll continue to pray for her." He started through the kitchen door. "Let me get you that plate of roast."

Zedd leaned his new cane against the wall and removed his hat after the man had left, tossing it on the table. The balding bard sat on a stool on a small platform, hunched over his lute as if permanently deformed around it, strumming with vigor and singing a spirited song about the adventures of a wagon driver; his journey along bad roads from one bad town to another with bad food and worse women, and how he loved the challenge of steep hills and twisting passes, driving rain and blinding snow.

Zedd watched one man, alone in a booth against the wall across the room, roll his eyes and shake his head as he listened to one improbable adventure after another. A whip lay in a neat coil on the table before him. Other men, at tables, thought the song a proper tale, and thumped their mugs as they sang along. Some of the drunker men tried to pinch the smiling serving girls that swept past, but caught only air.

At other tables sat nattily dressed men and women, probably merchants and their wives, talking among themselves and ignoring the singing. Fashionable nobility, wearing gleaming swords, sat at a few tables off to the quieter side of the room. In an empty area between the bard and the lone man in the booth, couples danced; some were serving girls and men who had paid them for the turn. Zedd noted with pique that while there were many men with hats, all the hats looked to be functional, and none were embellished with a feather.

Zedd reached into a pocket to count the gold coins. Two. He sighed. It was expensive playing the part of the wealthy. He didn't know how even the wealthy could afford it. Well, he would just have to do something about that if he was to get transportation all the way to Nicobarese. He couldn't have Adie riding that horse anymore; she was too weak.

358

Springing on light feet, Master Hillman swooped through the kitchen door. He set a gold-rimmed white plate heaped with roasted lamb in front of Zedd, pausing before he straightened to return a finger to each edge of the plate and turn it just so. Quickly producing a clean towel, he buffed a spot off the tabletop. Zedd decided that although he was hungry, he had better eat carefully, lest Master Hillman whisk out to wipe his chin for him.

"May I bring you a mug of ale, Master Rybnik? On the house?"

"Please call me Ruben, that's my name. A pot of tea would be splendid."

"Of course, Master Rybnik, of course. Anything else I could do? Besides the pot of tea?"

Zedd leaned a little toward the center of the table. Master Hillman did the same. "What's the current gold to silver exchange ratio?"

"Forty point five five to one," he answered, ticking the numbers off without hesitation. He cleared his throat. "I believe. At least, that's what I seem to remember." He smiled apologetically. "I don't keep track. But that's what I believe it is. Forty point five five to one. Yes, I think that's right."

Zedd made a show of considering this. At last he pulled out one of his two gold coins and slid it with one finger across the table toward the proprietor.

"I seem to be short of smaller coinage. If you would be so kind, could you exchange this for me? And I would like it divided into two purses. From one take one silver and exchange it for copper, and put that in a third purse. And please keep the odd bits for the house?"

Master Hillman gave two quick, deep bows. "Of course, Master Rybnik, of course. And thank you."

He swept the coin off the table so fast Zedd could scarcely see it go. After he left, Zedd dug into the lamb roast, watching the people and listening to the singing as he chewed. Near the end of the meal, Master Hillman was back, placing his broad, round back between Zedd and the crowd.

He set two small purses on the table. "The silver, Master Rybnik. Nineteen in the light brown one, and twenty in the dark." Zedd slipped them into his robes as the other set a heavier, green purse down, sliding it across the table. "And the copper in this."

Zedd smiled his thanks. "And the tea?"

The big man slapped his forehead. "Forgive me. In handling the exchange, I forgot." One of the noblemen was waving a hand, trying to get his attention. He snagged the arm of a serving girl coming from the kitchen with a tray of mugs. "Julie! Fetch Master Rybnik a pot of tea. And quickly, dear." She gave Zedd a smile and a nod before rushing on with her tray. Smiling, Hillman turned back. "Julie will see to it, Master Rybnik. If there is anything else I can do, please ask."

"Why, yes. You could call me Ruben."

Master Hillman chuckled absently and nodded. "Of course, Master Rybnik, of course." He rushed off toward the nobleman.

Zedd cut another piece of lamb and stabbed it with his fork. He liked the name Ruben. He shouldn't have told the man any more of it than that. While he pulled the meat off the tines with his teeth, he watched Julie cross the room, weaving between the crowded tables.

He chewed as he watched her plunk down mugs around a table of raucous men all wearing longcoats. As she set the last one before the last man, he said something to her. She had to lean over to hear above the din. The men suddenly burst into laughter. Julie straightened and thumped the man on the head with her tray. As she strutted away, he pinched her. She yelped but hurried on.

As she went past Zedd's table, she leaned toward him and smiled. "I'll be getting your tea for you right now, Master Rybnik."

"It's Ruben." He flicked a finger toward the table of noisy men. "I saw what happened. Do you have to put up with that all the time?"

"Oh, that's just Oscar. He's harmless, for the most part. But he has the foulest mouth I've ever heard, and I've heard my share. Sometimes, I wish that when he opened his mouth to spew some of his filthy talk at me, he'd get the hiccups instead." She huffed a wisp of hair back off her face. "And now he wants *another* mug. I'm sorry. I talk too much. I'll get your tea, Master Ryb . . ."

"Ruben."

"Ruben." She gave him a pretty smile before hurrying off.

Eating while he waited, Zedd watched the table of noisy men. A small wish. What could it hurt? Julie returned with the tea and a cup. As she set them on the table, Zedd crooked his finger, urging her to bend closer.

She leaned over, tightening the apron strings behind her back as she did. "Yes, Ruben?"

The wizard gently touched a finger to the underside of her chin. "You are a very lovely woman, Julie. Oscar shouldn't speak to you in foul language, or touch you again." His voice lowered to a slow, powerful whisper that almost seemed to make the air sparkle. "When you give him his ale, speak his name, and look him in the eyes, as I look into yours now, and you shall have your wish as you have spoken it to me, but you won't remember asking it, or that I have granted it."

Julie blinked as she straightened. "I'm sorry, Ruben, what did you say?"

Zedd smiled. "I said thank you for the tea, and I asked if anyone here has a team of horses, and perhaps a carriage for hire."

She blinked again. "Oh. Well . . ." She looked around as she pulled her bottom lip through her teeth. "Half the men in here, well, half the men who aren't dressed as fine as you, are drivers. Some hire out. Some haul freight and are regulars, just passing through." She pointed at a few tables. "They . . . and they, might hire out. If you can sober them up."

Zedd thanked her and she went to get the ale. He watched as she carried it back across the room and set it in front of Oscar. He leered up at her with a drunken grin. She stared into his eyes. Zedd saw her lips speak his name. Oscar opened his mouth to speak, but hiccuped instead. A bubble floated from his mouth, up into the air. It popped. Everyone at the table erupted in laughter. Zedd's brow pulled together in a frown as he watched. That's odd, he thought.

Every time Oscar opened his mouth to speak to Julie, he hiccuped, and bubbles floated up. The men roared with laughter, accusing her of soaping his ale. They all agreed that if she had, it would serve him right. She left the men to their laughter when the lone man in the booth caught her attention. She nodded after he asked for something and then headed for the kitchen.

Julie paused at Zedd's table, giving a nod back toward the lone man. "He might have a team. He smells more like a horse than a man." She giggled. "That wasn't kind. Forgive me. It's just that I can't get him to spend any money on ale. He wants me to bring him some tea."

"I have more than I can drink. I'll go share mine with him." He winked at her. "Save you a trip."

360

"Thanks, Ruben. Here's another cup, then."

Zedd put the last large piece of roast in his mouth as he surveyed the room. The men had quieted down, and Oscar had stopped hiccuping, as they all listened to the bard singing a sad song about a man who had lost his love.

Zedd picked up the teapot and cups, and started from his table. He cursed under his breath when he remembered his hat, and swept it up, noticing the cane and snatching that up, too. He deliberately passed close to Oscar, looking him over carefully. He couldn't figure out why he had hiccuped bubbles. Zedd gave a mental shrug. The man seemed normal enough, now, if a little too drunk.

The wizard paused next to the booth with the single man. He held up the pot and cups.

"I have more tea than I can drink. Could I share it with you?"

The man watched with a forbidding scowl from under bushy eyebrows. Zedd smiled. The man did indeed smell like a horse. He unfolded his huge arms, slid the coiled whip to the side of the table, and pointed for Zedd to sit before folding his arms again.

"Well, delighted, thank you. I'm . . . Ruben."

Zedd tossed his hat on the table and lifted his eyebrows in invitation to reply.

"Ahern," he said, in a deep, resonant voice. "What do you want?"

Zedd placed his cane between his knees with one hand and with the other tugged at the heavy robes as he sat on the bench, trying to pull a thick fold from under his bony bottom. "Well, I just wanted to share my tea, Ahern."

"What do you really want?"

Zedd poured the man tea. "I thought perhaps you might need some work."

"Got work."

Zedd poured tea for himself. "Really? What sort?"

Ahern unfolded his arms and sat back in the booth, appraising his new table companion's eyes, and nothing else. He wore a longcoat draped around his massive shoulders, over a dark green flannel shirt. His thick, mostly gray hair was long enough to nearly cover his ears, and looked to be infrequently pestered by a comb. His deeply creased, weatherworn face was splotched with pink, windburned patches.

"Why do you want to know?"

Zedd shrugged as he took a sip of tea. "So I can gauge if I can make you a better offer." Zedd, of course, could produce any amount of gold the man could ask for, but judged that not to be the best tack. He took another sip of tea as he waited.

"I haul iron from Tristen, down here to the smiths in Penverro. Sometimes over to Winstead. We Keltans make the finest weapons in all the Midlands, you know."

"I heard differently." Ahern's frown darkened. Zedd folded his hands over the silver-topped cane. "I hear them to be the finest swords in all the three lands, not just the Midlands." The bard started a new song about a king who lost his voice and had to command by written instruction, but had never allowed any of his subjects to learn to read, and so lost his kingdom, too. "Heavy loads to haul, this time of year."

Ahern gave the slightest hint of a smile. "Worse in the spring. In the muck. Then's the time we find out who can drive, and who can talk."

Zedd pushed the full cup a few inches closer to the man. "Steady work?"

Ahern finally took up the cup. "Enough to keep me fed."

Zedd lifted one coil of the braided leather. "I thought you looked to be a man familiar with the use of this."

"There's different ways to get effort from a team." He pointed with his chin in the general direction of the room. "These fools think they get what they want by laying to with the whip."

"And you don't?"

Ahern shook his head. "I crack my whip to get their attention, to let them know what I want, where to put their feet. My team works for me because I trained them to work, not because they get the whip. If I'm in a tight spot, I want a team that understands what I want, not one that jumps when they feel a whip. There are enough gorges strewn with bones of man and horse. Don't want to add mine to the lot."

"Sounds like you know your work."

Ahern gestured with his cup to Zedd's elaborate robes. "What line of 'work' you in?"

"Orchards," Zedd said, pointing a finger skyward. "The finest fruits in all the world, sir!"

Ahern grunted. "You mean you own land, and others work to grow you the finest fruits in all the world."

Zedd chuckled. "You have it true. Now, anyway. It didn't start that way, though. I started by myself, working, struggling, for years. Tending my trees day and night, trying to produce the best fruit anyone ever tasted. Many of the trees failed. Many times I failed, and went hungry.

"But I finally was able to do better. I saved every copper, and bought more land in the years I could. Planted, tended, picked, hauled, and sold it all by myself. Over time, people came to know my fruit as the best, and I became more successful. In the last few years, I've hired people to tend things for me. But I still keep my hand to the work, so that it lives up to what people know me for. Would you hope for any less success, in your work?"

Zedd sat back, smiling, proud of the story he had just invented on the spot. Ahern held out his cup for more tea.

"Where are these orchards?"

"In Westland. Moved there before the boundary went up."

"And why are you here now?"

Zedd leaned forward, lowering his voice. "Well, you see, my wife is not doing well. We're both old, and now that the boundary is down, she wants to visit her homeland. She knows healers there who may be able to help her. I'd do anything to help that woman. She's too sick to travel on horseback any longer, what with this weather, so I'd like to hire someone to take us to her healers. I'd pay any price, any price I can afford, to get her there."

Ahern's face softened, somewhat. "Sounds a fair enough journey. Where do you be headed?"

"Nicobarese."

Ahern slammed his cup down on the table. Some of the tea sloshed out. "What!" He lowered his voice and leaned forward, the table's edge pressing into his husky middle. "It's the dead of winter, man!"

Zedd ran his finger around the rim of his cup. "I thought you said spring was the worst."

Ahern grunted with a suspicious glare. "That's back northwest, the other side of the Rang'Shada Mountains. If you came from Westland, to go to Nicobarese, why would you cross the Rang'Shada first? Now you just have to cross it back again."

Zedd was caught off guard, and had to scramble to find an answer. At last he did. "I'm from up near Aydindril. We were going to go there for a visit to my homeland, before we went in the spring to Nicobarese. I thought to cross the mountains to the south, then go northeast to Aydindril. But Elda, that's my wife, she took sick, and I decided that, well, it would be better we go see her healers."

"You would have been better off to have gone to Nicobarese first, before you crossed the mountains."

Zedd folded his hands over his cane. "So, Ahern, do you know how to undo something done in error, so I may relive my life as you suggest?"

Ahern grunted a laugh. "Guess not." He thought a moment, finally letting out a tired sigh. "I'll tell you, Ruben, it's a long way. You're asking for trouble. I don't know that I want any part of it."

Zedd arched an eyebrow. "Really?" He made a deliberate survey of the room. "Tell me then, Ahern, if you find the task so formidable, which of these men here would be up to the job? Which are better drivers than you?"

Ahern regarded the crowd with a sour look. "I'm not saying I'm the best there is, but this lot's more boast than brains. Don't think there's a one of them that would make it."

Zedd shifted irritably on his bench. "Ahern, I think you're simply trying to boost price."

"And I think you're trying to lower it."

Zedd let his slightest smile touch his lips. "I don't think it as difficult a job as you make it."

Ahern's frown returned. "You think it easy?"

Zedd shrugged. "You drive in the winter now. I simply want you to drive in a different direction, that's all."

Ahern leaned forward, his jaw muscles tightening. "Well, the direction you want to go in is trouble! First of all, there are rumors of civil war in Nicobarese. Worse, the shortest way, unless you want to spend weeks going to the passes far to the south, is across Galea."

His voice lowered. "There's trouble between Galea and Kelton. I hear tell there's fighting along the border. Keltish towns have been sacked. The people here in Penverro are nervous, what with being so close to the border with Galea. It's all the talk. Going into Galea is sure trouble."

"Fighting? Wagging tongues of gossips. The war is ended. The D'Haran troops have been called home."

Ahern slowly shook his head. "Not D'Haran raids. Galean."

"Piffle!" Zedd snapped. "Keltans think it's a Galean attack every time a farmer knocks a lantern over and a barn catches fire, and the Galeans see Keltans every time a lamb is taken by wolves. I'd like to have the price of all the arrows that have been shot into shadows." He shook a finger at the man. "If either Kelton or Galea were to attack the other, the Central Council would have the heads of those who spoke the orders, no matter who they were!" He thumped his cane. "It would not be allowed!"

Ahern shrank back a little. "I don't know anything about politics, and less about those wicked Confessors. I just know that going through Galea can get a man shot full of arrows coming out of those shadows. What you want is not as easy as you think."

Zedd was tiring of the game. He didn't have time for this. Something Adie had said was nagging at the back of his mind. Something about light. Deciding to resolve the discussion one way or the other, he drained his tea in one gulp.

"Thank you for conversation, Ahern. But I can see you're not the man able to get me to Nicobarese."

He rose, reaching for his hat. Ahern laid a big paw on Zedd's arm and urged him down. He squirmed forward on his bench.

"Look, Ruben, times have been hard. The war with D'Hara disrupted trade. Kelton was spared the brunt of the war, but many of our neighbors weren't. It's hard to trade with dead people. There's not as much cargo as there used to be, but we still have more than enough men wanting to haul. You can't blame a fellow for trying to get his best price when an opportunity comes along." His eyebrows lifted as he leaned in a little more. "Trying to get the best price for the best fruit, as it were."

"Best fruit indeed." Zedd waved his hand impatiently toward the room. "Any one of these men will gladly offer to hire out. Any one of them can offer me a boastful story just as good as yours, as to why they would be the best driver. You're working up to asking top price. That's fair enough, but stop playing games with me, Ahern. I want to know why I should pay it."

With the tip of one thick finger, Ahern slid his cup to the middle of the table, indicating he wanted a refill. Zedd smoothed out his sleeves before obliging him. Ahern drew his cup into the protective shroud of his big arms as he leaned in. He glanced around the room.

Everyone was watching the bard sing a love song to one of the serving girls. He was holding her hand, singing words of eternal devotion. The girl's face was red. She held her tray behind her back with her other hand as she studied her feet and giggled.

Ahern extracted a chain with a silver medallion from under his green flannel shirt. "The reason I want top price is because of this."

Zedd frowned down his nose at the regal image on the medallion. "That looks to be Galean."

Ahern gave a single nod. "In the spring and summer, D'Hara laid siege to Ebinissia. The Galeans were slowly being choked to death, and no one would help them. Everyone had troubles of their own, with the D'Harans, and didn't want a piece of theirs. The people there needed weapons.

"I took loads of weapons, and some badly needed salt, up through some of the more isolated passes. The Galean guard had offered to escort any who would risk the run, but few took the offer. Those back passes are treacherous."

Zedd lifted an eyebrow. "Very noble of you."

"Nothing noble to it. They paid handsomely. I just didn't like to see them folks trapped like that. Especially knowing what D'Haran soldiers do to those they vanquish. Anyway, I reasoned that some Keltish swords might give them a better chance to defend themselves, that's all. Like I said, we make the best."

Zedd lifted a hand from where it was folded over his cane, and gestured to the medallion, now back under Ahern's shirt. "So what is that about?"

"After the siege was lifted, I was called before the Galean court. Queen Cyrilla herself gave this to me. She said I had helped her people defend themselves, and

I was always welcome in Galea." He tapped his chest, where the medallion hung under his shirt. "This is a royal pass. It says I may go anywhere I wish in Galea, unhindered."

"And so now," Zedd said, looking up from under his eyebrows, "you wish to put a price on something that is priceless."

Ahern's eyes narrowed. "What I did was a small bit; they bore the brunt of the hardship. I helped those people because they needed help, and because I was paid well. I'm not claiming to be a hero. I did it for both reasons. I wouldn't have done it for one alone. Now I have this pass, and if it will help me to make a living, well, I don't see anything wrong with that."

Zedd leaned back. "You're right, Ahern. The Galeans, after all, put a price in gold to your work for them. I shall, too, if I can. Name your price to take us to Nicobarese."

The tea cup looked tiny in Ahern's big hands as he rolled it back and forth. "Thirty gold. Not one less."

Zedd arched an eyebrow. "My, my. Don't we think a lot of ourselves."

"I can get us there, and that's my price. Thirty gold."

"Twenty now, ten more when you get us to Aydindril."

"Aydindril! You never said anything about Aydindril. I don't want anything to do with Aydindril, with their wizards and Confessors. Besides, we'd have to cross the Rang'Shada again!"

"You will have to cross anyway to come back here. So you cross in the north. It's hardly out of your way. If you don't like the offer, then I'll offer twenty to take us to Nicobarese, and I'm sure I can find someone there more than willing to take us to Aydindril for the other ten, if we even need carriage after my wife is healed. If you want all thirty, then I'll commit to it now, if you agree to take us all the way. That's my offer."

Ahern rolled his cup back and forth. "All right. To Aydindril. Twenty now, ten in Aydindril." He pointed a meaty finger in Zedd's direction. "But you have to agree to one condition."

"Such as?"

Ahern's finger moved, to point at Zedd's red hat. "You can't wear that hat. That feather will spook the horses sure."

Zedd's wrinkly cheeks spread in a grin. "One condition of my own, then." Ahern cocked his head. "*You* have to tell my wife that it's *your* condition."

Ahern grinned back. "Done." His grin vanished as quickly as it had come. "This isn't going to be an easy journey, Ruben, up into and across those mountains. I have a coach I bought with my earnings from hauling to Ebinissia. I can mount runners to it. Make easier going in the deep snow." He tapped a finger against the side of the cup. "Now, the gold?"

The bard's fingers danced across the strings, playing an enthralling tune without words. Practically every toe in the room was moving in time with it, adding a drumlike accompaniment. Zedd reached into his robes and put a hand around the two purses of silver coins. He watched the room without seeing it.

And then the wizard did again that which he had had to do far too often of late: he channeled a warm flow of magic into the bags of silver coins—and changed them to gold.

But what choice did he have? To fail in this endeavor was to see the world of

365

the living die. He hoped he was not simply providing himself justification for an act he knew was dangerous.

"Nothing is ever easy," he muttered under his breath.

"What was that?"

"I said I know it's not easy, this journey." He plunked the dark brown bag of gold on the table. "This should make it possible. Twenty now, as agreed."

Ahern pulled open the draw top and put two big fingers into the bag, counting, while Zedd idly watched people enjoying the food and drink and music. He was anxious to be off to Nicobarese.

"This some kind of joke?"

Zedd brought his attention back to Ahern. With two fingers, the big man drew a coin from the bag and flicked it across the table. The coin spun with a dull color before finally toppling over, making a sound just as dull. Zedd stared incredulously.

The coin looked just like an ordinary coin. Except it was wood instead of gold.

"I . . . I . . . well . . ."

Ahern had poured the rest of the gold coins into his big mitt and was now letting them tumble back into the purse. "And there are only eighteen here. You're two short. I'm not taking wooden coins."

Zedd smiled indulgently as he pulled the light brown purse from his robes. "I apologize, Ahern." He swept the wooden coin from the table. "It would seem I gave you the wrong purse, the one with my lucky coin. I would never give that away, of course. It's more valuable to me than gold."

He peered into his purse. Seventeen. And two of those were wood, too. There should have been nineteen, altogether. His mind reeled as he tried to make sense of it. Could Master Hillman have tried to short him? No, that would be too clumsy a theft. Besides, to carve a coin from wood, hoping to pass it off as gold, would be witless.

"My other two gold?"

"Oh yes, yes." Zedd pulled two gold coins from the purse and slid them across the table.

Ahern added them to his purse, jerked the drawstring tight, and stuffed the dark brown bag into a pocket. "I'm at your bidding, now. When would you like to leave?"

The silver coins that were turned to wood instead of gold did not concern the wizard; that could be explained. Somehow. But there were three coins missing. Vanished. That could not be explained. That did concern him. Concern him down to the bones in his toes.

"I would like to leave as soon as possible. At once."

"You mean tomorrow?"

Zedd snatched up his hat. "No, I mean at once." He glanced at the man's puzzled frown. "My wife . . . there is no time to waste. She needs to get to her healers."

Ahern shrugged. "Well, I just got back from Tristen. I'll need to catch a little sleep. It's going to be a long, hard run." Zedd reluctantly nodded his acquiescence. "First I'll put the runners on the coach. That'll take a couple of hours. Less if I can get one of these fellows to help me."

Zedd thumped his cane. "No! Tell no one what you're doing, or where you're going. Don't even tell anyone you're leaving." He snapped his mouth shut when he saw Ahern's frown, and thought he had better say something to ease it. "Those shadows you spoke of. Does no good to let them know where to point an arrow."

Ahern stared down suspiciously as he stood to his full, towering height, drawing his longcoat on. "First you talk me into taking you to the accursed land of wizards and Confessors, and now this. I think I asked too little." He flicked the ends of the coat's belt together into a loose knot. "But a bargain is a bargain. I'll get the coach set up, and get some provisions together before I snatch a little sleep. I'll meet you back here three hours before dawn. We'll be across the border and into Galea before midday tomorrow."

"I have a horse at the stables. We might as well take her along. Stop by and fetch her before you come for us." Zedd dismissed the man with an absent wave of his cane. "Three hours before dawn."

His mind was racing in other directions. This was more serious than he had thought. It was imperative that they have help as soon as possible. Maybe the woman in Nicobarese who had had the three daughters had studied somewhere, perhaps someplace closer. Maybe they could find what they needed without going all that way. Time was of the essence.

The light only knows, Adie had said, where the woman had learned about the skrin. The "light" was a common reference to the gift. It was also an obscure reference to something else entirely. He thumped his cane on the floor. Must Adie always speak in sorceress's riddles!

As Ahern headed for the door, the wizard rose and headed for the stairs.

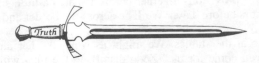

Z edd opened the door to be confronted by a haze of smoke that smelled of creosote. The window was opened, letting in icy cold air, and letting out the smoke. Adie sat on the bed, wrapped nearly to her neck in a blanket, brushing her straight, black and gray, jaw-length hair.

"What's going on? What happened?"

She pointed with the hairbrush. "I be cold. I tried to start a fire."

Zedd glanced to the hearth. "You need wood, Adie. You can't have a fire without wood."

He expected a scowl. Instead, it was a look of disquiet. "There be wood. I used magic, to try to light the fire from where I be in bed. But there be a big puff of smoke and sparks. I opened the window to let out the smoke. When I looked to the hearth, the logs be gone."

Zedd stepped closer to her. "Gone?"

She nodded and went back to brushing. "Something be wrong. Wrong with my gift."

Zedd stroked a hand down her hair. "I know. I had a similar problem. It must be the taint." He sat and took the brush from her hand, setting it down. "Adie, what can you tell me about this taint, about the skrin? We must have answers."

"I have already told you all I know. The skrin be force on the cusp between the world of the living and the world of the dead."

"But why won't the cut heal? Why won't my magic work to heal it? What made the logs disappear when you used magic?"

"Skrin be from both worlds. Do you not see?" She shook her head in frustration. "Skrin be magic, magic of both worlds, so it can work in both worlds. Additive and Subtractive. We be touched by that force. The taint be Subtractive."

"You mean that you think the taint of Subtractive Magic is corrupting our magic? Our gift?"

She nodded. "It be like you have just cleaned ashes from a hearth with your bare hands, and without washing them clean you try to hang up freshly washed white sheets to dry. Your hands be tainted with the ash, and it gets on the clean, damp, white sheets. Sticks to them."

Zedd silently considered the problem for a time. "Adie," he whispered, "we must somehow clean our hands. Wash the taint away."

"You have a talent for stating the obvious, old man."

Zedd checked his tongue and took a different tack. "Adie, I hired us a coach to take us to Nicobarese, but you're getting weaker, and I'm not going to be long behind. I don't know if we can wait. If there's another way, maybe someone else closer who can help us, I must know."

"There be no other way. There be no one else."

"Well, what about this woman who had the three daughters? Perhaps she studied somewhere closer to learn some of these things. Maybe we could go there, instead."

"It not be a help."

"Why not?"

Adie considered him a moment, and at last yielded. "She studied with the Sisters of the Light."

Zedd shot to his feet. "What!" He paced back and forth between the bed and the fireplace. "Bags and double bags! I knew it. I knew it!"

"Zedd, she studied with them to learn. Then she returned home. She not be a Sister. The Sisters not be so . . . unreasonable . . . as you think."

He halted to peer at her with one eye. "And how would you know that?"

Adie gave a resigned sigh. "The round skrin bone, the one that be given to me just before the woman died, the one I told you be important, the one we lost back at my house . . . the gifted woman who gave it to me be a Sister of the Light."

"And what was she doing in the New World?" Zedd asked in a level tone.

"She not be in the New World. I be in the Old World, at the time."

Zedd put both fists on his hips as he leaned toward her. "You crossed the Valley of the Lost? You went into the Old World! You're just filled right up full with little secrets."

Adie shrugged with one shoulder. "I told you I searched out women with the gift, to learn from them what I could. Some of them be in the Old World. I used my one passing through the valley and back to learn what I could of what I needed to know."

Adie snugged the blanket tighter around her shoulders. "The Sisters, some of them, taught me the little bits they knew. Important little bits. The Sisters view it as their province to know about the Keeper, the Nameless One as they call him, in order to keep souls from his grasp.

"I did not stay at their palace long; they would not let me stay unless I wished to be one of them, but for a time they let me study with them, study things in their vaults. There be Sisters in the palace I would not trust to cook me breakfast, but there be some who were great help."

Muttering, Zedd started pacing again. "The Sisters of the Light are misguided zealots. They make the Blood of the Fold look to be reasonable men!" He came to a halt. "And when you were there, did you see any of their boys? Did you see if they even had any with the gift?"

"I had my own learning to attend to. I not be there to argue theology with the Sisters. That not be a wise thing to do. They did not let me have anything to do with their charges, if indeed they had any. I be sure that if they had any boys, they be ones from their side.

"They know better than to risk violation of that truce. They strongly fear what wizards on this side would do if they did. They let me learn what I could from them, and let me study in the vaults, but they never let me see any boys, nor would they tell me if they had any."

"Well, of course they don't have any!" he snapped. "There are almost never any born with the gift, anymore. Too many wizards have been killed in the wars. We are a dying breed.

"And as First Wizard I would never turn down the teaching of one with the gift as happened thousands of years ago. Nor would any wizard I taught. And the Sisters know that! They know the rules! They may not take a gifted one unless every wizard declines to teach him. To go against the rules just once would mean a death sentence to any Sister that ever again crossed that valley."

"They know that, Zedd. They take that threat seriously."

"Well, they ought to know it! I met up with one of them once, when I was young, and I sent my warning to the Prelate." He flexed his fists as he stared off. "They are barbaric in their methods. They are children teaching surgery. If I knew how to get past those accursed towers, I'd go down there and lay waste to the Palace of the Prophets."

"Zedd, in that time past many with the gift died because there be none who would teach them to control it. Those with the power were possessive of it, and did not want to train another who one day might be a threat to their power. They abandoned those born with the gift, left them to die by the power of the thing they be born with but didn't know how to control. The Sisters didn't want to let those abandoned boys die. They just be doing what they think best to help people."

He cast her a withering glare. "The Sisters of the Light do only what is best for the Sisters of the Light."

"Maybe so, but they are sworn to follow the rules, the truce, just as you do, by letting them be when they come here."

He stared off, shaking his head. "To let those with the gift die, simply for their own selfish gain . . . If they had lived up to their responsibilities as wizards, the Sisters of the Light would never have come to be. Never been needed."

With his boot, he brushed a dead ember on the flagstone hearth back into the fireplace. "They would never think of allowing a wizard to teach a young sorceress to use her gift, yet they presume to teach a young wizard how to use his."

"Zedd, I believe as you, but listen to me: dead and buried causes and wars not be our concern. The veil be torn. The Stone of Tears be in the world of the living. Those be our concerns.

"I went to those women to learn. Magic I learned there, and have taught you, though insufficient to stop the taint, has been able to slow it. We must purge the taint before it claims us."

His mood cooled under the scrutiny of her white eyes. "Of course you are right, Adie. We have pressing problems to deal with."

She favored him with one of her little smiles. "I be glad you be wise enough to listen to wisdom."

He rubbed the ache in the back of his neck, squeezing the tight muscles. "Do you really think this woman with the three daughters would have known about this taint? It's a long way to go on a hunch and a hope."

"She studied with the Sisters of the Light many years. They liked her and wanted her to stay, to be a Sister. But she did not believe as they, and so finally went home. I don't know the extent of her knowledge, but if the Sisters know anything about the taint, and taught her, she would have taught her daughters. As much as I don't like the idea, they be in Nicobarese."

When Zedd saw Adie wrapping the blanket up around her shoulders, he closed the window. Kneeling at the hearth, he placed a handful of kindling on the grate and stacked on wood from the bucket to the side. He was about to use magic to start the fire, but thought better of it and instead lit a stick in the lamp. He squatted, touching the flame to the curls of the kindling.

"Zedd, my friend," Adie said in a quiet, gentle voice, "I not be a Sister of the Light. I know that be what you are wondering. I not be one of them."

That was exactly what Zedd had been wondering.

"And if you were," he asked without turning, "would you tell me?"

She was silent. He looked over his shoulder to see her smiling at him. "The Sisters of the Light value honesty above almost anything else. But to them, lying in the service of their Creator be a virtue."

The fire took a good start. Zedd stood before her, looking down without returning her smile. "That is no comfort to me."

She took hold of his hand, patting it with her other.

"Zedd, I will tell you the truth. I be in debt to some of them for the things they did for me, but I give you an oath on the soul of my dead Pell: I not be a Sister of the Light. I would never let them have one of the gifted from our side, as long as I knew there be a wizard to teach him. I would never allow a boy to be taken and subjected to their ways, had I a say."

Zedd smoothed the fringe of a carpet with his foot. "I know you're not one of them, dear lady. It's just that I hate the thought of those women doing those things to ones with the gift, when I can show them the joy of their talent. It's a gift. They treat it like a curse."

With a thumb, she rubbed the back of his hand. "I see you have yourself a dashing new cane."

Zedd grunted. "I hate to think what Master Hillman is scheming to charge me for it."

"And did you find us transportation?"

Zedd nodded. "A man named Ahern. We better try to get a bit of sleep. He's going to be here with a coach three hours before dawn."

He gave her a grim look. "Adie, until we get to Nicobarese and can rid ourselves of this taint, I think we had better consider the consequences very carefully before using magic."

"Are we safe here?"

A soft hand extended from the fog of dim light, brushing her cheek, comforting her.

*You are safe here, Rachel. Both of you are safe. Now, and always. You are safe.*

Rachel smiled. She did feel safe. Safer than she ever felt before. Not just safe like she felt when she was with Chase, but safe like she had felt in her mother's arms. She hadn't been able to remember her mother before, but she remembered now, remembered the encircling arms holding her to a breast.

The terrible fright she had shared with Chase while they raced to catch Richard was melting away. The bone-tired worry of whether or not they would catch him in time was melting away. The terror of the people who had tried to stop them, the fights Chase had had, the horror of the blood she had seen, all the blood she had seen . . . it was all melting away.

As she stood before the sparkling pool, the hands reached to her again. Reached to her from the gentle smiles of reassurance. The hands helped her undo the buttons of her dirty, sweaty dress, and pull it off. She flinched when her dress pulled against the bruise on her shoulder, the bruise she got when a man chasing them had knocked her down.

The smiles turned to sad looks of concern for her pain. The soft, gentle voices cooed comfort to her. The glowing hands caressed the shoulder, and when they lifted, the bruise was gone. The hurt was gone.

*All better?*

Rachel nodded. "Yes! It's all better. Thank you."

The hands pulled off her shoes and stockings. She sat on a warm rock and dangled her bare feet in the soothing water. It would be so wonderful to bathe and be rid of the dirt and sweat.

The hands reached for the stone hanging on the necklace around her neck. The hands drew back, as if afraid.

*We cannot remove this thing. You must do it without our help.*

Through the soothing warmth and security of the beautiful land around her, through the comfort of the peace she had found, through her desire to do as the gentle murmurs had asked, a voice rose up in her mind. It was Zedd's voice, telling her that she must not give the Stone to anyone, for any reason, telling her how important it was for her to guard it always.

She looked up, from the circles of ripples her feet made in the water, to the gentle faces. "I don't want to take it off. Can't I leave it on?"

The smiles returned and widened.

*Of course you can, Rachel, if that is what you wish. If that is what would make you happy.*

"I want it to stay on. That would make me happy."

*Then it will stay on. Now, and forever, if you wish.*

She smiled a smile of peace and security as she slipped into the soothing water. It felt so good. She floated and drifted. She felt all her troubles sloughing away with the dirt. One moment, it seemed she couldn't feel any more safe or happy, and then the next moment she did, and the next yet more.

She drew her arms through the healing, cleansing, golden water, swimming toward the other side of the pool, where she remembered leaving Chase. She found him almost up to his neck in the water, his head tilted back, resting on a soft mat of grass at the bank. His eyes were closed and he had a wonderful smile on his face.

"Father?"

"Yes, daughter," he whispered without opening his eyes.

She swam up beside him. He lifted an arm and she slipped under it. It felt so good to have his arm around her shoulders, comforting her.

"Father, do we ever have to leave this place?"

"No. They say we can stay forever."

She nuzzled against him. "I'm so glad."

She slept, really slept, like she couldn't remember ever sleeping before, so safe and sheltered, though she didn't know how long. When she dressed, her clothes were clean, and seemed to sparkle like new. Chase's clothes, too, were bright and shiny. She held hands and danced in circles with other children, glowing children, whose voices and laughter echoed. It made her laugh, too, laugh with happiness like none she had ever felt before.

When she was hungry, she and Chase lay in the grass, the warm fog and glowing, smiling faces around them, and ate things that were sweet and delicious. When she was tired, she slept, never having to worry about where she slept, because she was safe, safe at last. And when she wanted to play, the other children came to play with her. They loved her. Everyone loved her. She loved everyone.

Sometimes she walked alone. Filmy shafts of sunlight streamed through the trees. Glowing meadows were filled with wildflowers bowing in the gentle breeze, winking with bright specks of color.

Sometimes she walked with Chase, holding his hand. She was so happy that he was contented now, too. He never had to fight anyone anymore. He was safe, too. He said he was at peace.

He sometimes took her for walks, and showed her the woods where, he said, he grew up, where, he said, he had played when he was as little as she. She smiled with delight at the look of happiness in his eyes. She loved him and was fulfilled knowing he, like she, had found peace, at last.

She looked up, and a small smile touched her thin lips. She hadn't heard a sound, and she needn't turn to look in the near darkness. She knew he was there, on the other side of the door. She knew how long he had been there.

Her legs still crossed, she rose smoothly on a cushion of air, hovering above the straw-covered floor. The boy's limp arms swung as they dangled, like weighted fishing line. Lacking any life or rigidity, his back bent backward, draping over her arm. In her other hand was clutched the statue.

She unfolded her legs and stretched her slippered feet to the floor, settling her weight on them. As the boy slid from her arm, the dead weight of his head thunked against the floor. His arms and legs flopped askew to one side. His clothes were filthy. Disgusted, she wiped her hands on her skirts.

"Why don't you come in, Jedidiah." Her voice echoed from the cold stone. "I know you're there. Don't try to pretend you're not."

The heavy door squeaked slowly open and the shadowed figure strolled into the light of a single candle burning on a rickety, nearby table that was the lower room's only accoutrement. He stood relaxed, silently watching, as the orange glow faded from her eyes and they returned to the pale, pale blue shot through with violet flecks.

His gaze went to the statue in her hand. "The owner sent me to find that. She wants it back."

The thin smile grew. "Does she now?" She shrugged. "Well, I'm through with it." She held it out to him. "For now."

Jedidiah's face was a calm mask as he took the statue. "She doesn't like it when you 'borrow' her things."

She ran a finger down his cheek. "She is not the one I serve. I don't really care what she likes and what she doesn't."

"You would be wise to care a little more."

Her smile brightened. "Really? I could give her the same advice." She twisted, holding an arm out to the body on the floor. "He had the gift." Slowly, her hard eyes came back to his, the smile gone, as if one had never touched her features in all her life. Her voice came in a venomous hiss. "I have it now."

The slightest frown of puzzlement touched his cool expression.

"Think we must have the ceremony, Jedidiah? The ritual in the Hagen Woods?"

She slowly shook her head. "Not anymore. That is only the first time, because we are female, and female Han cannot absorb the male." Her voice lowered to a derisive whisper. "Not any longer. Now that I have the gift of a male, I can accept others without the ritual."

Her face glided to within inches of his. "So can you, Jedidiah," she breathed. "With the quillion, so can you. I could teach you. It's sooo easy. I simply showed him the joining rite, to try to show him his Han." Her cheek brushed his as she whispered into his ear. "But he didn't know how to control his gift. I created a vacuum in the quillion." She drew back to appraise his eyes. "It sucked the life right out of him. Sucked the gift right out of him. It's mine, now."

He studied her eyes a time before glancing down at the body. "I don't recall seeing him before."

She continued to whisper to him from only inches away. "Don't play games with me, Jedidiah. What you really mean is, where did I find him, and why haven't the Sisters, if he has the gift."

He shrugged nonchalantly. "If he has the gift, why isn't he collared?"

She cocked her head to the side. "Because he is so young. His Han is too weak to be detected by the other Sisters." She tilted her head to the other side. "But not by me." She touched her nose to his. "He was right here in the city. Right under their noses. Probably the offspring of a dalliance by one of you naughty boys."

"Very efficient. Saves having to bother with reports. Avoids awkward questions."

She glanced down at the body. "Be a good boy, and dispose of him for me. I found him living in squalor, down near the river. Dump him back there. No one will think anything of it."

He lifted an eyebrow. "You wish me to clean up after you?"

She ran a finger down his neck and across his throat, across his Rada'Han. "You make a serious mistake, Jedidiah, if you think of me as a mere Sister. I have the male gift now, same as you. And I know how to use it. You wouldn't believe how much that power increases when you add the Han of another."

"It would appear that you are becoming a Sister to be reckoned with. A wise person would take care with you."

She patted his cheek. "Smart boy, Jedidiah."

She gave him a little frown as she slipped her hands to his waist. "You know, Jedidiah, you may think of yourself as powerful in the gift, but I think you should worry about that. You have never had one to challenge your abilities before, your rightful place among the wizards here, but a new one comes. He will be here soon, and you have never seen one like this before. I think you may no longer be the pride of the palace."

His countenance showed no reaction, but his face slowly heated to red. He lifted the statue. "Well, you did say you would like to teach me."

She waggled a finger in front of his face. "Uh, uh, uh. He is mine. You may have another. Any gift will swell your power, but this one is mine."

He waggled the statue in front of her face. "She might have something to say about that. She has plans of her own. Plans for him."

She smiled with one side of her mouth. "I know. And you are going to keep me informed of her plans."

He lifted an eyebrow. "*You* have plans for *me*?"

The smile grew to both sides of her mouth. "Very special plans." Her hands roamed lower down the sides of his hips, feeling the firmness of his young muscles under his robes. "You're good with your hands, good at making things, making things in metal. I have something I want you to make for me. Something invested with magic. I hear that's one of your talents with the gift."

"You wish a trinket, an amulet, perhaps, in silver, or gold?"

"No, no, dear boy. You're to make it from steel. You're to gather the steel of a hundred sword points. Very special sword points. Sword points from the armory; old ones, ones that have been used. Ones that have pierced flesh in combat."

He arched an eyebrow. "And what is it you wish made?"

She slid a hand up the inside of his thigh. "We'll talk about it later."

She smiled at how quickly he responded to her touch. "You must be lonely, since Margaret ran away. Sooo lonely. I think you need a friend who understands you. Did you know, Jedidiah, that with the male Han comes a unique understanding of the male? I now understand in a new light what it is that men appreciate. I think we're going to be very special friends. As a special friend, you get the reward before performing the task."

She trickled a thread of magic into him, focusing it where it would do the most good. Her smile widened as his head rolled back. His eyes closed and he let out a throaty groan, and then gasped. Panting, he clutched his hands to her bottom, drawing her to him, and crushed his open mouth to hers.

She kicked the body out of her way as she let him force her to the straw-covered floor.

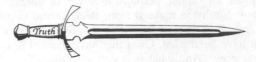

## CHAPTER 36

The wolverine grew larger in his vision. The arrow waited for the flat, dark head to lift. A low growl came from behind his left shoulder.

"Quiet!" Richard hissed.

The gar fell silent. The wolverine's head rose. With a zip, the arrow was away. Wings aquiver, the little gar bounced on the balls of its feet, its attention riveted to the flight of the arrow.

"Wait," he whispered. The gar froze.

With a solid thunk, the arrow found its target. The gar squealed in glee. Wings spreading and flapping, it bounced higher and turned to him. Richard leaned close and pointed a finger at the gar's wrinkly nose. The gar watched him attentively.

"All right, but you bring me back my arrow."

Head bobbing in quick agreement, the gar bounded into the air. Richard watched by the dim, early dawn light as it swooped down on the dead quarry, pouncing as if it were about to escape. Fur flew as claws ripped. The dark silhouette lowered, its wings folding against its back, as it hunched over the prey, growling and pulling its meal apart.

Richard turned from the sight and watched instead the streaks of cloud change color against the brightening sky. Sister Verna would be awake soon. He still stood his watch despite her insistence that it wasn't necessary.

She finally relented, but he knew she was angry because he wouldn't back down. *That* made her angry. What didn't? She was more angry than usual since coming through the valley the day before. She was silently livid.

Richard glanced toward the little gar to see it was still eating. How it had managed to follow him through the Valley of the Lost, he couldn't imagine. He had thought it was a mistake to keep feeding it before they reached the valley, but he felt responsible for it. Every night when he had taken his watch, it had come to him, and he had hunted food for it. He had thought he had seen the last of it when they crossed over into the Old World, but somehow, it had followed.

The little gar was passionately devoted to him when he was on watch. It ate with him, played with him, and slept at his feet, if not on them. When his watch was over, it hardly made a fuss about him leaving. Richard never once saw the gar at any other time. It seemed to instinctively know to stay away from the Sister, to avoid letting her see it. Richard was reasonably certain she would try to kill it. Maybe the gar knew that.

He was continually surprised by the intelligence of the furry little beast. It learned faster than any animal he had ever seen. Kahlan had told him that short-tailed gars were smart. Now he knew how right she was.

He had only to show it something once or twice to make it understand. It was learning to understand his words, and tried to imitate them, although it didn't seem to have the capacity for speech. Some of its sounds came strangely close.

Richard didn't know what to do about the gar. He thought perhaps it should strike out on its own, learn to hunt and survive, but it wouldn't leave; it followed, out of sight, wherever they went, even through danger. Perhaps it was too young to get by on its own. Maybe it saw Richard as its only way to survive. Maybe it saw him as a surrogate mother.

In truth, Richard didn't really want it to leave. It had become a friend as they had traveled through the wilds. It gave him unconditional love, never criticized him, and never argued with him. It felt good to have a friend. How could he deny the same thing to the gar?

The flap of wings brought him out of his thoughts. The gar thumped to the ground before him. It had gained a lot of weight since Richard had first found it. He would have sworn it had grown nearly half a foot, too.

The sinew under the pink skin of its chest and belly had become taut, and its arms were no longer all hide and bone, as they had been, but were thickening with muscle.

He was afraid to think of how big it would eventually get. He hoped it would be on its own by then. Hunting enough food to feed a full-grown short-tailed gar would be a full-time occupation.

After wiping the shaft on its fur-covered thigh to clean off the blood, the gar flashed Richard its hideous, bloodstained grin and held out the arrow. Richard pointed over his shoulder.

"I don't want it. Put it back where it belongs."

The gar reached over Richard's shoulder and slid the arrow back into the quiver that leaned against a stump. It contorted its features, seemingly to question if it had done it correctly. Richard smiled as he patted its full belly.

"Good boy. You did it right."

The gar flopped happily on the ground at his feet, contenting itself with licking blood from its claws and coarse fur. When it finished, it laid its long arms over Richard's lap, and rested its head on them.

"You need a name." The gar looked up, cocking its head to the side. Its tufted ears turned toward him. "Name." He tapped his chest. "My name is Richard." The gar reached out and tapped Richard's chest in imitation. "Richard. Richard."

It cocked its head to the other side. "Raaaa," it growled through sharp fangs, its ears twitching.

Richard nodded. "Rich . . . ard."

It tapped Richard's chest again. "Raaaa gurrrr," it said in its throaty growl, this time showing less teeth.

"Rich . . . ard."

"Raaaach aaarg."

Richard laughed. "That's close. Now, what are we going to call you?" Richard thought about it, trying to think of something appropriate. The gar sat, its brow bunched into deep furrows, watching him intently. After a moment, it took Richard's hand and tapped it against his chest.

"Raaaach aaarg," it said. It pulled Richard's hand to its own chest, tapping it against the fur. "Grrratch."

"Gratch?" Richard sat up straighter in surprise. "Your name is Gratch?" He tapped the gar again. "Gratch?"

The gar nodded and grinned as it tapped its own chest. "Grrratch. Grrratch."

Richard was a little taken aback; it had never occurred to him that the gar might have a name. "Gratch it is, then." He tapped his own chest again. "Richard." He smiled and patted the gar's shoulder. "Gratch."

The gar spread its wings and thumped its chest with open claws. "Grrrratch!"

Richard laughed and the gar leapt on him, letting out its throaty giggle as it wrestled him to the ground. Gratch's love of wrestling was second only to its love of food. The two of them tumbled across the ground, laughing and struggling to gently get the best of each other.

Richard was gentler about it than Gratch. The gar would put its mouth around Richard's arm, though, thankfully, at least it never bit. Its needle-sharp fangs were long enough to easily go all the way through his arm, and he had seen the gar splinter bone with those teeth.

Richard brought the wrestling match to an end by sitting up on the stump. Gratch sat straddling him, arms, legs, and wings wrapped around him. It nuzzled against Richard's shoulder. Gratch knew that at dawn Richard left.

Richard spied a rabbit in the underbrush, some distance off, and thought that perhaps Sister Verna would appreciate some meat for breakfast. "Gratch, I need a rabbit."

Gratch climbed off his lap as Richard took up his bow. After the arrow was off, he told the gar to bring him the rabbit, but not to eat it. Gratch had learned to retrieve, and was happy to do it; he always got what was left of the skinning and gutting.

After Richard was done and had bid Gratch good-bye, he hiked back to camp. His mind wandered back to the vision of Kahlan he had had in the tower, and the things she had told him. The sight of her being beheaded haunted him. He recalled her words:

*"Speak if you must these words, but not of this vision. 'Of all there were, but a single one born of the magic to bring forth truth will remain alive when the shadow's threat is lifted. Therefore comes the greater darkness of the dead. For there to be a chance at life's bond, this one in white must be offered to her people, to bring their joy and good cheer.'"*

He knew who the "this one in white" was. He knew what "bring their joy and good cheer" meant.

He thought, too, about the prophecy that Sister Verna had told him of, the one that said, "He is the bringer of death, and he shall so name himself." She claimed the prophecy said that the holder of the sword is able to call the dead forth, call the past into the present. He wondered, and worried, what that could mean.

At the camp, he found Sister Verna squatted at the fire, cooking bannock. The aroma made his stomach grumble. The sparsely wooded country was coming to life with sounds of animals and bugs heralding the dawn. Clusters of small, dark birds sang from the tall, thinly foliated trees, and gray squirrels chased each other up and down their branches. Richard hung the the skewer with the rabbit over the fire as Sister Verna continued to mind the bannock.

"I brought you some breakfast. I thought you might like some meat."

She gave only a grunt of acknowledgment.

"You still angry with me for saving your life yesterday?"

378

She carefully laid another small stick on the fire. "I am not angry with you for saving my life, Richard."

"I thought you said your Creator hated lies. Do you think he believes you? I don't."

Her face turned so red Richard thought her curly hair might catch fire. "You will not speak blasphemy."

"And lying is not?"

"You do not understand, Richard, why I'm angry."

Richard sat on the ground and, grasping his ankles, folded his legs in. "Maybe I do. You're supposed to be my protector. Not the other way around. Maybe you feel that you have failed. But I don't feel that you failed. We both just did what we had to, to survive."

"Did what we must?" Fine wrinkles radiated around her eyes as they narrowed. "As I recall from the book, when Bonnie, Geraldine, and Jessup led the people across the poison river, some of those people died."

Richard smiled to himself. "So you really did read it."

"I told you I did! That was foolhardy. We could have been killed taking that risk."

"We didn't have any choice."

"You always have a choice, Richard. That is what I am trying to teach you." She sat back on her heels. "The wizards who created that place thought they had no choice, but they made things worse. You were using your Han back there, and you were doing it without understanding the consequences."

"What choice did we have?"

Hands on her knees, she leaned forward. "We always have a choice, Richard. You were lucky, this time, that your use of magic didn't get you killed."

"What are you talking about?"

Sister Verna drew a saddlebag close and started rummaging through it, finally pulling out a green cloth bag. "You got some blood from that beast on your arm. Did any of the bugs bite you?"

"On my legs."

"Show me."

Richard pulled up his pant legs and showed her the swollen, red bites. She shook her head and, whispering to herself, pulled first one and then a second bottle from the bag.

With a stick found on the ground nearby, she dipped a white paste from one bottle and wiped it onto the flat of a knife blade. She threw the stick in the fire. Taking up another stick, she dipped a dark paste from the other bottle and mixed it with the light on the flat of the blade, then spread it along the edge. She threw the second stick, with some of the mixed paste on it, into the fire. Richard flinched when it exploded in a white-hot ball of fire that lifted skyward, dissipating as it rose, turning to a boiling cloud of black smoke.

She held up the knife to reveal a gray paste spread on the blade. "Light and dark, earth and sky. Magic, to heal what would otherwise kill you by tonight. You have a way of getting yourself out onto thin limbs, Richard. Each step you take only makes your predicament worse. Now, come over here, closer."

Richard dug his heels in and scooted around the fire. "Were you trying to decide whether or not you were going to help me?"

"Of course not. This is made from powerful magic, constructed magic, to smother the venom injected into you by the conjured creatures. Too soon, and the cure would kill you. Too late, the bites would kill you. It must be the right kind of magic, at the right time. I was simply waiting for the proper time."

Richard wanted to argue with her, but instead said, "Thank you for helping me." She frowned at him before leaning over his bites. "Sister, how was I making things worse?"

"You were being reckless. Using magic is dangerous, not only to others, but to the one who calls it forth as well."

Richard winced as she drew the edge across one of the bites, first one way, then the other, cutting an X on it. The sting made his eyes water.

"How can it be dangerous to me?"

She concentrated as she leaned over his leg, whispering an incantation while stroking the knife across his swollen flesh. He tried not to jump when she cut the next bite. She was only making light cuts, but they stung fiercely.

"It is like starting a fire in the center of a tinder dry wood. You find yourself in the center of the fire, in the center of what you have started. What you did was foolish and dangerous."

"Sister Verna, I was trying to stay alive."

She jabbed a finger at one of the painful bites. "And look what happened! If I don't heal you, you'll die." She finished with his legs and turned her attention to his arm. "When we were being attacked by those beasts, you thought to save us, but everything you did only increased the danger."

When she finished, she held the knife blade over the fire. A thin stream of white flame roared up from the steel, consuming the remaining paste. She held the blade to the fire until the paste, and the white flame, were gone.

"If I hadn't acted, Sister, we would be dead."

She shook the hot blade at him. "I did not say you were wrong to act! I said you acted in the wrong way! You used the wrong kind of magic!"

"I used the only thing I had! The sword!"

She pitched the knife. With a thunk, it stuck solidly in a piece of firewood. "Acting without knowing the consequences of the magic you call forth is perilous behavior!"

"Well, nothing you were doing was helping!"

Sister Verna rocked back on her heels, stared at him for a moment, and then turned to busy herself with replacing the bottles in the green bag.

"I'm sorry, Sister. I didn't really mean that. It didn't come out the way I intended. I only meant that you weren't able to sense the way, and I knew if we stayed, we would be killed."

The bottles clinked together as she moved them around in the bag. She seemed to be having difficulty getting them packed the way she wanted. "Richard, you think that controlling the gift, using magic, is what you are to learn with us. That is the easy part. Knowing what kind of magic to use, how much to use, when to use it, and the consequences of using it, that is the hard part. That is the meaning of everything. How, how much, when, and what if—just like the magic I have put on your bites."

She fixed him with a deadly serious expression. "Without that knowledge, you are a blind man swinging an axe in a crowd of children. You have no idea of the danger you invoke when you use magic. We try to give you sight, and some sense, before you swing that axe."

Richard picked at a clump of grass at his feet. "I never thought about it that way."

"Perhaps, if anything, I should be angry with myself for being foolish. I didn't think there was anything powerful enough to tempt me into a trap. I was wrong. Thank you, Richard, for saving me."

He wrapped a long stalk of grass around his finger. "I was so relieved to find you . . . I thought you were dead. I'm glad you're not."

She had pulled all the little bottles out of the bag and set them on the ground. "I could have been lost in that spell for all time. I should have been."

"What do you mean?"

There seemed to him to be more bottles than would fit into the bag, but then, he had seen them all come out. "We have tried to rescue Sisters before. We have seen some, and their charges, lost in those enchantment spells. I saw one, the first time I went through. We have never been able to get them out. Sisters have died trying." She started replacing the bottles. "You used magic."

"I used the sword. The sword has magic, you know."

"No. You didn't use the sword's magic. You used your Han, even though you didn't realize it. Using your Han through desire, without wisdom, is the most dangerous thing you can do."

"Sister, I think it was just the sword's magic."

"When you called to me, I heard you. We have tried to call to others, and they have never heard us. Not once."

"You just didn't know how. You couldn't hear me either, until I stepped through some sort of sparkling wall around you. Then you could hear me. You just have to step through that wall first."

She pushed bottles to each side to make more room as she spoke softly. "We know that, Richard. We have tried every sort of magic, and have never been able to pass through or break the wall of one of these spells, or been able to get the attention of one captured by it. No one has ever been brought out of an enchantment spell before." She replaced the last bottle and finally turned to face him. "Thank you, Richard."

He shrugged as he pulled the grass off his finger. "Well, it was the least I could do to make up for what I did."

"For what you did?"

Richard occupied himself with carefully rolling his pants back down. "Well, before I saved you, I kind of killed you."

She leaned closer. "You did what?"

"You were hurting me. With your magic. With the collar."

"I'm sorry, Richard. I was in the spell and didn't realize what I was doing. I didn't intend to hurt you."

He shook his head. "Not then. Before. In the white tower."

She leaned even closer and gritted her teeth. "You went into a tower? Are you mad? I told you what those towers are! How could you be so . . ."

"Sister. I had no choice."

"We have already discussed choice. I told you how dangerous those towers are. I told you to stay away from them!"

"Look, there was lightning all around. It was trying to strike me. I . . . well, I didn't know what else to do. So I dove through an archway, into the tower, for protection."

"Can't you follow the simplest instructions? Must you always act a child?"

Richard looked up from under his eyebrows. "Those were your exact words. You came into the tower. I was sure it was you. You were angry with me, much as you are now, and you used those exact words."

He gritted his teeth as he put a finger to the collar at his neck. "You used this. You used it to throw me against the wall, and pin me there with it. Can this collar do that, Sister?"

She sat much quieter. "Yes. We don't have the power of a wizard, the male Han. The collar amplifies our power, so we may be stronger than the one wearing it. So we can teach them."

His voice was deep with anger. "Then you used it to give me pain, like the pain you did for real, when you were in the spell. Only it was stronger, and went on and on. Can the collar do that, too, Sister?"

She pulled a clump of grass to her side and began cleaning her hands with it, avoiding his glare. "Yes. But that was a vision, Richard. I wasn't really doing it."

"I told you to stop hurting me or I would put a stop to it. You wouldn't stop, so I called the sword's magic and broke the bond of the power holding me. You were furious. You said that I had made my last mistake. You said you were going to kill me for fighting you. You were going to kill me, Sister."

"I'm sorry, Richard," she whispered as she looked up, "that you had to suffer that." Her voice regained some of its strength. "So, what did you do to me . . . to the vision of me?"

He leaned over and touched the edge of his first finger to the side of her shoulder. "I cut you in half with the sword. Right here."

Her hands stopped; she was stone still. Some of the color had left her face. Finally, she regained her composure.

Richard picked at the clump of grass by his foot again. "I didn't want to do it, but I was positive you were going to kill me."

She tossed the grass aside. "I'm sure you were, Richard. But that was only a vision. If it were real, it wouldn't have turned out that way. You would not have been able to do what you did."

"Who are you trying to convince, Sister? Me, or yourself?"

She met his glare. "The things you saw were not as they are in the real world. They were simply illusions."

Richard let it drop. He turned the stick with the rabbit to cook the other side, and slid the iron plate with the bannock to the side of the fire to let it cool.

"Anyway, when I saw you again, I didn't know if you were a vision, or real, but I truly hoped you were alive. I didn't want to kill you." He looked up and smiled. "Besides, I promised you that you would get through the Valley of the Lost."

She nodded. "Yes, you did. More desire than wisdom indeed."

"Sister, I was only doing what I could think of to survive. To help you survive, too."

She sighed and shook her head. "Richard, I know you're trying to do your best, but you must understand that what you think is best is not necessarily right. You're calling your Han without knowing what you're doing, or even realizing you're doing it. In so doing, you tempt danger you can't fathom."

"How was I using my Han?"

"Wizards make promises that their Han strives to keep. You promised me you would help me through the valley—save me. But in so doing, you have invoked prophecy."

Richard frowned. "I've given no prophecy."

"Not only given it, but used your Han without realizing it, used prophecy without knowing its form, to do something in the past to aid you in the future."

"What are you talking about?"

"You destroyed the horses' bits."

"I told you at the time why I did that. They're cruel."

She shook her head. "That's what I'm talking about. You think you did it for one reason, but it served another purpose. Your conscious mind is simply seeking to rationalize what your Han is doing. When we were running from the valley, I didn't believe in what you were doing, and I tried to turn my horse. Because he didn't have a bit, I was unable to."

"So what?"

She leaned closer. "Destroying the bits in the past satisfied a need of a promise in the future. That was using prophecy. You're swinging the axe blindly."

Richard gave her a skeptical expression. "That's a stretch, Sister. Even for you."

"I know how the gift works, Richard."

Richard thought about it, and finally decided he didn't believe her, but decided, too, that he didn't want to argue with her about it. There were other things he wanted to know.

"Is your little book full? I haven't seen you writing in it."

"I sent a message yesterday, that we have come through the valley. I have nothing else to write, that's all. The book is magic. With magic, we erase old messages. I erased all but two pages, but with what I added yesterday, there are now three pages full."

Richard tore off a corner of the hot bannock. "Who is the Prelate?"

"She charges the Sisters of the Light. She is . . ." Her eyes narrowed. "I've never mentioned her. How do you know of her?"

Richard licked the crumbs from his fingers. "I read it in your book."

Her hand flew to her belt, groping for the book. It was there, where it always was. "You've read my private writing! You have no right! I will . . ."

"You were dead at the time." Her mouth snapped shut, and he went on. "When I killed you, or the illusion of you, the book fell on the ground. I read it."

The tension left her muscles. "Oh. Well, that's simply part of the illusion. I told you, it's not as things are in life."

Richard tore off another corner of bannock. "There were only two pages with writing, just as the real book. Not until after we were through the valley did you add the third. Back then, there were only two."

She watched him eating the bannock. "Illusion, Richard."

He looked up. "One page said: 'I am the Sister in charge of this boy. These directives are beyond reason if not absurd. I demand to know the meaning of these instructions. I demand to know upon whose authority they are given. —Yours in the service of the Light, Sister Verna Sauventreen.' The second page said: 'You will do as you are instructed, or suffer the consequences. Do not presume to question the orders of the palace again. —In my own hand, The Prelate.' "

The Sister's face had drained of color. "You had no business reading something belonging to another."

383

"As I said, you were dead at the time. What instructions did they give you about me that made you so angry?"

The color came back to her face in a rush. "It has to do with a technicality. It's nothing you would understand, and anyway, it is not your business."

Richard lifted an eyebrow. "Not my business? You claim you are only trying to help me, yet you've taken me prisoner, and you say it's not my business? I have this collar around my neck, and with it you can hurt me, perhaps kill me, and you say it is not my business? You tell me I must do the things you say, that I must take them on faith, even though that faith is shaken with every new thing I discover, yet it's not my business? You tell me that the illusion I saw was not as things are in the real world, yet I find it was, and you tell me it's not my business?"

Sister Verna was silent. She watched him without emotion. Watched him, he thought, as if he were a bug in a box.

"Sister Verna, will you tell me one thing I've been wondering about?"

"If I can."

He pulled his legs up tighter under himself. He tried to keep any hostility out of his tone. "When you first saw me, you were surprised that I was grown. You thought that I would be young."

"That's right. We have ones at the palace who can sense one born with the gift. But you were hidden from us, so it took us a very long time to find you."

"But you told me just the other day that you had spent over half your life away from the palace, searching for me. If you've spent twenty-odd years looking for me, how could you expect me to be young? You would have expected me to be grown, unless you didn't know I had been born, and started searching for me long before anyone at the palace sensed me."

Her answer came in a cautious, quiet voice. "It is as you say. It has never happened this way before."

"So why would you come looking for me before any of you sensed that one with the gift had been born?"

She chose her words carefully. "We didn't know precisely when you would be born, but we knew you would be, so we were sent in search."

"How did you know I would be born?"

"You are spoken of in prophecy."

Richard nodded. He wanted to know about this prophecy and why they thought he was so important, but he didn't want to stray from the trail he was following at the moment. "So you knew it might be many years before you found me?"

"Yes. We didn't know when you would be born. We were only able to narrow it to a range of decades."

"How are the Sisters who are to be sent chosen?"

"We're selected by the Prelate."

"You have no say in the matter?"

She tensed, as if suspicious she might accidentally be slipping her neck through a noose, yet was unable to keep from voicing her faith. "We work in the service of the Creator. We would have no reason to object. The whole purpose of the palace is to help those with the gift. To be selected to save one with the gift is one of the greatest honors a Sister may receive."

"So, none of the others sent have ever had to give up so many years of their lives to rescue one with the gift?"

384

"No. I've never heard of it taking more than a year. But I knew this assignment could last for decades."

Richard smiled to himself in triumph. He leaned back, stretching his muscles. He took a deep breath. "Now I understand."

Her eyes narrowed. "What do you understand?"

"I understand, Sister Verna, why you treat me the way you do. I understand why we're always fighting, why we're always at each other's throats. I understand why you resent me. Why you hate me."

She looked like someone waiting for the trapdoor to fall out from under her. "I don't hate you, Richard."

He nodded, and pulled the catch on that trapdoor. "Yes, you do. You hate me. And I don't blame you. I understand. You had to give up Jedidiah because of me."

She flinched as if a noose had just tightened around her neck. "Richard! You will not speak to me in . . ."

"You resent me because of that. Not because of what happened to the other two Sisters. It's because of Jedidiah. If it weren't for me, you would be with him. You would have been with him for the last twenty years. You had to give up the love of your life to go on this accursed quest to find me. They sent you. You had no choice; you had to go. It's your duty, and it cost you your love, and the children you might have had. That's what I've cost you; why you hate me."

Sister Verna sat and stared; she neither spoke nor moved. Finally, she said, "The Seeker, indeed."

"I'm sorry, Sister Verna."

"No need to be, Richard. You don't know what you are talking about." She slowly lifted the rabbit from the fire, setting it on the iron plate with the bannock. For a moment she stared off into nothing. "We had better finish eating. We must be on our way."

"Fine. But I just want you to consider, Sister, that it's not by my choice. I didn't do this to you. The Prelate did. You should either be angry with her, or if you're so devoted to your duty, to your Creator, as you claim, then you should have joy in His service. Either way, please stop blaming me."

She opened her mouth to speak, but then instead fumbled with the stopper on the waterskin, finally getting it off, and took a long drink. Drawing deep breaths when she finished, she dabbed her sleeve to her wet lips.

Her unwavering gaze locked on his. "Soon, Richard, we will be to the palace, but first we have to pass through the land of a very dangerous people. The Sisters have an arrangement with them, to be allowed to pass. You will have to do a task for them. You will do it, or there will be great trouble."

"What will I have to do?"

"You will have to kill someone for them."

"Sister Verna, I promise you, I'm not going to . . ."

Her index finger rose from her fist, commanding silence. "Don't you dare swing the axe this time, Richard," she whispered. "You have no idea of the consequences."

She rose to her feet. "Get the horses ready. We must be leaving."

Richard stood. "Aren't you going to have your breakfast?"

She ignored his question and stepped close to him.

"It takes two to argue, Richard. You're always angry with me, with everything I tell you. You resent me. You hate me, because you think I made you put on that collar. But I didn't, and you know it. Kahlan made you put it on. It's because of her you wear the Rada'Han. If it weren't for her, you wouldn't be with me. That's what I've cost you, and why you hate me.

"But I think you should consider, Richard, that it's not by my choice. I didn't do this to you. Kahlan did. You should either be angry with her, or if you're so devoted to her, as you claim, then have joy in carrying out her wishes. Perhaps she has valid reasons for them. Maybe she has your interests at heart. Either way, please stop blaming me."

Richard tried to swallow, but couldn't.

The bloodred light of day's death oozed through the bones of trees lining the spine of the next ridge. Her green-eyed gaze left the well-hidden places where outposts of sentries were stationed. They were too far apart, she noted, or she would not be standing unnoticed where she was. She tallied the men in rank upon rank of tents marching up the valley floor below. Five thousand would be generous, she concluded.

Horses were picketed to her left, near supply wagons all neatly lined up. To the far side of the valley, latrines had been dug in the snow. Cook wagons stationed between the men and the supply wagons were packing up for the night. Colorful battle flags flew over the command tents. It was probably the most orderly army she had ever seen afield. Galeans did have a penchant for order.

"They look very nice," Chandalen said in a quiet voice, "for men about to be slaughtered." The two brothers gave nervous chuckles of agreement.

Kahlan nodded absently. That morning, they had seen the army these men were chasing. They were not neat. They were not orderly. They were not pretty. And their sentries were not stationed too far apart. Still, Chandalen and the two brothers had managed to get her close enough to see what she had wanted to see, and to take a tally.

She had guessed their numbers at fifty thousand. And that was not being generous.

She let out a long breath, its thin, white cloud drifting away in the cold air. "I have to stop this." She hiked her pack and bow up on her back. "Let's get down there."

Chandalen, Prindin, and Tossidin followed behind as she slogged down the hillside of fluffy snow. It had taken her longer than she had hoped to catch these men. A blizzard high in Jara Pass had left the four of them holed up in the shelter of a wayward pine for two days. Wayward pines always reminded Kahlan of Richard, and as she had lain in her fur mantle, listening to the howl of the wind, she had dreamed of him while she slept, and while she was awake.

She was furious that she had to lose valuable time on the way to Aydindril to stop this army from their suicide pursuit of the forces that had destroyed Ebinissia, but as the Mother Confessor she couldn't allow nearly five thousand men to die to no purpose. She had to stop them before they got close to the army that had plundered Ebinissia. They were too close now. They would surely make contact by the next day.

The army sprang to alert as the four figures in white wolf-pelt mantles marched toward them. Shouts erupted, and were repeated back through the ranks. Tent flaps were flung open and men poured out. Swords were drawn, sending the ring of steel into the cold, twilight air. Men with spears came running through the snow. Men with bows took up positions, nocking arrows. A wall of several hundred men put themselves between her and the command tents. More were coming at a run, pulling on clothes, shouting to others still in their tents.

Kahlan and the three men with her came to a halt. She stood tall and still. Behind her, Chandalen, Prindin, and Tossidin leaned lazily on their spears.

A man of rank tumbled out of the largest tent as he pulled on a heavy, brown coat. He made his way through the wall of men, shouting at the archers to hold their arrows. He was joined by two others of rank as he stumbled through the line of defenders. She recognized his rank as he approached. He was the captain. The two men with him, one to each side, were lieutenants.

When he drew himself to a panting halt before her, she let the hood of her mantle drop back. Her long hair fell across the white fur.

"What is the . . ." The captain's eyes went suddenly wide. He and the two lieutenants collapsed to a knee.

Every man as far as she could see fell to his knees. Every head bowed. The rustle of wool, the creek of leather, and the clang of steel fell silent. The three men with her cast one another glances of wonder; they had never seen the Mother Confessor greeted by anyone but Mud People before. The only sound was the slow creak of branches in the cold breeze.

"Rise, my children."

Accompanied by the renewed racket of movement, all came to their feet. The captain stood and gave her a smart bow, from the waist. He came up with a proud smile.

"Mother Confessor, what an honor!"

Kahlan stared in disbelief at his square jaw, his wavy light brown hair, his clear, blue eyes, his young, handsome face.

"You're a child," she whispered. She looked around to the hundreds, the thousands, of young, bright eyes all fixed on her. She blinked at them. She could feel the blood going to her face.

Her fists tightened as she shook with rage. "You're children! You're all children!"

The captain glanced back to his men with an embarrassed expression bordering on hurt. "Mother Confessor, we're new recruits, but we're all soldiers of the Galean army."

"You are all children," she whispered. "Children!"

Silence swept over the gathered recruits. Most looked to be fifteen or sixteen years. The captain and his two lieutenants shifted their weight and hung their heads. Some of the men couldn't help staring openly at Chandalen, Prindin, and Tossidin. They had never seen anyone like them before.

Kahlan grabbed the captain's lapels and began dragging him off. She growled to the two lieutenants. "You two come along with us." She glared over their heads. "Everyone go back to what you were doing!"

There was a rattle of swords being returned to scabbards and arrows to quivers as she dragged the captain out of earshot of his men. When she reached the trees, she pulled him toward a log and released him with an angry shove.

Kahlan flopped down on a snow-covered log as if it were a throne. She folded her arms. Chandalen stood to her right, Prindin and Tossidin to her left. They planted the butts of their spears and waited in silence.

She gritted her teeth. "What is your name, Captain?"

He fumbled with a brass button on his open coat. "I'm Bradley Ryan." His blue eyes came up. "Captain Bradley Ryan, Mother Confessor." He quickly glanced away to the man at his right. "This is Lieutenant Nolan Sloan." He pointed to the other side. This is Lieutenant Flin Hobson."

"How many *children* do you have along with you, Captain Ryan?"

He stiffened a little. "Mother Confessor, we may be younger than you, although not by much, and you may not think highly of us, but we're soldiers. Good soldiers."

"Good soldiers." She was hardly able to keep herself from screaming at him. "If you're such good soldiers, why was I able to walk, unnoticed, through your line of sentries?" His face reddened and he made a visible effort to remain silent. "And is there a one of these good soldiers, including you three, that is beyond eighteen?" He pressed his lips tighter and shook his head. "Then I repeat, how many children do you have along with you?"

"There are four and a half thousand under my command."

"And do you know, Captain Ryan, that you are about to stumble upon a force ten times your size?"

Captain Ryan lifted an eyebrow, and a little-boy grin grew out of one side of his mouth. "We're not about to 'stumble' upon anyone, Mother Confessor. We're about to catch them. We've been chasing them. I think we'll have them tomorrow."

She gritted her teeth anew. "Have them? Tomorrow, if I hadn't caught up with you, young man, you and all your 'men' would die. You have no idea of the army you are about catch."

He lifted his chin. "We know what we are chasing. We have scouts, you know. I get reports."

Kahlan shot to her feet, thrusting her arm to the right and pointing. "There are fifty thousand men around that mountain!"

"Fifty-two thousand, and a few hundred." He shrugged. "We're not stupid. We know what we're doing."

Her arm dropped as she glared. "Oh you do, do you? And just what were you going to do once you caught them?"

Captain Ryan smiled as he leaned in, sure that he could prove to her that he indeed did know what he was doing. "Well, they're about to come to a divergence in the pass. I'm going to send a force up there, around them, to come in from each fork. They'll think they're being attacked by a large force. We're going to drive them back this way, where we're going to be waiting for them, beyond the narrows just ahead.

"Then, we're going retreat back this way, to the narrows, then split the flank, let them in, until they have nowhere to go. The pikemen will be bunched in the narrowest place; they're called the Anvil. Archers to the sides will hold the enemy to the center. The force driving them is called the Hammer." His grin widened. "We'll crush them in the middle."

He flicked his hand in a casual manner as he straightened a little. "It's a classic tactic. It's called the Hammer and Anvil."

Dumbfounded, Kahlan stared at him. "I know what it's called, young man. The Hammer and Anvil is a bold maneuver . . . under the right conditions. Against a force ten times your size it's beyond foolhardy. You are a badger trying to swallow an ox whole."

"We were taught that with good timing, and determination, a small force of good men, in a tight place, like this valley . . ."

"Good men? You think that's going to count with the spirits? Is that what your pride and presumption leads you to think!" The captain's eyes descended to the ground. "You can't push a boulder with a stick! The only way to move them back this way is to frighten them into moving back." She thrust her arm out, pointing off toward the enemy again. "Those are experienced, battle-hardened men! They've been fighting and killing for a good long time. Do you think they don't know what a Hammer and Anvil is? Do you think that just because they're the enemy they are stupid?"

"Well, no, but I think . . ."

She jabbed a finger at his chest as she cut him off. "Do you want me to tell you what's going to happen, Captain? You don't have enough men to push them. When you send that detachment around them, they will accommodate you and move a little, and as they do they'll wing out to let your force in. That's called a Nutcracker. Guess who the nut is.

"Then they *will* move. For your anvil. They will be hounds roused to the scent of blood. After they've wiped out your Hammer, there will be nothing to contain them, nothing to keep their flanks from wheeling as they drive in. They have battle experience and know exactly what to do.

"They'll split your pikemen and their archers, and cut them off from their supporting swordsmen. A flying wedge protected by shields will drive into those pikemen. Crescents to the sides will trap them. Their armored cavalry will come at a full charge and rake down your wings of archers, who will by then have no pikemen to blunt the charge. You will all fight bravely, but you will be outnumbered perhaps twenty to one, because you've already sacrificed part of your force to be the Hammer, and they will all be dead by then.

"To fight a larger force, you must divide them, and conquer them one bit at a time. Instead, you will have done the opposite. You will have divided yourself in half for them, so they can kill half at a time. At their leisure."

The captain stood his ground. "We can make a good show of ourselves. You don't know how good we are. We're not novices."

"Every one of those children under your command will die! Have you ever seen anyone die, Captain? Not die like an old man in bed, but in battle? You will be run through with spears, shot through the eyes with arrows. Swords will hack off arms, split open ribs. Blades will rip your bellies open and spill your guts across the cold ground.

"Faces you know, your friends, these children, will look up at you in panic as they choke on their own blood and vomit. Others will be screaming for help as your enemy moves through the wounded on the ground and eviscerates them, to make them suffer a gruesome death. The ones who surrender will be executed while your enemy dances and sings about the great battle they have just won."

Captain Ryan's head finally rose. His lieutenants still stared at the ground. "You sound like Prince Harold, Mother Confessor. He has given me close to the same speech on a number of occasions."

"Prince Harold is a smart soldier."

Captain Ryan buttoned two of the brass buttons on his dark brown wool coat. "But that doesn't change my decision. Of all our choices, the Hammer and Anvil is the best chance we have against them. I believe we can make it work. We must."

Chandalen leaned toward her and spoke in his tongue. *"Mother Confessor, these men are the walking dead. We should be away from them so we do not get caught in their foolishness. They are going to die to a man."*

The captain frowned. "What'd he say?"

Kahlan leaned close to the young captain. "He says you are all going to die tomorrow."

Captain Ryan looked Chandalen up and down. "What does he know about battle? He's just a savage from the wilds."

Kahlan lifted an eyebrow. "Savage? He's a pretty smart man. He speaks two languages. His, and ours." Captain Ryan swallowed. "And he has fought in battles. He has killed men. How many men have you killed, Bradley?"

He glanced to his two lieutenants. "Well, none, I guess. Look, I'm sorry, I meant no offense, but I know about war."

"And what do you know about war, child?" she whispered.

"We're all volunteers. Myself, three years ago. Almost no man here has less than one year. We've all trained hard. Prince Harold himself has worked with us, taught us tactics. We've won mock battles against him several times. We may be young but we have experience. We were sent on this expedition as a final test before our assignments. We've been afield nearly a month, practicing war games and battle tactics. We know what we are about. Just because we're young, that doesn't mean we can't fight. We may be young, but that also means we're strong."

Chandalen laughed. "Strong? You travel like women." He cleared his throat when Kahlan lifted an eyebrow to him. "Well, some women. You are not so strong as you think. You are soft. You have wagons to carry your needs. That makes you soft. You will die tomorrow."

Kahlan turned back to the three soldiers. "My friend is wrong. You are not going to die tomorrow."

The captain brightened. "We're not? You believe in us, then?"

She shook her head. "You are not going to die tomorrow because I will not allow it. I'm sending you back. You are to take your division back to your command unit. That, Captain, is an order. I'm on my way to Aydindril to take care of this. I will put a stop to that army of killers."

Captain Ryan's expression hardened. "We have no command to return to. They were wiped out in Ebinissia. That was where we were training, but we were out on maneuvers. We have the trail of the ones who did it, and we are going after them."

"Those soldiers is Ebinissia were many times your number, and they were crushed by the force you chase."

"We know. Those were men we lived with, ate with, slept with. They were our teachers. They were our brothers, our fathers. They were our friends and companions." He shifted his weight and cleared his throat in an effort to keep his voice steady. "We should have been there with them. We should have been there to stand with them."

Kahlan turned her back to the three Galean soldiers. She put her fingers to her temples, closing her eyes as she rubbed in little circles. She had a headache from the worry of these young men all being slaughtered. She grieved for the friends of these men, friends and comrades who were killed defending their city. The faces of the young women floated before her mind's eye.

Kahlan spun around, looking into the eyes of the young captain. Eyes, she realized, that had seen more than she had at first thought.

"You were the one," she whispered. "You were the one who closed the doors.

You closed the doors in the palace. The doors on the rooms of the queen and her ladies."

He swallowed and then nodded. His blue eyes were wet. His lower lip quivered. "Why would they do that to those poor people?"

Kahlan answered in a gentle tone. "The object of a soldier is to make his enemy do foolish things. Either by making them too frightened, or too angry, to think. They do it to strike fear into your hearts, but more than that, to make you so angry you will do something foolish so they can kill you, too."

"Those men we chase are the ones who did that. We have no command to return to. It's upon us now."

"That is the foolish thing they want you to do. You will not. You will go to another command. You are not going to attack that army."

"Mother Confessor, I'm a soldier sworn to serve Galea and the Midlands. In my life, young though you think it is, I've never once entertained the idea of disobeying my commanders, my queen, or the Mother Confessor." Captain Ryan lifted her wrist with his finger and thumb and placed her hand on his shoulder. "But in this, I must disobey your orders. If you wish, you may take me with your power, but I will not otherwise do as you say."

Lieutenant Sloan spoke up for the first time. "And then you will have to take me, because I'll take his place, and lead our men to the fight."

Lieutenant Hobson stepped forward. "And then you'll have to take me."

"After the three of us," Captain Ryan said, "you will have to move through the officers and then every one of the men. If there is one left, he will attack, and die in battle if need be."

She drew her hand back. "I'm going to the Central Council and will take care of this. What you want to do is a suicide."

"Mother Confessor, we are going to attack."

"For what! For glory? You want to be heroes avenging the murdered? You want to die in a glorious battle!"

"No, Mother Confessor," he said in a quiet tone. "We saw what those men did to Ebinissia. We saw what they did to the soldiers they captured. We saw what they did to the women and children back there. Many of the men under my command had mothers and sisters back there. We all saw what was done to them, and what was done to our fathers and brothers. Our people."

He drew himself up tall and straight as he looked with resolve into her eyes. "We're not doing this for glory, Mother Confessor. We know it's a suicide mission. But we're all single; we have no families to leave without fathers. We're doing it because those men will go on to another city and do to them what they did in Ebinissia. We're doing this to stop them, if we can.

"Our lives are sworn to protect our people. We cannot shirk our responsibility. We must attack and try to stop these men before they kill any more innocent people. I pray to the good spirits that you succeed in Aydindril, but still, that will take too long. How many more cities will be plundered before you can bring the Midlands to bear on these men? One city is too many. We're the only ones in contact with these killers. Our lives are all that stand between them and their next victims.

"When I took the oath to serve, I swore that no matter the choices, no matter the orders, I would always put the protection of my people first. That's why I must disobey your orders, Mother Confessor—not for glory, but to protect the defenseless.

I wish to have your blessing in this, but I will try to stop those men with your blessing, or without it."

She sank to sit on the log again, and stared off into the distance, pondering the three soldiers. The six men waited in silence. Children indeed. They were older than she had thought. And they were right.

It would still take her some time to get to Aydindril and more time yet to raise armies to hunt down these killers. In the meantime they would go on killing. How many would have to die waiting for help from the Central Council?

She wished she could be anyone right now but who she was. The Mother Confessor. She disregarded her feelings and considered the problem as the Mother Confessor must; she weighed lives, those spent, and those spared.

Kahlan stood and turned to Chandalen. *"We must help these men."*

Chandalen pushed his hands farther up on his spear and leaned toward her. *"Mother Confessor, these men are foolish children, and they are going to die. If we stay with them they will bring a storm of killing around us. We will be killed with them. They will die just the same, and you will not reach Aydindril."*

*"Chandalen, these boys are like the Mud People. They are chasing their Jocopo. If we don't help them, then more will die like we saw back in the city."*

Prindin leaned in. *"Mother Confessor, we will do whatever you wish, but there is no way to help these boys. We are only four."*

Tossidin nodded. *"And then you would fail in your duty to reach Aydindril. Is that not important?"*

*"Of course it is."* She pulled some hair back off her face. *"But what if the army who killed everyone in that city were going next to the Mud People? Would you not want me to help if it were your people they would murder next?"*

The three men straightened. They twisted their spears while they thought, glancing over her shoulder occasionally, to the three soldiers who also stood silently.

*"What would you do to defeat this enemy,"* she asked as she moved her gaze among the three, *"if you had to?"*

At last Tossidin leaned in again. *"There are too many. It cannot be done."*

Chandalen angrily backhanded Tossidin's shoulder. *"We are Mud People fighters! We are smarter than these men who ride in wagons and murder women. Do you think them better fighters than us?"*

The two brothers shuffled their feet as they averted their eyes. *"Well,"* Prindin said, *"we know that the way they want to do it will only get them killed. There are better ways."*

Chandalen smiled. *"Of course there are. The spirits taught my grandfather how to do such things. He taught my father and my father taught me. The numbers may be larger, but it is the same problem. We know better than these men what to do."* He looked Kahlan in the eye. *"You, too, know better than these men what to do. You know you must not fight the way the enemy wants. That is what these men are about to do."*

Kahlan smiled at him and nodded. *"Maybe we can help these men protect other innocent people."*

She turned to Captain Ryan. He had been watching her speak in a foreign tongue with the three strange men.

"All right, Captain. We are going to go after this army."

He gripped her shoulders. "Thank you, Mother Confessor!" He jerked his hands back, realizing with a fright that he had actually touched her. He instead rubbed

393

his hands together. "It will work. You'll see. We'll have the jump on them. We'll surprise them and have them all on a pike."

She leaned toward him. He backed away. "Surprise them? Surprise them!" She grabbed him by his collar and pulled his face close. "They have a wizard, you idiot!"

The captain's face paled. "A wizard?" he whispered.

She released his collar with an angry shove. "You were at Ebinissia, didn't you see the hole melted through the wall?"

"Well . . . I guess I didn't pay attention. I only saw the dead." His eyes darted about, as if seeing them now. "They were everywhere."

She cooled at the pained expression on his face. "I understand. They were your friends and family. I can understand why you wouldn't have noticed. But that is no excuse for a soldier. A soldier must notice everything. Missing details can get you killed, Captain. This is a good example of a little detail that would have done you in."

He swallowed and then nodded. "Yes, Mother Confessor."

"Do you want to kill the men who destroyed Ebinissia?" The three soldiers spoke up that they did. "Then I am taking command of this legion. If you want to stop the men who are up there, then you will do as I say. And as Chandalen, Prindin, and Tossidin say.

"You may know about battle tactics, but we know about killing people. This is not a battle, Captain, this is killing people. We are only going to help you if you really want to stop those men. If you are interested in having a battle, then we will leave you right now so you can get yourselves slaughtered."

Captain Ryan fell to a knee. The two lieutenants followed his example. "Mother Confessor, it would be my greatest honor to serve under you. You have my life, and the lives of every one of my men. If you know how to stop those men from murdering any more people, we will do whatever you ask."

She nodded down to the three men. "This is no war game, Captain. For us to win, every man must do as he is ordered. Anyone who doesn't do as we order is aiding the enemy. That is treason. If you want to stop those men, then you all are going to have to turn command over to me, and you can't change your mind if the task becomes grim. Do you understand?"

"Yes, Mother Confessor. I understand."

She looked to the other two. "And you?"

"I am honored to serve under you, Mother Confessor."

"As am I, Mother Confessor."

Kahlan motioned them up and then drew her fur mantle closed. "I must get to Aydindril. It is of the utmost importance, but I will help you begin this. We will tell you what must be done. I can give you only a day or two; we will help you begin the killing, and then we must be on our way."

"Mother Confessor, what of the wizard?"

Kahlan looked at him from under her eyebrows. "You leave the wizard to me. Do you understand? He is mine. I will handle it."

"All right. What do you want us to do first?"

Kahlan walked between the captain and one of the lieutenants. "The first thing you have to do is get me a horse."

Chandalen leapt forward and gripped her arm, slowing her as he put his head close to hers. His tone was angry with suspicion. "Why do you want a horse? Where are you going?"

She came to a halt, pulling her arm free. She took in all six men. "Do you have any idea what it is I'm about to do? I'm about to choose sides. I am the Mother Confessor. If I choose sides, I choose sides for all the Midlands. I commit all the Midlands to war." She met Chandalen's eyes. "I cannot do that on the word of these men."

Chandalen erupted in fury. "What more proof do you need! You saw what they did back at that city!"

"What I saw does not matter. I must know why. I cannot simply declare war. I must know who these men are, for whom they fight." She had another reason to go, a more important reason, but she didn't speak it.

"They are killers!"

"You've killed people. Would you not want others to know the reason before they sought vengeance?"

"You foolish woman!" Prindin put a cautionary hand on Chandalen's arm, attempting to bring a little prudence to Chandalen's words. Chandalen angrily wrenched his arm away. "You say these men are foolish, and they have thousands. You are one! You have no chance to escape if they decide to kill you!"

"I'm the Mother Confessor. None may lay a weapon to me."

She knew it was an absurd pretext, but she had to do this, and could think of no other justification to allay his fears. Chandalen was too angry to speak. He finally turned away with a growl. She knew that in the past he would have been angry because if she were killed he couldn't return home; she thought that perhaps now he was genuinely afraid for her.

She didn't like the idea either, but had no choice. She was the Mother Confessor. She had a duty to the Midlands.

"Lieutenant Hobson, please get me a horse. A white or gray if you have one." He nodded and ran off to do as asked. "Captain, I want you to get all your men together and tell them what's happening."

Chandalen stood with his back to her. She stroked a hand down the white fur over his shoulder, over his father's bone knife. *"You are fighting for the Midlands now, not just the Mud People."* He let out an angry grunt. "While I'm gone, I want you three to start explaining to these men what must be done. I hope to be back before dawn."

When she saw Hobson returning with the horse, her knees tried to buckle. Dear spirits, what had she gotten herself into?

She turned to face Captain Ryan. "If I'm . . . If anything . . ." She took a breath and started again. "If I get lost and can't find my way back, you're to take your orders from Chandalen. Do you understand? You're to do as he says."

"Yes, Mother Confessor," he said in a quiet tone as he put his fist to his heart in salute. "May the good spirits be with you."

"From my experience, I'll take a fast horse instead."

"Then you have your wish," Lieutenant Hobson said. "Nick is fast, and he's fierce. He won't let you down."

The Captain cupped his hands, giving her a boost up onto the big warhorse. She looked down at the men as she gave the gray an introductory pat on his neck. Nick snorted and tossed his head. Before she lost her nerve, she pulled the big stallion around and urged him toward the slopes, toward a trail that would circle her around to come into the enemy camp from the other side.

**T**he snow-crusted trees loomed all about her in the eerie light. The moon would be down soon, but for the time being it gave the snow a luminescence that made the way easy to see. As she trotted her horse into the open valley, she was almost glad to be free of the pressing trees that could hide anyone intent on ambush. She made no attempt to conceal her approach, and the sentries saw her, but they made no move to stop a lone rider.

Ahead, the army's camp was alive with fires, men, and noise. As large as a small city, it could be spotted easily and heard from miles away. Confident in their numbers, they feared no attack.

With the hood of her fur mantle pulled up and drawn close around her face, Kahlan walked Nick among the confusion of men, wagons, horses, mules, tents, gear, and roaring fires. She sat tall on her horse, and above the din she could almost hear her heart thumping. The strong aroma of roasting meat and woodsmoke filled the still air. The snow had been trampled and packed flat by tens of thousands of feet, both man and beast, and by wagons of every sort.

Men were gathered around fires, drinking and eating and singing. Pikes were stacked upright in circles, leaning in, with their heads all resting together in bristling cones. Lances were everywhere, sticking up from snowbanks, looking like forests of stripped saplings. Tents sprouted all about without any order to their layout.

Men roamed far and near, stumbling from one fire to another to try the food, to join in song around men with flutes, to gamble at dice, or to share the drink. Sharing the drink seemed to be what occupied most of them.

No one paid any attention to her. They seemed too preoccupied to notice her. She kept her horse at a trot, and passed the ones who did stare up before they had a chance to wonder at, or confirm, what they had seen. The whole place seemed to be in an uproar of activity. Her warhorse didn't so much as flinch at the pandemonium all about.

From some of the tents in the distance she heard the screams of women, followed by the raucous laughter of men. Despite her attempt to stop it, a shiver ran down her spine.

Kahlan knew that armies like this one were accompanied by prostitutes who rode along in the supply wagons with other camp followers. She also knew that armies like this one took women as part of their plunder, considering them a simple privilege of victory, much as taking a ring from a dead man, and worth little more. Whatever the reasons for the screams, feigned delight or true terror, she knew she could do nothing about it, and so tried not to hear them, turning her attention instead to the men she passed.

At first she saw only D'Haran troops. She knew their leather and mail and armored uniforms all too well. Each of the breastplates bore an ornate, embossed letter *R*, for the House of Rahl. Soon though, she was able to pick out Keltans among the D'Harans. She saw one group of a dozen men from Westland, each with an arm around the next fellow's shoulders as they danced in a circle and at the same time drank from mugs. She saw men of other lands, too; a few from Nicobarese, some Sandarians, and to her horror, a handful of Galeans. Maybe, she thought, they were simply D'Harans in the uniforms of men they had killed. Somehow, she didn't believe that.

Sporadic quarrels were going on throughout the camp. Men argued over a lay of the dice, food, casks, or even bottles of drink. Some of the disputes erupted into fights with fists and knives. She saw one man stabbed in the gut, to the uproarious laughter of onlookers.

At last she spotted what she was looking for: the tents belonging to the commanders. Though they hadn't bothered to put up their flags, she knew by their size what they were. Outside the largest, a small table had been set up next to a roaring fire with spitted meat over it. Lanterns on poles surrounded the group of men gathered there.

As she approached, a huge man who sat with his feet up on the table was yelling, ". . . and I mean right now, or I'll have your head! A full one! You bring a full cask or I'll have your head on a pike!" When the soldier scurried off, the table of men erupted in laughter.

Kahlan brought her huge warhorse right up to the edge of the table. She sat tall and still as she appraised the half-dozen men sitting around the table. Four were D'Haran officers; the one with his boots resting on the table had been the man who had been yelling; one was a Keltish commander in an ornate uniform unbuttoned to reveal a filthy shirt soaked with wine and meat drippings; and one man wore plain, tan robes.

With a large knife, the man with his feet up on the table carved a long strip of meat from a bone. He tossed the bone over his shoulder to a snarling pack of dogs behind him. He tore the strip of meat in half with his teeth and pointed with the knife to his right, to the young man in plain robes, as he added a swig from a mug to the meat already in his mouth. He spoke around it all.

"Wizard Slagle here told me he thought he smelled a Confessor." He peered up with bloodshot eyes. "And where is your wizard, Confessor? Huh?" Everyone at the table laughed with him. Ale ran down his thick, blond beard. "Bring anything to drink, Confessor? We're nearly out. No? Well, not to mind." With the knife, he pointed over to the Keltish commander. "Karsh here tells me there's a nice city a week or so down the mountains, and they're bound to have some ale for us thirsty boys, after they welcome us to their town and swear allegiance."

Kahlan's eyes slid to the wizard. It was for him she had come. She coolly calculated whether or not she could make the jump from the horse to the wizard and touch him with her power before she was caught by that big knife. The man wielding the knife didn't look to be able to react too quickly. Still, she judged it to be poor odds. She was willing to give her life to the task, but only if she could be reasonably sure of success.

But it was for him she had come. The wizard was this army's eyes. He saw things before they could, and things they couldn't see, like her. And D'Harans feared things magic, and spirits. A wizard was their defense against magic and those spirits.

Her gaze moved from the wizard's deep-set eyes and drunken, leering smirk to what he was doing with his hands. He was whittling. Before him on the table was a pile of shavings. She remembered the piles of wood shavings in the palace at Ebinissia, outside the girls' rooms.

The wizard waggled the stick he had whittled. For the first time, she noticed what it was. It was a larger-than-life phallus. His smirk grew.

The man with the knife pointed it to the wizard. "Slagle's got something for you, Confessor. Been working on it for two hours, since he realized you were coming for a visit." He made a feeble attempt to hold back his laughter, but it came in fits through his restraint and he finally gave in to it.

Two hours. They had just told her the limits of this wizard's power. She had left the Galeans four hours ago, but nearly an hour of that had been spent at her task up on the ridges. That meant the Galean boys weren't yet close enough for the wizard to know of them, but were only concealed from discovery by a dangerously thin margin. Any closer, and the wizard would know of them. Long before they could bring any surprise to bear.

She waited for the D'Haran man's laughter to sputter out before she spoke. "You have me at a disadvantage."

"Not yet! But I will!" The men roared and hooted again.

With every beat of her heart, she became more calm. She pushed her hood back. She wore her Confessor's face. "What is your name, soldier?"

"Soldier!" He lurched forward and stuck the knife in the table. "I'm no soldier. I'm General Riggs. I'm supreme commander of all our troops. All our men, old and new, answer to me."

"And in who's name are you fighting, General Riggs?"

He swept his hand around. "Why, the Imperial Order is fighting a war on behalf of those who join us. A war against all the oppressors. Against all who fight us. Those who don't join us are against us, and will be crushed. We fight to bring order.

"Under the Imperial Order, all who join us will find protection, and in turn they will help protect all. All the lands will join with us, or they will be swept aside. It is a new order for which we struggle. The Imperial Order. They command all the lands, and I command them."

Kahlan frowned, trying to make sense of what she was hearing. "I am the Mother Confessor, and I command the Midlands, not you."

"*Mother* Confessor!" He clapped the wizard on the back. "You didn't tell me she was the *Mother* Confessor! Well, you don't look like any mother I've seen. But after tonight, you'll be a mother sure enough. You have my word on that!" He roared with laughter.

"Darken Rahl is dead." That brought the laughter to an end. "The new Lord Rahl has declared the war ended and called all the D'Haran troops home."

General Riggs rose to his feet. "Darken Rahl was a man of limited foresight, a man too much concerned with his ancient magic and too little concerned with order. He was too preoccupied with his own quests, his old religions. Magic, until it is eradicated, is a tool of men, not a master of them.

"Darken Rahl failed to use the opportunity he had. We will not fail. Darken Rahl himself, in the underworld, knows this, and repents. He is allied to our struggle, now. The good spirits have declared it! We no longer bow to the house of Rahl, but they, as all houses, districts, and kingdoms, to us. The new Lord Rahl will join us, too, or we'll crush him and any heathen dogs who follow him. We will crush all the heathen dogs!"

"In other words, General, you fight for no one other than yourself. Your purpose is simply to murder people."

"I do not fight for myself! This is a larger purpose than one man. We offer all the opportunity to join with us. If they don't join with us, it's because they're aligned with our enemies, and we must kill them!" He threw his hands up. "It's useless trying to explain such matters of state and canon to a woman. Women have no intellect for rule."

"Men have no exclusive talent to rule, General."

"It's profanity for men to bow down to a woman for protection! Right men concern themselves only with getting under a woman's skirts, not with hiding behind them! Women rule from their nipples, offering only their sympathetic pap. Men rule from their fist. They make and enforce the law. They provide and protect.

"Every king and patrician will be offered the chance to join with us, to bring his land and his people under our protection. All queens will be offered the chance to ply their wares in a brothel, or perhaps to be the humble wives of an indentured farmer, but either way make a proper use of themselves."

He swept his mug up from the table and took a few gulps. "Can't you see, woman? Are you that stupid, even for a woman? What has your Midland's alliance accomplished under the rule of women?"

"Accomplished? The alliance is to accomplish nothing but to let all the lands live in peace, to leave their neighbors' lands to their neighbors, and know that their own is safe from covetous hands, and that all will stand to protect each, even the weak and defenseless, so none will stand alone and naked."

He smiled in triumph as he looked to his comrades. "Truly spoken from the teat!"

He gestured with disgust. "You provide no leadership, no law; each land proscribes and pronounces as they see fit. What in one place is a crime, in another is virtue. Your alliance shies from bringing order to all. You're nothing but fragmented tribes, each jealously guarding what's his, with no thought to the union other than fits their own greed, and in so doing lets all be vincible."

"You are wrong, that is exactly what the Central Council in Aydindril is for, to bring all lands together for the common defense. The common defense against murderers like you. It is not a feeble union, as you seem to think, but one with teeth."

"A noble ideal. One, in fact, which I share, but one you only give pap to. You bring them together only timidly, not under common canon." He held his hand out to her, closing it into a fist as he sneered at her. "In so doing, you leave all lands ripe for the squeezing. You are lost souls in search of true leadership and in desperate need of protection.

"As soon as the boundaries fell, you were ravaged by Darken Rahl, and he was only halfhearted about it, seeking only his magic! Had he let the generals run as they would, there wouldn't be even a shell of this play alliance of yours left."

"And who is it we all need protection from?"

He stared off, whispering, almost to himself. "From the horde who will come."

"What horde?"

He looked up, as if he had just awakened. "The horde spoken of in the prophecies." He frowned at her as if she were hopelessly thick, and then held his hand out to the wizard. "The good wizard here has counseled us on the prophecies. You are one who spent your life with wizards, and you never sought their knowledge?"

"Your eloquent claim to want to join people in peace and law are high-minded words, General Riggs. But your atrocities in Ebinissia put the lie to them. For all time, Ebinissia will bear mute but irrefutable testimony to your true cause. You, and your Imperial Order, are the horde." Kahlan glowered to the wizard. "What's your part in this, Wizard Slagle?"

He shrugged. "Why, to assist and facilitate the joining of all people under the rule of common law."

"Whose law?"

"The law of the victors." He smiled. "That would be us. The Imperial Order."

"You have responsibilities as a wizard. Those responsibilities are to serve, not to rule. You will report at once to Aydindril, to take your place in that service, or you will answer to me."

"You?" he said with a derisive sneer. "You demand that good and decent men whimper and snivel before you, and at the same time you blindly let banelings have a free run of the land."

"Banelings?" She glowered at Riggs. "I suppose you would be foolish enough to seek council from the Blood of the Fold."

"They've already joined with us," General Riggs said, offhandedly. "Our cause is theirs, and theirs ours. They know how to expunge those who would serve the Keeper and thus our enemies. We will cleanse the land of all who serve the Keeper. Goodness must triumph."

"You mean your cause. It is you who would rule."

"Are you blind, Confessor? I rule here, now, but this is not about me; it's about the future. I simply fill the post for now, furrow the field so it may produce. It's not I who is the focus.

"We offer everyone the chance to serve with us, and every man with me has taken that offer. Others have joined our troops in our battle. We are no longer D'Haran troops. They are no longer troops of their homeland. We are all the Imperial Order. Any of right mind can lead us. If I fall in our noble struggle, another will rise up to take my place, until all the lands are joined under united rule, and the Imperial Order can flower."

Either the man was too drunk to know what he was saying, or he was mad. She glanced about at the dancing, drunken, singing men at campfires all about. Mad as the Bantak. Mad as the Jocopo.

"General Riggs." He had been muttering angrily under his breath, but stopped and looked up at her. "I am the Mother Confessor. Like it or not, I represent the Midlands. In the name of the Midlands I call upon you to to halt this war immediately and either return to D'Hara, or come to the council with your grievances. You may petition the Central Council with any dispute you have, and it will be heard, but you may not visit war upon my people. You will not like the consequence if you choose not to heed my orders."

He sneered up at her. "We make no compromises. We'll annihilate all who don't join us. We fight to stop the killing, to stop the murdering, as the good spirits have called upon us to do. We fight for peace! Until we win peace, we will have war!"

She frowned. "Who told you this? Who told you that you must fight?"

He blinked at her. "It's self-evident, you stupid bitch!"

"You cannot possibly be so stupid as to think the good spirits tell you to wage war. The good spirits do not act in such overt ways."

"Ah, well then, we have a disagreement. That is the purpose of war, is it not? To settle such matters? The good spirits know us to be in the right, else they would easily join against us. Our victory will prove they side with us or we could not win in our struggle. The Creator Himself wishes to see us triumph, and our victory will be proof of that."

The man was a lunatic. She redirected her attention to the Keltish commander. "Karsh . . ."

"General Karsh."

"You demean the rank, General. Why did you slaughter the people of Ebinissia?"

"Ebinissia was given the opportunity to join us, as will all be given the opportunity. Ebinissia chose to fight. We had to make an example of her heathen people, to show others what awaits them if they fail to join us in peace. It cost us nearly half our men, but it was a goal worth the cost. Even now, those lost are being replaced by others joining with us, and we will swell in rank to take in all the known lands."

"This, you call leadership? Extortion and murder?"

General Karsh slammed his mug down on the table. His eyes were fire. "We visit upon them what they visit upon our people! They raid our farms, our border towns. They kill Keltans as if we were bugs to be stepped on!"

"Yet we offered them peace. It is they who chose to shun our mercy. They were offered a chance at peace, a chance to join us; they chose war. In that way, they chose to aid us; they've made an example for others of the folly of fighting us."

"And what have you done with Queen Cyrilla? Did you slaughter her, too, or is she back there in your whores' tents?"

They all laughed. "She would be," Riggs put in, "if we'd found her." Kahlan almost sighed aloud with relief.

She looked back to Karsh, who was taking another swig. "What has Prince Fyren to say of this?"

"Fyren's in Aydindril! I'm here!"

So, perhaps the Crown wasn't a part of this. Perhaps this was little more than a band of murdering outlaws who fancied themselves as more.

Kahlan knew Prince Fyren, knew him to be a reasonable man. Of the Keltish diplomats assigned to Aydindril, he was the one who had done the most to bring Kelton forward into the alliance of the Midlands through the Central Council. He cajoled and persuaded his mother, the queen, to go the route of peace rather than conflict. Prince Fyren was a gentleman, in every sense of the word.

"Besides being a murderer, General Karsh, you are also a traitor to your own land and Crown. To your own queen."

He hammered his pewter mug down on the table. "I'm a patriot! A protector of my people!"

She leaned the slightest bit forward. "You're a treasonous bastard and an outlaw cutthroat without conscience. I leave to Prince Fyren the honor of condemning you to death. It will, of course, be a posthumous sentence."

Karsh pounded his fist. "The good spirits know of your treachery against the people of the Midlands! This proves their words true! They've told us we cannot be free as long as you live! They've called upon us to kill all those like you! All those who blaspheme! The good spirits will not abandon us in our struggle. We shall defeat all who do the Keeper's bidding."

"No real officer," she said, contemptuously, "would listen to the babbling of the Blood."

The wizard had made an angry-looking ball of liquid fire, and was slowly juggling it back and forth between his hands while he watched her. The flames spit and hissed, dropping little sparks. General Riggs belched and then put his knuckles on the table as he leaned toward her.

"Enough talking. Get down here, you little wench, so we can start the party. Us brave freedom fighters need a little fun."

General Karsh at last smiled. "And then tomorrow, or perhaps the next day, you will be beheaded. Our men, our people, will rejoice at your death. They will exult in our triumph over the Mother Confessor, the symbol of oppression by magic." His smile left as he turned red-faced once more. "The people must see your punishment to know that good can prevail! To have hope! When we have your head, our people can rejoice!"

"Rejoice that all you brave freedom fighters are strong enough to kill a single woman?"

"No," General Riggs said. He appeared for the first time sober as he looked up at her. "You miss the true meaning of what we do. You fail to see its significance."

His voice lowered, his tone softened. "It's a new age we enter, Confessor. An age that has no place for your old religions. The line of Confessors and their wizards is at an end.

"There was a time, three thousand years ago, when nearly everyone was born with the gift. Magic held sway over all things. That magic was used to vie for power. Wizards abused their power. In their greed, they killed one another. They killed others who had the gift, and so fewer lived to pass it on. Over time, those with the gift were culled from the race of men.

"Yet those left still contested for rule, and further thinned the ranks of those born with the gift. The magic, the other creatures of magic who were their charges, such as you, have been steadily stripped of their protection and fount of magic. Today there are almost none born with the gift. Magic itself is dying with them. They have had their chance to rule, just as did Darken Rahl with his magic, and they have failed. Their time, the time of wizards, is past.

"Their protection of the twilight beings is at an end, and so the age of magic is at an end. The time of man is upon us now, and there is no place in that world for the ancient, dying religion you call magic. It is time for man to take his place as inheritor of the world. The Imperial Order is upon the world, now, and if it were not them, it would be man by another name. It is time for man to rule, for magic to die."

Kahlan felt a sudden hollowness. An unexpected tear ran down her cheek. A choking feeling of true panic clawed at her throat.

"Do you hear that, Slagle?" she whispered hoarsely. "You have magic. The ones you aid would put an end to you, too."

He tossed the little ball of fire to his other hand, the light of its flames dancing across his grim face. "It is as it must be. Magic, chaste or foul, is the Keeper's conduit to this world. When I have helped extinguish magic in all its forms, then I, too, must die. In that way, I will serve the people."

Riggs gazed up to her, almost sorrowfully, as he went on.

"Our people must see the last living embodiment of that religion die. You are its symbol, the last creature of magic created by wizards. With your death, they will be filled with hope for the future, and be emboldened to extinguish all the remaining pockets of filth and perversion that are magic.

"We are the plowshare. Those lands now infested with magic will be freed of its taint, and can be resettled by pious people. Then, at last, we shall all be free of your dogmas, which have no part in the glory of the future of man."

He straightened, taking a drink from his mug. The harshness returned to his voice. "After we finish with you, then we'll bring Galea to heel, and the rest of the lands." He slammed the mug down. "Until complete and total victory is ours, we demand war!"

Rage swelled in her, banishing the momentary sensation of loss and panic, swelled on behalf of all those beings, the twilight beings, who depended upon her for voice and protection.

She nodded slowly as she held the general's gaze.

"In my capacity as Mother Confessor, the highest rank of authority in the Midlands, to whose mandate all must bow, I grant your wish." She leaned forward and spoke in a hiss. "Let there be war. On my word and office, not one of you shall be granted quarter."

Kahlan's fist came up to the wizard. It was for him she had come.

Her chest heaved with wrath, and with terror at the madness of these men. She let the magic surge within her, demanding release, demanding this wizard's death.

It was for him she had come. She must not fail. The Blood Rage screamed through her.

She called the lighting forth.

Nothing happened.

She froze for an instant in the panic of the failure of the magic. Then Riggs lunged for her leg.

Kahlan hauled back on the reins. The ferocious warhorse sprang into battle. He bellowed as he reared, kicking his front legs. Kahlan grasped his mane for dear life. A lashing hoof caught Riggs across the face, throwing him back. The thrashing hooves crashed down on the table, shattering it to splinters. Men in chairs toppled backward. Nick's front hooves crushed the head of one of the D'Haran officers, the leg of another.

The horse spun and kicked at the men. Kahlan gave him her heels, and he leapt into a gallop as the wizard was rising to his feet. Surprised men threw themselves out of the way. She took a quick glance over her shoulder to see the wizard throwing his hands out. A ball of wizard's fire exploded to life before him, turning in the air, awaiting command. He threw his arms out again, sending the fire on its way toward her.

The warhorse leapt over fires and men, kicking up both snow and flaming firewood. His legs caught tent lines, yanking them down. Kahlan spotted what she wanted, what she wanted more than life itself, and maneuvered the horse for it.

She could hear the wail of the wizard's fire coming for her. She could hear the screams of men unexpectedly caught up in it. She stole another glance to see the blue and yellow ball of flame tumbling through the tents and men, growing all the time, taking a course as drunken as the wizard. Wizard's fire had to be guided, and in his state, the wizard was having difficulty controlling what he had wrought. Were he sober, she would be dead by now.

*Dear spirits*, she prayed, *if I'm to die, let me have time enough first to do what I must.*

403

Kahlan reached her goal. As she galloped past, she yanked a lance from a snowbank and wheeled her horse. She dug her heels in, and Nick leapt ahead at a full gallop.

The ball of fire wailed toward her, setting tents and men afire. It grew and tumbled as the distance closed.

The lance was unexpectedly heavy, made for men who had more muscle than she, and she had to carry it upright to save her strength. The warhorse didn't flinch as he galloped, not at the noise, the confusion, the running men, or the wizard's fire. She pulled to one side and then the other, Nick's hooves digging into the packed snow. She dodged obstacles, weaving her way toward the wizard's fire at full speed. Toward the wizard.

Slagle tried to change the course of the fire, to block her advance, each time she wove in her headlong rush. His reactions were slow, but as the distance closed, she knew he wouldn't need to be fast to catch her up in it.

At the last instant, she wheeled her horse around to the right. The fire roared by so close she could smell burnt hair, and then she was racing again.

As she charged the horse ahead, the wizard's fire exploded behind, cascading across the ground like a burst dam. The horrifying death screams of man and beast caught in the conflagration filled the night air. Dozens of men, all afire, rolled through the snow, trying to put out the flames. But wizard's fire was not so easy to extinguish; it was alive with purpose.

The howls of pain panicked those around who didn't know what was happening. Men screamed in fear of spirits they thought were setting upon them. Swords were drawn and wielded, hacking at those running for their lives from the fire. Battle erupted out of nothing. The air carried not only the choking stench of burning flesh, but now blood.

She ignored the screams and sought the silence within.

The wizard stumbled backward and fell. He came to his feet whirling his arms. Fire formed in the air at the arc of his fingertips.

Though there was confusion all about, only one thing filled her vision. The wizard.

She couched the lance, tucking the base under her right armpit, jamming her grip tight against the leather stop. Gritting her teeth, she used all her strength to lift the heavy lance over Nick's bobbing head, to the left side, so as not to unbalance herself in the saddle.

Nick took her direction as if he could read her mind. She steered him at full speed, but it seemed to her that the last ten yards took hours, a race between her charge and the wizard calling forth fire.

Wizard Slagle looked up to direct the fire just as her lance caught him in the chest. The impact shattered the lance to splinters at midlength and nearly tore the wizard in half. She and her horse flew through a spray of blood.

Kahlan swung the half lance at a man lunging for her, catching him across the head. The impact tore the lance from her grip. She wheeled the horse and leaned forward over his withers as she galloped at full speed back through the confusion around the command tents. Her heart pounded as fast as the horse's hooves.

One of the D'Haran officers from the table was up and screaming for a horse. Men leapt onto horses bareback. As she began putting distance between them, she could hear him yell that if they failed to catch her they would be drawn and quartered to a man. A quick glance showed a good three dozen riders joining the chase.

Away from the command tents, back the way she had come, men didn't know what was happening, and saw a galloping rider as simply part of the drunken festivities. None moved to stop her. Men, tents, fires, polearms and lances stuck upright in the snow, stacks of pikes, horses, and wagons all flashed by in a blur.

Nick jumped anything he couldn't dodge. The threat of him not jumping or dodging had men diving for cover. Men at games tumbled out of the way, coin and dice flying into the air. Tents pulled up when their lines crossed Nick's legs flew up and billowed in a tangle behind, catching up her pursuers. Horses and riders crashed to the ground. Others ran over their own men in their frenzied attempt to keep her in sight.

Kahlan spotted a sword hanging in a scabbard that was fastened to the side of a wagon, and as she ran past, she pulled it free. Galloping past picket lines, she swung the sword, cutting the lead lines. She hacked the rump of one horse as she charged past. He kicked and screamed in fright and pain, panicking the rest of the horses. They bolted headlong in every direction. Lanterns on poles toppled onto tents, setting them afire.

The horses in pursuit balked at the fires, rearing and bucking, throwing their riders to the ground. A man lunged suddenly into her path, avoiding Nick's flying hooves and grabbing for her. Kahlan drove the sword home through his chest as she flew by. The hilt tore from her hand. She leaned forward and held on as Nick raced through the endless camp. The men chasing weren't as close, but they were still coming.

Suddenly, she was free of the camp, galloping through the open snow. Kahlan followed her own tracks across the flat by the waning light of the moon. The muscular horse plowed through the snow almost as if it weren't there.

She reached the trees at last, and before plunging in and ascending the steep slopes, she checked over her shoulder.

A good fifty men were not three minutes behind. She would be able to open the lead as she went up along the forest trail, but they would still catch her.

She would see to that.

$E$asy now," she cautioned. One hesitant hoof slipped. "Back, back, back. Come on boy, back."

From down the slope behind, she could hear the sounds of the chase; a man, probably one of the D'Haran officers, yelling angrily at the top of his lungs not to let her get away, and others urging their horses up the steep trail. When they reached the flat where she was, they would be in a full gallop again.

Kahlan tugged gently on the reins. Nick lifted his hoof from the ice and backed up, into the tight gap between the snow-crusted pines, back along his trail.

She found the long branch, with the forked end she had whittled to a pushing pole, stuck upright in the snow where she had left it beside the twin trunked spruce. She hefted it up, and started pushing the heavy, snow-laden branches. Her shoulder ached from having the lance shattered as she held it under her arm.

As she backed Nick between the trees, off her trail, she held the long push-stick out over his head, jostling the limbs. Relieved of their loads, they sprang up, partly screening the gap between the trees. More importantly, the snow tumbled to the ground, piling over her tracks. She pushed at a branch here, another there, sprinkling their snow over Nick's backing trail, covering it in, making it look natural, as if wind had simply freed the branches of their load.

She said a silent thank-you to Richard, for teaching her about tracks. He had said he would make a woods woman of her. She ached for Richard. She was sure he wouldn't approve of the desperate risk she was undertaking with the aid of what he had taught her.

But she couldn't allow these men to track her back to the Galean boys. There was a chance that some would carry word of what they had seen back, and then the Galeans would be slaughtered. If none of these men returned, it would be a long while before any more were sent, if ever.

Even if they were, by then it would be too late; she would have long been up and over the passes from which she had come, where the wind howled and drifted the snow constantly, and her tracks would be lost to them. They would not know where she had gone. From there, the mountains and forests went on in endless tracts, and her trail would have been last seen leading steadily away from her true destination. Those back at camp would have confidence that these soldiers would have her sooner or later, and with the prospect of plunder only days away, they would turn their attention to it instead.

The snow-muffled thundering of hooves brought her mind back to what she was doing. The men had reached the flat, and were charging at full speed again. Steadily, she worked her way back into the trees, shaking branches, covering her trail, backing toward the way she had come on her way to the army of the Imperial Order. The sounds of chase were almost upon her.

Kahlan leaned almost all the way over, stroking an arm along her horse's neck. She whispered toward his ears, and they swiveled back to the sound of her voice.

"Quiet now, Nick. Please don't move or make a sound." She stroked his sweaty neck again. "Good boy. Quiet now."

It sounded, to her, as if anyone would be able to plainly hear her heart beating in her chest.

The pursuers had reached her. As they charged along her trail, right in front of her, they broke through the screen of trees to her left, not ten yards away, at full speed. Kahlan held her breath.

She heard the clop of hooves as they hit the sloping ice hiding in the moon shadows beyond those trees, beyond her false trail. She had led her tracks between those trees, to the edge of a steep, rocky stream, where its water would tumble, were it not frozen, over a cliff.

It was a small stream, but as it froze, more water had bubbled and frothed over that which was already frozen, growing the area into an ice palace. Snow had been washed away as it fell, leaving the rounded, downward-sloping humps of ice bare and slick.

As the men broke through the trees, they had not twenty feet to halt their headlong rush before the cliff's edge, before the rock and ice halted, and only thin air lay beyond. And they had to do it on cascading mounds of ice. Were it flat ice, like a lake, the horses could have dug their iron shoes in, and tried to skid to a halt. But this was not flat, it was water slicked tumble-down ice, and as they slipped and slid and tripped and fell at a charge, they had no chance.

Kahlan could hear the pop of horses' legs breaking, as thousands of pounds of muscle moving at full speed could not be stopped by hooves catching in crevices. The bareback riders were helpless passengers.

The men shouted encouragement to their mounts, and the ones behind didn't recognize quickly enough the change in shrieking from anger to fright. Those behind crashed into those ahead, tumbling over and past each other. Bareback, with only halters and no aggressive battle bits, the riders didn't have the control they were accustomed to, and were carried helplessly forward.

Some leapt from their mounts as they came through the trees, and could see what lay ahead, but their momentum was too great, the distance too short, their fate beyond retrieval. The horses behind, their leg bones snapping, crashed down atop the ones already fallen, who were desperately grasping for a hold. There was none. It became a waterfall of living flesh, cascading over the edge.

Kahlan sat still, wearing her Confessor's face, as she listened to the screams of man and horse mingled together into one long wail as they disappeared over the mountainside. In the span of mere seconds, it was finished; more than fifty men and their mounts had plunged to their deaths.

When the night had been silent for a time, she dismounted and circled around, to keep her false trail free of any off-leading tracks, to the edge of the ice flow. In the dim light she could see the dark stains of blood over the ice mounds. Blood from broken legs, blood from cracked skulls. There were none of the enemy left on the cliff.

As she turned to leave, she heard low grunts of desperation. Kahlan pulled her knife and carefully inched her way to the source of the sounds, toward the edge.

Grasping a stout limb, she leaned out over the slanting ice flow. Forest debris was frozen in the ice; sticks and leaves had made a small dam at the edge, to be covered over as the ice grew. It left a few branches sticking out of the wall of ice.

Around one of these branches were clutched fingers. A man clung by his fingertips to the branch, his legs dangling over a drop of close to a thousand feet. He was grunting with effort as he tried to catch his feet up on the ice, but it was too slippery to give him any toehold.

Kahlan stood at the edge, holding the branch for support, as she watched him shivering. Dribbles of water bubbled over the ice, over his face, matting his hair and soaking his Keltish uniform. His teeth chattered.

He looked up to see her standing over him in the moonlight. "Help me! Please help me!" He couldn't have been past her age.

She regarded him without emotion. He had big eyes, the kind of eyes young women would surely have swooned over. But the young women in Ebinissia would not have swooned when they saw those eyes.

"In the name of the good spirits, help me!"

Kahlan squatted down, closer to him. "What is your name?"

"Huon! My name's Huon! Now please help me!"

Kahlan lay down on the ice, hooking a foot around a tangled root, taking a good grip on the stout spruce limb with one hand. She extended her other hand partway out, but not far enough for Huon to reach.

"I will help you, Huon, on a condition. I have sworn no mercy, and none shall be granted. If you take my hand, I will release my power into you. You will be mine, now and forever. If you are to live, it will be as one touched by a Confessor. If you would think to pull me over the edge with you before I can release my magic, let me assure you I would not make the offer were there that chance. I have touched more men than I can count. You will have no time. You will be mine."

He blinked icy water dripping down on him from his eyes, shook it from his face, and stared up at her.

Kahlan extended her hand toward him. "From now on, Huon, either way, your old life is ended. If you live it will not be as who you are now. That man will be gone forever. You will be mine."

"Please," he whispered, "just help me up. I won't hurt you. I swear to let you be on your way. It would take me hours to make it back to camp on foot, and you'll be long gone by then anyway. Please, just help me up."

"How many people in Ebinissia did you hear beg for their lives? To how many did you grant mercy?" Her words came as cold as the ice she lay on. "I am the Mother Confessor. I have proclaimed war without quarter on the Imperial Order. The oath stands as long as one of you lives. Choose, Huon. Death, or to be touched by my power. Either way, who you are dies."

"The people of Ebinissia got what they deserved. I'd rather take the hand of the Keeper himself than be touched by your filthy magic. The good spirits would never accept me to them if I were touched by your dark and profane magic." His lip curled in a sneer. "To the Keeper with you, Confessor!"

Huon threw his arms open and silently dropped away into the darkness.

As she rode back to the Galean recruits, she thought about the things Riggs, Karsh, and Slagle had told her. She also thought about the creatures of magic living in the Midlands.

She thought about the beautiful land of the night wisp, with open fields deep in ancient, remote forests, where the wisps gathered at twilight to dance together in the air above the grasses and wildflowers, like joyous fireflies. She had spent many a night lying on her back in the grass as they hovered above her and spoke with her of things common to all life: of dreams and hopes; of loves.

She thought about the creatures living in Long Lake, translucent things hard to see, seeming almost made of liquid glass, or of the water that was their home, with whom she had never spoken, but whom she had watched emerge at night to bask in the moonlight on rock and shore; creatures who had no voice, but with whom she had shared understanding, and had promised to protect.

She thought about the whispering tree people, whom she had spoken with in a hauntingly beautiful experience, frighteningly eerie, but somehow gently peaceful at the same time.

The whispering tree people were all joined as one, through their roots touching under the earth, and each spoke as if they were all but one, as if there were no individuals; yet each had a name to whisper to you if you made it promises of simple favors, a mass community that was at the same time all only one. To cut down a tree there would be to bring the pain of that one's death to all; they could not escape the contact they felt with each other. If people went into that land and cut down the trees, it would be torture to all. Kahlan had seen them in pain before. Their wails could make the stars cry.

There were other creatures, too, that were magic, and people, too, who possessed it. Sometimes it was hard to place a line between creatures of the wild and people. Some people of the Midlands were part creature, or perhaps some creatures were part people. They were strange and delightful, and very shy.

And so it went throughout various forms of magic, from the simplest things in the Howling Caves that could let you peek through solid rock to see their nests, to people like the Mud People, who had only simple magic that would do but one thing.

As Mother Confessor, all these, and many more, were her charges, and as Mother Confessor, she commanded all to protect these magic places, so no one people would bear the brunt of burden against others. It was an arrangement backed by Confessors and wizards extending back for thousands of years.

The twilight beings, Riggs had called them. That was the name given to these magical creatures by the Blood of the Fold, among others, because many of them came out only at night. For this reason, the Blood associated them with darkness, and so, out of fear, with the darkness of the Keeper of the Dead.

The Blood considered magic the force through which the Keeper extended his influence into this world, into the world of the living. The Blood were as unreasonable and thickheaded as any men alive. And they considered it their duty to send to the land of the dead any who they thought served the Keeper. That was just about anyone who disagreed with their view of things. In some lands the Blood were outlawed, and in some, like Nicobarese, they were encouraged and paid by the Crown.

Maybe Riggs was right. Maybe she should have brought the rule of law to stop men like this. But that had never been the intent of the council—to make all to bow in all things to one. The strength and beauty of the Midlands was in its diversity, even if some of that diversity was ugly. What was ugly to one was beautiful to another, and so it was that each land was to be left to rule itself, as long as it brought no force of arms to another. It was a tolerant suffering of things repugnant to allow things beautiful to blossom. It was a sometimes difficult and fine line to hold the council to: forcing lands to work together in some things, but allowing them to be autonomous in others.

But perhaps Riggs was right. People in some lands suffered the cruel or poor rule of their greedy or inept leaders, with no hope of matters being brought to change from without. Though the wise, but smaller, lands had not to live in fear of outside conquest. If the suffering of the people under less fortunate rule could be ended with wise central rule, would not matters be improved?

Yet when all lived under the same rule, every other form of existence was extinguished, never to have the chance to grow, though one of them might have been a superior way. The kind of single rule the Imperial Order represented was slavery.

Kahlan was surprised to encounter Galean sentries farther from their camp than before. They were no longer spread too far apart, and they were well hidden, popping up with drawn bows and bared steel when she was almost upon them. Chandalen, Prindin, and Tossidin had obviously been at work. The sentries put fists to hearts when they recognized her.

The dawn was turning the sky to a dark steel gray. It was warmer than it had been, with the clouds covering the land like a warming quilt. She was dead tired in the saddle as Nick plodded through the snow toward the camp, but as she came into sight of men rushing about, she came alert with the thoughts of what needed to be done.

Chandalen, Prindin, Captain Ryan, and Lieutenant Hobson were speaking with a group of men when they saw her riding toward the camp. The four came at a run to meet her at the edge of the activity. Men were cooking, eating, stowing gear, preparing weapons, and tending to wagons and horses. She spotted Tossidin, in his white wolf mantle, off some distance with Lieutenant Sloan, waving his arms in explanation as he talked to men who stood mute, with their spears all standing upright in the snow, the tight mob of them looking like a dark porcupine against the white ground.

Kahlan let out a weary moan as she dismounted before the four men who had come to greet her. Other men all around kept to their tasks, but moved more slowly as they watched her with great interest. The four before her stared openly with wide eyes. None said a word.

"What are you all staring at?" she said, a little short-tempered.

"Mother Confessor," Captain Ryan said, "you're covered in blood. Are you hurt?"

Kahlan stared down at the white wolf fur of her mantle, only it was no longer white. She realized for the first time that the skin of her face was tight with dried blood, her hair stiff with it.

"Oh," she said, in a quieter tone. "It's all right. I'm fine."

Chandalen and Prindin sighed with relief.

Lieutenant Hobson, still wide-eyed, swallowed. "What of the wizard? Did you see him?"

She lifted an eyebrow to him. "What you see on me is what's left of him."

Chandalen appraised her with a sly smile. "And how many others did you kill?"

Kahlan gave a tired shrug. "I was awfully busy. I didn't take the time to count, but all things considered, I would guess, including the fires, well over a hundred. The wizard is dead, that's what matters. Two of their commanders are dead also, and at least two more are wounded."

Captain Ryan and Lieutenant Hobson paled.

Chandalen's proud grin widened. "I am surprised you left any for others to kill, Mother Confessor."

She didn't return his smile. "There are plenty left." Kahlan rubbed her horse's nose. "Nick did most of the work."

"I told you he wouldn't let you down, Mother Confessor," Hobson said.

"That he did not. He was better aid than the good spirits. He kept me alive this day."

Kahlan lowered herself to one knee in the snow before the two Galean officers. She bowed her head.

"I find I must beseech your forgiveness." She took a hand of each in hers. "Though you are ignorant of how to accomplish what must be done, you have put your duty to the Midlands before my orders. That was courage of the highest order. I want you all to know I was wrong. You acted of noble intent." She kissed each hand. "I laud your righteous hearts. You have kept in mind your duty above all else. I beg you forgive me."

There was silence as she knelt on one knee. At last Captain Ryan whispered down to her.

"Mother Confessor, please. Get up. Everyone's watching."

"Not until you forgive me. I want everyone to know you did the right thing."

"But you didn't realize what we were doing, or why. You had only our safety in mind." Kahlan waited and he was silent in embarrassment a moment longer. "All right. I forgive you. . . . Don't do it again?"

She came to her feet, releasing their hands and giving them a small, humorless smile. "See that that is the last time you ever disobey me."

Captain Ryan nodded in earnest. "I will." He shook his head. "I mean, no, I won't, I mean I . . . We will do as you command, Mother Confessor."

"I understand what you mean, Captain." She let out a tired sigh. "We have a lot of work to do before we attack those men."

"We!" Chandalen shouted. "We were only to teach them some things, and then 'we' are to be on our way to Aydindril! We cannot become caught up in this battle. You have already taken enough chances! We must . . ."

Kahlan interrupted him. "I must talk to you three. Bring Tossidin. Captain, please collect the men, including the sentries. I want to speak to you all together. Please wait with your men. I will be with you shortly. And leave a tent up for me. I need a few hours' sleep while things are being prepared."

She walked off a ways, out of earshot of the camp, with Chandalen in tow, as Prindin went to get Tossidin. When they were all together, she turned to them. Chandalen was scowling, the other two waited without emotion.

"The Mud People," she began in a soft tone, "have magic."

"We have no magic," Chandalen argued.

"Yes, you do. You do not think of it as magic because you were born with it and it is the only way you know. You do not know of other peoples, of their ways. The Mud People can speak with their ancestors' spirits. They can do this because they have magic. You think this is simply the way things work, but they do not work so in other places, with other people. Your ability to do these things is magic. Magic is not some strange and powerful force, it's simply the way some people, some creatures, are."

"Others can speak with their ancestors, if they wish," Chandalen said.

"A few can, but most cannot. To them, it's speaking with the dead, and that is magic. Frightening magic. You, and I, know it is not to be feared, but you will never convince others that what you do is good. They will always think it evil. People believe as they were raised, and they were raised to believe that talking to the dead is evil."

"But our ancestors' spirits help us," Prindin said. "They never bring harm. They only bring help."

Kahlan laid a hand on his shoulder as she looked to his worried eyes. "I know. That's why I help to keep others away from you, so you may live as you wish. There are a few other people who talk with their ancestors, as you do, and they, too, have this magic. There are other peoples, and other creatures, that have magic different from you, but just as important to them as yours is to you." She looked to each. "Do you understand."

"Yes, Mother Confessor," Tossidin said.

Prindin nodded his agreement. Chandalen grunted and folded his arms.

"The important thing, though, is not if you believe what you have can be called magic. The important thing is for you to understand that others believe what you do is magic. Many fear magic. They think you are evil because you practice this magic."

Kahlan pointed in the direction of the army of the Imperial Order. "Those men, the ones we chase, the ones who killed all the people back at the city, they are joined in a cause. They wish to rule all the people of the Midlands. They do not want any to live as they wish, but to bow to their rule."

"Why would they wish to rule the Mud People?" Prindin asked. "We have nothing they would want. We stay to our lands."

Chandalen unfolded his arms and spoke softly. "They fear magic, and they wish us to stop speaking with our ancestors."

Kahlan squeezed his shoulder. "That's right. But more than that, they think it's their duty to the spirits they worship to kill you all. They are on a mission to destroy all who have magic, because they think magic is evil. They believe people like you have magic." She met Chandalen's eyes. "If they are not killed to a man, like the Jocopo, sooner or later, they will come and destroy the Mud People, just as they destroyed the city of Ebinissia."

The three men studied the ground in thought. She waited for them to weigh her words. Chandalen at last spoke.

"And they would kill the other people, those who wish not to have outsiders come to them, to live alone, like the Mud People?"

"They would. I spoke with the men of that army. They are like crazy men. They sound as if they have been visited by evil spirits, like the Bantak did. Like the Jocopo. They will not listen to reason. They think we are the ones who listen to evil spirits. They will do as they promise. You saw the city they destroyed and the size of the army defending it; it is not an empty threat.

"I must get to Aydindril so I can raise an army to fight these men. The councilors should already be doing that, but I must get there to make sure the extent of the threat is known, to make sure all of the Midlands joins together in this.

"But there are no forces at hand to fight these men, now, except these boys. There are cities that will be destroyed before help can arrive. Worse, the threat these men pose will convince some to join with them. Some see honor as an inconvenience and will side with the army they think will win. This will swell their ranks further.

"Before Aydindril can send troops to find and defeat these men, many will die. We must call upon these boys to join the fight now, before more innocent people are slaughtered. These boys volunteered to become fighters, like you, to protect their people, the people of all the Midlands. We must help them in this. We must not let this army of evil men escape to wander the Midlands, killing and destroying, and winning more to their side.

"We must begin the battle with these boys, help them, show them, to make sure they will know how to fight, and to know they will continue without us to lead them. We must lead them into the first battle, to give them confidence in the ways we teach them, before we can be on our way to Aydindril."

Chandalen gave her a level look. "And you will call the lightning to help us?"

"No," Kahlan whispered. "I tried last night, but it didn't come. It's difficult to explain to you, but I believe that because I invoked this special magic on behalf of Richard, it will not work except to protect him. I'm sorry."

Chandalen unfolded his arms. "Then how did you kill so many?"

Kahlan patted his arm where the bone knife was. "The same way as your grandfather taught your father, and he you. I did not do as they expected. I did not fight their way." The two brothers leaned in intently as she spoke. "They like to drink, and when they're drunk, they don't think so well, and they are slow."

Tossidin pointed behind with a thumb. "These men, too, like to have drink at night. They have a wagon of it among their supplies. We would not let them have any. Some were angry. They said it was their right."

Kahlan shook her head. "These boys also thought it would be right to march right up to an enemy who outnumbers them ten to one and have a battle in broad daylight. We must help them in this. We must teach them what to do."

"They do not like to listen." Prindin glanced back over his shoulder, at the men he had been trying to teach. "They wish always to argue. They say 'This is the way it is done' and 'We must do it so.' They are filled only with the way they were taught, and do not like to be told another way."

"Yet that's what we must do," Kahlan said. "We must lead them in the way that will work. That's why I need you three. I need you to help me in this, or many people, including, eventually, the Mud People, will die. I need your help in this. I must lead them into battle."

Chandalen stood mute and unmoving. The two brothers pushed snow with their feet, considering. Prindin finally looked up.

"We will help. My brother and I will do as you ask."

"Thank you, Prindin, but it's not you who must decide. Chandalen must be the one who agrees. It is for him to decide."

The two brothers took sidelong glances at him as he stood glaring at her. At last he let out an exasperated breath.

"You are a stubborn woman. You are so stubborn you will get killed if we three are not there to bring some reason to your head. We go with you to kill these evil men."

Kahlan sighed with relief. "Thank you, Chandalen." She bent and took up a handful of snow, using it to scrub the dried blood from her face. "Now I must go and tell these boys what they must do." She shook the snow from her hands when she had finished with her face. "Did you three get any sleep last night?"

"Some," Chandalen said.

"Good. After I speak with them, I need to get a few hours' sleep. You can begin showing them how to travel without their wagons. We must teach them to be strong, like you. We will begin the killing tonight?"

Chandalen gave a grim nod. "Tonight."

Kahlan climbed atop a wagon before the assembled men. They stood in brown wool coats, packed tightly together before her in the gray morning light. Captain Ryan, with his two lieutenants flanking him, stood at the front of the men. He leaned an arm on the wagon wheel, waiting.

Kahlan looked out at all the young faces. Boys. She was about to ask boys to die. But what choice did she have?

*Dear mother,* she wondered, *is this the reason you chose Wyborn as my father? To teach me what I am about to do?*

"I'm afraid I have only one bit of good news for you," she began in a quiet voice that carried through the cold air, out over the faces all watching her, "and so I will give you that first, to give you courage for the other things I have to tell you."

Kahlan took a deep breath. "Your queen was not killed in Ebinissia, nor did the men who attacked the city find or capture her. Either she was away when the attack came, or she escaped.

"Queen Cyrilla lives."

The boys seemed to take a deep breath, as if hoping she wouldn't add anything more, and then they erupted in wild cheering. They threw their arms in the air, shaking their fists at the sky. They yelled and hooted with joy and relief.

Kahlan stood in her blood-soaked wolf mantle, her hands at her sides, letting them have their time of celebration and hope. Some of the boys, forgetting for the moment that they were soldiers, hugged each other. She watched tears of happiness run down many a cheek as men leapt and shouted.

Kahlan stood feeling small and insignificant as the mob of boys poured out their adoration for her half sister. She couldn't bring herself to halt their rejoicing.

At last Captain Ryan climbed up onto the wagon next to her. He held his arms up, calling for silence.

"All right! All right! Hold it down! Stop acting like a bunch of children in front of the Mother Confessor! Show her what men you be!"

The cheering finally died out, to be replaced by grins and bright eyes. Captain Ryan clasped his hands together and cast her a somewhat sheepish look before taking a couple of steps away atop the wagon, to give her room.

"The people of Ebinissia," she went on, in the same quiet tone, "were not so fortunate."

The winter silence became brittle. Light breezes rustled icy branches on the trees ascending the slopes to either side of the flat valley pass holding their camp. The grins withered.

"Every one of you, at the least, had friends who were murdered there. Many of you had loved ones, family, who died at the hands of the men a few hours up this pass." Kahlan cleared her throat and swallowed as her eyes found the ground. "I, too, knew people who died there."

Her eyes came up. "Last night, I went to their camp, to discover who they were, and if they could be called upon to return to their homelands. They have no intention of doing anything but conquering all the lands and putting them under their rule. They have vowed to kill everyone who refuses to join them. Ebinissia refused."

The boys shouted and shook their fists. They, themselves, they said, would bring an end to the threat.

She spoke over their words, bringing them to silence as she did so. "The men who slaughtered your countrymen and countrywomen are called the Imperial Order. They fight on behalf of no country or land. They fight to conquer all lands, and to rule all lands. They answer to no government, to no king, to no lord, to no council. They believe themselves to be the fountain of law.

"They are made up of mostly D'Haran men, but others have joined them. I saw among them Keltans."

Waves of angry whispers swept back through the crowd. Kahlan let it go on for a moment. "I saw also, among them, men from other lands. And I saw Galeans."

This time shocked and angry voices called out that it wasn't true, and said she was wrong.

"I saw them with my own eyes!" They fell once more to silence. She quieted her tone. "I wish that it were not true, but I saw them. Men of many lands have joined with them. More men will join with them if they believe they can be part of the victory, part of the new law, if they believe they can be in on the plunder and awarded positions of authority and power.

"The city of Cellion lies hardly more than a hand of days ahead. The Imperial Order will have their surrender and allegiance, or their death.

"Other cities, towns, villages, and farms will suffer these men if they are not stopped. Eventually, all will come under their sword. I am going to Aydindril to marshal the forces of the Midlands against the Imperial Order, but that will take time. In that time, their numbers will swell with those who would think to be on the side of might. Right now, there is no one able to stop these men from killing everyone in their path who resists them.

"Except you."

Kahlan stiffened her back as she let what she had said sink in, and in preparation for what she was going to tell them next. She let the silence settle once more over the valley.

"As the Mother Confessor of the Midlands, and absent the luxury of conferring with the Central Council, I have had to do that which no Mother Confessor for a thousand years or more has had to do. On my authority, alone, I have committed the Midlands to war. The army of the Imperial Order is to be killed to a man. No negotiation or compromise will be offered by the Midlands. Under no circumstances will the Order's surrender be accepted.

"I have given an oath on behalf of the Midlands that no quarter shall be granted."

Astonished faces stared at her.

"Whether I live or die, this decree is irrevocable. Any land or people who willingly join with the Imperial Order cast their lot under the shadow of this edict.

"It is not in the name of Galea that I call upon you to fight. In the office of the

416

Mother Confessor, I call upon you to fight for the Midlands. For it is not Galea that is under threat, but all lands, and all free people."

There was confident grumbling that they were up to the task. Some in the ranks called out their assurance that they were the men to do it, that they were in the right, and would triumph.

Kahlan nodded to them all. "You think so? I want each of you to look to the faces around you." They mostly stared at her. "Do as I say! Look to all the faces around you! Look to your comrades!"

A little confused, they began looking around, twisting to see those to the sides and those behind, smiling and laughing among themselves, as if it were a game.

When they seemed to have finished with the task, she went on. "A few of you will remember the faces you have looked upon today. Remember, and grieve. The rest, if you take up this battle, will not be around to remember. They will die in the struggle."

In the cold silence, Kahlan heard the distant chatter of a squirrel, and then the sound of that, too, died away.

The smiles were all gone as she finally spoke again. "These men, the Imperial Order, are led by and are mostly D'Haran troops. D'Haran soldiers are trained from the time they are half your age. They fight internal conflicts in their land, put down riots and rebellions; they do not simply practice battle tactics, they live them day in and day out. They know only a life of fighting. They have been exposed to it in every form. I have taken the confessions of many D'Harans. Most do not know the meaning of peace.

"Since spring, when Darken Rahl sent them against the Midlands, they have been at what they do best: war. They have fought in battle after battle. All who have come before them have fallen.

"They relish fighting. They delight in it. They are as close to fearless as men come. They hold contests, often lethal, to win the right to be in the van of battle, to win the right to be the first to strike a blow at the enemy, to win the right to be the first to fall."

She surveyed the young faces. "You have confidence in your training, your battle tactics?" The faces nodded, looking to one another, smiling their knowing confidence.

Kahlan pointed to one, a sergeant by the look of his coat's braids. "Tell me then. You are now in the field of battle, having chased down these men, and here comes the enemy, back at you. You are in charge of the pikes and archers. Here they come. Thousands of them, yelling, running, coming to rend your force in two, to break your army's back. You see they have heavy spears, called by them argons, with long, thin barbs. If they pierce you, they are nearly impossible to remove. They cause ghastly wounds that are almost always fatal. Here they come, with their argons. Thousands of men. What is your tactic?"

The young man held his chin out, knowingly. "Form a tight rank of the pikes formed into a box or wedge to protect the archers. The pikemen face the pikes out and overlapping the shields, present the enemy with a tight, impenetrable wall. The shields protect the pikemen, who protect the archers. The archers take them down before they can get close enough to use their argons. The few who do fall on the pikes. Their drive is repelled and, in all likelihood, they have lost a good many men in the failed attempt, making another less likely."

Kahlan nodded, as if impressed. "Well stated." He beamed. The men around him grinned with pride in their knowledge of their business. "I have seen some of the

417

most experienced armies of the Midlands use those very same tactics when the D'Harans first came over, last spring, when the boundary went down."

"Well, there you have it," the man said. "They lose their charge against the archers and on the point of our pikes."

She gave him a small smile. "The D'Haran van, those men I told you about, the biggest, the fiercest, the ones who won the right to be the first at you? Well, they've developed special tactics of their own, for use against your plans. First of all, they have arrow shields, so as they run in, they're protected from the brunt of the archers' work.

"And I guess I forgot to tell you one other thing about those argons of theirs. These spears have iron-sheathed shafts for most of their length, and a unique purpose. As the enemy is charging in, mostly unaffected by your archers, they heave their argons at you."

"We have shields," the man pointed out. "Their argons expended, they will be on the point of our pikes."

She folded her arms, nodding to him. "The van, the men who won the right to be the first wave, are big men. I doubt the smallest has arms less than twice the average of yours. The argons are needle sharp. Thrown by those powerful arms, they penetrate and stick in your shields. The long barbs prevent them from being withdrawn."

The confident smiles were fading as she looked from face to face as she went on. "You now have argons stuck solidly in your shields. You drop your pikes, drawing swords to hack the heavy spears away. But the shafts are covered in iron, and don't yield. The spears are heavy, and the butts drag the ground. D'Harans can run almost as fast as their spears fly. As they reach you now, they jump on the shafts of the spears stuck in your shields, dragging them to the ground, leaving you on your knees, and naked to their heavy axes."

Arms still folded, she leaned toward them. "I have seen men split from scalp to navel by those axes."

Men glanced sideways at one another, their confidence shaken.

She nodded mockingly as she unfolded her arms. "I am not giving you conjecture. I've seen a D'Haran force take down an experienced army nearly ten times their size in just this fashion. In the space of an hour, the battle turned from a rout of the D'Harans to a rout of their foes.

"A D'Haran charge of the argon is almost as devastating as a classic cavalry charge, except they have far greater numbers than any cavalry. And their own cavalry is anything but typical. You don't even want to know about them.

"They lost half their number in the slaughter of Ebinissia, and they are in camp, now, singing and drinking. Would you, if you lost every other one of you, be of good cheer?

"I know you believe you can win a battle against a force ten times your size, and I know also that such a thing can be done. But it is those experienced D'Haran troops who, on a battlefield, fighting by the tactics of common war, could bring about such a feat.

"Please believe me, I mean no disrespect to your bravery, but in the field of war, you are not their equal. Not yet. You could not defeat an army half their size were the battle fought the way your enemy would fight.

"That does not mean you cannot win. It means only that you must do it in another way. I believe you can win, and I'm going to tell you what you must do, and lead you in the first strike, to start you in this. The Imperial Order is not invincible. They can be defeated.

"From this day forward, I shall never again call you 'boys.' From this day forward, you are men.

"You think of yourselves as soldiers of your homeland, Galea. But you are not. In this, you are not. You are soldiers, men, of the Midlands. For it is not just Galea who will be conquered, but all of the Midlands, if these men are not stopped. I call upon you to stop them."

The tightly packed crowd of soldiers, tempered by what they had heard, shouted that they would do the job. She watched from under her eyebrows as they confidently pledged to fight to the end. There were angry whispers from some in the crowd, to her right. Men were jostling each other and arguing. Some men wanted to speak, and others were seeking to prevent it.

"If you should choose to join in this battle, you will follow orders without question," she said. "But for this time only, you may speak your mind freely, without retribution. If you have something to say, then let all hear it now, or else hold it to your grave."

One man pulled his arm free of another. He glowered up at her. "We're men. We don't follow women into battle."

Kahlan blinked at him. "You follow Queen Cyrilla."

"She is our queen, we fight on her behalf. She doesn't lead us in battle. That's left to men to do."

Kahlan narrowed her eyes. "What is your name?"

He glanced around at his fellows, and then held his chin up. "I'm William Mosle. And we've been trained by Prince Harold himself."

"And I," Kahlan said, "was trained by his father, King Wyborn. King Wyborn was my father, too. I am half sister to Queen Cyrilla and Prince Harold."

There were astonished murmurs throughout the crowd. Without taking her eyes from Mosle, she lifted a hand to silence them. "But that does not count for command. You are soldiers. Your duty is to follow the orders of your commanders, and they the queen, and she must follow commands of the Central Council of the Midlands. The council of the Midlands follows the orders of the Mother Confessor.

"For now, I fill that office. My family name is, like your queen's, Amnell, but I'm of Confessor blood, first, and last. I am the Mother Confessor of the Midlands, and as such, if I say you're to march into a lake, then it's your duty to march until you're breathing water and seeing fishes. Does that make it clear enough for you, soldier?"

A few other men were shoving at Mosle, urging him to go on with their grievances. "It means you can order us, it doesn't mean you know what you're doing."

Kahlan let out a sigh and pulled some blood-stiffened hair back, hooking it behind an ear. "I don't have the time, today, to tell you of all the training I've had, or of all the fighting against impossible odds I've been through, or the men I've had to kill in that fighting.

"I would tell you only that last night, I went alone to the camp of the Imperial Order to save your life. The men of the Order, D'Harans, fear the things of the night, spirits, and for protection from that and to assist them, they had a wizard in their company. Had you, in your confidence of battle knowledge, tried to attack those men, that wizard would have known what you were doing, and probably used magic to kill you all."

Mosle's defiant expression didn't diminish, but some of the others broke into worried whispers. Fighting against steel was one thing, fighting against magic quite another.

Captain Ryan stepped forward. "The Mother Confessor killed the wizard," he said with pride. There were relieved sighs among the men. "If it hadn't been for her experience, we would have marched to our deaths without even having the chance to lay steel to steel. I, for one, intend to follow those I've sworn my life to serve: my land, my queen, the Midlands, and the Mother Confessor.

"We're going to stop this threat against the Midlands, and we're going to do it by following those we are sworn to follow. We go into battle under the command of the Mother Confessor."

"I'm a soldier in the Galean army!" Mosle seemed only to get more defiant. "Not a soldier in any Midlands army! I fight for Galea, not to protect lands like Kelton!" Kahlan watched as other men shouted their agreement. "This army, the Imperial Order, or whatever they call themselves, is marching toward the border. Cellion is a border city, and most of it's on the other side of the river, in Kelton! Most of its citizens are Keltish! Why should we die for the Keltans?"

Men in the crowd were starting to argue with one another. Captain Ryan's face was red. "Mosle, you're a disgrace to . . .!"

Kahlan held a hand out to silence him. "No, soldier Mosle is only speaking as he believes, as I asked him to. You men must understand me. I'm not ordering you to do this. I'm asking you to fight for the lives of innocent people of the Midlands. Tens of thousands of your fellow soldiers have already died in this battle. I would not ask you to lay down your lives for something you do not believe in. Most who go into this war will die.

"It's your decision to stay or not. You are not commanded to stay. But if you choose to stay, it will be under my command. I want no man with us who does not believe in what we do.

"Decide now, if you will be with us or not. If not, then you are free to go, because you will be of no help to your comrades."

Her voice turned as cold as the thin morning air. "If you decide to go with me into this war, then you will follow the orders of your superiors. In the Midlands, there is no one to outrank me. You will follow my orders without question, or your punishment will be unsparing. Too much is at stake to have to suffer men who can't follow orders.

"If I say you will do something, then you will do it, even if you know it's to cost you your life, because it's to save many more lives. I give no orders without sound reason, but I won't always have time to explain them. Your duty is to trust in your superiors and do as you're told."

She held out a finger and swept it slowly over their heads. "Choose, then. With us, or not. But choose this day for all time."

Kahlan drew her hands back inside her warm fur mantle and waited in silence while men discussed and argued among themselves. Tempers flared, and angry oaths were given. Men gathered around Mosle, and others moved away from him.

"I'm leaving, then," Mosle called out to the others. He thrust his fist in the air. "I'll follow no woman into battle, no matter who she is! Who's leaving with me!"

About sixty or seventy men gathered about cheered their support for him.

"Go, then," Kahlan commanded. "Before you become caught up in a battle you do not believe in."

Having made their choice, Mosle and the men with him cast her glares of contempt. He swaggered forward. "We'll leave as soon as we can get our things together. We'll not be rushed out on your word."

The men in the crowd pushed in. Before it came to blows Kahlan held her hand up. "Stop! Let them be. They've made their choice. Let them get their things and be gone."

Mosle turned and pushed his way back through the throng, his new men in tow. As they left the gathered soldiers, Kahlan carefully counted their numbers. Sixty-seven. Sixty-seven who would leave.

She looked out at all the faces. "Any more? Do any more wish to leave?" No one moved a muscle. "Then do all of you wish to join in this fight?" A united cheer went up. "So be it. I wish I did not have to call upon you men to do this, but there is no one else to ask. My heart weeps for those of you who will die. Know that none of those who live will ever forget the sacrifice you make for them and the people of the Midlands."

From the corner of her eye, she watched the sixty-seven men moving among the wagons, taking the supplies they thought they would need. "And now, to what must be done."

Slowly, she shook her head. "You men must understand what it is I call upon you to do. It is no glorious battle, as you think, where you move like pieces on a game board. No tactics to outwit an opponent in a grand engagement. We will not face them in the field of battle, but kill them in every other way."

"But Mother Confessor," someone near the front timidly called out, "it's the code of honor for soldiers to face one another in battle, to best him in a fair fight."

"There is nothing fair about having to fight in war. The only fair thing would be to live in peace. The purpose of war is singular: to kill.

"You must all understand this, for it's central to your survival. There is no honor in killing, no matter the method. Dead is dead. Killing your enemy in war is done to protect the lives of those for whom you fight. Their lives arc no better protected by killing your enemy sword to sword than by slaying him while he sleeps, but only put at risk by it.

"There is no glory in this task. It's an onerous deed. We do not intend to give them a chance to engage in pitched battle, to see who is the better at the game. Our chore is simply to kill them.

"If you have difficulty seeing the right of this, then I call upon you to consider the honor of the soldiers you are up against. Consider them as they stood waiting in gangs to rape your mothers and sisters. Consider what your mothers and sisters in Ebinissia thought of honor as they were tortured and raped and slaughtered."

The chill of her words sent visible shudders through the stone-silent men. Kahlan had to restrain herself from bringing any more horror to their eyes, but before her still floated the vision of the young women in the palace.

"If the enemy is looking the other way, so much the better, because they will not thrust a knife into you. If it is from a distance, with an arrow, so much the better, because they will not have a chance to impale you on an argon. If it is while they have food in their mouths, so much the better, because they will not be able to raise an alarm. If it is while they are sleeping, so much the better, because they will not have a chance to cleave you with their sword.

"Last night, my horse crushed the head of one of the D'Haran commanders. There was no glory in that, no honor, only the knowledge that perhaps that deed will prevent some of you from dying by his hand and wits. In that, my heart sings with joy. Joy that maybe it has saved some of your precious lives.

"What we do is done to save the lives of men and women yet alive and yet unborn. You saw what was done to the people in Ebinissia. Remember the faces of those dead. Remembered the way they died, and the horror they suffered before they did. Remember those soldiers captured, and beheaded.

"It is up to us to prevent that from happening to any more people. To do that, we must kill these men. There is no glory in the doing. Only survival."

In the back, two men gestured obscenely to those around them and walked off to join with Mosle's men. Sixty-nine. But the rest stood in firm resolution to take up the fight.

The time had come. She had dissuaded them from their raw thoughts of glorious battle, and told them of the true nature of their task. She had brought most to an understanding of the larger temper of the battle ahead. She had told them some of what must be done. She had brought them to a more focused understanding of their importance in the scheme of this struggle.

The time had come to charge them irreversibly to the burden, to forge them into an instrument of retribution that could annihilate the threat.

Kahlan opened her arms to the men before her, her blood soaked mantle hanging limp.

"I am dead," she called to the gray sky. Frowning, they all leaned in a little. "What has happened to my countrymen, my countrywomen—my fathers, sons, mothers, and daughters—has slain me. The agony of their slaughter has mortally wounded my heart."

Her arms spread wider as her voice rose in wrath.

"Only vengeance can restore me! Only victory can return my life to me!"

She gazed into all the wide eyes staring back. "I am the Mother Confessor of the Midlands. I am your mothers, your sisters, your daughters yet unborn. I call upon you to die with me, and live again only by avenging me."

Kahlan swept a hand out. "Those of you who join with me in this are dead with me. Our lives can be returned only through vengeance. As long as one of our enemy lives, we are dead. We have no life to lose in this battle, for our lives are already lost, here, today, now. Only when every one of the destroyers of Ebinissia is slain may we live once again. Until then we have no life."

She looked out at the solemn faces of the men gathered before her, watching, waiting for her next words. On a warm breeze, the bloody wolf fur rustled against her cheek. Kahlan pulled free her knife and held it up in her fist for all to see. She laid the weapon over her heart.

"An oath then, to the good people of Ebinissia who are now with the spirits, and to the good people of the Midlands!"

Almost all the men followed her example, holding their knives over their hearts. Seven did not, but, grumbling curses, rose to join with Mosle. Seventy-six.

"Vengeance without mercy before our lives are returned to us!" she pledged.

The sober voice of every man before her repeated the oath, joining with every other in unflinching unity.

"Vengeance without mercy before our lives are returned to us!" The roar of their words drifted away on the morning air.

Kahlan watched William Mosle cast a glance over his shoulder at her before following his men away, back up the pass.

She returned her attention to those before her. "You are all sworn in oath, then. Tonight, we begin the killing of the men of the Order. Let it be without quarter. We take no prisoners."

No cheer went up this time. The men listened in grim attention.

"We must no longer travel as you have been, with wagons to carry your needs and supplies. We must take only what we can carry. We need to be able to travel the woods, the small passes, so we can outmaneuver the men we hunt. I intend to sweep in at them from all directions and at will, like wolves at hunt. And like wolves, who hunt with coordination, we will control and direct them, as wolves control and direct their prey.

"You are men of this land. You know the woods and mountains around us. You have hunted them since you were children. We will use your knowledge. The enemy is in strange territory, and keeps to the wide passes with their wagons and great numbers. We will no longer be impeded as they. We will move through the country around them as do the wolves.

"You must divide up what you have in the wagons, and place what you can carry in your packs. Leave the heavy armor, it takes too much effort to carry, and we are not going to fight that way. Take only light armor you can wear at a forced march. Take what food you can.

"You are to take no liquor or ale. When you have avenged the people of Ebinissia, you may drink all you want. Until then, you will not. I want everyone alert at all times. We do not ever relax until our enemy is dead to a man.

"Some of the food that's left is to be packed into a few of the smaller wagons, without any arms or armor. We will need volunteers to give it to the enemy."

The men mumbled in surprise and confusion.

"The road divides ahead. When they are past the fork, and on their way to Cellion, the wagons with the food and all the ale are to take the other road, and then the smaller routes, to get ahead of them. You will lie in wait with these wagons until their advance guard nears, and then cross their path so they can see you. When their forward column spots you and gives chase, you are to abandon the wagons and escape. Let them have the food and drink.

"The Imperial Order is nearly out of ale, and tonight they will celebrate their luck. I expect they will get drunk. I want them to be drunk when we attack them."

The men cheered with that news.

"Know this: we're as a wolf pack, trying to bring down a bull. Though we are not strong enough to do it with one dispatching strike, we will harry him to exhaustion, drag him to the ground, and kill him. This will not be a single battle, but a constant nipping at his hide, taking small chunks of him at a time, wounding, weakening, and bleeding him all the while, until finally we have the advantage and can kill the beast.

"Tonight, under cover of darkness, we will slip into their camp and make a quick strike. This is to be a disciplined action, not random killing. We will have a list of objectives. Our aim is to weaken the bull. I have already partially blinded him by eliminating the wizard.

"The sentries and lookouts will be taken first. We will dress as many men as we can in their clothes. Those men will go into their camp and locate our targets.

"Our first need is to slow their ability to counterattack. I don't want us run down by cavalry. We need to bring ruin to their horses. There's no need to waste time killing them; breaking their legs is sufficient. We need to destroy their food. We're an army small enough to be able to get food by hunting, foraging, and buying from surrounding farms and villages, but one that size requires much. If we destroy their food, they will be weakened.

"We need to kill their arrow makers and fletchers, bowyers and blacksmiths, all the craftsmen who can make and repair bows, arrows, and other weapons. They will have sacks of goose wings for fletching arrows. They must be stolen or burned. Every arrow not made is one that can't kill us. Bow staves need to be destroyed. Wreck their bugles, if you find them, and the buglers. This will help take away their voice and coordination.

"Their lances, pikes, and argons will be stacked upright, together. Five seconds and a few swings with an axe or sword will destroy a great many. Heavy axes or hammers will at least bend the argons and render them useless. Every lance or spear broken is one that can't kill you. We want to burn their tents, to expose them to the cold, burn their wagons so they will lose supplies of every kind.

"Of most importance are their officers. I would rather kill one officer tonight than a thousand men. If we can kill their officers, it will make them dull and slow, and it will be easier to take this bull to the ground.

"If any of you can think of anything else that will weaken them, bring the ideas to me or Captain Ryan, or the other officers. The object tonight is not primarily to kill soldiers; there are too many. Our object is to disable them, make them weak, slow; to make them less sure of themselves.

"Most of all, our object is to put fear into their minds. These men aren't used to being afraid. When men are afraid, they make mistakes. Those mistakes allow us to kill them. I intend to terrify them. Later, I will tell you how.

"You have a few hours to get everything ready, and then we start moving. I want the sentries at double distance. Beyond them, I want lookouts and I want scouts to keep in contact with the Order. I want to know where they are at all times. I want constant reports. I don't want to be surprised by anything. I want to know of anything that you see or encounter, no matter how innocent it seems. If a rabbit jumps too high, I want to know about it. Just as we intend to trick them, I don't want them tricking us. Take nothing for granted.

"May the good spirits be with you. Now get started."

The men all began moving, the air coming to life with the sound of feet and talking. One of the two lieutenants stood near, unbuttoning his coat, giving orders to some men around him.

"Lieutenant Sloan." He looked up as the men he had instructed went to their tasks. "See to the sentries and lookouts at once. I want any of your men who know how to make white paint or whitewash to assemble the supplies they need. We will need large tubs of some sort. I want rocks heated, to warm the insides of tents."

He didn't question her strange instructions. "Yes, Mother Confessor."

"See that the small wagons with the ale and food are prepared, but hold them until I give the order to let them go."

He put his fist to his heart without comment and marched off to see to it.

Kahlan's legs felt as if they would give out at any second. She was so tired from having had no sleep, and from riding the better part of the night, to say nothing of the work she had done and the heart-pounding fright, that she could hardly focus her eyes anymore. Her shoulder hurt where the lance had been couched when it was shattered. The muscles in her left leg jittered with the effort of keeping her standing.

She was also mentally exhausted. Anxiety, over not only the enormity of her decision to take it upon herself to call all the Midlands into war, but also over her impassioned plea for these men to lay down their lives on her word, eroded her strength further. Despite the unusual warmth of the day, she shivered inside her fur mantle.

Captain Ryan stepped over to her. Chandalen, Prindin, and Tossidin were standing by the rear of the wagon, watching.

Captain Ryan gave her a sly smile. "I like it."

He jumped down and held his hand out for her. She ignored the hand and jumped down as he had done, and by luck more than anything, stayed on her feet. She could not accept his offer of help, not now, not with what she was about to do.

"And now, Captain, I must give you an order you are not going to like." She looked to his blue eye. "I want you to send men after Mosle and those who went with him. Send enough to be sure to accomplish the deed."

"Deed?"

"They must be killed. Send a force with instructions that they are to pretend to join with Mosle's men, so they don't scatter when your men approach. Send your cavalry behind, but out of sight, in case they're able to take to the woods. When they are surrounded, kill them. There are seventy-six. Count the bodies to make sure they are all dead. I will be *very* displeased if even one escapes."

His eyes were wide. "But Mother Confessor . . ."

"I take no pleasure in this, Captain. You have your orders." She turned to the three Mud People. "Prindin, go with the men he picks. Make sure those who departed are killed to a man."

Prindin gave her a grim nod. He understood the unpleasant necessity of what she was doing.

Captain Ryan tensed in near panic. "Mother Confessor . . . I know those men. They've been with us a long time. You said they were free to go! We can't . . ."

She laid a hand on his arm. He suddenly recognized the threat that represented. "I am doing what I must to save your lives. You have given your word to follow orders." She leaned a little closer. "Do not add yourself to those seventy-six."

He at last gave a nod and she removed her hand. His eyes told it all. Hate radiated from him.

"I didn't know the killing was to start with our own men," he whispered.

"It does not. It starts with the enemy."

Captain Ryan pointed angrily up the pass. "They're going in the opposite direction of the Order!"

"And did you think they would go to the enemy in plain sight of you? They intend to circle around." She turned and started off toward a tent that had been left up for her.

Captain Ryan, trailed by Chandalen, Prindin, and Tossidin, followed her, unwilling to concede. "If you were so concerned, why did you let them go! Why didn't you let the men kill them when they would have!"

"Because I had to give all those who would renounce us and abandon their fellows the chance to do so."

"What makes you think all the 'traitors' departed? There could be spies, or assassins, among us."

"Yes, there could be. But I have no evidence of that at the moment. If I find there are, I will have to deal with them then."

Kahlan came to a stop before the tent. "If you think I may be making a mistake about those men, I assure you, I am not. But even if I were, it is a price that must be paid. If we let them go, and even one of them betrays us, we could all be killed in a trap tonight. If we die, there will be none to stop the Order for a long time. How many thousands would die then, Captain? If those men are innocent, I'll have made a terrible mistake, and seventy-six innocent men will die. If I'm right, I will be saving the lives of untold thousands of innocent people.

"You have your orders. Carry them out."

Captain Ryan shook with rage. "I hope you don't expect me to ever forgive you for this."

"No, I don't. I expect only that you follow my orders. I don't care if you hate me, Captain. I care only that you live to do so."

He gritted his teeth in mute frustration.

Kahlan gripped the tent flap. "Captain, I'm so tired I can hardly stand. I need to get a couple of hours' sleep. I want a guard posted around this tent while I rest."

He glared at her. "And how can you be sure one of them might not be an enemy? They could kill you in your sleep."

"That's a possibility. But if that happens, one of these three men would avenge my murder."

Captain Ryan flinched and glanced at the three Mud People. In his anger, he had forgotten they were there.

Chandalen lifted an eyebrow to him. "I will first put sticks in his eyes, to hold them open, to be sure he sees what I do."

Lieutenant Hobson rushed up, holding a bowl out in his hands. "Mother Confessor, I brought you some stew. I thought you would like something to eat. Something hot."

Kahlan forced herself to smile at him. "Thank you, Lieutenant, but I'm so tired I'm afraid I wouldn't be able to keep it down. Could you keep it warm, until after I've rested?"

"Of course, Mother Confessor."

Captain Ryan's glare slid to his grinning lieutenant. "I have a job for you, Hobson."

"Two hours," Kahlan said, "and then wake me. You should all have enough to keep you busy in the meantime."

She pulled the flap aside and went into the tent, nearly collapsing onto the cot. She drew a blanket over her legs, and lifted the fur mantle over her head, shutting out the light. In her small, private darkness, she shook.

She would have given her life, right then, to have Richard hold her for just five minutes.

**S**he was kissing Richard, holding him tightly in her arms, her mind filled with no thought but peace and joy, when she started at the sound of shouting. Richard was gone. Her heavy arms were empty.

She sat up, pushing the blanket away, frantic for an instant, not knowing where she was, and then she remembered. She felt as if she might vomit.

She wished she could have a hot bath. She couldn't remember her last bath. She rubbed her eyes as Captain Ryan stuck his head inside the tent.

"How long?" Kahlan mumbled. "How long have I slept?" She threw the blanket aside.

"A couple hours, just about. There is someone out here for you."

Directly outside her tent waited a group of men, an ashen-faced Lieutenant Hobson among them. In their midst stood Mosle, bound and gagged and held at each arm by soldiers. His eyes darted about in panic. He tried to shout through the gag, but couldn't make himself understood.

Kahlan glowered over at Captain Ryan.

He stood with one thumb hooked in his belt. "I thought, Mother Confessor, that you would want to execute this man yourself. Since he seems to have personally offended you so." He held his knife out toward her, handle first.

Kahlan ignored the knife and turned instead to the men holding Mosle. "Release him, and stand away."

She felt as if she were still in a sleep, still in a dream. But she wasn't. There was no option.

As they stepped back, she reached out and snatched Mosle by his arm. He froze in fright for an instant, and then tried to back away.

But he had no time to escape. She was touching him now. He was hers. Her sleepiness vanished in a sucking rush as her power ignited. She gave no thought to what she was about to do; there was no choice. She was committed. She gave herself over to it.

The sounds of the camp—the jangle of tack, the grating of wooden boxes being skidded across wagon beds, the splintering of other boxes being pried open, the squeak of wheels, the whinnies of horses, the sound of thousands of feet shuffling, men talking, the clop of hooves, the sound of steel being sharpened, the popping of wood in fires, and the sound of her own heart beating—all faded away to silence.

In the silence of her mind, the power was all. She could feel Mosle's muscles tighten under her hand. But he had no chance. He was hers.

In the silence, in the quiet, in the peace of her mind, as she had done countless times before, she released her power, her magic, into the man before her.

There was a violent jolt to the air as it slammed into him. Thunder without sound. The snow around her and Mosle billowed away in a ring, rising and tumbling, until it dissipated and settled again.

Mosle, no more who he had been, dropped to his knees in the wet snow before her. His brow wrinkled with panic that, because of the gag, he would not be able to ask her to command him. He sucked air through his nose, trying to breathe with the terror that he might displease her. The camp around her had fallen into stunned silence, with her the heart of all attention. Kahlan pulled the gag from his mouth.

Tears of relief flooded from his eyes. "Mistress," he whispered hoarsely. "Please, Mistress, command me. Please tell me what I can do to serve you."

In trepidation, hundreds of stunned faces around her watched. Kahlan gazed down at the man on his knees before her. She wore her Confessor's face. "It would please me, William, if you would tell me the truth of what you planned to do after you left this camp."

He beamed with joy, more tears running down his cheeks, and would have clutched at her legs in gratitude had his arms not been bound behind his back.

"Oh yes, Mistress, please let me tell you."

"Tell me then."

It all came babbling out in a rush. "I was going to the camp of those other men, the Imperial Order you called them, and I was going to ask to join them. I was going to take all my men with me so they could join too. I was going to tell them of the presence of the Galean recruits, and of your plans, so they would be pleased with us, and would let us join with them. I thought they had a better chance than you, and I didn't want to die, so I was going to join with them. I thought they would be pleased if I brought them men to add to their ranks. I thought they would be pleased with us if we could help them crush you."

He burst suddenly in sobs. "Oh, please, Mistress, I'm so sorry I thought to do you harm. I wanted them to kill you. Oh, please, Mistress, I'm so sorry I intended you harm. Please, Mistress, tell me how I can gain your forgiveness. I will do anything. Please command me and it will be done. Please, Mistress, what do you wish of me?"

"I wish for you to die," she whispered in the icy silence. "Right now."

William Mosle crumpled forward, against her boots, and thrashed in racking convulsions. After a few long, agonizing seconds, he was still, his last breath rattling from his lungs.

Kahlan's gaze slid over a wide-eyed Captain Ryan, to Prindin, standing behind a still ashen Lieutenant Hobson. Chandalen was glaring at him, too. She spoke in his tongue.

*"Prindin, I told you to make sure they were all killed. Why did you not do as I said?"*

He shrugged self-consciously. *"They were of a mind to do this. Captain Ryan told them to kill the others but to bring this one to you. I did not know this when we left, or I would have told you. They had two hundred men on foot, and another one hundred on horses. As I told you, they were of a mind to do this, and I did not think I would be able to prevent it, except by killing him myself, and then I realized they might kill me for doing it, and then I would not be able to be near you, to protect you. Besides that, I knew you were right, and I thought it would do them good to learn a lesson."*

*"Did any escape?"*

*"No. I was a little surprised at how well they did the job. They are good men. They did a hard thing, a thing they wept to do, but they did it well. None escaped them."*

Kahlan let out a long breath. *"I understand, Prindin. You were right to do as you did."* She cast a sideways glance at Chandalen. *"Chandalen will be satisfied, too."* It was an order.

Prindin gave her a tight smile of relief. Her glare slid to Captain Ryan. "Satisfied?"

He stood stiff, pale and wide-eyed. "Yes, Mother Confessor."

She swept a glance over the gathered men. "Is everyone satisfied, now?"

There came from them all an uncoordinated, mumbled chorus of "Yes, Mother Confessor."

If there had been some before who were not terrified of her, there were none now who were not. The lot of them looked as if, were a twig to snap unexpectedly, they would bolt for the hills like frightened rabbits. This was probably the first time most had seen magic, and it wasn't wonderful, beautiful magic, but daunting, ugly magic.

"Mother Confessor?" Captain Ryan whispered. His arm was still held out, frozen, the knife he had offered her still in his hand. "What are you going to do to me for disobeying your orders?"

She looked to his bloodless face. "Nothing. This is your first day of being men in the war against the Order. Most of you didn't believe in the importance of what I had commanded. You have not fought in war before, and did not understand the need. I will be satisfied that you have learned something from this, and leave it at that."

Captain Ryan swallowed. "Thank you, Mother Confessor." With a shaking hand he slid his knife back in its sheath. "I grew up with him." He lifted the hand toward the body at her feet. "We lived about a mile apart, on the same road. We used to go hunting and fishing together all the time. We helped each other with chores. We always went to feast day in our best coats of the same color. We always . . ."

"I'm sorry, Bradley. There is nothing to ease the pain of betrayal, or loss, except time. As I told you, war is not fair. Were it not for the men of the Order making war, perhaps you would be fishing today, with your friend. Blame the Order, and avenge him, too, with all the rest."

He nodded. "Mother Confessor? What would you have done if you were wrong? What would you have done if Mosle wasn't going to the enemy?"

She regarded him until his gaze rose to meet hers. "I probably would have taken that knife you offered, and killed you."

She turned from his hollow expression and put a hand on the shoulder of the the man next to him. "Lieutenant Hobson, I know you had a difficult task. Prindin tells me you did it well."

He looked near tears, but still managed to stiffen his back with pride. She noticed that his beard hadn't even started to grow in earnest yet. "Thank you, Mother Confessor."

She looked around at the hundreds of men standing about, watching. "I believe you all have work?"

As if they had just awakened, everyone began moving again, slowly at first, and then with accelerating urgency.

Hobson gave a salute of his fist to his heart and turned to other business. The men who had brought Mosle lifted his body and carried it off. Others went to Chandalen and the two brothers, asking for instructions. Captain Ryan stood alone with her, watching as everyone went about their work.

Her legs felt limp and slack, like bowstrings left out in the rain all night. For a Confessor to use her power when she was rested and alert was taxing. To use it when she was already tired was perilously exhausting. She could hardly keep herself upright.

She had been dead tired from riding all night to the enemy camp and back, to say nothing of the fight with them. She needed more sleep than she had gotten, and using her power had cost her even the benefit of the short nap, and then some. She had used what strength she had left to do something that should have been done without her.

She thought maybe it must be the cold, and traveling in such difficult conditions, but she seemed more tired than usual lately. Maybe she could ask Prindin to make her some more tea.

"Could I speak with you for a moment, Mother Confessor?" Captain Ryan asked. Kahlan nodded. "What is it, Captain?"

He pushed his unbuttoned wool coat open, shoving his hands in his back pockets. He glanced away to watch some men filling waterskins. "I just want to say that I'm sorry. I was wrong."

"It's all right, Bradley. He was your friend. It's difficult to believe ill of a friend. I understand."

"No, that's not it. My father always told me that a man had to admit his mistakes before he could do right in this world."

He shuffled his feet and looked around, finally bringing his blue eyes to her. "The mistake I made was believing that you wanted Mosle killed because he wouldn't follow you. I thought you were being spiteful because he didn't want to follow you. I made a mistake, and I'm sorry. Sorry I thought that of you. You were trying to protect us, even though you knew we would hate you for it. Well, I don't hate you. I hope you don't hate me. I'm honored to follow you into this battle. I hope that someday I'm half as wise as you, and have the guts you do, to use that wisdom."

She released a quiet sigh. "I'm hardly older than you, yet you make me feel like an old woman. I'm relieved, you understand. It's a small pleasure in all this pain. You're a fine officer, and will do right by this world."

He smiled. "I'm glad we're on good terms again."

A man approached, and was waved forward by the captain. "What is it, Sergeant Frost?"

Sergeant Frost gave a salute of his fist to his heart. "We sent a few men out, and in an abandoned barn they found some crushed chalk and other things needed to make whitewash. We have some wooden tubs we can mix it in. You said you wanted it in something big. They're big enough to bathe in."

"How many of these tubs do you have?" Kahlan asked.

"A dozen, Mother Confessor."

"Put the tubs near each other, and pitch a tent around each. Use the largest tents you have, even if it is the command tents. Make the whitewash with hot water, and place the heated stones inside the tents, to keep it as warm as possible inside. Let me know when all this is seen to."

Keeping his obvious questions to himself, the sergeant saluted and rushed off to see it done.

Captain Ryan gave her a curious frown. "What do you want with whitewash?"

"We've just gotten back on good terms; let's not spoil it for a bit. I'll tell you after things are prepared. Are the wagons ready?"

"Should be."

"Then I must see to them. Did you send the sentries and lookouts?"

"First thing."

As she walked through the camp to the wagons, men came to her constantly. "The wagon wheels, Mother Confessor. As we destroy things we should stave in the wheels" and "Their battle standards, shouldn't we burn them, so they can't rally their men around them?" and "Couldn't we set fire to their baggage, so if the weather turns colder they'll freeze?" and "If we were to throw manure in their barrels of drinking water, they would have to waste time melting snow," and a hundred other ideas, from the absurd to the worthwhile. She listened to each with attention, giving her honest opinion, and, in a few cases, her orders to see it done.

Lieutenant Hobson came at a trot holding out a tin bowl. That was the last thing she needed.

"Mother Confessor! I kept some stew hot for you!"

Beaming, he handed her the bowl as she walked. She tried to act grateful. He walked along next to her, watching, grinning. She forced herself to take a spoonful, and to tell him how wonderful it tasted. It was all she could do to keep that one spoonful down.

After using her power, a Confessor needed time to recover. For some it was days; for her it took a couple of hours. Rest, if she could get it, was the best thing for a Confessor after using her power. The little rest she had gotten was now wasted. She could get no more now, and probably would get none this night either.

The last thing a Confessor needed while recovering her power was food. It diverted her energy to the food instead of returning her strength. She had to think of a way out of eating the bowl of stew or it would end up on the ground, to the embarrassment of all.

Thankfully, she reached the wagons before she had to take another mouthful. She asked Lieutenant Hobson to get Chandalen and the two brothers, and bring them to her. After he left, she set the bowl down on the splinter bar of the dray with the casks of ale and climbed up.

She motioned Captain Ryan up on the wagon as she counted. "Get some men. Unload the top rows so we can get at them all. Right the casks on the bottom row, and withdraw the plugs." As he motioned for men to help with the task, she asked, "Did Chandalen have you all make a *troga*?"

A *troga* was a simple, stout piece of cord or a wire with a wooden handle on each end, and long enough so that when it was given a twist, it made a loop that was the right size to drop over a man's head. It was applied from behind, and then the handles yanked apart. If it was made of wire, placed correctly at the neck joints, and the man wielding it had arms big enough, his *troga* could decapitate a person before the victim had a chance to make a sound. Even if it wasn't wire, or his arms were not that strong, the victim still made no sound before he died.

Captain Ryan reached behind his back, under his coat, and retrieved a wire *troga*, holding it up for her to see. "He gave us a little demonstration. He was gentle, but I'm still glad I wasn't the one he demonstrated on. He says he and Prindin and Tossidin will use these to take the sentries and lookouts. I don't think he believes we can sneak up on them like he can. But many of us have spent a lot of time hunting, and we're more clever . . ."

Captain Ryan leapt with a yelp. Chandalen had poked him in the ribs, having come up unseen behind him. The captain comforted his ribs and scowled at a smiling Chandalen. Prindin and his brother climbed up to help unload the barrels.

"You wish something, Mother Confessor?" Chandalen asked.

Kahlan held her hand out. "Give me your *bandu*. Your ten-step poison."

His brow wrinkled into a scowl, but he reached into the pouch at his waist and pulled out the bone box, leaning over to hand it to her. The brothers fished out their boxes, too, and handed them to her.

"How much will I be able to poison with it? How many casks can I make poison?

Chandalen stepped around Captain Ryan, balancing atop the sides of the round barrels. "You are going to put it in this drink?" Kahlan nodded. "But then we won't have any more. We must have it with us. We may need it."

"I'll leave a bit for emergencies. Every one we can kill in this way is one less to fight."

"But they might discover it's poison," Captain Ryan said. "Then we won't even have them drunk."

"They have dogs," Kahlan said. "That's why I want to send them food, too. They will throw the dogs some of the meat, to make sure it's good. I'm hoping they will be put at ease after testing the food on the dogs, and anxious enough for the ale that the idea of it being poisoned won't come into their heads."

Chandalen counted the barrels silently, and then straightened. "There are thirty-six. Twelve for each of our *bandu*." He scratched his head of black hair while he pondered. "It will not kill them, unless they drink much, but it will make them sick."

"How sick? What will it do?"

"It will make them weak. They will be sick in their stomachs. Their heads will spin inside. Maybe, some will die in a hand of days from the poison sickness."

Kahlan nodded. "It will be a great help."

"But this is hardly enough for all their men," Captain Ryan said. "Only some will drink this."

"Some will go to the unit who plundered it, and the rest will be divided among the men of rank first, with what's left going to the soldiers. The men of rank are the ones I'm after."

All the top rows were unloaded, leaving only the bottom row, which the men stood up so the plugs could be removed.

"Why are six of these barrels smaller?"

"They're rum," the captain said.

"Rum? The drink of nobility?" Kahlan smiled. "The commanders will take the rum first." She straightened from peering into one of the open casks. "Chandalen, will they be able to taste it? Will the taste give them warning, if I put more in some?"

He dipped a finger in a cask of rum, and sucked it clean. "No. This is bitter enough. Bitter things hide the taste of *bandu*."

Kahlan used her knife point to divide the poison from Chandalen's box into sixths. She swished each sixth off her knife point into the round opening in one of the smaller casks—those with the rum.

Chandalen watched what she was doing. "That much, in the smaller barrels, will probably kill them by morning, the next day for sure. But now you have none for the other six."

Kahlan handed Chandalen back his bone box with a little of the *bandu* left in the corners and climbed down from the dray. "Six of the casks of ale will have no poison so that we can be sure the rum will kill those who drink it." She put a knife point laden with poison from Tossidin's box into each of the next twelve. "Mix all the barrels up. I don't want the rum on the bottom. The commanders might not see it and take the ale instead."

Kahlan went to the last twelve and opened Prindin's box. She looked up. "You don't have very much. What have you done with yours?"

Prindin looked as though he wished she hadn't asked that question. He gestured vaguely. "When we left, I was not thinking so good. You were in a hurry, and so I forgot to see that my *bandu* box was full."

Chandalen put his fists on his hips and glared down from atop the wagon. "Prindin, how many times have I said that you would forget to take your feet could you walk away without them?"

"It doesn't matter," Kahlan said. Prindin looked relieved to have her interrupt Chandalen's questioning. "This will make them sick. That is all that matters."

As she was putting it in the barrels, she heard men in the distance hailing her. When she had swirled the poison into the last barrel, she looked up to see two huge draft horses trotting toward her. She frowned at seeing men riding them bareback, and calling out to her.

The two powerful draft horses looked shaggy in their thick, dun-colored winter coats, with heavy white feathering on their legs. They wore their harnesses and neck collars, but not their breeching. Several bends of chain were looped over the inside hame of each collar. The men about all stared at the odd sight.

When the horses came to a halt before her, the riders unhooked the loops of chain and dropped them to the ground. She realized then that the horses were connected by that chain, attached to the hame hooks on their collars. She had never seen such a thing. The two riders slid to the ground.

"Mother Confessor!" Their grins made their salutes look a little silly. The both of them were gangly, with short-cropped brown hair. Neither looked as if he could be fifteen. Their wool coats were unbuttoned in the warming day, and fit them like gunnysacks on lapdogs. They both looked about to burst with excitement. They halted before getting too close, but even their fear of her couldn't wither their breathless excitement.

"What are your names?"

"I'm Brin Jackson and this is Peter Chapman, Mother Confessor. We had an idea, and we wanted to show you. We think it'll do the job. We're sure it will. It'll work some clever it sure will."

Kahlan looked from one beaming face to the other. "What will do what job?"

Brin almost leapt with joy at being asked. He hefted the chain lying in the snow between the big horses. "This!" He lugged a wad of chain to her and held it out. "This will do it, Mother Confessor. We thought of it ourselves! Peter and me." He dumped the heavy chain on the ground. "Show her, Peter. Move 'em apart."

Peter's head bobbed as he grinned. He sidestepped his horse until the heavy chain lifted off the snow. The sag of chain swung to and fro between the hame hooks on the collars. Kahlan and all the men with her frowned, trying to understand what the peculiar rig was for.

Brin pointed at the chain. "You said we were going to leave the wagons, and we surely didn't want to leave Daisy and Pip behind. Them's our horses—Daisy and Pip. We're drivers. We wanted to help, and make a good use of Daisy and Pip, so we took some of the biggest trace chains and asked Morvan, he's the blacksmith, we asked Morvan to weld a couple of 'em together for us." He nodded expectantly, as if that should explain it.

Kahlan dipped her head toward him a little. "And now that he has?"

Brin held his hands open in excitement. "You said we needed to take out their horses." He couldn't help giggling. "That's what this is for! You said we're going to attack at night. Their horses will be tethered to picket lines. We gallop Daisy and Pip down the picket line, one on each side, and the chain'll break their legs out from under 'em! We'll take out the whole line in one sweep!"

Kahlan leaned back and folded her arms. She looked to Peter. He nodded, keen on the idea, too. "Brin, having horses chained together like that, at a gallop, and dragging a chain that will be catching things, heavy things, sounds to me very dangerous."

He wilted only a little. "But it could take out their horses! We can do it! We can get them for you!"

"They have close to two thousand horses."

Peter wilted more. Brin scrunched up his face as he looked at the ground for the first time. He scratched his shoulder. "Two thousand," he finally whispered in disappointment.

Kahlan glanced to Captain Ryan. He shrugged as if to say he didn't know if it would work or not. The other men standing about rubbed their chins and shuffled their feet as they pondered the rig.

"It will never do," Kahlan said at last. Brin's shoulders slumped more. "There are too many of them for you. You will need more horses set up like this." Brin and Peter's faces came up, their eyes widening. "Since you two know how to do it, I want you to get all the draft horses and their drivers together. This will be the best use of their skill.

"Use all the equipment off the wagons or breeching you need. We'll not be taking them anyway. Have the chains made up at once, and then I want you all to practice the rest of the day. I want you to set up things to drag the chains through. Heavy thing, so the horses will be used to what you're going to do. You need to practice so each team of men and horses can work together."

Peter came forward and stood next to a beaming Brin. "We will, Mother Confessor! You'll see! We can do it! You can count on us!"

She gave them each a sobering look. "What you want to do is dangerous. But if you can do it, it will be a great benefit to us. It could save many of our lives. Their cavalry is deadly. Take your gear and your practice seriously. Men will be trying to kill you when you do it for real."

They put their fists to their hearts, this time holding their chins up. "We'll see to it, Mother Confessor. You can count on the drivers. We won't let you down. We'll get their horses."

After receiving her nod, they turned to their horses. Heads together, whispering in excitement, they went to their task. Kahlan watched a lone rider, in the distance, galloping through the camp. He stopped to ask a group of men something. They pointed in her direction.

"They've only been with us a couple months," Captain Ryan said. "They're just boys."

Kahlan raised an eyebrow to him. "They are men, fighting for the Midlands. When I first saw you, I thought of you in much the same way you see them. Now I think you look a little older to me."

He sighed. "I guess you're right. If they really can do the job, it will be a brilliant achievement."

The galloping rider approached and leapt from his horse before it came fully to a stop. He gave a perfunctory salute. "Mother Confessor." He gulped some air. "I'm Cynric, with the sentries."

"What is it, Cynric?"

"You said you wanted to know about everything, so I thought I better report. We were just setting up the sentries about an hour out, between here and the army of the Order, near a road that crosses Jara Pass, and a coach came up the crossroad, from the direction of Kelton. We knew you didn't want anything unusual going on, so we stopped the coach. I thought I better find out what you wanted us to do."

"Who's in the coach?"

"An old couple. Wealthy merchants of some sort, or so they claim. Something about orchards."

"What did you tell them? You didn't tell them about us, did you? You didn't tell them that we have an army out here, did you?"

He shook his head vehemently. "No, Mother Confessor. We told them that there were outlaws in the neighborhood, and that we were a small patrol out looking for them. We told them they weren't allowed to pass until I checked with my commander. I said they had to wait until I returned."

Kahlan nodded. "That's quick thinking, Cynric."

"The driver's name is Ahern. He wanted to argue with us, and thought to give his team reins, until we showed him some steel. Then the old man came flying out of the coach, accusing us of trying to rob him. He started to swing his cane around at us, like he thought that would drive us off or something. Anyway, we drew arrows on him, and he decided he would get back in the coach."

"What is his name?"

Cynric shifted his weight to the other foot and scratched his eyebrow. "Robin, or Ruben, or something like that. Feisty old fellow. Ruben, I think. Ruben Rybnik, I think that's it."

Kahlan sighed as she shook her head. "They don't sound like spies. But if the Order catches them, and they know anything, they will tell it all before the D'Harans are through with them." She looked up. "What are they doing out here?"

"The old man says his wife is sick, and they're taking her to healers in Nicobarese. She didn't look well to me. Her eyes looked to be all rolled back in her head."

"Well, since they're on the road going northwest, going across Jara Pass, that shouldn't take them anywhere near the Order." She pulled some of her long hair back off her face. "But before I dare let them go, I best go speak with them."

Before she could take three steps, Sergeant Frost came running up behind. "Mother Confessor! The tubs of whitewash are ready. The tents are heated."

Kahlan let out a noisy breath. She looked from Sergeant Frost, to sentry Cynric, to other men waiting patiently to talk with her or ask instructions. She let out another breath. "Look, Cynric, I don't have the hour to ride out there, and another to ride back. I'm sorry, but I just don't have the time."

435

He nodded. "Yes, Mother Confessor. I understand. What do you wish done?"

She steeled herself to the orders. "Kill them."

"Mother Confessor?"

"Kill them. We can't be sure of the truth of who they are, and this is too important to worry about strangers running around loose. We can't take the risk. Make it quick, so they don't suffer."

She turned away toward Sergeant Frost.

"But Mother Confessor . . ."

She looked over her shoulder.

Cynric gathered up a length of reins. "The driver, Ahern, he has a royal pass."

Kahlan turned back and frowned. "A what?"

"A royal pass medallion. It's a medallion that was given to him by Queen Cyrilla herself. It says he was a hero to the people of Ebinissia in the siege, and in honor of his service he is to be given unhindered pass anywhere in Galea."

"The queen herself gave this pass?"

Cynric nodded. "I'll do what you command, Mother Confessor, but with this medallion the queen has promised him her protection."

Kahlan rubbed her forehead with her fingertips. She was so tired she could hardly focus her mind to think. "Since he has a pass given by the queen, we must honor it." She pointed a finger to the sentry. "But you tell him that he must be clear of the area immediately. Repeat what you told him about there being outlaws in the neighborhood. Tell him that you're hunting these outlaws, and that if you catch Ahern and his coach around here again, you're ordered to assume they are in with the outlaws, and you're to execute them on the spot. The road to Nicobarese goes northeast. Tell them to keep to it and not to stop before they're a good long distance from here."

Cynric clapped a fist to his heart as she turned to take Captain Ryan's arm and lead him toward the tents with the whitewash. Behind, she heard the sentry gallop off toward the coach he had found. The other men took the hint that they weren't to come, and went about other business.

She loosened the thong holding her mantle closed. The temperature had climbed above freezing, and the clouds had lowered nearly to the ground. The air felt wringing wet.

"Fog will move in by this afternoon," he observed. "This whole valley pass will be thick with it tonight." He glanced to her questioning frown. "I've lived in these mountains my whole life. When it takes a thaw like this in winter, the fog settles into the passes for at least a couple of days."

Kahlan surveyed the mountain sides ascending into the gray clouds. "That will serve us well. Especially for what I have in mind. It will be an aid to us in bringing terror to the enemy."

"So, are you ready to tell me what we're to paint?"

Kahlan let out a tired sigh. "We've devised a number of plans to strike targets that must be destroyed. Tonight will be our best chance of accomplishing those things, because they will be surprised. We will not have a chance of surprise like this again. After tonight, they will be expecting our next attacks."

"I understand. The men, too, know the importance of this. They will do well."

"We must also not lose sight of our intent. Our intent is to kill these men. Tonight, we will have the chance to do that as perhaps at no other time. We must take that opportunity.

"How many swordsmen do we have?"

He was silent a moment as he tallied the numbers in his head. "Nearly two thousand are swordsmen. Not quite another eight hundred archers, and the rest divided up among pikemen, lancers, and cavalry among others, including the rest of what an army needs, from drivers to fletchers to blacksmiths."

Kahlan nodded to herself. "I want you to select about a thousand swordsmen. Pick the strongest, the fiercest, the most eager for the fight."

"And what are we going to do with these men?"

"The men dressed in the uniforms of the sentries we kill will make an exploration of the enemy camp, and come back and give us the locations of our objectives. We have enough men to do the tasks we have assigned for those objectives.

"The swordsmen are for beginning our prime objective. Killing the enemy. They will first see to the enemy commanders, just in case they weren't poisoned, and then after that, they will kill as many men as they can in the shortest possible time."

They came to the dozen tents set up close together in a half circle. Kahlan checked inside them all to be sure they were equipped as she had ordered. Finished checking, she stood outside the largest and faced Captain Ryan.

"So, are you going to tell me, now, what it is we're to paint?"

Kahlan nodded. "Those thousand swordsmen."

He stared, dumfounded. "We're going to paint the men? Why?"

"It's simple. D'Harans fear spirits. They fear the spirits of the foes they kill, that's why they drag the bodies of their fallen comrades away from a battle site, like Ebinissia.

"Tonight, their fears are going to come to haunt them. They are going to be attacked by the thing they fear most: spirits."

"But they will recognize us as soldiers, simply with white clothes, not as spirits."

Kahlan looked at Captain Ryan from under her eyebrows. "They will not be wearing clothes. They will have nothing but their swords, painted white, just as are they. They will remove their clothes just before the attack."

His mouth dropped open. "What?"

"I want you to get the swordsmen together, now, and assemble them here. They're to go into the tents, remove their clothes, and dip themselves in the whitewash. After dunking themselves, they will stand near the hot rocks until dry. It won't take long. Then they can put their clothes back on. Until the attack."

Captain Ryan stood in shock. "But it's winter. They'll freeze without clothes."

"We have a break in the bitter cold. Besides, the cold will remind them to rush in and rush back out. I don't want them to stay in that camp very long. The enemy will recover from their shock in short order, and set upon any invader. I want our men to attack, kill terrified D'Harans, and escape.

"As I said, D'Harans fear spirits. When they see what they will at first think is their worst fear, they will be stunned. Their first thought will be to run, not to fight. Men die as easily from a sword through the back as through the front. Some will freeze in place, not knowing what to do. Even those who recognize the invaders as men painted white, and not as spirits, will be confused for a moment.

"Those few seconds of confusion, as we come upon each new group, are the seconds we need to run them through. In battle, the difference between killing, and being killed, is often a single moment of indecision.

"The swordsmen are not to engage in fights. If challenged, they're to run on to others. There are more than enough to kill; it's a mistake to waste time engaging in battle, if it can be avoided. I simply want enemy soldiers killed. After the commanders are dead, it doesn't matter which ones. I don't want our men fighting unless forced to; that only risks their lives needlessly.

"Rush in, kill as many men as possible, and rush out. Those are to be the orders."

Captain Ryan frowned as he considered. "I never thought I would hear myself say it, but I think it sounds like it might be an outlandishly successful tactic. The men aren't going to like it at first, but they'll follow orders. I'll explain it to them, and then I know they'll feel a little better about it.

"I've never heard of such a thing, and I'm sure the enemy hasn't either." He at last smiled a sly smile. "It's sure to surprise them, no doubt about that."

Kahlan was relieved he had come around to that much of it. "Good. I'm pleased to have the enthusiasm of a captain in the Galean army. In the Midlands army.

"Now, I want you to have my horse's saddle and tack brought here, and dipped in the whitewash. And please post some guards outside this tent, while I'm inside."

His eyes widened. "Your saddle? . . . You're not . . . Mother Confessor . . . You can't be serious."

"I would not ask my men to do something I myself would not do. They need to have a commander to rally around in their first battle. I intend to lead them."

Captain Ryan took a step back. He was aghast. He regained the step. "But Mother Confessor . . . you're a woman. And not in any way an ugly woman." Seemingly involuntarily, he took a quick glance the length of her. "In fact, you are . . . Mother Confessor, forgive me." He fell silent.

"They are soldiers with a mission. Make your point, Captain."

His face filled with blood. "These are young men, Mother Confessor. They are . . . Well, you can't expect . . . They are young men." His jaw moved as he tried to find words. "They won't be able to help themselves. Mother Confessor, please. You'll be embarrassed beyond all tolerance." He winced, hoping he wouldn't have to explain further.

She gave him a small smile to try to ease his horror. "Captain, have you ever heard the legend of the Shahari?" He shook his head. "When the tribes and lands now called D'Hara were being forged together, the method of conquest and joining were much the same as it is with the Imperial Order—join with them, or be conquered. The Shahari people refused to join into D'Hara, and they refused to be conquered.

"They fought so fiercely that they came to be greatly feared by the D'Haran troops, who outnumbered them many times over. The Shahari loved nothing more than fighting. They were so fearless and aroused about going into war that they went into battle naked and, well . . . aroused."

Kahlan looked up to see Captain Ryan staring, mouth agape. She went on. "The D'Harans all know the legend of the Shahari. They all, to this day, fear the Shahari." She cleared her throat. "If the men go into battle, and . . . that . . . happens, it will only bring greater fear to the men of the Order.

"I don't think, though, that the men need fear being embarrassed. They will have more pressing matters on their minds, like not being killed. And if it does happen, well then, they should know it pleases me because it will only strike greater fear into the hearts of our enemy."

Captain Ryan finally looked to the ground and pushed snow with his boot. "Forgive me, Mother Confessor, but I still don't like it. It puts you at danger for nothing of much gain."

"That's not true. There are two more important reasons I must do this. First, when I left the Order's camp last night I was being chased by about fifty men. The D'Harans have no doubt that those fifty men will catch me, and kill me."

The captain stiffened. "You mean there are fifty men roaming around looking for you?"

"No. They're all dead. To a man. But the men back at camp don't know that. When they see me, all white, like a spirit, they will think I was killed, as I should have been, and that it's my spirit in their midst. It will only frighten them further."

"All fifty . . .!" He peered up at her. "And what's the second reason?"

Kahlan stared at him for a moment. Her voice came softly. "When those men of the Order see me, whether they think me a spirit or they think me a naked woman on a horse before them, they will stare. While they are staring, they cannot kill our men. But we can kill them. It will divert their attention from the men, to me."

He gazed silently at her as she went on. "I would suffer any embarrassment on my part," she said, "if it will save the life of even one of our men. I must do this to help them, and to keep them alive."

He looked to the ground as he put his hands in his pockets.

"I never knew the Mother Confessor was a person who cared this much for her people," he whispered. "I never knew before, that she cared at all what happened to any of us." He looked up at last. "Is there anything at all I can say to talk you out of doing this?"

Kahlan smiled. "There's only one man in the world who could keep me from doing this, and you are not he." She laughed quietly. "In fact, if he knew what I was about to do, I'm sure he would forbid it."

His curiosity overcame his caution. "One man? Is he your mate?" She shook her head. "He is the one you will choose as your mate?"

Kahlan sighed pleasantly. "No. He is the one I'm to wed. At least I hope to wed him. He asked me to marry him." She smiled at the confused look on his face. "His name is Richard. He is the Seeker."

Captain Ryan stiffened and his breath cut off. "If I'm asking what I shouldn't, just say so, but I thought all Confessors used their power . . . I thought, your magic would . . . I didn't think Confessors could . . . marry."

"They can't. But Richard is special. He has the gift, and my power cannot harm him."

Captain Ryan smiled at last. "I'm glad. I'm happy for you, Mother Confessor."

Kahlan lifted an eyebrow. "But if you ever meet him, don't you dare tell him about this . . . pretending to be a spirit business. He has rather fusty views about such things. If you told him you let me run around naked with a thousand of your men, he would probably take your head off."

Kahlan laughed at the alarmed look on the captain's face.

"Captain, I need a sword."

"A sword! Now you're going to fight, too!"

Kahlan leaned toward him. "Captain, if I'm sitting there naked, and a D'Haran wishes to despoil my honor, how am I to defend myself unless I have a sword?"

"Oh. Well, I see your point."

He thought a moment. An idea brightened his face and he withdrew his own sword from its scabbard. He held the weapon out in both hands. It was an old sword, with a blade pattern wielded in the old fashion and acid etched in the fuller to display the wavy folds of steel.

"This blade was given to me by Prince Harold when I became an officer. He said it was his father's, that it was one that belonged to King Wyborn himself. He said King Wyborn held it once in battle." He shrugged self-consciously. "Of course, a king has many swords, and holds many of them in battle at least once, so they will be said to have been wielded by a king in defense of his kingdom. So it's not really valuable, or anything." He looked up expectantly. "But I would be honored if you took it as yours. It seems only right that, well, since you're King Wyborn's daughter, I guess, that you should wield his sword in battle. Maybe it has magic, or something, and will help protect your life."

Kahlan carefully lifted the sword from his hands.

"Thank you, Bradley. This means a lot to me. You are wrong; it is valuable. I will carry it with honor. But I will not keep it. When I'm finished, and leave for Aydindril in a couple of days, then I will return it, and you will have a sword wielded not only by a king, but by the Mother Confessor, too."

He grinned with the idea of that.

"Now, would you please post a guard outside this tent? And then see to the swordsmen?"

He smiled a little smile and brought his fist to his heart. "Of course, Mother Confessor."

As Kahlan went inside the warm tent, he was already returning with three men. He had a scowl on his face as serious as any scowl she had ever seen on any officer's face.

"And while the Mother Confessor is in her bath, you will keep your back to the tent, and not let anyone near. Is that clear!"

"Yes, Captain," the three wide-eyed soldiers said together.

Inside, in the warmth, Kahlan leaned the sword against the tub, slipped off the fur mantle, and then her clothes. She was so tired she felt sick. Her stomach felt as if it were rising and falling in waves. Her head spun so that she had to fight nausea that swelled in bouts.

She dragged her hand through the whitewash. It was hot, like a wonderful bath. But this was no bath. She lifted her legs over the edge one at a time, and eased herself down into the silky-smooth white water. Her breasts felt buoyant in the milky pool. For a few minutes, she draped her arms over the sides of the tub, closed her eyes, and pretended it was a hot bath. She wished so much that it could be a bath. But it wasn't.

It was something she did to keep some men alive, and to kill others. She would wear white as the Mother Confessor always did, but it would not be her dress, as always before.

Kahlan lifted her father's sword and held the hilt between her breasts, with the length of the blade running down her body, against her belly, and between her legs. She crossed her ankles and kept her legs apart so as not to slice her thighs on the weapon. She held her nose closed with her other hand, squeezed her eyes shut tight, took a deep breath, and then submerged herself.

Richard and Sister Verna continued on, through a dark and humid, dank and stifling tunnel of green, ascending the gently sloping road toward the humming, haunting sound of distant flutes. Branches holding not only their own leaves, but vines of every sort spiraling around and over them, and pale moss hanging in wispy curtains, filled the gaps between trunks to the sides, and nearly closed off the light from above.

Short walls to each side, looking to have been built in an attempt to hold back the tangled growth, were instead being snared by it and slowly enfolded into the creeping, leafy mat of life they sought to retain. From joints in the stone block, vines sprouted, surrounding and smothering whole sections of wall, bulging it in other places, pushing the occasional stone out to hang at a drunken angle, unable to fall to the ground because of the net of tendrils. The walls looked as if they were prey, being swallowed by a ponderous predator.

Only one part of the walls was untouched by the forest life—the human skulls. Atop the walls to each side, they were spaced at intervals of no more than three feet, each sitting on its own square of lichen-splotched stone, each clean of growth, looking like so many finials with eye sockets and toothy grins. Richard had lost count of the number of skulls.

His curiosity, his dread, failed to overcome his stubborn silence. He and the Sister had not spoken since their last argument. He had not even slept in camp with her, preferring instead to spend his watch, and the rest of the night, hunting and sleeping with Gratch. Sister Verna's angry silence was, at last, no match for his. He had no intention, this time, of being the one to make amends. They both contented themselves with looking at anything but each other.

Opening into sunlight, the road widened, splitting in the distance around a striated pyramid. Richard frowned, trying to see what made it look the way it did—a dotted, pale tan, with darker bands at evenly spaced intervals up its sides. He judged its height at three times his eye level from where he sat atop Bonnie.

As they approached, he realized the mound was constructed entirely of bones. Human bones. The dotted tan parts were skulls, and the bands were leg and arm bones placed end-out in layers. He guessed there must be tens of thousands of skulls in the orderly heap. He stared as they rode past; Sister Verna didn't seem to take notice.

Beyond the bone pile, the wide road led into a plaza of a dark and hazy city in the middle of the thick forest. The flat hilltop had been cleared of every tree, as had the terraced fields they had passed not an hour before.

The fields looked to be in preparation for planting. The ground was freshly turned, and there were stick people to scare away the birds when the seed was planted. It was winter, yet here, in this place, people planted. Richard thought it a wonder.

Rather than feeling open, this vast city, cleared of every bit of green that surrounded it, seemed even more closed and dark than the tunneled road. Buildings were square, with flat roofs, and faced with dingy plaster the color of bark. Near the roofs, and at each floor level, the ends of support logs stuck from the plastered walls. Windows were small, with never more than one in a wall. The buildings varied in height, but most were attached into irregular blocks. The tallest must have had four floors. None had the slightest variation in style, other than their height.

Haze and woodsmoke obscured the sky and the buildings in the distance. The plaza seemed simply an open place around a well in the center, and was the only open area of any size. It quickly terminated in narrow, dark streets with smooth walls rising up to each side, creating man-made chasms. Overhead, many of the blocky buildings bridged the streets, making them dark tunnels, and where there were none of the bridging buildings overhead, wash hung on lines between opposing windows. Some streets were cobblestone, but most were mud, running with fetid water.

People in drab, loose-fitting clothes filled the narrow streets, walked barefoot through the mud, stood with their arms folded, watching, or sat in groups in doorways. Women carrying clay water jugs on their heads, balanced with the aid of a single hand, moved tight against the walls to make room for the three horses. They made their way to and from the well in indifferent silence as Richard and Sister Verna passed.

A few older men sat in wide doorways, or leaned against walls. The men wore brimless, straight-sided, round, dark, flat-topped hats, with strange markings in light colors that looked to have been painted on with fingers. Many of the men smoked thin-stemmed pipes. Conversation fell silent as Richard and Sister Verna passed, and all watched the two strangers and three horses moving by. Some idly tugged on the long, dangling earrings they wore in their left ears.

Sister Verna led the way through the narrow streets, taking them deeper into the maze of drab buildings. When they at last reached a wider cobblestone street, she halted, turned to him, and spoke in quiet warning.

"These people are the Majendie. Their land is a vast, crescent-shaped swath of forests. We must travel the length of their land, all the way to the point of the horn of their land. They worship spirits. Those skulls we saw back there were sacrifices to their spirits.

"Though they hold foolish beliefs which are reprehensible, we do not have the power to change them. We need to pass through their land. You will do as they ask, or our skulls will end up with all the others on that pile."

Richard refused to give her the satisfaction of an answer or an argument. He sat with his hands folded over the pommel of his saddle and without emotion watched her until she finally turned away and started out once more.

After passing under a low bridge building, they entered a slightly dished, open square. Perhaps a thousand men milled about or clustered in small groups. Like the other men he had seen, these all wore the one long, dangling earring, though on the right side instead of the left. They also all wore short swords and black sashes. Unlike the other men, none of these wore hats on their shaved heads.

Off in the center, a raised platform held a circle of men sitting cross-legged, facing inward, around a thick pole. Here was the source of the eerie melody. A circle of women in black sat in a ring, facing outward, around the men.

Standing with her back against the pole, a big woman in a billowing black outfit slid the back of her hand up the pole and took hold of a knot in the end of a rope hanging from a bell. As she watched Richard and the Sister ride into the square, she rang the bell once. The Sister brought them to an abrupt halt as the piercing peal drifted across the square, hushing the men, and urging the flute players into faster strains.

"That is a warning," Sister Verna said. "A warning to the spirits of their enemies. The bell is also a call to the warriors present. Those are these men here in the square. The spirits have been warned, and the warriors called. If she rings that bell again, we die." Sister Verna glanced to his even expression. "This is a sacrifice ritual, to appease spirits."

She watched men come and take hold of the reins of their horses. The circle of women in black stood and began to dance and twirl to the haunting music. When Sister Verna glanced at him again, Richard, with deliberate care, checked that his sword was loose in its scabbard. She sighed and then dismounted. When she cleared her throat in annoyance, he finally dismounted, too.

Sister Verna drew her light cloak tight around herself as she spoke to him while watching the women in black dance and spin around the pole and the woman in the center.

"The Majendie live in a crescent around a land of swampy forest in which live their enemy. The people who live in the heart of that forbidding land are a wild, savage lot, and will not allow any of us through their land, much less guide us. Even if we could avoid them, we would become lost within an hour, and never find our way out. The only way for us to reach the Palace of the Prophets, which lies beyond these savages, is to go around them, along the crescent of land belonging to the Majendie. Our destination lies between the cusps of the crescent belonging to the Majendie, and beyond the savages in the center."

She glanced over, to make sure he was at least listening, before she went on. "The Majendie are at constant war with the savages who live in that swampy forest. In order to be permitted through Majendie land, we must prove we are allied with them and their spirits, and not their enemy.

"Those skulls we saw are the skulls of this enemy, who were sacrificed to the Majendie spirits. In order for us to be permitted to pass, we must help them in this sacrifice. The Majendie believe that men with the gift, like all men, carry the seed of life and soul, endowed by the spirits. More, they believe that one with the gift has a special, direct link with the spirits. A sacrifice made with the aid of a young man with the gift confers the sanctifying grace of their spirits upon all their people. They believe it breathes life, divine life, on their people.

"The Majendie require this participation when we bring young boys through for the first time, believing it links their spirits to those of the Majendie. This ceremony also insures that the people with whom they are at war will hate wizards, because they help the Majendie, and will never cooperate with them. This, the Majendie believe, denies their enemy a divine channel to the spirit world."

The men in the square all drew their short swords. Laying the swords on the ground with their points toward the woman in the center, they knelt with shiny heads bowed.

"The woman who rang the bell, the one in the center, is the leader of these

443

people. The Queen Mother. She is the one who is bound to the female spirits. She represents the spirits of fertility in this world. She is the embodiment of the receptacle of the divine seed from the spirit world."

The dancing women in black formed into a line and started off the platform in the direction of Richard and the Sister.

"The Queen Mother is sending her representatives to take you to the sacrificial offering." Sister Verna glanced up at him, then fussed with the corner of her cloak. "We are fortunate. This means they have one to be sacrificed. If we came here and they didn't, we would have to wait until one of their enemy was captured. Sometimes that can take weeks, even months."

Richard said nothing.

She turned her back to the approaching women in black and faced him. "You will be taken to a place where the prisoner is held. There you will be offered the chance to give your blessing. Not giving your blessing means you wish to precede the prisoner in sacrifice. If you don't give your blessing, it will only insure that you die, too.

"You give your blessing by kissing the sacred knife they will offer you. You don't have to kill the person with your own hand. You have only to kiss the knife to give your blessing, to give the spirits' blessings, and they will do the killing. But you must watch them do it, so the spirits will see the sacrifice through your eyes." She glanced over her shoulder at the approaching women in black. "The beliefs of these people are obscene."

She sighed in resignation and turned to face him again. Richard folded his arms and glared at her.

"I know you don't like this, Richard, but it has kept peace for three thousand years between us and the Majendie. Though it sounds a paradox, it saves lives, more lives than it costs. The savages who are their enemy make war not only on them, but also on us. The palace, and the civilized people of the Old World, are sporadically subjected to their raids and fierce attacks."

Small wonder, Richard thought, but he said nothing.

Sister Verna stepped aside to stand at his shoulder as the women in black formed into a dark knot before the two of them. All were older, perhaps the age of grandmothers. They were all portly, and their black outfits covered their hair and everything else except their wrinkled hands and faces.

With gnarled fingers, one drew the coarse black fabric tight at her chin. She bowed her head to Sister Verna. "Welcome, wisewoman. Our sentries have told us of your approach for nearly a day now. We are pleased to have you among us, for it is the time of the planting sacrifice. Though we had not expected your presence, it will be a great homage to the spirits to have the blessing in the sacrifice."

The old woman, who only came up to the height of his breastbone, looked Richard up and down, then she spoke again to Sister Verna.

"This is a magic man? He is not a boy."

"We have never before brought one so old to the palace of the wisewomen," Sister Verna said. "But he is a magic man, the same as the others."

The old woman in black looked into Richard's eyes as he watched her without expression. "He is too old to give the blessing."

Sister Verna tensed. "He is still a magic man."

The woman nodded to the Sister. "But he is too old to have others perform the sacrifice for him. He must do it himself. He must give our sacrifice to the spirits by his own hand." She gestured for a woman behind to come forward. "Lead him to where the offering waits."

With a bob of her head, the woman came forward and indicated he was to follow. Sister Verna tugged on his shirtsleeve. Richard could feel the heat of magic radiating from her fingers, up his arms, terminating in an uncomfortable tingling sensation at his neck under the Rada'Han.

"Richard," she whispered, "don't you dare swing the axe this time. You know not what you will bring to ruin."

Richard met her eyes before turning away without a word.

The round old woman led him off down a muddy street, past old men sitting in doorways, watching, and then turned them down a narrow alley. At the end she stooped through a low doorway. Richard had to bend nearly in half to follow.

Inside, carpets of intricate designs but dull colors covered the floor. There was no furniture except several low, leather-covered chests holding oil lamps. Four men with shaved heads squatted, rather than sat, on the rugs, two to each side of a passageway hung with a heavy tapestry instead of a door. Short spears with sharp, leaf-shaped iron heads rested across their knees. The unexpectedly high ceiling held a cloud of pipe smoke.

The men stood and bowed to the old woman. She bobbed her head to them and, as she did so, drew Richard forward.

"This is the magic man. Since he is the age of a man, the Queen Mother directs that the spirits take the sacrifice through his hands."

They all nodded and gave grim agreement that it was a wise decision, and prayed she would tell the Queen Mother that it would be done as directed. The woman in black bid them fair fortune in the task. She closed the rough spruce door behind herself after stooping through the low opening.

When she was gone, the men broke into grins. They all slapped Richard on the back, as if taking him into their confidence. The back of one man's shaved neck wrinkled in rows of furrows as he turned to glance at the tapestry-covered passageway. He put an arm around Richard's shoulder, giving it a squeeze with powerful fingers.

"You are fortunate indeed, lad. You'll like what we have for you." His sly smile revealed a missing, bottom tooth. "Come with us. You'll like this, lad. We can promise you, you will." He gave a hardy chuckle. "Today you'll be a man, if you're not one yet." The other three laughed with him.

The three pushed the tapestry aside, taking one of the lamps with them. The last man patted Richard's back, ushering him through. They all chuckled with anticipation.

The next room was much the same as the first, minus the pipe smoke. They led on through a sequence of rooms, each bare of decoration except for a few carpets scattered about. The men finally squatted beside a last covered passageway, planted the butts of their spears, and with a hand on them for support leaned toward him. They all shared the same cunning smiles.

"Careful now, lad. Don't be too anxious. Keep your head about yourself, and you'll have yourself a time with this savage."

They chuckled again with the private joke as they pushed the hanging aside and went through. Inside, the small, square room had a bare dirt floor. The ceiling was at least three stories high. A window near the top of one wall cast the small room in dim light. The place smelled of the chamber pot off to the side.

Crouched to the far left was a naked woman. She tried to push herself farther into the corner when she saw the men. Arms around her knees, she pulled them tight to herself.

She was covered with dirty marks and smears, cuts and bruises. Her mass of long, tangled, black hair frizzed out, framing her filthy face. Her dark eyes narrowed with loathing as she watched the four men. By their leering smiles, she had cause to know them.

Around her neck was a thick iron collar connected by heavy chain to a massive pin in the wall.

The men spread out around the room, squatted, and leaned their backs against the walls. Their fists held their spears upright between their knees. Richard imitated them, squatting and leaning against the wall to the woman's right.

"I wish to speak with the spirits," Richard said. The four men blinked at him. "I must ask them how they wish it done."

"There is only one way to do it," the man with the missing tooth said. "You must cut off her head. Now that the iron collar is around her neck, it's the only way to get her out. Her head must be separated from her body."

"Even so, it must be done in the manner the spirits wish. I must talk with them. I must know exactly how to do this . . . to please them."

They all considered this. The man with the missing tooth pushed his cheek out with his tongue as he pondered. Finally he brightened. "The Queen Mother and her women drink *juka* to speak with the spirits. I could bring you some *juka*, and then you, too, could speak with the spirits."

"Then bring me this *juka*, so I may speak with the spirits and do as they command. I would not want to make a mistake, and ruin your planting sacrifice."

The men agreed that this was a wise request, considering that Richard was to make the sacrifice himself instead of simply blessing it. One of the men hurried off.

The other three waited in silence, again leering at the woman. She moved her feet closer together to cover herself as she squatted in the corner, and glowered back.

One man pulled a thin-stemmed pipe and a long splinter from a pocket. He lit the splinter in the flame of the lamp, and used it to light his pipe. He puffed as he watched the woman, eyeing her in an intimate way. Her chin held defiantly up, the woman glared back. The smoke drifted up into the dim air as his steady puffing quickened.

Richard crouched, leaning against the wall, with his arms folded across his lap so as to partially hide his right hand draped nonchalantly near the hilt of his sword. The fourth man finally came back, carrying a round clay pot in both hands. The pot had a small opening in the top and white symbols painted around the sides.

"The Queen Mother and her women agreed, and sent this *juka* so you may call the spirits. When you drink this, the spirits will visit you." He set the pot in front of Richard and then, pulling a knife from his belt, held the green malachite handle out to him. It was carved with figures in obscene poses. "This is the sacred knife, to be used in the sacrifice." When Richard took the knife and slid the stout blade behind his belt, the man joined his fellows squatting against the walls.

The man closest to the woman, on the other side, seemed pleased that the Queen Mother had sent the *juka*. He gave Richard a knowing wink. Then he lifted his spearpoint to the woman's face.

"The magic man has come to offer you to the spirits." He smiled encouragement past her, to Richard. "But first, he would like to give you the spirits' gift of his seed." She didn't move. His smile transformed into a sneer as he thumped the butt of his spear to the dirt. "Do not insult the spirits! You will take their offering!" His voice lowered to a growl. "Now."

Her eyes never leaving him, she uncoiled herself and obediently lay down on the dirt, on her back. She opened her legs and cast Richard a defiant glance. She obviously knew the consequence of denying these men what they wished.

The man sprang forward and stabbed his spear into her thigh muscle. She screamed out and flinched back.

"You know better than that! You will not insult us! We are not stupid!" He feigned another jab. "Do it properly!"

Richard's fingers curled around the hilt of his sword, but otherwise he did not move. The woman made no effort to tend the bleeding gash on her leg, but instead obediently turned over onto her elbows and knees, sticking her bottom up in the air.

The men chuckled to Richard.

"You would not like to lie with this one face-to-face," the man with the missing tooth said. "She bites." The others nodded their certain knowledge of that. "Mount her this way, and hold her by her hair. She will not be able to bite you this way, and you can have all you wish."

The men waited. Neither Richard nor the woman moved.

"Can you fools not see?" the woman said. "He does not wish to mount me like a dog in front of you!" Her face lying against the dirt, she gave Richard a mocking smile. "He is shy. He does not wish you to see how little his magic stick is."

Every eye was on him. Richard's knuckles were white around the hilt. He strained to put an emotionless face over the rage of the magic searing through him from the sword. He struggled to maintain reason.

Letting the magic loose in here would accomplish nothing.

One of the men gave a playful elbow to another and laughed. "Perhaps she is right. He is a young one. Maybe he is not used to others watching his pleasure."

The seams around his control were strained near to bursting. Richard concentrated on keeping his free hand steady and making it move gracefully. He lifted the clay pot with the *juka*, showing it to them. He labored mightily to keep his voice even. "The spirits wish to speak to me of important matters."

The smiles all withered. The knew him as a magic man, but not a young one as they were used to seeing. They didn't have any idea of his power, but were obviously worried about it, worried about his smoldering, too quiet smoothness.

"We must leave him to his duty," one of the men said. "We should leave him to be with the spirits, and to take his pleasure from the savage if he wishes before he gives the spirits this offering." He bowed his shiny head to Richard. "We will leave you to your peace. We will wait in the room where you saw us first."

Solemn-faced, the four hurried off. After they were gone, and she could be sure they were a good distance away, the woman spat at him.

She arched her back like a cat in heat, sticking her behind higher in the air. "You may mount me now, like the dog you are. Come, magic man, prove you can mount a woman when she is held for you by a chain. You can do no worse to me than the other dogs." She spat at him again. "You are all dogs."

447

Richard extended his leg and shoved a foot against her hip, tipping her over. "I'm not like those men."

She rolled onto her back. She threw her arms and legs open and gave him a contemptuous glare. "So. You wish to have me like this, to prove you are better than they?"

Richard gritted his teeth. "Stop it. I'm not here for that."

She sat up. She lifted her chin, but her eyes filled with sudden terror. "So, you will sacrifice me now?"

Richard realized his hand was still gripping the hilt. He had forgotten to maintain a calm expression. He took his hand away, letting the magic recede and his rage cool. As she watched, he poured the *juka* on the dirt floor.

"I'm going to get you out of this. My name is Richard. What's yours?"

Her eyes narrowed. "Why do you wish to know?"

"Well, if I'm going to take you out of here, I need to know what to call you. I can't call you 'woman.'"

She surveyed him silently for a moment. "I am Du Chaillu."

"Do I call you Du? Or Chaillu? Or Du Chaillu?"

Puzzlement wrinkled her brow. "Du Chaillu. That is my name."

Richard gave her a smile of reassurance. "All right, then. Du Chaillu. Who are your people? What are they called?"

"We are Baka Ban Mana."

"And what does that mean, Baka Ban Mana?"

Her chin came up again. "Those without masters."

Richard smiled to himself. "I think you are worthy of your people. You don't look to be a woman to be mastered."

Chin still held up, she studied his eyes. "You say these words, but you intend to mount me as the others."

Richard shook his head. "No. I told you I wouldn't do that. I'm going to try to get you out of here, and back to your people."

"None of my people captured by the Majendie ever returns."

Richard leaned toward her. "Then you shall be the first."

Richard drew his sword. Du Chaillu scooted back against the wall, drawing her knees up to her chest, hiding her face. He realized that she had misinterpreted his action and expected the worst.

"It's all right, Du Chaillu. I'm not going to hurt you. I simply need to get that collar off you."

She shrank from him; then, thinking better of her shameful retreat, she lifted her head and spat at him. "Yes, by taking off my head. You do not speak the truth. You wish to kill me now, and just want me to meekly offer you my neck."

With his sleeve, Richard wiped the spittle off the side of his forehead. He reached out and put a comforting hand to her shoulder. "No. I'm not going to hurt you. I simply need to use this sword to get the collar off. How else can I get you out of here? You will be safe, you'll see. Let me get it off you?"

"Swords cannot cut iron!"

Richard lifted an eyebrow. "Magic can."

She squeezed her eyes shut and held her breath as he gently put an arm around her shoulder and rolled her facedown in his lap. He laid the sword's point to the side of her neck. He had seen the Sword of Truth cut through iron before, and he knew the sword's magic could do the job. She lay dead still as he slid the sword under the heavy iron band.

And then she lunged at him. In a blink, she had a fierce grip on his left arm. Her teeth clamped around his forearm, pinching the nerves.

Richard froze. He knew that if he were to try to yank his arm back, her teeth would probably tear the muscle from the bone. He still had his right hand on the sword. The rage of the magic pounded through him. He used the anger to help him block the pain and remain still.

With the sword under the collar as it was, it would be a simple matter to give it a twist and a push. It would cut her throat, if not decapitate her, and he would be free of her teeth. The pain from her locking bite was agonizing.

"Du Chaillu," he managed through gritted teeth. "Let go. I'm not going to hurt you. If it were my intention to hurt you, I could cut you right now with the sword to make you let go."

After a long moment, silent of everything but his labored breathing, she relaxed the pressure of her teeth, but didn't release his arm from her grip.

She tilted her head a bit. "Why?" Her eyes peered up at him. "Why do you wish to help me?"

Richard stared down into her dark eyes. He took a chance and removed his hand from the sword. He brought the hand up, and touched his fingers to the cold metal collar around his neck.

"I, too, am a prisoner. I, too, know what it is to be held by a collar. I don't like collars. Though I can't free myself in this way, I can try to free you."

Her ferocious grip on his arm relaxed. She cocked her head to the side as she frowned up at him.

"But you are a magic man."

"That's why I was taken prisoner. The woman I'm with is taking me to a place called the Palace of the Prophets. She says the magic will kill me if I don't go to this place."

"You are with one of the witches? From the big stone witch house?"

"She is not a witch, but one with magic, too. She put this collar on me to make me go with her."

Du Chaillu's eyes flicked over the collar around his neck.

"If you let me go, the Majendie will not allow you to go through their land to the big stone house."

Richard gave her a little smile. "I was hoping that if I helped you get back to your people, you would permit us to pass through your land, and maybe that you would guide us, so that we might reach the palace."

A sly smile spread on her lips. "We could kill the witch."

Richard shook his head. "I don't kill people unless I'm forced to. It would not help anyway. I must go to the palace to get my collar off. If I don't go there, I will die."

Du Chaillu looked away from his gaze. Richard waited while she glanced around her prison.

"I do not know if you speak the truth, or if you mean to cut my throat." She gently rubbed his arm where she had bitten him. "But if you kill me, I was to be killed anyway, and had no chance, and at least I will not be mounted any more by those dogs. If you tell the truth, then I will be free, but we must still escape. We are still in the land of the Majendie."

Richard winked. "I have a plan. At least we can try."

She frowned at him. "You could do this thing to me, and they would be happy, and you could go to the palace. You would be safe. Are you not afraid they will kill you?"

Richard nodded. "But I am more afraid to live the rest of my life seeing in my mind your pretty eyes and wishing I had helped you."

She gave him a sidelong glance. "Maybe you are a magic man, but you are not a smart man. A smart man would want to be safe."

"I am the Seeker."

"What is this, the Seeker?"

"It's a long story. But I guess it means I do my best to see the truth prevail, to see right done. This sword has magic, and it helps me in my quest. It's called the Sword of Truth."

She let out a long breath, and finally laid her head back in his lap. "Try then, or kill me. I was dead anyway."

Richard gave her filthy, bare back a pat of reassurance. "Hold still."

He reached under her neck and wrapped his fingers around the collar, holding it tight. With his other hand, the hand on the hilt, the hand through which the magic was coursing into him, he gave a mighty heave.

With a loud crack, the iron shattered. Hot shards of metal ricocheted off the walls. One large piece spun like a top in the dirt, finally wobbling and falling over. Silence settled over them. He held his breath, hoping none of the metal fragments had cut her throat.

Du Chaillu sat up. Her eyes wide, she felt her neck. Finding no injury, she broke into a wide grin.

"It is off! You got the collar off and my head is still attached!"

Richard feigned a touch of indignation. "I told you I would. Now we must get away from here. Come on."

He led her back through the rooms the way he had come in. When he reached the next to last room from where the men waited, he held a finger to his lips and told her to be quiet and wait for him to come back for her.

She folded her arms under her bare breasts. "Why? I will go with you. You said you would not leave me here."

Richard let out an exasperated breath. "I'm going to get you some clothes. We can't leave with you . . ." With a gesture, he indicated her bare condition.

She unfolded her arms and looked down at herself. "Why? What is wrong with me? I am not a bad shape to look upon. Many men have told me . . ."

"What is it with you people!" he whispered heatedly. "I have seen more naked people since I left my homeland last autumn than in the whole of my life! And not a one of you seems the least little bit . . ."

She grinned. "Your face is red."

Richard growled through gritted teeth. "Wait here!"

Smirking, she folded her arms again. "I will wait."

In the outer room the four men jumped to their feet when Richard came through the carpet-covered opening. He didn't give them any time to ask questions.

"Where are the woman's clothes?"

Confused, they glanced at one another. "Her clothes? Why do you want . . ."

Richard took an aggressive stride toward the man. "Who are you to question the spirits! Do as they say! Get me her clothes!"

450

All four flinched back. They stared at him briefly and then went to the low chests. They set the lamps aside and opened the lids, rummaging through the chests, tossing clothes aside.

"Here! I found them!" one of them said. He held up a garment that looked to be finely woven flax. Different-colored strips hung in rows from the light brown fabric. "This is hers." He held up a buckskin belt. "And this, too."

Richard snatched them from the man's fist. "You will wait here." He grabbed up a scrap of cloth the men had thrown on the floor as they had searched for the dress.

He went back through the opening before there was time for any questions. Du Chaillu waited, her arms still folded. When she saw what he held in his hands, she gasped. She clutched the dress to her breast. Tears filled her dark eyes.

"My prayer dress!"

She threw her arms around his neck and, raising up on her tiptoes, started kissing him all over his face. Richard mashed her mass of black hair flat against the sides of her head as he pushed her away.

"All right, all right, put it on. Hurry."

Grinning at him, she pulled the dress over her head, poking her arms through the long sleeves. Up the outside of each arm and across the shoulders was a row of little strips of different-colored cloth. Each was knotted on through a small hole beneath a corded band. The dress came to just below her knees. As she tied the belt at her waist, Richard noticed the blood still running down to her foot from where the men had stabbed her in the thigh.

He dropped to one knee before her and motioned with his hands. "Lift it up. Lift up your dress."

Du Chaillu looked down at him. She lifted an eyebrow. "I have just covered myself, and now you wish me to uncover?"

Richard pursed his lips. He waved the strip of cloth at her. "You are bleeding. I need to put this around the wound."

Giggling, she raised her skirt and held her leg out, rotating it from side to side, displaying it in a teasing manner. Richard quickly wrapped the cloth around her thigh, over the gash, and jerked the knot tight. She yelped with pain. He thought it served her right, but apologized anyway.

Taking her by the hand, he pulled her though the remaining rooms. As he passed through the last, he growled at the four men to stay where they were. Still holding Du Chaillu's hand tight, he led her back down the alleyway and streets to the open square. He saw the heads of the three horses sticking up above the sea of shiny, bald heads. He plowed his way through the throng, toward the horses.

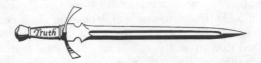

**A**lthough his sword sat in its scabbard, he was already drawing its magic. Rage surged into him. He summoned it ever onward, letting his barriers fall before its advance.

He was entering a silent world all his own. A world of grim committal to what he was.

Bringer of death.

Sister Verna paled when she saw him pulling Du Chaillu after, becoming even paler when she saw his demeanor.

Without a word to her, Richard snatched his bow off the side of his saddle. He grunted with the effort of swiftly stretching the bowstring to the bow. He yanked two steel-bladed arrows from the quiver hanging from Bonnie's saddle. His chest heaved with wrath.

The crowd had all turned toward him. Puzzled faces bobbed up as men behind jumped to get a view. The women in black all looked up in his direction. The Queen Mother watched.

Sister Verna's face was by now bright red. "Richard! What do you think . . .!"

Richard shoved her back. "Be quiet."

Bow and arrows in hand, he leapt up onto his saddle. The mumbling fell silent. Richard directed himself to the Queen Mother. "I have spoken with the spirits!"

The back of the Queen Mother's hand started sliding up the pole, toward the bell's rope. That was all the sign he needed. She had been offered a chance. The irrevocable commitment had been made.

He loosed the magic within himself.

In one swift motion, Richard nocked an arrow. He drew string to cheek. He called the target. The arrow was away.

The air hissed with the sound of the arrow's flight. The crowd gasped. Before the arrow reached the target, while the air still sizzled with its sound, Richard had the second arrow nocked and on target.

With a twanging thunk, the first arrow made a solid hit, dead-on where he intended it. The Queen Mother let out a clipped cry of surprise and pain. Penetrating the space between the two bones in her wrist, the arrow pinned her arm to the pole, preventing her hand from reaching the bell's rope. Her other hand started over toward the rope.

The second arrow sat rock solid in the invisible notch in the air, on target, waiting. "Move toward the bell, and the next arrow goes through your right eye!"

The gaggle of women in black fell to their knees, wailing. The Queen Mother became still. Blood trickled down her arm.

Inside, storms of anger thundered through him. Outside, he was stone. "You will hear what the spirits have commanded!"

Slowly, the Queen Mother let her free hand drop to her side. "Speak their words, then."

Richard still held the bowstring to his cheek, and had no intention of letting it relax. Though the arrow was aimed at one, his ire was directed at all.

Magic burned through him at full fury. The force of rage pounded through his veins. In the past, it had always been focused on an enemy, someone specific. This was different. It was open-ended rage, rage at all those present, at everyone involved in human sacrifice. This was nonspecific wrath.

That made it worse. It drew more magic.

Richard didn't know if it was the all-encompassing threat that drew more magic, or if it was because of all the practicing he had done with Sister Verna, enabling him to focus, but whatever the reason, he was calling forth more magic from the sword than he ever had before, more than he had known was there. The magic seethed with frightening power. The very air vibrated with it.

The men about stepped back. The wailing women fell into a hush. The Queen Mother's face was white against the black of her dress. A thousand people stood in silent terror of one.

"The spirits wish no more sacrifices! It does not prove your devotion to them, only that you can kill! From now on, you must show your respect of the spirits by showing respect for the lives of the Baka Ban Mana. If you do not, the spirits will vent their wrath by destroying you! Take their threat to heart, or they will bring starvation and death to the Majendie!"

He spoke to the men as they pressed forward. "If any of you makes a move against me or these two women, the Queen Mother dies." They all glanced to one another, seeking courage. "You may think to kill me," he told them, the target not wavering in the slightest, "but you cannot before the Queen Mother dies. You saw the shot I made. My hand is guided by magic. I do not miss."

The men backed away.

"Let him be!" the Queen Mother called out. "Hear what he has to say!"

"I have told you what the spirits have said! You will obey!"

She was silent a moment. "We will consult the spirits ourselves."

"You would insult them? You would be admitting you do not heed their words, but your own worldly wishes!"

"But we must . . ."

"I'm not here to bargain on their behalf! The spirits have ordered I give the sacrificial knife to this woman, so she may carry it back to her people, to show them that the Majendie will no longer hunt them.

"The spirits will warn you of their anger by taking the seed you plant, and only when you send representatives to the Baka Ban Mana and tell them you agree to the wishes of the spirits will you be able to plant your crops. If you do not follow the spirits' wishes, you will all starve to death!

"We are leaving now. I will have your word that we will be granted safe leave of your land, or you will die right now."

"We must consider . . ."

"I grant you until the count of three to give me your decision! One, two, three!" The Queen Mother gasped. The women in black gasped. The crowd gasped. "What have you decided!"

453

The Queen Mother held her free hand up, imploring he hold his arrow. "You may go! You have the word of the Queen Mother that you may leave our land unharmed!"

"A wise decision."

Her hand closed into a fist, one finger pointing toward them. "But this is a violation of our agreement with the wisewomen. The accord is at an end. You must leave our land at once. You are banished."

"So be it," Richard said. "But keep to your word, or you will reap the grim rewards of any imprudent action."

He released the tension from the bow. Standing in his stirrups, he pulled the sacred knife from his belt and held it up high for all to see.

"This woman will take this back to her people, and tell them of the words of the spirits. As to their part, the Baka Ban Mana may no longer make war on the Majendie. You may no longer make war on them. You will be two peoples at peace! Neither may harm the other! Heed the words of the spirits, or bear the consequences!"

His voice dropped to a fierce whisper, yet the wrath of the magic carried the words to the farthest corners of the square, and in the stillness, every ear could hear them. "Heed my orders, or suffer what I will bring upon you. I will lay waste to you."

Magic lay over the square like fog in a valley, ethereal yet real, a palpable manifestation of his outrage that touched everyone present, and all trembled at that touch.

Richard leapt off his horse. The men shrank back a few more steps. Sister Verna was speechless with rage. He had never seen her in such a state. She stood, as if paralyzed, with her fists out before her.

Richard leveled his glare, and his wrath, on her. "Get on your horse, Sister. We're leaving."

Her jaw looked ready to shatter under the pressure of how tightly it was clenched. "You are mad! We will not . . ."

Richard thrust a finger toward her. "If you wish to argue with someone, Sister, you may stay and argue with these people. I'm sure they will oblige you. I'm going to the palace to get this collar off. If you want to go with me, then get on your horse."

"There is no way! We cannot now travel the horn of the Majendie land! We are banished!"

Richard lifted his thumb to Du Chaillu. "She will guide us to the Palace of the Prophets, through the Baka Ban Mana's land."

Du Chaillu folded her arms and gave the Sister a self-satisfied smile.

Sister Verna looked from her to Richard. "You truly are mad. We cannot . . ."

Richard gritted his teeth with a growl, the sword's anger still at full fury. "If you wish to go with me to the palace, get on your horse! I'm leaving!"

Du Chaillu watched as Richard stuck the green-handled knife behind her buckskin belt. "I have charged you with a responsibility. You will live up to it. Now, get up on that horse."

Du Chaillu unfolded her arms in sudden worry, looking to the horse and back to him. She folded her arms again and put her nose in the air. "I will not ride on that beast. It stinks."

"So do you!" Richard roared. "Now get up on that horse!"

She flinched back. Eyes wide in fright at his glare, she swallowed, gulping air. "Now I know what a Seeker is."

She scrambled awkwardly up onto Geraldine. The sister was already atop Jessup. Richard vaulted up onto Bonnie.

With a last, warning look at the men gathered, he squeezed his horse's ribs and she sprang into a gallop. The other two horses took out after him. The men swept back out of the way.

The magic hungered for blood, raged for it. Richard wished someone would try to stop him. No one did.

"Please," Du Chaillu said, "it is almost dark. May we please stop, or at least allow me to walk. This beast is hurting me."

She was holding on for dear life, bouncing in the saddle as Geraldine trotted along. The little strips of colored cloth on her dress were all aflutter. He could hear Sister Verna's horse trotting along behind, but he didn't look back at her.

Richard glanced up at the sun setting beyond the thick tangle of branches. His rage was finally withering with the light. For a time, it had seemed as if he would never be able to put it down.

Du Chaillu pointed past him with her chin, to his right, afraid to lift a hand. "There is a small pond there, through the reeds, and a grassy place before it."

"Are you sure we are in Baka Ban Mana land?"

She nodded. "For the last few hours. This is our land. I know this place."

"All right. We will stop for the night."

He held her horse for her as she slid off. With a groan, she rubbed the flats of her hands on her bottom. "If you make me ride that beast again tomorrow, I will bite you!"

For the first time since they had left the Majendie, he was able to smile. As Richard went about unsaddling the horses, he sent Du Chaillu to get water in a canvas bucket. While she went off through the reeds and rushes to the pond, Sister Verna gathered wood and used her magic to set it afire. When he was finished caring for the horses, he put them on long tethers so they could graze on the grass.

"I guess introductions are in order," Richard said when Du Chaillu returned. "Sister Verna, this is Du Chaillu. Du Chaillu, this is Sister Verna."

Sister Verna seemed to have cooled, or at least put a mask over her anger. "I am pleased for you, Du Chaillu, that you did not have to die this day."

Du Chaillu glared. Richard knew she thought of the Sisters of the Light as witches.

"I do feel sorrow, however," the Sister added, "for all those who will die in your place."

"You are not pleased for me. You wish me dead. You wish all the Baka Ban Mana to die."

"That is not true. I wish no one to die. But I know I could not convince you of that. Think what you will."

Du Chaillu took the sacrificial knife from her belt and held the handle in front of Sister Verna's eyes. "They kept me on that chain for three moons." She looked to the green handle and pointed to one of the obscene couplings carved on it. "Those dogs did this to me." Sister Verna glanced to the knife as Du Chaillu tapped a finger to another scene. "And this. And this, too."

Sister Verna watched the other's chest heaving in ire. "There is no way I could convince you, Du Chaillu, how much I abhor what they did to you, and what they intended to do. There are many things in this world that I abhor, but can do nothing about, and in some cases, must tolerate, in order to serve a greater good."

Du Chaillu patted her belly. "I have lost my moon flow. Those dogs have put me with child! Now I must go to the midwives and ask them for herbs to shed the child of a dog."

Sister Verna clasped her hand before herself. "Please, Du Chaillu, don't do that. A child is a gift from the Creator. Please don't reject his gift."

"Gift! This great Creator has a wicked way of bestowing his gifts!"

"Du Chaillu," Richard said, "up until now, the Majendie have killed every Baka Ban Mana they have captured. You are the first to be freed. They will kill no more. Think of this child as symbol of the new life between your peoples. For that new life, for all your children, to flourish, the killing must stop. Let the child live? It has done no harm."

"The father has done harm!"

Richard swallowed. "Children are not necessarily evil, just because the father was."

"If the father is evil, then the child will be as he!"

"That is not true," the Sister said. "Richard's father was an evil man who killed many people, yet Richard seeks to preserve life. His mother knew that the guilt of crimes does not pass beyond the one who commits them. She did not spare her love because Richard's father raped her. Richard was raised by good people who taught him right. Because of that, you are alive today. You can teach the child right."

Du Chaillu's fury faltered as she looked to Richard. "Is this true? Your mother was treated as I, by an evil dog?"

Richard could only manage a nod.

She rubbed her belly. "I will consider what you say before I decide. You have returned my life; I will weigh your words."

Richard squeezed her shoulder. "Whatever you decide, I'm sure it will be for the best."

"If she lives long enough to decide," Sister Verna said. "You've made promises and threats that you cannot fulfill. When the Majendie plant their crops, and nothing happens, they will lose their fear of what you have told them today. What you've done will count for nothing and they will once again make war on her people. To say nothing of mine."

Richard pulled the leather thong with the Bird Man's whistle off over his head. "I wouldn't exactly say nothing is going to happen, Sister. Something is indeed going to happen." He hung the whistle around Du Chaillu's neck. "This was a gift to me, and now my gift to you, so that you can stop the killing." He held the carved bone up. "This is a magic whistle. It calls birds. More birds than you've ever seen in one place before. I'm counting on you to fulfill my promise.

"You are to go to their planting fields. Keep yourself hidden. Then, at sunset, blow on this magic whistle. You will hear no sound, but the birds will be called by the magic. In your mind, keep picturing birds. Think of all the birds you know as you blow on the whistle, and keep blowing until they come."

She touched the carved bone whistle. "Magic? The birds will truly come?"

He gave her a one-sided smile. "Oh, yes, they'll come. There is no doubt of that. The magic will call them. No person will hear the sound, but the birds will. The Majendie will not know it's you who calls the birds. The birds will be hungry and will devour all the seed. Every time the Majendie plant seeds, you call the birds and take it away from them."

She grinned. "The Majendie will starve to death!"

Richard put his face close to hers. "No. This is my gift to you, to stop the killing, not a gift to help you kill. You will call the birds to steal their seed until the Majendie agree to live in peace with you. When they have fulfilled their part of the bargain, you must fulfill your part, and agree to live in peace with them."

He put his first finger right in front of her nose. "If you misuse my gift, I will come back and use other magic against your people. I've placed my trust in you to do right. Do not fail my trust."

Du Chaillu averted her eyes. She gave a little sniff. "I will do right. I will use your gift as you say." She tucked the whistle into her dress. "Thank you for helping to bring peace to my people."

"That's my greatest hope. Peace."

"Peace," Sister Verna huffed. She directed a smoldering glare to Richard. "You think it's so simple? You think that after three thousand years you can simply decree that the killing will stop? You think all it takes is your mere presence, and the ways of people will change? You are a naive child. Though the crimes of the father do not pass on to the son, you have a simplistic way of seeing things that brings harm just the same."

"If you think, Sister, that I would be a party to human sacrifices for any reason, you are seriously mistaken." He started to turn away, but then turned back. "What harm have I brought? What killing have I started?"

She leaned toward him. "Well, for one thing, if we don't help ones with the gift, like you, it will kill them, as it would kill you. How do you propose we get those boys to the palace? We can no longer cross the Majendie's land." She glanced to Du Chaillu. "She has only given you pass through her land. She has not said we may bring others through." She straightened. "Those boys will die because of what you have done."

Richard thought about it a moment. He was exhausted. Using the sword's magic had wearied him as it never had before. He wanted nothing more than to sleep. He didn't feel like solving problems, or arguing. At last, he looked to Du Chaillu.

"When you make peace with the Majendie, before you let them plant once again, you must add another condition. You must tell them that in honor of the killing being brought to an end, in honor of the peace, they will let the Sisters cross their land." She watched his eyes a moment before she finally nodded. "Your people will do the same."

He narrowed his eyes at the Sister. "Satisfied?"

"In the valley, when you struck down a beast, a thousand snakes sprang forth from its corpse. This is no different.

"It would be impossible," she said, "for me to accurately recall all the lies you've told today. I've reprimanded you before for lying, and cautioned you not to do it again. I told you not to swing the axe today, and you did it anyway, despite my warning. I can scarcely tally all the commands you've managed to violate in this one day. What you've done has not finished the killing, but only begun it."

"In this, Sister, I am the Seeker, not your student. As Seeker, I have no tolerance for human sacrifice. None. The deaths of others are a separate issue. You cannot use it as a link to justify murder. There will be no compromise in this. And I don't think you want to punish me for stopping something I would wager you wish had been stopped long ago."

The muscles in her face relaxed. "As a Sister of the Light, I have no power to change things, and under obligation to save more lives, I had to uphold what has been for three thousand years. But I admit I hated it, and in a way I'm glad you have taken it out of my hands. But that does not negate the trouble it will cause, or the deaths. When you put the Rada'Han on, you told me that holding the leash to that collar would be worse than wearing it. Your words are proving true."

Her lower eyelids filled with glistening moisture. "You have made my greatest love, my calling, a misery.

"I am past wanting to punish you for your disobedience. In a few days we will be at the palace, and I will at last be finished with you. They will have to deal with you.

"We shall see how they handle you when you displease them. I believe you will find they are not prepared to be as tolerant as I have been. They will use that collar. And when they do, I also think they will come to regret holding your leash more than do I. I think they will come to regret trying to help you, as do I."

Richard put his hands in his back pockets as he stared off at the thick forest of oak and leather leaf. "I'm sorry you feel that way, Sister, and I guess I can understand it. Although I admit I have fought being your prisoner, this today was not about you and me.

"This was about what is right. As one who would wish to teach me, I would hope you shared that moral stance. I would hope the Sisters would not want to teach the use of the gift to one who could easily bend his convictions to the circumstance.

"Sister Verna, I was not trying to displease you. I simply could not live with myself if I allowed a murder to take place under my nose, much less participated in it."

"I know, Richard. But that only makes it worse, because it's all one and the same." She unclasped her hands and peered about at the fire and their supplies, finally pulling a cake of soap from a saddlebag. "I'll make a stew, and bannock." She tossed the cake of soap to him. "Du Chaillu needs a bath."

Du Chaillu folded her arms in a huff. "While I was chained to a wall, the dogs who came to mount me did not offer me water so I would smell pretty for you."

Sister Verna squatted down, pulling supplies out. "I meant no offense, Du Chaillu. I simply thought you would want to wash the dirt of those men off you. If it were me, I would want nothing more than to try to wash the feel of their hands from my flesh."

Du Chaillu's indignation faltered. "Well of course I would!" She snatched the soap from Richard. "You smell of that beast you ride. You will wash too, or I will not want to be near you and will send you off to eat by yourself."

Richard chuckled. "If it will keep the peace with you, I'll wash, too."

As Du Chaillu marched off toward the pond, Sister Verna called quietly to him. He waited next to her while she pulled a pot from a saddlebag.

"Her people have been killing any 'magic man' they could get their hands on for the last three thousand years. There is no time to give you history lessons." She looked up to his eyes. "Old habits spring to hand as easily as a knife. Don't turn your back on her. Sooner or later, she is going to try to kill you."

Her quiet tone unexpectedly raised bumps on his flesh. "I'll try to keep myself alive, Sister, so you can deliver me to the palace and at last be free of your onerous charge."

Richard hurried toward the pond and caught up with Du Chaillu as she was walking through the reeds. "Why did you call that your prayer dress?"

Du Chaillu held her arms out, letting the breeze ruffle the strips of cloth on her dress. "These are prayers."

"What are prayers? You mean the strips of cloth?"

She nodded. "Each is a prayer. When the wind blows, and they fly, each sends a prayer to the spirits."

"And what do you pray for?"

"Every one of these prayers is the same, from the heart of the person who gave me their prayer. They are all prayers to have our land returned to us."

"Your land? But you are in your land."

"No. This is where we live, but it is not our land. Many ages ago, our land was taken by the magic men. They banished us here."

They reached the edge of the pond. Puffs of breeze drew up ripples in dark patches. The bank was grassy with thick patches of rushes to each side, extending out into the water.

"The magic men took your land? What land?"

"They took our land from our ancestors." She pointed in the direction of the Valley of the Lost. "The land on the other side of the Majendie. I was going to our land, with our prayers, to ask the spirits if they would help our land be returned to us. But the Majendie caught me, and I was not able to take our prayers to the spirits."

"How will the spirits return your land to you?"

She shrugged. "The old words say only that we must send one every year to our land, to pray to the spirits, and if we do, our land will be returned." She untied her belt and slipped it to the ground. With unsettling grace, she tossed the green-handled knife aside, sticking it in the round end of a branch on a log.

"How?"

She gave him a curious frown. "By sending us our master."

"I thought you were the Baka Ban Mana, those without masters."

She shrugged. "Because the spirits have not sent us one yet."

While Richard was puzzling over this, she reached down, took hold of her dress, and pulled it off over her head.

"What do you think you're doing!"

She frowned. "It is me that I must wash, not my dress."

"Well, not in front of me!"

She looked down at herself. "You have already seen me. I have not grown any different since this morning." She looked up at him. "Your face is red again."

"Over there." He pointed. "Go on the other side of the rushes. You on one side and me on the other."

He turned his back to her.

"But we have only one soap."

"Well, you can throw it to me when you're through."

She came around to the front of him. He tried to turn again but she followed him around, grabbing at his buttons.

"I cannot scrub my own back. And it is not fair. You have seen me, so I should see you. That is why you are turning red, because you have not been fair. This will make you feel better."

He slapped her hands away. "Stop it. Du Chaillu, where I come from this is not proper. Men and women do not bathe together. It's just not done." He turned his back to her again.

"Not even my third husband is as shy as you."

"Third! You have had three husbands?"

"No. I have five."

Richard stiffened. "Have?" He turned to her. "What do you mean 'have'?"

She looked at him as if he had asked if trees grew in the forest. "I have five husbands. Five husbands and my children."

"And how many of those do you have?"

"Three. Two girls, and a boy." A wistful smile came to her. "It is a long time since I have held them." Her smile turned sad. "My poor babies will have cried every night, thinking I am dead. No one ever returned from the Majendie before." She grinned. "My husbands will be anxious to draw lots to see who will be the first to try to give me another child." Her smile faded and her voice trailed off. "But I guess a Majendie dog has already done that."

Richard handed her the soap. "It will all turn out fine. You'll see. Go bathe. I'll go on the other side of the rushes."

He relaxed in the cool water, listening to her splash, waiting for her to finish with the soap. A mist thickened over the pond, stealing slowly, silently, into the surrounding trees.

"I've never heard of a woman having more than one husband. Do all the Baka Ban Mana women have more than one husband?"

She giggled. "No. Only me."

"Why you?"

The water stopped splashing. "Because I wear the prayer dress," she said, as if it should be self-evident.

Richard rolled his eyes. "Well, what does . . ."

She came swimming through the rushes toward him. "Before you can have the soap, you must wash my back."

Richard let out an aggravated sigh. "All right, if I wash your back, will you then go back on your side?"

She presented her back to him. "If you do a proper job."

When she was satisfied, she finally went back to get dressed while he washed. She told him over the chirp of bugs and the trill of frogs that she was hungry. He was pulling his pants on while she called for him to hurry so they could eat.

He threw his shirt over his shoulder and ran to catch up with her as she headed toward the smell of cooking. She looked much better clean. Her hair looked like a normal person's, instead of a wild animal's. She looked no more like a savage, but somehow noble.

It wasn't dark yet, but getting close to it. The mist that had formed over the pond was drifting in around them from behind. The trees were disappearing in the gathering fog.

As the two of them stepped into the ring of light around the fire, Sister Verna

460

stood. Richard was putting his right arm through his sleeve when he froze at the wide-eyed look on Sister Verna's face. She was staring at his chest, at the thing he had never let her see before.

At the scar. At the handprint burned there. At the handprint that was a constant reminder of who fathered him.

Sister Verna was as white as a spirit. Her voice was so soft he had to strain to hear her. "Where did you get that?"

Du Chaillu was staring at the scar, too.

Richard pulled his shirt closed. "I told you before, Darken Rahl burned me with his hand. You said I was only having visions."

Her gaze slowly rose to meet his. Her eyes were filled with something he had never seen in them before. Unbridled fear.

"Richard," she whispered, "you must not show anyone at the palace what you have upon you. Except the Prelate. She may know what to do. You must show her. But no one else." She stepped closer. "Do you understand? No one!"

Richard slowly buttoned his shirt. "Why?"

"Because, if you do, they will kill you. That is the mark of the Nameless One." Her tongue wet her lips. "Sins of the father."

From the distance came the plaintive howl of wolves. Du Chaillu shuddered and hugged herself as she stared off into the deepening fog.

"People will die tonight," Du Chaillu whispered.

Richard frowned at her. "What are you talking about?"

"Wolves. When wolves howl like that in the mist, they are foretelling that people are to die violently in the night, in the mist."

## CHAPTER 44

They materialized out of fog and mist, the white fangs of death. The startled prey, at first immobilized by bone-chilling fright, jumped to flee before the white death. Fangs of white steel ripped into them without mercy as they bolted for their lives. Death squeals tore the night air with their terror. Hysteria sent them running heedlessly onto the waiting cold, white steel.

Fearless men tasted fear before they died.

Pandemonium spread on a wild uproar of noise. The ringing chime of steel, the splintering of wood, the ripping of canvas, the groan of leather, the pop of bones, the whoosh of fire, the crash of wagons, the thuds of flesh and bone hitting ground, and the screams of man and beast all joined into one long cacophony of terror. The wave of white death drove the tumult before it.

The sharp smell of blood washed through the air, over the sweet aroma of blazing wood, the acrid tang of igniting lamp oil, the smoky smack of flaming pitch, and the gagging stench of burning fur and flesh.

What wasn't wet with the cold mist was greasy-slick with hot blood.

The white steel fangs now were coated with blood and gore; white snow became a soggy mat of red splashes. The cold air was seared by gouts of flame that leapt up to turn the white fog an incandescent orange. Sinister, dark clouds of smoke hugged the ground while the sky burned overhead.

Arrows zipped past, spears arced through the air, splintered lances spun away into the mist, and severed pike heads whirled off into the darkness. Remnants of torn tents flapped and fluttered as if battered by a furious storm. Swords rose and fell in waves, driven by the grunts that accompanied frantic effort.

Men ran in every direction, like frenzied ants. Some tumbled to the ground, spilling their viscera across the snow. One of the wounded, blinded by blood, stumbled aimlessly until a white shadow swept by, a spirit of death, cutting him down. A wagon wheel bounced past, its progress quickly obscured from view by dark curtains of acrid smoke that drifted past.

No alarm had been raised; the sentries were long dead. Few in camp had realized what was happening until it was upon them.

The camp of the Imperial Order had lately been a place of noise and wild celebration, and for many, in their drunken state, it was hard to tell that anything of consequence was happening. Many of the men, poisoned by the *bandu* in the ale, lay sick around fires. Many were so weak they burned to death without trying to escape flaming tents. Others were in such a drunken stupor that they actually smiled at the men who drove swords through their guts.

Even the ones who were not drunk, or who were not drunk to the point of dullness, didn't truly appreciate what was happening. Their camp was often a place of raucous noise and confusion. Huge bonfires roared throughout the night, for warmth and as gathering places. They were generally the only reference points in the disorderly layout, so the fires of destruction caused little concern, except in the immediate area.

Among D'Harans, fighting in the camps was simply part of the revelry, and men screaming when they were stabbed in altercations was not noteworthy. What one had was only his if he was fierce enough to keep it from others who were always ready to take it. Alliances among D'Harans were shifting sands that could last a lifetime or, more commonly, for as little as an hour, when a new alliance became more advantageous or profitable. The drinking, and the poison, dulled their grasp of the sheer volume of screams.

In battle they were disciplined, but when not in battle, they were ungoverned to the point of anarchy. Pay, for D'Harans on expeditions, was in large part a share of the plunder—they had looted Ebinissia, despite all their talk of a new law—and having that new plunder made them perhaps less than single-minded in their devotion to duty. At battle, or the first sound of an alarm, they became a single unified fighting machine, almost an entity of one mind, but in camp, without the overriding purpose of war, they became thousands of individuals, all bent on serving their own self-interest.

Without an alarm to warn them, they paid the added noise and screaming little attention. Above the noise of their own business, trading, stories, laughter, drinking, gambling, fighting, and whoring, the unheralded battle a short distance away went largely unnoticed. The officers would call them if needed. Without that call to duty, their life was their own, and someone else's troubles were not theirs. They were unprepared when the white death materialized.

The sight of white spirits appearing among them was a paralyzing force. Many a man wailed in fear of the Shahari spirits. Many envisioned that the separation between the world of the living and the world of the dead had evaporated. Or that they had somehow been suddenly cast into the underworld.

Without the ale, both poisoned and unadulterated, it might not be so. As it was, the drink, and their confidence in their numbers and strength, left them vulnerable as they would never be again. But not all were drunk, or dull. Some rose up fiercely.

Kahlan watched it all from atop her dancing warhorse. In a sea of raw, unbridled emotion, she wore her Confessor's face.

These men were neither moral nor ethical; they were animals who lived by no rule but might. They had raped the women at the palace and had mercilessly butchered the people of Ebinissia, from the aged down to newborn babes.

A man lunged through the ring of steel around her, grabbing at her saddle for support. He gaped at her, crying a prayer for mercy from the good spirits. She split his skull.

Kahlan wheeled her horse to face Sergeant Cullen. "Have we captured the command tents?"

The sergeant signaled, and one of the white, naked men ran off to check as they drove deeper into the camp of the Order. When she spotted the horses, she gave the signal. From behind she heard the sound of galloping hooves, and the sharp rattle of chains: scythes of death, come to reap a crop of the living.

With a sound like a boy running past a picket fence with a stick in hand, the chain scythes being pulled at a full charge reaped a snapping of bone that meshed into a long, clacking roar. The beasts' screams and the dull thuds as they slammed the ground drowned out the sound of galloping hooves and breaking bone.

Even the drunken enemy turned from the white spirits to stare at the ghastly spectacle. It was the last thing they saw. Men stumbled from their tents, to watch without understanding what it was that was occurring before their eyes. Others wandered aimlessly, mugs in hand, as if at a fair, drunkenly looking from one sight to another. There were so many, some had to wait a bit for their turn to die.

Some were not drunk and saw not spirits but men painted white. They saw an attack, and understood well-honed blades coming for them. A pocket of fierce counterattack was surrounded and broken, but not without cost. Kahlan rallied her men and drove her wedge of white steel deeper into the heart of the enemy's camp.

She saw two men on huge draft horses—she couldn't see who they were—having cut down all the horses they could find, take to charging down a line of tents, reaping havoc as well as helpless men. The chain caught something as solid as bedrock. It whipped the horses around into a brutal collision. The riders went down. Men with swords and axes swarmed over them.

A man with sword to hand, and sober, she was alarmed to note, appeared suddenly next to her leg. He looked up with a fierce glare. His sharp eyes made her feel suddenly nothing more than a naked woman sitting on a horse.

He took all of her in. "What the . . ."

A foot of steel erupted from his breastbone, driving a grunt from his lungs.

"Mother Confessor!" The naked man behind yanked his sword free and pointed with it. "The command tents are over there!"

A movement to the other side caught her attention. With a backhanded swing, she caught the side of a stumbling drunk's neck.

"Let's go! To the command tents! Now!"

Her men abandoned the enemy they were decimating to follow her as she jumped Nick over men and fires and crumpled wagons. As they followed, they didn't stop to slaughter the confused, panicked, and drunken D'Harans everywhere, but cut down those they could if it didn't slow their pace. Where necessary, they engaged the sporadic resistance.

The large command tents were surrounded by her white Galeans. They held a small group of about fifteen men at swordpoint. Before them lay a neat row of at least thirty bodies on their backs in the snow.

Others of her men were throwing battle standards and flags atop a large pile already smoldering and burning in the fire. Empty casks lay scattered in the snow. When their army had come under attack, the commanders had issued no orders. The army of the Imperial Order was without benefit of direction.

Lieutenant Sloan pointed with his sword to the line of bodies. "These officers were already dead. The poison did its work. These others were still alive, although not in the best of health. They were all lying about in their tents. We could hardly get them up. They asked us for rum, if you can believe it. We've held them, like you said."

Kahlan surveyed the faces of the bodies in the snow. She didn't see what she wanted. She looked to the faces of the captured officers. He wasn't there either.

She directed her Confessor's face to a Keltish officer at the end of the line. "Where's Riggs?"

He glared at her, and then spat. Kahlan lifted her gaze to the man holding him.

She drew her finger across her throat. He didn't hesitate. The officer went down in a heap.

She looked to the next officer. "Where's Riggs?"

His eyes darted about. "I don't know!"

Kahlan drew her finger across her throat. As he went down, she looked to the next man, a D'Haran commander.

"Where's Riggs?"

His eyes were wide, but not at the two bleeding bodies beside him. His horror was for her. A spirit before him. He wet his lips.

"He was hurt, by the Mother Confessor. I mean, by you. Before." His voice trembled. "When you were . . . alive."

"Where is he!"

He winced, shaking his head vigorously. "I don't know, great spirit! He was hurt, his face was cut by the horse. He is being tended to by the surgeons. I don't know where their tents are."

"Who knows where the surgeon's tents are?"

Most trembled and shuddered as they shook their heads. Kahlan stepped her horse down the line of officers. She stopped before one she knew.

"General Karsh. I am *very* pleased to see you again. Where's Riggs!"

"Wouldn't tell you if I knew." He grinned as he leered up at her. "You look better naked than I fancied. Why are you whoring with this lot? We could do you better than these boys."

The man holding him twisted his arm until he cried out. "Show respect for the Mother Confessor, you Keltish pig!"

"Respect! For a whore holding a sword? Never!"

Kahlan leaned toward him. "These 'boys' have you under their blades. Every one is a better man than you, I would say.

"You wanted war, Karsh. You have your wish. You have war, now. A real war, not a slaughter of women and children, but a war led by me—the Mother Confessor. A woman. War without quarter."

She sat up straight in her saddle, letting his eyes linger on her breasts. "I have a message, Karsh. A message for the Keeper. You will be with him presently. Tell him I said to make plenty of room; I'm sending all his disciples home."

Her gaze swept down the line of men holding the officers. She drew her finger across her throat in a quick gesture. The response was just as quick.

As the bodies tumbled forward, she cried out, her hand darting to her neck. A stinging pain jolted her. It was in the exact same place . . .

It was the pain of Darken Rahl's lips on her neck, the pain she had felt when he had come to them in the spirit house, when he had burned Richard with his hand. When he had kissed her neck and silently promised her unimaginable horrors.

Men rushed forward. "Mother Confessor! What is it!"

She took her hand away. Blood coated her white fingers. She couldn't say how she knew, but she knew without doubt that the blood was drawn by the perfect, snow white teeth of Darken Rahl.

"Mother Confessor! There's blood on your neck!"

"It's nothing. I'm all right. I must have just been nicked by an arrow, that's all." She gathered her wits and courage. "Put the head of every officer on a pole, for all their men to see, to let them know they are without leaders. And hurry."

By the time the last dripping head was hoisted up, D'Harans were pouring in

465

from all sides. Most were drunk, laughing as if it were nothing more than a drunken brawl. But inefficient and clumsy as they were, their numbers were alarming. They were like a swarm of bees; for every one knocked down, ten replaced him.

Her men fought fiercely, but they were no match for the overwhelming numbers sweeping in. Men she had talked to, reassured, inspired, yelled at, and smiled to were falling with cries of pain and terror. They had been here too long.

Ahead, a pitched battle erupted. The Galeans were being driven back. If they were driven back, they had no chance of escape. They couldn't go back the way they had come, back to men who would have had time to have been sobered by the carnage around them, to gather their senses, and their spirit.

Without surprise, they were nothing but a bunch of naked boys and one woman. If they tried a second time what had worked once, they would all die. They had to cleave their way through the Order, to the other side of the valley. D'Harans hacked in at the white forms. Her ankle was grasped by a powerful hand. She hewed it off and shook her foot to shed the disembodied hand.

They were in danger of being swallowed into the belly of this beast.

Disregarding the death cries of her men, disregarding her promise not to leave the protective ring of the fiercest Galean swordsmen, disregarding her promise not to deliberately put herself into peril, Kahlan charged Nick into the thick of the battle, and beyond—into the enemy.

Her sword stabbed to each side, into any enemy close enough. Teeth gritted, she swung at flesh and bone. Her wrist tingled from the jarring impacts, and her arm was so weary she feared she would not be able to lift the sword much longer.

Frightened that she would be taken down, her men poured ahead, toward her, with renewed resolve. They drove the dark wave back, rolling over it as she urged her horse forward into the sea of dark leather uniforms.

She stood in the stirrups, holding her sword high. "For Ebinissia! For her dead! For her spirit!"

It had the desired effect. Men of the Order who were confused by the white enemy, but were nonetheless determined to crush them, whatever they were, stopped and stared openly at a white, naked woman atop a horse suddenly in their midst. Their faith, that the attack was from men and not spirits, faltered. They gaped in open astonishment. She swept her gaze around at all the eyes peering up at her.

She swung the white sword in a circle over her head as a breeze ruffled her white hair back off her shoulders. "In the name of their spirits, I have come to avenge them!"

Leather-clad men fell to their knees, dropping their swords, pressing prayerful hands together. They held those hands up to her. They wailed for protection. They called for her mercy. They cried for forgiveness. Had they been sober, she wondered, would the illusion be so convincing? As it was, the effect was apocalyptic.

"We grant no quarter!"

As all faces stared up toward her, as eyes shed tears of trepidation, weapons set upon them from behind. The sudden, violent, merciless wave of hard steel terrified them, convinced them that the spirits would have them all. They broke and ran, dropping weapons, screaming in fear of the underworld.

They had done what they had come to do. Time was now against them. They needed to escape.

They charged onward, a deadly, swift river of white that poured over and around the tents and fires and wagons and men, surprising ever more of the lethargic enemy, killing as many as they could while rolling ahead. White death moved into the mist once again.

Kahlan glanced behind, and saw the pairs of draft horses, their riders holding the chains up between them. She waved them into the stream of white, urging them to move faster. They started unhooking one end of the chains from the hame hooks and looping the chain over the horn on the other horse, to give each horse freedom, now that they needed to make a quick escape.

In the distance, in the fog to the right, she saw a line of picketed horses. She saw Brin and Peter come together, snap the end of the chain over the other hook again and urge Daisy and Pip into gallops. She thought to scream at them, to order them to keep with the others, that they couldn't hope to get them all, that they had done enough and must leave now, that it was too late. But she knew they wouldn't hear her.

Brin dropped the loops of chain. They spread the horses to pull the steel taut as they peeled away toward the picket line of horses. The hooves of the big horses thundered across the ground. She took a last look at Brin and Peter, knowing it would be the last time she ever looked upon them in this world, and then turned her attention ahead.

She pointed with her sword. "There are the rest of the supply wagons!"

The men knew what to do. As she charged the column past, the wagons were doused with lamp oil. Wheels were staved in, and torches thrown. The wagons erupted in flame. More torches set fire to tents. The men brought awake by the noise and fire found blades sweeping at them. The fires faded into an orange glow in the mist behind as they plunged onward into the fog.

Suddenly they broke free of the camp, and were in open snow. Now that they were away from the camp, and its fires, the darkness pressed around them. The men in front faltered, looking about as they jogged.

"Scouts forward!" she yelled. "Where are the scouts!"

Two men charged through the ranks, to the fore, pointing out the direction of the pass they sought. She looked for the others, turning from side to side. None came. She galloped Nick to the van, after the two scouts.

"Where are the others! They were ordered to be in the lead!"

The round, wet eyes that looked up at her answered her question without words.

"All right," she said, "you two know the way. Get us out of here."

Fifty men had scouted the pass they wanted. Fifty, to be sure there would be a good number left to show the way. Two were left.

With a silent growl she cursed the spirits. Shamefaced, she called the curse back. They had at least left her those two; without them, they would be left to wander in the fog, freezing and vincible to the men of the Order chasing them.

She pulled Nick to a halt beside the stream of naked men. She swooped her arm frantically.

"Move move move! Run, curse you, run! They'll be on top of us!" The men on the draft horses, Brin and Peter not among them, came abreast of her. "Drivers! Watch for the scout ahead! He'll show you the stakes to follow." They nodded that they remembered.

Men in D'Haran uniforms, with white cloth swatches sewn into their epaulets to show that they were in fact the Galean men who had infiltrated the enemy camp in the uniforms of the sentries, ran past. "Don't forget to pull up the stakes before you get up on the horses."

They were to double or triple up on the draft horses and ride to one of the other small camps established around the enemy. Earlier in the day, they had made trails all over the valley so that without the sticks stuck in the snow to mark the proper trail, none would know the way to those camps.

The trail through the snow from all the men on foot would be easy for the enemy to follow. But they had plans to take care of that.

In the distance, back toward the Order, she saw the rear guard engaged in a pitched battle. Lieutenant Sloan was supposed to keep that from happening, and keep the rear moving. Cursing anew, she galloped her horse back. Without pause, she charged between the two forces, spun and charged through again, separating the two sides. The leather-clad D'Harans fell back at the sight of the white spirit woman atop a white horse.

She waded in among the Galeans. "What's the matter with you! You know the orders! Run, or you won't make it!"

The men started moving, trying to drag a body with them.

"Where's Lieutenant Sloan! He's supposed to be back here!"

The men nodded to the body they were dragging. The side of the head was gone, and she could see the exposed brain. It was Lieutenant Sloan. The D'Harans charged in again. She pulled the reins and Nick reared. The D'Harans fell back once more.

"He's dead! Leave him! Run! Run, you idiots! If any of you stops again for anything, I'll make you fight the rest of this war naked! Now run!"

This time they took off in earnest, kicking up snow, running for their lives. Again she swept past the line of drunken D'Harans, causing them to stumble backward and fall over one another in panic. She had to stall these men to give her own time to gain enough of a lead.

She ran Nick through the D'Harans, trampling those who got in the way. The men scattered in momentary dread of the white spirit woman, some calling to the spirits for protection. But others came back swinging weapons. If they caught Nick's legs . . .

She fought back with her sword and her warhorse, as they closed around her. Her men were fading into the fog. *Run*, she bid them, *run*. She swung the sword at men who reached out. The next time she glanced back, she saw nothing but dark fog and mist. She was losing her sense of direction as she wheeled Nick around, charging at the men, trying to buy her own men the time they needed to escape.

She tried to break away, but the enemy swarmed around her, with more coming all the time. Some yelled at the others that she was just a woman, and not a spirit, and they weren't going to let a woman get away. She felt more naked than she had felt all night.

Men threw themselves around Nick's legs, and although he reared and kicked them off, even more took their place, staggering the big horse with their weight. Kahlan hacked furiously at the men, shearing off arms, splitting skulls, and stabbing bodies.

With a sea of men all around her, she suddenly realized that her situation was untenable. She knew that if they got her off her horse, she was finished, and her horse was being hobbled. Try as she might, she couldn't get the men away.

For the first time that night, she truly feared she wasn't going to make it. She was going to die, here, in the snow, in this mist-shrouded valley. She would never see Richard again.

She felt an abrupt, icy pain in the bite on her neck. Darken Rahl's bite. She thought she heard quiet laughter in the air.

She slashed away at the men grabbing for her. Powerful fingers clutched her legs. The pain of those fingers urged her into frantic stabbing. Nick managed to spin, the men's feet flying outward, but they held on tight. She slashed and hacked the arms. More caught hold of her horse's bit, taking control from her. A horse was valuable plunder, and they didn't want it killed, as long as they thought they were in control of the situation.

A big soldier grabbed the horn of her saddle, dragging himself up. "Don't kill her! It's the Mother Confessor! Don't kill her! She must be alive when she's beheaded!"

She slashed the side of his neck, A fountain of hot blood gushed across her thigh. Another yelled, "Don't kill her! Bring the bitch down!" A cheer went up from the reaching men.

She swung at the grasping hands. Fingers raked her legs. Eyes all around leered up at her. She slashed wildly as Nick stumbled sideways, trying to pull his head free, but the men held his bit tight.

A man leapt up from behind and snatched her by the hair. She let out a cry as he yanked her backward off the saddle. Hands grappled her as she tumbled to the ground. Everyone went down in a pile under her. Big hands seized her by her legs, her waist, her ankles, and her breasts.

Fingers wrapped around the blade, trying to wrench it from her. She twisted the hilt, severing the fingers. She swung and stabbed ferociously. Bodies pressed her to the cold ground, pressed the wind from her lungs. She bit the fingers covering her mouth. A huge fist struck her across the jaw.

They finally seized her flailing arms.

There were too many.

*Dear Richard, I love you.*

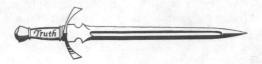

**K**ahlan struggled to draw a breath, but with the weight of men on her, she couldn't. Tears stung her eyes. More men piled on. A beefy elbow in her middle pressed into her, feeling as if it would squash her in two. Drunken breath bathed her face.

Her vision dwindled to a small spot. Everything around the center was going black, and the center was shrinking. She swallowed a mouthful of blood. Her own.

She heard what sounded like the distant rumble of thunder. At first, she could only feel the vibration in her back against the ground, but then the sound swelled, growing louder, sharper. The screams of men reached her ears.

Some of the men over her looked up. Their weight lifted a bit, and she sucked air into her lungs. It was the sweetest breath she had ever drawn.

As the giant of a man atop her, the one who had struck her face, turned to the sound of thunder, turned his fierce eye from her, she saw that his other had a scar across it, and down his cheek. That empty eye was sewn shut. Somehow, her left hand squirmed free. She seized his throat.

She heard a metallic rattle. The thunder, she suddenly realized, was horses' hooves. Erupting out of the fog, Brin and Peter, atop Daisy and Pip, galloped at a full charge down the line of D'Harans, mowing them down with the chain. They raced toward her like a landslide felling trees. The men stared in frozen shock. Kahlan's fingers clutched around the one-eyed man's throat.

And then she released her power.

The magic slammed into him.

Thunder without sound rattled all the chain mail.

The staggering jolt made the men flinch back. They all cried out with the pain of being so close as the magic was loosed. A ring of snow lifted, sweeping outward in a circle.

Nick was standing over her, and he jumped with the pain, too. His hind leg came down on a man's head right next to her ear. Bone crunched under the weight. Hot blood and gore splattered the side of her face.

The one eye of the man above her gaped at her. "Mistress!" he whispered. "Please command me."

"Protect me!" she screamed.

He sat up abruptly, his massive muscles bulging. He held the hair of a man in each fist. He tossed them back as if they were mere children.

Her sword arm was free. She swung at a man to the other side, the blade ruining his face. The one-eyed man roared as he tossed men aside. The draft horses rushed onward at a full charge.

She was free of the hands. She leaped to her feet. The chain was almost upon them.

"Help me up on my horse!"

The one-eyed man grabbed her ankle in his big fist and, with one arm, boosted her up into the saddle. Somehow she still had the sword in her hand. She leaned forward and swung it at the man holding the bit, holding his prize. The sword's tip sliced open the side of his face and half the length of his arm. He staggered back with a shriek. She snatched up the reins. The one-eyed man bellowed as he lopped off heads and ripped open chests with his huge war axe.

"Go, Mistress! Escape! Orsk will protect you!"

"I'm going! Run, Orsk! Don't let them get you!"

The D'Harans abandoned her and her horse to turn to the new threats—Orsk and the chain. She thumped Nick's ribs with her heels, urging him into a gallop just as Brin and Peter caught up with her. She stuffed her bare feet into the stirrups as the three of them raced away.

She spotted the trail that hundreds of feet had left in the snow and followed it across the valley, into the mist, leaving the men of the army of the Order to collect their wits. It took them mere seconds. They charged after her. There were more than enough still alive. Thousands.

Peter unhooked the chain that must have broken hundreds of bones and necks. The end of the chain bounced behind. Brin's bony fingers drew in the dragging slack and coiled it over the hame.

As she galloped into the night, she thought she could hear the sound of soft laughter fading behind. She shivered with the memory of the kiss Darken Rahl had left on her neck. She felt suddenly very naked again.

Though the mist was icy cold, feeling like sparkling flecks all over her, she was sweating. Blood ran from her swollen lip.

"I never thought I would see you two again," she yelled over the sound of hooves.

Brin and Peter, in their too-big coats, grinned in the darkness. "We told you we could do the job," Brin said.

She smiled for the first time that night. "You two are a marvel."

She just caught sight of the hindquarters of the other draft horses disappearing into the fog. She pointed. "There are your men. Good luck." With a wave, they turned away from her.

She galloped on alone, and a short distance later caught up with the men on foot. She first saw only one. He had a horrific gash on his leg and had fallen far behind. She knew she should leave him. She knew she should. The D'Harans were right behind.

As she rode up to him, he turned his head up as he struggled through the snow. He knew she had to leave him. Those were the orders. Her orders. Keep up, or be left behind. No exceptions.

As she rode by, she leaned over, extending her arm down. They clasped wrists and she yanked him up behind her.

"Hold on, soldier."

He held his arms out, trying to balance as the horse ran, afraid to touch her. "But . . . where?"

"Around my waist! Put your arms around my waist!"

He still held his arms out as he bounced. "But . . ."

"Haven't you ever put your arms around a woman before?"

471

"Yes . . . but she had clothes on," he whined.

"Do it, or you'll fall off, and I'm not coming back for you."

Reluctantly, carefully, he put his arms around her waist, stiffly trying to keep them away from anything important, or unfamiliarly exotic. Kahlan gave the back of his hands a pat of reassurance. "When you brag about this, don't make it more than it is." He let out a small, worried groan that made her smile.

As they rode on, she could feel his warm blood running down the back of her leg, dripping from her toes in the stirrup. She could hear the shouts of the enemy chasing behind.

He was losing a lot of blood. In exhaustion, he laid his head against the back of her shoulder. If they didn't tie his wound closed, he would bleed to death in short order. She was naked, and had nothing to use as a bandage, even if they had the time to stop.

"Hold the wound closed with a hand," she said. "Clamp it closed as tight as you can. And hold fast to me with your other arm. I don't want you falling off."

He took one arm from her waist and held the gash closed as she rode right on the heels of the men at the end of the line. They were cold and fatigued. The men of the Order were not far behind. As she looked back, they came into sight. She was shocked by the numbers. They hooted and hollered.

"Run! Run or we will be caught!"

A wall of rock, with scraggly trees growing from cracks and clefts, loomed up before them. The men ran up the narrow pass as if their lives depended on it. And they did.

As they began the climb up the rift, she rang the flat of her sword three times on the rock, giving the signal.

A man ahead turned as he ran. "We're not there yet! It's too soon! We'll be caught along with the enemy!"

"Then you better run faster! If we wait too long, they will get through, too!"

She rapped the rock wall three more times, the ringing sound carrying into the dark, damp air. She hoped it would work; there, of course, had been no way to perform a test. The men ahead scrambled up the trail. Nick's hooves slipped in places on the snow-covered rock.

At first, she could only feel it, a rumbling deep in her chest, too low to hear, but too powerful not to be felt. She looked up along the mist-slicked rock that disappeared above into the dark and fog. She couldn't see it yet, but she could feel it.

She hoped the man was wrong, that it wouldn't be too soon. When she heard the battle cries of the men coming from behind, she knew they had no choice.

And then she could hear it: a booming roar, as if the ground itself were moving. She could hear tree trunks snapping. The thundering growl reverberated off the surrounding mountain walls. The ground vibrated.

"Run! Can't you run any faster? Do you want to be buried alive? Run!"

She knew they were going as fast as they could, but they were on foot, and from atop her horse, it seemed painfully slow. Deadly slow.

Overhead, the rumbling roar grew louder as uncountable tons of snow crashed down toward them. She was thrilled that the men on top had been successful in starting an avalanche on command; but she was also terrified that she had given the command too soon.

A lump of wet snow slapped her face; another smacked her shoulder. Little clods

rattled through the trees above them and bounced out
fluffy snow misted her face. The roar was deafening.

A flow of thundering white sluiced over the ledge
it, like running through a waterfall. Behind her, a tree
spinning out over the precipice. They just cleared the
snow.

The men of the Imperial Order behind were not
charged with timber and boulders, cascaded down w
were swept away in the tumbling white death. The fu
of men it carried away, rolling them into the pounding

Kahlan sagged with relief. They could not be followed now.
entombed.

The panting men slowed, but they couldn't slow too much, or they would freeze.
Their pace kept them warm. Their feet, she knew, despite being wrapped in white
cloth for a little protection, were not warm. They had given her their best effort.
They had given the Midlands their best effort. Many had given their lives.

Kahlan was so exhausted from lack of sleep, as well as the fatigue of battle,
along with the emotional drain of fright, and the effort required to use her power,
that she could hardly stay upright. Soon, she told herself, she could rest. Soon.

She patted the hand on her stomach. "We made it, soldier. We're safe, now."

"Yes, Mother Confessor," He whispered groggily. "Mother Confessor, I'm sorry."

"For what?"

"I only killed seventeen. I'm sorry. I promised myself I'd get twenty. I only got
seventeen," he mumbled.

"I know heroes of battle, decorated men, who have not bested half that number
in combat. You have made me proud. You have made the Midlands proud. Feel
only pride, soldier."

He mumbled something she couldn't understand.

She patted his hand again. "You'll be to help soon. Hold on. You'll be fine."

He didn't answer. She looked behind, down the trail, and saw only white, and
heard only silence. In the distant, dark mountains, a wolf yipped.

A short time later, on a high plateau, they reached the camp. The men ahead in the
line were already wrapped in blankets as they shivered around fires, warming their
feet. Some were pulling on their clothes under the blankets. More men threw blankets
around the men coming in ahead of her and tended the wounded. Some of the
wounded were groaning in pain, feeling it for the first time, now that the heady
furor of combat and escape had evaporated. She began to feel a throbbing in her
lip.

In the flickering light of small fires, she could see Prindin and Tossidin, some
distance away, running around searching the new arrivals. When they saw her on
the horse, they both sighed with relief, giving her twin smiles.

Captain Ryan, dressed in a D'Haran uniform and with a bandage around his left
hand, ran over. Other men took the reins, and yet others extended their hands to
take the man behind her as she held him by an elbow, lowering the limp form down.

Prindin ran to meet her, her mantle in hand. He stood, holding it open for her, rattled through the trees above them and bounced out over the edge. A cloud of fluffy snow misted her face. The roar was deafening.

A flow of thundering white sluiced over the ledge above. They drove through it, like running through a waterfall. Behind her, a tree trunk bounced on the trail, spinning out over the precipice. They just cleared the leading edge of the bulk of snow.

The men of the Imperial Order behind were not so lucky. The plunging snow, charged with timber and boulders, cascaded down with ever-gathering power. They were swept away in the tumbling white death. The fury of sound muffled the screams of men it carried away, rolling them into the pounding slide, burying them alive.

Kahlan sagged with relief. They could not be followed now. The pass was entombed.

The panting men slowed, but they couldn't slow too much, or they would freeze. Their pace kept them warm. Their feet, she knew, despite being wrapped in white cloth for a little protection, were not warm. They had given her their best effort. They had given the Midlands their best effort. Many had given their lives.

Kahlan was so exhausted from lack of sleep, as well as the fatigue of battle, along with the emotional drain of fright, and the effort required to use her power, that she could hardly stay upright. Soon, she told herself, she could rest. Soon.

She patted the hand on her stomach. "We made it, soldier. We're safe, now."

"Yes, Mother Confessor," He whispered groggily. "Mother Confessor, I'm sorry."

"For what?"

"I only killed seventeen. I'm sorry. I promised myself I'd get twenty. I only got seventeen," he mumbled.

"I know heroes of battle, decorated men, who have not bested half that number in combat. You have made me proud. You have made the Midlands proud. Feel only pride, soldier."

He mumbled something she couldn't understand.

She patted his hand again. "You'll be to help soon. Hold on. You'll be fine."

He didn't answer. She looked behind, down the trail, and saw only white, and heard only silence. In the distant, dark mountains, a wolf yipped.

A short time later, on a high plateau, they reached the camp. The men ahead in the line were already wrapped in blankets as they shivered around fires, warming their feet. Some were pulling on their clothes under the blankets. More men threw blankets around the men coming in ahead of her and tended the wounded. Some of the wounded were groaning in pain, feeling it for the first time, now that the heady furor of combat and escape had evaporated. She began to feel a throbbing in her lip.

In the flickering light of small fires, she could see Prindin and Tossidin, some distance away, running around searching the new arrivals. When they saw her on the horse, they both sighed with relief, giving her twin smiles.

Captain Ryan, dressed in a D'Haran uniform and with a bandage around his left hand, ran over. Other men took the reins, and yet others extended their hands to take the man behind her as she held him by an elbow, lowering the limp form down.

Prindin ran to meet her, her mantle in hand. He stood, holding it open for her, waiting for her to dismount so he could put it around her shoulders. He grinned at her.

Without moving from the saddle, she slowly extended her hand. "I have had enough eyes on my flesh to last me the rest of my life. Throw it up here!"

Prindin shrugged self-consciously and tossed the mantle up to her. Tossidin swatted the back of his brother's head. Silence fell over the gathered men. They all looked away in embarrassment as she put the mantle around her shoulders and tied it.

She slid down, finding her legs barely up to the task of holding her. She used the sword still in her hand as a cane. She had to pause a moment until everything stopped spinning. She glanced to the man lying in the snow at her feet.

"Why isn't someone helping this man? Don't just stand there, help him!" No one moved. "I said help him!"

Captain Ryan stepped closer to her. He kept his eyes on the ground. "I'm sorry, Mother Confessor. He's dead."

Her hand tightened into a fist. "He's not dead! I was just talking to him!" No one moved. She beat her free fist against his chest. "He's not dead! He's not!"

Everyone looked away. No one said anything. She finally glanced at the men around the small fires, at all the hanging heads. Her hand fell to her side.

"He killed seventeen of them," she said to Captain Ryan. "He killed seventeen of them," she said louder, to the rest of them.

Captain Ryan nodded. "He did well. We are all proud of him."

She watched the faces as they all finally came up. "Forgive me. All of you, please forgive me. You have all done a good job." The fury had gone out of her. "You have all made me proud. You are heroes, in my eyes, and in the eyes of the Midlands."

The men brightened a bit. Some went back to eating, while others started passing around tin bowls and spooned beans from pots on the fires. Some tore off chunks of flat camp bread to dunk in the beans.

"Where's Chandalen?" she asked as she pushed her feet into the boots Tossidin handed her.

"He went with the archers. I imagine that he's probably shooting arrows into D'Harans right now." Captain Ryan leaned toward her, as the brothers moved away, and lowered his voice. "I'm glad these three are on our side. You should have seen them taking out the sentries. Prindin, especially, is like death itself, with that *troga* of his. It was eerie, they way they were first here, and then over there, and you never even saw them move. I never heard a thing. They just appeared with the sentries' uniforms."

"You should see them do that out in the open grassland, in broad daylight." Kahlan looked him up and down. She managed a small smile. "Quite handsome. You wear it well."

He pulled at his shoulder. "I don't know how they wear this heavy mail all the time." He fingered a slash in the leather. "But I was glad to have it on."

"How did everything go? How many men did you lose?"

"We got nearly everything we went after. In these uniforms, we didn't have to do much fighting. Hardly anyone noticed us, except the ones we killed. We only lost a few men." He glanced back over his shoulder. "Looks like you caught the worst of it. I took a rough count as you came in. We lost close to four hundred of the thousand swordsmen who went in."

She stared past him, at the men around the fires. "We came close to losing them all." She brought her attention back to the captain. "But they did themselves proud. The drivers, too."

He cradled his bandaged hand. "From the ones I talked to, I don't think many took less than ten of the enemy, and many took a lot more. We took quite a chunk out of the Order's hide."

Kahlan swallowed. "They took quite a chunk out of ours."

"Did the men do like I told them?" he asked. "Did they keep any trouble away from you?"

"They kept the enemy so far from me I couldn't tell you what they looked like. I'm afraid I wasn't able to add much honor to your sword, though it was a comfort to have along. I pray you will at least be honored that I carried it in battle."

He frowned, leaning to the side, trying to get a better look at her face in the firelight. "Your lip looks cut." He glanced at her warhorse as the men were taking the tack off. "That horse is covered in blood. You're covered in blood, too, aren't you?" It was an accusation, not a question.

Kahlan stared off at a fire. "Some drunk threw something at me. It cut my lip. That wounded soldier I was bringing in bled to death on my horse, and on me." Her eyes drifted among the young faces around fires. "I wish I could have done half as well they. They were magnificent."

He grunted suspiciously. "I'm just relieved to see you."

"Is everything else in order? The archers, the cavalry? We must make the best use of our opportunity while they're drunk and sick with the poison. We must make the most of this weather, too. We can't let up for a moment. One lightning strike after another. No engagement. Glancing attacks, always from a different place."

"They all know their jobs, and are waiting their turn. The archers should be finished soon, then the cavalry, then the pikemen. We're ready for their sentries, when they send them out. Our men will sleep in turns, but from now on, the Imperial Order will get no sleep."

"Good. These men need rest. In the morning, it will be their turn again." She lifted a finger to the captain. "Remember the most important thing." She quoted her father, " 'The weapon that most readily conquers reason is terror and violence.' Don't forget that. It's the tool they use, and now we must turn it on them."

Prindin came back into the firelight. "Mother Confessor. My brother and I made you a shelter, while we waited for your return. We have your clothes there, and hot water, so you may wash yourself if you wish."

She tried not to show how eager she was to wash off the reek of war. "Thank you, Prindin."

He held his arm out, showing her the way to the small clearing. The brothers had built a roomy shelter of balsam boughs covered over with snow. She crawled through the low opening to find candles inside. The snowy ground was covered with a mat of boughs, too, giving the shelter the pleasant aroma of balsam. A steaming bucket of water had just been set next to hot rocks placed in the center. She warmed her fingers over the rocks.

The brothers had made her a warm and snug home for the night. She could have wept at their thoughtfulness.

Her pack was there, and her clothes folded in a neat pile. Kahlan took off her necklace, the one Adie had given her, the one with the round bone. It was the only thing she had worn into battle. She clutched it to her cheek a moment before she washed it. It reminded her of the one her mother had given her.

She dunked her whole head in the bucket, washed her hair, and then methodically washed the rest of herself. It was only a sponge bath, but it still felt wonderful to wash off the blood, and the feel of the hands. She had to force herself to think of other things as she washed, to keep from being sick. She thought of Richard, thought of his boyish smile that never failed to make her grin, thought of his gray eyes that could look right into her. When she finished washing, she lay down, drying her hair on the rocks.

She desperately needed sleep. She still hadn't recovered her Confessor's power since using it on the one-eyed man, Orsk. She could feel the emptiness in the pit of her stomach, a hollow where the power belonged. It would be a while longer until it was restored. She wouldn't be able to shake the sick, dizzy exhaustion, though, until she had sleep.

She longed to lie down in her bedroll and sleep. It had been so long, and she was so sleepy. But she couldn't. Not yet.

She put the necklace back over her head and then laboriously pulled on her clothes. From her pack she recovered an unguent and spread it on her cut lip. When she replaced it, she saw the bone knife Chandalen had given her, and tied it around her arm again.

She was so tired she could hardly force herself up, but she had something to do before she slept; she had to be with her men. She wouldn't let them think she didn't hold their interest highest in her heart. They had offered their lives; the least she could do was show her appreciation, on behalf of the Midlands.

Clean, her long hair full and shiny once more, and dressed at last in layers of warm clothes and her mantle, she wound her way among the campfires. She listened with serious attention to the babbling stories of some, and the quiet, brief words of others. She spoke with all who had questions, gave smiles of reassurance, and let them all know how proud she was of what they had done. She knelt by the wounded, checking to see if they were warm enough, and laid a hand to their cheeks, giving comfort, and wishing them good health and quick healing. She, too, felt relief when they were calmed by her touch.

At a fire surrounded by ten silent soldiers, one young man was trembling, but she didn't think it was from the cold.

"How are you doing? Are you all right? Are you getting warm?"

Her presence surprised and brightened him. "Yes, Mother Confessor." A racking shiver rattled his teeth. "I never thought it would be like that." He composed himself, and indicated the others. "These are my friends. Six didn't come back."

She held her mantle closed with one hand and brushed the hair back off his forehead with the other. "I'm sorry. I, too, grieve for them. I just wanted you men to know that you made me proud. You were as brave as any soldiers I've ever seen."

He chuckled nervously. "We'd all be dead if it wasn't for you. We were being driven back, hacked to pieces, and then you charged right into the enemy, all by yourself. They all turned their attention to you, and then, while they were confused, we counterattacked. What you did saved us."

He shook his head. "I wish I had killed half as many men tonight as I saw you kill." They all nodded their earnest agreement. He brushed trembling fingers across his face. "Thank you, Mother Confessor. If it weren't for what you did, we would all be dead, too." He gave her a twitch of a smile. "If I had the choice, I'd choose to follow you into battle over Prince Harold himself."

"Pretty good with a sword, is she?"

She started at the voice. The soldier turned to see Captain Ryan standing behind her.

"I think she could teach us swordsmen a thing or two. You wouldn't believe what she . . ."

Kahlan patted his shoulder. "Have you had something to eat?"

He pointed to the pot of beans on the fire. "Would you share some with us, Mother Confessor?"

She almost lost control of her queasy stomach. "You men eat. You need the strength. Thank you for the offer, but I must first see to the others."

Captain Ryan followed her away. "I had thought you might have some trouble handling a sword. The men who unsaddled your horse told me they found dismembered hands and fingers caught in the girth strap, and a few other places."

Kahlan smiled at men she passed. They lifted a hand or bowed their heads in greeting. "Have you forgotten who my father was? He taught me the use of a sword."

"Mother Confessor, that doesn't mean . . ."

"Lieutenant Sloan was killed."

He fell silent a moment. "I know. They told me." He put a hand under her arm when she stumbled. "You don't look so good. Some of those men who were poisoned looked better than you."

"It's just that I haven't slept for so long." She didn't tell him that she had also used her power again. "I'm dead tired."

Back outside her shelter, Tossidin offered her a bowl of beans. Her fingers covered her mouth as her eyes winced closed. She thought she might faint at the sight and smell of food. Tossidin seemed to understand and took it away.

Prindin put a hand under her other arm. "Mother Confessor, you must eat, but you need rest even more." She nodded her agreement. "I made you some tea; I thought it might be a comfort." He pointed with his chin to the shelter. "It is inside."

"Yes, tea might help settle my stomach." She gave the captain's arm a squeeze. "Wake me in the morning, when it's time for the next attack. I'll go with the men."

"If you're rested enough. Only if . . ." She cut him off with a look. "Yes, Mother Confessor. I'll wake you myself."

Inside the cozy shelter, she sipped the hot tea, and shook. Her head was spinning. She could only take a few swallows before she fell into the bedroll. She would be better, she told herself, when she was rested. She could feel her power coming to life at last, swelling with its familiar force within her chest.

She curled up under her fur mantle, thinking of the thousand things that needed to be tended to. She worried about the men who were at that moment attacking, and the ones who would go next. She fretted for them all. They were so young.

She worried about what she had started. War.

But she hadn't started it. She had only refused to abandon the lives of innocent people to a sure death. She'd had no choice. As the Mother Confessor, she had a responsibility to the people of the Midlands. If the Imperial Order wasn't stopped, untold thousands would die at their hands, and those who lived would live as slaves to the Order.

She thought about the young women at the palace in Ebinissia. Their faces floated and spun through her mind's eye. She was too weary to weep for them. When they were avenged, there would be time enough to weep.

She seethed with a lust for vengeance. She resolved that she would hound the army of the Imperial Order to their graves. In the morning, she would once more lead her men against the enemy. She would see it through. She would see those girls, and all the others, avenged.

If the Imperial Order wasn't stopped, not only would innocent people be slaughtered, but all magic, good and bad, all the creatures of magic, would perish.

Richard had magic.

Her mind drifted to Richard. And then she did weep, weep in the hope that he would not hate her for what she had done. She prayed that he would be able to understand and forgive her. She had done the best for him, to save him, to save the living. Her tears slowed, finally sobbing to a stop.

Her thoughts of Richard swept the jumbled, tangled, flashing images from her head. Her mind focused, for the first time in days, it seemed, on things other than fighting and killing.

Focused on who she was, who Richard was. Focused on important matters floating in the fog at the back of her awareness.

Thinking about Richard brought back to her the things that were important, but which she seemed to have forgotten. There were things other than the Order that were important. Very important. It seemed as if this war had distracted her from higher imperatives, from those important matters.

She thought about Darken Rahl. Darken Rahl had marked Richard. The Sisters of the Light had taken him. She was supposed to be going to Aydindril, to help Richard, to get Zedd to help Richard. . . .

Richard had to stop the Keeper.

Kahlan frowned in the darkness under her mantle. The veil to the underworld was still torn. She shouldn't be running around, swinging a sword at D'Haran troops.

She remembered Darken Rahl's laughter.

She touched her neck, and felt the swollen, broken skin. It had been real. He had laughed at how foolish she was.

Kahlan sat up. What was she doing? She had to help stop the Keeper. Shota had said the veil was torn; so had Darken Rahl and Denna. Kahlan had seen a screeling, a creature straight from the underworld. She had spoken with Denna. Denna had taken Richard's place with the Keeper so that he could live to repair the tear in the veil.

Kahlan was supposed to be going to Zedd. She shouldn't be running around playing at soldier.

But if the Imperial Order wasn't stopped . . .

But if the veil was torn . . .

She had to get to Aydindril. She had to get to Zedd. These men could fight a war without her. That was their job. She was the Mother Confessor. She shouldn't be running around foolishly risking her life, when the Midlands—the world of the living—was in danger.

That was what Darken Rahl was laughing at: her foolishness.

She picked up the cup of tea Prindin had made for her and held it in her hands, letting it warm her fingers. She was the leader of the Midlands and had to act like a leader, and tend to the most important things above all else, to the things that she, and only she, could do. She downed the rest of the tea, making a face at the bitter taste.

Kahlan lay down again, holding the teacup on her stomach. The faces of the dead women again floated before her eyes. The weapon that most readily conquers reason is terror and violence; that was what the enemy had done to her—the horror of what they had done had conquered her reason.

That very day, she and her men could have been lost if the scouts had all been killed. Without those guides, they would have been lost, and vincible to the enemy.

That was what she was: a guide. She was a guide to the Midlands. She belonged in Aydindril, guiding the council, pulling everyone together against the threat. Without that guidance, they would be ignorant, and lost in the fog of what was happening.

She was also Richard's guide, for the help he needed. It was up to her to get Zedd's help. Without that guidance, Richard, and all the living, were lost.

She sat up, staring into the candle flame.

No wonder Darken Rahl had been laughing at her. She had been letting the enemy conquer her reason. She had almost been diverted from her duties, and given the Keeper time to work his plans.

She knew now what she had to do. She had done enough to get these men started, had shown them their responsibility, and how to carry it out. Now they had the knowledge they needed to conquer the enemy. What she had done was right, but now they had their jobs, and she had hers.

This army knew what to do, now. She had to get to Aydindril.

Having decided, it felt as if a great weight had been lifted from her, but at the same time she felt infused with purpose. Richard, even though he wasn't with her, had helped her find the truth in all the confusion, and helped her to see her true duty.

She looked in the teacup, but she had drunk the tea, and the cup was empty. Her head felt fuzzy. Her eyes wouldn't stay open. She was so tired she could no longer sit up.

As she flopped back down, she wondered what Richard was doing, where he was. Probably with the Sisters, learning how to control the gift. She prayed to the good spirits that they would help him realize how much she loved him.

Her arm, suddenly too heavy to hold up, fell to the side, and the cup rolled away.

Sleep was as dreamless as death.

**S**he plunged into a void, a wasteland of brutal blackness bereft of all sense of time or awareness of place. She was lost to the world. The dark deprivation was beyond understanding, or comfort.

Drifting in the depths of that void, she felt something. That there was something to feel sparked hope in her, hope of escape from this forsaken nowhere. With that tingling of sense, she snatched desperately at substance, as if clutching a rock in a vast, dark river. Trying to fight back from the suffocating darkness brought sensation to her body.

She floated back, her head throbbing with a dull ache, and numbly she tried to understand what it was that was happening to her. Someone called to her. Mother Confessor, they called. No, that wasn't her name.

It came to her. Kahlan. That was her name. Hands shook her. Someone was calling to her, and shaking her.

She returned from a great distance.

Kahlan's eyes opened, and the world spun. Captain Ryan was gripping her shoulders, shaking her, calling to her.

She drew a deep breath of cold air into her lungs. She twisted her arms away from him, but then had to put her hands back on the ground for support. Concern creased his features.

"Mother Confessor, are you all right?"

"I . . . I . . ." She looked about. Tossidin was there, too. She sat up the rest of the way and put her cold fingers to her forehead. "My head . . . What time is it?"

"It will be light soon." With a look of concern, he glanced back over his shoulder at Tossidin. "We came to wake you, as you told me to. The swordsmen are ready to go."

Kahlan pushed her mantle off. "I'll be ready in a moment, and we can . . ."

She remembered her decision to get to Aydindril. She had to get to Zedd. She had to get help for Richard. If it was true that the veil was torn . . .

"Mother Confessor, you don't look well. You've been through a lot, you hadn't slept in days, and you've only just gotten a few hours of sleep. I think you need more."

Yes, she did. Though she could feel that her power was back, she definitely did not feel recovered. She put a hand on his arm.

"Captain, I must leave for Aydindril. I must . . ."

He gave her a little smile. "You rest. You're not rested enough to travel. Stay here and rest. When we get back, you'll be rested and you can leave."

She nodded, still clutching his sleeve for support. "Yes. And then I must leave.

I thought about it last night. I must get to Aydindril. I'll rest until you get back, but then I must leave." She looked about. Only Tossidin was there with the captain. "Where's Chandalen, and Prindin?"

"My brother went to check on their sentries, to make sure that they didn't place any," Tossidin said, "so that our attack will be without warning."

"Chandalen is attacking with the pikemen," Captain Ryan said. "I'm to meet him with the swordsmen for the next attack."

Kahlan comforted her sore lip. "Tossidin, tell Chandalen that when your attack is finished, we must leave. You three be careful. You must get me to Aydindril." She could hardly keep her eyes open. She could hardly bring forth the energy to speak. She knew she wasn't able to travel, yet. "I'll rest until you return."

Captain Ryan sighed with relief that she wasn't going with them, that she would be safe, here. "I'll leave some men to stand guard while you rest."

She gestured with her hand. "This camp is well hidden. I'm safe up here."

He leaned forward insistently. "Ten or twelve men are not going to make any difference to us, and I would be better able to put my mind to our task if I'm not worrying about you all alone back here."

She didn't have the energy to argue. "All right . . ."

She flopped back down. With a troubled frown, Tossidin pulled the mantle up over her. She was sinking back into the blackness as the two of them crawled out the opening. She tried to keep herself from going into that unfeeling place, but she was helplessly swept away.

The crushing weight of the void closed in around her. She tried to escape its grasp, tried to come back up, but the darkness was too thick, like being encased in mud. She was trapped, still being sucked deeper. She felt a surge of panic.

She tried to think, but could not form thoughts into coherent concepts. She had the sense that something was wrong, but could not bring her mind to bear on the solution.

This time, instead of surrendering, she focused all her strength on thoughts of Richard, on her need to help him, and the darkness then was not a total void. She had an inkling of time, sensing its incremental passing. She felt as if she were sleeping her whole lifetime away as she tenaciously kept Richard in her thoughts.

Her concern for him, and her anxiety over the strangeness of the depthless sleep, let her slowly, methodically, claw her way back. Yet it seemed to take hours.

With a desperate gasp, she came awake. Her head swirled with a throbbing ache. Her whole body tingled with sharp little pricks of pain. She laboriously pushed herself up, to sit, staring about her dark shelter. The candle was burned almost all the way down. Quiet hummed in her ears.

She thought maybe she needed cold air to wake up. Her arms and legs felt thick and heavy as she crawled through the opening of the shelter. Outside, it was dusk. She looked up at the first stars winking through the trees. Her breath fogged before her face as she stood on wobbly legs.

Kahlan took a step, and promptly tripped over something, falling on her face in the snow. Her cheek still against the ground, she opened her eyes. Inches away, glassy eyes were staring at her. The side of a young man's face was lying against the snow, close to hers. It was his leg she had tripped over. It felt as if her bones wanted to leap out of her skin and run.

His throat was gaping open, his neck nearly sliced in two, letting his head bend back from his body at an impossible angle. She could see the opening of his severed windpipe. Clotted blood covered snow. A bloom of bile rose up into her throat. She swallowed, forcing it back down.

Slowly lifting her head, she saw the dark forms of other bodies. They were all Galean. Every sword still rested in its scabbard. They had died without the chance to fight back.

Kahlan's legs tensed, wanting to run, but she strained to be still. In the dull fog of the halfsleep she couldn't throw off, she struggled to think. Her mind seemed to be mired in a dreamlike stupor, unable to concentrate. Someone had killed these men, and could still be around; she somehow had to force herself to think.

She touched her fingers to the dead soldier's hand. It was still warm. This must have just happened. Maybe that was what had wakened her.

She peered up, among the trees. Men moved in the shadows. They had seen her, and were moving into the clearing around her. They laughed and hooted as they came forward, and she saw who they were—close to a dozen D'Harans, and a couple of Keltans. Men of the Imperial Order. With a gasp, Kahlan sprang to her feet.

One man, the one closest, had a puffy red wound down the left side of his face, from his temple to his jaw, where Nick's hoof had caught him. Ragged stitches held the black and red flesh closed. He gave a sneering smile with the good side of his mouth. It was General Riggs.

"Well, well, I have found you at last, Confessor."

Kahlan flinched with the rest of the men when a dark form screaming a battle cry crashed through the underbrush. As the men turned, Kahlan bolted the other way.

Before she turned, she had seen the fading light glint off a huge war axe. The crescent-shaped blade struck down two men in one swing. It was Orsk. He must have been searching for her, too, so he could protect her. One touched by a Confessor never gave up.

Her legs felt thick, and tingled as if she had slept on them, but she ran as hard as she could. Yelling and screaming erupted behind her. Steel rang against steel. Orsk roared as he tore into the men after her.

Spruce branches slapped her face as she staggered through the trees. Dead limbs and brush snagged her pants and shirt. Dizzy, she stumbled through the drifts. Snow splashed against her face as she crashed through drooping boughs. She couldn't make her legs run fast enough.

The man on her heels grunted as he dove for her. His arms snared her legs and she went down hard. She spit snow out as she kicked and struggled to get away. The man clawed his way up her legs, grabbing hold of her belt and throwing himself on top of her.

The red face with the angry wound down one side hovered right over hers. In triumph, he grinned wickedly. Back through the trees, she could hear the sounds of furious battle. She and Riggs were alone as she struggled to squirm away.

One fist grabbed her hair and held her head to the ground. His other fist punched her in the side, knocking the wind from her lungs. He hit her again. Nausea swept through her in a hot wave as she fought to get her breath.

"I've got you now, Confessor. You'll not get away again. You may as well resign yourself to it."

He was alone. What was he thinking? She slapped a hand to his chest. It seemed a puzzle to her that a lone man would think he could take a Confessor.

"You have no one, Riggs," she managed to say under the weight of him. "You've lost. You are mine."

"I don't think so." He sneered. "He said you can't use your power, now."

He lifted her head and thumped it against the ground. Her vision blurred. She tried to concentrate on what she needed to do. He lifted her head again to bang it against the ground. Though she was bewildered by what he had said, she had to do it now, before he knocked her unconscious, before it was too late. Now, when time was hers.

In the silence of her mind, as he lifted her head, she let her Confessor's power sweep through her. She released her restraint.

There was thunder with no sound. The impact of power, of magic, made Riggs flinch. Tree branches all around shook with a jolt. Snow dropped down, splattering on his back and her face.

His eyes went wide, his jaw slack. "Mistress! Command me."

With the last of her strength, she managed to ask, "Who told you my power couldn't harm you!"

"Mistress, it was . . ."

The bloody point of an arrow exploded from the prominence on the fore of his throat. The broad steel point stopped a scant inch from her chin. His eyes teared as his mouth moved and blood frothed, but no words came forth. As his breath rattled from his lungs, he began slumping onto her.

A fist gripped the shoulder of his uniform and pulled Riggs away. At first, she thought it would be Orsk, but it wasn't.

"Mother Confessor!" A worried Prindin peered down at her. "Are you hurt? Did he hurt you?"

He hastily rolled the general off her and offered his hand to help her up as his eyes glided down the length of her lying on the snow. She stared up at him, but didn't take his hand. Using her power had left her exhausted and limp as never before.

His customary grin spread on his face as he shouldered his bow. "I can see you are not hurt. You look very fine."

"You didn't need to kill him. I had already used my power on him. He was mine. He was just about to tell me who it was that said I could not harm . . ."

Her whole body tingled with apprehension at the way his eyes took her in. His familiar grin ran a cold shiver up her arms and the back of her neck, making the fine hairs stand stiffly out.

Orsk crashed through the trees. "Mistress! Are you safe?"

She could hear others coming in the woods behind him. She heard Chandalen's voice. Prindin swiftly nocked an arrow. Orsk lifted his axe with one big fist.

"Prindin! No! Don't hurt him!" Prindin drew his bow. "Orsk! Run!"

The big man spun without question and darted back into the brush. An arrow followed him in. She heard the arrow strike something solid. She could hear Orsk stumble through the barren undergrowth, breaking branches and saplings. The snapping of twigs died out, and then she heard him hit the ground.

She tried to stand, but feebly fell back. It felt as if she had no bones and her muscles were melting. Her strength was gone. The blackness was trying to suck her back in.

Prindin turned his grin back to her as he shouldered his bow once more.

Kahlan strained to bring forth the strength to speak. It came in a breathy whisper. "Prindin, why did you do that?"

He shrugged. "So we can be alone." His smile widened. "Before they chop off your head."

Prindin. Prindin had told Riggs her power wouldn't hurt him, so she would expend it on him, and would have nothing left. Her legs trembled with the effort of trying to lift herself. She fell back again as he watched.

A voice came through the trees. It was a breathless Chandalen, calling to her. In another direction, she heard Tossidin calling. She tried to scream to them. Only a weak, hoarse complaint came from her throat. Darkness pressed into her.

Maybe she was still asleep, she thought. She could hardly speak, hardly move, just like a nightmare. She wished it were.

But she knew it was no dream.

Prindin turned to the insistent calls. Kahlan dug her heels into the snow and, with a mighty effort, managed to scoot herself back. Her hand fell on a stout maple limb lying on the ground.

Prindin rushed to her. She focused all her fear, her dread, her pain and horror at what was happening, into action. It took everything she had. Prindin reached for her.

Kahlan came up swinging the stout limb. Prindin ducked and snatched her would-be club, wrenching it from her grip. He spun her to him and curled his arm around her head, over her mouth, as she tried to warn Chandalen. Though he wasn't big, she knew Prindin to be incredibly strong, but in her present state, even a child could have had his way with her.

Chandalen ran up behind them, a knife in hand. Kahlan bit into Prindin's arm. She cried out as Prindin spun with impossible speed and strength, catching Chandalen across the side of the head with the branch. The sound of the hollow thunk was sickening. The blow knocked Chandalen into the boughs of a fir tree. As she twisted from Prindin's grip, she saw blood on the snow around Chandalen.

Tossidin, breathing hard, burst through the trees. "What is happening! Prindin!"

He saw them and stopped in his tracks. He looked to Chandalen and then to Prindin.

Prindin peered back over his shoulder at his brother, speaking in his own tongue. *"Chandalen tried to kill us! I came here just as he tried to kill the Mother Confessor. Help me. She is hurt."*

Kahlan collapsed to her knees, crying out. "No . . . Tossidin . . . no . . ."

Tossidin ran toward them. *"What is this trouble Chandalen told me of? What is wrong with you, brother? What have you done?"*

*"Help me! The Mother Confessor has been hurt!"*

Tossidin gripped his brother's shoulder and spun him around. *"Prindin! What have you . . ."*

Prindin slammed a knife into his brother's chest. Tossidin's eyes went wide in surprise. His mouth opened but no words came. With a wheeze, his legs buckled and he crumpled to the ground. Kahlan cried out. He had been stabbed through the heart.

Chandalen sat up with a groggy groan. He put his hands to his bleeding scalp. Keeping an eye to the wounded man, Prindin pulled a bone box from his waist pouch. He had a full box of *bandu*. He hadn't given her all his poison.

Helpless to stop him, Kahlan saw Prindin wipe a generous gob of poison onto the arrow's point. Dazed, Chandalen held his head in his hands as he tried to gather his wits. Prindin drew the bowstring to his cheek. She knew he was aiming for Chandalen's throat. Just as Prindin released the arrow, she managed to throw herself against his legs, making the arrow go astray from its target. It still hit Chandalen in the shoulder.

The back of his fist across her face sent her sprawling. Powered by sheer terror, Kahlan started scrambling away on her hands and knees. The snow was freezing her fingers. The knees of her pants were soaked and icy wet. She concentrated on the cold to try to revive herself. She glanced over her shoulder as she clambered away.

Prindin drew another arrow from his quiver, and wiped it in the poison as he watched her struggle. As he had watched Chandalen. A cry came from her throat as she staggered to her feet and ran. A nightmare. It had to be a nightmare.

The arrow felt like a club hitting the back of her left leg. She screamed and fell to her face. Her leg flamed in hot pain. A tingling, prickling sensation spread through the muscle. The pain seared through the bone, into her hip.

Prindin was suddenly over her. He knelt down and gripped the arrow sticking from the back of her leg. He put his other hand against her bottom to hold her, and yanked the arrow free. Kahlan could feel the tingle of the poison going up her leg.

*"Don't worry, Mother Confessor, I did not use much poison on your arrow, like on Chandalen's, just enough to make sure you will give me no trouble. He will be dead in another minute. You will live long enough to have your head chopped off."* His hand stroked her bottom. *"If they do not wait too long."* Prindin leaned over her. *"It is too cold out here. We will go back."*

He took hold of her wrist and started dragging her across the snow. In her mind, Kahlan fought him; she struggled, she shrieked, she hit, but she couldn't make her body obey. She was as limp as a rag doll being dragged over the snow. She could feel the poison spreading to her ribs.

Tears streamed down her cheeks. Orsk. Tossidin. Chandalen. Her. How could Prindin do such a thing? She sobbed as her face slid over the snow. How could he? His own brother. He had stabbed his own brother as if it meant nothing. Who could do such a thing? How could anyone do such a thing? How could anyone but a . . .

Baneling.

She gasped with the realization. She had never fully believed in banelings, before. Wizards had told her they were real, but she never believed the wizards knew for sure. She had always thought it might be superstitious nonsense that sent people hunting things in the dark, things from the underworld, things bidden from the Keeper's own dark whispers.

But now she knew. She was in the grips of a baneling. Dear spirits, how could no one know? He had helped her so many times. He had befriended her.

So he could be close to her, and keep track of her for the Keeper. He was a baneling. Darken Rahl had laughed at her. Because she was so stupid.

She knew now, without a doubt—the veil was torn. Darken Rahl had promised her such things. He had come to tear the veil the rest of the way, and she had foolishly thought she was in control of what she was doing, but all the time Darken Rahl, and the Keeper, had watched her through Prindin's eyes.

But why wait until now? Why let her fight in this war, let all these people die, before he snatched her?

Kahlan knew why. The Keeper was of the world of the dead. Bringing death to the world of the living was what he wanted. He resented the living. That was why he wanted the veil torn—so he could bring death to the world of the living.

He coveted this world's breath of life. He enjoyed watching people die. He did not wish to stop it too soon, stop the suffering, the fear, the pain.

It felt as if her arm might tear from its socket as Prindin tugged her through the brush, and over a log half covered over with snow. The tingling of the poison had spread across her chest.

Her left leg had gone numb. At least, she thought, she couldn't feel how much the arrow wound hurt. The round, iron point had hit the bone, and Prindin had not been gentle about pulling it out. At least it was numb, now.

When they reached the shelter, she could see bodies all about, not only the Galean men, but the men of the Imperial Order that Orsk had killed. Soon, when Prindin was finished with her, he would turn her over to the army of the Order, and she would be beheaded. It would be over, and there was nothing she could do to stop it. She couldn't even fight back. She would never see Richard again. Dear spirits, he would never know how much she loved him.

Prindin dragged her through the opening to the shelter and heaved her onto the mat of boughs. As he lit two more candles from the one that was almost burned down, she struggled to breathe, to remain conscious.

*"I wish to be able to see you,"* he explained with a lecherous smile. *"You are very fine to look upon. I wish to see all of you."*

She had always liked his smile. She didn't like it now.

Prindin took off his fur mantle and tossed it aside. His smile vanished. His eyes were wild. He didn't speak in her tongue anymore, but only his own.

*"Take off your clothes. I wish to look upon you, first. To be aroused by the sight of you."*

Even if he had held a knife to her throat, she wouldn't have been able to obey; she couldn't move her arms. "Prindin," she managed to whisper, "the men will be back soon. They will catch you here."

*"They will be busy. They are having a fight like they never expected."* His smile returned. *"They will not be back soon, if at all."* The smile changed in an instant to a twisted expression of hot rage. *"I said take off your clothes!"*

"Prindin, you are my friend. Please. Don't do this."

He crawled on top of her, yanking at her belt. *"Then I will do it for you!"*

Tears, over her helplessness, over the loss of a friend to this madness, to the Keeper, ran down her cheeks. "Prindin, why?"

He sat up, as if surprised by the question. *"The great spirit said I may have you before he takes your spirit to the underworld. He said I am to have a reward, for the work I have done. The great spirit is pleased with me for delivering you to him."*

The bite on her neck stung with prickling pain. She shivered with sorrow for Tossidin and Chandalen. She shivered at her own desolate, hopeless situation. The tingling from the poison had spread across her shoulders. She could feel the slight twinge of its first touch moving up her throat.

He squeezed her under him as he kissed the place on her neck where Darken Rahl's lips had been, where the bite was. The pain, the visions, sent a silent shriek through her.

*"Prindin . . . please . . . after you have me . . . let me go?"* She hoped that hearing her words in his tongue would mean more to him. *"Please?"*

486

He lifted his head away, looking into her eyes. *"It would do no good for me to leave you. You have been poisoned, by the tea, and by the arrow. You will die soon, anyway. You must be beheaded before you die of the poison. It will be better. You will not suffer the poison's end. That is my mercy to you."*

Prindin grinned as he started to bend over her again, kissing her neck. Tears ran down her cheeks.

*"I hate you,"* she wept. *"You and your great spirit."*

He sprang up, standing, as best he could in the small shelter, with his fists at his sides as he glared down at her.

*"You are to be mine! I have been promised! I will have you! Your power cannot harm me, I saw to that. It is used up for now. You are to be mine! If you will not give yourself to me, I will take you! You brought your hateful magic to my people, your hateful ways! You are evil, and I will take you, to conquer your wickedness! The great spirit has said it shall be so!"*

Prindin pulled his buckskin shirt off over his head, off his wiry frame. He leapt full onto her, landing with a grunt. His face was right above hers.

They stared at each other in surprise.

He had no idea what had happened. She knew *what* had happened, but had no idea *how*.

She could feel his warm blood flowing over her fist. His pupils expanded. He coughed, splattering little droplets of blood across her face. With a long, slow gurgle, he went limp as his last breath left his lungs.

Tears ran down Kahlan's face. She didn't have the strength to push him off her; she could hardly breathe under his weight.

And so she lay still, feeling his blood drain over her hand between her breasts and soak into her shirt. The tingling of the poison had risen up her neck.

In the tingling blackness, her lip hurt. Something was jabbing against the cut, making it throb. Something was in her mouth. She thought it felt like a finger, poking into her mouth.

"Swallow!"

Kahlan frowned in the darkness, in her sleep.

"Swallow! Do you hear me? Swallow!"

Making a sour face, she did as commanded. The finger pushed more of the dry things into her mouth.

"Swallow again!"

She swallowed, hoping the voice would leave her alone, now. It did. She sank back down into the tingling void. She drifted in the nowhere place, unaware. She had no concept of time, no idea how long she floated.

With a gasp, her eyes opened. She blinked around at her shelter. The candles were burned halfway down. Her fur mantle was covering her.

Chandalen leaned over, peering down at her. A broad smile spread on his lips. He let out a long sigh of relief.

"You are back," he said. "You are safe, now."

"Chandalen?" She tried to make sense of what she was seeing. "Am I in the underworld, or are you are not dead?"

He laughed quietly. "Chandalen is hard to kill."

She worked her tongue, trying to wet her dry mouth. She was awake, really awake, for the first time in as long as she could remember. It seemed she had forgotten what it was like to be awake, how vibrant it felt. Still, she did not move, afraid the blackness would return.

"But, Prindin shot you with a ten-step arrow. I saw it."

He turned a bit, looking away in chagrin. She could see that his black hair was matted with dried blood. He flipped his hand, as if uneasy that he had to explain.

"Remember I told you that our ancestors took *quassin doe* before they went into battle, so that if they were shot with a ten-step arrow, the poison would not kill them?" She nodded. He tenderly tested his wounded scalp. "Well, in honor of my ancestors, my warrior ancestors, I ate some of the *quassin doe* leaves before I went to fight. The *quassin doe* you gave to me back at that city." His eyebrows lifted, as if further justification was needed. "It was to honor my ancestors."

Kahlan smiled warmly to him as she put a hand to his arm. "You have done your ancestors proud."

He helped her sit up. In the dim light, she saw that Prindin lay next to her, on his back.

The bone knife, the bone knife made from Chandalen's grandfather's bones, the one she had worn at her arm, jutted from Prindin's chest. The black feathers fanned out around the hilt end, draped like a shroud over the fatal wound. Somehow, she had managed to put that knife between them when Prindin had leaped on her. Somehow.

She remembered her numb, helpless plight. She remembered the tingling feeling of the poison, and that she couldn't move. She remembered her terror. She remembered Prindin's leap onto her.

But she didn't remember pulling the knife.

Her voice trembled. "I'm so sorry, Chandalen." Her fingers covered her mouth. "I'm so sorry that I killed your friend."

Chandalen glared at the body. "He was not my friend. My friends do not try to kill me." He put a comforting hand to her shoulder. "He was sent by the great, dark spirit of the dead. His heart was taken by evil."

Kahlan clutched his sleeve. "Chandalen, that great, dark spirit of the dead is trying to escape from behind the veil. He wants to pull us all behind the veil, into the world of the dead."

His brown eyes studied hers. "I believe you. We must get you to Aydindril, so you may help stop him."

She sagged with relief. "Thank you, Chandalen. Thank you for understanding, and for saving me with the *quassin doe.*" Kahlan clutched his arm. "The men! Prindin set a trap for them! What time is it?"

He made a comforting, hushing sound. "When Captain Ryan came to Tossidin and me before the attack, I asked where you were. I knew you would want to be with them. He told me that you were sick. That you could not wake. It sounded to me like *bandu.*

"Captain Ryan said you would not eat, and would have only tea Prindin made for you. I knew then, what was happening. I knew you had been poisoned, and the only thing you had was tea.

"Tossidin and I were greatly worried for you. We checked to see if the enemy had changed position. We saw that they were waiting for the attack where we had planned it at first. I made the men change the attack, and come from a different place than expected. As soon as I gave the new orders, we rushed back here.

"I knew Prindin had betrayed us, but Tossidin thought there must be some other explanation. He trusted his brother and did not want to think evil of him. He paid for his trust, his mistake, with his life."

Kahlan looked away in the uneasy quiet. She frowned back at him. "What of the arrow? What of the wound on your head? We must see to your wounds."

Chandalen pulled the neck of his buckskin shirt to the side, revealing a bandage over his left shoulder. "The men returned in the night. They stitched my head. It is not as bad as it looks. They also took out the arrow."

He winced as he pulled the shirt back up on his shoulder. "I taught Prindin well. He used a bladed arrow. Bladed arrows do more harm coming out than going in. One of the men, the one who cuts and sews the wounded, cut out the arrow, and stitched me together. The arrow hit the bone, so it did not go in too far. My arm is stiff, and I will not be able to use it for a time."

Kahlan felt her leg. There was a bandage under her pants. "Did he stitch my leg, too?"

489

"No. It did not need sewing, just to be wrapped; I did that. Prindin used a round point on you. That is not like I taught him. I don't know why he would do that."

Kahlan could feel the presence of the body next to her. "He wanted to be able to get it out of me, after he shot me with poison," she said quietly. "He wanted it out of his way. He was going to rape me before he gave me to the enemy."

Chandalen watched the body, not wanting to look at her, and said he was glad that had not happened.

She touched his left hand. "And I'm glad it was your shoulder, and not your throat."

He frowned. "I taught Prindin how to shoot. He would never miss my throat from that distance. Why did he not shoot my throat?"

She shrugged, feigning ignorance. He grunted suspiciously.

"Chandalen, why is his body still in here? Why didn't you drag him out?"

He moved his wounded arm a bit with his other, making it more comfortable. "Because Grandfather's spirit knife is still in him." He regarded her with a serious expression. "You have used the aid of Grandfather's bones, his spirit, to protect yourself, to take another life. Grandfather's spirit is bonded to you now. No other may touch his bone knife, now. It is yours, and only you may touch it. You must remove it."

Kahlan momentarily contemplated whether or not she could just leave the knife where it was, and bury it with the body. She thought maybe the bone knife should be put to rest, too. But she discarded the thought. To the Mud People this was powerful spirit magic. She would insult Chandalen if she rejected the knife.

She thought, too, that maybe she would be insulting the spirit of Chandalen's grandfather if she didn't take back the knife. She wasn't entirely sure that it wasn't the spirit in the bone knife that had killed Prindin to save her. She didn't know how the knife had gotten into her hand.

Kahlan reached out and wrapped her fingers around the round end protruding from Prindin's chest. It made a sucking sound as she pulled it from the body. She wiped it clean on the balsam boughs covering the floor.

Kahlan brought the round end to her lips and kissed it lightly. "Thank you, spirit grandfather, for saving my life." Somehow, it seemed the right thing to do.

Chandalen smiled as she slid the bone knife into the band on her arm. "You are a good Mud Person. You knew what to do without me telling you. Grandfather's spirit will watch over you always."

"Chandalen, we must get to Aydindril. The veil to the underworld is torn. We've done what we must to help these men. I must do my job, now."

"When we first found these men, I did not want to stay with them. I wanted to be away from their fight so that you would be safe." He stared off at nothing. "Somehow, I forgot that thought, and all I wanted to do was fight and kill the enemy."

"I know," she whispered, "that happened to me, too. I forgot all about what I was supposed to be doing. It's almost as if we, too, listened to the great, dark spirit. The veil is torn. Maybe that's why we were distracted."

"You think that this veil is torn, and because of that we forgot what we were to do, and wanted only to kill?"

"Chandalen, I don't know the answers to these things. I must get to Aydindril. The wizard will know what to do. Richard needs help. We have taken enough time here. We must not waste any more. We must talk to the men, and then be on our way. Are they out there?" He nodded. "Then let's get going."

She started to rise, but he put his good hand to her arm and stopped her. "They have been waiting outside your shelter all night. I would not let them come inside."

He took his hand back as he seemed to search for the right words. "I feared greatly that you would die this night. I didn't know if I had given you the *quassin doe* in time. Prindin had been giving you poison without our knowing it, for a long time. You almost went to the spirit world.

"If you had died, I would never be able to return to my people again. But that is not why I am glad you live. I am glad because you are a good Mud Person. You are a protector to our people, the same as Chandalen. We each fight in our own way." He lifted an eyebrow. "Lately, you have been fighting too much like Chandalen fights. You are good at it, but you should leave that to me, and fight in the way you are meant to fight."

Kahlan smiled. "You're right. Thank you for sitting with me all night. It was good to have you near. I'm sorry you were hurt."

He shrugged. "Someday, when I find a woman for myself, I will have scars to show her, so she may see how brave Chandalen is."

Kahlan laughed. "I'm sure she will be impressed with your bravery when you were shot with an arrow."

Chandalen gave her a crooked look. "It does not prove I was brave because I was shot with an arrow. Anyone can be shot." He lifted his chin. "I am brave because I did not cry out when the the arrow was cut from me."

Someday, Kahlan thought, some fortunate woman would have her hands full with this one. "I'm glad the good spirits watched over you, and you are with me."

He narrowed his eyes as he peered at her. "I do not know what happened, but I think Prindin missed my throat because you were watching over me, too."

She only grinned. When she looked to the body, her grin withered. She stroked the fur of her mantle. "Poor Tossidin. He loved his brother. I'll miss him."

Chandalen glanced to the body. "I have known them since they were young boys. They both followed me around, begging me to teach them. Begging to be one of my men." He hung his head in silence. Finally, he returned his attention to her. "The men are worried greatly about you. They are waiting."

Kahlan followed as he crawled out on his knees and one hand. She dragged the sword with her. Outside, in the light, there was a sudden rustle of sound as men rose to their feet.

Captain Ryan rushed forward, but a big man, with one arm in a sling, thrust his good arm across the captain's chest, stopping him cold. He held a monstrous war axe in his fist.

"Orsk? You are alive, too?"

His eyes were red from weeping. Kahlan remembered the way her father had wept when her mother, his mistress, was ill.

"Mistress!" Tears sprang anew to his eyes. "You are well! What do you wish?"

"Orsk, these men are all my friends. None of them will hurt me. You do not need to keep them away. I'm safe. It would please me if you just sat quietly for now."

Instantly, he flopped to the ground. Kahlan gave a questioning frown to Chandalen.

Chandalen shrugged. "I saw him fight to protect you, and Prindin wanted to kill him, so I gave him *quassin doe*. The men dug the arrow from his back. I am not sure how badly he is hurt; he has no interest in his wound, only in you. I was only

491

able to keep him out of the shelter by telling him you needed to be left alone or you might not recover, but he would not leave this spot as long as you were inside."

Kahlan sighed as she gazed at the grisly face staring silently up at her. She could hardly stand to look at the jagged white scar, and the one eye that was sewn shut. She returned her attention to an impatient Captain Ryan, and the hundreds of faces behind him.

"How goes the war?"

"The war! Dash the war! Are you all right? You had us scared to death!" He cast a hot glance at Chandalen, and then at Orsk sitting in the snow. "These two wouldn't even let me have a peek at you, to see how you were."

"That's their job," Kahlan said. She gave them a warm smile. "Thank you all for your concern. Chandalen has saved me."

"Well, what happened? This place was a mess. The dozen men I left here were slaughtered. By a *troga*. Prindin and Tossidin are dead. And there were dead men of the Order. We feared they killed you."

Kahlan realized Chandalen had told them nothing. "One of the dead men, off in that direction, is General Riggs, of the Imperial Order. Orsk here," she pointed down to the one-eyed man, "killed most of the men of the Order. They came here to get me. Prindin killed our guards, and his brother, and he tried to kill me." Whispers and gasps spread among the men.

Captain Ryan's eyes looked like they would pop from his head. "Prindin! Not Prindin. Dear spirits, why?"

She waited until silence settled over the men. She spoke in a quiet tone. "Prindin was a baneling."

Stunned silence was all she heard for a moment, and then the worried whispers of "baneling" spread back through the ranks.

"You men are doing a fine job. But now you must fight on without me. I must get to Aydindril." Disappointed murmurs filled the air. "I would not leave you if I did not know you were up to the task. You have all proven your worth and your heart in battle. You are men the equal of any."

The men stood a little taller. They listened intently to her, as if hearing their general.

"I am proud of each and every one of you. You are heroes of the Midlands. This army of the Imperial Order, threat though it is, is representative of a larger threat to the Midlands, to the world of the living. That the Keeper would send a baneling to stop me is proof of that.

"I believe the Imperial Order is aligned with the Keeper. I must now turn my attention to this threat. I know you will fight on, as you have sworn, and show the enemy no quarter. I know the days of the Order are numbered."

Kahlan realized that her neck didn't hurt. She touched her fingers to the bite. It was gone. Suddenly she felt that perhaps she had escaped the Keeper's grasp in more ways than one.

With a serious demeanor, she regarded the young faces that intently watched her. "Though you will fight on without quarter, you must not let yourselves become what you are fighting. The enemy fights to kill, and to enslave. You fight for life, and freedom. Keep that always uppermost in your hearts.

"Do not let yourselves become what you hate. I know how easy it is to do. It almost happened to me."

Kahlan put a fist into the air. "I promise to never forget a one of you. Promise me that when this is finished, both the threat from the Imperial Order, and the threat from the Keeper, that you will one day all come to Aydindril, so the Midlands may honor your sacrifice."

The men all lifted a fist in pledge. A cheer went up.

"Captain Ryan, please tell the men at the other camps my words. I wish I could speak to them all myself, but I must leave at once."

He assured her it would be done. Kahlan lifted the sword in both hands, holding it out.

"King Wyborn wielded this sword in battle to protect his land. The Mother Confessor has wielded it in defense of the Midlands. I now place it in capable hands."

Captain Ryan's fingers carefully lifted the sword from hers. He held it as if holding the crown of Galea itself. A beaming grin lit his face.

"I will carry it with pride, Mother Confessor. Thank you for everything you have taught us. When you first found us, we were boys. Thank you for making us into men. You have taught us not only to fight better but, more importantly, what it means to be soldiers, and to be protectors of the Midlands."

He took the hilt in his fist and held the sword skyward as he turned to his men.

"Three cheers for the Mother Confessor!"

As she listened to the three wild cheers, Kahlan realized that in all her life she had never heard anyone cheer the Mother Confessor before. She had to strain to keep her surprise from showing. She lifted a kiss on her fingers and thanked them all.

"Captain Ryan, I wish to take Nick, and I will need two other horses, also."

Chandalen lurched forward. "Now, why do you need horses!"

She lifted an eyebrow to him. "Chandalen, I have an arrow wound in my leg. I can hardly stand, much less walk. I need to ride, if I'm to get to Aydindril. I hope you do not think me weak because of it."

His brow knotted up. "Well, no. Of course you cannot be expected to walk." His eyes turned angry again. "But why do you want two other horses?"

"If I ride, you must, too."

"Chandalen does not need to ride! I am strong!"

She leaned close and spoke in his tongue. *"Chandalen, I know the Mud People do not ride horses. I would not expect you would know how. I will teach you. You will do fine. When you return to your people, you will have a new skill that none of them have. They will be impressed. The women will see that you are brave."*

He grunted suspiciously as he scowled. "Then why do we need the third horse?"

"We're taking Orsk."

"What!"

Kahlan shrugged. "You can't draw a bow until your arm recovers. How will you protect me? Orsk can wield an axe with his one good arm, and you can throw a spear with yours."

He rolled his eyes. "I am not going to be able to talk you out of this, am I?"

"No," she said with a small smile. "Now, we better get our things and be on our way."

Kahlan surveyed the men one last time. Her men. She gave them a salute of her fist to her heart.

They all silently returned the salute.

She had lost much with these men. She had gained much.

"Take care. Each and every one of you."

493

S o, when are we going to meet your people, the ones who will guide Sister Verna and me to the palace?"

Du Chaillu glanced back over her shoulder, pulling her mass of black hair out of the way to peer at him. She was leading her horse. Richard had grown tired of her complaints, and when she finally refused to ride any longer, he decided not to make an issue of it and let her walk. Richard had decided to walk for a while himself. Sister Verna rode behind them, watching Du Chaillu like an owl from atop her horse.

"Soon." Her cool, distant expression disturbed him. "Very soon."

Her attitude had slowly changed since they had left the Majendie land, as they went deeper into hers. She was no longer chatty and open, but had grown haughty and distant. Sister Verna rarely took her eyes from Du Chaillu, and Du Chaillu, in turn, didn't miss a move the Sister made. They were like two cats with their fur standing on end, silent and still, but ready to spring. It wouldn't have surprised him if soon he saw their teeth bared.

Richard had the feeling the two of them were constantly testing each other, but in ways he couldn't see. By the Sister's attitude, he didn't think she was pleased about what she was discovering. Richard could tell, from experience, when the Sister was touching her Han. He recognized the shroud of it in her eyes. She was touching it now.

In the gathering darkness, Du Chaillu turned abruptly from the wide forest trail, leading them on a narrow path through the thick, tangled growth. Dark water holding dense thickets of reeds and broad-leafed plants with pink and yellow trumpet-shaped flowers lurked to the sides. Richard's eyes scanned the shadows among the trees.

Du Chaillu came to a halt at the edge of a sandy, open area. She lifted the reins of her horse to Richard. "The others will join us in this place. Wait here, magic man."

The term she used to address him lifted his hackles. He took the reins. "Richard. My name is Richard. I'm the one who saved your neck. Remember?"

Du Chaillu looked at him thoughtfully. "Please don't ever think I do not appreciate what you have done for me, for my people. Your kindness will be always in my heart." Her eyes seemed to go out of focus, and her voice softened with regret. "But you are still a magic man." Her back straightened. "Wait here."

She turned and disappeared into the forest around the clearing. Richard stood watching her vanish as Sister Verna dismounted. She took the reins to all three horses.

"She is going to try to kill you now," she said, as if telling him that she thought it would rain tomorrow.

Richard glared at her. "I saved her life."

Sister Verna started leading the horses to the trees. "You are a magic man to these people. They kill magic men."

Richard didn't want to believe her, but he did. "Then use your Han to prevent it, Sister, to preserve life, as you told Du Chaillu she should do with her new child."

Sister Verna stroked her horse's chin. "She has use of her Han, too. That's why the Sisters have always avoided these people; some of them can use their Han, but in a way we don't understand.

"I've tried little things on her, to test her. The spells I send at her disappear like pebbles dropped down a well. And they do not go unnoticed. Du Chaillu knows what I try to do, and somehow is able to annul it. I told you before, these people are dangerous. I have fought every step of the way to prevent this. I warned you not to swing the axe. You saw my efforts as misguided."

Richard gritted his teeth. His left hand gripped the hilt of the sword. He could feel the bumps of the word *Truth* woven into the wire, and through it the heat of its rage.

"I have no intention of killing anyone."

"Good. Keep the anger of the sword out. You are going to need it if you're to survive. They are surrounding us as we speak; that much my Han can tell me."

Richard felt as if things were suddenly spinning out of his control. He didn't want to hurt anyone. He hadn't saved Du Chaillu just to have to fight her people. "Then I suggest you call on your Han, Sister Verna. I am the Seeker, not an assassin. I'm not going to kill your enemies for you."

She took a few strides toward him. Her voice was tight and controlled. "I told you, my Han is not going to be able to help. I would end the threat if I could, but I can't. Du Chaillu has power against magic. I'm begging you, Richard, defend yourself."

His eyes narrowed. "Perhaps you just don't want to help. You're angry that I spoiled the arrangement the Sisters had with the Majendie. You plan on watching, like you always do, just to see what I'll do."

She slowly shook her head in frustration. "Do you really think, Richard, that I would spend half my life in my duty to find you and carry you safely to the Palace of the Prophets, only to watch you killed when we're on the doorstep of my home? Do you actually believe that I wouldn't stop this if I could? Is your opinion of me that low?"

His impulse was to argue with her, but instead he considered her words. What she said made sense. Richard gave an apologetic shake of his head, then quickly glanced into the shadows. "How many are there?"

"Perhaps thirty."

"Thirty." In frustration, he folded his arms. "How am I to defend against thirty, by myself?"

She looked out into the darkness a moment, then cast her hands forward. A wind rose, carrying a veil of sand and dirt outward into the blackness. "That will slow them for a short time, but not stop them."

She turned her brown eyes on him once more. "Richard, I have used my Han to seek an answer. The only thing my Han tells me is that you must use the prophecy to survive. You've named yourself the bringer of death, as the prophecy foretells. The prophecy is about you.

"You must use the prophecy if you are to defeat that many. The prophecy says the holder of the sword is able to call the dead forth, call the past into the present. Somehow, that's what you must do in order to survive—call forth the dead, call the past into the present."

Richard unfolded his arms. "We're about to be overrun by thirty people you say are going to try to kill me, and you give me riddles? Sister, I told you before that I don't know what it means. If you want to help, then tell me something I can use."

She turned away, walking back toward the horses. "I have. Sometimes prophecies are meant to give aid to the one named by sending help across time, providing a key that may open a door to enlightenment. I believe this prophecy is such. This prophecy is about you; you must find its use. I don't know its meaning."

She stopped and turned to look back over her shoulder. "You forget, I tried to keep us out of the hands of these people. You said that in this matter, you were not my student, but the Seeker. As the Seeker, you must use this prophecy. You are the one who got us into this. Only you can get us out."

Richard stared after her as she gentled the nervous animals. He had thought about this prophecy before, wondering, ever since she had told it to him, what it could mean. Sometimes he had felt as if he was on the verge of insight, but the feeling always slipped away from him before coming to fruition.

He had used the sword many times, and knew its capabilities. He also knew his own limitations. Against one, the sword was virtually invincible, but he was flesh and blood. He was no expert swordsman; in the past he had always depended on the sword's magic to make the difference. But he was only one man, and they were many. The sword could only be in one place at one time.

"Are they good fighters?" he asked.

"The Baka Ban Mana are without peer. They have special fighters, blade masters, who train from sunup to sundown, every day. And then they train by the light of the moon. Fighting is almost a religion to them.

"When I was young, I saw a Baka Ban Mana blade master who had gotten into the garrison in Tanimura kill nearly fifty well-armed soldiers before he was taken down. They fight like they are invincible spirits. Some people believe they are."

"That's just great," he said under his breath.

"Richard," she said, without looking to him, "I know we don't get along. We could look at the same thing and each see something different. We're from different worlds, both of us are headstrong, and neither of us likes the other very much.

"But I want you to know that I'm not trying to be obstinate about this. You spoke the truth in that this is about you as the Seeker, not as my student. In a way I don't understand, it's also bundled up with prophecy. You are riding a ripple in events. I am but a bystander in this. If you die, however, I die, too."

She at last lifted her eyes to his. "I don't know how to help you, Richard. There are people closing around us, to watch what will happen, and I know that if I try to interfere, I will be killed by them. This is about prophecy, you, and the Baka Ban Mana. I play no part in it, other than to die, if you do.

"I don't know what the prophecy means, and I realize you don't either, but keep it in mind, and maybe its use will come as you need it. Try to use your Han, if you can."

Richard stood with his hands on his hips. "All right, Sister, I'll try. I'm just sorry I'm no good at riddles. And if I'm killed, well, thank you for trying to help me."

He looked up at the sky, at the thin veil of clouds that dimmed the moon. The darkness helped hide those who came. There was no reason it couldn't be used to his advantage, too.

Richard was a woods guide, at home in the darkness of the woods. He had spent countless hours at games like this, with other guides. This was his element, too, not just theirs. He didn't have to do it their way. Crouching, he moved off, away from the Sister and their horses, and became one with the moon shadows.

He found the first of them looking the wrong way. Still and silent, he watched the dark form wrapped in loose clothes, squatted on one knee, watching the Sister. Clutched tightly in one fist was a short spear, its butt planted in the sand. Two more spears lay on the ground.

Richard concentrated on controlling his breathing to keep from making a sound as he glided closer. Moving, stopping, moving again, he approached ever closer. His hand reached out. Inches from the spear, he froze as the head turned.

The figure sprang up, but Richard was close enough. He snatched the spear away. As the man whirled, Richard spun the spear and whacked him across the side of the head. He went down before he had a chance to raise an alarm.

One down, Richard thought as he straightened, and without having to kill him. At least, he hoped he hadn't killed him.

Slipping out of the darkness, a figure appeared. To the side, another. And then another. Richard turned about and saw more appearing. Before he could move away, he was surrounded.

The forms were wrapped in bark-colored loose clothes so they would blend in with the surrounding country. Cloth wound around their heads hid all but their dark eyes, which shined with grim determination.

There was nowhere to run. Richard sidestepped into the clearing as the circle of forms moved with him. More were closing in all about. Richard turned, watching them as they formed two rings around him.

Maybe he could still do this without killing. "Who speaks for you?"

The inner ring of robed figures dropped their round shields and cast their extra spears to the ground, points toward Richard. Each clasped their remaining spear in two hands like a staff. Their eyes never left him. The outer ring of warriors cast their shields and all their spears to the ground and put their hands to their sword hilts, but didn't draw them.

A soft rhythmic chant began, and the two circles slowly began moving in opposite directions.

Richard walked backward in a tight circle, trying to keep watch on all of them. "Who speaks for you!"

The slow chant continued in time with their sideways steps.

A figure wrapped from head to foot like the others rose up on a rock beyond the outer circle.

"I am Du Chaillu. I speak for the Baka Ban Mana."

Richard could hardly believe this was happening. "Du Chaillu, I saved your life. Why would you want to murder us?"

"The Baka Ban Mana are not here to murder you. We are here to execute you for stealing our sacred lands."

"Du Chaillu, I've never even seen your land before. I had nothing to do with whatever happened."

"Magic men took our lands from us. They laid down our laws. You are a magic man. You bear the sins of those magic men before you. You even bear their mark, to prove it. You must do as all before, who we could catch. You must face the circle. You must die."

"Du Chaillu, I told you the killing must stop."

"It is easy to proclaim the killing must end, when you are the one about to die."

"How dare you say that to me! I risked my life to stop the killing! I risked my life for you!"

She spoke softly. "I know, Richard. For that I will always honor you. I would have borne your sons, had you asked it of me. I would lay my life down for you. For what you have done, you will live on as a hero to my people. I will tie a prayer to my dress, that the spirits take you tenderly to their hearts.

"But you are a magic man. The old law says that we must practice every day, and be better with a blade than any other people born. We have been told that we must kill every magic man we can catch, or the Spirit of the Dark will take the world of life into the dark."

"You can't go on killing magic men, or anyone else! It must stop!"

"The killing cannot end because of what you have done. It can only end when the spirits dance with us."

"What does that mean?"

"It means we must kill you or what has been spoken will be brought to pass— the Dark Spirit will escape his prison."

Richard pointed with the spear. "Du Chaillu, I don't want to kill any of you, but I will defend myself. Please stop now, before anyone else is hurt. Don't make me kill any of you. Please."

"Had you tried to run, we would have put spears in your back, but since you choose to stand, you have earned the right to face us. You will die anyway, as have all before whom we have caught. If you do not fight us, it will be made quick, and you will not suffer. You have my word."

She turned her hand in the air and the chanting started again. The outer ring of men drew their swords—long, black-handled weapons, each with a ring at the pommel holding a cord that looped around the swordsman's neck to keep the sword from being lost in battle. Each blade was curved, widening toward the clipped point.

The men spun the swords, passing them from right hand to left, and back again. The blades never stopped spinning. The two rings began moving in opposite directions again. The inner circle of men began twirling the spears like staffs.

Richard had known guides who carried staffs. No one ever bothered a guide with a staff. These people were better than any guide he had ever seen. The shafts of wood were a blur in the moonlight, the steel points a circle of dull reflection.

Richard broke the spear shaft over his knee and drew his sword. The sound of steel rang above the sound of the whistling spears and blades.

"Don't do this, Du Chaillu! Stop it now, before anyone else is hurt!"

"Do not fight us, witch man, and we will grant you a quick death. I owe you at least that."

Richard's chest heaved; the muscles in his jaw flexed as he gritted his teeth. The chanting increased in speed, and the circles of men moved faster.

Richard glared at Du Chaillu as she stood on the rock. "I disavow responsibility for what is to happen, Du Chaillu. It is you who presses this. What happens is your responsibility. You bring it!"

She spoke softly, her voice filled with regret. "We are many. You are but one. I am sorry, Richard."

"Only a fool would have confidence in those odds, Du Chaillu. They are not what they seem. You cannot all come at me at once. You can only attack one, or two, or at most three at a time. The odds are not what they seem to your eyes." Richard wondered dimly where his own words had come from.

He could see her nod in the moonlight. "You understand the dance of death, witch man."

"I'm not a witch man, Du Chaillu! I am Richard, the Seeker of Truth. I'm not going with this Sister to learn to be a witch man by choice. I'm a prisoner. You know that. But I will defend myself."

Du Chaillu watched him in the moonlight. "The spirits know I am sorry for you, Seeker Richard, but you must die."

"Don't be sorry for me, Du Chaillu. Be sorry for those of you who are going to die this night, for no good reason."

"You have not seen the Baka Ban Mana fight. We will not be touched. Only you will taste steel. Dismiss your concern; we are safe. You will have no killing to regret."

Richard loosed the sword's magic, the rage.

The two circles moved and chanted faster, spun their weapons faster. The storm of the sword's anger thundered through the Seeker. Even in the grip of the rage, the wanton need to kill, he knew it wasn't going to be enough. They were too many. And he had never seen anyone handle weapons the way these people did.

Heedlessly, he pulled more of the magic to him. Pulled until the mercilessness of the hate pounded in his head and nearly made him sick. He drew it into the depths of his soul.

Richard stood still in the center of the moving circles. He touched the gleaming blade to his forehead. The steel was cold against his hot skin, against his sweat.

"Blade, be true this day."

He called the magic onward. Before he even realized what he was doing, he pulled off his shirt and threw it aside, to be free of any hindrance to his movement. Why would he think to do that? It seemed the right thing to do, but he had no idea where the thought came from. He drew the blade up straight before him. His muscles flexed and tightened, glistening with sweat.

He found the center of himself, that place of quiet, of focus. He sought his Han within the white-hot center of his rage.

*Use what you have,* a voice within him said. *Use what is there. Let it loose.*

In the quiet of his mind, Richard remembered the time he had stood on Zedd's wizard's rock, to use its magic to hide the cloud that Darken Rahl had sent to track him. The rock had been used by many wizards before Zedd. As Richard had stood on it, calling the magic onward, letting it flow through him, he had felt the essence of those who had come before. He remembered the way it had felt to feel the things they had felt, to know the things they had known. It had given him insight into those who had once used the magic.

Suddenly, he knew what the prophecy meant.

He wondered how it was possible to have used the sword before without seeing it, without seeing what the magic held. Just like the wizard's rock.

Others had used the Sword of Truth's magic, and in the bargain, the magic retained a memory of their talents at fighting, of every move in which it had ever been used. The talent of untold hundreds who had wielded this blade, men and women alike, was there for the taking. The skill of both the good and the wicked was bound into the magic.

In his stillness, he saw the first come from the left.

*Be a feather, not a rock. Float on the wind of the storm.*

Richard unleashed the magic and spun with the attack, letting it sweep past him. He didn't strike, but let himself float with the press of the charge. He let the sword's magic guide him. The attacker tumbled to the ground when he didn't make the expected contact.

Instantly, another came, twirling his spear. Richard spun around again, and as the attacker passed, he used the sword to splinter the shaft in two. A spearpoint thrusted toward him. Without stopping, he glided past it and brought the sword up, cutting the shaft in half. Another charge came from behind. He met it with a foot to the chest, throwing the man back.

Richard gave himself over to the magic from the sword, and to the peace within himself. Things he didn't even understand, he was doing without thought.

He controlled the rage to keep from killing. He used the flat of the blade to strike the back of a head here, used his feet to trip an advance there. The faster they came, the faster he reacted, the magic feeding off their energy. Fluidly, he slipped among the attackers, splintering spears when he could, trying to disarm the Baka Ban Mana without killing them.

"Du Chaillu! Stop this before I have to hurt them!"

Yelling at her was a mistake. It distracted him. It allowed a spear through his flowing defense. He had a choice as the rage instantly exploded at the threat. He could kill the attacker, or do only what was necessary to stop him.

His sword spun, its tip whistling through the air, and lopped off the hand that thrust the spear. Blood and fragments of bone filled the air. The scream was a woman's.

Some of the Baka Ban Mana were women, he realized. It didn't matter. They would kill him if he didn't defend himself. Losing a hand was better than losing your head. First blood brought the rage, the need to kill, boiling up within him, hot and thirsty for more.

He fought the attackers and fought the things within himself that wanted to press the attack to those around him. He didn't want to press the attack. He only wanted them to stop. But if they didn't stop . . .

When he broke their spears, they picked up others and threw themselves at him again. He slipped among them like a phantom, conserving his energy as he let them wear themselves out.

The outer ring, who had continued to circle while the inner one had attacked, stopped, and then, swords awhirl, began advancing. Those with the spears—the ones who were still standing—stepped back through the outer ring as it came forward.

Swords spun in the air. Instead of waiting for them to come to him, Richard went to them. They flinched in surprise as the Sword of Truth shattered two of the flashing blades.

"Du Chaillu! Please! I don't want to kill any of you!"

The ones with the swords were faster than the ones with the spears. Too fast. Talking, and trying to disarm them without killing, was a dangerous distraction. Richard felt a hot pain flash through the flesh over his ribs. He hadn't even seen the blade coming, but he had moved by instinct and received a shallow slash instead of a killing cut.

His own blood being drawn summoned the sword's magic to his defense—the rage, the skill of those who had held it before him. Their essence seared through him, and he couldn't hold it back. There was no choice anymore. It overwhelmed his restraint. He had given them every chance. He was beyond retrieval, now.

Bringer of death.

The swordsmen rushed in a deadly wave.

He loosed the magic with a vengeance. The stalling was over. The barriers down, he danced with death, now.

The night erupted in a warm mist of blood. He heard himself screaming and he felt himself moving; he saw men and women falling, as disembodied heads tumbled across the ground. The lust for it raged through him.

No blade touched him again. He countered every strike as if he had seen it a thousand times before, as if he had always known what to do. Every attack brought a sure and swift death to the attacker. Bone fragments and blood exploded through the night air. Gore sluiced across the ground. The horror of it all melted together into one long killing image.

Bringer of death.

He only realized he had his knife in his left hand and his sword in his right when two came from opposite sides at once. He hooked his arm around the neck of the one on the left and slit his throat while at the same time running the one on the right through with the sword. Both collapsed to the ground as Richard stood panting.

Quiet echoed around him. There was no movement, except for one on her knees, holding herself up with one hand. Her other hand was missing. She rose to her feet, pulling a knife from her belt.

Through his glower, Richard watched the determination in her eyes. She ran for him with a scream. Richard stood deathlike in a cold cocoon of magic. The rage pounded as he watched her come. She raised the knife.

Richard's sword whipped up and impaled her through the heart. The dead weight of her pulled the sword down as she slid off it to the ground, her last breath gurgling out as her fingers grasped the blade, sliding down its wet red length as she slipped into the hands of death.

Bringer of death.

Richard lifted his smoldering glare to the woman standing on the rock. Du Chaillu stepped down, unwrapped her head, letting the long cloth hang down, and went to one knee in a bow.

Richard, his rage burning hotly, strode to her. He lifted Du Chaillu's chin with the sword's point.

Her dark eyes stared up into his. "The *Caharin* has come."

"Who is the *Caharin*?"

Du Chaillu looked unflinchingly into his eyes. "The one who dances with the spirits."

"Dances with the spirits," Richard repeated in a flat tone. He understood. He had danced with the spirits of those who held the sword before him. He had called the dead forth, danced with their spirits. He almost laughed.

"I will never forgive you, Du Chaillu, for making me kill those people. I saved your life because I abhor killing, and you have brought the blood of thirty to my hands."

"I am sorry, *Caharin*, that you must bear this burden. But only through the blood of thirty Baka Ban Mana could the killing stop. Only in this way can we serve the spirits."

"How is killing serving the spirits!"

"When the magic men stole our land, they banished us to this place. They placed upon us the duty of teaching the *Caharin* to dance with the spirits. Only the *Caharin* can stop the Dark Spirit from taking the world of the living. The *Caharin* is given to the world as a new born babe, who must be taught. Part of this duty is placed upon us—to teach him to dance with the spirits. You have learned something this night, have you not?"

Richard gave a grim nod.

"I am the keeper of the laws of our people. It was our calling to teach you this. If we were to ignore what the old words tell us we must do, then the *Caharin* would not learn what is within himself, and he would be defenseless against the forces of death. In the end, death would have everyone.

"The Majendie sacrifice us, to remind us always of our duty to the spirits, and to remind us to practice with the blades. The witch women to the other side aid the Majendie, so that we will be surrounded, with no way of escape, and nowhere to go, so that we will always be under threat, and unable to ever forget our duty.

"It is proclaimed that the *Caharin* will announce his arrival by dancing with the spirits, and spilling the blood of thirty Baka Ban Mana, a feat none but the chosen one could accomplish except with the aid of the spirits. It is said that when this happens, then we are his to rule. We are no longer a free people, but bound to his wishes. To your wishes, *Caharin*.

"The old words say that if every year the one who wears the prayer dress goes to our land, to give our prayers to the spirits, then one year, they will send the *Caharin*, and if we carry out our duty, then he will return our land to us."

Richard stood, as if in a dream, glaring down at the woman. "You have taken something precious from me this night, Du Chaillu."

She came to her feet, straightening before him. "Do not speak to me of sacrifice, *Caharin*. My five husbands, whom I loved, whom my children loved, who have not seen me since I was captured, were among the thirty you have just killed."

Richard sank to his knees. He felt like he might be sick. "Du Chaillu, forgive me for what I have done this night."

She gently put a hand to his bowed head. "It has been my honor to be the spirit woman of our people when the *Caharin* has come, to be the one to wear the prayer dress and bring him to his people. You must do your duty, now, and return our land, as the old words tell us."

Richard lifted his head. "And do the old words say how I am to accomplish this task?"

She slowly shook her head. "Only that we are to help you, and that you will. We are yours to command."

In the dark, Richard felt a tear run down his cheek. "Then I command that the killing stop. You will do as I have already ordered. You will use the bird whistle to bring peace with the Majendie. While you are doing that, you will do as you promised, and have someone guide us to the Palace of the Prophets."

Without looking up, Du Chaillu snapped her fingers. Richard realized, for the first time, that people in the shadows surrounded the bloody clearing. All were on their knees, bowed toward him. At the snap of her fingers, several sprang forward.

"Guide them to the big stone house."

Richard stood before her, looking into her dark eyes. "Du Chaillu, I'm so sorry I killed your husbands. I begged you to stop it, but I'm so sorry."

Her eyes bore the timeless look he had seen in the eyes of others; Sister Verna, Shota the witch woman, and Kahlan. He knew now that it was the gift he was seeing. A ghost of a smile came to her lips. He didn't know how she could smile at a time like this.

"They fought as hard as any Baka Ban Mana have ever fought. They had the honor of teaching the *Caharin*. They have given their lives for their people. They brought honor to themselves, and will live on as legends."

She reached out and placed her hand on his bare chest. On the handprint there. "You are my husband, now."

Richard's eyes widened. "What?"

She gave a curious frown. "I wear the prayer dress. I am the spirit woman of our people. You are the *Caharin*. It is the old law. You are my husband."

Richard shook his head. "No, I'm not. I already have . . ."

He was going to say he already had a love. But the words caught in his throat. Kahlan had sent him away. He had nothing.

She shrugged. "It could be worse for you. The last one who wore the prayer dress was old and wrinkled. She had no teeth. I hope that I bring at least some pleasure to your eyes, and maybe someday a song to your heart, but I belong to the *Caharin*. It is not for you, or me, to decide."

"Yes it is!" He looked about and then snatched up his shirt. As he put it on, he saw Sister Verna at the edge of the clearing, watching him, like a bug in a box. He turned to Du Chaillu.

"You have a job to do. You will do it. The killing is ended. The Sister and I must get to the palace so I can get this collar off."

Du Chaillu leaned over and kissed his cheek. "Until I see you again, Richard, Seeker, *Caharin*, husband."

R ichard and Sister Verna sat on their horses, anchoring long, thin shadows, as they looked down from the grassy prominence. Trees meandered along the low places among some of the hills, and blanketed others in dusky green. The vast city below lay awash in a straw-colored haze that muted the colors into a mellow monotone. The distant tiled and shingled roofs shimmered in the rays of the setting sun like points of light on a pond.

Richard had never seen so many buildings laid out in such an orderly array. Off to the edges they were smaller, but toward the core they seemed to grow, both in size and in grandeur. The faraway sounds of tens of thousands of people and horses and wagons drifted all the way up to them on the hill, carried on the light, salty breeze.

A river meandered through the collection of countless buildings, dividing the city, with the part on the far side twice as large. At the edge of the city, docks lined the banks along the mouth of the majestic river. Boats of all sizes were not only moored there, but dotted the river, their white sails filled with air. Some of the boats, he could just make out, had three masts. Richard had never imagined that such large boats might exist.

Despite being there against his will, Richard found himself fascinated by the city, by all the people and all the sights it must hold. He had never seen such a place. He imagined a person could probably walk around for days and days, and not begin to see it all.

Beyond, shimmering with golden sparkles and reflections, lay the sea, stretching to a knife's-edge line at the horizon.

Dominating the city, near the center, rising up on an island of its own, stood a vast palace, its imposing, crenellated west wall bathed in the sun's golden rays. Baileys and ramparts and towers and sections and roofs, all of grand design, joined together into a complex structure that held labyrinthine courtyards with trees, or grass, or ponds. The palace seemed to be stretching its stone arms, jealously trying to enclose the whole of the island atop which it sat.

Seen from this distance, with the thread-thin streets radiating out from the the island at the core of the city, and strandlike bridges spanning the river all around, the palace reminded Richard of nothing as much as a fat spider sitting in the center of its web.

"The Palace of the Prophets," Sister Verna said.

"Prison," Richard said without looking to her.

She ignored the comment. "The city is Tanimura, and through it, the River Kern. The palace itself sits on Halsband Island."

"Halsband." His hackles rose. "Is that some kind of sardonic joke?"

"What do you mean? Does Halsband have significance?"

Richard raised an eyebrow. "A halsband is a collar used to launch a hunting hawk on an attack."

She shrugged dismissively. "You read too much into things."

"Do I? We shall see."

She let out a small sigh as she lifted her hips, starting her horse down the hill, and changed the subject. "It's been many years since I was home, but it looks as it always has."

The two Baka Ban Mana men who had guided them through the swampy, trackless forest for the last two days had left them that morning, once Sister Verna was at last in familiar territory. Although he never lost his sense of direction, Richard could easily see how people could become disoriented there. But he was at home in such places of vast desolation, and was more likely to become lost in a building than in dense woods.

The two men had spoken little over those two days. Though they were swordsmen as fierce as those Richard had fought, they were in awe of him. Richard had to shout before they would stop all the bowing. No amount of shouting, though, could make them stop calling him *Caharin*.

One night, before he went to stand his usual watch, Sister Verna had told him, in a quiet tone, that she was sorry that he had had to kill those thirty people. A little surprised by her sincerity and the seeming lack of meaning other than that stated, and haunted by the memory, he had thanked her for understanding.

Richard scanned the fertile hills and valleys. "Why isn't this land farmed? With all those people, they must need to plant food."

Sister Verna lifted a hand holding the reins and indicated the land on the other side of the city. "Farms cover the land on that side of the river. On this side, it's not safe for man nor beast." Tilting her head back, she indicated the land behind. "The Baka Ban Mana are always a threat."

"So they don't farm here because they're afraid of the Baka Ban Mana?"

She cast a glance to her left. "Do you see that dark forest?" She watched him as he took in the fringe of the dense tangle in the next valley. Huge, old, gnarled trees were packed close together, covered with vines and moss, and harboring gloomy shadows. "This edge runs for miles more toward the city. It's the Hagen Woods. Stay far away from it. All who let the sun set on them in the Hagen Woods die. Many who set foot there die before they have a chance to wait for the sun to go down. It's a place of vile magic."

As they rode, he kept glancing toward the Hagen Woods. He felt a longing for that gloomy place, as if it complemented his dark mood; as if he belonged in there. He found it hard to draw his eyes away.

Up close, the streets of Tanimura were not the orderly place they appeared from a distance. The fringes of the city were a confusion of squalor. Men pushing or pulling carts laden with loads of rice sacks, or carpets, or firewood, or hides, or even garbage, wove around and past each other, sometimes clogging the way. Lining the road were hawkers of every sort, selling everything from fruits and vegetables and strips of meat cooked on little sticks over tiny smoky fires in impromptu stone hearths, to herbs and fortunes, to boots and beads. At least the cooking gave spotty relief from the reeking stench of tanneries.

Huddled groups of men in worn, dirty clothes shouted with excitement or burst into laughter around games of cards and dice. Side streets and narrow alleyways were clogged with people and lined with ramshackle huts of tarp and tin. Naked children ran and played among the flimsy shelters, splashing in muddy puddles and chasing each other in games of catch-the-fox. Women squatted around buckets, washing clothes and chatting among themselves.

Sister Verna muttered to herself that she didn't remember the squalor and the unhoused multitudes. Richard thought that, despite their condition, they looked happier than they had a right to.

Despite having lived out-of-doors, and being a little dirty and rumpled, Sister Verna, compared to these people, looked like royalty. Anyone coming close bowed in reverence to the Sister, and she prayed for the Creator's blessing on them in return.

The timeworn buildings, some faced with faded, crumbling plaster, some with age-darkened wood, were just as packed as the streets. Colorful wash hung from the rusty iron railings of nearly every tiny balcony. A few held pots of flowers or herbs. Laughter and the hum of conversation came from taverns and inns. A butcher shop displayed fly-covered carcasses on the street out front. Other shops sold dried fish, or grain, or oils.

The farther he and the Sister went, the cleaner the city became. The road widened, even the side streets were wider, and none had huts leaning against the buildings. The shops had bigger windows with painted shutters, and better-looking wares, many displaying colorful, locally woven carpets. By the time the wide road became lined with trees, the buildings were grand. The inns looked elegant, with doormen standing in red uniforms before them.

On the stone bridge over the Kern, men were lighting lamps hung on poles to show the way in the gathering darkness. In the river, below the bridge, fishermen in small boats with lanterns rowed through the dark water. Soldiers in ornate uniforms with gold-trimmed white shirts and red tunics, and carrying polearms, patrolled each side of the river. As the horses' hooves clopped along the cobblestone, Sister Verna finally spoke.

"It's a great day, at the palace, when a new one with the gift arrives." She cast him a brief, sideways glance. "It's a rare and joyous event. They will be happy to see you, Richard, please remember that. To them, this is an event of note in their calling. Though you feel differently, their hearts will be warmed by the sight of you. They will want you to feel welcome."

Richard thought otherwise. "Make your point."

"I just did. They will be delighted."

"What you are saying, in other words, is you would like me not to horrify them right off."

"I didn't say that." She glanced with a small frown at the soldiers guarding the bridge. She finally looked back to him. "I am simply asking you to realize that these women live for this very thing."

Richard stared ahead as he rode past more guards in dress uniforms. "A wise person, a person I love, told me once that we all can only be who we are, no more, and no less." His gaze swept the top of the wall ahead, noting the soldiers there, and what arms they carried. "I'm the bringer of death, and I have nothing to live for."

"That's not true, Richard," she said in a quiet tone. "You're a young man, and you have much to live for. You have a long life ahead of you. And though you may have named yourself the bringer of death, I have seen you do nothing but strive to stop the killing. Sometimes you will not listen, and make matters worse, but it's through ignorance, not malice."

"Since you abhor lies, Sister, I'm sure you wouldn't want me to pretend to feel other than I do."

She sighed as they went through a huge gate in the thick, outer bailey wall, the horses' hooves echoing inside the long, arched opening. Beyond, the road meandered among low, spreading trees. Windows in the buildings rising up all around were aglow with soft yellow light. Many of the buildings were connected by covered colonnades, or enclosed halls with arched openings covered over with latticework. Benches dotted the far side of the courtyard, against a wall with a frieze carved with figures on horses.

Through archways with white-painted gates, they came to the stables. Horses browsed in a field beyond. Boys dressed in neat livery, with black vests over tan shirts, came to hold the horses as he and the Sister dismounted. Richard gave Bonnie's neck a scratch and then started taking down his belongings.

Sister Verna brushed out the wrinkles in her divided riding skirt and straightened her light cloak. She fussed at her curly hair. "No need for that, Richard. Someone will bring your things."

"No one touches my things but me," he said.

She sighed and shook her head, and then told the boy to have her things brought in. He bowed to her, and then hooked a lead line on Jessup. He gave a sharp snap on the line. Jessup balked.

The boy brought a whip around on the Jessup's rump. "Move, you dumb beast!"

Jessup bellowed as he tried to yank his head away.

The next thing Richard knew, the boy was flying across the walkway. He slammed up against a flimsy wooden wall and landed on his seat, as a glowering Sister Verna loomed over him.

"Don't you dare whip that horse! What's the matter with you? How would you like it if I did that to you?" In shock, the boy shook his head. "If I ever hear of you whipping a horse again, you will be without a job, after I whip your skinny bottom."

The wide-eyed lad gave a quick nod and apology. Sister Verna glared a moment longer and then turned, whistling for her horse. When Jessup trotted up, she scratched him under his chin, comforting and calming him. She led him inside to a stall and saw that he had water and hay. Richard made sure she didn't see his smile.

As they walked across the courtyard, she said, "Just remember, Richard, there isn't a Sister here, or even a novice, who, while at the same time as she was yawning, couldn't throw you across a room like that with her Han."

Inside a wood-paneled hall with long yellow and blue carpets running under ornate side tables, three women waited. They became all atwitter at the sight of Sister Verna. Sister Verna was a head shorter than he, and none of these three women were as tall as she. They smoothed their full, pastel skirts, and tugged at the white bodices.

"Sister Verna!" one cried out as the three rushed up. "Oh, dear Sister Verna, it's so good to see you at last."

A tear or two ran down their rosy faces. Their smiles looked about to burst their cheeks. Each looked a good deal younger than Sister Verna. She surveyed the big, wet eyes.

Sister Verna tenderly stroked the sniffling face before her. "Sister Phoebe." She touched another's hand. "And Sister Amelia, and Sister Janet. It's so good to see you again. It has been a long time indeed."

The three giggled with excitement, at last composing themselves. Sister Phoebe's round face looked about, past Richard.

"Where is he? Why haven't you brought him in with you?"

Sister Verna lifted her hand toward Richard. "This is he. Richard, these are friends of mine. Sisters Phoebe, Amelia, and Janet."

The smiles transformed into astonished looks. They blinked as they took in his size and age. They stared in open amazement before finally sputtering over each other's words about how glad they were to meet him. They tore their eyes from him at last and returned their attention to Sister Verna.

"Better than half the palace is waiting to greet you both," Sister Phoebe said. "Everyone has been so excited since we received word that you would arrive today."

Sister Amelia smoothed back her fine, light brown hair, flipping back the ends that barely brushed her shoulders. "No other has been brought in since you left for Richard. All those years, and no other. Everyone is so eager to meet him. I guess they are in for a 'big' surprise," she said as she blushed, glancing sideways at him. "Some of the younger Sisters, especially. A pleasant surprise, I would say. My, but he is big."

Richard remembered a time, when he was little, when he had been imprisoned in his house by a pouring rain. His mother had some women friends visiting to help in the making of a quilt, and to pass the time in conversation. As they sat and sewed while he played on the floor, they discussed him as if he weren't there, talking about how he was growing, and his mother had told how much he ate, and how good he was at reading. In similar discomfort, now, Richard shifted his pack up higher on his shoulder.

Sister Phoebe turned to him and just beamed. She reached out and touched his arm. "Listen to us go on! We shouldn't talk about you like you weren't here. Welcome, Richard. Welcome to the Palace of the Prophets."

Richard silently watched the three Sisters blinking up at him. Sister Amelia giggled, and said to Sister Verna, "He doesn't talk much, does he."

"He talks enough," Sister Verna said. Under her breath, she added, "Thank the Creator he is quiet for now."

"Well," Sister Phoebe said, in a bright voice. "Shall we go?"

Sister Verna frowned at her. "Sister Phoebe, who are the troops I saw, the ones in the strange uniforms?"

Sister Phoebe's brow wrinkled in thought a moment, then her eyebrows lifted. "Oh, those troops." She dismissed it with a wave. "The government was overthrown, a few years back. I guess it must have been while you were away. The Old World has a new government, again. We have an emperor, now, instead of all those kings." She looked to Sister Janet. "What is it they call themselves?"

Her brow creased in thought, Sister Janet's eyes turned toward the ceiling. "Oh, yes," she said in a demure voice. "The Imperial Order. And you are quite right, Sister Phoebe; they have an emperor." She nodded. "Yes, the Imperial Order, led by an emperor."

Sister Phoebe shook her head in wonder. "Such foolishness. Governments come, and governments go, but the Palace of the Prophets always remains. The Creator's hand shelters us. Shall we go greet the others?"

Following behind the three, they passed through warmly decorated passageways and halls. As far as Richard was concerned, he was in hostile territory. Threat always caused the magic of the Sword of Truth to try to seep into him, to protect him. He let in a trickle, keeping the anger on a slow burn. Sister Verna glanced sideways occasionally, as if measuring the growth of his glower.

At last, they went through a pair of thick walnut doors that opened into a vast chamber. They had to pass under a low ceiling and between white columns with gold capitals, before entering under a huge, vaulted dome painted with immense scenes of people in robes surrounding a glowing figure. Two levels of balconies with ornate stone railings ringed the circular room. Stained-glass windows lit the top balcony from behind. The floor of the room was made up of small, light and dark wood squares laid out in a zigzag pattern. The hum of well over a hundred voices echoed around the chamber.

Women stood in bunches around the floor and more lined the balconies. Scattered among the women on the second level were some men and boys. The women, all Sisters of the Light, he presumed, were dressed in finery. There seemed to be no pattern; their dresses were of every color, with designs ranging from conservative to revealing. The boys and men were dressed in everything from plain robes to coats as elaborate as Richard imagined any lord or prince would wear.

The buzz of talking died out as everyone began turning to the new arrivals. As the room fell to silence, applause started, swelling into a roar.

Sister Phoebe took a few steps toward the center of the room, raising her hand, calling for silence. The applause died out in spurts.

"Sisters," Sister Phoebe said, her voice trembling with excitement, "please welcome Sister Verna home." The applause roared again and, after a few moments, the hand brought it to silence once more. "And may I present our newest student, our newest child of the Creator, our newest charge," she turned, holding her hand out, wiggling her fingers, indicating she wanted Richard to step forward. He took three strides to her, Sister Verna going with him.

Sister Phoebe leaned close and whispered. "Richard . . .? Do you have any more to your name?"

Richard hesitated a moment. "Cypher."

She turned back to the crowd. "Please welcome Richard Cypher to the Palace of the Prophets."

The clapping started again. Richard glowered as every face watched him. Women near pressed closer, to get a better look at him. There were women of all ages and descriptions in the crowd, ranging from some who looked old enough to be kindly grandmothers to some hardly old enough to be called women, with those of every age in between. They ranged from plump to skinny, with hair as different as their dress, with every color from blond to black. Their eyes, too, were of every color.

He noticed one woman who stood near him. She had a warm smile on her reed-thin lips, and strange, pale blue eyes with violet flecks through them. She was looking at him as if he were an old, dear friend, whom she loved, and hadn't seen in years. She was applauding enthusiastically, and elbowing a haughty woman next to her to join in the clapping, until the other finally did.

Richard stood with his arms at his sides as he studied the layout of the room, noting exits, passageways, and placement of guards. As the applause died out, a young woman in a dress the same shade of blue as Kahlan's wedding dress worked her way through the crowd. The blue dress had a round neck, decorated with white lace that ran down to the narrow waist and matched that on the cuffs.

She approached, coming to a halt right in front of him. Perhaps five years younger than he, and a head shorter, she had full, soft brown hair that reached to her shoulders, and big, brown eyes.

She gaped at him. With each slow breath, her bosom swelled at the lace. Her hand floated up. Her delicate fingers brushed his cheek, and stroked down his beard. She seemed transfixed as she stared up at him, stroking his beard.

"The Creator has indeed heard my prayers," she whispered to herself.

She seemed to suddenly remember where she was and snatched her hand back. Her face flushed red.

"I'm . . . I'm," she stammered. She regained her composure, her face recovering its smooth complexion. She clasped her hands before herself and turned, as if nothing had happened, to address Sister Verna. "I am Pasha Maes, novice, third rank. I am next in line to be named. I have been placed in charge of Richard."

Sister Verna gave her a small, tight smile. "I think I remember you, Pasha. I'm pleased to see you have studied hard and done well. Richard is passed out of my hands, now, and into yours. May the Creator gently hold you both in His hands."

Pasha smiled proudly and then turned to Richard. She cast a glance down the length of him. She looked up, batted her eyelashes at him, and gave him a warm smile.

"I'm pleased to meet you, young man. My name is Pasha. You are assigned to me. I'm to help teach you, help with whatever else you may need in your studies. I'm a guide of sorts. Any problems or questions you have are to be brought to me, and I will do my best to help you. You look like a bright boy; I'm sure we are going to get along just fine."

Her smile faltered under the heat of his gloves. She smiled again and continued. "Well, first of all, Richard, we don't allow boys to carry weapons here at the Palace of the Prophets." She held her hands out, palms up. "I'll take your sword."

The trickle of rage from the magic had turned to a torrent. "You are welcome to my sword, when I am no longer breathing."

Pasha's gaze flicked to Sister Verna. The Sister gave a slow, slight shake of her head in stern warning. Pasha's gaze returned to Richard and her frown transformed to a smile.

"Well, we'll talk about it later." Her brow bunched together. "But you need to learn some manners, young man."

Richard's voice came in a tone that took some of the color from Pasha's face. "Which one of these women is the Prelate?"

Pasha gave a bubble of a laugh. "The Prelate is not here. She is much too busy to . . ."

"Take me to her."

"You do not see the Prelate when you wish. She sees you when she has reason to see you. I can hardly believe Sister Verna has not taught you that we do not allow our boys . . ."

Richard put the back of his hand against her shoulder and swept her aside as he took another stride into the room, redirecting his glare to the hundreds of eyes watching him.

"I have something to say."

The vast room fell to a hush. From two different places in his mind, the same thought had come forward at the same time. He recognized each origin. One was

510

*The Adventures of Bonnie Day*, the book his father had given him, and the other was the sword's magic, the knowledge of the sword, the spirits he had danced with.

The memory and message were the same: *When you are outnumbered, and the situation is hopeless, you have no option—you must attack.*

He knew what the collar was for. His situation was hopeless. He had no options. He let the quiet ring in the chamber until it was uncomfortable.

His fingers tapped his Rada'Han. "As long as you keep this collar on me, you are my captors, and I am your prisoner." Murmurs hummed in the air. Richard let them trail off before he went on. "Since I have committed no aggression against you, that makes us enemies. We are at war.

"Sister Verna has made a pledge to me that I will be taught to control the gift, and when I have learned what is required, I will be set free. For now, as long as you keep that pledge, we have a truce. But there are conditions."

Richard lifted the red leather rod at his neck, the Agiel, in his hand. Beyond the rage of the magic, the Agiel was only a dim tingle of pain. "I have been collared before. The person who put that collar on me brought me pain, to punish me, to teach me, to subdue me.

"That is the sole purpose of a collar. You collar a beast. You collar your enemies.

"I made her much the same offer I am making you. I begged her to release me. She would not. I was forced to kill her.

"Not one of you could ever hope to be good enough to lick her boots. She did as she did because she was tortured and broken, made mad enough to use a collar to hurt people. She did it against her nature.

"You," he looked to all the eyes, "you do it because you think it is your right. You enslave in the name of your Creator. I don't know your Creator. The only one beyond this world I know who would do as you do is the Keeper." The crowd gasped. "As far as I'm concerned, you may as well be the Keeper's disciples.

"If you do as she, and use this collar to bring me pain, the truce will be ended. You may think you hold the leash to this collar, but I promise you, if the truce ends, you will find that what you hold is a bolt of lightning."

Dead-still silence rang in the room. Richard rolled up his left sleeve. He drew the Sword of Truth. The distinctive sound of steel filled the silence.

"The Baka Ban Mana are my people. They have agreed to live in peace with all people from now on. Anyone who harms one of them will answer to me. If you do not accept this, do not let the Baka Ban Mana live in peace, our truce will be ended."

He pointed back with the sword. "Sister Verna captured me. I have fought her every step of this journey. She has done everything short of killing me and draping my body over a horse to get me here. Though she, too, is my captor and enemy, I owe her certain debts. If anyone lays a finger to her because of me, I will kill that person, and the truce will be ended."

From the corner of his eye, Richard could see Sister Verna's eyes close. Her hand covered her white face.

The crowd gasped as Richard drew his sword across the inside of his arm. He turned it, wiping both sides in the blood, until it dripped from the tip.

His knuckles white around the hilt, he thrust the blade into the air.

"I give you a blood oath! Harm the Baka Ban Mana, harm Sister Verna, or harm me, and the truce will be ended, and I promise you we will have war! If we have war, I will lay waste to the Palace of the Prophets!"

511

From the far balcony, where Richard couldn't see its source, a mocking voice drifted out over the crowd. "All by yourself?"

"Doubt me at your peril. I am a prisoner; I have nothing to live for. I am the flesh of prophecy. I am the bringer of death."

No answer came in the silence. He slammed his sword home into its scabbard.

Richard held his arms out as he gave a gracious bow. He came up smiling. "Now that we all understand each other, understand the truce, you ladies may go back to your celebration of my capture."

He turned his back on the stunned crowd. Sister Verna's head was lowered, her hand covering her face. Pasha's lips were pressed so tightly together they were turning blue.

A stout, stern-faced woman crossed in front of him, stopping before Sister Verna. The woman held her nose in the air until Sister Verna lifted her head and straightened her back.

"Sister Verna. It is obvious you have neither the talent nor skill to be a Sister of the Light. Your failure is quite beyond the pale. As of this moment, you are broken to novice, first rank. You will serve as a novice until such time as, and if the Creator wills, you earn the title of Sister of the Light."

Sister Verna lifted her chin. "Yes, Sister Maren."

"Novices do not speak to a Sister unless asked to! I did not ask you to speak!" She held out a hand. "Surrender your dacra."

Sister Verna flicked her hand, the silver knife appearing from her sleeve. She twirled it, presented the handle to the other woman, and then stood silent, her eyes straight ahead.

"At dawn tomorrow, you will report to the kitchens. You will scrub pots until you are judged worthy to attempt something more demanding of your intelligence. Do you understand!"

"Yes, Sister Maren. I understand."

"And if you even look like you are going to give me any back talk, it will be the stables instead of the kitchens, cleaning stalls and hauling manure!"

"In that case, Sister Maren, I will report directly to the stables, instead of the kitchens, and save your ears what it is I would say to you."

Sister Maren's face reddened. "Very well, novice. The stables it is."

Sister Maren paused before Richard, giving him a tight smile. "I trust that does not break your truce." She lifted her chin and stormed off.

The room was silent. Richard looked to Sister Verna, but the Sister stared straight ahead. Pasha, her face set in a scowl, suddenly put herself between them.

"Verna is no longer your concern. Your arm is bleeding. Since you are my charge, I will tend to it."

She took a calming breath as she twined her fingers together before her waist. "There is a big banquet, to welcome you, beginning in the dining room. Maybe you will feel better about all of us after the banquet. Everyone is looking forward to it. Everyone wants a chance to personally welcome you." She shook a finger at him. "And you will be on your best behavior, young man!"

Having put the sword away, he had put most of the anger away. Most, but not all. "I'm not hungry. Show me to my dungeon, *child*."

Her fists tightened on her blue skirts. With a dark look, she considered him a moment. "Very well. Have it your way. You can just go to bed without your supper, like a spoiled child." She turned on her heel. "Follow me."

Sister Verna put her hand to the brass lever. The room was shielded. She took a controlled breath and then knocked.

A muffled voice behind the heavy door answered. "Come."

The shield dissolved. She opened the right side of the double doors and stepped in. Two women sat, each at her own desk, to each side of the door beyond. Both were writing in ledgers. Neither looked up.

"Yes," the one to the left said as she continued writing, "what is it?"

"I have come to return the journey book, Sister Ulicia."

Sister Ulicia wet her finger and flipped a page. "Yes, just put it on the desk. Shouldn't you be at the banquet in honor of your return? I would think you would want to get reacquainted with old friends."

Sister Verna clasped her hands. "I have more important matters to attend than banquets. I wish to give the journey book to the Prelate, personally. And I wish to speak with her, Sister Ulicia."

They both looked up. "Well," Sister Ulicia said, "the Prelate does not wish to speak with you, Sister Verna. She is a busy woman. She can't be bothered with unimportant matters."

"Unimportant! It is not unimportant!"

"Do not raise your voice in this office, Sister Verna," the other warned. She dipped her pen in an ink bottle and bent back over her writing.

Sister Verna took a step forward. The air between the desks, before the door beyond, shimmered suddenly with a powerful shield that hissed and crackled in warning.

"The Prelate is busy," Sister Ulicia said. "If she deems your return of consequence, she will send for you." She pulled a candle closer and bent back to her book. "Just put the journey book on my desk. I will see that it's returned to her."

Sister Verna controlled her voice as she gritted her teeth. "I have been broken down to novice." They both glanced up. "Broken to novice, because I followed the orders of that woman. Despite my pleas and appeals, she forbade me to do my job, my duty, and because of that, I am to be punished! Punished for doing as the Prelate ordered me to do! I will at least hear the reasons!"

Sister Ulicia leaned back in her chair and then turned to the other woman. "Sister Finella, please send a report to the headmistress of the novices. Inform her that novice Verna Sauventreen came to the Prelate's office without authorization or invitation, and further, she carried on in a tirade unbecoming of a novice hoping one day to be a Sister of the Light."

Sister Finella shifted herself in annoyance as she glared up at Sister Verna. "My, my, *novice* Verna, your first day in your pursuit of higher calling, and already you've earned a letter of reprimand." She clicked her tongue. "I do so hope you learn to behave yourself, if you ever hope to be a Sister of the Light."

"That will be all, novice," Sister Ulicia said. "You are dismissed."

Sister Verna turned on her heel. She heard the snap of fingers. She looked back over her shoulder to see Sister Ulicia tapping the corner of her desk.

"The journey book. And I don't believe that is the way a novice departs when she is dismissed by a Sister. Is it, novice?"

Sister Verna pried the small black book from behind her belt and gently set it on the corner of the desk.

"No, Sister, it is not." She curtsied. "Thank you, Sisters, for your time."

Sister Verna sighed to herself as she closed the door against her back. She stood for a moment, considering.

Eyes to the floor before her, she made her way back through the palace, down halls both opened and closed, both stone and paneled, across floors carpeted and tiled. Rounding a corner, she came suddenly upon someone. She looked up into a face she had been hoping not to see.

He smiled in a familiar manner. "Verna! How good to see you!"

His young, square-jawed face looked unchanged. His wavy brown hair was worn a little longer over his ears than before, and his shoulders were broader than she remembered. She had to restrain herself from touching his cheek, from falling into his arms.

She bowed her head. "Jedidiah." She gazed up into his brown eyes. "You look fit. You look . . . the same as you have always looked. You wear the time well."

"You look . . . I guess . . ."

"The word you are searching for is old. I look old."

"Ah, Verna. A few wrinkles—" He glanced down her body. "—a few pounds, do not diminish a beauty such as yours."

"I see your tongue is still in good form around women." She glanced to his plain, tan robes. "And I can see you've been a good student, as always, and have managed to advance yourself. I'm proud of you, Jedidiah."

He shrugged off the compliment and pressed his fingers together. "Tell me about the new one you brought in."

Her eyes narrowed. "You've not seen me in twenty-odd years, since I rose from your bed to go on my journey, and that is your question for me? Not, how have I fared? Not, how do I feel about you after all this time? Not, has your heart found another? Well, I guess the shock of seeing how I've aged has made those questions fly right from your head."

The sly smile stayed on his lips. "Verna, you're not a silly girl. Surely you must realize that in the passing of so much time, neither of us could be expected to . . ."

"Of course I know that! I had no delusions of us. I had simply hoped to return and be treated with a little tact and sensitivity."

He shrugged again. "I'm sorry, Verna. I always thought of you as a woman who appreciated candor, one who had no use for word sports." His eyes went out of focus. "I guess I've learned so much about . . . life . . . since back then, when I was so young."

She removed her glare from his handsome face and started away. "Good night, Jedidiah."

"What of my question?" His voice had an unpleasant edge to in. He softened it. "What's the new one like?"

She halted, but didn't turn. "You were there. I saw you. What you saw of Richard is what he is."

"I also saw what happened to you. I'm gaining a little influence among some of the Sisters. Maybe I can do something to help you with your situation." He gestured vaguely with a hand. "If you're open with me, and satisfy my curiosity, maybe I can help you out of your unfortunate predicament."

She started out again. "Good night, Jedidiah."

"I'll be seeing you around the palace, Verna. Think on it."

She couldn't believe how ignorant she had been all those years ago. She remembered Jedidiah as caring and sincere. Maybe her memory was addled.

Maybe she was just thinking of herself, and hadn't given him the chance to be kinder. She must look a mess. She should have cleaned herself up, put on a nice dress, at least fixed her unruly hair, before she saw Jedidiah. But she had not had the chance.

Maybe if she had touched his cheek, he would have remembered the spark of something, maybe remembered the tears he shed the day she left, and the promises he had made. Promises she knew the moment they left his lips would be broken before their echo faded, so long ago.

She came to the hall that led to the novices' apartments. She stood looking down at the doors. She was tired. Sunup to sundown in the stables was going to be exhausting. She turned the other way, instead. She had one other thing to do before she slept.

Pasha came to a stop before a doorway with a casing of stone, carved to look like vines. Nestled in the center of the stone vines was a large, round-topped, fumed oak door.

Pasha lifted an eyebrow to him. "Your dungeon."

"There's no bolt on the outside of the door. How will you lock me in?"

She seemed surprised by the question. "We don't lock our boys in. You're free to come and go as you please."

Richard frowned. "You mean I'm free to roam this building?"

"No. You're free to go wherever you wish. You may go most anywhere in the palace, or into the city, if you wish. Most of the boys spend a great deal of their time in the city." Her face reddened a little at the last of what she said, and she looked away from his face.

"What about the country around the city?"

She shrugged, and then pulled the shoulder of her blue dress back up a little. "Of course. I don't know why you would want to go into the countryside, none of the other boys do, but there's nothing stopping you from going outside either the palace or the city."

A worried wrinkle came to her brow. "But you must stay clear of the Hagen Woods. It is extremely dangerous. Were you warned about the Hagen Woods? Were you shown where it is while you journeyed to the palace?"

Richard nodded. "How far may I go into the countryside?"

"The Rada'Han will prevent you from going too far afield; we must be able to find you, but the limit is a good number of miles in a radius around the Palace of the Prophets."

"How many miles?"

"Farther than you would want to go. I expect almost all the way to the land of the savages."

"You mean the Baka Ban Mana."

She nodded. "Nearly that far, I would expect."

"Unguarded?"

She put her hands on her hips. "You are assigned to me. I will accompany you most everywhere you go, for now. After our boys are more experienced, they go off on their own when they wish."

"Whenever I want, I can simply wander around?"

"Well, you live here, at the palace, of course. And you must be around for your lessons. I will give you lessons, and so will a number of the Sisters. We will teach you to touch your Han, and then once you are able to do that, we will begin to teach you how to control it."

"Why different Sisters? Why not just one, or you?"

"Because sometimes the Han of certain people works better together. Also, the Sisters have more experience than me, have more knowledge. There may be one or several of us who are better able to help you, and so different Sisters give you lessons, until we discover with whom you work best."

"Will Sister Verna be one of those?"

Pasha gave him a look from under her eyebrows. "Verna is no longer a Sister. She is no longer entitled to the appellation. She is a novice, now, and should be addressed simply as Verna. Novices, other than the one assigned to you—that is me—are not allowed to give lessons. Novices of the first rank, like Verna, are not allowed to have anything to do with our boys. The duty of a novice is to learn, not to teach."

Richard didn't think he could ever think of Sister Verna as simply Verna. It sounded too strange to him. "When will she be a Sister again?"

"She must serve as a novice, and advance as any other novice. I started scrubbing pots in the kitchens when I was little. It has taken me this long to be given this chance. One day, if Verna works as hard as I have, then she, too, will have the chance to be a Sister of the Light. Until then, Verna is a novice."

Richard fumed at the thought of Sister Verna being demoted on his account. By the time she was again a Sister, she would be an old woman. He changed the subject. "And why are we allowed to roam around?"

"Because you are not a danger to the people. Someday, when you learn to control your Han, then you begin to have limits placed on where you may go. The people in the city are afraid of boys who can wield the power—unfortunate incidents have happened in the past—and so once a boy becomes skilled at handling his Han, he is then restricted from the city. As the boys advance as wizards, they are placed under more restrictions, until near the end, and their release, when they are confined to certain areas of the palace.

"But for now, you're free to go almost anywhere you wish. I will know where you are all the time, by your Rada'Han."

"You mean any Sister can find me by this cursed thing?"

"No, only the one who gave it to you, because she held it and recognizes its power, and since I'm in charge of you, I must be able to know where you are at all times, so I will need to allow my Han to recognize your Rada'Han's unique feel."

She pushed the door open and went into the dark room. With a sweep of her arm, lamps set all around the room sprang to flame.

"You must teach me that trick," he muttered.

"It's not a trick. It's simply my Han. And that's the simplest of many things I will teach you."

The ceiling of the huge room was painted around its molding with different-colored lines in intricate patterns. The walls were paneled in cherry of a warm color. Tall windows hung with rich, deep blue moire drapes looked out on the night. There was a fireplace, with a white column to each side. Most of the wood floor was covered with thick carpets. Comfortable-looking chairs and couches were placed about the room, and arranged in front of the fireplace.

Richard thought that his whole house would fit twice into the room. He slipped the pack off his back and leaned it against the wall next to the fireplace. He stood the quiver of arrows and the unstrung bow beside it.

He went to the right, to a set of double doors made up of small panes of glass and covered over with sheer, cream-colored curtains. Beyond the doors was an expansive balcony overlooking the city. Stone urns filled with flowers were set about the slate floor of the balcony. He put his fingers to the marble railing as he looked to his right, past the sparkling lights of the city, to the hills from where he had come.

"The sunsets are beautiful from this balcony," Pasha said.

Richard wasn't interested in sunsets. He studied the courtyard below, the gates, the roads, the patrolling soldiers, and the bridges to the city and the hills beyond. He tried to fix a map of it all into his head.

He went back inside and marched to the other end of the room, to the doorway there. Beyond was a bedroom almost as large as the first room. It held the largest bed he had ever seen, covered with a deep purple quilt. Another pair of glassed doors led to another balcony, but this one looked south, out over the sea.

"It's a beautiful view," Pasha said. "A romantic view." She saw that he was looking to the sections of the palace below. She pointed. "Across that courtyard are some of the women's quarters, where most of the Sisters' rooms are." She shook the finger at him. "You will stay away from them, young man!" She turned away. "Unless a Sister invites you to her room," she added under her breath.

"What do I call you," he asked. "Sister Pasha?"

She giggled. "No. I'm a novice, though I hope to become a Sister if I prove myself with you. Until then, I am simply Pasha."

Richard turned to her, directing a glare to her eyes. "My name is Richard. Do you have trouble remembering it?"

"Look here, you are assigned to me and . . ."

"If that is too difficult for you to remember, you have no chance of ever becoming a Sister, because if you insist on trying to demean me by calling me by other than my name, I will see to it that you quickly fail in your test." He leaned over her as he glowered down at her wide eyes. "Do you understand, Pasha!"

She swallowed. "You will not raise your voice to me, young . . ." She lifted her chin a little. "You will not raise your voice to me, Richard."

"That's better. Thank you." He hoped she would leave it at that; he was in no mood to be kind if she was not.

517

He turned away. This balcony held less of a view of the things he was interested in, and so he went back into the bedroom.

She followed on his heels. "Look here, Richard, you will learn some manners or else I will . . ."

That was the end of his indulgence. He spun to her. She lurched to a halt, almost colliding with him.

"You've never been in charge of anyone before, have you?" She didn't move. "I would say that this is the first time you have been given responsibility, and you are terrified you will muck it up. Since you are inexperienced, you think acting like a tyrant will fool people into thinking you know what you are doing."

"Well, I . . ."

Her voice trailed off as he leaned down, putting his face close to hers.

"You should not be frightened of letting me see that you are inexperienced at commanding people, Pasha. What you should be frightened of is that I will kill you."

Her eyes narrowed with indignation. "Don't you dare threaten me."

"This is a game to you. A way for you to fulfill some arcane rules by prancing around, pulling your little puppy around by his collar, and training him to lick your hand, so you may gain a new rank."

He gritted his teeth as he lowered his voice. "It is not a game to me, Pasha. It's a matter of life and death. I am a prisoner, held in a collar, as a beast, or a slave. I have only as much control of my life as you people allow. I know I am to be tortured by you as a way of breaking my will.

"You are wrong, Pasha, if you think that I'm making a threat. I'm not. I am making a promise."

"I'm not what you think of me, Richard," she said in a small voice. "I want to be your friend."

"You are not my friend. You are my captor." He held a finger up in front of her face. "Don't you ever turn your back on me, because I will kill you, just as I killed the last person who held me prisoner in a collar."

She blinked up at him. "Richard, I don't know what happened to you before, but we're not like that. I want to be a Sister of the Light to help people see the Creator's goodness."

Richard was dangerously close to letting the magic slip from his control. He struggled to maintain his grip. He had other things to do. "I am not interested in your theology. Just remember what I told you."

She smiled. "I will. I apologize for making you angry by calling you other than by your name. Please forgive me. I've never done this before. I was only doing as I thought I should, following the rules, as I was trained."

"Forget the rules. Just be yourself, and you will have less trouble in life."

"If that would help you believe that I'm only trying to help you, then that's what I shall do." She pointed. "Here. Sit on the edge of the bed."

"Why?"

Though she didn't move, he felt a gentle push. He fell back, to sit on the edge of the bed. "Don't . . ."

She stepped between his legs, close to him.

"Hush. Let me do my job. I told you before, I must let my Han come to know your Rada'Han, so I will know where you are at all times."

She put her hands to each side of his neck, over the collar. She closed her eyes.

Her breasts were right in front of his face, moving with each breath. He felt a soft tingling sensation that sank all the way to his toes and then came back up through him. It was slightly uncomfortable, but not unpleasant, and in fact the longer it went on, the better it felt.

When she took her hands away, the absence of the sensation was agony for a moment. The world seemed to hum and spin. He shook his head.

"What did you do?"

"I simply let my Han come to know your Rada'Han." She looked a little dazed. She swallowed as a tear ran down her cheek. "And something of your Han, your essence."

She turned away. Richard stood.

"Does that mean that you will always know where I am, now? By my collar?"

She nodded weakly as she strode slowly across the room. Her voice regained its control. "What are your preferences, for food? Your special requirements?"

"I don't eat meat."

She stopped in her tracks. "That's one I've never heard before."

"And, I guess I don't like cheese anymore, either."

She considered a moment, and then walked on. "I will tell the cooks your special requirements."

A plan was forming in his head, and she wasn't part of it. He needed to get rid of her.

Pasha went to a tall, pickled-pine wardrobe. It was filled with fine clothes. There were trousers of a smooth weave, at least a dozen shirts, mostly white, some with ruffles, and coats of every color.

"These are yours," she said.

"If everyone was surprised I was grown, why are they a size of a grown man?"

She inspected the various items, feeling the fabric, taking some out and holding them up for a better look. "Someone must have known. Verna must have told them."

"Sister Verna."

She put a black coat back. "I'm sorry, Richard, but it is just Verna, now." She pulled out a white shirt. "Do you like this?"

"No. I would look foolish wearing fancy things like that."

She smiled coquettishly. "I think you would look very handsome in it. But if it doesn't please you, there are coins on the table over there. I'll show you some shops in the city, and you may purchase whatever you like better."

Richard glanced to the marble-topped table. There was a silver bowl of silver coins, and next to it, a gold bowl heaped full with gold coins. If he worked his whole life as a guide, he would never earn even half that much gold.

"It's not mine."

"Of course it is. You're a guest of the palace, and the palace provides whatever our guests require. If you use that up, it will be replaced." She pulled out a red coat with gold brocade on the shoulders and cuffs. Her eyes brightened. "Richard, this would look simply grand on you."

"Even if you cover a collar with precious gems, it's still a collar."

"This has nothing to do with your Rada'Han. What you're wearing is disgusting. You look like some savage from the woods." She held the red coat open. "Here, try this on."

He snatched the coat from her hands and threw it on the bed. Gripping her by the arm, he marched her to the door in the front room.

"Richard! Stop it! What are you doing!"

He pulled the door open. "I'm tired, it's been a long day. Good night, Pasha."

"Richard, I'm only trying to help you look better. You look uncivilized in that outfit. You look like some huge beast."

He went calm as he took in her blue dress, blue the color of Kahlan's wedding dress.

"That color does not become you," he said. "Does not become you at all."

She stood in the hall, staring at him with big brown eyes. He kicked the door shut.

He waited a few minutes, and then checked the hall. There was no sign of her. He went to his pack, beside the fireplace, and started taking things out. He wouldn't need everything. No need carrying all his extra clothes.

As he was stretching the string to the bow, there was a soft rap at the door. He crept across the carpets, listening. Maybe she would go away if he didn't answer it. He didn't need her hanging around, telling him what to wear. He had important things to do.

The soft knock came again. Maybe it wasn't Pasha. Richard pulled his knife. He yanked the door open.

"Sister Verna."

"I just saw Pasha, running down the hall in tears. I'm surprised at you, Richard." She lifted an eyebrow to him. "I didn't think it would take you that long. I've been hiding around a corner, afraid I would be caught while I waited." A shawl capped her curly hair and spread down over her shoulders. "Did you have to make her cry?"

"She is fortunate I didn't make her bleed."

She lifted the shawl from her head and settled it around her shoulders. A small smile touched her lips. "May I come in?" He held out his arm in invitation. "And it is simply Verna," she said as she stepped through the threshold. "I am not a Sister."

He slipped the knife back into its sheath. "I'm sorry, but I don't think I could bring myself to call you anything else. To me, you are Sister Verna."

"It is not proper to address me as Sister." She looked around the room as he closed the door. "How are the accommodations?"

"They would not embarrass a king. Sister Verna, I know you won't believe me, but I'm really sorry about what happened. I didn't mean to bring my troubles down on you."

A broad grin spread on her face. "You have been a constant trouble to me, Richard, but, for once, this trouble was not caused by you. Another brought this trouble upon me."

"Sister, I know I caused you to be broken to a novice. I didn't intend that. But the part about you being sent to work in the stables, that was your own doing."

"Things are not always as they seem, Richard." There was a twinkle in her eye. "I hate scrubbing pots. When I was a novice, when I was young, I hated that more than anything else. I'm not happy in a kitchen, and less so with my hands in scalding water.

"I like horses much better. They don't talk back, or argue with me. I like being around horses. More so, since you destroyed the bits and I became friends with Jessup. Sister Maren thought she held the reins, as it were, but she was doing what I wished."

520

Richard smiled with one side of his mouth. "You are a very devious woman, Sister Verna. I'm proud of you. But I'm still sorry you are put back to novice because of me."

She shrugged. "I am here to serve the Creator. It matters not how. And this is not your doing; the Prelate's orders are what caused me to be broken to a novice."

"You mean the orders she wrote in the book? She forbade you from using your power on me, didn't she?"

"How do you know that?"

"I figured it out. You were often angry enough to spit fire at me, but you never used your power to stop me. I don't think that would have happened unless you were under orders to watch but not to interfere. After all, if the Rada'Han is used to control, why else would you not use that control?"

She shook her head to herself. "You are a very devious person yourself, Richard. How long have you known?"

"Since I read the book in the tower. Why are you here, Sister?"

"I wanted to see if you were all right. Starting tomorrow, I won't get the chance again. At least not for a very long time—not until I'm raised to Sister of the Light again. First-rank novices aren't allowed to have anything to do with young wizards. The penalty is quite severe."

"Your first day as a novice, and already you're breaking the rules. You shouldn't be here. You'll be up to your elbows in scalding water and dirty pots if they catch you."

She shrugged. "Some things are more important than rules."

Richard frowned at the distant look in her eyes. "Why don't you sit?"

"I don't have time. I only came to keep a promise." She pulled something from a pocket. "And to bring you this."

She lifted his hand and placed something in it, then closed his fingers around it. When Richard opened his fingers and looked, his knees almost buckled.

It was the lock of Kahlan's hair he had thrown away.

Sister Verna clasped her hands together. "The first night, the first night we were together, I found that."

Without looking up, he whispered, "What do you mean, you found it?"

She leaned back and looked up at the ceiling. "After you fell asleep, after you decided not to kill me, I went for a walk, and I found it."

His eyes slid closed. "I can't take this," he managed to make himself say. "I have set her free."

"Kahlan made a great sacrifice to save your life. I promised her that I would not let you forget that she loves you."

Richard's strength had vanished. The muscles in his legs quivered. His hand shook.

"I can't take this. She sent me away. I have set her free."

Sister Verna spoke softly. "She loves you, Richard. Please, as a favor to me, take it. I have violated the rules to bring this to you. I made a promise to Kahlan to make sure you know she loves you. I was reminded again today what a rare thing real love is."

Richard felt as if the whole weight of the palace had fallen down on him.

"All right, Sister. As a favor to you. But I know she doesn't want me. If you love someone, you don't ask them to put a collar around their neck; you don't send them away. She wishes to be free. I love her, and so I have set her free."

"Someday, Richard, I hope you will realize how much she has sacrificed, and the truth of her love. Love is a precious thing, and should not be forgotten. I don't know what your life holds in store, but someday you will find love again.

"But, I think you need a friend more than anything else right now. I'm sincere in my offer, Richard."

"Will you take this collar off me?"

She was silent a moment. Her voice came heavy with regret. "I cannot, Richard. It would bring you to harm. I have a duty to preserve your life. The collar must stay on."

He nodded. "I have no friends. I am in enemy territory, in enemy hands."

"That's not true. But I'm afraid that, as a novice, I won't have the chance to convince you otherwise. Pasha looks like a nice young woman. Try to make friends with her, Richard. You need a friend."

"I can't make friends with someone I may have to kill. I meant every word I said today, Sister."

"I know, Richard," she whispered. "I know. But Pasha is almost your age. Sometimes, it's easier to make friends with those your own age. I think she would like to be your friend.

"For a novice, this is as important a time as it is for a young wizard. The relationship between a novice and the wizard she is assigned is unique. The bond that will grow is very special, and will last the lifetime of each.

"She, too, is frightened. Her whole life, she has been a student, a novice. Now, for the first time, she is the teacher. Not only the boy learns, but the girl, too. They both are entering a new life. It is a very special thing, for both."

"Slave and master. That is the only bond."

She sighed. "I doubt any novice has ever faced a task like the one Pasha will have. Try to be understanding of her, Richard. Pasha is going to have her hands full with you. The Creator knows the Prelate herself would have her hands full with you."

Richard stared off at nothing. "Have you ever killed anyone you loved, Sister?"

"Well, no . . ."

Richard lifted the Agiel in his fist. "Denna held me by my magic, as do the Sisters. She kept a collar around my neck, as do the Sisters.

"They had tortured her until she was mad enough to do the same to me. I understood how she could do it, because I would have done anything she said, to keep from being hurt anymore."

He was hardly aware of the pain from the Agiel ripping through him.

"I understood her, and I loved her." A tear ran down his face. "That was the only way I was able to escape. She controlled the rage of the sword. Because I was able to love her, I was able to turn the blade of the Sword of Truth white."

"Dear Creator," Sister Verna whispered, her eyes wide, "you have turned the sword's blade white?"

Richard closed his eyes and nodded. "I had to take the love of her into my heart. Only then could I turn the blade white. Only then could I run it through her while she looked lovingly into my eyes. Only because I loved her, could I kill her, and escape.

"As long as I live, I will never be able to forgive myself."

Sister Verna embraced him protectively. "Dear Creator," she whispered, "what have you done to your child?"

Richard pushed her away. "Go, Sister, before you get into trouble." He wiped his eyes. "I'm being foolish."

She gripped his shoulders. "Why didn't you tell me this before?"

He wiped his sleeve across his nose. "It's not something I'm proud of. And you are the enemy, Sister." He looked to her wet eyes. "I've told you the truth, I told the other Sisters the truth today; I will kill anyone I must. Sister, I'm capable of killing anyone. I'm the bringer of death. I'm a monster. That's why Kahlan wanted me sent away."

She brushed his hair back from his face. "She loves you, Richard. She was trying to save your life. Someday you will see that." She sighed. "I'm sorry. I must go. Will you be all right?"

His smile was empty. "I don't think so, Sister. I think there is going to be war. I think I'm going to end up killing Sisters. I hope you aren't one of them."

She wiped her fingers across his cheek. "We never know what the Creator has in store for us."

"If this Creator of yours has any power, I think you'll be restored to Sister a lot sooner than you think, Sister."

"I must go. Good luck to you, Richard. Have faith."

As soon as she was gone he threw his cloak around his shoulders and put on his pack. He had to act now, while they were still afraid of him, while they were still unsure. He checked that the sword was clear in its scabbard. He hooked the quiver on his pack and shouldered his bow as he moved out onto the balcony.

With a running knot, Richard attached the rope to the stone railing. He put his knife between his teeth, and then slipped over the edge, into the darkness, into his element.

Night didn't seem to diminish the number of people on the streets of Tanimura. The little fires cooking meat on sticks still burned, and the hawkers still conducted a brisk business. Men called to him to come throw dice with them. Once they saw his collar, people tried to entice him into buying everything from food to shell necklaces for his lady. He told them that he had no coins. They laughed, saying that the palace would pay for anything he wanted. Richard hunched his shoulders and kept walking.

Women dressed in flimsy, revealing clothes pressed against him, giggling and smiling as they ran their hands over him, trying to get fingers into his pockets. They made him offers he could hardly believe. Pushing didn't get them away. His glare did.

Richard was relieved to leave the city behind, to leave the lights of torches, lamps, candles, and fires behind, to leave behind the smells and the noise. He breathed easier when he was into the moonlit country. He glanced over his shoulder at the twinkling lights while he climbed the hills.

He was constantly aware of the collar around his neck, and wondered what would happen if he went too far, though, from what Pasha had told him, that was many more miles than he intended to go. Still, he worried she might be wrong, and that the slack in his chain might suddenly snap tight.

Finally, he reached a satisfactory spot. He surveyed the grassy prominence overlooking the city in the distance. A little way off to the side, in the swale, he could see the dark shapes of old trees looming up in the moonlight. Shadows black as death lurked in the gaps.

Richard stared at the menacing gloom for a time, transfixed by a faint, lingering desire to go into the waiting folds of its night. Something in him hungered to go in there, and call forth the magic. Something in him lusted to bring forth the rage, to let it vent its wrath, vent his wrath.

It felt as if his frustration at being held against his will, his anger at being a helpless prisoner, his fear at not knowing what was going to happen to him, and his heartache for Kahlan, all needed to be let out, like pounding a fist against a wall when you were angry. Somehow, those woods promised him that release.

Richard finally turned from the Hagen Woods and set about collecting firewood. With his knife, he whittled a pile of shavings into a bare spot he had scooped out with his boot. Striking steel and flint, he started the shavings to smoldering, and once they had taken with a good flame, he piled on some wood. Once the fire was going nicely, he set out a pot, poured in water, and started cooking rice and beans. While he waited for it to cook, he finished a small piece of bannock he still had left.

He sat, his arms curled around his knees, and watched the dark woods, the Hagen Woods. He watched the city shimmering in the distance. The sky overhead was a sparkling canopy of stars. He watched the sky, too, waiting to see a familiar shape blacken a patch of stars.

After a time, he heard a soft thud behind him. He laughed when the furry arms grabbed him and tumbled him onto the ground. Gratch gurgled with his throaty laugh, his arms and legs and wings trying to enwrap his opponent. Richard tickled his ribs, and Gratch roared with a deep, growling laughter. The tussle ended with Gratch finally on top, hugging Richard with arms and wings. Richard embraced the little gar tightly.

"Grrratch luuug Raaaach aaarg."

Richard squeezed him tighter. "I love you, too, Gratch."

Gratch put his wrinkly nose to Richard's. His glowing green eyes looked down, and he let out in a throaty giggle.

Richard wrinkled his nose. "Gratch! Your breath smells!" He sat up, holding the gar in his lap. "Did you catch some food on your own?" Gratch nodded enthusiastically. Richard hugged him again.

"I'm so proud of you! And you did it without blood flies. What did you get?" Gratch cocked his head to the side. His furry ears turned forward.

"Did you get a turtle?" Richard asked. Gratch giggled and shook his head. "Did you get a deer?" Gratch sagged with a regretful growl. "Did you get a rabbit?" Gratch bounced and shook his head, enjoying the game.

"I give up. What did you have to eat?"

Gratch covered his eyes with his claws, peeking out between them.

"A raccoon? You got a raccoon?"

Gratch nodded with a toothy grin, then threw his head back and roared as he pounded his chest.

Richard patted the beast's back. "Good for you! Very good!"

Gratch gave a gurgling giggle and then tried to push Richard back for more wrestling. Richard was relieved that the gar was finally able to start catching his own food. He made Gratch sit still and settle down while he checked the rice and beans. He held the pot out.

"You want some of my dinner with me?"

Gratch leaned close and carefully smelled the pot. He knew it was hot. He had gotten a burn before and was careful now when Richard cooked things. He wrinkled his nose at the rice and beans. He made a croaking sound and rolled his shoulders. Richard knew that meant he wasn't enthusiastic, but if nothing better was forthcoming he would have some.

Richard poured him some in his own bowl. "Blow on it. It's hot."

Gratch held the tin bowl to his face and pursed his leathery lips. He blew air and spit between his fangs as he tried to cool his snack. Richard ate with a spoon as he watched the gar trying to lick the rice and beans from the bowl. Finally, Gratch rolled onto his back and, holding the bowl with his claws and feet, poured its contents in his mouth. In three swallows it was gone.

Gratch sat up and flapped his wings. He scooted close. With a plaintive babble, he held out his bowl to Richard. Richard showed him the empty pot.

"All gone." Gratch's ears wilted. He put a hooked claw to Richard's bowl and gave it a little tug. Richard pulled his bowl away and turned his back. "Mine. It's my dinner."

Gratch resigned himself to waiting patiently while Richard finished eating. When Richard pulled his knees up and wrapped his arms around them as he watched the city, Gratch squatted and tried to imitate the pose.

Richard pulled the lock of hair from his pocket. He twirled it in the moonlight, staring while he watched it turning. Gratch thrust out a claw. Richard elbowed it away.

"No," he said in a low voice. "You can touch, but only if you're gentle."

Gratch reached out tentatively, slowly, carefully touching a claw to the lock of hair. His glowing green eyes looked up, studying. He stroked the claw down Richard's hair.

Gratch touched Richard's cheek. Touched a tear rolling down. Richard sniffed and swallowed. He put the lock of hair back in his pocket.

Gratch put a gangly arm around Richard's shoulder and laid his head against him. Richard put his arm around Gratch, and they watched the night for a time.

Finally deciding he had better get some sleep, Richard found a spot of thick grass on which to spread a blanket. He lay down with Gratch curled up close, and the two of them fell asleep together.

Richard woke when the moon was nearly down. He sat up and stretched. Gratch made fists and imitated Richard, adding wings to the yawning stretch. Richard rubbed his eyes. It would be dawn in an hour or two. It was time.

He stood, Gratch coming up beside him. "I want you to listen to me, Gratch. I have some important things to tell you. Are you listening?"

Gratch nodded, his wrinkly face set in a serious cast. Richard pointed to the city.

"You see that place, with all the fire, all the light? I'm going to live there for a while." Richard tapped his chest and then pointed to the city. "I'm going to be down there. But I don't want you to visit me there. You must stay away. It's a dangerous place for you. You stay away." Gratch watched Richard's face. "I'll come up here to visit you. All right?" Gratch thought a moment, and then nodded.

"You stay away from the city. And you see the river down there? You know what a river is; I've shown you water. You stay on this side of the water. This side. Understand?"

Richard didn't want the gar hunting the livestock on the farms on the other side of the river. That would surely get him in trouble. Gratch looked from Richard's face to the city, and then back. He made a sound from deep in his throat to express his understanding.

"And Gratch, if you see any people," Richard tapped his chest and pointed to the city, "people like me, don't you eat them." He put a finger in front of Gratch's face. "People are not food. Don't eat any people. Understand?"

Gratch growled in disappointment, and then nodded. Richard put an arm around the gar's shoulders and turned him toward the Hagen Woods.

"Now listen. This is important. You see that place down there? Those woods?"

A low, menacing growl rose from the gar's throat. His lips drew back from his fangs. The glow in his green eyes intensified.

"You stay out of there. I don't want you going into that place. I mean it, Gratch. You stay away." Gratch watched the woods, the growl still in his throat. Richard gripped a fistful of fur and gave him a shake. "You stay away from there. Understand?"

Gratch glanced over and finally nodded.

526

"I have to go in there, but you can't follow. It's dangerous in there for you. Stay out."

With a plaintive pule, Gratch put an arm around Richard and pulled him back a step.

"I'll be safe; I have the sword. Remember the sword? I showed you my sword. It will protect me. But you can't come with me."

Richard hoped he was right about the sword; Sister Verna had told him that the Hagen Woods were a place of vile magic. But he had no choice. It was the only plan he could think of.

Richard gave the gar a tight hug. "You be a good boy. Go hunt yourself some more food. I'll be coming up here to see you, and we'll wrestle. All right?"

Gratch grinned at the mention of wrestling. He pulled hopefully on Richard's arm. "Not now, Gratch. I have something I must do. But I'll come back on another night and wrestle with you."

Gratch's ears wilted again. His long arms wrapped around Richard in a good-bye hug. Richard collected his things and, with a final wave, headed down into the swale. Gratch watched as the dark woods swallowed him up.

Richard walked for close to an hour. He needed to be deep enough into the Hagen Woods to make sure his plan would work. Limbs draped with moss and vines looked like arms reaching out to snatch him. Sounds drifted through the trees—guttural clicking and long, low whistles. Off in stagnant stretches of water things splashed at his approach.

Warm, and breathing hard with the effort of the walk, he came to a small clearing, high enough to be dry, and open enough to afford him the view of a small patch of stars. There was no rock or log in the clearing, so he flattened a thick clump of grass and sat down beside his pack, crossing his legs. He closed his eyes and drew a deep breath.

Richard thought about home and the Hartland Woods. He longed to be back in his woods. He thought about the friends he missed so much, Chase, and Zedd. All the time he had grown up with the old man, Richard had never known Zedd was his grandfather. But he had known he was his friend, and that they loved each other. He guessed that was what mattered. What difference would it have made, anyway? Richard could not have loved him more, and Zedd could not have been more of a friend.

It had been so long since he had seen Zedd. Although he had seen him at the People's Palace, in D'Hara, he hadn't really had much time to talk with him, to catch up on things. He shouldn't have left so soon. He wished he could talk to Zedd now, to seek his help and understanding.

Richard had no idea if Kahlan would go to Zedd. Why should she? She was rid of Richard, and that was what she wanted.

He wished with all his heart it weren't so.

He missed her smile, her green eyes, the soft sound of her voice, her intelligence and wit, her touch. She made the world alive for him. He would have given his life at that moment just to hold her for five minutes.

But she knew what he was, and had sent him away.

And he had set her free.

It was for the best. He wasn't good enough for her.

Before he realized what he was doing, he was seeking the peace within himself, seeking his Han, as Sister Verna had taught him. He had practiced almost every day when he had been with her, and although he never felt his Han, whatever it was, it had always felt pleasant to seek it. It was relaxing, and brought peace. It felt good to do that now. He let his mind find that place of peace, and let his worries drift away.

In his mind, as he always did, he pictured the Sword of Truth, floating in space before his mind's eye. He saw every detail of it, felt every detail of it.

In his peace, in his meditation, without opening his eyes, Richard drew his sword. He wasn't quite sure why, except it felt the right thing to do. The unique ring of steel hung in the night air, announcing the blade's arrival to the Hagen Woods.

He laid the sword across his knees. The magic danced with him in the place of peace. If anything came, he would be ready.

Now, he had to wait. It would be quite a while, he was sure, but she would come.

When she realized where he was, she would come.

As he sat still and quiet, the night returned to its normal activity around him. While he concentrated on the picture of the sword, Richard was vaguely aware of the chirps and clicks of bugs, the low, steady croaks of frogs, and the rustling of mice and voles among the dry debris of the forest floor. The air occasionally whirred with a bat. Once, he heard a squeak as an owl caught its dinner.

And then, while in the dreamlike haze as he sat and pictured the sword, the night became still.

In his mind, he saw the dark shape behind him.

In one fluid movement, Richard was up and spinning, the sword tip whistling through the air. The flowing shape pitched back, and lunged again when the sword was past. Richard felt a thrill that he had missed, that it would not be ended so soon, that he could dance with the spirits, that he could let the rage free.

It moved like a cape in the wind, dark as death, and just as quick.

Around the clearing they darted, the sword glinting in the waning light of the moon, the blade slicing the air, the dark shape's bladelike claws flashing past. Richard immersed himself in the sword's magic, in its wrath, in his own. He freed his anger and frustration to join with the sword's own fury, reveling in the dance with death.

Across the clearing they spun, like leaves in a gale, one avoiding the blade, the other, the claws. Lunging and ducking, they used the trees for cover and attack. Richard let the spirits of the sword dance with him. He immersed himself in the magic's mastery, he let himself do as the spirits counseled, and he watched, almost in a detached state, as they spun him this way and that, had him skim across the ground, dodge right then left, leap and thrust.

He hungered to learn the dance.

*Teach me.*

Knowledge, like memory, flowed forth, forged by his will into the completing link.

He became not the user of the sword, the magic, the spirits, but their master. The blade, the magic, the spirits, and the man were one.

The dark shape lunged.

Now. With a solid thwack, the blade halved the shape. A spray of blood hit the trees close by. A death howl shivered the air, and then all was still.

Richard stood panting, almost sorry it was over. Almost.

He had danced with the spirits of the dead, with the magic, and in so doing, had found the release he sought; release not only of some of his feelings of helpless frustration, but release, too, of darker needs deep within himself that he didn't understand.

The sun had been up for nearly two hours when he heard her coming. She was blundering through the brush, huffing indignantly at branches that snagged her clothes. He could hear twigs snap as she staggered up the rise. Tugging her skirt free from a thorn, she stumbled into the clearing before him.

Richard was sitting cross-legged, with his eyes closed and the sword resting across his knees. She came to a panting halt before him.

"Richard!"

"Good morning, Pasha." He opened his eyes. "Beautiful day, isn't it?"

She held her long, brown skirt up a little in her hands. Her white blouse was damp with sweat. Her hair had burrs in it.

Pasha blew a strand of hair from her face. "You have to get out of here at once. Richard, this is the Hagen Woods."

"I know. Sister Verna told me. Interesting place; I rather like it."

She blinked at him. "Richard, this place is dangerous! What are you doing here!"

Richard smiled to her. "Waiting for you."

She peered around at trees and dark shadows. "Something smells awful in here," she muttered.

Pasha squatted down in front of him, smiling a little smile as a person might to a child, or to someone she thought was insane. "Richard, you've had your fun, your nice walk in the country; now, give me your hand and let's get out of here."

"I'm not leaving until Verna is restored to Sister again."

Pasha shot to her feet. "What!"

Richard took his sword in hand and rose in front of her. "I'm not leaving here until Verna is restored to the rank of Sister, the same as she was before. The palace must choose what's more important to them—my life, or keeping Sister Verna a novice."

Pasha's mouth fell open. "But the only one who can remove Verna's sanction is Sister Maren!"

"I know." He touched his finger to her nose. "That's why you're going to go and tell Sister Maren she must come here, in person, and give me her solemn pledge that Verna is once again a Sister, and agree to my terms."

"You can't be serious. Sister Maren will not do that."

"I'm not leaving this spot unless she does."

"Richard, we'll go back and see if Sister Maren will discuss this, but you can't stay here. It's not worth dying for!"

He regarded her with a cool expression. "It is to me."

Her tongue wet her lips. "Richard, you don't know what you're doing. This is a dangerous place. I'm responsible for you. I cannot allow you to stay here!

"If you won't come away with me, then I will have to use the collar and make you come with me, and I know you don't want that."

Richard's grip tightened on the sword's hilt. "Sister Verna is being punished in retaliation against me. I have made a vow to myself to restore Verna to Sister. I can't allow the sanction to stand. I'll do whatever I must, die here if I have to.

"If you use the collar to hurt me, or drag me off, I'll fight you, with everything I have. I don't know who will win, but if that happens, I am sure of one thing: one of us will die. If it's you, then the war will have started. If I die, then your test to become a Sister will end on the first day. Sister Verna will still be a novice, but that is where she stands now. At least I will have done my best."

"You would be willing to die? For this?"

"Yes. It's that important to me. I will not allow Sister Verna to be punished because of what I have done. It was unjust."

Her brow wrinkled. "But . . . Sister Maren is the headmistress of the novices. I'm a novice. I can't go to her and tell her she must reverse the order—she'll skin me alive!"

"I am the cause of the trouble; you are simply the messenger. If she punishes you, I would not stand for it, any more than I will stand for what was done to Sister Verna. If Sister Maren wishes to start a war, then let it start. If she wishes to keep my truce, then she will have to come to me, here, and agree to my terms."

Pasha stared at him. "Richard, if you are here when the sun goes down, you will die."

"Then I would suggest you hurry."

She turned, holding her arm out toward the city. "But . . . I must go all the way back. It took me hours to get here. It will take me hours to go back, and then I must find Sister Maren, and then convince her that you're serious, and even if I could get her to agree to return with me, we must still get back here."

"You should have ridden a horse."

"But I ran here as soon as I realized where you were! I wasn't thinking about a horse, or anything else! I knew there was trouble and just came after you!"

He gave her an even look. "Then you made a mistake, Pasha. You should have thought before you acted. Next time, maybe you will think first."

Pasha put a hand to her chest as she gulped air. "Richard, there is hardly time . . ."

"Then you had better hurry, or your new charge will be sitting here, in Hagen Woods, when the sun goes down."

Her eyes moistened with frustration and concern. "Richard, please, you don't understand. This is no game. This place is dangerous."

He turned a little and pointed with the sword. "Yes, I know."

Pasha peered around him, to the shadows, and gasped. Hesitantly, she stepped to the thing by the trees. Richard didn't follow. He knew what was there; two halves of a creature from a nightmare, its guts spilled across the ground.

Its sinuous head, like a man's half melted into a snake, or lizard, was a picture of wickedness itself; covered in a glossy, tight, black skin, smooth down to the base of the thick neck where it began welting up into pliable scales. The lithe body was shaped much like a man's. The whole of the creature seemed made for fluid speed, deadly quick grace.

It wore hides covered with short, black hair, and a full-length, black, hooded cape. What Richard had taken for claws were not claws, but three-bladed knives, one in each webbed hand, with crosswise handles held in the fist. Steel extensions went up each side of the wrist for support when a strike was made.

Pasha stood dumbstruck. Richard finally went to stand by her, looking down at the two halves of the thing. Whatever it was, it bled, the same as any other creature. And it smelled, like fish guts rotting in the hot sun.

Pasha stood trembling as she stared at the thing. "Dear Creator," she whispered. "It's a mriswith." She took a step back. "What happened to it?"

"What happened to it? I killed it, that's what happened to it. What sort of thing is a mriswith?"

Her big brown eyes came to his. "What do you mean, you killed it? You can't kill a mriswith. No one has ever killed a mriswith."

Her face was a picture of consternation.

"Well, someone has killed one now."

"You killed it at night, didn't you."

"Yes." Richard frowned. "How do you know that?"

"Mriswith are rarely seen outside Hagen Woods, but there have been reports over the last few thousand years. Reports given by people who somehow managed to live long enough to tell what they saw. The mriswith always take on the color of what is around them. In one report, one rose up in the tidal flats, and was the color of mud. One time in the sand dunes, it was the color of the sand. One report noted that in the light of a golden sunset, the mriswith was golden. When they kill at night, they're never seen, because they are black, like the night. We think they have the ability, maybe the magic, to assume the color of their surroundings. Since this one is black, I guessed that you killed it at night."

Richard took her arm, gently pulling her away. She seemed transfixed by the creature. He could feel her trembling under his hand.

"Pasha, what are they?"

"Things that live in the Hagen Woods. I don't know what they are. I've heard it said that in the war that separated the New World from the Old, the wizards created armies of the mriswith. Some people believe the mriswith are sent by the Nameless One.

"But the Hagen Woods are their home. And the home of other things. They are why no one lives out in the country on this side of the river. Sometimes, they come out of the woods, and hunt people. They never devour their kills, they seem simply to kill for the sake of killing. Mriswith disembowel their victims. Some live long enough to tell what got them; that is how we know as much as we know."

"How long have the Hagen Woods, the creatures, been here?"

"As far as I know, at least as long as the Palace of the Prophets, nearly three thousand years."

She took a fistful of his shirt. "In all that time, no one, not once, has ever killed a mriswith. Every victim said that they never saw it until after it slashed them open. Some of those victims have been Sisters, and wizards, and not even their Han warned them. They said they were blind to its coming, as if they were born without the gift. How is it you were able to kill a mriswith?"

Richard remembered seeing it coming in his mind. He took her hand from his shirt. "Maybe I was just lucky. Someone was bound to get one sooner or later. Maybe this one was just a half-wit."

"Richard, please, come away with me. This is not the way to have a test of wills with the palace. This could get you killed."

"I'm not testing anyone's will, I'm taking responsibility for my actions. It's my fault Sister Verna was demoted; I've got to set it straight. I'm taking a stand for what's right. If I don't do that, then I am nothing."

"Richard, if the sun sets on you in the Hagen Woods—"

"You are wasting precious time, Pasha."

It was late afternoon when he heard them coming. He heard the sound of only one horse, and Pasha's voice calling out the direction. At last they broke into the clearing.

Richard sheathed his sword. "Bonnie!" He gave the horse's neck a scratch. "How you doing, girl?"

Bonnie nuzzled his chest. Richard pushed his fingers in the side of her mouth and felt the bit while Sister Maren frowned at him.

"I'm glad to see you use a snaffle bit, Sister."

"The stableboys said they couldn't find the spade bits." She glared down at him suspiciously. "Seems they vanished. Mysteriously."

"That so?" Richard shrugged. "Can't say I'm sorry."

Pasha was panting with the effort of having kept up with the Sister on her horse. Her white blouse was soaked with sweat. She fussed hopelessly with the matted, tangled mess of her hair. The Sister must have made Pasha walk, as punishment. Sister Maren, in her plain brown dress buttoned to her neck, looked cool and comfortable atop the horse.

"So, Richard," Sister Maren said, as she dismounted, "I am here, as you requested. What is it you want?"

She knew very well what he wanted, but Richard decided to restate it in a pleasant tone. "It's quite simple. Sister Verna is to be restored to Sister. At once. And you are also to return her dacra to her."

She gestured dismissively. "And here I thought you would want something unreasonable. This is simple. It is done. Verna is returned to Sister. It makes no difference to me."

"And when she asks why, I don't want you to tell her about this business with me. Just say you reconsidered, or something, and decided to reinstate her. If you want, you can tell her you prayed for guidance from your Creator, and it came to you that she should remain a Sister."

She brushed some of her fine, sandy hair back from her face. "That would suit me. Are you satisfied? Is everything to your liking?"

"That would end it, and keep our truce."

"Good. Now that the trifling matters are dispensed with, show me this dead bear. Pasha has half the palace in an uproar with some babble about you killing a mriswith." Pasha furiously studied the ground as Sister Maren directed a scolding frown in her direction. "The foolish child never sets her slippered foot on anything that hasn't been swept, scrubbed, or polished. The only time she sticks her head out-of-doors is go see the latest bolt of lace to come to Tanimura. She wouldn't know a rabbit from an ox, and she certainly wouldn't know a . . . What is that smell?"

"Bear guts," Richard said.

He held out his arm, showing her the way. Pasha deferentially stepped aside. Sister Maren straightened her dress at her hips and marched toward the trees. Pasha peeked up at him, and when they heard Sister Maren gasp, her head came the rest of the way up and she smiled.

When Sister Maren stepped backward to them, her face white as bedsheets, Pasha resumed her study of the ground.

Sister Maren's trembling fingers lifted Pasha's chin. "You have spoken the truth," she whispered. "Forgive me, child."

Pasha curtsied. "Of course, Sister Maren. Thank you for taking the time to witness my report."

Sister Maren's haughty attitude had vanished, to be replaced by sincere concern. She turned to Richard. "How did this creature die?" Richard lifted the sword clear of its scabbard a half foot and then slid it home. "Then what Pasha said is true? You killed it?"

Richard shrugged. "I spend quite a lot of my time out-of-doors. I knew it was no rabbit."

Sister Maren returned to the creature, mumbling to herself. "I must study it. This is an unprecedented opportunity."

Pasha looked to Richard and wrinkled her nose in disgust as the Sister ran her finger over the lipless slit of a mouth, touched the ear holes, and ran her hand across the glossy black skin. She tugged at the hide clothes, pulling them this way and that as she inspected them.

She rose to her feet, peering down at the entrails. Finally, she turned to Richard. "Where is the cape? Pasha said it had a cape."

When the mriswith had lunged, and he had sliced it in two, the cape had been billowed open and so it was undamaged. While Richard had been waiting for Pasha to return with the Sister, he had accidentally learned the astonishing thing the cape could do. After that, he had washed it clean of blood, hung it over branches to dry, and then stuffed it away in his pack. He had no intention of giving that cape away.

"It's mine. It is a prize of battle. I'm keeping it."

She looked perplexed. "But, the knives . . . don't men fancy things like that as prizes of battle? Why would you want a cape instead of the knives?"

Richard tapped the hilt. "I have my sword. Why would I want knives that have proven inferior to my sword? I've always wanted a long black cape, and it's a fine one, so I'm keeping it."

The furrows of her scowl stole back onto her face. "Is this another condition of your truce?"

"If need be."

The furrows softened. She sighed. "I guess it doesn't matter. It is the creature that is important, not its cape." She turned back to the reeking corpse. "I must study this."

While she bent back to the mriswith, Richard hooked his bow, quiver of arrows, and pack to the front of the saddle. He put his foot in the stirrup and sprang up onto Bonnie.

"Don't stay after the sun goes down, Sister Maren."

She glanced over her shoulder. "My horse. You can't have my horse."

Richard smiled apologetically. "I twisted my ankle fighting the mriswith. I'm

533

sure you wouldn't want the palace's newest pupil limping all the way home, now, would you? I might fall and crack my skull."

"But . . ."

Richard reached down and gripped Pasha's arm. She gasped in surprise as he yanked her up, sitting her behind him on Bonnie. "Please don't let the sun set on you here, Sister. I hear it's dangerous in the Hagen Woods after dark."

Pasha hid her face from the Sister, and he could feel her giggling softly against his back.

"Yes, yes," Sister Maren said, her eyes already lost to the mriswith, "all right. You two go on back. You have done well, both of you. I must study this creature before the animals get to it."

Pasha held him so tight that he could hardly breathe. It was distracting to feel her firm breasts mashed against his back. Her fingers gripped his chest, trying to get a better hold on him, as if she was afraid she might fall at any moment.

When they were clear of the woods, and into the open hills, he slowed Bonnie to a walk and pried Pasha's hands off.

She clamped them right back. "Richard! I might fall!"

He pulled her hands loose again. "You're not going to fall. Just hold on easy, and let your hips move with the horse. Use your balance; you don't need to cling for dear life."

She gripped his sides. "Well, I'll try."

The sky was turning golden as they descended the rounded hills toward the city. Richard swayed with Bonnie's steps as she went over rocks and across shallow ravines, and thought about the mriswith, and his hunger to fight it. The craving to go back into the Hagen Woods still burned in the back of his mind.

"Your ankle isn't really twisted, is it?" Pasha asked after a long ride in silence.

"No."

"You lied to a Sister. Richard, you must learn that lying is wrong. The Creator hates lies."

"So Sister Verna has told me."

He decided he didn't want to ride anymore with her holding on to him, so he dismounted and lead Bonnie by the reins. Pasha scooted forward into the saddle.

"Then why did you do it if you know it's wrong?"

"Because I wanted to make Sister Maren walk back. She made you walk all the way out there again as punishment for something that was not your fault."

Pasha slid off Bonnie and came up to walk beside him. She raked her fingers through her hair, trying to arrange it to her satisfaction.

"That was very nice of you." She put a hand on his arm. "I think we're going to become good friends."

Richard pretended to turn and look around as he walked so that her arm fell away. "Can you get this collar off me?"

"The Rada'Han? Well, no. Only a full Sister is able to remove a Rada'Han. I don't know how."

"Then we are not going to be friends. I have no use for you."

"You have gone to great risk for Sister Verna. She must be your friend. A person only does such things for friends. You went out of your way to see that I had a horse to ride back. You must hope we can become friends."

Richard watched the country ahead as he walked. "Sister Verna is not my friend.

I did as I did only because what was done to her was my fault and was unjust. That is the only reason.

"When I decide to get this collar off, only those who help me will be my friends. Sister Verna has made it clear that she will not help me get the collar off. She intends that it remain on me. When the time comes, if she stands in my way, I will kill her, the same as I will kill any other Sister who tries to stop me. The same as I will kill you, if you stand in my way."

"Richard," she scoffed, "you're a mere student; you shouldn't brag about your powers so. It's unbecoming to a young man. You should not even joke about such things." She took his arm again. "I don't believe you would ever hurt a woman. . . ."

"Then you believe wrong."

"Most young men have trouble adjusting at first, but you will come to trust in me. We will become friends, I'm sure of it."

Richard yanked his arm away and spun to her. "This is no game, Pasha. If you get in my way when I decide the time has come, I will cut your pretty little throat."

She peered up at him with a coy smile. "Do you really think I have a pretty neck?"

"It's a figure of speech," he growled.

He moved on, tugging Bonnie ahead. Pasha hastened her step to keep up. She walked in silence for a time, busying herself with pulling little knots and burrs from her hair.

Richard was in no mood to be pleasant. Killing the mriswith had brought him a strange feeling of fulfillment, but it was fading now, and his frustration with his situation was returning, and it brought with it the anger.

Pasha's face brightened. She put on a pleasant smile.

"I don't know anything about you, Richard. Why don't you tell me about yourself?"

"What do you want to know?"

"Well, what did you do . . . before you came to the palace? Did you have some kind of skill? A profession you worked at?"

Richard scuffed his boots through the dirt. "I was a woods guide."

"Where?"

"Where I grew up, in Hartland, in Westland."

Pasha pulled the white blouse away from her chest, trying to dry it. "I'm afraid I don't know where that is. I don't know about the New World. Someday, when I'm a Sister, maybe I'll be called upon to go there, and help a boy."

Richard didn't say anything, so she went on. "So you were a woods guide. That must have been scary, being out in the woods all the time. Weren't you afraid of the animals? I'd be afraid of the animals."

"Why? If a rabbit jumped out of a bush, you could just burn it to ashes with your Han."

She giggled. "I'd still be frightened. I like the city better." She pulled some hair back from her face and looked at him as they walked. She had a funny way of wrinkling her nose. "Did you have a . . . well, you know, a girl, a love, or anything?"

Richard was taken by surprise at the question. His mouth opened, but no words came out. He snapped it closed. He was not about to discuss Kahlan with her.

"I have a wife."

Pasha missed a step. She hurried to catch back up. "A wife!" She considered a moment. Her voice now had an edge to it. "What is her name?"

535

Richard kept his eyes straight ahead as he walked. "Her name is Du Chaillu."

Pasha twisted a strand of hair around her finger. "Is she pretty? What does she look like?"

"Yes, she is pretty. She has thick black hair, a little longer than yours. She has attractive breasts, and the rest of her is shapely, too."

From the corner of his eye he could see Pasha's face glowing red. She picked at the end of the strand of hair. Her voice came quiet and cold, despite her trying to layer indifference over it.

"How long have you known her?"

"A few days."

Her hand fell away from her hair. "What do you mean, a few days? How could you only know her a few days?"

"When Sister Verna and I went to the Majendie land, a few days ago, they had her chained up. They were going to sacrifice her to their spirits, and they wanted me to do the killing. Sister Verna said I was to do as the Majendie wished, so we could pass through their land.

"Instead, I disobeyed Sister Verna, and shot an arrow at their Queen Mother, pinning her arm to a pole. I told them that if they didn't let Du Chaillu go, and make peace with the Baka Ban Mana, I would put the next arrow through the Queen Mother's head. They wisely agreed."

"She is one of the savages?"

"She is Baka Ban Mana. A wisewoman. She is not a savage."

"And she wed you because you were her hero? Because you rescued her?"

"No. Sister Verna and I had to go through her land, to come here. When we were there, I killed her five husbands."

Pasha snatched him by the arm. "They are blade masters! You managed to kill five of them?"

Richard started walking again. "No, I killed thirty of them." Pasha gasped. "Her five husbands were among the thirty. Du Chaillu is their spirit woman, and said I was now the leader of her people. She said that since she was the spirit woman, and I their leader, their *Caharin*, I was now her husband."

Pasha's smile crept back. "Then you aren't really her husband. She was just telling you some of her savage . . . some of her Baka Ban Mana spirit babble."

Richard didn't say anything. Pasha's smile evaporated. Her scowl returned. "Then how do you know what her breasts, and the rest of her, looks like?" She looked the other way and gave a sniff. "I suppose she rewarded you for your valor."

"I know because when they sent me in to kill her, she had a collar around her neck and she was chained to a wall. She was held naked in that collar so that men could rape her whenever they wanted." Pasha swallowed and looked away again. "She is with child, now, by one of those men. I guess that because the people to be sacrificed are held in a collar, the Sisters never gave a thought to putting a stop to it. I don't guess the Sisters care much what happens to someone in a collar."

"The Sisters care," Pasha said in a small voice.

Richard didn't argue. He walked on in silence. Pasha looked cold as she folded her arms beneath her breasts. The sky was turning a deep purple, but it was not getting cold; it was still warm.

After a time, Pasha's step regained a bit of its bounce. She glanced over, the smile back.

"So, what about you? You have the gift. Did your father have the gift, too? Is that where it was passed down from?"

Richard's mood sank like a rock in a well. "Yes, my father had the gift."

She looked up hopefully. "Is he still living?"

"No. He was killed a short time ago."

Pasha smoothed the front of her skirt. "Oh. I'm sorry, Richard."

Richard's hand tightened on the reins. "I'm not. I'm the one who killed him."

She froze. "You killed your father? Your own father?"

Richard's glare locked on to her. "He had me captured, and put in a collar to be tortured. I killed the beautiful young woman who held the leash to that collar, and then I killed him."

She had no trouble mistaking the threat in his voice, his words, or his eyes.

Her lower lip began to quiver, and then Pasha burst into tears, turned, and ran. Holding her skirts up in her fists, she went around an outcropping of rock and ran off over the edge of the hill.

Richard let out a long sigh as he tied the reins to a slab of granite. He patted Bonnie's neck.

"Be a good girl. Wait here for me."

He found Pasha sitting on a rock with her arms wrapped around her knees as she cried. Richard came around to face her, but she turned her face away. Her shoulders shook as she gasped in racking sobs.

"Go away!" She put her forehead against her knees as she wailed. "Or did you come to slice me to bits?"

"Pasha—"

"All you care about is killing people!"

"That's not true. I want nothing more than to end the killing."

"Oh, sure," she cried, "that's why you speak of nothing else!"

"That's only because—"

"I've been praying for this day nearly my whole life! All I ever wanted was to be a Sister of the Light. The Sisters help people. I wanted to be one of them!" She succumbed to her tears. "I'm never going to be a Sister, now."

"Sure you will."

"Not according to you! From what you keep telling us, you intend to kill us all! From the first moment, all you have done is threaten us!"

"Pasha, you don't understand."

Her tearstained face came up. "Don't I? We had a big banquet to make you feel welcome, bigger even than the harvest banquet. I had to go without you and tell everyone you were ill. They all stared at me! The other novices get boys who want to learn. My friends have come to me before, complaining that their young charge brought them a frog or a bug in his pocket. You bring me a mriswith!"

"Sister Maren said we did well today. She hardly ever says that. It's not something she does unless she really means it.

"You were cruel to Sister Maren. She has been headmistress of the novices ever since I came here. She is strict, but that's because she cares about us. She watches out for us."

Pasha gasped back a sob. "When I was little, the first day I came to the palace, I was scared. I had never been away from home. Sister Maren drew a little picture for me. She told me it was a picture of the Creator. She put it on my pillow and told me He would watch over me in the night, so I would be safe."

Pasha tried to stifle the tears, but couldn't. "I've always kept that picture. I wanted to give it to my boy on his first night, so he wouldn't be afraid. I had it with me yesterday. When I saw you, saw that you were grown, I knew I couldn't give it to you. I didn't want to embarrass you.

"And when I saw you, I thought, Well, Pasha, he's not a young boy, like all the other novices get, but the Creator has given me the handsomest man I ever saw. I was so glad I had on my prettiest dress, the one I had been saving for that day." She gasped for air. "And then you tell me I'm ugly!"

Richard's eyes slid closed. "Pasha, I'm sorry."

"No you're not!" she cried. "You're nothing but a big brute! We had everything prepared for you. We gave you one of the nicest rooms in the palace. You didn't care. We provided you with money for whatever you might need or want, and you act as if we insulted you. We had fine new clothes for you, and you turn your nose up at them!"

She wiped her tears, but more replaced them. "I'd be the first to admit that there are some Sisters who think too much of themselves, but most are so kind they wouldn't even step on a bug. And you hold up a bloody sword in front of them and vow to kill them!"

She held up fists full of her skirt and covered her face as she convulsed in sobs. Richard put a hand on her shoulder but she pushed it away.

Richard didn't know what to do with his hands. "Pasha, I'm sorry. I know it must seem like—"

"No you're not! You're not sorry at all! You want the Rada'Han off, but that's what my job is, to teach you to use your gift so you can get the collar off. But you won't let me! Without the collar, you would have died.

"Two Sisters have given their lives for you. They will never come home to their friends. Those friends wept in secret, and put on a smile to welcome you. In return for trying to help you, trying to save your life, you threaten to kill us all!"

Richard put a gentle hand to her head. "Pasha . . ."

"I'm never going to be a Sister. Instead of getting a boy who wants to learn, I get a madman with a sword. I'll forever be the object of laughter at the palace. Young girls will be told to behave themselves or they'll end up like Pasha Maes, and be put out like she was. My dreams have come to ruin."

It hurt him to see her sobbing in such pain and sorrow. Richard took her up in his arms. She fought him at first, trying to push him away, but when he pulled her against him and put her head to his shoulder, she went limp and cried all the harder. Richard held her tight and rubbed her back as she trembled and cried. He rocked her gently in his arms.

"I only wanted to help you, Richard," she sobbed. "I only wanted to teach you."

He hushed her. "I know. I know. It will be all right."

She shook her head against his shoulder. "No it won't."

"Yes it will. You'll see."

Finally, her hands came up, clutching his shirt as she cried. Richard didn't try to stop her tears, he simply held her, trying to give her comfort.

"Do you really think that you could teach me to use the gift, and that then the Sisters would take the collar off?"

She sniffled. "That's my job. That's what I've been training for. I wanted so much to show you the beauty of the Creator, of his gift to you. That's all I wanted."

538

Her arms circled him. She clung to him, as if trying to soak up succor. He stroked her hair.

"Richard, when I touched you yesterday, when I touched your Rada'Han, and felt something of your Han, I felt some of your feelings. I know you hurt inside. It made me hurt just to feel a little of it."

Her hand came up to the side of his neck, as if to comfort him. "I don't know of many things that can cause that much hurt. Richard, I'm not asking to take her place."

Richard's eyes closed as his head sank down on her shoulder. He swallowed back the pain. She ran her fingers through his hair and held his head to her.

After a time, he found his voice. "Maybe it wouldn't hurt me to occasionally wear one of those outfits."

She pushed away a little, looking up through her tears. "Maybe just to the dining room, with the Sisters?"

He shrugged. "That would be a good use of them, I guess. You pick one you would like me to wear. I don't know anything about fancy clothes." He managed a small smile. "I'm just a woods guide."

Her face brightened. "You would look handsome in the red coat."

Richard winced. "The red one? Does it have to be the red one?"

She ran her finger down the Agiel hanging from his neck. "No, it doesn't have to be that one. I just thought it would look good on your broad shoulders."

Richard sighed. "I will feel foolish in any. It might as well be the red."

"You will not look foolish; you will look handsome." Pasha grinned. "You'll see. All the women will be batting their lashes at you." She lifted the Agiel. "Richard, what is this?"

"Just sort of a good-luck charm. You ready to go back? I think you need to get started teaching me. The sooner you start, the sooner I get this collar off. Then we'll both be happy; you will be a Sister, and I will be free."

He put his arm around her shoulders and she put hers around his waist as they walked back for Bonnie.

539

On the bridge to Halsband Island, in a pool of light under a lamp, a crowd of boys and young men mobbed them. Many were dressed in fine clothes, some wore robes, and each had a Rada'Han around his neck. They all excitedly asked questions at the same time, wanting to know if it was true that Richard had killed a mriswith, and what it looked like. They wanted to tell Richard their names, and clamored for him to draw his sword and show them how he had vanquished the legendary monster.

Pasha spoke to the most persistent boy at her hip. "Yes, Kipp, it's true that Richard killed a mriswith. Sister Maren is studying it now, and if she deems it appropriate, she will tell you of its nature. But I can tell you true that it is a fearsome-looking beast. Now, off with you all. It's nearly dinnertime."

Despite their disappointment that no more information was forthcoming, they were excited by what they had heard. They ran off in a bunch to tell others.

After leaving Bonnie at the stables, Richard walked with Pasha down halls and through vast chambers, trying to memorize the layout. She pointed out the boys' dining halls, and the dining hall where the Sisters and some of the older young men ate. She also took him past the kitchens, where the aromas of cooking wafted through the surrounding corridors.

Pasha pointed through a lattice-covered archway to a graceful stone wall running under the spreading branches of trees. The wall was veiled in places by vines. Large white flowers dotted the green.

"That's the Prelate's offices, and quarters," Pasha said.

"Will she be at dinner tonight?"

Pasha giggled softly. "No, of course not. The Prelate doesn't have time to have dinner with us."

Richard turned out of the hall and down a walkway toward a gate in the wall.

"Richard! What are you doing? Where are you going?"

"I want to meet the Prelate."

"You can't simply go visit her!"

"Why?"

She hurried along beside him. "Well, she's a busy woman. She can't be bothered. They won't let you see her. The guards won't even let us through the gate."

He shrugged. "It won't hurt to ask, will it? Then, afterwards, you can pick an outfit for me, and we'll go to have dinner with the Sisters. All right?"

The offer to let her pick his outfit gave her pause. Pasha stuttered that she supposed it wouldn't hurt just to ask and struggled to keep up as he marched toward the guard. The guard stepped before the iron gate, spread his feet, and hooked his thumbs on his weapons belt as Richard strode right up to him.

Richard put a hand to the man's shoulder. "I'm so sorry. Forgive me. Please? I didn't get you in any trouble, did I? I hope not. She hasn't come out to yell at you, yet, I hope."

The man frowned in confusion as Richard leaned closer. "Look . . . what's your name?"

"Swordsman Andellmere. Kevin Andellmere."

"Look, Kevin, she said she would send the guard at the west gate to get me if I was even one minute late. She probably forgot to send you out. It isn't your fault. I promise I won't mention your name. I hope you're not angry with me."

Richard put his back to Pasha and leaned even closer to the guard. "You understand." He rolled his eyes meaningfully toward Pasha and then gave the man a wink. Kevin glanced to Pasha as she fussed with her tangled mat of hair. "Eh? You understand, I'm sure. Look, Kevin, say you'll let me buy you an ale. Will you? I better get in there before I get you in trouble, but before I go, promise me you'll let me buy you an ale, to make it up to you?"

"Well, I suppose I could let you buy me an ale. . . ."

Richard clapped Kevin on the shoulder. "There's a good man."

Pasha was right on Richard's heels as he stormed past the guard and through the gate. He turned and gave Kevin a wave and a smile.

Pasha leaned close. "How did you do that? No one gets through the Prelate's guards."

Richard held the door into the building open for her. "I just gave him too much to think about, and a worry he feared might be true."

When an answer came to her knock, they stepped into a dimly lit room with two desks, and two Sisters.

Pasha curtsied. "Sisters. I am novice Pasha Maes, and this is our new student, Richard Cypher. He was wondering if he might meet the Prelate."

Both Sisters glowered at her. The one on the right spoke. "The Prelate is busy. Dismissed, novice."

A little pale, Pasha curtsied again. "Thank you for your time, Sisters."

Richard gave a little bow. "Yes, thank you, Sisters. Please give the Prelate my kindest regards."

"I told you she wouldn't see us," Pasha said on the way out.

Richard hiked his pack up higher on his shoulder. "Well, we gave it our best try. Thanks for indulging me."

He had known that Pasha had been right, that the Prelate wouldn't see them, but he had seen what he had come to see. He had only been interested in knowing the layout of the building and grounds for future reference.

Richard hadn't changed his mind about his captivity, but he had decided to try a different approach for a while. He would bide his time, and see what they could teach him. Nothing would please him more than to be released from the collar without having to hurt anyone.

In the building that housed his room, Gillaume Hall, named after a prophet, Richard had learned, a young man came hesitantly out of the shadows on the lower level, before the wide marble stairs. His head of curly blond hair was cut short at the sides. His hands were stuck into the opposite sleeves of his violet robes. Silver brocade circled the cuffs and neck. He looked smaller than he was because of the way he hunched over.

His head bowed to Pasha while his blue eyes searched for a safe place to settle.

"Blessings on you, Pasha," he said softly. "You look lovely tonight. I pray you are well."

Pasha squinted in thought. "Warren, isn't it?" His head bobbed, surprised that she knew his name. "I'm fine, Warren. Thank you for asking. This is Richard Cypher."

Warren smiled shyly at Richard. "Yes, I saw you before the Sisters, yesterday."

"I suppose you, too, want to know about the mriswith," Pasha said with a sigh.

"Mriswith?"

"Richard killed a mriswith. Isn't that what you wanted to ask about?"

"Really? A mriswith? No . . ." He turned back to Richard. "I wanted to ask if you would care to come down to the vaults sometime, and look at the prophecies with me."

Richard didn't want to embarrass the young man, but he had no interest in prophecies. "I'm honored by the offer, Warren, but I'm afraid that I'm not much good with riddles."

Warren diverted his eyes to the floor. "Of course, I understand. Not many of the others are much interested in the books, either. I just thought that maybe, well, I just thought that since you mentioned that particular prophecy yesterday, that maybe you would want to talk about it. It's a unique piece of work. But I understand. I'm sorry to have bothered you."

Richard frowned. "What prophecy?"

"The one you mentioned at the end. About you being, well"—Warren swallowed—"the bringer of death. It's just that I don't think I've ever met anyone from the prophecies before." He blinked in awe. "Since you are in the prophecies, I thought, well, I thought maybe . . ." His voice trailed off. He looked down at the floor as he started to turn away. "But I understand. I'm sorry to have . . ."

Richard gently caught hold of Warren's arm and turned him back. "Like I said, I'm not very good with riddles. But maybe you could teach me something about them, so I wouldn't be so ignorant. I do like to learn."

Warren's face brightened. His whole body seemed to swell. When he straightened, he was almost as tall as Richard.

"I'd like that. I would really like to talk to you about that prophecy. It's a real conundrum. To this day, the argument over it has never been settled. Maybe with your help . . ."

A broad-shouldered man in plain robes, and wearing a Rada'Han, slipped up silently, took a fistful of Warren's robe at the shoulder, and moved him aside. His eyes were locked on Pasha the whole time. He gave her a smooth smile.

"Good evening, Pasha. It will be dinnertime soon. I've decided to take you." His eyes glided down the length of her and then back up. "If you can get yourself cleaned up. And do something with your hair. You look a mess. You better get to it."

He started to turn away. Pasha put her arm through Richard's.

"I'm afraid I have other plans, Jedidiah."

Jedidiah gave Richard a cursory glance. "What, this country boy? The two of you going to go chop wood, or maybe skin rabbits?"

"You're the one," Richard said. "I remember your voice. You're the one who called down from the balcony, yesterday, asking, 'All by yourself?' "

Jedidiah's condescending smile looked to come easily to him. "An appropriate question, don't you think?"

Pasha lifted her chin. "Richard killed a mriswith."

Jedidiah's eyebrows went up in mock wonder. "Well, how brave of the country boy."

"You've never killed a mriswith," Warren spoke up.

Jedidiah slowly turned a withering glare on Warren. Warren shrank away. "What are you doing above ground, Mole?" He turned back to Pasha. "And did you see him kill it? I would wager he was alone when he claimed to have killed it. He probably found a mriswith that had died of old age, stabbed it with his sword, and then bragged to you, to try to impress you." He redirected a smirk to Richard. "Isn't that about the way it happened, country boy?"

Richard grinned. "You've caught me cold. You have it right."

"As I thought." He twitched a small smile to Pasha. "Come to me later, child, and I'll show you some real magic. A man's magic."

Jedidiah strode away imperiously and disappeared around a corner. Pasha put her fists to her hips.

"Why did you say that! Why did you let him think that!"

"I did it for you," Richard said. "I thought you wanted me to stop causing trouble and act a gentleman."

She folded her arms in a huff. "Well, I do."

Richard turned to Warren, still shrunk back against the marble newel post. "If he does anything to you, Warren, I want you to come tell me. It's me that's the thorn in his pants. If he takes it out on you, you come tell me."

Warren brightened. "Really? Thank you, Richard. But I don't think he would bother with me. And I'll be seeing you down in the vaults, when you have the time." He cast a shy smile at Pasha. "Good night, Pasha. So nice to see you again. You look lovely tonight. Good night."

She smiled. "Good night, Warren." She watched him scurry off down the hall. "What a strange young man. I almost couldn't remember his real name. Everyone calls him the Mole. He almost never comes up from the vaults under the palace."

She glanced sideways to Richard. "Well, you've made a friend tonight who can be of no help to you, and an enemy who can harm you. You stay away from Jedidiah. He's an experienced wizard, close to being released. Until you learn to defend yourself with your Han, he can hurt you. He can kill you."

"I thought we were one big happy family."

"There is a pecking order among wizards. Wizards with the strongest power vie for dominance. It sometimes gets very dangerous. Jedidiah is the pride of the palace, and does not take well to the idea that another may challenge his supremacy."

"I'm hardly a challenge to the power of a wizard."

Pasha lifted an eyebrow. "Jedidiah never killed a mriswith, and everyone knows that."

Feeling decidedly uncomfortable in the red coat Pasha had selected, Richard tried to enjoy the lentil porridge they had prepared especially for him. Pasha wore a stunning dark green dress that did more to reveal her figure than cover it. Richard thought it revealed more of her breasts than was prudent. The young men there as guests of Sisters or their novices did little eating, and a lot of watching. None missed a move Pasha made.

Many of the young men in collars came by and introduced themselves to Richard, saying they wanted to get to know him better. They promised to show him the city and some of its more interesting sights. Pasha's face reddened at the last. Richard

543

asked if they knew where the guards went for ale, and they promised to take him there whenever he wished.

Sisters of every age, shape, and size came to greet him. They all acted as if the events of the night before had never taken place. When Richard asked Pasha why, she said all the Sisters understood the difficulty a young man had in making the adjustment of coming to the palace. She said they were accustomed to such outbursts of emotion, and didn't take them to heart. Richard kept to himself the thought that this time they should.

Some of the Sisters smiled and said they hoped they would be given the opportunity to work with him, and a few scowled and promised they would be seeing him, and promised not to be tolerant of anything less than his best efforts. Richard smiled and said he would give them nothing less than his best. He wondered to himself what he was committing to.

Near the end of the meal, two attractive young women, one in a satiny pink dress, the other in yellow, rushed in, stopping at various tables, speaking in whispers to other young women. They at last came to the corner where Richard and Pasha sat.

One bent close to Pasha. "Have you heard?" Pasha stared with a blank look. "Jedidiah fell down a flight of stairs." Her eyes sparkled with the telling of the gossip. She leaned closer with the titillation of what she had to tell next. "Broke his leg."

Pasha gasped. "No! When? We just saw him a while ago."

The woman giggled and nodded. "Yes, it's true. It just happened, not but a few minutes ago. The healers are with him now. No need for concern; he'll be back to good by morning."

"How did it happen?"

The woman shrugged. "Just clumsy. Tripped on the carpet and tumbled down." She lowered her voice. "He was so furious he flamed the carpet to ash."

"Wizard's fire!" Pasha whispered incredulously. "In the palace? Such a high crime . . ."

"No, no, not wizard's fire, of course not, silly girl. Even Jedidiah is not that brazen. Just simple fire. But it was one of the oldest carpets in the palace. The Sisters are not pleased at his display of temper. They ordered the bone, and the pain, not be mended until morning, as punishment."

Their gossip finally expended, the two young women's eyes and smiles settled on Richard. Pasha introduced them as two friends of hers, Celia and Dulcy, two novices with charges of their own. Richard was polite, complimenting them on their pretty dresses, and the way their hair was curled. Their smiles widened.

Taking his arm when they finally left, Pasha thanked him.

"For what?"

"I've never been permitted to eat with the Sisters, or with the novices who have a young man to train. This is the first time I've ever been to dinner just like I was a Sister. You were pleasant and considerate of everyone; I was so proud to have you with me. And, you look very handsome in those clothes."

"In that dress, I would imagine you could easily get someone better bred than me as a dinner companion." Richard pulled open the fancy shirt collar. "I've never worn a shirt this ruffled, or white. Nor a coat this red. I think I look foolish."

A self-satisfied smile spread on Pasha's face. "I can promise you that Celia and

Dulcy do not think you look foolish. I'm surprised you couldn't see them glowing green. I thought maybe they might decide to sit right down on your lap."

Richard thought that if Celia and Dulcy liked the red coat so much, they could have it, but he kept the thought to himself. "Why doesn't an important wizard like Jedidiah wear fancy clothes?"

"Only beginning wizards wear clothes like this, and are permitted to go into the city. At certain milestones in a wizard's advancement, they change to a particular form of dress. The further a wizard progress, the more modest his dress. That's why Jedidiah wears simple tan robes, because he has nearly reached the end of his training."

"What's the purpose of such an odd rule?"

"To teach humility. Those with the nicest clothes, the most freedom, and unlimited money, are those with the least power. No one respects them for these things. It's meant to teach the young men that mastery comes from within, not from external trappings."

"Then, wearing these things is a demotion for me. I was already wearing humble clothes."

"You are not yet entitled to wear humble robes. You may wear your own clothes occasionally, if you wish. If they were simple robes, though, it would not be allowed.

"The people in the city know a wizard's abilities and power by his dress. No wizard who wears simple robes is permitted to go into the city." She smiled. "Someday, when you have advanced enough, you will be permitted to wear the robes of a wizard."

"I don't like robes. I like the clothes I was wearing."

"When you have your collar off, and leave the palace, you may wear what you wish. Of course, most come to respect the robes of their profession, and wear them the rest of their lives."

Richard changed the subject. "I want to go see Warren. Tell me how to get down there."

"Now? Tonight? Richard, it's been a long day, and I must give you your first lesson yet tonight."

"Just tell me how to get down there. Will Warren be down there this late?"

"I don't know that he is ever seen anywhere else. I think he must sleep on the books. I was surprised to see him up in the palace today. That in itself will be gossip for weeks."

"I don't want him to think I forgot him. Just tell me how to get down there."

"Well," she sighed, "if you insist on going, we will go together. I'm supposed to escort you wherever you go in the Palace of the Prophets. For now, anyway."

Ln the core of the Palace of the Prophets, they began their descent down into the vaults. The stairways on the upper levels were elegant. Lower down, the stairs became utilitarian stone, with their leading edges worn round and smooth. The maidservants he had seen on the upper levels were nowhere to be seen.

Paneled walls gave way to stone. In some places he had to duck under huge beams. Lamps were no longer stationed on the walls, but, instead, widely spaced torches lit the way. Sounds of palace life were left far behind, to be replaced by dead silence. Some of the hallways were wet with leaking water.

"What's in these vaults?" Richard asked.

"The books of prophecy. Books of history, and records of the palace are also kept there."

"Why are they way down here?"

"For protection. Prophecies are dangerous to the untrained mind. All novices study books of prophecy, but only certain Sisters are permitted to read them all, and work with them. Young wizards who show that their gift gives them an aptitude for prophecy are taught by these Sisters.

"There are a few young men who work and study in the vaults, but Warren is to the vaults what Jedidiah is to other forms of magic. Every wizard has a specialty. We will work with you to discover what your innate ability is. Until we can learn this, it will be hard to take your training very far."

"Sister Verna told me something about that. So, what do you think my talent is?"

"Usually, we can tell by the personality of the boy. Some like to work with their hands, and end up making things of magic. Some like to help the sick or injured, and become healers. Things like that. We can usually tell."

"So what about me?"

She glanced briefly in his direction. "None of us has ever seen anyone like you before. We have no idea, yet." Pasha's face brightened. "But we will."

A huge, round stone door, as thick as Richard was tall, stood open in the gloom. Beyond it were rooms carved from the bedrock that the palace sat atop. Lamps did little to brighten the place. There were a number of long, timeworn tables with books and papers scattered about on them, and shelves in rows that extended into the distance to each side. Two women sat at the tables, taking notes as they read by the light of candles set close.

One of them peered up and addressed Pasha. "What are you doing down here, child?"

Pasha curtsied. "We came to see Warren, Sister."

"Warren? Why?"

Just then, Warren came scurrying out of the darkness. "It's all right, Sister Becky. I asked them to come."

"Well, the next time, please let someone know in advance."

"Yes, Sister, I will."

Warren burrowed between the two of them and took their arms, leading them into the shelves. When he realized he was touching Pasha he jerked his hand away and turned red.

"You look . . . dazzling, Pasha."

"Why, thank you, Mole." She flushed red herself. She put a hand to his shoulder. "I'm sorry, Warren . . . I didn't mean anything by that. I meant to call you Warren."

He smiled. "It's all right, Pasha. I know people call me the Mole. They think it a pejorative, but I take it as a compliment. You see, a mole can find its way in the dark, where others are blind. That is much like what I do; I find the way where others see nothing."

Pasha sighed in relief. "I'm glad, Warren. Mole, did you hear that Jedidiah fell down a flight of stairs and broke his leg?"

"Really?" He searched her eyes. "Maybe the Creator was trying to teach him that when you hold your nose so high in the air, you can't see where you are going."

"I don't think Jedidiah paid any heed to the Creator's lessons," Pasha said. "I heard tell that he was so angry he burned a prized carpet to ash."

Warren still held her eyes. "You are the one who should be angry, not Jedidiah. He said cruel things to you. No one should say cruel things to you."

"He is usually kind to me, but I admit, I did look a mess."

"Some of these books look a mess to people, but it is what's inside that matters, not the dust on their covers."

Pasha blushed. "Why, thank you, Mole . . . I think."

Warren looked to Richard. "I didn't know if you would really come. Most people say they will, but they never do. I'm so pleased you did. Come this way. Pasha, I'm afraid you must wait here."

"What!" She leaned forward, and Richard thought that maybe her breasts might spill out if she didn't straighten up. "I'm going, too."

Warren's eyes widened. "But I must take him into one of the back rooms. You are a novice. Novices are not allowed."

She smiled warmly as she did straighten up. "Mole, if a novice is not allowed, how could a new student be allowed?"

Warren's eyes narrowed. "He is in the prophecies. If the prophets saw fit to write about him, they could hardly intend he not see it."

Warren seemed considerably more confident down here in his element than he had been up in the palace. He stood his ground with confidence. Pasha rubbed his shoulder. He glanced down at the hand.

"Warren, you're the Mole; you show others the way. I'm the one in charge of Richard; I show him the way. I would be neglecting my duty if I allowed him to go somewhere without me this soon. I'm sure you can make an exception for me. Can't you, Warren? It's to help Richard, to help understand the prophecy and how he is to serve the Creator. Isn't that what's important?"

Warren finally took his eyes from her and told them to wait. He went off to the two Sisters and spoke with them in hushed tones. He finally came back wearing a smile.

"Sister Becky said it would be permitted. I told her you understand a bit of High D'Haran. In case she asks, say you do."

"What's High D'Haran? Warren, you want me to lie to a Sister!"

"I'm sure she will not ask." Warren turned his face away. "I told the lie for you, Pasha, so you would not have to."

She leaned closer to him. "Warren, if you're caught telling lies about such things, you know what they will do."

He gave her a small, haunted smile. "I know."

"What will they do?" Richard asked, suddenly suspicious.

Warren waved impatiently. "Never mind. You two come along."

They had to hurry after him as he scurried off into the darkness. They went past rows of shelves placed tight together, coming at last to a solid wall of rock. Warren put his hand to a metal plate, and part of the wall moved away, revealing another chamber beyond. Inside the small room sat a table and maybe a dozen rows of shelves. Four lamps made it seem bright inside, by comparison.

Inside, Warren touched another plate and the section of wall slid closed, entombing them in stone and silence. He pulled out a chair for Pasha and had Richard sit to her right. Finally, he pulled a leatherbound book from the shelves and carefully placed it before Richard.

"Please don't touch it," Warren said. "It's very old and fragile. Of late, it has been getting more use than usual. Let me turn the pages."

"Who's been using it?" Richard asked.

"The Prelate." A smile twitched across Warren's lips. "Whenever she is to come down here, her two big guards come first and make everyone leave. They clear the vaults, so the Prelate can have the place to herself, and people won't know what she reads."

"Her big guards?" Pasha asked. "You mean the two Sisters in her outer office?"

"Yes," Warren said. "Sister Ulicia, and Sister Finella."

"We saw them today," Richard said. "They didn't look that big to me."

Warren lowered his voice meaningfully. "If you ever cross them, you will think otherwise. They will seem very big, indeed."

Richard took pause at Warren's expression. "If the place is cleared out, how do you know she has been reading this book?"

"I know." He turned to the book on the table. "I know. She has been doing most of her reading in this room, of late. I live with these books. When someone touches them, I can tell. You see this smudge in the dust? It's not mine. It's the Prelate's."

Warren carefully lifted open the cover and, with both hands giving support, turned the yellowed pages. Richard didn't recognize any of the words, or some of the letters for that matter. On one of the pages that Warren flipped, Richard thought he recognized something: a drawing. It sparked a deep memory. Warren flipped over more pages, finally stopping. He leaned over Richard's shoulder, pointing.

"This is the prophecy you spoke of." Warren moved around to the right side of the table. "This is the original, in the prophet's own hand. Few have ever seen it. Do you understand High D'Haran?"

"No. It just looks like scribbling to me." Richard glanced over the meaningless writing. "You said there was argument over its meaning."

Warren's eyes had an intense gleam. "There is. You see, this is a very old prophecy, perhaps as old as the palace, maybe older. This is the original prophecy.

548

It's in High D'Haran, as is everything in this room. Very few people understand High D'Haran."

Richard nodded. "So people have only read the translations, and there is reason to believe that those translations may not be accurate."

"You understand," Warren whispered. His movements became more lively. "Yes, yes, you see the problem. Most don't. Most think one thing in one language must mean a certain thing in another. In order to complete the translation, they settle on an interpretation that fits their view of the meaning, but in so doing, they create a conspectus that may or may not be the meaning of the prophecy."

"But that doesn't take into account possible different meanings," Richard said. "So when they translate it, they give it only one version. They can't translate its ambiguity."

Warren thrust himself forward in excitement. "Yes! You have it! That's what they can't understand, and so they argue over the various translations, as if there is a right way and a wrong way to do it. But this is High D'Haran . . ."

Warren's words trailed off. Richard was staring at the page. The images there were drawing him in. It was almost as if they were murmuring to him. He had never seen such words before, but somehow they resonated with something deep within him.

His hand slowly reached out, drawn to one of the words. His finger came to rest on it.

"This one," Richard whispered, as if from a trance. The strokes of the letters seemed to lift from the page, as if alive, and coil around his finger, the dark lines caressing, fondling, with intimate familiarity. Before his eyes, too, floated the image of the Sword of Truth.

Warren's white face came up from the book. "*Drauka*," he whispered. "That's the word that is the center of the controversy. *Fuer grissa ost drauka*—the bringer of death."

Pasha leaned over. "So what's the controversy? You mean those words can be translated differently?"

Warren made a vague gesture with his hand. "Well, yes, and no. That's the literal translation of the words. It's their meaning that is in dispute."

Richard pulled his hand back. He banished the image of the sword. "Death. It has different meanings."

Warren practically laid on the table as he leaned over. "Yes! You understand!"

"Death is plain as pie," Pasha said.

Warren straightened and rubbed his hands together. "No, Pasha. Not in High D'Haran. The weapon the Sisters carry, the dacra, its name comes from this word. *Drauka* means death, as in dead, like if I were to say 'the mriswith Richard killed is dead.' *Drauka*. Dead. But it has other meanings, too. *Drauka* also is a word that represents the souls of the dead."

Pasha leaned forward with a frown. "Are you saying that *drauka*, in that sense, can make it mean 'the bringer of souls'?"

"No." Richard said. He whispered the second meaning of the word. "Spirits. The bringer of spirits."

"Yes," Warren said in a quiet voice. "That is the second interpretation."

"How many of these different meanings to *drauka* are there?" Pasha asked.

*Three,* Richard thought.

"Three," Warren said.

Richard knew the third. "The underworld," he whispered as he stared at the word *drauka* on the page. "The place of the dead. That's the third meaning of *drauka*."

Pale as a spirit, Warren leaned toward him. "But you don't understand D'Haran?" Richard slowly shook his head, his eyes fixed on the page. Warren's tongue darted out to wet his lips. "Please tell me you don't have D'Haran blood."

"My father was Darken Rahl," Richard said softly. "He was the wizard who ruled D'Hara, and before him, my grandfather, Panis."

"Dear Creator," Warren whispered.

Pasha put a hand to Richard's arm as she leaned toward them both. "Underworld? How could it mean underworld?"

"Because," Warren said, "the underworld is the world of the dead."

Her brow knit tighter. "But how could it mean 'the bringer of the underworld'? How can you bring the underworld?"

Richard stared blankly ahead. "You tear the veil."

The silence echoed around the stone room. Pasha looked from one face to the other. She finally broke the silence.

"But I was taught that for a foreign word in a prophecy that had different shades of meaning, you had only to interpret it in context. It should be a simple matter of seeing how it is used to decipher its meaning."

Warren lifted an eyebrow. "That's what the argument is about. You see, in this prophecy, it speaks of things that could pertain to each of the three possible meanings of the word *drauka*. Depending on which meaning was intended, it changes the meaning of the prophecy. That is why it cannot be interpreted with surety. It's like a dog chasing his tail. The more you try, the more you just end up going round and round.

"This is why I'm so anxious to know the intended meaning of the word *drauka*. If I could know that, then I might be able to decipher the rest of the prophecy accurately for the first time. I would be the first in three thousand years to understand it."

Richard pushed his chair away from the table. "Well, as I said, I'm not very good with riddles." He forced himself to smile. "But I promise to think on it."

Warren brightened. "Would you? I would be so appreciative if you would be able to help me."

Richard squeezed Warren's shoulder. "You have my word."

Pasha rose. "Well, I guess we better get to Richard's lesson. It's getting late."

"Thank you both for coming. I rarely have visitors."

Pasha leading, the three of them went toward the door.

As she passed through the doorway, Richard slapped his hand to the metal plate on the wall.

The door grated closed. Pasha beat her fists to the stone, as the slit had become too small for her to come back through. She shouted for them to open the door. As the stone sealed closed, her words were cut off, leaving Richard and Warren in silence.

Warren stared at the metal plate. "How did you do that? You are just a beginning wizard. You should not be able to effect a shield with your Han for a very long time yet."

Richard didn't have an answer for the question, and so he ignored it. "Tell me what you meant about knowing what the Sisters would do to you if they caught you telling that kind of lie."

Warren's hand went to his collar. "Well, they would hurt me."

"You mean they would use the collar's magic to give you pain?"

Warren nodded as he took a knot of his robes in his fists.

"Do they do that often? Give us pain with the collar?"

Warren twisted the knot of robe. "No, not often. But to be a wizard, you must pass a test of pain. They come from time to time and give you pain with the Rada'Han, to see if you have learned enough to pass the test of pain."

"And how do you pass the test?"

"Well, I can only imagine that when you can endure the pain without begging them to stop, you pass. They never tell me what must be done to pass." His face had gone ashen. "I've never been able to keep from begging them to stop. Once you learn to endure what they give, they give more."

"I thought it might be something like that. Thanks for telling me." Richard stroked his beard. "Warren, I need your help."

Warren lifted the sleeve of his robes and wiped it at his wet eyes. "What help can I give?"

"You said there are prophecies about me. I want you to study everything about me you can find. And about the Towers of Perdition, the Valley of the Lost. I also need to know everything I can about the veil." Richard pointed at the book on the table. "There was a drawing a few pages before you stopped on the prophecy. It was a teardrop shape. Do you know what it is?"

Warren went to the book and turned the pages back. "This?"

"Yes. That's it." He remembered seeing it around Rachel's neck, in his vision of her and Chase in the Valley of the Lost. An image of Zedd came into Richard's mind. His heart thumped faster. "That looks like the thing I saw. What is it?"

Warren gave him a puzzled look. "The Stone of Tears. What do you mean you saw it?"

"What is the Stone of Tears?"

"Well, I'm not sure. I'd have to study about it, but I think it might have something to do with the veil, if *drauka* could be interpreted to have something to do with the underworld. What do you mean you saw it?"

Richard ignored the question for a second time. "Warren, I also need to know about the Stone of Tears, and everything you can find about the people who used to live in the Valley of the Lost. The Baka Ban Mana. Their name means 'those without masters.' And about one they call the *Caharin*."

Warren stared dumbly at him. "This is all a lot of work."

"Will you help me, Warren?"

Warren looked down, picking at his robes. "On a condition. I never get out of this place. Not that I don't like working with the prophecies, you understand, but people think that I have no interest in anything else. I'd like to see the country around the palace—the woods, the hills."

He twisted his fingers together. "I'm afraid of big places. The sky is so big. That's the other reason I stay down here, because it feels safe to me. But I'm sick of living like a mole. I would like to try going outside and seeing it. Would you, well, show me the countryside? You look to me like someone familiar with the out-of-doors. I think I would feel safe if you went with me."

Richard smiled warmly. "You've come to the right person, Warren. I was a woods guide, before all this started. I don't know all the country around the palace yet, but I surely intend to. I'd really enjoy guiding you around. It would be just like old times."

Warren's expression brightened. "Thank you, Richard. I look forward to seeing open places. I need some adventure in my life. I'll start right away on the things you want, but the Sisters give me work, so I must search when I can find the time. And I'm afraid that I must be honest; it will take a long time. There are thousands of volumes here. It will take months, just to get a good start."

"Warren, this may be the most important thing you ever studied. You may be able to save time if you start by reading everything the Prelate has been reading."

A sly smile came to Warren's lips. "I thought you said you weren't good with riddles. That is what I was thinking." His smile turned to a concerned frown. "Why do you want to know these things?"

Richard studied the other's blue eyes for a long moment. "I am *fuer grissa ost drauka*. Warren, I know what it means."

Warren clutched his fingers to the sleeve of Richard's red coat. "You know? You know which is the correct translation?" His fingers trembled. "Would you tell me?"

"If you promise not to tell anyone else, for now." Warren nodded eagerly. "No one has been able to figure out which one of the three is the true translation because in trying to justify one, they invalidate the whole." Warren frowned. Richard leaned toward him. "They are all true, Warren."

"What?" he whispered. "How can that be?"

"I have killed people with this sword. I am the bringer of death in that sense. That is the first meaning of *drauka*.

"In order to prevail against otherwise impossible odds, such as defeating the mriswith, I use the sword's magic to bring forth the spirits of those who have used it before me. I have called the dead forth, called the past into the present. In that way, I am the bringer of spirits. That is the second meaning of *drauka*.

"As for the third meaning, bringing forth the underworld, I have reason to believe that I may have somehow torn the veil. That is the third meaning of *drauka*."

Warren gasped.

"It's very important that you find out the information I asked you about. I don't think I have a lot of time."

Warren nodded. "I'll try. But I think you put too much faith in me."

Richard lifted an eyebrow. "I have faith in a man able to break Jedidiah's leg."

"I did nothing to Jedidiah. Jedidiah is a powerful wizard. I would never dare to oppose one of his powers."

"Oh, come on, Warren. There are ashes of the burned carpet on the shoulder of your robe."

Warren brushed frantically at his shoulder. "There is no ash there. I see no ash."

Richard waited for Warren's eyes to come up. "Then why are you brushing at your robes?"

"Well, I . . . I was . . . I just . . ."

Richard put a reassuring hand on Warren's back. "It's all right, Warren. I'm a believer in justice. I think Jedidiah got what he deserved. I won't tell anyone. And you must not tell anyone about any of this."

"I must warn you, Richard, you did a very dangerous thing yesterday when you told all the Sisters that you were the bringer of death. That is a well-known, and hotly debated, prophecy. There are Sisters who believe it means you are one who kills. They will try to comfort you. There are others who think it means you will bring forth the dead, call the spirits. They will want to study you." He leaned a little closer. "There are others who think it means you will tear the veil, and bring the Nameless One to swallow us all. They might try to kill you."

"I know, Warren."

"Then why would you let them know you are the one in the prophecy?"

"Because I am *fuer grissa ost drauka*. When the time comes, I will kill any of them I must in order to get this collar off. I had to give them fair warning first, give them the chance to live."

Warren touched his fingers to his lower lip. "But you wouldn't hurt Pasha. Not Pasha."

"I hope to hurt no one, Warren. Maybe with the information you help me with, I won't have to hurt anyone. I hate being *fuer grissa ost drauka*, but that is who I am."

Warren's eyes teared. "Please, you wouldn't hurt Pasha."

"Warren, I like her. I think she is a lovely person, inside, like you said. I only kill to protect my life, or the lives of innocent people. I don't believe Pasha would ever give me cause, but you must understand that if I am right, and the veil is torn, then more is at stake than any one person's life. Mine, yours, or Pasha's."

Warren nodded. "I have read the prophecies. I understand. I will search for the things you need."

Richard tried to reassure him with a warm smile. "It will be all right, Warren. I'm the Seeker; I'll do my best. I don't want to harm anyone."

"Seeker? What is the Seeker?"

Richard slapped his hand to the metal plate. "I'll tell you about it later."

Warren glanced down at the plate as the door slid opened. "How are you able to do that?"

Pasha was standing calmly, waiting, her face making a good effort at not showing her anger.

"And just what was that all about?"

Richard stepped through the doorway. "Boy talk."

Pasha stopped him with a hand to his arm. "What do you mean, boy talk?"

Richard looked into her warm brown eyes. "I was twisting Warren's arm, making him tell me about the test of pain. You failed to mention it, so I had to ask him about it. Or were you planning on waiting until you came to do it, before you told me?"

Pasha rubbed her bare arms, as if to warm them. "I do not do that, Richard. I'm only a novice. Full Sisters must do it."

"Why didn't you tell me about it?"

Tears welled up in her eyes. "I don't like to see people hurt. I didn't want to frighten you about what may not come for a long time. Sometimes the waiting can be worse than the actual experience. I didn't want you to have to wait in fear."

"Oh." Richard let out a long breath. "Well, I guess that's a good reason. I apologize, Pasha, for what I was thinking of you."

She forced a smile. "Shall we go start your lessons?"

Above ground again, they passed down halls and through several buildings until they finally reached Gillaume Hall, where his room was. The fabric of Pasha's dress made a swishing sound as they climbed the wide marble stairway. The walls and columns were a matching tan, variegated marble.

It was a beautiful place with elegant rooms, but it was not as impressive as the

People's Palace, in D'Hara. Before he had seen that magnificent edifice, he would have been astonished by the opulence of this place. Now, he simply noted its layout in reference to everything else. Upstairs, as they went down another wide, carpeted hall, he saw several other young men wearing Rada'Han. At last they reached his room.

Richard caught her wrist as she reached for the door handle. She looked up in puzzlement.

"There's someone inside," he said.

I    t is my job to watch over you," Pasha said.

She used her Han, breaking his hold on her wrist and throwing him aside as if with an invisible hand, and then charged through the door. Richard rolled, finishing on his feet, drew his sword, and flew in after her. Only the small flames from the hearth gave light to the otherwise dark room. They both stumbled to a halt in the near darkness.

A voice came from a chair beside the fire. "Expecting a mriswith, Richard?"

"Sister Verna!" Richard slid his sword back into its scabbard. "What are you doing here?"

She rose to her feet and swept her hand in the direction of a lamp, bringing the wick to flame. "I didn't know if you heard." Her face was unreadable. "I'm once again a Sister of the Light."

"Really?" Richard said. "That's great news."

Sister Verna clasped her hands in a relaxed manner. "Since I'm a Sister, again, I wanted to come and speak privately to you for a moment." She glanced to Pasha. "About some unfinished business Richard and I have."

Pasha looked from the Sister to Richard. "Well, I guess this dress is, well, not the most comfortable thing to give lessons in. Why don't I go change." She curtsied to Sister Verna. "Good night, Sister. I'm so happy for you; you should be a Sister. And Richard, thank you for being such a gentleman tonight. I will return after I change."

Richard stood facing the door once he had closed it behind Pasha.

"Gentleman." Sister Verna said. "I'm delighted to hear it, Richard. I would also like to thank you, for my being returned to Sister. Sister Maren told me what happened."

Richard laughed as he turned to her. "You've been around me too long, Sister. But you need more practice at telling lies; you're not yet totally convincing."

She couldn't keep a small smile from coming to her lips. "Well, Sister Maren told me that she had prayed for guidance, and decided I would serve the Creator best if I were a Sister, in view of my experience." She lifted an eyebrow. "Poor Sister Maren; lying seems to have become infectious since you arrived here."

He shrugged. "Sister Maren did what was right. I think your Creator would be pleased with the outcome."

"I heard that you killed a mriswith. News spreads through the palace like a blaze through dry grass."

Richard walked to the hearth. He leaned on the dark granite mantle and stared into the flames. "Well, I had no choice."

Sister Verna stroked a hand tenderly down his hair. "Are you all right, Richard? How are you doing?"

"I'm fine." Richard pulled the baldric over his head and set it and the sword aside. He tossed the red coat on a chair. "I'd be better if I didn't have to wear these silly clothes. But I guess it's a small price to pay for peace. For now. What did you want talk to me about, Sister?"

"I don't know what you did, how you got me returned to Sister, but thank you, Richard. Does this mean you would like for us to be friends?"

"Only if you will take this collar off me." She looked away from his eyes. "Someday, Sister, you will have to make your choice. I hope when the time comes, you choose to be on my side. After all we've been through, I would hate to have to kill you, but you know what I am capable of. You knew what my answer would be; surely, you came here for more than that."

"I have told you before how you are using your Han without knowing what you are doing, remember?"

"Yes, but I don't think I'm using my Han."

She lifted an eyebrow. "Richard, you killed a mriswith. As far as I know, that has not been done in the last three thousand years. You had to use your Han to do that."

"No, Sister, I used the magic of the sword to kill it."

"Richard, I have observed you, and learned a little about both you and your sword. The reason no one has ever been able to kill a mriswith is because they never knew it was coming. Even the Han of Sisters and wizards could not sense its approach. Your sword may have killed the mriswith, but your Han let you know it was coming. You are calling on your gift, but without control."

Richard was tired. He didn't feel like arguing, so he didn't. He flopped into a plush chair. He remembered the way he had seen the mriswith in his mind, had seen it coming. "I don't understand what I'm doing, Sister. The mriswith came, and I protected myself."

She sat in a chair opposite. "Look at it this way, Richard; you killed a beast as deadly as anything walking the land, yet that little girl with the big brown eyes, and about as much power compared to you as a sparrow compared to a hawk, just used her Han to throw you down the hall. I hope you will study hard so you may learn to control your Han. You need to get it under control."

She looked at him intently. "Why did you go into the Hagen Woods, after I told you that they are dangerous? The real reason. Not the justification, but the deep-down-inside reason. Please tell me the truth, Richard."

Richard stretched back, looking up at the ceiling. He finally conceded with a nod. "It was like something drew me in. It was a need. A hunger. It was like I needed to pound my fist against a wall, and that was the way to do it."

He thought she might launch into a lecture, but she didn't. Her tone was sympathetic.

"Richard, I've been talking to a few friends of mine. None of us knows everything about the magic of the palace, and especially the Hagen Woods, but there is reason to believe that the Hagen Woods were placed there specifically for certain wizards."

Richard studied her quiet expression, the creases in her face, the sincerity in her eyes. "Are you saying, Sister, that if I need to pound my fist against the wall, maybe I should do so?"

She gave a slight lift to her eyebrows. "The Creator gave us hunger so we would eat, because eating is necessary."

"What would be the purpose of a hunger like mine?"

She shook her head. "I don't know. For a second time in as many days, the Prelate has declined to grant me an audience. But I'm going to try to find some answers. In the meantime, just please don't let the sun set on you in the Hagen Woods."

"Is this what you came to tell me, Sister?"

She looked away, and paused, rubbing her forehead with two fingers. She looked uncertain. He had never seen her like this. "Richard, there are things going on that I don't understand, and they are connected to you; events are not happening as they should." She saw his curious look. "I can't talk about them just yet."

She cleared her throat. "Richard, I don't want you to trust every one of the Sisters."

Richard lifted an eyebrow. "Sister, I trust none of you."

That brought a short-lived smile to her face. "For now, that would be best. That was what I wanted to tell you. I'm going to find the answers, but for now, well, let's just say that I know you will do as you must to stay safe."

After Sister Verna left, Richard thought about what she had said, and about the things Warren had told him. Mostly, he thought about the Stone of Tears.

It puzzled him that the magic in the Valley of the Lost would present him with a vision of something he had never seen before, and put it around Rachel's neck. The other visions seemed to have been anchored in his longings and fears. Maybe because he missed seeing his friend, Chase, he saw the vision of Rachel, too; she would be with Chase. But why would the vision put around her neck something he had never seen before, which turned out to look like a drawing in a book?

Maybe they weren't the same thing. He told himself they couldn't be, but an uneasy feeling inside said otherwise.

As much as he missed Chase and Rachel, it was the stone around Rachel's neck that had captured his attention. It was as if Rachel were bringing it to him for Zedd, and Zedd had been there with him, urging him to take the stone.

Pasha's knock at the door brought him out of his brooding. She was wearing a plain, brownish gray dress with small, pink cloth buttons up the front, all the way up to her neck. Though it didn't show the expanse of flesh the green dress had, it was tailored so that it revealed nearly every detail of her shape. The fact that it covered everything only made what it covered all that much more intriguing. The color somehow brought out the softness of her brown hair.

Pasha sat cross-legged on the floor, on the blue and yellow carpet in front of the fireplace. She draped her dress carefully over her knees and then looked up.

"Here. Sit like me, in front of me."

Richard sat on the floor and folded his legs. She motioned him to come closer until their knees touched. She took his hands and held them lightly as they rested across both their knees.

"Sister Verna didn't do this when I practiced."

"That was because the Rada'Han had to be within the circle of influence of the magic of the palace before we could practice in this way. Until now, when you have practiced touching your Han, it has been alone. Most of the time from now on, I, or a Sister, will use our Han to assist you." She smiled. "It will help you progress faster, Richard."

"All right. What do you want me to do?"

"She told you how to try to reach your Han? How to concentrate on finding that place within yourself?" Richard nodded. "That is what I want you to do. While you search for that place, I will use my Han, through the Rada'Han, to try to guide you."

Richard squirmed a little, getting more comfortable. Pasha took back a hand and fanned her face.

"This dress seems so warm, after wearing the other."

She unbuttoned the top five buttons of her dress and then took his hand up again. Richard glanced at the fire, to check the logs, so he would know how long it had been when he opened his eyes again. He could never seem to judge the time while he searched for his Han. It always seemed like mere minutes, but it was usually at least an hour.

Richard closed his eyes. He brought forth the image of the Sword of Truth on a plain background. As the quiet settled over him, as he sought the peace within, his breathing slowed. He took a long breath, and then let himself sink into the calm center.

He was aware of Pasha's hands holding his, of her knees touching his, and of her even breathing coming into harmony with his. It felt good to have her holding his hands. He didn't feel isolated the way he had always felt before. He didn't know if she really was using the magic of his collar to go with him, but he felt himself spiraling deeper than he had before.

He drifted in the timeless place without thinking, without effort or worry. Whatever his Han was, he didn't see or feel anything he hadn't seen or felt before. Other than feeling more relaxed than before, and the comforting feeling of having Pasha with him, it was no different. He was dimly aware of his body starting to feel cramped, and of the warmth from the fire. The cold steel of the sword seemed to be a core of ice in the heat.

At last, he opened his eyes. Pasha opened her eyes with him. Richard glanced to the fire. The logs had been reduced to glowing coals. Two hours, he judged.

A trickle of sweat ran down Pasha's neck. "My, but it's warm tonight."

She unbuttoned buttons. A lot of buttons. More of her was showing than had shown in the green dress. Richard made himself look back up into her soft eyes. Pasha gave him a small, self-assured smile.

"I didn't feel anything," Richard said. "I didn't sense my Han. Although, I don't know what it is I'm supposed to sense."

"I didn't, either, and I should have. Strange." She sighed to herself with a puzzled expression. Her face brightened. "But it takes practice. Did you feel my Han? Was it any help?"

"No," he admitted. "I didn't feel anything."

She made a little quirk with her mouth as she frowned. "You didn't feel anything of me?" He shook his head. "Well, close your eyes and try again."

It was late, and Richard didn't want to practice anymore; it was tiring. But he decided to do as she wished. He closed his eyes. He concentrated on trying to bring back the sword.

Suddenly he felt Pasha's full lips against his. His eyes opened as she pressed against him. Her eyes were closed, her brow wrinkled. She grasped his face with her hands.

Richard gripped her shoulders and pushed her away. She opened her eyes and licked her lips.

She smiled coyly. "Did you feel that?"

"I felt it."

She hooked an arm around his neck. "Apparently, not enough."

Richard gently put a hand against her as she tried to lean in. He didn't want to embarrass her, so he tried to keep his voice pleasant. "Pasha, don't."

She rubbed her free hand around on his stomach. "It's late. No one will be around. If it will make you feel more comfortable, I'll shield the door. You shouldn't worry."

"I'm not worried. I just . . . don't want to."

She looked a bit hurt. "You do not think I am pretty enough?"

Richard didn't want to offend her, and he didn't want to make her angry. But he didn't want to encourage her, either.

"It's not that, Pasha. You're very attractive. It's just that . . ."

She unbuttoned another little button. Richard reached out and took ahold of her hand to stop her. He realized the situation was becoming hazardous. She was his teacher. If he angered or humiliated her, things could become dangerously complicated. He had things to do, and couldn't afford to turn her antagonistic.

She pulled her dress up her legs and put his hand against her thigh. "You like this better?" she asked in a breathy voice.

Richard froze at the firm, sensual feel of her flesh. He remembered what Sister Verna had said, that he would soon find another pair of pretty legs. These were certainly that, and Pasha was leaving precious little to the imagination. He pulled his hand away. "Pasha, you don't understand. I think you're a beautiful young woman. . . ."

Her eyes fixed on his face as she ran her fingers down his beard. "I think you're the most handsome man I've ever seen."

"No, you don't. . . ."

"I love your beard. Don't ever cut it off. I think a wizard should have a beard."

Richard remembered the time Zedd had used Additive Magic to grow a beard and teach him a lesson, and then had shaved it off, explaining he couldn't make it vanish with magic because that would take Subtractive Magic, and wizards didn't have Subtractive Magic. Subtractive Magic was of the underworld.

He caught her wrist and pulled her hand away from his face. To Richard, his beard was a symbol of his captivity. It meant he was a prisoner. Prisoners don't shave, that was what he had told Sister Verna. But he didn't think now was the time to explain that to Pasha.

She kissed his neck. Somehow, he was unable to stop her. Her lips were so soft, and he could hear her insistent breath close to his ear. It felt as if the kiss went all the way through him, down to his toes, something like the feeling he had had when she had put her hands to his Rada'Han. The tingling numbed his brain. Inside, he groaned. His resistance was being dissolved by her kisses. . . .

When he had been held in a collar by Denna, he had had no choice—not even death could rescue him from whatever Denna wanted—but he still felt shame for what he had done.

He was in a collar again, and Pasha was using some sort of magic on him, but he knew that this time he had a choice in the matter. He forced himself to hunch his head and get her lips from him. He gently pushed her back.

"Pasha, please . . ."

She straightened a little. "What's her name, this girl you love?"

Richard didn't want to tell her Kahlan's name. It was his life. It was private. These people were his captors, not his friends. "That's not important. That's not the issue."

"What does she have that I don't? Is she prettier than me?"

You are a girl, Richard thought, and she is a woman. But he couldn't say that. You are a pretty candle, he thought, and Kahlan is the sunrise. But he couldn't say that either.

If he spurned Pasha, he would have war on his hands. He had to get out of this without making her feel resentful or rejected.

"Pasha, I am honored, I'm flattered, I really am, but you have only known me a day. We've really just met."

"Richard, the Creator gives us urges, and pleasure from acting on them, so we will come to know His beauty through His creation. There is nothing wrong with this. It is a beautiful thing."

"He also gave us a mind to decide what is right and what is wrong."

Her chin lifted just a little. "Right, and wrong? If she loved you, she would be with you; she wouldn't have let you go. That's what is wrong. She thinks you aren't good enough for her. She must wish to be free of you; if she cared she would have kept you with her. She's gone. I'm here and I care. I would fight to keep you. Did she fight?"

Richard's mouth opened, but no words came through the hurt. He felt as if his will to go on had drained right out of him, leaving nothing but a hollow, dead shell.

Pasha reached out and touched his cheek. "You'll see that I care, Richard. I care more than she does. You'll see. It's right if a person cares as I do." Her brow creased in worry. "Unless you think I'm unattractive. Is that it? You've seen many women, and you think that in comparison, I'm ugly?"

Richard cupped a hand to the side of her face. "Pasha . . . you are ravishing. It's not that." He swallowed the dryness, trying to make his words sound sincere. "Pasha, could you just give me some time? It's simply too soon. Can you understand? Could you really care for a man who would forget his feelings so easily? Could you just give me some time?"

She wrapped her arms around him and laid her head against his chest. "I knew yesterday, when you held me so tenderly, that it was another sign that the Creator had sent you to me. I knew then that I would never want another. Since I'll be yours forever, I can wait. We have almost nothing but time. We have all the time you could possibly want. You'll see that I'm the one for you. You just tell me when you are ready, and I'll be yours."

Richard sighed as he closed the door behind her. He leaned his back against the door, thinking. He didn't like deceiving Pasha, letting her think that with time he could come to feel differently about her, but he had had to do something. How shallow could Pasha's understanding of people be, for her to think that one could win love by invoking lust?

He took out the lock of Kahlan's hair, spinning it in his fingers as he watched it. The things Pasha had said about Kahlan not fighting for him made him angry.

560

Pasha could never know the struggles he and Kahlan had been through; the hardships they had had to overcome, the anguish they had suffered together, the battles they had fought together. Pasha probably couldn't conceive of a woman of Kahlan's intelligence, strength, and courage.

Kahlan had indeed fought for him. She had more than once selflessly risked her life for him. What could Pasha know of the terrors Kahlan had bravely faced, and conquered? Pasha wasn't woman enough to serve Kahlan tea.

He stuffed the lock of hair back into his pocket. He forced his thoughts of Kahlan from his mind. He couldn't endure the pain. He had other things to do.

Going into the bedroom, he positioned the ash-framed standing mirror, and then retrieved his pack from the corner. Richard pulled out the black mriswith cape. He threw it around his shoulders, and stood inspecting his image in the mirror.

It looked like a normal cape. He thought it quite handsome, actually. The cut and length was right; the mriswith had been about his size. The heavy fabric was inky black, almost as black as a night stone that Adie had given him to help him across the pass, almost as black as the boxes of Orden. Almost as black as eternal death.

But the pleasing cut of the cape was not what intrigued him.

Richard moved back against the light-brownish wall. He pulled the hood up, cowling it around his face, and drew the cape closed. As he watched his image in the mirror, he concentrated on the wall he was standing against.

In the span of a breath, his image vanished.

The cape had become the color of the wall he stood against, to such a degree that only if he stared, focusing on the edges of the cape, could he distinguish himself standing against the wall. If he moved, it was only slightly easier to pick out his shape against the wall. Though his face was exposed, somehow the magic of the cape, or possibly the cape's magic along with his own, served to mask it, too, to enfold it somehow into the concealing color.

This explained why the mriswith appeared to be different colors.

Richard moved objects behind himself, to discover what effect they had. He stood in front of the wall and partly in front of a chair with his red coat draped over it. The cape produced a blotch of red that did a good job of mimicking the color and shape behind. Though it wasn't as flawless as when he stood before a plain wall, it would still be easy to miss him if he stood still.

Movement would distort the complicated images, as the cape changed to accommodate new conditions, though it still fooled the eye into missing him, but if he stood still, he virtually vanished in front of anything. The effect, at times, could be dizzying to watch. When he stopped concentrating, the cape would return to black.

This, he thought as he looked at himself in the mirror standing in a simple black cape, was going to be useful.

As the weeks passed, Richard was constantly busy.

He remembered that Kahlan and Zedd had told him that there were no wizards with the gift left in the Midlands. Small wonder; they seemed to all be at the Palace of the Prophets. There were well over a hundred boys and young men at the palace. From what Richard could discover, a goodly number of the older ones, at least, were from the Midlands, with some even from D'Hara.

Killing a mriswith had earned Richard celebrity status among the younger boys. Two of them, Kipp and Hersh, were the most persistent. They followed him around, begging to hear stories of his adventures. At times they exhibited the maturity, almost wisdom, of old men. At other times they, like all boys, seemed interested in nothing more than mischief.

The object of this mischief was usually a Sister. The boys never seemed to tire of thinking up new tricks to pull on them. Most of the pranks appeared to involve either water, mud, or reptiles. The Sisters only occasionally erupted in anger when caught up in the boys' antics, and even then, they quickly forgave them. As far as Richard could tell, the boys never earned more than a stern lecture.

In the beginning, the young boys thought to number Richard among their targets. Richard had things to do, and had no time or patience for it. When the boys learned that Richard was neither shy nor slow with discipline, they quickly moved on to other targets with their buckets of water.

The fact that Richard set limits made Kipp and Hersh like him all the more. They seemed starved for older male companionship. Richard rewarded them with adventure stories, or sometimes, when he was going from one place to another, and their presence wouldn't impede his progress, he taught them about the woods, tracking, and animals.

They coveted staying in Richard's good graces, so when he wanted or needed to be alone, and signaled with a finger or a nod, they vanished. Richard let them be around often when he was with Pasha, since he couldn't do more important tasks then anyway. Frustrated, because she couldn't seem to find time alone with him, Pasha was somewhat mollified when Richard got her excluded from the boys' list of targets. She appreciated not having her fine dresses drenched or having to worry about discovering a snake in her shawl.

Richard occasionally asked Kipp and Hersh to preform little errands, just to test them. He had plans for their talents.

The other young men in collars wanted to show Richard the city. Two, Perry and Isaac, who lived in Gillaume Hall with him, took him into the city and showed him the tavern where many of the guards drank, and he soon after bought Swordsman Kevin Andellmere the ale he had promised him.

Richard discovered that most of the young men spent their nights away from the palace, staying in various fine inns around the city. It didn't take Richard long to figure out why. They were provided money, the same as he, and they were practiced at spending it. They bought themselves fancy clothes, dressing like princes, and on their overnight stays they picked the finest accommodations.

There was no shortage of women wanting to share those accommodations. Astonishingly beautiful women.

When Perry and Isaac took him to the city, they were always quickly surrounded by attractive women. Richard had never seen women this brazen. Every evening, the two men would each select a woman, sometimes several, and buy them presents, maybe a dress or a bauble, and then depart for their rooms.

The two told him that if he didn't want to bother with spending time buying gifts, he could simply go to any of the houses of prostitution, but they assured him that those women were not as young, or nearly as pretty, as the ones who approached them on the streets. They admitted, though, that they went to prostitutes sometimes when they didn't feel like wasting time being sociable for no more than a simple coupling.

When he was spotted with a collar, Richard drew women the same as Perry and Isaac did. Richard was beginning to see in a new light what Sister Verna meant about him soon finding another pair of pretty legs. The other two men thought Richard was mad to turn down all the offers. Sometimes, Richard wondered if they might not be right.

Richard asked Perry and Isaac if they weren't afraid of a woman's father cracking their skulls. They laughed and said that fathers sometimes brought their daughters to them. Richard threw his arms up and asked if they weren't concerned about getting some woman they didn't even know pregnant. They explained that if a woman "got herself" pregnant, the palace would provide for her and the child, even her whole family.

When Richard had asked Pasha what was behind such a bizarre convention, she folded her arms across her breasts and presented her back to him while she explained that men had uncontrollable urges, and those urges would be a distraction to learning to use their Han, so the Sisters encouraged the men to satisfy their needs. That was why she didn't go to the city with him at night. She was restricted from interfering with his . . . needs.

She had turned back to him and begged him to come to her with his needs, saying she would see to it that he had no desire to go to other women, or if he did go to the city, to at least allow her to be one of the women he slept with. She told him that she could satisfy him better than any other woman, and offered to prove it.

Richard was dumbfounded by such talk, to say nothing of the behavior. He told Pasha that he only went to the city to see the sights. Having grown up in the woods, he had never roamed around in a city before. He told her that where he came from it wasn't right to treat women in such a way.

He promised that if he was ever overcome with need, he would come to her first. She was so happy to hear this that she didn't mind when he reminded her that he wasn't ready yet. She had no idea that there were times when he felt so lonely that he was sorely tempted to give in to her. She was unquestionably alluring, and it was sometimes difficult for him to make himself keep her at arm's length.

Richard had Pasha show him everything she could of the palace. He had her show him some of the city, and take him on a tour of the docks, to see the big boats. She said they were called ships, because they went to sea. Richard had never seen anything that large afloat. She told him that they brought trade from cities of the Old World farther down the coast.

Pasha went with him to the sea, and they sat for hours, watching the waves, or explored the tide pools. Richard was astounded to learn that the sea went up and down, with tides, all by itself. She assured him that it was not the magic of the palace, but did such a thing everywhere. Richard was spellbound by the ocean. Pasha was content to simply sit with him. But Richard couldn't afford to sit and watch the ocean too often. He had things to do.

Pasha wasn't permitted to go with him to the city in the evening, in case he chose to be with a woman. He had to constantly reassure her that that was not why he went out at night. Since it was the truth that he wasn't sleeping with any of the women, he had no difficulty being sincere and convincing her. He did not tell her the truth, however, about what he really was doing.

Richard decided that as long as the palace wanted to provide him with money, he was going to allow them to finance their own undoing. He spent the palace's money wherever it would help him. He became a regular at the taverns and inns the palace guards frequented. Whenever he was around, they never paid for a drink.

Richard made an effort to learn all their names. At night, he would write down the name of any new guard he had met, and everything he could discover about him or any of the other guards. He paid the most attention to those who guarded the Prelate's compound, and any other place he discovered he was forbidden access. He stopped by their posts whenever he was at the palace, and inquired idly about their lives, their girlfriends, their wives, their parents, their children, their food, their problems.

Richard bought Kevin special expensive chocolates that his girlfriend favored, but which Kevin could ill afford on his wages. The chocolates earned Kevin favors from his girlfriend. Kevin always brightened at Richard's approach, even when he looked tired from the favors.

Richard loaned money to any guard who asked, knowing it would never be repaid. When a few made excuses as to why they didn't have the money to pay back, Richard would not hear their reasons, telling them that he understood and that he would feel bad if they were to worry about it.

Two of the toughest, who guarded a restricted area on the west side of the palace, would let him buy their ale, but wouldn't warm to him. Richard took it as a challenge. He finally struck on the idea of hiring them the services of four prostitutes—two each, just to get their attention. They wanted to know why. Richard told them how the palace provided him with money and he didn't see why only he should enjoy it. He told them that since they had to stand up all day guarding the palace, he thought it only fair for the palace to pay to put a lady under them when they lay down.

The offer was too much for them to resist. They were soon giving him surreptitious winks when he passed. Once they became amenable to his offers, he saw to it that they had reason to give him the winks on a more frequent basis.

As Richard knew they would, the two guards began bragging about their romps. When some of the other men found out that Richard had been willing to provide those two with the services of ladies, they pointed out to Richard that it wasn't fair to the others that they should be excluded. Richard conceded that he saw the logic of their argument. He soon discovered that he didn't have the time to handle individual requests, so he struck on an idea.

He found a mistress of a brothel open to an inventive business arrangement. He put the establishment on retainer, open only to his "friends." He calculated that in this manner he was actually saving the palace money, over a piecemeal arrangement.

He wanted the men to remember to whom they owed their gratitude, so required they give the mistress the code phrase "a friend of Richard Cypher" before they would be granted admittance. There were no other restrictions. Richard gave the mistress a healthy raise in the retainer when she complained to him that business was steadier than she had anticipated.

Richard soothed his conscience about the morals of what he was doing by reminding himself that he couldn't change what people chose to do, and it might save him from having to kill the guards when the time came. In that light, it made sense.

One day when Pasha was with him, and a man gave him a wink, she asked why. He told her it was because he was with the most attractive woman at the palace. She smiled for an hour.

Richard accustomed the guards to seeing him in the black cape of the mriswith. He kept Pasha happy when he was with her by frequently wearing the red coat she liked best. Sometimes he wore the others: the blue, the dark blue, the brown, or the green. Pasha most liked taking him to the city, but she went for hikes in the surrounding countryside to try to be a part of his interests.

Richard learned that the guards were soldiers in the Imperial Order, on special detachment to the palace. The Imperial Order ruled all of the Old World, but seemed to have a nonintervention policy with the Palace of the Prophets. They never interfered with any Sister, or any man wearing a Rada'Han.

The guards were stationed at the palace to handle all the people who came to Halsband Island. Every day, people poured over the bridges to come to the palace. Sisters saw petitioners of every want. Some requested charity, some intervention in disputes, and some wished to be guided in the Creator's wisdom. Others came to worship in the courtyards scattered throughout the island. They viewed the place where Sisters of the Light lived as hallowed.

Richard learned that the city of Tanimura, vast though it was, was merely an outpost of the Old World, at the fringe of the empire. Apparently, the emperor of the Imperial Order had an arrangement with the palace to provide guards, but not law. Richard suspected that the guards were the emperor's eyes in an area of his empire where he was denied dominion. Richard wondered what the emperor received in return for this arrangement.

Richard also learned that in at least one of the restricted areas, the Sisters had a "special guest" who never came out, but he was unable to discover any more.

Richard began testing the guards' loyalty to him with simple, innocuous requests. He told Kevin that he wanted a special rose for Pasha that grew only in the Prelate's compound. Richard made a point of parading Pasha, wearing the yellow rose, past Kevin. Kevin smiled with pride.

At other restricted areas, Richard used the flower excuse, or said that he wanted to get a view of the sea from atop a particular wall. He made sure to remain in sight at all times, to reassure the guards and dull their sense of caution.

It wasn't long before he had all the guards accustomed to his forays. After a time, he was coming and going almost as he pleased. He was their friend—a trusted and valuable friend.

Since he was collecting so many rare flowers from the restricted areas, he used them to an advantage—he presented them to the Sisters who practiced with him. They were puzzled as to why he would give them flowers from restricted areas. He explained that he considered the Sisters who trained him to be special, and he therefore didn't want them to have just any flowers, but those that were special, and artfully obtained. Besides making them blush, this explanation also disarmed an otherwise inevitable suspicion if he frequented restricted areas.

Though, as near as Richard could tell, there were close to two hundred Sisters, only six worked with him.

Sisters Tovi and Cecilia were older, and as kind as doting grandmothers. Tovi always brought cookies or some other treat to their sessions. Cecilia insisted on combing his hair back off his forehead with her fingers and planting a kiss there before she left. Both blushed furiously when he gave them rare flowers. Richard had difficulty thinking of either as potential enemies.

The first time Sister Merissa showed up at his door, Richard almost swallowed his tongue. Her dark hair and the way she filled her red dress made him stumble over his words like a fool. Sister Nicci, who never wore any color but black, had the same effect on him. When Sister Nicci locked her blue eyes on his, he had trouble remembering how to breathe.

Sisters Merissa and Nicci were older than Pasha—his age, or maybe at most a couple of years older. They carried themselves with confidence and slow grace. Though Merissa was dark, and Nicci blond, they seemed to be cut from the same rare cloth.

The power of their Han radiated from each, making them almost seem to glow. Richard sometimes thought he could almost hear the air crackle around them. Neither walked. Both glided—like swans, serene and cool. Yet he was sure either could smelt iron ore with their placid glances.

Neither ever grinned. They bestowed small, subdued smiles. And only while looking him in the eye. Richard could feel his heart thumping faster when they did.

Once, he offered Sister Nicci one of his rare flowers from a restricted area. His explanation of where it had come from and the story of why he was giving it to her flew right out of his head. She took the white rose gingerly between a finger and thumb, as if it might soil her hand, and while her gaze held his, she gave him one of her subdued smiles and said in an indifferent tone, "Why, thank you, Richard." What Pasha had told him about boys bringing Sisters frogs came to his mind. He never gave either Sister Nicci or Merissa a flower again. Anything less than priceless jewels seemed an insult.

Neither ever offered to sit on the floor for their sessions. In fact, the very idea of Sisters Merissa ar Nicci sitting on the floor seemed ludicrous to him. The older Sisters, Tovi and Cecilia, sat on the floor, the same as Pasha, and it seemed perfectly natural. Sisters Merissa and Nicci sat in chairs, and held his hands across a small table. It somehow seemed an erotic experience. It made him sweat.

They both spoke with a quiet economy of words that added an air of nobility to their bearing. While neither ever made a clear offer, they managed to somehow leave no doubt in Richard's mind that they were available to spend the night with him. Richard could never pin down anything specific in what they said to confirm the impression, but he had no doubt. Their oblique words left him room to feign missing their intent, and neither ever deigned to clarify what she had said.

He prayed that they would never make the offer any more explicit, because if they did, he knew he would have to bite his tongue in half to keep from saying yes. Both brought to mind what Pasha had told him about men having uncontrollable urges. He had never been around anyone who could make him stammer and fumble and in general make himself appear a fool as those two did. Sisters Merissa and Nicci were the embodiment of pure, unadulterated lust.

When Pasha found out that Sisters Merissa and Nicci were two of his teachers, she gave a small shrug, and said that they were very talented Sisters, and she was sure they would help him reach his Han. But her cheeks broke out in red blotches.

When Perry and Isaac found out about Sisters Merissa and Nicci, they both nearly succumbed to apoplexy. They said they would give up all the women in the city, forever, just to have one night with either. They said that if Richard was ever offered the opportunity, he had to take it, and tell them every detail. Richard assured them that women the likes of those two would never be interested in a woods guide like him.

He dared not say out loud that the offer had been made.

The fifth Sister, Armina, was older, a mature woman who was pleasant enough, but all business. When he had no more luck finding his Han with her than any of the others, she told him that it would come with time, and not to feel disappointed, but perhaps he should try to put more effort into it. Over time, she warmed to him, and smiled more. She was surprised and flattered by the special flowers. She blushed at her own blushes. Richard liked her straightforward personality.

The last Sister, Liliana, was Richard's favorite. Her easy smile was disarming, her plain, bony looks somehow alluring because of her open, friendly nature. She treated Richard like a confidant. Richard felt relaxed with her, sometimes spending more time than he could afford, talking with her late into the night, simply because he enjoyed her company. Though he had no friends among his captors, she came closer than any.

When Richard gave her the special flower, she hooked some of her brown hair behind an ear and leaned in. Her eyes were wide with mischief, wanting to know how he had gotten past the guards. She giggled when he told the story he invented of sneaking behind their backs. She stuck each rose proudly through a buttonhole, and wore it until it wilted or he gave her another.

When she touched him in a friendly way, it somehow seemed the natural thing to do. He found himself laying a hand on her arm in the same manner when he told her funny stories about when he had been a guide. They roared with laughter together, holding their ribs and getting tears.

Sister Liliana told him how she had grown up on a farm, and loved the country. Several times Richard invited her on a picnic out in the hills. She was comfortable and happy in the countryside. She didn't care if she got her dress dirty. Richard couldn't imagine either Sister Merissa or Nicci setting a foot to dirt, but Sister Liliana would flop right down on the ground with him.

She never made an offer to sleep with him. That in itself put him at ease. She never displayed any pretense; she seemed to genuinely enjoy her time with him. When he opened his eyes after a session with her and admitted he felt no Han, she would squeeze his hands and tell him that it was all right, and that she would try harder the next time to help him.

Richard found himself telling her things he told none of the others. When he confided how much he wanted the Rada'Han off, she put a hand to his arm as she gave him a wink, and told him that she would see to it that he had his wish, that when the time came, she would do it herself. She said she could understand his feelings, and for him to have faith.

She promised that if one day he was at the end of his tolerance, and he truly could stand it no longer, she would help him, she would remove the collar. But she wanted him to know that she had faith in him, and wanted him to put in his best effort to learn to control his Han before she even considered it.

She said that other young men tried to forget their collar by bedding every woman willing. She told him that she could understand urges, but she hoped that if he chose to sleep with a woman it would be because he liked her, and not because he was trying to forget the collar. She told him not to go to the prostitutes because they were dirty and he would catch something.

Richard told her that he was in love with someone, and didn't want to be unfaithful to her. She grinned and clapped him on the back and said she was proud of him. Richard didn't tell her that Kahlan had sent him away, but he wanted to. He knew that someday, if he could stand it no longer, he could tell Liliana and she would listen, and understand.

Because he was so comfortable around her, he felt that if anyone could help him find his Han, it would be her. He hoped it would be her. Richard had had only a brother, and didn't know what it would be like to have a sister, but he imagined that if he did have one, she would be like Liliana. The name Sister Liliana had a different meaning to him than was intended. She seemed his soulmate.

Still, he couldn't let himself open up completely to her. The Sisters were his captors, not his friends. They were the enemy, for now. But he knew that when the time came, Liliana would side with him.

Richard's lessons with the six Sisters took up at most two hours a day. A waste of two hours as far as he was concerned. He was no closer to touching his Han than he had been the first time Sister Verna had him try.

When Richard could manage to be alone, he explored the land around the palace, and found the limits of his invisible chain. When he reached the farthest distance the collar would allow him to go, it felt like trying to walk through a ten-foot-thick wall of mud layered over solid rock. It was frustrating to be able to see beyond, without obstruction, yet not be able to continue walking.

It happened, as near as he could tell, about the same distance from the palace in any direction. It was a good number of miles, but once he found the limit, his world began to feel very small indeed.

The day he found his boundary, the limits of his prison, he went to the Hagen Woods, and killed a mriswith.

His only true solace was Gratch. Richard spent most nights with the gar. He wrestled with his furry friend, ate with him, and slept with him. Richard hunted food for Gratch, but the gar was learning to hunt on his own. Richard was relieved to learn that; he didn't have the time to be with him every night. Hungry or not, Gratch was always distraught when Richard missed a night.

Richard was worried that Pasha would know where he went all the time, by his collar, but quite by accident he discovered something else his mriswith cape did— it masked from Pasha his whereabouts. When he wore the cape, she couldn't find him by his Rada'Han, by his Han.

She was puzzled by his blanking out from her sense of where he was, but didn't seem too concerned, offering that perhaps it had an explanation that she would come to figure out one day. She seemed to think it was a deficiency on her part. Richard never offered her the solution.

He realized that this was the reason none with the gift ever knew a mriswith was coming. Richard wondered why he had been able to see the beast in his mind. Maybe it was as Sister Verna said, that he was using his Han. But Sisters and wizards knew how to use their Han, and couldn't detect the mriswith.

Richard had an easier time when he could go where he pleased, and know Pasha would not know where he was; it saved thinking up explanations. He worried that if she ever discovered the reason, she would destroy his cape, so he hid a second for that contingency.

Gratch seemed to be bigger every time Richard saw him. By the end of Richard's first month at the palace, the gar was a head taller than Richard, and significantly stronger. When they wrestled, Gratch learned to be careful not to hurt him.

Richard also spent some of his time with Warren, getting him used to going outside. At first, he took Warren out into the courtyards at night. Warren told him that the size of the sky and landscape frightened him, so Richard reasoned that night would show him less of the landscape, at least to start.

Warren said that the Sisters had had him down in the vaults for so long that he thought he just became used to being closed in, but he was tired of it. Richard felt sorry for him, and wanted to help him. He really liked Warren. He was about as smart as anyone Richard had ever met. There didn't seem to be anything that Warren didn't know at least a little about.

Warren was nervous about being away from the safety of the palace, but was reassured by Richard's presence, and the way Richard never ridiculed his fears. Richard was always considerate, never taking Warren farther than he felt comfortable. Richard told him that it was just like after you were injured and had been laid up for a while: it took time to stretch the old muscles.

After a few weeks of their nighttime forays, Richard started taking Warren out in the daylight, first just up onto the walls to look at the vastness of the sky and ocean. Warren was always close to a stairway that led back into the palace, so he was reassured by having an escape route close by if he felt he had to go back inside. A few times he did, and Richard always went with him, and talked about other things to take his mind away from the uncomfortable feeling. Richard had Warren bring a book outside with him, so he could be distracted by reading. Letting Warren forget about the size of the sky helped.

On a bright, sunny day, after Warren had become comfortable out-of-doors, Richard decided to try taking him out into the hills. Warren was a bit giddy at first, but as they sat on a rock high in the hills, overlooking the countryside and the city, Warren said that he felt as if he had mastered his fear. He said that he still felt uncomfortable, but he felt the fear was under control.

He grinned at the vast landscape spread out below, enjoying the sight that for so long his fears denied him. Richard told him that he was happy that he was the one to have been able to guide him out of his mole hole. Warren laughed.

Warren said he needed adventure in his life, and this felt like the beginning.

As far as Warren's search for information was going, he had been able to find out precious little. He had so far found only a few references in old books that talked about the Valley of the Lost, and the Baka Ban Mana, but what he found was intriguing. The information made reference to the power the wizards had given the Baka Ban Mana in return for taking their land, so that they could someday have their land restored. It said that when the completing link was joined with this power invested in their spirt woman, the towers would fall.

Richard thought about Du Chaillu saying that he was the *Caharin*, and that they were now husband and wife. That was a linking of sorts. He wondered if over the intervening time the meaning of this joining could have been taken to mean marriage, instead of its original intent.

As they sat watching the vast landscape, Warren said, "The Prelate has been reading prophecies and histories that talk about 'the pebble in the pond.'"

Richard's ears perked up. He remembered Kahlan singing him a song about screelings that mentioned "the pebble in the pond." Warren hadn't studied those prophecies before, and hadn't been able to piece together their importance as of yet.

"Do you know what the Wizard's Second Rule is?" Richard asked.

"Second Rule? Wizards have rules? What's the first?"

Richard looked over. "Do you remember that night Jedidiah broke his leg, and I told you that you had carpet ash on you? And you tried to brush it off? I was using the Wizard's First Rule." Warren frowned. "You think on it, Warren, and let me know what you figure out. In the meantime, it's important that you speed up the search for the information I asked you about."

"Well, it will be a little easier, now that Sister Becky is sick every morning, and won't be looking over my shoulder. She's pregnant," he said in answer to Richard's questioning frown.

"Do many of the Sisters have children?"

"Sure," Warren said. "What with all the young wizards around who can no longer go to the city. The Sisters help out with their needs, so they can study."

Richard gave Warren a suspicious look. "Is Sister Becky's child yours?"

Warren blushed furiously. "No." He kept his eyes to the city. "I'm waiting for the one I love."

"Pasha," Richard said.

Warren nodded. Richard looked down at the Palace of the Prophets, and the city that surrounded it. Needs.

"Warren, do all the children of men with the gift inherit it?"

"Oh no. It's said that many thousands of years ago, before the Old and New World were separated, many had the gift. But over time those in power methodically killed off young ones with the gift, so they would have no one to threaten their rule. They also withheld the required teaching. It used to be that fathers taught their sons, but as fewer were born with the gift, and it skipped more and more generations, those who knew the way jealously guarded their knowledge. That's the reason the Palace of the Prophets was created—to help those with the gift, who had no teacher.

"As time went on, the gift was bred out of the race of man, the way you breed a trait out of an animal. This gave the wizards who held power less and less opposition all the time.

"Now that the trait is so bred out, one born with the gift is exceedingly rare. Maybe only one child in a thousand fathered by a wizard is born with the gift. We're a dying breed."

Richard looked to the city again, then to the palace.

His eyes locked on the palace, Richard slowly rose to his feet. "They're not seeing to our 'needs,' " he whispered, "they're using us as breeding stock."

Warren stood. His brow wrinkled. "What?"

"They're using the palace, the young men at the palace, to breed wizards."

Warren's brow furrowed deeper. "Why?"

Richard's jaw muscles flexed. "I don't know, but I intend to find out."

"Good," Warren said with a grin. "I need an adventure."

Richard gave him a cold look. "Do you know what adventure is, Warren?"

Warren nodded, the smile still on his face. "An exciting experience."

"Adventure is being scared to death, and not knowing if you will live or die, or if the ones you love will live or die. Adventure is being in trouble you don't know how to get out of."

Warren fumbled with the braiding on his sleeve. "I never thought about it like that."

"Well, you think on it," Richard said, "because I'm about to start an adventure."

"What are you going to do?"

"The less you know, the less adventure you'll have to worry about. You just find out the things I need to know. If the veil is torn, we're all going to have a never-ending adventure."

"Well," Warren said with a twinkle in his eye, "I found out at least one thing of help, then."

"The Stone of Tears?"

Warren nodded with a grin. "I found out there is no way you could have seen it. It's locked behind the veil. In a way, it's part of the veil."

"Are you sure? Are you sure I couldn't have seen it?"

"Positive. The Stone of Tears is the seal that keeps the Nameless One locked in his prison of the dead, in the underworld. He can rule the souls of the dead there with him, but he cannot come to this world. The Stone of Tears seals him there."

"Good," Richard said with a relieved sigh. "That's great, Warren. Good work." He gently gripped Warren's robe and pulled him closer. "You're sure. There's no way the Stone of Tears could be in this world."

Warren confidently shook his head. "None. It's impossible. The only way for the Stone of Tears to be in this world would be for it to come through the gateway."

Richard felt his flesh beginning to tingle. "Gateway? What's the gateway?"

"Well, the gateway is what the name implies. A passage. In this case, a passage between the world of the living and the world of the dead. It's magic of both worlds, a passage constructed of magic. The gateway can only be opened with both Additive and Subtractive Magic. The Nameless One has only Subtractive, since he is in the underworld, so he can't open the gateway. The same way someone in this world could not open it, because we have only Additive Magic."

Bumps were rising on Richard's arms. "But someone in this world, someone with both forms of magic, could open the gateway?"

"Well, sure," Warren stammered. "If they had the gateway. But it has been lost for over three thousand years. It's gone." He gave Richard a self-assured smile. "We're safe."

Richard wasn't smiling. He grabbed Warren's robes in both hands and yanked his face close. "Warren, tell me the gateway isn't called the Magic of Orden. Tell me the gateway isn't the three boxes of Orden."

Warren's eyes slowly expanded to the size of gold pieces. "Where did you hear that name for it?" he whispered in a disquieted tone. "I'm the only one in the palace besides the Prelate and two other Sisters who are permitted to read the books that call the gateway by its ancient name."

Richard gritted his teeth. "What happens if one of the boxes is opened?"

"They can't be opened," Warren insisted. "They can't. I told you, it takes both kinds of magic, Additive and Subtractive, to open a box."

Richard shook him. "What happens!"

His eyes still wide, Warren swallowed. "Then the gateway between the worlds is opened. The veil is breached. The seal is off the Nameless One."

"And the Stone of Tears would be in this world?" Warren nodded as Richard tightened his grip on the robes. "And if the box were to be closed, that would close the gateway? Seal the breach?"

"No. Well, yes, but it can only be closed by one with the gift. It takes the touch of magic to close the gateway. But if one with the gift closes the box, the gateway, then it ruptures the balance, because he has only Additive Magic, and the Nameless One escapes the underworld. More correctly, this world would be swallowed into the world of the dead."

"Then how can the box be closed to keep the worlds separated!"

"The same way the gateway is opened. With both Additive and Subtractive Magic."

"And what about the Stone of Tears?"

"I don't know. I would have to study."

"Then you better study fast."

"Please," Warren whined, "you don't mean that you know where the boxes are. You haven't found them, have you?"

"Found them? The last time I saw the boxes, one was opened, about to suck my bastard father into the underworld."

Warren fainted.

Under the impotent rays of the late-day sun, an old woman was spreading wood ash on the ice covering the vast expanse of stairs. Kahlan walked past, relieved that the old woman didn't look up to see that the person in the heavy clothes, white fur mantle, and carrying a pack and bow was the Mother Confessor returned to Aydindril.

She was in no mood for starting a celebration tonight. She was exhausted. Already, before coming home to the palace, she had climbed up to the Wizard's Keep on the mountainside, but the Keep was stone cold and dark as death. The shields were in place, though a Confessor could enter, but no one was inside.

Zedd was not there.

The Keep sat now as the last time she had seen it so many months ago, when she had left to find the missing great wizard. She had found him, and helped stop the threat from Darken Rahl, but now she needed the great wizard again.

Since leaving the Galean army nearly a month before, she had been struggling to reach Aydindril, and Zedd. Storms had raged for days at a time. Passes had been rendered impassable by the weather and snow, forcing them to backtrack and find alternate routes. It had been a frustrating and tiring journey, but the despair at reaching her goal and not finding Zedd was withering.

Kahlan had made her way through the side streets, avoiding Kings Row. The palaces on Kings Row housed dignitaries, staffs, and guards of the lands that were represented in Aydindril. The kings and queens and rulers of those lands stayed in their palaces when they came to address the council. The palaces were a matter of pride for each land, and each was magnificent, although none could begin to compare to the Confessors' Palace.

Kahlan had avoided Kings Row because she would be recognized there, and she didn't want to be recognized right now; she wanted only to find Zedd and, failing that, speak to the council, so she headed toward the service area to the side, near the kitchens.

Chandalen was out in the forest. He didn't want to come into Aydindril; the size of the city and the multitudes of people made him uneasy, though he denied it, and claimed only to be more comfortable sleeping outside. Kahlan couldn't blame him; after being alone in the mountains for so long, she, too, was uneasy going into the city, even though she had grown up in this place and knew its streets and majestic buildings as well as Chandalen knew the plains around the Mud People village. The people everywhere made her feel closed in as never before.

Chandalen wanted to go home to his people, now that she was delivered safely to Aydindril. She could understand his desire to be off, but asked him to rest the night, and say good-bye to her in the morning.

She had told Orsk to spend the night with Chandalen. His presence was wearing; his one eye following her everywhere, his jumping to help her with everything, his constantly standing ready to do her bidding at the slightest indication. It was like having a dog continually at heel. She needed a night away from that. Chandalen seemed to understand. She didn't know what she was going to do about Orsk.

A stifling blast of warm air hit her as she went in through the kitchen entrance. At the sound of the door, a thin woman in a sparkling white apron spun to her.

"What are you doing in here! Get out, you beggar!"

As the woman lifted her wooden spoon in a threatening manner, Kahlan pushed back the hood of her mantle. The woman gasped. Kahlan smiled.

"Mistress Sanderholt. I'm so pleased to see you again."

"Mother Confessor!" The woman fell to her knees, clasping her hands together. "Oh, Mother Confessor, forgive me! I didn't recognize you. Oh, good spirits be praised, is it really you?"

Kahlan pulled the wiry woman to her feet. "I've missed you so, Mistress Sanderholt." Kahlan held out her arms. "Give me a hug?"

Mistress Sanderholt fell into Kahlan's arms. "Oh, child, It's so good to see you!" She pushed away, tears running down her face. "We didn't know what had become of you. We were so worried. I thought I might never see you again."

"It has been a long and difficult time. I can't tell you how good it is to see your face again."

Mistress Sanderholt started pulling Kahlan toward a side table. "Come. You need a bowl of soup. I have some on now, if these featherbrains who do what scarcely passes for cooking haven't ruined it with too much pepper."

The welter of cooks and help caught the words and kept their heads down, applying their attention to their tasks. The sounds of whisks and spoons on bowls stepped up. Men picked up sacks and hurried away. Brushes worked at pots with greater zeal. Butter hissed in hot pans, and bread in ovens and meat on spits suddenly needed checking.

"I don't have time, right now, Mistress Sanderholt."

"But I have things I must tell you. Important things."

"I know. I have things to tell you, too. But right now I must see the council. It's urgent. I've been traveling a long time, and I'm exhausted, but I must see the council before I rest. We will talk tomorrow."

Mistress Sanderholt couldn't resist another hug. "Of course, child. Rest well. We will talk tomorrow."

Kahlan took the shortest route, through the immense hall used for important ceremonies and celebrations. Fires in the large, magnificent fireplaces set around the room between fluted columns sent shadows of herself spiraling around her as she crossed the green slate floor. The room was empty, now, allowing her footsteps to echo overhead from the intricate lierne vaulting with the wavelike, sweeping ribs. Her father used to set thousands of walnuts and acorns, representing troops, all over the floor of this room, to teach her battle tactics.

She turned down the hall at the far end, toward the corridor to the council chambers. In the Confessors' private gallery, groups of four glossy black marble columns to each side supported a progression of polychrome vaults. At the end, before the council chambers, was a round, two-story-high pantheon dedicated to the memory of heroines: the founding Mother Confessors. Their portraits, in frescoes between the seven massive pillars ranging to the skylight, were twice life size.

Kahlan always felt like a pretender to the post in the presence of the seven stern faces that overlooked the room. She felt they were saying, "And who are you, Kahlan Amnell, to think you could be the Mother Confessor?" Knowing the histories of those heroines only made her feel all the more inadequate.

Grabbing both brass levers, she threw the tall, mahogany doors open and marched into the council chambers.

A huge dome capped the enormous room. At the far end, the main vault was decorated with an ornate fresco celebrating the glory of Magda Searus, the first Mother Confessor. Her fingers were touching the back of the hand of her wizard, Merritt, who had laid down his life to protect her. Together, now, for all time in the colorful fresco, the two oversaw the Mother Confessors who followed and sat in the First Chair, and their wizards.

Between the colossal gold capitals of the columns thrusting up around the room were sinuous, polished mahogany railings at the edge of balconies that overlooked the elegant chamber. The arched openings, set at intervals around the room and leading up to the balconies, were decorated with sculpted stuccos of heroic scenes. Beyond were windows looking out over the courtyards. Round windows around the lower edge of the dome also let light into the glistening chamber. At the far end was the semicircular dais where the councilors sat, behind an elaborate, curved desk. The opulent First Chair in the center was the tallest.

A clump of men were gathered around the First Chair. By the numbers, Kahlan judged about half the council to be present. As she strode across long swaths of sunlight on the patterned marble floor, the heads began to follow her progress.

Someone was sitting in the First Chair. Although not enforced in recent times, it was a capital offense for a councilor to take the First Chair, as it was considered tantamount to a declaration of revolution. The conversation hushed as she approached.

It was High Prince Fyren, of Kelton, sitting in the chair. His feet were up on the desk, and he didn't take them down as he watched her draw near. His eyes were on her, but he was listening to a man with smoothed-down dark hair and beard, streaked with a touch of gray, leaning over whispering to him. The man's hands were in the opposite sleeves of his plain robes. Strange, she thought, for an advisor to be dressed so, like a wizard.

Prince Fyren lifted his eyebrows in delight. "Mother Confessor!" With deliberate care he took his polished boots down and came to his feet. He put his hands to the desk and leaned over, looking down. "So good to see you!"

Before, Kahlan had always had a wizard; now, she had none. No protection. She could not afford to appear timid or vulnerable.

She glared up at Prince Fyren. "If I ever again catch you in the chair of the Mother Confessor, I will kill you."

He straightened with a smirk. "You would use your power on a councilor?"

"I will slit your throat with my knife, if I have to."

The man in the plain robes watched her with unmoving dark eyes. The other councilors blanched.

Prince Fyren pulled his dark blue coat open and rested a hand on his hip. "Mother Confessor, I meant no offense. You have been gone for a long time. We all thought you were dead. There has been no Confessor in the palace for . . . what?" He looked

575

to a few of the other men. "Four, five, six months?" Hand still on his hip, he held his other out and gave a bow. "I meant no offense, Mother Confessor. Your chair is returned to you, of course."

Kahlan eyed the remaining men. "It is late. The council will meet in full session first thing in the morning. Every councilor will be present. The Midlands is at war."

Prince Fyren lifted an eyebrow. "War? On whose authority? We have not discussed such a grave matter."

Kahlan swept her gaze over the councilors, letting it finally settle on Prince Fyren. "On my authority as the Mother Confessor." Whispering broke out among the men. Prince Fyren never let his eyes leave hers. When she glowered at the men who were whispering, it sputtered out. "I want every councilor here, first thing in the morning. You are adjourned, for now, gentlemen."

Kahlan turned on her heel and marched from the room. She didn't recognize any of the guards she saw throughout the palace, but then she wouldn't; Zedd had told her before how most of the Home Guard had been killed in the fall of Aydindril to D'Hara. She missed the old faces.

The center of the Confessors' Palace in Aydindril was dominated by a monumental eight-branched staircase, lit, from four stories overhead, by natural light that came through the glass roof. The vast square was surrounded at midlevel by arcaded corridors, their arched openings separated by polished columns of wildly variegated gold and green marble standing on square plinth blocks, each decorated with a medallion of a past ruler of one of the lands of the Midlands. The hundreds upon hundreds of glistening, vase-shaped balusters had been turned from a mellow yellow stone that seemed to glow from within. The square newels, made of a dusky brown granite, were nearly as tall as she, and each was capped with a gold-leafed lamp. Florid carvings in stone covered expansive panels under the complex bands of dentil moldings that ran in mitered bands over the tops of the capitals. The center landing held statues of eight Mother Confessors. Kahlan had seen modest palaces that would fit within the space the staircase occupied.

The monumental staircase and the room that held it had taken forty years to build, the expense borne entirely by Kelton, in partial recompense for their opposition to the joining of the lands into the Midlands, and the war it spawned. It was also decreed that no leader of Kelton could ever be honored with a medallion at the base of the columns. The staircase was dedicated to the people of the Midlands, and was to honor them, not those who built it as penalty. Kelton was now a powerful land of the Midlands in good standing, and Kahlan thought it foolish to rebuke a people for something their ancestors had done centuries ago.

As she reached the central landing and turned up the second flight toward her room, she saw a phalanx of servants waiting at the top of the stairs. They all bowed as one when her eyes fell on them. She thought it must look absurd—nearly thirty sparkling, combed and buffed people in clean, crisp uniforms, all bowing to a filthy woman in wolf hides, carrying a bow and heavy pack. Well, this could only mean one thing: word of her arrival had swept through the whole of the palace already. There wasn't likely to be a gardener in the farthest greenhouse that didn't by now know the Mother Confessor was home.

"Rise, my children," Kahlan said when she reached the top of the stairs. They moved back to make way for her.

And then it started. Would the Mother Confessor like a bath, would the Mother Confessor like a massage, would the Mother Confessor like her hair washed and brushed, would the Mother Confessor like her nails buffed, would the Mother Confessor care to take any petitioners, would the Mother Confessor like to see any advisors, would the Mother Confessor like any letters written, would the Mother Confessor like, wish, want, need, or require a whole list of things.

Kahlan addressed the mistress of the maidservants. "Bernadette, I would like a bath. Nothing else. Just a bath."

Two women rushed off to see to the bath.

Mistress Bernadette's eyes made an involuntary flick down at Kahlan's attire. "Would the Mother Confessor like to have any of her clothes mended, or cleaned?"

Kahlan thought about the blue dress in her pack. "I guess I have a few things that need cleaning." She thought about all the rest of her clothes, most soaked with blood from one battle or another. "I guess I have a lot of things that need to be washed."

"Yes, Mother Confessor. And would you like me to lay out your white dress for tonight?"

"Tonight?"

Mistress Bernadette reddened. "Runners have already been sent to Kings Row, Mother Confessor. Everyone will want to welcome the Mother Confessor home."

Kahlan groaned. She was dead tired. She didn't want to greet people, just to tell women how fine their hair looked all pinned and decorated, or men how fine the cut of their coat was, or to listen patiently to supplications that invariably involved the distribution of funds and always sought to prove that the appellant was in no way seeking advantage, but only relief from the inequitable situation in which he was mired.

Mistress Bernadette gave her a corrective look, as she had done when Kahlan was little, as if to say, "Look here, young lady, you have obligations, and I expect no trouble about it."

What she said, though, was "Everyone has been fraught with concern over the safe return of the Mother Confessor. It would do their hearts good to see you safe and well."

Kahlan doubted that. What Mistress Bernadette really meant was that it would do Kahlan good to remind people that the Mother Confessor was still alive and in charge. Kahlan sighed. "Of course, Bernadette. Thank you for reminding me people have kept me in their hearts and been worried."

Mistress Bernadette smiled as she bowed her head. "Yes, Mother Confessor."

As the rest of the servants rushed off, Kahlan leaned toward Mistress Bernadette. "I remember when you would have added a swat on my behind for having to remind me of things."

Mistress Bernadette's smile returned. "I think you are too smart, now, for that, Mother Confessor." She rubbed an invisible spot from the back of her hand. "Mother Confessor . . . did you bring any of the other Confessors home with you? Will any of the others be returning, soon?"

Kahlan's features slid into her Confessor's face, as her mother had taught her. "I'm sorry, Bernadette, I thought you knew. They are all dead. I am the last living Confessor."

Mistress Bernadette's eyes filled with tears as she whispered a prayer. "May the good spirits be with them always."

"Why should they commence now," Kahlan said tersely. "They didn't bother to be with Dennee the day the quad caught her."

The fireplaces in her rooms were all blazing, as she had known they would be, and would have been every day she had been away, month after month. The fires in the Mother Confessor's rooms would never be allowed to go out in the winter, in case she returned. There was a silver tray on a table, with a fresh loaf of bread, a pot of tea, and a steaming bowl of spice soup. Mistress Sanderholt knew spice soup was her favorite.

Spice soup reminded Kahlan of Richard, now. She remembered making it for him, and he for her.

After dropping her pack and bow to the floor, Kahlan crossed the plush carpets and went into the next room. She stood, idly rubbing her fingers on one of the great, polished posts at the foot of her bed, staring, remembering that she was supposed to be here with Richard. The day they arrived in Aydindril they were to already have been wed. She had promised him this big bed.

Kahlan remembered the joy in her heart the day they talked about being wed and coming to Aydindril as husband and wife. She felt a tear roll down her cheek. She gasped a deep breath against the hot pain that burned through her chest, and wiped the tear away with her fingertips.

Kahlan went to the glassed doors, opening them out onto the expansive balcony. She put her trembling fingers to the broad, icy railing and stood in the cold air, looking up the mountainside to the Wizard's Keep, its dark stone walls standing out in the last golden rays of the sunset.

"Where are you, Zedd?" she whispered. "I need you."

He came awake with a gasp as he slid and thumped his head. He sat up, blinking. An old woman with straight, black and white, jaw-length hair was sitting opposite him, cowering in a corner. The two of them were inside a coach. It rolled abruptly, sliding him across to the other side. The woman was staring in his direction. He blinked in surprise at her. Her eyes were completely white.

"Who are you?" he asked.

"Who be you?" she asked right back.

"I asked first."

"I . . ." She drew her cloak around her fine, green dress. "I don't know who I be. Who be you?"

He held a finger skyward. "I'm . . . I'm . . ." He let out a thin sigh. "I'm afraid I don't know who I am, either. Don't I look like anyone you recognize?"

She pulled her cloak a little tighter. "I do not know. I be blind. I cannot see what you look like."

"Blind? Oh. Well, I'm sorry."

He rubbed his head where he had hit it on the side of the coach. Looking down, he saw that he was wearing fine clothes; a maroon robe with black sleeves that had three rows of silver brocade around them. Well, he thought, at least I must be wealthy.

He picked a black cane off the floor, giving its fine silverwork a look. He turned and thumped it against the roof, in the direction of where the driver must be sitting, up top. The old woman jumped with a fright.

"What be that noise!"

"Oh, sorry. I was trying to get the driver's attention."

The driver must have heard. The coach slid to a stop, and then rocked as someone climbed down. When the door drew open and he saw the size of the man in a longcoat sticking his windburned face in, he clutched his cane and slid back.

"Who are you?" he asked, brandishing the cane.

"Me? I'm just a big fool," the big man growled. His deeply creased face softened into a little smile. "Name's Ahern."

"Well, Ahern, what are you doing with us? Have you kidnapped us? Are we being held for ransom?"

Ahern chuckled. "More like the other way around, I'd say."

"What do you mean? How long have we been asleep? And who are we?"

Ahern looked to the sky. "Dear spirits, how do I get myself into these things?" He let out a sigh. "You've both been asleep since late yesterday. You've slept last night, and all day today. Your name is Ruben. Ruben Rybnik."

"Ruben?" He harrumphed. "Ruben. Well, that's a fine name."

"And who be I?" the woman asked.

"You are Elda Rybnik."

"Her name is Rybnik, too?" Ruben asked. "Are we related?"

Ahern hesitated. "Yes and no. You two are husband and wife. Sort of."

Ruben leaned toward the big man. "I think that needs explaining."

Ahern gave a sigh, and a nod. "Your name's Ruben, and hers is Elda. But that's not your real names. You told me that for now, it would be best if I not tell you your real names."

"You have kidnapped us! You've knocked us on the head and spirited us away!"

"Just calm down, and I'll explain."

"Then explain, before I give you a thrashing with my cane."

"It isn't worth it," Ahern mumbled to himself. "How did I ever get into this? Gold, that's how," he answered himself.

Ahern pushed into the coach, sitting next to Ruben. He pulled the door closed against the flying snow.

"Well, just invite yourself right in," Ruben said.

Ahern cleared his throat. "All right, now, you two listen to me. You both were sick. You had me take you to see three women." He leaned closer to Ruben and scowled. "Three sorceresses."

"Sorceresses!" Ruben yelped. "No wonder we don't know who we are! You took us to witches and had a spell put on us!"

Ahern put a calming hand on him. "Be quiet and listen. You are a wizard." Ruben gawked at Ahern. Ahern turned to Elda. "And you are a sorceress."

Ruben waved his arms around with a flourish. "No I'm not," he snapped, at last, "or you'd be changed to a toad."

Ahern shook his head with a grumble. "Your power is gone."

"Well," Ruben asked as he straightened his back, "was I a talented wizard?"

"You were good enough to put those cursed fingers of yours to the side of my thick head and put it in my mind to help you. You said wizards had to use people sometimes, to do what must be done. The burden of a wizard you called it. You said helping you was something I would have done anyway, that you were only calling on the 'goodness' within me to hurry my thinking along. Anyway, that, and more gold than I've ever seen, convinced me to do something I ought to know better than to get tangled in. I surely don't like anything to do with wizards and magic."

579

"And I be a sorceress?" Elda asked. "A blind sorceress?"

"Well, no, ma'am. You were blind, but you could use your gift to see—see better than I can see with my eyes."

"Then why be I blind, now?"

"Both of you were sick. Sick with some kind of evil magic. The three sorceresses agreed to help you, but in order to cure you, they had to . . . well, they had to give you both something that would make your magic, your gift, go away. You made me wait outside, so I don't know what they did. I just know what you told me before you went back in for the last time to have it done."

Ruben leaned in. "You're making this up."

Ahern ignored him and went on. "The sickness you two had was feeding on your good magic. I don't know the way magic works, and the spirits know I don't want to know, I only know what you told me, the way you explained it to me, when you came out and convinced me to help you. You said that in order to help you, the three sorceresses had to give you something to make your magic go away. Only in that way could you two heal. The evil magic wouldn't wither and die, and your wounds heal, as long as it had the good magic to latch on to, to feed on."

"So now we have no magic?"

"Well, I don't know how it all works, but as I understand it, you can't really get rid of your magic. What the three women did was make you forget everything about yourselves, so you wouldn't know you had any magic, so the evil magic wouldn't know, either, that it was there. So that's why neither of you knows who you are, or how to use magic. That's why Elda is blind."

Ruben squinted. "Why would the sorceresses agree to help us?"

"Mostly because of Elda. They said she was a legend among the sorceresses of Nicobarese. Something about what she did when she was younger and used to live here."

Ruben stared at the big man. "It has to be true." He turned to Elda. "It has to be true. No one could invent such an absurd story. What do you think?"

"I think as you. I think he be telling us the truth."

"Good," Ahern said. "Now comes the part you aren't going to like."

"What about our magic? When does it come back? When do we remember who we are?"

Ahern raked his meaty fingers through his shaggy, gray hair. "That's the part you aren't going to like. The three women said they doubt you two will ever get it back. You may never remember. You may never get your magic back."

The silence echoed in the coach. Ruben finally spoke. "Why would we agree to such a thing?"

Ahern picked at his fingers. "Because you had no choice. You were both sick. Mighty sick, Elda more than you. She would have been dead by now, and you within another day or two, at most. You had no choice. It was the only way."

Ruben folded his hands over the silver head of his cane. "Well, if that is so, then we had to. If we never remember, we will just learn to be Ruben, and Elda, and start our lives over."

Ahern shook his head. "There's a problem about that. You told me that the three women said that if the evil magic finally left you, then you might be able to get your memory, and your magic, back. You told me that it was imperative that you get it back. You said that there was great trouble in the world that you had to help with. You said that it was a matter of grave importance to every person alive. You said you had something you must do."

"What trouble? What is it I must do?"

"You didn't tell me. You said I wouldn't understand."

"Well, how do we get our memories, our magic, back?"

Ahern glanced to each. "It may not come back. The three women didn't know if it ever would, but if it is to come back, it will only come back with a shock. A great emotional jolt, or shock."

"An emotional shock? Like what?"

"Like maybe anger. Maybe if you are angry enough."

Ruben frowned. "So . . . what? You are to slap me, to make me angry?"

"No. You said that you didn't know how, but something like that wouldn't work. You said it required a great emotional shock, but you didn't know what it could be, or how to bring it about. You also said that if something did bring on the anger, it would be violent, and terrible, because of the magic. You said you had no choice, though, because you would die if you didn't do this."

Ruben and Elda sat in silence and thought while Ahern watched them. "So, where are you taking us? Why are we in this coach?"

"Aydindril."

"Aydindril? Never heard of it. Where is it? How far?"

"Aydindril is the home of the Confessors, clear on the other side of the Rang'Shada Mountains. It's a long journey: weeks, maybe a month. It will be close to winter solstice, the longest night of the year, before we get there."

"Seems a long way to go," Ruben said. "Why did I want you to take us there?"

"You said you had to go to the Wizard's Keep. You said that it takes magic to get in, but you don't have any magic, now, so you told me how to get you in. Seems you were a troublesome child, and had a secret way to sneak in and out of the Keep without triggering the magic."

Ruben drew his finger and thumb down his smooth jaw. "And you say I told you it was urgent?"

Ahern gave a grim nod.

"Then we'd best be on our way."

---

Just as she had been smiling to people all evening, Kahlan smiled to the woman in an elaborate dark blue gown before her. The woman was relating how concerned everyone had been for the Mother Confessor. Her insincerity was as transparent as the hypocrisy from everyone else. Kahlan had spent her whole life listening to duplicitous people try to mask their avaricious nature with words of altruism and amity. It sickened her.

Kahlan wished that just once, one of these people she lived and worked with would have the honesty to admit how strongly they hated her and how it infuriated them that she wouldn't allow them to rape the Midlands and its people for their own benefit. She admonished herself that they were not all like that.

Kahlan idly wondered, as she half listened, what this dignified wife of an ambassador would think if instead of seeing the Mother Confessor standing before her in a sparkling white dress, wearing a choker of jewels worth half her kingdom, she were to see her on a horse, naked, painted white and drenched in blood, as she hacked with a sword at the faces of men trying to kill her. Kahlan decided the woman would probably faint.

When the woman finally paused for a breath, Kahlan thanked her for her concern, and moved away. It was getting late and she was tired. She had an early appointment with the council. Seeing herself as she passed a mirror, Kahlan felt as if she had been dreaming for a very long time, and had awakened, the same as she was before, the Mother Confessor, in her white Confessor's dress, at the Confessors' Palace in Aydindril.

But she wasn't the same as the last time she had been here. She felt a hundred years older. She smiled; at least the bath had been wonderful. She couldn't remember finding a bath so luxurious. She had almost forgotten what it was like to be clean.

Near the doorway, another finely dressed lady approached. A twitch of a frown touched Kahlan's brow. The woman's sandy hair seemed too short—out of character with the other women's hair, which brushed their shoulders. But her dress certainly was in character; it was a costly looking black gown, letting her shoulders, and the sparkling emerald necklace, show.

The woman blocked the doorway just before Kahlan stepped through. She dropped a hurried curtsy, her blue eyes darting about as she came up.

"Mother Confessor, I must speak to you. It's urgent."

"I'm sorry, but I'm afraid I don't remember you."

The woman's blue eyes never looked up; they were constantly checking the other people. "You don't know me. We have a friend in common. . . ."

When the woman caught sight of a sour-faced, older woman looking in their direction, she put her back to the woman.

"Mother Confessor, did you come to Aydindril alone, or did you bring someone with you?"

"I have a friend, Chandalen, who came with me, but he is in the woods to the south for the night. Why?"

"That is not the name I was hoping to hear." She looked up into Kahlan's eyes. "You must . . ."

Her words trailed off. Her intense blue eyes slowly opened wider. She stood as if turned to stone.

"What is it?" Kahlan asked.

The woman seemed to be seeing specters. "You . . . you . . ."

The color had drained from her in a sickening rush. The woman staggered back a step. The sudden whiteness of her shoulders against the black fabric of her gown made her look like a spirit in a dress. Her jaw trembled as she tried without success to bring words forth. Her face was a mask of terror.

Her blue eyes rolled back into her head. Too late, Kahlan reached out for her. The woman crumpled into a heap on the floor.

People nearby gasped. Kahlan, along with others, bent to the woman. Men and women crowded around, murmuring to each other about too much wine.

The sour-faced woman elbowed her way through to the front. "Jebra! I thought it was Jebra!"

Kahlan looked up. "You know this woman? And who are you?"

The woman abruptly realized who she was speaking to. She flashed a sudden smile and curtsied awkwardly. "I am the Lady Ordith Condatith de Dackidvich, Mother Confessor. I'm so pleased to meet you, at last. I've been wanting to talk . . ."

Kahlan cut her off. "Who is this woman? Do you know her?"

"Know her?" Her sour expression returned. "She is my body servant. Her name is Jebra Bevinvier. I'll have the lazy wench thrashed!"

"Body servant?" a man said. "I don't think so. I've had dinner with Lady Jebra, and I can assure you, she is a lady."

Lady Ordith sniffed. "She's an imposter."

"Then you must pay her well," the man said sarcastically. "She stays in the finest inns, and pays with gold."

Lady Ordith gave the man another haughty sniff and snatched a guard's arm. "You! Take this wench to my quarters. I'm staying at the Kelton Palace. I'll get to the bottom of this."

Kahlan came to her feet and gave the Lady Ordith a withering glare. "You will do no such thing. Unless you are presuming to tell the Mother Confessor what to do in her own palace?"

Lady Ordith stammered an apology. Kahlan snapped her fingers to the side while holding Lady Ordith's gaze. Guards jumped forward.

Kahlan turned. "Take Lady Jebra to a guest room. Have a servant bring her some ginger tea, cold towels for her head, and anything else she wants. I do not want her disturbed by anyone, and that includes the Lady Ordith. I'm retiring for the night, and I do not wish to be disturbed by anyone, either. I have an early session with the council. After I meet with the council, I want Lady Jebra brought to me."

The guards saluted and bent to Lady Jebra.

When Kahlan reached her room, she was brought out of her troubled thoughts by the sight of two Keltish guards, from the Kelton Palace, at the doors to her room. When the guards saw her, one of them coolly tapped on the door with the butt of his spear. Someone was in her rooms. Kahlan glared at the impassive guards as she stalked through the doors.

No one was in the outer room. She stormed into the bedroom. When she saw him, she froze to a halt. Prince Fyren was standing on her bed, with his back to her.

He gave her a smirk over his shoulder while he urinated in the center of her bed.

When he was finished, Prince Fyren turned while he buttoned his trousers.

"What in the name of the spirits do you think you are doing?" she whispered.

He lifted an eyebrow to her as he strutted past. "Just letting the Mother Confessor know how happy we all are to have her home." His coat was open. He smoothed the ruffles on the front of his white shirt as he paused at the door. "Sleep well, Mother Confessor."

Kahlan yanked six times on the bell cord. Six breathless maidservants met her as she was charging down the hall.

"You wanted something, Mother Confessor?"

Kahlan gritted her teeth. "Take my mattress and bedcovers outside to the courtyard and burn them."

The girl blinked. "Mother Confessor?"

"Drag the mattress from my bed, along with all the bedcovers, out into the courtyard below my balcony, and set them on fire." Kahlan clenched her fists. "What part don't you understand!"

The six flinched back a step. "Yes, Mother Confessor." They stood trembling, their eyes wide. "Now, Mother Confessor?"

"If I wanted it done tomorrow, I would have called you tomorrow!"

Kahlan reached the stairs over grand entrance just in time to see Prince Fyren joining the man in plain robes waiting there for him. His dark eyes met hers for a long moment.

"Guards!" She screamed down toward the doors. The men in uniform looked up as they came running. "Diplomatic privilege is suspended! If I see that Keltish pig or any of his personal guard in this palace before the council session tomorrow morning, I will personally skin you all alive after I kill him!"

They saluted. Kahlan saw Lady Ordith in the hall leading to the entrance, watching everything that had just happened.

"Lady Ordith." Lady Ordith was already staring up. "I believe you said you were a guest of the Kelton Palace. Get out of mine."

She was stammering her good-byes as Kahlan spun on her heel and headed back to her room. She picked up a handful of guards on the way.

Outside her rooms, she waited until they were lined up before her doors. "If anyone comes into my room tonight, it had better be over your corpses. Do you understand?"

The all saluted to indicate that they did. Inside, Kahlan threw the white mantle around her shoulders and went out onto the balcony, into the bitter cold night. She stood with her back straight, near the railing, as she looked down on the scene in the courtyard below.

She wanted to run, but she couldn't. She was the Mother Confessor. She had to do what all the Mother Confessors before her had done—protect the Midlands. She was alone, and had no one to help her in her duty.

Tears rolled down her cheeks as she watched flames leap up from her bed; the bed she had promised Richard.

The reflections of the Mother Confessor, in her white dress, rotated around the polished black columns as she marched down the gallery, the Mother Confessor's private entrance to the council chambers. Kahlan was an hour early. She planned to be sitting in the First Chair as she watched all the councilors arrive. She didn't want them talking among themselves before she was present.

She froze to a halt as she threw the doors open. The room was packed. Every council chair was occupied. The galleries were all packed with people—not only officials, administrators, staff, and nobility, but ordinary people: farmers, shopkeepers, merchants, cooks, tradesmen, wagon drivers, and laborers. Men and women of every sort. Every eye was on her as she stood before the doors.

Across the huge room, the councilors all sat in their chairs. No one made a sound. Someone was sitting in the First Chair. From this distance, she couldn't see who it was, but she knew.

Kahlan touched her fingers to the bone necklace at her throat and prayed to the good spirits for protection and strength. Her boots echoed off the marble as she strode through patches of sunlight. There was something on the floor before the dais, but she couldn't tell what it was.

When Kahlan reached the curved desk, the man sitting in the First Chair was not the one she expected. Stretched out on a litter before the dais lay the body of Prince Fyren. His skin was pasty. His arms were folded, his hands laid over the blood-soaked ruffles of his shirt. His sword rested across his body. Prince Fyren's throat had been sliced open nearly to his spinal column.

Kahlan looked up to the solemn, dark eyes watching her. He came forward from the back of the First Chair and folded his hands together on the desk. A quick glance revealed what she hadn't noticed before: a ring of guards around the room.

She glared up at the man with the dark hair and beard. "Get out of my chair, or I will kill you myself."

The room rang with the sound of swords being drawn. Without taking his dark eyes from her, the man gestured with a flick of his hand. Every sword went hesitantly back into its scabbard.

"You are done killing people, Mother Confessor," he said in a quiet voice. "Prince Fyren was your last victim."

Kahlan frowned. "Who are you?"

"Neville Ranson." Still, his eyes did not leave her as he turned his hand up. A ball of flame ignited above his palm. "Wizard Neville Ranson."

Still, his eyes did not leave her as he cast the ball of flame skyward. It rose obediently toward the peak of the dome, where it broke, with a pop, into thousands of sparkles. Astonished gasps filled the room.

Wizard Ranson leaned back and drew open a scroll. "We have a great many charges, Mother Confessor. Where would you like to begin?"

Without turning her head, Kahlan's eyes took a sweep of what she could see of the room. There was no chance of escape. None. Even if the man before her were not a wizard.

"Since they will all be invented, I guess it doesn't matter. Why don't we just dispense with the mockery, and simply proceed to the execution."

The room remained dead silent. Wizard Ranson did not smile. His eyebrows lifted.

"Oh, no mockery, Mother Confessor, but serious charges. We are here to get to the truth of them. Unlike the Confessors, I refuse to put an innocent person to death. Before we are finished today, everyone here will know the truth of your treason. I want the people to know the full extent of your vile tyranny."

Kahlan clasped her hands together as she stood with her back straight. She wore her Confessor's face. The people all leaned forward a little.

"Since it is a long list," Ranson said, "we might as well begin with the most serious charge." He glanced down. "Treason."

"And since when is defending the people of the Midlands treason?"

Wizard Ranson slammed his fist to the desk as he shot to his feet. "Defending the people of the Midlands! I have never in my life heard such filth from the mouth of a woman!" He smoothed his tan robes at his stomach and then sat back down. "Your 'defense' of the people was to plunge them into war. You would condemn thousands to die, to assuage your dread that someone other than yourself would rule. And rule with the unanimous agreement of the council, I might add."

"It is hardly unanimous if the Mother Confessor dissents."

"Dissents for her own selfish motives."

"And who is it that you would have rule the Midlands? Kelton? Yourself?"

"The saviors of all people. The Imperial Order."

A prickling sensation rose up her legs. Kahlan felt as if the whole of the dome overhead were collapsing down on her. Her head spun. She thought she might be sick right there, in front of everyone. She forced her stomach to behave.

"The Imperial Order! The Imperial Order slaughtered Ebinissia! They crush all opposition to steal rule for themselves!"

"Lies. The Imperial Order is dedicated to benevolent rule. They simply wish to put your murderous intents to an end."

"Benevolent! They raped and butchered the people of Ebinissia!"

Ranson chuckled. "Come, come, Mother Confessor. The Imperial Order has murdered no one." He turned to a man Kahlan didn't recognize. "Councilor Thurstan, has your crown city been harmed by anyone?"

The jowly man looked surprised. "I have just arrived two days ago from the beautiful city of Ebinissia, and they know nothing of their slaughter."

The crowd chuckled with him. Ranson smiled petulantly at her.

"Did you not expect, Mother Confessor, that we would have witnesses to expose your preposterous stories? This is simply a fiction meant to inflame people's fears, and stir them to war."

Ranson snapped his fingers. A woman in drab, worn clothes came in and stood to the side. Ranson gently told her not to be frightened, and to tell her story. The woman told of how her children had to go to bed hungry, because she had no money. She said she had been forced into prostitution to feed her children. Kahlan knew it was a lie. There was no scarcity of charitable people and groups who would help anyone truly needing it.

For the next hour, one witness after another was paraded in, and each told a story of hunger and want, and how the palace would not give them money to feed and clothe themselves, not caring if their children starved. The people in the balconies listened with rapt attention to the sad stories, some weeping with the witnesses.

Kahlan recognized a few of the people testifying. She remembered Mistress Sanderholt offering them work in the past. She had told Kahlan that when they had come in, they scoffed at the things they were asked to do. Mistress Sanderholt ended up having to do many of the tasks herself.

Wizard Ranson rose to his feet, after the last witness had told his tearful story, and turned to each side, addressing the people gathered. "The Mother Confessor has a vast treasury, and she intended to use it to finance a war against the people of the Midlands who would wish to be free of her rule. She first takes the food from your mouths, and the mouths of your children, and then, to keep you from thinking about the gnawing hunger in your gut, invents an enemy, and starts a war with your hard-earned money, which she has stolen for her already wealthy friends.

"While you people go hungry, she eats well! While you need clothes, she would buy weapons! While your sons would bleed to death in battle, she lounges in the lap of luxury! When your family members are unjustly accused of crimes, she uses her magic to make them confess to crimes they did not commit to silence their protests against her tyranny!"

People were weeping. A few cried out with anguish at the last part. Still more angrily demanded justice. Kahlan began to doubt that she would be beheaded. This mob would probably tear her apart before she ever made it to the block.

Ranson held his arms open to the people gathered. "As a representative of the Imperial Order, I direct that the people get what they really need. The treasury of Aydindril will be put to its best use. It will be turned back to the oppressed. I direct that every family shall be entitled to one gold piece a month, to clothe and feed your children. There will be no starvation allowed under the rule of the Imperial Order."

Cheering erupted in the great hall. The wild applauding and huzzahs went on unabated for a good five minutes. Ranson sat and steepled his fingers while he listened to the celebration. He never took his eyes from Kahlan, nor she from his.

Kahlan knew that life's hardships were not that simple to eradicate. She knew that seeming kindness could in truth be cruel. She calculated that the payments would take, at most, six months to empty the treasury. She wondered what would happen the following month, when the money was gone, and people would have by then stopped working, or planting, to provide for themselves. Then there certainly would be hunger and starvation—in the guise of generosity.

At last the noise died out. Ranson leaned forward.

"There is no way of telling how many people have gone hungry, or starved to death, or died in war, by your command, Mother Confessor. It is obvious you are guilty of treason against the people of the Midlands. I see no reason to draw the evidence out, as we could, for weeks." The other councilors all voiced yeas of agreement. Ranson slapped his hand to the desk. "Guilty of the first charge then: treason."

The people cheered, again. Kahlan stood with her back stiff, wearing her Confessor's face. Ranson read off charges she could scarcely believe could be read with a straight face. Witnesses came forward and testified to atrocities that Kahlan thought anyone with common sense would laugh at. No one laughed.

People she had never met before confided their intimate knowledge of what Confessors did in secret. A lump rose in Kahlan's throat as she heard what people thought of her. People repeated irrational fears and rumors of every sort of outrage committed by Confessors, and the Mother Confessor in particular.

For her whole life she had sacrificed everything, as had the other Confessors, to protect these people, and the whole time they believed these monstrosities instead. Kahlan thought, when she heard a witness testify that in order to retain their magical power, Confessors had to dine regularly on human flesh, that there would be laughter at the charge. Instead, wide-eyed people leaned forward and gasped. She had to bite the inside of her cheek to keep from bursting into tears, not because she was being charged with such things, but because people truly believed them of her.

Kahlan finally stopped listening. As Ranson listed charges, brough forth witnesses, and the council found her guilty of charge after charge, she thought about Richard. She tried to remember all the moments she had spent with him, all the times he had smiled, all the times he had touched her. She tried to remember every kiss.

"You think it amusing!" Ranson railed.

Kahlan looked up. She realized she was smiling. "What?"

A woman was standing to the side, weeping into a kerchief. Kahlan blinked at her, and then looked up to Ranson.

"I'm sorry, I guess I missed her performance."

The crowd grumbled in anger. Ranson leaned back in his chair with a disgusted shake of his head.

"Guilty, of practicing your Confessor's magic on children."

"What? Are you insane? Children?"

Ranson held a hand out toward the woman, who broke into wild wailing. "She has just testified that her child is missing, and has told how other women have had their children disappear, too, and how it is common knowledge that the children are taken so that Confessors may practice their magic on them. As a wizard, I can verify the truth of this." The crowd howled with rage.

Kahlan blinked up at him. "I have a headache. Why don't you just chop it off for me."

"Uncomfortable, Mother Confessor? Uncomfortable that the people would be given the chance to face their oppressor, and hear the extent of her heinous crimes?"

Kahlan held her Confessor's face to keep from tears. "I am sorry only that I have given my whole life to the people of the Midlands. Had I known they would be so ungrateful, and believe instead such filth after what I have sacrificed for them, I would have been more selfish and left them to true tyranny."

Ranson scowled down at her. "You have worked your whole life for the Keeper." The crowd gasped again. "That is who you serve. That is what you work for. You offer the souls of your people to your master, the Keeper, in the underworld."

People in the balconies wailed with terror. Cries of anger and calls for vengeance echoed in the dome. Shaking their fists, the crowd on the main floor tried to push forward, but the guards spread their arms and held them back. Ranson lifted his hands, calling for calm and quiet.

Kahlan moved her gaze over the people to each side.

"I give you to the Imperial Order," she called out in a loud voice. "I work no longer to save you. You will be punished for your unthinking willingness to believe these lies. Punished by what your own selfish desires will bring upon you. You will come to regret the torment you have willingly cast yourselves into. I am joyful that I will be dead, so I will not be tempted to help you. I regret only that I have ever shed a tear for your suffering. To the Keeper with all of you!"

Kahlan glared up at a smirking Wizard Ranson. "Get on with it! Chop off my head! I'm sickened with this travesty of truth! You and your Imperial Order win. Kill me, so I may be rid of this life, and go to the spirit world, where I will not have to suffer to help anyone. I confess to everything. Execute me. I am guilty of it all." She looked down at the body at her feet. "Except killing this Keltish pig. I wish, now, that I had killed him, but unfortunately, I can't claim credit."

Ranson lifted an eyebrow. "A liar to the end, Mother Confessor; you cannot even admit the truth of this murder."

Lady Ordith came in, her nose in the air, and testified that she had heard Kahlan threaten Prince Fyren only the night before. The council all spoke up, that they, too, had heard her threaten to cut his throat.

"This is your proof?" Kahlan asked.

Ranson gestured to the side. "Bring in the witness. You see, Mother Confessor, we know the truth. One of your former friends wanted to help hide the truth of your ways, and we had to use extreme measures to make her cooperate, but in the end, she did."

A shaking Mistress Sanderholt was led into the chamber. Guards stood to each side of her stooped, thin frame. Her face was drawn, her red eyes heavy with dark bags underneath. Her familiar vitality was gone. Swaying slightly, she looked as if she could hardly stand without aid.

Mistress Sanderholt held her mangled hands out, in fear they would touch anything. All her fingernails had been pulled off with tongs. Bile rose in Kahlan's throat.

A stern-faced Neville Ranson looked down at the woman. "Tell us what you know of this murder."

Mistress Sanderholt gazed unblinking up at him. She bit her lower lip. Her eyes filled with tears. It was obvious she didn't want to speak.

Ranson slammed his fist on the desk. "Speak! Or we will find you guilty of aiding the murderer!"

"Mistress Sanderholt," Kahlan said softly. The woman's eyes came to her. "Mistress Sanderholt, I know the truth, and you know the truth; that is all that matters. These people are going to do as they plan, with or without your help. I do not want you to suffer on my account. Please tell them what they wish to hear."

Tears rolled down her face. "But . . ."

Kahlan straightened her back. "Mistress Sanderholt, as Mother Confessor, I command you to testify against me."

Mistress Sanderholt gave her a twitch of a smile. She turned her face up to the council. "I saw the Mother Confessor sneak up behind Prince Fyren. She cut his throat before he knew she was there. She offered him no chance to defend himself."

Ranson smiled down and nodded. "Thank you, Mistress Sanderholt. And you were her friend, but you came forward and agreed to testify, because you wanted the council, and the people, to know the truth?"

More tears streamed down. "Yes. Though I loved her, I had to tell the people the truth of her murderous ways."

After she was escorted out, and the council had unanimously found Kahlan culpable, Ranson stood, lifting his hand for silence before addressing the people.

"The Mother Confessor has been found guilty of all charges!" Everyone hooted and hollered their satisfaction. They shouted for an immediate execution. "The Mother Confessor will be executed, but not this day." He held his hand up angrily against the protests. They quieted. "She has committed crimes against all the people. They must be given a chance to hear of justice being done. They must be given a chance to come to the beheading. It will be held in a few days, when everyone harmed by this criminal has had a chance to come to see her executed."

Neville Ranson stepped down and came around the dais. He stood in front of her, looking into her eyes. He spoke quietly, to her, and not to the crowd.

"You would think to use your power on me, Mother Confessor?"

That had been exactly what she had been thinking, to use her power knowing she would die in the process. But she said nothing.

Ranson's smile was cold and cruel. "You shall not have the chance. I am going to strip you of three things. First, your power and its symbol. Second, your dignity. Third, your life."

Kahlan threw herself at him. He stood, his hands clasped, and watched as she was able to move only inches before she was mired in a thickness of air that held her tight. She fought unsuccessfully against the staggering power that held her.

The wizard lifted his hands. Kahlan saw a flash. She cried out as she felt a cold shock flood through her body. It felt as if she had plunged naked into an icy river. She shivered violently. The sting of cold brought tears to her eyes. The cold pain felt as if it could grow no worse, could hurt no more, but then it did.

It felt as if her insides ripped, as if her heart were being torn from her chest. She screamed in pain. Stunned by the shock of it, she realized she was on her knees. Ranson was holding his hands out, over her head.

When the pain lifted, she felt tingling panic.

Her power was gone.

Where she had always felt it before, without even being aware of it most of the time, she now felt a forlorn emptiness.

She had so often wished to be rid of it, but never realized what it would feel like to be without her magic. She cried out again. Tears streamed down her cheeks at the forsaken, vacant desolation. She felt naked before the mob of people.

She forced herself to stop the tears. She would not let these people see the Mother Confessor cry. No—she would not let these people see Kahlan Amnell cry.

Ranson drew Prince Fyren's sword from its scabbard. He stepped behind her. He took up her hair in his fist and pulled it out tight as she knelt on the cold floor.

With the sword, he sliced her hair off, close, right at the nape of her neck. The shearing felt almost as shocking to her as having her power taken. The hair Richard loved so. She bit back tears.

Neville Ranson held up the severed handful of her hair to wild cheering. Kahlan knelt, numbly staring at nothing, as soldiers tied her wrists behind her back. Ranson grasped her arm, under her shoulder, and hauled her to her feet.

"The first of it, then, Mother Confessor. You have been stripped of your power, and its symbol. As I promised you. Now to the rest of it."

Kahlan was silent—there was nothing to say—as Ranson and a cluster of grinning guards led her down through the palace. She didn't pay any attention to where she was being taken. She was thinking about Richard, hoping he would remember her love for him. She lost herself in memories of him. She let the world around her go. She would soon let the world of life go, too. The good spirits had deserted her.

She was numb to what was happening. The emptiness of being without her power left her feeling half dead already. She had never known how much it meant to her, how much a part of her the magic was, until it was gone. She wondered if this dull bleakness was the way people without the power felt all the time. She couldn't imagine living without the magic.

She longed for death, now, to end this dead feeling. Only Richard had accepted her with her power. She never completely accepted it herself, but Richard had. Now it was too late. She grieved more for the loss of her magic than her life. She knew, now, what the other creatures of magic would feel, when it happened to them. She grieved for them.

Ranson's hand on her arm jerked her to a halt, jerked her to awareness, before an iron door in a dim corridor. One of the guards worked at a rusty lock on the iron door. Kahlan recognized the door. She had taken confessions down here.

"And now, to my second promise, Mother Confessor," Ranson said with a sneer. "You will be stripped of your dignity."

Kahlan gasped as his fist grabbed what was left of her hair and jerked her head back. As she was held helpless, her wrists bound painfully behind her back, and her hair in his fist, Ranson kissed her neck.

Right where Darken Rahl had kissed her neck.

The same horrors coursed through her mind as when Darken Rahl had done it. She shuddered with revulsion, with the horror of the visions. In her mind, she saw the young women in Ebinissia, only this time, she was one of them.

"I would rape you myself," Ranson whispered in her ear, "but I find your sense of honor disgusting."

The door squeaked open, and without any further word, Ranson shoved her through the doorway, into the pit.

## CHAPTER 59

**K**ahlan gasped at the feeling of falling through space, but before she had a chance to fully consider what would happen when she hit the floor, rough hands caught her. They pushed her down to the cold stone. She saw the light of the doorway above disappear when the door clanged closed. In the light of a sputtering torch in a bracket, she saw grinning men all about, pushing in at her.

The rope cut into her wrists. Her feelings of terror and helplessness gave way to desperate action. Kahlan kicked a man in the groin. She was on her back on the floor, so she had leverage to do damage. She rammed her heel into the face of another man leaning over her. He fell back with a cry. She kicked frantically at the others.

The grasping hands caught her ankles. She kicked her legs but the men held tight. She rolled to the side, breaking the grip, and skittered into a corner. Her freedom was only momentary. They seized her flailing legs again.

In the back of her mind, as she fought, Kahlan desperately tried to think. A spark of thought tried to get her attention. It was something about Zedd, but she couldn't think clearly.

The men fighting to get at her pushed her white dress up her legs. Hands pawed at her thighs. Big, meaty fingers hooked her smallclothes, stripping them down her legs and off her feet. She felt rough hands and cold air on her flesh. She fought the men and, at the same time, her own panic.

Two men were on the floor; one holding his crotch, the other sprawled out, blood gushing from his ruined face. His nose was crushed. There were ten others, all trying to get at her at once. They threw each other back, trying to force themselves on top of her, the biggest working his way in. Kahlan couldn't get her breath.

With frantic effort, the spark of thought sprang forth. She remembered asking Zedd if he could remove her power. She had wanted to be free of it so she could be with Richard. Zedd had told her that it wasn't possible to rid a Confessor of her power, that she was born with the magic, and it couldn't be separated from her as long as she was alive.

How could Ranson have stripped her of her power? Zedd was a wizard of the First Order; there was no wizard with more power than a wizard of the First Order. Why wouldn't Ranson have wanted to rape her first? He said she disgusted him. But he said he wanted to strip her of her dignity. Why wouldn't he want to do it?

Unless he was afraid.

Afraid she would figure it out. Figure what out?

It came to her. The Wizard's First Rule.

People would believe anything, if they wanted to believe. Or if they were afraid it was true. She was afraid it was true that he had stripped her of her power. Maybe he had used magic to give her pain and mask her ability to sense her own magic, to try to trick her into believing what she feared.

As the men groped at her, she groped for her power. She tried to find the calmness, the place of her magic, but it just wasn't there. All she felt was emptiness. Where she always felt the swell of magic before, she now felt only a numb, hollow void.

She wanted to cry at the feel of the men's hands on her legs, and between them, but she couldn't allow herself to lose control, her only chance. Try as she might, she couldn't find the magic, couldn't call it forth. It was simply gone. She desperately wanted her hands free.

"Wait!" she screamed.

The men all stopped for a moment, their faces pulling back, looking at her. She gasped to catch her breath.

Talk, she ordered of herself, while you have the chance. "You're doing it all wrong!"

They laughed. "We think we'll figure it out," one said.

Kahlan struggled to control her fear, and think. They were going to do what they were going to do, and she couldn't stop them. Fighting them in this way was going to accomplish nothing, except to feed her panic. She had only one chance, and that was to use her head. She had to slow them down and give herself time to think.

"If you do it this way, you will just be denying yourselves the full satisfaction of it."

They frowned. "What do you mean?"

"If you're all fighting each other, and me, you won't be able to really enjoy me as a woman. Wouldn't it be more enjoyable if I cooperated?"

They all looked at one another. One to the side spoke up. "She has a point. The queen wasn't nearly so much good after she went numb on us."

"Queen?" Kahlan asked. "What queen? You men are just bragging on me. You've had no queen."

"Queen Cyrilla," a different man said. "She fainted on us, then went feebleminded. Just lay there the whole time, like a dead fish. But we had her anyway, had a queen. Still . . ."

Kahlan fought back the scream, fought to keep the meaning of what she had just learned from making her start kicking again. That would only get her the same as Cyrilla.

Her only chance was to use her head. She needed time to search for her magic, and if she somehow did find it, she needed the men separated. Otherwise, nine men would overpower that one. She had to have things organized first, in case the magic worked. And, she needed the strongest to be the one.

For an instant, she abandoned her idea, fearing it wouldn't save her, and worse, fearing she wouldn't have the nerve to do it. But then she bleakly realized that even if it didn't work, it didn't matter. They were going to rape her one way or the other. Her only chance was to try. She had nothing to lose.

"That's what I mean. Wouldn't you rather have my cooperation? I'm going to be down here for days. You'll each have more than your share of time on me. Wouldn't you rather I helped? That way, you could all have what you want." She thought she might vomit.

"Keep talking," the biggest man said in a gruff voice.

Kahlan stiffened her resolve. "I've never . . . had a man before." They all hooted

593

at their luck. She waited until their leers came back to her. She fought back the urge to shriek at the looks in those eyes. "Like I said, I've never had a man. I know you men are going to have me, and I can't stop you. If it's going to be done anyway, I'd rather . . . enjoy it."

Their hungry smiles widened. "Yea? Well, what do you think you'd enjoy most, little lady?"

"If you did it one at a time. Wouldn't that be better for you, too? If you weren't fighting each other, if you waited your turn, then you could concentrate on enjoying everything a real woman has to offer."

A couple of the men grabbed at her legs, pulling them apart. They growled that they would have what they wanted their own way. The biggest, the one with the gruff voice, hauled them back, throwing one against the wall. His head banged with a loud thunk.

"Let her talk! She makes sense!" He turned his vicious eyes on her. "Let's hear your offer."

Kahlan tried to slow her voice down, and sound like she might be intrigued by the idea. She tried to sound self-confident as she shrugged.

"If you do it my way, I'll give you whatever you want. I'll make sure you enjoy whatever you like."

Some of the men chuckled. The big man's eyes showed his suspicion. "Why? And how do we know you mean it?"

"Because I'll be able to enjoy it, too, that way." Kahlan swallowed back her fear. "Untie my hands, and I'll show you I mean it."

She leaned forward as he untied her hands, another man taking the opportunity to fondle her breasts. She remained still. At last, her hands were untied. She rubbed her aching wrists and then smiled at the big man as she ran her fingers down his cheek.

He slapped her hand away. "You're running out of time. You better show us you mean what you say."

Kahlan steeled herself as she leaned back against the wall. She pulled her dress up above her waist, drew her knees up, and spread her legs. She looked to the big man. "Touch me."

Three of the other men reached for her. She slapped their hands away. "I said one at a time!" She looked the big man in the eyes, when they came up. He towered over the other men. "What's your name?"

"Tyler."

"One at a time. You first, Tyler. Touch me."

The stone walls echoed with the sound of heavy breathing. The big man reached out and stroked her. It took all her strength to keep her knees apart. She forced herself to breathe. She prayed he couldn't see her shaking.

A grin spread on his hulking face as his husky hand groped her. She coyly pushed his hand away and put her knees together.

"See? Isn't that better that some delicate woman who faints at the first touch and lies on the floor like a dead fish?"

The other men agreed that it surely was. Tyler gave her a suspicious look.

"You look like one of them Confessors."

Kahlan sputtered a laugh. "Confessor!" She pulled out a short strand of hair. The feel of how short it was almost made her cry out in anguish. "Does this look like I'm a Confessor?"

"No . . . but that dress . . ."

"Well," Kahlan said, "she wasn't wearing it, so I borrowed it."

"Last I heard, they don't behead people for stealing a dress. What did you do to get yourself thrown in with us?"

She held her chin up. "I didn't do anything. I'm innocent."

The men laughed. They said that they, too, were innocent. Tyler wasn't laughing with them. He had a dangerous look in his eyes. She knew she had to do something, and quick.

With her heart thumping so hard she thought it might come right out of her chest, she took Tyler's hand in both of hers, and put it back up between her legs, pressing her thighs to it.

Tyler's leering grin swept the caution from his face. "So what is it you want us to do?" he asked.

"I'll make myself available here, and the rest of you all go over there, while I'm with each man in turn. That way I'll feel safe enough to enjoy it, and at ease enough to make sure you do, too." She looked back to the big man and licked her lips as she smiled. "And I have one other condition. I want you first. I've always wanted a really big man."

She shivered at the look in his eyes. She told herself that she was the Mother Confessor; she had to keep her head. She licked her lips again as she wiggled herself against his hand.

Tyler burst into laughter. The others all chuckled nervously with him. "You lofty ladies all act better than everyone else, but when it comes to it, you're just a whore, like all the rest."

His smile vanished in a way that made her heart skip a beat. "I wrung the neck of the last whore what acted like she was better than me, and decided to change her mind. That wizard told us what he'd do if we were to kill you, but that don't mean we won't make you regret it if you go back on your word." Kahlan could only manage a smile and a nod. "Let's get to it."

A sweep of his arm scattered the others to the opposite side of the pit, while she was desperately seeking the feel of her magic. He told them they could decide among themselves who went next. And then he turned to her. He started unbuckling his pants.

Kahlan wildly searched her mind for a stall. She needed time to figure out how to find her power. "How about a kiss, first?"

"I don't need no kiss," he growled. "Open your legs, like before. I liked that."

"Well, it's just that a kiss from a big, handsome man gets a woman randy to please him."

He paused a moment, then put his right arm around her shoulders and slammed her to the floor beside him. "You better get randy real quick, before I lose my patience."

"I promise. Just kiss me a bit first."

Tyler pressed his lips to hers. She gasped when his other hand suddenly went up between her legs, but this time with forceful insistence, instead of a gentle touch like before. He thought the gasp was cooperation, and pressed his lips harder to hers. She wrapped her arms around his neck. The smell of him almost made her sick.

Kahlan tried to concentrate on finding the calm, as she always had before when she used her power. She could not find the place. She desperately sought the swell of magic, but found nothing.

Failure brought tears of frustration. Tyler's breathing was becoming emphatic. He was pressing so hard that it was hurting her lips against her teeth. She pretended to savor it.

It was almost impossible to concentrate with the terror of what his hand was doing between her legs, but she dared not stop him. Panic rose in her throat as she forced herself to hold her legs open for him. Her heels pressed harder to the floor and her feet trembled in her boots.

Kahlan reprimanded herself. She was the Mother Confessor. She had used her power countless times. She tried again, but nothing happened. Her memory of the young women in Ebinissia was keeping her from being able to focus.

And then she thought of Richard. She almost wailed with longing for him. If she was ever to have a chance of seeing Richard again, she had to use her magic. She had to be strong. She had to do it for him.

Nothing happened. She realized she was whimpering in frustration against Tyler's mouth. He took it for passion.

His face pulled back a few inches. "Spread your legs more, so they can all see how much a fancy lady wants Tyler."

She submissively drew her heels closer to herself and spread her knees wider. The men all hooted their approval. She could feel her ears burning. She remembered what Ranson had said about taking her dignity. Tyler pressed his lips back to hers. Tears seeped from the corners of her eyes.

It wasn't working. She couldn't find her power—if it was even there. She had no choice. She was going to have to follow through with what she had offered the men. Failure to do so now would only bring her a beating on top of it. There was no escape.

She thought about the poor women in Ebinissia. That was what was going to happen to her. It was hopeless. In her mind, she gave up. She surrendered to what was going to happen.

Something her father had told her sprang to the front of her mind—*If you ever give up, Kahlan, you are lost. Fight with every breath. With the last, if you must, but don't give up. Not ever. Don't hand them victory. Fight with what you have to the last breath.* She wasn't doing that. She was giving up.

Tyler sat up. "Enough kissing. You're ready."

She had run out of time. She wondered if Richard would hate her for this. No. He would know she had no choice. He would be disappointed only if she felt shame for being a victim. He had suffered unimaginable pain before Denna had done what she wanted. He knew what it meant to be helpless. She did not blame him for what was forced on him. He would not blame her. He would comfort her.

If it didn't work with this man, she told herself, then maybe it would work with the next. She would keep trying with each. She would not give up. She would keep trying to find her power with each.

"Keep your legs open," Tyler growled as he undid his trousers. She realized she had unconsciously put her knees together. She obediently spread them again as a tear rolled down the side of her face.

*Dear spirits*, she prayed, *help me*.

No. The good spirits had never helped her before. They had never come to her

596

aid before, despite her efforts on their behalf, despite her pleas. They would not come now.

To the Keeper with the worthless good spirits.

*Don't cry, girl*, she told herself. *Fight them. With your last breath if need be.*

"Please," she said. "Just one more kiss?"

"You had enough kissing. Time to do as you said. Time for me, now."

Kahlan pulled her heels up against herself, spread her legs as wide as she could, and wiggled her bottom as he leered. "Please? Your kisses are the best I've ever had. Just one more? Please?" She watched his chest heave. "Then I'll please you like no woman ever has. Just one more kiss."

He flopped down on her, between her legs. His weight drove the wind from her lungs. "One more, and then you deliver."

He crushed his whiskered face to hers. He was out of control. His lips were cutting hers against her teeth. She tried to ignore the burning heat of him pressing painfully against her.

Kahlan slapped her hands to the sides of his muscular neck. Her lungs burned for air. This was her last chance. Her last breath. Fight with it, she told herself. Fight.

For Richard.

As she had done countless times, she released her restraint, although she felt no power pushing against it.

It was like leaping into a dark, bottomless pit.

There was thunder but no sound.

The violent jolt to the air brought down a shower of stone dust.

The men all cried out with the pain of being so close when her power was released.

Kahlan almost screamed with joy. She could feel the magic in her middle again. It was weak, from having just been used, but she could feel it again. It was back. It had never left; Ranson had used magic to make her believe a lie.

Tyler's jaw had gone slack as he pulled back, looking down into her eyes. "Mistress!" he whispered. "Command me."

The other men were scrambling toward them.

"Protect me!"

Heads cracked against the walls, sending splashes of blood across the stone. Tyler snapped a man's arm. Wails of pain echoed around the room. There was a furious battle for a few minutes, until Kahlan was able to direct Tyler in accomplishing what she wanted—a truce.

She didn't want him to fight all the men; if they succeeded in getting the better of him, then she was finished. She wanted them separated, the men keeping their distance, and Tyler guarding her. That was her best chance of surviving until she could recover her power.

She screamed orders to the men, as well as Tyler. Six were left standing, in fighting form, and enraged. One was writhing on the ground, screaming in pain, a shattered bone jutting from his forearm, and the other four, including the one she had kicked in the face, were not moving.

Kahlan told the men that she would keep Tyler at bay as long as they stayed in their corner. Reluctantly, they moved to the opposite side, dragging the others with them. The screams kept them convinced that they should bide their time before

597

taking on the big man with the wild eyes. She made them throw her her smallclothes, under threat of sending Tyler to get them.

Kahlan sat in the corner, her back against the wall. Tyler stood before her, in a half crouch, dancing on the balls of his feet, his arms out and ready. The men watched as they rested against the other wall. Kahlan knew that this uneasy truce could not go on for days. Sooner or later, Tyler would run out of energy. Then they would have him. Then they would have her. The men knew that, too.

The night wore on, with the men watching, and Tyler guarding her. She caught a few moments of uneasy sleep from time to time. Kahlan had no idea what time it was, but she judged it to be between the middle of the night and close to dawn.

Though she was afraid, and knew that they were going to come to behead her sooner or later, she felt joy that her power was back, and that she had beaten them with that much of it. The good spirits hadn't helped her; she had helped herself. She felt self-satisfaction at what she had done. She had not given up.

And the good spirits had left her to it, as they always did. Kahlan was furious with the good spirits. Though she had lived her whole life to see their ideals upheld, they never once helped her.

Well, no more. She was finished with the good spirits, as she was finished with trying to help the ungrateful people of the Midlands. What had it gotten her? She had learned in the council chambers what it had gotten her. It had gotten her the undying hatred of her people. The very people she fought for thought she harmed children. People didn't like Confessors, and were afraid of them for a variety of reasons, but she had been stunned to learn what people really believed about her.

From now on, she was going to worry about herself, her friends, and Richard, and to the Keeper with the rest of them. He could have them all. She was through with it all.

She was the Mother Confessor no longer. She was Kahlan.

The torch sputtered out, plunging the pit into blackness.

"Thank you again, good spirits!" she screamed at the top of her lungs. Her words echoed around the pit. "To the Keeper with you!"

The men set upon Tyler in the dark. Kahlan didn't know what was happening. She could hear grunts and screams and thuds.

She heard an echoing, banging sound. She couldn't understand what it was. And then she heard a muffled voice calling out her title. The familiar voice was coming from above.

"Chandalen! Chandalen! I'm down here! Open the door!"

"Mother Confessor!" came the voice from beyond the door. "How do I open the door!"

Kahlan let out a shriek when a hand snatched her ankle and pulled her from her feet. Chandalen called out at the sound of her scream. Tyler grabbed the fingers around her ankle and bent them back until they snapped. The man screamed in the dark.

"Chandalen! You need a key! Use the key!"

"Key? What is this key!"

"Chandalen!" She shoved a head away from her middle. "Chandalen! Remember when we were in the city with the dead people? Remember the queen's room that was locked? Remember I showed you a key to open the door? Chandalen, one of the guards up there has a ring on his belt! It has the key! Hurry!"

Kahlan recognized Tyler's grunt as he was slammed to the wall. She could hear the bone-jarring blows of his fist. She could hear a metallic noise from above.

"Mother Confessor! It will not turn!"

"Then it's the wrong one! Try another!"

Someone crashed into her, knocking her to the floor. She clawed at his eyes. He punched at her middle.

A sudden shaft of light descended into the pit. Tyler saw the man on her and threw him off. A ladder dropped down.

"Tyler! Keep them away from the ladder!"

Kahlan threw herself onto the ladder and scrambled up. The men piled on Tyler. She heard him groan and then his neck snap. Her foot slipped through a rung when a fist punched the back of her calf. Hands grabbed at her ankles. Kahlan kicked the face of the man right behind and then clambered up. He tumbled back, taking the others with him. They charged back up in a rush.

Kahlan stretched for the hand extended down. Chandalen clamped onto her wrist and yanked her through the doorway. He stabbed the man right behind her. As the man toppled back, Chandalen slammed the door closed. Panting, she fell into his arms.

"Come, Mother Confessor. We must get out of this place."

There were dead guards everywhere, all killed silently, from behind, by Chandalen's *troga*. He held her hand as they ran through the dank, dark halls and up stairs. She wondered how Chandalen had managed to find his way down here. Someone must have shown him the way.

Around a corner, they came to the sight of a bloody battle. Bodies were sprawled everywhere. Only one man was standing. Orsk. His great battle-axe dripped with gore. Orsk nearly leapt out of his skin with joy when he saw her. She was almost thrilled to see his scarred face.

"I made him wait," Chandalen explained as he pulled her through the bloody mess. "I told him that I would bring you, if he waited and guarded this hall."

Chandalen frowned at her. Kahlan realized he was staring at her hair, or what was left of it. He said nothing, though, and she was glad for that. It felt more than strange not to feel the weight of her hair; it was heartbreaking. She had loved her hair; so had Richard.

Kahlan bent and took a war axe from one of the dead guards. With her power not yet recovered, she felt better with a weapon in her hands.

Chandalen, dragging Kahlan along by her hand, with Orsk protecting the rear, burst through a door. Directly outside, the captain of the guards had a woman pressed up against the wall. Her arms were wrapped around his neck as she kissed him; his hands were up her dress.

As they charged past, and the startled captain looked up, Chandalen drove his long knife into the man's ribs.

"Come!" he said to the woman, "We have her!"

The woman fell into line with the rest of them as they wound their way up through the palace. Puzzled, Kahlan looked back. The woman in the hooded cloak was the woman who had fainted—Jebra Bevinvier.

"What's going on?" Kahlan asked Jebra.

"Forgive me, Mother Confessor, for fainting. I had a vision of you being beheaded. It was so horrifying that I fainted. I knew I must help, so that the vision would not come true. You told me that you had a friend in the woods. I went and found him."

They all flattened up against a wall and waited for a patrol to pass through an adjoining room. When their echoing footsteps faded, Chandalen turned with a hot look to Jebra.

"What were you doing with that man!"

She blinked in surprise. "He was the captain of the guards. He was making the rounds with a whole detachment. I convinced him to send the guards away for a while. I did the only thing I could think of to keep fifty men from trapping you down there."

Chandalen grumbled that maybe it made sense. As they headed on, Kahlan told Jebra that she had done a brave thing, and that she understood what courage it took to do it. Jebra protested that she was no heroine, and didn't want to be one.

At an intersection with a vaulted corridor, Mistress Sanderholt was waiting. Letting out a cry, Kahlan threw her arms around the woman. Mistress Sanderholt held her bandaged hands out.

"Not now, Mother Confessor. You must escape. This way is clear."

As the others rushed in the direction Mistress Sanderholt indicated, Kahlan went the other way. They all turned and ran after.

"What are you doing!" Chandalen yelled. "We must escape!"

"I have to get something from my room."

"What could be more important than escaping!"

*"Grandfather's knife,"* she said as she ran.

When they realized they were not going to be able to change her mind, they all followed after as she led them up through the labyrinth of smaller and less frequently patrolled halls. Several times they did encounter guards. Orsk fiercely hacked them to pieces when they charged after her.

As she came around a corner at the top of a stairway, a surprised guard spun to her. With all her strength, Kahlan buried her axe in the center of his chest. His sword skittered across the floor as he went down on his back.

As he thrashed on the floor, Kahlan put a foot against his heaving stomach and tried to pull the axe out. Bubbles of air and blood frothed forth, but the axe was stuck tight in his breastbone, so she scooped up his Keltish sword instead. Chandalen lifted an eyebrow. Before they reached her room, she had cause to use the sword, and with similar, deadly effect.

The others waited in the outer room, recovering their wind, while she rushed into her bedroom. She froze when she saw her blue wedding dress. She swept it up and held it to her breast. That was what she had come for. She didn't want to leave it; she was never returning to this place. Kahlan shed a tear on the dress, rolled it into a tight bundle, and stuffed it in her pack.

All the other clothes from her pack were cleaned, too, and laid out for her. She stuffed them in the pack after strapping the bone knife around her left arm. She threw the mantle around her shoulders. Hurriedly, she strung the bow.

She swept through the outer room, her pack and quiver on her back, and her bow on her shoulder. She had everything she wanted. Everything that meant anything to her. She paused a moment, looking at her room for the last time as she idly turned the round bone on her necklace, and then led the others out and down a back way, headed for an outside door.

She lost count of how many men Chandalen took out with his *troga* or knife. When a big guard charged out of a side hall and tried to roll them down, Kahlan ran him though with the sword. The four of them were grim death moving through the palace. The alarm bells rang frantically in the tower.

On the landing leading to the great staircase, Orsk lopped off a guard's head. The body rolled down the stairs, spilling a trail of blood, as if unrolling a red carpet for them. The headless man flopped to a stop against the statue of Magda Searus, the first Mother Confessor.

They ran down the stone steps, the sound echoing in the vast chamber. Near the bottom, a sudden stab of pain took Kahlan's feet out from under her. She tumbled down the last few steps. The others shouted and rushed to her, wanting to know how she was hurt. She told them that she had just stumbled.

She hadn't stumbled.

Kahlan pulled her bow off her shoulder and pointed with it. "Down that hall. All of you, head down that hall. Turn right at the end. I'll catch up with you. Go."

"We're not leaving you!" Chandalen insisted.

"I said go!" Kahlan stood against the blistering pain in her legs. "Orsk, get them moving, now. I'll catch up. I will be displeased with you if you fail to get them out of here."

Orsk raised his axe and growled. The other two backed toward the hall as they pleaded with her. They protested that they had risked their lives to rescue her, and they would not leave her, now.

"Orsk! Get them out of here!"

"Why!" Chandalen and Jebra yelled together.

Kahlan pointed with her bow. Across the great chamber, up in one of the distant arcades, stood a shadowed figure. "Because otherwise he'll kill you."

"We must escape! He will kill you, too!"

"If he lives, he will hunt us down, with magic, and kill us all."

A bolt of yellow lightning arced across the broad room. Stone crashed down, nearly covering the opening where the others stood.

Kahlan drew one of Chandalen's flat-bladed, man-killer arrows from her quiver.

"Mother Confessor!" Chandalen screamed. "You cannot make that shot! I could not make that shot! You must run!"

She didn't tell them that the wizard was sending slashing shards of pain through her, and she couldn't run. It was all she could do just to stand. "Orsk! Get them out! Now! I'll catch up!"

Another bolt of lightning sent stone flying everywhere and the three of them running down the hall, Orsk pushing them along.

Kahlan put a knee to the floor to steady herself as she nocked the arrow. She drew the string to her cheek. The blade of the arrow was horizontal in her line of sight. She could hardly see Ranson, he was so far away, and the pain was blurring her vision.

But she could hear him laugh as he sent violent splinters of magic ripping through her. It sounded like Darken Rahl's laugh. She bit the inside of her cheek against the pain, against the scream trying to fight its way out. She couldn't hold back the clipped whimpers.

"An archer, Mother Confessor?" he called from the distance. His laughter echoed off the stone around her. "Your freedom was brief, Mother Confessor. I hope it was worth it to you. You will spend a good long time in the pit, thinking about it."

He was too far away. She had never made a shot from this far. Richard had. She had seen him do it. *Please, Richard, help me. Show me how, like you did that day. Help me.*

Stone vines tore from the panel next to her and whipped around her middle, squeezing. The shearing pain made her shriek.

She brought up the bow again. With her last breath, if need be, she told herself. Her arms shook. She could hardly see the wizard. He was too far away. The vines held her tight. She couldn't run, even if she wanted to.

*Help me, Richard.*

Another brutal wave of pain seared up her legs and through her insides. Burning tears ran down her cheeks as she shuddered and gasped. She couldn't hold the bow up.

Lightning arced around the great staircase. The sound was deafening. Stone chips whistled past. Clouds of dust rose as a column collapsed with a crash.

She heard Richard's words in her mind: *You have to be able to shoot no matter what is happening. Just you and the target, that's all there is. Nothing else matters. You have to be able to block everything else out. You can't think about how afraid you are, or what will happen if you miss. You have to be able to make the shot under pressure.*

She remembered how he had whispered to her, whispered for her to call the target.

With a jolt, the target came to her, as if the wizard were standing right in front of her. She could see the flashes of liquid light jumping from his fingertips.

She could see her target—the bump in his throat bobbing up and down as he laughed. She let her breath flow out, as Richard had taught her. The arrow found the notch in the air.

As gentle as a baby's breath, the arrow left the bow.

She saw the feathers clear the bow. She saw the string hit her wrist. The stone vine wrapped around her throat. She kept her eyes on the target. She watched the feathers of the arrow as it flew. The pain tearing her insides rose with his laughter.

The wizard's laughter cut off abruptly. Kahlan heard the thunk of the blade hitting his throat. When the stone vine suddenly dropped away, she fell forward on her hands and knees, tears dripping from her face, as she waited for the pain to melt away. It went with merciful swiftness.

Kahlan staggered to her feet. "To the Keeper with you, too, Wizard Neville Ranson!"

There was an earsplitting crack, like a lightning strike, but instead of a flash of light, a ripple of total darkness swept across the room. Bumps rippled up her arms. The lamps flickered back on.

Kahlan knew—the Keeper had indeed taken Wizard Neville Ranson.

She heard a grunt, and turned just in time to see a guard leaping down the steps toward her. Kahlan ducked and came up under him as he landed. She used his momentum to loft him over the railing, into the well below.

He snatched at her as he went over, but his fingers caught only her necklace. It tore from her, and went down with him. Kahlan bent over the railing, seeing him smack the stone floor, three flights down. She saw the necklace tumble from his hand when he hit, and slide across the floor.

"Curse the good spirits," she growled.

Kahlan started for the stairs to retrieve her bone necklace, but skidded to a stop and looked up at the sound of boots on stone. More guards were coming. She hesitated for a moment, looking down, and then ran for the hallway instead. The spirits hadn't helped her; what good was a necklace going to do? It wasn't worth her life.

Kahlan caught the others as they made the outside doors. They all sighed with relief to see her, and to hear that the wizard wouldn't be coming after them. Kahlan led as they ran out into the night. The four of them raced down the expanse of steps to the relentless sound of the alarm bells behind. She headed south—the shortest distance to the woods.

A breathless Jebra caught her arm, dragging her to a stop. "Mother Confessor . . . !"

"I am not the Mother Confessor any longer. I am Kahlan."

"Kahlan then. But you must listen to me. You cannot run away."

Kahlan turned back to the path through the courtyard. "I'm through with this place."

"Zedd needs you."

Kahlan spun back. "Zedd? You know Zedd? Where is he?"

Jebra gulped air. "Zedd sent me to Aydindril. The day after you left D'Hara. He said he had to go get a woman named Adie, and then he would come to the Wizard's Keep. He sent me here to help you and Richard, and have you wait. Zedd needs you."

Kahlan gripped Jebra's shoulders. "I need Zedd. I need him very badly."

"Then you must let me help you. You must not leave. They will expect you to run, and will search the countryside. They will not expect you to remain in Aydindril."

"Remain? Stay in Aydindril?"

She thought a moment. She was known in Aydindril. No, not exactly. Her long hair was known. People other than councilors, ambassadors, staff, and nobility rarely saw the Mother Confessor up close, and when they did they mostly stared at her long hair. She no longer had that hair.

The thought of her loss made her insides knot up. She hadn't known how much her power, and her long hair, meant to her—until they were gone.

"It might work, Jebra. But where would we hide?"

"Zedd gave me gold. No one knows of my involvement in your escape. I will rent rooms and hide you, all of you."

Kahlan considered it a moment, then smiled. "We could be your servants. A lady like you would have servants."

Jebra shrank back. "Mother Confessor, I could not do that. I am nothing but a servant myself. Zedd made me pretend to be a lady. But I could not pretend that. You are a true lady."

"Being a servant does not make you less than me. We all can be only who we are, no more, no less." Kahlan started them all off again, toward a part of Aydindril with quiet, secluded, and exclusive inns. "And it is startling to learn what you can do when you have to. We will do what we must. But if you keep calling me Mother Confessor, you are going to get us all killed."

"I will do my best . . . Kahlan. All I know is that we must wait until Zedd returns to Aydindril." She tugged insistently on Kahlan's sleeve. "Mother Confessor, where is Richard! It is vital!" Her voice lowered with unease. "No slight intended, and I pray none is taken, but it is Richard that is important. Zedd needs Richard."

"That is why I need Zedd," Kahlan said.

Richard grabbed an arm of each boy. "Slow down," he said in a low voice. "I told you, I have to go first."

Kipp and Hersh sighed impatiently. Richard checked around the corner, peeking down the hall, and then pushed the two boys up against the wall. Frogs kicked in their pockets.

"This is serious. I picked you two because I know you're the best. Now, you do as I told you, the way we planned it. Stay here, with your backs to this wall, and count to fifty. You don't so much as peep around the corner until you get to fifty. I'm depending on you to do it right."

They grinned. "We're your men," Kipp said. "We'll get them out of there."

Richard squatted and put a finger close to each face in turn. "This is serious business. This isn't just some game. This time you could get in real trouble. Are you sure you want to do this?"

Kipp put his hands in his pockets, feeling the frogs. "You came to the right men. We can do it. We want to do it, Richard."

They were excited because they had never made it past the guards before. This was uncharted territory for their specialty. Richard knew they didn't appreciate the danger involved, and he hated to have to use them in this manner, but it was the only thing he could think of.

"All right then, start counting."

Richard rounded the corner and swept down the hall, his mriswith cape billowing open. When he reached the proper door, he stood against the white marble wall opposite the double doors and drew the hood up. He pulled the cape closed and concentrated on the marble behind him.

He stood motionless. The boys burst around the corner, yelling and screaming at the top of their lungs as they ran down the hall. They stopped in front of the double doors, looking both ways. They didn't see him standing behind them, and he knew they were wondering where he was hiding.

As they had been instructed, they threw the doors open and, giggling with excitement, began pulling frogs from their pockets and pitching them into the room. The two Sisters were frozen in surprise for only an instant. Richard watched as both came flying around their desks, one snatching up a rod. The boys heaved their last frogs with a squeal and raced away in opposite directions, shouting taunts of "Can't catch us! Can't catch us!"

Sisters Ulicia and Finella slid to a stop on the polished marble floor outside the doors. They almost slid right into him, and were only inches away. Richard held his breath.

The Sisters saw the boys make the turns at opposite ends of the hall. They threw their hands out. Pictures crashed to the floor as flashes of shimmering light knocked them from the walls at the end, but they missed the boys. Growling in anger, the Sisters parted, one dashing after each boy.

Richard waited until they had turned the corner, and then he stepped away from the wall, letting his concentration relax, letting the cape return to black. He wondered what it would look like if someone were to see it happen, to see a person seem to materialize out of the air.

The outer room was empty. Before the door between the desks, the air seemed to sparkle and hum. Experimentally, Richard put his hand into it. The air felt thick, but it seemed to have no harmful effect. He pressed himself through the sparkles and went through the door beyond.

The room inside, not quite as large as his own outer room, was dimly lit, and paneled in rich, dark wood. In the center sat a heavy walnut table piled with papers and books, and three candles. Down the length to each side were floor-to-ceiling bookshelves crammed full of disheveled books, and a few other odd objects.

An old woman, one of the cleaning staff, in a heavy, dark gray work dress, was standing on a stool, dusting a top bookshelf. She turned with surprise as he came to a halt. She glanced to the door, and then back to him.

"How did you . . ."

"I'm sorry, ma'am. I didn't mean to startle you. I just came to see the Prelate. Is she about?"

The woman squatted, her foot searching for the floor. Richard gave her his hand. She smiled her appreciation as she brushed a wisp of graying hair back from her face. Most of it was drawn into a loose knot at the back of her head. Once she was standing on the floor, the top of her head only came up to the lower tip of his breastbone. Her body was on the wide side, as if she had once been taller, and a giant had put his hand on the top of her head and squashed her down a good foot.

She looked up, giving him a curious frown. "Did Sisters Ulicia and Finella let you come in?"

"No," Richard said as he looked about the comfortably cluttered room. "They stepped out."

"But they would have left a shield. . . ."

"Ma'am, I must speak to the Prelate." Across the room, Richard saw doors to a courtyard standing open. "Is she about?"

"Do you have an appointment?" she asked in a quiet, gentle voice.

"No," he admitted. "I've been trying to get one for days. Those two wouldn't cooperate, so I made my own appointment."

She put a finger to her lower lip. "I see. But you must have an appointment. Those are the rules. I'm sorry."

Richard started for the open doors. He was getting impatient, but kept his voice calm, as he didn't want to frighten the old maidservant. "Look, ma'am, I must see the Prelate, or we are all going to have an appointment with the Keeper himself."

Her eyebrows lifted in wonder. "Reeeeally." She clicked her tongue. "The Keeper, is it. My, my, my."

Richard stopped suddenly. He winced and let out a groan. He turned on his heel. "You're the Prelate, aren't you?"

An impish grin came to her face, her eyes twinkling with it. "Yes, Richard, I guess I am."

"You know who I am?"

She chuckled. "Oh, yes, I know."

Richard sighed. "So you're the one who runs this place?"

She laughed louder. "As I hear it told, you seem to be running it now. Been here hardly a month, and you have half the palace wound around your will. I've been thinking about asking for an appointment to see *you*."

Richard gave her a friendly scowl. "I would have granted it."

"I've been looking forward to meeting you." She patted his arm. "From now on, you may come to see me whenever you wish."

"Then why wouldn't you let me in before?"

She folded her hands together beneath her ample, rounded breasts. "A test, my boy. A test." She smiled up at him. "I am impressed. I expected it to take you another six or eight months yet."

The door burst open. Richard was jerked from his feet, yanked back by his collar, and smacked up against the wall. He was stuck tight, the wind knocked from his lungs. Two irate Sisters stood just inside the doorway with their fists on their hips.

"Now, now," the Prelate said, "stop that, you two. Let the boy down."

Richard thumped to the ground, glaring at the two Sisters. "I am the one who talked those two boys into doing as they did. What they did is my fault. If there is any revenge, it had better be against me, and not them. If you harm them, you will answer to me."

One of the Sisters took a step toward him. "Their punishment has already been ordered. This time, for once, they will learn a lesson." She angrily pointed a stout rod at him. "You are going to have your own punishment to worry about."

"Yes, Sister Ulicia," the Prelate said, "I think punishment is in order." The Sister gave Richard a self-satisfied smile. "Yours," the Prelate said.

Sister Ulicia gaped. "Prelate Annalina?"

"Did I not give you specific instructions that Richard was not to be allowed in here?"

The two Sisters straightened. "Yes, Prelate Annalina."

"And here he is. Standing in my office."

Sister Ulicia pointed at the door. "But . . . we left a shield! He could not . . ."

"Oh? Could not?" The Sister's hand dropped at seeing the Prelate's wrinkled brow. "Seems I see him standing here. Do I not, Sisters?"

"Yes, Prelate Annalina," the two said as one.

"And so now your idea is to reward your own failure by going back to your posts, as if nothing had happened, and punish their success?" The Prelate clicked her tongue. "You two will take the punishment you have ordered for the two boys."

The Sisters blanched. "But Prelate . . ." the second whispered. "You can't have that done to a Sister."

"Really, Sister Finella? What did you order for the boys?"

"To have their bottoms strapped . . . publicly . . . tomorrow morning, after breakfast."

"That sounds fair. You two will take their place."

"But Prelate," Sister Ulicia whispered in astonishment. "We are Sisters of the Light. That would be humiliating."

"Learning humility never harmed anyone. We are all humble before the Creator. For your failure, you will be strapped in their place."

Sister Ulicia stiffened. "And if we fail to submit, Prelate Annalina?"

608

The Prelate smiled. "Then you would be telling me that you no longer deserve to be trusted, and further, that you no longer wish to be Sisters of the Light."

They both bowed. When the door closed behind them, Richard lifted an eyebrow to the Prelate.

"I hope never to get on your wrong side, Prelate Annalina."

She chuckled. "Please, call me Ann. That is what my old acquaintances call me."

"I'd be honored to call you Ann, Prelate, but I'm not an old acquaintance."

"You think not?" She smiled. "My, what a knowledgeable boy. Well, no matter. Call me Ann, anyway. Do you know why I punished them? Because you took responsibility for your actions. They did not recognize the importance of that. You are learning to be a wizard."

"What do you mean?"

"You knew it was dangerous to cross those two, did you not?" Richard nodded. "Yet you used those boys, knowing that it was a possibility they could be hurt."

"Yes, but I had to do it. It's that important, and it was the only thing I could think of."

"The burden of a wizard. That's what it is called. Using people. A wise wizard understands that he cannot do everything himself, and that if the matter is important enough, he must use other people to accomplish what must be done. Even if it is to cost those other people their lives. It's a rare ability, and vital to being a good wizard. Perhaps, to being a Prelate, too."

"Ann, it's urgent. I must speak with you."

"Urgent, is it? Well, then, why don't we go for a walk in my garden, and we can talk about this urgent business."

She placed her arm in his, and walked him through the open doorway. Outside, in the moonlight, was a grand, expansive courtyard, with trees, paths, flower beds, wild areas, and a lovely pond. The beauty of the garden didn't register in Richard's mind. He had hardly been able to eat or sleep since he had had his talk with Warren. If the Keeper escaped, he would have everyone, including Kahlan. Richard had to do something.

"Ann, there is great trouble in the world. I need your help. I need this collar off so I may go help."

"That's what I am here for, Richard. To help. What is the trouble?"

"The Keeper . . ."

"The Nameless One," she corrected.

"What difference does it make?"

"Calling him by his name calls his attention."

"Ann, it's just a word. It's the meaning of the word that matters, not an arrangement of letters. Do you think that when you call the Keeper the Nameless One, instead, that he would be fooled into thinking you weren't speaking of him? It's a mistake to assume your enemies are ignorant, and you are clever."

A hearty laugh rose from in her chest. "I have been waiting for a very long time for someone to figure that out."

She paused with him at the edge of the pond, and he asked, "What is 'the pebble in the pond'?"

She gazed out over the water. "You are one, Richard."

"You mean there are more than one?"

A small stone floated through the air, up into her hand. "Everyone has an effect on others. Some people inspire others to do great things. Some take people into crime with them. Those with the gift affect those around them even more. The stronger the Han, the stronger the effect."

"What does that have to do with me? What does that have to do with a pebble in a pond?"

"You see all the duck weed floating on the surface? Say that's the other people, the world of life, and this pebble is you." She tossed the stone into the pond. "See what happens? The ripples caused by you affect everyone else. Without you, all those ripples would not have happened."

"So they float up and down, on the ripples. But the stone sank."

She gave him a humorless grin. "Don't ever forget that."

The answer gave him pause. "I think you invest too much faith in me. You don't know anything about me."

"Perhaps more than you think, child. And what is it that concerns you about the Keeper?"

"Something must be done. He's about to escape. One of the boxes of Orden has been opened, the gateway is open. The Stone of Tears is in this world. I need to do something."

"Ahh." She smiled as she drifted to a stop. "So you, who was just thrown up against a wall by the Han of a mere Sister, wants to go off and battle the Keeper himself?"

"But things have happened. Something must be done."

"I see you have been talking to Warren. A very bright young man, Warren. He is still young, though. Sometimes he needs direction. Guidance." She tipped a branch closer. "He studies hard, and loves those books. I think he must know every smudge on them."

She was inspecting a flower on the branch. As he watched her in the moonlight, he decided he might have thought himself more clever than he was. Warren, too.

"So, what about the Keeper? What about the Stone of Tears?"

She put her arm back through his and walked him on. "If the gateway is open and the Stone of Tears is in this world, Richard, why does the Keeper not have us? Hmm?"

"Maybe he's about to swallow us all at any moment."

"Ahh. So you think that maybe he is busy with his dinner, and when he is finished, and wipes his chin clean, he will get around to swallowing the world of the living, so you want to rush off and close the gateway before he picks his napkin from his lap? Is this the way you think the worlds beyond ours work? In the same terms as this world?"

Richard nervously raked his fingers through his hair. "I don't know. I don't know how it all works, but Warren said . . ."

"Warren does not know everything. He is but a student. He has a talent for the prophecies, but he has much to learn.

"Do you know why we keep the prophecies down in the vaults, and restrict who may read them? For the very reason we are having this discussion. Because prophecy is dangerous to the untrained mind, and sometimes even to the trained mind. There is more to things than you see, or the Keeper would have us already."

"Are you saying we're not in danger?"

She smiled a sly smile. "We are always in danger, Richard. As long as there is a world of the living, there will be danger. All life is mortal."

She patted his arm again. "You are an important person, a person in prophecy, but if you go off foolishly, you can cause more harm than good. The Stone of Tears being in this world cannot, in itself, allow the Keeper to escape through the gateway. The Stone is a means to that end."

"I hope you're right," he said as they walked on.

She glanced up. "How is your mother doing?"

Richard looked off into the darkness. "She died when I was young. In a fire."

"I'm sorry, Richard. And your father?"

"Which one," he muttered.

"Your stepfather, George."

Richard cleared his throat. "He was killed by Darken Rahl." He darted her a sidelong glance. "How do you know my stepfather?"

She gave him one of those timeless looks that he had seen from others before; from Adie, Shota, Sister Verna, Du Chaillu, and Kahlan. "I'm sorry, Richard. I didn't know he had died. George Cypher was quite a man."

He came to a stop, his flesh atingle. "You," he whispered. "You are how my father got that book." He left the statement vague enough that she would have to fill in the details to confirm it.

A little of her smile came back. "Afraid to say it out loud? The Book of Counted Shadows, that is the book you are speaking of." She gestured to a stone bench. "Sit down, Richard, before you fall down."

Richard slumped to the bench. He looked up as she stood before him. "You? You gave that book to my father?"

"Actually, I helped him get it. You see, Richard, as I told you, you and I are old acquaintances. Of course, the last time I saw you, you were bawling your head off. Only a few months old, you were."

She smiled distantly. "If your mother could see you now. She was bursting with pride over you. She said your were the blessing to balance the curse. You see, Richard, balance is what the world of the living is all about. You are a child of balance. I have much invested in you."

Richard's tongue seemed stuck to the top of his mouth. "Why?"

"Because you are a pebble in the pond." Her eyes seemed to go out of focus. "Over three thousand years ago, wizards had Subtractive Magic. None since has been born with it. We have been hoping, but none, until now, has come into this life. A few have had the calling, but not the gift of it. You have the gift for both Additive and Subtractive Magic."

Richard shot to his feet. "What! Are you mad!"

"Sit down, Richard."

The quiet power of her voice, her penetrating gaze, her presence, made him sink to the bench. For some reason, she seemed suddenly very big to him. She was the same size as before, but it felt as if she towered over him. Her voice became imposing, too.

"Now, you listen to me. You are causing me a great deal of trouble. You are like a bull that keeps knocking down fences and trampling the crops. Too much is at stake to have you acting without knowing what you are doing. I know you think you are doing right, but so does the bull. Your problem is lack of knowledge. I intend to give you an education.

"Though you will not believe some of what I have to tell you, you had better come to accept it, or you will be in that collar a good long time, because it cannot come off until you accept the truth."

"I was told the Sisters took the collar off."

The look in her eyes made him wish he had kept his mouth closed, or that he could trade places with the two Sisters who were to take a public strapping.

"Only when you accept yourself, accept your ability, your true power, will it come off. You put the Rada'Han around your own neck. We don't have the power to take it off until you can help us, with your own power. The only way you can do that is to learn, and to accept who you are.

"Now, first of all, you must understand about the Keeper, and the Creator, and the nature of this world. Your problem, the problem most people have, the problem Warren has, is that you try to understand the worlds beyond in terms of this world.

"Good and evil, the Creator and the Keeper, are chaos divided into two opposing forces. Although each abhors the other, they are interdependent, and cannot exist one without the other. They define each other. The struggle, our struggle in this world, is maintaining the balance."

Although Richard kept his mouth shut, he couldn't keep the frown from his face.

"From the Creator springs life, the soul of life. It blooms into this world. Without the Keeper, without death, there can be no life. Without death, life would be open-ended.

"Can you even imagine a world in which no one ever died? Where every child born lives? Forever? Where every plant that sprouts flourishes? Where every tree lives forever, and every seedling sprouts and grows to a tree?

"What would happen? How could we eat, if we could kill no animal, or harvest no crop, if it all lived forever and could not die? A never-ending life of gnawing, ravenous hunger? The world of the living would be consumed by chaos, and destroy itself forever.

"Death, the underworld as some call it, is eternal. You think of it in terms of this life. In eternity, time has no meaning, no dimension. To the Keeper, a second, or a year, has no meaning.

"It is through those in this world, who serve him, that the Keeper is given the dimension of time. It is their urgency that drives his struggle, because they understand time. He needs the living if he is to succeed. His promises to those who help him are seductive, and they hunger for his triumph."

"So what part do the living play in this?"

"We divide and define the chaos with order, and keep it separated: light and dark; love and hate; good and evil. We are the balance.

"We are like the duck weed floating on the surface of the pond. The air above is the Creator, the depths below, the Keeper. The souls of the living, which have come down from the Creator, blossom to life in this place, and when they die, they descend to the world of the dead.

"But that does not mean it is evil. Evil is a judgment we put on it. The Keeper is like the muck at the bottom of the pond. Spirits of the dead reside anywhere from the depths of that chaos and hate, near the Keeper, to near the living, near the light of the Creator. It is the hope of the living to spend eternity in the warmth of that light.

"It is we, the living, who separate, and define the worlds to each side of life. Magic is the element that gives this world the power to do that. Magic is the balance point.

"The Keeper would like to swallow the world of the living, to triumph. To do that, he must eliminate magic. But at the same time, in order to triumph, he must use magic to tip the balance."

Richard struggled to keep his head above the murky waters of confusion. "And wizards have the power to influence this balance?"

She was still leaning over him. She held up a finger. "Yes. You have both sides of the magic." Her smile evaporated in a way that took his breath with it. "That makes you an extremely dangerous person, Richard.

"You have both sides of the gift; you have the power to mend, or destroy the veil. There are good people who, if they knew of your power, would kill you in a twinkling for fear you might destroy us all, if not deliberately, by accident."

"And you? Are you one of those?"

"If I were, I would not have helped your father get the Book of Counted Shadows. Your involvement stopped the immediate threat, but it also fed the gateway magic, and chances greater danger in the future. It was a risk I had to take, because the consequences of not doing so would have been disaster. But if what has happened is not fixed, it will be greater disaster in the end."

"What is the veil? Where is it?"

She reached out and tapped his forehead. "The veil is within those of us with magic. We are are its custodians. That is why balance means so much to those with the gift. When the veil is torn, the balance is tipped. The further it tips, the more the veil tears.

"The Creator rules his domain, the Keeper, his. The Keeper needs the Creator to feed him life, the Creator needs the Keeper to allow it to be renewed. The veil keeps the balance."

Her face was grim. "This view would be considered blasphemy by many. They see the Keeper only as evil that must be destroyed. But to do so would ultimately accomplish the opposite—all life being swept away like a sandbar in a river flood."

"Just for the sake of argument, what if I did have both kinds of magic? What is my power for?"

"Most wizards have a talent that leans in a particular direction. Some are healers, some make things of magic, more rare are prophets. The most rare are war wizards. There has not been one born in over three thousand years. Until you."

Richard wiped his sweaty palms on his pant legs. "I don't like the sound of that."

"*War wizard* has two meanings which balance each other, as in all things magic. The first meaning is that they can tear the veil, bring destruction and death—war. And the second is that they have the magic needed to fight against the powers of the Keeper. Being a war wizard does not mean you are evil, Richard. Many who fight do so to protect those who are defenseless. It means you have the capacity to care enough to fight, to defend the innocent."

" 'Lest he who's born true can fight for life's bond. And that one is marked; he's the pebble in the pond.' " Richard quoted.

She lifted an eyebrow. "For one who professes to scoff at prophecy, you seem to know some of the more pivotal passages. If I'm not entirely addled, I expect you have been marked."

Richard could feel the scar on his chest as he nodded. "Are you saying that my life is already marked out? That I'm just meant to live it out, as it has been preordained?"

"No, Richard. Life is not predetermined. The prophecies mean only that you have potential. You have the ability to influence events. That's why it is so important for you to learn.

"Of most importance is that you learn to accept yourself. If you do not do this, you will harm the most vital part of yourself: your free will. If you act without understanding, you could cast yourself into the chaos.

"I let you live when you were born because you have the potential for doing good. Within you is the hope of life. But until you truly accept both sides of your magic, you are a danger to every living thing."

Richard desperately wanted to change the subject. He felt as if the world were crushing him. "What is the Stone of Tears?"

She gave a little shrug. "In the world of the dead, it exists as a force. In this world, it exists as an object with power, representing that force.

"The Stone of Tears is like a weight that holds the Keeper at the infinite end of his world, where his influence here is diminished to the point of balance."

"Then if it's here, off him, he is freed from his prison."

"If that were true, we would all be dead. Hmm?" She lifted a questioning eyebrow, but Richard didn't say anything. "It's one of the seals that locks the Keeper beyond. There are others, that still hold. Magic helps hold him back, for now.

"The Stone of Tears has the power, though, to destroy the balance, to tear the veil and free the Keeper, if it is used in this world, by such as you, in the wrong way. You see, the Stone has the power to banish any soul to the infinite depths of the underworld. But if it were used in that way, through hate, through selfishness, it would feed power to that side, and destroy the veil.

"The veil can only be restored by one with the gift for both sides of the magic. The Stone must be put back where it belongs.

"We must struggle to keep the other seals intact until the day when one such as you can restore this lock while there is still time. Meanwhile, the Keeper gains strength here. His minions struggle to break the other seals. There are other ways to free the Keeper."

"Ann . . . are you sure about me? Maybe . . ."

"You proved it just tonight, by walking through that shield. Our shields are made of Additive Magic. The only way for you to penetrate it was for your Han to use Subtractive."

"Maybe my Han, my Additive Magic, is just stronger."

"When you came through the Valley of the Lost, you would have been drawn to the towers. To both towers. Am I right?"

"I could have just come across them by accident."

She let out a tired sigh. "The towers were created by wizards who had both kinds of power. In the white tower, there is white sand. Sorcerer's sand. I doubt you would have taken any."

"That doesn't prove anything. And what is sorcerer's sand?"

"Sorcerer's sand is extremely valuable, nearly priceless. It is only gathered by chance happenings across the tower. Sorcerer's sand is the crystallized bones of the wizards who gave their life into the towers. It's a sort of distilled magic. It gives power to spells drawn with it—good, and evil. The proper spell drawn in white sorcerer's sand can invoke the Keeper.

"You took, instead, some of the black sand, did you not?"

"Well, yes. I just wanted a little bit, that's all."

She nodded. "Just a little bit. Richard, no wizard since the towers were built has been able to gather any black sorcerer's sand. It cannot be taken from a tower by any but those with Subtractive Magic. Guard that black sand with your life. It's more valuable than you can imagine."

"Why? What will it do?"

"Black sorcerer's sand is the counter to the white. They nullify each other. The black, even one grain of it, will contaminate a spell drawn to invoke the Keeper. It will destroy the spell. A spoonful of it is a weapon worth kingdoms."

"Still," he said, "it could just be that—"

"The last wizards born with both kinds of magic invested the Palace of the Prophets with their magic. The prophets of that time knew one would be born again with both sides of the magic, a war wizard, and so they created, too, the Hagen Woods, and the mriswith. One born with the Subtractive would be drawn to that place. Drawn to do battle there.

"The collar keeps the Additive gift from killing you. The Hagen Woods provide an outlet for the other side of your power. It is something the Sisters cannot provide."

"But I used the Sword of Truth." His voice sounded to him like a plea into a gale. "It was the sword."

"The Sword of Truth was also created by wizards with the gift for both sides of the magic. Only one born the same could bring out the full range of its magic. Only you can use the sword to its full potential. And you have not done so yet.

"It is an aid to you, but even so, you do not need it to kill the mriswith. Your gift is enough. If you do not believe me, leave your sword, and go into the Hagen Woods with just your knife. You will still kill the mriswith."

"Others have used this blade. They didn't even have the gift, much less Subtractive Magic."

"They were not truly using the sword's magic. The blade was made for you. It's an aid, much as prophecy is an aid, much as the mriswith are an aid, sent down through time."

"I don't think I could be one of these war wizards."

"Do you eat meat?"

"What does that have do do with anything?"

"You are a child of balance. Wizards must balance themselves, the things they do, their power. War wizards rarely eat meat. Their abstinence is a balance for the killing they sometimes must do."

"I'm sorry, Ann, but I just can't believe I have Subtractive Magic."

"That's why you are such a danger. Every time you encounter magic, your Han learns more about how to protect you, to serve you, but you are not aware that it is learning. The Rada'Han helps it grow, though you're not aware of the process.

"You do things without knowing the importance, or the reason, like when you were drawn to the black sorcerer's sand and took it, or when you took the round skrin bone from Adie."

Richard's brow pulled together. "You know Adie, too?"

"Yes, she helped your father and me get through the pass, so we could retrieve the Book of Counted Shadows."

"What round bone are you talking about?"

Richard saw the slightest twitch of alarm in her eyes.

"Adie had a round bone, carved all over with beasts. It's an object of great power. Your Subtractive Magic would have drawn you to it."

Richard remembered seeing the round bone on a high shelf. "I saw such a thing at her house, but I didn't take it. I wouldn't take something that didn't belong to me. Maybe that means I don't really have Subtractive Magic."

She straightened. "No, you noticed it. The fact that you didn't take it means only that since you did not have the Rada'Han on yet, your power had not developed enough to draw you to the skrin bone, the way it drew you to the black sand."

Richard hesitated. "Is this some kind of problem?"

She smiled. It looked forced to him. "No. Adie would protect that bone with her life. She knows how important it is. You can recover it in the future."

"What does it do?"

"It helps protect the veil. When used by a war wizard, like you, with both powers, it invokes the skrin. The skrin are a force that helps keep the worlds separated. You might say they are guardians of the boundary between worlds."

"What if the wrong person got their hands on it? A person wishing to help the Keeper?"

She pulled on his shirt, urging him up. "You worry too much, Richard. I have work to do. You must leave me to it, now. Do your best, child, and study. Learn to touch your Han, to get control of it. You must learn if you are to be of any help to the Creator."

Richard turned back to her. She was staring off.

"Ann, why does the Keeper want the world of the living? What will it gain him? What is the purpose?"

Her answer came in a soft, distant voice. "Death is the antithesis of life. The Keeper exists to consume the living. His hatred of life has no bounds. His hatred is as eternal as his prison of death."

**R**ichard was in a world of his own as he headed for the stone bridge. He had been cloistered in his room for days, thinking. When the Sisters came to give him his lessons, he put in only a halfhearted effort. He now feared he just might touch his Han.

Warren was busy day and night in the vaults, checking what Richard had told him and looking for more information. There had to be at least some truth to what the Prelate had told him—why else would the Keeper not yet have used the gateway, if he could.

He needed to go for a walk. He felt as if his head were about to burst. He just wanted to be away from the palace for a while.

Pasha suddenly appeared at his side. "I've been looking for you."

He stared ahead as he walked. "Why?"

"I just wanted to be with you."

"Well, I'm going for a walk in the country."

She shrugged. "I wouldn't mind a walk. May I come along?"

Richard looked over. She was in her wispy maroon dress, the one with the V-shaped neckline. The day was chilly. At least she had on a useful-looking violet cloak. She was wearing big gold loop earrings. Her belt matched her necklace, with the same kind of gold medallions. She looked alluring in the outfit, but they weren't exactly hiking-in-the-country clothes.

"Are you wearing those useless slippers?"

She held a foot out to show him her tooled leather boots. "I had them made special, just so I could go for walks with you."

Made special, he grumbled to himself. Richard remembered how hurt she had been that time he had told her that the blue dress didn't become her. He didn't want to hurt her feelings by sending her away. She was only trying to please him. Maybe, he thought, the company of a smiling face would do him good.

"Well, all right then. I guess you can come along, as long as you don't think I'm going to entertain you in conversation."

She grinned and took his arm. "I'd be happy just to walk with you."

At least having Pasha on his arm kept most of the women away from him as they passed through the city. The ones who did boldly approach earned a glare from Pasha. The ones who braved the glare earned something else: a touch of her Han. They yelped from the invisible pinch and made themselves scarce.

Richard understood, now, why the palace was breeding wizards. They were trying to get one with Additive and Subtractive Magic.

And now they had one.

They walked silently up into hills bathed in the golden light of the late-afternoon sun. Richard felt better out in the open, rocky hills overlooking the city. Though it was an illusion, he felt free. He suddenly wished Pasha weren't along. He hadn't come out to see Gratch in days. Gratch was probably frantic.

He was at a loss as to what he was going to do next. He didn't know if everything the Prelate had said was true, and he didn't know which he feared more—that it was a lie, or the truth.

Pasha's hand on his arm tightened in a way that brought him out of his brooding thoughts and made him draw to a halt. She glanced about nervously. He could tell by the way she was breathing through her mouth that she was frightened.

"What's wrong?" he whispered.

Her gaze searched the surrounding rocks. "Richard, there is something out here. Please, let's go back."

Richard drew the sword. Its unique ring filled the still afternoon air. He felt nothing, no sense of danger, but Pasha's Han obviously felt something that frightened her.

Pasha let out a little shriek. Richard spun. Gratch's head poked up above a rock. Pasha backed away.

"It's all right, he won't hurt you."

Gratch gave a tentative grin, showing his fangs, as he stood to his full, towering height.

"Kill it!" she screamed. "It's a beast! Kill it!"

"Pasha, calm down. He won't hurt you."

She backed farther away. Gratch stood looking from Richard to Pasha, not knowing what to do. Richard realized she might use her power to hurt the gar, so he put himself between the two.

"Richard! Move! It must be killed! It's a beast!"

"It won't hurt you. I know him. Pasha . . ."

She turned and ran, her violet cloak flying behind. Richard groaned as he watched her leap from the top of one rock to another, making her way down the hill. He scowled back at Gratch.

"What's wrong with you! Did you have to scare her! What are you doing showing your face to people!"

Gratch's ears wilted. His shoulders slumped, and he began to whine. When his wings started quivering, Richard went to him.

"Well, it's too late now to be sorry. Come on and give me a hug." Gratch cast his eyes to the ground. "It'll be all right."

He put his arms around the big, furry creature. Gratch finally responded. He threw his arms and wings around Richard, gurgling his happiness. In a moment, he pulled Richard off the rock and wrestled him to the ground. Richard tickled his ribs and wrestled until Gratch was giggling in glee.

After they had settled down, Gratch put a claw tip in the pocket where Richard kept the lock of Kahlan's hair. He looked at Richard from under hooded eyebrows as big as axe handles. Richard finally figured out what Gratch meant.

"No. No, that's not the same woman. It's a different person."

Gratch frowned. He didn't understand. Richard didn't feel like trying to explain that the lock of hair he was always looking at was not from Pasha. At Gratch's urging, Richard instead wrestled with his woolly friend.

It was twilight when Richard made it back to the palace. He was going to have to find Pasha and explain to her that Gratch was his friend, and not a dangerous beast. Before he had gone far, Sister Verna found him, instead.

"Did you feed that baby gar back in the wilds, the one I told you to kill? Did you let that beast follow us!"

Richard stared at her. "It was helpless, Sister. I couldn't kill something that was no harm to me. We've become friends."

Muttering, she wiped a hand across her face. "As absurd as it sounds, I suppose I can understand; you needed companionship, and you certainly didn't want it from me."

"Sister Verna . . ."

"But why would you let Pasha see it!"

"I didn't. He just popped his head up. I didn't know he was there. Pasha saw him before I knew."

She let out an exasperated sigh. "The people around here fear beasts; they kill them. Pasha went screaming to the Sisters that there was a beast in the hills."

"I'll explain it to them. I'll make them understand. . . ."

"Richard! Listen to me!" He backed away a step and stood silently while he waited for her to go on. "The palace believes that 'pets' are a hindrance to learning to use your Han. They believe it diverts feelings away from them, to the creature. I think they are being foolish, but that is beside the point."

"What is the point? You mean they will try to keep me from seeing him anymore?"

She put an impatient hand on his arm. "No, Richard. They think it's a vile beast that could turn on you. They think you are in danger. The Sisters are forming a search party as we speak. They intend to hunt it down and kill it, for your own good."

Richard stared at her concerned expression for only a second, and then he was running. He charged over the bridge and back into the city. People gaped as he flew past. He leapt over carts that wouldn't move out of the way fast enough. He knocked over a stand selling amulets. People hollered at him, but he ran on.

His heart thumped in his ears as he raced up the hills. Several times he stumbled over ditches or rocks, but he rolled to his feet, gasping for air, and rushed on. In the darkness, he leapt from rock to rock as he crossed ravines.

At the crest of a round-topped hill near where he had been with Gratch earlier, he yelled, between panting. His fists at his sides, he tipped his head back and screamed Gratch's name. His voice echoed off the surrounding hills. Only silence answered when the echoes died out.

Exhausted, Richard fell to his knees. They would be coming soon. The Sisters would use their Han to find the gar. Gratch wouldn't know what they intended. Even if he kept his distance, their magic could reach out and kill him. They could knock him from the air, or set him afire.

"Graaaatch! Graaaatch!"

A dark shape blackened a patch of stars. The gar thumped to the ground and folded his wings. He cocked his head and gave a purling gurgle.

Richard grabbed Gratch's fur in his fists.

"Gratch! Listen to me. You have to go away. You can't stay here any longer. They're coming to kill you. You must leave."

Gratch let out a questioning whine that rose in pitch. His ears perked forward. He tried to put his arms around Richard.

Richard pushed him away. "Go! You understand me, I know you do! Go! I want you to go away! They will try to kill you! Go away and never come back!"

Gratch's ears wilted as he cocked his head to the other side. Richard pounded a fist to the gar's chest. He pointed north.

"Go away!" He threw his arms out and pointed again. "I want you to go away and never come back!"

Gratch tried to put his arms around Richard again. Richard pushed them away again. Gratch's ears lay down against his head.

"Grrratch luuug Raaaach aaarg."

Richard wanted more than anything to hold his friend and tell him that he loved him, too. But he couldn't. He had to make him go in order to save his life.

"Well I don't love you! Go away and never come back!"

Gratch looked to the hill Pasha had run down. He looked back at Richard. His green eyes were filling with tears. He reached out for Richard.

Richard shoved him away. Gratch stood with his arms out. Richard remembered the first time he had held the furry beast. He had been so little then. He was so big now. But as he had grown, his friendship, and his love, had grown, too.

He was Richard's only friend, and only Richard could save him. If Richard really loved him, he had to do this.

"Go away! I don't want you around anymore! I don't want you to ever come back! You're just a big dumb bag of fur! Go away! If you really love me, then you'll do as I ask, and go away!"

Richard wanted to keep yelling, but the lump in his throat caught the words. He backed away. Gratch seemed to wither in the cool night air. His arms came out again with a pitiful, forlorn wail. He called with a plaintive, keening cry.

Richard took another step back. Gratch took a step toward him. Richard picked up a rock and heaved it at the gar. It bounced off his huge chest.

"Go away!" Richard cried. He threw another rock. "I don't want you around anymore! Go away! I don't ever want to see you again!"

Tears ran from the glowing green eyes, over the wrinkles of his cheeks. "Grrratch luuug Raaaach aaarg."

"If you really love me then you will do this! Go!"

The gar looked again to the hill Pasha had run down, turned, and spread his wings. With a last look over his shoulder, he bounded into the air and flew off into the night.

When he could no longer see the dark shape against the stars, or hear the sweep of wings, Richard crumpled to the ground. His only friend was gone.

"I love you, too, Gratch."

He cried in racking sobs. "Dear spirits, why have you done this to me? He was all I had. I hate you. Every last one of you."

He was halfway back when it hit him. He froze in his tracks, his mouth hanging open. In the stillness of the night, his shaking fingers reached to his pocket.

The lights of the city flickered in the near distance. Rooftops shimmered in the moonlight. Distant sounds of the city drifted out to him at the edge of the hills.

He pulled out the lock of Kahlan's hair.

*If you really love me*, she had said, *you will do this*. That was what he had told

Gratch. In a flash of understanding, it all came to him. The jolt of comprehension took his breath.

Kahlan had not been sending him away, she had been saving his life. She had done for him what he had just done for Gratch.

The pain of having doubted her took him to his knees. It must have broken her heart. How could he have doubted her?

The collar. He had been so afraid of the collar he had been blinded to it. She loved him. She didn't want to be set free, she wanted only to save his life.

She loved him.

He threw his arms open and turned his face up to the sky.

"She loves me!"

He knelt, staring at the lock of hair she had given him to remind him of her love. In his whole life, he had never felt a sense of relief this great. The world came back to life for him.

Richard's mind swirled in a confusion of conflicting emotions. He felt heartsick that he had sent Gratch away, that Gratch thought Richard didn't want him around anymore, but at the same time, he felt overwhelming joy that Kahlan loved him.

In the end, joy won out. He decided that someday Gratch might come to understand, as he had, that it had been necessary. Someday, he would have the collar off, and he would find Gratch, and make it up to him. And even if he didn't, the gar was better off living as a gar should, hunting and searching out its own kind. It would come to have its own happiness, as had Richard.

Although he wanted more than anything to throw his arms around Kahlan, hug her tight, and tell her how much he loved her, he couldn't. He was still a prisoner of the Sisters, but he would study, and learn, and get the collar off. He would get the collar off, and return to Kahlan. He knew without a doubt that she would be waiting for him. She had said she would always love him.

When he met the search party of Sisters at the edge of Tanimura, he told them that they needn't bother, that they would find the beast gone. They didn't believe him, and went on into the hills. Richard didn't care. Gratch was gone. His friend was safe.

Richard bought a gold necklace from a street hawker. He didn't know if it was real gold, but he didn't care, it looked pretty. He trotted the rest of the way to the palace.

Pasha was pacing up and down in the hall outside his room.

"Richard! Richard, I was so worried. I know that right now you're furious with me, but in time you will see that . . ."

He grinned. "I'm not angry, Pasha. In fact, I brought you a present, to thank you."

She smiled in coy surprise as he offered her the necklace. "For me? Why?"

"Because of you, I figured out that she loves me, and always has. I was just being a blind fool. You helped me see that."

She regarded him with a frosty look. "But you are here, now, Richard. You will forget her in time. You'll see that I'm the one for you."

He smiled happily at her. "Pasha, I'm sorry. It's nothing against you. You're a beautiful young woman. In time, you'll find the one for you. You can have your pick of nearly any man. Everyone likes you. But I'm not the one for you. Maybe if I lived to be a hundred, but short of that . . ."

Her sly smile returned. "Then I will wait."

He kissed the top of her head before going through the door. He didn't think he would be able to sleep while he was this excited, but all the walking and running had left him exhausted. His last thoughts before he drifted off were of Kahlan. He pictured her in his mind, as if she was there with him: her special smile, her deep green eyes, and her radiant long hair. He drifted into the best sleep he had had in months.

In the days following, Richard felt as if his feet hardly touched the ground. Everyone was puzzled by his good mood. They frowned at him at first, but were eventually caught up in his cheer. Some of the Sisters giggled when he told them they looked as beautiful as a sunny day.

He urged the Sisters who came to practice with him to try harder, to help him reach his Han. He had them stay longer than usual. Sisters Tovi and Cecilia bubbled with enthusiasm, Merissa and Nicci bestowed small smiles of pleasure, Armina was cautiously pleased, and Liliana delighted. He wanted his collar off, and until he could do what they wanted, he knew it would stay on.

Having not seen Warren in a while, he finally went down to the vaults to see how his search was coming. Sister Becky was off retching, and the other Sister giggled when he winked at her.

Warren was pleasantly surprised to see him and exhilarated about some of the things he had found. He could hardly wait to tell Richard. When the door to one of the back rooms had grated closed, he started opening volumes on the table.

"What you told me has been a great help. Look here." Warren pointed at words Richard couldn't understand. "Just like you told me. This says that the Stone of Tears being in this world, in itself, does not free the Keeper."

"So what significance does it have?"

"Well, it's as if there are a number of locks on his prison door, and this turns the key in one, but it does not free him. There are a number of ways for it to help him, a number of objects of magic to help. But the Stone of Tears itself must be used by one from this world, one with the gift for both Additive and Subtractive Magic, to free the Keeper. Those with only the gift for Additive can cause harm, tear the veil more, but not free him with it.

"I think," Warren said with a twinkle, "that we're safe with that black stone in this world as long as we're careful."

"It's not black. I never told you it was black. I just described the shape and size."

Warren touched a finger to his lower lip. "Not black? Then what color is it?"

"Amber."

Warren slapped his hands to his chest with a groan of relief. "Thank the Creator." He let out an uncharacteristic whoop. "That's the best news I've heard all year! Amber means it was touched by a wizard's tears. That repulses the Keeper. It's like rotten, festering meat would be to us. His agents won't touch it!"

Richard's grin widened. It had to be Zedd who had done it. That was why he felt Zedd's pull from the stone. This, on top of his discovery about Kahlan, was just too much. He couldn't keep the happiness to himself. "Warren, I have other good news. I'm in love. I'm going to be wed."

Warren gave another whoop, but then his smile wilted. "It's not Pasha, is it? If it is, that's all right, I will understand. You two will make a handsome . . ."

Richard lightly touched Warren's shoulder. "No, it's not Pasha. I'll tell you about her some other time. She's the Mother Confessor. I didn't mean to interrupt you. What about the other things?"

"Well." He pulled another book across the table. "There are precious few references to the round bone you spoke of, and the skrin. One of them is in a forked prophecy having to do with the winter solstice coming up in a couple of weeks. It's a complicated juncture of forks and crossovers. We've only recently learned that the prophecy about that woman and her people is the descendent of a true fork. . . ."

Whenever Warren went off on his talk of forks and junctures, Richard always started getting lost. About the only thing he understood was winter solstice.

"What does the winter solstice have to do with anything?"

Warren looked up. "Winter solstice. The shortest day of the year. Shortest day, longest night. See what I mean?"

"No. What does that have to do with the skrin?"

"The longest night of the year. Longest night, most darkness. You see, the Keeper has certain times when he can exert greater or lesser influence in this world. His is the world of darkness, and when we are in the period of the longest darkness, the veil is at its weakest. That's when he is able to do the most harm."

"Then we're in danger in a few weeks, at winter solstice."

Warren's eyebrows lifted in delight. "Yes. But you've given me the information to solve an upcoming prophecy, along with what we now know to be the true fork involved along with it. You see, with this winter solstice, there is a prophecy about the danger to the world of the living.

"The Keeper has to have a number of elements in place for it to be a true fork, such as an open gateway, but he needs an agent in this world—" Warren leaned forward in delight. "—and he in turn needs the skrin. If he has the skrin bone you told me of, he can invoke the guardian, and destroy it. If the guardian is destroyed, the Keeper can come through the gateway."

"Warren, that sounds pretty frightening to me."

Warren lifted his hand with a dismissive wave. "No, no. Many prophecies sound ominous, like this one. But the elements are rarely all in place, so they turn out to be false forks, as most do. The books are clogged with false forks, because—"

"Warren, get to the point."

"Oh, yes. Well, you see, you told me that your friend has the bone that can invoke the skrin. And the Keeper would need an agent, but he doesn't have one. Without the skrin bone, and with the upcoming fork which we know must be passed correctly, and we think it will, this is just another false fork, so we're safe!"

Richard felt a distant tingling of apprehension, but Warren's bubbly confidence overwhelmed it. He was caught up in Warren's enthusiasm. He gave the young man a clap on the back.

"Good work, Warren. Now I can concentrate on learning to use my Han."

Warren beamed. "Thank you, Richard. I'm so glad you've been able to help me. I've made more progress than I ever thought I would before I met you."

Still grinning, Richard shook his head in wonder. "Warren, I've never met anyone that was so smart, yet so young."

Warren laughed as if that was the funniest thing he had ever heard.

"What's so funny?"

"Your joke," Warren said, wiping tears from his eyes.

"What joke?"

Warren's laughter slowed to a frowning chuckle. "About me being young. It was funny."

Richard held his polite smile. "Warren, why is that funny?"

Warren's chuckle died down to a grin. "Because I'm one hundred and fifty-seven years old."

Richard's flesh prickled. "Now you're making a joke. That's a joke. It is a joke, Warren, isn't it?"

Warren's good humor evaporated. He blinked. "Richard . . . you do know, don't you. They must have told you. I was sure they would have told you by now. . . ."

Richard's arm swept the books aside. He scooted his chair closer. "Told me what? Warren, don't you say something like that and then go silent on me. You're my friend, you tell me."

Warren cleared his throat and then wet his lips with his tongue. He leaned in a little. "Richard, I'm sorry. I thought you knew, or I would have told you myself a long time ago. I would have."

"Told me what!"

"The magic. The magic of the Palace of the Prophets. It has Additive and Subtractive elements to it that are tied to the other worlds. That makes time move differently here."

"Warren," Richard said hoarsely, "do you mean it affects all of us? All those wearing the collar?"

"No . . . everyone at the palace. The Sisters, too. This place is spelled. As long as the Sisters live at the palace, they age the same as we do. The spell makes us age more slowly; makes time seem different to us."

"What do you mean, 'different'?"

"The spell slows our aging process. For every year we age, those outside age between ten and fifteen years."

Richard's head was spinning. "Warren, that can't be true. It can't." He tried desperately to think of proof. "Pasha. Pasha could only be . . ."

"Richard, I've known Pasha for over a hundred years."

Richard slid the chair back and stood. He raked his fingers through his hair. "That doesn't make any sense. It has to be some kind of . . . Why would it work like that?"

Warren took Richard's arm and sat him down. He pulled his own chair close. He spoke in a soft, concerned voice, as one would when breaking calamitous news to a someone.

"It takes a long time to train a wizard. Outside, in the rest of the world, over twenty years had gone by before I was even able to touch my Han. But because I live here, I had aged less than two years. Twenty years had passed here, too, but I aged only two. If the palace did not slow our aging, we would all die of old age before we could even light a lamp with our Han.

"I have never heard of it taking less than two hundred years to train a wizard. Commonly, it takes near to three hundred, and sometimes even as much as four hundred.

"The wizards who created this place knew that, and so they tied the magic here to the worlds beyond, where time is meaningless. I don't know how it works, just that it does."

Richard's hands shook. "But . . . I have to get this collar off. I have to get to Kahlan. I can't wait that long. Warren, help me. I can't wait that long."

Warren glanced to the floor. "I'm sorry, Richard. I don't know how to get our collars off, and I don't know how to get by the barrier that keeps us here. I know how you feel, though. It drove me into the vaults for the last fifty years. Some of the others don't seem to care, and say that it just gives them more time with women."

Richard slowly rose. "I can't believe it."

Warren turned his face up. "Richard, please forgive me for telling you. I'm sorry I was the one to hurt you. You've always been . . ."

Richard put a hand to Warren's shoulder. "It's not your fault. You didn't do it. You simply told me the truth." His voice felt as if it were coming from the bottom of a well. "Thank you for the truth, my friend."

All he could think, as his feet shuffled toward the door, was that his dreams were all dying. If he couldn't get the collar off, everything would be lost.

Sisters Ulicia and Finella both stood in warning as he came through the doors. They backed away, the same as the guards had, when they saw the look on his face. A sparkling shield went up before the door. He went through it without slowing. The door beyond burst open for him, without him touching it, part of the frame splintering. It somehow never occurred to him to use the knob.

The Prelate was sitting with her hands folded on the heavy walnut table. Her solemn eyes watched him come. Richard pressed up against the table, towering over her.

"I must admit, Richard," she said in a somber tone, "that I have not been looking forward to this visit."

His straining voice broke. "Why didn't Sister Verna tell me?"

"I ordered her not to."

"And why did you not tell me?"

"Because I wanted you first to learn some significant things about yourself, so you would be better able to understand your importance. The burden of a wizard, and of a Prelate, too."

Richard sank to his knees before her desk. "Ann," he whispered, "please, help me. I must have the Rada'Han off. I love Kahlan. I need her. I need to get back to her. I've been gone a long time. Please, Ann, help me. Take the collar off."

She closed her eyes for a long moment. When they opened, they were heavy with regret.

"I spoke the truth, Richard. We cannot get the Rada'Han off until you learn enough to help us. That will take time."

"Please, Ann, help me. Isn't there any other way?"

Slowly, her eyes staying on his, she shook her head. "No, Richard. Over time, you will come to accept it. They all do. It is easier for the rest, because they come here as boys, not understanding, and grasp it only over time. We have never had to tell one grown, like you, who could understand the significance."

Richard couldn't make himself think clearly. It felt as if he were stumbling in a dark dream. "But, we'll lose so much time together. She will be old. Everyone I know will be old."

Ann smoothed her hair back as she averted her eyes. "Richard, by the time you are trained and leave here, the great-great-great grandchildren of everyone you know will have died of old age and been buried in the ground for over a hundred years."

He blinked at her, trying to comprehend the math of the generations involved, but it all turned to mush in his mind. He suddenly remembered what Shota had warned him of—a trap in time. This was that trap.

He had been stripped of everything by these people. Everything he loved was gone. He would never see Zedd again, or Chase, or anyone he knew. He would never hold Kahlan again. He would never be able to tell her that he loved her, that he understood the sacrifice she had made for him.

**R**ichard looked up from where he sat on the floor to see Warren in the doorway. He hadn't heard the knock. When he said nothing, Warren rushed over and squatted down beside him.

"Listen, Richard, something you said made me think. You said that you were going to wed the Mother Confessor."

Richard's mind came out of the daze and his eyes suddenly came up. "The prophecy is about her, isn't it. The prophecy you said would come on winter solstice."

"I think it might be. But I don't know enough about her, about Confessors, to tell. Does the Mother Confessor wear white?"

"Yes. The Confessors are born to find the truth. She is the last one."

"Richard, I think that is good news. I think she is to find happiness, and bring it to her people, on winter solstice."

Richard remembered the vision he had had in the Tower of Perdition. He remembered the horror of what he had seen. The words Kahlan had spoken were burned into his memory. He quoted it to Warren.

*"Of all there were, but a single one born of the magic to bring forth truth will remain alive when the shadow's threat is lifted. Therefore comes the greater darkness of the dead. For there to be a chance at life's bond, this one in white must be offered to her people, to bring their joy and good cheer."*

"Yes! That's it! I believe that the 'greater darkness' means both the Keeper, and winter solstice. I think that means . . . Richard, where did you read that prophecy?"

"I didn't read it. It was brought to me in a vision of her."

Warren's eyes grew big, the way they tended to do when he was astonished. "You had a vision of prophecy?"

"Yes, she brought me the words, and also brought a vision of what it means."

"What does it mean?"

Richard brushed at his pant leg. "I can't tell you. She said that I could speak the words, but not of the vision. I'm sorry, Warren, but I dare not violate that warning without knowing the consequences. But I can tell you that the results of this prophecy coming true would not be joyful for her, or for me."

Warren considered a moment. "Yes. You are right." He looked over out of the corner of his eye. "Richard, there is something about prophecy I think I should tell you. Hardly anyone knows this, but the words don't always reflect the true intent."

"What do you mean?"

"Well, a few times when I have read prophecies, I've had a vision. The vision turns out to be true, and so does the prophecy, but not in the way you would think from reading it. I believe that the true way prophecy is meant to be understood is through the gift, through the visions."

"Do the Sisters know this?"

"No. I think this is what it means to be a prophet. Richard, if you had this vision, and heard the words, and saw the meaning, maybe that means you are a prophet."

"According to the Prelate, I have a different talent. If she is right, then having the vision might just be part of my ability for what I truly am."

"Which is?"

"The Prelate said I'm a war wizard."

His eyes widened again. "Richard, war wizards have the gift for both Magics. None with the gift for Subtractive, too, has been born in . . . in thousands of years. Maybe the Prelate is wrong."

"I hope she is, but it would explain some things. From what a friend of mine told me, Additive Magic is using what is, adding to it, multiplying it, altering it; the doing of things. Subtractive Magic is the counter, the undoing of things.

"All the shields are put up by the Sisters. They have only Additive. Even those with the gift cannot easily go through them, or break them, because they also have only Additive. Power against power. But somehow I'm able to walk right through the shields around here without even trying.

"Subtractive Magic would explain that. Subtractive would counter the Additive of the shields; undo it."

"But you said you tried to go through the barrier that keeps us from leaving. That's a shield, too. Why can't you go through that shield, then, if you really have the Subtractive?"

Richard lifted an eyebrow and leaned in. "Warren, who put those shields in place?"

"Well, the ones who placed the rest of the magic of the palace, the wizards of old . . ."

"Who you said had Subtractive Magic. That shield is the only one placed by them. It's the only one I can't go through. It's the only one my Subtractive Magic, if I truly have it, wouldn't counter. See what I mean?"

Warren sat back on his heels. "Yes . . ." He rubbed his chin as he thought. "Well, that would make sense. It might fit with some of the prophecies about you. If you really are a war wizard, and are the one born true."

"And do these prophecies say I will prevail?"

Warren hesitated. He glanced over at the Sword of Truth lying on the floor nearby. "If I said 'white blade,' would that mean anything to you?"

Richard let out a heavy breath at the memory. "I can turn the blade of my sword white, through magic."

Warren wiped his hand over his face. "Then I think we might be in trouble. There is a prophecy that says, *'Should the forces of forfeit be loosed, the world will be shadowed yet by darker lust through what has been rent. Salvation's hope, then, will be as slim as the white blade of the one born true.'"*

"Through what has been rent. The open gateway," Richard said.

"That would make 'the darker lust' be the Keeper."

"Warren, I have to do something about the prophecy. The one about the one in white. It's important. Do you have any ideas?"

Warren watched him, as if trying to decide something. "I do. I don't know if it will help." He put weight on his hands as he rubbed them on his thighs. "They

628

have a prophet here, at the palace. I've never seen him. I want to, but they won't let me. They say it's too dangerous for me to talk to him until I learn more. They promised that when I learn enough, they will let me talk with him."

"Here in the palace? Where?"

Warren pulled a fold of his robes from under his knees. "I don't know. It would have to be one of the restricted areas, but I don't know which one, and I don't know how we can find out."

Richard stood. "I do."

Richard knew he had gone to the right guard when Swordsman Kevin Andellmere turned white as a spirit at the mention of the Prophet. He was reluctant, feigning ignorance at first, but when Richard gently reminded him of all the favors, Kevin whispered the location.

The compound Kevin had divulged was one of the most heavily guarded. Richard knew where all the guards were stationed because he had gathered white roses there, and had been up on the wall, to "look out at the sea." He also knew all the guards. They were frequent visitors to the prostitutes he provided.

He didn't slow at the outer gate, but simply gave a nod to the wink the guards gave him. The guards at the rampart were considerably more reticent, stammering and holding out a hand to halt him. He shook the hand, pretending that he thought that was what was meant by it. They finally sighed and resumed their post as he marched away, his mriswith cape billowing open.

At the end of the rampart was a small colonnade, and at the end of that, winding stairs that led down to the Prophet's quarters. The guards at the door he wanted were the two he had had trouble winning over at first, and the first to receive his gift of female company. They stiffened when they saw him.

Richard casually made for the door between them. "Walsh, Bollesdun, how you doing?"

They crossed their pikes over the door. "Richard, what are you doing down here? The roses grow up top."

"Look, Walsh, I have to go see the Prophet."

"Richard, don't put us in this spot. You know we can't let you in. The Sisters would skin us alive."

Richard shrugged. "I won't tell them you let me in. I'll say I tricked you. If anyone finds out, which they won't, just tell them I snuck by, and you didn't know until I was on my way out. I'll back your story."

"Richard, you're really . . ."

"Have I ever done anything to cause trouble? Have I ever done anything but help all you men? I buy you drinks, I loan you money when you need it, I let you have free access to the girls, and it never costs you a copper. Have I ever asked for anything in return?"

Richard had his hand on the hilt of the sword. One way, or another, he was going through that door.

Walsh pushed a stone chip with his boot. With a heavy sigh, first one, and then the other, pulled their pikes up. "Bollesdun, go make your rounds. I'm going to the privy for a sit."

Richard took his hand from his sword and gave the man a pat on the shoulder. "Thanks, Walsh. I appreciate it."

Halfway down the inner hall, Richard felt layers of resistance, shields, like the ones that were outside the Prelate's door, but they only slowed him a bit. The room inside was as spacious as his own, but perhaps more elegantly appointed. One wall held large tapestries, and another expansive bookshelves. Most of the books, though, seemed to be scattered about the room, on chairs and couches and covering the blue-and-yellow carpets on the floor.

Richard could see the back of a man in the chair beside the cold hearth.

"You must tell me how you do that," the man said in a deep, powerful voice. "I would be most interested in learning the trick."

"Do what?" Richard asked.

"Walk through shields as if they weren't there. Burns the flesh right off me if I try."

"If I ever figure it out myself, I'll let you know. My name is Richard. If you're not busy, I would like to speak with you."

"Busy!" The man's shoulders shook with his hearty laugh. When he stood, Richard was a little surprised at how big he was. His long white hair had made Richard think he might be old and shriveled. Old, he was, shriveled he was not. He looked strong and full of vitality. His smile was welcoming and threatening at the same time. He wore a Rada'Han, the same as Richard.

"My name is Nathan, Richard. I've been looking forward to meeting you. I didn't expect you would find your way in alone."

"I wanted to come alone so we could talk freely."

"And do you know that I am a prophet?"

"I didn't come here to learn to bake bread."

Nathan's smile widened, but he didn't laugh. His brows pulled together like a hawk's. His voice took on a hiss. "Would you like me to tell you of your death, Richard? How you are to die?"

Richard flopped down on the couch and plunked his feet up on a table. He returned the hawklike glare and threatening smile in kind. "Sure. I'd love to hear all about it. And then when you're done, I will tell you how you are to die."

Nathan lifted an eyebrow. "And are you a prophet?"

"Enough of one to tell you how you are to die."

The frown turned curious. "Really. Tell me then."

Richard took a pear from a bowl on the table, polished it on his pant leg, and took a bite. He spoke as he chewed. "You are going to die right here, in these rooms, of old age, without ever seeing the outside world again."

The creases in Nathan's face deepened as his expression sagged. "Seems you are a prophet, my boy."

"Unless you help me. Maybe if you help me, I'll be able to come back here and help you get out, too."

"And what is it you want?"

"I want this collar off."

A sly grin spread on Nathan's face. "Seems we share a common interest, Richard."

"But the Sisters say I will die without it."

The sly grin widened. "They demand truthfulness from others, but rarely inconvenience themselves with it. The Sisters have their own agenda, Richard. There is more than one path through the woods."

"The Sisters say I must learn to use my Han, in order to get it off. They don't seem to be helping much in that."

"It would be easier to teach a stump to sing than for a mere Sister to teach you to use your Han. You have Subtractive Magic. They can't help you."

"Can you help me, Nathan?"

"Perhaps." Nathan sat down in his chair, leaning forward intently. "Tell me, Richard, have you ever read *The Adventures of Bonnie Day?*"

"Read it? It's my favorite book. I read it until my eyes nearly wore the words off the page. I'd love to meet the person who wrote it, and tell him how much I liked the book."

A broad, childlike grin stole onto Nathan's face. "You just have, my boy. You just have."

Richard came forward from the back of the couch. "You! You wrote *The Adventures of Bonnie Day?*"

Nathan quoted a few passages, to prove his intimate knowledge. "I gave the book to your father, to give to you when you were old enough to read. You were just born, at the time."

"You were there with the Prelate? She didn't tell me that."

"I doubt the truth occurred to her. You see, Ann doesn't have the power to get into the Wizard's Keep in Aydindril. I helped George get in, so he could get the Book of Counted Shadows. They have some very interesting books of prophecy there."

Richard stared in astonishment. "Seems we are old acquaintances, then."

"More than acquaintances, Richard Rahl." Nathan gave him a meaningful look. "My name is Nathan Rahl."

Richard's mouth dropped open. "You are my . . . great-great-something-or-other?"

"Too many 'greats' to count. I am nearly a thousand years old, my boy." He waggled a finger in the air. "I have had an interest in you for a long time. You are in the prophecies.

"I wrote *The Adventures of Bonnie Day* for some of those who had potential. It is a book of prophecy, of sorts. A primer of prophecy, one you would be able to understand, so it would help you. It did help you, didn't it?"

"More than once," Richard said, still having trouble keeping his jaw up.

"Good. I'm pleased then. We gave the book to a few, special boys. You are the only one still alive. The rest died in 'inexplicable' accidents."

Richard finished the pear while he thought. He definitely didn't like the part about Subtractive Magic. "So can you help me with using my power?"

"Think, Richard. The Sisters have not given you pain with the collar, have they."

"No. But they will."

"Fighting the last war, Richard. What did Bonnie Day tell the Warwick troops guarding the moors? That the enemy would not come the same way as they had before. That they were foolishly wasting their energy trying to fight the last war." Nathan lifted an eyebrow. "You seem to have missed the lesson. Just because something happened to you before, that does not mean it will happen again. Think ahead, Richard, not behind."

Richard hesitated. "I . . . had a vision in one of the towers. A vision that Sister Verna used the collar to hurt me."

"And it brought the anger forth."

Richard nodded. "I called the magic and killed her."

Nathan gave a small, disappointed shake of his head. "The vision was your own mind trying to tell you something, trying to show you that you could defend yourself if they did that, that you could defeat them. It was your gift and your mind working together, trying to help you. You were too busy fighting the last war to heed the message."

Chagrined, Richard kept his mouth shut. He had worried about them hurting him, to the exclusion of everything else. He had ignored the true meaning of what Kahlan had done, because he had been so afraid of the past coming to life again. Think of the solution, not the problem; that was what Zedd had taught him. He had been blinded to the future by the past.

"I see what you mean, Nathan," he admitted. "What did you mean about the Sisters not giving me pain with the collar?"

"Ann knows you are a war wizard, I told her before you were born. I told her near to five hundred years ago. She would have given orders to the Sisters. Giving pain to a war wizard is like kicking a badger on his rump."

"You mean that pain is somehow the secret to my power?"

"No. The result of pain. Anger." He gestured to the sword at Richard's hip. "You use the sword in that way. Anger calls forth the magic. Actually, you call the magic, it brings you anger, and so the magic works. Would you like me to show you how to touch your Han?"

Richard scooted forward. "Yes. I never thought I would say that, but yes. I need to be able to get out of here."

"Hold up your palm. Good." He seemed to pull an aura of authority around himself. "Now, lose yourself in my eyes."

Richard stared into the hooded, deep, dark, azure eyes. The gaze drew him in. Richard felt as if he were falling up into the clear, blue sky. His breath came in ragged pulls, not of his own will. He felt Nathan's commanding words more than heard them.

"Call forth the anger, Richard. Call forth the rage. Call forth the hate and fury." Richard felt it, just as when he drew the sword; as he felt his breath being drawn for him, he felt the anger being drawn. "Now, feel the heat of that rage. Feel the flames of it. Good. Now focus those feelings in the palm of your hand."

Richard funneled the rage of the magic to his hand, directed its flow, feeling its force. His teeth gritted with the power of it.

"Look in your hand, Richard. See it there. See what you are feeling."

Richard's eyes moved slowly to his hand. A ball of blue and yellow fire tumbled slowly above his outstretched palm. He could feel the energy flowing from himself, into the fire. He increased the flow of rage, and the angry ball of flame grew.

"Now, cast the rage, the hate, the anger, the fire, at the hearth."

Richard threw his hand out. The slowly tumbling sphere of flame stayed with his hand. He looked to the hearth, focusing the rage outward, casting it away from himself.

The liquid light howled as it streaked to the hearth, exploding there with a crack, like lightning.

Nathan smiled with pride. "That is how it's done, my boy. I doubt the Sisters could teach you that in a hundred years. You're a natural. No doubt about it. You are a war wizard."

"But Nathan, I didn't feel my Han. I didn't sense anything different. All I felt was angry, like when I use the sword. For that matter, like when I shut my finger in a door."

Nathan nodded knowingly. "Of course not. You are a war wizard. Others have only one side of the gift. They use what is around them; the air, heat, cold, fire, water, whatever they need.

"War wizards aren't like others. They instead tap the core of power within themselves. You don't direct your Han, you direct your feelings. The Sisters teach the 'how' of how everything is done. That is irrelevant to your power. For you, results are all that are important, because you draw power from within. That is why the Sisters cannot teach you."

"What do you mean that's why they cannot teach me?"

"Have you ever seen a seamstress miss a pincushion? The Sisters want you to watch your hand, the pin, and the pincushion. That's the way other wizards use their magic. War wizards don't watch, they just do. Their Han acts instinctively."

"Was that . . . wizard's fire?"

Nathan chuckled. "That was to wizard's fire what an annoyed moth is to an enraged bull."

Richard tried again, but the fire wouldn't come. The anger wouldn't come. He could draw the sword's anger, but it wasn't the same kind he had done with Nathan, from within himself.

"It won't work. Why can't I do it again?"

"Because I was helping you, showing you with my own power what it's like. You are not yet able to do it on your own."

"Why?"

Nathan reached over and tapped Richard's head. "Because it must come from in here. You have yet to accept yourself, who you are. You don't believe. You still fight who you are. Until you accept yourself, until you believe, you won't be able to call forth your Han, your power, except in great anger."

"What of the headaches that came from my gift? The Sisters said they would kill me without the collar."

"The Sisters nibble around the truth as if it were gristle in a piece of meat. They only eat it if they're starving. They want us prisoners so they can bring us to their ways.

"What they attempt to do when they train with you is what I have just done. The headaches are dangerous, but only if a young wizard is left alone with his power. When you had the headaches, were you ever able to make them go away?"

"Yes. Sometimes when I concentrated on shooting arrows, or when something inside warned me of danger, or when I was angry and used the magic of the sword, then they went away for a time."

"That's because you were bringing the gift into harmony with your mind. The only thing required to keep the gift from harming you is a bit of instruction—like I just gave you.

"Teaching wizards should be a wizard's business. For a wizard, bringing your mind into harmony with your gift is a simple matter, because it's the male gift teaching the male gift. What I have just done with you is enough to keep the gift from harming you for a good long time—without the Rada'Han.

"In the future, joining with a wizard will take you the next step, and protect you until you reach the following plain. It's only important to have help available when you need it. The Sisters need a hundred years to show you what I have just done.

"They use the collar as an excuse to take us prisoner for their own purposes. They have their own ideas about the training of wizards. Their idea is to control wizards."

"Why?"

"They think wizards are responsible for all the evil that has befallen mankind, and if they collar the power, control it, and indoctrinate it, they will bring the light of their theology to the people. They are zealots who believe they are the only ones who know the true way to eternal reward in the Creator's light. They feel justified in using any means to gain that end."

"You mean that what you have just showed me, with my power, is enough to keep the gift from killing me, without the collar?"

"It's enough to keep the gift from killing you, but it would take many more lessons to teach you to be a real wizard. All I have done is to hold the stallion's bit, so he won't buck you off. It would take much more work to teach you to ride with grace."

Richard could feel the muscles in his face draw tight. "If this is true, then they are kicking the rump of a badger. Thank you, for helping me." Richard rubbed his fingers together. "Nathan, there is great trouble coming. Coming very soon. I need to know a few things. Do you know the Wizard's Second Rule?"

"Of course. But you must learn the first, before you have the second."

"I already know the first. I killed Darken Rahl with the first. It states that people can be made to believe any lie, either because they want to believe it's true, or because they are afraid it's true."

"And the counter to it?"

"The secret is that there is no counter. I must be always vigilant, knowing that I, too, am vulnerable, and never arrogantly believe I am immune. I must always be alert that I can fall prey."

"Very good."

"And the Second Rule?"

Nathan's white eyebrows hooded his azure eyes. "The Second Rule involves unintended results."

"So, what is it?"

"The Second Rule is that the greatest harm can result from the best intentions. It sounds a paradox, but kindness and good intentions can be an insidious path to destruction. Sometimes doing what seems right is wrong, and can cause harm. The only counter to it is knowledge, wisdom, forethought, and understanding the First Rule. Even then, that is not always enough."

"Good intentions, or doing right, can cause harm? Such as?"

Nathan shrugged. "It would seem kind to give candy to a small child, because they like it so. Knowledge, wisdom, and forethought tell us that it would make the child sick if we continued this 'kindness' at the expense of good food."

"That's obvious. Anyone would know that."

"Say a person hurts their leg, and you bring them food while they heal, but after time they still don't wish to get up, because it hurts at first. So, you continue to be kind and bring them food. Over time, their legs will shrivel, and it will be even more painful to get up, so you are kind and continue bringing food. In the end, they will be bedridden, unable to ever walk again, because of your kindness. Your good intentions have brought harm."

"I don't think that happens often enough to be a problem."

"I'm trying to give you obvious examples, Richard, so you will be better able to extrapolate to more difficult problems, and understand an obscure principle.

"Good intentions, being kind, can encourage the lazy, and motivate sound minds to become indolent. The more help you give them, the more help they need. As long as your kindness is open-ended, they never gain discipline, dignity, or self-reliance. Your kindness impoverishes their humanity.

"If you give a coin to a begger because he says his family is hungry, and he uses it to get drunk, and then kills someone, is it your fault? No. He did the killing, but had you given him food instead, or gone and given his family food, the killing would not have happened. It was a good intention that resulted in harm.

"Wizard's Second Rule: the greatest harm can result from the best intentions. Violation can cause anything from discomfort, to disaster, to death.

"Some leaders have preached peace, saying that even self-defense is wrong. It seems the best of intentions to shun violence. In the end, it often leads to a slaughter, where their threat of violence in the beginning would have prevented attack, and resulted in no violence. They put their good intentions above the realities of life. They accuse warriors of being bloodthirsty, when the warriors would have actually prevented bloodshed."

"Are you trying to say I should feel no shame at being a war wizard?"

"It does the sheep no good to preach the goodness of a diet of grass, if the wolves are of a different mind."

Richard felt as though he were having a conversation with Zedd. "But kindness can't always be wrong."

"Of course not. That's where wisdom comes in. You must be wise enough to foresee the consequences of your actions.

"But the problem with the Second Rule is that you can't always tell for sure whether you are violating it, or simply doing right. Worse, magic is dangerous. When you add magic to the good intentions, violation of the Second Rule can lead to catastrophe.

"Using magic is easy. Knowing when to use magic is the hard part. Every time you use it, you can bring unexpected ruin.

"Do you know, Richard, that it's the weight of one flake of snow that is one too many, and causes an avalanche? Without that one, last flake, the catastrophe would not happen. When using magic, you must know which is the one snowflake too many before you add its weight. The avalanche will be out of all proportion to what you think the weight of that flake could invoke."

Richard rubbed his thumb on the hilt of his sword. "Nathan, I think I may have torn the veil because I violated the Wizard's Second Rule."

"You did."

"What did I do?"

"You used your magic, through the Wizard's First Rule, to win. In so doing, you fed magic to the boxes, the gateway, tearing the veil. You did it through ignorance. You didn't know that the unintended results of doing what seemed right could be the destruction of all life. One snowflake indeed. Magic is dangerous."

"How can I fix it?"

"The Stone of Tears must be put back on the Keeper. The lock, the seal, must be restored. The Stone of Tears must be sent back to its rightful place, in the underworld, where it will serve to restrain the Keeper's power in this world. To do that requires both powers.

"The key must then be turned in the lock, so to speak, by closing the gateway. This also requires both Magics. Doing any of this with only one side of the magic would rip the veil, so a wizard with the gift for only the Additive, such as myself, would be of no help. Only one such as you can accomplish the task.

"Until it is done, we are in terrible danger. If you act wrongly, use the stone for your own reasons, you have the power to destroy the balance and tear the veil the rest of the way, sending us all into eternal night."

Richard stared at the table while he thought. "Do you know what an 'agent' is?"

"Ah. You must be talking about the trouble with the upcoming winter solstice. An agent is one who trades favors with the Keeper, favors such as the innocent souls of children, in return for knowledge of the use of Subtractive Magic."

He gave Richard a dark look. "But that would not be a problem, because you sent Darken Rahl to the underworld, where he has no power here. Darken Rahl is in the underworld, is he not?"

Richard felt a gnawing pain in the pit of his stomach. He had not only torn the veil, but in violating the Second Rule again, by trying to help with a gathering, he had brought an agent, Darken Rahl, back to this world where he could act to tear the veil. It was all Richard's fault. He felt hot and dizzy. He thought he might be sick at any moment.

"Nathan, I have to get this collar off."

Nathan shrugged. "I can't help with that."

Richard had come here for a specific reason. He decided he had to try to get the answer. He cleared his throat.

"Nathan, there is someone very important to me. She is in danger, and I must help. There is a prophecy about her that is written down, but it also came to me in a vision."

"Which prophecy?"

*"Of all there were, but a single one born of the magic to bring forth truth will remain alive when the shadow's threat is lifted. . . ."*

In his deep, powerful voice, Nathan finished the prophecy. *"Therefore comes the greater darkness of the dead. For there to be a chance at life's bond, this one in white must be offered to her people, to bring their joy and good cheer."*

"Then you know of it. Nathan, I saw the meaning of the prophecy. I was told not to speak of the vision, but it's not a joyful outcome as far as I'm concerned."

"She is beheaded," Nathan said in a quiet voice. "That is the true meaning of that prophecy."

Richard put his arm across his churning stomach. That was what he had seen in the vision. His world started spinning again.

"Nathan, I have to get away from here. I have to stop that from happening."

"Richard, look at me." Richard looked up, managing to hold the tears back. "Richard, I must tell you the truth. If this prophecy does not happen, there is nothing beyond. We all die. It will be the end of all life. The Keeper will have us.

"If you use your power to stop it, you will rip the veil asunder and allow the Keeper to swallow the word of the living."

Richard shot to his feet. "Why! Why would she have to die to save the living! It makes no sense!" His fist tightened around the hilt of the sword. "I have to stop it! It's just a stupid riddle! I won't let her die for a riddle!"

"Richard, a time will come when you have to make a choice. I have been hoping for a very long time now that when that time comes, you will be wise enough to make the right choice. You have the power to destroy us all if you choose wrongly."

"I will not stand here while you tell me I must let her die. The good spirits have done nothing to help. I must. I will."

Richard stormed from the room. Cracks ran along the walls beside him as he marched down the hall. Chunks of plaster rained down behind as he went. Richard only dimly noticed, but it pleased his temper. When he went through the shield, the paint on the walls to the side charred and curled.

Richard's thoughts ran wildly in all directions at once. He knew now that his vision had been of what was going to happen if he didn't stop it. It was going to come true if he couldn't get away from the palace. Maybe that was what the prophecy meant, that he would be held prisoner there, and he wouldn't be able to help, and Kahlan would die.

In the courtyard below, Richard saw a commotion. Guards were running from everywhere. When he got closer, he saw one of the Baka Ban Mana blade masters. There had to be close to a hundred worried-looking guards surrounding him in a ring, holding their distance. The man in loose-fitting clothes, in the center of the ring, looked unconcerned.

Richard pushed through the throng. "What's going on?"

The man bowed to Richard. "*Caharin.* I am Jiaan. Your wife, Du Chaillu, has sent me to give you a message."

Richard decided not to contest the wife part. "What is it?"

"I am to tell you that she has followed her husband's instructions. We have brought the Majendie to a peace with us. We no longer make war with them, or the people here."

"That's wonderful news, Jiaan. Tell her I am proud of her, and her people."

"Your people," Jiaan corrected. "She wants you to know she has decided to bear the child. And she also sends message that we are ready to return to our homeland. She wishes to know when you will come to take us there."

Richard glanced around at the people. Not only guards were gathered, but Sisters, too. He recognized a few of his teachers watching; Sisters Tovi, Nicci, and Armina. Pasha stood nearby. At the far edge of the crowd he saw Sister Verna. On a balcony in the distance, beyond the walls, he saw the squat figure of the Prelate.

Richard turned back to Jiaan. "Tell her to be ready, that it will be soon."

Jiaan bowed. "Thank you, *Caharin*. We will be ready."

Richard spoke to the guards in a circle around them. "This man has come in peace. He is to be left in peace."

Jiaan strode away, unconcerned, as if he were alone on a walk, but the ring of guards moved with him, as Richard knew they would until he was well clear of the city. The crowd started drifting away.

Richard's head was pounding. He had brought his father back from the underworld by violating the Wizard's Second Rule a second time in the spirit house; he had tried to do the right thing and instead had brought harm. Warren had told him that the Keeper needed an agent to escape, and Richard had provided one.

His mind reeled. He had just found out that Kahlan loved him and life seemed good again, only to discover that he was to be trapped here for hundreds of years, and if he couldn't escape, Kahlan would die on winter solstice. His thoughts went around and around in a desperate tangle.

He had to do something. Time was running out. He decided to find the one person who might be able to help him.

**S**he heard the voices in the outer office, and hoped it was who she thought it would be. She was not looking forward to this, but she was running out of time. Richard would have surely found a way to see Nathan by now, and Nathan would have done his part. Now it was time to do hers.

She couldn't completely trust Nathan, but in this, he would have done what was required. He knew the consequences of failure. His had been a task she didn't envy—adding the weight of that snowflake.

With a flick of her fingers, the door swung open. She had had to have the carpenters fix the doorframe. Richard had shattered it with his Han, without even being aware of what he had done. And that was before he had even gone to Nathan.

The curt speech cut off as the door opened, and the three faces looked in, awaiting instruction.

"Sister Ulicia, Finella, it's late; why don't you two run along to your offices and tend to your paperwork. I will see her. Sister Verna, please come in."

Ann stood as Sister Verna strode in. She liked Verna. She abhorred what she was going to have to do to her, but she was running out of time. Hundreds of years to prepare, and now time and events were slipping through her fingers.

The world was at the brink.

Verna bowed. "Prelate Annalina."

"Please, Verna, sit down. It has been so long."

Verna pulled a chair close to the opposite side of the table. She sat with her back straight and her hands folded in her lap. "How good of you to take your valuable time to see me."

Ann almost smiled. Almost. *Dear Creator, thank you for sending her to me testy; though it won't make my job any less onerous, it will surely make it easier.*

"I have been busy."

"So have I," Verna snapped. "For the last twenty-odd years."

"Apparently not busy enough. We seem to be having difficulty with a boy you collected, and should have brought to task before he ever arrived."

Verna's face turned scarlet. "Had you not forbidden me from doing my duty, using my skills, I would have done so."

"Oh? Are you so barren of resourcefulness, Verna, that you could not function with minor restrictions? Pasha, a mere novice, seems to be having better success, and she functions under the same restrictions."

"You think so? You think he is under control?"

"He has not killed anyone since Pasha took over."

Verna stiffened. "I think I know something of Richard. I would advise the Prelate caution in her confidence."

Ann looked down, moving papers about, as if devoting attention to words she was not seeing. "I will take your advice under consideration. Thank you for coming, Verna."

"I'm not finished! I haven't yet begun!"

Her eyes came slowly up. "If you raise your voice to me again, you will be, Verna."

"Prelate Annalina, please forgive my tone, but there are matters of grave importance I simply must raise."

Ann sighed, feigning impatience. "Yes, yes, then please do get to it. I have much work to do." She folded her hands on the desk and gave Verna a blank look. "Go on then."

"Richard grew up with his grandfather. . . ."

"How nice for him."

Verna paused in annoyance at the interruption. "His grandfather is a wizard. A wizard of the First Order. His grandfather wanted to teach him."

"Well, we will see to his teaching. Is that all?"

Verna's eyes narrowed. "I do not need to remind the Prelate that it is a direct violation of the truce to take a boy from a wizard who would teach him. I was told that there were no wizards left in the New World to teach boys. I was lied to. I was used. We have been stealing boys. You made me a part of that."

Ann smiled indulgently. "Sister, we serve the Creator, so all may learn to live in his light. Now, in view of our duty to the Creator, what is a truce with heathen wizards?"

Verna was struck speechless.

*Dear Creator, I like this woman so. Please give me the strength to break her.* Nathan had added his snowflake, she had to add hers.

"I have been sent on a twenty-year chase, without knowing the reason, I have been deceived, my two companions died, one at my hand, I have been forbidden use of my power to do my job . . ."

"Do you think I forbid your use of your power capriciously? Is that what's bothering you, Verna? Very well then, if you must know the reason, it was to save your life."

Verna stiffened in caution. "If I remember my lessons in the vaults, there is only one reason such restriction would save my life."

Inwardly, Ann smiled. Verna wanted it spoken aloud. "Indeed. Richard has Subtractive Magic."

"You knew that? You had one with Subtractive Magic collared? You would risk that? You would have him brought here, to the palace?" Her hands unfolded and she leaned in a bit. "Why?"

Ann held the other's gaze. "Because there are Sisters of the Dark in the palace."

She didn't twitch. She knew. At least, she suspected. *Bless you, Verna, you are a bright one. Forgive me for what I must do.*

"Is this room shielded?" Verna asked in an even tone.

"Of course." She left unsaid that her shield would not protect against these Sisters.

"Do you have proof of such an accusation, Prelate?"

"I do not need proof, right now, because this conversation is restricted. You will not speak of it. Unless you plan to bring charges. If you do, I of course will deny it, and say a bitter Sister was trying to accuse the Prelate of blasphemy for personal gain. And then we would have to hang you. Neither of us wants that, now do we?"

Verna sat stiff and still. "No, Prelate. But what does that have to do with bringing Richard here?"

"When your house is overrun with rats, the only thing you can do is bring in a cat."

"This cat sees us all as rats. Maybe with good reason. Some might say that perhaps you were not bringing in a cat for your rats, but bait. Richard is a good person. I would not like to think he is being sacrificed."

"Do you know why you were selected to go after Richard?"

"I had thought it was your vote of confidence."

Ann shrugged. "In a way, it was. Although I'm not sure that there are Sisters of the Dark in the palace, and I have no idea who they are if it's true, I had to assume that if it is true, then since Grace and Elizabeth were at the top of the list, they would be Sisters of the Dark. I knew from prophecy, that only my eyes have seen, that Richard probably has Subtractive Magic, and further, that he would refuse the first two offers. I knew the first two sisters would die.

"If the Nameless One's disciples knew any of this, they would want the third name on the list to be one of theirs, too. I used my prerogative as Prelate to pick the third Sister."

"You chose me, because you had faith that I was not one of them?"

What Ann wanted to say was *I have known you since you were a child, Verna. I know your quick mind, your heart, and your soul. You, of all the Sisters, were the one I trusted with the fate of the world. I knew Richard would be safe in your hands.*

But she could not say that.

"I chose you, Verna, because you were far down on the list, and because, all in all, you are quite unremarkable."

The room rang with silence for a long moment. Verna swallowed. "I see."

Ann affected dispassionate objectivity. Inside, her heart was breaking.

"I doubted you were one of them. You are a person of little note. I'm sure Grace and Elizabeth made their way to the top of the list because whoever directs the Sisters of the Dark considered them expendable. I direct the Sisters of the Light. I chose you for the same reason.

"There are Sisters who are valuable to our cause; I could not risk one of them on such a task. The boy may prove a value to us, but he is not as important as other matters at the palace. He may be a help. It was simply an opportunity I thought to take.

"If there had been trouble, and none of you made it back, well, I'm sure you can understand that a general would not want to lose his best troops on a low-priority mission."

Verna's breathing looked forced. Her voice sounded it. "Of course, Prelate Annalina."

Ann shuffled her papers impatiently. "I have important matters to get back to. Is there anything else, Sister?"

"No, Prelate."

When the door closed, Ann lowered her face into her shaking hands. Tears dripped onto her papers.

She appraised his eyes for a long moment. Richard didn't know if she would say yes or not, but he had had to tell her much of what he had learned just to get her to agree to listen to his plea. He couldn't afford to fail. He needed help. He had to trust someone.

"All right, Richard. I will help you. If half of what you say is true, I must help you."

Richard sighed as he closed his eyes in relief. "Thank you, Liliana. I'll never forget you for this. You're the only one around here who will listen to reason. Can we do it now? Time is critical."

"Now?" she whispered harshly. "Here? Richard, if what you say about you having Subtractive Magic is true, it won't be a simple matter to remove your Rada'Han. I will need to retrieve an object of magic that the Sisters keep guarded. It's an aid, used to amplify power. Maybe through that, and with your help, it will be enough to get the collar off.

"Not only that, but if the Nameless One is involved, there is no telling what ears, or Han, might be paying attention."

"Then, when? Where? It has to be soon."

She wiped her fingers over her eyes as she considered. "Well, I think I can retrieve the object before tonight, so we could try tonight. But where? It can't be in the palace. It would be too dangerous."

"The Hagen Woods," Richard said. "Everyone avoids the Hagen Woods."

Liliana looked up. "Richard, you can't be serious. It's dangerous there."

"Not for me. I already told you how I can tell if the mriswith are coming. We'll be safe enough, and we won't have to worry about any Sisters, or Pasha, stumbling by while we're trying to get this cursed thing off my neck."

She let out a frustrated breath. At last she laid a hand on his shoulder and, giving it a squeeze, smiled. "All right. The Hagen Woods, then."

With a stern look, she gripped his shoulder and held him out at arm's length. "I'm violating a whole stack of rules by doing this. I know it's important, and the right thing to do, but if they catch us before we can do it, they will make sure I never get near enough to you to ever again try."

"I'm ready now, let's go."

"No. I must try to retrieve the aid first." She cocked her head to the side as she frowned. "And I just thought of something else. They keep telling you not to let the sun set on you there. Why?"

Richard shrugged. "Because it's dangerous."

"And after everything you've learned, you believe them? You trust them? Richard, what if they don't want you to let the sun set on you there because you might learn something useful? You said the Hagen Woods were placed there by the wizards of old who had Subtractive Magic, in order to help those like you. What if the Sisters don't want you to have that help? What if they are just trying to make you afraid, so you won't discover it?"

Wizard's First Rule. Were they deceiving him? Was he believing a lie? "You may be right. We'll go before sunset."

"No. We don't want to be seen together. And it will take me some time to steal the aid. Do you know where the long, split rock sits in the stream to southwest corner of the Hagen Woods?"

"I know the place."

"Good. You get there before the sun sets; you are the one the magic is for. Go in the woods by the split rock. Tie strips of cloth to branches so I can follow where you went, and find you. I'll meet you there, in the woods, when the moon is two hands in the sky. And Richard, don't you dare tell anyone about this, or you will be risking not only my life and yours, but Kahlan's too."

Richard nodded with a smile of thanks. "On my word. Tonight, then."

He paced his room after she left. He was anxious to get this over with, and be off. He was running out of time. If Darken Rahl had the skrin bone, they were already out of time. But that was just foolish. How would he get it? He was a spirit. Maybe it was as Warren said, that the elements were rarely all in place.

It was Kahlan he was worried about. He had to help her.

A knock brought him out of his thoughts. He thought it might be Liliana come back, but when he opened the door, a distraught Perry pushed into the room.

"Richard! I need your help." He pulled out a fistful of robes. "Look at this! They promoted me!"

Richard glanced down the length of the simple, brown robes. "Congratulations. That's great, Perry."

"It's a disaster! Richard, I need your help!"

Richard frowned. "Why is it a disaster?"

Perry threw his arms in the air, as if it should be obvious to anyone. "Because I can't go into the city! I'm restricted in these robes! I'm not allowed to go over the bridge!"

"Well, I'm sorry, Perry, but I don't see how I can help you."

Perry took a deep breath to calm himself. He looked up pleadingly. "There's a woman in the city . . . I've been seeing her steady of late. Richard, I really like her. I'm supposed to meet her tonight. If I don't show up, so I can explain, if I never show up again, she'll think I don't care about her."

"Perry, I still don't see what I can do about it."

Perry grabbed him by his shirt. "They took all my clothes. Richard, you could lend me some of yours. Then no one would recognize me, and I could sneak into the city, and see her. Please, Richard, lend me some of your clothes?"

Richard thought a moment. He didn't care if he was violating some obscure rule of the palace, it seemed insignificant compared to what he was doing, but he still worried for Perry.

"The guards all know me. They will see it's you in my clothes and tell the Sisters. Then you'll be in for trouble."

Perry glanced away, frantically thinking. "Night. I'll wait until night, and then I'll go. They won't see so clearly who it really is at night. Please, Richard? Please?"

Richard sighed. "It's fine by me, Perry, if you want to risk it. Just don't get yourself caught. I'd hate to know I helped get you in trouble." He gestured to the bedroom, where the wardrobe was. "Come on. Take whatever you like. You aren't quite my size, but I guess you're close enough."

Perry added a grin to his sidelong look. "The red coat? I can have the red coat? She'd like me in that."

"Sure." Richard led a giddy Perry toward the bedroom. "If that is what you would like, take it. I'm glad someone will enjoy wearing the red coat."

Perry sorted through the wardrobe, looking for a pair of pants and a shirt he thought would look dashing.

"I saw Sister Liliana leaving your room, just before I came." He pulled out a ruffled, white shirt. "She one of your teachers?"

"Yes. I like her. She's the nicest of the lot."

Perry held up the shirt in front of himself. "How does this look on me?"

"Better than on me. You know Liliana?"

"Not really. She just always gave me the shivers. Those strange eyes of hers."

Richard thought about Liliana's pale, pale blue eyes shot through with violet flecks. He shrugged. "I thought they were strange, too, at first. But she's so bubbly and friendly that I don't even notice them anymore. She has such a warm smile that it's hard to see anything else."

Richard sat quietly with his legs folded and the sword across his knees. He wore his mriswith cape so that Pasha and Sister Verna wouldn't know where he was. He didn't want either to know the sun had set on him in the Hagen Woods. Either would surely come after him if they knew what he was doing.

He had found a small clearing, high enough to be dry, and had waited there since the sun had gone down. He could see the full moon through the tight tangle of branches, and judged it about two hands high. He didn't know what was supposed to happen in the Hagen Woods when the sun set on you there, but so far it seemed as it always had when he had been there before at night.

He returned Liliana's call, and she came out from behind a fat oak. She looked about at the woods. It wasn't a tentative glance, but a confident appraisal.

She sat before him, crossing her legs. "I got it. The aid I told you about."

Richard smiled in relief. "Thanks, Liliana."

She pulled it from her cloak. In the moonlight, he could see it was a small statue of a man holding something clear as glass. She held it up, showing it to him.

"What is it?"

"The crystal, this clear part here, has the power to amplify the gift. I don't have the power to get your Rada'Han off, if it is true that you have Subtractive Magic, because I have only Additive. You will hold this in your lap. When we join our minds this will help amplify your power, so I can use it, and be able to break the hold."

"Good. Let's begin."

She pulled the statue back. "Not until I tell you the rest."

He looked into her pale, pale blue eyes, at the dark flecks spread through them. "So tell me."

"The reason you can't help get the collar off is because you don't have the training to use your gift. You don't know how to direct the power. This will overcome that deficiency. I hope."

"You're trying to work up to warning me about something."

She gave a single nod. "You don't know how to control the flow, so you be will at the mercy of the aid. But the aid doesn't understand pain. It simply does what it must. What I need."

"So you're telling me it might hurt. I'm prepared to endure pain. Let's get started."

"Not 'might.' " She held up a cautionary finger. "Richard, this is dangerous. It will hurt you. It will feel like your mind is being torn apart. I know you want to do this, but I don't want to deceive you. This will make you think you are dying."

He felt a trickle of sweat run down his neck.

"It must be done."

"I will be directing my Han to try to break the hold of the collar. The aid will be pulling power from you, to do as I need to overcome the Rada'Han. It will hurt you."

"Liliana, I can take whatever is necessary. It must be done."

"You listen to me, Richard. I know you want to do this, but you listen. I will be pulling the gift from you, to help break the collar. Your mind will feel like I'm trying to pull the very life from you. Your inner mind may interpret that as me trying to suck the gift, the very life, from you.

"You will have to endure the feeling of having your life ripped from you. You will have to endure it until the collar breaks. If you try to stop it when my power is in you, trying to do as I must . . ."

"So what you are saying is that if it's too much, and I want to stop, I can't. If I try to stop the pull on my magic, it will kill me."

"Yes. You must not resist. If you do, you will die." Her expression was as serious as he had ever seen it. "You must trust me, and not try to stop what is happening to you, or you will die, and then Kahlan will die. Are you sure you can do that?"

"Liliana, I would do anything, endure anything, to save Kahlan. I trust you. I will put my life in your hands."

She at last nodded and placed the statue in his lap. She gazed into his eyes a long moment, and then kissed her finger. She touched the kissed finger to his cheek.

"Into the void, then, together. Thank you for your trust, Richard. You will never know what this means to me."

"Nor to me, Liliana. What do you want me to do?"

"The same as we have always done before. You just try to touch your Han, as always, and I will do the rest."

She wiggled forward until their knees were pressed together. They held hands, letting them rest over their knees. Each drew a deep breath, and closed their eyes.

At first, it was the same as it always was, just deep relaxation as he concentrated on the image of the Sword of Truth. The pain, at first, was simply an uncomfortable tingling. It spiraled deeper, settling at the base of his spine, feeling like a pulled muscle. The pain worked its way up his back.

Abruptly, it erupted everywhere at once, something like the pain of the Agiel; a hot ache searing through the marrow of his bones. Denna had taught him to endure pain. He said a silent thank you to Denna, for what she had done. Maybe it would be what he needed to endure this, to save Kahlan.

The twisting torture took his breath. His back stiffened. Sweat instantly drenched his face. His lungs burned for air. With the greatest of effort, he drew a breath.

Shattering pain exploded through his mind, plunging him into a timeless place of ripping, unending agony. He struggled to hold the sword in his mind. Tears ran down his face. He had to do this.

It felt as if every nerve in his body were exposed and being held to a flame. He thought his eyes might burst. He thought his heart might burst. He flinched with each agonizing tug of pain. It was torture beyond endurance.

And then it seemed as if what he had felt had not yet been the beginning of it. He was unable to scream, to breathe, to move. It seemed his very soul was being ripped from him.

As Liliana had warned him, it seemed as if his very life was being pulled from him. He felt a wash of panic that this was killing him. He felt dark death soaking into the void left by what was being ripped from him. He dimly worried that this wasn't right. Terror burgeoned deep within him, and then that too was pulled into the swirling torrent erupting outward.

He wanted nothing more than to scream, as if it would somehow ameliorate the agony. But he could not. His muscles seemed to be losing their life along with the rest of him. He could not breathe, or even hold his head up.

*Please, Liliana, please hurry. Please.*

He struggled not to resist what she was doing. He prayed that he would not fight her. He had to get to Kahlan. She needed him.

His eyes were open, he realized, when he recognized the statue in his lap. His head was hanging. The crystal was beginning to glow a dull orange. A dim part of him thought that that must mean it was working, doing its job. His head felt as if it were coming apart. He expected to see blood dripping down, but he saw only the orange glow increasing.

*Please, Liliana, hurry.*

Blackness was enveloping him. Even the insufferable pain was beginning to seem distant. He felt life slipping from his grasp. He felt an emptiness coming upon him that was more ghastly that anything he thought possible.

In the fading recesses of his mind, he felt a presence.

Mriswith.

He felt them near. His level of alarm rose. They were around him, closing in.

And then he heard, as if from a great distance, Liliana's voice. "Wait, my pets. You may have what is left, when I am finished with him. Wait."

He could dimly see the mriswith in his mind, as he always had when they came to him. When Liliana spoke, they moved back.

Why would she say that? Why would the mriswith move back at her command? What did she mean? Maybe the pain had driven him insane, and it was only a mad illusion.

He felt a presence at his back. Not a mriswith. Worse. More gruesome by ten. He felt its fetid breath on his neck.

Liliana's voice came in a dangerous hiss. "I said wait." The presence receded a bit, but not as far as the mriswith.

What did she mean, they could have what was left? He was dying, that was what she meant. He could feel it. He was dying.

No. Liliana said he would think that. It was simply happening as she had said, that was all. He had to be strong for Kahlan. But he had so little left to give. He was dying. He knew he was. The statue in his lap was glowing brighter.

The hot breath returned to his neck. He heard a low growl from the loathsome thing. He vehemently wanted it away from him.

Liliana's menacing voice came again. "Wait. I will be finished in a moment, and then you may have his body. Wait."

In that instant, something deep within him told him that if he was ever going to save himself, this was the last chance. It had to be now. The decision to act was sudden desperation.

From deep within, from the core of his mind, from the core of his being, from the core of his soul, he wrenched his will to action, and by force of will, with frantic, colossal effort, he yanked his power, his life—himself—back.

A thundering boom sounded, and an impact sundered the air, throwing the two of them apart. Richard landed on his back at one edge of the clearing, Liliana at the other. The Sword of Truth was in the center. The mriswith and the other creature melted back into the darkness among the trees.

Richard gasped for air. He sat up and shook his head. The statue lay on the ground in the center, near his sword. The orange glow was gone.

Liliana floated upward without effort. It looked as if an invisible hand had lifted her gently to her feet. The sight raised hackles on the back of his neck.

She smiled wickedly. Richard hadn't thought Liliana to be capable of such a vile grin. It made his toes curl in his boots.

"Oh, Richard, I was so close. I've never experienced anything like it. You have no idea of the glory of what you have. But I will have it yet."

Richard glanced to the sides, trying to decide which way to run. He felt like a fool, and at the same time was overcome by a sense of profound loss. "Liliana, I trusted you. I thought you cared for me."

She lifted an eyebrow. "Did you?" The slow smile returned. "Maybe I did. Maybe that's why I was doing it the easy way. Now we do it the hard way."

Richard blinked. "What do you mean, the hard way?"

"The quillion would have been the easy way. I have taken on the gift from many a male. But you resisted where they could not. Now I must skin you alive to have your gift. First, I will have to disable you. You will lie helpless, as I do it."

She held out a hand. A sword floated out from behind the big oak, out of the darkness, and into her hand.

With a shriek, she swept across the clearing toward him. Her sword flashed in the moonlight.

Without thinking, Richard lifted his hand, calling his sword and its magic. The response was instant. The anger inundated him. He felt the hilt slam into his palm as Liliana swung her sword. The sword, the magic, the spirits, were with him. He brought the blade up, blocking her strike.

Dimly, Richard wondered why his sword didn't shatter hers. But then he was moving. The dance with death had begun.

He countered her strikes, and she his. He evaded attacks that should have had him, and she thwarted attacks that should have had her. She spun like the wind, slipping away at the last instant. He felt as if he were fighting a shadow. No human could move the way she did. He could not move the way she did.

Behind, he felt the sudden, loathsome presence. He checked the thrust of her blade, and spun, bringing the sword around with lightning speed. For an instant, he saw a snarl of fangs, and a malicious glare, and then the sword made solid contact, and what was there was rendered unrecognizable as it disintegrated.

He felt her blade coming, and dove over the falling hulk. Rolling to his feet, he returned the attack. The night air rang over and over with the sound of steel on steel.

Richard realized that her blade must somehow be like his. She had a weapon the match of the Sword of Truth. Besides that, she had command of magic he could only imagine. He didn't have to imagine long.

As the battle wound its way across the clearing, both straining with all the fury they could bring forth, she leapt back, and sent a bolt of fire racing toward him. He dodged at the last instant, and it flew past, hitting a tree. The trunk exploded in a shower of splinters. The top of the tree crashed down around him, some of the branches knocking him from his feet.

Liliana slashed through branches as thick as his arms to get at him. They splintered the way the trunk had. Richard scrambled out from under and fought her back into the thick woods.

As they clashed over and over again while descending a steep hill, he began to analyze her tactics. She fought ferociously, but without grace—like a soldier in combat among the lines. He didn't know how he knew that, except it had to come from the spirits of his sword's magic.

The way she attacked, slashing and swinging, left her open for a thrusting counterattack. Richard pressed that attack at her, but when he finally managed to thrust at her middle, the strike that should have found its mark slid to the side. She was protected, somehow. She had the use of magic he didn't understand.

Richard was exhausted, and was fighting on the pure rage and fury of the magic. She didn't even seem winded. "You can't win, Richard. I will have you."

"Why! You can't win in the end!"

"I will have my reward."

He ducked behind a tree, just missing a swing that sent wood chips flying. "If you help the Keeper escape, he will swallow all life!"

"You think so? You think wrong. He will reward those who serve him. He will grant me things the Creator never could."

He stabbed at her, but the sword slid to the side. "He's lying to you!"

Her blade whistled past his face. Her calm, deliberate attacks were relentless. "We have a bargain. My oath seals it."

"And you believe he will keep his end?"

"Join with us, Richard, and I will show you the glory that awaits those who serve him. You can live forever."

Richard leapt to the top of a rock. "Never!"

She looked up with a cold detachment. "I thought this would be pleasurable, but I find I am growing bored."

Liliana swept a hand out. Twisting, snaking lightning came from the hand, but it was not like any lightning he had ever seen before.

It was black lightning.

Instead of a bolt of light and heat, it was an undulating void, as dark as the night stone, as dark as the boxes of Orden, as dark as eternal death. The dim, moonlit scene seemed a sunny day in comparison.

Richard knew: he was seeing Subtractive Magic.

Liliana swept the black lightning across the rock beneath his feet. It effortlessly sliced a smooth-edged void through the rock. The remaining part he stood atop collapsed onto the half below. Trees behind for a good distance, severed in the same way, by the same black bolt, crashed to the ground in a roar of noise.

Richard lost his footing and toppled backward onto the steep slope, tumbling down the hill. He threw his arms out to stop himself when he hit the flat at the bottom, and immediately rolled over onto his back. He looked up and gasped.

Liliana was standing right over him, her sword held high in both hands. By where she was looking, he knew she intended to cut off his legs. He froze at seeing her sword commence its descent.

What he was doing was not working. He had to do something else, or he was going to die.

Her blade was a blur in the moonlight. He released himself, gave sanction to his inner self, his gift. He would surrender to whatever was there, or he would die. It was his only chance. He found the calm center within, and did its bidding.

He saw the Sword of Truth thrusting upward. His knuckles were white with effort. The sword was a white glow in the gloomy light.

With all his force, he drove the hissing white blade into Liliana, under her ribs. When the tip severed her spine, coming out her back between her shoulder blades, she went limp. Only his sword and strength held her upright.

Her mouth dropped open in a gasp. Her sword fell, sticking in the ground to the side. Her wide, pale eyes stared down at him.

"I forgive you, Liliana," Richard whispered.

Her arms twitched in an uncoordinated manner. Terror filled her eyes. She tried to speak, but only blood frothed forth.

There was an earsplitting crack, like a lightning strike, but instead of a flash of light, a ripple of total darkness swept through the forest. Its touch made his heart skip a beat. When it lifted, the moonlight seemed dazzling, and Liliana was dead.

Richard knew—the Keeper had taken her.

Before, he had called the sword's white magic knowing full well what it meant. This time, he had done as Nathan had told him, and let his instinct, his gift, call it forth. It had been a surprise to him, both the instant calling of the white magic, and the fact that he had not consciously done it.

Something within had known that that was what was needed to counter the Keeper's hate that filled Liliana. Richard was left stunned by what had happened. He stared down at Liliana as he withdrew his sword. He had confided in her. He had trusted her.

He realized that he was still where he had started—with the collar around his neck, and no ideas of how to get it off. Collar or no collar, he had to get through the barrier that kept him here. He decided that he would go get his things from the palace, and then he would find a way through the invisible wall.

As he wiped the sword clean on her clothes, he recalled how it had been in the center of the clearing, a good distance from him. He had somehow called it to him, along with the magic. The sword had flown through the air, and come into his hand.

He set the sword on the ground, and experimentally called its magic. The anger, the fury, filled him, as always. He held his hand out and willed the blade to come to him. It lay rock-solid on the ground. Try as he might, it would not so much as twitch.

Frustrated, he returned it to its scabbard. He pulled her sword from the ground and broke the blade over his knee. When he threw it aside, he noticed something white nearby.

White bones gleaming in the moonlight were mostly all that remained of the desiccated corpse. Only the top half was there. He assumed animals must have gotten the rest, but then he found the pelvis and legs, some distance away. Tattered remains of a dress that matched the top half still surrounded the leg bones.

Richard knelt, inspecting the upper body. Animals had not touched it. There was not a single tooth mark on any bone. It remained now as it had fallen.

With a frown, he saw that the bones of the lower spine were shattered. He had never seen bones splintered in such a way. It was as if this woman had been blown in half, while alive.

He knelt silently, staring, wondering. Someone had killed this woman. Somehow, he knew: magic had killed this woman.

"Who did this to you?" he whispered down at the corpse.

Slowly, a skeletal arm rose toward him in the moonlight. The fingers uncurled. A thin chain dropped down, dangling from the bones of a finger.

Richard, his hair feeling as if it were trying to stand on end, carefully took the chain from the fingers. There was a single object on the chain. He held it up in the moonlight and saw it was a lumpy piece of gold, formed into the letter *J*.

"Jedidiah," Richard whispered, now knowing what made him do so.

As Richard approached, he noticed a commotion on the stone bridge. A crowd lined one edge, everyone looking down to the river. At the center, he eased his way through toward the low, walled railing. An he did, he saw Pasha at the crown, too, leaning out over the stone, looking down.

"What's going on?" he asked as he came up behind her.

Pasha spun at the sound of his voice. She flinched when she saw him. "Richard! I thought . . ." She looked back over the railing, down to the river, and then back to him.

"You thought what?"

She threw her arms around his middle. "Oh, Richard! I thought you were dead! Thank the Creator!"

Richard pried her arms off and then leaned over, looking down to the dark river below. Several small boats, each with a lantern, were towing a body tangled in their hand-casting nets. In the flickering yellow light, he could see the red coat.

Richard ran over the bridge and down the banks, reaching the shore as the men were landing the boats. Grabbing the nets from a man, he hauled them and their load up onto the grassy bank.

There was a small, round hole in the lower back of the red coat. He rolled the body over and looked into Perry's dead eyes. Richard groaned.

*Wizard's Second Rule.* Perry had died because Richard had violated it. He had tried to do something good, with the best of intentions, and it had brought harm. It was Richard the dacra had been meant for. It was he they thought they were killing.

Pasha was standing on the bank behind him. "Richard, I was so afraid. I thought it was you." She started crying. "What was he doing in your red coat?"

"I loaned it to him." He gave her a quick hug. "I have to go, Pasha."

"You don't mean the palace. You didn't really mean what you said about leaving. I know you didn't. You can't leave, Richard."

"I meant every word. Good night, Pasha."

He left the men to their grisly task and headed for his room. Someone had meant to kill him, and it hadn't been Liliana. Someone else was trying to kill him.

As he was loading his things into his pack, he heard a knock at his door. He froze, a shirt half-folded in his hands. Then he heard Sister Verna's voice beyond the door, asking if she could come in.

Richard yanked the door open, preparing to launch into a tirade, but the look on her face caught the words in his throat. She stood woodenly, staring off at nothing.

"Sister Verna, what's wrong?" He took her arm and led her into his room. "Here, sit down."

She sank to the edge of the chair. Richard knelt in front of her and took her hands.

"Sister Verna, what's wrong?"

"I've been waiting for you to return." Her puffy, red eyes finally sought his. "Richard," she said in a subdued voice, "I could really use a friend right now. You are the only one who came to mind."

Richard hesitated, she knew his condition, though he now knew she couldn't get the collar off.

"Richard, when Sisters Grace and Elizabeth died, they passed their gift to me. I have more power than any Sister at the palace, any normal Sister. I know you won't believe this, but I doubt even that will be enough to remove your collar. But I wish to try."

Richard knew that she couldn't remove it. At least he was told that she couldn't. Maybe Nathan was wrong.

"All right. Try then."

"There is pain involved. . . ."

Richard's brow drew together in a suspicious frown. "Why do I not find that surprising?"

"Not for you, Richard. For me."

"What do you mean?"

"I have discovered that you have Subtractive Magic."

"What would that have to do with it?"

"You locked the Rada'Han on yourself. It locks on by using the magic of the one it is attached to. I have only Additive Magic. I don't think that will be sufficient to break the bond.

"I have no power over your Subtractive Magic. It will fight what I try to do, and that will hurt me. But don't be frightened. It won't hurt you."

Richard didn't know what to do, what to believe. She put her hands to his neck, at the sides of his collar. Before she closed her eyes, he saw a glazed look he recognized. She was touching her Han.

Muscles tense, with his hand on the hilt of his sword, he waited, prepared to react if she tried to harm him. He didn't want to believe Sister Verna would harm him, but then, he hadn't thought Liliana would ever hurt him either.

Her brow wrinkled. Richard felt only a pleasant, warm tingle. The room vibrated with a dull hum. The corners of carpets curled up. Windows rattled in their frames. Sister Verna shook with effort.

The standing mirror in the bedroom shattered. Panes of glass in the doors exploded as the doors to the balcony banged open. The curtains billowed outward as if in a wind. Plaster fell from the ceiling, and a tall cabinet toppled over with a crash.

A low moan of pain issued from her throat as the flesh on her face trembled.

Richard seized her wrists and pulled her hands from his collar. She sagged forward.

"Oh, Richard," she said in a mournful voice, "I'm sorry. I can't do it."

Richard took her in his arms and held her tight. "It's all right. I believe you, Sister. I know you tried. You have found a friend."

She squeezed him tight. "Richard, you have to get away from this place."

He sat her back in the chair as she wiped her fingers at the lower lids of her eyes. Richard rocked back on his heels. "Tell me what's happened."

"There are Sisters of the Dark in the palace."

"Sisters of the Dark? What does that mean?"

"The Sisters of the Light work to bring the light of the Creator's glory to the living. Sisters of the Dark serve the Keeper. It has never been proven that they even exist. The accusation, without proof, is a crime. Richard, I know you aren't going to believe me. I realize this sounds like I'm just—"

"I killed Sister Liliana tonight. I believe you."

She blinked at him. "You did what?"

"She told me she was going to take my collar off. She had me meet her in the Hagen Woods. Sister Verna, she tried to take the gift from me, for herself."

"She can't do that. A female cannot take on the gift of a male, or the other way around. It isn't possible."

"She said she had done it many times before. It seemed possible to me when she was trying. I could feel her pulling the life, the gift, right out of me. She almost succeeded. I came close to death."

She brushed back her curly hair. "But I don't see how . . ."

Richard pulled out the statue. "She was using this. The crystal started glowing orange when she was doing it. Do you know what it is?"

Sister Verna shook her head. "I think I've seen it before, somewhere, but I can't remember. It was so long ago. Before I left the palace. What happened then?"

"When that didn't work, because I used my power to stop her, she called a sword from the shadows. She wanted to wound me. She said she was going to skin me alive, and then steal my gift for herself. She tried to cut off my legs. Somehow, I got her first.

"Sister Verna, she had Subtractive Magic. I saw her use it. Not only that, but someone else is trying to kill me. I loaned my red coat to Perry. They just dragged his body out of the river. He had been stabbed in the back with a dacra."

She grimaced. "Oh, dear Creator." She twined her fingers together in her lap. "The palace knows you have Subtractive Magic. They're using you to flush out the Keeper's disciples." She took his hand. "Richard, I've been a part of this. I should have long ago questioned things that were wrong, but I didn't. I instead did as I thought was right."

"Questioned what?"

"Forgive me, Richard. You should never have had a Rada'Han put around your neck. It wasn't necessary. I was told there were no wizards in the New World to help boys. I thought you would die without our help. Your friend, Zedd, could have kept the gift from harming you. The Prelate knew there were wizards to help you. She let you be stolen from your friends and loved ones for her own selfish reasons. You didn't need the Rada'Han to save your life."

"I know. I talked to Nathan. He told me."

"You went to the Prophet? What else did he say?"

"That I have more power than any wizard born in three thousand years. But I have no idea how to use it. And that I have Subtractive Magic. He said that the Sisters could not remove the collar."

"I'm so sorry I brought this upon you, Richard."

"Sister Verna, you were deceived, as was I. You're a victim, too. They've used both of us.

"There is worse trouble. There is a prophecy that says that on winter solstice, Kahlan is going to die. I must stop that from happening. And Darken Rahl, my father, an agent of the Keeper, is in this world. You saw the mark he burned on me. He is an agent who can tear the veil if he has all the elements in place, though I doubt he does.

"Sister Verna, I have to get away from here. I must get through the barrier."

"I'll help you. Somehow, I'll help you get through the barrier. Your problem will be the Valley of the Lost. I don't think you can get through the valley again. Now that the collar has helped your Subtractive Magic grow, you will call the spells to you. The magic will find you, this time."

"I might have a way. I must try."

Sister Verna thought a moment. "The Keeper would want to stop you, if there is a possibility for this prophecy about his agent to come to pass. The Sisters of the Dark will work to stop you. I am sure Liliana wasn't the only one."

"Who placed her as my teacher?"

"The Prelate's office assigns teachers. But the Prelate probably wouldn't have done it herself. Such matters are usually handled by her administrators."

"Her administrators?"

"Sisters Ulicia and Finella."

"I thought they were her guards."

"Guards? No. Maybe in a bureaucratic sense. The Prelate has more power than they. She doesn't need guards. Some of the boys think of them as guards, because they are always turned away from the Prelate's door by the two Sisters. They do some of their work in the Prelate's office, and they have their own offices where they handle a variety of administrative tasks."

"Maybe the Sisters of the Dark came after me, decided they had to act now, because they had been discovered."

"No. The Prelate told me no one but she knows."

"Could anyone have overheard?"

"No. She shielded the room."

Richard leaned in. "Sister Verna, Liliana had Subtractive Magic. The Prelate's shield would not have worked against that. One of those two administrators assigned Sister Liliana to me."

She drew a sudden breath. "And the other five. If one or both of those two in the outer office heard what the Prelate knows, then the Prelate . . . Sister Ulicia's office—that's where I saw that statue!"

Richard grabbed her wrist and yanked her from the chair.

"Come on! If they tried to kill me, they may try to kill the Prelate before she warns anyone else!"

The two of them raced down the stairs and out of Gillaume Hall. They crossed the lawns in the darkness, ran down halls and through passageways. Kevin wasn't there, another guard was on duty, but he didn't stop them, as he, too, knew Richard, and Sisters were not restricted.

Richard knew they were too late when he saw the charred doors to the Prelate's office broken from their hinges. He slid to a stop on the slick marble floor of the hall. Papers and ledgers were scattered out into the hall.

Sister Verna was still running down the hall as he went into the office with his sword drawn. It looked as if a thunderstorm had been turned loose inside. What was left of Sister Finella lay on the floor behind her desk. The rest of her was splattered across the wall. He heard Sister Verna gasp as he kicked in the door to the Prelate's office.

When the door swung back Richard dove through and rolled to his feet with his sword in both hands. The Prelate's room was more of a mess than the outer room. Papers were nearly a foot deep over most of the floor. It looked as if all the books from the shelves had exploded, throwing the pages everywhere. The heavy walnut table was in splinters against the far wall. The room was in near darkness. Only the doorway behind and the open doors to the moonlit garden let in any light.

Sister Verna lit a bright flame in her palm. In the sudden illumination, he saw a form at the far end of the room near the overturned table. The head came slowly up. The eyes locked on his. It was Sister Ulicia.

Richard dove to the side as a bolt of blue lightning blasted through the room, ripping open the wall behind. Sister Verna returned the attack with a searing gout of yellow flame. Sister Ulicia dove through the doorway into the courtyard to avoid the fire. Richard went after her. Sister Verna ran to the overturned, splintered table, pawing scraps away.

"Duck!" Richard screamed back to her.

A twisting rope of the black lightning sliced through the walls right over his head as he flattened to the floor. Severed bookshelves crashed down. He could see through the void sliced by the black lightning into the next room, and the rooms beyond. Plaster and lath and stone collapsed down, raising boiling clouds of dust.

In a fury, without thinking, Richard came to his feet when the black lighting ceased, and ran outside. He saw a dark form running down the path.

Again, black lightning arced from the shadows. The snaking void raked the courtyard. Trees toppled over, limbs snapping and popping as the trees fell. A stone wall collapsed when it was sliced in two. The noise was deafening.

When it stopped, Richard sprang to his feet again. He was just about to start running down the path to find her, when an invisible hand snatched him, yanking him back.

"Richard!" Sister Verna's growl was as strong as he had ever heard it. "Get in here!"

He returned to the Prelate's room, panting when he stopped over Sister Verna. "I have to go . . ."

She shot to her feet and grabbed his shirt in her real hand. "Go what! Go get killed? What good will that do? Will that help Kahlan? Sister Ulicia is a master of powers you cannot even imagine!"

"But she might get away."

"At least you will be alive when she does. Now come help me with this table. I think the Prelate is still alive."

Hope leapt to life in him. "Are you sure?"

Richard started pulling the broken pieces away, throwing them behind. He found the body at the bottom of the debris. Sister Verna was right. The Prelate was alive, but looked seriously hurt.

Sister Verna used her power to lift heavy pieces of the table and bookcases clear while Richard carefully pulled lesser chunks off the small woman. She was wedged into the bottom bookshelf against the wall, and covered with blood.

She groaned when Richard gently put his hands around her and drew her out. He didn't think she was long for this life.

"We have to get help," he said.

Sister Verna's hands played over the Prelate's body. "Richard, this is very bad. I can feel some of her injuries. It's more than I can help with. I don't know if anyone will be able to help with this."

Richard lifted Ann in his arms. "I can't let her die. If anyone can help her, it's Nathan. Come on."

Guards and Sisters came rushing, having heard the deafening roar of the power Sister Ulicia had unleashed. Richard didn't stop to explain as he made for Nathan's compound. He tried to hold Ann gently as he ran, but he knew by her groans that he was hurting her.

Nathan came in from his courtyard when he heard them call. "What was all that noise? What is it? What's happened?"

"It's Ann. She's been hurt."

Nathan led him into the bedroom. "I knew that stubborn woman was asking for trouble."

Richard laid Ann gently on the bed and stood near as Nathan experimentally glided his spread fingers over the length of her. Sister Verna waited and watched from the doorway.

Nathan pushed up his sleeves. "This is serious. I don't know if I can help her."

"Nathan, you have to try!"

"Of course I do, boy." He made a shooing motion with his hands. "You two go wait out there. This will take a while. At least an hour or two before I know if what I can do will help enough. Leave me to it. You can be of no help."

Sister Verna sat with her back stiff while Richard paced.

"Richard, why do you care so much what happens to the Prelate? She had you taken when she shouldn't have."

Richard combed his hair back with his fingers. "I guess because she had the chance to take me when I was little, and she didn't. She let me grow up with my parents. She let me have their love. What else is there to life, but the chance to be nurtured by love. She could have taken that, too, but she didn't."

"I'm glad, then, that you are not bitter."

Richard paced and thought. He didn't pace for long.

"Sister, I can't sit here doing nothing. I'm going to talk to the guards. We need to know where those teachers of mine are, and what they're doing. The guards will find out for me."

"I suppose it couldn't hurt. Go talk to the guards. It will make the time pass more quickly."

Richard strode down the dark, stone corridors, deep in thought. He needed to find out where Sisters Tovi, Cecilia, Merissa, Nicci, and Armina were. Any—or all—could be Sisters of the Dark. Who knew what they were planning next. They could all be looking for him. They could all be . . .

Stunning pain hurled him back. It felt as if he had been whacked across the face with a club. He staggered to his feet, the world spinning and tipping. He dumbly felt for blood, but there was none.

Another blow smashed into the back of his head. He pushed himself up on his hands, trying to decipher where he was. His thoughts came thick and slow. He struggled to understand what was happening.

A dark shadow stood over him. With an effort, and halting movements, he came to his feet again. He groped for his sword, but couldn't remember which hand to use. He couldn't make himself move fast enough.

"Out for a walk, country boy?"

Richard looked up at a smirking Jedidiah, standing tall with his hands in opposite sleeves. Richard found the hilt of his sword. He sluggishly worked at drawing it. He lurched back as he battled to bring the magic forth.

As the rage flooded into his foggy brain, Jedidiah pulled his hands out. He had a dacra. His arm lifted, the silver knife in his fist. Richard wondered what he should do, and if this was real. Maybe he would wake and find it only a dream.

At the apex of his swing, light seemed to come from within Jedidiah's eyes. Slowly at first, and then with gathering speed, Jedidiah toppled forward, slamming face-first to the stone floor.

A ripple of heart-stopping darkness swept though the corridor.

When the torchlight returned, Sister Verna was standing behind where Jedidiah had stood. She had a dacra in her hand. Richard collapsed to his knees, still trying to gather his wits.

Sister Verna rushed forward, putting her hands to the sides of his head. Alertness jolted into his mind. As he came to his feet, he glanced down at the body, seeing a small, round hole in the back.

"I thought I had better go talk to some of the Sisters," she explained. "I realized that the more people who know about the Sisters of the Dark, the better."

"He was the one, wasn't he? He was the one you loved."

She slipped the dacra back up her sleeve. "He wasn't the Jedidiah I knew. The Jedidiah I knew was a good man."

"I'm sorry, Sister Verna."

She nodded absently. "You go talk to the guards. I'll talk to the Sisters. Meet me back in Nathan's room when you're through. I think it best if we catch a few hours' sleep there, instead of our rooms."

"I think you're right. We can get our things when it's light, and then be off."

When he heard Nathan come into the room, Richard sat up in the chair and rubbed his eyes. Sister Verna rose more quickly from the couch. Richard blinked, trying to banish the haze of sleep.

They both had been up late. The whole palace was in an uproar. What had happened in the Prelate's office was proof enough of the mythical Sisters of the Dark. Doubters had only to take one look at the smooth-edged voids that lined up through a dozen walls, or the cleanly sliced trees and stone, to know that nothing short of Subtractive Magic had been used.

Richard had sent the guards out to look discreetly for the six Sisters: Sister Ulicia and his five teachers. The Sisters were searching, too. He had also gone to talk to Warren, to tell him what had happened.

Richard stretched his legs as he stood. "How is she? Is she going to recover?"

Nathan looked haggard. "She's resting more comfortably, but it's too soon to tell. When she has rested, I will be able to do more."

"Thank you, Nathan. I know Ann could be in no better hands than yours."

He added a grunt to his sour expression. "You're asking me to heal my jailer."

"Ann will appreciate it. Perhaps she will rethink your being held. If she doesn't, I'll come back and see what I can do."

"Come back? Going somewhere, my boy?"

"Yes, Nathan, and I need your help."

"If I help you, you might get it in your obstinate head to go off and destroy the world."

"And do the prophecies say you were sent to stop me?"

Nathan let out a tired sigh. "What is it you want?"

"How can I get through the barrier? My collar stops me."

"What makes you think I would know?"

Richard took an angry stride toward the towering old wizard. "Nathan, don't play games with me. I'm in no mood and this is too important. You've been through. You went with Ann to get the book from the Wizard's Keep in Aydindril. Remember?"

He smoothed his sleeves down. "It's a simple matter of shielding the Rada'Han. Ann helped me through; Sister Verna can do the same for you. I'll tell her how."

"And what of the Valley of the Lost? Can I get back through that?"

Nathan, his eyes suddenly intent with a dark look, shook his head. "You have called too much power to yourself. The collar has helped it grow. You'll also call the spells. Sister Verna can't pass again; she has been through twice already. Additionally, she has too much power now. With passing twice, and taking the gift of the other two Sisters, she is locked here."

"Then how did you ever get through three times? You're from D'Hara, that's once. You went to the New World again with Ann, and came back. That makes three times. How did you do it, if it can't be done?"

A sly smile came to his lips. "I did not go through the valley three times. Only once." He held up a hand to silence Richard's arguments. "Ann and I didn't go through the valley. We went around the obstacle. We sailed around the ambit of the spells, far out to sea, landing finally in the southernmost reaches of Westland. It's a long journey, and not easily done, but we made the crossing. Not many do."

"By sea!" Richard glanced back to Sister Verna. "I don't have that kind of time. Winter solstice is not even a week away. I have to go through the valley."

"Richard," Sister Verna said in a soft voice, "I can understand how you feel, but it will take almost that much time just to reach the Valley of the Lost. Even if you find a way through, there is no time to get where you want to go."

Richard controlled his rage. "I am inexperienced at being a wizard. I cannot count on my gift. For that matter, I don't care if I ever learn to use it.

"But I am also the Seeker. In that, Sister Verna, I am not so inexperienced. Nothing is going to stop me. Nothing. I've made a promise to Kahlan that if I must go to the underworld and battle the Keeper himself, in order to protect her, I will do it."

Nathan's expression darkened. "I have warned you, Richard. If that prophecy is not allowed to take place, the Keeper will have us all. You must not try to stop it. You have the power to hand the world of the living to the Keeper."

"It's just a meaningless riddle," Richard growled in frustration, though he knew better.

Nathan's scowl was the scowl of a Rahl, the scowl Richard had inherited. "Richard, death is intrinsic to life. The Creator brought it to be, too. If you make the wrong choice, all the living will pay the price of your pertinaciousness.

"And Richard, don't forget what I told you about the Stone of Tears. If you misuse it to banish a soul to the depths of the underworld, you will destroy the balance between everything."

"Stone of Tears?" Sister Verna said in a suspicious tone. "What would Richard have to do with the Stone of Tears?"

Richard turned back to Sister Verna. "We're running out of time. I'm going to my room to get my things. We need to be on our way."

"Richard," Nathan said, "Ann has put her faith in you. She let you have the love of your family, so that perhaps you will better understand the true meaning of life. Please consider that when the time for choice is upon you."

Richard looked up at Nathan for a long moment. "Thank you for your help, Nathan, but I won't let the one I love die for a riddle in an old book. I hope to see you again. There is much for us to talk about."

Richard dumped the bowl full of gold coins into the bottom of his pack before stuffing the rest of his things in. He reasoned that if it helped him save Kahlan, then it was the least the palace could do, after all they had done to him.

The gold had been a kindness that lulled the rest of the young men at the palace into laziness. It harmed their humanity, as Nathan had said. Maybe that was why Jedidiah turned to promises from the Keeper.

Richard doubted that any of the young wizards, except Warren, had done a day's work since they had come here and had ready access to unlimited gold, but no knowledge of its value. Just one more way the Palace of the Prophets destroyed lives. He wondered how many children of young wizards that gold had spawned.

Richard went out onto the balcony to take stock before he left. Guards were patrolling the grounds. Sisters, too, were diligently searching every building and covered corridor. The Sisters would have to somehow deal with those six. He certainly had no idea how to contain their power.

When he heard the door in the front room, he assumed it would be Sister Verna. They had to get going. When he turned and looked, he had no time to react.

Pasha was storming through the room toward him. She threw her hands up. The doors blew off their hinges and over the balcony railing, falling the thirty feet to the stone-paved courtyard below.

The impact of the solid wall of air threw him back. Only the railing prevented him from being thrown over with the splintered doors. The wind had been knocked from his lungs, and a sharp pain in his side prevented him from taking another breath.

As he staggered away from the edge of the balcony, another blow threw him back once again, this time hammering his head against the stone railing. He saw a shocking spray of blood hit the stone before the slate floor collected him.

Pasha was screaming in a rage. At first, her words were nothing but an incoherent buzz in his mind. He pushed himself up with his hands. Blood was running from his head. A pool of it spread beneath him. Reeling, he toppled to his side.

He managed to sit up and flop back against the railing. "Pasha, what . . ."

"Keep your filthy mouth shut! I won't hear any of it!"

She was standing in the doorway, fists at her sides. One fist held a dacra. Tears streamed down her cheeks.

"You're the Keeper's spawn! You're an obscene disciple of the Keeper! You do nothing but hurt good people!"

Richard put his hands to his head. They came away covered with blood. He was so dizzy he had to fight the urge to be sick.

"What are you talking about?" he managed to mumble.

"Sister Ulicia told me! She told me you serve the Keeper! She told me how you killed Sister Liliana!"

"Pasha, Sister Ulicia is a Sister of the Dark . . ."

"She told me you would say that! She told me how you used your vile magic to kill Sister Finella and the Prelate! That's why you were always wanting to go to the Prelate's office! So you could kill our leader in the Light! You are filth!"

The world swam before his eyes. He saw two of her, moving around and around each other. "Pasha . . . that's not true."

"Only the Keeper's tricks saved you yesterday. You gave someone else the coat I loved, to humiliate me! Sister Ulicia told me how the Keeper whispers in your ear!

"I should have killed you when I saw you on the bridge; then none of this would have happened. But I foolishly thought I could save you from the Keeper's clutches! Those Sisters, and the Prelate, would be alive now had I finished the job. I failed the Creator when you tricked me into killing Perry, but that will not save you again. Your vile underworld tricks will not save you again!"

"Pasha, please, just listen to me. You're being lied to. Please listen. The Prelate isn't dead. I can take you to her."

"You wish to kill me, too! That's all you ever talk of—killing! You profane us all! And to think I could have ever thought I loved you!"

She raised the dacra and, with a scream, ran for him. Richard somehow managed to pull the sword, woozily wondering which image of her to try to stop. The anger, the magic, of the sword brought strength to his arms. He brought the sword up as she dove for him, dacra first. The two images of her converged.

The sword never touched her. With a shriek, she was propelled over the railing above him. She screamed all the way down. Richard's eyes winced shut when he heard her scream terminate as she hit the stone.

Richard opened his eyes to see a stunned Warren standing in the doorway. He remembered Jedidiah's fall on the stairs.

"Oh, dear spirits, no," Richard whispered.

He levered himself to his feet and took a quick glance over the edge. People rushed from different directions toward the body. Warren was shuffling woodenly toward the railing. Richard stopped him halfway there.

"No, Warren, don't look."

Tears welled up in Warren's eyes. Richard put his arms around his friend. *Why did you do that,* he thought, *I could have done it. I was going to do it. You didn't have to.*

Over Warren's shoulder, Richard saw Sister Verna standing in the room.

"She killed Perry," Warren said. "I heard her admit it. She was going to kill you."

*I could have done it,* Richard thought, *you didn't need to.* But instead he said, "Thank you, Warren. You saved my life."

"She was going to kill you," he cried against Richard's shoulder. "Why would she do that?"

Sister Verna put a comforting hand to Warren's back. "She was lied to by the Sisters of the Dark. The Keeper filled her mind with lies. She heard the whispers of the darkness. The Keeper can make even the good listen to his whispers. You did a brave thing, Warren."

"Then why do I feel so ashamed? I loved her, and I killed her."

Richard simply held him as he wept.

Sister Verna pulled them back into the room. She made Richard bend over as she examined his head. Blood was dripping all over the floor.

"This must be tended to. I can't fix this much damage."

"I can," Warren said. "I'm fair at healing. Let me do it."

When Warren had finished, Sister Verna made Richard hold his head over the basin while she poured the ewer of water over him, washing off the blood. Warren sat on the edge of a chair, his head in his hands. Richard thought that he was going to need the basin.

Warren's head came up when the Sister finished. "I figured out the rule you told me about. People will believe a lie because they want to believe it's true, or because they are afraid it is. Just like Pasha believed a lie. Am I right?"

Richard smiled. "You are, Warren."

Warren managed a weak smile. "Sister Verna, can you take this collar off me?"

Sister Verna hesitated. "You would have to pass the test of pain, Warren."

"Sister," Richard said. "What do you think he just did?"

"What do you mean?"

"The young wizards sent back through the valley are able to pass because they don't have sufficient power to draw the spells to them, they are not full wizards. Zedd told me that wizards have to pass a test of pain.

"Over the millennia, the Sisters have convoluted that into making them endure physical pain. I think they're wrong. I think the test Warren just passed is more pain than the Sisters could ever give. Am I right, Warren?"

He nodded, his face going white again. "Nothing they ever did hurt like this."

"Sister, remember when I told you how I turned the blade white, and killed that woman by loving her? Maybe that, too, was a form of the test of pain. I know how much that hurt."

She spread her hands in dismay. "Do you really think that one with the gift must kill someone they love to pass the test? Richard, that can't be."

"No, Sister, they don't have to kill someone they love. But they must prove they can make the right decision. They must prove they have what it takes to choose the greater good. Would one with the gift be a good servant to this Creator of yours, to the hope of life, if they could act only for selfish needs?

"Giving someone pain, as the Sisters do, doesn't prove anything except that the victim does not die. Wouldn't serving the light of life, and loving life, require that the person prove instead that of their own free will they would choose right, choose that light of life and love for all people?"

"Dear Creator," she whispered, "have we had it wrong all this time?" Her hand covered her mouth a moment. "And we thought we were bringing the Creator's Light to these boys."

Sister Verna's back straightened with resolve. She stood before Warren, putting her hands to the sides of his Rada'Han. As she stood with her eyes closed, her hands to the collar, there was a humming vibration in the air. After a moment, silence settled over the room, and then Richard heard a snapping sound. The Rada'Han cracked and fell away.

Warren looked positively giddy at the sight of the broken collar. Richard wished it could be that easy for him.

"What are you going to do now, Warren?" Richard asked. "Are you going to leave the palace?"

"Maybe. But I wish to study the books some more first, if the Sisters will allow it."

"They will allow it," Sister Verna said. "I will see to it."

"Then, maybe I would like to travel to Aydindril, to the Wizard's Keep, and study the books and prophecies you told me were kept there."

"That sounds a wise plan, Warren. Sister, I must be going."

"Warren," she said, "why don't you come along until I reach the valley? You are free, now." She glanced to the balcony. "I think it would do you good to get away from here for a time, and think of other things. And I could use some help when we reach the valley, if Richard accomplishes what he thinks he will."

"Really? I would like that."

As the three of them lugged their gear toward the stables, three guards—Kevin, Walsh, and Bollesdun—spotted them and ran to catch up.

"We may have found them, Richard," Kevin said.

"May have? What do you mean? Where are they?"

"Well, last night, the *Lady Sefa* set sail. We talked to people down at the docks who said they saw some women, maybe the Sisters, go aboard. Most agree they saw six women go aboard in the darkness, just before she sailed."

"Sailed!" Richard groaned. "What's the *Lady Sefa*?"

"A ship. A big ship. They left with the tide late in the night. They have a good lead, and from what I hear, there isn't a ship in port that can catch the *Lady Sefa*, or go as far to sea."

"We can't go after them, and do your other task," Sister Verna said.

Richard shifted his pack in annoyance. "You're right. If it's really them, they're gone for now, but I know where they're going. We'll have to deal with them later. At least the Palace of the Prophets is safe. We have more important things to tend to right now. Let's get the horses, and be on our way."

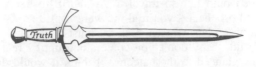

**K**ahlan ran down the dark stone corridors and through the tomblike chambers. The first rays of light splashed golden patches against the coarse, dark gray granite wall opposite the windows as she raced up an east stairway. Her heart pounded with the effort. She had not stopped running since Jebra had told her that she had spied a light in the Wizard's Keep: that Zedd was back.

She remembered what it felt like to run with long hair: the weight of it, the way it streamed out behind, flowing with her strides. She felt none of that now. But it didn't matter; she felt only desperate elation that Zedd was back. She had been waiting so long. She screamed his name as she ran.

Bursting into the cluttered reading room she stumbled to a panting halt. Zedd stood behind a table with books and papers scattered over it, just as she remembered it from the last time she had seen it, months ago. Candles on stands gave the small room an intimate glow. The reading room had but a single window, facing the still murky western sky.

A big man with bushy eyebrows, mostly gray hair, and a weathered, creased face looked up from a walking stick he was inspecting. Adie sat in a chair to the side, her head flitting toward sounds. Zedd cocked his head with a curious frown.

"Zedd!" She gulped air. "Oh, Zedd, I'm so relieved to see you."

"Zedd?" He turned toward the big man. "Zedd?" The big man gave a nod. "But I like Ruben."

"Zedd! I need your help!"

"Who be there?" Adie said from the chair.

"Adie, it's me. Kahlan."

"Kahlan?" She twitched her head toward Zedd. "Who be Kahlan?"

Zedd shrugged. "A pretty girl with short hair. She seems to know us."

"What are you talking about! Zedd, I need help! Richard is in trouble! I need you!"

Zedd's brow wrinkled in bewilderment. "Richard. I know that name. I think . . ."

Kahlan was frantic. "Zedd, what's the matter! Don't you know me? Please Zedd, I need you. Richard needs you."

"Richard . . ." He rubbed his smooth chin as he stared in thought at the table. "Richard . . ."

"Your grandson! Dear spirits, don't you know your own grandson!"

He stared at the table, thinking. "Grandson . . . I seem to remember . . . no, can't say I do."

"Zedd! Listen to me! The Sisters of the Light have him! They've taken him away!"

Kahlan stood silently catching her breath. Zedd's hazel eyes rose slowly to meet her gaze. His face lost its curiosity as his eyebrows drew in to hood his glare. "The Sisters of the Light have Richard?"

Kahlan had seen wizards angry, but she had never seen a look in any wizard's eyes like the look in Zedd's eyes.

"Yes," she said. She wiped her sweaty palms on her hips as she watched a crack run up the stone of the wall behind him. "They came and took him."

Zedd put his knuckles to the table and leaned toward her. "That's not possible. They couldn't take him unless they got one of their cursed collars around his neck. Richard would not put a collar around his neck."

Kahlan's knees were beginning to tremble. "He did."

His seething expression seemed it might ignite the very air. "Why would he put their collar around his neck, Confessor?"

"Because," she said in a small voice, "I made him put it on."

The candles on one of the stands close to him abruptly melted, dripping their wax to hissing puddles on the floor. The iron arms that had held the candles drooped down, like a plant needing water. The big man shrank back toward the wall of shelves.

Zedd's voice came in a dangerous whisper. "You did what, Confessor?"

The room echoed with silence as she stood quivering. "He didn't want to. I had to do it. I told him that he had to put it on to prove he loved me."

Kahlan thought she felt herself hit the wall. She couldn't understand why she was sprawled on the floor. She pushed herself up with shaking arms. She gasped as she was suddenly jerked to her feet and slammed against the wall again.

Zedd, his eyes wild, was right in front of her. "You did that to Richard!"

Kahlan's head spun. Her own voice sounded distant. "You don't understand. I had to. Zedd, I need your help. Richard told me to find you, and tell you what I had done. Please Zedd, help him."

In a rage, Zedd backhanded her across the face. She skinned her hands on the stone floor as she went down. He yanked her to her feet and slammed her to the wall once more.

"I can't help him! No one can! You fool!"

Tears ran down her face. "Why? Zedd, we have to help him!"

She brought up her arms in front of her face to ward him off when he drew his hand back again. It didn't help. Her head smacked the wall again. The room spun. She shook all over. She had never seen a wizard in a rage so out of control. Kahlan knew he was going to kill her for what she had done to Richard.

"You fool. You treacherous fool. No one can help him now."

"Please, Zedd. You can. Please, help him."

"Not even I. No one can get to him. I can't pass the towers. Richard is lost to us. All I had left is lost."

"What do you mean, lost to us?" With trembling fingers, she wiped blood from the corner of her mouth. She didn't wipe the tears. "He will be back. He has to come back."

Zedd's eyes never left hers as he slowly shook his head. "Not while any of us are alive. The Palace of the Prophets is in a spell of time. Richard will be there for the next three hundred years while they train him. We will never see him again. He is lost to this world."

Kahlan shook her head. "No. Dear spirits, no. That can't be. We will see him. It can't be true!"

"True, Mother Confessor. You have put him beyond any help. I will never again see my grandson. You will never again see him. Richard will not return to this world for another three hundred years. Because of you. Because you made him put on that collar to prove he loves you."

He turned his back to her. Kahlan fell to her knees. "Noooo!" She beat her fists on the floor. "Dear spirits, why have you done this to me!" She cried in choking sobs. "Richard, my Richard."

"What happened to your hair, Mother Confessor?" Zedd asked in a menacing voice, his back still to her.

Kahlan sat back on her heels. What did it matter anymore. "The council convicted me of treason. I have been sentenced to be executed. To be beheaded. The people all cheered at the pronouncement of sentence. They all wanted to see it done. But I escaped."

Zedd nodded. "The people shall have their wish." He grabbed what was left of her hair in his fist and started dragging her from the room. "For what you have done, you shall be beheaded."

"Zedd!" she screamed. "Zedd! Please, don't do this!"

He used magic to drag her down the hall like a sack of feathers.

"Tomorrow, at the winter solstice festival, the people shall have their wish. They shall see the Mother Confessor beheaded. As First Wizard, I will see to it. I shall see it done."

Kahlan went limp. What did it matter? The good spirits had abandoned her. They had stripped her of everything that mattered.

Worse, she herself had condemned Richard to three hundred years of the thing he feared most.

She wanted to die. Death couldn't come fast enough for her.

Richard stood with his hands on his hips as he watched the dark clouds made by spells in the distance, in the Valley of the Lost. They looked beautiful in the sunrise, with golden edges and striations of glowing rays. But he knew they were deadly.

Du Chaillu put an affectionate hand to his arm. "My husband makes me proud this day. He returns our land to us, as the old words have foretold."

"I've explained it to you a dozen times, Du Chaillu; I am not your husband. You have simply misinterpreted the old words. It only means we must do this together. And we haven't done it yet. I wish you would have come with me without bringing everyone else. I don't even know if this will work. We could be killed."

She patted his arm reassuringly. "The *Caharin* has come. He can do anything. He will return our land." She left him to his thoughts and started back to the camp. "All our people should be with us. It is their right." She stopped and turned back. "Will we be leaving soon, *Caharin*?"

"Soon," Richard said absently.

She started off again. "I will be with our people when you are ready for me."

The entire Baka Ban Mana nation was camped behind them. Thousands upon thousands of tents were spread out over the hills, like mushrooms after a month of rain. He hadn't been able to talk them out of coming, to convince them to wait, so they were all here, with him.

Richard sighed. What difference did it make? If he was wrong, and this failed, he had no reason to worry about all the Baka Ban Mana being disappointed in him. He would be dead.

Warren and Sister Verna quietly came up behind.

"Richard," Warren said, "can we talk to you?"

Richard continued to stare out at the storms. "Of course, Warren." He cast a glance back. "What's on your mind?"

Warren pushed his hands up the opposite sleeves of his robes. Richard thought it made him look very wizardlike when he did that. Warren was going to someday end up being Richard's idea of what a wizard ought to be: wise, compassionate, and charged with knowledge Richard could only wonder at. If they didn't all die, that was.

"Well, Sister Verna and I were talking. About what happens after you get through the valley. Richard, I know what you want to do, but we have run out of time. There never was enough time to begin with. Tomorrow is winter solstice. It can't be done."

"Just because you don't know how to do something, that does not mean it can't be done."

"I don't understand."

Richard smiled at them. "You will. You will understand in a few hours."

Warren looked away toward the valley. He idly scratched his nose. "If you say so, Richard."

Sister Verna said nothing. Richard was still trying to get used to her not arguing with him whenever he said something oblique. He wasn't sure she didn't want to.

"Warren, about the prophecy, the one about the gateway and the winter solstice. Are you sure it's about this winter solstice?" Warren nodded. "And if there were an agent, with an open box of Orden, and the skrin bone, are those the only elements needed to open the gateway, to tear the veil?"

A hot breeze ruffled Warren's hair. "Yes . . . but you told me Darken Rahl is dead. There is no agent."

It sounded more like a worried question than a statement.

"Must the agent be alive?" Sister Verna asked.

Warren shifted his weight to the other foot. "Well, not in principle, I guess. If he were somehow called back into this world, but I don't see how that could be done, but if it were done, that would be all that was needed."

Richard sighed in frustration. "And then this spirit agent could do the things the living agent would have done?"

Suspicion crept onto Warren's face. "Well, yes and no. It would require another element. A spirit cannot perform the physical requirements necessary to complete the covenant. He would need a coadjutor."

"You mean the spirit could not perform certain of the tasks needed, so he would need hands that would work in this world."

"Yes. With a helper, a spirit could do what was needed. But how could an agent be called back into this world? I don't see how that could be accomplished."

Sister Verna glanced away. "You had better tell him."

Richard pulled his shirt up and showed Warren the scar. "Darken Rahl burned

667

me with his hand, when I unintentionally called him back into this world. He said he was here to tear the veil."

Warren's eyes opened wide. His worried gaze darted to the Sister, and then back to Richard. "If Darken Rahl is an agent, as you said, and he has someone to help him, then we are only one element away from destruction—the skrin bone. We need to know."

Richard pushed the mriswith cape back over his shoulder. "Sister Verna, would you help me?"

"What is it you would like me to do?"

"The first time you told me how to try to touch my Han, I decided to concentrate on a mental image of my sword. But that time, the first time, I used a background to put it against. It was something from the book of magic I told you about. The Book of Counted Shadows.

"When I tried to touch my Han, with the sword on that background, something happened. I was somehow in D'Hara, in the People's Palace, where the boxes are. I saw Darken Rahl. He saw me, too, and spoke to me. He told me he was waiting for me."

Sister Verna's eyebrows lifted. "Did this ever happen again?"

"No. It frightened the wits out of me. I never used that background again. I think if I use that background now, I may be able to see what is happening there."

She folded her hands together before herself. "I've never heard of such a thing. But it may have something to do with the Magic of Orden. It would not be the first thing about you that astonished me. It could be real, or just a fear, like a dream."

"I need to try. Would you sit with me? I'm afraid of not being able to pull back."

"Of course, Richard." She sat down on the ground and held up a hand. "Come. I will be with you."

Richard pulled the mriswith cape around himself as he sat down, folding his legs. "This thing hides my Han, maybe it will work to keep Darken Rahl from seeing me this time."

Richard relaxed himself as he held hands with Sister Verna. He concentrated on the mental image of the sword against the black square with a white border, as he had done the first time. As he concentrated, seeking the calm center, something began to happen.

The sword, the black square, and the white border all began to shimmer as if seen through heat waves, the same as the first time. The solid form of the sword softened, becoming transparent, and then vanished. The background dissolved. Once again, Richard was looking into the Garden of Life, at the People's Palace.

He searched the filmy image, seeing white bones where before he had seen burned bodies. He remembered them lying over the short walls, in bushes, and sprawled on the grass. They were much as he remembered, only now they were mostly exposed bones.

Richard saw the white, glowing figure of Darken Rahl, but he was not standing before the stone altar, before the three boxes of Orden. He was near the circle that had held white sand. The sand had not been there the last time he had seen this vision.

A woman in a long, brown skirt and white blouse knelt at Darken Rahl's feet, bent over the circle of sand. Richard willed himself closer. She was drawing lines in the sparkling sorcerer's sand. Richard remembered some of the symbols she was drawing; Darken Rahl had drawn them before when he had opened the box.

Richard watched her hand moving slowly, carefully, as she drew the lines of spells. Her right hand, he noticed, was missing the little finger.

In the center of the circle, in the center of the sorcerer's sand, sat a round object. Richard went closer. It was carved all over with beasts, just as the Prelate had described.

Richard wanted to scream with rage.

Just then, Darken Rahl lifted his face, and looked right into Richard's eyes. A smile slowly spread on his lips.

Richard didn't know if Darken Rahl was really looking at him or not, but he didn't wait to find out. With desperate effort, he forced the image of the sword back into his mind, like slamming a door, at the same time banishing the black-and-white background.

With a gasp, Richard forced his eyes open. His chest heaved.

Sister Verna's eyes came open, too. "Richard, are you all right? You've been at it an hour. I felt you trying to pull back, so I pulled with you. What happened? What did you see?"

"An hour?" Richard was still trying to catch his breath. "I saw Darken Rahl, and the skrin bone. He had a woman there, helping him draw spells in the sorcerer's sand."

Warren leaned over Richard's shoulder. "Maybe it was just a vision of a fear. It may not have been real."

"Warren could be right," Sister Verna said. She drew her lower lip through her teeth as she thought. "What did the woman look like?"

"Wavy, shoulder-length brown hair, maybe about your size. She was bent over, drawing in the sand, so I couldn't see her eyes." Richard pressed his fingers to his forehead as he thought. "Her hand. She was missing the little finger on her right hand."

Warren groaned. Sister Verna's eyes slid closed.

"What? What's the matter?"

"Sister Odette," she said. "That's Sister Odette."

Warren nodded confirmation. "She has been gone for close to six months. I thought she went to get a boy."

"Curse the spirits," Richard said under his breath. He sprang to his feet. "Warren, run and get Du Chaillu. Tell her we must leave right now."

He ground his teeth in frustration. He had thought he had all the time he needed. Well, he still had enough time, if he hurried.

Du Chaillu seemed in a trance as Richard pulled her forward by the hand. With the Sword of Truth in his other hand, Richard was in a world of his own, too. His thundering rage was a match for the angry black clouds. The spells of magic circled them like a pack of dogs around a porcupine, angry and insistent, but holding their distance as they searched for an opening.

Wisps of light emerged from the darkness and whirled around them, spiraling down to vanish into an aura that surrounded Du Chaillu. She seemed to be absorbing the magic, as Sister Verna told him she had done before. Together, they were the completed link Warren had told him the old books said would contain the power and bring the towers down.

Through the waves of heat and the boiling mist, Richard saw the first tower. He pulled Du Chaillu onward, toward the glistening black wall that disappeared into the darkness overhead. Dust and dirt lifted around them as they rushed toward the arched opening in the wall. Spells snatched at them, but their light was sucked to Du Chaillu.

Richard acted without thought, not knowing what drove him onward, and not trying to stop it. If he was to succeed, if he was to save Kahlan, he had to let those things within himself guide him. He had to hope that if he truly had the gift, it would react on instinct, as Nathan had told him, and do what was needed.

Du Chaillu seemed not to notice the sparkling black sand they stood on in the center of the tower. She seemed lost in a private spell of her own, in the power passed down to her from those who built the towers and took her people's land. So far, she had done her half of what was needed; she had protected him. Now Richard had to do his part.

On impulse, holding her hand tight in his, he lifted the sword high in the other, pointing it straight up. He lost himself in the fury of the magic, letting it overwhelm him. He felt the heat of it in the calm center he had always sought. He let the rage fill the void.

Lightning exploded from the sword, arcing up into the darkness overhead, jumping from one wall to the other, bathing them all in liquid light. The noise was deafening.

Fire raced through the black stone until the whole of the tower glowed, the stone turning white in the heat of the luminous discharge.

Richard felt as if the lightning were passing through him, too. It seared him with its power, erupting outward, and up through the sword. Only his rage enabled him to endure the ferocity of the onrushing force coming from within.

Flickering webs of lightning cascaded down the walls and across the black sand, until everything was alive with it. The black sand turned white, as had the walls, and the world burned with pulsing fire and light.

Abruptly, it ended. The lightning cut off, the fire winked out, and the roar of noise ceased, leaving silence ringing in his ears. The polished black stone of the tower was left a blinding white gloss.

Du Chaillu seemed still not to notice what was around her, and Richard pulled her onward, to complete the task for which they both had been born.

In the white tower, as he held the sword high, he expected the flash of heat and light again, but it did not come. Instead, the counter to it, the balance to it, exploded forth.

Concussion ripped the air, threatening to strip flesh from bone, as black lightning blasted upward, a void in the light. Like the lightning before, Richard felt the might of the power erupting from deep within himself, as if his very soul were pouring it forth. The snaking void in the light raked the walls, and, with a thunderous roar, pierced a void into the darkness above.

As the black lightning twisted into the darkness overhead, shadows oozed down the white walls, making it seem as if they were melting into the depths of eternal night. Darkness reached the ground and flowed toward them, soaking into the white sand, turning it black.

Richard never gave thought to trying to escape the encroaching night. When it reached them, he felt as if they were being plunged into icy water. Du Chaillu, her eyes closed, shivered with the touch of it. Richard noted it, but through the wrath of the sword's magic, it was a distant sensation that only fed the anger.

It seemed the whole world had vanished forever into inky obscurity. Light, and vision, were beyond even memory.

Richard felt the undulating, twisting rope of the black lightning, the void in the world of life, cut off. Sudden silence replaced the cacophony. He could hear himself breathing hard. He could heard Du Chaillu doing the same. Light and life and warmth emerged from the cold void.

Outside, through the arches in the stone, now glossy black where it was once white, Richard could see light coming through the thinning fog. The ground that before was baked and barren was now green and lush. Still holding hands, he and Du Chaillu stood in the archway, watching the haze and smoke lift on a world no one had seen in thousands of years.

Hand in hand, they walked out into the cool air, across the thick grass, and through shafts of sunlight. The storms of spells were gone, the dark clouds they spawned evaporating as they lifted. The air smelled fresh and clean. The feel of life vibrated around them.

The valley off to the pale blue line of mountains in the distance was lush and green. Groves of trees were gathered in places along meandering streams. Gentle rises overlaid each other in differing shades of green.

Richard could understand why the Baka Ban Mana would want their land back. It was a place that simply looked like home. This was a place of light and hope that would have stayed in a people's heart throughout all the dark centuries. It was not a place that belonged to them—it was they that belonged to this place.

"You have done it, *Caharin*," Du Chaillu said. "You have returned our home from beyond the mist."

Richard saw a few people scattered about in the distance, those who had been trapped in spells for untold years. They wandered aimless and confused. He had to find two he knew.

Sister Verna and Warren galloped toward them, bringing his horse. Before they had completely stopped, Richard was up on Bonnie. Du Chaillu thrust a hand up. She wanted to go with him. Reluctantly, he pulled her up behind.

"Richard," Warren said, "that was astonishing! How did you do it?"

"I haven't the slightest idea, Warren. I had been hoping you could explain it to me."

Richard galloped Bonnie off in the direction he remembered seeing Chase and Rachel when he had been through the valley the first time. Warren and Sister Verna followed after. It wasn't long before he found them sitting on the bank of a brook. Chase, with his arm around Rachel's shoulders, and his usual look of strained tolerance nowhere in evidence, looked confused.

Richard swung his leg over Bonnie's neck and leapt down. "Chase! Are you all right?"

"Richard? What's going on? Where are we? We were coming to get you. You can't go . . ." He looked around. "You can't go into the valley. Zedd needs you. The veil is torn."

"I know." Richard handed the reins to Sister Verna and quickly introduced everyone. "My friends will explain it all to you." He put a knee to the ground in front of Rachel. The dark, amber-colored Stone of Tears hung on a chain around her neck, just as he remembered it. "Rachel, are you all right? How do you feel?"

She blinked up at him. "I was in a nice place, Richard."

"This is a nice place, too. You will be fine, now. Rachel, did Zedd give you that stone?"

She nodded. "He said you might want it, and I was to keep it for you, until you came to get it."

"That's why I'm here, Rachel. May I have it, then?"

She smiled and pulled it over her head. Richard unclasped the chain and pulled the Stone off. Holding it in his hand, he could feel its warmth, and Zedd's presence.

The chain was too small for him. He handed it back to Rachel, telling her it looked prettier on her than it would on him, and then strung the Stone onto a leather thong he had ready.

He hung the Stone of Tears around his neck, along with the Agiel and the dragon's tooth. From the corner of his eye, he watched the distant dot growing in the sky.

"Richard," Warren said, "after seeing what I just saw, with the towers, I have no doubt you can do what you say you can do, but you have no time to reach where you must go. Tomorrow, the world is going to end if you don't get there. What are you going to do?"

"Where is it we are going, my husband?" Du Chaillu asked.

" 'We' are not going anywhere, Du Chaillu. You are staying here, with your people."

"Husband?" Chase said, a scowl finally starting to creep onto his face.

"I am not her husband. It's just some silly idea she got in her head." Richard watched the red shape growing, high up in the sky. "Look, I don't have time to explain it. Sister Verna and Warren can tell you about it."

Sister Verna, a suspicious frown on her face, took a step toward him. "What are you going to do? Warren was right, you have no time."

In the distance, the red wings spread wide as the dragon plunged into a dive. Richard unhooked his pack from Bonnie, slinging it onto his back. He gave Bonnie's neck a good-bye hug. He hooked on the quiver, and slipped the bow over his shoulder. From the corner of his eye, he watched the dragon plummet straight down.

"I'm going to have time. I must leave you now, Sister."

"What do you mean you are leaving? How?"

At the last instant the dragon pulled out of the dive. Her long neck stretched out. Wings spread wide, she shot toward them at incredible speed, skimming along just above the ground.

"I have only one chance to reach my goal in time. I must fly."

"Fly!" Warren and Sister Verna shouted together.

Scarlet swept up with a roar. Everyone else saw her for the first time. Immense wings beat to slow the dragon's speed.

Their clothes flapped in the sudden burst of wind. The grass all around flattened in the gusts. Warren, Sister Verna, and Du Chaillu stepped back in surprise. Scarlet settled to the ground as her forward speed was brought to a halt by her beating wings.

"Richard," Sister Verna said as she slowly shook her head, "you have the oddest pets of anyone I've ever met."

"Red dragons are pets to no one, Sister. Scarlet is a dear friend."

Richard trotted toward the huge red dragon glistening in the sunlight. Scarlet snorted a small cloud of gray smoke.

"Richard! How good to see you again. Since you called me so urgently with my tooth, I presume you are in trouble again. As usual."

"Trouble indeed, my friend." Richard patted a glossy red scale. "I've missed you, Scarlet."

"Well, I've already eaten. I guess I must instead give you a ride in the sky to work up an appetite. Then I will eat you."

Richard laughed. "Where is your little one?"

Her ears twitched. "Off hunting. Gregory is not so little anymore. He misses you, and would like to see you."

"I would like to see Gregory, too. But I'm in a terrible hurry right now. I'm running out of time."

"Richard!" Du Chaillu ran toward him. "I must go, too. I must go where my husband goes!"

Richard leaned toward Scarlet's ear as she lowered her head and peered at him with one yellow eye. "A little flame, Scarlet," he whispered. "Just for effect. Don't hurt her."

Du Chaillu leapt back with a squeal as a burst of fire charred the grass at her feet.

"Du Chaillu, your land is returned to your people. You must stay with them. You are their spirit woman; they need you. They need your guidance. I would ask something else of you: protect the towers that are on your land. I don't know if they can bring any harm, but as the *Caharin*, I order that no one shall ever enter them. Guard them, and keep all others out, too.

"Live in peace with others who would live in peace with you, but continue to practice with the blades so you may protect yourselves."

Du Chaillu drew herself up tall. The little strips of cloth on her prayer dress fluttered in the breeze, along with her thick black hair.

"You are wise, *Caharin*. I will see that it is as you say, until you return to your wife and your people."

"Richard," Sister Verna said. Her face held a serious look. "Do you know where Kahlan is?"

"Aydindril. She would have gone there; the prophecy takes place before her people. She will be in Aydindril."

"The time of choosing is upon you, Richard. Where are you going now?"

He looked long into her steady gaze.

"D'Hara."

After appraising him silently for a moment, she at last embraced him in a warm hug. She kissed his cheek. "And then?"

Richard raked his fingers through his thick hair. "Somehow I will stop what is to happen in D'Hara, and then I must get to Aydindril before it's too late. Take care, my friend."

She nodded. "Warren and I will see to the people here who have been released from the spells. They will need guidance. I have been a Sister of the Light for nearly two hundred years. All I ever wanted was to help people who needed it. But you had help. There is no excuse for taking you, or others. I want to try to set some of this right."

Warren gave Richard a firm hug. "Thanks, Richard. For everything. I look forward to seeing you again."

Richard winked. "Try not to have any adventures."

"I'll go with you," Chase said.

"No." Richard wiped a hand over his face. "No, go home, Chase. Take Rachel to her new mother, and her brothers and sisters. Emma will be worried sick by now. She hasn't seen you in ages. Go home to you wife and family. I'll need to be returning home soon, too."

Richard turned back to Sister Verna. "We must do something about those six Sisters. They're sailing for Westland. The people there have no protection against magic. In Westland, those Sisters will be like hawks in a hatchery."

"I think that journey will take them some time. You have time enough for them, Richard."

"Good. Kahlan will want to wed before the Mud People. Then I may need to come and get some advice on how to handle those six. Talk to Nathan, and Ann. We can decide what to do then."

"Be careful," Warren said. He stood stoically with his hands in the opposite sleeves of his robes. "And I don't just mean with yourself. Don't forget the things Nathan and I have told you. Don't forget that everyone else is in danger from what you can do with the Stone of Tears. I don't think you have yet reached your time of choosing."

"I'll do my best."

Scarlet lowered herself so he could climb up onto her shoulders. He gripped the black-tipped spines and hauled himself up. Richard gave a slap to a red scale.

"To D'hara, my friend. Again."

With a roar of flame, Scarlet launched into the sky.

In the distance, in the predawn gloom, he could see the green glow. It rose from the People's Palace, through the glass roof of the garden of life, like a beacon. Richard had seen that color of green from only one place. The underworld.

The icy wind tore at his clothes as Scarlet's wings beat with a steady cadence. She had put strenuous effort into the flight to D'Hara. She understood the danger posed by the Keeper. The underworld would take her, too. And she hated Darken Rahl. He had stolen her egg before and used it to enslave her.

As she began her descent, she peered back, her ears turning toward him. "There will be enough time, Richard. We can still make it to Aydindril. It is only just dawn."

"I know you'll get me there, Scarlet. I'll try not to give you too much time to rest."

Scarlet banked to the left, steepening their descent down toward the courtyard where they had been before. It was a place the huge dragon could land in the dark with room to spare. The palace's vast jumble of roofs and walls rushed up toward them with frightening speed. Richard's toes tingled with the feeling of floating off her back as she plummeted.

Suddenly, from the darkness below, a blinding flash of lightning crackled up all about them. It left yellow lines of afterimage in his vision. Before Richard could make sense of it, another came.

Scarlet roared in pain and pitched to the left. They dropped into a sickening spiral toward the ground. Richard gripped her spines as the huge dragon tried to recover.

On the vast steps rotating below, he saw the woman illuminated by the light of the next bolt of lightning she sent forth from her hands. Once again, Scarlet roared in pain. He couldn't see the woman in the darkness when the lightning cut off.

Scarlet struggled to check the uncontrolled descent. Richard knew that another bolt of the lightning would finish her. He tore the bow from his back and yanked an arrow from the quiver.

"Scarlet! Make fire so I can see her!"

As Richard drew the string to his cheek, Scarlet let out a fiery roar of pain and anger. In its red glow, he saw the woman raise her arms again. Before he could call the target, the spiral took her out of his line of sight.

"Scarlet! Look out!"

Scarlet drew back her right wing, and they tipped the other way. The yellow lightning streaked past to the left, just missing them. The ground was coming up fast.

In the flickering red light of the dragon's blast of fire, Richard saw her raise her hands again. He drew the bowstring and twisted his body with their motion to keep her in sight.

Before she could disappear again, he called the target. The instant it came to him, the arrow was away.

"Turn!"

Scarlet beat her right wing, making them wobble in the air as the yellow bolt erupted past, between the dragon's neck and wing. Almost before it began, the lightning cut off.

A ripple of total blackness passed over them. The arrow had found its mark. The Keeper now had Sister Odette.

With a hard jolt, they hit the ground. Richard was thrown off, and tumbled across the ground. He sat up and shook his head, then sprang to his feet.

"Scarlet! Are you hurt bad? Are you alive?"

"Go," she groaned in a deep vibrating voice. "Hurry. Get him before he has us all." She held her trembling left wing out.

Richard stroked her snout. "I'll be back. Hang on."

Richard drew the sword as he charged up the hill of steps. He didn't need to call forth the anger; it was with him before he had even touched the hilt. He ran in a blind rage toward doors between the colossal columns.

As he ran through the doors, a handful of soldiers charged out of the darkness. Without pause, Richard scythed into them. His blade flashed in the torchlight coming from the vast halls inside. Richard danced with the spirits. His blade was fluid grace among the hacking soldiers.

The first, he cut in half, breastplate and all. Every charge was met with swift steel. In a matter of moments, the fifteen men lay scattered across the bloody floor, and then Richard was moving again.

So much for his welcome back. He remembered the D'Haran army pledging their loyalty to him the last time he had been here, when he had killed Darken Rahl. Maybe they just didn't know who he was. More likely, they knew precisely who he was.

Richard chose a hall that led in the direction of the Garden of Life. Three levels of balconies looked down on the hall. Most of the torches were dark. He saw no people as he ran past a devotion square with white sand raked in circles around a pitted rock.

From a staircase at the side, a half-dozen Mord-Sith charged down, running toward him. Each wore her red leather uniform, and each had an Agiel in her hand. Through the rage, he realized that he couldn't use the sword on them, or they would capture him by its magic. He was furious. He needed to get to Darken Rahl. He didn't need to have to deal with these deadly women.

Reluctantly, Richard sheathed his sword and drew his knife. Denna had told him once that if he had just used his knife instead of his sword, he would have had her. He was not going to be able to outrun them; he was going to have to kill them.

The biggest, a blond-headed woman at the lead, held her hands out as he went for her. "Lord Rahl, no!"

The other five slid to a stop behind her. Richard slashed at her, but she lurched back into a half crouch with her hands held out to the sides.

"Lord Rahl! Stop! We are here to help you!"

Though he had put the sword away, he had no shortage of rage of his own. He had to get to Darken Rahl if he was to get to Kahlan. "Help me in the afterlife—you will be there shortly!"

"No, Lord Rahl! I am Cara. We are here to help you. You cannot go that way. That hall is not secure."

Richard stood panting, knife in hand. "I don't believe you. You want to capture me. I know very well what Mord-Sith do to their captives."

"I knew Denna, your mistress. You wear her Agiel. Mord-Sith do not live to hurt their captives any longer. You set us free. We would never hurt the one who set us free. We revere you."

"When I left here, I told the soldiers to burn all those outfits and give you new clothes. I ordered the Agiel taken from you. If you revere me, why have you not followed my orders?"

A sly smile touched her lips as she lifted an eyebrow over a cold, blue eye. "Because you cannot free us just to enslave us in a life you choose. We are free to choose for ourselves. You made that possible.

"We chose to fight to protect our Lord Rahl. We have sworn to lay down our lives for you, if necessary. Not only the men of the First File can protect you. We have chosen to be your personal bodyguards. Not even the First File dared argue with us. We take orders from no one but Lord Rahl."

"Then I order you to leave me alone!"

"I'm sorry, Lord Rahl, but we cannot follow that order."

Richard didn't know what to believe. This could just be a trap. "I'm here to stop Darken Rahl. I have to get to the Garden of Life. If you don't get out of my way, I will have to kill you."

"We know where you go," Cara said. "We will take you, but you must not go that way. We do not hold all the palace. That way is not safe. In fact, this whole section of the palace is in the hands of the insurgents. The First File would have lost a thousand men to come down here. We told them we would go, that it would be less risk to you. For that reason only, they agreed."

Richard started angling around the women. "I don't believe you, and I can't risk what you would do if you are lying. This is too important. If you try to stop me, I will have to kill you."

"If you go that way, Lord Rahl, you will die. Please, let me whisper a secret message in you ear." Cara handed her Agiel to a woman behind her. "You may hold your knife to me. I am without a weapon."

Richard gripped her hair in one fist, and held the razor-sharp knife to her throat. If she so much as flinched, he intended to cut her throat. Cara put her mouth close to his ear.

"We are here to help you Lord Rahl," she whispered. "It is the . . . toasted toads' truth."

Richard straightened. "Where did you hear such a thing?"

"Do you know its meaning? Commander General Trimack said that it is a coded message from First Wizard Zorander, so that you would know we are loyal to you. He told me to tell no one but you."

"Who is General Trimack?"

"The commander general, First File of the palace guard. They are loyal to you. The First File is the ring of steel around the Lord Rahl. Wizard Zorander told General Trimack to guard the Garden of Life at all cost.

"Two days ago that magic woman came. She killed nearly three hundred of our men getting into the Garden of Life. We tried to stop her, but we could not. We have no magic against her. She killed close to a hundred on her way out, tonight.

"We followed her out, and watched from a window on the third level. We saw her send lightning to strike your dragon from the sky. We saw you kill her. Only the true Lord Rahl could do that.

"Please, Lord Rahl, terrible things are happening in the Garden of Life. Let us take you there, so you may stop the evil spirit."

Richard had no time to waste. They had to have gotten that message from Zedd. He had to trust them.

"All right, let's go. But I'm in a hurry."

Grins came to each woman. Cara took back her Agiel and grabbed him by the shirt at one shoulder. Another of the Mord-Sith gripped his shirt at the other shoulder. They started running, dragging him along with them. Cara whispered that he should be as quiet as possible. The other four spread out in front, scouting the way.

They took him quickly, but silently, through small side halls and dark rooms. While the scouts slipped up narrow servants' stairs, Cara and the other pressed him up against the wall, crossing their lips with a finger, waiting until they heard a short whistle, then dashed up the stairs, pulling him along by his shirt.

At the top of the stairs, he nearly tripped over the body of one of the four Mord-Sith who had gone ahead. Her face had been split open by a sword. Eight D'Haran men in armor were sprawled in contorted positions down the hall, blood running from their ears. Richard recognized death caused by an Agiel.

One of the women in red leather at the end of the hall motioned them onward. Cara pulled him around a corner where the woman pointed, and up another staircase. He felt like a sack of laundry the way they yanked him this way and that, jamming him up against walls and in corners while others scouted a clear course.

He could hardly keep up with them as they ran down halls, still gripping his shirt at each shoulder, hauling him along. Richard lost track of where they were going as they went up stairs and through countless rooms. A few of the rooms had windows, and he could see that the sun was coming up.

Richard was winded when he finally recognized the broad corridor they entered. Hundreds of men in uniforms of mail and shiny breastplates all dropped to a knee when they saw him. The clatter of all their armor and weapons echoed down the wide hall. Every man put a fist over his heart. When they came up, one stepped forward.

"Lord Rahl. I am Commander General Trimack. We are close to the Garden of Life. I will lead you there."

"I know where it is."

"Lord Rahl, you must hurry. The rebel generals have launched an attack. I don't know if we will be able to hold this position long, but we will hold it to the last man while you are beyond."

"Thank you, General. Just hold them off until I send that bastard Darken Rahl back to the underworld."

The general gave a salute of his fist to his heart as Richard started moving. He trotted down a polished granite hall he remembered. It took him to the huge, gold-covered doors to the Garden of Life.

Nearly in a trance of rage, Richard burst through the doors, into the garden. The sun was up. Its first rays lit the treetops in the garden. Richard marched down the path, past the short, vine-covered walls, and out onto the grass.

In the center of the garden was a circle of white sand—sorcerer's sand. The round skrin bone sat in the center, with complicated lines drawn in the sand that encircled it. Beyond was the altar with the three boxes of Orden—the gateway to another world. Each was beyond black, seeming as if it would suck the light from the room.

From the opened box, a shaft of green light poured forth, up through the glass roof, and into the sky. Whatever Darken Rahl had been doing was opening the gateway. Sparkling light, blue, yellow, and red, spiraled around the shaft of green light.

The white, glowing form of Darken Rahl watched him stride across the grass. Richard stopped before the circle of sorcerer's sand, opposite him. A small smile spread on Darken Rahl's lips.

"Welcome, my son," came the hiss of his voice.

Richard felt the scar of the handprint heat on his chest. He ignored the pain of it. Darken Rahl's glowing blue eyes moved to the Stone of Tears hanging from Richard's neck.

Darken Rahl's gaze locked on Richard's. "I have spawned a great wizard. We would like you to join with us, Richard."

Richard said nothing. He seethed with wrath as he watched Darken Rahl's smile widen. Through the fury of anger, the pounding wrath of magic, he watched, and he sought the calm center, too.

"We can offer you what no other can, Richard. What the Creator Himself cannot offer. We are greater than the Creator. We would like you to join with us."

"What could you possibly offer me?"

Darken Rahl spread his glowing arms. "Immortality."

Richard was too angry to laugh. "When did you succumb to the delusion that I would believe anything you would have to say?"

"It is true, Richard," he whispered. "We have the power to grant it."

"Just because you managed to get some of the Sisters to believe your lies, that does not mean I would."

"We are the Keeper of the underworld. We control life, and death. We have the power to grant either, especially to one of your magic. You can be the master of the world of life. As I would have been, before you . . . interfered."

"Not interested. Got anything better to offer?"

Darken Rahl's cruel smile widened. His eyebrows lifted. "Oh, yes, my son," he hissed. "Oh, yes."

He swept his hand out, over the circle of sand. Shimmering light formed into a person kneeling forward. The light coalesced into a recognizable form.

Kahlan.

She was in her white Confessor's dress, kneeling forward. Her hair was cut short, just as in the vision he had had in the tower. A tear fell from her closed eyes as the side of her face pressed to the block. She mouthed his name, and that she loved him. Richard's heart pounded violently.

"The dragon is wounded, Richard. She cannot take you to Aydindril. Your time has run out. You have no option left but to let us help you."

"What do you mean, 'help?' "

Rahl's smile retuned. "I told you, we have the power over life and death. Without our help, this afternoon, before her people, this is what will happen."

His glowing hand swept out again. The blade's broad edge glinted in the air above her. The axe descended, thunking into the wooden block, sending out a spray of blood. Richard flinched.

Kahlan's head tumbled away. Bright red blood spread beneath her, soaking into the sand, into the white dress, as her body toppled to the side.

"Noooo!" Richard screamed, his fists at his sides. "Noooo!"

Darken Rahl swept his hand over the body, and it vanished into sparkling light and faded away.

"Just as I have taken away the vision of what will happen this day, we can stop the reality. We can offer immortality not only to you, but if you join with us, to her, too."

Richard stood stunned. It sank in, really sank in, for the first time. Scarlet was wounded. She could not fly him to Aydindril. This was winter solstice. Kahlan was going to die this day, and he had no way of getting to her. His breath came in ragged gasps.

The world was ending for him.

This was the meaning of the prophecy. If he took this offer, if he chose to stop her death, then the world would end for everyone else.

He thought of Chase, taking Rachel home to meet her new mother. He thought of all the happiness she would have in that life with love around her. He thought of his own life, with his father and mother, of the love, the happy times together, even the not so happy times, and how much it had meant to him.

He thought about the time he had spent with Kahlan, and the joy of being in love with her, and all the other people who must have had such joy, and would in the future. If there was a future.

"You can walk hand in hand with her, Richard. Forever."

Richard's eyes came up from the white sand. "Hand in hand, through the ashes of death. Forever."

What would it do to Kahlan, to her love for him, if he offered her such a selfish destiny. She would be horrified. Then whenever she looked at him, she truly would see a monster. Forever.

He would live forever with her revulsion, not her love. Thus, in trying to save her, he would destroy not only everyone else, but her heart, too.

The price was too high, even for his love.

But this would end his life, his love, too.

Richard was consumed with rage and calm at the same time. He stared into the glowing eyes of evil. "You would poison our love with your taint of hate. You don't even know the meaning of love."

The wrath swelled to a wild storm within him. At least, he would extract his price for this. His vengeance.

Richard lifted the Stone of Tears in his fist. Darken Rahl staggered back a step.

"Richard, think about what you are doing."

"You will pay for this."

Richard pulled a handful of black sorcerer's sand from his pocket and cast it onto the circle of white sand.

Darken Rahl threw his arms open. "No! You fool!"

The white sand writhed, as if alive, as if in pain. The symbols drawn in it twisted, contorting around themselves. The ground shook. Steaming fissures raced across the grassy ground.

Lightning flared up from the sparkling white sand, flicking about the Garden of

Life. The room thundered with a riot of noise and blinding light. The sorcerer's sand melted into a liquid pool of blue fire. The air shuddered with violent concussions.

Darken Rahl shook his fists to the sky. "No!"

His head came down, and when he saw Richard coming slowly toward him, the Stone of Tears held out in his fist, he went still. His hand came up in forbidding.

Richard staggered to a stop, the pain of the scar on his chest taking his breath. The agony seared through him. From deep within, he pulled resolve and made himself move despite the torment. Each step only increased the pain. It felt as if his flesh were burning off his bones and the marrow itself were boiling. In the calm at the center of the storm of anger, he was able to ignore it.

Richard pulled the Stone of Tears off over his head. He held the leather thong out in his hands, the Stone dangling before Darken Rahl's face. Rahl shrank back.

"You will wear this in the depths of death. Forever." Richard stepped closer. "Kneel."

The glowing form sank to its knees. The glowing eyes stayed on the Stone in the air above. Richard lowered the leather thong, to hang it over the head of his father's spirit. He paused.

Over Darken Rahl's head, behind him, he saw the altar that held the boxes. The open one in the center, alive with things beyond knowing, was sending its green light upward in a beacon.

Richard remembered what Ann, Nathan, and Warren had told him. If he used the Stone for selfish reasons, for hate, it would tear the veil. He wanted more than anything to send Darken Rahl to the depths of the underworld, to punish him forever for what he had done. But that would only accomplish what he had already decided was beyond price.

Besides, he had brought this on himself. That he had not done it intentionally made no difference. Life was not fair, it simply existed. If you accidentally stepped on a poison snake, you got bitten. Intentions were irrelevant.

"I have caused my own grief," Richard whispered. "I must suffer the consequences of my own actions. I cannot make others pay for what I have caused, intentionally or not."

Richard hung the Stone of Tears back around his own neck. Darken Rahl came to his feet in alarm.

"Richard . . . you don't know what you're saying. Punish me. Hang the stone around my neck. Have your vengeance!"

Richard turned partway toward the center of the Garden of Life and held out his hand. The round skrin bone, in the pool of blue fire, hurtled to his palm. His magic protected him.

He held the skrin bone up high. In the grip of rage, in the grip of calm, he called the power onward. It erupted from his fist.

Lightning, yellow and hot, shot forth into Darken Rahl.

Lightning, black and cold, shot forth into Darken Rahl.

They twisted together in the unleashed wrath of the skrin.

A ripple of total darkness swept across the room, and when it lifted, the lightning, and Darken Rahl, were gone. The skrin bone felt cool in his fist.

The green light from the box glowed brighter, making the room hum. Richard pulled the Stone of Tears from his neck. The leather thong fell away as the Stone turned to black in his palm.

Richard thrust out his hand. The Stone of Tears flew to the green light, floating in it a moment, rotating in the beam. The green light faded as the Stone of Tears sank toward the box, becoming transparent, until it passed from existence. The beacon of green light vanished, plunging the Garden of Life into silence.

Richard held the skrin bone out in his fist, and once again the twin lightning erupted, thundering across the distance. Flashes of white-hot light and ice-cold blackness washed over him. When it ended, and silence rang in his ears once more, the three boxes sat on the altar.

Each was closed.

Richard knew they could not be opened again without the book, and the book existed only in his head. The boxes of Orden, and the gateway they represented, would remain closed for all time.

Richard heard a metallic snap. He felt something brush at his neck, felt something fall at his feet.

He looked down to see the collar, the Rada'Han, on the ground. It was off his neck. He was free of it.

The pain, too, was gone. He felt his chest. The scar was gone.

In the silence, Richard stood dazed. He wasn't sure what had just happened. He didn't know how he had done it.

It was over.

For him, everything was over.

Kahlan was going to die this day.

And then he was running. The day wasn't over yet.

As he emerged from the doors of the Garden of Life, the five Mord-Sith surrounded him. He ignored them as he ran. In the corridor beyond, a sweaty, dirty General Trimack waited with hundreds of men just as grimy-looking. Many were bloody.

With a cacophony of clanging armor and weapons, the men as far as he could see down the smoky corridor fell to their knees, fists clapped to hearts. General Trimack returned to his feet. As he took three long strides toward Richard, Cara moved protectively in front of him.

"Get out of my way, woman!"

Cara didn't budge. "No one touches Lord Rahl."

"I'm his protection just as much as . . ."

"Stop it, both of you."

Cara relaxed and stepped to the side. General Trimack gripped Richard by the shoulders. "Lord Rahl, you've done it. It took a long time, but you did it."

"Done what? What do you mean it took a long time?"

His eyebrows lifted. "You've been in there most of the day."

Richard's breath faltered. "What?"

"We fought them fiercely for hours, but we were being pushed back. We were outnumbered ten or fifteen to one. Then you sent the lightning. I've never seen anything like it.

"Wizard Zorander told me that the palace is a huge power spell drawn on the ground of the plateau, drawn to protect and give power to the Lord Rahl. I never would have believed it until I saw it myself. The whole of the palace was alive with lightning. It flickered through every wall in the place.

"Every one of the those bastard generals who was loyal to Darken Rahl was cut down by the lightning. Their troops who fought on were ripped apart by it, too. Those who laid down their weapons and joined us were unharmed."

Richard didn't know what to say. "I'm glad, General, but I can't take credit. I

682

was in there the whole time. I'm not even sure what I did in there, much less what happened out here."

"We are the steel against steel. You did your part. You were the Lord Rahl, the magic against magic. We are all proud of you." General Trimack gave Richard a clap on the shoulder. "Whatever you did, you must have chosen right."

Richard put his fingers to his forehead, trying to think. "What time is it?"

"Like I said, you were in there most of the day, while we fought out here. It's near to late afternoon."

Richard clutched at his chest. "I have to go."

He started running. Everyone charged off after him. Before long, he was confused by the huge, converging halls. He slid to a stop on the slick marble floor and turned to Cara at his hip.

"Which way!"

"To where, Lord Rahl?"

"Where I came in! The fastest way!"

"Follow us, Lord Rahl."

Richard ran behind the five Mord-Sith. Behind him came what seemed to be the entire army of the palace. The racket of all the armor and boots echoed off the walls and ceilings high overhead. Columns, arches, staircases, devotion squares, and intersections of halls flew past. They raced down halls and down stairs.

Richard was winded when nearly an hour later he went through the doors between the giant columns and out into the cold air. Soldiers poured out behind. He ran down the steps four at a time.

Scarlet lay on her side in the snow, the glossy red scales rising and falling with her labored breathing.

"Scarlet! You're still alive!" Richard rubbed her snout. "I was so worried."

"Richard. I see you have managed to survive. It must not have been as difficult as you thought." She struggled to give a dragon's grin. It faded. "I'm sorry, my friend, but I cannot fly. My wing is injured. I tried, but until it is healed, I'm afraid I'm stuck on the ground."

Richard shed a tear on her snout. "I understand, my friend. You got me here. You saved the world of life. You are a heroine more noble than any in history. Will you be all right? Will you be able to fly again?"

She managed a weak laugh. "I will fly again. But not for a month or so. I will recover. It is not so bad as it seems."

Richard turned to the officers behind. "Scarlet is my friend. She has saved us all. I want you to bring her food. Whatever she needs, until she is recovered. Protect her as you would me."

Fists went to hearts.

Richard grabbed the general's arm. "I need a horse, a strong horse. Right now. And I need to know how to get to Aydindril."

The general turned. "Get a strong horse, now! You, go get maps to Aydindril for Lord Rahl!"

Men started running. Richard turned back to the dragon.

"I'm so sorry you're suffering, Scarlet."

Scarlet's chuckle rumbled deep in her throat. "The injury is not so painful. Look over there, around the side."

Her head, at the end of her long neck, followed him around. Richard was astonished to see an egg nestled in a crook of her tail.

683

A big, yellow eye peered at him. "I just gave birth. That is most of my weakness. Just as well I'm to be aground."

She played fire over the egg. Tenderly, she stroked her talons over it. As Richard watched, he thought about the beauty of life, and how happy he was that others could continue to have it.

But the vision of the falling axe kept playing over and over in his head. He couldn't stop the horror of it. His hands shook. It could be happening at that very moment. His breathing came in ragged pulls.

At last a man came running with a map. He held it out and pointed. "Here, Lord Rahl, is Aydindril. This is the fastest route. But it will still take you several weeks."

Richard stuffed the map in his shirt as another soldier galloped up on the horse. Richard retrieved his pack and bow from the snow where they had fallen when Scarlet had come to ground.

General Trimack held the reins to the muscular horse while Richard quickly lashed his things to the saddle. "There is food in the saddlebags. When will you return, Lord Rahl?"

Richard's mind was in a fog, racing in a thousand directions at once. All he could see was the axe falling.

He leapt up into the saddle. "I don't know. When I can. Carry on until then. And continue to guard the Garden of Life. Don't let anyone go in there."

"Safe return, Lord Rahl. Our hearts are with you."

Fists went to chests as he urged the powerful horse into a gallop and charged at full speed through the huge gates that stood open for him.

Richard cursed under his breath when the horse dropped dead under him. He picked himself up, when he had stopped rolling through the snow, and started pulling his things off the lifeless, lathered beast. He felt an ache of sorrow for the horse; it had given him everything it had.

He had lost count of how many horses had died under him. Some simply stumbled to a stop and refused to move anymore. Some dropped to a walk and would run no more. Some gave everything until their hearts quit.

Richard had known he was being too hard on them, and had tried to pace them, but he simply could not bring himself to go slow enough. When a horse died, or quit running, he managed to find another. Some owners were reluctant to sell, thinking they would haggle with him. Richard threw a fistful of gold at them, and took the horse.

He was near dead with exhaustion himself. He had slept and eaten little. Sometimes he had walked while his mount recovered. When he had had to find a new horse, he had run.

Richard hoisted the pack onto his back and started trotting off. It had been two weeks since he had left D'Hara. He knew he had to be close to Aydindril.

The fact that it was two weeks past winter solstice somehow didn't seem as important as his rush to reach Kahlan. It somehow seemed to him that if he could hurry fast enough, it would save her, that if he put in his best effort, it would somehow make time wait for him. He could not accept that he was too late.

He came to a panting halt at the top of a rise in the road. Ahead, in the sparkling sunlight, lay Aydindril. On the wall of mountains to the far side of the city he could see the gray walls of the Wizard's Keep. Richard ran on through the snow.

The streets were crowded with people, people hurrying through the cold afternoon air, and people standing about, stomping their feet to keep warm as they hawked their wares. Richard rushed past them all. When he saw people were staring at him because of the Sword of Truth, he pulled the mriswith cape over it.

A hawker ahead stood by the side of the road with a short pole resting on the ground. It had a crossbar with wispy strips hanging from it. When Richard realized what the man was calling out, he came out of his mental fog with a jolt.

"Confessor's hair!" the man bellowed. "Get a lock of the Mother Confessor's hair! Right off her vile head! Don't have many left! Show your children the hair of the last Confessor!"

Richard's eyes locked on the long hair. It was Kahlan's. He swept the lot of it off the pole and stuffed it in his shirt. When the man thought to fight for it, Richard slammed him up against the wall. He gripped the man's shirt in his fists, and lifted him clear of the ground.

"Where did you get this!"

"The . . . the council. Bought it from them to sell. Bought it fair after they cut it from her. It belongs to me." He shouted for help. "Thief! Thief!"

When an angry crowd pressed in to defend the man, the sword came out. People scattered. The hawker ran for his life.

Richard's fury was building despite his putting the sword away as he headed for the Confessors' Palace. He saw it rising up on the vast grounds ahead. He remembered Kahlan telling him how magnificent it was. He knew it almost as if he had seen it before.

He remembered, too, Kahlan telling him about a woman there, a cook. No, the head cook. What was her name? Sand something. Sanderholt, that was it. Mistress Sanderholt.

The aroma of cooking led him to the kitchen entrance. He charged through the door. A roomful of working people shrank back at the sight of him. It was obvious that no one wanted any part of whatever he was about.

"Sanderholt!" he called out. "Mistress Sanderholt! Where is she!"

People nervously pointed to a hallway. Before he had gone more than a dozen strides down the hall, a thin woman came rushing from the other direction.

"What's the trouble! Who's calling me?"

"I am," Richard said.

Her frown withered to a look of consternation. "What is it I can do for you, young man," she said in an uneasy voice.

Richard worked at keeping threat out of his tone. He didn't think he was very successful. "Kahlan. Where can I find her."

Her face turned nearly as white as her apron. "You would be Richard. She told me of you. You look like she said."

"Yes! Where is she!"

Mistress Sanderholt swallowed. "I'm sorry, Richard," she whispered. "The council sentenced her to death. The sentence was carried out at the winter solstice festival."

Richard stood staring down at the thin woman. He was having difficulty deciding if they were talking about the same person.

"I think you misunderstood," he managed. "I mean the Mother Confessor. Mother Confessor Kahlan Amnell. You must be talking about someone else. My Kahlan can't be dead. I came as fast as I could. I swear I did."

Her eyes were filling with tears. She tried to blink them away as she stared up at him. Slowly, she shook her head.

She put a bandaged hand to his side. "Come, Richard. You look as if you could use a meal. Let me get you bowl of soup."

Richard dropped his pack, bow, and quiver to the floor.

"The Central Council sentenced her to death?"

She gave a weak nod. "She escaped, but was caught. The Central Council reiterated the sentence before the people at the behead . . . at the execution. And then the members of the council all stood smiling while the people cheered them."

"Maybe she escaped again. She's a resourceful woman. . . ."

"I was there," she said in a broken voice, tears running down her face. "Please don't make me tell you what I saw. I've known Kahlan since she was born. I loved her."

Maybe there was a way to go back somehow, and get here in time. There had to be a way. He felt hot and dizzy.

No. He was too late. Kahlan was dead. He had had to let her die to stop the Keeper. The prophecy had beaten him.

Richard gritted his teeth. "Where is the council."

At last she managed to take her eyes from him. She pointed a bandaged hand down the hall and gave him directions.

She turned back. "Please, Richard, I loved her, too. Nothing can be done now. You can accomplish nothing."

But he was already moving, the mriswith cape flying behind as he swept down the hall. He saw only enough of what was around him as he moved swiftly along to follow the directions she had given him. He moved toward the council chambers the way his arrows flew to the target when he called it.

Guards were everywhere, but he paid them no heed. He had no idea if they paid him any, nor did he care. He flew single-mindedly toward his target. He heard the movement of men-at-arms around him, in the side halls. He barely noted them on the balconies.

At the end of a column-lined hall stood the doors to the council room. As he marched down the hall, men moved in front of the doors. He only dimly noticed them. He saw only the doors.

His sword still hadn't left its scabbard at his hip, but the magic was coursing through him at full fury. The soldiers closed rank before the doors. He didn't slow, the black cape billowing open, his brow set in a glare, as he charged ahead.

They made their move to stop him. Richard marched on. He wanted them out of his way. The power came by instinct, without conscious effort. He felt the concussion. In his peripheral vision he saw blood hit the white marble.

Without missing a stride, he emerged from the ball of flame in a gaping hole twice the size the doorway had been. Huge chunks of stone hurtled through the air, trailing smoke. Debris rained down about him. One of the doors spiraled through the air in an arc; the other spun like a top as it skittered across the floor of the council chamber along with ragged pieces of armor and shattered weapons.

At the far end of the room, men behind a curved desk rose angrily to their feet. As he advanced relentlessly onward, Richard drew the sword. The unique sound of steel rang in the huge room.

"I am Supreme Councilor Thurstan!" the one in the center, at the tallest chair, said. "I demand to know the meaning of this intrusion!"

Richard was still coming. "Be there one of you who did not vote to sentence the Mother Confessor to death?"

"She was sentenced to death for treason! Legally, and unanimously, sentenced by this council! Guards! Remove this man!"

Men came running across the vast floor, but Richard had already closed on the dais. The councilors drew knives.

Richard leapt to the top of the desk with a scream of rage. The blade cleaved Thurstan in two, from ear to crotch. A swing to each side took off heads. Several of the men tried to stab him. They weren't close to fast enough. The sword found every robed figure, including the ones who tried to run. It was over in seconds, before the guards had made half the distance.

Richard leapt back atop the desk. He stood in the grip of unbridled wrath, holding the sword in both hands. He waited for them to come. He wanted them to come.

"I am the Seeker! These men have murdered the Mother Confessor! They have paid the price of murder! Decide if you wish to be on the side of dead cutthroats, or on the side of right!"

The ring of men slowed their advance, looking tentatively to one another. Finally they stopped. Richard stood panting.

One man looked back at the hole in the wall where the doors had been, and then glanced over the debris scattered across the floor. "You are a wizard?"

Richard met the man's eyes. "Yes. I guess I am."

The man sheathed his sword. "This is wizard's business. It's not our place to challenge wizards. I'll not die for something that's not my place."

Another sheathed his weapon. Soon, the room rang with the clatter of steel being returned to hangers and scabbards. They began leaving, the room echoing with the sound of their boots. In a matter of moments, the vast council chamber was empty but for Richard.

He sprang down from the desk and stared at the tall chair in the center. It was about the only thing not dripping with gore. That would have been the Mother Confessor's chair, Kahlan's chair. She would have sat in that chair.

Woodenly, Richard sheathed the sword. It was over. He had done everything there was to do.

The good spirits had deserted him. They had deserted Kahlan. He had sacrificed everything to see right done, and the good spirits had done nothing to help.

To the Keeper with the good spirits.

Richard dropped to his knees. He thought about the Sword of Truth. It had magic; he decided that he couldn't count on it working for what he needed now.

Instead, he drew the knife at his belt.

He had done everything there was to do.

Richard put the point of the knife to his chest.

With cold precision, he looked down, to make sure it was pointed at his heart. Kahlan's hair, the hair he had taken from the hawker, stuck from his shirt. Richard pulled the lock she had given him from his pocket.

She had given it to him to remind him she would always love him. He wanted only to end his uncontrollable agony.

"She is awake," Prince Harold said. "She is asking for you."

Kahlan finally pulled her gaze from the flames in the hearth. She darted a cool glance at the wizard sitting next to Adie on a wooden bench. Though Zedd had recovered his memory, Adie had not. She still thought of herself as Elda, and was still blind.

Kahlan crossed the dark dining hall. When they had arrived, the inn had been deserted, as had the rest of the town, for fear of the advance of the Keltish forces. The empty town was a good place to rest in their run from Aydindril. Two weeks on the run had left them all in need of a rest, and a little warmth.

A week out of Aydindril, their little company, Zedd, Adie, Ahern, Jebra, Chandalen, Orsk, and Kahlan, had been intercepted by a small force led by Prince Harold. Prince Harold and a handful of his men had escaped the slaughter of his forces in Aydindril, and had lain in wait. When Queen Cyrilla was taken out to be beheaded, he made a daring raid, and in the confusion of people come to see the execution, he snatched his sister from the axeman.

Four days after joining with Prince Harold, they encountered Captain Ryan and his remaining nine hundred men. They had wiped out the Imperial Order to a man. It had cost them dearly, but they had carried out their mission.

Even her pride in them failed to rally her spirits, though she refused to betray that to those men.

After she wrung out a cloth in the basin, Kahlan sat on the edge of her half sister's bed. Cyrilla was aware, as she was from time to time, though she always slipped back into the dazed stupor before long. When she was in that state, she saw nothing, heard nothing, and said nothing. She simply stared.

Kahlan was heartened to see her tears now, as it meant she was awake. When she was alert, only Kahlan could talk to her. The sight of men sent her either into a screaming fit or back into a stupor.

Cyrilla clutched Kahlan's arm as Kahlan wiped the cool cloth over her brow. "Kahlan, have you thought about what I said?"

Kahlan pulled the cloth back. "I don't want to be the queen of Galea. You are the queen, my sister."

"Please, Kahlan, our people need a leader. I am not fit to do it now." She clutched her hand tighter to Kahlan's arm. Tears poured forth. "Kahlan, you must do this for me, for them."

Kahlan wiped the tears with the cloth. "Cyrilla, things will turn out well, you will see."

She clutched a fist over her belly. "I cannot lead, now."

"Cyrilla, I understand. I do. Though they did not do to me what they did to you, I was in that pit. I understand. But you will recover yourself. You will, I promise."

"And you will be the queen? For our people?"

"If I agree, it would only be temporary. Only until you have regained your strength."

"No . . ." she moaned. She sobbed, hiding her face against the pillow. "Don't . . . Please. Dear spirits, help me. No . . ."

And then she was gone again. Gone into the visions. She went limp, still as death, staring up at the ceiling. Kahlan kissed her cheek.

Prince Harold waited in the darkness outside the door. "How is my sister?"

"The same, I'm afraid. But have faith. She will recover."

"Kahlan, you must do as she asks. She is the queen."

"Why can't you be king? That would make more sense."

"I must fight on for our people, for all the Midlands. I cannot devote myself to the struggle if I'm burdened with concern over being king, too. I'm a soldier, and I wish to serve in the way I know. It is what I was meant to do. You are an Amnell, daughter to King Wyborn; you must be the queen of Galea."

Kahlan started to flip her long hair back over her shoulder, but it wasn't there. It was hard to forget the habits of a lifetime, to remember that her hair was chopped short.

"I will think on it," she said, as she started off.

She stood once more before the fireplace, the only source of light in the dining hall, staring into the flames, watching the once living things turn to ash. Everyone avoided her, and left her to herself.

After a time, she realized Zedd was standing beside her. She was only now beginning to get used to him in those fancy robes.

He held his cup out. "Why don't you have a sip of spiced tea."

She didn't look up from the flames. "No, thank you."

He rolled the cup in his palms. "Kahlan, you can't go on blaming yourself. It is not your fault."

"You wear lies poorly, wizard. I saw the look in your eyes when I told you what I had done. Remember?"

"I've explained that to you. You know I was under the spell cast by the three sorceresses, and only great emotional shock could break it. Anger could do the task, but once anger is brought on, it must be allowed to rage uncontrolled if it is to break the spell. I have told you how sorry I am for what I did to you."

"I saw the look in your eyes. You wanted to kill me."

He watched from under his eyebrows. "I had to do that, Mother Confessor. . . ."

"Kahlan. I told you, I am no longer the Mother Confessor."

"Call yourself what you will, but you are who you are. Denying the name does not make it so. And as I told you, I had to do that, too. To bring on a death spell, the person to be spelled has to be convinced they are to die, or it will not work.

"Once the anger brought back my memory, I knew I had to use a death spell, so I simply used what was happening to do what had to be done. It was an act of desperation. Had I not done it in that way, people would not have believed they saw you beheaded."

Kahlan shuddered at the memory of that magic. As long as she lived, she would never forget the chill touch of the death spell.

"You should have used magic to destroy that council of evil, instead. You should have saved me by killing those men."

"And then everyone would have known you were still alive. Everyone there was under the madness of hate. Had I done that, then we would have had the entire army, and tens of thousands of people, chasing after us. This way, no one chases us. We can now proceed with what must be done."

"You can proceed. I have quit the cause of the good spirits."

"Kahlan, you know what would happen if we were to give up. It was you yourself, last autumn, who came to Westland to find me and tell me that very thing. You helped convince me that if we abandon the side of magic, of right, of helping those who are powerless, then the enemy is handed an uncontested victory."

"The spirits saw fit to leave me without help. They stood by as I delivered Richard into the hands of the Sisters of the Light; they let me hurt him, let him be taken from me forever. The good spirits have chosen their side, and it is not with me."

"It is not the good spirits' job to govern the world of the living. It is our job, the job of the living, to tend our own world."

"Tell it to someone who cares."

"You care. You just don't realize it at the moment. I've lost Richard, too, but I know that I cannot allow that to deter me from right. Do you think Richard would love you if you were really the kind of person who could abandon those who needed your help?"

She said nothing, so he pressed the attack.

"Richard loves you partly because of your passion for life. He loves you because you fight for it with everything you have, with the same ardor as his. You have already proven that."

"He was the only thing I ever wanted out of life, the only thing I asked the good spirits for. And look what I have done to him. He thinks I betrayed him. I made him put a collar around his neck, the thing he feared more than death. I am not fit to help anyone. I only bring harm."

"Kahlan, you have magic. I have told you, magic must not be allowed to die. The world of life needs magic. If magic is extinguished, all life will be impoverished, and could even be destroyed.

"No one knows about the forces we have. We will go to Ebinissia, no one will expect that, and pull the Midlands forces together from there to strike back against them. No one will know we have brought Ebinissia back from the ashes of death."

"All right! If it will still your tongue, I will be the queen. But only until Cyrilla is better."

The fire crackled and popped. Zedd spoke in quiet admonition. "You know that is not what I mean, Mother Confessor."

Kahlan said nothing. She bit the inside of her cheek to keep from crying. She would not let him see her cry.

"The wizards of old created the Confessors. You have unique magic. It has elements to it that no other magic has, not even mine. Kahlan, you are the last Confessor. Your magic must not be allowed to die with you. Richard is lost to us. That's the way it is. We must go on. Life, and magic, must go on.

"You must take a mate and give the world that magic into the future."

Still, she stared into the flames.

"Kahlan," he whispered, "you must do it to prove Richard's love and faith in you."

Slowly, she turned to the room behind. Orsk sat cross-legged on the floor, beside Chandalen. Only he looked at her, with his one eye, the scar across the other looking white and angry in the firelight. He watched every move she made. Everyone else in the room tried to appear furiously engaged in their own business.

"Orsk," she called.

The huge man sprang to his feet and crossed the room. He stood hunched before her, waiting word whether he was to fetch her a cup of tea, or kill someone.

"Orsk, go up to my room and wait for me."

"Yes, Mistress."

After he had bounded up the stairs, she slowly crossed the room. She could hear the bed creak when he sat on it, waiting.

As she put her hand to the newel post, Zedd put his over it, stopping her. "Mother Confessor, it does not have to be him. You can surely find one more suited to your likes."

"It makes no difference. I have already touched him with my power. Why harm another, for no more than this?"

"Kahlan, I'm not saying it has to be now. Not this soon. I am saying only that you must come to accept it, and at some point it must be."

"Today, tomorrow, next year. What does it matter? It will be the same in ten years as it is today. Wizards have been using the Confessors for thousands of years. Why should I be any different? I may as well get it over so you will be content."

His watery gaze stayed on hers. "Kahlan, it's not like that. This is the hope of life."

691

She felt a tear roll down her cheek. She could see the pain in his eyes, but she showed him no mercy for it.

"Call it what you will. That does not change what it is. It is rape. My enemies could not accomplish it; it took my friends to rape me."

"I know, dear one. How well I know."

She started up the stairs again, but his hand on her arm stopped her.

"Kahlan, please, do just one thing for me first? Go for a little walk to think things over, and ask the spirits for guidance. Pray to the good spirits, seek their direction."

"I have nothing to say to the good spirits. It is they who wish this; they have sent you, to give me 'guidance.'"

His thin hand stroked her short-cropped hair. "Then do it for Richard."

She stood staring at him. Finally, she glanced out the back door, to the small, frozen garden at the back of the inn. It was just dusk outside.

Kahlan stepped down. "For Richard."

Richard sat in Kahlan's tall chair, stroking the long locks of her hair. He had pulled them out of his shirt, not wanting to stab himself through her hair. He didn't know how long he had been sitting there, touching her hair, lost in memories of her, but he noticed it was just turning dark out the windows.

Richard laid the hair carefully over the arm of the chair, and picked up the knife once more. In a daze of anguish, he put the point to his heart. His knuckles were white around the handle.

It was time.

At last it was going to be over. The pain would end.

His brow creased. What was it Mistress Sanderholt had said? Kahlan had told her of him? He wondered if Kahlan had told Mistress Sanderholt anything else. Maybe a last message for him, before she died. What could it hurt to ask? He could die, then.

Richard pulled Mistress Sanderholt from her kitchen, into a small pantry lined with stores. He closed the door.

"What have you done, Richard?"

"I killed her murderers."

"Well, I can't say I'm sorry about that. Those men did not belong on the council. Let me get you something to eat?"

"No. I don't want anything. Mistress Sanderholt, you said Kahlan told you of me. Is that right?"

She didn't look like she wished to dredge up the memories, but at last she took a deep breath and nodded. "She came home, but things had changed here. Kelton had . . ."

"I don't care what happened here, just tell me about Kahlan."

"Prince Fyren was murdered. She was convicted, wrongly, of that crime and a whole list of others, including treason. The wizard in charge sentenced her to be . . . executed."

"Beheaded," Richard said.

She gave a reluctant nod. "She escaped, with the help of some of her friends, killing the wizard in so doing, then went into hiding. But she got word to me, and I visited her. At those visits, she told me of all the things she had been through. She told me all about you. She liked to talk of nothing more."

"Why didn't she escape? Why didn't she run?"

"She said she had to wait for a wizard named Zedd. To help you."

Richard's eyes closed as pain tightened in his chest. "And so they caught her while she waited."

"No. That's not how it happened." Richard stared at the grain patterns on the wood floor while she went on. "The wizard she waited for returned. He is the one who turned her in."

Richard's head came up. "What? Zedd came here? Zedd wouldn't turn Kahlan over to be executed."

Her back stiffened. "Turn her in he did. He stood on the platform before the cheering crowd and ordered it done. I watched as that vile man gave the nod to the axeman."

Richard's mind spun in confusion. "Zedd? A skinny, old man, with long, wavy, white hair sticking out in every direction?"

"That is he. First Wizard Zeddicus Zu'l Zorander."

For the first time, a spark of hope ignited in him. He didn't know everything about Zedd, but he did know him capable of similar things. Could it be?

He grabbed her by her shoulders. "Where is she buried?"

Mistress Sanderholt took him out into the dusk, to the secluded courtyard where Confessors were buried. She told him that Kahlan's body had been burned in a funeral pyre, supervised by the First Wizard. Then she left him to be alone with the immense marker stone over her ashes.

Richard ran his fingers over the letters carved in the gray granite. KAHLAN AMNELL. MOTHER CONFESSOR. SHE IS NOT HERE, BUT IN THE HEARTS OF THOSE WHO LOVE HER.

"She is not here," he said aloud, quoting from the marker.

Could it be a message? Could she be alive? Had it been a trick by Zedd to save her life? Why would he do it?

Maybe, maybe, to keep them from chasing after her.

Richard fell to his knees in the snow before the monument. Dare he hope, just to have his hopes crushed?

He put his trembling hands together and bowed his head.

"Dear spirits, I know I have done wicked things, but I have always tried to do right. I have fought to help people and to uphold your principles of honesty and right.

"Please, dear spirits, help me.

"I've never prayed to you in earnest for anything before. Not like this. I've never meant anything like this before. Please, if you never again help me, help me this one time.

"Please, dear spirits, I can't go on if I don't know. I've given up everything to see right done. Please grant me this. Let me know if she is alive."

His head hanging, tears dripping from his face, he saw flickers of light on the ground before him.

Richard looked up. A glowing spirit towered over him.

When he recognized who it was, he went rigid.

Kahlan had walked around the garden countless times. Part of her hesitation was dread that she might be granted confirmation of her fear. Finally, she she knelt down and folded her hands together on a rock before her. She bowed her head.

"Dear spirits, I know I am not worthy, but please grant this. I must know if Richard is all right. If he still loves me."

She swallowed back the burning sensation in her throat. "I must know if I will ever see him again.

"I have been disrespectful, I know, and I have no excuse but my own failing as a good person. If you grant me this, I will do whatever the good spirits require of me.

"But please, dear spirits, I must know if I will ever see my Richard again."

Her head hung as he cried. Tears dripped from her face. Before her, on the ground, flickers of light danced.

Kahlan looked up, into the face of the glowing spirit towering over her. She felt the warmth of the calm smile from the face she knew.

Slowly, involuntarily, Kahlan rose to her feet.

"Is it really . . . you?"

"Yes, Kahlan, it is I, Denna."

"But . . . you went to the Keeper. You took the mark Darken Rahl put on Richard. You went to the Keeper in Richard's place."

The glowing smile of peace swelled Kahlan's heart with joy.

"The Keeper was repulsed by what I had done. He rejected me. I went instead to be with what you think of as the good spirits.

"In much the same way that what I did earned me peace I never expected, the sacrifices you and Richard have selflessly made for others, and each other, have merited the granting of this peace to the two of you. Because you each possess both sides of the magic, and are linked to me by deeds, before I pass beyond the veil I am empowered to bring you together, for a brief time, in a place between the worlds."

Denna, draped in long, flowing robes, spread her arms wide. The luminous folds hung from her arms all the way to the ground.

"Come, child. Come into my arms, and I will take you to Richard."

Trembling, Kahlan stepped under Denna's outstretched arm.

Richard stood under the illumination of Denna's arm as it came tenderly around him. The world vanished into the radiance. He didn't know what to expect, only that he wanted to see Kahlan more than life itself.

The overpowering, white blaze dimmed to a mellow glow.

Kahlan appeared before him. She gasped, and then threw herself into his arms. She wailed his name as she clutched him.

They embraced, without words, just feeling the presence of each other. He felt her warmth, her breathing, her quaking. He didn't want to ever let her go.

They sank to the soft support under them. He didn't know what it was, and he didn't care; it was solid enough to hold them. He wanted her arms around him forever. She finally stopped weeping, and put her head against his shoulder as he held her tight.

At last, she looked up to his face, her beautiful green eyes gazing deeply into his. "Richard, I'm so sorry I made you put that collar around your . . ."

Richard put his finger to her lips. "It was all for a reason. It took me time to understand how foolish I was being, and how brave you are. That is all that matters. It makes me love you all the more, because you sacrificed your own needs to save me."

She shook her head. "My Richard. How did you get here?"

"I prayed to the good spirits. Denna came."

"Me too. Denna made a sacrifice for you, too. She took the power of the mark, so you would live. Denna gave your life back to me. She is at peace now."

"I know." He ran his hand down her head, down her short hair. "What happened to your hair?"

"A wizard cut it off."

"A wizard. Well then, I guess a wizard will have to restore it to you."

Richard ran his hand lovingly down her hair. He remembered the way Zedd had stroked his hand down his own jaw to make his beard grow. It seemed as if from having seen Zedd do it, he knew how to do it, too. With each stroke of his hand, her hair lengthened. Richard continued to pull from the calm center within him, and her hair continued to lengthen. When it was the same as before, he stopped.

Kahlan lifted a long lock of her hair, looking at it in wonder. "Richard, how did you do that?"

"I have the gift, remember?"

She beamed with her special smile, the smile of sharing she gave no other. Kahlan ran her hand down his cheek.

"I'm sorry, Richard, but I don't like your beard. I like you the way you were before."

He lifted an eyebrow. "Really? Well then, since we set you back to right, we will just have to do the same for me, too."

Richard drew his hand down his jaw, again pulling the power from the calm center.

Kahlan gasped in astonishment. "Richard! It's gone! Your beard is gone! You made it vanish! How did you do that!"

"I have the gift for both sides of the magic."

She blinked in surprise. "Subtractive Magic? Richard, is any of this real, or am I just dreaming it?"

And then he kissed her, long and deep.

"Feels real to me," he said breathlessly.

"Richard, I'm afraid. You're with the Sisters. I will never again be able to be with you. I can't go on if you are going to be taken from . . ."

"I'm not with the Sisters. I'm in Aydindril."

"Aydindril!"

He nodded. "I left the Palace of the Prophets. Sister Verna helped me. Then I had to go to D'Hara."

Richard told her everything that had happened since he had left her, and she told him all she had been through. Richard could hardly believe the things she had done.

"I'm so proud of you," he said. "You truly are the Mother Confessor. You are the greatest Mother Confessor that ever lived."

"Go back to the hall before the council chambers, and you will see big paintings of Confessors who were greater than I will ever be."

"That, my love, I doubt."

He kissed her again. A hot, passionate kiss. She kissed him back, desperately, as if she needed nothing so much from life as to be in his arms kissing him. He kissed her cheek, her ears and her neck. She moaned against him.

"Richard, is the scar, Darken Rahl's mark, really gone?"

He pulled his shirt open to show her.

Her hand stroked his chest. "It's really true," she whispered.

Tenderly, she kissed his chest. She ran her hand over him, kissing where it had been. She gave a sucking kiss to his nipple.

"Not fair," he said breathlessly. "I get to kiss anything on you that you kiss on me."

Kahlan looked him in the eye as she unbuttoned her shirt. "Bargain struck."

She started pulling at his clothes as he trailed wet kisses down her soft flesh. Her breathing quickened with each.

"Kahlan," he managed to say as he pulled away, "the good spirits may be watching us."

She pushed him onto his back and kissed him. "If they truly are good spirits, they will turn their backs."

The feel of her warm flesh made his head spin. The feel of the shape of her made him moan with need. Around them, the mellow glow pulsed with their breathing. It seemed to be an extension of their heat.

Richard rolled over on top of her. He gazed down into her green eyes. "I love you, Kahlan Amnell. Now, and always."

"And I you, my Richard."

As they pressed their lips together, she wrapped her arms around his neck, and her soft legs around his.

In the void between worlds, in the soft glow of a timeless place, they were one.

Kahlan strolled back into the inn. She stood in the shadows at the end of the hall leading into the dining room. She still felt the glow, the warmth, the mind-numbing joy and fulfillment. Everyone looked up when they heard her footsteps.

Zedd shot to his feet. "Kahlan! Bags, girl, where have you been all night! It's just turning to dawn! You've been missing since dusk! We've been searching the town all night for you! Where did you go?"

She turned and held her hand out. "To the little garden, out back."

Zedd stormed across the room. "You were not in the garden!"

She smiled dreamily. "Well, that was where I went, but I left that place. I went to be with Richard. Zedd, he escaped from the Sisters. He is in Aydindril."

Zedd slowed to a stop. "Kahlan, I know you have had a hard time of it, but you have simply had a vision of something you wished."

"No Zedd. I prayed to the good spirits. She came and took me to Richard. To be with him in a place between the worlds."

"Kahlan, that is simply not . . ."

Kahlan stepped out of the shadows, into the firelight. Zedd's eyes went wide.

"What . . . what happened to your hair?" the wizard whispered. "It's long again."

Kahlan grinned. "Richard made it right. He has the gift, you know." She held out the Agiel hanging from her neck. "He gave me this. He said he doesn't need it anymore."

"But . . . there has to be some other explanation. . . . ''

"He gave me a message to give to you. He said to thank you for not closing the opened box of Orden. He said he was glad his grandfather was wise enough not to violate the Wizard's Second Rule."

"His grandfather . . ." Tears ran down his wrinkled face. "You saw him! You really saw him! Richard is safe!"

She threw her arms around him. "Yes, Zedd. Everything is going to be all right, now. He restored the Stone of Tears to where it belongs, and closed the box of Orden. He called it the gateway. He said it takes both Additive and Subtractive Magic to do it or it would have destroyed all life."

He gripped her shoulders and held her out. "Richard has Subtractive Magic? Impossible."

"He had a beard, and made it vanish. He said to remind you of the lesson you gave him, that only Subtractive could do that."

"Wonder of wonders." His sharp features came closer. "You're all in a lather, girl." He put a sticklike hand to her forehead. "You don't have a fever. Why are you sweating?"

"It was . . . hot, in that other world. Quite hot."

He peered at her hair. "You hair is all tangled. What kind of wizard would grow hair back all tangled? I would have grown it back straight. That boy has a lot to learn. He didn't do it right."

Kahlan's eyes went out of focus. "Believe me, he did it right."

He turned his head, appraising her with one eye. "What were you doing all night? You've been gone the whole night. What have you two been doing?"

Kahlan could feel her ears heat. She was glad she had long hair again. "Well, I don't know. What do you and Adie do when you are alone together all night?"

Zedd straightened. "Well . . ." He cleared his throat. "Well, we . . ." He lifted his chin and pointed a finger skyward. "We talk. That's what we do, we talk."

Kahlan shrugged. "That's what we did, too. Just like you and Adie do all night. We talked."

A sly grin stole onto his face. He hugged her tightly in his thin arms, patting her back. "I'm so happy for you, dear one."

Zedd took her hands in his and danced around the room. Ahern smiled and pulled out a little flute, playing a bouncy tune. "My grandson is a wizard! My grandson will be a great wizard! Just like his grandfather!"

The celebration went on for a few minutes, with everyone joining in the laughing. They all clapped in time with the tune as Zedd danced with her around the room.

Kahlan saw one person not joining in. Adie sat in a rocking chair in the corner. She had a small, sad smile on her face as she turned her ear to follow them.

She went to the old woman and knelt before her. Kahlan took up her frail hands. "I be happy for you, child," Adie said.

"Adie," Kahlan said in a soft voice, "the spirits sent a message for you."

She shook her head regretfully. "I be sorry, child, but it would mean nothing to me. I not remember being this woman Adie."

"I promised to deliver the message. It's important to one beyond that you have it. Will you hear the message?"

"Tell me then, though I be sorry I won't know its meaning."

"It's a message from one named Pell."

The room was silent behind her. Adie's rocking came to a halt. She straightened the littlest bit. Her eyes filled with tears.

Adie's hands tightened around Kahlan's. "From Pell? A message from my Pell?"

"Yes, Adie. He wants you to know that he loves you, and that he is in a place of peace. He said to tell you that he knows you never betrayed him. He knows how much you love him, and he is sorry you have had to suffer. He said to tell you to be at peace, knowing all is well between your spirits."

Adie turned her ear away and looked at Kahlan with her white eyes. Tears rolled down her cheeks.

"My Pell knows I did not betray him?"

Kahlan nodded. "Yes, Adie. He knows, and loves you as always."

Adie pulled Kahlan into her arms as she wept. "Thank you Kahlan. You could never know how much this means to me. You have given me back everything. You have given me back the meaning of life."

"I know how much it means, Adie."

Adie stroked the back of Kahlan's head as she held her close. "Yes, child, perhaps you do."

Jebra and Chandalen cooked breakfast while the rest of them talked and planned.

Though it would be a grisly job clearing Ebinissia of all the bodies, at least it was still winter, and not the task it would be in spring. From Ebinissia, they would pull the Midlands back together.

Kahlan told them that Richard would try to meet up with them in the Galean Crown city, and that he said that then he might need to take Zedd back to Westland, to see about the Sisters of the Dark. But for now, they were safely out to sea.

After a good meal, filled with joy and happy conversation that had been missing for so long, they started packing up their things. Chandalen, with an uneasy expression, pulled Kahlan aside.

"Mother Confessor, I wish to ask you something. I would not ask you, except I know no one else to ask."

"What is it, Chandalen?"

"How do you say 'breasts' in your tongue?"

"What?"

"What is the word for breasts? I wish to tell Jebra that she has fine breasts."

Kahlan rolled her shoulder self-consciously. "Chandalen, I'm sorry, but I meant to have a talk with you about that. I guess with everything that happened, I never got around to it."

"So talk now. I wish to tell Jebra how much I like her fine breasts."

"Chandalen, with the Mud People, that is a proper thing to say to a woman. It's a compliment. But in other places, it is not taken as a compliment, but as improper. Very improper, until two people know each other."

"I know her well."

"Not well enough. Will you trust me in this? If you really like her, then you must not tell her this, or she will not like you."

"But, women here do not like to hear the truth?"

"It's not that simple. Would you tell a woman in your village you would like to see her with the mud washed from her hair, even though it is the truth?"

He lifted an eyebrow. "I see what you mean."

"Do you like other things about her?"

He nodded enthusiastically. "Yes. I like everything about her."

"Then tell her you like her smile, or her hair, or her eyes."

"How do I know which is the proper thing to compliment?"

Kahlan sighed. "Well, for now, just stick to anything that isn't covered by clothes, and you will be safe."

He nodded thoughtfully. "You are wise, Mother Confessor. I am glad you have Richard back as your mate, or you would surely have chosen Chandalen."

Kahlan laughed and gave him a hug. He returned it warmly.

Outside, she saw to the men: Captain Ryan, Lieutenant Hobson, Brin and Peter, and others she knew. They were infected by her smile and good cheer.

In the stables she checked on Nick. Chandalen had stolen him back when they fled Aydindril. The big warhorse neighed softly at her approach.

Kahlan rubbed his gray nose as he nudged his head against her. "How you doing, Nick?" He nickered. "How would you like to carry the queen of Galea to the palace in Ebinissia?"

Nick tossed his head enthusiastically, anxious to be out of the stables and off into the brightening day.

Water dripped from melting icicles at the edge of the stable roof. Kahlan looked out over the hills. It was going to be a rare, warm day in the winter. But soon it would be spring.

Mistress Sanderholt was surprised when Richard took another bowl of soup and chunk of bread.

"Mistress Sanderholt, you make the best spice soup in the world, after mine."

In the kitchen beyond, the help was busily going about breakfast preparations. She closed the door.

"Richard, I am pleased you are so much better. I was worried you would do something terrible last night, you were grieving so. But this is too much of a change. Something must have happened to make you have such a turnaround in spirit."

He looked up at her as he chewed. He swallowed the bread. "I will tell you if you promise to keep it a secret, for now. It could cause serious trouble if you told anyone."

"I promise, then."

"Kahlan is not dead."

She stared blankly at him. "Richard, you are worse than I thought. I myself saw . . ."

"I know what you saw. The wizard you saw is my grandfather. He used a spell to make everyone think she was executed, so they would not be hunted down, so that they could escape. She is safe."

She threw her arms around his neck. "Oh, dear spirits be praised!"

"Indeed," Richard said with a grin.

Richard took the bowl of soup outside to watch the dawn. He was too exhilarated to be cooped up indoors. He sat on the vast steps, looking around at the magnificent palace soaring up all around him. Towers and spires and sweeping roofs loomed in the early dawn light.

As he ate his soup, he watched a gargoyle atop the edge of a nearby, enormous frieze supported by fluted columns. The pink clouds were just beginning to glow behind it, silhouetting the grotesque, hunched shape.

Richard had just put a spoonful of spice soup in his mouth when he thought he saw the gargoyle take a deep breath. Richard set the bowl down. He rose to his feet, his eyes never leaving the dark shape. It moved again, just a little twitch.

"Gratch! Gratch, is that you!"

The shape didn't move. Maybe it was just his imagination. Richard held his arms open wide.

"Gratch! Please, if that's you, forgive me. Gratch, I've missed you!"

It was still a moment, and then the wings stretched out. It leapt from the corner of the building and swooped down in a glide toward him. With a flutter of wings, the huge gar landed on the steps a short distance away.

"Gratch! Oh, Gratch, I've missed you!" The gar watched with glowing green eyes. "I don't know if you can understand, but I didn't mean what I said. I was only trying to save your life. Please, forgive me? Richard loves Gratch."

His wings fluttered. A cloud of breath came from between long fangs. His ears perked up.

"Grrratch luuug Raaaach aaarg."

The gar bounded into Richard's arms, knocking him to the steps. Richard hugged the furry beast, and Gratch enfolded him in arms and wings. Each stroked the other's back, and each grinned in his own way.

When they finally sat up, Gratch hunched down, staring curiously at Richard's face. With the back of a huge claw, he stroked Richard's jaw.

Richard felt his smooth face as he smiled. "It's gone. I'm not going to have a beard anymore."

Gratch's nose wrinkled in disgust. He let out a gurgling growl of displeasure.

Richard laughed. "You'll get used to it." They sat together in the quiet of the dawn. "Do you know, Gratch, that I'm a wizard?"

Gratch gurgled a laugh and frowned dubiously. Richard wondered how a gar could know what a wizard was. Gratch never failed to astonish him with what he knew, with what he could grasp.

"No, really. I am. Here, let me show you; I'll make fire."

Richard held his palm out. He called the power from the calm center. Try as he might, nothing happened. He could not make so much as a spark. He sighed as Gratch howled in a roar of laughter, his wings flapping with the joke.

A sudden memory came to him—something Denna had told him. He had asked her how he had done all those things with magic. She had looked at him with that all-knowing smile of peace, and said, *Be proud you made the right choices, Richard, the choices that allowed to happen what came about, but do not call arrogance to your heart by believing that all that happened was your doing.*

Richard wondered where the line was. He realized he had a lot to learn before he was a real wizard. He wasn't even sure he wanted to be a wizard, but he now accepted who he was—one born with the gift, born to be the pebble in the pond, son of Darken Rahl, but lucky enough to have been raised by people who loved him. He felt the hilt of the sword at his elbow. It had been made for him.

He was the Seeker. The true Seeker.

Richard's thoughts again touched the spirit who had brought him more happiness than in life had brought him pain. He was deeply gratified that Denna had found peace. He could want nothing more for her, for someone he loved.

He came out of his thoughts and patted the gar's arm. "You wait here a minute, Gratch. I'll get you something."

Richard ran into the kitchen and retrieved a leg of mutton. As he ran back down the steps, Gratch danced from one foot to the other in excitement. Together, they sat on the steps, Richard eating his soup, and Gratch tearing into the meat with his fangs.

When they had finished—Gratch had even eaten the bone—Richard pulled out a long lock of Kahlan's hair.

"This is from the woman I love." Gratch considered, then looked up as he gently reached out. "I want you to have it. I told her about you, and what you mean to me. She will love you just as I love you, Gratch. She will never chase you away. You can be with us whenever you want, for as long as you want. Here, give it back a moment."

Gratch held out the length of hair. Richard took off the thong holding Scarlet's tooth. It would do him no good any longer; he had already called her with it. He tied the long lock of hair to the thong, and then hung the whole thing over Gratch's head.

With a claw, Gratch stroked the long hair. His grin wrinkled his nose and showed the full length of his fangs.

"I'm going to go to her now. Would you like to come along?"

Gratch nodded his enthusiasm, his head bobbing, his ears twitching, and his wings fluttering.

Richard looked down on the city. Troops were moving about. A lot of troops. Imperial Order troops. It wouldn't be long before they gained the courage to investigate the death of the council, even if it was at the hands of a wizard.

Richard smiled. "Then I guess I better find a horse, and we can be on our way. I think it best if we were away from here."

He looked out on the brightening day. A breeze with a hint of warmth ruffled his mriswith cape. Before long it would be spring.